MW00380311

In behalf of the author,
I thank you for reading
Sasha's story –

Death to Reach a Star

Karmic wishes,
Jim Gagnon

Death to Reach a Star

a novel

by

J. Maris Gagnon

Twin Omega Press
Seattle, Washington

for L.T.

DEATH TO REACH A STAR

 Published in the United States of America by *Twin Omega Press,* Post Office Box 55697, Seattle, Washington 98115.

Library of Congress Catalog Card number: 92-62096

ISBN 0-9634840-0-1 (hardcover)
ISBN 0-9634840-1-X (softcover)

Death to Reach a Star is a work of historical fiction. Aside from historical personages/places/events depicted herein, any resemblance to actual events, places, or persons living or dead is purely coincidental.

CONTENTS

PRINCIPAL PLAYERS

Aleksandr Mikhailovich Sekovsky, known as *Sasha* (affectionately, *Sashenka*)

Count Mikhail Sergeyevich Sekovsky (Sasha's father), an owner of land situated along the northeast shore of Lake Ilmen in Novgorod *oblast* (province), south of the provincial capital, also known as Novgorod. The late *Lady Melissa Devon-Tyler (Countess Sekovskaya)* was Sasha's mother

Sir Edward Devon-Tyler is *'Uncle Ned',* Melissa's brother

Nikolai Petrovich Zhelanov, sometimes called *Kolya*, is Sasha's first cousin and the son of Count Mikhail Sekovsky's sister

Princess Sofiya (Sophie) Sergeyevna Sekovskaya Zhelanova, Nikolai's mother, a well-to-do St. Petersburg society matron. The late *Prince Pyotr Kondratyevich Zhelanov (Uncle Petya)*, renowned cellist, was Nikolai's father

Anna (sometimes called *Anyuta*), is Nikolai's sister. Nikolai's other sisters are: *Nina* and *Natalya (Natasha),* who are twins, *Tatyana,* and *Eugenia*

Boris Timofeyevich Zhelanov, is Nikolai's first cousin on the Zhelanov family side

Vladimir Denisovich Rykazian, (called *Volodya*), is a beekeeper of Russian/ Armenian descent employed by Count Sekovsky on the Ilmen farm

Viktor Ilyich Bulyarin, (called *Bulya*, or affectionately, *Vitya*), is a ledger clerk employed by Count Sekovsky on the Lake Ilmen farm and the son of *Ilya Isayevich Bulyarin*, an influential member of the Novgorod *zemstvo* (provincial council)

Semyon Ilyich Bulyarin is Bulya's brother

Valenti Appollonovich (called *Vliny*), his wife *Marina Ivanovna* (called *Marnya*), and her daughters *Eva* and *Tereza*, are all (along with Eva's husband *Rolfe*) servants in the Sekovsky estate household

Ilarion Pavlovich Sheremetev, also known by the first name *Pierre* and surname of *Pavlovsky*, is an illicit Moscow merchant and whoretrader in the underworld

Yevgeny Ivanovich Mrenitsev, and his sister, *Lyubov Ivanovna*, (also called *Missy*), are servants to Sheremetev

Grigor Fokimovich Mrenitsev is paternal uncle to Yevgeny and Lyubov

Zhenya Grigoryevna Mrenitseva is the daughter of Grigor and Lyubov

Count Makar Serafimovich Byelov is the neighbor and lessor of the Zhelanovs' seaside bungalow in Yalta

Sergei Pavlovich Diaghilev, Vaslav Nijinsky, Mikhail Fokine, Tamara Karsavina, Anna Pavlova, and *Igor Stravinsky* are all noted historical personages associated with the *Ballet Russe*

PLEASE NOTE:

(1) This work contains occasional graphic depictions of both homosexual and heterosexual sex.

(2) Regarding measurements:

one *verst* equals approximately 2/3 of a mile
one *desyatin* equals approximately 2 & 3/4 acres

(3) Regarding calendars:

Until February 1918, Russia followed the old Julian calendar system, which in the Twentieth Century lagged thirteen days behind the Gregorian calendar system used in Europe and the U.S. Correspondents sending letters/cables to or from Russia often included both dates as a matter of course.

(4) Regarding transliteration of Russian names/words:

Herein use is made of a combination of System I, approved by the U.S. Board on Geographic Names (considered closest to popular usage) and System II, the Library of Congress System, used by most libraries and scholarly journals. For names of common usage in the West, Western spelling has been retained (e.g., Tchaikovsky in lieu of Chaikovsky, Rachmaninoff instead of Rakhmaninov, Moscow over Moskva, etc.). The letter 'o' in Russian orally fluctuates between an 'a' and 'o' sound, depending upon the word and inclination of the speaker; in the few instances where such words do occur within the text of *Death to Reach a Star,* the author has attempted the most prudent transliteration.

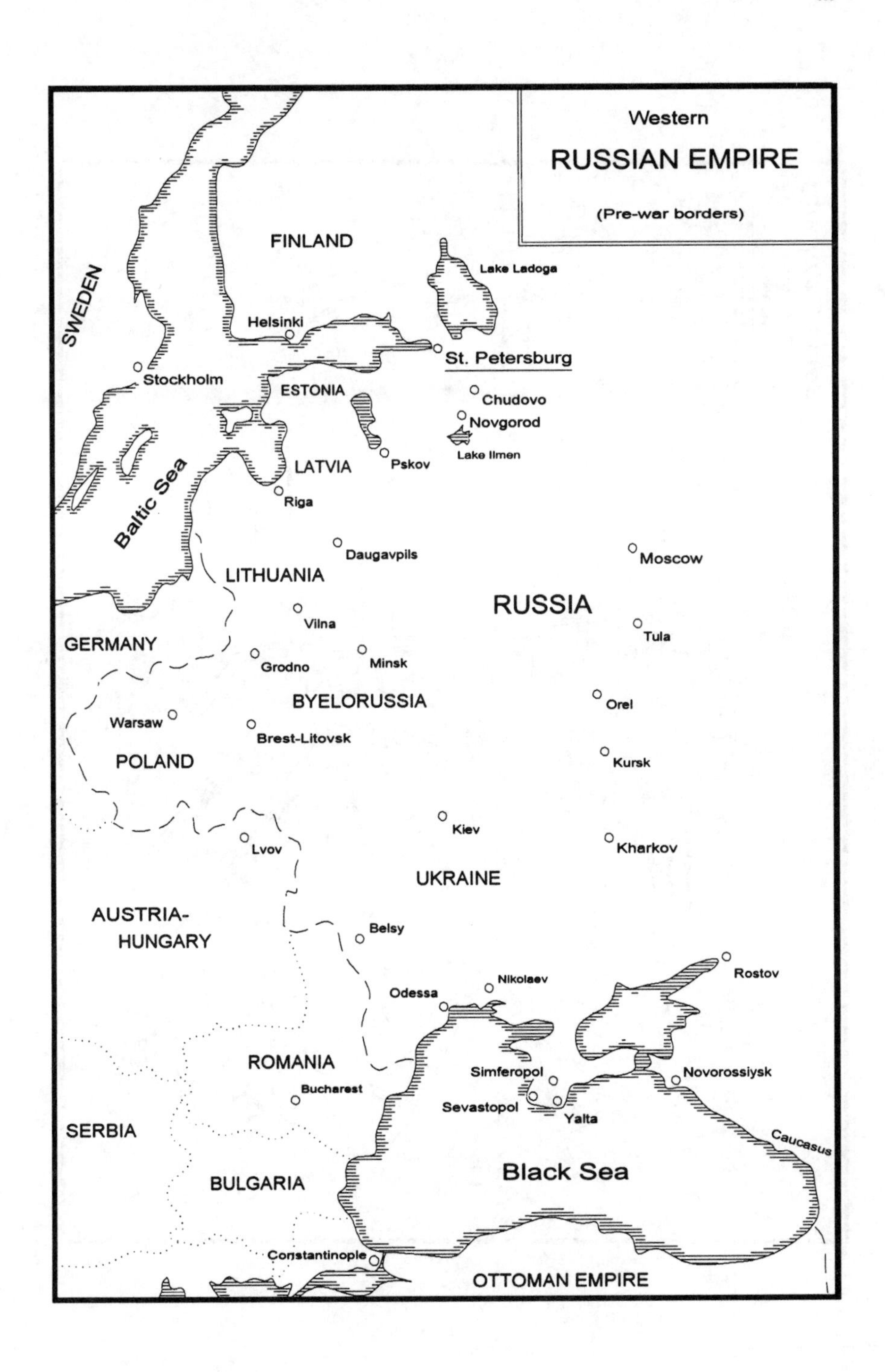
Western
RUSSIAN EMPIRE
(Pre-war borders)
FINLAND
Lake Ladoga
SWEDEN
Helsinki
St. Petersburg
Stockholm
ESTONIA
Chudovo
Novgorod
Lake Ilmen
Pskov
LATVIA
Baltic Sea
Riga
Daugavpils
Moscow
LITHUANIA
RUSSIA
Vilna
Tula
GERMANY
Grodno
Minsk
BYELORUSSIA
Orel
Warsaw
Brest-Litovsk
POLAND
Kursk
Kiev
Lvov
Kharkov
UKRAINE
AUSTRIA-
HUNGARY
Belsy
Rostov
Nikolaev
Odessa
ROMANIA
Simferopol
Novorossiysk
Bucharest
Sevastopol
Yalta
SERBIA
Caucasus
Black Sea
BULGARIA
Constantinople
OTTOMAN EMPIRE

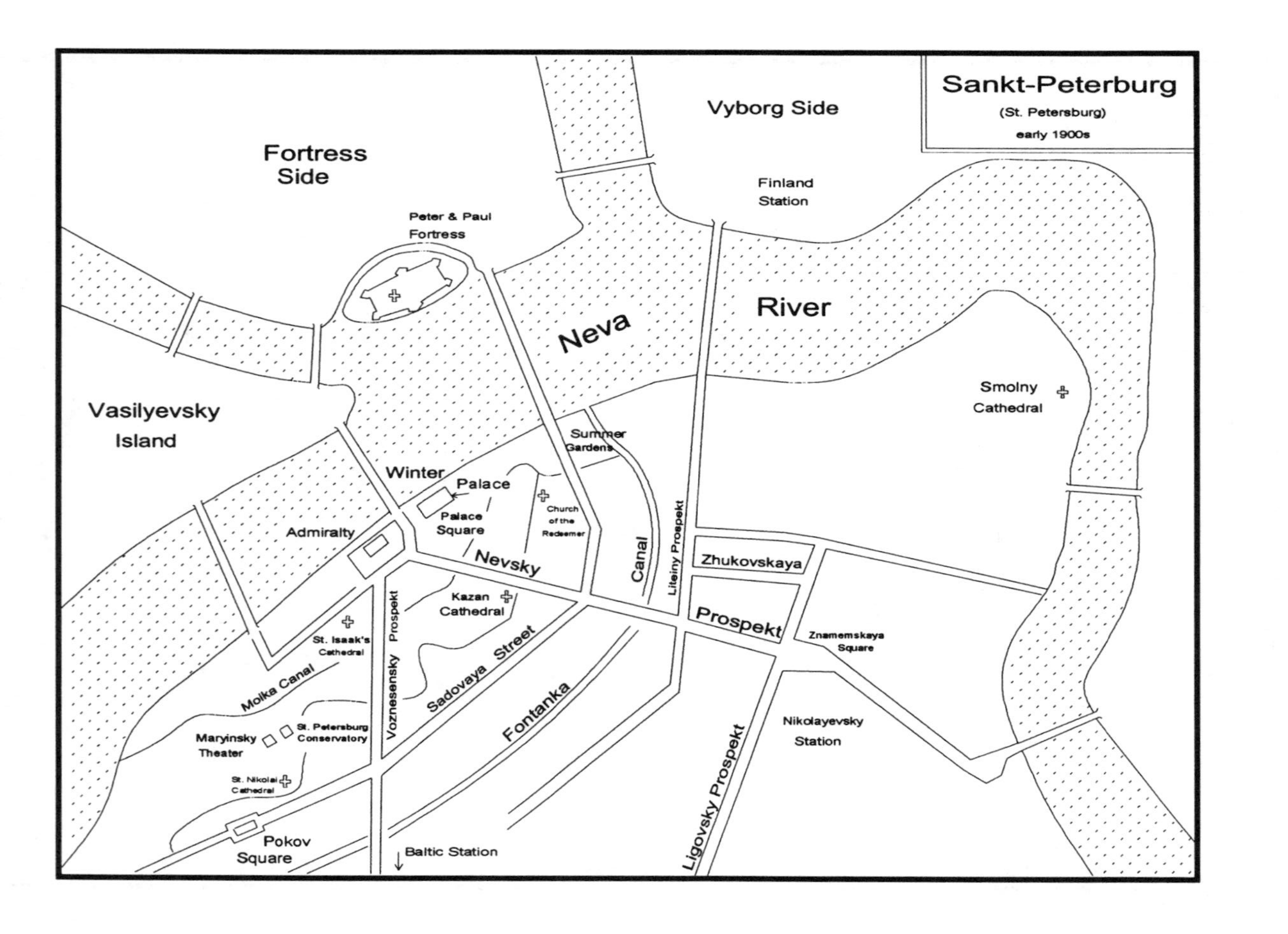

Sankt-Peterburg
(St. Petersburg)
early 1900s
Vyborg Side
Fortress Side
Finland Station
Peter & Paul Fortress
Neva
River
Vasilyevsky Island
Smolny Cathedral
Summer Gardens
Winter
Palace
Church of the Redeemer
Palace Square
Admiralty
Nevsky
Canal
Liteiny Prospekt
Zhukovskaya
Kazan Cathedral
Prospekt
Znamemskaya Square
St. Isaak's Cathedral
Voznesensky Prospekt
Sadovaya Street
Moika Canal
Fontanka
Nikolayevsky Station
Maryinsky Theater
St. Petersburg Conservatory
St. Nikolai Cathedral
Ligovsky Prospekt
Pokov Square
Baltic Station

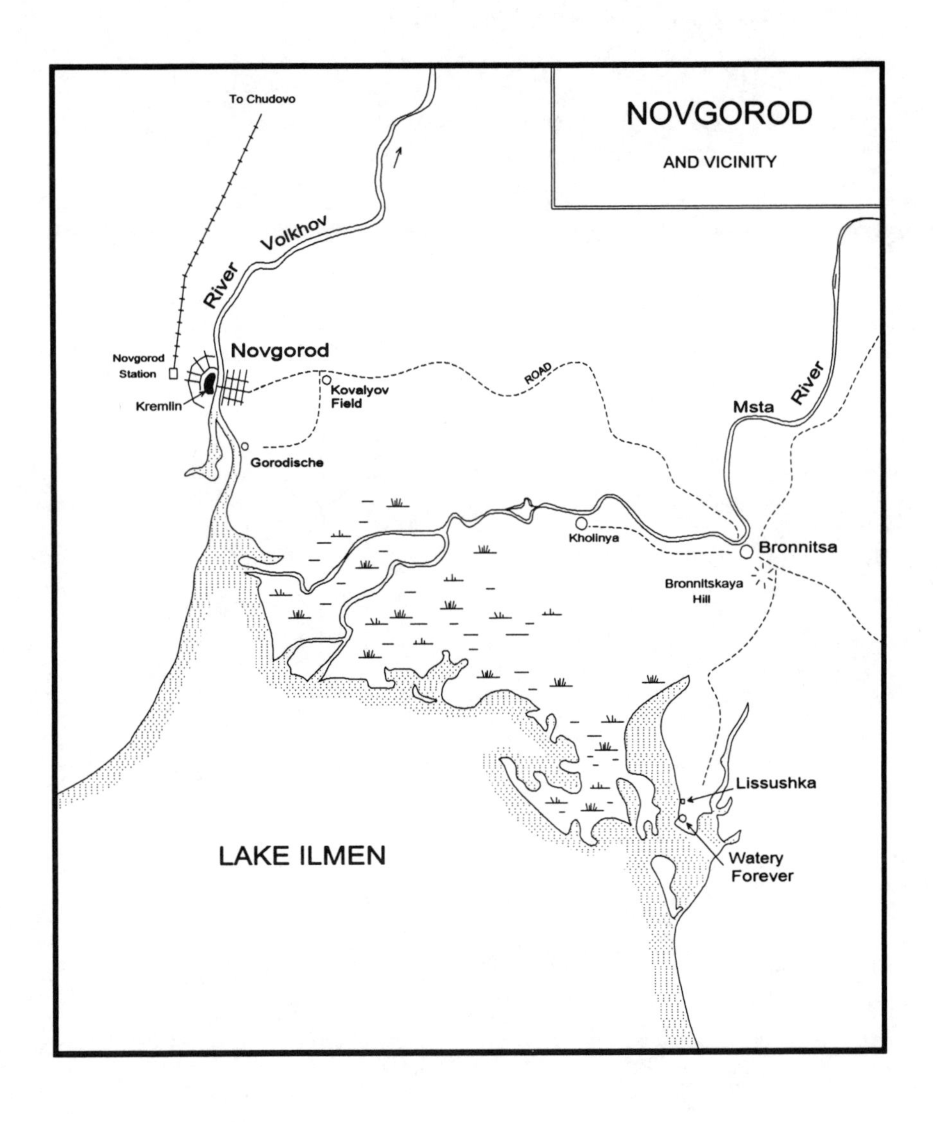
NOVGOROD
AND VICINITY
To Chudovo
River Volkhov
Novgorod
Novgorod Station
Kremlin
ROAD
Kovalyov Field
Gorodische
Msta River
Kholinya
Bronnitsa
Bronnitskaya Hill
Lissushka
Watery Forever
LAKE ILMEN

PROLOGUE

Lost wayfarer lies essayed to death,
Obscured above its stoic caption.
I'm not sure
Where it was taken or by whom,
Or if, at the time, I was even paying attention.
Our gaunt faces spell history
Near starved,
Preying on the last entrails of primitive survival,
Fighting pathos in the early Twentieth Century.
I stand on the edge,
At the far right side of the motley group in the picture:
Hollow face, dark eyes, ermine hat, wire glasses,
Bundled up to my neck in rags
Against that winter's nightmare of disgrace,
My frozen fingers
Grasping a bayonet
Amongst a sea of bayonets, pistols, revolvers,
Picks, hoes, shovels—anything
We could possibly get our hands on
To wage our war with.
Then, our war seemed so damned important.
Now, only this photograph does—
This image of a face not my face yes my face—
Mesmerized in an old reality of bruises.
My body did not survive
(even the bones could not be found).
My name failed to propagate in my own country.
My home was burnt to the ground.
My farm was razed; my wife
Killed herself
In an empty, sunken morning of despair.
Mourning
Is so hard to shake off; sometimes still,
Even after all this time, such sadness envelopes my soul,
Until I realize, remember that it is my soul,
Yes, my soul,
That has survived, my own essence
Haunting me in playful peeks of tantalization,
Cast up from timeless orbs of two dark eyes
Staring back from an antique picture. . . .

CHAPTER ONE

Solo Wind

Conspiracy of whispers. Hastened footprints trampled through the pine boughs. Red armbands, a white banner: premonitions etched in tar; stilted stabs at crude, barely literate Russian. Despite shouts from the peasant elders, admonishing them to stop, the young men are all lining up, sullen-eyed and determined. Unmistakable. There is going to be another demonstration.

Father will be furious this time! Not that he harbors any great love for the Tsar—but they risk his ire for certain, Father warned them: one more demonstration, and he would have their heads!

Through the sliver of fading light, I glimpse the war of shovels and scythes hoisted wrathfully upward, blades in silhouette waving portents of doom high throughout the air. Dipped low behind them in the western sky, bands of yellow melting ruddy orange usher in last rounds of stragglers from the hemp fields, weathered men all shouting curses against the protest as they tramp cakes of mud from twine-wrapped leggings or pairs of mismatched boots. Scuffles of contention then breed havoc in a plague across the yard, shoves and punches erupting at long and bloody last into a wild, dozen-strong fistfight—whereupon women start screaming, their children shrieking; a pale old babushka grapples low to the ground, begging for intercession of the Saints. Two brawny oafs bound out from the granary and attempt in vain to crack an aged wooden flax-break over a third fellow's head. And then some fool sets one of the hayricks afire.

Following upon lead of the last time, a group of loyal stewards attends to speedy dousing of the flames. Undaunted, scores more youths surge past them, all intent upon joining the fist-waving rabble led by a giant of a blond-headed peasant stalking about with the barrel of a firearm poked through blousoned folds of his shirt. "What devil's caught

Rykazian?" the man shouts, pausing to make a scanning search of the farmyard for the second time. "Was all his idea from the start, yes?" he demands, seizing hold of the banner yet again and helping the others hoist it high. "Hey!" he roars on. "Where the hell's Rykazian?"

Then more cursings, shovings, rantings; three drunken plowhands stumble in triumphantly from the southface woods with news of another hayrick somewhere set aflame . . . while all the while above the whole rampant din, one of the peasant elders—blessed with an overpowering, squeaky voice bent on raking shuddering chalkboard tremors over other people's monotones—continues squalling up unto the loft of heaven with nary a pause for breath: "Break it up, I tell ye—break it up! The Count himself is comin', by God's breath, I tell ye! Blessed Virgin save us all, ye rascals, ye blitherin' nitwits! Ye'd best all hurry along, fergit about this politickin' nonsense, an' break it up! . . ."

Brow pressed to the doorjamb, I stare beyond to the crimsoning glare of August evetide sun, its play of color caught in spectacular host against outer horizon's turbulent cloudy-blue depths. But against both beauteous sight and transpiring tumult, I slam shut wary eyes, gulping back a shudder of fear. A torched arrow of pain carves through my ankle as I at last ease closed the door, wincing as light's final ray of hope extinguishes forever, the bolt clanging solidly down into the old iron latch. And then I seize my cap off in a fury and pummel it to the ground—only to stand afterward gawking, grumbling, struggling for balance, and shaking my head in disbelief. "Oh, dear God," I mutter out between a desperate moan and clammy clenching of fists. "Lord's holy shit . . . !"

From the upper gratings, a soft breeze hung with the scent of birch and pine starts shifting through the air, swift hint of dusk's chill gripping cooler each and every eve as the season winds down through the tail end of summer. Yes, my father—the crusty old doctor, the respected landowner, the Count—is due homeward any moment. And if he finds me in here, if he learns what I have been up to, he is going to have *my* head.

Both sidewall panels, ready daytime exits, remain locked shut; have been for over an hour. While the door—the one and only door—lies now within tell-tale sight of everyone. A one-and-only-door behind which stands an apiary milked in a mist of murky twilight, its transformation from haven of familiarity into a pit of terror drastic and complete. Six rows of seven across, forty-two hive body-boxes—each layered full unto overflowing with thousands of bees—bar my way to the back window.

'Fear o' bees is only the demon queen dancin' in the eye o' yer fettered mind,' Pavel said. 'Fer hundreds o' years, yer kinfolk have tended the hives. Is in yer blood, boy! How can ye fear?' And he laughed at me, like he always does, hardly able to believe it—his mirth ringing gently, good-naturedly, a teasing, quipping grandfatherly row soon enough souring, yellowing, festering away into the sarcastic hackles of none other than that no-good, rabble-rousing half-Armenian snake, Volodya Rykazian: 'What's a'matter, Carrot-top? Eh? Lost your nerve? You scaredy-puss, 'fraidy-cat? Eh? Of naught but a few bees? Jesus, and here I been tendin' these hives since I was half your height, ha! Ha, ha, ha, ha, ha . . . !'

Cursing him, I stare through an eye-widened cringe of panic from wall to farthest warehouse wall, telling myself: *They are not going to swarm; you just fastened the last of the lids back on, for Christ's sake!* Despite such laments, cold beads of sweat start seeping into my collar and soaking beneath my armpits, my every breath rattling into labored requiem against the murmuring all-pervasive drone: of a million yellow-jacketed sand pebbles ticking one by one through the sieve of hell's hourglass. Plaintive and desperate, my moans drift softly upward toward the air vents in the ceiling, unheard by the unsung god. For God is always unhearing and unsung—when, no matter what the situation, one has to get out: of the building, your house. Your current ruse, meanest lie. Latest third-story-window-escapade. Your skin. Or whatever else it is.

Shit.

Well?

Inscrutable to the naked eye, tickling my clairvoyant instinct to its inner core, the cue of intuition sings into my ears again—the Phantom of Indifference apparently now quite intent upon proving me quite wrong—by shrugging His shoulders, and musing with tepidity: *So. You propose to spend the rest of your life in there?*

Uh-huh.

With resolution, I fetch up my cap and slap it back on my head, yanking the brim down low and snug to my brow. And—solely for His amusement—I cross myself in good measure.

Then, forcing calmness, I begin a cautious, limping trek along the dirt floor past the rows of hives.

Of course, the infamous legend about Great Uncle Dmitri lends scant little comfort. So far away from home, so lost away in time I was: on school leave with my mother's family, five summers ago in England, when I first heard the whole of it—and amongst all the strangeness, the tale seemed even more spooky! I was only ten and very impressionable, and it was during the summer solstice, when we all made the annual trek to Stonehenge, and the nights danced full with hollow stars. On and on Uncle Ned kept ranting with that bleary gleam in his eye, swearing on the Gospels for it sure to be the truth, about how fifty years ago—close to this time of year, the summer harvest!—my Great Uncle Dmitri was found one day outside the apiary warehouse: face down on the ground, cold dead and stark naked. And covered from head to toe with at least a million—'at least a million!' Uncle Ned swore—raging, swarming bees: 'I say! Drones as big as your fist, boy . . . stingers on the queen bugs long as the length of your thumb . . . aye, your mum saw much of Russian bees . . . wrote me of Dmitri just before she passed on, that she did . . . of course you have never seen them! Not a single hive will your papa let you near, will he? Such monstrous bees could swallow up a mite like you in three quick gulps, that they could . . . well, of course 'tis the bloody truth, boy! By Jove, killer bees is what your papa's kin has been raising back there in Russia, am I telling you. . . .'

An eternity seems to pass away before I grapple at last for the ledge of the back window, crushing it beneath a vise of shaking fingers. Although behind, my father's hordes of honeybees continue humming away in hive after layered box-hive, all settled into combs for the night, entranced with feeding—a sated army of millions surrounded day in and day out by scores of people about whom they could care not a livid whit. *See? God, Uncle Ned, years of foolish nightmares—and for what? Outrageous tavern stories! Lord in Heaven, I could just kill you!*

Letting out a heave of relief, I peel back the screen and push out through the open crag of the window. But as my left foot—always dragging these days—catches a bump on the ledge, I topple out head first, landing with a hurtful, walloping thud in the weeds. The dirt cakes up like flour dough, sticking in clumps to the honey dabs on my fingers.

"Well, well!" booms out a familiar shout closing in fast above my head. "And just lookey what we got here."

Eyes twinkling, his smirk stretched from ear to ear as if ready to call my bluff again at a game of cards, that no-good, rabble-rousing half-Armenian snake—Volodya Rykazian—saunters on up, widely straddles the ground, hooks both thumbs into his coverall pockets, and grins down at me. "Stealin' honeycombs again!" he bellows with a loud guffaw, laughing. "Eh, Sasha?"

"You go and piss in a sty, Volodya," I warn him, shoving up to my feet.

"Hey!" he counters back, "and just who was it first taught you how to fish a hive? Huh? Ha! Oh, and I know what you were doin' in there," he then proclaims, leering, grinning knowingly. "Uh-huh, snuck yourself 'nother sticky little love-token for Katya, eh? Yes, Sekovsky?"

"Blast it, Rykazian! You mind your own business."

"My boy," he drawls out low with emphasis, his grin darkening into a churlish frown, "beehives are my business."

The blow comes swiftly, expertly glanced—hurtling me straight back into the warehouse wall. Stunned, catching sharp splinters in my shirt as I slide past all clumsy effort down to the ground, I glare up at Volodya through the stream of hazy ashen dust, choking, sputtering out: "H-How dare you!"

"Shut up!"

And then—bursting forth from the hidden folds of his dirty smoke-stained coveralls—the barrel of a pistol blazes across my incredulous, cornered horizon of errors.

Volodya points it straight into my face.

And cocks the hammer.

"Rykazian! Have you lost your mind?"

"I said shut up!"

Turning off to the side, he pokes two fingers into his mouth and spews off a piercing whistle. A near stampede unto the death responds, gangs of plowhands dashing with eager shouts and hurried waves from around both corners of the apiary warehouse. Protest banners long cast unto forgotten winds, straight around Volodya they all crowd in a frenzy, hoots and jeers emitted upon sight of me and climbing in a gleeful refrain of enthusiasm accompanied by a banging chorus of picks, hoes, and scythes.

"What's it all about?" cries the giant blond one from earlier, his gun still stuffed like a badge of glory within his white cotton shirt, his eyes scouring me from head to toe with sinister lip-smacking relish.

"Stealin'—honeycombs from the apiary!" roars Volodya.

"Akkh, stealin'!" returns a battle cry intoned.

"Stealin' honeycombs, by God," shouts the giant one above the others yet again. "Let's take the runt then, Boss!" he urges Volodya. "We can string him up in the granary—eh, lads? We should string the little runt up!"

Catching my breath, I stare up at Volodya—his grin vanquished to a past epoch now. Point-blank aim kept straight and true, he holds the gun steady, his dark Armenian eyes bereft of all emotion and starkly holding mine.

So—this is what it comes to after all.

I should have listened. Father warned that something like this could happen. 'Stop your fraternizing with the peasants,' he insisted last summer.

All on account of Bloody Sunday.

Over a year and a half ago, it was. An entire year and a half now since, late on the eve of that fateful January ninth, the shocking news trailed in from Petersburg—impossible, incredible!—that hundreds, perhaps even a thousand demonstrators had been slaughtered by crack Imperial troops that day in Palace Square. While, some say, the Tsar himself stood like a vulture, watching the whole ravenous scene from his balcony window in the Winter Palace above. Never will I forget my father's haunted face, his murmur of: 'And so it begins,' as he slowly raised his snifter, acknowledging my Uncle Petya's worried frown from across the room with a solemn toast.

Father's observation was not without merit; indeed, can perhaps even be claimed prophetic. Some have even begun calling Bloody Sunday the 1905 Revolution!

Since that sorry turn of events, no more bouts of cards with Volodya and his wily friends out in the tool shed during the heady nights of summer. In the past year alone, four demonstrations have disrupted my father's secluded provincial life of farming and keeping bees at our lakeside Novgorod estate. And—carefree harvest-time torching of hayricks entirely aside—ever since the leaders of the Petersburg Workers' Soviets were arrested down to their every last man last December, scores of peasant uprisings have overtaken the provinces, estate houses sometimes burned, whole fields of crops razed unto waste. Only to be followed in the cities by the strikes, the riots. I know. Since late spring, when I last boarded at school in Petersburg, dozens more such disturbances have occurred.

Across this turbulent edge of squares, Volodya and I now stare one another down, two old friends wrenched forever apart, birthrights tearing us headlong away into separate worlds.

"String him up, Boss! Yaaa!" Laughing and hissing, several of the youths keep pushing Volodya toward me, nodding their affirmations with vehemence, like drooling dogs, the scent of blood thickening up in their nostrils.

"Little more than a worthless half-breed, that he is!" one of them taunts from behind. "Yaaa, not even true Russian. The lad is little better than the bastard runt o' the old man an' some English whore."

"Lies!" I shout back, again scrambling upward. "Naught but filthy peasant lies—"

"I told you to shut up, Sekovsky!" Volodya yells, banging me with another fierce, sneering shove down to the ground.

In defiance, I hold his gaze—but my breath begins rasping forth in stinging heaves. Such predicament demands decisive action—soon. I could try to make a run for it. But with this sore ankle, I scarce get around like a young colt; they would be right on me for certain. And I have seen pack hunts.

They are nasty.

Nonetheless, I start plotting a path for flight past various farmyard buildings—the apiary, the tool shed just beyond, then the smokehouse, the dairy barn—until Volodya waves his pistol off through the air, pointing with triumphant glee over all our heads. "Akkh! Forget this thievin' runt!" he bellows out to the plowhands. "We've matters of greater import to attend upon right now, haven't we lads?" With a wink this time, he glances back down at me, grinning.

Undeterred, the gang assails him in protest, pleading: "But, Boss . . . !"

"Or—shall we string the Count's son up for his petty larceny?"

"Yaaa!" they shout out behind him in boisterous, hearty refrain. "String the runt up fer stealin'! Stealin' he did plain and true!" Their grumbling roar wafts up through the air upon a rumble of determined foot-stomping—while I brace back against the wall, stifling a gasp and readying to tear off into a run.

"Akkh, hold your tempers!" Volodya shouts out across the whole lot of them, sarcasm bloating his laughter as he shoves the pistol down into my face once again. But this time, he releases the hammer with an easy flick of his thumb. "It's skin off the Count's nose, not ours," he yells on. "What do we care? After all, we are tolerant men, we are men of heart! And in this case," he shouts on, laughing, "ha!—heart is sorely needed! Now, now, hear me out, lads, hear me out! So this spoiled little runt of the Count's litter took another honeycomb—ha!—and so he did. But, hey!" he thunders out, projecting his voice like a stage echo above all the noisy chaos in the farmyard for everyone in the entire world to hear: "With his sooo-pretty looks, how else can poor, tame little Sasha ever hope to woo the girls?"

The burst of laughter is deafening—swelling into a raucous, knee-slapping roar—followed by the inevitable rash of hoots and screeching whistles as they all start meandering off after Volodya, who winks at me yet again and hollers back: "Akkh, darlin'! Spent your whole summer baskin' out in the sun again, that you did! Now, with all them freckles—I swear to God!—you've grown even more fetchin'! Ha, ha, ha, ha, ha!"

"Where's the milkmaid?" somebody else then yells.

"Yaaa! Hey, wait'll the lake freezes over, wait'll skatin' time comes! Then guess what, lads? We all got te decide which one of 'em gets te be the fairy princess! Ha, ha, ha, ha, ha!"

Doubled over now with heaves of hysteria, the stragglers, most of them the rougher looking ones with bulging muscular arms near twice the size of my own, shuffle off, gloating back with further torrents of insults: "Akkh! Have a go at it, Carrot-top! Little Doe-eyes thinks he's in love! Ply yer wares again with the milkmaid, Doe-eyes! The milkmaid, ha, ha, ha! Akkh! If wares the lad even has! Ha, ha, ha! She loves me, she loves me not, she loves him, ha, ha, ha! Katya, the milkmaid, loves you! . . ."

After the longest aching eternity of my entire life, the last of them finally disappear around the corner of the apiary.

Reddened to a near match with my hairline, my ears gone hotter than flaming ash, I snatch my cap back from the weeds and hoist once more up to my feet. And then slam my fist into the warehouse wall.

In lieu of circumvention, such outburst only magnifies the crush of rage, throbs of agony coursing as if to burst through my every finger. Cursing the Unsung God sitting so smugly up within His unhearing heaven, I throw back my head and dare Him with every last ounce of my will for a bolt of lightning, a quake of boulders—any swift phenomenon of destruction, obliteration, deliverance. But then a banging thud over by the far end of the smokehouse—loud enough above the brawling farmyard roar to distract even my anguished, self-absorbed attention—reminds me that, impossible as it may seem, my lot in life—so long despised, night after lonely, sleepless night; so endlessly bemoaned, day after mirror-glass avoiding day, ever since I was first old enough to fathom the truth about my looks—could be worse.

Fat ledger notebooks tumble off in all directions as Viktor Ilyich Bulyarin—the bespectacled, lovesick inventory clerk—runs the back end of the buckboard rig into the cornerpost of the smokehouse again. For no less than the third time this month.

Once more I flatten back to the wall as yet another group of men rushes heedlessly past me with their shovels. "Bulya, you idiot!" I shout, cupping my hands against the blaring noise. "Can't you ever watch where you are going?"

Scrambling down in an apologetic fluster, Bulya begins hurtling the ledgers with resounding thuds back into the rig. Then, without even bothering to tether the poor horse, he sprints off in a blinding run, charging straight past me, his eyes gone wide with amazement as he gawks at the tumult of chaos continuing to erupt unchecked throughout the farmyard. "Sasha!" he exclaims, wildly waving both arms as if I must be totally oblivious to the whole mounting torrent all around. "It's a demonstration!"

"Bulya, wait!" I shout after him. "Have you seen my father? One of the beekeepers has a pist—"

But before I can finish, Bulya disappears around the corner of the warehouse like a runaway locomotive.

As the shouting escalates unto a fever pitch, everyone else is running in that direction, too. Except for me. Father's threat was exaggerated, but his mandate still fully clear: that—torched hayricks notwithstanding—he would positively attempt to flay me should I ever be caught so much as near any one of these demonstrations.

So dutifully, I slap my cap back on yet again and limp off for the direction of the dairy barn, all the while attempting to shrug off concern about renewed whiffs of smoke trailing through the air. But a growing sense of uneasiness only continues pervading my every thought: *not common and not good, for the peasants to be shouldering so many weapons, setting so many fires. Not good at all.*

But—surely Volodya was merely showing off? . . .

Oh, of course he was. That Armenian mischief-maker is always showing off! And would never have shot me. Who else but Volodya was good enough to teach me how to dig into the hives when I first wanted to? And who else but Volodya, past all the other lads, ofttimes sneaks me some cigarettes, and takes pause to share a smoke and trade an occasional barb or two behind the apiary, the barn, the tool shed whenever I pass? No, those plowhands would never have harmed me, either; they were simply spoiling for a bit of fun. After all, the Feast of the Assumption is only five days past; it is near unto the harvest; everyone always gets a bit giddy at the closing heights of summer. Volodya never would have shot me! Probably he traded for the gun last month at the hawkers' fair, most likely without any live shells.

Always like Volodya: seize the drama of the moment without paying heed to life's practical details. Or indeed to the consequences. For a certainty.

For a certainty, nothing is going to happen! Of course not! My father—Count though he remains—is also a doctor, a tolerant man, and greatly respected in the village, in the towns of Kholinya, Bronnitsa, and in Novgorod-proper itself. Of course, by nature the old lug ever remains haughty and aloof, an attitude only befitting his rank. But in any medical emergency any time of the day or night, Father always goes to any lengths whatsoever to help the people. Ofttimes I have been with him: whether on our way home from the railway station or from town, upon so many journeys have we been diverted; so many times have we been awakened by the frantic poundings of some desperate soul upon our front doors in the middle of the night. Always Father goes, distractedly waving off any and all apologies. The peasants know this. The result has been that, of all the local landowners, we seem to have experienced the least trouble of any with these endless incidents and demonstrations. Grateful souls do not forget.

Cap in hand, at last I lean into the door of the dairy barn, cracking it open halfway—and glance in to find, stacking up the milk pails, a wonder of wonders, vision of visions, stray dark curls peeking out coyly from the knotted nape of her brightly embroidered kerchief, her every step echoing the elegant grace of a prima ballerina at the Bolshoi. My heartbeats begin to thud in wild spurts, all my anxiety about the farmyard disruptions entirely forgotten.

"Katya," I call in softly.

The last pail drops into the stack with a resounding clang. "Sasha Sekovsky?" she cries. "Are ye truly there? Lord help me, where have ye been? Seems like I been waitin' here all day long!"

Scampering through the hay, Katya rushes out, spinning around from the doorway with one hand clasped about the wooden jamb, eyes widened and her smile radiant. "What took ye so long?" she demands, her laughter lilting softly through the air. "I been stallin' fer over an hour. Everybody else has run off to that idiot demonstration!"

"Forgive me, Katya." Dismayed, I feel my ears threatening to heat up murderously as I murmur in explanation: "I had some trouble getting back out from the apiary. Here." Handing over the butcher's paper with the honeycomb wrapped up in it, I swallow hard and stare back down to the ground, taking care with my steps in an effort to prevent her from noticing my limp.

"Oh, ye precious black-eyed thief!" Katya gasps upon sight of the honeycomb. "Oh, no, but look!" she then exclaims, grabbing outward for my hand. "Ye've taken stings all over yer fingers again."

I snatch them quick away from her, protesting: "It is nothing, Katya—no, stop! Don't fret over it all so. I tell you, is naught but a few stings . . . all right, all right! Yes, I promise—I shall fetch some aloe for it later from Father's cabinet."

"As soon as ye git home!" Katya orders with a frown. But as she glances back upward, the frown melts away once again into her ready smile. "Oh! An' I have so much to tell ye, Sasha!" she cries, giggling. "But heaven bless ye by all the Saints fer this delicious comb o' honey! Why, I shall—oh, yes—I shall bake for ye the most splendid cake o' *kulich* ye'll ever taste in yer life."

"Oh, no, Katya—please! I can fetch a honeycomb whenever I want. Use it to make something for your old grandfather."

"But—it is yer Birth Day this day! Is it not?"

My mouth drops; back at her, I stare in complete astonishment.

"Well!" Hands bending to her hips, Katya peers at me like one of the scowling old babushkas always seen tweaking children's ears over in the village. "Ye tell me the truth and don't fudge, now!" she demands. "It is yer Birth Day this day, yes?"

"Well, as a matter of fact, it is. But—"

"So now we are the very same age?"

To my mortification, the lobes of my ears abruptly go ablaze with their hottest fire. "F-Fifteen, yes," I stammer out. But after a moment, no longer can I contain my joyful smile. "Heavens, Katya!" I cry, laughing. "How did you know?"

"Oh, because," Katya answers matter-of-factly, "Natasha said ye read the other day fer Viktor Ilyich."

My voice rasps out thick and dry as straw: *"What?"*

"So me and her, we rode into town yesterday to see Lyudmilla, the Gypsy teller, so Natasha could get her own readin'. An' we couldn't believe what Lyudmilla said about ye! That ye were born this very day on one of the mystic spheres! That ye're one o' the *volkhvi*—"

Oh, shit! . . .

"—one o' the ancient high priests!" Her voice racing on between enthusiastic, breathless gasps, Katya starts tugging at my sleeve as I try, uselessly, to slink away. "An' that ye pray with numbers!" she exclaims, her high pitched drawl carrying on in whining sing-song testament far over the rampant farmyard din. "That ye're an honest te

God augur!" she gasps on. "An' that ye ply the winds with spells from yer number-prayers! Oh! Is it true, Sasha? That ye're a wizard, one o' the 'hidden ones?'"

"No, it is not true!" I shout, once again pushing her eager hand away. "I am not one of your 'ancient high priests!' That is all naught but a spiel of harebrained nonsense!"

"But, Sasha—ye read for Viktor Ilyich! And Lyudmilla said—"

"Never you mind what Lyudmilla said, I am not one of those sorcerers! And that Bulya was hardly supposed to go off and *tell* anybody."

"But when Lyudmilla read the Tarot cards for Natasha, it came up the very same as what ye read the other day fer Viktor Ilyich. Well, Lyudmilla said so! See, Viktor Ilyich gave Natasha the paper where ye wrote down the meanings o' yer cards, and Lyudmilla swore unto her dyin' grave that all her cards was near unto the very same. An' so, do ye know what happened last evetide then, right after supper? Viktor Ilyich finally worked up the nerve te speak te Natasha's father, an' now it is all arranged! Jest as ye foretold, Sasha: now Viktor Ilyich an' Natasha are betrothed!"

"Oh, for God's sake!" I blurt out, rolling my eyes toward the heavens in a quandary mixed between delight and disgust.

"So, it must be true!" Katya raves on, still beaming up at me in worshipful wide-eyed rapture. "Ye are one of the *volkhvi!"*

"No!" I storm back at her, "I am not one of the *volkhvi!* Now, will you stop all this senseless, foolish talk? And that is all Lyudmilla ever does, anyhow: talk, talk, talk! And how can she presume unto knowing such things? I have never even met the nosy old yapping woman—and am not one of those *volkhvi* black magician-heretics!"

Backing down at last, Katya crosses her arms in a pouting huff, her eyes flashing forth blue-hot sparks of indignation. "Then," she murmurs with a knowing nod, "perhaps ye'll admit te bein' a white magician?"

I stare to the ground. And then back up at her, unable to proffer any answer.

"Ye will not deny it?

To the walls, the ground, to the glowing sunset, I search for recourse, my heartbeats pounding to thunder.

"Uh-huh! Jest as Lyudmilla said," Katya declares smugly. "Told me te come out and ask ye te yer face. Said were ye in truth a white magician, ye'd never dare deny it."

"Ha!" I yell back, pointing her down. "That Lyudmilla is naught but a mangy old gossip with her fat nose stuck in too many kitten litters! Humph! Now will you stop hounding me so? Bulya was never supposed to tell anybody, he promised! And now what have I to show for my effort? You! Following me all around the farmyard and blabbing in the loudest voice imaginable to everyone within earshot about these things! Blast it—both you and Natasha should simply leave everything well enough alone from now on!"

Katya responds to my angry tongue-lashing by promptly, bitterly bursting into tears.

"Oh, Katya!" I groan out, "don't! I meant not to make you weep, don't! Please . . . ." Gently, I hurry her back along with me to just inside the doorway of the dairy barn; gallantly, I make her a loan of my handkerchief, although cold frustration once more rends good intention unto a hapless end. Always it ends up like this with Katya, despite the harmony, the sheer romantic poetry of all last winter—when, every chance we could steal away, she and I dashed out upon the lake, flinging one another all over the ice and dancing around through single, sometimes double loops, our synchronization so uncanny, so artistic that even those very same peasants goading me with such mercilessness just moments ago all rose up and cheered! But every time I make the effort to pause and simply talk with this girl, it only ends up always like this: all arguments and awkwardness, near unto nigh impossible!

At last Katya dries her eyes, accepts my profuse apologies, and as the uproar from the demonstration begins encroaching its way back toward the barn, I urge her inside the door with me and push it shut, murmuring in a hushed undertone: "Look, Katya, the truth is that—"

The truth. The problem with the truth is that I simply cannot bring myself to utter the truth's actual incriminating words.

"—the truth, Katya, is that—I am—oh, Lord!" In surrender, I throw up both hands. "The truth is," I go on in a whisper, "that I am simply not at all a good liar."

A deafened silence spreads out between us in spite of more roaring shouts from the farmyard tumult breaking just beyond the barn door. "Then," Katya whispers back, "it is true. Ye are one o' them white magicians. One o' the *volkhvi.*"

I fix my gaze downward into flaxen depths of the straw, murmuring: "What else did Lyudmilla tell you?"

"That ye cast spells with numbers and songs on the wind."

"That is wrong! I never 'cast spells.' Nor do I 'pray' with numbers. I only ascribe to their study, to contemplation. My beliefs include an acknowledgment of the vastness of numbers and sound, and assent to the power of their dual forces within the universe. Casting spells and abusing power is only the way of the black sorcerers—like those beady-eyed shamans from the *Khlysty*, the stragglers from the mutilation cults ofttimes said to be wandering the hills south of the lake. He who cloaks himself in truth's mantle forever abhors their ways—never, never forget that!"

"How does one pray with sound?" Katya inquires, staring at me solemnly.

In response, I manage a wry smile and pull both arms upward to my right, fingers fluttering out as if pressing a row of keys.

"Oh, but o' course!" she gasps with delight, "yer flute! Why, some o' the village lads swear ye must be half-mad, playin' the way ye do for so many endless hours. But why, Sasha? If ye cannot, as ye have told me, cast spells? What good is studyin' numbers, playin' sounds if ye can cast no spells with yer magical power?"

"The voices of the numbers must provide direction and comfort of and within themselves, and nothing more. But occasionally, one may attempt to help other seekers along the way. That is why I read the cards for Viktor Ilyich."

As Katya looks at a complete loss, I go on, explaining: "Every one of the cards in the Tarot deck corresponds to the meaning of a particular number."

"Oh."

"Katya, have you and Natasha told others of your friends about these things Lyudmilla said?"

With a sharp intake of breath, Katya cowers away from me once more, hiding her face within her hands. "Now ye will be angry with me all over again, Sasha!" she cries, her voice muffled through trembling fingers.

"Katya, no! I am not angry with you. Truly, honestly, sweetheart, I am not. I am angry," I go on with a sigh, "because lynchings are still not entirely uncommon in these parts. Do you understand? Lynchings of upstarts like me, those who shun the Orthodox ways, those who are known to be involved in some of the things that I do."

"Oh, no—Lord in Heaven, Sasha! I meant ye no harm."

"I know."

Blue eyes widened with spears of regret, Katya presses her hand upon my chest—and lets forth another gasp, her fingers curling around the amethyst crystal hidden beneath the placket of my shirt.

"This is a talisman?"

When I stare away, she goes on: "Lyudmilla said many of the *volkhvi* ofttimes wear one! Does it have magical powers?"

Once again I sigh, wondering indeed if the girl has grasped any part of my carefully worded explanation. "No, it does not possess magical properties!" I cry in exasperation. "And I am telling you, Katya, for the final time: I do not cast spells! I only wear this stone around my neck because it is a keepsake. The crystal once belonged, God rest her soul, to my mother."

"Oh, yes. I am sorry. Never casts spells does he, the white sorcerer." This Katya murmurs more to herself than to me, her eyes gone distant and dreamy and set aloft on faraway worlds.

"Look," I whisper on, "I must hurry back and tell my father—one of the beekeepers has a—"

But my voice chokes to a halt as, lips curling upward in a mischievous smile, Katya starts inching her hand teasingly up my chest along the links of the crystal's hidden chain. With a gentle eagerness, she smooths her cool fingers against my hotly flushed face.

"Happy Birth Day," she murmurs.

And kisses me: shy and soft and just like the first time.

The only other time.

She draws away, and I watch her lashes flutter, two black fans shielding the most precious jewels of cosmic wonder as she nestles her head in against my shoulder. My fingers, trembling but somehow still heedless of my rising inner panic, begin winding themselves beneath her kerchief and into the luxuriant bound-up braids of her hair. Rasping forth upon the outermost verge of self-control, a voice that seems scarce my own soon murmurs low against her ear: "Can we do that again?"

"Oh, yes!"

Katya lets me kiss her, another soft brush of my trembling against her trembling. She lets me kiss her again, allowing my arms to wrap fully around her this time—while I press closer and urge in a little firmer, her mouth opening beneath mine with just the slightest pause of yielding and anticipation. As her arms slide upward around my neck at last, I smooth my cheek against hers, slamming shut my eyes and heaving in the heady rose-water fragrance of her hair, gulps of breath hacking in ferocious little pops all the way down my throat. "Katya,"

I moan out, my voice gone hoarse and prickly as a coat of wool. "Oh, blessed *Katya . . . .*"

And then, half-crazed with yearning, I seize her: pin her flat back against the dairy barn door, my hands clamped around her waist and sliding slowly upward on each side for the springy touch of her breasts; my knee shoved in between both of hers as calico ruffles and white petticoats billow up all around my legs; my mouth ramming into hers, dividing her lips outward, piloting mine inward, my tongue slashing across her teeth like a wave upon the wind, my mind spinning past every care and thought of reason in the world unto a whirling, blurry chasm of haze . . . *oh, God! I am so hard! And she is so soft. . . .*

"Nooo!" sears the scream into my ear. "Stop it—unhand me, ye moron!" Punching away, she manages to latch onto the rim of a stray milk pail, slamming it with a cry of vengeance flat into my wrist.

"Oww!" Doubling over, I clamp my hand around my arm and let her go—and then attempt to shield away continued brunts from the pail, my ears cringing beneath her high-pitched shrieks of outrage. "Ye sick-minded, double-crossin' cad!" she wails out at the top of her lungs. "I thought ye were respectable, mannered, an' proper. But, no! Ye're naught but scum, jest like all the others! Jest what do ye think I am, Sasha Sekovsky, ye devil, ye greedy, leechin' monster? Ye think me naught but a—*a romp*, do ye? A wanton, one o' the little strumpet tarts from that horrid tavernhouse in town? Is that all ye think I am?"

"No! Of course not, and will you stop hitting me?" Diving for it, I wrench the milk pail away from her grasp and heave it with a wood-splintering thud into the far barn wall.

"Well, then—ye can take this, too!" Katya yells, snatching the honeycomb out from her pocket and wrathfully smashing it down into the dirt.

"What did I do?" I shout back, throwing up both hands before her in a confused fluster. "You said I could kiss you! Is not as if I neglected to ask permission."

"Kiss!" Past her stare of horror, Katya's gaze shifts downward, alighting upon the bulge stretching the fly of my trousers. "The kind o' kiss *ye* happen te want starts with a betrothal, ye filthy, hot-blooded leech!" she declares, pointing. "I don't care whether ye be landed, titled, uppity Count's son or no—nobody tries such hanky-panky business with the likes o' me!"

In emphasis of her point, another milk pail whizzes bare inches past my nose, and I duck for cover, landing in a mound of hay—where I attempt to shield my head and my embarrassing display of passion alternately with either hand. "Katya, stop throwing all the pails, for God's sake!" I yell up at her. "I was scarce attempting to force myself upon you, I promise, for love of the Saints! And I meant not to insult you, nor—"

"Oh! Indeed!" And then she starts in with a further ranting tirade of accusations—while I shove up to my feet and snatch out a hoe from the side rack just in time to begin deflecting the literal wall of angry pails that starts crashing in upon me from every direction.

"I was not going to force you!" I shout back. "I would never, ever contemplate such a thing! You are the one who has been batting eyes, following me around every day with your friend Natasha and teasing me to no end! Don't you know you have both been driving me half-mad all summer long? Oww! And will you stop throwing all these pails at me?"

"No!" Unconvinced, the girl seizes several more, hurling them nonstop—while, past guilty affirmations clanking steadily one atop another within as well as without, all I can recall for some reason are the words of Volodya, something I heard him whispering to one of his chums last week when I was nosing around the wall on the south side of the apiary: 'Akkh! Men, women: what the hell's the use sometimes? Never goin' to meet each other halfway, to anybody's likin'! Women: think they got to have themselves a knight in shinin' armor! And men, ha! All we ever want in the end is a good juicy whore. . . .'

I suppose Volodya was right about what I want.

And Katya is perhaps more than justified in branding me a cad. Indeed, how many nights have I lain tormented by her image, hour after hour, all the way until first breath of the morn's blue dawn? How many nights have I lain throbbing, hurting, near set unto bursting out of my skin's seams; how many times have I lain sweating and moaning beneath my twisted sheets, driven past every reasonable bound of my senses into acts of gasping, solitary desperation—while praying that Father has not heard the slamming of the headboard into the wall yet another time again? Always the devil of lust rages, unchecked, unquenched, unsatiated; blacker and blacker ever it rages, always despite each next desperate, tearful prayer for absolution—coarse, fleshly desire hounding me far into the depths of so many bitter, torridly sleepless nights—cold curse on a lifetime of achings—hot pulse on a thousand triggers—wicked, sinful lecher that I am ever clamoring out through my every pore in shameful, merciless volleys of shots. . . .

Shots!

Her hand grasping another pail, both of mine still clamped upon the hoe, Katya and I stare at one another through a lull of gaping silence, all life cut from our argument by the quick snap of reality's noose. From outside, the click-a-tat staccato again sounds through the stillborn air.

Followed by roaring prelude—and then an avalanche of screaming.

"Lord in His Heaven!" Katya cries, pail-handle slipping from her grasp. "What was it? I thought I heard—"

"No!" I shout, dropping the hoe. "Oh, dear God!" Tearing past her, I bound limping for the door, my words—for a few brief seconds—lapsing instinctively back into frantic quavers of English: "Lord Jesus help us—I knew it, I simply *knew* it: the demonstration! Father—Volodya—*the pistol!"*

* * *

Bereft of the clattering buckboard rig, Bulya seems lost in the sea of faces, but I stumble into him at the outer fringe of the crowd. "Hold your tongue!" he bellows, wrenching me fast to his side through a mass of elbows, his explanations scarce audible above the torrent of screaming and commotion. "What do you mean," I shout back, "go not a step farther? What happened?"

"Sasha! Will you just hold your—"

"I will have silence!" My father's voice roars out above all heads, and I catch sight of his revolver shoved up into the air. Two more shots ring out, hollow thunderbolts of warning crashing off into the crimson-colored sky.

A hush of awe blankets over the crowd within the same moment that I at last glimpse the object of the frantic women's screams. Sprawled out upon the ground before the gang of youths still clutching shovels, picks, scythes, and their tar-laced banner rests the body of the blond-headed giant—his chest covered in blood from a fatal wound, his gun resting inches away from his open, unmoving palm.

And beside the body stands Volodya, his whole darkened countenance etched in fear—but his pistol, gripped with both hands, aimed straight into the face of the angry lone horseman in the yard.

My father.

Whose head is bare, his hair mussed, thick white tufts wafting out lazily through the breeze. To me, his expression is only far too painfully familiar: the broad, handsome face reddened near to a pulp, dark eyes gone ablaze with fury, his jaw set with grim resolution as he struggles to contain his rage.

"I wonder which of us is quicker, Vladimir Denisovich," Father states to Volodya, his rich baritone booming out across the farmyard in a tone of trenchant calmness. "My weapon," he observes dryly, "is yet cast unto the air; yours remains aimed without question at its target. As you can see by the fate of your friend on the ground, only a fool judges a man's dexterity by his age. So—just how game are you today? A little roulette? You wish to risk it? Or no?"

I shove away from Bulya, but he seizes me back, clapping his hand over my mouth—and my scream is caught only unto throes of silence, silence.

"All weapons to the ground, everything! Now!" Father roars, his gaze still locked unceasingly upon Volodya, his knuckles whitening upon the grip of his revolver yet held aloft within the air.

The moment stands fixed in a horrible vise of indecision, stark challenge to the ticking straits of time as the peasants, unmoving—some with faces grimacing in anger, others biding time's fortune with merely wary and watchful glances—stare back at their infuriated landlord. But the pause is brief enough; as if the yard was suddenly bathed in a fan of cool water, the tight hinge of tension dispels as, from somewhere in the back, the first shovel goes down. Then, one by one, all the farm implements begin going down. The banner, wrinkling its pitiful misspelled demand of *STOP TAX, GEEVE LAND* into an obedient flutter of oblivion, is brought back down. At last Volodya remains the only one left standing in defiance.

"Well?" Father demands.

After letting forth a stream of muffled curses, Volodya finally smashes his weapon away into the dirt. Pavel, the overseer, and several other of the stewards jump for him, and in response to Father's angry nod, they lead him off toward the row of rotting posts from the fence once used to separate the apiary from the dirt road winding off toward the nearby village.

All remaining rumblings in the crowd still beneath a renewed murmur. The young men involved in the demonstration start to slink off toward their kinfolk gathered near the walls of the various farm buildings, and the crowd at last breaks up, everyone shying away from the open yard and strewn-out collection of tools, the body, and the banner.

It is only when Father dismounts, revolver still dangling in his hand as if in silent warning to everyone, that I catch sight of the blood—a veritable crimson icing trickling down his left arm and seeping into rivulets of honey stained upon the sleeve of his cotton work jacket. "Oh, my God!" I gasp out. "Papa!"

"Sasha, no!" Bulya orders, attempting a desperate clinch. "No, wait—"

But he cannot pin me back this time; arms flailing with all my strength, I tear through the crowd, shoving against people, knocking them into one another in my attempt to outwit Bulya as he continues latching out for me from behind.

"Now, I regret," announces Father, "the increase in the blasted taxes." Appearing entirely oblivious to the wound, he stoops and retrieves his cap from the ground, dusting it off against his knee before slapping it back onto his head. His face then assumes an attitude of tightened patience, his voice rattling off his recitation from memory as he begins to explain—exactly as during all the previous demonstrations earlier this year—about his lack of control over taxation rates, which of course involve no decision of his, as such are set by decrees from none other than the Tsar in Petersburg.

"Blast it, let me go!" I hiss at Bulya, spearing my elbows back into his ribs. "Can't you see he is hurt?"

"No! His Honor told me that no matter what happened, to keep you back."

Father's monologue breaks off abruptly, his dissertation interrupted amidst a sentence upon his spying of the two of us jostling with one another at the edge of the crowd. "Sasha," he murmurs in a drastically lowered tone, "do not concern yourself with it just now. It is only grazed."

"But—"

"Stay with Bulya. Move back over by the west wall of the apiary."

"But, Father!"

"Sasha! As of yet, I am the only target. Do you understand?"

I stare at him, disbelieving my ears—having heard naught but English.

And then, as if nothing at all is amiss, Father turns again to the attentive crowd and continues his droning speech in Russian.

English! Inwardly, I confirm every precious word of his last two sentences to myself yet once again. *And in front of all of them!* But this situation cannot have gotten so out of hand! Matters are again coming under control. These people all appear positively docile! But—I know I did not mishear his last words, definitely spoken in English!

Our normal language of conversation. Always. Ever since I can remember, my first words as a child being those he insisted I be taught in proper English. Russian he included not much later, of course, as a local necessity—along with French and some Italian, both obligatory for school and reading. Of late, though, to multilingualism has attached one rule fast and resolute: English only in the house, or when within close proximity to one another; never again in front of the peasants—not anymore. 'Oh, the devil with your oafish friends, your all-night card games,' Father admonished me over a year ago. 'I tell you, boy, for your own good: the peasants are not to be trusted, these are dangerous times, this Bloody Sunday was much more than another mere isolated revolutionary incident. From this time forward, you and I must blend in, become as agrarian, as Russian as possible. I know this is difficult for you, Sasha, to stifle away the language of your mother's heritage, upon which your papa has always rhetorically insisted. Trust my judgment, please! From this time forward, the only circumstance ever warranting some breach of this pact between us is if the peasants absolutely must not understand—only if either of us is in some type of danger. So, will you please stop trying to impress your friends with fancy books in Latin letters, and do as I ask?'

I did as he asked.

With an obedient nod, I do as he asks now, and along with Bulya, who continues hovering at my side like an anxious mother hen, I back off toward the west wall of the apiary.

"Now." Rapidly pulling to a conclusion his discourse to the crowd about the taxes, Father retrieves a ratty-edged ream of folded papers from the pocket of his jacket. "This," he announces, waving the pages outward on a heightened gust of evening wind, "with the updates appended chronologically in order of their decree, is the Emancipation Proclamation. . . ."

And he starts reading out excerpts about the rights to land negotiations, much of his words again recited straight from his memory as well as from mine as he reminds the peasants—many of whom begin shunning his gaze with obvious pangs of guilt—about numerous past examples of generous leasehold grantings from our lands.

Sighing, I begin scanning over faces in the crowd. Although pockets of stragglers, mostly women, start wandering off to stoke up stoves for evening meals, a throng yet boasted in the dozens strong remains clustered around fringes of the yard. Near all young and old alike hail from the tiny southshore village known affectionately as 'Watery Forever' by virtue of its many surrounding bogs and marshy quagmires. Amongst the rows of faces, I glimpse Katya's, her eyes cast demurely downward, her shoulders nestled beneath the protective wing of her grandfather's arm. Closely behind them, the village Orthodox priest hovers like a stalwart reed of ancient tradition, waves of his graying beard caught gently to the wind, folds of his immaculate white cassock flanked in sharp contrast to the profusion of dark homespun fabrics worn by remaining penitents. Their faces hung with grim humility, many of the elderly people continue crossing themselves while nodding back reverent salutations toward the priest, although a fair amount of attendant sons and grandsons maintain growling, surly expressions. But most particularly interesting to note is the reaction of the majority of the women—whose eyes with few exceptions remain riveted upon my father.

Not, I know from long experience, on account of even one of his words. Instead, as the speech slowly rambles on, near unto every female, young and old, continues staring dreamily at my father's expressive face. For a handsome devil the man ever has been—and so remains now, yet proud of carriage and lacking obvious wrinkles, stray streaks of ruddy auburn evincing a youthful robustness, laced so they still are through heavy whitened side whiskers betraying not near the advent of his whole seventy-four years. Never does it fail to amuse me how the poor man must always fend off the women in droves, even at his age. Small matter whether they be daughters of the local peasantry, of neighboring landowners, or even—on those rare occasions when he does venture northward—of the aristocracy in Petersburg.

But for years, my father has made his position of disinterest quite clear. He will not marry again, ever; he has said so, and I have seen him write it with tired impatience numerous times. Because forever, he will love only one woman: Lady Melissa Devon-Tyler.

Whom, I realize—considering that today is my Birth Day—I had best forget in entirety. Best, actually, for me to start praying to all the Saints: that Father himself does not perchance remember.

Business, of course, affords swift tonic for bygone woes. "Bulya," I whisper, nudging him, "why was Father so late in returning this afternoon?"

"Kolinsky's farm. Forty versts 'round the lake. Remember? The hive sale."

Oh, of course. Kolinsky's overseer wanted to make appropriations to take farther south, or so I was told when I helped Bulya ready the books for it. To sell on commission, which makes him some money and saves Father, or more likely, Pavel, travel time into more remote areas where fewer of the railroads run.

"Thirty-five hives!" Bulya whispers with enthusiasm. "Can you imagine? Five years since we've closed a sale this big."

I nod mutely as he fills in ledger details regarding the sale. Thirty-five hives probably involved the entire afternoon for bargaining and winding up any remaining business. Father has been gone since early this morn. And who would be more privy to such information than a beekeeper? Naught but the perfect opportunity for Volodya and his group of plowhands to rile up a bunch of peasants into starting another demonstration.

"From this point on, I want no more disturbances on my lands!" Father blares on. "We are attempting to run a farming operation here. We have twenty, twenty-five days perhaps, until the first frost. Can't you people understand that if we interrupt work for even one more afternoon this season, it could threaten the entire harvest? Don't you remember, near unto two decades ago during the early nineties, the bounding depths of the starvation? Or are your memories that short?"

The crowd responds to this admonition with pious, nodding heads and murmurs of condescension. I note scores of peasant youths, many of them familiar faces from Volodya's earlier convergent gang, sulking under upbraiding glares from their own fathers.

"Now, the final matter," Father goes on with a long sigh, "is that I will not tolerate the illegal possession of firearms on my lands. And today I intend to set an example to once and for all make this completely understood."

Nodding toward Pavel and the stewards, who with some effort continue restraining Volodya, he says: "Tie him up to the fence posts." Then, his revolver remaining yet unholstered, Father hurries from the center of the yard with long purposeful strides as another expectant hush filters out over the crowd.

"Thirty lashes," he orders out loudly just upon reaching my side.

My mouth drops. From Bulya to Father, I stare—once, twice, and then back again—certain that I could not possibly have heard correctly. But the set of Father's jaw remains grim and resolute, unequivocally confirming his intention. And across the yard, Pavel—gentle grandfather of a growing horde of gleefully screaming grandchildren; minstrel troubadour of accordion serenades during the holiday festivities of Christmastide, of *Maslenitsa*, and the joyous Easter Season; Pavel the ready accompanist whenever large groups of us gather together to skate out upon the lake—dark and stony-eyed, his expression as grimly determined as Father's, Pavel begins unraveling, to my horror, one of the thickest bullwhips.

"My God!" I gasp, whirling back upon Father. "Thirty lashes? *Flogging?* Father, have you lost your senses?"

His finger—first warning count against me, stunned adversary in his four-cornered ring—shoots upward.

"Father, please!"

Swift as a bullet, his arm lashes outward, banging my head back against the warehouse wall, his fingers clutched about my collar in a strangling throat-hold. "From you," he whispers—again in English, his mouth looming a bare hair's sliver away from mine, "I will tolerate not another single word. Understood?"

I stare at him through a seeping wave of horror, cringing away from the odor of brandy laced all over his breath.

"Understood?"

Only when I lower my eyes does he at last release his hold on my throat. But calling over to Pavel, he shouts: "All right, make it twenty lashes, then! But Lord, be quick about it, man! The sun's near gone, for devil's sake."

The blows begin instantly: *one.*

Two, three . . . .

Arms strung out tautly between two of the fence posts, Volodya quivers in anguish as the blood starts oozing in glistening wet stripes across his bare back. As never before, he starts earning my most profound admiration. Because he makes not a sound of acquiescence—not a single, solitary sound.

Four . . . five . . . six . . . .

One would think these peasants gathered in the yard would be outraged. For hundreds of years the common people have struggled to regain their rights, ever since Kievan times when serfs first became bound to their lands. But in lieu of any protests, heightened murmurs and spews of barely contained laughter follow upon each gruesome slash of the whip—some of the men pointing, others shaking their heads with guffaws and gloated bellows as flasks of vodka start making the rounds despite hardened stares of the old babushkas. Piercing through dusky embers of the twilight, countless children's screams spill forth with eager delight in response to this unexpected, graphic dose of entertainment. Beside me, Bulya checks his pocket watch with a sigh of boredom and mumbles something about the chickens having broken loose again. Several women, toddlers tugging joyfully at their long skirts, hurry off toward the profusion of clucking noises emanating from the direction of the coophouse.

Nine . . . ten . . . eleven . . . .

Lord God have mercy! I am the one who earlier stared down the barrel of the gun; later saw that same gun pointed at my own father! Yet am I the only one who gives a damn at all about what they are doing to Volodya?

I want not to look, nor to watch. But I must.

Because my reaction to this hideous spectacle is being scrupulously noted. Swallowing hard against the gritty knot welling up in my throat, I neither turn, nor avert my eyes; instead, keep my stare fixated upon Volodya and the whip and the blood. Because I will not allow him the satisfaction!

Fourteen, fifteen . . . .

"Humph!" Rudely knocking against my shoulder, Father brushes past with a satisfied grunt. To Bulya, he says: "Both of you follow behind. I want today's sale recorded on the cash books, now—before either of you locks out for the day. Understood?"

"Yes, Your Honor—consider it done!" Bulya snatches at my numbed arm, urging: "Sasha, come."

By the time we round up the rig, and Father mounts his horse, the noise from the whip abates at last. I have been keeping count. Bless his dear old heart, Pavel had the gumption to stop at eighteen.

It is only at the frazzled end of hellfire's rope that bare whimpers at last escape Volodya's iron will—to be followed by shudders of agony coursing across every last reach of the farmyard in plaintive, gasping sobs.

The stewards drag him away. The muddied banner is rent to shreds as a small group of icon-waving mourners and several men with shovels converge upon the body of the hapless blond giant. Armloads of farm implements strewn all about the yard are quickly gathered up and brought to the sheds as everyone else starts heading off toward pillars of chimney smoke wafting up from village huts in the distance. Once more life's basic truth prevails, the prospect of food in one's belly assuming its rightful hedge of importance over the afternoon's political nonsense and paltry failed demonstration.

As Father charges off through the woods just far enough ahead to be out of earshot of our whispers, Bulya takes full advantage of my captive attention and begins chattering on without pause about his betrothal to Natasha and the supposed 'miracle' of the Tarot reading. But despite the livid tongue-lashing I have been storing up for him in return for yapping about this to everyone, I cannot respond any further than with grunts or wary wide-eyed nods.

Up ahead, the Sekovsky estate house soon looms into view before us through a lush frame of feathered pines.

Such an idyllic scene: music of the ever-temperate muses, a steady piccolo sonata trickles away day in, day out past heathery waving cattails dotting the nearby lakeshore. Heady with the scent of roasted duckling, the pungent tang of woodsmoke rolls upward, bidding welcome from double kitchen chimneys towering above two spacious stories wrapped in ruddy varnished pine boards. Above the broad, spotlessly polished cathedral windows, fading glimmers of day's last light shine upward in a fan of fleeting prism lines upon the grooved wooden spire of the house's solitary cupola. Lissushka, he has named this place, our home.

After my mother.

With its stately architectural magnificence and delightful proximity to the lake and the woods, the beauty of this place—Lissushka on Ilmen near the village of Watery Forever, its walls modeled with exacting interpretive finesse upon wooden outlays of the famous log churches on the northward isle of Kizhi—inspires lavish compliments from everyone who ever visits here.

Little do they know about the secrets. And the lies.

It is all very simple: Vliny, my father's trusted man-servant for the past fifty years, and Marnya, his wife, and her daughters, who help run the household, live in separate comfortable quarters downstairs past the woodroom. Upstairs, facing the eastern range of the woods, my room lies across the hall from Father's study, his haven boasting peaceful, quiescent view of the lake—where he works, eats, and sleeps still on the divan that has never been replaced in all of these fifteen years. Because no one is allowed into the locked room at the opposite end of the hall. No one. Ever.

That is the room that belongs to her. The ghost.

Reckoning hails justice, its time swinging fast on the approach. Up ahead, Father rides with such a steadied sense of ease upon his Arabian mare. One would think he had just arisen early in the morn, refreshed and wide awake. Truly amazing it is how, when he succumbs to what must be his only, and yet greatest weakness, scarce a soul on earth can ever tell.

Even I can rarely ever tell. I could not tell at all—not until he moved up to my face, his breath searing into mine so closely that it could not help but reveal why he was so insistent about the flogging.

Because he had been drinking.

My attempts at reassurance only result in frantic jumbles of words tripping one after another upon themselves within my head: *Father is a tolerant man! A generous man! A benevolent man!*

Generally.

He is a doctor! And cares deeply for the people—for all people! He would never harm a soul!

Usually.

Generally and usually, such attributes describe the character of my father, Count Mikhail Sergeyevich Sekovsky, down to its stoic, predictable core.

Except when he drinks.

And there is only one reason—only one reason in the ill-fated, languishing scroll of all earth's time—that my father ever drinks.

Me.

* * *

The grandfather clock out in the hallway clock strikes nine.

It strikes ten.

Dutifully, I have been attempting to squeeze in another hour of practice. But as I huddle upon the tufted cushion spread across the window seat in my room, my flute lying carelessly within my arms, I realize that I have only been staring, for how long I cannot recall, at engraved letterings of the words *Boehm & Mendler* etched upon the instrument's silver corepiece. My mind's visions, however, retain naught of fleeting woodwind legacies, nor of the arrays of musical notations dotting numerous stacks of orchestrations lying scattered about my feet. Instead, the spectacle conducted earlier out in the farmyard, blurred through a mounting vortex of anger, continues burning through my every thought—juxtaposed upon memories of two summers ago. When I learned the truth about love.

Love: so transitional, so illusional. Love for oneself, for one's country, one's heritage, for a song, a dream. Love of a man for a woman. Love of a father for his son.

Two summers ago, I learned the truth about love at four o'clock in the morning during one of the humid, sleepless nights of early August. Always had I been an extremely pudgy child—'my dumpling' Marnya ofttimes still calls me. Never very tall, during those last seven months of my twelfth year, I had grown a full five inches, sprouting out thin as a reed whistle, and I was ravenous, constantly. And so again at four o'clock in the morning, I had stolen off downstairs into the kitchen, clad in naught but a dressing gown, where I was stuffing myself with black bread, pickled mushrooms, and cold potatoes left over from our supper of the previous eve. That spring at May's boarding school in Petersburg, I had allowed my hair to grow out long past my ears—the better, so I had reasoned, to hide the haunting, hollow face always staring back at me from the dormitory mirror-glass. As I had shunned the barber's shears all summer long as well, by August the unruly mop had grown near unto my shoulders, dark and straight as a wreath of crimson flax—long strands of it hanging, to my continued irritation, in vision's way as I crouched over the book from which I could not tear away my eyes for even one bloody second.

Victorian Platitudes it was named—or some other such mawkishly deceptive title as I can scarce recall now, having long since misplaced it—but I remember the book. My cousin, near two years my senior, had procured it during his latest swing through Paris that summer. Only Nikolai—my dear cousin never more than a room away from his prized Eighteenth Century Guarnerius violin, his own locks sun-washed so blond and lanky-fine, they sorely tempt me like a girl's, so much I sometimes yearn to reach out and caress my fingers through those pale strands . . . yes, only Nikolai Zhelanov, rakish devil that he is, could ever happen upon such a gem! Two months earlier in Petersburg, I had passed with flying colors the little initiation test he had arranged: twenty paces. Loaded Brownings. We shot each other's cuff links off. At last willing to take me further into his brotherly confidence, he began to relate the first of what since then has become only one of the many stories of his numerous exploits through whorehouses both in Europe and in Petersburg. While I stared at him in wide-eyed, gasping shock, he thrust the book into the pocket of my jacket, stressing pointedly: 'Never show Uncle Misha or Maman, ever!' But then, laughter husky and titillating beneath his breath, he whispered: 'High time you acquired what we call a 'real' education, little Sasha!'

Education, indeed! The book detailed incident after scathing sexual incident, culminating in a panoramic forty-page-long Dionysian orgy, with atrocities recounted of such a bizarre nature that I had never imagined such feats to actually be possible: not only were scenes graphically depicted of men bedding women, but of women bedding women and men bedding men!

Fascinated and horrified, in the early hours of that summer morn, I was tearing through the book for the second time.

A guffaw from somewhere far across the familiar reaches of the walls jolted abrupt clamors of reality through my transfixed stupor. Father was up. As the boards creaked over my head in the kitchen ceiling, I could hear his steps up above in the water closet.

While stowing the food back into the pantry, I felt suddenly overcome with cold—for two hours had I been downstairs, reading under mounting shivers of perspiration. From a drawer, I fetched one of Marnya's old crocheted shawls and draped it about my shoulders, stuffing the book beneath my arm before making for the stairs.

For a certainty, I thought I had waited long enough for Father to return to bed. But at the top of the stairwell, before I could even catch my breath, he materialized like a ghost through a haze of shadows from the open doorway of the guestroom—standing there unmoving, his face aghast, his eyes gone wild as a madman's, as if he had just seen some vision come straight out of hell.

'Lissa!' he then rasped out.

I froze—at first scarce fathoming what he had said, what it meant. And then a piercing shudder chilled down my spine as I remembered that 'Lissa' was the name he had once called my mother.

'Lissa, it truly is you!'

Paralyzed, I began shaking my head in profuse denial, and gripped the shawl more tightly about my shoulders—only to realize far too late that that was precisely what a woman would do!

'Lissa, my darling—wait! Don't back away from me! Lissa . . .!'

Furious protests stuck in my throat, and the book toppled to the floor unheeded as he lunged for me, ripping the shawl away, his voice moaning out: 'Lissa, my God, my God!' I lashed back fiercely, punching with both fists, but he was far too strong and wrenched me back into his arms, his murmurs pouring forth unchecked between gasps of joyous laughter: 'Oh, little Lissa! My one and only precious, forever beloved little Lissa! How long have I waited, how long have I loved you—Lissa, bless God, bless God!' Breath searing agony and passion against my earlobes, his hot kisses started in upon my neck—my cold, terrified neck which never in all my life had colored beneath any such kind of kiss from anyone! Like brands of fire, his lips began inching their way upward along my throat—until I finally struggled partway free of his iron grasp, screaming out like a netherworld banshee into the bowels of the blackened night: *'Papa, nooo!'*

It awakened the entire household. Within seconds, candle tapers appeared, along with a couple of handheld lamps, at the foot of the staircase. Vliny, Marnya, her daughters, the elder daughter's husband—the French cook Vliny had brought in on a whim that summer—everyone rushed in from the servants' quarters at the back end of the house. Their fear was obvious and justified: that there was a fire, for long centuries the primordial bane of countless Russian wooden structures. But instead, the whole group only found itself staring in dumb amazement as Father and I gaped at each other in horror from opposite ends of the upstairs hall.

He dismissed them momentarily after making some offhanded explanation, and slammed his study door shut with such a torrent of force that it near blasted the hinges off.

I locked myself into the water closet and was sick until dawn.

Of course, I knew he had not meant it. Was all naught but a terrible, horrid mistake; he had thought me, in all actuality, to be my mother!

I have always wondered what would ever possess a man so fully rendered unto duty and service of his country to literally turn his life upside down at the age of fifty-eight, and wed a girl of barely seventeen past the near universal, stupendous outcry of scandal and social outrage. Melissa Devon-Tyler was a sumptuous English beauty and heiress, who, so my aunt continually reminds me, was so headstrong and impertinent as to pursue him—instead of the other way around—much to the chagrin and hopeless consternation of her own parents, and indeed Father's kin as well. But marry they did. Whereupon he brought her here to Novgorod, and Marnya says their love filled this house with echoes of joy for months on end. Apparently, Melissa exulted in everything Russian and endeared both the peasantry and neighboring landowners to her heart forever with charitable gifts and lavish tea parties, dances, and dinners. Incredible! I can never imagine such *fêtes* of gaiety taking place in this lonely, somber house. Sometimes one can still catch a rare mention of my mother's name in town amongst groups of the elderly folk. In their stories, she is always referred to as 'the little English countess.'

So crushed, so utterly devastated he must have been when she perished within less than two years.

'You are a child of anguish, of so much anguish,' Marnya mutters sometimes in spite of herself when in one of her melancholy moods. But then, as if always attempting to convince me, she never fails to counter with repeated reassurances of how for so long my father had earnestly wanted a son. That night, after Melissa died in his arms, I guess they almost lost me too, the babe she had borne of scarce four pounds. Night after night, I am told, he remained by the side of the cradle, not sleeping at all for weeks on end, watching my every movement, continually hounding the wet nurse, pacing the floor like a lunatic, wrapping me up and carrying me in his arms and cajoling and singing French and Russian lullabies and forcing me, through what must have seemed naught more than the sheer strength of his will, to live.

As a young child, I remember feeling showered with that love. When all of my cousins bore down with the flux during my fifth Easter, he broke off our annual holiday trek into Petersburg, fearing that I too would catch ill. Instead, together we sought out the Liturgy in town. Never will I forget how he bounced me upon his knee the whole time as we rode into Novgorod in our rickety closed carriage with the old family crest carved into the door. Utterly enthralling was the ancient Holy Cathedral of St. Sofiya, the highest of its six shimmering domes crowned by the proud bronze statuette of Novgorod's legendary dove. Inside, I remember being held fast in the grip of a child's awe by the majesty, above, of the grand golden-lit candelabrum; by the glittering beauty, below, of the many chalices adorning the altar behind embroidered vestments and crowned miters of the priests as they paced back and forth swinging their bejeweled, smoky censers. Singing *a cappella*, the choir ensconced within the cathedral's high balcony above rained haunting melancholy tribute down to the loftiest of treasures towering upward from below: an array of haloed, hollow-eyed faces each framed in hues of red, deep forest green, and stark traditional burnt umber. The Saints Peter and Paul, Georgi, Vasili the Great, Saint John the Baptist, and the Blessed Virgin all from either side flanked the triumphant Holy Christ Himself, graced as the very center portrait of Sofiya's famous Assumption iconostasis wall. Throughout the somber, crowded celebration, as the musky scent from countless votive candles filled my nostrils, and I practiced with inept fingers at imitating everyone I saw in making the sign of the cross, Father stood off in a corner, balancing me upon his shoulder while whispering fairy-tale nonsense into my ear, his voice as deep and richly evocative as those of the chanting priests and swollen with pride as, one after another, various townsfolk and acquaintances approached and made virtually the same undeviating remarks about the obvious resemblance between the two of us: 'Oh, yes, Yer Honor—the little one has the very same black-Russian eyes, that he does. An' by the Saints alive, good luck it is, too! Jest lookey that mass o' red hair. . . .'

But as I grew older, he grew away; matters with certain of his investments dictated frequent sojourns to Munich and Paris. From nannies and governesses, I graduated to hated Petersburg boarding schools, and during the summers was farmed out with visits to my mother's family in England.

However, two years ago, during the summer when I turned thirteen, everything changed. The Tylers were still far away on a voyage to the American eastern seaboard and Caribbean isles. So, in lieu of my Uncle Ned railing east for Baltic Station in Petersburg to whisk me off for another of our laughter-filled, card-playing train rides to Berlin, instead it was Father who arrived to bring me back for the summer to these solemn walls of Novgorod, his ever-stern expression breaking with a fluster of surprise as he caught his first glimpse of me debarking from the cab I had taken from school. I thought he was only staring so strangely because I had grown taller and so thin.

Unquestionably, from the moment of that summer's awful incident in the hall, I learned the painful truth behind his odd stare—because at last I knew whom I truly resembled. Her. Sumptuous English beauty and all.

A week later, during some petty argument about the amount of time I was being forced to spend working on the ledgers with Bulya—the task he had set me to that summer to occupy my restless spirit—the core of truth manifested with dogged finality: that love is a diabolical double-edged sword. Wrenched through the blinding sieve of hurt and shame, beauty becomes ugliness; affection, contempt. And love—love becomes naught but a swift expedient to hate.

That was when he first struck me. And that night, his drinking, far beyond the nuances of any recreational pursuit, began in deadly earnest.

And still, he is drinking. Up the steps from the downstairs pantry I have just heard him stomp yet again—for the third time since supper. With yet another flask of his *Napoleon* brandy.

Flickering back and forth across the confines of the room from its perch upon my desk, the glow of the oil lamp lends mockery to my loneliness, the mirror-glass hung above the bureau glimmering with hated shadowy snatches of my reflection.

I avoid looking at it. Of course, the bruises from the last time, a week ago, are scarce visible. The man is a doctor. Even in his worst drunken rages, he knows where to hit, how to hurt—in crafty ways, belying any obvious later evidence. Even in broad daylight.

Sighing, I press my cheek against the cold pane of glass. My room's window rests lower than every other on the second story; from prior experience, I know I could reach the ground outside with only two bedsheets. But in an attempt to prove some semblance of responsible maturity, I have avoided such temptation all summer long, ever mindful of his unquelled fury since the spring, when I injured my ankle during a similar bungled fiasco at school.

Unquelled fury, however, continues raging through my own heart as well—and at last I hover in the hallway before his door, hurtful gasps raking into my lungs and cold sweat fringing up beneath the hair on the back of my neck. 'Poor, tame little Sasha!' Tame? Indeed! Damn Volodya and his uncanny knack for so easily discerning the truth! And so now am I supposed to remain sitting meekly by, saying not a single word, and thereby possibly making way for the occurrence of even further atrocities than what my father ordered today?

One matter it is for him to expunge his wrath upon me. To a certain extent, I can understand. But as far as the flogging, I have my suspicions that what he ordered done out there today was not entirely legal.

"Get in here and speak your piece, then!" he bellows gruffly from behind the door.

My fist unclenches from its poised position, fingers dropping down to rest upon the knob. It happens this way almost every time. Rarely do I need knock.

"Well?"

Through florid puffs of tobacco smoke, he glares at me morosely from his leather chair, his feet, still shod in their boots, hoisted up upon the seat of the velvet-cushioned divan. His fingers, stiff and whitened, continue slamming the rod inward and outward—inward and then outward again, over and over. Apparently, for near unto two hours now, he has been doing naught but cleaning his gun.

Father's study, boasting a bay window framing grand view of the lake and a massive collection of East Indian teak and mahogany furniture, a room filled with books in dozens of languages lined up to the ceiling on all four walls, has forever intimidated my wary soul, his papers and personal accessories so neatly stacked and set out to the minutest detail in their proper places. Stark comparison with my own cluttered shambles of an inner sanctum lying across the hall. Past renewed pangs of slovenly guilt, my voice comes out very small, much like a child's, as I inquire about his bandaged arm.

"As I said during supper, you needn't be concerned!"

"Y-Yes, sir!" I back off to the door—but hesitate.

"Well?"

The sharpness of his tone causes me to near jump from my skin. Nonetheless, I clear my throat, nervously, murmuring: "The, uh, the flute was not disturbing you?"

He looks away, his gaze suddenly gone distant, alighting upon his fingers with a hint of reverence. "You know your flute never bothers me," he replies in a lowered tone. "Comforts, as a matter of fact. Think it's the only sound in the world that ever renders me peace of mind anymore. Keep practicing, young maestro. Play your Bach all night, if you like—or your Mozart, your Tchaikovsky—or all, every blessed ethereal one until the morn, if you choose. Be assured I'll not be disturbed."

I nod mutely, my eyes cast downward—but when I make no move to absent myself from his presence this time, he roars out again: *"Well?* I said get out with it and say your piece! Oh, yes, I know you: simply chock-full to the death again of all that damn socialist rhetoric! Which is the only reason you have bothered to intrude like this and trouble me at all. Yes?"

"I—merely wished to raise one question."

"Well, dammit, boy—raise your one question, then!"

"There will be a meeting of the *zemstvo*, the village council?"

"Yes, yes! Of course there will be another worthless, inane meeting."

"And they will—perhaps—order a hearing?"

"And perhaps order a hearing! And just what, my young prodigy—who should be in his room, practicing!—is your concern with any of this nonsense?"

"Pardon any presumption on my part, Father, but is it not your intention for me to be the one running this estate someday?" I turn on him sharply, hard put, despite the growing fear of his sour mood, to contain my own irritation. "And it is not entirely legal; in fact, it is not *at all* legal anymore, flogging as a means of punishment! Docking pay or imposing a fine would have been more in order. Don't you think?"

Father slams his gun down onto the desk as if his fingers had just caught afire. "What's the matter, Sasha?" he growls, his face darkening with a taunting, sarcastic leer. "You're not man enough to stand the sight of a little blood?"

Hands grappling for the knob to the door, I near clear the room before he pounces for my back, tearing my grip away and shoving me around to shout down into my face: "If there is anything I scarce appreciate right now, it is an upbraiding by an arrogant little fourteen-year-old of a count's son who does naught but embarrass his poor father before the whole of Petersburg with capers in mindless folly from third-story school windows!"

Guiltily, I struggle out from his grasp and stare to the floor.

"How could you ever pull something so foolish?" he bellows on with scarce a breath's pause in between words. "Fracturing your ankle! And would you stay off it long enough? No, of course not! You had to be tramping around with nary a care in the world bare of two weeks hence—and now, look at you. You think all this eve I've taken not any notice of that limp? By the Saints, Sasha! Why must you be such a burden to me, day and night, year after year without ever any end to it, why? How long have I prayed that someday, somehow, you would learn from the example of your cousin! Why on earth can you not be more like him? Nikolai—prize pupil of the St. Petersburg Conservatory, at sixteen, one of the most promising young violinists in all of Russia! And do you emulate him at all, and work studiously at polishing your technique, as I have begged for years? Oh, no—not you! You only gallivant on unceasingly with foolish schoolboy escapades, although you have assured me time and again that you do wish to follow in your cousin's footsteps. Well, that has now become a distinct possibility. Just this morn, I received a letter from the headmaster about an opening for this coming autumn. But do you spend enough time practicing? No—instead, all summer long, you've had upon your mind only one prospect: impressing that damn peasant girl!"

"You are wrong, Papa! I have been practicing! You have heard me—"

"I'll believe it adequate when I see you pass the audition."

"I will pass the audition! I'm good enough to pass the audition now—well, I am! And I practice as much time as I can manage past all the ledger work you and Bulya heap upon me!"

"Humph!"

Heart pounding in quickened spurts, I cross my arms, fearing but unable to help glaring at him. For months now, his chagrin over the matter has bristled on unabated—and it was only a hairline fracture! While all this time, I have been simply itching to inform him that the sole reason I took to sliding down bedsheets from the window at school in the first place was in order to attempt to find my way across town to see Nikolai.

But ever protective of my promiscuous cousin, again I hold the guarded information in.

Raking his hands through his hair in exasperation, Father crosses back over to his desk and starts loading up his pipe with more tobacco, stuffing in the flakes with uncharacteristic heedless jabs, half the contents of the pouch scattering over the carpet, while he continues muttering on in between his teeth: "Damned headstrong, impertinent English blood! I found the impetuosity charming in my wife. But I swear for all the love of God that I cannot bear the likes of it in my son! Cursed I am, cursed I swear—saddled with a sulking, trying, insufferable prankster of a fourteen-year-old! . . ."

"Fifteen!" I blurt out, my voice bounding across the room in a squall of defiance.

"What?"

"Fifteen!"

Father's eyes widen in dawning realization, and I breathe in with a horrified gasp, immediately regretting the foolish words. But it is too late; in half a bound, he charges back across the study floor, his angry grip near wrenching my arm from its socket as he bellows: *"What* did you just say?"

"Nothing, sir! Not a blessed thing!"

"What did you just say?"

"Y-You heard me," I choke out in a helpless gasp.

"Ahh, yes!" he roars out at the top of his lungs. "Fifteen—that is correct, today is the day! Fifteen years, is it?"

"Father! Don't—"

"Fifteen godforsaken years ever since that day, when my whole life was reduced to naught but a parody in hell!"

"F-F-Father . . . !"

He grapples for my shoulders, his fingers crushing into my collar bone, his face crimsoning in a bloody spate of rage. "Fifteen years of senseless disappointment, fifteen years of endless trouble and pain! You have been naught but a torment all of my life!" he shouts. "Naught but a burden of sorrows from the first moment I ever laid eyes upon your wretched face!"

His knuckles slam for my ear as I shout: "Father, no—please!"

"Shut up!"

Rock-hard, his fists plow into my shoulders and chest as I scream out helplessly: "Stop it! Father—*Papa!* Please, *no!"* Gasping, I attempt to keep from doubling over upon the floor.

"I told you to shut up, you whining little good-for-nothing cur!"

The force of the next blow sends me staggering toward the wall—and I slide, whimpering, down against the heavy glass doors of an old curio cabinet, several small Chinese urns set atop it wavering in precarious balance as I collapse upon the floor.

Harsh silence then engulfs the room. Past enormous difficulty, I attempt to focus my eyes—until the object upon the floor at which Father continues staring in such mortified, open-mouthed shock converges into view.

An antique gold-cast chain. Between the broken links of which lies my mother's amethyst crystal.

Oh, Jesus Blessed God!

I swoop for it—only to end up splayed out on all fours across the carpet, while he glares down at me, his breath hacking up a storm, the crystal dangling precariously above my face from his shaking fingers as he shouts downward: "Where did you find this? Answer me!"

Shaking my head in desperation, I stagger upward, mumbling: "I—"

"You have let yourself into her room!"

"No, Papa! I mean—"

"Don't you lie to me, Sasha!" he roars, wrenching me up to my feet. "Answer me! How on earth did you ever manage to let yourself into her room? Who told you where I keep the key? Dammit, who told you? Answer me!"

His fist slams into my ear again, and I crumple into the side of the desk, clutching my throat and choking desperately for air. "Father, no!" I scream, ducking my head into my arms.

But the brunt of his hand plows into my temple—once, twice, four times, six times—the force of his voice shattering up through the roof: "Who told you where I keep that key? No one else knows where I keep that blasted key except—wait a moment! Vliny! Damn him, I will have his head!"

"Father, wait! No, don't blame Vliny! He's not the one who told me where the key was, I swear!"

At this, he stops short in the doorway, glancing over his shoulder and demanding: "Who, then?"

Shaken from head to toe, again I bury my head into my arms, coarse sobs making their timely, welling threat.

"Who told you where it was, Sasha?" he shouts, wrenching me up to him again. "You blasphemous, sniveling little thief! You tell me who told you where that key was, or I am going to drag Vliny up here, and I swear I will knock both of you senseless until dawn! Who told you where to look for that damned key? Who told you?"

Shaking, shaking, he keeps shaking, will not stop shaking me! . . .

"Tell me, Sasha!"

"Uh—uh—Un—cle—N-Ned!"

My sobs shatter forth then in an uncontrollable burst—and through the blur, I glimpse the startled pall of realization dawning upon his face. "You! he roars downward, punching for me once again before whirling around on his heel.

"Father, no! Wait!"

I scramble upward, charging after him into the hall—but already he has flung the door open with a crashing bang, the sanctity of my room invaded—and ravaged irreparably as desk drawers fly out and schoolbooks, papers, pens and pencils, icons, and precious little trinkets tumble off in all directions. "Where is it, Sasha?" he demands, coloring to purple amidst the rampage. "I tell you, I will find it! Where is it?"

"Papa, stop! You are making the worst mess of—"

"Mess? A mess is this shambles you forever keep stacking up without ever letting Marnya in for even an hour to clean! And look at this! Fifteen hundred marks I paid for this flute—and here you leave it sitting out dangling half-off the window seat, as if naught but a child's toy!"

"Forgive me, Papa!" Falling upon it, I twist the delicate silver joints apart; hurriedly tuck the pieces back down into their velvet-lined slots in the case.

"Sloppy, careless!" he rages on. "A mess is what you are, all the way down to that untrimmed mop of hair you forever leave hanging in your face! Now, you tell me—where is it?"

"I do not know what you are talking about! Please stop ransacking my desk!"

"Ah-ha!" In triumph, he swings around, holding out my crease-lined deck of Tarot cards. "What a fool I was!" he shouts, seizing onto my collar and throwing me roughly upon the bed. "I let all those crazy stories from the village simply pass me right on by. You know the rumors—yes, Sasha?"

"N-No! No, I don't—"

"The ones about the beauteous red-headed witch? Ha! And I thought they were talking about a woman, some new tart taken up with one of the shopkeepers again in town. Never on earth did I imagine they were speaking about my own son!"

"It is not witchcraft!" I scream back.

"Don't you tell me what witchcraft is!" he yells, smashing down the Tarot pack and sending loose cards scattering all about the floor. "Witchcraft is the only way Ned could ever have found out where I keep that key!"

"That is not true in the least! The man is merely a clairvoyant."

"Oh, hell! I am not going to stand about here arguing with you over definitions."

After rummaging further through the bottom drawer of the desk, he uncovers the true object of his search at last. Lumbering up to the bed, he shoves the book into my face, roaring: "I knew it, I bloody well knew it—by dammit to hell!"

"Papa! Don't take it, please!"

"Look at this innocent excuse for a title!" he yells on. *"The Science of Numbers,* by Edward Devon-Tyler, Baronet of the Realm. So he could parade it past naive noses everywhere as a mere mathematics text! Think you that I know not what this truly is? The man had his persuasive claws all over Melissa's mind, too."

Fending off my protests, Father yanks the book open and begins leafing through the first section. "Look at this," he snorts derisively, "begins not until page thirty-two, so one must suffer past a long-winded introduction in order to detect the true gist of this folly. *The number one,"* he begins reading. *"This is the male principle, the Yang. Quite aptly illustrated in the ancient Tarot as the vibration of the solitary Magician. . . ."*

"That does not mean it to be witchcraft!" I shout, swiping outward but again entirely missing the book.

"And look at all this in the back!" he goes on, brandishing the book high up in the air from my reach and tearing through the stiffened pages. "Small wonder you've slackened off so in your practice time—this entire volume is filled top to bottom with your notes: *numerology,* it says. Oh, by the Saints alive! And look at this collection of pitiable back-slanted writing! How many hours, how many years did I spend shoving the spoons, the pencils, everything you ever got your grip on back into your right hand, Sasha—and still you must remain contrary to everyone else, and never learn it, and go on using your left. Only to continue tormenting me like a changeling from hell, I swear to God!"

"What difference should it make whether I be right or left handed?"

"I suppose the next question you'll ask is what difference should it make whether or not you be a witch!"

"I am *not* a witch!"

"No, you are not. Because this book and these cards are going straight into the kitchen stove—now."

"Father, no!"

With a renewed surge of energy, I fling myself through the air and grapple with him wildly, at last coming up with the book. "Papa, you cannot! It is two years of work! Father, you cannot burn my book—"

"Let go of it!"

"No! You cannot burn my book!"

"Goddamn you!" Again his fist rams out, pummeling me into a flattened heap upon the floor, before he at last stomps away past a string of muttered curses, the book stuffed securely beneath his arm.

"W-Would it have mattered if she had lived?" I shout out after him, sobbing. "Or—would you have beaten her, too?"

Father halts in the doorway, his back to me, the whitened hairs brushing his collar glistening into beady lines of sweat, his shirt stretched tautly across his broad angry shoulders. But he says not a word, only indicating having heard through the vengeful, heavy rasping of his breath.

"Perhaps you should go to bed, Sasha," he murmurs softly at last.

"And—and perhaps you should go and fuck yourself in hell!"

I shove up quickly to my feet, but all I can see is the window—his hand—and shards of shattering glass . . . the window . . . his hand . . . and naught else but simply untold shards of shattering glass. . . .

* * *

Cooing and quiet, night sings with a nesting chorus of crickets and bullfrogs, the trees humming with bleated hootings of the owls. But from somewhere far off beyond the maze of pine-scented, birch-strewn wooded clusters, eerie, plaintive moans of some horribly injured animal tear apart all cover of darkness; near tear apart every bone in my ears. At last my tongue touches my front teeth. My whole mouth tastes like dirt. . . .

Voices. From the shadows, Father's horrified cries: "Sasha! My God, what have I done?"

And then Vliny: "This time it has gone too far, Misha."

"Fool, don't you think I can see that? Quick, have you a tie, a belt—anything! I have got to stop all this blood. And I need my bag! My bag, by dammit—hurry!"

Vliny runs off, while Father yells after him: "And iodoform! From the storeroom chest, at least two bottles. And from the woodroom—hurry!—we'll need boards for splints!" Then he turns to me, his hands tenderly—tenderly?—cradling my head: "It is going to be all right, I promise you, my Sasha. . . ."

Dumbfounded, I stare upward, wholly unable to fathom the drastic change in his temper. Then suddenly, I hear Marnya's wailing, and Father shouting back at her: "Blast it woman, take all of these icons back out of here! No one is going to be saved by Saint Georgi now. Oh, blasphemy, my blessed arse! You want to do something to help me, go clear everything off the kitchen table—yes, everything! Put both leaves in and scour the whole thing off clean. And hurry!"

The animal moaning in the background mounts shrilly—painfully—as Vliny rushes back. For some reason, I cannot peel my gaze away from his spindly graying moustache. For years now, every eve, the man has lingered at table in the kitchen after supper, attempting with one of Marnya's crocheting needles to coax the drooping hairs into loops as if a Chinese. Wrathfully, he continues glaring at Father as he hands over sour-smelling medicinal bottles, his tone full of grumbling recrimination: "Too far this time." And I know he is talking about the beating, about all the beatings, and this I cannot understand. Up until now, no matter how desperately I have begged, he has never, ever intervened.

Father's words begin clanging like crashing cymbals in my ears: "Set it? Going to set it right now, by God. Yes, here! Have you found a small piece of wood? Put it in his mouth—here, like this." Coarse fibers stick onto my lips as Father's fingers grope inward, shoving my tongue into the back of my throat. "Simply bite down upon it, Sasha—yes, that's good," he murmurs, patting my head, the tone of his voice melting into a monologue of reassurance, as if . . . as if he was working on someone, just like when he is ministering as a doctor. . . .

"What?" I mumble disjointedly. "Papa, w-what on earth is happening?"

"Sasha, do not fight me!" Father implores. "Keep that stick in your mouth and try not to talk."

"But—"

"Keep your head down."

"Keep yer head down, Sasha! Don't try te look at it!" Vliny yells, pushing me backward.

But not before I catch the barest glimpse of my leg.

Or—what was once my leg. My left leg. The one beset with the ill-begotten hairline fracture in the ankle.

Now only a pitiful protrusion of blood and splintered bone.

"Sasha," Father murmurs softly, "it is going to be all right. . . ."

The moaning from the frightened animal then escalates from afar into a hideous primal scream of terror, and I suddenly realize that the scream has come from none other than my very own throat . . . the animal is—*oh, God!*—the animal is me.

And then the night strikes white, my screams go black. . . .

* * *

Moaning sounds: that loathsome animal again. *No! I do not want to hear it! . . .*

"Hush . . . hush, now! Shhh . . . ."

Kisses at my temples. A small, soft hand running through my hair. I try to focus through the steeping blur. "Tereza Ippolitovna?"

"Shhh! Quiet yourself, little brother. Try not to talk."

"Hold him still!" Father's voice, as if from some other world—a chaotic, powerful void hung far in the distance.

She is Marnya's younger daughter. "Tereza!" I gasp out, "why am I lying upon this table? Why are you holding my head like this? Heavens! It feels very nice. . . ."

"Lord Almighty! Hush!" I hear the embarrassed laugh, sense the blush of the girl, barely nineteen.

"Tereza?" I whisper on. "Did you find where he put my book? He's not thrown it into the fire, has he? The book Uncle Ned gave me. Did you find it?"

"Shhh!"

"And the crystal? Did you find my mother's amethyst crystal?"

To this issues no response: only coughing, a couple of nervous gasps.

"Why was he so infuriated?" I cry out, clinging desperately to her hand. "Is it so wrong of me to want something of hers? I was doing no wrong with the crystal, I swear! I was merely wearing it. Is it so wrong to want to keep a part of her close and cherished to me? She was my mother, do you hear? Melissa Devon-Tyler was my mother! She was! Why will he not allow me the crystal? He stored away all the picturegraphs; he'll not permit me to gaze upon her image anymore, nor to speak of her in his presence, ever . . . is it so wrong? To want a small piece, a tiny part of my mother—my real mother—to hold dear to me? Is it so wrong? Is it? . . ."

"Misha . . . ." Vliny's voice, shuddering as if with tears. His arm spans the air, crossing my body, his hand grasping hold of the broadened shoulder hunched in a stooped bend over my leg. But fiercely, the shoulder shakes him off—and then I see the white head bent, clumps of hair stuck to his brow with grizzled beads of sweat, his eyes remaining fastened downward in a riveted spell of concentration. "Only the morphine talking," the gruff voice murmurs, face twitching not a muscle. From his fingers, a gossamer silver thread winds straight upward. Then it goes back down, comes back up again. "Tereza!" he barks out with irritation, "tuck his head back down, try to calm him. Maryna, will you help her? I don't care—anything! Tereza, kiss him on the mouth if you have to, he should like that. Well! I don't know, simply try to calm him. He must lie still! I daren't give him anymore, not yet. . . ."

* * *

'. . . ho, ho! I daren't give him anymore, not yet!'

They are talking about *kvas*—the raspberry flavored ale, cool like a burst of fresh spring water in my mouth. Marnya laced the foam with newly cut mint sprigs from the summer herb garden. I want more from Papa's mug, I want more!

It is 1896. The belt is crisp and snug; the leggings lambswool, my cotton tunic sporting a high starched collar.

I am five.

And chasing him. The game is hide-and-seek. He is making me practice in between my French and English letters. 'Papa, are you there?'

'Français, français!' His chuckles filter out, hearty and resonant from around the alcove past the kitchen corner.

I repeat in French: 'Papa, are you there? Papa!'

But it is into Marnya that I run as she scurries back inside with a basketful of shucked peas from the porch. Laughing, she swoops me up into her arms, and I snatch the kerchief from her head, letting loose two massive sable braids flocked with specks of gray. 'Maman! Tell me, you must tell me where my papa is!'

'Oh, dear! Please say yer words again in Russian, precious little soul, my dove, my little angel dumplin'! Because ye know yer real mama had to go away. And Miss Nanny Emily is outing with her young man for the afternoon, but to return by suppertime, we promise. Afraid Marnya-mama talks only in old peasant Russian, sweetest heart.' She kisses me, and bursts into giggles as I gleefully swipe at her head with the scarf.

'Matushka! Why did real mama have to go away? Did she talk in French like Papa? Oh! Everyone says my real mama was a princess, that she came from a fairy-land, and had dark golden curls, and was very, very beautiful! My papa will not go away, will he? Oh, Matushka, tell me! You must help! I must find Papa—we are hiding and seeking! . . .'

'Well, look!'

Scarce do I catch the glimpse—back of a shoe turning around the corner stove. I barrel after him, shrieking with delight: 'Papa! Papa, I have found you—I win! Papa! Papa? Are you there? . . .'

* * *

". . . Papa? Are you there?"

"I am here, Sasha." The grip comes warm, firm, pressed full with reassurance, his reach long from the end of the table. From his other hand still dangles the needle, the gossamer thread. "Hold on, my Sashenka. Only a little while longer. Vliny, the time?"

"Almost dawn."

"Surely the elders from the *zemstvo* will be here. Lord, how could I ever have been such a fool?"

Utter silence. Then Vliny replies coldly, in broken French: "Mikhail Sergeyevich, what is done is perhaps done. But the *zemstvo* must be reckoned with before . . . ."

Vliny apparently does not want the women to understand. But Father answers him in Russian anyway: "Yes, yes, I know! Well, you are going to have to stall them regardless. Yes, at least until next week. If they'll not believe you, bring them in here, and I will show them his leg! Well, it will have to be an impromptu meeting then, and brief. I am not leaving him for a moment. Oh, Sweet Jesus—as if I've never broken the law before! Retribution is only my middle name. Now, don't you start in on me about that travesty after the War. How many times did I bail you out? And leave off with the holy formality, will you?

'Mikhail Sergeyevich,' my blessed arse. Marnya, bring the lamp a bit closer—there, thank you. Sasha, hold on, and try to remain still. I know this must be hurting you dreadfully. I am near finished with the stitches; I promise there will not be many more."

"Papa, no! Don't let go—"

"Hush, little brother!" Tereza's quavering voice again. "Yer papa cannot tend to yer leg and hold yer hand too! Here, I will hold yer hand. Rest yer head back here against the pillow, and I will hold both o' yer hands in both o' mine. See? There."

"Oh, Tereza! Your hands feel very, very nice! . . ."

* * *

Voices: Father, Vliny, Marnya. And others: shouting, arguing. Broken to fragments at last by Father's thundering roar.

I cringe away, bursting into sobs. "Precious dumplin', no!" Marnya rocks my head. "Yer papa is not angerin' at ye anymore—them's only visitors. Listen, ye hear the clink of the glasses? Is all settled, they are taking vodka together with him. See? Is all settled—hush, my darlin'. Here, ye hold these: here's the lovely icon o' the Blessed Virgin, an' o' course the one o' yer very favorite, the Great Nevsky hisself, yer very own namesake Saint, remember? Prince Aleksandr, God's Protector and Patriarch over our ancient sovereign land, called itself Lord Novgorod the Great. Such a precious artifact this icon is, an' passed down long over more years o' yer fine family than anybody kin scarce remember! Ye say yer prayers rightly, now—go ahead—and yer old Marnya-mama will rock ye to sleep. . . ."

Night: the blur goes white—nymphets chasing the wind upon heels of threatening killer ghosts from the isle of Circe—no, wait. Only the breeze. Gauze curtains fluttering from the open drawing room windows above figurines on the chess table. Windsong accompanied by wracking sobs—from the outside? No, from inside, from close by. From—right here?

My leg. Spears of ice piercing through balls of flesh condensed inside a mass of ballooning marble, pounding and pounding past waves of nauseating agony. More terrified, primordial moans: the lone animal dying, half-mired yet in consciousness, its carcass picked off by the greedy vultures, sharp beaks sapping away the last of my strength. My fingers, shaking, tear like claws at the coverlet, coming up with a shock of white hair.

I cling to the grasp of his hand.

His sobs, shaken to the very depths of reason: "Anything, dearest blessed God in Heaven, anything Thou might ask . . . stop the infection, bring the fever down, please! Forgive an old man, a blundering, steel-hearted fool, I beg Thee, I beseech Thee! Forgive this sinner whom penance is upon now with this awful consequence of his own drunken rage . . . never again will it come to anything like this, I swear to Thee, oh, dear Lord! By all the Blessed Saints in Heaven, forgive this wretched sinner! Take me—make me the one to grovel in shame at Your feet if you must—but not this child, take not my son from me away to Your Bosom yet, please! Not my poor Sashenka, whom I have hounded for years with a madman's rantings, all on account of some foolish mistake one lonely night in a darkened hallway . . . oh, God, please bring the fever down! I have tried comfrey, yarrow—everything that I know how, yet still he is burning up . . . you cannot mean to take him now—oh, please! For centuries have we known Your mercy . . . past near all the others in the old medieval times, You spared us the wrath of the Awesome Ivan's lechery, You saved us from his yoke of shame and Muscovy exile—and a score of generations have my fathers borne You since in reverent gratitude. You cannot mean for the line to end now with my Sashenka, You cannot! Oh, dear Lord, save him, I beg You! I will do anything You ask of me, forevermore—until the end of time . . . dear God, please! Please . . . ."

Morntide. Of a later, perhaps thousand-million years. Dawnlight's glimmering beckons, orange-red fringes of the sun bordering at the sill of the window. And yet the sobs continue, his throat now sore and wordless, prayers uttered only with a shaking head, repeated motions of his hand making the sign of the cross over himself. Over me. Moaning, I squint through a gashing headache, vision splicing gradually back together from a seeming spread of the aeons, my eyes, after days—weeks?—coming into blurry focus. My hand edges outward tentatively into the narrow void.

"Papa? Are you there?"

He can say nothing—only nod his head in grateful spurts of affirmation, his shoulders coursing through a violent shudder, his hand gripping like an iron press and causing me to cry out as he crushes mine near unto death.

"Come away now, Mikhail Sergeyevich," Marnya demands authoritatively, dragging him off, her stout arm gripped firm about his waist. She guides him across the room toward Vliny, who awaits open-armed within the shadows. "Ye see the fever is down," Marnya prattles on. "Yes, I will watch, I promise I will awaken ye if there is even the slightest thing, yes—go! Ye must go to bed now—ye must."

She thrusts something into my mouth—cool tea that trickles down each side of my chin. I seize the glass from her gnarled fingers, gulping frantically, desperate for the sweetness of chamomile against the chalky residue of comfrey coating my tongue. Suddenly, the room's heavy odors converge and hit me like a leaden blow: dried blood; putrid puss from the bandage. The stench from the chamber pot shoved just beneath the table. Although wiped clean, the smell still lingers, abounding all around, diminished not even by the breeze.

"Here, there is plenty more tea, precious dumplin' love. Are ye hungry? Let me bring ye some food."

"No, Matushka—wait." The voice trails off, dwindling away into shaking rasps. "I—I merely want to sleep. . . ."

* * *

"Aleksandr Mikhailovich," says Doctor Friedrich, straining for my gaze.

But I continue staring past him. Not for one second do I take my eyes away from Father's tortured face.

"Aleksandr Mikhailovich," Friedrich pleads again.

"I hear you."

My lips taste dry as salt. I wet them with the tip of my tongue. Father's gaze does not waver from my stare for a single instant. We both know what the German doctor is going to say.

"My opinion is—"

Friedrich stops, his mouth pursing inward, thin lips disappearing into his sunken, narrow face. At the two of us, he gapes with a long sigh, his mood clearly caught midway between confusion and exasperation. Beneath the hearth, the fire crackles, logs tussled about in breaking snaps and sharpening emphasis to the man's unspoken words. To the edge of the brick mantle, its shelf lined from end to each end with Marnya's hollow-eyed, somber collection of antique icons, Father grasps his hand, scarred wounds of his anguish laid out bare for all the world to see in the depths of his Russian-black eyes—two saddened orbs prostrated low before me in the most humble, abject lament of regret: *I am sorry—sorry! So terribly, utterly sorry . . . .*

"My opinion," Friedrich reiterates loudly, "is that you will never again be able to walk on that leg. Despite your father's attempt at surgical repair. Which, I might emphasize," he adds, nodding deferentially in Father's direction, "is intrinsically in itself a fine piece of work. But to walk, well . . . too many ligaments were torn. Too much bone was splintered away. Try to set your full weight back, and it will only shatter like an eggshell. My recommendation, therefore, is amputation."

Father breaks his stare away from mine at last and runs both hands roughly across his face, pressing weary fingers across his furrowed brow. "Doctor," he murmurs, turning on Friedrich with an affronted glare, "I beg to disagree."

"Doctor Sekovsky! Have you not considered whether your emotional involvement in this case has seriously affected your professional judgment?"

My tall tea glass shatters into the fireplace like a tempest blown out of the night sky. The saucer goes flying in after it, disjointed clinking of its scattering pieces stabbing apart the room's sudden hush of silence. A paperweight crashes in next, breaking into only a quartet of chunks, mismatched shards thudding clumsily across the hearth's stone bricks before coming to rest at last beside Father's feet on the carpet.

My hand gropes across the table in its now vain search for something else close enough to throw.

"Doctor Friedrich, I need to speak with my son privately for a few moments," Father says in a hurried rush. "My housekeeper is renowned throughout the province for her brewing of speciality teas. Perhaps you would care to take a glass in our parlor? I promise not to keep you waiting long—and wish you to know how greatly I appreciate the time you have taken to journey here to Lake Ilmen all the way from Moscow."

Grumbling, Friedrich stuffs his stethoscope back into his rounded leather bag. "Aleksandr Mikhailovich," he murmurs, nodding again toward me.

I nod back, lowering my eyes.

As Father conducts him to the parlor, once more I yank off the quilt and attempt examination of my leg. Which has been temporarily bound in a makeshift cast of paste-soaked, stiffened burlap, roll after roll of fabric lashed around six wooden splints supporting the sides. Friedrich is here because Father wanted a second opinion. And because today this cast comes off—for either better or worse.

The door clicks shut softly, and he comes and stands above me, arms crossed, his eyes fastened to the floor, his jaw unmoving.

"I hate you!" I spit out at him. "I would wrench out your filthy guts and spread them bloody thick across every wall, floor, and corner of this awful house—although such fate for a certainty would match naught of the true hell that you deserve!"

"Sasha—"

"No, stay away from me!" I yell, deflecting away his arm. "So help me God, if you ever lay your stinking hands upon me again, I swear I will kill you!"

Father expels a heavy sigh, eyeing the cast. "Going to be a bit difficult, don't you think? Considering?"

"You know what I mean!"

Across the sofa, he reaches for my right arm, but I snatch it angrily back—upon which his hand shoots upward toward my cheek. Fully expecting the familiar sting of the slap, I cower away, attempting to stifle the hoarse scrape of fear sawing through my throat. But instead—to my surprise—I open wary eyes in response to the touch, warm and gentle, as he tucks a loose strand of hair back behind my ear.

"Your arm," he murmurs. "It is time to retape it."

My right wrist was sprained in the fall. I cannot help but wince back a shudder as he starts peeling off the tape: *No, I do not want him to touch me, ever again! Not in anger; not with warmth, either. All I want from now on is to hate him. . . .*

"How did you ever come upon so many bee stings?" he asks. "I noted several on your other hand, too."

"Blast it!" I blurt out in exasperation. "I happen to live on a bee farm."

"But usually only the keepers acquire so many—"

"Must you only continue to hound me?"

"All right." Again that great heaving sigh. "Look," he goes on in a lowered tone, "Friedrich is waiting. We have a decision to make." Securing the tape back, he grasps up my fingers, interlacing his within mine.

Angrily, I snatch my hand away. "Send the dumbskull German krauthead back to Moscow!" I shout, pointing toward the southern end of the room. "It takes two of you to perform a decent amputation, yes? Which is the only reason why you have asked the fool here today, is it not? Consider your effort futile! I have already made my choice. You are not taking my leg away from me on top of everything else, *Papa.*"

He ignores my sarcastic emphasis, answering: "This is not a decision to be made by a child, Sasha."

"I am not a child!"

"I know! So do you think that, for perhaps five minutes, you could quiet down like a reasonable young adult, and listen while I explain your options?"

I cross my arms, glaring at him in livid reply. He motions Marnya for some tea; to bring two more glasses. "What options?" I demand finally, spitting the words up into his face.

"If we amputate—now, please listen to me! If we amputate, you can be fitted with a prosthesis. I am not talking about a stick or a stump; very sophisticated methods are employed in their manufacture now. It could be measured with a great degree of accuracy against the length of your other leg, and you would be able to walk for a certainty. Perhaps without even much of a noticeable limp."

In practically one gulp, I down my tea to the bottom, and again—while Father rolls his eyes—I send the glass hurtling, delicate pieces of another heirloom crashing against the fireplace grating in jarring, singing spikes. "And?"

"Your leg was broken in basically two places," he goes on softly. "First, at the hairline fracture in the ankle, and fortunately, that one came very clean. But as far as the other: the shinbone was twisted apart, and literally crushed back upon itself; you landed straight atop it. I spent that entire night attempting to piece it back together as best I could. But—there were so many loose bone fragments, in so many tiny pieces. . . ."

Father's words break off, and from his pocket he snatches out his handkerchief and covers his face, shaking his head back and forth in a moan of grief. Abruptly, he rises; turns from me and loudly blows his nose. Reaching outward, he then grasps hold of my right leg, left hand cupped above my knee, his other palm braced beneath the arch in my foot as I roar out indignantly: "And exactly what do you think you are doing?"

"The one with the cast is not our sole concern," he whispers out with difficulty, attempting to clear his throat. "Muscles will atrophy, could have begun already. Lord, what has it been—near unto two weeks? Come now, move it up for me, Sasha—that's right. . . ."

The soreness stretches all the way to my toes as he flexes my good leg repeatedly upward and then downward again, gently guiding with both hands.

"As for the left one," he goes on, "I know not if you can tell, but it will definitely heal up shorter, by at least two fingers' width. Perhaps even three. I am sorry. I told you I did the best I could in piecing it back together. So little remained with which to work. I am more sorry than you can ever know, my Sasha."

"So." Again I cross my arms, the effort stupendous to keep my voice reasonably even. "You also recommend amputation?"

Father abruptly abandons the therapy and drops down to his knees, facing me at eye level as he reaches for my arm across the sofa. "No! Because I think you have the determination, and the gumption—hell, if anyone has the gumption!—to walk again if you so want. But—it is not going to be easy."

This time, I do not shrug off his fist, clenched again with dogged urgency over mine.

"The pain will be immense," he continues in a hushed tone. "The permanent cast must stay on at least through Christmastide, perhaps even longer. I imagine by February, when the *Maslenitsa* fairs start up, you can be rid of it for a certainty. After that, resting even an ounce of your weight upon that foot will be excruciating at first. But there are innovative methods I have seen work. A fellow suffered a similar injury when I was in Si—"

Suddenly, such a fit of coughing seizes Father that I almost end up calling out to Marnya in a panic. "I mean," he goes on, "ahem!—I mean, I worked with a similar injury when I was stationed at the field hospital in Sevastopol during the Crimean War. With this patient, the kneecap was shattered also. What we did was use a compress bottle in a large bucket of water. I supported most of his weight at first, and we made the attempt several times a day, until he finally regained enough strength in his leg to stand completely, first in the buoyancy of the water, then upon the hardwood floor. After that, walking again was a whole new test of his will and endurance. But he was able to do so eventually. I think such a method could work in your case. But it is going to take time and patience, and—most importantly—nothing less than your complete cooperation. Despite the fact that by now I know you thoroughly detest me to hell's end."

Letting go my hand, he pushes up from the sofa. "So, Aleksandr," he says. "Does your original choice still stand?"

I stare into embers of the fire, whispering: "I'll walk."

"Remember my words! It is hardly going to be easy."

"I swear to you, Father—it scarce matters if I do naught else of any import in my entire life! I want to walk. On my own leg."

"Cooperation is going to be imperative."

"Cooperation you can be assured of! I want to walk. Between us—by your modern medicine, by gifts of my white magic, we will bend the fates! I will walk."

"Oh, that reminds me."

To my astonishment, he then sets my mother's amethyst crystal—its gold-cast chain appearing to have been painstakingly repaired—down upon the empty saucer on the table.

"I have been a hard-hearted fool," he murmurs. "Not to allow you to keep something of hers."

Next, he lays my pack of Tarot cards and Uncle Ned's book down beside the crystal. "On the condition," he states flatly, "that you keep these 'studies' of yours entirely to yourself."

"Papa! I know what all the village has been saying about Bulya, but all I did was attempt to help a friend."

"Your intentions are beside the point, Sasha. You have heard me bemoaning the Black Hundreds and their scouring of the land, their stringing up of Jews and any other leftist sympathizers upon whom they can possibly set their filthy hands. Unfortunately, I have reason to believe that a few local *zemstvo* members are actually involved in the awful dealings, at least with some of the pogroms. But in the past, witches, fortune tellers and the like have also been found amongst their victims. We must squelch such rumors without delay. Understood?"

Somehow, I knew my gnawing fear of Katya's and Natasha's gossiping was not without warrant. Catching my breath, I grip both hands together, murmuring: "Y-Yes, sir."

"Now. I will go back out to the parlor and attend to dismissing Friedrich. Then we are going to put you up on the kitchen table again in order remove the stitches. That in itself will not hurt overly much; it is dealing with the casts that will. Afterwards, I want to plaster on the permanent one. I do not feel it wise to allow you any more morphine; I am certain it was the cause of that frightful headache you suffered after the surgery. Some people respond adversely to the ungodly stuff, and you seem to be amongst them. But I will pour you a small draught of brandy."

"I do not care for any of your brandy!" I shout shrilly. Never, it seems, shall I ever forget that awful night, the horrid stench of the liquor on his breath.

"All right. We can use cognac, then."

"No! I'll not have any bedeviled tonics dulling my senses, do you understand? I do not want anything!"

"Well," Father replies softly, glancing back over his shoulder as he heads off toward the door, "perhaps you care not for a drop to dull the pain now. But believe me, Sasha—the hour will come when you will."

* * *

"Bless you, Your Honor, dear Lord in Heaven! I never expected—"

"Now, now, Viktor Ilyich," croons Father in a gruff, embarrassed tone, patting Bulya's arm and once again urging him with a pointed finger to tuck away in his pocket the conspicuously fat envelope stuffed with paper rubles. "You have served us well—please stop carrying on so! Consider it a wedding bonus. And our most humble salutations to you and your new bride."

"Bless you! Bless you, Mikhail Sergeyevich . . . ."

Basking within Bulya's radiant glow along with everyone else, I cannot help but wonder: *Have I done such an awful thing? Such a horrid, blasphemous thing?*

I no longer think so, not now. For here stands Bulya: gawky, buck-toothed Viktor Ilyich Bulyarin, burdened so with anxious eyes and wire spectacles, and for the longest time a favorite practical joke target of Volodya and his plowhand gang. Good old dependable, stick-in-the-mud Bulya: always so clumsy and awkward, that in all the years I have known him, never have I seen the fellow able for more than a few moments to stay astride a horse! Here is the same man who can never manage to collect his pencils or papers, whose notebooks spring off desks, tables, or from the buckboard rig at the slightest provocation—here stands Bulya with a grin stretched from ear to ear, his face sparkling with a jaunty roguishness beneath his high top hat, pressed cuffs of his woolen trousers lapping at polished wing-tip shoes, his high-buttoned frock coat broadening out narrow shoulders into manly sturdiness as, beaming with pride from head to toe, he squeezes his arm about the waist of his Natasha. And yet but two months ago, he remained terrified of approaching her, and this after two-and-a-half years of daily ravings about the girl in Pavel's office—until one day, wholly unable to concentrate upon my work because once every five minutes the fool would burst out with another spiel of lovesick lamentations, I threw down the Pskov market ledger in a pique of frustration and shouted: ‘Well, for Lord’s sake, man—then why do you not simply go and speak to the girl?’

‘Oh, but I cannot! What if . . . !’

And then followed an entire four days of ‘what if this?’ and ‘what if that?’ What if he was overly tempting the fates? What if she poked fun at him? And then what if Volodya and his group of snickering buddies found out that she had spurned him? And then what if, after that, he could never face her—or any other woman—again for the rest of his life? And on and on and on!

In an effort to salvage my sanity, I employed an age-old method to uncover the truth about Natasha’s feelings. Not magic, nor witchcraft. Merely a simple trick of common sense gleaned after lifelong exposure to the gossipings of Marnya and her two daughters: I asked one of the women.

Katya.

‘Of course she’s set on him! We spent the entire summer takin’ every chance te pass by the two of ye in Pavel’s office. Hasn’t he even seen her? Well, she don’t care about him bein’ ten years older! Hasn’t he even noticed her moonin’ for him until every blessed eve? Oh, but I fear is all hopeless, Sasha—she’s even shyer than he is! Lord, how we can git the two of ’em together?’

In reply, I made mention of an idea, fended off her excited pleas of curiosity, and asked her to wait a couple of days.

So the Tarot reading was not some spell I had conjured up like an ancient shaman out of earth’s astral abyss. I merely turned around a couple of the inverted cards, spoke in a convincingly mystical tone, and related to Bulya what I had already learned on the side.

“Bless you, Sasha, bless you!” he continues bellowing on, pressing my hand repeatedly until my knuckles begin to smart. “This miracle never would have occurred without the readin’ of the Tarot you performed that day! God be praised, we are so happy.”

“Bless ye, indeed, Aleksandr Mikhailovich,” Natasha murmurs shyly, her tall headdress draped high with clattering blue freshwater pearls and swaying forward precariously as, for about the twentieth time, she once again she bows her head. “May the Saints always smile upon yer way. Me and my husband will stay forever in yer debt.”

“Please, Natalya Alekseyevna,” I reply, sweaty palms tightening about the handholds of my crutches. “In truth, naught so extraordinary did I accomplish. And please, as I asked of you both earlier: we really must speak of it no more.”

"Indeed," I hear Father say gruffly, his tone caught with distraction as his arm slips with protective firmness about my shoulders once again.

To my relief, the bridal pair wanders off. Past the raucous group of merrymakers throwing one another about the floor in a wild Cossack dance while at the same time tossing back and forth several full foaming bottles of champagne, Father's stare remains fixed upon the small group of men clustered off in the alcove leading to the small house's adjoining room. Bulya's eldest brother, Semyon—a dashing opposite in character, who as a one-time groomsman, taught me to ride scarce before I could even walk—stands beneath the archway, conversing with several members of the local *zemstvo* council, including his and Bulya's father, Ilya Isayevich, a churlish man with a balding head and sniveling voice for whom I have always felt the greatest repugnance. His replies shave across the blaring music in loud guttural snatches, the latest of which causes my heartbeats to stab into my throat: "Priestly sorcerers, my ass!" he grumbles out. "We'll have none o' them slitherin' *volkhvi* ne'er-do-wells 'round these parts! Bet yer life on it, we'll smoke that witch out, wherever he or she is. We'll set the dogs on such waywards 'til they make for the Urals. What, red hair? By the devil—oh, hush, woman, is hardly good luck! Red hair's naught but a portent o' all the Evil One's doins, that it is! An' probably naught better than dyed mash on some slut, only that it is, too. . . ."

"Never mind," Father whispers close to my ear. "The man is merely blowing off steam. And only drunk as a pig." His grip again tightens around my stiffened shoulders.

Suddenly, there sounds a loud guffaw, and across the frantic back-and-forth windings of the dancers, old Bulyarin doffs his hat in a groveling display of formality and bows down low in our direction, bleating out coarsely: "Akkh! To be beggin' yer pardon, gents! No offense intended, Yer Exc'lency! Aleksandr Mikhailovich."

As I stare, flushing, to the floor, Father waves him off with a joking laugh and once again raises his glass. Across the noisy room, the two of them then shout out hearty toasts to the bridal couple and bolt down their champagne. But as old Bulyarin yells: "Once agin, no offense!" before turning back to Semyon and the others, a chilling fear lances to the inner core of my soul, spurred on by the hint of menace lingering in the man's gaze. *Could I be mistaken? Or was his tone bordering blatantly upon the sarcastic?*

Perhaps not such a terrible thing have I done—but definitely not a very wise thing. Not wise at all.

"Father, I cannot keep standing anymore." Unable to stop myself, I shift my full weight back into his girth, again clamping rigid hold down upon both crutches.

"I know. I sent Rolfe for the troika a few moments ago; he should be waiting outside. You wish for me to carry you?"

"Please God, no! Not in front of all of these people."

"Well, let us steer you toward the door then. I'll be right behind."

Not an easy task: so many village folk have crowded into the small peasant house, all laughing and dancing off their liquor, that it is almost impossible for us to elbow our way through. But to my relief, Vliny spots us and shoves out in front of me. "I'll round up the women," he tells Father, walking backwards with outstretched arms to clear a pathway to the door.

"You shall do no such thing!" Father protests loudly. "Why do you think I insisted upon bringing both troikas? Get back with Marnya and the girls and down yourself another bottle of that fine Bordeaux champagne, my old friend!" As we reach the door, Father claps Vliny upon the shoulder, winking at his old companion's widening gap-toothed grin. "Rolfe's free to turn around and head back should he choose. I know Eva will have a fit to be stuck here without him. It is simply that Sasha's exhausted, and I must get him home."

The whiff of night air from the outside jars into the stuffy room with cool, tingling freshness, flecks of new snow scattering in about the pinewood threshold as we shove open the door. Vliny pulls aside, and I am almost through when the sound of my name—echoing from somewhere off in the crowd with the strangest lilting sense of familiarity—catches my ear. Turning, I encounter, dwarfed beneath a smaller but no less imposing pearl-studded headdress, another of the fairy princesses from the wedding party.

"Aleksandr Mikhailovich!" she cries again, halting with a sudden gasp of embarrassment as Father peers down at her, his eyebrows raised, his glare harshly critical of such boldness which must appear, indeed, unseemly in his eyes: a mere peasant girl shrieking her heart out across the room to the landlord's son.

"Yekaterina Dmitryevna," I reply, going short of breath and scarce remembering to bow my head in polite greeting.

"Oh, I am sorry—ye're tryin' te leave! I jest wanted ye te know, Aleksandr Mikhailovich, that our prayers go with ye."

Blushing with embarrassment, she nods in the direction of my leg.

In truth, I had not expected Katya to ever take notice of me again after our row that day in the barn. Still, unable to help it, all eve long I have been stealing glances, watching her dote upon the arm of her new beau, a sturdy peasant fellow with a lean gait and long, graceful legs. A skater, obviously. With resignation, I tell myself again to share, not envy, her happiness. Never will I be able to skate again—not with her, nor anyone. Father has insisted it will be strictly out of the question.

"Thank you, Yekaterina Dmitryevna," I say to her.

"Katya!" Laced with irritation, an appalled matronly wail flies across heads of the crowd. "Heaven have mercy on our souls! What do ye think ye're doing, botherin' the Count?"

"Christ's name!" Father grumbles, rolling his eyes as Katya scurries back to her mother.

Abruptly, dizziness begins overpowering me. "Come along!" Father urges, his hands already guiding beneath my arms. "Only two more steps, only one more step—and through the door—"

"Lord God be praised!" I exclaim. Both crutches tumble off sideways into the snow just as Father's grip closes firm about my chest. Eyes not moving for one second away from the dangling cast, he hoists his other arm up beneath my knees, lifting me to him like a fragile doll. Impatiently, he signals for Rolfe to wind the troika in closer between the groups of tethered horses and numerous sledges packed into the clearing.

"Thank you for waiting until we reached the outside," I murmur gratefully, hanging on for dear life, my arms clamped fast around his neck.

"Yes, yes—and how my Sasha would have died of embarrassment! Well, supposing I was fifteen with such a fair lass chasing me across a noisy wedding crowd, I'd near kill myself too, and try to clear the door before anyone could see me being carried off by my papa like a babe in arms." He shakes his head, hearty laughter rumbling across his chest. "One o'clock in the morning, or thereabouts, surely," he goes on, gazing upward and eyeing the moonless black sky. "Makes quite a long day, my boy. Actually, I think you managed pretty damn well."

All day I have been blessing the Saints that October, over September, is one of the most favored months for weddings—for had it been any earlier, I would certainly have missed seeing Bulya in all his glory, and Natasha coiffed in her puffed sleeves and rolls of pearls, gleaming like a little firebird shot straight from the ancient legends' winds. But between the morntide procession of the families throughout the village, the long afternoon of Holy Sacraments, then these evetide revelries at the bride's father's house lasting clear into wee small hours of the next starry morn, the festivities have drained the precious reserve of energy I had built up in anticipation. My first true outing since the accident could perhaps have been much more temperate in nature, indeed.

Bells jingling, the troika shears off in a blinding burst of speed through the woods toward the estate house. As I sigh with relief, Father wraps old furs closely up about the two of us; loosens his cravat. Helps to loosen mine.

"Old Bulyarin," I say, my voice trailing off through a weary shudder. "The Black Hundreds."

"Yes."

"He knows. Father, he knows it's me!"

"Calm yourself." Pulling out his pocket watch and squinting at its shiny face in the darkness, Father shakes his head and wraps an arm about me closer, murmuring: "Of course he knows it's you."

"Well, dear God in His Graces! Then how can you sit and so casually—"

"Because I bought him off."

"What?" Head lapping against his shoulder, I stare upward through a haze of confusion in the star-laced darkness.

Father snorts derisively. "He knows it's you, and I bought him off. I bought off the priest, too."

"The Orthodox priest!" Small wonder the man kept eyeing me so strangely all during the wedding ceremony.

"Bulyarin is naught but an old gaffer," Father goes on. "Pay his words no heed. Neither of them will bother us about it again."

"But how can you be so sure?"

"Because I bought them both off. Vodka talks quite loudly in this country. Along with gold. Or had you never noticed?"

Unconvinced, I seize his collar, pleading: "But, Papa—I tell you, Bulyarin is different, I can sense it! Vindictive, the man is, utterly self-serving—and possessed, I think, of a reactive temper putting to bloody shame even staunch Orthodox fanatics."

"I know. That is why, after I bought him off, I told him I beat hell's guts out of you when I found out about your witchcraft dabbling. Which is the truth, yes?"

Uncomfortably, I look away.

"And then, by way of further explanation, I made mention about how you took the fall—accidentally, I told him—out of your bedroom window. Told him it was just and due punishment meted out by the Good Lord Himself for anyone, Count's son or no, involved with any pagan blasphemy."

In response, I stiffen away from him, the troika bells lashing on through a jarring glare of silence.

"Oh, you needn't start sulking!" he exclaims, yanking me back to his side. "And worry your head no more over Bulyarin. His Black Hundreds have more interest in stringing up leftist upstarts like your old friend Vladimir Denisovich than in plying their vengeance upon gentry sons who stick their noses into a little trouble now and then. You must remember that power is the object; the status quo of the old aristocratic system is what the bastards are attempting to ensure, methods deplorable as they are. I suppose should the socialists ever triumph, Bulyarin and his toady fools will simply gravitate to the opposing side and carry on their terrorizing from there. Little in politics ever changes. Whatever the case, it is just as well to remember what I told you: keep that book and those cards put away in your room, show them to no one else. For your own good, Sasha."

"Yes, sir."

Up ahead, the onion-domed outline of the estate house cupola swings into view. Again I lift my head from Father's shoulder and peer up at him through the darkness, murmuring: "Volodya was not at the wedding, was he?"

"Took off soon as he could after the flogging, so they tell me. Probably caught the train to Pskov, or Petersburg, even." A long sigh heaves forth, speared with pangs of regret. "Damn foolish," he mutters to himself. "Drunken, foolish thing to do."

He presses his arm close, and I lean into him again, vaguely wondering—past his stilted answers offered to my profusion of questions at the time—about how matters truly resolved themselves last month during the hearing, when he was forced to make his explanations to *zemstvo* council. The first time since the accident that he ventured much farther than earshot distance away from the house. And even then, his trepidation was obvious in leaving for so long. Wholly on my account.

With my arms wrapped around his neck again, Father waves Rolfe and the troika away, and with light-footed, youthful ease, carries me through the brisk cover of the *parosha,* winter's first layering of snow, and on into the house. Upstairs in my room, his touches are gentle and endearing as he assists me with undressing for bed, at last tenderly tucking the heavy quilts and furs up about my neck. "Good night, my Sashenka," he murmurs, planting a kiss upon his finger and stamping it to the tip of my nose just as he once did every night for a time when I was very young.

Dreamily, I smile up at him—and touch a kiss to my own finger, pressing it warmly against his hand. "Good night, Papa."

And again we are drawn closer—another night, another barrier broken down; another bridge of the old fierce ravings torched clear unto ashes scarce remembered. In the past weeks, thread by reluctant, fraying thread, astute resistance has been slowly untangling the spool of my anger wound to such a bitter torque last month when he plastered on the permanent cast. Ever since then, our house has been filled with more generous warmth and talk and laughter than in many a long frigid year—for our nightly quarrels have ceased in entirety. Instead, my father's words and every action have become therapeutic, gentle, and kind—just as when I was a child! Now, in spite of my leg and the pain; in spite of the many punishing years to which I have been subjected beneath his hand, I can see that, in the end, it will perhaps be unthinkable to hold firm to my angry resolution to feel only hatred for this man, Mikhail Sergeyevich Sekovsky—haughty Count, old country doctor—my father, who in truth appears only to love me more than I could ever have imagined.

* * *

For three more days waning on into three more nights, he continues to dote upon me his warmth and caring. But then I make the mistake of asking the wrong thing—one meager offhand suggestion—and our lull of peace shatters apart again irrevocably, the renewed horror of confrontation threatening through Vliny's widened eyes and frantic voice as he bursts raggedly after me into the drawing room, hollering as if to save his life: "Sasha, fer yer own good, ye git back over on that sofa, and by the devil's arse, ye stay there!"

"No!" I protest, toppling over in my effort against him several French provincial chairs. "Hey! Why, you miserly old lout! You give me back my crutches!"

"Watch the cast!" Father roars from the doorway, his taut finger pointing concern above rage across Marnya's head—while she continues lashing out at him like a banshee consumed with the switch from the kitchen broom.

"Foolish weddings!" I shout back at Father as Vliny struggles to keep me pinned down. "Merely get one all garbled up, looney and sentimental as an old cross-eyed, bubble-headed babushka! Lord! What a fool I was to imagine you care one whit about me at all! To ever hope you might see some light of reason . . . you know what you can do, *Papa?* You—you can go and drink the piss of the devil!"

"Sit down there, Sasha, and shut up!" Vliny roars into my ears, grabbing a fat pillow and stuffing it into my face. Behind him, Father's voice thunders up into every board of the rafters: "Insufferable, curse-beladen Tyler blood! England! I wish to God I had never set foot in England!"

"Mikhail Sergeyevich, no!" Swinging the broom with all her strength, Marnya shoves flat into him, blocking his path again with her body as he tries in vain to surge past her.

"Misha!" Vliny doubles around to assist Marnya, his arms flailing out in desperate stabs of admonition. "Blast it, man—will ye git control o' yerself? Don't ye see what the lad is doin'? Ye told me this would happen when the child started gittin' better—remember? Ye told me we could only expect this."

"Give me back my crutches!" I shout again, stabbing out for anything—first a candy dish, another tea glass, two small porcelain statuettes. One after another into the fireplace they go, shattering into heaps of smithereens.

"Sashenka, stop it!" Marnya lumbers up to the table, clearing all other objects—whether filled with liquid or no—off into her apron with one fell-swoop of her arm.

"Thief!" I shout on at Father, shaking at him a white-gripped fist of defiance. "Robber-baron of all affection—you and your godforsaken shrine to a dead woman's memory . . . well, at least you had decency enough to change the linen! When I finally peeked into that room last year, I thought I'd find her stinking blood and all the birthing water left exactly as it was, crusted up over the sheets."

At this, the three of them freeze in their tracks, jaws dropping as they stare at me dumbly, all gasping in shock.

"Why—why you little acid-tongued viper from hell!" Father rasps out finally, his face glowering livid purple with rage.

In reply, I haul off and spit at him through the air.

"Misha, *nooo!*"

Ramming past Vliny and Marnya, Father dives for the sofa—but they both leap after him, each clamping onto an arm. "Ye see what he is doin'!" Vliny screams frantically. "Misha! Don't ye see what the boy is doin'?"

"Yes, by God—I see what he is doing! What he has always done, all his life: driving me out of my senses!"

"And ye remember what I said to do when it happened! Do ye remember, man?"

Wrathfully, Father turns upon Vliny. "All right, then! But answer me this: are you aware of any other father with any other son, city or country, noble or peasant, who ends up with a literal war breaking out in his house every single time he exercises his parental prerogative and utters the word 'no?'"

"Misha—"

"Whatever happened to respect for one's elders? Whatever happened to respect for members of one's own family! You want to know the first golden rule Russian children learn, Sasha?" Father shouts, whirling around and pointing me down. "Respect for their elders—particularly their fathers!"

"Indeed!" I shout back. "Ever since the Awesome Ivan impaled his own son to death!"

"Oh, by the Saints alive!" Father's fist slams down onto the fireplace mantle with such a blast of force that half of Marnya's icons fly off, startled jumble of holy faces clattering noisily down to the hearth.

"Misha!" Vliny pleads on, violently shaking Father's arm. "What did I say to do?"

"All right, man—so I am going, and I am doing it!"

Rattling off a torrent of mumbled curses, Father tears off his shirt, sending half the buttons flying, and shoves it into a wad in Vliny's arms. Then he disappears out the drawing room archway, heels of his boots pounding down the hall in furious banging thuds as Vliny charges after with a colorful cursing spiel of his own. From the woodroom then sounds the crashing of tools, muffled sounds of their angry voices.

"I am sorry she died!" I holler at the top of my lungs, cupping my hands and widely projecting my voice.

"Sasha, no!" Marnya exclaims.

"I am sorry she died! God on all of heaven's earth, you have no idea how sorry I am, Father! How do you think life bids for me—looking almost exactly like her, looking like a girl? I tell you, I am sorry your Lissa was the one who died . . . and not me!"

"Sashenka!"

Again I shake Marnya off. "And now, on top of everything else," I shout on, "my own father throws me out a second-story window! My own father makes me a cripple!"

"Stop it!" Marnya demands, shaking me up and down. "Stop tormentin' yer poor father so!"

"Give me back my crutches!" I hiss at her.

Small eyes screwed up to tiny holes in her heavily lined face, Marnya crosses her arms and draws herself up to her full height, glaring down at me and barking: "No!"

"You meddling old bitch."

In quick response, the back of her hand plows straight across my face.

"W-Why, you!" I gasp out, stunned, glaring up at her.

"If ye ever talk te me in such words agin, Aleksandr Mikhailovich," she yells, seizing my shoulder and sinking her nails in until the pain forces me to cry out, "I swear I'll fill yer filthy, disgustin', gutter-seepin' mouth full te the brim with ash from the sooty hearth an' scrub 'til the very whites of yer teeth scour off! Do ye hear me?"

Cringing back into the cushions of the sofa, I bring my hand up to my stinging jaw. *I can't believe she hit me! I can scarce believe it!*

Father then reappears in the doorway, drenched with sweat, auburn-white hairs glistening across his heaving chest like drops of darkened blood. Pointing across at me just as I open my mouth, he shouts: "Shut up, Sasha! *Nobody* is going into Melissa's room."

My protests to this latest rebound stick hard within my throat—for with horror, I stare downward to the object grasped so passionately within his hand.

An axe.

Then Vliny shoves back in past Father—but with his own tone greatly calmed. "Jest remember, Misha," he repeats, "it's only 'cause the boy is gittin' better. Ye knew it would be like this. Remember?"

"Humph!" Slinging the axe up over his shoulder, Father turns and again bangs down through the hallway, his shouts trailing fiercely after him: "Cursed I am, cursed I swear! The devil take England!"

Outside, a splintering crash shatters into the still night, followed in earnest by steady rhythmic poundings as Father begins chopping wood.

After a long pause filled with shrugs and quirky, indiscernible hand gestures to Marnya, Vliny wanders out again after Father.

Ears smarting black fire, I keep my arms crossed and my eyes glued upon sight of the thick woolen stocking topped over the toe of my cast.

Marnya's shadow stoops; I note the swish of the broom, the clinking of glass into the dustpan as for several tense, silent moments she busies herself with the cleaning up. Finally, she once again moves to the side of the sofa. "I will give ye yer crutches now," she murmurs, retrieving them from the floor.

"You hit me," I rasp out, biting my lip.

"And ye hurt my feelins greatly!" she retorts. "Sayin' what filth ye said."

"I cannot recall you ever hitting me."

"Ye were nine and a half. Somethin' like this: all yer rotten curse words. After bein' with yer cousin agin in Petersburg."

"Well," I murmur hoarsely. "All right, then. I—I am sorry. I apologize, Matushka."

"I'm sorry, too. Do ye want these crutches, or no?"

As I take them, her hand edges toward a gentle motherly squeeze of reconciliation—but I fling it angrily away, choking out: "Simply leave me alone! Please?"

"Humph! Very well," says Marnya, stonily averting her gaze.

The dustpan clatters loudly in rhythm with the splitting of the wood outside as she grumbles her way back into the kitchen.

Bare of five minutes later, it sounds: a frantic onslaught of fist-pounding upon the front doors. I hear Marnya scurrying to answer it and catch a glimpse of Vliny bursting back through the hall and tearing at his hair, exclaiming: "Lord in Heaven, not tonight! My head's achin' bad 'nough as it is! What on earth, now?"

Voices ensue, and they retrieve Father, axe and all, from the back. I hear his pointed questions: "How long ago—yesterday? How many? I thought you had Shchabikov for a doctor there. Oh, for the love of Christ! You mean he took a fall in it, too? Well, why in the world did you neglect to come sooner? Oh, no—my son is much better. Of course I can . . . ."

Momentarily, he strides into the drawing room, pulling on another shirt, a thick sweater, and then his tie and formal hunting jacket as Marnya hands them over. "I have to ride down the lakeshore, Palandin's estate, twenty versts south of Kolinsky's," he says in a tightened murmur. "There's been another sledding accident. Damn these people for always building their infernal ice slides up far too high."

I offer no response; merely continue staring straight ahead as he again rechecks the cast and proceeds hurriedly through the daily therapy with my legs.

"You will ask Vliny to help you run through this?" he then says. "It is very important, Sasha. Do it least four, better five times each day. For the pain, you can continue taking cognac in your tea, and also the valerian drops whenever you feel the need. But above all, be careful of the cast—promise me, no recklessness, please. I know not how long I will be gone."

Reluctantly, I nod, avoiding his glance.

"Are you going to be all right?" he then asks.

And pauses, waiting.

Gaze still locked upon the sight of my toes, I reply: "Do you want to know what I think? That you wish the wood you have been chopping out there so fervently was, in truth, my head. So why don't you simply bring the axe back in here, and have done with it, and absolve us both of our misery?"

Whirling around, Father storms away without reply, and out in the hallway, I hear his further dictated instructions regarding my care made to Vliny, to Marnya. And then the front doors slam shut with a shuddering bang, at last leaving the house in an abrupt vacuum of peace.

Outside, bells of a troika fade tinkling into the night, horses' hooves lumbering off through the snow far into the distance.

* * *

"And there we was!" Vliny exclaims, sinking back beside me into the cushions of the sofa. Laughing, he hoists his feet up upon the ancient trestle-table and begins postulating scenic emphasis through the air with the aid of one of Marnya's crocheting needles. "Guns blastin' and cannons roarin' right out o' the very righteous bowels o' death!" he goes on. "But me, I'm quartermaster, an' all I'm thinkin' is, these boys—the one's that's left, anyway—been passin' hardtack gutters fer days; got te git somethin' decent te eat. So I starts headin' back—an' lo and behold, he near runs smack into me, an' I yell: 'Hey, Doctor! Ye lost yer mind? Git back behind the line, fer God's sake! Can't ye see this is the grimin' battlefield?'"

I shoot Vliny a frosty glare: *I know what you are trying to do. And it is not going to work.*

"Akkh, quit yer grumblin', minstrel!" And he grabs my cap from the table and slaps it back onto my head, pulling it down on each side low to my ears.

"Papa!" The two sisters, Eva and Tereza, spring forward from their chairs, chiding him in unison: "Stop teasin' poor Sasha all the time! Let him play."

"Yaaa, Papa!" Marnya grins at me and hurls another ball of yarn into Vliny's face. "Stop interruptin' God's songs o' Heaven! Let the child play."

Grumbling agreement, I yank off my cap and start smacking Vliny soundly in the shins, but he only continues poking for my ribs—while again Marnya and the sisters protest: "Papa, stop it! Let him play."

"Akkh, women! Every boy needs a fair amount o' wrestlin' now and then." Giving in at least for the moment, Vliny hurls the yarn ball back at Marnya, allowing me to retrieve my flute and pick up again on the soft background flutter of a Handel sonata.

"Anyways," Vliny goes on, "I knew who he was, always takin' provisions to the infirmary and all, and I run after him, yellin': 'Doctor! Ye crazy fool—git down, fer the righteous love o' God! Git down!' But do ye think the man would listen fer even one second? Oh, no! 'Stead, he runs straight away, tryin' te git a better view. I could scarce believe it! I mean, bullets are flyin' straight 'round the two of us everywhere! So I run after him, yellin' first in Russian, and then in French—hopin' maybe that would catch his attention—but no, he's still runnin'; runs all the way te this poor lad half-sunk in the sand. Starts checkin' fer the signs o' life, and I yell: 'Dead, I tell ye! He's dead!' Course, then he yells back about hearin' a heartbeat, but two seconds more, an' it don't matter: mortar blast fells three more of 'em on top o' this first one, and near blows the doctor's head off, too. 'There's no hope fer it—git back te the one's ye kin help!' I tell him, an' I grab his arm and drag him off with me, tryin' to find cover. Course, he struggles straight away, an' I think, Lord in Heaven! Got te be right out o' Petersburg, no kind o' horse sense at all! Next thing I know, there he is, best target ye ever saw in yer whole blitherin' life with all that flyin' red hair, standin' up on a mound in front o' the water wagon an' watchin' the row o' cannon go off, yellin': 'God Almighty! Just look at the sight of it!'"

Vliny, Marnya, Eva, and Tereza all burst into roar of hysterical laughter, and unable to help myself, I become caught up in it, too. With the skill of a carnival ventriloquist, Vliny has every inflected nuance of Father's speech down to mimicked perfection, and it sounds exactly like him.

"'God Almighty! Just look at the sight of it!'" he bellows out again. "An' I'm after him, screamin': 'Git down! Git down!' An' jest as I land on top o' the man, the mortar hits fer sure, blastin' into the barrels o' the water wagon behind us, chunks o' board flyin' out in all directions and water gushin' everywhere, drenchin' both of us head te foot!"

This inspires another round of screeching, choke-filled laughter. "And then what happened?" I ask, wiping at my eyes as Marnya winks at me.

"Then? Well, figurin' we was both stuck together right to our skins an' covered with mud, we did what any decent gents would do: introduced ourselves. First thing he says to me is: 'You're from Pskov? Well, by God—that makes us chess partners, then.'"

I begin closely examining the keys on my flute. "So. And what happened after that?"

"What? Well, after that, we got us back over te the infirmary, an'—"

"No, Vliny. I mean, what happened to the two of you after all that? After the War?"

Of details of Father's and Vliny's adventures after the Crimean War, I have been in continual pursuit for ages. But no matter who or how I ask, no matter when or where, little ever results but vague, shallow answers.

"We toured Europe together! Akkh, now there was a high-rollin' time, back in them days."

"Vliny—"

"An' then he met yer mum."

"That was over thirty years later! What happened in between?"

"Akkh, youth!" he bellows, waving me off. "Fer all that fancy schoolin' yer papa's been shovin' ye full of, still don't know nothin', do ye? Man's got te make a livin', that he does! Think all our lives have jest been full o' boozin' war stories? Makin' a livin', settin' yer nose te the grindstone, that's what life is." Breaking into an enormous grin, his eyes dancing with mirth, Vliny points across at Marnya, proclaiming loudly: "Somethin' that poor fool Ippolit never learned."

Sighing, I look away. Of course, the perfect response is always to change the subject. Vliny wiggles out of it this way every time.

"Really, Papa!" Eva cries, glaring across at Vliny. Drawing the bunting up close about her infant son, she nestles him into the crook of one arm, while with the other she begins profusely crossing herself. The other two women follow ready suit, but Marnya—that old self-satisfied smirk overtaking her face—grunts out matter-of-factly: "The man choked te death."

Tereza then bounds to her feet and hovers over Marnya with a glower of indignation, exclaiming: "Mother! Must ye sit there an' gloat so about it?"

"Oh, sit back down!" Vliny yells, laughing as he boots Tereza back into her chair with a nudge at her backside from his foot.

"Papa!"

"The man choked te death," Marnya repeats, nodding as if having uttered a holy affirmation.

Beneath the affronted perusal of both Eva and Tereza, I attempt without much success to subdue my own chuckles. Common knowledge around the village of Watery Forever has it that Vliny was carrying on wildly with Marnya while she was still married to Ippolit, a horrible drunkard trapper who forever gambled away all his earnings and beat her incessantly every time he pulled back into town with a new load of pelts. The girls were still toddlers when one day, much to the convenience of everyone involved, Ippolit happened to choke to death on a fat piece of gristled bone that somehow 'accidentally' got cooked into a meat pie.

Marnya and Vliny married bare of a month later.

"The man choked te death!" Marnya declares again with the same smug, almost imperceptible smile.

"Akkh, Strudel-nibblins!" Vliny swoons, clasping his hands together and gazing tenderly over at Marnya. "Yer cookin's got te be most renowned all o' this side o' the Urals. An' jest what a man could die fer!"

"Papa!"

The girls pounce upon Vliny, and the dispute breaks out in full swing once again. Both waving their arms, Tereza and Eva shout down into their step-father's face as, laughing uproariously, he defends himself with pillows from the sofa.

Cuddling her grandson, cooing and whispering baby-nonsense to him, Marnya glances up toward me and winks again.

"Hope I never vex you that sorely," I whisper across, laughing.

"Akkh, dumplin'!"

The girls, now shrieking with laughter themselves, both begin pummeling Vliny with pillows. Scooting away from the blows, I start disconnecting my flute, easing the pieces down into their velvet troughs in the case. Despite the ever generous show of familiarity from these dear people—yet again evidenced by Marnya's pointed finger and her admonitions of: "Stay, Sashenka! Stay!"—I have begun to feel quite the intruder, privy to a wedge of family closeness in which I truly have no place.

Father has often become cross with me for spending as much time as I do with them in their quarters. But unlike many of the issues about which we disagree, in this case, his point never prevails for long. Many a night he wanders back in here himself for awhile; he and Vliny always have both a chess and a card game brewing constantly. Warm and darkly rustic is the abode at the back corner of the house, the wood furniture draped with homespun pillows and endless layers of Marnya's brightly crocheted afghans, the scent of hickory and tallow from the old candles they still prefer to use lingering with a pungent bite throughout the air. Stark contrast it is indeed to the environs of the main house, its lofty, spacious downstairs parlor always sprayed with a shower of light from the many rows of high cathedral windows. Eclecticism reigns supreme in Lissushka's primary rooms all boasting French provincial furniture, the curio cabinets filled with my mother's English china and Father's oriental porcelain artifacts, the walls hung with many a modern painting from Holland or Italy or England. Much like Western Europe, to a large extent, are the rooms of the main house. And totally like Russia is the backward portion comprising the servants' quarters.

But the house breathes Russia, too—everywhere awash in icons, mica-tile, amber-inlaid frames of mirror-glasses, and large family portraits. Passed down over long generations, the somber eyes of my forefathers reflect fortitude and strength, staunch courage emanating from the determined placement of their hands, unbridled will of the ancient Novgorodian traditions, self-rule and democracy—although subjugated now for so many long centuries—yet lurking in the proud, spirited hold of their heads.

It is heritage, and it is mine—yet only partly. The other half lies past a long line of Elizabethan courtiers far back in legendary adventures of medieval Plantagenet England. Knights in shining armor and Slavic warriors bearing the black eyes of Tartars. England and Russia. Unlike Vliny and his family, rooted in traditions of singular Slavic peasantry, I remain forever torn between two opposing reaches of the world, never quite certain of my true place.

"Akkh—stay, dumplin'!" Marnya continues urging as I reach for the crutches.

"Is that Rolfe?" Eva suddenly exclaims, pillow poised over Vliny in the air.

Everyone quiets, listening: from the yard outside, the sound of hoofbeats barely echoes, faint poundings of hope thudding through the snowpack in the distance.

In a fit of haste, I ram up on my crutches and bound along with the rest of them for the window. “Sasha!” cries Vliny from behind me, “will ye simply slow down an’ take some care?”

Once he slides open the window and pries back the shutters, we stare outward at a lone horseman. Rolfe. But no other with him, nor any troika in sight.

“Perhaps he has word,” Vliny murmurs in my ear.

“I scarce voiced any concern!” I snap, glaring around at him.

“Ye don’t have te. The longer he’s gone, the more it’s written all over yer face.”

“Oh, piss on it, Vliny.”

Marnya shoots me a raised eyebrow for swearing, but Vliny ignores it and heads outside.

At last Rolfe bursts into the yard, near flying from the saddle in his haste to dismount the horse. Stomping the snow from his boots when he reaches the threshold along with Vliny, whose face is long, he nods in my direction, and without even doffing his heavy sheepskin greatcoat, he starts toward me, attempting with effort to fend off the flurry of kisses from Eva. “No sign,” he says, shaking his head with sad apology. “Not at Shchabikov’s, nor at Palandin’s, which he left five days ago. Not even northward at Novgorod. I am very sorry, Aleksandr Mikhailovich. I must’ve checked at four or five other places, talked with near unto twenty people. No sign.”

I stare away to the window. The pane, the outer shutters remain covered with a thickened coat of frost. Outside, the snowbanks have crested to almost four feet. Although the blizzard of the last week has subsided to a mere fraction of its former tumult, since sundown yet another chill-wind has begun lashing fiercely against the forested side of the house, ever dreaded portent from the Siberian east.

And still he is gone—out there. Somewhere.

Today is the ninth day.

* * *

“I’m tellin’ ye, Sasha,” Vliny says for the near-hundredth time, “the man jest would o’ holed up somewhere. Would o’ waited it out. Would never be fool enough te try gittin’ through this kind o’ storm.”

"I know, I know." In a pique of frustration, I slam my pencil down, and stare with a weary sigh at the littering of orchestrations spread out in all directions to farthest reaches of the kitchen table.

"So jest go back in there an' try te git some sleep."

"I can't."

"Look," Vliny goes on in a paternal tone, "I know ye hate sleepin' in the drawin' room every single night. But I am not lettin' ye back up them stairs 'til he gits back. If he finds out ye been up there on them crutches without him, he'll have my head!"

"It is not that."

"Well, what then?"

"It's been twelve days. What if he never comes back, Vliny? Never, ever again?" *God! Twelve whole days . . . .*

"Sasha, of course yer papa is comin' back!"

"Vliny, you and I both know that he has never been away for this long before, not on an unplanned call." Once again I rake trembling fingers through my hair. "No matter how fierce the storms," I whimper on, "no matter how cold the nights, he's never been away doctoring before for all of twelve days! What on earth will I do if he never comes home again? Oh, dear Lord God . . ."

"Sasha!" Vliny squeezes fast hold of my arm. "Calm yerself, lad. I think ye underestimate yer old papa greatly! Why, I remember when . . ."

But Vliny's stories render me no solace now.

What if Father does not return? The only reason would be if he could not return. At all.

Which would mean that, somehow, somewhere—on some lonely, godforsaken country road, in some frozen bog or remote stretch of the snow-covered woods somewhere—something has happened to him.

And if something has indeed happened to my father, it would mean many things.

I would inherit the title: become the owner, the landlord. *The Count.*

A thought of which I have always been terrified. Little desire have I to become a farmer, ever to fret continually over the keeping of the bees and harvesting of the flax and hemp. For dealing with the peasants and their plows and harrows, for hedging politics with others of the gentry or members of the local *zemstvo*, I fear I possess precious little talent. Our family can scarce be compared to the Morozovs, the Vorontsovs, or the Sheremetevs, their vast landed holdings scattered across sixteen or seventeen different provinces with thousands of peasants within easy tenure. Were that the case, my duty would be less profound, for I could simply hire someone to oversee the whole tedious enterprise and have done with such tiresome worrying! But my father's title derives only from an inheritance gleaned long ago in a greater historic far away—and this, his only remaining estate, is small by relative comparison to land tracts held these days by other even minor gentry. And Lissushka's domain yet continues to gradually diminish, year by year, as more tracts of land are bequeathed out to leaseholders. And for years now, the farm has steadily been losing money.

I know. I work on the ledgers. Only the revenue from our investments in Germany and France—vineyards Father owns jointly with several partners in the wine country of Bordeaux and Cologne—offsets the continual loss from the farming operation and provides our family with a secure source of income. Peeled deep from the pocketbook, Father's wedding gift to Bulya was, indeed, a true gift of his heart. In society, appearances must always be kept up, and this we manage decently enough, for we are not poor; we are comfortable. But only that. Cravats and tails and top hats we abscond from the finest of English tailors. But working clothes worn on a daily basis—cotton jackets and flannel shirts and trousers and even woolen underdrawers—suffer through many a mending time and again, for a constant balancing act it all is. And were something to happen to Father, then I would be thrown into the quandary of contending—as he now must—with every little financial contingency constantly, all the time!

Which burden I would not relish even were I not now near immobilized with this broken leg.

Perhaps on my part is due some attempt at selflessness over selfishness. For generations, sons everywhere, peasant or noble, city or country, have followed without any question in the footsteps of their fathers. But my father's way has never been mine. My way has been crystal clear ever since I was a child of nine and first wrapped my fingers around those silver keys.

All I have ever wanted to do is play the flute in an orchestra.

"Ye should go to bed," Vliny commands gruffly from behind, apparently having realized that I have caught not a single word of his rambling story.

But I shake my head at him, once again snatching up a ratty stack of orchestrations. "No. It is only half-past eleven. I must finish this. No one knows what is going to happen. You are certain this is all of them from upstairs? You checked under my bed, yes? I know several had been tossed beneath there."

"Sasha! I looked under three times, fer God's sake."

"All right. Thank you."

He stares in silence as, still fraught to distraction, I continue sorting through the mounds of manuscripts.

"Oh, hell! I s'pose I can't sleep, neither," he blurts out finally. "What kin I do te help?"

"Well." Stifling another yawn in spite of myself, I squint through the bare glow of the lamplight and murmur: "I am attempting to break these into groups by composer. Lord, I'd never realized I had accumulated this many. So let me see—"

I hand over half my stack.

"But!" Vliny protests loudly, "I don't know none o' these fancy—"

"Simply read off the titles, and I'll tell you where to put them. Most all are in French."

"But—"

"Oh, come, Vliny! I know you sneak books from Father's library. I know bloody well that you can read French."

"Humph! Oh, all right." His brow furrowed, he peers down at the first manuscript with a critical glare and grumbles beneath his breath: "*A Little Night Music.*"

"Mozart." I point across the table. "Here, second stack on the left."

"Humph! All right, uh . . . *Concerto in C Major for Flute and Orchestra.*"

"Also Mozart."

"Akkh! Well, then, this next one seems te be missin' a title. Got a name, but I can't read yer writin': 'Quo . . . Quant . . . .'"

"Quantz. Johann Quantz. Beside the Mozart stack."

"Humph! Uh, let's see now . . . *Dance of the Blessed Spirits* from *Orfeo ed Euridice.*"

"Christoph Gluck. Right here, by my arm. Thank you."

"Akkh! Uh, next is *Leonore Overture Number Three.*"

"Beethoven."

"Oh, now I heard o' him!"

"Uh-huh. Set it over between Quantz and Mozart—yes, that stack. There."

"Humph! Now, here's a bunch from Bach: *Orchestral Suite Number Two in B-Minor; Concerto in G-Minor for Flute and Strings; Flute Sonata Number Two in E-flat Major . . . .*"

With him grunting and me pointing, we continue sorting out the manuscripts. In the process, Eva, her two silky chestnut braids dangling down to her waist, wanders in sleepily and begins searching through the pantry for some porridge to spoon to the baby, who is teething. "Both lost yer senses, sortin' papers like that at this hour!" she murmurs under her breath, laughing, as she disappears back down the hall.

"Git back te yer bed, woman—this is all educated hankerins goin' on in here!" Vliny yells after her in a boisterous puffed-up voice. "Humph! Now, let's see—this next one's interestin'. No title, no name, not even any printed-up bars on it, jest a bunch o' lines an' all the notes set down in real fancy writin'."

"Let me see." I scan over the paper, immediately noting the familiar stylish hand. "Uh-huh. This is something of Nikolai's."

"He writes music?" cries Vliny, astonished.

"Oh, yes. You know my cousin is a formidable talent." With care, I fold up the paper and tuck it into the pocket of my shirt.

"Well, that so I understand, but—"

"You've heard him play, Vliny. The Zhelanovs are the ones who visit near every Christmastide. Although last year, only the youngest of the sisters, Anna and Eugenia and Tatyana, came along with Uncle Petya and Aunt Sophie and Nikolai. Remember the venison and sweetbreads we feasted on then? Eh? Damn!" I go on bemusedly, chin rested upon my fist. "And remember Christmas before last, what Nikolai had begun working on, the cascading triplets from *Sheherazade?* Lord, I'll never forget those moments: watching, listening, feeling caught in his wizard's spell, loath to budge away from the sound of that violin for the rest of my life! Ambitious he is, too—insists he's bound for a first section chair in the Maryinsky Orchestra. If anyone can accomplish such a feat of triumph, it is certain to be Nikolai."

"Sounds a rash proud te me," Vliny retorts, screwing up his face. "Humph! Musicians . . . ."

Unable to suppress a smile, I point to the stack in his hands.

"Oh! Here's the next one: *Midsummer Night's Dream*."

"Mendelssohn. Next to Quantz—over there."

"Humph! This one here says *Meditation* from *Thaïs.*"

"That's Jules Massenet—over here, beside the Gluck stack.

"Akkh, the *Nutcracker Suite!* Now, I know who this is."

He searches around the table and finds the Tchaikovsky pile just as I point it out.

"Humph! Now here's another one with all kinds o' written-out notes, but scribbled out back-handed. Got a title, though. Says: *Solo Wind."*

Letting out a gasp, I jolt upward in my chair and snatch out for the paper—but Vliny bounds close to the dome of the oil lamp, already intently inspecting the notations. "Hey!" he yells out with a widening grin. "This is yer writin'!"

"Vliny! Give me that—"

"Akkh! Heavens te bless my name, thanks be te God, praise all the merciful Saints! Never woulda imagined it—our Sasha is a composer!"

"I am not!"

"But—two whole pages! Lookit all this. . . ."

"Will you please give it to me?" At last I manage to wrest the pages from his grip, yelling: "And will you stop becoming so all worked up out of sorts? This is hardly extraordinary! Over half the themes in the piece are Nikolai's."

"Lord in Heaven!" Entirely ignoring me, Vliny continues crossing himself with glee, imparting mumbled blessings up to the ceiling with his hands.

"Vliny!"

"Saints be praised! Sweet Virgin be gloried!" he bellows on. "Our own Sasha—the one I been bouncin' on my knee and ribbin' all these years, the one that's so scared unto his very death o' bees—our own Sasha is one o' them highbrowed composers! Watch out, big ole St. Petersburg Conservatory of Music—our own Sasha's goin' te come an' take the whole town by storm!"

"Oh, *hell!"* I choke out in response, slamming my pencil once again to the table.

Vliny's eyes follow mine to the sight of the cast, propped up upon two pillows on an adjoining kitchen chair.

"Did you have to remind me?" I shout out at him.

"Well!" he retorts, his expression greatly subdued. "I was meanin'—well—next year."

"And most certainly, it could have been this year. I could be studying in Petersburg now, right this very moment, like I was supposed to! If *he* hadn't broken my leg."

In response, Vliny screws up his eyes at me, demanding: "Ye got te be so damned disagreeable all of the blessed time?"

"Oh, Lord God! Let's not have you start in on me, too." Glaring up at him, I wave across the table with spearing accusations of my pencil, exclaiming: "I am pained unto bloody death at hearing about my shortcomings. That is all everyone ever does—fling my every fault back into my face past oaths invoking the word: 'England!'"

"Oh, fer devil's sake! Pipe down, will ye, boy?" In a blustery huff, Vliny shoves the stack of orchestrations back into my arms. "Know where I'm not so welcome," he mumbles, heading off to return to bed. But at the threshold, he pauses to turn around, and informs me flatly: "Ye're wrong, Sasha."

"About *what?*"

"Ye're not so much like yer mum as ye think."

"Oh, no?" I snap in reply. "I have a father who will debate you into the barren ground over that contention."

"Indeed, he would. An' ye—not me—would be the one yellin' back, an' the whole house would be eruptin' into a flamin' mess agin, jest like the last time. An' ye know why?"

Caught off guard by his sudden empathetic tone, I meet his glance mutely, and shake my head.

"'Cause it's not Lissa Tyler that ye take so much after. No, it's more 'cause ye're jest like him."

Past hollow flickerings of the lamplight, my stare fixes upon my hands. Long slender fingers. Hands of a flutist, yes. Or hands of a surgeon—indeed, much like Father's. A very great deal.

"Well. It's the truth," Vliny mumbles, shrugging.

His footsteps then clod wearily down the hall.

I let out a sigh and rub both thumbs unto my brow as another broad gust of wind lashes against shutters of the kitchen window. The storm has not abated, not entirely. Not yet.

Guiltily—and acutely aware that I only take the trouble to show due reverence when pausing to ask favors—I stare upward.

But the Unsung Hero imparts only appropriate response, hovering far above in a cosmos of silent reprimand, murmuring low notes through waves of the astral aeons about regret. And immaturity.

Shuddering from head to foot, I bury my head into my arms upon the table, unmindful now of all of my carefully sorted orchestrations. "Please, dear Lord," I whisper out, "I beg you! Let Papa come home. I swear to You, I ask not for all the selfish reasons, my worries over the farm . . . perhaps Vliny is right. I must come to some understanding with my father, at least once during this pitiful, painful lifetime. Please, I promise to take back every hateful word I have ever said, because deep down, I—I do care about my father, a great deal . . . oh, God, please! Please let Papa come home soon. . . ."

* * *

I awaken in a stupor, lost in a trail of murky hovering light. To find the lamp all run out of oil, candle tapers on the table melted down into little round pods of wax. My reach, thrust blindly outward, sends several piles of orchestrations flying off into billowing scatters across the floor. From far off, Vliny's loud guffaws and grunts follow upon a squealing eruption of women's voices. I grope through every pocket, at last find my watch in the most unlikely one, its face reading seven.

Then, in a foot-stomping stampede, Vliny, Marnya, and Tereza tear through the kitchen—all three waving wildly and shouting as they rush by: "There he is!"

From the foyer archway, I watch as Father bursts inside, his ice-encrusted coat and hat and a thick bundle of crocheted scarves shoved into Marnya's joyfully awaiting arms. Smacking Vliny upon the shoulder, he shouts out upon a boastful swell of laughter: "Rook spears Knight across the board, my good fellow—I made it back, by damn!"

But his smile extinguishes instantly upon sight of me.

"For all of God's Wrath in Heaven!" he roars, his arm thrusting outward like a shot toward my face, his dark eyes gone ablaze with furious accusation.

Bracing for defense, I seize my grip upon the crutches—but before I know it, he has half-carried, half-dragged me across the floor and over to the boot bench, forcing my legs out prone upon it over a rash of prideful, sleepy protests. "For God's sake, Sasha—look at you!" he bellows out. "So gaunt and pale, even your freckles are fading away; so thin, Lord! Look at these two hollow eyes staring back at me from such sunken depths . . . blast it, Marina Ivanovna!" he yells off after Marnya—who, with Vliny, wisely makes a retreat for the kitchen, "have you not even been feeding this child? Valenti Apollonovich, you come back out here and face me like a man, you yellow-bellied vagabond scoundrel! Have you spent not a single moment of my prescribed therapy with this poor boy?" Shaking his head in disgust, Father begins poking with relentless worried stabs at the muscles in my legs.

"Papa, stop!" I plead as he continues thundering out at Vliny and Marnya in vehement interrogation. "We have followed your every instruction to the letter. Yes, of course—sometimes even six times a day. Of course they're feeding me! I promise I'm a greedy pig. Well, I suppose I am rather tired, afraid I've not caught much sleep."

"And why not?" And again he starts ranting: at Marnya for not bringing down enough blankets and pillows from my room; at Vliny for not riding in to the apothecary in town for more bottles of valerian drops; at Tereza and Eva for neglecting their share of the household chores—his anger sputtering steamily on, until I at last manage to interject loudly: "Papa! They have scarce been negligent, I swear! In fact, they've all been quite wonderful. It's simply that you have been gone for twelve whole days."

"Oh."

Letting out a gruff cough, he pushes to his feet and thrusts both hands into his pockets, towering above me with a suddenly tender, almost boyish awkwardness. "Forgive me, Sashenka. Lord, so perplexing it is at times, how events turn quickly one right after another."

He starts to pace, the heels of his boots tapping in comforting spurts of rhythm across the pinewood floor. "After I brought Shchabikov back to his house from Palandin's," he says, "the first storm hit, so I stayed put for a couple of days. Then I met an old Army friend, and storm or no storm, the next thing I knew, we had both ambled down south to Staraya Russa to stay for another couple of days, drinking just like old times. Upon return home, I had originally intended to swing back north through Novgorod for attending upon some errands in any case, so instead, from Staraya, I simply took the west way around. Of course, renewed brunts from the storm slowed me. Then while upon the road through Vorobeika, just south of town, I found myself being tailed by one of the many midwives I happen to know, the woman wailing on with such a squall of hysteria that I could scarce understand her—although, of course, from the moment I saw her face, I knew exactly what the trouble was, and followed straight after." Halting in the center of the floor, Father pauses long to stare outward toward the frame of slender windows built about the front doorway, their thickened panes lit past the wooden shutter slats with tiny orange streaks from the glow of the rising sun. "In my youth," he goes on, "my ambition was one-pointed to a fault: cavalry, and naught else. So after taking my higher-school colors, I sought immediate commission in the Tsar's elite Horse Guards. No other notion would I entertain—much to your grandfather's chagrin, I might add, and he forced me into the Medical Academy nonetheless! With such skill in surgery, the scalpel blade, not the saddle, became my theater of expertise. Ultimately, I decided it a worthy compromise. But look at me fifty long years apart! How the fates turn somersault effects of irony upon one's life. Never did I intend upon becoming the near busiest baby doctor in the province. Ahh, yes," he murmurs with a wistful sigh, "when the midwives find themselves in a tangle, to me they come a'screaming.

Anyhow, in this case it was the usual calamity: over twenty hours of birthing pains, everyone positively beside themselves. After I arrived, mortal hysteria went on for another two hours, but in the end, mother and baby daughter survived just fine. I must have stayed close to four days with them, though, on account of the second big storm. When that finally let up, another husband started pounding upon the door—the woman's sister was close to deliver, twins, they suspected. And so I ended up involved there for another couple of days. I suppose, though," he concludes, a reflective grin spreading over his face, "that I must admit to a certain amount of pride in my acquired occupational gamut. After all, I've lost neither mother nor child in a breech birth since—"

His words stop. My eyes lock onto his; his onto mine—the split-second tearing out between us through the old fifteen-year-long waning lapse of hellfire and regret.

Bereft of sound, my lips involuntarily form his sentence's finishing word: "Melissa."

Father abruptly embarks upon close examination of the floor, long stabs of time ticking by in silence as my leg begins to throb with its usual dull morning burst of pain, my stomach growling insatiably toward the mounting promise of kitchen breakfast odors.

"Look," Father says at last, hunting for my upward gaze. "Someday, I promise, you, Sashenka, I shall allow you into your mother's room. But—not yet. I must reconcile fully to God's will first. I suppose I never have forced myself to face everything squarely—and it makes me naught, perhaps, but an old blundering fool. Forgive me—forgive me for blaming you all these years. None of what happened the night Melissa died was your fault, Sasha—none of it. But will you please be patient about investigating her room, until I feel ready? And I would prefer that we speak of the matter no more until I am able to—until I can—"

His voice breaks off, and with an abject sigh, he plops down upon the bench beside me, shaking his head and grumbling into clasped hands.

"All right, Papa. I will not bother you about her room again. I promise."

"Here." After shuffling into the folds of his shirt, he produces a small thin packet bound tightly in butcher's paper, which he begins to unwrap. "Peace offering," he says, whipping it outward.

A beautiful little wood-carved, amber-inlaid piccolo with tungsten keys.

"Peace offering accepted!" I gasp, seizing it up. "By the stars! Where on earth did you ever happen upon such a treasure?"

"The smith in town. His old grandfather carves. Can you imagine? Back of the shop, behind the tack and all the shoeholds."

Immediately, I start testing off the keys, smatterings of birdsong spiraling away with joyful abandon into encroaching warmth of the new morn.

"Of course, you already have the silver one matched to your flute," he says. "But I thought you might prefer something lighter to carry around."

"For that, it is perfect! This will fit right down the shaft of my boot. Father, I thank you!"

With a slap to my shoulder, he bellows: "Well! Come then, put it away, young man. First some breakfast, wouldn't you agree? We must build that strength of yours back up. And, Marnya!" he yells off teasingly, cupping his hand. "Is that sausage burnt up to a ready crisp yet? Better be blackened sooty just to my liking, by God! Snow's so deep, I had to start riding from Novgorod two full hours before dawn."

Marnya yells back something about *bliny* mountains piled two heads higher than a man's stance, and Father bounds up, retrieving my crutches and thrusting them into my hands. "Oh, I near forgot," he then says, another search through his pockets producing a thick rumple-edged envelope.

"Looks like from You-Know-Who," he cries, teasing a poke into my ribs before hurrying off for the kitchen.

The return address swims before my eyes into an inky blur:

N. P. Zhelanov . . . 22 Zhukovskaya Ulitsa . . .

With a gasp of joy, I tear it open—only to be stung to the core by his angry, hurriedly dashed-off words:

Cad! You mean, save for another sorry anecdote misled from your housekeeper, you cannot send even one gracious sentence of news or inquiry in reply? And three times I write, virtually robbing my bow of scarce precious time for the effort, mind you! Aleksandr Sekovsky, are you so truly base a fellow, and not the proper gentleman you have been brought up to be past such painstaking trials upon your family's fortitude? Have you no appreciation? No true and proper manners? Not a shred of honest, decent common sense?

Just as I ready to crumple up the letter in a flush of rage, I spy the next sentence:

Ha! Got you—barbed wire to a barbed ass! And how dare you write me such a note, and say: 'Upon pain of death, open not in Rimsky's, but in Auer's class!' So there I sat with the finicky old bald-headed brute breathing down my neck—while, captivated, I tore like wildfire through your yarn about talking sturgeon in the Volkhov. Sheer indecency, I am telling you—a lark of larks spiced throughout the entire page with such filthy jokes as I have never heard! Did I ever get rapped on the knuckles for that one! Yes, yes, and there you are—engulfed in hysteria. I can hear you literally all the way from here. . . .

Doubled over with laughter, I wave Vliny off as he pokes his head through the kitchen door, full of demands about what is so bleating funny.

But from the remainder of the letter, of course, escapes the inevitable crush of sadness:

. . . and did you know how close you came? Your old tutor, Lauforte, sent the Maestro a four-star letter of recommendation. For some reason, flutes are scarce this term. I swear you'd have been snatched up like bandits' gold. Of course, snatched up to where is the question (you know what I mean). Well, Silver Fingers—it has got to be next year (I hope to God they let us back into school by then)—otherwise, I fear I shall go mad at the fault of Maman. Rooming at home is tedious to no end, and she can be such a frump sometimes! So unlike school. My precious cousin, there is no life, there is no existence worth bearing upon this earth of dark mournful winters without the diversion of our pranks! I miss you terribly, insanely. We all pray nightly for your leg to heal, and this very moment, I just found Anna in the midst of writing you another sorrowful ten-page letter

(sorrowful, ha! Love-letter is more like it). But seriously, how on earth did you manage to fall through your window—you, the window-winging expert of the world? That is some fair distance, and the extent of your injury surprised none of us, considering. So difficult it must be for you, dear heart—such a constant, daily ordeal of pain. Uncle Misha has regularly kept us informed about how you continue to act so very brave. . . .

Past the personal meanderings, my cousin's letter proves more significant for the news it does not impart: no word at all of the strikes, which have been rumored to be mounting and causing shortages of bread and even power for the city's gaslamps; no hint about the long-awaited granting of constitutional assembly and convening of the so-called 'Duma of Popular Hopes;' and past his barest alluded mention, no word at all about the Conservatory—which, having been embroiled in student protest ever since the Bloody Sunday massacres, has been closed down by the Tsar for the past year, students taking their lessons at instructor's houses and only permitted to gather openly for occasional examinations. Nikolai is wise. Political discussions these days remain best left to the realm of private conversation, not tangible postings so readily liable to perusal of the Tsar's censors. But despite the lack of news, he does manage to mention several scattered social tidbits that whet my appetite, beginning with a mouth-watering description of the latest concoction they have whipped up over at Donon's before making sly mention of Tamara Karsavina, the Maryinsky prima ballerina whom he knows had long ago stolen away my heart before she ever became the flushest talk of the town. . . .

Petersburg. Where I have spent my many school-terms—and indeed near unto half of my life. Petersburg: home to Venetian bridges, corniced palaces, grand rolling vistas, and glinting violet nights ever teasing at the breath of summer's dawn; Petersburg of the ballets, operas, symphonies, and endless applauding bejeweled throngs; Petersburg of dancing until the heady throes of dawn, its taverns filled with fortune tellers, fire-eaters, and Nikolai's luscious, beguiling whores. Petersburg, that wondrous citadel of golden spires where, beyond the somber, musty walls of this small house on an obscure bee farm, I once lived a far different life.

Next week, two days after Hallowmas, Nikolai turns seventeen. He and his sisters will celebrate until long past the stroke of midnight with my Aunt Sophie at her spacious townhouse rooms on Zhukovskaya Street. And for the first time that I can remember ever since I was a toddler, I will not be there.

Instead, I shall be here: struggling past daily curses with crutches, straining through hours of music practice, toiling through my other lessons with staunch effort and Father's help. An entire winter to be spent entombed, entrapped, obliterated, isolated from all thought of frivolity past attempts to keep hold of a steady bar on a temperate keel within my burgeoning river of pain. And from this lonely abode in Novgorod, I know I shall count every day, hour, minute, second, and tiny facet upon every shining star in the sky—until I can at last converge back again upon true course with my own solo wind; until I can return to again behold the dear face of my cousin Nikolai—in Petersburg. . . .

CHAPTER TWO

Petersburg: Fallen Angel

Curly black side-whiskers slicked down past the brim of his sheepskin hat, the conductor nods throughout the rail coach, bellowing in a melodic Cossack shout over our rows of bobbing heads: "Ten minutes! Petersburg! Nikolayevsky Station, St. Petersburg! Ten minutes!"

"Your move," says Father, pen gripped tightly in one hand, while with the other, he continues leafing through medicinal advertisements in the back pages of the newspaper.

Nose pressed to the window-glass, I barely hear. Long past are the quaint creaky rows of peasant huts and lonely wayside rail stop platforms. Scores of corniced buildings are flashing by in droves now, distant cupolas peeking in translucent hues across horizon's lengthy span of muted blueness, high spires of gold from cathedrals at every turn catching fair glint of the sun and beckoning to the lustful lull of the train as if with the sly flick of a harlot's invisible fan. The city seems enormous, ten times vaster than I remember, rolling out before my eyes on a magic carpet of space, and again my throat aches dry in swallows of anticipation. Novgorod, that ancient sovereignty, its legacy of a thousand years spanning back unto the time of the great Lawgiver Ryurik and the first wanderings of the medieval *Rus,* lurks quietly behind now, one hundred sixty versts south-to-the-southeast. St. Petersburg, castle of the Neva, maiden of countless twinkling palace lights, looms before us, closing in to the barest brush of breath, two angelic arms outstretched to encircle me, her lover, in throes of tearful reunion after these silent months of absence. Solid and steadfast, sworn to my code of honor wherever I may go, my birthplace—crust of the earth, its bones of my ancestors buried in surrounding rifts of the taiga forest—will remain forever bound to my soul, for she is Novgorod. My wife. But this place—throne of the sun, jewel of heaven dazzling and wondrous, unattainable beauty of its waters, its canal bridges, its quays of palaces dancing ever the faintest step away from grasping mortal reach—this place is my elixir, my potion, my inescapable sin. For she is Petersburg. My mistress.

"Sasha!" Father's brow creases yet once more with a frown of wearied patience. "Do you intend to move, or shall I fold it up again?" He holds the paper out, his fountain pen rolling precariously back and forth atop it amidst renewed jolts from the train.

Neither of us can tolerate playing chess for any great length of time at the board. Forever it stands, figures fully loaded in mockery of our mutual sloth of wit, like a blank page taunting a columnist who can think of naught to say. But move ten steps from the damn thing, or ten moments away, or ten versts down the road, and we each rankle forth simultaneously with a wealth of conspiring moves. Hence the necessity for carrying the game around—one game lasting ofttimes for weeks on end—on a piece of paper. "Bishop takes rook's pawn," I say, budging not one speck from the window. "Check."

"Check?" Bolting upward from the velvet-cushioned seat, Father yanks the chess paper back out to its full size, almost ripping it in half. "Sasha, you can hardly . . . oh, wait a moment—Christ's socks! Why, you're right. Oh! Pardon, M'sieur, M'mselle." In a fluster, he nods in quick apology for his loudness to the fashionably dressed young couple, both of whom look up with some dismay from their reading. Apparently a brother and much younger sister, they have remained seated across from us ever since we boarded after changing trains at Chudovo.

"Check," I repeat, hard pressed to stifle my grin as Father whacks a playful clap on my arm with the end of his rolled-up newspaper. After marking in the new move, he settles forth with elbows upon his knees, mumbling: "Caught myself in a pickle of a quandary now." Stretching the chess paper out once more, he peers downward with a studious sigh, his dark eyes dancing into the challenge as he attempts to plot his next move.

"Five minutes!" Again the conductor breezes through. "Claims tickets to the baggage coach; debark to Nikolayevsky Station . . . five minutes!"

I grasp firm my flute, packed in its leather traveling case, slip on my derby, and reach for my walking stick.

"You know," Father observes, glancing at me with a fond smile as he tucks the chess paper back into the pockets of his coat, "you can scarce even tell."

"You," I reply, "are sincere but biased profoundly. But, thank you." I nod at the walking stick's ornate brass-encased handle, murmuring: "At least these are in the height of fashion."

Thanks be to God, my leg healed straight. The limp, however, lingers in obvious awkwardness. Only for two weeks have I been walking free of the single crutch, strict caution pervading as a second nature pattern for every step taken wherever I go. But as the train slows upon approach into the station, everyone gathering up coats and bags and elbowing for space within the aisle, the steady reminder of the limp—despite sympathetic glances I receive from several onlookers—holds no specter of tragedy. To be walking at all courts the pinnacle of holy triumph after so many months of agonizing pain—the tumultuous effort of attempting to stand, of bearing even a little weight, of learning the muscle movements again—then to take one step, two steps, the thousand steps beyond.

His encouragement and watchful fatherly prodding shored me up past the insurmountable waves of despair, he dashing to the rescue each and every time I tumbled down the stairs or crumpled yet again into tears outside in a drift of snow. All winter long he bore the brunt of my misdirected anguish, ofttimes not succeeding in an entirely gentle manner himself despite stoic efforts at maintaining patience. For my horns are growing like the long-stunted sprigs of a fresh young buck—while his, regal and massive, have not yet succumbed to brittleness. And so we have locked and locked and locked, tussling for forage, ramming for the does, pounding and hurtling and squaring off again and again, battling one another constantly for finite reaches of individual territory and precious, private mental space. But never again since that fateful day has he ever struck me, although his numerous chopping episodes piled up enough wood outside through the winter to last past twice the amount of our household needs. And through the months, as he watched, and I struggled past all odds and observed him gazing back upon the gradually manifested results of his diligent care, I began to realize that my father and I had gained toward one another, after these long years, a startling new camaraderie of mutual respect.

So triumph meets its summit now as I walk, the train grinding to its grease-wrenching, smoky halt. Row by row, the chattering passengers pour for coach doors momentarily opening wide unto quays of architectural symmetry and ribbons of icy-white canals criss-crossing the grand embrace of my dear Lady Petersburg.

I nod over my shoulder, glancing up at Father with the barest wisp of a smile, appreciation flooding through my heart as never before upon the joy of this long-awaited moment. "Thank you, Papa."

Wide grin escaping him, Father squeezes my arm, the profusion of tiny wrinkle-lines spread across his broad, ever-handsome face swollen with beaming pride. "I'll see about the baggage—go!" he orders, laughing. "Go and find your cousins, Sasha."

Hobbling outward, I keep careful eye between coach floor and platform. "And tell the porter careful of the portmanteau with Anna's gift in it!" I call after Father once we debark. But he ignores me, his eyes glued in fixation once again upon the chess paper as he wanders off.

Another week and a half will bring Eastertide and the yearly celebration of ice-breaking upon the great River Neva. Thus the many long wooden platforms, the concourse, the high blue and white corniced archways of Nikolayevsky Station stand filled with scores of harried people. Most especially are ladies parading about in their latest Parisian finery—hats, feathers, and parasols capping a foray of cremes, blues, pinks, and yellows of springtime, willowy dresses nipped into tiny waists and draped with brooches or modest strands of pearls beneath short sable coats or ermine capes whipping little tails about the air. But it is lavender batiste I spot across the rash of giddy footsteps still jostling out from the coach doors—and the face of the young girl seated across from us while upon the train.

Attentively, two eyes of speckled hazel beckon for mine, alighting with amusement when she senses my returned glance. A slow smile curves upon pouting lips; black lashes begin to flutter coquettishly from beneath the brim of her broad, gaily feathered hat.

"M'mselle," I murmur politely, tipping my derby. But no sooner does she take a step in my direction, than does also her menacing top hatted brother, striding out protectively beside her. With a haughty glare toward me, he snatches up her arm and drags her off, pirating her back down the platform amidst a flurry of squealing protests. Alhough the girl manages to sneak one look back.

During which, I swear, she blows me a kiss!

Blessing the stars to have at last achieved return unto the delights of Lady Petersburg, I stare around through a giddy haze, attempting to catch my breath. Then I begin a precarious limping trek through the bustling crowd, scaling creaky platform boards in watchful tentativeness as I make for the grand old stationhouse building itself. Once past its beveled doors and rows of busy ticket booths, I turn about and gaze back outward, hand shaded to my brow. Through the throng of people, however, I find biding for due attention not the familiar faces of my cousins, but instead my own image as reflected back from the wide stationhouse windows.

The suit, of course, is a holdover from last year, the trouser hems once again let down painstakingly by Marnya because I had grown. But the collar and cuffs of my shirt are spanking new, high and rounded in the latest style, and the derby is flawless, for since last spring I have not had occasion to wear it much. The brim hides enough of my hair slicked down beneath that, at least since we left, Father has ceased his grumbling about the length—for still he complains endlessly, although my trips to the barber have courted dogged regularity since Christmas. I suppose I am not a bad sight; the walking stick lends a dashing air. Small wonder she blew a kiss! Small wonder I have missed the joys of this sparkling city so very much, indeed.

Suddenly, I hear my name shouted across heads of the crowd, and scarce do I turn before confronting a double-winded tornado: two pale-headed bullets racing one another down the concourse and through the stationhouse doors straight toward my collision, their shouts blaring on past frenzied gasps of joy.

But I freeze with a gulp of panic, yelling back: "No, wait, the both of you! Wait a moment—Nikolai! Watch the flute!"

Instead, my cousin Nikolai near topples the both of us flat into three passing matrons and one of the scheduling boards. Then he swings around, remembering, his arm joining mine in protective shield of the flute's shoulder case. "Sasha!" he roars out. "For endless months have I waited—Anna, look! Our Sasha is here at last!"

"Here with a numskull!" I snap back in a huff. "Lord Almighty, have you entirely lost your senses? Had I bumped your Guarnerius so, you would have—"

"Countered with a ploy for murder, surely!" he retorts, bowing low in profuse, genuine apology. But then he breaks into a rakish grin. "And have I ever missed you to death!" he shouts on, throwing wide both arms to sweep me into a rough embrace, his smother of kisses darting back and forth between my cheeks.

Laughing, returning a like smother of kisses, I add a hard pinch to his arm in retaliation, and nod toward his sprouting moustache, exclaiming: "Lord, I am insanely jealous!"

"Of me? Ho, but have a look at you: brand new derby, brand new collar. Strut around like a fop you do, I swear by the devil's arse."

"Kolya!" Anna cries in dismay, whacking him soundly in the shins with her parasol. "One mustn't curse so."

"Curse? Young lady, I shall curse whenever and however I bloody well please."

Shoving Nikolai away, I cast both arms out wide toward Anna, and moan in my best teasing tone: "Anna Petrovna, Princess Zhelanova—Face to Launch a Thousand Ships unto the Throes of Hades! I beg thee upon my knees, I beseech thee unto thy heart—humor a poor bumbling country oaf! Kiss me, Anyuta."

Of course, our love-letter promises were only meant half-jokingly. Though at eighteen a year older than Nikolai, Anna has always seemed more like a year younger, and hence our closeness. Blushing a deeper hue of red than even my hair, she backs away—while her brother and I burst into a conspiring peal of uproarious laughter. "You two insufferable mischief-makers!" Anna yells back hoarsely, grinning in spite of herself as a wealth of stray golden ringlets tumbles outward from her large feathered hat.

"And this you term the latest fashion?" I retort. "Carrying about upon your head a gigantic fruit basket?"

Sticking out her tongue in reply, Anna turns her jabbing parasol upon me, demanding sarcastically: "Halt the persecution, M'sieur and Madame Fashion-Plate, the both of you! And the way you two forever promenade around to no blessed end, like a couple of rutting peacocks."

In reply, Nikolai collapses low into another bow and starts waving his derby at Anna past a mocking glare of indignation.

"Oh, put that back on!" I order with an elbow poked into his ribs as he bursts into another round of laughter. "Come, truly," I then say to Anna. "Give your cousin a welcome-home kiss."

"I can't. Kolya will not let me."

"And what have you to say about it?" I demand, whirling upon Nikolai.

"She has the most horrid sore throat! I shall kill her should you catch it and be unable to play."

"Oh, it is true," admits Anna, nodding. "Perhaps Uncle Misha has a tonic that might help. I shan't bear missing tonight at the Maryinsky."

"You managed tickets for *Godunov?*" I cry, amazed.

"Stood in the gallery line for four hours." Grasping his derby over his heart, Nikolai eyes the heavens beseechingly, moaning: "And how we sell our souls for art! Or perhaps, how I have sold my time."

"Well, everyone has become bored unto death with sitting home during Lent," Anna explains, her parasol clapping Nikolai's shin with another chiding whack. "Concert tickets have become scarce, those for the ballets after Easter even more so."

"Oh, no!" I gasp, "I have been waiting for months!"

"Not to worry, he managed ballet tickets, too."

"Sasha is in love with Pavlova!" Nikolai declares, snickering.

"You are in love with Pavlova!" I blast back.

"Then you are in love with Karsavina!"

"Well . . . ."

"And do you two Don Juans intend to do naught but swoon day and night over ballerinas all the way until Eastertide, just like last year?" Haughtily, Anna pulls closed the frog-button fastenings of her white ermine capelet and again rescues her sliding hat. "Your ballets will resume soon enough!" she proclaims with a toss of her head. "In the meantime, we must prepare for the balls. I have shopping to do! For a new pair of gloves, for toilet water—at Cabussue's, at Brocard's, today."

"On the way, we can stop at Filippov's," I add with relish.

"And is food ever your only thought?" Nikolai pokes me in the ribs.

"Crab meat *pirozhki*, so I heard on the train. You think you can come upon crab meat, in winter, in Novgorod?"

"One mustn't eat crab meat during Lent, Sasha," Anna fires at me with an accusing gasp.

"But crab meat is fish," I insist.

"It is not."

"Oh, for devil's sake!"

"And you stop cursing, too!"

Shoving in between, Nikolai waves us both down, ordering: "Anna, let him be! The poor lad's been stuck out in the country for months. Allow him his indulgences."

"And who put you in charge, Kolya?"

"And stop calling me that! We'll stop by Cabussue's and Filippov's, and wherever else anyone desires. And by the bookstores, too. I've another order come in at Smirdin's." Stepping away with disdain as if from two spoilt children, Nikolai frowns and slips out his watch from his waistcoat pocket, murmuring: "Heavens, where is Maman?"

Following his gaze, I scan through the stationhouse windows back toward the concourse, but detect yet no sign of my aunt. Then Anna starts coughing. "How miserable for you!" I cry, giving her shoulder an affectionate squeeze, our dispute forgotten in entirety. "Father will set you to rights, sweetheart. Ask him to whip you up some of our best black honey with eucalyptus."

"Oh, is not quite so treacherous as this morn," she replies. "But no easy matter for you, I would imagine, to play the flute with a sore throat. So I daren't kiss you at all, Sashenka, darling. Kolya, you kiss Sasha again, this time for me."

"Blast it, Anna," Nikolai fumes back, "stop calling me that!" Face darkening, he whirls around, yanking his derby low to his brow, his flinty gray eyes sweeping through the beveled windows and down the station platforms in a brooding mire of storm.

"Oh, poo!" Anna chides in retributive glee, whacking at him once more with her parasol. "And why not? Kolya, Kolya, Kolya!"

"Stop! You know how I hate that name! The devil can take it!"

"Kolya! Don't curse."

"Sasha!"

As Nikolai and Anna pounce for one another with a vengeance, the next two eldest sisters, Eugenia and Tatyana—both in their early twenties—rush past them, throwing decorum to the winds, and engulf me in a veritable hurricane of embraces and cheeky kisses.

"Look at him, Tatyana! Oh, Sasha, you poor darling, your leg . . . ."

Brushing off glances of sympathy with a grin of nonchalance, I begin to relate stories of my plight during the last few months—much to fawning responses and wide-eyed "Ooos!" and "Ahhs!" At the same time, I keep an eye peeled for Father, who is as yet nowhere to be seen. At last the girls let loose of me, Nikolai and Anna wind up their stinging little spat, and Aunt Sophie—head held high, her stance as regal as that of the Queen of England—appears waltzing down the concourse with two besotted porters at each side. "Darling Sashenka!" she drawls in French as she glides past the stationhouse doors, holding wide her arms and catching my hand into both of hers. "How we have worried and prayed for you these long months! Praise Heaven's Name that you are walking again at last."

Normally, I would not hesitate to kiss my aunt's cheek. The problem is the hat, barring my way with a low burgundy brim encased in rolling veils of black polka-dot netting. As an alternative, I press my lips upon Aunt Sophie's kid-gloved fingers—whereupon, amidst cries of "How gallant! How chevalier!" the voices of the girls burst into a chorus of squealing feminine delight. Nikolai, grinning with disgust, shakes his head and rolls his eyes toward the high overhead ceiling.

"Now, now!" Aunt Sophie, her hands spread as if attempting to quiet a den of barking puppies, calms the girls back unto trills of restrained giggles. "Where is he?" she then demands with a wide smile, tugging at my arm. "I imagine the old lout remains as unbearable as ever?"

Laughing, I reply: "Well, he has at last permitted me use of my left hand while supping in his presence. Next, he'll be off siding with the liberals in the Duma."

This inspires another heady outburst of laughter; Father's insistence about right-handedness has been a family joke for years. Draping her arm about my shoulders, Aunt Sophie—with enthusiastic interjections from both of the older girls—begins to relate an amusing anecdote about her exploits with Father during their younger days.

Between them, he the eldest, she the youngest, eight other siblings intervened, but only the middle two—Aunt Vera and Uncle Ivan, both long ago immigrants unto England—also survived beyond childhood. At fifty-six, Aunt Sophie, despite tiny wrinkles evidenced in profusion upon her face behind the hat veils, yet remains possessed of a svelte, swan-like litheness imbued with an easy sense of warmth. Every one of her daughters has inherited the same unbridled carefree loveliness, and for me it is near intoxicating within the sumptuous gathering of gaily chattering blue-eyed blondes. Especially on account of Anna. Noon's radiant golden light, streaming through the stationhouse windows and bouncing unabashedly through snatches of her untamed curls, likens the girl to none other than a fashion model from the picture-cover of a French magazine.

Remembering politeness, again I steal my eyes away, turning to ask of Aunt Sophie: "And how are the twins?"

"Oh! Natasha writes regularly from New York, although I still cannot imagine what she possibly sees in that diplomat fellow she married—Americans, ugh! And Nina, well . . . ." Pulling out her peacock-feathered fan, Aunt Sophie sighs heavily, although she seems, as always, rather amused by Nina's unorthodox meanderings. "Berlin was the last stop. Prague and then Budapest to be next, so I heard. Twenty-five years old and still no husband! Flits from place to place—a free spirit, like a bird, she says. Thinks she is Jenny Lind. Saints in Heaven help us."

Crossing herself, Aunt Sophie begins fluttering forth in a bored manner with the fan.

"Anna," I say, warmly grasping up her arm, "we must find Father and the portmanteau. I have the loveliest gift for you, from a woodcarver's shop in Novgorod—"

I stop abruptly, catching, just from the corner of my eye, the sight of Nikolai.

From some length away, he merely continues staring—his penetrating gray gaze searing into mine across confines of the air, no longer the glance of my friend and near-brother, my long-loved, ever-cherished cousin. Instead, scathing indictment exudes as if from a near total stranger taken aback by a startled, dawning glimmer of recognition.

Only once before have I seen such a stare—last February, when the cast finally came off—and when, over Father's hysterical objections, I first climbed back atop my mare, Jespa, and rode off straight away from our stormy tirade with my crutches lashed tight across the saddle horn. Upon passing outside one of the Orthodox sanctuaries in Bronnitsa, the village set upon the western roadside way from Lissushka into Novgorod, I encountered an almost identical assault of piercing scrutiny—from an old babushka, her eyes astonished and unyielding. And I heard the voice, wary tremors of suspicion lacing through the shadows upon the import of one fearfully uttered word: *volkhvi*.

"Sasha!" Anna cries, tugging at my sleeve. "A gift for me? You were saying?"

Nikolai's stark perusal vanishes within the next instant: again the broad grin. The casual, friendly air. But tremors of the mood linger; averting his gaze, he shoves his hands stiffly down into his trouser pockets and turns upon his heel, murmuring: "I suppose I should go and assist Uncle Misha with the baggage."

"Sasha?" Anna pleads on.

Heart sinking, I watch Nikolai's hunched figure pounding back out the stationhouse doors and down the concourse.

"Never you mind," Aunt Sophie whispers in my ear, her gloved fingers pressing a reassuring squeeze upon my arm.

"What on earth has come over him?" I cry.

"Not a thing. You know how Kolya is. One moment, the most inspired flashes of wry humor; the next, utter depths of abject melancholy! At least he is becoming more adept at quickly recovering his composure. Lord help me, Kolya is so like his father, your Uncle Petya." Aunt Sophie's sigh chokes her voice into a halt, and she pauses long, crossing herself once more. The three girls and I do the same, following with low murmurs of: "God rest his soul."

Late last spring, Prince Pyotr Zhelanov, the cellist Aunt Sophie married, passed away in his sixty-fourth year. Nikolai would scarce talk to me, or anyone for that matter, for months after the funeral. Of the entire lot of them, it seemed to affect him most of all. Even more greatly than Aunt Sophie.

"Come!" she motions to the two elder girls. "Never you mind about Kolya's sour face, Sasha. We will chase on after him and find out what has been keeping Misha."

With difficulty, I turn away from the stationhouse windows, attempting to shrug off dark forebodings spawned by the fading image of Nikolai. "Father was involved in plotting a chess move," I tell Aunt Sophie. "I put him in check."

"Well! In that case, he's probably sitting on some stump somewhere and entirely forgotten about the baggage! Oh, heavens—Anna, stay here. I know you have been yearning to talk to Sasha for months."

"Maman!" Anna blushes near to burst.

"Oh, poo!" Aunt Sophie waves Anna's schoolgirl blustering off, and with the porters still hovering closely after, starts back through the stationhouse doors with Tatyana and Eugenia flanking her fondly one on each side.

"Is this true, Anna?" I ask, turning to her with renewed enthusiasm. "That you have been yearning—yearning, she said—to talk to me for months?"

She allows me to hold her hand. It is not entirely improper; we are, after all, cousins. At last she surrenders to the pull of the hat, tucking the large bunch of ribbons and netting in beneath her arm. As a result, golden curls drift in a luscious tumble down her back, settling about her like the web-spun frame of an enchantress. "Pity about your leg," she murmurs, slowing her steps so as not to hurry me. "And will it never go away? The limp?"

"I am afraid not."

"Sasha," she then asks, "how on earth did you ever manage to fall out your upstairs window?"

Aunt Sophie, I believe, is somewhat privy to the dark side between myself and my father, knowing him so well. But to the cousins, white lies tell easier than scarred blurs of truth. "Prone to clumsiness, I suppose," I reply—and abort her next inquiry by grasping up her hand and gazing warmly into her eyes, murmuring: "And did you truly miss me so?"

"Of course!" Lashes fluttering, she looks coyly away, smiling and adding: "But honestly, I think Kolya missed you even more than I. Tired and cranky as an old sputtering bear has he become over these past months, ohh! And listless in his studies, save for his music. Ofttimes it seems he does naught but storm about all day long, muttering about the lack of diversions."

"I see." I look away from her, unable to restrain my creeping grin.

In quick response, Anna whirls upon me, eyes flashing stark blue torrents. "Oh, I thought so!" she cries, waving an accusing finger. "You two must already have something thought up! Please, Sasha—nothing so dreadful as the last time, that live frog in the salmon mousse, now you promise!"

"Anna!" I protest with widened eyes, "how can you say such a thing? That was over a year ago! Nikolai and I are all grown up."

"No, the two of you will never grow up! Now, you promise to tell me when it is coming," she demands, not believing a single of my denials. "So that I can absent myself from the room!"

"Anyuta, sweetheart! We would never try anything so dreadful as that again, not during dinner, I promise!"

"Well, you had best not! And certainly not tonight. Maman has invited several guests, including Count Orlov, even the Grand Duke."

"Indeed?" Chuckling under my breath, I grasp her arm through mine, replying with reassurance: "Oh, stop worrying your pretty little head about such trivial matters, Anyuta. Your brother and I intend to behave like the most perfect gentlemen, you have my earnest word! Now come, *ma cousine*—we must hurry along and catch up with the others."

* * *

Aunt Sophie remains the only woman in the world possessed of the ability to melt Father's heart into buttery little pieces.

I duck around the corner as I detect the echoes again, his voice simpering on like a drooling court lackey's: "Ahh, Sofya—my angel, my gem! The most sumptuous meal I have ever feasted upon in my entire life—superb it was, I tell you! *Magnifique!"*

"Oh, Misha . . . ."

"Ahh, Sofya . . . ."

Oh, brother!

Such plaudits, however, boast no exaggeration; supper was delicious. I near sated myself on cold salads and the variety of pickled mushrooms at the appetizer bar, and during the main course of the meal, scarce mourned our Lenten plight, the absence of butter at the table, about which I have been complaining nightly for weeks. Instead, blending into obscurity amongst the dozens of other guests, I picked idly at chunks of broiled halibut and focused all attention upon the most unforgivably roguish of endeavors: two entire hours spent casting devilish winks at Anna. She, in turn, spent her whole meal staring in mortification between me, her plate, and down into the *décolleté* of her gown—cut far too low and constantly slipping from her lovely white shoulders. Every time she gasped and hiked the bodice back up, Nikolai would catch my eye or jab into my toe with his, breaking into torrents of snickers.

'Well!' I attempted to explain sheepishly afterward, 'we meant to conduct ourselves like perfect gentlemen—but how do you expect us to react then you show up at table in only half a gown?'

'Humph!' As soon as the servants began retrieving our empty plates, the ladies herding children into the drawing room and a core of gentlemen retiring to the study for their sherry and flavored vodkas, Anna, with her whacking fan, was in my hot pursuit throughout every upstairs hallway, finally stomping off indignantly before I could offer any further mirthful attempts at explanation.

"Ahh, Sofya . . . *magnifique! Extraordinaire!*"

Always a strange colloquial mixture of Russian and French holds sway in Father's and Aunt Sophie's conversations, neither of them staying solidly in either language sometimes even through the end of a word. Long have I wondered how he ever so skillfully mastered English—which she speaks quite brokenly, with a heavy French accent, apparently never having had the proper schooling to absorb the idioms any further.

Suddenly, as they bound around the corner, Father runs smack into me, reams of orchestrations flying out from my arms.

"And what mischief are you up to?" he asks, glancing upward with an utterly daffy expression from the sketch paper he has been carrying, Aunt Sophie's hand yet again drawn through his arm.

"Not a thing, Papa!" I answer in a rush, steadying my hand upon the walking stick and tightening my other arm about the stack of orchestrations, attempting not to drop any more. "Nikolai and I were simply readying to review our repertoire," I tell him, fixing my gaze downward.

"Well, you'd best hurry, darling," Aunt Sophie says, mercifully handing over the collection of loose manuscripts from the floor. "That is, if you wish to take desert before leaving for the Maryinsky. Baked fig cakes are being set out, along with pineapple compote, and the fresh oranges Cook found this morn at market. And they will be mixing the rum punch presently."

"Why are you wearing your woolen jacket in the house?" Father then inquires, his gaze waning upward only with reluctance from his notes. "You've not caught Anna's sore throat, have you?"

"Oh, no, sir! We—uh, Nikolai and I just stepped in from the balcony. We were, uh, stargazing."

"Oh. And this is Anna's gift?"

I catch my breath as he nods at the bulge from the parcel hidden beneath the sleeve of my jacket.

"Uh, yes! And I meant to thank you, Papa, for keeping your eye so watchfully upon the portmanteau." I scan over his paper, desperate to change the subject. "Is that your next move?" I ask, assuming it to be a fresh copy of our continuing game.

"That is hardly chess, darling," Aunt Sophie interjects in a placating tone. "Misha has drawn up another choreography layout, or some such thing." Toying back and forth between her drop earrings and the beads of her shimmery coral necklace, she nods bemusedly in the direction of Count Orlov, who—from the swell of angry voices mounting in the study—appears to be involved in a heated political debate with several other gentlemen about Prime Minister Stolypin and the so-called 'Second Duma of Popular Anger.'

"These sketches comprise the *Spanish Dance* scene in *Swan Lake,*" Father murmurs, puffing proudly on his pipe, his stare once more intent upon his paper.

Tchaikovsky's wondrous ballet is first on our agenda soon after Easter. But I had assumed Father would not accompany us; forever has he detested such Petersburg society outings. "Since when did you become interested in choreography?" I ask, paying only the slightest attention, again struggling with my sagging bundle of orchestrations.

"1853," he says—and then, despite the profound disaffection with which I know him to regard political discussions, he follows after Aunt Sophie, who wanders off at the beckoning of Count Orlov and his rancid cigar.

I gape after Father with a growing frown. Several times since the accident has he uttered such strange answers to my seemingly idle questions—pieces of a puzzle manifesting gradually from the part of his life about which I still know so very little. In 1853, he would only have been twenty-two.

Paying cautious heed to my steps, I move along the mica-tile-inlaid hallway to its farthest corner—the rendezvous point. Back flattened against the wall, Nikolai awaits as expected, his own bundle of orchestrations clutched within his arms. But as I edge up beside him, he whispers in warning: "Nix it! Tatyana Alert!"

With a sharp intake of breath, I pull my jacket lapels close around my manuscript stack, attempting to conceal the parcel.

"Sasha! Kolya!" Fan fluttering, blonde hair swept up within a wreath of emerald-accented pearls, Tatyana, swathed in ribbons and ivory lace, floats past upon the arm of Ivan Feodorovich, her fiance, a snooty uniformed dandy from the Semyonovksy Guards. "And when do you two aficionados intend to demonstrate your talents for us?" she demands, peering down with narrowed eyes from across the top of her fan, addressing us as if we were naught but mere servants.

"When you allot us a scarce five minutes for practice!" Nikolai mutters, shooting her a scowling glare.

"Oh, poo! And must you ever drown in your dire moods, Kolya?" Fortunately, she lets the matter drop, and once they bend to whisper endearments into each other's ears, she and her doting paramour wander off toward chatterings of the desert crowd now gaining swift momentum in the drawing room.

"Not much time left." Nikolai's sigh tests the air.

"Anna made me promise to tell her when it was coming," I reply, spying down the length of the hall. At last, save for the servants, not another single person in sight.

"And did you?"

"Of course not."

Seizing my arm, Nikolai leans in close, the warmth of his breath grazing across my temple. "'Anna's gift in the portmanteau!'" he whispers, mimicking my voice. "A wooden jewelry box, entirely unbreakable! So—you said it would be good. What have you brought for us?"

We both deposit our stacks of orchestrations—which we have both only been carrying around as a diversion—onto the floor. And from the folds of my jacket, I pull out the curing jar.

Full of eighteen live spiders.

"I love you!" Nikolai gasps, delighted, his fingertips crushing my arm.

"Marnya allowed me to keep them in the hotbed all winter. Bless her heart, she never asks why. So," I say, inclining my head toward the drawing room. "The punch?"

"Yes, perfect!"

"Damn! I love rum punch." But then I break into a peal of laughter, while he continues desperately trying to contain his own. "But sacrifices we must make, yes?" I cry, nudging my elbow into his. "For sake of the cause!"

"Indeed! All for one and one for all—or in this case, both for either: the cousins Sekovsky and Zhelanov, ever compatriots in crime, united and unflappable!"

"Who never let by any Easter Season without at least one infamous little stunt!"

"Stunt? *Mon cousin,* we are the ones who concocted the word!" He pulls out his watch. "Twenty minutes until we leave for Maryinsky. I assume you want me to do the honors?"

"You'll have to. I daren't let go of this walking stick, and besides, the guests stare so at my limp. I would be far too obvious."

"Very well. I shall sneak from the study into the drawing room through the sliding doors. Can you reach the lower vestibule downstairs within two minutes? We'll dash out the front doors and catch ourselves a cab ride in the first *drozhki* we can flag down."

Again—now hanging arm to arm—we break into a near uncontrollable tirade of snickers, which we attempt without much success to stifle. "For a certainty, Sasha," he goes on, dabbing at his eyes, "make sure you clear the stairs in time. I know my sisters, revenge is their hallmark. They'll probably try to tickle us both to death."

"Go!" I whisper hoarsely, shoving him away from the wall with an insistent laugh. "And put the jar in a spot where we can find it later! Marnya made me promise to return it."

After a grinning salute back to me, Nikolai scurries off with the jar toward the doorway to the study.

All the way down the stairs, several of the elegantly attired servants—some speeding by with stacks of crystal goblets and dishes, others carting off empty silver trays—continue inquiring about my welfare: "Some assistance with the steps, M'sieur? You are not taking it too quickly, M'sieur? You are going out, M'sieur? Your hat, your coat, M'sieur?"

"Thank you, no—I am quite proficient!" With impatience, I wave off more worried, patronizing stares, supposing that Aunt Sophie must have given some special instructions on my behalf. But despite descending one step at a time, I manage quite nicely—and reach the lower vestibule, my hand still resting upon the balustrade, when from above, the drawing room erupts in a volcano of screams.

"Now, now!" I hear Nikolai shout—his feet pounding like leaden drumbeats into the upstairs floor. Bursting into the hallway, he jostles precariously past a maid carrying a tray of freshly filled champagne glasses, missing her by the merest hair's breadth. Then, in a breach of propriety that leaves even me gaping upward at him in a stunned squawk of delight, he heaves himself—to the astounded stares of the servants—straight upon the banister, sliding all the way down it in a fraction of a second, an act for which years ago we both suffered repeated chastisement while still in primary-school. "Go!" he shouts, clamping onto my arm and rushing us toward the doors. "Come along—Anna was nowhere to be seen! I think she took the cut-off down through the kitchen."

"Hey, wait will you? I cannot keep up!"

"Well!" Through the front doors we stumble, the both of us coatless, into the stark night cold, Nikolai dragging me with him across the slippery pack of ice and up to the curbstone. *"Drozhki, drozhki!"* he yells, wildly waving both arms toward the street.

From depths of the yellow gas-lit night, four cabs converge in a tangle of flying harnesses upon the spot—just as Anna jumps us.

"Fiends! Cads! Criminal saboteurs!" Her hand closes fast upon my collar, wrenching me backward along with Nikolai.

"Take no prisoners! Execute the two heartless, scheming mischief-makers!" Storming up from behind in an engulfing rustle of taffeta, Eugenia starts whacking her fan at us with unrestrained glee.

"Anna, Eugenie—stop it!" shouts Nikolai, smacking back at the both of them, pale strands of his neatly-combed hair flying off in all directions.

With a yelp of triumph, Anna pounces upon me, seizing away my walking stick. "Now, that is not fair!" I exclaim, latching for safety back onto Nikolai's arm.

"No *drozhki!"* she yells past our heads, waving the stick out beyond our reach and brandishing it furiously at the cabs.

"Give it back!" As she bursts into a peal of giggles, we both grapple with her in a huff for the cane, only wrenching it away when the shoulder of her gown starts sliding off again and the last of the cabs shuffles back toward the distant hovering darkness of Ligovsky Prospekt.

"Hear ye! Hear ye! Bring them in for their punishment!" Tatyana's voice sounds gloatingly over the group of chuckling guests now gathered within the townhouse's elegant front entryway. Amongst them, Aunt Sophie hovers yet upon Father's arm, her laughter lilting forth behind that of the girls with its usual bubbling gaiety. "Oh, Misha!" she cries, wagging a remindful finger upward into his face. “You old bloat! And some of your school-days pranks Mother and I laughed over years later.”

“Pranks, indeed—naught but endless pranks!” Father shoots me a simmering glare as I shrug, attempting to look past him. But eventually, his expression softens, and he shakes his head, a reluctant smile edging upward in between puffs on his pipe.

“Bring in the prisoners! Bring in the prisoners!” Flanking us on either side and shrieking like a platoon of shews, the girls drag us back from the curbstone into the townhouse.

“Why could you not have simply waited for Anna to show back up in the drawing room?” I whisper crossly over to Nikolai.

“They were readying to serve the punch! What else did you expect me to do?”

“Oh, hell!”

In the drawing room at the baby grand piano, two glasses of rum punch, each full to the brim with a froth of crawling spiders, are shoved into our faces. “Oh, verily indeed!” I snort over at Anna, sticking out my tongue.

“Proceed with the punishment!” then rings the assembled chorus of voices.

And as if from nowhere, my flute, fully assembled, is pushed into my hands. And Nikolai’s violin and bow shoved into his.

“Now, wait a just one moment!” he protests loudly.

“We have been informed that the proper punishment for your crime is this!” Eugenia calls out, triumphantly holding forth a piece of newspaper within both hands and reading as if from a formal decree. “You two tasteless bards, who have had the gall to ruin our cherry-rum punch, will now proceed to entertain the Esteemed Household of Zhelanov with naught but the finest music in all the land, while we—your Imperial Slavemasters—sample our dessert!”

Amidst the reaction of roaring shouts, clapping, and laughter, I whisper over to Nikolai: “But—I cannot play in front of such a large crowd of people!”

“We haven’t our music!” he calls in a fist-waving shout to Eugenia, haughtily shaking back his head, his nose thrown to the air.

“Indeed!” The massive stack of our combined orchestrations then lands with a plodding thump down at our feet.

Tatyana, grinning down at us, wipes her hands with staid satisfaction.

“Looks as if we’ve no choice, *mon cousin,*” Nikolai murmurs to me, shrugging. And in perfect ease, he starts applying rosin to his bow.

"But, Nikolai!" I gasp, tongue freezing in my throat.

"Oh, Sasha—come now," he replies, gauging my stricken glance. "Is not as if you've never before given a recital."

In response, I glare back at him, reddening. Scores enough recitals have I given in my time—at least once a week during the many winter months in school. Which is precisely the point; *ages* have intervened since those long months at school. "Nikolai, I've not caught chance to practice for an entire day," I go on, my neck going clammy against the hot swelter of bodies crowding into the room. "And—all these people!"

"Day's going to come when you'll play in front of dozens more people than this, little cousin." Cocking an eyebrow, Nikolai casts me a sidelong glance past his jaunty grin.

"Nikolai, I'm serious!"

But to my acute dismay, he waves me off, and starts thumbing nonchalantly through the stack of orchestrations.

"Nikolai, will you please listen? I've not played before any such group in months—almost a year, in fact—since I last boarded at school in Petersburg. And you know that, even then, I was never at my best before large crowds."

"Sasha, after playing that flute for near unto seven years, I think you've scarce any call to panic."

"But—we've not even had chance to test our interpretation on all these!" With emphasis, I shove my finger down at the stack of orchestrations.

"Well, it's not as if that's the end of the world. I have been writing you quite faithfully—once a week, in fact—about every one of them ever since last October."

"Nikolai, it matters little how many times we've hashed over the manuscripts in the letters! We must find some chance to practice together in person."

Brows pursing together in a frown, Nikolai stares off into the crowd. The uproar has escalated to such a point that we can hardly hear one another. "All right—look," he says finally. "We'll do the Massenet; we both know it by heart, and it's always a favorite."

"But, Nikolai!"

"Sasha, for God's sake—will you please trust me? How can you ever expect to play professionally if you lose your wits in front of a little gathering like this? I'll play lead through the whole blessed piece if you want! Simply back me up and blend in."

Unable to do much else, I nod and let out an aching breath, actually admitting to some relief. Leave it to Nikolai to maintain perfect poise under such an unexpected torrent of pressure. Obviously, his training under Maestro Auer at the Conservatory has encompassed much more than the mere niceties of honing his bow technique.

"Please! Please!" he calls with a grinning wave to the crowd, urging them to simmer down. Then he announces: "Massenet's *Meditation* from *Thaïs*."

The predictable response ensues: delighted nods, shouts, and a renewed round of applause.

Never one to tempt the fates during a performance, I manage to fish the music for the piece out from our stack of manuscripts. Setting it upon the piano stand, I then proceed to adjust the hand position from the quick assembly of my flute.

Although it has indeed been fitted together perfectly. "I hope you were the only one who touched this!" I call to Father, pointing, my meaning getting across room's uproar more in gestures than in words.

Father nods back, his stern frown breaking into a another reluctant smile as, under Aunt Sophie's continued prodding, he at last starts clapping along with everyone else.

"Please! A moment to warm up, please!" Nikolai shouts with another insistent wave.

Before cueing in with long readying notes, I sound an 'A' a couple of times on the piano and follow with my own 'A,' allowing Nikolai to tune.

As the first tremors from the violin pierce across the laughter and clapping, the crowd's boisterousness only increases further, the chorus of voices goading us to: "Play! Play!" with such an onslaught of revelry that at last there is no more hope of any time to stall. Attempting past all exasperation to calm my quavering fingers, I silence my tones and nod to Nikolai, who arches upward into position with his bow.

And then—just as during countless other times—my fear vanishes within an instant.

Massenet's *Meditation* is, even under the most ordinary of circumstances, a work of haunting lyrical beauty, but rendered now—in this room stunned into an abrupt hush of silence by none other than the evocative ghost, Merlin's musical apprentice—the notes defy imagination, searing spades into every heart from the second that bow bites melody across the strings.

Upon which Nikolai's whole being entirely transforms: into that of someone I do not know—for the mask he wears before the world shatters away like a screen of so much corrupted fleshly dust. Eyes riveted upon the inward symphony acted out at behest of his fingers, he abruptly ignites the room with nothing less than a consecration unto the Most Holy—for Nikolai, my cousin, is God's chameleon.

Listening, enthralled, I almost quiver apart in pain.

By the time my opening measure starts, I have shaken off my nervousness, and settle with ease into automatic patterns. Not for mere idle fancy have I spent almost seven years, untold hours of each day, endless wanings into every night, practicing—and so I follow through upon my meager exercises, doubling over the peal of the violin as it wafts up into hollow mountings of the scales. But that is *all* I can do, to double, to follow—and prostrate my plodding technical competence before the artistry of this greater power with the most humble, reverent capitulation.

And as such, for hours could I but remain, utterly entranced, held immobile as stone by sight of his every sweeping, graceful stroke carved across virgin confines of the air. Indeed, for days on end, for weeks without a pause could I lock myself in a room with Nikolai and feast upon no other morsel, drink from no other vessel but the sight and sound of him playing his violin. Musicians in the dozens have I had some chance in my life to observe at close range, but never have I seen *any* instrument played by any other mortal with such daring, poignance, and fervency of focus culled *without exception* into each and every spell-bound, devotional attack. Perhaps envy of such prodigiousness and extraordinary mastery I should feel, but I simply cannot. Instead, it is privilege to exult within, much less accompany, my cousin's gifted presence.

As shimmering glassy tones begin to captivate every ear in the room, Nikolai's bold bow-strokes angle out into the *Meditation's* long whispers of *legato* moanings, chords of anguish coaxing my flute's timid accompanying phrases toward heights of ecstasy against the violin's climactic singing lull. Fighting back a lump welling up in my throat, I almost cannot continue to play, the augur's alchemy wavering onward measure by the raw, aching depth of each next upward measure toward the very summit of the Holy Grail's ageless universal quest. Rent irreparably, my own coarse temporal fabric courts shadows in an unearthly flux as if transformed into bare spirit thrust outward unto the freshness of autumn's first chill-wind to die in joy upon a silent burst of light. For just as during the many Christmastides and happy Easter frolics of years long past, when I have as well borne witness to this ever-growing marvel, sighs of awe against such glory of sound lure a steadied tread of hoofbeats crashing from my chest up to my ears: *oh, my God, dear holy Jesus God! This sound is absolutely breaking... my heart....*

Then at last, relief—as high glowing strokes of the finale cascade aloft in triumph. Dashing the bow off into the air like a primeval sorcerer flashing his wand in hallowed worship unto the sky, Nikolai then whirls around and shoves down it to the floor, its tip barely grazing the narrow gleam of naked pine in a muted hovering thrill. For the briefest second afterward as he flexes away his hand, the violin hangs beneath his chin, dangling in a wavering flutter of death-defying balance—before he cradles the neck back up again with a wistful, undying caress of love.

And then his face changes back—and my cousin, the eternal hooligan, returns to us from the netherspace of his wanderings up in the ethereal clouds. Grinning with rakish abandon and dragging me up from my chair along with him, he swings off into a pompous bow before tempestuous roars of: "Bravo! Bravo!"

Past the echoes of violin music ringing in my ears, I scarce detect the heady rush of applause. My glimpse of Father reveals him standing with Aunt Sophie across the room near the hearth, both of them a stark contrast of darkened colors against peach-brocade musings of the window draperies. Arms wrapped together, they each continue beaming from ear to ear with widened smiles of parental pride.

"You are on your way, Solo Wind," Nikolai whispers—and I gasp in surprise to feel him so near, his hand closing upon my wrist.

"Y-You only flatter me, Maestro!" I stutter out, gazing overlong into his face. "And, please—you mustn't call me that."

"Ha! As long as you refrain from calling me 'Kolya!'" he jokes, wincing, wrinkling up his nose.

Head still spinning, I yet barely hear. "You know I've not called you by that name for years," I murmur haltingly, amazed that in the miracle of these moments he can remain so concerned with such triviality.

"And much appreciated!" he replies, laughing, and adding with a nod between the crowd and my flute: "You will get used to it."

"I will never get used to you. And to that!" I declare, staring at his incomparable Guarnerius with the sudden mortifying realization that my voice has ground to breaking, emotion catching me forever at its precarious crossroads. Stabbing into my pockets, I recover my handkerchief, muttering: "Praise the stars, Nikolai! I swear by the dear Lord—you are a magician."

With a sly wink, Nikolai gives my wrist another affectionate squeeze; lets go. His shout then bounds out far above the excited audience din: "Enough, you free-hoarding spider-rum guzzlers! And might I take this opportunity to announce the debut of M'sieur Sekovsky—my stalwart friend and co-conspirator in crime—next Thursday morn, at nine o'clock sharp, before M'sieur Glazunov and the inevitable entourage at the St. Petersburg Conservatory of Music!"

"Nikolai!"

Flushing into a angst of scarlet, I manage to snatch back enough presence of mind to bow graciously before the renewed round of applause. But wholly ignoring my glare, Nikolai only continues on, shouting: "An audition which constitutes only a mere formality, I assure you!"

"Will you stop!" I cry, laughing through gritted teeth, my fingers pinching into his arm.

"Told you—best get used to it," he whispers back with a teasing poke of his elbow. "Now, come along!" he then insists. "You and I and a fair group of these ravishing *demoiselles* must be off for our long-awaited rendezvous at the Maryinsky."

* * *

Fighting for breath, I pad through lushly carpeted hallways of the Maryinsky Theater, my ears cringing against the shrill tempest of soprano notes yet echoing in distant snatches from the auditorium. There is stark difference, I am beginning to find, between the ability to walk and the ability to walk fast. As I hobble along, sympathetic glances follow, to my acute chagrin, from other truants lingering in the outer foyers to gossip or take a smoke.

The third act has already begun, but little do I care anymore. All the alcoves, the hat racks, the coat-withdrawing rooms have I checked, but I cannot find him—which only causes me to hurry faster, hot beads of sweat drenching into my stiffened collar, a ring of cold starch chafing fresh paper-cuts into the back of my neck. The knot clinching my stomach again worsens, continuing its twisted, cruel vise.

At last, in the men's water closet, I find him splashing cold sprays from the tap upon his face. After which he glares up at me from the basin.

"For God's sake!" I cry, knuckles stretched to the bone upon the handle of my cane. "What did I do?"

"Just go back and enjoy the performance, Sasha."

"No! Blast it, you have to be so damned inscrutable all the time?"

"Blast it, you have to be so damned emotional all the time?"

Reflected through the mirror-glass, Nikolai's glare bores hollow rivets into mine. I sigh in exasperation, in confusion, blurting out: "What on earth do you mean?"

"'Breathtaking!'" he mutters in harsh reply, a baiting sarcasm stung into every syllable of the word. Drying his hands, he lights a cigarette with unsteady fingers and whirls upon me for the kill, his eyes two gleaming spheres of hematite wracked with poisonous arrows of accusation. "Every aria, every bloody phrase!" he exclaims, vehemently blowing out smoke, "you have to snatch up my arm and sit clinging to me like a simpering fool, babbling on without ever any end to it: 'Breathtaking! Breathtaking!'"

My gaze wanders to the floor. Granted, I have heard better renditions of *Godunov.* More like a concert than a full-scale opera this performance is—for everyone, theater buffs included, remains beholden to strictest observance of the Lenten fast. But the voices echo yet with holy resonance despite absence of the costumes, the lavishly adorned sets. "I—I love music," I offer at last by way of pitiful, halting explanation.

"I am not talking about music!" Nikolai shouts—and slams his fist down upon the counter with such a ferocious bang that one of the attendants pokes his nose through the doorway, checking for a mishap.

"Oh, for Christ's sake, it's nothing!" he barks at the man, who scurries off amidst a flood of apology. Then, through another hazy stream of smoke, that ever-dreaded, glassy glare settles upon me once again—in the exact same way as this morn after my arrival at the railway station. "Breathtaking, Jesus God!" he snaps, turning away in disgust. "Breathtaking, indeed."

"Nikolai, what are you *talking* about?"

"Obviously, naught that you could ever understand! So why don't you simply get the hell out, and stop following me around like—like my whining little brother?"

I sprint back out through the door faster than even I had imagined possible.

"Sasha!" I hear him calling straight after. "Wait—"

Wrathfully, I pound down the hall, soft velvet hues of the theater's wealth of Nattier-blue hangings swimming before my eyes into the purest virulent sea of red.

"Sasha—"

He grapples me to a stop just before the central auditorium archway. "Take your hands off me!" I spit out at him through clenched teeth.

Catching his breath, Nikolai lets up on my arm. "I am sorry," he whispers loudly, as I glare heatedly across at him. "Sasha, please—don't shrug away without listening!" he chokes on. "I am truly sorry—forgive me, please."

Not without vindictiveness do I take note of tiny beads of moisture fringed all about his brow and collar, his watch dangling from its chain long trailing from his waistcoat pocket, his tie gone pitiably askew, taut fingers yanking apart the folds with sharp impatience in an attempt to quell his desperate spate to breathe.

"Sasha," he murmurs on, "you are my favorite cousin in all the world! Look, I—I know not what comes over me in my spells of gloom. From the bottom of my heart, I beg you to forgive me, please!"

From the tie, I glance back upward toward my cousin's eyes. No longer the accusatory glare; only Nikolai, the puzzlement, the changeling. The chameleon in so many other ways than merely with the violin.

Guiltily, he averts his gaze; fumbles with retying his tie.

Snatching through a billowing haze of blue velvet curtains, I stomp back into the auditorium.

Back at our two gallery rows, an awkward silence hangs amongst the group of cousins. Up on the stage, the soprano finishes at last, and the tenor starts forward. Through the crowd's rustlings, I detect one of the girls, either Tatyana or Eugenia, whispering something to the other about: "Where there be two flints, surely sparks will fly. . . ."

"Sasha, please—you know I scarce meant a word I said!" Nikolai whispers loudly, jabbing into my arm for about the twentieth time as, for about the twentieth time, I smack his hand away. And say nothing.

"Don't you pull that famous silent treatment on me!" he pleads on. "Oh, for God's bloody sake! . . ."

* * *

"And what foolishness is the row about this time?" Towering through the small room's doorway with a frown, Anna plants both hands upon her hips, yet again refusing to leave me be. "Sasha!" she cries indignantly. "You've scarce spoken to anyone else in the past three days, either. The least you can do is talk to me."

"Fine. I will talk to you—as long as we avoid discussing why I will not talk to him."

"Oh!" Anna lets out an exasperated sigh, groaning: "You are just as insufferable as my insufferable brother!"

Shrugging, I continue playing my flute.

"And will you stop that?"

"No! I happen to be readying for my audition next week, remember? If my playing appalls you so, leave."

'The Quarry' we call this room—an extra maid's room carved into the upstairs corner niche of the townhouse with scarce any view down into the quaint inner courtyard just outside. In a normal house, this room would be the attic with the angled dormers, and as such, stands piled to the walls with boxes, old toys, broken furniture, musty trunks stuffed with discarded clothing, and knickknacks with which no one can seem to bear parting. "I came in here to be alone," I inform Anna pointedly, then making a lengthy examination of the flute while adjusting its headjoint tuning.

In response, Anna tosses her head, her crown of wavy ringlets floating in a dusky web against slivers of afternoon sunlight pouring through the window. "Kolya's still at class," she says. "Why don't you come downstairs and join our parlor games? Maman said we could all read Gorky again later. And you know such difficulty as it is to convince her into allowing us to read Gorky! This time, you can take the part of Vaska. Or even Luka—"

"Ha, Luka the prophet!" I burst out. "An enigma of truth waltzing through an indiscernible veil of half-lies. Is that what you take me for—a puzzlement, a chameleon?"

Anna stares as if unfamiliar with the meaning of half my words.

"Well, it is your brother who is simply impossible, Anna Petrovna—not I!"

"Sasha, I did not say you were an enig—a whatever."

"Look, will you simply please leave? I have scarce any intention of coming downstairs until dinner. Well, I do not care a livid whit whether your brother is yet at class or not, Anna! Lord—there are simply too many people."

Indeed, so many people are staying over for Easter—a veritable platoon of cousins continually traipsing throughout the house, half at least under the age of ten and driving me into livid fits. Besides which people have been sleeping everywhere, crammed several to a room, pillows, featherbeds, and blankets strewn all over the townhouse floors. Others seem not to mind it so, all accustomed to the lazy casualness of such frequent family gatherings. Every Easter and Christmastide my memory neglects me, sharp reminders stabbing back only after the first few days: noise everywhere, and such a preponderance of blazing lights upon every chandelier in every room, constantly, that I beg penance for the many times I have cursed rural remoteness and the impossibility for having our house wired for the only modern convenience we yet lack in Novgorod. Give me an oil lamp, give me back my rustling water from the lakeshore, anything but all these lights, the continued noise . . . and so I have stolen up to a litter-strewn attic in my search for solitude, hopefully to hide away and scratch back some semblance of inner peace.

Despite my deliberate brusqueness, Anna refuses to leave. "And must you forever loll about like a farm peasant?" she says, laughing, her toe stubbing at my boot-heel with a teasing prod.

Some ordinary cotton clothes I packed along because always I begin to suffer immeasurably after the first few days, becoming sick unto death of starch, ties, and collars. "And must you forever dress like the lowliest trollop?" I shoot back. Again another velvet dress, far too intricately styled for even the late afternoon, with the same type of dangerously plunging neckline.

Instead of bristling at my rebuff and absenting herself, as I had hoped, Anna drops down to her knees beside me—and to my profound dismay, heaves her bosom out flauntingly. "Oh, it bothers you!" she whispers in a husky lilt. "Despite all the teasing, the eyes you and Kolya bat at me every night during supper."

Mortified, I slide across the floor as she again dares perilously close, her lips yawning eagerly toward mine.

"Anna!" Heart hammering into my throat, I attempt to duck away—but before I can protest any further, she throws both arms around my neck and crushes her mouth across mine in a blistering kiss.

"Blast it—don't!" I shout, roughly shoving her away.

"Shhh! You want everyone else to hear? And stop cursing so."

"By blood of the Saints!" I gasp in reply. "Are you crazy? All those letters, those poems I wrote—I was lonely, and in pain, for months, Anna. I never truly meant that you and I should—should ever—"

From the floor, the answer peals up in a capricious tirade of giggles.

"Oh!" I bark at her self-righteously, "and I suppose you think this is all naught but a joke!"

"Oh, poo! You needn't fret so, little cousin. My sore throat is much better. And forgive me," she goes on mockingly, heaving herself up from the floor. "I had forgotten you are still only fifteen. And such a child."

"I am *not* a child!"

"Humph! Kolya said you were."

Cursing her and 'Kolya' wordlessly under my breath, I duck back into the corner and start easing apart my flute.

Still in no hurry to allow me any hope of peace, Anna wanders across the room and throws open one of the old storage trunks, its lid clanging back loudly upon the floor, the odor of cedar and mothballs lifting through the air. From it she pulls out an old ermine stole—the kind yet possessed of the little ears and eyes, tails fluttering at the ends—and wraps it up about her neck and shoulders in coquettish mirth. "You like me better covered up?" she teases, giggles still hounding through the air.

"Humph!" I snap the flute case shut with a determined click.

Waltzing across the floor, Anna dangles the tails of the stole from her hands while impishly swinging her hips.

"Is he due to return presently from class?" I demand in exasperation—although I know him still to be gone; no hint of the violin's magic has yet sounded from down the hall.

Without answering, Anna extracts from the trunk a long lace veil and bunches it up upon her head, the ends cascading down her back in a showy train. "Perhaps," she observes, "I shall be like an American bride, dress as Natasha did for her wedding."

"You have a suitor in mind?" I reply absently—but unfortunately, once I catch her look, the drift is obvious. "Well, cousins have been known to marry!" she proclaims past my horrified flush, again bursting into peals of giggles.

"Oh, for the love of God, Anna!" I plead, rolling my eyes toward the heavens. "Will you simply leave off it all already?"

Tossing her head coyly, Anna yanks another keepsake from the trunk, this time a tattered old gown of Aunt Sophie's adorned with a ridiculously fat silken bustle. "Oh!" she cries out happily. "Eugenie and I used to have such fun in here every summer, playing dress-up."

One after another, more old gowns come flying out from the trunk as Anna, seeming at last to have forgotten her little charade with me, starts humming to herself with dreamy girlish sighs of contentment.

Grumbling, I heave myself upward with walking stick and flute case in hand and start off for the door.

A loud clank then rattles up from the bottom half of the trunk, causing us both to stop and peer down past the mess of rumpled fabric and bands of old lace littered about the floor. “What was that?” I demand.

Frowning, Anna follows my gaze. “I don’t know. Sounded a bit too heavy for jewelry, yes?” Grinning upward with a wicked wink, she beckons me to join her. “Oh, come—these old keepsakes are such frolic—let’s see what it is. Oh, I promise I’ll not try to kiss you again, Sasha! I was only teasing.”

Warily, I retrace my steps and crouch down onto the floor beside her; then together we start searching through the trunk. Beneath the next old gown lies a neatly packed row of threadbare shirts and work-worn trousers. Strangely, the hues of the shirts seem mismatched somehow, as if at one time each shirt had actually been different in color. But now, all lie muted into the same overworn blend of threadbare gray.

“Good heavens!” Anna exclaims with startled curiosity, digging her hands throughout the pile. “Why on earth would Maman want to keep? . . .”

And then she stops abruptly, going white as a sheet while whispering out: “Oh, no!”

“Anna—what is wrong?”

“We—we must put these clothes away—”

“Why?” As she leans hurriedly across, attempting to shut the trunk, I block the lid with my arm, demanding: “Anna! What in heaven’s name has come over you?”

“I am telling you—we must put these clothes away!”

“Not until I see why you are acting so queerly about them, we don’t.”

“But, Sasha!”

Shoving her off, I wrestle out one of the shirts. The flap over the left breast pocket boasts bare thread markings, dozens of scarred little holes, as if from ripped-up embroidery. Gripping the shirt between both hands, I stare at it long and sharply catch in my breath, a cold shudder of dread splicing through my heart.

“It’s naught but a frayed old shirt!” Anna whispers in frantic dismay. “We should put it away—”

"What was sewn here?" Turning upon her, I point to the pocket. "A name? Numbers?"

"I—I don't know!" Drained of all color, she attempts to bang the lid down again, but once more I elbow her off. A further exploration of the trunk reveals the trousers to resemble the shirts in their washed-out, muted grays of former colors. "What was that clanking sound we heard?" I then ask with harsh insistence. "Hardly jewelry." Past her whimpering protests, I dive headlong into the trunk.

"Sasha, it's all naught but a bunch of old work shirts! Who can possibly care? Let us go—I think they're readying for reading Gorky downstairs."

In a fit of haste, she starts piling up the old ballgowns.

"No, don't stuff all those back in here! I am not going anywhere until we find an answer to this mystery." At last, at the very bottom of the trunk, I uncover the chain.

Thick links of brittle iron, rusted near unto the core.

As I ease it out, the metal rattles ominously within my hands, tinny reverberations drifting to the doorway, probably echoing down the hall and across the remainder of crowded third-story rooms. A concave flap of solid iron, broken off into a clump of jagged pieces, swings upon its end. "What is this?" I murmur hoarsely, staring upward, aghast. "A part of a leg iron?"

In answer, Anna's eyes darken, guilty as sin.

"Blast it!" I shout, grappling for her arm. "You know all about this—and you are not telling me!"

"No, I do not know a thing about any of it!" she cries, attempting to slap me off.

"Whose leg iron is this?" I yell into her ear.

"I don't—"

"Whose leg iron is it?"

Giving her a roughened shake by the shoulders, I force her to meet my eyes; defiant, her stare lashes back, taut blue wariness laced with stubborn refusal to yield. "Is—is it my father's?" I rasp out at last.

Gasping, Anna buries her face into her hands.

"Answer me!" I shout, again shaking her. "Does this leg-iron belong to my father?"

"All right—yes! It—it is, indeed, Uncle Misha's."

"Why?" I choke out, desperate to fend off the anvil of terror slamming apart my soul. "Why in God's name would Father keep a leg-iron in a trunk in Aunt Sophie's attic?"

"I think a—a souvenir. From the War."

As I search her face with suspicion, she stammers on: "Well! Is t-true, no? That after fighting on the battlefield, men ofttimes keep such strange things?"

Too many of just such stories have I heard from Vliny to proffer any rebuttal on that point. "So?" I demand. "Do you know why he kept it?"

"Someone who was wearing it saved his life. Or something like that."

"And the clothes? What about the clothes?"

"Sasha! Will you stop with your insistent inquiries? I truly do not know!"

Breaking free from my grasp at last, she scurries from the room in a billow of rustling taffeta petticoats, slamming the door soundly shut behind her.

Frowning, I glance back to the heaped pile of clothes, folds of fabric swimming into a maze of tormented colors before my eyes. After a long moment, I start to gather the shirts and gowns back up into the trunk; then, winding up the chain, I return it to its place at the bottom and snap the lid softly shut.

Thirty years. Over half of Father's lifetime about which I still have virtually no clue.

I could ask him. Half an hour ago, he countered with a move that put me in check, and part of my solitary sojourn up here was for pondering upon my next strategy. He is sitting down there now in the drawing room beside Aunt Sophie, reading the newspaper, smoking his pipe, and listening to Tatyana pick like a bird at the piano keys. How heartless, how irreverent for me to simply wander in and interrupt the settled placation he has made of his life: 'Yes, Father, Knight takes your Rook—and by the way, does this piece of a leg iron happen to belong to you?'

Sighing, I rub quivering palms at my temples. Perhaps once more I am simply overreacting; perhaps it is merely as Anna said: that the chain belonged to someone who saved his life. After all, a field doctor spends his time attempting to save soldiers' lives; if circumstances should reverse, and someone happen to save his, the event would indeed be memorable.

But such would still give no explanation for the shirts—all far too narrow in the waist to have ever fit portly Uncle Petya.

* * *

"What do you mean, Knight takes Rook?" Father storms, glaring rank perturbation down into my face. "You are simply handing over the game!"

"Perhaps."

His grip wrenches powerfully into my arm, and toward the half-open doors of the dining room, from which the after-supper chatter continues twittering on, he nods with his most vehement warning, rasping out beneath his breath: "Just what is irking you so, Aleksandr? This little spat still? With Nikolai?"

I whip my tie off with a vengeance.

"Humph!" Father snorts. "At least tonight you had the decency to dress for dinner."

Last night was grandly humorous. Without thinking, I appeared at table in my boots and belted peasant tunic, causing a sensation of whispers amongst the girls.

"You will stifle your impertinence for the remainder of our visit here!" Father reiterates under his breath.

"Will I?"

His fist crushes into the chess paper, and I watch his other at his side, hovering against the outer limits of patience. Before the accident, such boldness would have merited an instant clapping behind my ear, and another brawling fight between us would have ensued. Ever since then, he has done well with containing his anger—he promised never to strike me again, and he has kept his word. But periodically, I cannot resist testing him.

"Put that back on!" he orders, pointing at the tie dangling from my fingers. "You are coming along with me back into the drawing room, where you will proceed to conduct yourself like a perfect gentleman, while the ladies serve desert."

"No, I am going up to Uncle Petya's library to read."

"But you have spent the last three nights in there!"

"So? Scarce difference it makes, Father, past all the people here—noisy children crawling like insects out of the woodwork at every turn! Christ, is it wrong to seek a bit of peace?"

At last he releases my arm. "I suppose not," he murmurs, sighing with heavy agreement.

"Besides," I go on in a more subdued tone, "Uncle Petya's shelves boast a full collection of Dostoevsky's books. I am reading *Crime and Punishment."*

"Again?"

"The plot is quite fascinating." Shrugging away from him, I shove my hands into my pockets and stare at the floor.

"Oh, all right." In exasperation, Father glares up to the ceiling, exclaiming: "Youth!" His stare again drawn to the chess paper, he waves it toward me as he backs away, insisting: "I am not marking this in until you decide to renew serious play, Sasha. It is hardly like you to give up the game."

Avoiding his eye, I continue staring at the floor.

"I wish you'd smooth matters over," he murmurs from the doorway. "With Nikolai."

Noncommittally, I nod. Past necessary affirmations or negations, not a word have I traded with my cousin for four entire days—an awkward situation, bedded down as he and I are in the same room together, and ironic because this was supposed to be a joyous time after our long separation of so many months. But small use proves close proximity now, the both of us each night feigning sleep—while staring for hours across the darkness in a mutual ambush of frosty silence.

"Oh, let the devil take your sulking, Sasha!" Father implores me. "I tell you, scarce before you know it, you'll be near unto eighty years old, and despising yourself for cold-shouldering friends long dead."

"May I be excused to go up to the library?"

Father throws up his hands, and past familiar distraught mutters about England, disappears back into the dining room.

Dishes clank. Feet shuffle against the drone of feminine chatter as family and guests all file toward the drawing room for desert. Above them, my lumbering footsteps pound the stairs and echo sadly into the wooden floor as I limp down the third-story hall.

I know not why I should spend months yearning to return to Petersburg, only to do so and then suffer such a bout of homesickness that I can scarce wait for return unto Novgorod. Perhaps spending the entire autumn and winter honing independence amidst the quiet atmosphere of home in lieu of adhering to rigid dormitory rules has forever spoiled me. Or perhaps apprehension over the audition, scheduled for one week from today, yet reigns supreme—surely Glazunov and the other distinguished professors will only laugh at my incompetence. The Conservatory, after all, has been home to marvels: Tchaikovsky, Rachmaninoff, Rimsky-Korsakov. Currently, they sponsor such prodigies as Nikolai. Who am I to even entertain the thought of meeting such grand expectations as a performer or student of composition? Ridiculous! I had best return straight away to Novgorod and become a doctor like my father. Or more likely—and perilous as it still seems!—become a bee farmer.

Uncle Petya's small library is the only room in the house besides the Quarry where no one has been bedded down, and for the past three eves, I have stolen into it like a thief snatching back precious time from the grip of duty's devil. And so again I turn the antique brass handle on the door, relishing the thought of waning away another span of hours humored blackly by Dostoevsky's melancholy musings.

Black humor lasts for not another second—as the door bends open, a strong hand pulls me through, fingers clamping up roughly over my mouth. A second arm seizes in a Titan's vise across my chest, forcing me into the room, the door slamming shut with a solid kick.

Back against the wall Nikolai pins me, his hollow-gray eyes boring outraged tunnels into mine. "We have to talk!" he exclaims.

"How dare you!" I roar, landing a furious punch into his neck.

He punches back, knocking the wind flat out of my lungs.

"Nikolai!" I gasp, heaving for breath. "G-Goddamn it!"

Forcing me around, he spews shrill anguish into my face: "Sasha Sekovsky, you are the only brother I have ever known. Seven years ago down on the banks of your Lake Ilmen, recall you not our dares of foolishness? Slicing gashes in our fingers, mixing up our blood—childish scars still borne with rash pride by each of us unto this day! And now you presume we have naught left to say to one another?"

Morosely, I glare away to the wall.

"Look," Nikolai goes on, cheeks paling near to the washed hue of his flaxen hair. "Again I ask your forgiveness for my outburst of the other night. You want me to fall down upon my knees and beg your acceptance of my apology? Here—"

He drops down to the floor, seizing me about the ankles.

"Oh, for God's sake, Nikolai—get up!"

"Well!" Sheepishly, he stumbles back upward, spreading both hands out wide. "Dear Lord, Sasha," he cries, "my only wish in the world is to talk to you! I mean, last night, what did you do? Showed up at table decked out like a frigging Hussar! I swear, was all I could do to contain my mirth! Talk about outdoing the spider stunt in the grandest fashion! You should have *seen* the expression on Uncle Misha's face—not to mention Maman's. But could you take part in any of the fun? Oh, no—you only continued sulking like a spoilt child! I spent the entire two hours tugging at the tablecloth, ramming your toe, trying everything I could think of to catch your eye, but would you give a damn at all?

No, not a hint, not a word! My God, Sasha—what do you want from me?"

"An explanation, I suppose!" I rasp out hoarsely. "For that remark you made in the Maryinsky water closet."

"Sasha, was all simply a slip of the tongue! You know how I have been stewing day and night like a madman over this Mendelssohn piece, preparing for tomorrow's recital. You know the poor footing I'm on with Auer—have been ever since the day the old brute took me on! I swear, I can do naught to please the man."

"Nikolai, at least you haven't an interview next week upon which hinges the entire rest of your life."

"I know." His hand closes around mine; squeezes it.

Roughly, I snatch my arm away, turning on him ferociously: "Have you any idea how long I waited to attend the *Godunov* opera with you? And can you even fathom how heartbroken I was months ago when you all left straight away for Paris the day after Christmas—again? Through ages of pain and frustration have I struggled with this leg, mostly without a speck of company from anyone close to my own age! The only one of the peasants I ever got on with was Volodya; he was eighteen. And I tell you—despite the taunts he'd rankle at me in front of his mangy friends, he and I managed quite nicely when we stole off alone together—used to play cards every night, and he showed me how to fish honeycombs from the hives! But you know how Father took care of that little fledgling friendship for me, ha! And so in the meantime, where the hell have you been? The Crimea, Paris, Genoa, Berlin—or here in Petersburg, enjoying yourself immensely amidst applauding audiences, your schedule so full to the brim that, save for Christmas, you could spare not even one meager side trip out to Novgorod during all the remainder of the winter!"

"Dammit, Sasha! Have you forgotten that I wrote you at least a five-page letter *every* single week?"

"Then why my first night back here do you treat me like the bastard runt of some lowly Vyborg beggar?"

"I said I was sorry!" Nikolai rasps out, his gaze searing rank holes of frustration into mine once more. "Jesus Christ! *What else do you want me to say?"*

"I don't know!"

Fortunately, he takes a backward step at last—otherwise, I fear I would literally breathe pure dragon's fire into his heart.

"Look," he murmurs, staring down to the floor and ruffling a hand through his hair, "I meant not to take my inner turmoils out upon you, dearest cousin. You are my best friend, one I would never hurt for all the world! I simply do not know what comes over me sometimes. Is like a jinx, a blackened demon ever chewing at my soul."

Sighing, I step over to the corner table, flick on the reading lamp, and stare across at him through the faint halo of light, asking: "Is that why you look at me so strangely sometimes?"

Nikolai frowns, his eyes taking on a solemn pensiveness. "What do you mean?"

I clear my throat. "The way you keep staring at me," I go on haltingly. "As you did at the station. Before you left to help Father with the baggage. You don't remember?"

"No." Betraying only confusion, his gaze wanders to the floor.

"But—the same thing then happened in the water closet at the theater."

"I have no idea what you are talking about, Sasha!"

I feel my face flush. Despite the sharp bite of his denial, Nikolai does seem just as bewildered as I about the whole matter. "Oh, never mind!" I cry, exasperated, rolling my eyes.

In response, he holds out his hand, murmuring: "I take back my heartless remark. Will you accept my apology?"

As I let out another lengthy sigh, he adds: "Look, I can scarce any longer bear this. Eight days is the most you have ever gone without speaking to me at all, two years ago after I soaked you with whipping cream in the dormitory."

"Oh, God in Heaven!" I exclaim wrathfully. "I swore to never so much as come near you again after that." But in spite of myself, the chuckles well up in fond, lingering remembrance.

Imbued with the old gaiety, Nikolai's gaze meets mine again, and I cannot help but proffer out my hand. Both of his own he clamps fast around it, urging: "Come! We have decided to fetch a troika and go racing on the Neva. I've heard that ice-breaking will be in two or three days, so tonight could be our last chance!"

I cock a wary eyebrow. Despite my love of driving at blinding breakneck speed, the bells jingling, the wind slashing about our heads, I cannot help but remember where we finally ended up the last time.

"Oh, come along!" Fully gauging the expression of stiff reluctance upon my face, Nikolai grins and starts fingering his moustache—an irritating, vain little habit I've noticed him to have acquired during these last several nights at dinner. "You are not going to chicken out on me, now—are you, little brother?" he goads, winking devilishly.

"I am not your little brother, and I am *not* chicken!"

"Good! Then come—we've hidden away four bottles from Uncle Misha and Maman, the best chilled champagne!"

* * *

Had I wholly forgotten how enchanting the Petersburg nights can be? Northward sprawls the vast outlying Fortress of Peter and Paul, its high cathedral spire hungering skyward to mark the marble tombs of the Tsars. Both west and eastward shimmers the ageless Neva mirror-glass; southward stand row upon row of regal palaces bearing combs of window tapers, countless tiny lights sparkling against rounded outlines of Redeemer's cupolas and St. Isaak's massive golden dome looming up in either direction. And below, the ice taunts us, dares us; we taunt and dare it, all four of us shrieking like a squall of nether-spirits casting spells within a magic white cave. . . .

"Faster!" Nikolai shouts, snagging the cork from yet another bottle of champagne to send the foam spurting out across the floorboards of the troika, much to our frantic screams of delight.

"Sasha, *s'il vous plaît!"* demands Anna, making a pointed production of thrusting her crystal goblet into my hand. "One always serves the ladies first," she insists.

"Oui, M'mselle," I rasp out hoarsely, snatching up the neck of the bottle and sloshing champagne into her glass.

"You're drunk!" she exclaims.

"I am not."

"Oh, so what if he is?" Nikolai uncorks yet another bottle, which he and I then proceed to share, passing it back and forth between ourselves and gulping each of us straight from the neck amidst bursts of laughter at the horrified reaction of the girls.

"Faster!" I call up ahead to the driver—who responds by bursting out into yet another woeful love song to his three prancing Arabian steeds. Once more we careen around, speeding off into a breathless headlong rush of icy wind.

"Yes, do take us back around again!" Nikolai adds, waving his arm and promising ten extra rubles as a tip. "All the way back down to the Winter Palace—and hurry!"

With so many sleighs and troikas jammed onto the Neva, all flying along the river-ice at manic breakneck speed, it is a wonder there have yet been no collisions. Up ahead, making a vain attempt to ignore us and our gleeful shouts of "Wherefore art thou, Romeo?" Tatyana rides in a cozy sleigh beside her doltish, hawk-nosed lieutenant. Upon hearing the screeching giggles of Anna and Eugenia as we again careen around them, the fur-bundled, love-struck pair makes another attempt at feigning ignorance of our presence as their driver, signaling a rash of obscenities to ours, pulls short into a perilous turn.

"Le virage, fair Montague!" I shout out as we pass. "Three horses clear the curve ten times better than one!"

"Hey, Romeo!" Nikolai yells in agreement, "only troikas take giddy turns! Best leave off that sorry sleigh and fetch you an honest troika—eh, Romeo? Hey! Wherefore art thou, Romeo?" he bellows on, bursting into another peal of laughter as he downs in scarce three gulps near unto a third more of the bottle of champagne.

"Indeed!" Anna whispers coyly in my ear. "Wherefore art thou, Romeo?"

Nervously, I attempt to disentangle her arm, although, entwined with Nikolai's, it has again wound behind my neck—but she only shoves right back, scrunching her body against mine, her warm breath nuzzling into my ear.

"Stop it, Anna."

"Oh, poo! Hush, little cousin—and drink all of your champagne."

I glance beyond her, but find Eugenia gaping out of the troika with a bemused grin, appearing more tipsy than any of us. In her struggle with retaining her oversized sable muff, she scarce takes notice. Trying the opposite direction again, I slam my elbow once more into Nikolai's ribs, leveling another vindictive glare at him for forcing me to relinquish my usual claim. It is ever an old rivalry between us, the possession of the end seat, whether it be in a classroom, coffeehouse, or sleigh. But he only winks back in stealthy triumph—while nudging me even more snugly into Anna's eager embrace, almost as if in full cahoots with her attempt at my seduction. "Oh, down some more champagne!" he shouts, shoving the neck of the bottle straight into my mouth. Banging his foot then onto the floorboards, he admonishes the driver to press on with more boisterous shouts of: "Faster! Faster!"

With a terrifying burst of speed, we abruptly fly off all the way down the full course of the Neva ice, rushing by other sleighs and troikas with a ferocity that forces us all to grip one onto another for dear life.

Once we slow at last, I snatch the champagne bottle back from Nikolai again. "We lost Tatyana," I mumble, peering around as the troika winds into yet another perilous turn.

"Over there!" Nikolai calls breathlessly, pointing across my head. "Over there! They're heading back toward the Summer Gardens."

"Oh, who cares about Tatyana?" Anna exclaims, her voice slurred, both arms winding once more around my neck.

"Anna—stop!"

"No! Hush and kiss me."

Whereupon she attempts to do just that—as I back away in desperation, shoving to no avail. "Anna, blast you!" I gasp in mortification, tearing my mouth away from hers.

In response, she and Nikolai burst into a derisive chorus of laughter.

"Oh, ha!" I shout back in fury, glowering at them both. "And I suppose you two planned this from the beginning?"

"Thought so!" Nikolai calls across my head, grinning over at Anna. "That he never has been kissed."

"I will consent to be your special tutor, country cousin!" Anna declares. "Poor starved provincial soul." Erupting in giggles, she again yanks up, beneath the wrap of furs, the sagging shoulder of her gown.

"Anna!" I shout. "Nikolai! Let go of me!" But he only continues pushing me toward her.

"This is how it is done, my innocent sweet!" Anna whispers, her laughter grazing my ear.

Another steaming, heady kiss she plants across my mouth—until wrenching gleefully away to leave me gasping for breath in throes of near-asphyxiation.

As the sleigh flies down the ice past more rows of gleaming palaces toward our breakneck rendezvous with the Summer Gardens, I hear Nikolai's laughter mixed with Anna's squeals of conspiring delight. "Kiss him again!" he urges her, once more shoving me against her swollen bosom, its pale hollows of temptation peeking out without any trace of decorum from the sliding bundles of fur coverings.

"Shall we kiss you again, country cousin?" Anna cries, blonde curls dangling mischievously from beneath her new blue fox hat. Impatiently, she yanks it off, sending her long mane tumbling down between the two of us in a teasing billowy cascade.

"Humph! I'll show you how to bloody well kiss again!" I stutter hoarsely, seizing hold of her arms.

"Oh, look at this!" she retorts, throwing back her head, laughing. "So he thinks he is true Romeo after all! Ha, ha—"

Her voice muffles into a stifled whimper as, wrenching her to me roughly, I seize her into a kiss of kisses brandished with every last ounce of my strength.

At first, I hear Nikolai bursting into another torrent of laughter behind me. But as the moment drags on into another, and yet another, and still I refuse to let Anna go—tightening my hold like a pair of pincers down around her waist despite the sudden desperate flailing of her arms—I feel his grip prying into my shoulder, attempting to pull me back. "Sasha!" he shouts, his tone half-laughing, half-serious. "Enough already, you're—she's—*Sasha!* Stop it, you're hurting her!"

Cursing, he at last tears me away from her—and the instant we break free, the back of Anna's hand plows into my cheek with a stinging slap.

"Get out!" she screams, her face flushed like a livid melon, blue eyes flashing though peeled slits of rage.

"You were the one who kept baiting me the whole time!" I shout back, pointing at her.

"Stop the troika!" she commands the driver.

"Oh, Anyuta—come!" Nikolai interjects. "Was all naught but a simple joke—"

"Stop the troika!"

Over Nikolai's heated objections, the driver follows Anna's orders, pulling off to the nearest boat launch east of the Summer Gardens.

"Now, get out!" Anna wails again, her breath hacking forth unevenly as she struggles against tears. Snatching back the coverings of furs, she draws them up to her neck in haughty repose and starts kicking at the both of us until we stumble, upon a flood of curses, out from the sleigh.

"Blast you, Anna!" Nikolai yells back at her. "Can't you hold up your end of coaxing out a bit of fun?"

"Humph! Both of you can go to—to hell! Back to the Winter Palace!" she shouts at the driver.

Nikolai, at foolish risk to his arm, swipes in and manages to seize the last unopened bottle of champagne—just before Anna, Eugenia, and the troika blast off amidst a flurry of watery shavings down the long plane of ice.

"Showed her a taste of passion, indeed, my friend," my cousin then says into my ear, his laughter bit into taunting frost rings as his breath laces over mine through the stark night air. "I take it back," he adds with a snort of approval. "You are not quite the innocent I had thought."

"Ha! I take due note that tonight you've no further qualms about my catching her sore throat."

"Drozhki!" he calls upward toward the street, ignoring my continued glare as we bid our way up the slippery ice-encrusted cobblestones of the boat launch.

In the commotion, I scarce managed to fetch my walking stick as Anna booted us from the troika, but navigating my way up the slope of the boat launch is still difficult. Albeit reluctantly, I find myself forced to cling fast hold of Nikolai's arm until we reach the more level curbstone of the street. Then I shove angrily away, snarling: "You conniving sneak! You arranged this whole dastardly little affair—yes?"

"I beg your pardon?"

"And yesterday? When you were off to class? I'd retreated to the Quarry; was attempting to get in some practice. She scarce let me alone. So—did you promise to buy her that new hat if she'd kiss me? Did you convince her into faking a sore throat—so I'd want her even more? What is this, Nikolai? Another asinine 'initiation' test?"

Eyes hooded, he peers at me cooly through shadows of the yellowy gaslight, murmuring out barely above a whisper: "I have no idea what you are talking about, Sasha."

"Humph!"

A couple of cabs whisk up to the curb across the mix of ice and watery slush. "And now," I go on, "I suppose we'll be off to the usual place?"

"We want over to the Vyborg side," Nikolai tells both drivers. He then proceeds to become embroiled in the inevitable haggle between their boisterous pleadings over the fare. Finally, he drags me along with him into the closest cab, and the universal love song to the steed begins in a bellowing baritone as we charge off, huddled against one another somewhat uncomfortably in the compact snugness of the tiny two-seater.

"You neglected to answer my question," I remind him at last.

"Need I? It is what you want. Yes?"

Nose thrown disdainfully to the air, Nikolai settles the champagne bottle in between his knees. And whispers: "Because you still never have. Have you?"

I lurch away, my neck hot and chafing. Shaking his head, he lets out a short laugh and lights up a cigarette.

"You wish to fetch yourself a citing?" I warn him crossly. Street smoking prohibitions may be old, but in some places, especially Novgorod—possessed of so many wooden structures with the ever present danger of fire—are still law.

"Ha! You provincial idiot—you have been in the country too long! Petersburg rescinded such ordinances decades ago. Coppers these days are far too overrun with strikers and bloody bombing terrorists to cite some poor fellow for an idle flick of ash! Besides, we're going across the river. Who fucking cares?"

But I note the effort he takes to keep the ash from grazing the street, flicking it to the floor of the drozhki about our boots.

"Give me one," I demand then, grabbing for his case.

He snatches it quick away. "No, have you gone daft? And wholly forgotten that you play a wind instrument?"

Glaring at him in reply, I cross my arms and watch smoke rings flutter from his mouth against teasing rushes of the wind.

But I choose not to press the matter, having far enough with which to contend—my heart racing, my mind fraught with undulating spasms of panic. And the hailstorm of last year's visions from the place to which I am certain we are going.

* * *

Tawdry as its name, this place—at least the upstairs portion—is called Violetta's. From Murzhinsky's Tavern below, the noise continues blaring upward: balalaikas, horns, drums, songs of the Gypsy dancers; laughter, curses, the clanking of bottles and glasses; repeated shouts of "Vodka!" and *"Kvas! Kvas!"*; the crashing of chairs amidst angry scuffles and a brewing legacy of fistfights. Despite the infestation of cockroaches and dank smell pervading from the slums all around, the tavern downstairs is the place I would prefer to be.

There were two fire-eaters down there. Ever long have I been both fascinated and repulsed by watching them toss the flaming pins down their throats with nary a care, their sidekicks ever riling all the gawkers. At this point, the unobtrusive stance of a silent gawker I would welcome with relief—but instead, I remain captive hostage to untold yards of gauzy red draperies hung amidst shadows of a confining maze. No separate rooms exist as such at Violetta's, only partitioned-off little alcoves and cubicles—all without doors—sporting old divans and hastily made-up beds. Unfortunately, up here, one is expected not to be a gawker.

Up here, one is expected to absolutely relish in the fullest efforts at participation.

"Oh, come, dahling!" the woman whispers to me again, her hands inching downward, long pointed nails plucking open the second button of my shirt.

But once more I shove her off, shouldering my way along the wall, breath stabbing into my lungs like searing spikes of fire.

Nikolai bursts into another round of hooting laughter, telling her: "Just keep at him, Tisha; truly a shy one, yes?"

Then he buries his face again into the neck of the toothy redhead with whom he has been much busy, yards of her tightly curled tresses wound up about his bare shoulders. I watch the muscles in his back tensing, untensing, tensing again as she starts toying with his belt, unhooking it, yanking it off, her hands easing into the waist of his trousers. With furious, trembling fingers, he then wrenches away her corset, his lips sliding downward from hers to the molded softness of her heavy breasts. Cupping one in each hand, he begins kissing first from one swollen nipple and then to the other, his mouth working back and forth in sucking twists as her arms wrap around his head, her sighs shuddering against him in soft, low moans.

Together, they collapse upon the bed.

"Sweetest," Tisha murmurs again, warm fingers tickling against my clammy throat. She attempts another kiss as I dodge away again.

"You don't like me?" she whimpers, her mouth pursing in a childish pout.

"Quite the contrary!" I gasp. The fact is, the girl is beautiful: oriental, delicate as a jade flower with wide slanted eyes, high narrow cheekbones, straight hair falling in a long black sheath across her flimsy silken gown. Little does it matter. Unlike my precocious cousin Anna, unlike the graceful Katya who so long ago allowed me to kiss her inside the barn, the whores know wily, intimidating moves that make me quiver like a plodding fool, and the more beautiful they are, the more fretful I steadily become.

"Here." I pull from my pocket several kopek pieces and a ruble note, insisting: "Please, go fetch me another drink."

"Dahling, aren't you drunk enough already?"

"I scarce asked for your opinion. Go and fetch me another drink."

With an exasperated sigh, Tisha takes the change and pads off for the stairs. Warily eyeing the swaying movements of her hips as she waltzes off, I down last sips of ice from my tumbler and call after her in a shaking voice: "And tell them honest Scotch whiskey this time, the kind from the bloody Isles, not that watery home brew! Do you hear me?"

Backing off then into the shadows, I slink past the partition to steal another look at Nikolai and his plyings with the whore.

To find both lying completely naked, kissing and hacking at one another like two banshees possessed of an electric charge. Panting for breath, he pushes on top of her, his hand gliding across her thigh. She spreads her legs out as far as they will stretch, and his three fingers, forced together rigid as a knife, thrust straight forward into the moist, hairy warmness of her.

Slamming shut my eyes, I flatten back to the wall, the old spell again suffocating my resolve, stern intent of proving my manhood once and for all cast off in a vortex of high seas—and leaving me deserted somewhere in between a flood of exhilaration and lapping waves of nausea.

Two years ago, my first look at a woman naked hardly lent itself to profound aesthetic appreciation of the female body. The summer I turned fourteen, playful vacation frolics in Europe had become assigned to distant memory; due to the growing fiscal problems, I was needed more than ever on the farm again for book work when the school term ended. For the first time, I took the train all the way from Petersburg to Novgorod by myself, but no sooner had Father met me at the station than were we diverted by a frantic midwife, and in the ensuing inevitability of the following four hours, I found myself drafted into service along with everyone else, exchanging bandages, proffering forceps and the like. Only afterward, when Father found me with my head literally slung in a pail outside in these people's outhouse, did it appear to dawn on him that, at my age, I was not quite so prepared as he for the bloody spectacle involved in the birth of a child.

Of course, he apologized profusely—only informing me then that, had I wished, I certainly could have left the room.

Scant help that was to me after the fact. Or is now.

"Here, dahling!" Tisha rasps out eagerly, shoving another sloshing tumbler into my hand. "Now," she whispers, her soft breath cooing against my cheek, "shall we?"

Reaching into my billfold, I slip out a five-ruble note; hand it over to her and whisper back: "Go away and leave me alone."

"Akkh! But, dahling! Are you sure?"

I slip out another five-ruble note; down half my drink and whisper again: "Go. Leave me."

The girl sighs, stuffing the bills into her plunging *décolleté.* "Have it as you will, then," she says with a disdainful shrug—and saunters off, black hair swishing in a liquid fan behind her as she disappears off toward another of the cubicles.

In one burning gulp, I down the remainder of my drink; then inch up again along the wall and attempt to remain unnoticed while narrowing every tremulous thought upon the sight unfolding on the bed.

Nikolai is ready to take the whore now. Virtuoso in sex as well as music, my cousin never simply bangs off a whore. Instead, he always takes the time to build the suspense up into a stinging aria, teasing the women mercilessly with his fluttering, prodding fingers. And sure enough, he has done it again with this one; eyes languid and imploring, her nails raking across his lower back, she seems to want him even worse than he wants her. At last he pushes in between her legs, hovering upon his knees and grinning down at her slyly, his engorged penis lancing outward like the teasing shaft of conductor's baton—until her hand closes upon it, and then his hand closes upon her hand closing upon it, and then together they shove him in. . . .

Heart thundering in my ears, I shut my eyes again, shuddering against a drench of sweat while stiffening in mortification against the squeeze of my own desperate, sneaking fingers, both fists clutched scarce a wily inch away from the growing bulge in my own crotch . . . *oh, God! You pitiful, senseless fool! You know you've seen him like this dozens of times before. . . .*

And just like the other times, I sneak a peek again, and there they are . . . curving, arching, twisting, rolling against thunder . . . torturing flits in the shadows . . . I wonder if he even realizes that I am watching . . . if he knows that all I have ever done is watch . . . and *watch* . . . always with both hands quaking at my sides, fists ever clenching, unclenching, threatening to take on a life of their own. . . .

No! Damn you—don't!

In agony, I slam both fists again back into the wall.

Good God, Sekovsky! What the devil has come over you? Dozens of whorehouses, dozens of times like this with Nikolai—and before that, all the inane, childish little feats: who can pee farthest into the lake? Whose is longest? Quick, find the measure-tape—*oh, God! I am sick, perverted . . . base beyond all description . . . but simply cannot stop demon fingers from inching forward . . . no, dammit—don't you dare!*

So long have I borne my nightly agony of sin: bid Father good-night . . . pray for my mother's soul . . . wrestle both fists beneath the fur-trimmed coverlet . . . succumb to the thrusting dirty devil of desire . . . so what if I give in a little early? No one will care in the least; this is a fucking bordello, dammit! But what if Nikolai, or someone else sees . . . *oh, sonuvabitch, Sekovsky! Can't you even jack yourself off in a filthy whorehouse without winding up in another moralistic inner debate?*

"Uh-huh . . . some of us simply like to watch."

This time, I snatch back my hands with an audible gasp of horror—and a knowing elbow nudges into mine, soft chuckles brushing through the air as the voice adds: "Some fellows just gotta fuck the hell out of the whores. But others of us, we're voyeurs, eh? The ones who simply like to watch."

Mouth dropped, I stare at him aghast: waves of long black hair, dark olive skin, sinewy figure shoved brazenly in beside me against the wall. Recognition at last prevails as I recover the farthest fraction of my voice, stammering out: "M-My God! *Volodya?"*

I gape at him, stunned.

"In the flesh—and at your service, Count Sekovsky," he proclaims sarcastically. With a mischievous grin, he nods past the partition toward the bed. "Your cousin, the violinist, I presume?"

"Just how in hell do you know?" I snap, still petrified with amazement.

"Whoa, simmer down! Christmastide a year and a half past. Surely you remember? News of his talent spread like wildfire all across the village—and a ready group of us soon huddled outside, listenin'. A lofty rendition from our very own Rimsky-Korsakov, I believe?"

Still shaken, I turn away with a begrudging nod.

Eyeing in triumph the sight of Nikolai and the girl, Volodya then whispers: "I see he plays the ladies with the same artful finesse."

"Why don't you *shut up?"*

"Ha! And why don't you afford your cousin a bit of privacy?" Casting me a gloating leer, he waltzes off, breaking into a wealth of snickers permeating down the length of the shadowy hallway.

After a guilty glance back toward the bed, where Nikolai and the girl continue to go steamily at it, I duck out from the cubicle and follow after Volodya.

"What am I doin' here?" he cries. "Me? That was the question I was about to ask you. Or have you made it your habit, dallyin' in Vyborg slums? There aren't more respectable bordellos over on Sadovaya, near the Haymarket, on your side of the river?"

To his derisive laughter, I reply: "Places that cost a literal arm and a leg, yes."

"Oh, forgive me! So true it is, then, survival on a mere pittance. The poor schoolchildren of Russia's impoverished nobility!" Chuckling as I shoot him a tepid glare, he shrugs and nods toward the stairwell. "Oh, come! I meant no offense. Let me buy you a drink."

With some reluctance, I stare back toward the direction of Nikolai's cubicle.

"I assure you he's still quite busy," Volodya whispers with a loud guffaw.

"Humph! Well . . . ." Against the back of my aching neck, I rub my hand, admitting: "I suppose I could use another drink."

"So—hurry it up, then!" Grasping up his perfectly pressed lapels, Volodya saunters off down the hall, murmuring backward: "I owe you one, you know."

In a fluster, I round up my jacket and walking stick, and hurry after him, calling: "What do you mean, owe me one?"

Downstairs, I find him seated at a corner table tucked away from most of the boisterous confusion of the tavern. Over two large tankards of vodka, he explains:

"I'd be dead save for you."

"Whatever do you mean?"

"Thirty lashes can finish a man. I heard you interfered and whittled it down to eighteen. I'll never forget."

Dark eyes twinkling merrily, he raises his glass in a toast of appreciation.

Exaggeration appears to remain Volodya's favorite hallmark. Thirty lashes might well finish a dog, but hardly a young, robustly healthy man. Still, after all the tumult of that fateful day, I never thought about the fact that my influence lessened the harshness of Father's penalty. "I only 'whittled' it down to twenty," I reply, lifting my glass to meet his. "Pavel's doing made it eighteen."

"Pavel always was a soft-hearted old bastard. Well! Let us drink a toast to him also."

Again our tankards clink.

Volodya must be nineteen by now—although he appears at least five years older with his swaggering, self-assured gait, his cocky grin. "You seem to have done rather well for yourself," I say, nodding at his suit, the quality of its linen fabric and superb fit garishly paling the second-hand tailoring on mine.

"Indeed, so I have," he replies, winking at me past a sidelong grin. "But tell me," he goes on, his expression mellowing into a serious frown, "just what the devil happened to your leg?"

I pick my fingers across splintery wooden ridges in the table; stare long at bare trestlework. "Retribution, I suppose," I blurt out at last with a shrug. "He had to expunge his wrath upon someone." The admission, the ease with which it slips out, surprises even me. So forthright. So helplessly honest.

"Murderous beast, the man is!" Volodya mutters, his bitter glare piercing off into the distance.

"Volodya, that is not entirely true."

"Humph! What is true is that every man is biased when it comes to his father. As I still am when it comes to the Armenian drunkard who is mine."

Unable to resist a reluctant nod of agreement, I stare off aimlessly toward the fire-eaters and the bar.

"Well?" he goes on. "I'd heard rumors about some kind of 'accident.' But nothin' more. You want to tell me what happened?"

My first instinct—to counter instead with inquiries about his activities of these past months—dissolves unto infinity as I stare vacantly into my memories through the glassy tankard of vodka.

And then the next thing I know, I start talking nonstop—vocal chords stretched to the rasping limits as they have not been in days, weeks, months—telling him everything about the accident and afterwards: every incident, every little crushing defeat and joyful spin of triumph in learning to walk again; all the moments, hours, endless days spent within the bloated sphere of pain; all my pending apprehension involved with next week's audition at the Conservatory—the things that, in truth, I wanted to sit down and say to Nikolai, despite having written about it all to such great length in the letters. It matters not; I yearned so to sit down with him and simply say these things. But there has been no time. Or at least the right time.

Volodya proves a far better listener than I would ever have credited him, and in the process of so rashly baring my soul upon his patient ears, the hurtful thudding of my heart at last slows, twisted visions of Nikolai's romp with the whore upstairs at last receding far enough from my mind's eye to afford my breathing a bit of evenness, my nerves a lull of peace.

"Honestly needed that drink, didn't you?" Volodya's laughter mixes into the banging chaos of tavern music as he once more pours vodka from his tankard into mine.

"Oh, no, please—I mustn't." Protesting, I press cold fingers to the rising squall of pain searing across my brow.

"And so—will you come?"

I glance upward, mumbling: "I'm sorry?"

"To my flat. I just asked if you'd care to stop by and see my new flat."

"You did?"

"As I said, is not far," he goes on with hurried enthusiasm. "Scarce down the street. Quite proud to have acquired my own place. Let me show it off to you!" Again winking across at me jovially, he grasps up his lapels. Then, beckoning to a serving maid, he passes her a ten-ruble note. "Upstairs, blond hair, his name is Prince Zhelanov, he's with Glafira—you know, the redhead. Tell him that his cousin Sasha has sated himself so with Tisha's favors that he is takin' an early cab home."

The girl answers Volodya with a knowing grin. "Far too generous ye are, Vladimir Denisovich!" she says, greedily eyeing the note.

"You know her?" I stammer, attempting to focus my eyes upon the girl's wavering form as she wanders off.

"Oh, yes. One can make the greatest strides in life from working with the oddest assortment of people." Chuckling, Volodya nudges my arm. "Come, let us go," he murmurs, his voice cool with reassurance. "You seem as if you could use a spell of rest. I know I could. And besides, there is something I want to show you."

* * *

Above a dress shop the flat is: four blocks down from the deafening noise of the tavern, three floors up, squalid and dark, filled with scattered clothing, papers, and books, bereft of furniture save for a table, an oil lamp, a solitary mattress. Warm and crackling with a rush of heat the quick fire burning in the stove is, soft snaps punctuating rasps of breath across baiting shadows of the air. Graceful and powerfully lithe as a jungle cat he is—stealthy, stalking—tension poised in every cautious step eased toward his virgin prey. Hollow-eyed, pale, and transfixed as a ghost I am, staring ahead at the shock of my image in the mirror-glass, no longer able to breathe.

His hand edges outward again—shyly, tentatively—this time up to my neck. My cheek.

"No—damn you, Volodya! Stop!"

"No!"

He shoves in behind me, fingers gripping about my shoulders, forcing me back against him. "Look at it, Sasha—yes!" he cries passionately, pointing straight ahead. "This is what I wanted to show you: this marvel, this jewel. Blast it, stop fightin' me so! Look at the face in the mirror-glass! . . ."

I shake my head with frantic, violent stabs; cringe away in a whimper.

"Look!" he commands again. From behind, his hands clamp upon either side of my head until I quiver to a standstill at last, panting to catch my breath. As I shut my eyes against the sight of us, he starts winding his fingers through strands of my hair, his voice grating into a soulful whisper. "Don't you realize," he intones softly, "that when I said you'd grown even more fetchin', I meant much more than a mere passin' joke?"

"You are mad!" I scream, slashing out at him. "Stop it, damn you! Let me go!"

"Pavel said you took after your mother!" Volodya exclaims, enthrallment still dazzled within his eyes despite the angry pummeling I hurl at him with both fists. "Used to hear it far and wide, from all the elders in the village, the legend of her beauty. Just like you—oh, dear God, Sasha! Don't you know how long I've been haunted, how long I have waited . . . ."

His hand cups behind my neck.

"Volodya, no! God, please! I beg you—"

Then he does it—*oh, God, I can't believe it; he does it, truly does it!*—a crush, a kiss like nothing I've ever known: desire unfathomable, thirst unforgivable, rending furious words into a long slough of trailing, pathetic whimpers.

I jab my fist for his throat, but he is ready for it; easily deflecting the blow, he pulls away from me, laughing, pointing back in triumph: "Ha! You liked it, Sasha—holy shit! I even think you kissed me back."

"You are sick!" Barreling past him, I bound out the door; stumble down the dimly lit hallway—only to be thwarted at the head of the stairs by the growing pervasiveness of my limp. Wincing against the steely gnaw of pain, I clutch for balance onto the banister—and turn to find him sauntering gaily after me, my walking stick proffered forth within his hand. But his expression is serious. "Go, if you wish," he urges, handing over the cane with an amicable nod. "You'll be back, I wager. After all—I saw what you underlined in that book."

With an affected sigh, Volodya then jams both fists into his pockets, tosses his head, and marches smugly back down the hallway to the door of his flat.

"What book?" I shout after.

The door slams.

"Dammit, Volodya!" Against every rattling murmur of better judgment in my head, I rush full-speed after him, my fists pounding into the door as I yell: *"What* book?"

The door flies open and he yanks me through.

"Don't you remember?" he whispers, hot lips grazing my throat.

"Stop it! You filthy—" I punch savagely at him. *"What* book?"

"Victorian Soiree—or whatever the hell the name was supposed to be . . . you know. The book about the orgy. Or perhaps I should say, orgies?"

My eyes widen in dawning horror. *Oh, God. That book!*

"Found it in the apiary," he goes on, spurts of his breath slicing ragged heaves against my hair. He snatches up my wrists; the walking stick bangs between us onto the floor. "Right beside one of the front-end hives," he whispers on. "Never knew I could read French, did you? Ahh, God bless old Vliny for never bein' able to shut up. He's the one taught me, you know. I saw all the passages you underlined in that book. You know which ones I mean, don't you, Sasha?"

"Shut up!"

"Honestly should keep a better hold on your possessions, don't you think? What if your illustrious father had found that book?"

"Shut up!"

"Along with all them underlines? You know, beneath the passages about the men? The queers?"

Gasping, I try to wrench away—but he only pulls me closer, dark eyes dancing with spears of mirth, the tip of his tongue moistening at both corners of his lips. "Admit it, Sasha," he whispers hoarsely. "You want to kiss me again! . . ."

My fist swings out in another punch, but he snatches it up, and after planting a nuzzling kiss upon my palm, he eases my fingers upward to his face, caressing my knuckles across the prickly-warm shadow of his beard. "You like touchin' me this way, don't you?" he murmurs with a rattling laugh. "You like touchin' another man this way, don't you, Sasha Sekovsky? Admit it!"

"Stop it!" I shriek at him, my throat choked dry as parchment, my head shaken back and forth in desperate wracking stabs of denial.

But he only continues rubbing my hand against the velvety coarseness of his face until I can no longer force the effort to pull away.

"Stop torturin' yourself, Sasha. You know what I am; I know what you are. I saw you in the whorehouse. You were scarce lookin' at any of the women—oh, no. You were lookin' at your cousin."

"N-No!" I blurt out.

"Yes!" He clips two fingers under my chin, demanding: "Look at me."

Slamming for his chest again, I bury my head into both hands.

"You want to kiss me, don't you?"

"No!"

"Liar."

"I do *not* want to!"

"Fucking little liar! Look straight into my eyes and tell me, then!" Jerking me around, he glares down into my face, shouting: "Look into my eyes and see the truth of yourself, damn you! See the truth of all them underlines—and all the little stars, every exclamation point you scribbled in that book! Look straight into my eyes and see if you can still deny you want to kiss me then!"

"I do not want to kiss you!" I scream out murderously, cringing from the thought that by now the neighbors can surely hear us.

"Right, you don't want to kiss me—ha!" Volodya retorts, his tone at first derisive, then amused. "Bluffs at kissing, bluffs at cards! Blast you, Sasha Sekovsky—you always were naught but the most pitiful liar in the world."

Then—before I can stop it—he throws both arms back around my neck, his mouth yawning in a cave onto mine again.

"Volodya, *no! . . .*"

. . . nooo! I cannot; we cannot . . . it is white blindness! . . . black lust . . . the holy wellspring of eternal damnation . . . torturing, hounding, predicating every thought . . . every move . . . every single day . . . ever since the first page of that wonderful—horrible!—vastly illuminating book . . . .

Knees buckling, we collapse together onto the floor.

"Oh, Sasha," Volodya babbles on, "the Saints help me! Three long, lonely, desperate years! Goin' senseless at every sight of you; knew it could never happen on the farm. A godsend, this night, a blessed stroke of fate, a miracle it is!" More kisses sear down past the collar of my shirt; as it comes off, his hands caress me everywhere . . . in back . . . in front . . . .

"Volodya!" I gasp out as his fingers seize swiftly downward, unhooking my belt. "For the love of God!"

"Lie back," he urges, his lips again grazing into my neck, his hand sliding from the folds of my trousers down into my underdrawers.

"Volodya—*no!*"

"And are you tellin' me you don't want to?" he then shouts, sprung back abruptly upon his knees, his glare fixed upon me in a flush of torment. "Huh? Are you? You don't want to? Is that what you truly want to tell me?"

I stare at him long through an eerie lull, shivering all over with apprehension and the dark anguish of yearning; at last slide along without further protest as he guides the both of us over onto the floor mattress. "Kiss me," I whisper, reaching for him with harsh insistence and slamming shut my eyes, bending my mouth unto his.

"Kiss you I will then, and how. . . ."

The back of my head meets the stiff edge of the mattress, and his mouth closes fast upon mine, blunt urgency belying velvet, sucking unto frenzy. Again and again I dissolve away unto rapturous oblivion within the coveted unfamiliar warmth of another person's arms, swallowing bliss through every heady, grinding embrace—only to rear up with the shock of renewed misgivings once I feel the fabric ease, buttons poking apart one by one as he manages to peel open my fly. "No, Volodya!" I gasp, shuddering in panic against him. "No, wait—"

"Oh, hush, my lovely! You like when we kiss, yes? You like when we rub, yes? Well, I guarantee you'll like this part ten times as much as either." Urging me back downward, caresses of reassurance warm across my chest and back; slither down both my thighs. . . . "Yes, yes, lie down," he whispers. "Hush, shhh . . . it will be all right. Close your eyes—that's right, Sasha, my darlin'. Simply take a slow deep breath, and close your eyes. . . ."

My hail of protests chokes to a squall of silence upon utterance; eyes slammed shut once more, I close my hands about the wavy blackness of his head just as his mouth closes over the thrusting madness of my entire world.

Oh, Jesus God!

It goes all the way down his throat. I almost scream—spinning off into the furnace of the volcano . . . begging him to stop, praying for him to go on . . . while his head I crush into an iron vise between both shaking hands . . . while my penis I pound into his mouth—past the terrorizing fear that I am choking him . . . strangling me . . . unto *death . . . oh, thank God . . . !*

. . . thank God I never take long . . . never, ever take very long . . . .

Soft laughter, hovering light. Low chuckles blend through fissures of muted reckonings. Curling up beside me upon the mattress, Volodya coos tender nonsense into my ear as I drift back and forth between snatches of numbing sleep—and as I jolt up out of that sleep again, staring, wide-eyed, into his face.

Grinning down at me, he guides my hand onto the swollen bulge of his own crotch.

"The first thing one learns," he murmurs, hurriedly unbuttoning his fly, "is that reciprocity is the law of nature."

With a gentle brush of fingers through my hair, he urges my head onto his lap.

From the pall of the window, moonlight glints in elusive feathered prisms across his face. "And now, my lovely," he whispers with a conspiring wink, "now, as you can see—it is your turn."

* * *

Four o'clock in the morning: Volodya walks me to the downstairs vestibule of the apartment building.

"You realize about things that can happen?" he murmurs, handing over my derby.

I take it and nod, following his gaze up the street. At the corner, several burly youths slouch huddled about a oil-barrel fire, warming themselves.

"Tomorrow?"

"Yes."

"Be careful!"

"I will."

He pats my shoulder. The door shuts between us—softly, silently—his footsteps tapping off through the narrow vestibule into the cool night.

I drag off the stub of my cigarette; stomp it out. Fish another from the case he lent me—but the glare from the uniformed officer manning the sidewalk station abruptly forces a change of mind. Apparently, parts of Petersburg still hold fast to the old laws, for whatever the reason. Stuffing the case away, I spread both hands out in placation, murmuring: "All right, all right!"

Grumbling, twirling his nightstick, the copper turns back inside the station door.

Such is irony. The corner youths have begun craning their heads, sizing me up. For a certainty, should they decide to pursue a little fun at my expense, the copper would most likely make not a move to stop them.

From shadows in the taverns, I have watched it many a time: whole gangs converging upon some poor lout, bone-shattering punches plowing him down amidst shrieking roars of that leering, forbidden word: *cocksucker* . . . .

A cab rounds the corner, and I snap my fingers, calling: *"Drozhki!"*

The horse pulls up short to the curbstone, but the driver hesitates. "Where?" he shouts, glancing for his watch, his expression uncharacteristically surly for a driver, full of tired impatience as he complains: "It's late, and it's cold."

I nod southward toward the array of distant yellow-globed gaslamps, Petersburg's Trinity Bridge looming in protective dominance over her silent, icy-white Neva. Cupolas from the Redeemer Church and from the dome of St. Isaak's play in barest silhouette behind tiny palace lights sparkling in immense rectangular patterns through misty layers of fog. "Zhukovskaya," I tell him with my eye still peeled lovingly upon the view. "Across the river."

Literally the same as if I had brandished a fat roll of rubles.

"Sit, then!" he barks back—though with deference this time, indicating the seat with a toss of his head.

Safe in the cab, I settle into the wrap of furs and shut my eyes, remembering the warmth, his taste . . . *Volodya* . . . .

So much more I did than I ever thought I would: took him deep down into the well of my throat; slathered my tongue all up and down the mucousy-hard wetness of him; lovingly, wantonly drank the salt of the earth. . . .

Now, if only my fingers would stop shaking. If only the knot in my stomach would uncurl; if only choirs of guilt would stop ringing down in thundering accusation from every murky cloud in the sky. Tentatively, I brush the back of my hand once more across my mouth; wipe over my chin for the near hundredth time with the end of my handkerchief.

If somehow I could simply remain in Vyborg, stay forever with Volodya, all thought of shame would dissipate away. But now, like a lamb headed for the slaughter, I must return. To that outer world filled with a wealth of judgmental mannequins from the inexorable past: Father. Aunt Sophie. The girls, and . . . .

Oh, God. Nikolai . . . .

* * *

"Have you not a shred of decency?" Aunt Sophie wails, flushed and breathless, little red blotches seeping through the peachy mask of powder dusted over her face. "No respect for the sensitivities of myself and the girls? The Saints help me, I near fainted straight away! Here I thought you to be in bed, and you waltz in from a cab, disheveled as a street urchin, in the midst of breakfast! I have never been so shocked and humiliated in my entire life! Really, Kolya!"

"Maman, please! For the hundredth, for the thousandth time—I am sorry!"

Blanched as a ghost, Nikolai dashes after her with another sheepish string of profuse, abjectly mumbled apologies.

Quite illuminating has it been to see Aunt Sophie so distraught. For years, I have rarely ever heard the woman raise her voice! Three days now, and still she will not let the matter rest. Poor Nikolai. Last week I would not speak to him, and now his mother barely will.

At ten o'clock Saturday morning, while we gathered about the buffet table munching down pastries, and I was still mortified about catching anyone's eye, not knowing whether I had been heard coming in so late, Nikolai attempted to sneak up the stairs after catching a cab back from the whorehouse.

Ever since then, all the attention focused upon his blundering escapade has made everything so easy.

"Your leg," Father says, catching up with me in the study. "Is the aching any better?"

"I tell you, there is no time!" I reply, choking back my laughter. "But I meant to thank you, Papa. The balm you whipped up helped immensely."

"What is so damned funny?"

I shove the chess paper back into his hand. "You wanted serious play, so here you are! Bishop takes your Queen. Checkmate."

Open-mouthed, he stares at the paper.

"Well!" I offer, shrugging. "You insisted that I not throw away the game."

Father scratches his head, and with a long sigh, blurts out: "Christ's beard! I must have surrendered unto senility."

Gloating with mirth, I hold out my open palm.

"Oh, hell!" he grumbles, snatching out his billfold. "I can see the headlines in the society pages now: 'Obscure Novgorodian Count Bankrupted By Own Son.'"

Shaking his head and puffing effusively on his pipe, he slips three ten-ruble notes into my hand.

And turns the paper over. "All right!" he cries with relish. "Go again for forty this time. What's your first move?"

From the portmanteau, I snatch out a fresh shirt and fluff it flat across the bureau top, attempting to smooth out the creases. "Oh, I do not know. As I said, there is no time! In ten minutes, we must leave for the *soirée.*"

"Another *soirée?*"

I stare across at him with some impatience. Already he has donned his slippers and velvet smoking jacket, quite set for another quiet eve curled up by the parlor fire with Aunt Sophie and their shared collection of French, English, and German newspapers. "Heavens, Papa!" I cry, staring around distractedly in an effort to spot my cuff links and the studs to my shirt. "And were you not ever young? Did you never go out on the town?"

"Oh, I suppose," Father replies, inspecting the moves written over the chess paper but watching me wryly from the corner of his eye. "But I was never much for palace-hopping in this infernal city," he goes on. "Hobnobs, snubnosery, everyone sizing up everyone else all the time—as if one makes his mark in life by how much he pays his tailor! And I daresay, you'd best not let the foolish snobbery go to your head, either."

"Papa, this is merely a little *fête* over at Madame Polinskaya's."

Father bursts into a roaring laugh. "Indeed? I would hardly say that over a hundred people is merely a 'little *fête.*'"

"Shhh!" Warily, I glance toward the open door. From the hallway, Aunt Sophie can still be heard on the rampage. "There will be an orchestra," I whisper over at Father, pressing a finger to my lips. "Tchaikovsky: fate of my life, eternal plight of my heart!"

Sighing and humming the melody, I cast my arms into the air and start waving into a conducting tempo of the *Flower Waltz.*

"Humph! And dancing?" Father cocks a conspiratorial eyebrow. "During Lent?"

I shrug. "Oh, Papa, you know I cannot dance in any case. Oh, Father! Stop acting as if I had defied the Liturgy. Even could I dance, I assure you, I would not break Lent, I promise. The only reason we are going is for a chance to spy upon the orchestra."

"Who is she?" he then asks, grinning.

I freeze.

"I could not help but notice," he says, moving in behind me, his warm fingers pressing upon my shoulder. Heart pounding, I glance upward at last; meet his gaze reflected behind me in the mirror-glass.

"Last week, it was all mournful silence, a passionate Dostoevsky vigil!" he cries, hand flung to the air in mock exasperation. "This week, it is recitals, *premières, soirées*—every blessed night! Ahh, but such a sparkle my Sasha has in his eyes," he goes on, chuckling. "Haven't seen you look quite so content in the longest time. So, who is she? A ballerina, perhaps?" he teases. "A grand duchess?"

Blushing, I stare to the floor. But then I catch his eye again with a shy wink. "No," I murmur softly. "Better than a ballerina. Or even a grand duchess."

"Oh, indeed?"

"Of course!"

"So, then who is she? What is her name?"

"Lady Petersburg."

So easy. So nonchalant. So perfectly, innocently treacherous.

Laughing softly, Father shuffles for the door. "I see. Well, not to be out too late, my young swain, do you hear? That Thursday morn audition will descend before you know it, and I want you good and ready."

"I practiced from dawn until supper again, Papa."

"Yes, yes, I know, I heard. And I commend you. Simply keep it up, is all I am saying."

"Yes, sir."

The newspaper whacks rhythmically against his thigh as he pads back down the hall.

I have not been entirely untruthful. She *is* Lady Petersburg.

Stolen moments spent at Pluchard's and at the Smirdin, eyeing scores of magazines and the latest editions of newly printed books. Sweet afternoons of quayside strolls with Anna—who has forgiven my wayward troika behavior after a literal inundation of imported daffodil bouquets—

the two of us ever promenading over quaint little Fontanka Canal bridgeways, there to purchase cones of fruit ice from street vendors or stop briefly within one of the many avant-garde teahouses. And afterwards, the hours spent with Nikolai after school, churning out riveting crescendos between my flute and his violin until practicing ourselves into a collapse of giddy exhaustion upon the sofas. And then, we have talked—just as I have wanted for so long: about God and music; about ambition and music; about the theater, ballerinas, the latest reviews, best orchestras, and most of all, our music—the two of us constantly bumbling in late for supper, much to Aunt Sophie's ever-rising chagrin.

Almost frightening it is, because all has been far too easy, my settling back into quaint routine and ordinary 'cousin Sasha' normality—every day turning on charm I never even thought I possessed to find myself bantering back and forth with quick-witted repartee and duly impressing all the girls.

Each day I sink further into the role, becoming more and more proficient an actor.

And each night—eventually, somehow, after slipping away, after inventing yet another ingenious excuse—I have returned to Volodya, relishing each breath of his warm and sensuous mouth, shuddering unto ecstasy beneath every touch of his roaming hands to drown within the aching taste of my silent, secretly growing sin.

I was wrong about Nikolai. It has been me, all along.

I am the one who has been the chameleon.

"Maman, if you do not mind, I should like to dress now!"

Roughly, Nikolai slams shut the door.

"There is no forgiveness in the woman!" he exclaims, raking his hands in a fluster through his hair.

Covering my mouth, I attempt to muffle another bevy of snickers.

"Oh, shut up, Sasha!" he bellows, wrathfully banging open bureau drawers. "Christ, I am a grown man! I shall stay out all night whenever I damn well please. Why is she after me like such a shrew this time? And I tell you, I am not the only one—she was in a horrid tiff at Uncle Misha earlier, too. Well, I do not know what about. Lord! Thank God we are on our way to see an orchestra, otherwise I think I would literally explode!"

"Tchaikovsky," I murmur worshipfully—and whipping off my shirt, I pull on the fresh one.

Nikolai lights a cigarette. "Sasha is in love," he declares, eyeing me, at last managing a grin.

Again I start waving the conductor's act through the air, tightly shutting my eyes. "Can you hear it?" I ask him, my baton yet swept with the glory of the music. "I swear, I have been stranded with this waltz climbing in my head all day long."

"Oh, yes," he murmurs, his expression gone serious. "I can hear it."

"Somehow, I thought you could."

"That is why you and I get on so well together: connected heads, twin hearts. Out amongst all those floating phrases. At least—most of the time."

I smile at him, laughing. Our little spat now seems like so many long, tiring years ago.

"Best grant me Rimsky, though," he adds with a knowing wink.

"Oh, I grant you Rimsky! The heights, the depths: hold me in the bosom of thy Persian yearnings, torture me within thy wandering medieval soul . . . I salute thee, Rimsky!"

Spearing off the finale with a bleating sigh, I stop conducting and stare, breathless, into the mirror.

Behind me, Nikolai rolls his eyes. And starts changing his clothes.

I swallow hard, forcing the effort not to watch him. Music and truth. Two overlapping illusions crossed indiscernibly upon swift heartbeats in time. How long? Until he catches an unguarded look in my eye? Detects the shadow past my cautiously perfected countenance of gaiety? Uncovers the truth about my secret?

What if he knew? What if Father, Aunt Sophie, if the any of the girls knew?

Such thought sends splicing arrows down my throat. I cannot imagine how I would face all of them, any of them. Ever again.

Back and forth it glints, the amethyst crystal, shallow warning beacon peeking out from behind the placket of my open shirt. My fingers curl around it with the relief that least *she* will never know.

Shame is being unable to meet one's own eyes in the mirror.

And for the first time in one's life, feeling content that one's mother is dead.

* * *

From the outside, the Polinsky mansion seems subdued, appearing almost darkened out for the night—but inside, chandeliers blaze everywhere, the staircases wreathed in vast spinnings of woven electric lights, the porticoes and high frames of the doorways lined with fluttery backdrops of mauve-silk hangings and overflowing pots of fuchsias, begonias, and fragrant lilacs, sweet breath of endless soft blossoms dancing through the air upon the piquant odor of flavored vodkas and spiced mint punch. A *'fête,'* not a 'ball,' the invitation read—but in truth, a ball by any other name, Lent or no. Nikolai was able to squander an invitation because Madame Polinskaya once commissioned cello solos from Uncle Petya.

"Ahh, now here it comes!" he says, eyes glued with mine upon the orchestra, his right hand positioned into the anxious conductor's lull before the triumphant burst of glory.

There proceeded no polonaise, nor onslaught of introductions, as is the custom. Two or three couples simply wandered out hesitantly onto the floor, all eyes averted with shame-faced guilt for entertaining the thought of dancing during Lent. But once the music started, no one any longer cared. Now once again the ballroom lies entranced, filled to capacity with uniforms, black tuxes, white ties, and the silks, taffetas, and shimmery brocades of the ladies fluttering beneath heathery wreaths of bounded, braided hair encased in diamonds, emeralds, rubies, and freshwater pearls. Everyone hovers in position, hands held high, manly fingers clasping smaller daintily-gloved ones, the entire hall poised in a stiffened pause upon the heightened thread of tension. And then the conductor dashes down his baton, the bows spring up, horns and woodwinds rise, the waltzes from *The Sleeping Princess* beginning once again.

"Oh, yes!" I cry, chills fluttering up and down my spine, my fists slammed wrenchingly together. "Oh! Take my heart, save my soul, Pyotr Ilyich Tchaikovsky: slay me, slay me!"

"Praise God, Praise Heaven, Praise the Mother, Praise Every Blessed Living Thing!" Eyes creased shut, Nikolai lets out a deep moaning sigh. Then he snatches up my arm, nodding. "Now, this is the *Rose Adagio*—"

"Yes!" I reply, latching onto him. *"Pas d'action—*

"—in twelve/eight time—"

"—*maestoso*—woodwind and harp cadenza—the four princes ask for the Princess Aurora's hand on her birthday. Wait, now—here comes the harp! Ohhh . . . why, look at that fool with the piccolo. How can one ever expect to play decently at such a poor angle as that?"

"Think that's poor, check the third row, second section," Nikolai declares, pointing across at the violins. "That fellow's all slumped forward. Now, is that any way to perform such glory? I tell you: pride, confidence one must possess! Like this."

Tossing back his head disdainfully, Nikolai snaps into his bow position and silently demonstrates the proper technique.

"Oui, oui, Maestro!" I start clapping at him. "Superb! *Magnifique!"*

"Shhh!"

We burst into laughter as several frumpy overweight matrons, all hovering near the punch bar and munching down appetizers, haughtily glare down their noses at us.

Nikolai elbows me, snickering. "They disapprove of your boots, country cousin."

"By your ass," I reply crossly, glaring at him. Our heated discussion about my boots on the way over in the cab almost escalated into another full-blown argument.

Which he will not let pass. "Whoever heard of wearing boots with a evening tux!" he snorts, laughing.

"I find it much easier to walk in boots than in shoes!" I storm angrily, crossing my arms. "And it looks not so awkward, the cuffs fit over very nicely. Father even said so! And just what do they care? What do you care?"

Obviously, not much anymore—waving me off, Nikolai steadies his attention onto a group of beribboned, giggling young ladies who continue staring over at the two of us from shadowed confines of the punchbowl group. "Looks as if they mind your boots not one little bit," he jokes, jabbing me again with his elbow. "Perhaps you have introduced a new fashion trend."

"Oh, shut up."

To my relief, he drops the matter at last, and renews our discussion of the waltz.

I know I would be much more clever to simply shrug the entire episode off, but the boots remain a sensitive issue. The greater ease with which they permit me to walk is only the first reason for my insistence upon wearing them. The second is that I have started carrying a knife.

Vyborg is, after all, a rough neighborhood for forays and nightly escapades. One cannot be too careful.

So far, I have been lucky.

As Nikolai starts mimicking the violins again, I tell him: "I am going to fetch myself some punch."

"And spy upon the ladies!" he replies loudly, continuing to mimic string mountings without opening his eyes.

"You are the one who is besotted unto his death with the ladies!" I retort hotly. "Going to break Lent! Going to dance—yes?"

"Oh, no—not with Maman this peeved at me already." Without pause, his invisible bow dashes up and down through the air.

"Humph!" Glaring at him, I seize my walking stick and pound away.

The punch, a sweet cocoa-mint laced with a touch of cognac, I find burningly delicious, and down two goblets before wandering back in between the groups of laughing chatterers hidden within shadows of the porticoes and curtains. Flirts continue eyeing one another behind the ruse of fans, giggles, and the lavish, greedy swish of taffeta, all the young girls responding amicably to the strutting nods and feverish, bold glances from the uniformed clusters of men.

Acutely conscious of the flush warming into the back of my neck, I weave amongst them awkwardly, wishing to God my limping would not draw such sympathetic notice. Across the room, I see that Nikolai has struck up a conversation with one of Madame Polinskaya's daughters. Shoulders drawn up to his full height, his grin rakish and charming, he teases her along into a swell of blushing laughter before collapsing down into an elegant bow, whereupon he plants a kiss onto her daintily gloved hand.

I stare across with narrowed eyes, unable for some reason to tear my thoughts away from the sight of his hair, which soon will begin to lighten up even more, for always in the summer months it becomes streak-washed as if with the quiescent kiss of the sun. His moustache, however, will probably shadow in still a bit darker, yet beholden to winter's murky towhead lull. As he flirts with the girl, he fingers it carelessly and tosses back his head, his serious gray eyes sparkling with delight—and yet, when he looks away from her and out to the orchestra, the change is striking: a solemn, prayerful vigil spanning off into stillborn distance, focused far beyond the length of the physical room—as if it is music, fleshly-embodied, that he sees hovering beyond. I follow his quick glance to the orchestra; look back once more—and discover the girl, her hand now resting upon his arm.

Again.

Hurtfully catching in my breath, I shove both hands into my waistcoat pockets and turn away, my mind wincing back sharp bites from Volodya's words: 'You were scarce lookin' at any of the women—oh, no! You were lookin' at your cousin. . . .'

Leaning back against the portico, I shut weary eyes and attempt not to think.

Minutes wane by, and the music rolls on—much of my joy in it long since dissipated. Looking back at last, I find that Nikolai has disappeared, apparently gone looking for me. The check of my watch reveals it early yet. Anxious to save him the trouble of searching me out, I take up the walking stick again, setting my hand upon it with the firm resolution of somehow concocting another excuse and setting off to leave soon for Volodya's. Then the blustery feminine conversation rattling on just beyond the curtain—to which I have been listening these past few moments with half an ear—stops me cold.

"Sekovsky, his name is, yes?"

"What? No, Pasekovsky. Or at least, I thought—"

"No, I am certain it is Sekovsky. They have some sort of connection, cousins or such, to the Zhelanovs. You know, Tatyana? Who is betrothed to Captain Ivan Orlinsky?"

"Now, there is a good match."

"Indeed! Would be perfect, in fact, had only her family not such close connection with the Sekovskys. I know—oh, yes, I wholly agree with you. What did you say, Marie?"

"Mikhailovich," a flat voice states authoritatively. "But I do not know his first name. A beekeeping farm near Novgorod, I believe. His father—"

"Was once quite a large estate, near unto a whole town in itself, or so I heard. But I guess of late—"

"But such a pity! Whatever happened to his leg?"

"Probably some farming accident, ugh!" the authoritative voice sneers. "And whoever could stand living like such pigs as they do in the provinces?"

"Oh! But he is so—so—"

"You've gone daft, Tasha! Heavens, I swear he is prettier than you are."

"He is not!"

A yelping chorus ensues, full of embarrassed, rankling laughter.

"But what were you saying about his father?"

Abruptly, Nikolai bumps into me, chiding: "Where have you been? Everywhere I have been searching! They are beginning the *Panorama Waltz.*"

"Shhh!" I press a quick finger to my lips, urging: "Listen."

"Oh, ho!" He spies the girls and lets out a short laugh. "My cousin, the eternal eavesdropper."

The authoritative voice starts in again, chortling with disdain. "Oh! You will never believe what I heard about his father. Why, I can't imagine how he'd even have such gall as to show his face here—unless the poor child simply does not know. Anyhow, rumor has it that his father, Mikhail Sergeyevich . . . ."

Whirling upon me, his expression gone cold as death, Nikolai exclaims: "Sasha! Let us go."

"What? No!" I cry, flinging off his arm. "I want to hear this."

"But, Sasha—"

"Let go of me!"

" . . . his father, Mikhail Sergeyevich . . . he must be in his seventies, now. Terrible scandal—he married a seventeen-year-old English girl . . . old enough to be her grandfather! Can you imagine? And after thirty years . . . although I must admit to hearing something about his sentence being commuted. All the way to Irkutsk, it was . . . yes, in Siberia . . . ."

"What?" I choke out as Nikolai wrestles hold of my arm, urging me away.

" . . . can you imagine? Court-martialed! From the elite Horse Guards . . . and of course from the medical service . . . high scandal at the field hospital in Sevastopol. . . ."

"That is a lie!" I exclaim, seizing upon Nikolai's lapels, barely managing to keep my voice down.

"Sasha, *come.*" Again latching on a furious hold, Nikolai drags me with him to the closest hallway entrance leading beyond the punchbowl.

"That is impossible!" I shout, tearing at him wildly. "I have never heard such slander in my entire life! My God! Did you hear what that woman said? Siberia! My father, *court-martialed?* That is preposterous, ridiculous, insane!"

Heaving for breath, I stop short as Nikolai's somber gaze meets mine. "Dear God!" I roar out at him as the whole room blurs into a chasm of dank light and withering hypocrisy. "Why are you looking at me like that? You cannot possibly believe—*Nikolai!"*

White as a sheet, Nikolai shuts his eyes; opens them; stares off into the glare climbing between the curtains and porticoes and the music.

Once more I clamp onto his lapels. "Nikolai, dammit!" I shout in desperation. "Look at me!"

When he finally does, it is through a threatening well of tears as he rasps out: "Sasha . . . I am sorry."

I stare at him, horrified.

Behind us, the music of the *Panorama Waltz* descends from its thundering blare of notes into a crash of sickening off-key cymbals . . . the laughter and gay chattering of the couples gradually begins heckling forth in droves of ironic smirks from every corner of the room as the truth hits like a bomb: thirty years . . . about which I know virtually nothing, save for some clothes in a trunk . . . stuffed atop clattering remnants of a leg-iron . . . .

"Oh, my God!" I scream out. *"Oh, my God!"*

"Sasha, wait!"

In a blood-pounding rush, I charge out the nearest palace door with him close upon my back. Hacking at my sleeves, he yells: "Wait, let us at least fetch our coats!" Tears choke at me; drums blast spikes of shrapnel into my ears . . . I never even realized I possessed some ability to run. . . .

"You dirty double-crossing snake!" I roar once Nikolai catches up, my left hook plowing into his chin and trouncing him off in a quaking spin toward the curbstone snow.

"Look!" he pleads, panting, jostling around on one arm and pointing upward at me. "I understand why you are so angry—"

"You scarce understand *shit!* Blood brother, blood sucker—dearest cousin, best friend in the whole wide fucking world! J-Jesus Christ! How on earth could you know something like this—and then *keep* it from me?"

"Because I made a promise!"

"To whom?"

"Your father!"

Caught with a spell of shivers, Nikolai trudges clumsily back up to his feet.

Through the quivering frost of silence, I haul off and spit at him.

Normally, upon such provocation, my cousin's fist would slam like thunder into my face. But it certainly does not now.

Instead, he guiltily begins shaking the slush from his sleeves.

"I hate you!" I rasp out between clenched teeth.

"Sasha, please—"

"Go to hell!"

Still shouting my name, he claws after me as I bound into the street after the nearest cab.

* * *

Once cozy and inviting, tempered along polished balustrades and high sweeping walls with warm wood accents and mauve-hued undertones, the townhouse now looms overwrought in a maze of startling black and white contrasts, a Golgotha burdened beyond holy conception with doomed silence and widened space, the chatter of the girls near nonexistent, my shadow cast long and large through waning echoes of light as I blast through the door, struggle up the stairs, and pound down the hallways, determinedly following my nose.

After the pungent trail of Father's tobacco smoke.

With a start of surprise, he stares up from his easy chair, the newspaper yet caught within his lap, his pipe dangling loosely between wizened fingers. "God's teeth, boy!" he exclaims, stealing a quick glance over to the sideboard mantle-clock. "A bit early, no? For you to be . . . *Sasha?"*

His jaw drops.

"Liar!" I scream, my fist bounding out across the yawning gulf of the room in a flying pronouncement of accusation.

Stifling a gasp, Aunt Sophie crosses herself and slowly eases upward from her armchair.

Groping to his feet, his mask of complacency at last expunged, Father proffers the newspaper forth as pitiable defense between us as my voice cracks into a froth of haggard gulps. "And you, Papa," I shout out, "are the one who taught me about honor!"

"Oh, Misha—you insufferable old fool!" Hands shaking uncontrollably, Aunt Sophie throws down her embroidery and turns upon Father, the pearly quiescence of her face drowned in a flush of rage. "And was I not trying to warn you all this week?" she cries, choking back tears. "Just this very morn, was I not *again* reminding you about how the gossips carry on in this town?"

"Stay out of this, Sofya!" Father roars, slamming the newspaper to the floor.

"No! You know you should have told the poor child by now—"

"Uncle Misha!"

In a breathless rush, Nikolai bursts in through the drawing room doors, his muddied footprints trailing tiny wet puddles across flower patterns of the Persian carpet. From the shoulders downward, he stands covered with sludge, his evening tux ruined for a certainty. When he tried to climb after me into the *drozhki,* I threw him back out of it again, straight down into the mired slush of the street. "Uncle Misha, I am sorry!" he tells Father, his eyes sunken with grief, both hands clasped placatingly together, begging forgiveness. "There was naught that I could do! He overheard—"

"Then it is true!" I shout, whirling back upon Father.

"Sasha, listen to me—"

"Irkutsk it was, yes?"

Father's face blanches into a sickened shade of yellow.

"Siberia!" I rage on hoarsely. "The mining camps."

Numbly, he stares back at me through the crash of silence.

"Lord Almighty God!" I shout on. "No wonder the years of secrecy—along with the pieces of that leg iron I found in the trunk upstairs!"

Tears streaming down both cheeks, Aunt Sophie abandons the futile rummage through her pockets for her handkerchief and flees the room.

"Sasha, *listen* to me!" pleads Father.

"Court-martialed!" I rant on, lashing out at him with both fists. "Unto what sentence? Twenty-five years? Thirty years? Hard labor? Upon what charge? Murder? Treason? Blast it, Zhelanov—let go of me!" Punching hard, once more I fend off my cousin's encroaching hands and halting attempts at explanation, while Father shouts back: "Sasha! Was not all for such reasons as you may think!"

"And whatever *the hell* does it matter what the reasons were? My God—what about honor? Our family's score of generations: Uncle Dmitri; Grandfather Sergei; ancient, revered Dmitryevich—Peter the Great made him a count, remember? And before him, all the valiant others, such courage borne against the bloody terror of the 1570 purge . . . . with their portraits have I grown up, the eyes of ages courting Lissushka's every wall . . . my God! How could you do this to me—to us!—to our heritage? How could you ever foul our family name with such disgrace?"

My voice breaks then, choked sobs shattering off into the stillness, tears of irony reverberating back from concave reflections of the walls, doors, floorboards—from every gleaming, polished surface of the house.

Face coarsened into a weary grimace, Father begins inching slowly forward. His hand hovers outward, dark blue veins stretched tautly across white flesh in swollen cords of agony, a peace offering of uneasy, tentative inquiry, his fingers brushing gingerly across my arm, his voice going very soft, intonations breaking scarce above a whisper: "Sasha," he urges, "listen to me. Let me explain. . . ."

"No!"

"Listen to Uncle Misha!" Nikolai implores again.

"You go and fuck yourself in a pismire, Nikolai!"

"Sasha!" Father cries in consternation.

"And you!" I shout on, turning once more upon him, "can go and do naught but the very same!"

"Blast it, boy—I know you are furious!" he counters. "But will you simply pause and listen to what I am trying to tell you?"

"Indeed! And just what other lies have you told me?" Lunging wildly away from the both of them, I clutch through a bleary haze for the door. "Or truths have you hidden from me, *Father?"* I spout on hatefully. "Was my mother, the Lady Melissa, truly an English heiress as you have said? Or—or was she simply some whore?"

The hall, the stairs, the vestibule: I tear through angled corners of imagined barricades like a hunted criminal fleeing the dogs, boots pounding ferociously out the door and into the slushy, muddied mire of the street upon frantic screams of: *"Drozhki! Drozhki!"*

Father and Nikolai halt up short at the townhouse doorway as I clamber into the cab—and I hear his voice, wracked with mournful resignation as he tells Nikolai firmly: "No. Let him go."

* * *

The instant the apartment's door shuts behind us, I pin Volodya back against it in a furor of kisses until he squirms away, stuttering out between gasps of delight and bewilderment: "S-Saints alive! Whatever has come over you?"

"Not a thing!" I insist, seizing hold of him again, my lips scouring fast into desire's heady thralldom past the pounding pressure of my rage.

"Oh, no? Ha! You storm in here like a madman: no hat, no overcoat, your suit half-covered with mud. What the hell happened?"

Instead of answering, I clamp both hands onto the collar of his woolen tunic, begging: "Please! Simply kiss me . . . again and again!"

Through wavering shadows of the lamplight, Volodya peers back at me with a frown. But at last his lips curl once again into their familiar mischievous grin. "Must admit, Black-eyes," he murmurs, pulling me to him and nuzzling soft kisses against my throat, "I like you this way."

"Good," I whisper back. "Then fetch the butter."

Eyebrows shooting upward, Volodya gasps with stunned delight and steps back, searching my face, murmuring: "Are you sure?"

"Fetch the butter."

Still I felt overwhelmingly reluctant when he suggested such diversion from our recent repertoire last night. It is, after all, the last avarice to which one can succumb. A finality from which there is no turning back upon this road, once taken.

Dragging deeply off a cigarette, I watch through hooded eyes as he fishes the crock from the pantry. "This is the purest, the softest, the whitest!" he exclaims with the blustery enthusiasm of a street vendor, his hands cupped around the mound of butter as if about a holy relic. "I tell you, we use this—"

He stops in the middle of the floor, catching his breath as I start throwing off my clothes.

"We use this," he goes on softly, "and I promise you, Sasha—will hurt not even the slightest bit. . . ."

"Good. Then let us fuck the hell out of each other until we can no longer think."

* * *

"Sasha, I care for you—honestly, I do. A great deal. Which is why I have to tell you, that you can't—"

I stare up to the doorway.

"You can't stay here." With a hardened frown, Volodya snatches on his sheepskin greatcoat.

"I told you twice already," I reply in a low murmur. "Only until Thursday morn, my audition for the Conservatory. Then I'll board in a rooming house."

"With what?" he exclaims, dark eyes lancing me with a scowl of perturbation. "No clothes, save a muddied suit and those I have lent you? No money? And—no flute?"

"I have the piccolo." Again I slip it out from the shaft of my boot.

"And that is what you intend to play in the Imperial Orchestras? A mere toy purchased from a woodcarver's shop in Novgorod?"

I turn away.

Scarce does it matter. *My own father.* Imprisoned; exiled to the mining camps in Siberia. Through such shame, I could never hope to show my face before anyone in Petersburg, in Novgorod, ever again.

My only consolation is that, to my immense surprise, Volodya seems privy to not even the slightest hint of the whole dastardly affair.

"I grant you, the man is a murderous beast," he continues rankling on, his words hedging perilously close to the stymied, blackened corners of my thoughts. "And whatever caused this row between the two of you the other night, I am certain he is entirely to blame! But you have got to return home, Sasha. Else, how are you goin' to—"

"I am *not* going back." With a vengeance, I slam my fountain pen to the floor. And for the third time, tear up the list I have been writing.

Always it is the last stab, my final clutch at any sense of congruity, of normalcy: during a crisis, come up with a next step, devise a plan, write everything down with calculating mathematical precision. Start making a list.

Volodya sighs mutely, staring as more tiny rifts of paper billow to the floor.

"I'll go see that idiot banker Frolov again come the morn," I tell him, sputtering curses as I tear off the last sheet of paper from the tablet. "The old fool is only worried about protecting his own ass. That money is mine, all eight thousand rubles; the account is written in my own name! Blast it, three summers have I spent waning away in Bulya's office, piled up to high over my head in bookwork. Father promised me that money when the time came, and there should be no reason why he need visit the bank personally to sign it over."

"Unless he's as stubborn as you are."

I slam the pen to the floor and cross my arms.

"Unless he'll hold onto that money as a way to get you back."

"I am not going back! I do not give a bloody damn about him anymore."

Volodya cocks a wary eyebrow, and with a sidelong glance into the mirror, adjusts his derby.

"I only care about you," I add softly.

"And that is the other matter."

My limbs go cold. I know what he is going to say. Inevitability is written all over his face. "What other matter?"

"Don't fall in love with me, Sasha," he murmurs with urgency. "Don't you dare."

The door slams behind him. I listen to his footsteps, dark echoes chasing seismic contortions of my heart all the way down the hall.

Cursing my voracious tendency for blushing upon the slightest cue, I crush out the stub of my cigarette; light another. Then crush that out too; grab the empty case and hurl it across the lid of the stove and into the rest of the rubbish, piled up high now and reeking of fish-rot and vegetable peelings in the room's farthest corner.

I have got to stop: the incessant smoking, incessant worrying. Nonstop for near unto two straight days now, haunting all of my waking hours, pirating away any hope of sleep—my only solace found in tumults of the kisses and ecstasies of the passion, the strange closeness of lying beside Volodya in his bed during the night, listening to the steady onward beating of his heart beneath my ears. In here, I could hide away and lose myself forever, living only to touch, to taste, to enjoin with him again and again—for now, this bedeviled, aching closeness with my one-time farmyard adversary seems almost everything in life for which I could ever wish.

But he is right. I cannot stay in these filthy, vagrant slums of Vyborg. Without pause, visages from my window musings hound me. Stoop-shouldered, blank-eyed, many of them wrapped up in little more than burlap rags, dregs from the factories trudge in continual weariness up and down these forbidding streets. During later evetide hours, they gather around open bonfires and fight with one another for scraps of food foraged from refuse bins tucked within the litter-strewn courtyards and alleyways of nearby tenement buildings and taverns.

Such is not my world. Yet after this disaster, neither can Petersburg society be my world anymore.

The piccolo. Through twisted poundings of my broken shame, I stare at it again as the long moments begin their nightly climax into lonely, dreadful hours. Fingers pressed dutifully upon the keys, I flatten my chin into the curve of the embouchure plate, but it no use. No sound emits; no music remains within the recessed caverns of my heart. With a heavy sigh, I ease the slender instrument back into its felt pouch in my boot. Incredible, it now seems—how I prayed and worried, how overjoyed I was upon Father's return last year after those twelve horrendous days of the blizzard. 'A lighter one to carry around,' he said upon proffering the gift. And carry it around I have, like a beloved talisman.

Ever since.

The other night, upon the realization that I yet retained the miserable thing in my possession, I near hurled it into the wall in a flush of rage before Volodya wrestled it out of my hands. And wisely, too—for now this gift from the man I should forever disown has become my sole earthly possession, save for my billfold and its stash of sixty-four rubles. The borrowed clothes are simply that—borrowed and conspicuous, hanging far too loosely on my narrow frame, the sleeves of the tunic too long, legs of the trousers dragging out no matter how many times I stuff them back into the shafts of my boots.

Confusions, worries—and now morbid fears have begun to haunt me. Each night, between the hours of ten and about three or four in the morning, Volodya disappears. To where, he will not tell me, and he forbids my coming along. When asked if this was his work, the method by which he maintains his living, he admitted as much in such a derisive, sarcastic fashion that my curiosity died upon the tip of my tongue.

Somehow, instinct told me that the less I knew about any of it, the better.

Instinct proves me right. As I tear up yet another list and start my search across the mess of the room for more scratch paper, clues to Volodya's secret wanderings begin to manifest with almost prophetic tenacity.

First I find, amazingly, what appear to be ledger notebooks filled with lists of strangely written names like 'Cupid' and 'Fairy-Tail' and 'Kharkovian Princess'—some followed by check-marks and some not, but all with triple and sometimes quadruple ruble-figures marked in several columns across the page.

Frowning, I stare with a critical eye at haphazardly kept journal entries that would most assuredly try any prudent accountant's patience. Upon further perusal of the pile, I find two other near identical notebooks—before, to my horror, discovering the pamphlets.

Scores of them. In a twine-tied stack hidden beneath a mound of seemingly harmless newspaper advertisement clippings. Stilted stabs. This time of immaculate, professionally typeset Russian:

Cherish the land! Till peasants' souls! Hail victory to V.M. Chernov's Socialist Revolutionary Party!

"Oh, no!" I gasp aloud. Clutching my hands to my throat, I cast an apprehensive glance over my shoulder at yet invisible evil-eyed agents of the Tsarist police before huddling back over the pile.

Which contains sheet after sheet of revolutionary propaganda from the illegal presses of *Izvestia* and *Russian Gazette*—along with accounts of past, agendas for prospective demonstrations; lists of numerous meetings; names of new members, amongst them: 'Vladimir Denisovich Rykazian.'

Oh, hell! To become involved in any of this dissent is utter foolishness; an entire year the Conservatory is shut down by the Tsar after only the tiniest fraction of students even hint at progressive leanings! How on earth did Volodya ever manage get himself mixed up with . . . ?

Memory duly interrupts with its wisely stabbing elbow: red armbands. A white banner. Father's revolver, dangling with such casual readiness from his fingertips. Volodya's bloodied back—the snap of the whip—his quivering arms lashed in between two fenceposts . . . .

Indeed. What else leads a man to such insanity, save for insanity itself?

Each night have I kissed across his back, tracing long lines over every one of the scars, attempting to ease the hurt away. Not solace enough, I can see now.

Shit! I have got to get out of here—my God! A person can get arrested for even carrying around these kind of flyers, much less storing bundles of them in his flat. . . .

I jump, catching my breath—somehow detecting the rush of footsteps long before their sudden ominous pounding down the hall. Hurriedly, I shove the pamphlets back beneath the stack of clippings.

Volodya blasts into the room panting with sweat, his long coat hurled out behind him like the cloak of an avenging angel. Wrenching shut the door behind, he slams down both locks while screaming frantically: "Sasha! Get into the wardrobe-cupboard!"

"The wardrobe-cupboard? What do you mean, get *into* it? It's scarce even large enough to—"

"There is no time for debate, dammit! Just shut up and get in there!"

The top shelf of the room's meager, wood-chipped cupboard he roughly yanks out, nails and all, before shoving me down into its tiny breadth of space. "Don't breathe, don't think, and don't move!" he orders, slamming shut the door.

"But, Volodya!"

"Sasha, shut up, damn you, if you value your ass—"

His protests dissolve into the dust of an explosive wood-splintering crash. To my horror, I realize that the front door has been kicked in, fastened double-locks and all. *Damn, I was right about getting out of here! I should have left long before this. . . .*

Shaking from head to foot, I cup both hands over my mouth and attempt not to breathe.

"J-Jesus Christ!" I hear Volodya stammer out, his voice pitched high with terror. "Pierre!"

"Shut up, Rykazian."

A thudding shove plows into the wall . . . repeated whacks and thuds . . . whimpering from Volodya; his plaintive, whining cries of: "Pierre, no, please!" Interlaced with bellowed curses and rude tauntings from at least two other men . . . .

The sound of him being beaten.

"Ahh, Vladimir Denisovich—tsk, tsk!" At last a mincing voice shrills sarcastically across the room. "Volodya, my angel heart," the man lauds on, "how clever you must think you are! And such high hopes I held for your potential in this business. A partner's position I had surely entertained—Lord, cherish the thought!—so duly impressive appeared the extent of your entrepreneurial ability."

"Pierre!" Volodya begs between breathless, shuddering gasps. "I can explain."

"Indeed? Well, such explanation should prove most interesting. Particularly as we have been keeping a tail on you ever since Saturday night. All right: Yevgeny, Stefanovich—let up on him, good souls."

As if sucked into a vacuum, the tumult in the room careens into a void of silence.

"Where is he?" Pierre then harshly demands.

Volodya starts coughing, guffawing. "I—I honestly don't know what you are talkin' about—ooohhh!"

The sound of him crumpling to the floor.

Followed by the furious order: "Tear the place apart!"

Oh, God! Forcing a damper to my every breath, I huddle in close underneath the shelf, both arms plastered over my head as sounds of the search crash brazenly through the apartment. For the barest instant, I open my eyes, coming nose to nose with a grimy black cockroach—the last thing I see before the rickety door bangs open and two stout, heavily-muscled arms punch in to drag me out upon gloating utterances of: "Ah-ha!"

The man looms huge, near unto a head and a half above my height, his cap pulled flat to his eyebrows over a greasy mound of dishwater hair, a whitened scar running down the length of his right cheek and testifying to a history of rigorous brawny prowess. His hand clamps like an iron vise around my left wrist just as I thrust my knife upward from the shaft of my boot. I cry out; the knife clatters to the floor.

Grinning with relish, the man calls out, laughing: "Ha, ha! Got one here with a bit o' spunk, Exc'lency, that we do!"

One arm he clamps around my chest, the other around my mouth, before dragging me out toward the others.

"Pierre, I can explain!" Volodya shouts with frantic pleas of desperation in between repeated blows from the other henchman. "He is not one of the roundups, but a friend!"

"A friend?" Pierre drawls, mocking him. "Oh, for bloody God's sake, Rykazian! Spare me such insidious trysts at sentimental—"

"Who the hell do you think you are?" I roar, jabbing furiously back with my elbows the instant the giant man lifts his hand away from my mouth.

Fat as a cannonball, the clenched fist flies upward, readying to slam into my face. "Shut up, you little—"

"Wait!" Pierre commands shrilly.

I feel my blood start draining into bitter water the instant I catch my first glimpse of Pierre—then to stare at him, benumbed.

Like two onion-bulbs stuck in a scarecrow, his eyes loom hideously large, stung with limpid, greenish malice. Round and pasty, his face bears florid dimples from wealed scars and faded pockmarks, but his carriage proves straight and stern, a smart top hat neatly setting off his wispy mound of thinning hair, his suit elegant, tailored from the finest Scottish wool, stark contrast to the greasy slovenliness of his two peasant henchman.

"By the devil!" he gasps out in a low voice, staring through a silent haze of shock.

At me.

A gleaming smile then overtakes the man's puffy face. Without a second's pause for shame, his eyes languidly rake up and down my form past the lull of eerie silence before he inches forward, stepping adroitly upon his toes. Chills flash up and down my spine as, finger by finger, he begins fastidiously picking off his long white gloves.

"Pierre, you do not understand!" Volodya gasps from the floor, still stooped and clutched over from the blows. "This one is not from the roundup! Indeed, he comes from one of the ancient boyar families. He is not one of your idle misfits, Pierre—for God's sake, please! I tell you, you cannot take him, you *cannot!* He is a coun—"

On the barest flick of a snapped finger, Volodya doubles over in an agonizing scream from another blow.

"Incredible," Pierre blurts out with amazement, his eyes still locked upon my face. "Absolutely incredible!" he repeats again, lolling each word out lazily on his tongue as if tasting over every syllable.

Shaking, I cringe away as his hand edges toward my cheek. "Twenty years of running the auction block," he goes on, wide-eyed, "and never—*never* have I seen such astounding beauty. . . ."

Oh, God!

His cold-tipped finger runs slowly from the corner of my jaw all the way into the hollow of my throat.

"Skin like porcelain!" he laments on. "And the profile: Aphrodite of the Ages!" Again the same finger: traced from crown of head to brow and down the bridge of my nose . . .

"Stop it!" I rasp out hoarsely.

"Shut up, you little whinin' cur!" the giant blares wrathfully in my ear, his threatened muscle-hold wrenched like iron shafts around my arms. "Or I'll break 'em both, do ye hear me?"

Gritting my teeth against the soaring pain, I struggle into a reluctant nod.

Pierre continues with his gloating finger-winding inspection. "Ahh, yes!" Cupping his knuckles under my chin, he turns my head from side to side as if inspecting an animal purchase at market. "The truest black eyes," he murmurs with reverent satisfaction. "A little Tartar blood, *n'est-ce pas?"*

My angry retort comes squelched again from behind by the treacherous muscle-hold on my arms.

"Oh, save your pride, darling!" Pierre croons close into my ear. "Mother of God, they invade for two hundred years, what do you expect? So we all inherited a little slant-eyed debauchery. But you: a bit of English, I daresay. Or Scottish blood, perhaps? Indeed, I know breeding when I see it. But the hair: look at this, Yevgeny, masses of it! And red as dark fire . . . ."

"Yaa, Exc'lency!" the man called Yevgeny answers with feigned enthusiasm from behind. "A fine one he is, if ye say so, indeed."

"Fine enough to take for my very own this time," Pierre murmurs softly to himself.

"No!" Volodya shouts from across the room. "I tell you, Pierre—you *cannot!"*

Once more he doubles over, screaming, kicked this time straight in the groin.

Pierre spares Volodya not so much as a sidelong glance. "Ahh, yes, sweeting," he whispers again into my ear, his clammy palm sliding over my cheek again as I wince violently away. "A great mystery it is, the origin of the word *Rus*. But you and I are both quite privy such lofty obscure meaning, yes?"

I shake my head numbly through a quaking rise of nausea.

"Never listen to what the foppish old historians write in their schoolbooks!" he admonishes with a sharply wagging finger. "The word *Rus* means 'fire,' darling. It means 'red-haired.'"

And again his hand cups under my chin, his lips near grazing mine as he goads tauntingly: *"N'est-ce pas?"*

Abruptly, he turns on his heel—just as Yevgeny's hand clamps back over my mouth, his fat fingers hideous and suffocating, reeking of stale olives and vodka.

With a beckoning glower of malice, the other henchman hoists Volodya up from the floor. "Which is the hand that touched my goods?" Pierre demands, looming over him, pointing.

"No!" Volodya rasps out, ducking both arms behind his back. "Please!"

"Which is the hand that touched my merchandise? This one?"

He yanks out Volodya's right hand.

"Pierre, *no!"*

"You were warned! About what fate befalls dealers who ply their sticky little fingers into my property, Vladimir Denisovich."

"Pierre, *nooo! P-Please! I beg you!"*

Pausing, sighing as if with reconsideration, Pierre makes a long show of lighting up a cigarette caught in a stylish mother-of-pearl-enameled holder. Then impatiently, he starts swishing back and forth with his long white gloves.

"Pierre!" Volodya shouts, "I'll make it up to you, bring in twice the quota for next month, I promise!"

The two henchman stare across the room, awaiting orders.

"Oh, have done with it, Stefanovich," Pierre at last mutters, rolling his eyes.

Past shrieking howls of protests, Stefanovich shoves his charge roughly back down to the floor, pinioning Volodya's left arm behind, his right wrist forward to then one by one spread out all five fingers flat against the floorboards. After which the henchman reaches across for the object Pierre disdainfully whips out from his waistcoat.

A meat cleaver.

Yevgeny's hand again tightens over my mouth as he whispers low into my ear: "Ye value yer own fingers, pretty little Carrot-head?"

Catching the harsh, bare glint from the kitchen bulb, the meat cleaver's square blade flashes through the air.

"Pierre—nooo!" Volodya screams.

"Then watch what happens to thems that disobey!" Yevgeny utters warningly.

The blade slams down—straight across all four tips of Volodya's knuckles.

Past the screams, past the whirling, suffocating haze of horror, I stare aghast at the blood . . . four little stumps of flesh . . . slivers of bone and skin and muscle oozing out rancidly across the floor . . . tearing my gaze away, I reel to a stop before the image in the mirror-glass: Yevgeny towering behind, his evil gap-toothed grin gloating in triumph upon his face, his one arm still clamped like a bear's paw across my chest, the other plastered over my mouth—while above it, my eyes stare outward, hollow with fright, black as two shining coals. Big as saucers.

Agonizing sobs from Volodya continue hounding unheeded throughout the room.

"All right," Pierre then urges in a tone of boredom. "Let's have done with the rest of it, then."

With a quick glance at me, he again snaps his fingers.

"Jest hold still, now—don't give us no trouble," Yevgeny orders from behind.

Heartbeats blasting in my ears, I stiffen with a jolt, elbowing back into him with all my strength—to no avail. Yevgeny's grip remains unyielding, holding me taut and fast. From Pierre's coat, I catch the barest glimpse of the bottle—*oh, my God!*—shudder as he uncaps it—*no! Jesus Christ, they cannot, they cannot!*—the sickeningly sweet stench permeates across the room as they moisten the handkerchief—*no, they mustn't; no, please! It—it is dangerous; Father never uses it; people have died in the chair having teeth extracted!* Yevgeny's hand springs away from my mouth. . . .

"No, please!" I sob, gulping, hacking, begging with shameful ineptitude the moment the handkerchief comes up. "No, you cannot—*no, please! No! Stop!* N-Not c-chlo . . . ro . . . f-form . . . ."

CHAPTER THREE

Apprenticeship in the Arts Unwary

High torches blaze in righteous triumph throughout the darkness, the inevitable chants of "Constitutional democracy!" and "Freedom!" gushing forth in a unison of screaming voices, and all up and down the street, the stomping continues. There must be two hundred of them by now, a rippling wave of felt hats and sheepskin coats curling around their bearded leader like a swarm of bees. Hoisted high upon his comrades' shoulders, the man of the hour beats his fists through the air and inspires a wave of curdling shouts, encouraging the crowd's growing revelry with hearty curses against the Tsar.

Near the curbstones, the Cossack regiment remains waiting in shadowy abeyance, all eyes trained upon their captain. On several occasions during the past two years, I have, along with Nikolai, been distant witness to just such a scene. Neither of us has ever been foolhardy enough to risk infiltrating the crowd, but we have also never been unable to resist securing the best perches all about Petersburg from which to survey the mounting incidents of revolutionary disturbance. This time, as with the others, the sequence portends to be the same: if the captain's saber goes up, the Cossacks will charge; if it remains down, they will not. So far, the blade rests at the man's side, hovering—as so many other matters do these days—in the throes of political indecision.

Obviously, the Cossacks have been given orders not to interfere with the demonstration unless deemed absolutely necessary.

"Constitutional democracy!" the people again start chanting—over and over, their voices trained into an undulating core: "Grant us true democracy! And freedom!"

Again I shove through the iron bars, grappling for the window sash, but it is no use. A fist's width is as far as the pane will open.

Apparently, its construction was specifically designed to allow ventilation but thoroughly prevent escape.

With blinded rage, I grip the bars for the seeming millionth time, shaking them in hot-tempered, rolling heaves like a madman purged of his wits. But the heavy rails scarce budge from their iron frame fastened upon the wall. Already have I checked: forty-eight tightly sunken screws, twelve each side around, aptly secure the bar-plate across the breadth of the room's single window. It would take days, a week perhaps, to loosen the wretched thing—that is, if I can be lucky enough to find, in the scrupulously neatened tidiness of this room, a coin misplaced somewhere, or a perhaps a piece of discarded metal small enough to fit into the tiny grooves.

And then to the street, it looks to be about five stories down.

No matter—I would risk five stories. I am good at window escapades; I would think of something! Had I my pocket knife, I could make quick work of the damn screws securing the bars. But the pocket knife is missing. Along with my belt. My mother's amethyst crystal. And the piccolo.

Through the crack of the window, my frantic shouts for help again become drowned into sad waters of oblivion, melting unheard into the roaring street noise below. As the tumult continues blaring upward, I shut my eyes wearily against the noise and press my brow yet once more against the icy bars. All those people screaming their hearts out for freedom. At least they yet possess the privilege of walking about unhampered down on the street.

Turning on my heel too swiftly, I careen with a thud into the side of the bureau. No walking stick, no cane, nor other decent substitute has been left anywhere in proximity. Only a little over three weeks have I been walking without the aid of a shoulder crutch. Normally, shut in against my will, ready to tear out my hair, I would pace—limp or no limp—back and forth, rote tonic for a racing mind. But now, without a cane to reassure my tentative footing, I dare not even do that.

As many times as I have tried the window, I have also tried the door—which remains locked from the outside, no response ensuing no matter how fiercely I scream, pound, or shake upon the knob.

In the half-hour since awakening, I have been able to discern two things. The first is that whoever owns this palace must be very, *very* rich.

The walls are encased in marble: heightened black rivers and snowy peaks strewn in a flighty spray of earth's molten beckonings across rich blankets of dark green jade—opulence generally reserved for the exquisite frames of icons, pieces of precious jewelry, or treasured heirloom trinkets. Never have I seen the likes of such used in an entire room's four walls. Even the commode, the sink in the large lavatory stand cast in the same grandiose, reflective slabs of marble—as I would suspect the tub is, although for some reason, that too has been partitioned off behind locked doors.

Although sparse, the furnishings are yet richly adorned—the frame of the bed thick with gleaming spires of brass, the tufted chairs inlaid with tiny carvings of amber, turquoise, garnets, and onyx set in curved moldings of rich mahogany and polished oak. The olive-colored, crest-emblazoned carpet reflects only the finest quality in traditional Persian weavings, and seems expertly matched to the eerie tone of the walls.

Strange paradox it is, such richness, such majestic splendor in a room obviously meant only to house a prisoner.

The second thing I have learned, far more foreboding than this wealth of inner surroundings, is the expansive wealth of the view just outside.

When I first awoke, faint glimmers of sunset hung upon encroaching phantoms of the darkness, just enough dusky light escaping in a long band off the horizon to permit faint recognition of a few buildings.

A few were enough. Everyone in Russia knows, either from old paintings or the modern picturegraphs, the image of that gargantuan onion-domed monstrosity, and as I peer back through the window, searching out the garish outlines of St. Vasili's Cathedral yet again, I clutch at my head, my heart crushed to blank beats of pounding stone in my chest, my throat torn with spasms of panic. *Impossible!* I keep telling myself—and yet, stark evidence only continues abounding all around, stern fortresses towering up on every side with all the menace of the old wars. Ever readied as battlement, the massive walls of the ancient kremlin encapsulate St. Vasili's; flank dozens of other shimmering golden domes with Mother History's sword of staid protection, a scourge raised high against my Novgorodian nakedness as I grovel before her in literal obscurity, wholly bereft of my internal traveling passport, or any other proof of identity. Along with my rail credit vouchers and my cash, the passport remains within my billfold—which is most probably still lying at this very moment down upon the floor beside the mattress in Volodya's flat in Petersburg.

A key cracks in the lock, and I jolt around as the door begins to creak open through the hollow silence.

"What the hell am I doing in *Moscow?*" I shout wrathfully into the barrel of a gun.

"Git back!"

To my surprise, the wary captor is not the huge Yevgeny, nor the stodgy Pierre; instead, a young woman. "Git back, I'm tellin' ye! I'll not be puttin' up with no guff from the likes o' ye, do ye hear?"

Reluctantly, I lower my hands down to my sides.

Revolver still leveled at me, the girl cautiously steps her way into the room. Perhaps not any older than her late teens, she is tall, taller than I am in fact, thin and gaunt with a steady morosity of purpose, her apron hanging in oversized billows over her long skirt as if a set of pleated draperies wholly unsuited for a coarsened window. Her kerchief also seems caught in too many layered folds upon her small head. Sensing my perusal, she adjusts it self-consciously, poking back stray strands of escaping straw-colored hair. But it is her mouth that most conspicuously draws my attention: at first, I think it to be a harelip, but as her image sharpens beneath the blaze of overhead lamplight, I surmise it instead as a brownish birthmark slicing up in a hideous triangular pattern to the tip of her nose.

Coughing, I avert my stare.

Glaring me down through narrowed eyes, she sets the tray she has been carrying behind her with a loud clang upon the table; steps back and pulls off the silver lid. "Eat!" she commands authoritatively, motioning toward the table with the gun.

Were this Yevgeny or Pierre, in an instant I would smash the food to the floor and make a desperate launch for freedom. But my surprise is so acute at the sight of this willowy waif of a girl, I simply cannot help letting out a short laugh. "And?" I say to her, shrugging. "I suppose you'll shoot me if I don't?"

Instead of answering, she nervously fingers up the trigger.

"All right!" In surrender, I wave both palms through the air. "I suppose," I admit with a sigh, "that I am a tad hungry."

She stares at my leg with a strangely mixed expression as I guide my hand along the wall for balance while hobbling over to the small table. Upon the tray rests a plate of herring and smoked salmon, cold tomatoes in aspic, and a generous chunk of warm black bread. From a carafe, the girl pours fresh lemonade into a silver goblet before returning quickly to her guard-like stance at the doorway, the revolver still trained stiffly in her hand.

Against the low buzzing roar from the continuing commotion outside, the girl and I lock stares, sizing up one another. At first, I proceed with deliberate slowness, wondering if I can possibly stow the fork away in my pocket afterwards without her taking notice. Later I might be able to manage the window-bar screws with the edge of the tines. But after a couple of bites, my fancied musings toward escape evaporate into a different type of desperation: the food is delicious, and I find myself absolutely ravenous, finally wolfing down everything to its last scattered morsels with all the sloppy relish of a common plowhand.

"I can bring more if ye're still hungry," she murmurs, eyes glancing briefly to the plate. "There's skewered swordfish, potatoes, and cheese dumplins, too. But Cook thought it best te start ye out slow from a dose o' chlor'form."

"You have a name?" I ask, peering upward at her.

"Call me Missy, if ye want. Everybody else does," she answers with a sneer.

"Missy," I repeat thoughtfully. "But such is not a true name."

"Yaa, and ye'd best not be givin' yer true name neither te nobody 'round this filthy den o' thieves."

"And why is that?"

"Ha! Ye truly are as naive as they all said." Moving in closer from the door, she smiles with a tender, curious expression, looking me up and down with widened eyes. "An', like they said," she goes on in a hushed tone, "ye're jest as beautiful."

Flushing scarlet, I slam the fork down upon the table and stare at the empty plate, my heart racing in my ears. No longer does any use remain in asking what they want of me. That answer was unequivocally provided back in Volodya's flat by Pierre's disgusting, stroking fingers.

"What day is it?" I demand, holding my gaze fast unto my hands.

"Wednesday."

Lord Jesus! Near unto twenty hours. All last night, all this following day have I slept, knocked into blinded senselessness from the chloroform. "And why," I go on tersely, hard put to contain my rage as I spit out each stilted word, "did they have to bring me all the blessed way to Moscow?"

The girl shrugs, and says, as if seeing no reason why anyone should care: "Pierre prefers keepin' his business dealins here."

"And just who is this Pierre, that he can kidnap anyone he wants upon a moment's whim, and bring him halfway across the country without any prior say-so?"

Drawing up proudly to her full height, Missy declares with passion: "His Honor, Ilarion Pavlovich Sheremetev!"

"What?"

"Yaa, ye heard right. Bastard son o' the great family he is! An' rich as the Tsar, or else fair close."

Staring about the room, I nod in mute agreement. If such fineries adorn a cell meant solely for captivity, just how grand are Pierre's personal living suites? And small wonder he could transport an unconscious prisoner all the way from Petersburg to Moscow without arousing the slightest suspicions of porters or conductors. The man probably maintains his own private railway coach.

"Ye're not from Vyborg, are ye?"

It is now with trepidation that I return her gaze. In scores of provinces across the Empire, the Sheremetevs command vast scattered holdings, their name synonymous not only with money, but with power—power that can, with the flick of a pen, make or break the teetering finances of an obscure Novgorodian count. Power that, upon the merest studied frown at a luncheon with the right people, might ruin the career of an aspiring musician.

"Thought so," she goes on. "Ye don't talk like the scum from Vyborg or Vasilyevsky, the others Rykazian brings in."

"Y-You know Volodya?" I stammer out with a gasp. "Do you know what happened to him?"

"What, 'bout the fingers? Oh, sure. Word gits 'round. Nobody crosses Pierre. Course, I only know Rykazian by his name, not his face. I never been te Petersburg."

"No—I mean, do you know if he's all right? They did not kill him, did they?"

"Oh, I scarce think so." Again she shrugs. "Doin' that would be no good fer business."

"Did they bring him here with me?"

"Not far as I know. They'll keep him in Vyborg, prob'ly. Pierre's short on dealers in Petersburg."

"What do you mean, 'dealers?'"

Blushing, Missy stares to the floor as if having already revealed far too much. Awkwardly, she lopes across the room and extracts the silver tray from beneath my hands, her gun still held in steady warning. "I'll go git ye some o' that swordfish now, if ye like."

At least this Sheremetev bastard appears to feed his captives well. "Would you?" I reply, managing a faint smile while noting with sharpened watchfulness her stabbing, awkward gait as she heads back for the door. Tall she may be, but entirely lacking in any grace. And in body size, the girl actually matches me fair enough. "Also," I say to her quickly, "could I ask for one more thing?"

She pauses, frowning.

"Just a cane. As you can see, it's a bit difficult for me to walk without one."

"Did Yevgeny hurt yer leg in the scuffle at Rykazian's?" Her question seems tinged with amazement.

I shake my head, murmuring: "No, it is an old injury."

Missy sighs with relief. "Pierre'd have the oaf's head fer any harm done te ye. Well, I don't know if they'll let ye have a cane. But I'll see what I kin do."

The key turns expertly the instant the door shuts behind her, my hands lunging upon the knob far too late to wrench it back open.

"Damn!" I flatten back to the wall. The solution is the cane, then. Loath as I am to hit a girl, if I could simply knock her down, hopefully without hurting her too much, at least I would be out the door and that much farther on my path to escape.

After that, escape to where is the question. Do I return to Petersburg? And to my father? And my interview, at the Conservatory, is tomorrow morning! Can I reach Petersburg by tomorrow? But of course, the audition could be rescheduled. If I can just get there.

A difficult task without money, without a traveling passport. Perhaps I could find a telegraph office, send a wire—something, somehow. There has got to be some escape!

The thought of the alternative—Pierre—only heightens a lingering wave of nausea.

In desperation, I fumble once more in my pockets for my watch, the sole possession left me along with my handkerchief. The face reads a quarter to eight. Upon the table, I spy the heavy silver-plated carafe Missy has inadvertently left behind and quickly swipe it up in my hand as faint echoes of her returning footsteps begin sounding in the hall just beyond the door.

Bracing back behind the doorjamb, I poise the carafe high overhead and hold my breath.

The key turns in the lock again—but this time, the door swings wide open, crashing with a shower of splinters back into the wall. Without any pause for thought, I lunge forward, hurtling the carafe with all my strength—and stumble straight into the gleefully awaiting arms of Yevgeny.

"Sneaky little bastard!" he shouts, throwing me with a rattling bang back onto the table.

"Ye bumblin' fool—don't hurt him!" Missy warns from behind.

The door—last avenue to my escape—slams shut behind her with a solid, plodding thud of finality.

"Now, ye listen te me, an' listen good!" Yevgeny roars down into my face, both fists gripped like meaty claws upon my collar. "Ye touch one hair on the lass—so much as even a scratch goes on her from ye—and I'll cut ye te pieces!" Shoving me flat onto my back, he yanks a massive hunting knife out from his belt and starts brandishing it back and forth in front of my nose with lustful, leering guffaws. "And don't think I've no heart fer it neither, Black-eyes. Pierre may be quite taken with ye, but I'm no fag. Don't give a hoot for yer pretty freckled face! But ye see," he goes on, wrenching me hurtfully back upward, "what I am is a man who does like souvenirs."

From his pocket, he pulls out a pitiful crusty stub of human flesh, the nail-bed sunken to a gruesome blotch of blackened purple. Once, as far as I can tell, it must have been someone's thumb.

And then poisonous waves of horror start to course through my every vein. My eyes go wide, focusing in disbelief on the tiny balled wad of bone and blood—before I meet Yevgeny's glare again with a sickened gasp. "Akkh, yes!" he bellows triumphantly—and I realize, shaking like a leaf all the way down into my boots, that this not merely any human thumb.

It is Volodya's thumb.

I slam shut my eyes, groping for the last fading shreds of sanity, wondering idly if a man can bleed to death simply from the loss of his thumb and fingers.

"Be warned!" Yevgeny yells, throwing me back once more onto the table.

"Yevgeny Ivanovich, that's enough!" Missy implores.

"Akkh, ye're soft as mash, woman!" Garnering his massive body upward in a blustering heave for breath, Yevgeny seizes a last grip upon my collar. "Remember, ye sneakin' little black-eyed tart: the lass is my own blooded sister. An' dear te me!" he yells.

"I—I'll not touch her, I promise!"

"Ivanovich! Ye've had yer fun—now, git out," Missy orders, pointing.

"Oh, an' by the way," he mutters absently, wrenching back open the door. "He said ye could have this."

To my astonishment, Yevgeny throws the piccolo into my grasp. "An' ye try sneakin' out this door while Missy's workin', it's me ye'll deal with—understand?" he bellows again, shaking his fist in a swipe of fury through the air. "Steady watch I'll be keepin', so don't try nothin'—don't even think it!"

Finally, after a reverent nod in the direction of his sister, he bounds, grumbling, out the door.

"Are ye all right?"

The girl helps me up from the top of the table and shoves a cane into my trembling hands. "Here, sit down," she orders—and numbly, I collapse onto the chair, watching through a blank-eyed haze as she bustles about my feet, sweeping up the mess of littered tableware.

"Skewered swordfish," she then announces, removing the silver lid from a new tray with a dramatic flourish.

I stare at it, murmuring hoarsely: "Uh, I think I have quite lost my appetite."

The lid clangs back down. "I'm sorry. I wouldn't o' brought him, 'cept I knew ye was goin' te jump me. Don't ever try it agin—do ye hear?"

Desperate to contain my ragged gasps of breath, I proffer forth an obedient nod.

"Here's fresh peaches and some ripe glass-apples. I'll leave 'em for later."

An amply layered fruit bowl she sets down upon the center of the table. With quickened strides of purpose, she then heads back into the lavatory, from which the gush of water spouts on; spouts off; spouts on again. A harsh jangling echo sounds from a set of keys.

Fighting off further shudders at the thought of Yevgeny's knife and Volodya's pitiful severed thumb, I clutch the piccolo up to my chest, fingers of both hands running lovingly up and down its row of tungsten keys. "Father, remember when you gave me this?" I murmur softly to myself, my heartbeats flooding out to him across imagined skies, full of prodigal pleas intertwined with abject admissions of forgiveness. I care not a whit anymore about the fiasco in Siberia. All I want in the world now is to see his dark-eyed, handsomely weathered face again, to throw my arms wide around his broad shoulders and hang on for dear life just like the other times he has carried me home. "Father? Can you hear me far off in Petersburg across these spiteful tangents of the wind? Father—God—anybody out there, do you hear me? Show me the way out of this nightmare: somebody interfere, call the police, come looking for me! *Please . . . .*"

"I'm settin' up the shower," Missy murmurs softly, startling me as she brushes aside my arm. Making an effort to avoid my gaze, she wipes her hands with a thick cotton towel.

"What do you mean, 'setting up' the shower? And why do they keep it locked?"

"Same reason they took yer belt and pocket knife. Same reason there's no razors in here."

I stare at her dumbly. *Suicide? They think I might try to kill myself?*

"Come along." She nods toward the lavatory. "Let's git yer clothes off."

"Get my *clothes off?"* I blurt out incredulously.

"Oh, an' don't think I never seen a naked man before! Come along, Red—we scarce got all night. Ye want te risk gittin' yer hide beat with Pierre's leather switch?"

"I hardly intend to disrobe in front of you!" I retort, glaring at her and making awkward, stabbing threat with the cane.

"Ye want me te call Yevgeny back in here?" she yells in retaliation, pointing back toward the door.

I shake my head with vigorous denial. "All right! But why the great urgency about bathing right now?

"'Cause it's time te git ye ready fer Pierre."

* * *

"I will not!" I shout, pushing away from her in horror.

Lips pursed, dainty brows creased in an impatient frown, the girl Missy only continues unlocking the bureau.

An ingenious contraption: in reality, not a clothing bureau at all, but instead a woman's vanity equipped with false drawers that pull out to collapse into a low-tufted, swiveling seat. Beyond, a wide mirror-glass emerges, heretofore entirely hidden against the wall.

Onto the vanity top slams Missy's lacquer tray, its contents of tiny color-pots and fragile horsehair brushes rattling like a coven of malicious demons consumed with twinkles of mirth. Whirling around, she shoves both fists onto her hips, points at the vanity seat, and shouts: "Git over here!"

"I will not let you paint my face!" I shout back, quivering livid white in defiance.

"Pierre'll be furious if I don't! Ye want me te git Yevgeny back in here?"

"You do whatever the devil you want! I will *not* let you paint my face!"

Her high-pitched whistle follows through the air with such a piercing shriek that I wince away in pain, clapping both palms over my ears.

Snarling curses under his breath, Yevgeny bangs open the door and stomps back into the room, his vodka flask quickly stuffed into his jacket pocket.

"I am not a woman!" I shout at him, frantically shaking my head back and forth in denial. "Don't let her do this to me! *Please!"*

"Sit down, and shut up!" Clamping onto my shoulders, Yevgeny hurls me with one angry, swinging swipe of his fat hands onto the vanity bench. Missy, hurrying up beside, starts retrieving paint pots and brushes from the lacquer tray.

"No!" I shout on, rearing back—but Yevgeny's grip blocks any hope of struggling away. "I will *not* let her paint me up to look like a woman!" I rage on at him. *"I will not!"*

Seizing a fierce hold onto my wrist, Yevgeny slams it flat down to the countertop and pulls out his knife. "Ye goin' te cooperate?" he whispers softly. "Or do I git me another souvenir?"

He pries the thumb out deftly from my stiffened ball of a fist, adding with a curt, guttural laugh: "Great prize te go with Rykazian's, eh?"

I shove at him, punching and gasping, near flinging my arm from its socket with trying to yank away. No use.

"Ye goin' te sit still?" he demands again, the blade of his knife pressing its sharp mark into the flesh of my hand.

Choking for breath, I grope out with my other arm, hoping desperately for some reprieve from Missy—but from far off to the side and out of my reach, she only murmurs: "What's it to be, Red?"

In answer to my furious glare, Yevgeny mumbles: "Well, I guess I'll jest take my ready due." With a shrug, he increases the pressure on the knife, the tiniest pin-prick searing into my thumb to produce a hovering, watery drop of blood.

"No!" My next proud words sputter off into tinny rantings of a cornered animal. "All right—oh, please God!" I stammer helplessly. "I'll—I'll do whatever you want."

Rolling his eyes, Yevgeny lets up at last and sheathes his knife.

But he remains towering guardedly above at the side of the bureau, his heavy-lidded eyes fixing upon me with a disdainful sneer. Yanking the brim of his cap low to his brow, he leans back against the wall, fumbles with three or four bad matches, and finally lights himself a cigarette.

Avoiding his gaze, I duck away from the acrid odor of the smoke, wishing to God not to so crave the taste of his cheap tobacco.

"Look at me," Missy demands.

She starts wiping over my face with a dampened towel, her fingers grasping two small brushes loaded up with kohl-darkened face-paint. "All right. Now shut yer eyes."

Cringing from her touch, I struggle to sit calmly as she slathers the kohl onto my face. As if the degradation I have already been forced to suffer through has not been enough: the woman near climbed into the tub with me before I angrily barked her down, but still she would not let me alone, shoving in soap, the brushes, a sickeningly sweet perfumed rinse for my hair. Afterwards, clucking and sputtering around like an overwrought mother hen, she was everywhere with the towels, roughly scrubbing my whole body as if attempting to buff up a prize piece of furniture. That is all I am to them, I can see now: a valuable market commodity to be cared for, a piece of property. Pierre's play-toy. *Oh, God. I can't believe this is happening to me! I simply cannot believe it. . . .*

"There!" Missy announces at last. "Scarce so bad, now." With a pat to my shoulder, she tosses the paint pots back into the tray and snatches up a larger brush, which she begins raking vigorously through my hair.

Warily, I open my eyes and spy a peek into the mirror.

I expect to look like some horribly made-up sideshow freak at a summer carnival. Instead, the gracious subtlety of her efforts comes as a true surprise: the lids of my eyes have merely been darkened in a bit, the barest hint of a black line extended out across each temple. My lips have been rouged up also, but not with any more detail than the minimum posturings required for the faces of tenors or male dancers to stand out beneath stage lights at the opera or ballet.

But this is *not* the ballet. Save for a sheer lavender robe, I sit shivering in nakedness—and am being primped up for a man who appears to be a professional whoremonger.

"Gorgeous," Missy murmurs with envy as she continues brushing out my hair.

Squinting shut my eyes again, I curse my lazy habit of allowing it to grow. Curse myself for my foolish affair with Volodya, for managing to become mixed up in this whole dreadful catastrophe. And most of all, more than anything else, I curse my face. *Damn you, Melissa Devon-Tyler! Why must I ever suffer for the sin of your death? Why did I have to be the one to inherit your face?*

"Hmmm." Chucking her fingers up under my chin, Missy rechecks her work with critical detachment. "Perhaps I'll jest buff on a bit more—"

"No," Pierre interrupts from the doorway. "The child is exquisitely beautiful just as he is."

I freeze—and feel my heartbeats hammer away into crashing shatters of oblivion.

"Yaa, Exc'lency!" In a hurried fluster, Missy snatches up the paint tray, shoves me away from the bench, and motions Yevgeny to lock up the vanity. With respectful nods, the two of them acknowledge Pierre and then rush from the room in a clatter of boot-heels, neither uttering another word.

The door slams ominously shut upon their quick footsteps fading down the hall.

From across the room, Pierre eyes me up and down with a sigh of anticipation and breaks into a taunting grin. White and perfect as ocean pearls, his teeth gleam with a strange, almost artificial luminescence beneath slanted quivers of the lamplight. "Ahh, yes," he murmurs. "A nymph, an angel you are, indeed!"

Plucking at each finger as if at petals of a cherished rose, he begins slowly easing off his long white gloves.

I glare at him through wrathfully hooded eyes. Bereft of his top hat, clad merely in a dressing gown and cuffed trousers falling about his bare feet in loosely tailored folds of emerald silk, he seems much smaller, far less imposing than the poshly suited businessman barking out orders to his peasant henchmen two nights ago in Volodya's flat. Sizing him up with caution, I begin to wonder if I might be able to take him. I am at least thirty, perhaps even forty years younger. His age is difficult to discern; his face, though puffy and pockmarked, remains devoid of many wrinkles, but his hair proves gray and most pitifully wispy, greasy strands combed with diligent care across a growing bald spot at the crown of his head.

"Take it off," he orders, tossing his gloves onto the bed. "It's high time for me to see what my newest prize looks like." His eyes indicate my robe.

"No!"

He answers with a scathing laugh, gliding across the carpet on the balls of his feet in an easy burst of grace. "Well, I see you intend to make this little *tête-à-tête* rather—oh, how shall we say? Interesting—yes, indeed, darling! Such arresting beauty . . . coupled with such proud, haughty defiance."

I lunge for the table lamp, urging myself on: *he is scrawny as a wizened old lizard; Yevgeny, no one else is near; I can take him. . . .*

The lamp, table, chairs, my fists—all crash at him through the air. I fling pillows from the bed, attempt to trip him up by strewing the silken quilted coverlet out across the floor; slash at his feet, stomp for his toes, claw at his hair, stab with my elbows, try repeatedly to land a solid punch; kick, bite, and scream like a banshee . . . all of it incredibly to no avail . . . for my bad leg slows me . . . while Pierre only continues dwarfing my pitiable efforts with the callous, eager anticipation of the strong hound circling in upon a helplessly ravaged fox, his laughter rattling ever closer in my ears each time I back up, each time I try once again to fend him off.

"Touché!" he gasps with delight, at last muscling me to the floor. "I knew I'd never land such a heady looker as you without an old-fashioned, brawling fight."

"Let me go!"

In response, his fist slams like an anvil into my jaw.

Stunned, I gape around at the reeling room. *How could I have so underestimated him? Surely the man cannot be that strong. . . .*

Smearing his cheek into the blood running down my chin, he murmurs against my mouth: "Even more lovely like this, you are, darling! Oh, yes—young blood is so tantalizingly delicious. . . ."

His lips clamp down upon mine in a furiously suffocating kiss.

"Nooo!" I tear myself away, stabbing out wildly, punching hard for his ribs.

"Ohhh!" Although he clutches at his side, the man seems virtually unfazed. "Ha, ha! Not much of a boxer, are you?" he bellows out, laughing. "Oh, you'll bend to me soon enough, Black-eyes."

"I shall do no such thing, ever!" I shout, adding sarcastically: "Ilarion Pavlovich!"

"So. They told you. Damn the peasants—always talk, talk, talk. Well, save your syllables, my sweet. All servants in my palace—as well as all guests—have leave to address me solely as 'Pierre.'"

"I am not your servant, nor your guest!"

"Oh, yes, you are. And from now on, I expect you to start to act like the servant you indeed are." The brunt of his hand slams once more into my face.

Totally stunned by his massive strength, I crumple yet again to the floor, hacking for breath while fighting back a mortified rush of tears.

With a harsh jolt, Pierre yanks me back upward by both wrists. "There is no use in continuing to fight so, my love," he says, torrid laughter lancing into my every breath. "I quite assure you: you are dealing with an expert who has tamed many a hot young colt in his time. You see, breaking in reluctant virgins is my prerogative as the director of this—oh, how shall we say?—illustriously lucrative operation. And reluctant you may be, but you are no virgin. Are you, darling? Damn that crafty Armenian snake! I pay him to recruit, not to train. But I must say, I never take on a dealer not possessing an eye for quality, who has no personal inclination for this business. You get my drift, *n'est-ce pas?* Surely Rykazian taught you a little something about—oh, how shall we say?—the more splendid niceties of life? Tell me, did you like it? When he fucked you? Did you like fucking him?"

I reply by spitting into his face.

He hits me again; again pulls me back upward, his lips closing upon mine in another smothery, salivating kiss.

"Nooo! Dammit, stop!"

Pierre deflects my angry punches and cups his palm around the back of my neck, murmuring: "Ahh, yes—most haunting, soulful eyes I have ever seen. . . to be honest, I scarce ever trouble myself with soiled merchandise. But you are so beguiling, this time I simply could not resist. . . ."

"Goddamn you, *stop!"* I shout out at the top of my lungs—but despite my pummeling blows, his lips move from my throat to the lobes of my ears before he pulls back again, chuckling with an evil smile, his gaze fastened with studious inquiry upon my hands. "Beautiful all the way down to the fingertips!" he exclaims, grasping them up, his breath caught in an aching sigh. He turns them over and examines my shaking palms; turns the knuckles back up again. "Look at the long fingers—how poised, yet how fragile these are!" he exclaims. "As if those of an artist. Or perhaps—a musician?"

Stifling a gasp, I shake my head back and forth in violent gusts of denial, attempting—with hopelessly clumsy ineptitude—to scoot out from under him.

"You see, my precious," he gloats on, grappling me to a halt with an iron-clad grip, "I know my way around musical instruments. And I saw that piccolo."

"You go to the devil's filthy hell!" I scream, flushing, punching out at him once more as he eyes the piccolo lying aside my watch upon the bedside table.

"I made a detailed examination of that piccolo," he goes on, again wrenching me up close to his chest. "Oh, yes—at first it looks quite the toy. Until one takes some measurements, *n'est-ce pas?* Until one checks to see that it has endured significant use. Along with fastidiousness in care. So—tell me, you feisty red-headed progeny of the ancient *Rus:* you also play the flute?"

Choking on my furious retort, at last I manage to land a stinging left hook into his jaw.

"Goddamn it!" he chokes out. "Why—you beastly, savage little—"

"Thought you enjoyed defiance!" I rasp out sarcastically. "Ilarion Pavlovich!"

"I believe in this case the novelty is beginning to wear off!"

With a heaving ferocity of abandon, he lashes out again, his fist slamming repeatedly into my cheeks, eyes, nose . . . slap after pounding, back-handed slap, he pummels me into the floor . . . until at last I lie limply, sapped of all remaining strength and desperate to stifle my childishly shameful whimpers.

"Oh, I see!" he exclaims, breathless and panting, victorious gladiator hovering above in triumphant, sweaty-hued flush of conquest. "A pity," he then cries, laughing. "Indeed—which finger is the most imperative for keying near unto every single note?"

Roughly wrenching out my right hand, he clamps his entire fist around my pinky finger. And starts bending it back.

"Nooo!" I scream. *"No, please!"*

"Then stop fighting me, you little flit! Or I'll snap it straight off your hand—and you'll never play again. Do you hear me?"

He wrenches my finger back farther . . . and even farther . . . .

"All right!" I choke out. "Let go, *please God!* I—I'll do anything you want! J-Just don't ruin my hands!"

He lets up then and tilts backward upon his heels, grinning down with a gloating sneer. "That's much, much better," he murmurs. "Now, I want you to tell me. Who you are."

I stare at him through a blurred, frozen haze.

"No common peasant enunciates his words with such impeccably lilting crispness," he declares with an impatient wave of his hand. "Could be from the English Quarter, even, I daresay! You come from a family of civil servants, artisans, merchants—what?"

Wiping the back of my hand across my mouth, I smear off more blood and peer at him with widening tremors of suspicion. If my true identity should be ascertained, rumors could fly through Petersburg drawing rooms and salons like flaming target arrows, no matter the relative obscurity, whether my father, the political ostrich, spent half of his life exiled to Siberia or not. The old cunningly familiar voice of conscience—intuition—God—whatever—continues drumming its steady blare into my head without a second's pause for rest: *Do not, under any circumstances whatsoever, tell him who you truly are!*

"Y-Yes, m-m-merchants," I rasp out finally. "Merchant-artisans . . . in w-wood carvings. Some musical instruments: piccolos, flutes, balalaikas." *Oh, God! Please let that be enough to steer him off the track. . . .*

"And exactly where in Petersburg are you from?"

"Uh, lower Sadovaya, south of the Haymarket. My mother, God rest her soul, was an English governess."

"And your father?"

"Never knew him."

He laughs derisively, muttering: "Excellent!"

Good. Let him think I am some bastard orphan, then. Never must my family learn of this abduction, nor of this shameful atrocity, my being forced to surrender unto this man and his filthy whims. *Never!*

"And your name?"

"Khulinov," I tell him quickly.

"I see, Khulinov. You have a first name?"

"I prefer if people call me 'Piccolo.'"

At this, his eyes narrow in on me with a patronizing leer. "All right, darling!" he snorts. "You want to play name games, fine. Go ahead and keep your precious secret."

Then in one swift, impatient movement, he hoists me to my feet—while at the same time loosening the sash to the robe, its soft fabric fluttering off in a languid billow to my ankles as his hands glance across my bare shoulders.

Entirely unheedful of my mortified flush of shame, Pierre stoops down and begins a thorough inspection of my bad leg's winding lines of blotchy, mottled scars. Ruefully shaking his head, he mutters as if to himself: "Pity. Will bring the price down."

My heart stops, hot color draining away into a cold blanch of panic. *Price? He intends to sell me?*

"And I suppose your gait holds neither any hint of grace?" he demands flatly, his brow furrowed with a critical frown.

"I—I need the cane."

"Well, you shan't need it now. Get into bed."

Catching my breath instead, I try to back away.

"Blast you!" he yells, yanking down the switch cord to the lights. "Enough of this impertinent stalling! I see the time has come to teach you a badly needed lesson!"

Bursting across the room in one furious long stride, he throws me, against a rush of screaming protests, down upon the bed—and starts tying my hands together in front of my face with the sash from the lavender robe.

"Nooo!" I scream. "Don't! *Please!"*

"Goddamn it—*shut up!"*

Around a post in the footboard of the bed; back around my wrists, the sash winds—until, with a grunt of satisfaction, Pierre yanks the ends into a firm, insoluble sailor's knot.

"You can't tie me up like this!" I shout, kicking out at him with every last ounce of my strength. "You filthy, lecherous old—"

"Shut up!" he roars down into my ear. With a renewed ferocity of passion, he starts beating me all over again, his fist slamming repeatedly down into my face . . . I thought he had drained me past all earthly endurance already, but I was wrong . . . *oh, God! I thought my father used to beat me, but it was never anything like this. . . .*

And then his blows, my screams—all of it abruptly stops. Coming to rest upon my shoulders, his hands caress down my back, smooth up the backs of my legs—until his two eager thumbs crease in a separation of my buttocks. . . .

Oh, Jesus God!

With a fierce tug, I thrash back from the bedpost like a demon possessed, yanking both wrists against the pull of silken bindings—but the sash remains wound so tightly that the fabric sears into my flesh, raw little slivers of skin and blood chafing up and down my arms. "Pierre, no!" I rasp out hoarsely. "No, wait—anything but this! Pierre, please—oh, my God, *nooo!* Pierre, don't! *Please!"*

But his hands seize like claws around my belly, hot breath searing against the back of my neck as he rams inside me.

"Oh, little Piccolo!" he mumbles, his palm clamping across my mouth to stifle the screams. "Tight as a maid you still are . . . delicious! Now, now—you will get used to it. . . ."

Swallowing hard, I shut my eyes and fight back flashing images of the mounds of butter we used; how ecstatically intoxicating it all felt the first time—the second time—all the times . . . how gentle, how tender Volodya was with me, and I with him . . . how there was not the slightest trace of pain. . . .

Untold hours seem to drag on mercilessly as Pierre keeps ramming in—over and over, oblivious to my curses, heedless of my whimpers. Shrouded in a ghostly pall of darkness, the room starts tilting in rolling glassy angles before my eyes, strangely severed images from the past galloping to-and-fro as I stare numbly into the night: Father astride his Arabian mare, whacking his cap down upon his knee one day with a boisterous laugh as Pavel and Bulya beat a horribly dissonant old peasant melody out on two sadly battered balalaikas . . . Marnya, full of impatience while chopping garlic and turnips in the kitchen, snatching the fat wooden ladle from the soup tureen, holding it up to my lips, and yelling: 'Ye knucklehead! Course it got enough salt!' . . . Katya, winking and grinning at me from behind the dairy barn butter churn, her nose buried a bunch of lilacs I had stuffed into a jar and left for her after that glorious summer day of our first kiss . . . Nikolai, lying flat upon my bed in my room, deliberately squalling out a lewd old peasant song, his violin propped up between his knees as he played it backwards—while, overcome with hysteria from my perch at the window seat, I chimed in with the chorus, waving the flute at him like a drunken conductor, our laughter, as always—just like our music—binding the two of us together in a perfect wedge of harmony. . . .

I wince back my final cry as Pierre finishes at last and draws back out with an exhausted shudder. His arms collapse around my shoulders, and long moments tick by in eerie, rasping quiet until our sweat begins to blend cold. Finally, he pushes roughly off, and with a preoccupied frown, strides out of the room.

As the door slams shut behind him, faintly diminished rumbles echo in from the still-open window. Apparently, the workers' demonstration outside has been allowed to run its course without any Cossack interference.

And then I realize with a shock that, for the first time that I can remember since awakening here, the door is not locked.

Oh, Lord in Heaven! Why now? While I am tied up to this bed!

Cursing, gritting my teeth, I twist in frantic, chafing heaves against the bedpost, curling my arms around, pulling and yanking in every direction, but it is no use; my thumbs scarce reach the knots. *Oh, Jesus Christ—why must silk be so strong? What are they going to do, leave me tied up in here until the bloody morn?* Pressing my hot cheek against my hands, I attempt to coax some sense of feeling into my icy fingers; attempt to swallow back the avalanche of pain gnashing at the base of my skull.

At last the soft padding of shoeless feet echoes just outside in the hall, and the door swings back open.

Sighing with relief, I look up, expecting to see Missy. Instead, it is Yevgeny—clad only in thick stockings and his woolen underdrawers—looming over me with his knife.

"Oh, no!" I rasp in terror. *"Oh, God, please—nooo!"*

"Shhh!"

The knife slices down; I stare at my fingers: all my dreams, all my music, all the years, all the hopes . . . doomed forever . . . *oh, God! Here they go. . . .*

But to my amazement, the blade only slashes through the bindings, freeing my arms from the bedpost.

As I stare after him, dumbfounded, Yevgeny disappears into the lavatory and re-emerges with a cold washcloth—which he pats up to my face, murmuring: "Ye all right, lad?"

His tone, though gruff, comes yet tinged with startlingly gentle concern.

Jaw dropped, I gape at him in disbelief as he continues swabbing the cloth over my face.

"W-Why y-y-you?" I demand finally. "Why not h-her?"

"Woman needs her sleep. Think ye're the only one she's got te care for?"

I watch blankly as he blots dried blood from the cloth into the tin water pitcher.

"He'll not beat ye so rough if ye give in te him," he then mutters, sighing.

Shooting him a glare through the silvery moonlight, I start pounding my fists together, flexing my fingers against their flood of little needle-stinging waves. "Ha! And were you in my place, would you give in without a fight?"

"Me, in yer place?" Yevgeny chokes on an incredulous laugh, proclaiming: "I'm scarce a fag!"

I grab the washcloth from his hand with a vengeance and fling it onto the floor. "And just what makes you think I am?" I yell, suddenly no longer afraid. The fact that the man had the decency to come in and untie me makes him loom far less fearsomely than before.

"Don't try puttin' no gall over on me, Black-eyes!" he snaps in reply. "We saw ye an' Rykazian carryin' on together. Watched ye come an' go fer a whole three nights."

"So? You think that makes me fair game for you to spirit off against my will in the middle of the night? To force me to become Pierre's whore?"

"I'll take my rubles wherever I kin earn 'em," he answers quietly, averting his gaze.

Past an embarrassed cough, he scoops up the quilt from the floor and throws it over my naked shoulders.

"Why the hell did you come in here?" I shout, seizing the quilt up angrily and collapsing in exhaustion back upon the bed.

"'Cause Missy heard ye screamin' from all the way down the hall!"

"Humph!" I wince away from the memory of her hand patting my shoulder, as if she actually cared, the moment before Pierre came in. "And because I'm little to either of you but a piece of barter merchandise!" I yell up at Yevgeny. "A slave to be sold to the highest bidder, yes? For that indeed is the filthy business in which Pierre and all of you peasant scum are involved?"

He turns away.

I bury my face into a pillow, sobbing: "Get out!"

Hesitant, Yevgeny remains standing at the bedside. "Ye bleedin' anywhere else, lad?" he asks after a long moment.

"No, damn you! Take your foul questions and go rot in the reeking pit of hell!"

Sighing, he extracts a small goatskin pouch from his sock and sets it down onto the bedside table, muttering: "Aloe juice balm, if ye want it. Helps bruises, helps bleedin'." Then he stomps off, grumbling in a florid huff about the sins of youth and ingratitude.

The door slams shut behind him, the key turning swiftly in the lock.

I swipe up another pillow and pull it over my head, stifling the rush of cold sobs, and start praying with the most fervent desperation ever summoned forth in my entire life: to wake up, come the morrow, safe and tucked into bed in my own room in Novgorod—drenched in the fragrance of springtime and basking in the love of Eastertide, a thousand lifetimes far away from this appalling ungodly nightmare.

* * *

Missy sighs, frowning at the sight of my bruised face. "Not much help fer it, I'm afraid," she says, shaking her head. After one last conciliatory stroke at my eyelid, she tosses the horsehair brush back into the lacquer tray.

I keep my eyes fastened upon the counter of the vanity, careful to avoid the battered reflection lurking in the mirror-glass.

"Ye're not goin' te talk te me at all?" Missy then demands again, the third time she has postured the question in as many days.

Yesterday was Easter Sunday. Last night, for hours, I searched out scores of illuminated belfries past the barrier of the iron bars. When midnight ushered in Resurrection's triumph at last, I wept to hear the wondrous roaring peal of the bells.

"Ye could say somethin'," chides Missy past another moping pout.

And then a million songs, all birdsong one, erupted from high towers of the churches—followed by the blasting gunshots of military salutes, incantations of the priests, and prayers of the pilgrims rising up in chants of joy from the long processions winding through the streets below.

So petty now seem my childish lamentations at missing the gluttony festivities of *Maslenitsa*. Back in February, before Lententide, I had begged Father to allow my escape unto Petersburg to celebrate the licentious revelries of Butter-Week with my cousins. But as I had only just begun walking on my left leg, he forbade it profusely—promising that come Easter, he would do naught to prevent me from riding carousels and watching puppet shows, from sledding, swinging, and stuffing myself with a train load of butter, eggs, sugared pastries, and twice as much partridge and roasted pork loin as the year before. After ranting past his denials, I finally gave off my begging for a railway ticket with brooding resignation, for on top of everything else, during the three-day carnival held in Lissushka, he even refused to allow me up with Vliny and Tereza on the ice slides.

"Do ye mind?"

I jump, startled, as Missy motions me away from the vanity, and as she locks it up, I wander dazedly over to the window.

Just when I was beginning to marvel that my prayers had been answered, that the horror of four nights ago was truly naught but a hideous dream, Missy, after taking back the supper tray, returned tonight with the face-paint.

Such ministrations have done little good, not with two blackened eyes, the near dozen purplish bruises. Three days have I been left unto myself, but without much sleep, the pain gnawing continuously at my face and joints, the scattered, unruly dreams bidding welcome through my each nodding-off only unto lonely, blank-eyed hours.

With a strangely idle sense of detachment, I begin to wonder what occurred during my ill-fated interview time on Thursday morn at the St. Petersburg Conservatory.

"I'm tellin' ye agin," Missy admonishes from behind. "Don't fight him, and ye won't git beat. Ye think it's goin' te do ye any good, gittin' so dreadful hurt? If ye want my advice—which I git the sense that ye don't, but I'm givin' it te ye anyway, so ye'd best listen—my advice is, ye might try savin' up some o' yer strength."

Shutting my eyes away from her, I press my brow once more to the cold iron emptiness of the window bars.

"Look," she says, suddenly from very close—and when her hand comes to a tentative rest upon my arm, I jerk angrily away. "Oh, jest listen te me, Red! Truth 'bout Pierre is—" She stops abruptly, stealing a guilty peek toward the door. "Truth is," she goes on in a hushed whisper, "Pierre goes more fer the curly-headed, angelic-blondie types. Ye're jest a lark for him, Red—way too earthy lookin' a one fer his true taste. Ye git my drift? Akkh, jest give it a bit o' time! What are ye, fifteen? Sixteen? The man never takes any much older. Always gives up once their beard starts settin' in."

At this, I seize upon her with a virulent glare, flushing bright as a beet. All those stolen early morning tirades locked in the upstairs water closet with Father's straight razor, mowing it over my cheeks and chin—yet still, the hairs lie fine as raw-spun silk, barely willing to grow. "And then what happens?" I retort sullenly. "I shall be sold to some other vile charlatan? At a public auction?"

"God be Praised!" Missy exclaims, crossing herself in a fluster of arm-waving enthusiasm. "Three days o' silence, morn until eve. I thought the child had gone mute!"

Inwardly cursing her, I press back into the iron bars.

"I'm only tryin' te ease matters for ye, Red," she says softly, her hand again brushing my shoulder.

"Ease matters!" I gaze off toward the hovering lights of the darkened Moscow skyline, telling her: "If you truly want to ease matters, you would help me to escape."

"I can't do that."

"Why not? You certainly seem like a decent enough soul. The other night, you were the one who sent Yevgeny in here, yes?"

Snatching back her hand, Missy scrunches it into her mouth, and avoids my gaze.

"I want to go home!" I cry out in desperation, grasping up her arm. "Don't you understand? I am not some wayward urchin of the streets! I have family, people to whom I must return. Please, Missy—or whatever on earth your real name is—you must help me!"

"No, I can't! Now, stop it—let go o' me." Swinging out roughly, she shakes me off and bounds back across the room, where she starts gathering up the paint pots into the lacquer tray.

"Then to bloody hell with you!" I shout after her. "By the devil, you and Yevgeny—despite your caring little pats on my shoulder, always asking if I'm all right—all you truly care about is rubles, what price I'll bring! You know something? Neither of you is any better than that monster Pierre!"

In muffled silence, Missy hurries from the room and locks up the door.

Choking back vengeful tears, I stare off into the starlight and the shrouded image of my father's face. *Is he even looking for me? Does he any longer care?* But I was the one who ran off that awful night like such a fool in the *drozhki,* thundering away from his pleas for understanding; I was the one who left. Did Nikolai try to catch up with me? Had it been him, I know I would have followed, later. Do they even care that I have not come home? Do they have the faintest clue about this abduction?

The key turns in the lock once more, and the door whisks wide open: to reveal, in emerald-swathed, gloating brilliance, the smirking visage of Pierre.

In his fist, he grasps a short leather switch, beaten with steady rhythm into his opposite palm. His eyes leer across at me, half-open colorless agates of hotly beckoning desire. "So, my little Piccolo," he murmurs with a sharp intake of breath. "You have had a few days to rest and nurse your bruises. Tonight, I expect repayment for my patience, whether through passivity or violence. Which is it going to be?"

In his palm, the knot of the switch snaps over and over like deathly metered tickings of a clock.

Violence. *How I yearn to tear him from limb to limb with my bare hands! . . .*

'Save yer strength,' Missy said.

And the woman is right. Renewed beatings will only drain away precious energy, dull the sharpened alertness I must maintain for any laxity in their security measures. Further resistance will only hamper the physical fitness required, particularly in light of the handicap of my bad leg, during any possible chance for escape.

"Well?" Pointedly, Pierre clears his throat, hissing: "What is the answer, Piccolo? You keep me waiting."

Without a word, I let slip from my shoulders the silken robe, avert my eyes, and grip the handle of the cane, taking slow steps in the inevitable direction of the bed.

* * *

Hungry, frantic tweaking sounds out upon the sill once again.

I stretch through the bars, toss bread crumbs to the sparrows.

Days have melded into weeks. My life remains forever juxtaposed between imminent disaster and a mundane structure of outward routine: an ample breakfast of pastries and eggs always come late in the morn; a light meal following two to three hours after, predecessor to an extravagant supper of the finest French cuisine served up in grandiose style, sparkling crystal goblets and all, during the hour of sunset. Missy and Yevgeny are the only servants I ever see, although ofttimes droves of other people can be heard shuffling to-and-fro just outside the door. Every third or fourth night, around eightish, Pierre arrives to extract his due from my body, and as long as I refrain from fighting much, he no longer resorts to the beatings, although sometimes—as if still relishing the bloody mire of conquest—he simply cannot seem to resist lashing my wrists about the bedpost before proceeding yet again in the throes of quasi-sadistic fantasy. Fortunately, Yevgeny always makes it a point to check in afterward to see if I am all right, and if need be, he cuts me loose.

The food is excellent, my new clothes of soft, fresh-pressed cotton and lightweight serge fit with scrupulously tailored perfection; the room is luxurious and kept warm on cool nights by advent of a large steam furnace that hums with steady abandon into the wee small hours. But still, the shower-tub Missy locks off after every use, nothing sharp or breakable is ever left anywhere about, and guarded pleadings for return of my mother's amethyst crystal have been met with stern denial, and finally the renewed threat of Pierre's leather switch. The door is always immediately locked whenever anyone departs, and my attempts at distracting Missy's attention for long enough to make a run for it have ever proven futile, for although not much my elder in years, she seems all the wiser to every fresh trick I happen to think up.

And not once, even as the days of spring stretch longer and lighter toward brightly dawning fringes of summer, have I been allowed to leave the room, even under guard, and venture outside.

Today the sun is blazing, the air heady with the scent of newly sprouted lilacs. Which only seems to spur on more bleated, hungry, gulping little beaks.

I stretch through the bars, toss bread crumbs to the pigeons.

I have been given dozens of Russian and English books, including Dostoevsky's *Crime and Punishment,* in which yesterday I was able to pick up where I had left off so long ago in Uncle Petya's study during the days just before Easter. First, Pierre casually left off a couple of boxed sets of volumes one night, without any inquiry as to the extent of my ability to read. Now, every few days, Missy brings another large basketful of classics from his library.

Soft linen cloths have been provided me for cleaning my piccolo, and every day, for hours, I play *études* by Debussy, concertos by Quantz—and Massenet's wondrous *Meditation*, every note always piercing unrequited longing for the sound of my cousin Nikolai's voice through the shattered core of my heart. . . .

For I have been given no hope at all of freedom—save for Missy's continued hints of Pierre's fickleness, and his search begun amongst prospective supplicants for the highest price.

Outside the window, the spires of Moscow dance through a radiant splash of sunlight, the banded cupolas of St. Vasili's Cathedral yet startling up into the sky as they have for hundreds of years; as they will for hundreds of years more. Not since I was nine, when we traveled here with the Zhelanovs for a special performance of Tchaikovsky's works at the Moscow Conservatory, have I been to this strange city hovering upon the gilded fringe of the Orient. Scarce remembering the trip, now I long like a vagabond to traverse the streets, drink in the air, gaze at all the unfamiliar sights.

But the bars continue to prevent any tourism, escape, or daring freedom-flight. Only two screws have I loosened thus far, and those just barely. The others are hopeless.

Last night, Yevgeny told me the date: June twenty-fourth. *Two months.*

If I must stay entombed within this room much longer, I fear I shall go mad. . . .

Swallowing hard, I stretch out to the sill again, toss bread crumbs to more sparrows.

* * *

I *have* gone mad.

In the beginning, it was naught but a mere cloud of the imagination, the barest wedge of silver light peeking through the panes. And now, it—she—hovers before the window, yards of lanky tresses cascading to the floor in a honey-golden wreath, her slender nymphet's form draped in a blanket of sun-washed robes. Howling wind crashes about her; thunderbolts shimmer through the air; the sound of water courses through a flood of rapids, roaring far above my head.

Oh, God—no more dreams! Please—no more disjointed, terrifying dreams . . . .

"I am not a dream, Sasha."

I slap both hands across my eyes and start muttering prayers to the stars, God, Christ, Buddha, the Virgin, Saint Georgi, and to any and every other possible phantasm in the universe for the spell to *stop* . . . but when I look up, she is still there, insisting: "I am not a dream—"

"Get out! Leave me be, whoever, whatever you are!" Scrambling out from bed, I stumble for the door, near wrenching apart the knob while shaking it up and down in its wooden frame. "Missy, Yevgeny Ivanovich—*please!"* I scream. "Someone come and let me out of here!"

"They cannot hear you from our distance, Sasha."

"Dear God in Heaven—how do you know my name? Who, *what* are you? Hey! No, let go of me!"

My mind goes dead blank.

Her hand is white fire.

The blur becomes the old, familiar room: framed in the corner, the window seat still faces the house's crusty eastern edge. Piled stacks of ratty-edged papers and notebooks filled with orchestrations litter the oversized desk; Uncle Ned's treatise about the power of numbers, with several markers in it, has been tossed upside down upon a heap of old clothes stuffed into a basket on the floor. My flute, minus its footjoint, lies tucked carelessly within rumpled folds of the fur throw strewn across the bed.

Wearing my own clothes, I am in my own room, grasping a hand of white fire, listening to a soft purr that settles about my head, murmuring: "Sasha, you know who I am."

Despite the fearful striving to catch my breath, at last I cannot help but step back and stare in awe at the sight of her face.

Perhaps once, perhaps twice in a lifetime does one ever happen upon such a woman. Oh, there are beautiful women: primped and posed, demure grins and sultry winks aptly beckoning past veiled efforts spent rendering plain features unto fairness. But this woman: hollow of cheekbone, exquisite of profile, and poised of a regal, haughty grace—with eyes like dewdrops of amber fire and the smile of a wicked angel—this woman is every man's fantasy . . . Godiva and, Lord forgive me, the Blessed Virgin melded together as one! This woman could cause a collision at a railway junction, on the streetcar bridges, at the corner of the busiest Petersburg prospekt: cabs, harnesses, and neighing horses all piled one upon another in a tangled heap of scrap—while the drivers, stunned and mopping brows with their caps, stare gaping past befuddled grins at her poetic footsteps prancing down the quay. . . .

I seize her hand: cool as dawn's breath. "M-My God!" I stammer out. *"Melissa?"*

"Yes, my little dove." She kisses my cheek through the gulf of time, as if naught but a bedroom door has ever left us separate. "Yes, my darling, my cherished angel Sasha. I am your mother."

Indeed, this woman is none other than Melissa Devon-Tyler, clad now as in all the treasured picturegraphs: curled honey ringlets gleaming about the crown of her head, a mass of willowy braids caught within a long spun-golden net. Her dark taffeta gown sets off sheer lace sleeves, a round rose-petal bustle tucked demurely into the small of her back. Her bosom, faintly swollen, pales beneath double strands of sparkling blue sapphires and tiny river pearls. And her gaze: one of such profound, aching love, the hurt sears straight into my knees. "Melissa!" I gasp out. "I mean—pardon me, M-Mother! What—when—how?"

"Shhh!" With an impish grin, she presses a finger to her lips, whispering: "We shall play a surprise on your papa! Oh, he will be so thrilled."

"Father!" I shout to the door, grasping up her fingers within my own. "You must hurry up here to see this!"

"Oh, no, Sasha—you mustn't tell Misha yet. You and your papa yet have much to share. In the way of redemption, time is of such essence . . . oh, my poor darling—how I have missed your life! How I have yearned to hold you in my arms and kiss away every hurt, but you must try to remember, and understand current impetus: ofttimes, we must sacrifice the all for the one, then the one for the all."

"Sacrifice? Impetus?"

"Behold a virgin shall conceive!" she goes on breathlessly. "And shall bear a son . . . except a man be born again, he shall not enter the kingdom of heaven . . . behold the I Am, which becomes I Am That . . . which becomes I Am That I Am. . . ."

"Wait—you speak in naught but riddles!"

She touches my face, her smile wet with tears. "Ponder upon my words, Sasha," she murmurs fervently. "Wait until the triangle forms, whence understanding comes."

"Melissa—Mother—such words make no sense!" I back away, shaking my head in confusion, chills flashing up and down my spine in an eerie, fearful rush. "Father!" I gasp out hoarsely. *He must come up and explain this! Did she truly die when I was born—or was that the dream? Or is this? Which is the illusion? And which is reality?* Once more I lunge with a surge of desperation at the doorknob, shouting: "Father, please God! Come upstairs!"

The door flies open—not out to the hallway, nor the familiar yellow glint of lamplight peeking beneath the crack of Father's study door, but unto a concave, blackened sky laced across the entire arc of time with thousands of glittering, star-like flames. . . .

"You will brave the threshold presently, my darling."

I whirl around, screaming: "Melissa!"

Only to see vast folds of the white robes engulfing her yet again, her long hair streaming in billowing waves to the floor. Blinking in prisms of feathery pink light, a golden triangle hovers in repeated flashes above her head. And then, past the grip of my outstretched arms, her image vanishes into a spinning speck of dust.

Moaning, I crouch back against the door, cover my head with both hands, and slide down to my haunches upon the floor.

Bare walls of emerald marble leer back through shadowy confines of the moonlight. The door remains shut, locked; the window emerges again encased in its menacing frame of iron bars, the pane raised scarce a fist's width open, gauzy curtains fluttering back and forth against whispers of the summer breeze.

It is three A.M.—*and madness, naught but madness!* Shivering in my nightshirt, I crouch huddled down upon the floor, going mad in Sheremetev's palace. . . .

* * *

At breakfast, Missy brings a child with her.

"Now, ye sit down there, an' I won't have no actin' up!" she yells crossly at the little girl—who crouches, whimpering, into a corner. "An' ye leave him alone, too," she adds, pointing over at me.

"Is she yours?" I ask, amazed. Hardly more than a child herself, Missy scarce seems old enough to have one of her own. "How old is she?"

Shrugging off my question, Missy says: "We heard ye bangin' on the door agin' last night." With a pursed frown, she hoists the silver-domed breakfast tray up on the table. "What was it, 'nother nightmare?"

The new promise of this summer's morn, its fresh dewy scent so enthralling bare moments ago at the window, snaps back abruptly into the harsh reality of truth and imprisonment. "What do you want?" I retort, bristling, once again pressing both thumbs to my eyes, weary from the lack of sleep. "A vivid depiction of my dream? So you and Yevgeny can gloat about my secret terrors?"

Seizing the dome-cover from the tray, Missy slams it onto the floor with a furious bang, shouting: "Fie on it, Red! Now ye know there's no truth te such as that."

In response, I glare away. The sight of the little girl, peeking warily up at me through a tangled mess of black curls, softens the bitterness of my mood. "How old is she?" I ask again.

"Four and a half," Missy snaps reluctantly.

Fist now dripping with saliva and crammed into her mouth, the child stares back with widened violet eyes—and not for a moment does her gaze waver, the spell of fascination apparently having been inspired by my piccolo.

Snatching it from my pocket, I play a quick scale. "You like that?" Grinning, I crouch down and crook my finger, urging her over.

"Don't encourage her!" Missy yells, fists flying past all patience to her hips.

"And why not? I don't bite. Contrary to what you seem to think."

"I never said that ye bite."

"No, but you certainly act like it. All the time."

"Humph! An' how do ye think ye act?" Missy bursts out, waving an accusatory fork toward my face. "No matter what I do, ye don't like it. Every day, I try te set this food up with fancy glasses and fresh cloth napkins, so yer meals'll be pleasin' te ye. Every eve, I make sure the bathwater's pipin' hot and that ye always git plenty of it, cause showerin' seems te be yer high pleasure in life. An' I keep bringin' ye more heavy basketloads full o' books from the library room, but do ye ever give a thought te once in a while sayin' 'thank ye?' Oh, no, not ye—ye whinin' little leech! Ye jest sit in that chair an' mope an' pout worse each an' every time I come in here, always glarin' at me like I was the most vermin-plagued sight ye'd ever set eyes on!"

At last she stops, shaking and breathless, her voice closing in upon a sob, her mouth trembling, a tiny fringe of perspiration glistening across her upper lip.

As she wipes at it with the back of her hand, I gape at her, stunned.

Then, to my continued astonishment, she whirls away from me, hunches her shoulders, and starts dabbing at her eyes with a handkerchief.

The little girl, sensing the dower shift in mood, lets out a appropriate bawling wail.

"An' now look at what ye've done!" Missy storms on. Blinking past more angry tears, she rushes over to the child and scoops her up in her arms, glaring back as if I must be the most villainous cad on the planet.

Sighing, I slip the piccolo back into my pocket and hurry toward them. "Here, I'll take her," I murmur to Missy, reaching outward.

"Oh, no, ye don't!"

"You have work to do, yes?"

Darting away, she yanks her kerchief low to her brow, her eyes appraising me with wary suspicion.

"I promise I'll not bite. Let me hold her awhile."

At last, although still hesitant, Missy hands the child into my arms.

The little girl lets off whimpering as I start crooning nonsense into her ear. "So," I venture after a moment, "what is her name?"

Again Missy balks.

"Oh, come! You want to keep your true name from me, fine. But at least tell me hers."

"Humph! All right: Zhenya. Zhenya Grigoryevna."

"That's a beautiful name! Heavens, I don't know why you need be so frightened of telling me yours."

"Noticed ye won't tell me yers."

Avoiding her gaze, I nod instead toward the child. "Why did you never bring her with you before?"

"She was with her father."

"I scarce realized you were married."

"I'm not."

My ears twinge scarlet.

"Oh, an' jest what are ye so tweaked about?" Missy snaps, rolling her eyes. "Never seen a woman with a bastard child before?"

Turning in a huff, she starts making an overt, noisy show of setting out the breakfast tableware.

Zhenya looks upward with a shy grin and starts mumbling as I gently swing her back and forth and turn us around in playful circles. Such a wondrous, profound relief it is to nestle my head in close to hers—to hold, to cradle in my arms someone who merely wants to hold me back with naught but a child's desire, wholesome and unmenacing. "She's a lovely little girl," I say to Missy with genuine admiration.

"Well." Smoothing her rough work-worn hands over the folds of her apron, Missy lets out a wistful sigh. "S'pose matters could be worse," she says, lifting the covers from the steaming breakfast dishes and casting me a somber sidelong glance. "At least the poor babe escaped bein' born with the mark."

So accustomed have I become to the daily sight of Missy that the birthmark, once having seemed so hideous with its purple gash marring her upper lip, now rarely catches my attention. "You know," I tell her, "you could actually be quite pretty if you'd use some of that face-paint to blot out the mark a bit."

"Humph!" Her lips curl into a sarcastic sneer, and she rasps out: "Shut up! Will ye?"

I bite back my ready retort, but still cannot help returning her glare—after all, my observations are not entirely unfounded. With little else to do, I watch the woman all the time behind her back, make my scrutinies when she is unaware. Like her daughter, she has the loveliest violet-colored eyes. And when calmer, a glow like the ripened sod of fresh-plowed earth after a new spring rain—not wholly unattractive. Even to me. "Well," I go on with a burst of emotion escaping my voice, "you would be pretty if you'd simply put a bit of effort into it. And would help immensely if you'd stop carrying on like a nagging fishwife all the time."

"Me? Ha! *Ye* are the one who nags te no end!"

"Because you're keeping me prisoner here! Or have you entirely forgotten that circumstance?"

"I am not keepin' ye prisoner, Pierre is!"

"And you do his bidding, yes? So what difference is there? You are keeping me prisoner just as much as he is—"

"I am not!"

"Yes, you are!"

We stare each other down again across more trembling, white-hot space.

At last, biting her lip, Missy looks pointedly away.

"You—you care!" I find myself stammering out to my own astonishment. "Lord be Praised—I think you care about me! Don't you?"

Her face blushes into crimson fire. "Ha! Men!" she chokes out with a forced laugh. "Always full o' themselves and harebrained idiot ideas. . . ."

"I think you positively detest keeping me prisoner like this!" I shout back. "And that Pierre's actions appall you so that you might be persuaded to help me escape!"

Cursing me wordlessly, Missy whirls around and scoops Zhenya back out of my arms. "Sit down and eat yer breakfast!" she commands harshly, pointing.

Instead, I follow her over to the armchair, imploring for help while she flings off my clasped hands with a stinging whack. "I could pay you, Missy!" I go on nonetheless. "Honestly, I could! I have a tidy stash of rubles sitting in a bank account in Petersburg."

"I can't do that!"

"And why not?" Collapsing upon my knees before the chair as she sits down, I grasp up the hem of her apron, burying my face into its roughened burlap folds. "Missy, help me get out of here, I beg you, I know you could, I know you want to! Please!"

"No! Now, will ye stop it? By the devil's arse!" Her sigh hangs heavily in the air. "For love o' the Saints, Red!" she cries out gruffly. "Don't ye understand? Pierre'd have our hides if I helped ye try te escape."

I had neglected to think of that. Mournfully, I look away, and start patting my hand aimlessly over Zhenya's long black curls.

"An' is not only fear o' his wrath," Missy goes on in a hushed voice. "Me and Yevgeny, we owe Pierre. Don't ye have any idea what happens to souls born like I am?"

I shake my head, confused. "What do you mean?"

"The mark, Red." Missy points to her face—and begins to relate how, from their tiny village near Smolensk, she and Yevgeny were hounded out, soon after her birth, with their widowed mother—from town to town the three of them drifting, never staying long, forever hungry, barely clothed, always deprived of acceptance. All solely on account of the birthmark.

The tale is sad, but not surprising. Superstition runs rampant amongst the country peasants. Other rumors have I heard of children born with marks, in some regions left in baskets to flow down the rivers to an icy death, or worse yet, burned alive in stoves on account of even the tiniest facial scar, sacrifices to the ungodly devil of ignorance.

"Mother passed on when Yevgeny was eight, and I was four," Missy concludes, rocking Zhenya back and forth in her lap, her voice tinged with sadness. "Yevgeny Ivanovich may not look like he's got any wits about him most o' the time, but believe me, he does. He managed, at that age, te git us both here te Moscow on the train, knowin' it was only in the city that we'd ever survive. The Saints smiled upon us. One o' Pierre's maids took us in. Both strong, we both worked, even then. Pierre agreed we could stay on in the house if we'd earn our way. And so we have. Ever since."

After a long moment, I search out her gaze. "I would have to say that such a story makes me feel quite fortunate," I admit. "Despite present circumstance."

Shyly, Missy's hand slides across Zhenya's shoulders to mine, and she grasps my fingers up in a roughened squeeze. "Breakfast is gittin' cold, Red," she says.

I run a final fond tug through Zhenya's curls and laugh—the first time, it seems, that I have laughed in the longest silence of forever—watching with delight as the child's groping fingers impatiently push away my own. Again the little girl reaches in fascination for my piccolo. "Can you bring her with you the next time you come?" I implore Missy earnestly. "I tell you, the sight of your little Zhenya is a salve to my weary heart."

Missy smiles wistfully, her glance marked with some surprise. "All right," she murmurs, nodding, her expression alighting upon me with a tender softness. "I think I will."

* * *

Twirl me into hurricane, hurl me into storm,
Suck me into craving, spawn me into warm,
So warm . . . .

"You kissed me back, Piccolo!" Pierre exclaims with a gloating laugh, wrenching himself upward triumphantly on his elbows.

Staring at him aghast, I feel my cheeks color in a blaze of purple and start shaking back and forth my head.

"Admit it—you kissed me back!"

"I did not!" Slapping at him, I heave across the bed.

He seizes my arm, insisting: "And I think you want more."

"I do not!"

"I think you want much, *much* more!"

"Nooo!"

The struggle is futile, my strength dwarfed against the powerfully trained muscles behind his grip, my cold resistance squaring off against a much more formidable enemy—for the adversary is no longer only this flesh-peddling charlatan's desire, but the raw, uncharted hemispheres of my own. Dry swallows of secret yearnings again tempt away the ploy of constant struggle, sentencing my soul to an angst of shame against his insistent prodding, his carefully engineered caresses, his constant enticements at prying open my mouth, ever clamped so tightly shut—*oh, God! If only I was not always so damned hungry. . . .*

"Ahh," Pierre croons, panting with satisfaction, a beady trickle of saliva webbing out between his lips and mine. "So. Little Piccolo does not find his master so abhorrent after all."

"Let me go! You bloody-fucking—"

His hand flashes upward, sting of the readied blow wilting off into thin imaginings of the air—for instead, he pulls me breathlessly up to him yet again.

"Ilarion Pavlovich, stop!"

His lips barely graze mine.

"Ilarion Pavlovich, don't!"

And press a little firmer.

"Ilarion Pavlovich—"

And firmer . . .

"Nooo!" I shout. "Please—for the love of God!"

As I tear away, Pierre bursts into laughter, his watery eyes twinkling merrily beneath their lazy, half-closed lids. With a quick snatch of my wrist, he foils yet another plunging escape attempt, his hot palms smoothing with fondling caresses across my bare shoulders, his moans grating tirelessly on and on: "Give into your lust, my love. Succumb to those shivers of desire—for me, yes, little one? *N'est-ce pas?"*

"Ha! F-Flatter yourself if you must!"

"Flatter myself? Oh, *do* I?" Again he reverts into French, a habit he has cultivated of late during our encounters, despite my stoic defiance of always answering in Russian. "Ha! How my little Piccolo loves to play his games." He catches my eye with a knowing wink. "Games with words, with names," he goes on sarcastically. "Games with languages:

English, French, Italian. Always my clever little fire-headed gem plays the pretender, acting as if he scarce understands, when he does; acting as if entirely daft of all the tricky foreign words. Naive little fool! Think I know not what a prize you truly are? You, not I, are the one drowning in a mire of delusion. Ha! And you think I'm blind to your passionate kisses masking such hot-blooded anguish—oh, you don't believe me? Here, allow me to show you."

His hand swipes downward, fingers wrapping firmly around a rock-hard penis.

Mine.

"Goddamn you to the bleeding devil!" I rasp out, shoving him. *"Let go!"*

"Oh, no! You see, darling—contrary to what you were beginning to believe, thinking me naught but a selfish, gluttonous old brute bent only upon sating myself with your tender little ass—contrary to what you were beginning to conclude about this entire situation, I truly had much more in mind! Something closer to—oh, how shall we say? A tutorial relationship—ahh, yes! And I see such would suit your liking also, *n'est-ce pas?* Oh, stop pushing at me so—admit that you like it! Admit it! You see, darling—with you I have only just begun. . . ."

"Dammit, *stop!"*

But he pushes on top of me, burying his face into my chest, his lips brushing with prodding insistence against every inch of my skin . . . his tongue gliding ever so softly over each of my nipples . . . .

"Ilarion Pavlovich!"

. . . warm mouth opening, closing . . . wet kisses slathering all the way down my belly . . . .

Oh, God!

. . . and pressing down between my legs . . . moistness, firmness, hotness . . . *madness!* . . . sucking down into prickly hairs of the scrotum . . . slowly licking back up the quivering shaft of my penis . . . .

Slamming shut my eyes, I rake ferocious fingers into frayed strands of his hair, choking out: "Fuck you to bloody-burning hell, Ilarion Pavlovich Sheremetev! *G-Goddamn you . . . ."*

* * *

Flames . . . black wood . . . hot sparks . . . red glowing cinders chafing twixt a shadowed play of billowy clouds caught in the light of a Hallowmas moon . . . .

"Heretics!" the rioters yell, their swarm of torches blazing at the foot of the mound. "By the Blessed Virgin, by Saint Vladimir, deliver us! Save us from the likes o' bloody Sodomite heretics. . . ."

Wild rantings and fervent prayers cap scores more angry epithets curdling forth on a chanting, frenzied wave: "Naught but bloody witch-mongers, they are! Blessed God, Saint Georgi have mercy! Save us from devil-feeder Sodomite heretics! . . ."

Heretics . . . echoes of the word pound without mercy into my aching skull, the rows of faces descending as if from a grisly, hellish dream: swarthy features, bulging eyes, unkempt beards and long straggling hair, blackened soot, ratty field grime, the stench of musty layers and days of unwashed filth, ragged kaftans bound with rope and fringed pieces of cotton twine, gold-flecked eyes catching tiny pinions from the flames, blank stares menacing savagely all around through a glassy wall of hysteria. . . .

Flames begin licking at my toes.

"Nooo!" I try to wrench away, but the ropes hold fast, secured tautly about my shoulders, ankles, and hips—my arms lashed behind the tall wooden tower of a stake . . .

I thrust my hands backward, stabbing, gripping for something, anything—and come up with *another* pair of hands.

His hands.

Love . . . oh, ancient. So hollow-holding in your arms forever and evermore—*oh, God, so real* . . . love like a wash of light, the purest lilting song transposed across all measures of earth, water, fire, air—and even time itself. Love of the aeons . . . love of the hundred-hundred lifetimes . . . love . . . *oh, my love . . . my one and only twin-bound, pledged-ray soul-love . . . .*

"Close your mind to the shouting, Sasha!" he calls back hoarsely. "Concentrate on the mantra!"

"The mantra?" Past the crowd's heaving roar, I can scarce detect his words.

"Listen to me!" he shouts on. *"Concentrate* on the mantra!"

"But they will kill us!"

"Sasha, the mantra is our only hope now: *Nurture me with longing, kindle me with tears; I will love you always . . . in a hundred-hundred years . . . ."*

"But the flames!" I scream, wrenching backward. "My feet!"

"Sashenka, pay the flames no heed! Simply say the mantra with me!"

"But we are going to die!"

"There is no death!"

"Christ in Heaven!" I sob. "How I so want to believe that!"

"Then say the mantra with me, damn you! *Nurture me with longing—"*

"N-Nurture me with longing—"

"Kindle me with tears—"

"I—I will love you always—"

"In a hundred-hundred years . . . ."

His fingers crush mine desperately; the flames whirl up around us as he shouts on and on: "Concentrate on the mantra, only the mantra! . . . "

Shuddering away into the fiery sieve of pain, my voice seeks his, shaken and sobbing: "It matters naught which was foresaid! I love *only* you . . . forever and evermore. . . ."

The wall of flame spews upward.

Thundering and victorious, shouts of the crowd ring out in righteous triumph far above our heads: "Heretics! Sodomites and heretics! . . ."

* * *

"Oh, God, oh, my God . . . *nooo!"* Screaming in agony, I tear against the blistering pull of the ropes: *no more fiery, searing flames . . . God, please! I do not want to be burned alive! . . .*

"Will ye jest hold still fer one bloody second!" shouts Yevgeny, looming above me with his knife.

"Jesus Christ!" Again I scream.

"Akkh! Ye looney little snivelin' bastard! Will ye jest shut up and quit blastin' my eardrums all te hell? By the Blessed Saints—the way ye carry on all the time, it's past belief!"

His knife slashes, cutting loose the bindings strapping my wrists to the footrest of the bed.

I stare up at him in shock. As he sheathes his knife, a guilty expression overtakes his squinty-eyed face. Still fully clothed, apparently he has gotten in quite late—and drunk—from his Saturday night rounds of carousing at the gaming houses and taverns.

"Well!" he mutters out sheepishly, glancing down toward the silken fragments of the sash now littering the floor. "Stop lookin' at me like I was some criminal lowlife, already! Ye're lucky I even come in here te cut ye loose at all, ye whinin' little fag!"

Muttering angry curses under his breath, he stomps back out of the room.

I scavenge across the bedside table and knock several half-open books onto the floor before coming up at last with my pocket watch in violently shaking hands: two o'clock in the morning.

The stake, the fire: naught but a dream!

But then—*how* so real?

And that other stake, the man tied behind me: not anyone I can recognize, nor have ever known, but—*Lord in Heaven!* Such love . . . an aching, tormented memory . . .

Oh, it was love, all right.

Just like the Melissa dream.

"Oh, God!" Seizing a pillow, I smother it over my head, but no matter how tightly I squeeze shut my eyes, fresh images of the furious crowd start blazing forth anew. Caught against the fading echoes of Yevgeny's footsteps pounding down the hall, my voice scrapes pitifully into depths of the broken night: "Madness! Sheremetev's palace . . . Moscow . . . Sheremetev's palace . . . and naught but utter *madness!* . . ."

* * *

Through the window bars, I stare down at glimmering flickers of the gaslamps. The police are tearing down a banner, arresting yet another group of demonstrators, the shouts of "Death to the Tsar!" and "All power to the Workers' Soviets!" hammering high into the air. Scores of nightsticks ram into dulling thuds of flesh; shots blast out and two bodies stagger, falling limply, while wary bands of onlookers scatter hurriedly away. At last, upon a wave of ruthless jabs and pounding blows, several defiant, cursing men are hounded at bayonet point into the paddy wagon.

I wonder if their fate will prove any worse than mine.

"So—I assume this is goodbye?" I snap, clammy fists clenched to my sides as I once more glare over at Missy.

The vanity shelves slam shut. Eyes fastened rigidly before her, she replies without emotion: "Make sure te take yer piccolo. And yer watch."

I cross my arms. "And my amethyst crystal?"

Missy shakes her head.

"Blast him! He cannot take that from me, he *cannot!*"

She does not answer.

"How can you do this?" I go on, bounding across the room toward her in a breathless, panting rush. "How can you see this travesty clear unto its ugly, despicable head? How can you simply stand aside and allow him to *sell* me?"

"Back off, Red!" Yanking out the silver-plated tray, still left over from supper, she holds it out across her apron, a ready shield.

"And I thought you were my friend!"

Looking sharply away, Missy jams the keys into the vanity lock with furious, stabbing motions, saying not a word. Still averting her gaze, she hands over my watch and the piccolo, saying: "Put 'em in yer boot."

"Missy, *please!*"

"I said put 'em in yer boot!"

Dejectedly, I do so—and throw myself in a heave upon the bed, burying my head within my arms.

Only yesterday afternoon, she and Zhenya were both so happy. For over a month now, near every time she has come during the day, Missy has always brought along her little Zhenya, a laughing mite-sized savior to my heart, a gentle boon to my long spans of loneliness and bouts of waning sanity. And yesterday after lunch, the two of them brought up a bucket of blueberry fruit-ice from one of the street vendors down below, blessed solace for us all against the continuing swelter of languid August heat. We made half a dozen ice cones in sticky rolled-up pastries, laughed our heads off by trying to outdo each other's outrageous stories . . . so comforting it was, the laughter, the gaiety. I almost felt peaceful, content. . . .

In these past four months, time has flown and yet stood still. Easter, the Maytide festivals—the wondrous violet quiescence of the Petersburg White Nights—all have continued a million aeons away in far seas of a distant outside world—while unbeknownst to anyone, Sheremetev has forced me to become his whore. In the interim hours, having been foiled to blank frustration's end at any physical escape, I have tried my utmost to build a psychic haven—by tearing in one heedless rush after another through so many books that now I suffer from a constant straining squint, forever induced to hold the pages yet closer and closer; by playing the piccolo until my fingers, aching so, can no longer press the keys—and by becoming a fast friend to this woman, and ready twaddling playmate to her little girl. None of which now seems to matter for naught.

Still, she is fully prepared to do her duty and deliver me over to the wolves.

I was beginning to suspect that something like this was about to occur. Near unto two weeks has it been. Apparently, the challenge has diminished, the taming of my spirit no longer holding such a heady lure—for Pierre has not returned, not once since that awful night after backing me straight into seduction's corner and forcing quick surrender to his ingenious plyings with my body's own treacherous whims.

No flowing silken robe has been provided me against shame's nakedness tonight. Instead, I have been ordered into much more theatrical prisoner's garb: light gauzy trousers, a belted tunic adorned with pearly rows of buttons and a ridiculously oversized pair of blousoned sleeves. And Missy has taken extraordinary care in making me up with more than twice the usual amount of face-paint, glimmers of cherry-rouge dabbed with painstaking skill and filling out my lips; svelte lines of darkened kohl drawn in feathery almond shapes, accentuating the doe-look of my eyes—a shameful and foolish masquerade, trappings fit for none better than a slave-hand eunuch on the stage-set of *Arabian Nights!*

And in these four months, they have repeatedly refused me the services of a barber, no matter how desperately I have implored. Its length now thwarting my original intent of facial subterfuge—longer than even during that awful night when I was thirteen and Father mistook me for his ghostly Melissa in the hall—the hair hangs in an unkempt mass straight to my shoulders, marking my resemblance to a girl more than ever.

"Missy, I am begging you! Don't turn me over to Sheremetev and the others!" Shoving off from the bed, I attempt to corner her one more time, following behind and snatching at her apron strings, pleading my heart out until she whirls angrily around, shouting: "Oh, fer the Lord's bloody sake! Will ye jest *shut up?"*

Then we both jump back, startled, as the door bangs wide open.

Peering into the room with a preoccupied frown, a dark-haired, swarthy-featured man nods and informs us: "Five minutes."

Upon which the door abruptly slams shut again.

Reddening in a flush of embarrassment, Missy steals the barest peek in my direction before swiping the face-paint tray up under her arm.

"That—that was Zhenya's father!" I blurt out in amazement.

Turning back upon me in lividly choked fury, she yells: "So?"

Always I had assumed the man to be some distantly mired phantom in the woman's saddened past, not tangible, not visible—not alive—and definitely, not here. "F-For love of the Saints!" I stammer out in self-righteous indignation. "Why doesn't the thieving cad marry you?"

"'Cause he can't!"

"And why not?"

"What business is it o' yers, Red?"

"Were Zhenya my child, I'd marry you!"

Missy's blush deepens effusively into her cheeks as she stares back at me in shock. "Ha! I suspect ye would!" she then rasps out, rolling her eyes, shaking her head as if wholly unable to believe her ears.

"Indeed, I would!" I shout on. "And you know why? Because where I come from, we happen to possess some semblance of honor!"

At this, she bursts into a peal of stunned laughter.

"What is so blessed funny?"

"Ye! And yer high-minded ideals!"

With determination, I snatch onto her arm, insisting: "Help me get out of here, and I *will* marry you—here, tonight, anywhere you want in Moscow."

"Ye're only fifteen!"

"Sixteen in two weeks!"

"Oh, an' that is what ye truly want, Red? A wife an' child te care for, at age sixteen? Ha! I told ye before, and I'm tellin' ye agin': I am not helpin' ye te escape out o' here tonight! I have my job te do. We been all over this before, at least a dozen times! Now will ye quit harpin' at me so, and leave off it already? Hey, let go!"

Deflecting her angry palm, I bury my face into her shoulder, continuing to beg for mercy without pause, while she shouts on and on: *"No!"*

As she shoves me away once more, the door swings open yet again.

"They're almost ready." The swarthy man looks in with a point of his finger to Missy—but then, nudged on the shoulder, he turns to someone speaking to him just outside.

Again I clamp fiercely onto Missy, she still my sole hope from certain drowning death in hell's whorehouse quicksand—but the struggle is useless; she obviously has no intention of helping me at all now. In spite of that, I cannot keep myself from demanding in a high-pitched, childish squall: "J-Just one last thing, Missy—please! Tell me your name."

"Oh, Blessed Christ, Red!"

"Please! Tell me your *true* name."

Her eyes search mine mutely across the infinite gulf of space spread a bare hand's width between us—while from the doorway, the swarthy man loudly clears his throat.

"Lyubov," she whispers softly.

And her face becomes a question, waiting.

"Sasha," I whisper back.

"Goodbye, Sasha."

I shut my eyes, trembling in the scant breath of the moment as, with a tender, fleeting gentleness, she plants a kiss upon my cheek.

The swarthy man again clears his throat, a flush of irritation deepening into his tone this time. "And are you quite finished now, *Lyubov?"* he says to her sarcastically, spitting out both syllables with slow decisiveness as if he normally never calls her that, his lips curling upward in a darkly amused sneer.

Eyes blazing, she stares him down in hot defiance—but as she hurries for the door, her gaze remains riveted on his, his on hers—a hazy chord of passion and taut vehemence spawning out between them. And I can see that, despite everything—whatever it all has been about—he is still intimate with her, and she with him. . . .

Heart pounding in mortification, I fix my gaze down upon my quivering hands.

Which ropes instantly lash around, the man having crossed the room in two quick strides. "Let's go," he orders with a harsh tug, and I stumble after, protesting: "But I need the cane!"

As he drags me through the doorway, I search around for Missy—Lyubov—hoping for her to remind him about my leg, but it is no use. She is no longer anywhere to be seen.

Instead, save for the servants—groomsmen clad in peasant garb; stewards swathed in primped layers of emerald-velvet finery and hurrying to-and-fro with steaming bowls full of shellfish and crispy morsels of *pirozhki* spread out on gleaming silver trays—save for a smattering of servants, from end to long winding end, the hallway is literally teeming with whores.

Whores by the gallivating, risque dozens: men and women, boys and girls—many of the children scarce reaching to the height of my shoulders—all of them jostling about with one another gaily as if nothing is amiss, as if descent into such throes of physical degradation constitutes naught but the dull waning of ordinary routine. Without exception, all faces are painted up in varying degrees of gaudy eye-batting extravagance, everyone clothed in such a dazzling array of jewels, vibrant colors, and filmy flowing fabrics that the gathering resembles the promenade at a Petersburg Hallowmas costume ball.

Amongst them all, I would fit in perfectly—save for being dragged past with the ropes.

Stares turn in our direction, but few linger; fans swish lavishly; giggles rattle up the majestic rose-hued marble encasements of the walls. Shrieks of gossips echo in piercings of triumphant glee high toward ivory-crested paintings in the palace's rounded ceiling domes, and from a widened alcove where a large group of women—or rather, *men* dressed as women—huddle amidst taut whisperings of soft falsetto voices, corks blow simultaneously off several bottles of champagne.

"My God—what *is* all this?" I gasp out, wide-eyed.

Noting my struggle with the limp, the swarthy man slows his pace and crooks his hand up under my arm, saying with a wistful shake of his head: "Believe me, lad—is a far better fate for them all. No life is it to wish for, the putrid stench of the factories. The certain death of the mines."

"You mean—all these people are here *willingly?"*

He gives no answer; scarce has to.

The fact is obvious.

At some distance from the bulk of the crowd, we halt before a grand set of amber-inlaid double-doors. "I am sorry we have to do this," the man then murmurs beneath his breath into my ear—all the sarcasm, the menacing glower of his prior demeanor wholly cast off as if naught but a carefully construed act. "Every so often, Pierre sets his sights on one like you," he goes on ruefully. "Pity about your fetching looks. Not to my liking, none of this is, forcing one into a such a life against his will. . . ."

"Then, stop now!" I implore him, grasping unto desperation for this last vague semblance of a new ally—my fingers crushing into his hands, eyes lancing for his eyes.

"No," he retorts sharply. "Business is business."

His hand moves toward the knob.

"Wait!" I cry, clamping onto his wrist—and catching in that same stunned instant sight of the pince-nez tucked within his pocket—accessory of an educated man, who reads. Acutely obvious it is now, his difference from the others, the absence of the peasant slur in his speech, the subtly tailored cut of his clerk-like clothes.

"No help for it, lad—Pierre's orders are his orders. We have no choice."

"Wait a moment—we? Who the hell is *we?"*

The latch clicks open with sharp emphasis beneath his fingers. "The Revolution!" he whispers back in a breathless rush.

Then the door swings wide open, and he hurries me into the room, his passionate revelation retreating into a blank-eyed stare of silence.

"Well, well!" exclaims Pierre, grinning with satisfaction, the ball of the leather switch snapping back and forth lazily in his open palm. After making a critically heightened survey of my flushed face, he declares: "Superb! Tell Missy her skill with the pencils truly does exceed all admirability."

Replying with only a stiffened nod, the swarthy man remains mute behind me.

In a booming voice, Pierre continues: "As you see, gentlemen, when I promise a prize, I exceed even my own expectations! And deliver naught but the very halo of perfection."

He steps away and drapes his hand out in a rolling motion toward the two of us, making an exaggerated bow of presentation.

Three elegantly-suited men, seated behind a wide table at the window, stare in weighty perusal.

"Bidding starts at one-five," Pierre then announces.

"You bloody-fucking turd of a cow's ass!" I shout out—before the hand, from behind, clamps over my mouth.

"As you can see, he is quite a spirited one!" Overcome with a round of chuckles, Pierre fishes his handkerchief from his upper waistcoat pocket and begins dabbing at his eyes. "But, observe." Again he approaches, rams his fist up under my chin, and nods at the swarthy man to let up on the restraint. "I daresay," Pierre babbles on giddily, "the proud lift of the head, the arresting Irish-Saxon features—as you can see, gentlemen, for his face alone, this one is a treasure indeed. *N'est-ce pas?"*

I struggle wrathfully, but Pierre's fist holds tight, jamming my lower teeth into the uppers, smothering me into a clinch of furious silence.

"In actuality, I had grown quite fond of this child," he continues on, staring straight into my eyes and saying pointedly: "Oh, you can be assured, gentlemen—he is quite aptly versed in the many accoutrements of love, and wildly spurred on by his own passions—ahh, yes! A little tiger in bed, this one, he is. In addition," Pierre adds—still clamping my chin, but glancing with a detached mercantile stare back to the group of men: "I consider this particular shade of hair to be at the highest premium, a rarity stemmed from the old Nordic bloodlines, and beauteous as a ripened henna of autumn leaves it is, as you can well see. A fine addition this one would make to any of your collections, gentlemen, *n'est-ce pas?* As to the incidentals: the boy is about fifteen, says his name is Khulinov, orphan of an English governess, who taught him well. I suspect him conversant in French as well as English, and possibly Italian. His training in music, probably by some charitable grandfatherly soul, is obvious; his mastery of the piccolo is impeccable, and he well knows the classics, along with the more popular works from our Russian masters. As we agreed, a prize I promised, and a prize I have delivered. As I said, gentlemen: bidding starts at one-five."

The second his grip lifts away, I scream: "The devil take you to the flaming depths of hell's bowels, Ilarion Pavlovich Sheremetev! You blood-sucking, piss-drinking, filthly bastard of a—"

Pierre's fingers snap; from behind, a wound-up kerchief gags in between my teeth. Tying the knots roughly behind my neck, the swarthy man growls out with profound irritation: "Dammit, shut up! You think this is going to help either of us any? Hold your tongue and keep still!"

Still sputtering dry curses against thick wads of the cloth, I shove my elbows back into his ribs, but he locks his arms around my chest and crushes me in a determined vise, while Pierre declares proudly to the group of men: "You see? I told you this one came with a hefty dose of passion—just like a steamy little race-colt he is, ha! Spirit, indeed."

"Far too much for me." With a curt nod, one of the men behind the table snatches up his cane and derby and strides off for the doorway.

"The money or the barbs, Larshinsky?" Pierre quips after him, laughing.

"Both!" Muttering back something about a preference for blonds in any case, the man fades off into the glittering hallway amongst the whores, the heavy doors of the room moaning back to their creaking close behind him.

"The injury to the boy's leg, Ilarion Pavlovich. You inflicted this yourself?"

It is the tall, thin man seated at the other end of the table who speaks, his Russian imbued with the barest trace of a foreign accent—although for the life of me, I cannot determine whether its exact source be German or English.

"Certainly not!" Pierre bellows, glowering at him, affronted. "I do not deny that proper punishment is meted unto my charges when justly earned, M'sieur. But you can hardly think me fool enough to mar valuable goods in such a dastardly manner! No, I assure you: the injury already plagued the boy when I first acquired him—a childhood accident, or some such folly. Was no doing of mine, nor of any of those in my employ."

"Very well, then I shall take him at one-five."

"Not so fast."

The other man at the table—short and balding, a succulent watery grin spreading across his face to reveal a mouthful of rotten, cigar-stained teeth—opens out a leather case and retrieves a fat wad of bound-up ruble bills, muttering in my direction: "One-five-five."

Regarding his own stack of bills with careful consideration, the tall man counters: "One-six."

Oh, God! I shut my eyes, praying with all my heart and soul for a miracle, for some deliverance from this ghastly nightmare, but God—again—remains unhearing and unsung, and the crazy language of the bidding builds on: *one-six-five . . . one-seven . . . .*

I struggle ferociously, but the swarthy man scarce allows me to breathe.

One-seven-five . . . one-eight . . . .

Staring across the room, I start to grow dizzy; at last begin to drink in the sweet tonic of variety laced across patterns of the draperies, a rose-hued feast for weary eyes after the singularity of wallowing emerald fixations strung across my one-roomed prison of these past four months. Through the window, specks of light beckon to my aching heart with visions of the far-off glimmering outlines of Moscow's onion-domed cathedrals. My gaze drifts numbly downward: on a sideboard table, a samovar—gilt-edged with painted rivers of snowy-white and china-blue penciled along its porcelain-inlayed sides—steams pleasantly, an arrangement of glassy tea-cups encircling it in a homey, inviting row. I wonder if it was Lyubov who set the table with such tidy care; I wonder about how these people can so easily continue with the bland domesticity of what they call their normal lives—while banishing a fellow soul to naught but certain death in some travesty of a whorehouse hell. And I wonder about the swarthy man, about his mysterious pince-nez and strange whisperings of revolution; I wonder about the tangled circumstances between him and Lyubov, between him and Sheremetev, between him and all the rest of the scattered fragments that I simply cannot piece together. And as my eyes continue to wander, I wonder about the endless teak inlays set with such painstaking craftsman's care into the alabaster walls of this room, showcased frames edged in hexagonal patterns and imbedded with scores of rounded agates and tiny slivers of jeweled amber, all riveting and stupendous. Even one of those dozens of panels would be worth the entirety of a year's cash crop on my father's farm . . . *goddamn Sheremetev! Goddamn him and his flagrant, stinking wealth . . . goddamn this whole whoring palace with its tainted opulence and filthy splendor. . . .*

"One-nine-five . . . two? Two! Shall we call it, then? Then, sold! To M'sieur Greifmann!"

After casting a mocking sigh of regret in my direction, Pierre bows toward the tall man with a flourish, announcing: "For two hundred thousand rubles!"

I gape at them both, stunned. Two hundred *thousand? Rubles? Mother of God!*

"All right," the swarthy man mutters with harsh warning into my ear. "There's not going to be any trouble for it, now."

The ropes lash around my ankles. . . .

No, sonuvabitch! Now I'll never get free—

. . . the hood wraps over my head. . . .

—Goddamn them! The trip from the palace would have been my only chance!

"Hold still, damn you!"

I cannot see! No eyeholes in the hood; I start ramming back into him with every ounce of my strength. . . .

"Well," I hear Pierre say, "prudence perhaps dictates administering a dose of chloroform in this case again."

"Nooo!" I scream, the sound droning through muffled wads of the gag.

"In truth, I would prefer to dispense with any tonics," the tall man tells Pierre.

"Nooo! Please don't!" I try to scream again.

"If you don't want the chloroform, hold still!" the swarthy man orders from behind.

With overwhelming reluctance, I force myself to do as he says.

Then, like a common sack of potatoes, he hoists me up over his shoulder and begins to carry me from the room . . . blood rushes into my head against the giddy hacking of Pierre's laughter echoing away in the background. Distant chatters flit back and forth from the profusion of whores still gathered in the hall; footsteps pound menacingly over floors, stairs, encasements of wood, malachite, and marble; doors swing open and slam shut one after another against the incessant barking of setters and the hunting hounds that rich men keep in tow for country sport—until finally, sounds of the street prevail. In desperation, I choke through the weave of the gag for some real breath of live outside air—to be assailed with the smell of horses, the sound of doors creaking open on squeaking hinges. The swarthy man dumps me onto the hard wooden bench of a closed-in carriage; doors slam shut, and upon a stiff fling of the reins, the driver's goadings to his steeds snap like sour notes into my ears.

And we start moving.

A hand inches up along my neck and attempts to loosen the folds of the hood slightly as I flinch away in revulsion. "Can you breathe?" It is the same voice, the stilted Russian of the tall, thin man.

I hesitate for a moment before deciding to nod *yes*—upon which I start wrenching my body back and forth, letting out another string of ferocious muffled curses.

"You might as well contain your excitement. I am only a messenger," the man replies.

Across from me, I hear him sigh in a bored tone and open out a newspaper.

Half-heaving myself from the seat, I try kicking out at him with both bound-up legs—and end up slamming my left ankle flat against the metal window-pull.

Shuddering with pain, I dig my nails into my palms, cursing him, cursing Sheremetev, cursing the folly, the utter blinded foolhardiness of hitting my bad leg. Teeth gritted, I cling for dear life onto sanity's last fading shreds, while all remaining strength slowly starts ebbing away drop by drop.

"Best sit back and enjoy the ride," the man tells me. "We'll arrive quite shortly."

And then what? Another walled-in, towering prison without air, trees, or sky? Another fate of groveling to some heavy-handed master's sickening, perverted whims?

Near in tears, I fight back myriads of visions floating in and out of my head in poignant snatches of fleeting memory: tall birch trees, the graceful wooden cupola of my father's house in Novgorod; the white majestic spires of St. Petersburg circling like lofty falcon's wings unto the silver-violet sky; eerie ruins of old Roman legacy at the tiny village of Penzance in Cornwall, where crashing waves of the Atlantic heave up in dancing abandon upon England's high-cliffed, mossy shores. The faces follow: Uncle Ned, Aunt Sophie, Anna, Nikolai, Father . . . *oh, God!* Never, never shall I visit any of my cherished places, see any of my beloved people, ever again . . . how foolish I was, bemoaning my father his austerity, pitying my plight with a crippled leg, thinking I had known despair. I was wrong—*oh, God! Terribly, horribly wrong . . . .*

The visions shatter into one stabbing piece as the carriage jolts to an abrupt halt.

The thin man opens the door. Clambering in like an ox, a grunting servant heaves me up roughly over his shoulder, his arms wrapping uncomfortably about the backs of my knees, his movements awkward and plodding. With effort, I attempt to keep my nose from banging into his back upon his every step. Apparently right on the heels of the tall man, he carries me off to the gates of my new prison.

But somehow, the sounds seem strange. Once we clear the door, tiny bells ring up a storm from carts whisking by on squeaky little wheels. We pass through to the shock of breathless gasps and startled utterances of women's voices wholly unused to such gruesome spectacle—for groups of people seem gathered, gawking as we pass by. In the distance, lids of cases continue snapping shut, echoes of old train travels ringing in my mind with the soft click of Father's tapestry-woven portmanteau. Then we seem to cross an unusually wide breadth of space, and my mind reels, juggling for answers: could this possibly be a lobby? In a hotel?

Sure enough, our destination is a modern elevator lift, creaking slowly up at least three floors.

The door to a room swings open scarce before the tall man knocks. Depositing me in an unceremonious heap upon the floor, the grunting servant stands stalling for his tip. Then the door slams shut, and low murmurs tread the air in accented voices—again German or English—until at last the crisply sounded exchange of paper money follows mutual murmurs of agreement.

Upon which the tall man seems to take his leave—while ominous, heavy footsteps pound in my direction.

With a searing slash, a knife ribbons through the ropes binding my feet and hands; urging me upward, insistent fingers loosen and then whip off the hood. I stare dumbly into the shock of light as nimble fingers reach behind and make quick work of the knotted gag, finally slipping its stifling folds away from my mouth.

After a moment of hesitation—and a groan of disgust—the silence shatters upon the quick-clip of a proper British accent and the English-spoken words: "Are you quite all right?"

Stepping backward, a stylishly-attired middle-aged gentleman starts looking me up and down.

My eyes focus at last; my jaw drops in shock; I shake my head up and down, back and forth, small gasps of emptiness spawning out from someplace where, long ago, there was once a voice. Both arms flung out wide, I then lunge after him in a full heaving charge, grappling up about his neck and near hurtling the both of us back onto the floor—while shouting out at the top of my lungs: "Oh, my God—*thank blessed Jesus God! Uncle Ned!*"

CHAPTER FOUR

Penance

Laughing, flinging out the reins, I shout: "Hurry, Sunnyrae—faster! Come, straight into the surf, now—take me back into the wash of heaven. Yaaa!"

Once more—as I shriek with delight—we charge into the crashing waters of the Atlantic Ocean.

"Oh, Sunnyrae, you are such a prize! As dear as my own little Jespa back home, do you hear?"

Shaking her head up and down as if with cognizant agreement, the mare whinnies heartily and nuzzles her snout toward my pockets as I slide from the saddle into the wet surf.

"Well! Do you think that deserves a sugar cube? Oh, I say!" I cry out, laughing, mimicking Uncle Ned. "By Jove, my little neighing pucker-lass—you deserve all remaining sugar cubes on earth!"

Much to the mare's whinnying approval, I snatch an entire handful from my pocket and let her feast upon the whole lot. Hanging onto the saddle horn, I steady my balance against her girth and stare off into the roaring waters meeting blue horizon.

My love affair with the sea began six summers ago, upon my first trip to Cornwall. Forever could I traipse up and down the spare, sandy beaches—basking in the sun, drinking in the wind, splashing through the dancing surf, old songs of jaunty seaman's tales echoing from every barge, pleasure craft, or fishing trawler seen skimming across the frothy span of blueness.

But never has such joy of salt air been more invigorating than now—each breath of it heady with the trembling of love's first kiss, each taste sparkling with a numbing glow like a draught of the finest French champagne. Oh, how blessed it is to ride free, to stand outdoors, to walk the air, to run the land unhindered! Forevermore will I gulp in every fleeting scent without cruel constraint, absolved of Pierre's hurtful, prying hands and those torturous iron bars.

Easing my cap low to my brow, I shade my spectacles with my hand and scan up and down the rugged coastline before gazing dreamily back out to sea again. Take a ship due west, and after the voyage of a lifetime, you will happen upon Newfoundland and the Gulf of St. Lawrence's snaking vein winding into French Canada. Follow your heart across forest lands of burgeoning frontier, head north, and find American Alaska, its wealth of pirating adventures luring toward the Klondike's tempting legends of stolen gold. Test the ice and your daring wit, your courage and your stamina, and set off with sleds and a dozen dogs across tundra fields toward the Bering Sea, beyond which blooms a vast empire called . . . Russia.

I repeat the precious word once, twice, what seems a thousand times; shut my eyes and bury my head—and my breaking heart—into Sunnyrae's mane.

"Sasha!"

The water, lapping in lazy waves about my bare feet, has become ice cold. I know it is time to go in, but I dare not. Not yet—for past Sunnyrae's head, I stare up to the precipice of the mossy bluff. Appearing no larger than a doll, Uncle Ned bounds to the ledge in his familiar impatient guise, hands cupped to his mouth as continues calling down my name.

In the rendering of which he always insists upon stressing the second syllable over the first, as if naught but some unutterable foreign anomaly. But to Uncle Ned, everything Russian is some strange foreign anomaly. Incredible it was, seeing him in Moscow; the man can scarce speak more than three or four words of the language!

"Sasha!"

"Yes! Sir?"

The waves crash, punctuating the awkward pause.

"Bring Sunnyrae in!"

"But—"

"I said bring her in! Time has come for us to talk."

His tone is adamant—and portends no more protestations.

Reluctantly, I remount the horse and head for the path to the steep incline up the bluff.

1903 it was, the last time I beheld this wonder of Cornwall. Four years.

The ocean, the charming little artist's town of Devonbury hugging the hills above the coast: both are just as I remember. Winnebar, the magnificent rambling country house boasting an incomparable ocean view, remains as I remember. But Uncle Ned is not as I remember.

For I am not as he remembers.

Never will I forget that first expression upon his face: withering revulsion. At the sight of his very own nephew—clad in pearly, swishing gauze, and dolled up with rouge and heavy face-paint. Long hair grazing my shoulders, I flung it back, anxiously, with trembling hands, my husky voice—an anomaly against the ruse of my girlish appearance if there ever was one!—coursing out past a wave of shudders and reassuring him, over and over, that it truly was me.

I know the reason. He expected to see the giggling twelve-year-old cherub again. Not some red-headed faggot whore—bearing such striking resemblance to his long-dead, ever-cherished younger sister, Melissa.

It scarce mattered, I told myself. Once I stripped off the clothes, rid myself of the trappings, he would be like old Uncle Ned again. So relieved was I at being rescued, I slept near unto the entire two days that it took us to reach Paris by train—ages, years it had seemed, since I had stowed away a decent night's sleep. By the time we boarded the ferry at Le Havre, I had procured decent Scottish woolens, a derby, and—far too embarrassed to venture into a barber's—a scissors. In the terminal water closet just before we boarded, I hacked off the hair, trimming it shorter than I ever have in all these four years. Then, bothered to wit's end by my pursed squint as I attempted in vain to read the newspaper—another blessed token of freedom, for books Pierre may have allowed me in abundance, but never a newspaper—all too aware of my continued struggle with the blurred lines of print, I purchased a pair of wire-rimmed spectacles in an apothecary shop when we stopped for the night in Southampton, and have been wearing them ever since.

However, none of my outer changes seem to have wrought any difference. Uncle Ned's tone continually remains gruff with irritation, his whole demeanor harsh, and not a thing I can do—no matter what it is, even if it is something he *tells* me to do!—meets with his approval.

In an attempt to prolong my escape from this 'talk' he keeps insisting we need to have, I drop Sunnyrae off at the stables, and much to the consternation of the stuttering stall-hand, rub her down myself, taking my sweet time with the whole operation, sorting out the tack and all.

"I say, upstairs!" I hear Uncle Ned call sharply, from far off, the moment I sneak through the downstairs side door back into the house.

Taking pains to avoid the servants while grumbling against the inevitable confrontation, I shrug off my new Norfolk jacket and lay it dutifully across my arm, smooth back my hair, and tighten my grip upon the brass-inlaid handle of my cane.

Uncle Ned maintains also his main residence at Plymouth in Devonshire, and a townhouse in London. Winnebar, only a country retreat, is near twice the size of Lissushka in Novgorod, and in lieu of my father's stern eye for sleek lines and elegant posturings, stands cluttered to the hilt with a profusion of mismatched bric-a-brac of every possible imaginable kind: garishly fringed sofa-chairs, tables draped with beads and scores of tapestry hangings, the floors strewn with boar rugs, overdone burgundy Persian carpets, and hunting prizes of fur coverlets. Several rugs lined with souvenir Indian-feathers muffle the many balconies' wiry wrought-iron facades. Oval mirror-glasses and framed oil paintings peeking past a half-dozen teakwood and paper-filigree oriental screens cover every wall from the side door entrance unto two floors upward, while black and cherry wood lacquer trays set upon every bureau overflow unto sheer riotous contagion with papers, pens, pencils, pieces of jade from the Orient, ivory keepsakes from Africa, and Aunt Mary's endless collections of prize-winning miniature thimbles from both Britain and America. About every one of the house's quaint, stuccoed archways beckon massive brass and porcelain Chinese urns, each containing pots full with palms, tropical rubber-plants, and feathery aspidistras waving through the salt-air breeze. Black and white, large and small, both busts and full-bodied statuettes of every Greek statesman, playwright, and philosopher history ever coughed up line the tops of bookshelves and mantles of the hearths, four visages alone of Socrates and at least two of Plato gracing the curve of the balustrade as, frowning with distaste, I weave amongst the conglomeration of scattered objects and make my way to the foot of the stairs.

"And good riddance to you, too!" I whisper sarcastically upon passing the last of the statues, sticking out my tongue.

I cannot thwart irreverence. It seems utter paradox, an exercise in senility itself, the thrusting of such Grecian stateliness in amidst this gaudy tumult of Victorian junk!

Father has always complained that my slovenly housekeeping habits were inspired by Uncle Ned. But four years ago, Winnebar never seemed this over-burdened with clutter! Perhaps, though, I simply do not remember.

"In the study!" my uncle orders once I reach the head of the stairs.

As I step through the doorway, Uncle Ned's hand waves outward from just beyond it, smacking a friendly clap to my shoulder—and causing me to whirl back away from him with a breathless, wincing shove.

"Sasha?" Staring wide with surprise, he exclaims: "I say, my boy! Whatever is wrong?"

"No, please—*don't* touch me!" I cry, smacking back his hand as he reaches out for me again.

Shuddering from head to foot, desperately stifling my urge to turn tail and run straight away, I fasten my eyes upon the floor to avoid meeting his stare.

Uncle Ned steps back, frowning, scanning me from head to foot. "I see," he says at last, nodding, turning on his heel.

I watch his back and steadied shoulders, cursing myself and my damned involuntary reflexes. Just the same as in the hotel in Moscow: as he struggled with his revulsion at the sight of me, I struggled with mine at the sudden engulfing swarm of his flesh, shoving away with horror the instant after throwing myself so foolishly into his embrace.

"Is scarce personally meant," I offer by way of ear-reddened, sheepish explantion as he indicates a chair.

"I understand."

He understands, he says. *Oh, yes—I understand: my nephew has been made into a whore. And can no longer bear to have a soul on earth touch him . . .* must his tone sound so patronizing? *Must it?*

With shaking fingers, I ram the rims of my spectacles back up on the bridge of my nose and swallow hard. *Goddamn it: no one touches me without asking . . . ever again!*

"You wished to see me?" I manage to force a conciliatory tone at last.

Uncle Ned nods, although still not deigning not to take a chair. Instead, he remains standing by the hearthside, continuing to survey me while puffing away lazily on his pipe. Although not a tall man, he seems now to loom like a giant over the entire room, the crown of his graying head bent, his shadow cast long across intricate patterns of the Persian carpet by the slow tilt of the fading sun.

"Supper will be presently," he states, fumbling in his waistcoat pocket to remove his watch. Overlong he stares at its face—almost as if, now that he has detained me for this 'talk' he insists we must have, reluctance precludes his proceeding.

"And that is why you called me in to see you?" I say, cocking an eyebrow. "I am quite aware that supper is served precisely at six, Uncle Edward." Already, although it has only been a week, the stiff formality observed in this household is driving me into fits. Seven servants, manners impeccable sunup to sundown, all dressed prim and proper in fluffs and tails, continually hover about to the point of nuisance, ministering to the needs of a mere three people. Ties and jackets are required even for riding; Uncle Ned himself, although I understood no business meetings were scheduled for today, is still attired in his dapper waistcoated suit, as if ready to attend the opera. Why did it all never bother me so four years ago?

Wistfully, I sneak a glance up at him—yearning selfishly to be treated as the child I once was so long ago—and not like such a steadfastly responsible adult.

At last Uncle Ned tucks away his watch. "I have tried to let you alone this past week to afford you some much needed rest," he says. "And recreation: every day, so I've noticed, you head for the beach with Sunnyrae. A fine choice—she is a wonderful animal: foal of Chrissyrae, a mare of which I was most fond in my youth. Most fortunate is this balm of summer. The weather has been truly hospitable, wouldn't you agree? Of course, we are always blessed in Cornwall, I daresay! So—I take it, after the spells of riding, that you are feeling more yourself?"

That is debatable. But I answer with politeness: "Yes, sir."

"Good. Then there is much we need discuss."

He crosses the room, and from a leather satchel, removes a parcel wrapped up in dark tissue paper. Turning, he holds it up in the air, looks down at me, and says dramatically: "I believe this belongs to you."

With a frown, I murmur: "I beg your pardon?"

Uncle Ned hands me the package, insisting: "Open it."

Shrugging, I do so—wondering idly at what sort of joke he has concocted. Stiff and proper though he is, in the typical dichotomy of the British, Uncle Ned is often at the forefront with oddball stories or the most outrageous, quirky jokes.

But this is no joke: I tear off the paper—uncovering, to my horror, my leather billfold.

Last seen on the floor of Volodya's flat in Petersburg.

Ocean wind whips fragrantly through the room's sheer linen curtains; the clank of kitchen utensils rattles up in squeaky, grating refrain from the downstairs. "Is it yours?" Uncle Ned demands finally.

Eyes clamped shut, lip bitten near to the sting of blood, I nod *yes*.

"I had assumed so. It contains your Russian traveling passport," he tersely replies.

Not only does it still contain the passport, but also my rail credit vouchers; amazingly, even the sixty-four rubles left behind at the time remain within the billfold, undisturbed. "W-Where did you find this?" I rasp out, my voice gone stiff as chalk.

"It was not I who found it. It was your cousin, Nikolai Zhelanov."

I clamp my hand over my mouth. *Oh, my God.*

"In a flat in the Vyborg district—leased to the name of one Vladimir Denisov," Uncle Ned states dryly, searching out my gaze across the room, while I continue scrupulously avoiding his. With irritation, he begins pacing the floor, the room filling up with a stream of pungently layered smoke-rings from his pipe. "Whose legal name, in actuality, is Vladimir Denisovich Rykazian," he goes on. "Following your stormy confrontation with your father, your cousin searched the city far and wide. Eventually, he began asking questions at the tavern adjoining the bordello you two had been frequenting that past week. He bribed a serving wench, who swore she saw you there with Rykazian; it was she who led him to the apartment. To his profound dismay, there he discovered your billfold, your soiled clothes, and a great deal of dried blood."

I shut my eyes again. This past week, on account of my exhaustion—and my uncle's seeming displeasure with my every move—I have avoided him as much as possible. And avoided answering, as well as asking, any questions.

Which can be withheld no longer. "I take it," I mumble out, harshly clearing my throat, "that they contacted you after that?"

"It was your Aunt Sophia who wired me. You father left straight away for Novgorod, after scarce speaking to anyone, so I understand."

Slouching forward, I stab both elbows to my knees and lower my head into my hands . . . *oh, God!* "W-Who—who told him? About the abduction? About Sheremetev?"

"I do not believe that your father has the slightest clue as to what transpired between you and Sheremetev," Uncle Ned replies.

Astonished, I jolt upward, staring with my mouth gaping as he continues past an exasperated shrug: "Actually, I think your father assumes you to be dead. He refuses to answer any of my letters. Were this anyone else, I'd be at my wit's end attempting to explain such deplorable, erratic behavior—but this is Count Mikhail Sekovsky with whom we find ourselves contending, humph! After all—sixteen years ago when your mother passed away, he reacted in near the exact same way: would not communicate with a soul on earth; shut himself up in that farmhouse in Novgorod to care for you nonstop night and day—and no one, not even your Aunt Sophia, learned of the tragedy of Melissa's death for over a month! You can imagine how appalling it was for us, especially for both of your grandparents here in England, anxious as we all were about Melissa's health and your impending birth."

"So, you are saying that my father will answer *no one's* inquiries?"

"That is correct. Six times have I wired; every telegram has been received. He refuses to sign for any of them; refuses to send any answer."

"Well, has anyone traveled to Novgorod to check and see if he is well?"

"Oh, yes. Your cousin Nikolai has made the journey there twice. Each time, I am told—after ascertaining that there was no further news of you—your father refused to speak to him."

I sigh loudly. Stubborn retreat into the depths of private hermitage sounds just like the crusty, hard-headed old lout. "But why would Father refuse to answer your letters?"

At this, Uncle Ned manages the first smile I have seen cross his face in the entire past week. "Sasha, certainly you must recall: your father and I—and all the Tylers, for that matter—have never exactly been on the best of terms."

Again I sigh. Supposing that some obscure grandfatherly Russian count took to courting my seventeen-year-old sister—had I a sister—I imagine I would look upon the man with little favor, either.

"The Zhelanovs," I go on, sorting aimlessly through the items in my billfold in order to have something with which to occupy my hands. "I assume they know I am here?"

"I sent a wire just before we left the hotel in Moscow. As overcome with exhaustion as you were, I decided it best to bring you straight here in lieu of staying at the hotel any longer and awaiting a reply."

"So—has Nikolai returned to Novgorod, and informed Father?"

"I am afraid that has been quite impossible," Uncle Ned replies, frowning. Crossing over to the desk, he begins refilling tobacco into his pipe. "The Zhelanovs left for the Crimea almost immediately after Easter. Your late uncle, I believe, kept a country house there?"

"Near Yalta, yes. Actually, they lease the bungalow from an old friend, and travel there near every summer season—but why on earth would they leave so soon? Aunt Sophie never misses the White Nights Festivals come June. And Nikolai would have been preparing for spring term examinations at the Conservatory."

"Nikolai joined them at the end of May when his studies were concluded. Your cousin, Anna, is ill."

A blinding chill chokes my heart near to an abrupt stop. "Anna? Ill?"

"The doctors are unsure. She continues to worsen: chronic shortness of breath, a lingering sore throat."

"Oh, dear Lord!" I cry out. "Not tuberculosis!"

Uncle Ned's hand waves sternly through the air. "Calm yourself. The outlook is scarce that bleak—not yet, in any case. Sore throat is not a common symptom of the consumption. But they felt it prudent to remove Anna to a warmer climate as soon as possible. According to her latest letter, your aunt seems quite hopeful. The child's health has improved greatly, particularly in the past few weeks."

From the desk, Uncle Ned hands me Aunt Sophie's letter.

I attempt to read it over, but the writing swims before my weary eyes into an unintelligible, scrawly French blur. "The trip bid well for the Zhelanovs," Uncle Ned goes on gently, nodding as I frown away and pass the letter back into his hands. "The shock of your disappearance affected them all greatly. I understand Nikolai himself was quite indisposed after the whole affair. The poor young man was frantic with worry over you, and rather fraught with exhaustion between his studies, my continued demands for information, and his trips into Novgorod for dealing with the idiosyncrasies of your father."

"Have you since received a reply from the wire you sent the Zhelanovs before we left Moscow?"

Uncle Ned hands me a telegraph copy that says in English:

Bless you, Sir Edward—thank God!

Princess Sofiya Sergeyevna Zhelanova
Yalta
11/24 August 1907

I stare at the paper until the words meld into an inky black line, at last murmuring: "So, my father still does not know that I am alive? And here?"

"That, apparently, is the case."

"And the Zhelanovs? Did you tell them where I happen to have spent the last four months?"

"Of course not. They know nothing beyond the obvious fact, conceded by the sending of the telegraph wire, that you were in Moscow. I have made no mention to anyone of Sheremetev. Quite honestly, I saw no reason to distress the Zhelanovs any further. I also took into consideration the fact that, were I in your place, I would want the utmost secrecy maintained regarding the entire affair."

I search out his gaze gratefully. "Thank you."

Uncle Ned nods.

"So," I go on, "how on earth did you find me?"

His eyes narrow, his stare hardening to the floor. "Greifmann, the messenger who brought you to the hotel. In June, I retained his services with the objective of tracking you down. His real name is Greisenbaum. Normally, he deals with disentangling lovers' spats, bringing home straying wives, those sorts of matters. He is one of Petersburg's finest private detectives."

I watch my feet, frowning, as he continues: "Your cousin made some mention of this Rykazian fellow; said he'd been an apprentice on your farm until just last year, that he'd stolen away for the cities after one of those infernal demonstrations, or some such nonsense. Instinct told me that following Rykazian's trail a little farther would lead straight to you. Of course, the man himself disappeared off into the slums somewhere, but Greisenbaum followed up on some ledger records your cousin had found left behind in the apartment. It took us some time to decipher these, and once we implicated Sheremetev, we were forced to await an opportune moment to intervene; Sheremetev must own virtually half the Tsarist police. Fortunately, we learned the news of the impending auction—at considerable cost, I might add—from a very reluctant woman informant."

In response, I practically leap out of my chair, demanding eagerly: "Did she have a facial scar? A birthmark under her nose?"

"I have no idea. Greisenbaum related that the woman always took pains to cover herself.

"Was her name Missy?" I ask. "Or—Lyubov?"

"She would only identify herself to us by the name of 'Gypsy.'"

I shift back, sighing, disappointed. Lyubov was definitely very blonde, and no Gypsy.

"I assume," Uncle Ned goes on, "that you never revealed to Sheremetev—or anyone else there—your true identity?"

"Are you *insane?*" I cry, appalled. "Scandalous rumors would have flown like wildfire all through Petersburg!"

"I understand, Sasha," Uncle Ned says pointedly, his hand again raised in the air, waving to calm me. "Did you know that Rykazian was working for Sheremetev?"

"Of—of course not!" I stammer out, red-faced. "I—he—we merely had a drink together! Just as Nikolai told you: Volodya and I knew one another from the farm. He was the beekeeper Father flogged that day last summer; remember I wrote you of it in my Christmas letter? That was why he ran off."

"So, you crossed paths with this Rykazian fellow in the tavern, and later had a drink with him?"

"Yes."

"Sasha, what on earth possessed you to go to Rykazian's flat after the confrontation with your father?"

"Well!" I snap at him, my cheeks burning up to my earlobes. "And wherever else was I supposed to go? No one ever *told* me that Father spent thirty years in Siberia!"

"I happen to be fully aware of that, Sasha."

"Oh, Lord God! The whole living world was fully aware of it! And I suppose he made you swear, also, to never tell me the truth? Christ help me!" I blurt out angrily as Uncle Ned nods in affirmation. "Blast all you people, keeping this from me, making me a veritable laughing-stock of all Petersburg!"

"About Rykazian," Uncle Ned interrupts.

"And why do you continue hounding me so about him? I knew not a thing about Sheremetev, nor about any of the filthy goings-on, I swear!"

"Did you know that Rykazian was a homosexual?"

The hot buzz foaming through my ears shatters into a crash of silence.

"According to Greisenbaum," Uncle Ned says stiffly at last, "Sheremetev only employs 'dealers' who are themselves homosexuals."

He lets the statement hang strangling in the air, a gradually coagulating web, its wily scorpioid closing in for the kill.

Scarce daring to breathe, I keep my eyes riveted upon my billfold and my hands—for if I look up and meet his gaze, the man is going to see through to the bloody truth. He will know that the experience with Sheremetev was scarce my first.

And if there is one avarice on earth for which I know my uncle has absolutely no tolerance—despite his progressive scholarly musings in numerological study and leanings toward the Hindu-inspired tenets of Theosophy—if there is one failing in anyone, friend or foe, that I know my uncle positively will not stand for, it is any kind of proclivity toward sexual aberration. Product of the rigid, morally strait-laced primers of his youth, the man is as vociferously opinionated about such matters as the most committed Puritan; from four years ago, his biting comments about the Oscar Wilde scandal yet sting within my memory. And the second he meets my eyes, the truth, dancing naked and ashamed, will betray me flat out in front of his face—for I am what I am. The Sheremetev fiasco entirely aside.

"I repeat the question again." His voice blasts ramparts of cold scorn across the room, showering me with frosty pellets of disdain. "Did you know that Rykazian was a homosexual?"

There is no help for it. He is going to learn the truth eventually; Uncle Ned is a gifted clairvoyant. How else could he, from oceans away, pinpoint the exact location of the key to Melissa's room, hidden in an old shoe tucked behind some trestle-boards in the closet to Father's study? We might as well have done with whole row, because that is what it is going to be.

We might as well have done with it all right now.

Swallowing hard, I open my eyes and level my stare into his, culpability—and my defiance—searing out like a flaming tong of iron between us.

"M-My God!" stammers Uncle Ned in response, his cheeks crimsoning in a virulent flush of rage. "Why, you bloody . . . you filthy, despicable little . . . !"

In two quick strides, he bounds across the room to my chair, his mouth working in tortured gasps. Flexing and unflexing, his fist trembles at his side, and as if of its own accord, at last springs upward, the brunt of his hand hovering menacingly in the air above my face.

Reaching upward, I take care with removing my wire spectacles and tuck them into my shirt pocket. "Go ahead," I tell him without emotion, nodding up at his hand. "Of late, I have grown accustomed to nightly beatings."

Whirling around, he undertakes great effort to restrain himself and glares away to the floor.

I slip my spectacles back on and arise from the chair, murmuring: "I assume you are quite finished with your questions?"

"Indeed! You just answered the next question I meant to ask. Get out of my sight, Sasha!"

My feet pound in stark hauntings of reply across the room's gleaming cedar floorboards. "That," I shout, before slamming the study door soundly shut behind me, "is precisely what I intend!"

* * *

"I'd make it worth your while, Doe-eyes."

The man whips a five-pound note out from his jacket pocket and waves it through the air.

"No."

"I'd make it doubly worth your while."

Now, a ten pound note.

"I said no, blast it! Leave me alone."

Shrugging, mumbling: "'Ave it your way, 'umph!" he saunters off toward other shadowy groupings of tables clustered within the inn-house.

I slump back over my soup, spooning it slowly, wishing to God for some taste of meat past all the knuckles and muttony pieces of gristle. I wish to God that my profile did not so resemble a girl's, that I had not cut off so much of my bloody hair.

"Twenty shilling, laddie!" the innkeeper's daughter then calls upon a slew of giggles from the doorway to the kitchen. "Wait, I take it back—for the likes o' you, so young and all, an' prob'ly your first time, I bring me price down to fifteen!"

Groaning, I roll my eyes. Do these people think of naught but satiating their filthy carnal desires, one way or the other?

The girl, slyly toying with tawny ringlets caught at the nape of her neck as she scans back and forth across the parlor of the inn for other prospective takers, can scarce be more than twelve or thirteen.

Nervously, I finger the grip of the pistol tucked away just inside the sleeve of my jacket, my gaze riveted upon the man who called me 'Doe-eyes'—his heavy muscular form now crowded in with two other burly louts at the farthest corner table. Their conversation, sprinkled with grunts and low rankling chuckles over plates of stew and kidney pie, continues with enthusiastic punctuations made by the man's stabbing fork, pointed once again in my direction.

Fortunately, as they turn their attention to the food, their loud guffaws begin to dwindle off, and the innkeeper's daughter at last busies herself with a far more responsive mark on the other side of the long hearth. Gulping down my soup to its last watery spoonful, I sponge through the bowl hungrily with the crust from my chunk of sourdough bread. Then, from the shadows, a grimly lurking figure emerges past the flank of my elbow scarce before I even see him.

"One more step, and you're risking a whole helluva lot more than your ass!" I hiss out, swiftly cocking the pistol and leveling it for the man's groin.

"Humph! And must you insist upon peppering your language with such insufferable vulgarities?"

Hands cast to the air in a mocking guise of surrender, Uncle Ned moves into widening flickers of the lamplight.

Not moving a muscle, I keep the pistol aimed straight for him.

"Are you going to proceed to shoot me?" he asks. "Or might I sit down?"

Sighing harshly, I uncock the hammer, but blurt out before I can help myself: *"Sukin suyn!"*

"Sasha—"

"Zhestoky zayebanyets, zhestoky sebyalyubyets! Kak vas nenavizhu! . . ."

Chafing with obvious displeasure, his thin lips tightly pursed, Uncle Ned settles into the chair opposite mine. "I suppose such heated rebuttal means the same in any language," he observes after a long pause.

Without answering, I hang my head into my hands shamefully, quivering against an unchecked froth of rage and the urge to spew out at this man—whom I have for so long respected and loved—more hateful, anguished declarations laced with Russian epithets by the dozens.

"You care to explain to me what you are doing here?"

Tersely, I remind him: "You ordered me out of your sight. I thought I had complied with your request."

Letting out a long sigh, Uncle Ned snatches off his derby and his dark leather gloves. "I hardly meant for you to depart Winnebar, Sasha!" he bursts out, glaring at me with exasperation. "And not for over an entire week! Good Lord God—I just spent near unto four months searching all over Russia for you. Now you expect me to chase you half across England as well?"

"I have scarce fled half across England!" I counter. "I simply rode a few miles into town. And I do not expect you to do anything more for me than you already have."

Grumbling, he begins to survey the mildewy walls of the inn with acute sniffles of distaste. "And must you stow yourself away in such a mournful rat-hole?" he demands, cocking an eyebrow.

"It is an affordable rat-hole."

"Speaking of money—you care to explain to me how you procured the combination to the lock of the safe?"

I stare into my empty bowl, inspecting the whorl patterns ground into its chipped clay pottery. "I took no more than I thought I would need," I insist, reddening. "Only twenty pounds. Oh, for the Lord's sake, stop looking at me like that! I left you all the rubles from my wallet, left you a signed I.O.U.."

"One I cannot even read."

"I always sign my name in Russian!" I snap back at him. "Perhaps you would understand—if you cared half a decent whit about your own heritage."

In response, Uncle Ned's fist slams onto the table, his bearded cheeks coloring with outrage as he chokes out: "How dare you mouth off to me in such a tone, young man!"

"You think the pistol," I retort, pointing at him, "the money were the only revelations I came upon in that safe?"

He stares away, peering far off into the dusky half-light of the parlor.

"Yes, perhaps you should explain about the pedigree charts, Uncle Edward," I sputter out vehemently. "And why you keep them hidden in the safe. Perhaps you should tell me about *her:* Marie Devon-Tyler, your mother, my grandmother. Marie Zhelanova Devon-Tyler."

Uncle Ned covers his mouth with the back of his hand.

"Everyone, all my life," I go on, "particularly my father, has blamed all of my peculiarities on being half-English. When in reality, I am only a quarter English—yes, Uncle Edward?"

"All right," he mumbles after the longest pause. "I suppose that is true."

Like a hammer, my spoon plows into the table. "Blast it! Why did no one ever tell me?"

"She was born in Lynton," he says defensively. "Her mother was a Willoughby—Jesus, how much more bloody English can you get? Her father simply happened to have been born in Pskov."

I glare away from him, and beneath his harshly disapproving stare, light up a cigarette. "So. I assume I am cousin to Pyotr Zhelanov's family in more ways than one?"

"My grandfather was a distantly related cousin to the Petersburg Zhelanovs, yes," he admits, then pointedly clearing his throat. "You still have not answered my question as to how you managed to open up the safe."

Guiltily, I look away from him again. Such a lark it all was when I first began my daredevil plyings—in Father's study, Pavel's office—that first summer three years ago spent cooped up doing book work on the farm. After the endless days of pencil-pushing, when boredom drove me near into fits of tears, Volodya cornered me repeatedly, goading me out of my fear of getting caught. After which he taught me how to test my ears, showed me how to pick apart the locks.

Of course, I never took anything. Otherwise, they might have found me out!

"I suppose you scarce intend to enlighten me," Uncle Ned observes at long last.

In reply, I blow a smoke ring through the air, shrugging.

"Are you now ready to return with me to the house?" he then demands.

"Return to the house? You called me filthy—despicable. Somehow, I obtained the notion that you abhor the merest sight of me." I stare off in the opposite direction toward the sudden brusque sound of clanking pots in the kitchen.

With an exasperated sigh, Uncle Ned starts drumming his fingers across the table. "I'll admit I might have been a bit harsh," he replies, his voice lowering. "I suppose it is not entirely unheard of, for properly-bred young men to—to occasionally dabble in such pursuits. The Oscar Wilde travesty notwithstanding, humph!" he snorts disdainfully. "But if you want my advice," he goes on, wagging an emphatic finger toward my face, "at your age, I'd scarce construe one haphazard, isolated little incident into life's immutably foregone conclusion. Most probably, before we both know it, you'll be all agog over some willowy young lady, and we'll both have long forgotten about the whole affair."

I frown doubtfully. Tired as I was, I knew where my blushing stares were gravitating, while we were aboard the trains, the ferry: definitely not toward the young women. The only woman I can seem to think of with any kind of tenderness, odd as it seems, is Lyubov. But night after night, urge after urge, in between the haze of sweaty, grappling dreams—just as in all these past months—my body hungers after only one naked visage: Volodya's.

"I spoke with a clockmaker about taking on work in town," I say abruptly, flicking cigarette ash onto my saucer. "He begged of need for a decent ledger-clerk, and I was able to demonstrate for him my three years of summer work experience. My room here costs ten shillings a night."

"None of this will be necessary, Sasha."

"Oh, yes, it will. I happen to owe you two hundred thousand rubles."

Two hundred thousand rubles. Near unto nine thousand pounds sterling! Its debt weighing on my every breath, day in and day out, like a runaway trainload full of bricks.

"You owe me not a pence of it, Sasha," Uncle Ned's voice echoes as if from some faded, conical distance. "You see, that money was your inher—"

"Uncle Edward! Believe me, I truly appreciate, more than you can ever know, all the time and effort you have expended these past months on my behalf. But I will not take charity—not from you, nor anyone else."

"Sasha, will you please listen to what I am trying to tell you? That money was part of your inheritance."

A faint smile creases Uncle Ned's lips as he pulls a sheaf of papers from his waistcoat pocket and begins untying the silken binding. "I thought this subject would arise, so I brought the documentation along. These are the deeds of trust to your mother's dowry," he explains, indicating a rash of signatures, including my father's, scrawled across several pages of official printed lines. "The total amount of fifteen thousand pounds—"

"Fifteen *thousand* pounds?" I gasp, jaw dropping.

"Oh, yes. Your Grandpa Will was always most adamant about finances. He saw to it that your mother was well-provided for; set up the dowry several years before she ever met your father. Upon the marriage, the amount was roughly divided into thirds: one-third vesting to your Father; two-thirds held in trust for any offspring, to revert to your father, if no issue, upon your mother's death. About a year after you were born, your father returned here to Cornwall after one of his

Parisian trips, and we re-formalized the agreement. The sum of ten thousand pounds was to revert to you either at the age of twenty-five, or whenever I felt it prudent to sign over my trusteeship. See, your name appears right here," he says, pointing to its English-spelled version typed in on one of the bottom-most lines of the deed. "So," he goes on, "if you remain as determined to restore to me those expenses incurred in your 'rescue,' and prefer not to be bound to years of drudgery as some common paper-shuffling clerk, you can make your restitution to me through dissolution of the trust. If you wish." Hunching over the papers, Uncle Ned dons his reading spectacles and starts checking over the long lines of figures. "At the current exchange rates, subtracting an amount equivalent to two hundred thousand rubles—in addition to a miniscule sum for my incidental expenditures involved in this, uh, matter, would leave—oh, I would say—about thirteen-hundred pounds or so in the account."

As I continue staring at him, stunned, he says: "Sasha, I would be happy to forfeit my trusteeship in entirety, and allow you that money as well at this time, to do with as you will. And perhaps somehow," he adds, "you will eventually recover the remainder of your mother's inheritance from Sheremetev."

Still numbed with amazement, I stare back and forth between my uncle and the stack of papers. Dolefully, I had resigned myself to the bleak prospect of remaining in this English seaside town, perhaps for an untold period of years, in order to work off the massive amount of the debt. Father made some mention once of an 'inheritance'—but from the offhanded way with which he spoke of it, I had assumed it to be only a nominal amount, some mere pittance useful for my university expenses upon once reaching the age of majority. For a certainty, I had not a clue that the amount hedged anywhere close to ten thousand pounds! As I glance over the formal-appearing papers, the tangible reality of such an incredible sum as even the thirteen-hundred remaining continues to entirely elude me. Looking back at Uncle Ned with lingering suspicion, I attempt to decipher his motives for such sudden willing forfeiture of the trust. The man took his degree in the law, and from the appearance of these papers, I doubt if I could contest his guardianship or the continued abeyance even if I so chose. Yet, his eyes now blurred with a weary exhaustion never yet evidenced during these past turbulent weeks, my uncle seems much more intent on smoothing out the prickly situation between the two of us than with maintaining leverage over administration of the funds.

The greatest irony, however, is that—in addition to my mother's amethyst crystal—Sheremetev now has the majority of her dowry.

But at least with this amount, I am rich! Well, not rich—but could definitely afford to treat myself to a bit more than knuckle-bone soup and day-old crusts of bread. And perhaps someday, sooner than I had ever dared dream, I could return home to Russia.

"You may keep the Webley pistol," Uncle Ned informs me, nodding toward the humped bulge beneath the shoulder of my jacket. "In fact, if you would accompany me back to Winnebar, I shall be happy to complete the gift with the match to the pair, an old Webley vest-pocket model. I say, you should find it a tad more convenient to tote around over the larger one. Both, I should hope," he murmurs with emphasis, glancing off into the shadows toward the group of boisterously guffawing men, who continue to eye me, "will provide protection enough to see you back across the Continent unmolested. Because you do want to return home—yes, Sasha?"

Stubbing out my cigarette, I attempt to shrug noncommittally while toying with my spoon in the empty soup bowl.

Uncle Ned pulls another sheaf of papers from his pocket. "This is a letter to your father," he states, holding a fountain pen out toward my hand. "I want you to address the envelope."

"Me? Why?"

"Because I am certain that this is the only way the old fool will finally accept the bloody letter!" he exclaims loudly.

As I frown, confused, he adds: "Because I think—for once, in lieu of complaining—that your father will be overjoyed at the sight of your wayward back-handed script."

"Oh." Hesitantly, I stare between the pen, the envelope, and the letter.

"You may read it, if you wish. The note is quite brief," he says, nodding.

Indeed, the letter is short, and to the point:

Dear Mikhail Sergeyevich:

As you can well see, he is alive, and yes, has been staying with us these past weeks in Cornwall. He has a great many questions, and harbors considerable resentment, about your sequester in Siberia. As to his flighty taking of leave and subsequent adventures, well—you know how young men are, running off to conquer the world in search of God, Peace, Truth. I suspect, however, that he will readily return home if so encouraged.

Your faithful servant,

Edward Devon-Tyler, Esq.,Bart.
4 September 1907

"Is there anything you care to add?" Uncle Ned asks, watching closely as, with trembling fingers, I tuck the letter back into the envelope.

I stare down at the rough-hewn boards of the table for the longest time; at last take the sheet of paper he offers and scrawl hurriedly:

I should like to return home. Will you permit it?

S.
Cornwall
22 August/4 September 1907

Barely does Uncle Ned seal my postscript inside the envelope but do we both jump near straight from our chairs. Across the room, the group of men bursts into a tirade of raucous, brawling shouts, coins clattering onto their table in a slew of bet-hedging as they leer over at us, pointing and snickering.

"I believe it now most prudent for us to return to Winnebar," Uncle Ned urges, his menacing scowl searing righteous indignation across the parlor.

I survey my fingers, cringing at the alternative: the door to my room, upstairs, possesses no lock. But still, perhaps foolishly, stubborn pride manages to intervene. "Uncle Ned, truly I must insist upon not taking anymore charity."

"Oh, Good Lord, Sasha—you are my nephew!" he bellows in reply, rising from the table. "I say, you are family, and welcome to stay at Winnebar for as long as you wish. I have already tethered Sunnyrae to the carriage outside, so hurry along and gather up your things."

* * *

I stare into the rounds of images lurking in my tea. "So, you do not think it was entirely foolhardy of me?"

"On the contrary!" With a sly grin, Uncle Ned tucks his fingers into his waistcoat pockets, toying with his watch and cache of change as he paces back and forth before the open window. "I say, Sasha! There is hope for you yet."

"But—they acted as if I had performed some sort of miracle!"

"Only ignorance, my boy. Knowledge is the seed of all power, never forget that! Actually," he goes on, chuckling and shaking his head, "the methodology of the reading you performed for your friend Viktor Bulyarin adheres to sound principles of occult practice—note that I said 'sound' principles. Certainly, we have our bloody quacks, just as in any other field. Unfortunately, a greater proportion seem to proliferate in our case. How I wish we could have done with half-crazed palm-reading women committing literal usury day in and day out with coaxing refrains of: 'You are coming from darkness into light; you must pay me twice as much and come now three times each week for the next two years,' et cetera!"

Laughing, I stir sugar cubes into my tea and toss back my head, gulping in another heady breath of the brisk salt air while following my uncle's gaze out the window toward the crashing waves.

"Common sense," he goes on pointedly, "using, not abusing, the factors of the world in reaching conclusions—this is the hallmark of the white magician." Turning from the window, he winks over at me with amusement. "I mean, what did you do? Went and asked the gossipy servant women to find out if the girl had a liking for your friend. I say, positively ingenious! In truth, my foremost surprise is to find you possessed of such acute perception at so young an age."

Reddening, I tell him: "Well, in any case, they married last October. Heavens, near unto a year ago now."

"Perhaps they will name their first child after you."

"Uncle! Please!"

Waving off my wide-eyed protests, Uncle Ned wanders over to his tapestry-strewn desk and begins refilling his pipe from his favorite ruby-inlaid snuffbox, a keepsake in which is always stored an extra stash of prime American tobacco. "So much the world has yet to learn," he mutters, staring once more with bemusement out the window. "Of late, I have been pondering a great deal," he goes on. "For instance, what exactly is meant by the phrase: 'He died for your sins?' Oh, how the ignorant so shirk responsibility, fancying themselves redeemed by the so-called 'Jesus!' Now, you tell me," he orders with insistence, pointing across the room at me with his pipe. "Who, to you, is the Christ?"

"Well . . . ." With some effort, I attempt to speak plainly despite imagined eavesdropping demons from the stalwart Russian Orthodoxy. "Not 'the Savior,'" I answer at last. "You know what I think deep down about Name Days holding greater import than the anniversary of one's birth and Holy Days dragging on for over a third of the entire year. The grip the Church has upon the people in my country is frightening, ridiculous! Thank goodness, last year when I refused to any longer take Holy Communion, Father finally let off on his forcing me to suffer each and every week through untold hours of the Liturgy. But as far as the Christ—there can be no disputing that the postulate of 'do unto others as you would unto yourself' is perhaps the most important lesson of all time. Definitely, amongst the greatest of teachings."

"Yes, the Christ played a most special role amongst such as Solomon, the Buddha, Confucius, Lao Tzu, Pythagoras. I believe he was chosen to specifically illustrate to the Western world the pathway of Obligatory Pilgrimage."

"'Obligatory Pilgrimage?'"

Squinting off into the dusky sunlight, Uncle Ned pauses long before answering. "'The Path of Sorrows,'" he continues at last. "'The Dark Night of the Soul.' Such euphemisms refer to the universality of 'the Christ experience.' Perhaps you will understand more readily if I return to my earlier train of thought—now, remember to think in the context of the Cycle of Incarnation and Cycle of Karmic Law. What, precisely, is meant by the phrase: 'He died for your sins?'"

Again I study the reflection of my tea for clues to the answer. Always I become so enraptured with the whole cascading vortex of metaphysics whenever my uncle and I become engaged in these lively discussions. The air gains raw momentum from our combined presence and eager thrashings of bold words, the preponderance of new ideas bouncing back and forth between us like saucers tossed across the room, new quests and old realities reverberating ever skyward. "'He died for your sins,'" I begin, drumming my fingers across the table, lost in thought.

"Rid yourself of all ritualistic archetypes!" Uncle Ned cries. "Think of the lesson in terms of Karma."

Finally, I mutter: "Each man dies for his own sins?"

"Essentially, correct!"

"But," I protest, "then why the mesmerizing image of the crucifixion haunting us throughout history? Could it be that, each lifetime that we live, we suffer through pain and tribulation, or work off negative Karma, to hopefully have less trouble—that is, less unresolved Karma—with which to be burdened in upcoming lifetimes?"

"Yes, the experience of the Christ was indeed an example of such basic truth of Karma. But in essence, I believe it was also much more. The Christ, apparently, died for all of his own sins."

"You mean—he worked off *all* of his remaining negative Karma? In one lifetime? But I thought such a momentous feat takes scores of lifetimes! What happens after a person completes such final Karmic absolution?"

"The vessel is purified—and so begins the Obligatory Pilgrimage."

"But—that would seem more the end of a pilgrimage than a beginning."

"The end of the Obligatory Pilgrimage *is* the beginning," Uncle Ned declares with an impish grin.

"You speak in paradoxes, Uncle!"

"Of course it is a paradox. All of life is paradox! Recall you not the basis of our earliest discussions, when you first came to Cornwall so many years ago? Reality is illusion; illusion, reality. Hence, life is duality—which leads to another favorite truth, the concept of triplicity in nature. The idea of Sacred Triad has a direct bearing on the Obligatory Pilgrimage: yours, mine, and ours. Past, present, and future. Father, Son, and Holy Spirit. The Sacred Three eclipse the 'birth in Christ,' so to speak. Another way to phrase it is thusly: the 'I Am' becomes the 'I Am That'—which becomes the 'I Am That I Am.'"

Somehow, it seems as if I have heard this all before—and I rustle through the cobwebs of my brain, searching for comprehension—but only end up shaking my head, even more confused. "I still do not understand much of this, Uncle."

"Give it time, Sasha. You are as yet very young; these are rather testy concepts we are bantering about with such carefree abandon here today. In sum, the Obligatory Pilgrimage is another term for what is meant by 'dwelling in Christ' or the 'birth in Christ.' But I agree, the whole matter remains stubbornly abstruse despite all attempts at explanation. Experience remains the best source for insight. For now, brood not over such things; merely rely upon your growing intuition, and concentrate on your path as you continue to see it. The instance of the Tarot reading performed for your friend was the type of example I had hoped you would report to me. The white magician is part of the world, not a force alien from it. And remember my earlier mention of the Shinto. Oh, how I wish our species would have done with racial antagonisms, the white man coursing about the world—subjugating, colonizing, setting himself up as the supreme manifest. No good will come of any of it ten, twenty years from now, you mark my words."

"When you say 'the Shinto—'"

"The Shinto of Japan are of particular significance. A great truth it is, the concept of worship unto antiquity, the development of the mantra: 'We *are* our ancestors.'"

"In other words, you presume that souls reincarnate repeatedly within the same family? So, hundreds of years ago—perhaps—I was a Sekovsky? Just as I am now?"

"Well, surnames—and many other factors, of course—evolve over time. Who knows? Perhaps you were a Tyler! Perhaps, in another time, a Sekovsky. Both are undeniably plausible."

"Then why can I not remember?"

"Ahh, Sasha, just as I said—you are still so young."

"But you remember past lifetimes: Athens, Atlantis! And Uncle Ned, I so want to remember who I was, where I have been, what I have done! But always either blankness or confusion disrupts my meditations, vague dreams riddle my sleep. How does one tell the difference? Between a dream and an actual past life 'memory?'"

"When you experience a memory in lieu of a dream, Sasha, believe me, you will know. Besides, cultivating 'blankness' during meditation is not entirely unfortunate, my questing young prodigy! Keep in mind that, when you begin to experience actual past life memories, the first visions usually encountered are of the death—which only follows the natural sequence of events. Remember back to when you were a child? Remember back to your birth? If you could accomplish that, and then go farther back, the first memory you will encounter is of your previous death. In some instances, not an altogether easy prospect with which to live."

"I suppose not," I reply, for once feeling some relief that I possess none of my uncle's skill in mastery of the teachings.

"Of course," he counters jovially, "then one can proceed with our conclusive discussion of yesterday, the illusionism of linear time: that all events, past, present and future, are occurring all at once, right now!"

"Oh, please!" I cry, laughing, throwing up both hands. "I'd much prefer retiring tonight *before* sunrise."

Letting out another round of hearty chuckles, Uncle Ned wanders back over to my side at the table.

For his perusal, I present the paper upon which I have been most studiously working, and he dons his spectacles, scanning over the delineations. "A numerology for your name based upon the alphabet of thirty-three letters," he murmurs, nodding. "In the Russian. Well, I would say, Sasha—particularly as you always sign your name in Russian—that the numerology for your chart should be derived from that same language as well."

"And you think I should discard the one you did for me four years ago? In English?"

Uncle Ned shrugs. "Language is a complex irony, the ultimate repository of culture. For instance—a table, in Russian: *stol,* correct? Obviously, those letters reduce to different vibrations than the letters of the word 'table' in English. Therefore, a table to a Russian must mean something different, albeit perhaps ever so slightly, than a table to an Englishman. Just as our English tea differs so markedly from your—ahem!—overpowering Russian *chai,* or tea. In the chart of a person who speaks only one language, lives in one culture, no problem ensues. It is when we run into someone like you, Sasha—multilingual, and also brought up amongst a confluence of competing heritages—that it becomes difficult to pinpoint which numerological basis applies in respect to one alphabet or another. My advice simply follows here as in everything else: when in doubt, follow your heart."

"And," I remind him, "if I do indeed follow my heart, and cast the numerology for my name in the Russian, I take on a destiny number of sixteen. The Tower."

"The vibration of the Tower is much like that of the number thirteen, the Death card," he reminds me. "Supplicants literally blow their stacks whenever it appears in a Tarot reading. But more often than not, both denote constructive, not destructive force. Rejuvenation in life always follows upon some sort of symbolic 'death,' if you will. I would say that the Tower card in your case predicates significant challenges for your life—but it also grants possibilities for rich reward."

I sigh wistfully, hoping him to be right—for a certainty, I would have been at my wit's end had I encountered the Tower card when I read the Tarot for Bulya.

"Well," I go on, "the other interesting result of following the Russian numerology for my name is that, according to the calculations

I have extrapolated for my cousin Nikolai's name, he and I possess the same outer path: the sixty-three, or Nine of Swords."

"Ahh, yes—nine swords point to the eastern light, a dawn of new beginnings. Your cousin is very dear to you, yes, Sasha?"

I nod. "He has always been as a brother to me."

"Then without a doubt, your lives will be closely intertwined," Uncle Ned observes. "Particularly with the unbridled interest you both share in music."

"What about the birth date and problem of the competing calendars?" I then ask. "Upon which life lesson number should I base my chart: the forty-seven, which results from the Russian calendar, or the twenty-nine, which occurs under the European method?"

"Here, I think, we have less of a dichotomy than with those vibrations deriving from the alphabet," he replies with assurance. "The Russians may yet adhere to the Julian calendar, but it has been proven far less accurate astrologically than the Gregorian. So, follow the European calendar, and use the twenty-nine. It is the Three of Wands—significant for your life lesson, I believe. Recall the triplicity aspects we were discussing earlier."

"The Three of Wands, triplicity of spiritual power," I murmur thoughtfully. "That makes me born in September instead of August, Uncle Ned," I groan. "A Virgo! And all this time, I had assumed my Sun to be in the sign of Leo."

"Perhaps your Moon is in Leo, Sasha. But as far as numerology goes, follow the twenty-nine. It reduces to the same vibration as the word 'light.'"

"Indeed?" Snatching up more paper, I scrawl out the word 'light,' assigning each letter its given number as per the English alphabet. Sure enough, Uncle Ned's assessment is quite correct.

"Yes, light," he goes on, chuckling with amusement. "Flickering, unstable, fraught with spasms of fiery energy. That is, the word 'light' as written in the English."

"Edward! Sasha!" Breeze whipping away at the skirts of her ivory-taffeta shirtwaist, Aunt Mary bursts into the room, her face agog with excitement. "Oh, my heavens!" she exclaims, waving about both arms. "Haven't either of you heard me? Or are you two involved in one of those impossible discussions about the origins of the universe again? For the past five minutes, I've been calling from the yard! Sasha, the postman is waiting with a parcel."

"A parcel!" Swarms of papers scatter across the table to the floor as I snatch up my cane and dash out of the room, close on Aunt Mary's heels all the way downstairs to the porch.

"Are you Alek—Alexander Chekobsky?" the postman demands, closely scrutinizing the letter. "Er, Shekowsky?"

"Sekovsky, yes."

"Registered letter; sign here."

Doing so, I stare dumbly at the word 'Novgorod'—wondrous, delectable stabs of sparsely written Russian smudged across the lines of the return address—as the postman trudges off.

"Open it, darling!" Aunt Mary exclaims breathlessly. "All the way from your dear papa, truly, is it now? Oh, how it seems as if we have been waiting forever!"

Forever, indeed, has it seemed that I have waited, longed, and hoped, the waning weeks passable only by wading through the intricate abstractions of my discussions with Uncle Ned. Meanwhile, the leaves outside have darkened unto a parade of autumnal harvest gold, ocean waves mounting behind in a ferocity of abandon toward the steady charge of certain winter. Each night have I prayed earnestly for Father's answer—only, until now, to watch the postman arrive empty-handed each and every day.

The letter contains no salutation, and only one line:

Of course I will permit it! No questions asked.

M.S.S.
Novgorod
15/28 September 1907

"My goodness, darling!" Aunt Mary cries, fanning herself with her gloves. "Such a short letter! Scarce but a note, really."

"Indeed," Uncle Ned observes with a stern frown, glancing over my shoulder. "I say! Why on earth did the man bother to send it registered post?"

From another pocket deep within the folds of the padded envelope, I extract a long stub of crisply stapled papers.

"Oh, my word!" Aunt Mary cries, peering toward it. "Whatever has he sent you, darling?"

"It's a ticket. For the steamer."

* * *

Stinging, icy flakes begin to fall, fleeting gusts whipping about the loaned horse's prancing hooves as clumped nettles of moss, branches, pine boughs, and loose ferns cartwheel through the dampened forest floor, spurred on by the teasing ploy of winter's first chill-wind.

I pull close the reins, slowing to a walk again—not for lack of rest, but merely to stop and gaze about while breathing in every precious sight with added sighs of wonder.

All the way from Petersburg, I kept my nose pressed to the train windows, marking the stations: Slavyanka, Tosno, Ryabovo, Babino . . . all the way from Chudovo, I sat with fingers clenched onto the padded velvet armrests, scarce taking a breath nor making a move for the entire hour and a half, so engrossing was the endless panorama of pine flanking birch, linden nestled in alder, dark cupolas of the village churches ranging up beyond the trees only to disappear again town by town, one after another, through the jolting pane of glass.

And now, as if to cap perfection, fresh dewy snowflakes have joined into the grand choreography cascading through the ratty brush, the first sentinels of winter grazing across the grounds of my home in a poignant bid of welcome.

Always so tantalizing it is when the first snow blankets across the woods, frosting all the branches, stilling low hoots of the owls and eager rustlings of the squirrels, a faint hush quieting over the vibrato of wandering forest life like a magical layer of dust infused from a eerie glass dream.

Brushing wet snowflakes from my thighs, I peer off through the tall branches of the woods. Caught in the spoils of the dusk's fading light, Lissushka's solitary wooden cupola glimmers through outlines of the cragged trees, while billows of thick smoke belch out behind the spire from the house's double chimneys. Apparently, Marnya is cooking up quite a storm.

And as if sensing my pangs of hunger, the mare lets out a loud whinny, impatiently tossing her head.

"Ahh, take it easy, lass—I'll fetch you a nosebag in no time," I murmur, patting her neck—but unable to help myself, I continue reining her in, contentedly staring off through the expanse of the woods.

A good two hours it takes to ride all the way home, ofttimes longer in inclement weather, west as the railway station lies from town. But today, despite the brimming threat of snow, I could not help but slow my pace down to a lazy sinner's fault, easing aimlessly all morn through green grassy moats and the lush surrounding park-like lands of the Novgorod kremlin grounds set high upon western banks of the sprawling River Volkhov. For hours, it seems, I stood out past the Sofiya side shoreline gates, staring down the whole vast length of the river's southern tributaries, a rise of cupolas from the Yuryev Monastery and Church of the Redeemer at Mount Nereditsa shimmering in teasing plays of gold upon horizon's tree-filled edge. Later, after crossing river, I spent the afternoon wandering through near every churchyard on the town's eastern side, there to gawk at countless bell towers, spires, and cupolas as if upon architecturally studious holiday. Afterward, I strayed in my musings from as far north as Kovalyov field to as far south as Gorodishche, before turning off at last to follow old trails along the Msta River's confluence of fertile fishing grounds, where once I caught a prize sturgeon as a child. At the Church of Peter and Paul at Kholinya, at the Transfiguration of Our Savior in roadside Bronnitsa, I paused each time far overlong—staring skyward, thanking heaven—while nearby peasants surveyed me as if a moron half-crazed of his wits. Most of the remaining afternoon I lingered up at Bronnitskaya, the low hill rising up just to the west of its namesake town and graced with the proper, but yet somehow eerily blue-domed Chapel of the Presentation set so oddly at a place still brimming full with legends of the old *volkhvi* sorcerers. Staring long and hard from the crest of the hill unto the clear glassy water of the lake, I could not help but marvel at how I had once been so eager to leave this place, this paradise where I first came into the world and spent my early years. And now, with Watery Forever's peasant huts risen upon close distance, and Lissushka's outlines beckoning suddenly so near, a scant half-verst away through a tangled brush of woods, it all seems too good to be true, and that I deserve no part of this triumph in return, I who spent near all of last winter here grumbling and complaining, so absolutely set on my heels to leave.

The joy, however, remains incomplete. Doubt continues gnawing away the shivers of gladness tickling at my spine: will he be truly pleased to see me? Or will it worsen again between the both of us, and become as life bid before the accident: long days of my rantings, endless nights of his beatings—years of hating him, hating myself, barely wishing to live?

Sighing past old glooms and fresh pinions of trepidation, I attempt once more to shrug off my fears, catch up the reins, and guide the mare back out onto the main village road.

Upon which a voice shouts from afar: "Whoa, girl—whoa! Hey, you! Yaa, you, up there—look out! Cart out of control, cart out of control! Clear the roadway—oh, no—*look out!"*

Screaming frantically, my mare rears up before I can stop her—while a peasant's knotty buckboard rig, loaded up to overflowing with hay and oversized sacks of grain, near topples over upon its frontal wheels before slamming to a clattering halt.

"Down, girl—down!" I shout, harshly lashing back the reins and seizing a grip onto the saddlehorn.

Bundled up to his eyes in scarves and ratty patch-marked woolens, the rig's hapless driver jumps down, shouting a slew of angry curses at his horse.

"You blundering, dim-witted fool!" I exclaim, pointing furious accusation down at him. "Think you own the road? I am the son of Count Mikhail Sekovsky, proprietor by landed right for seventeen desyatins up the rim of the shore! Who the hell do you think you are, all loaded down and driving like a drunken troika cabby, for love of the Saints?"

"Your Honor! Forgive me!"

"And just where are you headed on my father's lands with all of this—" I stop in mid-sentence as the man at last yanks the heavy layers of scarves from his face. "Oh, dear Lord!" I gasp out. *"Bulya?"*

"At your service, sir!" Bulya bows down low to the ground.

"For God's sake, Bulya—get back up! Forgive me, I scarce knew it was you."

"I am very sorry, Sasha Mikhailovich!" Bulya cries sheepishly, pointing toward his mare's head. "She got spooked just down the road a bit. Wheel caught a chuck-hole, and I couldn't rein her in."

"My old friend, you ever have a charmed way with horses."

Bulya breaks into a wide grin, exclaiming: "Damn my infernal brother's hide! You remember those pranks Semyon would pull when he was first workin' His Honor's stables, first teachin' you how to ride. Threw me up on Jespa stomach-first and hogtied me over her saddle one day—she still wasn't all the way broke in back then, you know. Guess I never been able to bear the beasts much since!"

We both burst into laughter, Bulya scrambling over from the rig just as I slide from the saddle—but before he can suffocate me into one of his wrenching bear-hugs, I squirm uncomfortably away. "Akkh! And what's come over you?" he cries, punching for my ribs. "You've no joy in seein' me?"

"Oh, of course—but heavens!" I point over at the rig. "Why are you so loaded down with hay and grimy oat sacks? I mistook you for one of the farm peasants."

"Barter units for the tax assessment," he says, glancing up toward the estate house. "I'm on my way to pick up my father. He's been conferring with His Honor all afternoon about last week's meetin' of the *zemstvo* council."

I break into my own grin in response. "Which, more likely than not, 'His Honor' made no attempt to attend?"

"Of course not! Your father has been awaitin' you like a hawk for an entire week. And so have I! Did you enjoy your holiday in England? Lord! I remember the last time. Did you again visit the famous ruins at Stonehenge?"

"As a matter of fact, yes."

"My, but your uncle sounds like such a progressive fellow! And how was your trip on the steamer, cold as it's been?"

"Bless the stars, we made Petersburg just before the ice hit harbor." Gazing yearningly back up toward the estate house, I add: "Well, I suppose I'd best go expiate Father of his anxiety."

"Sasha, might I ask a favor of you? Will you come back with me to my cottage for a few moments?"

"Whatever for?"

Waving his arms in an insistent fluster, Bulya climbs back up into the rig. "There's not much time; we've got to hurry, but you must come, Sasha—oh, you must!"

* * *

Beaming from ear to ear, Natasha brings the swaddled bundle out from the tiny pine cradle.

"Oh, dear Lord!" I cry, quickly doffing my cap.

"And is he not the most marvelous, miraculous, beautiful child upon which you've ever set your eyes?" Bulya exclaims—and dozens more superlatives gush forth from him nonstop as Natasha, after settling the squirming dark-haired infant into its father's arms, remains standing over the two of them with diligent motherly watchfulness.

"C-Congratulations, Natalya Alekseyevna," I manage to stammer out gruffly, still wholly astounded.

"Thank and bless ye, Aleksandr Mikhailovich. Vitya scarce had te drag ye all the way over here, what with ye jest returnin' and all."

"Oh, hush, woman!" Bulya cries, smacking at her playfully and giving her arm an affectionate squeeze.

Easing the infant back to Natasha, Bulya winks over at me and says: "And perhaps our Young Master would now care to hold his namesake child?"

"Oh, no!" I gasp out, blushing into an angst of scarlet. "Bulya!"

With a joyful smile, Natasha brings the bundle over to the door. "Course, my own brother's named 'Aleksandr'—so was sort of a double-christenin', for both ye and him."

"Bulya!" I protest on, "you truly never should have—"

"Oh, fie on it, man—I won't hear no embarrassed complaints! Come Tasha," he urges his wife, "let Sasha Mikhailovich hold his namesake child." But as Natasha hesitates, Bulya becomes most insistent, saying: "Oh, come now! I'm sure the Young Master's health is much better."

Searching my face with wary, soulful eyes, Natasha clutches the child up to her bosom protectively, murmuring: "Forgive me, Aleksandr Mikhailovich, but I—I—"

"Tasha!" Bulya implores her.

"But, Vitya! Couldn't he still be catchin'?"

As I stare between the both of them, frowning in bewilderment, Bulya bellows: "Of course not, woman! The strep don't stay contagious after all them months!" Extracting the bundle from her with some effort, he hustles the infant over into my arms, admonishing: "Oh, Tasha—stop your frettin' like an old babushka! The warm weather cured Sasha Mikhailovich for a certainty. Look at him: straight and tall, healthy as a horse!"

Sighing, smiling in apology, Natasha mumbles in reply: "Oh, I s'pose ye speak truthful 'nough, my husband." Shyly, she comes to stand at my side, her gaze meeting mine only for an instant before dropping adoringly back down to her son. "Aleksandr Mikhailovich," she then asks, "are the Crimea lands truly as beautiful as all the sayins? With strawberries grazin' all the hillsides, and winegrapes draggin' out in verst-long vines, and lilacs bloomin' in the very dead o' winter's snow?"

"The Crimea?" I blurt out.

"Lord, such a shame it was about the Music Conservatory!" Bulya exclaims, nodding at me. "And after them long months of preparin'. Everybody in Watery Forever knows how much you'd practiced, that flute music pipin' everyday for hours through windows of the Lissushka estate house. Yet, it certainly must've been the most prudent course, headin' southward," he observes. "Semyon caught the strep four years ago; went to Sochi straight away and took the cure within two weeks! Such a pity, though—and I understand one of your cousins was also taken ill?"

"Uh, yes. My cousin Anna Zhelanova."

"Bless the Saints that you're both better! We were rather surprised, though, that His Honor did not accompany you on the journey."

"Oh, well." Having rocked the child for an obligatory amount of moments, I hand him back over to Bulya. "You know how Father hates to be away from the farm any more than necessary," I manage to say after searching through my mind's daze for some excuse. "And he has never been overly fond of the Crimea. Ever since the War."

When Bulya frowns, incomprehending, I add: "No, no—not the Japanese War. Father fought long before that, during the Crimean War."

"Oh, yes. Of course."

After a quick glance toward their mantle clock, I pull back on my cap. "Again, congratulations to you both! And thank you for inviting me into your home, Bulya. It was very good to see you once again, Natalya Alekseyevna, but I think I had best hurry homeward now before the sun goes."

"Oh, no—the estate house!" Bulya jumps up and almost bangs his head against the low rafters of the cottage ceiling, gasping out: "Lord in Heaven, I near wholly forgot—I was supposed to pick up my father!"

* * *

"Viktor Ilyich Bulyarin!" Vliny shouts, angrily flinging open both front doors. "Ye turd-brained, nit-witted whelp of a foreman's nightmare! Ye ever slam that rig into the side o' this house agin, an' I'll tan yer—"

He stops, gaping wide-eyed and open-mouthed, his hand flattening against his balding head.

"Oh, by the Blessed Saints!" he then yells. "Mama! Misha! Mama, ye'd best git out here an' see what sail the wind jest blew in, Lord be praised! Misha! Give off blabberin' about the roadway tokens, an' git yerself out here! Mama! Ye're not goin' te believe—"

"What are ye hankerin' at Viktor so much fer, ye bat-blind, cuss-simperin' old fool!" Marnya grumbles, smearing greasy fingers across her sackcloth apron as she bounds in a fit of impatience from the kitchen. "And why are ye yellin' at me like such a drunken lout? Can't ye see I'm up te my neck in buttered noodles an'—*oh, my Lord!"*

The ladle she has been waving at Vliny with such vindictiveness bangs unceremoniously onto the floor.

"Sasha!"

And then—before I can utter the slightest protest—they both engulf me in a swarm of embraces and kisses.

"V-Vliny!" I stammer. "Matushka, honestly, I—" Nervously, I attempt to extricate myself, but to no avail. Vliny starts yelling to Father at the top of his lungs, while Marnya continues pattering all over with pecking motherly smacks to my hands and face, crooning on and on: "My angel, my little dumplin', my precious baby dove! Lord Almighty, look how tall ye've grown, how like a man ye've come te be! Akkh! Bless the godly Saints, bless Mother Russia, bless the sweet earth, an' all the high twinklin' stars! Bless ye, Sweet Virgin Mother, fer watchin' over my baby dove fer these long worryin' months! Bless ye, Saint Georgi be praised, fer deliverin' our precious angel back to us whole and safe! Praise be to God! Our own Sashenka has returned!"

"What in the blessed world is the commotion about out there?" I hear Father roar from the open drawing room doorway. "You two think this is Friday night vodka-guzzling in the village tavern? Ilya Isayevich and I are trying to talk! Can't you folks manage to get those grain sacks loaded back into that rig without—"

Stomping out of the room like a riled bear, he stops cold in front of the kitchen archway, staring in a sudden grip for breath as, from either side, Vliny and Marnya part away from me at last.

Bulya's father—Ilya Isayevich Bulyarin, ever-prominent despot of the local *zemstvo* council—emerges from behind at Father's elbow. Screwing up his eyes in his heavily jowled face, he peers at me in critical bemusement, and finally cannot seem to resist breaking the silence by muttering: "Well, well—and so the prodigal son returns."

I swallow hard. Apparently, not everyone well abides the concocted story about my illness. "Ilya Isayevich," I murmur, forcing politeness.

"Aleksandr Mikhailovich." He nods with averted eyes. "Well, Mikhail Sergeyevich," he goes on to Father, "I s'pose we quite wrapped up our business fer the day. I shall be awaitin' your reply te the road proposals. All votes from the noble houses have te be accounted fer."

"Yes, yes!" Father stammers with impatience, waving him off while muttering beneath his breath: "Sorry politics! I assure you," he goes on, "that this time, there shan't be any delay, Ilya Isayevich—the papers will reach your office by the deadline."

"Good. Then as our day's business is done, I shall be lettin' ye get on with yers," old Bulyarin replies, casting a meaningful glance in my direction.

Everyone scatters: Marnya to the kitchen; Vliny and the two Bulyarins to the east side of the house to check the fate of the hapless rig—leaving me alone at last in the hallway vestibule with Father.

He has allowed his beard to grow back lush and snowy-white, only the sparsest traces of ruddy auburn tucked into the hairs grown about his ears and chin. Not since my primary-school days do I remember him wearing a full beard past the more fashionably thickened mutton-chop side-whiskers. Elegantly trimmed, it somehow takes long years away from his age, but closer scrutiny reveals a scarred weariness about his eyes, heavy rings darkened beneath in dull morbidity as he continues holding my stare.

At last he nods acknowledgment, saying: "Well. I see you have grown into quite the young man. Make you appear rather bookish, I daresay. The spectacles."

With fingers caught atremble, I push the wire frames back up the bridge of my nose, murmuring haltingly: "Books forced me into the quandary, all right. Far too much reading."

"Indeed? And with what else have you been occupying yourself these past months?" Father then inquires, studying my face. "Did you find God? And Peace? And Truth?"

I close my fist around the handle of the cane, wondering, between my flesh and the brass-enameled knob, which is more icy. And I wonder why, for the love of God, I cannot go over to him and at least shake his hand; wonder why he, standing so stiff and straightly formal with his back held against the wall, cannot bring himself to bound toward me with the same carefree, welcoming joy as Vliny and Marnya. But I suppose there remains much for which we must yet forgive one another. "I thought," I say tersely, staring to the floor, "that you promised there would be no questions."

"Oh, yes," he replies, nodding. "Of course."

And then he does come—with the slightest smile, a signaled effort at ready tolerance overtaking his rugged features as he shuffles across the floor toward me. Awkward, boyish it is almost, the way he extends his hand. "I suppose, under the circumstances," he murmurs, "that it is my place to make the first move."

I shake that hand hurriedly, too impatiently, as if only wanting to cast him off—then to outwardly do so, cringing away with a piercing shriek the moment he squeezes hold of my arm.

Drawing back in shock, Father harshly surveys me up and down before politeness checks his glance—but within the vast cognizant breadth of that tiny instant, his eyes seem to ken all the shame, horror, and depravity of my experience with Sheremetev without his ever being told. "For God's sake, Sasha!" he bellows out flush-faced, at last recovering a remnant of his voice. "What on earth has come over you? Can a father not reach to embrace, to welcome his son home after a faraway journey?"

In a cane-pounding flurry, I shove away, stumbling blindly back for the front doors.

"Sasha!"

"No!" Flinging off his arm once, and then twice more, I seize fast hold of the doorjamb in a pitiful stance of defense, rasping out in a voice ground near unto breaking: "Per-Perhaps it was a mistake! For me to even have thought of returning home—"

"Sasha!"

"Let me alone! Will you, *please?* I do not want to answer your questions—nor to sink into any embraces!"

Feet skidding across the ice-pack out upon the front porch, I grapple onto the closest wooden post and grip hard for balance, staring down to my shaking toes, panting to catch my breath.

"All right!" Father cries insistently, waving out his hands. "You care not to embrace your old papa upon arriving home, fine—and as I promised before, no questions will be asked! Now, will you please simply come back inside?"

But I remain clinging stubbornly to the post, biting my lip against stiff shivers of trepidation, yet wholly unable to meet his gaze past my burning flush of shame.

Stepping back within the open doorway, Father looks me cautiously up and down once again before tearing his eyes away with a long painful wince; at last shoves his fists down into his trouser pockets and stares to his feet. "Very well," he begins softly. "Then I will say my piece right here and now, if you will not come in from the porch. What I have yearned to say to you for so very long now, my Sashenka, is that I am sorry. And beg your forgiveness, for everything. I understood perfectly well why you ran away that awful night. That is why I told Nikolai to go ahead and let you go. I mean, God Almighty, had my father kept from me so many years of ugly truth, I'd have wanted the man's head on a bloody pike and his ass in a spit as well! Sasha, I can scarce make much explanation for my secretiveness, my obstinacy, my never telling you about Siberia, and I hardly expect you to try to understand when I can scarce fathom my deplorable behavior myself. But what matters now is not my disgraceful past, nor whatever foolish business in which you have dallied during these past months. All I wish in the world, for the sake of the both of us, is for you to know Lissushka as your home again, with no hard feelings from me. So, please—I am begging you! Do not run away like this, now that you are barely here. Allow me, at the very least, to provide shelter and sustenance, and if I can, a bit of comfort for your soul. For God's sake, Sasha, you are my son! And no matter what rifts have occurred between us, or what else will happen—ever—I want you to know that you are always beholden to my heart until my utmost dying breath. And even if you wish to never speak a word to me again, at least allow me to fulfill my parental duty, my primary obligations to you—and to the memory of your dear mother."

Fingers gripped like talons onto the post of the porch, at last I hedge a glance up at his face.

"Please, Sasha," Father whispers on, sharply looking downward, fragments of his voice torn with a sob. "Come back into the house. You must be famished after riding all the way from the railway station in the cold. Let us go and break bread together once again as a true family—it has been so long! Marnya has been cooking all day, you know. Can't you smell the swan? I know how you love roasted swan."

"Papa—"

"What? Ask anything, Sasha—I will grant whatever you wish!"

After sucking in deep frosty breath, at last I meet his eye squarely, saying with some effort: "I will come back into the house and eat supper with you now, Papa."

As he sighs with profound relief, I begin inching my way back inside.

But when Father offers his hand out for assistance across the threshold, I freeze, staring down at his fingers. I look up to his face; look back down to his hand again.

Coughing with embarrassment, he pulls it quickly back to his side.

Toward the direction of the dining room, I then nod, murmuring: "After you."

Whereupon I follow him in, take my seat at the table—and somehow manage to endure the overwhelming commotion made over me during the five courses of the meal by Marnya, Vliny, Tereza, and Eva, the four people with whom I have grown up, and who all seem to think that I can merely walk back into this house and pick up my life again as if everything in the world was yet as innocent and carefree as before.

Finally, I can admit that it is not. No matter the lushness of Novgorod, the beauty of Lissushka. No matter the warm coziness of these cherished, familiar walls.

During my first heady days of freedom spent riding the beaches for hours and basking within the sunny delights of Cornwall, I thought I had become my old self again. When autumn's winds began lilting briskly through the air, and I became so enamored in the philosophy discussions with Uncle Ned, I thought I had somehow miraculously regained the self-composure rent to such bitter shreds by Sheremetev's aptly scored physical and psychic lacerations. And today when I first saw Bulya, and joined in the excitement over his newborn child, I yet felt supreme upon stretched wings of optimism, so confident was I that the entire filthy, sordid ordeal would dissolve like torched embers from my mind, the vestiges of my old life beckoning once more in abundance, ready and waiting to be slipped on again as if naught but a favorite set of old clothes.

But upon confronting my father, and his sad dark eyes that somehow seem to sense—beyond all hesitant, apologetic talk—that somewhere, sometime in these last months, something has been, and still is, terribly, horribly wrong; upon having to face him—the one person on earth whose opinion I respect and value above all others—with my wounded pride, cold shame, and the miserable truth of everything, I realize that nothing is the same.

Nothing is ever going to be the same again. At all.

* * *

It becomes a curious camaraderie of silence, devoid of any and all but the rudimentary posturings and salutations.

He takes me with him to Kolinsky's farm, fifteen versts as the crow flies south along the lake, but actually forty or so by road. More hives are pending sale, this time late in the season, and he felt it prudent to gauge the honey stores again and recheck other matters for the wintering. All the while, he keeps me in close tow, his voice always pattering on in an instructive monotone of reassurance—while Kolinsky's overseer stares with a cocked eyebrow. Unsure of what to make of Count Sekovsky's son's stony reticence, he continues to regard me warily while listening to Father ramble on about the peculiarity of such sunny weather for the early weeks of November.

The next day, we ride together up to Bronnitskaya Hill and then down into the thatch-roofed village itself, somehow unconsciously tracing the path of my earlier homeward vigil. Afterward, we continue our way along the river roads toward the tiny village of Kholinya, then to ride from there farther west amidst dense forests and marshy bogs to reach Novgorod-proper by the time the sun tops noon. Through the eastern part of town, we slow to a walking pace, easing our way toward the Volkhov bridge past high glinting domes of the Transfiguration, the Assumption, the St. John, St. Georgi, St. Nikolai, and at least a dozen other monasteries and stucco-white cathedrals.

Long before sight of the bridge, clusters of ruddy brick-peaked watchtowers—grim sentinels from wars of old—loom up in plays of slanted wooden roofs and eerily darkened vacant windows from Novgorod's western side, nine massive bastions in all built each at strategic corner sightlines along the vast rounded enclosure of the ancient kremlin wall. Once across the chilly span of the Volkhov, we tether our horses just outside the kremlin's arched eastface gates. With my stare held firm upon the swift, smart heels of my father's boots, I trudge along after him into the park-like grounds of the kremlin itself, the lawns and walkways bathed everywhere in half-melted, icy mounds of slush. We make due haste past the flat-roofed buildings of the renowned antiquities museums, and I watch shyly from behind as he makes the required deferences to quick salutes and respectful nods emitting from all sides as we pass, two richly-tailored shadows in ruddy ermine weaving soon through the gathered market-day throngs of gray sheepskin coats and frayed felt hats worn more commonly by townsfolk and the peasants.

Straight to the vast, wizened bell and grand historical countenances of Mikeshin's Thousand Year Monument he strides, pulling up short to commence the usual parental lecture about Ryurik of Old facing south, toward Kiev; Peter the Great facing north, toward Petersburg—and on and on he prattles, although not overbearingly so, about near all of the monument's one-hundred-twenty-nine dark, painstakingly sculpted historical figures. Turning around, he then bids me with him back across the lawns toward the kremlin's most ancient and revered monument of all, our Holy Cathedral of St. Sofiya, where he points up at the highest cross and bronze dove statuette capping its central dome. I shade my spectacles against the glint of golden apse tiles, all shining near white as the stuccoed facade of the building itself beneath a harsh glare from the high noon sun. "Staunch and true, Lord Novgorod remains until the dove flies away!" he announces proudly—and throwing back his head, squaring his shoulders, he dashes off a quick salute to the legendary bird. Through the archway linking the cathedral with the provincial theater hall, he then waves me along with him again, following the meandering pathway leading back toward Sofiya's towering west-side entrance and her famous Korsun Doors.

The renowned frescoes, gilt of bronze in raised relief, are cast in murals depicting scenes of saints and battles from the Old and New Testaments, with both Latin and Slavonic inscriptions carved in above haloed heads of the figures. "Originally commissioned by Wichman von Magdeburg for the Cathedral of Plozk," Father informs me, eyeing the artwork and whispering beneath his breath as if we are both privy to some preciously guarded secret. "To this day, no one has any idea how these damned German doors ended up in Novgorod!" And he lets forth a stream of hearty chuckles, shaking his head past certain visions of the plottings of our wily, cunning ancestors.

We skirt then for lazy, waning moments around the rear side of the cathedral, lingering long at each of its elegant arched stone windows, wavers from within of countless votive candles flickering acquiescence from both high and low alike as he relates old folk tales about every single crevice, cornice, and tempered iron window-grating. Through the northside doors, we venture inside upon attendance to daily Liturgy, and for the first time in many months, I accompany him without overriding complaint, the smoke from the censers delighting my nostrils, the old choral hymns pealing down from the balcony in soothing rhyme and somehow bequeathing unto my heart a sense of peace. I even utter prayers, following with the sign of the cross made in meek obedience to Father's frowning, insistent nods. Afterward, we pause again outside to make due inspection of Sofiya's high blue and white eastface bell tower row, staring up the both of us at its solitary shimmering cupola with nods acknowledged in reverence unto architectural grandeur. A further historical discourse about Prince Aleksandr Nevsky and the ancient feudal republic itself called Lord Novgorod the Great emits then at colorful length on his part, and we linger once more overlong upon the walkway winding so invitingly through snow-soaked peekings of the grass. Only as the sun begins hailing fast toward afternoon do we at last amble our way, with considerable reluctance, back toward the eastface kremlin gate to fetch our horses.

Across the river again on the town's eastern side, we pause in a noisy teahouse to lunch and warm ourselves. Rambling on in low amiable tones at last no longer about history and heritage, but instead about Anna's improving health, he begins to speak of the holiday we must someday make to the Zhelanovs' bungalow in the Crimea. All the while, he watches without comment as I wince against the squall of balalaika music and stare through the windows, continuing to light up and stub out cigarette after cigarette. After a few more moments, the brandy flask peeks out again from behind the heavy flap of his coat, and he pours another draught into his glass of tea. And then nods, with questioning eyes, toward mine.

I stare back in a choke of silence—but at last shrug, and nod, and watch as, with a snort of approval, Father pours some of his brandy into my glass.

Back out in the cold again, I cannot help but steal glances at him: his worn, gray weariness has disappeared like a forgotten shadow in the two days since I have come home. A jaunty twinkle catching his eye as we cross the street to retrieve our mounts, he proceeds to hold up all cart-horse traffic right in the center of the main town roadway while pausing to banter back and forth with a couple of other gentlemen farmers of old acquaintance—before taking strident pains, over my awkward protests, to introduce me to them with a beaming, proud regard that I have never known. At last, as we veer off for home, I cannot help but gape after him, careening between flutters of delight and dismay while attempting to make some sense of his incredible behavior. Never in my life has he encouraged me to drink with him. Never has he been able to tolerate my quirky assignations with cigarettes—and never have we been able to ride together for any great length of time without erupting into the inevitable shouting confrontation about my preference for mounting on the right flank over the left. But all this day, as we have made our way from place to place—mounting, dismounting, remounting again and again—he has scarce spared a second glance, leaving me stranded with my once-beriddled left-handedness in blinkings of confusion, for my argument was freshly readied to countermand his first off-handed comments with the harsh reminder that, due to his own inadvertent bidding and the injury caused my leg, I hardly any longer have a choice.

Even when we stop to pee in the river, he seems to understand—hurrying along first and then leaving me alone at the bank—for it is only alone now that I can accomplish my necessities, anxiously thwarting off old images of Sheremetev's lewd-eyed stares while making certain that no one, from anywhere around, happens to be watching.

As winter's ebbing sun begins waning low in the western sky, we leave Novgorod, the Rivers Volkhov and Msta, Kholinya, and at last Bronnitsa and its haunting blue-domed chapel on the hillside all behind, the two of us galloping together in amiable silence down the narrow dirt road leading lakeside toward Watery Forever and Lissushka. Before rounding the final bend for home, he stops—as I had fully expected—and inclines his head toward the shortcut path winding from the road through the woods. "Perhaps best pay our respects," he murmurs wistfully. "After all, we missed chance for our usual remembrances after Eastertide."

Murmuring agreement, I dismount and follow him along the overgrown walking trail toward the fence setting off tangled thickets of forest brush from the grassy lawn of the family cemetery. Again he embarks afresh upon another discourse, this time about the architectural wonders awaiting our inspection on the isle of Kizhi: "One of these Petersburg jaunts, we'll manage a side trip up there, Sashenka. If you've a yen for architecture, you will be utterly enthralled, I tell you. The view is stupendous, and if you think Novgorod holds towers that stun the eye, well! Nineteen I was, and still at university, when I first beheld those gable-ridged *kokoshnik* domes, and I said to myself: 'By God, Misha Sekovsky! You are going to build yourself a stately house with a fleck-carved wooden cupola hungering up for the sky, just like one of those grandiose churches, someday.'"

Only half-hearing, I halt as he does, tether my mare, and wander through the ancient iron gate, nodding deferentially toward Uncle Dmitri's and Grandfather Sergei's steep Orthodox markers. But it is toward the western end of the cemetery that I turn in earnest, there to kneel down before my mother's granite headstone. *Countess Sekovskaya,* inscribed in haughty Russian letterings, sprawls across its milky grayish plaque of Italian marble, with the acknowledgment, *Beloved Melissa,* carved in English beneath. The dates, *1872-1891,* hovering below, seem so harshly absolute, so short, so final.

Father stops talking and kneels down beside me, and we both cross ourselves.

I place down at the base of the marker a bunch of heather carried in my coat since early this morn, along with a white rose purchased at a seller's stall in town.

"God rest her soul," Father mumbles, finishing off his prayer, rising.

Still kneeling, I continue staring at the stone.

"Come, Sasha," he urges, pointing back toward the horses. "I know the snow hasn't taken yet, but the ground is damp. You could catch a chill."

"Papa? Why did you never tell me?"

I look up at his face.

To see him turn away with a roughened clearing of his throat, as if caught off guard by my actual utterance of a sentence after the stoic, silent spell maintained over the last two days. Awkwardly, he begins fumbling with the brim of his elegant fur-skin hat—although, well-fitted, it scarce requires adjustment.

"Papa?"

"Come, Sasha—please, get up! You'll get your knees soaked." Grasping up my arm, Father pulls me to my feet as, with concerted effort, I attempt not to recoil from his touch, crying with insistence: "Papa, you could at least have told me!"

Leaves crackle, whipped up by the fresh chill-wind, and scatter across the forest floor through long gusts of time spanning the uncharted wilderness always holding the two of us so separate.

Father shoves both hands into his coat pockets and begins pacing back and forth a short distance in front of the grave, his eyes—with all the cragged, rugged emphasis of his solid seventy-six years—again taking on their old hollows of weariness. His head remains bent as he continues his inspection of the toes of his shiny leather boots, one silent footstep after another.

I lean upon my cane and watch the rhythm of his feet as well, waiting.

"Suppose," he begins finally, again roughly clearing his throat, "suppose you had a son—"

I swallow hard, reddening, yet astutely watching his feet pound back and forth.

"—whom you adored."

He stops pacing, and stares over at me. "Oh, yes," he declares, shaking his head at my expression of bewilderment. "That is precisely what I said." His voice lowers then to a softened whisper: "My son—"

"Papa, I—" I catch my hand to my mouth.

"—whom I positively *adore.*"

Choking back stiff pangs of guilt and a well of tears threatening at the back of my throat, I look sharply away.

"And suppose," Father goes on, "that you realized one day, that—proud of an old cuss as you were—you were naught but a stinking, yellow-bellied coward. Because you shrank from telling this sensitive, talented, much-adored young son of yours anything of your long-guarded, dreadful secret. Because, knowing the boy's flighty temperament so well, you feared that he might run away."

From the ground, he retrieves a branch of new-cut birch, stoops down upon his haunches, and starts tracing doodle-patterns with it across the dampened, mossy earth. "I know you probably can scarce believe that your papa truly does adore you, Sashenka," he murmurs, not looking up at me.

Past him, I stare to the marker, Melissa's poignant letterings merging into a well of numbness before my eyes.

"Yes, I understand," he says, rising, but still holding onto the stick. "Lost in confusion, the youth searches his heart with ever-oblique questions: 'So, why did the old fart beat me near to a bloody pulp? Night after wretched night?'"

In answer, he follows my rigid stare to the grave. "Because I suppose, Aleksandr Mikhailovich Sekovsky," he answers bemusedly, pointing at the marker, "I suppose you are not so much like our Lady Melissa after all. Oh, no—quite the contrary! You are not at all so much like her, as you are like me—"

"Papa, you—you needn't say all this!"

"—stubborn, independent, hog-headed, foul-mouthed, vain to a fault; a young man far too intelligent for his own good. Who sticks his nose far too easily into other people's business where it does not belong. And all while being far too consistently pleased with himself right up to the scraping little crawdad-pincer still stuck up his ass."

As my jaw drops, he grins sheepishly. "Well!" he bellows upon a roaring laugh. "A correct assessment in every regard, yes?"

Flushing scarlet, I stare away—although after a heart-hammering pause, I can no longer contain my urge to smile.

"I never told you about my adventure in Siberia because you used to be too young to understand. As you grew older, believe me, I tried. I cannot tell you how many times, whether it be at supper-table or in the stables or wherever, that I almost said something. I certainly did not want you to find out about it the way you did. But in the end, I was always afraid that you would be so heartbroken and outraged that you would forever forswear me, and run away. And I was right."

My smile extinguishes. I stare back to the grave.

"I suppose, all this past year, I've been dropping hints here and there," he goes on sadly, "especially after we spent so much time together tending to your leg. But surely, Sashenka, you must know," he continues with emphasis, pointing across at me with the stick, "that your father—who, as you so earnestly reminded me that horrible night on Zhukovskaya, has tried his utmost to teach you the sacred meaning of the word 'honor'—surely you, of all people, must know that your father would never do anything to disgrace his country."

Grimacing, Father flings the stick far over the fence into ratty tangles of the forest brush. "I was sent to Siberia on a falsified charge," he says. "A certain very well-connected young lady, for whose favors I—along with droves of other young gentlemen; yes, I was young then, this was in 1856—anyhow, this particular young lady, for the affections of whom I and many others had been vying with some effort, quite suddenly found herself with child. Upon which she demanded that I marry her."

Again my jaw drops. "And you refused?"

"Of course I refused!" he shouts out vehemently. "I would be damned if I, Mikhail Sekovsky, heir to a score of generations of proud Novgorodian lineage, was going to raise another man's son."

"You mean," I gasp, "you and she—you two never—"

"Of course not!" he roars. "I might have had my designs on the girl, but I was scarce any fool! And my father taught me the same code of honor as I have attempted to teach you."

Blinking in confusion, I drag my ermine hat off and shake out my hair, which is already becoming long again, ruffling my fingers through it with impatient stabs. "I do not understand, Father. Since when does refusal to marry someone incur a sentence to Siberia?"

"Recall what I said. This certain young lady was very well-connected."

"But—*Siberia?*"

"Oh, Irkutsk was scarce the penalty for refusing to marry the girl—God forbid! But if I never give you another piece of advice, Sasha Sekovsky, do take this: do not ever, *ever* tangle with a woman scorned, do you hear me? Anyhow, I suppose I was the one 'chosen' to accept the blame for this young woman's little 'mishap,' because three months before that time, I had happened, while on leave to Petersburg, to pay her a brief visit—at about the same time that she apparently received a much more intimate caller than myself. Upon returning to my post at hospital in Sevastopol, I received a letter with her outrageous demand. When I replied that I would have no part of it, she stunned the life out of me with her conniving threats, swearing that she would use her influence to ruin me. I had some hint of what was coming, and rushed back north to Petersburg, retained an attorney, and hurriedly divided up every trace of my real property, signing half over to Sofya and half to Vera in temporary abeyance; much too smugly, I felt certain that I had outwitted this woman and her vindictive paramour at their own game, that they legally could no longer cause me ill. Then your Uncle Dmitri suffered his famous heart spasm in the apiary, and I inherited the old Ilmen estate—that's what we called this place in those days. So this—ahem!—young lady and her co-conspirator in love and angst went straight for my jugular vein."

I stare up long and hard from my hat. "Father, please forgive me, but I still do not understand."

He laughs as if still hardly able to understand it all himself. "Oh, yes!" he goes on, shaking his head. "It is an effective, useful ploy—most brilliant chess strategy ever devised, I daresay! It is why, when compared to the gentry in Britain, in Germany—to all the other European houses—we Russians possess not one whit of political power. Through the guise of autocracy, they utilize the tactic whenever some cocksure, headstrong upstart like me becomes a bit too pleased with himself, believing he has outfoxed them. In a nutshell, what was ordered of me was to shut down the entire Ilmen estate—which they knew to then be my largest inheritable piece of property—and move, uprooting farm, hives, clerks, serfs, and all; I mean, all the families, the whole damn tweaking village, mind you—to some inconspicuous, rotting outpost near Tashkent."

"You mean—you were ordered to forfeit, to surrender our lands? *In entirety?*"

"Exactly."

"That ludicrous!" I cry, my ears steaming for revenge.

"Indeed. It is also how Russian nobles have been kept in strict tow in this country for several centuries."

"But that can only be ordered by the Tsar!"

"Correct again."

"But—who was this woman? And just whose child *was* this, that she could arrange for an order of estate forfeiture if you refused to marry her? The—the only person possessing that kind of power is the Tsar!"

I stop, mortified, the guilty words catching deep within my throat.

Father rolls his eyes, shrugging, nodding with exasperation. "Yes, Sasha," he blurts out. "I know!"

"M-My God!" I stammer out. "The child was the *Tsar's?"*

Again he shrugs. "Such was my conclusion as well! Oh, hell—I can't say I have any tangible proof about the whole pitiable affair—who ever could? But who else can send a man to Siberia for thirty long years for something so trivial as spurning a capricious, spirited young lady suddenly finding herself in need—rather quickly, mind you—of a well-educated, appropriately-born young husband?"

Sighing, I turn my hat over, staring into the ring of fur mounded about the crown. "Siberia," I murmur haltingly. "Thirty years."

Father's dark eyes go somber and silent, focused into a long tomb of memories dancing in the woods far off past the headstone of Melissa's grave.

"And the court martial?" I inquire at last.

"Humph! Like a fool, I thought that through it all, I would be able to retain my position in the Guards. I'd just taken first lieutenant's bars, you know." Leaning back against the fence, he frowns and crosses his arms. "I had no idea that this whole ordeal was going to resolve itself so drastically until the day I was served with the order to appear before the Commandant. From there, they took me to the brig, and suddenly I realized that my whole life was as well as over. There was this lieutenant-colonel—also a physician—onto whose bad side I had managed to thoroughly entrench myself after a card game one slow Saturday night out at the medic's station in the field. With his cooperation, they concocted some unthinkable trumped-up charge about my insubordination that supposedly resulted in the deaths of two officers while at hospital in Sevastopol."

Black fire begins to char the greenery of the forest to cinders all around me. "Who was this lieutenant-colonel?" I demand, hairs bristling up on the back of my neck.

Father pushes off from the fence and hurries toward me, resolutely shaking his head. "No, Sasha—"

"I swear, I'll wring the man's filthy, lying neck!"

"No!" Father's hand grips into my arm, steadying it. "No names, no revenge, Sasha—no axes to grind, no more prices to pay—please. Besides, the man's dead thirteen years now. The woman who started this whole business is long dead also—and dear God forgive me, the Tsar certainly met his just deserts. I think I was even more pleased to see him blown to bloody bits than the Narodnaya revolutionaries! Please, Sasha, don't nurse any vengeful yearnings over this. I have found that the only way to keep one's sanity intact in this world is to simply try to proceed with one's life. It is enough for me that the next Tsar Aleksandr was gracious enough to grant my petition for pardon. I was indeed quite lucky to have my title and my rights restored: the malicious lieutenant-colonel had duly discredited himself in another back-stabbing medical scandal a couple of months before my release—although I wish to God he had had the decency to do so a few years sooner! Ahh, well . . . ." Taking a sharp breath of the icy-crisp air, Father sighs, dreamily scanning about the forest. "At least I finally got this wondrous place back!" he says with a smile. "The Crown confiscates all your earthly possessions once they send you packing off to the East, you know."

"Is it true," I ask, mournfully searching his face, "that the condemned walk to Siberia?"

"Ahh, yes . . . the ancient posting-road," Father says with a sigh, staring back up through the trees. "Yes, Sasha—the long trek there on foot causes the death of many."

"My God, Papa! How on earth did you ever survive?"

He laughs. "Luck! And a bit of wit, I suppose. They were in dire need of a doctor for the mine encampment. Prisoners were dropping like flies from the cholera when I arrived there. Near died of it myself—that is the whole point of the Siberian camps: they haven't the guts to string a man up on a gibbet in front of his accusers, and instead sentence him to slow wasting death. But as things happened, I was fortunate. When one's business is saving lives, the recipients of your ministrations ofttimes show profound gratitude. Such indeed saved my sanity and my soul—one of the lives I nursed along through the plague of that first winter was that of a prison guard, the Major in charge of discipline throughout the camp. All the other *plenniki* scoffed at me, called me a madman, said that I should simply let the swine die and bid him good riddance—but I helped the man, got him back up on his feet, and he never forgot it. For thirty years thereafter, he made certain that whenever assignments changed, I was never posted much farther than a building's distance beyond his reach. And he helped me procure supplies and the medicines I needed for the sick, often when official channels were clogged beyond all hope. He even snuck me extra rations of food, all from his own table, during the times when my own health was shaky and the prison gruel not fit for feeding a dog. Loath as I was to accept favors over the other *plenniki,* I took what I needed to survive. Because that is what one does in Siberia, Sasha—what one must. In order to survive."

"For the whole thirty years, this man helped you?"

"Oh, yes. I know I would never have walked out of there, save for his mercy. People may suffer through five, perhaps even ten years in the camps—but of how many have you ever heard, managing to stay alive to come home and talk about thirty years of Siberian imprisonment?"

Shyly, I lay my hand upon Father's arm. "Do you know if this man is still alive, Papa? Could you tell me his name? Perhaps I could write a letter, or in some other way send some expression of a son's gratitude."

"When we return to the house, you can thank him in person, if you want. The name you know him by is Vliny. Yes, yes—our own Vliny! He's scarce left my side since I helped him out that sickbed almost fifty years ago, Sasha."

Dumbfounded, I start shaking my head. "But all those stories about the War! The two of you in the Crimea—"

"Are precisely that. Simply stories."

"But—Vliny and Marnya . . . then what about all the jokes about Ippolit?"

"Oh, they cooked a hog-shank into a meat pie, all right!" he replies, laughing uproariously and smacking his hand to his knee. "All the tales about the way they got rid of Ippolit are true to the mark! And then Vliny married Marnya, about a year after I married your mother."

With a harsh sigh, I clutch weary fingers to my brow, attempting to rub back the sudden enormity of new truths. "Are there any more startling revelations, Father? Or is this finally the last of them?"

He claps me on the shoulder, chuckling, and shoves his hands down into his pockets again. "Well, uh—there is one further—ahem!—tiny confession I suppose I must make to come completely square with you, Aleksandr." Loudly, he clears his throat. "You see, your grandmother, Melissa's mother—"

"—was a Zhelanov."

"Ned told you?"

"I found out."

"Oh, my!" Father exclaims. "I hope you did not become too terribly angry—"

"Positively furious!"

Throwing back his head, Father bursts into another pealing roar of laughter.

"Is not all so bleating funny!" I shout out, pummeling him with my hat.

Still laughing, he swipes the hat from me with both hands and crams it flat onto my head.

"Hey!"

"All right—come, my slightly over half-Russian, smirking, squirming progeny!"

"Exactly five-eighths Russian!" I yell, pounding for his ribs.

He grabs my arm, urging me back toward the horses. "Yes, yes—you exactly five-eighths Russian, three-eighths British, acid-tongued, rampaging heathen of a black-eyed warlord—then mount that prancing Arabian steed and take the whole blithering Empire to task, by damn! Is high time you escorted your old papa back home to his supper."

Mounting hurriedly, I whirl around, pointing down at him. "Papa! You'd best not ever again taunt me about England!"

Doffing his hat, Father swoops down into a low bow in front of Jespa's jittery hooves. "Sasha, you have my solemn word," he cries, laughing. "From now on, I shall bless the day I went to England!"

* * *

"No!" he roars, his fist slamming like an anvil down onto the corner of the desk.

"And why *not?*" I shout back, glowering hot sparks back at him.

"Because I *said* so, Sasha!"

"Dammit! You know what you are? Naught but an insufferable, asinine, vile old hypocrite!"

His hand flies upward toward my face; slams instantly back down onto the desk. "Will you kindly make some effort to curb your cursing tongue while living in my house, Aleksandr?"

"Not until you explain your reason for saying 'no!'"

"I have more than enough reason for saying 'no,' and am under no obligation to explain any of my motives to you!"

"Indeed! Exactly as you have never explained anything else of import to me: about Siberia, nor about my mother! For my whole blessed life!"

"Blast it, Sasha!" he shouts, springing to his feet. "Get out of here; I am telling you for the last time: no one is going into Melissa's room!"

Whirling around, I storm out of the study, slamming the door ferociously behind. Flinging open the door to my own room, I stomp inside and slam that shut too, sending quaking shivers across every eastern plank of the house. Half-blinded by rage, I hoist up my cane and smash it clattering across the floorboards—and then cursing him, cursing my own foolishness, I snatch it back up again with angry, stumbling awkwardness and throw myself upon the cushions of the window seat, curling up into its farthest corner.

In the hall, I soon hear Vliny's coaxing voice; Father's continuing angry protests. Again the study door slams—and from inside, I hear them talking in low wrangling undertones, the sounds muffled and indistinguishable.

Lifting my head, I peer through folds of the curtains into the stark, still night. All through supper, all through the elaborate dessert course of *sharlottka* pastries dressed with Marnya's famed raspberry-spice topping, he was so jovial, so open, so downright refreshing to converse with—as if overwhelmed with relief at having at last come completely honest with me after these many long years of veiled, guarded allusions. But once I make my tentative request, he completely flies into a rage, like a lunatic, upon hardly the slightest provocation!

Is it so outrageously inhuman of me to want to go into my mother's room?

Muttering another slew of curses against the continued existence of my father's soul, I yank out the dark velvet-lined case and angrily start fitting together the joints of my flute.

As soon as I flatten my chin into the curve of the embouchure plate, a hesitant knock sounds upon my door.

In response, I straight away attack *fortissimo* high 'C'—forcing the tone into a piercing, chalk-screeching wail that howls far off across the space of the rafters for as long as my lungs can sustain it.

Unfazed, the knock sounds again at my door.

"Come in—if you think your ears can tolerate what your patience can't!" This time, I attack high 'B'.

As Father slips through the door, I ease the flute down into my lap and cross my arms, demanding sarcastically: "Yes? *Sir?"*

Eyes riveted to the floorboards, he slowly approaches the window seat, and murmurs without looking at me: "All right. Go in, if you want—I no longer care."

And to my astonishment, he then lays down before my feet on the window-seat cushions the key to Melissa's room.

Back by the door, he glances over his shoulder. "Forgive me, Sashenka," he whispers in a hoarsened undertone. "I am, as I have told you before, an insensitive, pig-headed fool—a man who has spent near all of his adult life looking out, by necessity, for his own welfare above that of all others. For someone like me, there is inevitably great difficulty in catering to the whims of a wife. Or to those of a son."

The door shuts softly behind him.

With a deep sigh, I stare down to the key; glance back over to the door. Look down once more at the incredible gleaming sight of the key.

Hot with shame, my flute in one hand, the key in the other, I stumble back out into the hall—and stand hesitating for what seems like untold hours just outside his study door.

"Father?" I venture at last.

"Come in, Sasha."

Head bent over his massive mahogany desk, he sits intensely studying a manuscript which he has been translating into French from the Sanskrit. "Yes?" Wearily, he looks up at me.

With trembling fingers, I set the key down before him on the desk, guiltily avert my eyes, and clutch up my flute with both hands, saying low under my breath: "I had entertained the hope, Papa, that we could venture into Melissa's room together."

Father picks up the key and holds it out in front of my face. "Sasha, you take this key and go into her room whenever you want. But please do not insist that I go in with you."

Frowning, I demand: "Why not?"

The pen with which he has been writing slams down onto the desk. In exasperation, he shuts his eyes. "Because," he rasps out, creasing his fingers to his brow, "if I go into that room, I may never come back out."

"Never come back out?" I gasp after him incredulously.

Waving me off, he cups his head into both hands, moaning, murmuring: "She's in there."

"Who's in there?"

"Liss. Your mother."

"What?"

Astounded, I search across the sorrowful angles of his face—attempting to piece together the meaning of the joke—but his expression, somber and bent determinedly onto the pointy fountain-tip of his pen, remains deadly serious. "Father!" I blurt out at last. "That is crazy!"

"Of course it is crazy!" he storms back. "Why do you think I refuse to go back in there?"

"Oh, for God's sake! Melissa—Mother is not in that room!" I stammer nervously. "She's dead, Papa: in the ground, buried, laid to rest. Today, we visited her grave."

"Of course your mother is dead! And buried, and in the ground in that grave! Everywhere *except* in that room. In there, she's still waiting for me," he insists, his voice lowering into a hushed, awe-struck whisper. "In the bed."

Shaking my head furiously, I point my flute at him, exclaiming: "Good God! You've gone daft, Papa!"

"Perhaps. You don't believe me? Go ahead and take that key and go in there and see for yourself."

"Papa!"

"And will you stop waving that flute around like a toy conductor's baton?" he demands, wincing as he watches me. "Fifteen hundred marks!" he then mutters, rolling his eyes.

Wholly at a loss for words, I stand frowning, gaping down at him.

"Well!" he cries. "I knew you'd never believe me." Again he holds up the key. "Go ahead! Go in there. I tell you, Melissa is waiting for me in the bed."

"No one was awaiting me when I snuck in there three years ago!" I shout.

"No, but you were scarce looking for her like a lovesick swain, now, were you?"

A slow chill gnaws its way into the core of my heart as, uncomfortably, I begin to recall my strange dream about Melissa that summer night not so long ago at Sheremetev's palace.

"Go ahead!" Father bellows on with insistence. Slamming the key back onto the desk, he stares down at it, wide-eyed. "Go on into her room, Sasha—and see what I mean."

Following his gaze, I reply: "Perhaps come the morn, Papa. Right now, I, uh, think I had best go practice."

"She's in there, Sasha. I swear to you, it is God's honest truth! I never told you anything about it before because I knew you would never believe me."

"Uh-huh."

I shuffle for the door.

"Sasha?"

Stiffening, I press my brow against the knotty pinewood jamb, my stomach churning in anticipation against the next preposterous, utterly inconceivable thing he might say. "Yes?"

"Why don't you practice in here? I cannot tell you how much I've missed the sound of your music in this house all these past long months."

"But, Papa! I've scarce had a chance since I've been back! The headjoint pitch must be completely flat."

Again Father's pen slams wrathfully down onto the desk. Moaning in exasperation, he starts raking his hands through his hair. "Can I not make but one request of my son!" he yells out. "Mind you—not an order! Not an Imperial directive—merely a simple request! Can I not make but one request of my son that will *not* result in a renewed threat of all-out war between him and his father?"

Begrudgingly, I shut the study door and take a seat over on his divan, and after my obligatory long tones, I say haltingly: "And? Your pleasure?"

Father glances up from his writing with a wary nod. "Do you think," he murmurs, "that we might—perhaps—actually be able to agree upon the *Andante Cantabile?* Tchaikovsky's Fifth?"

I cannot help but smile. "Papa," I assure him, "you know I will never take you to task over Tchaikovsky's Fifth."

As I start playing, the pain in his face eases away into a tired, mellow contentment. Casting away the pen, he cries out: "Wait!" The brandy carafe and two snifters quickly cradled up within his grasp, he hurries over toward me, pouring a generous draught into each glass.

I hesitate only briefly before taking the delicate crystal snifter from his hand with murmured thanks.

"Forever to Tchaikovsky's Fifth, then!" he exclaims, grinning, as our glasses clink. "Eventually the fireworks simmer down. Welcome home, Sasha."

* * *

Of course, it was inevitable that he would come, and of course, it was inevitable that with his coming, so many expectations would follow.

"What do you mean, you will not go?" Father demands, his jaw dropped, his fork slamming onto the table.

"Exactly what I said."

"But I have already written to Glazunov!" he roars, his face reddening with a burning flush. "I have already requested another interview."

"Then you might as well write back and withdraw your request!" I warn him. "I am not going."

Stare held to the table, Nikolai begins refolding the corners of his napkin in a fidgeting, impatient rush. "If you would both excuse me," he says softly, "I think I shall go and check if I packed my rosin."

Seeking escape as well, I storm over to the window, glaring after my cousin's crisply pounding footsteps, only far too aware that his rosin is always the first item he packs, even before a choice of repertoire, before he travels anywhere, whether it be across town or across the Continent.

Guiltily, I scan past Father's head and the dining room entrance to ascertain that Nikolai has indeed exited the hallway, and then sneak a cigarette with shaking fingers, ever mindful to seize any opportunity away from my cousin's scolding scrutiny. "You may continue your rampage, Father, all night, should you choose," I declare, spewing out a stream of smoke and turning my back upon him. "I have chosen not to enter the St. Petersburg Conservatory."

"Sasha, my God—you have spent years preparing to go!"

"Well! I have changed my mind."

To my surprise, he does not answer—and when I glance over my shoulder, it is to find him staring forlornly down at his empty supper dishes, hand to his brow, seemingly drained of all further combative energy.

"You—you are ashamed of me," he finally says.

My heart catches in my throat. "Oh, Papa, no—of course not! It is simply that I—"

"You are ashamed to return, to mix in Petersburg society again. Because of me."

"Father, no! You are terribly, horribly wrong!" I cry, bounding over to him. "I could never be ashamed of you, nor of all that you have been through! Dear Lord, after everything you have told me over the past few days, there is no one of whom I could be more *proud.*"

"Well! Then why do you not wish to further your studies at the Music Conservatory?"

Again I whirl around, seeking refuge at the window.

"Dammit, Sasha!" he bellows, rising from his chair. "Answer me!"

"You will not understand."

"Oh, Christ in Heaven! I just knew that I never should have told you of any of it!"

"That is not the reason!"

"Just what else can the reason be?"

"Blast it, Father! I am not ashamed of you; I am ashamed of me!"

"Well, God's teeth, boy! Whatever the hell for?"

"Because of what happened in Moscow!"

Our roaring voices moan into a vacant gulf of silence.

"M-Moscow!" he stammers out, incredulous. *"Moscow! That* was where you were all these past months?"

Taking scrupulous pains to avoid his gaze, I cross my arms and glare sullenly back out the window.

"What in hell's name possessed you to go to Moscow?" he rages on, pushing off from the table in such a tempest of fury that half the flatware flies scattering across it in all directions. "If I told you once, Sasha, I told you a thousand times: if there is anyplace on earth that a Novgorodian blueblood had best keep his ass away from, it is that veritable monstrosity of a barbarian city!"

"Father, I would appreciate, for once, your sparing me the history lesson."

"And Aleksandr, I would appreciate, for once, your coming halfway honest with me!"

"Dammit!" I shout, slamming both fists onto the window sill and whirling around. "You promised there would be no more questions!"

"But, Moscow!" he continues ranting on. *"Moscow!"*

Heartbeats pounding up into my ears in wild, hurtful spurts, I snatch off my spectacles and press back to the window, a trembling fist caught to my brow in an attempt to stave off continued remnants of the nightmare, Sheremetev's poisonous owl-eyes ever lurking just outside past every dusky, snow-flecked swaying of the birch.

In supplication, Father's hand grips my arm, and I flinch away, shouting: "Don't! Let go of me! Dammit, I said *let go!"*

After an exasperated sigh, he does so as I whirl back upon him with angry warning: "I do not wish to speak any further about Moscow! And I would appreciate if you would stop pressuring me to audition for the composition program at the St. Petersburg Conservatory."

Shaking his head with a woeful frown of misgiving, Father follows the lowered direction of my stare. "All right," he murmurs at last. "I promised there would be no questions. You do not wish to attend the St. Petersburg Conservatory, I will not insist upon it, will not force you to go, if you are so set against it. If it is not what you truly want."

Stunned at this ease of acquiescence, I steal a quick glance up to his face.

To find his eyes lingering long upon me, an aching pang of sadness escaping before he abruptly looks away, seeking out his own phantasms of memory lurking far beyond the frosty pane of glass.

Finally he says: "And? Will you go back to May's?"

"Oh, please," I beg him, groaning, "do not force me to return to that wretched school!"

"All right, so? You do not wish to enter the Conservatory, you refuse to return to May's. Just what exactly *do* you want, Sasha?"

I allow the pause to drag on almost to infinity before risking my answer: "I wish to stay here."

"What? In Novgorod? But, Sasha! The town has no adequately suited preparatory school."

"Can you not assist me with my studies, Papa?"

Taken aback, Father tucks both hands into the pockets of his velvet smoking jacket. "Well, I suppose I could," he replies with a startled smile. "But as far as graduation exams—"

"Oh, for Christ's bloody sake!" I blurt out. "Who cares about such drivel as diplomas?"

"Education ensures social ranking, Sasha!" he declares staunchly.

"Well! I have been tutored in harmony and notation, as well as woodwind technique, since I was nine. I am well-versed in all the literatures, I speak three languages—and thanks to Uncle Ned and his numerical treatise, I have been pursuing self-study in mathematics for the past three years, clear up to the workings of Euclidian geometry! Does education, as you see it, hinge solely upon a near meaningless scrap of paper? Oh, all right!" I cry, ducking away from his imploring nod. "I am not insisting upon never returning to my studies, Papa. It is simply that, for this year, at least, I need a spell of peace."

Father rolls his eyes. "Oh, very well, Sasha—I suppose I can assist you. The current term has dragged on for far too long in any case to allow you catch up in a reasonable amount of time. But if you are going to remain here," he goes on, wagging an insistent finger, "I expect help with the book work in Pavel's office. Lord knows, the postings are yet overdue. Bulya was short-handed with the ledgers all last summer. And next summer, we will resurrect this conversation in its entirety, because despite the endless talk and damn revolutionary incidents piling up one after another, the St. Petersburg Conservatory has been producing fine composition graduates for years, and I'd be loath to see you forfeit all your years of study and training on a mere youthful whim."

I nod with relief, murmuring: "Yes, sir."

From out in the drawing room, the 'A' sounds on the piano, and Nikolai can be heard tuning up his violin.

Father inclines his head toward the doorway. "I think it best now for you to go join your cousin," he says softly. "You know he can only stay for this one night. And all these months, the poor lad has been starved for your company, Sasha."

As Marnya hurries in to retrieve the supper dishes, Father stalls to joke with Vliny in the woodroom, leaving me alone with my trepidation as I stub out my cigarette in a saucer and make my way haltingly toward the drawing room, and Nikolai.

My cousin has greatly changed. No longer is he so intent upon impressing me clear unto mortification with his whorehouse stories, which used to hold such sway over our reunions after long periods of separation. Likewise, although eighteen now, taller, and befit of a burnished, rugged handsomeness quite strikingly resembling my father's, he has shaved the moustache off, and no longer seems so affected with his vanity. Instead, every movement of his hands, every glance of his somber gray eyes comes edged now with an inscrutable yearning sadness, as if some alien force beyond the world's reach has cruelly touched and stung him to his deepest core. Earlier, when he first arrived and dashed toward me out of the slowing troika, his sable hat flying off into the snow and his arms outstretched with the boundless, laughing affection we have fawned upon one another for so many happy years, I know he was hurt when I shrunk from returning his embraces. And all during our afternoon conversations, then during supper, he and Father have continued eyeing one another cautiously in between their mutual glances at me, guilty stares darting back down to their hands or plates again whenever I would take note—as if between themselves these past months there has grown some sort of secret understanding and strange new closeness in which I cannot share, and yet, ironically, of which I am the very cause.

In the drawing room, I find him with his head bent, the blond-white streaks his hair has gleaned over the summer blending into murky hues of wintery towhead-ash as, in studious concentration, he leans over from his seat on the piano bench, tuning Uncle Petya's cello, which he has brought with him, and upon which I have never seen him lay a hand since his father's death nearly a year and a half ago.

Without looking upward, he murmurs: "So. I take it you will not come."

I shrug, intensely studying the handle of my cane. "It is for the best."

"I'll miss you."

"I know."

Uncomfortably, I watch his steadied testings of the strings, and at last clear my throat. "You, uh, never told Father. Whence Uncle Ned's first telegram about me came?"

Head still bent, Nikolai answers gruffly: "Uncle Misha was already half-mad with fright for you. I thought it best not to impart any further distress. And you know how he feels about Moscow."

"Indeed, so I have yet been reminded again." Letting out a long sigh, I nod toward the cello. "So. You finally decided to try your hand at the old girl?"

Stare kept to the strings, Nikolai replies: "Had to expiate my demons. First I lost Father. Then I thought I lost you."

He looks up at me.

"The bloodstains in that apartment where I found your billfold," he reminds me. "We thought you were dead."

Stiffening away from his inquiring stare, and wishing to God that we could all somehow magically forget about my unfortunate disappearance, I lean back against the sideboard of the piano, whispering: "So did I."

Nikolai sets the cello back against the bench and comes to stand awkwardly beside me. "Look," he says, wringing his hands together, "I'll make every effort to travel here as often as I can steal away until you resume your studies in Petersburg. You will need someone to help keep you musically on your toes. And it was I, after all, who insisted upon our frequenting Murzhinsky's Tavern during that foolhardy week. To tell you truly, Sasha, when it comes to your disappearance, I feel directly responsible. And I know you are still loath to discuss the matter, but if you ever wish to, please be assured—I would listen."

"Thank you for your concern, Nikolai," I cry, reddening. "But I would simply prefer not to dwell upon it!"

"Well," he says, pointing over toward my flute case, "will you at least play harmony with me, then?"

With a smile of relief, I open out the case and begin piecing the joints together. "Harmony I'll play anytime you ask, Nikolai Zhelanov! Every chance with you is a true privilege."

"Oh, posh on it!" he cries, laughing, managing an embarrassed grin at last.

"So? And on what have you been working of late?" I nod toward the notebook of manuscripts he has brought with him.

Suddenly aglow with a burst of his old enthusiasm, he flips open the leather portfolio. "Do you remember when we were corresponding last year, the arrangement we had worked over for the opening *Largo,* Rimsky's *Sheherazade?"*

"Oh, yes!" I point down to the notations. "In unison, flute and violin expound the stormy notes of the Sultan's brutal wrath, followed by the solo in triplets: you take it first, as written; I follow up on the cadenza and then we banter back and forth, doubling each other into the chase back upon the full-scale melody."

"Excellent, I was so hoping you'd remember!"

"Oh, I could never forget this. Next to Tchaikovsky's Fifth, and most assuredly the *Pathetique Overture*, it is my utmost favorite."

By the time we finish warming up, Father, Vliny, Marnya and Eva, along with her infant son, have taken seats in the drawing room. Both perched upon the French provincial chairs with their right legs identically crossed, Father and Vliny continue their mimicry by smoking away on their pipes and making twin gestures of easy, besotted contentment. After pinning up her braids, Eva begins bouncing the wide-eyed bundle on her knee—while amidst the voluminous swarm of her crocheting, Marnya swoons over and over: "Akkh, Blessed Virgin—a concert! A concert!"

"Perhaps not a concert, as such, Marina Ivanovna," Nikolai tells her, laughing. "But we shall attempt to please." Pointing across at me in a teasing stab with the bow, he then says: "Shall we?"

Upon his count, we both pound into the low tempestuous tones of the Sultan's overture—and then I drop off as Nikolai takes up his solo discourse of Sheherazade's lilting voice, promising her wealth of Sinbad's tales and begging the Sultan for mercy through the sweet glassy prayer of the violin.

Watching Nikolai play never fails to astound me, and particularly this piece: spiced with exotic flavors of twirling Eurasian melodics, Sheherazade's pleading is the bared heart of Rimsky, and the scarred soul of longing, hurting, questing, and triumphing that is so unequivocally

Russian. Cascading up and down the scales in poignant, hovering encore, luring every other trivial sound on earth away from my enraptured ears, the music pulls me along into its lover's trance until I stand gaping in awe at the violin—just like all the other times: stunned to silence, worshiping bare spires of sound, drawfed by the magnificence of Nikolai's gifted presence, my flute dropped to my side, my cue entirely forgotten.

He repeats the encore once again and then, with a frown of impatience, glances up at me, barking: "Sasha!"

"Yes?" The image of the dancing bow swims before my eyes, the whole room gone entirely aglaze.

"This *is* where you come in," Nikolai replies, sharply tapping his foot, pointing with the bow to the manuscript.

"Oh!"

From across the room, both Father and Vliny burst into a ruckus of guffaws and knee-slapping laughter, Vliny bellowing out: "Looks dumb-struck te me!"

"Love-struck is what I'd call it," snorts Father, grinning mischievously over at Nikolai.

"You two fools!" I shout, flushing near to my feet. "Is scarce Nikolai; is on account of the music!"

"Sasha!" Nikolai exclaims, grinning over at Father. "Do you intend to naught but stand around forever trading quips with these two barbarians?"

At this, Father lets out a derisive, laughing hoot—while Nikolai turns back to me and continues: "Or are we actually going to play this piece?" Imperiously, he starts tapping the music stand with his bow.

"You bet your boots we are going to play this piece! Catch up if you can, Maestro!" Wrathfully, I snatch up my flute and spring back into the melody.

Never one to be caught off guard, Nikolai leaps again into the *Largo* with me, although continuing to grin over at Father while muttering across his stringings: "Never know about these hot-aired woodwind players—tsk, tsk!"

Ignoring the reply of howling laughter, I set my concentration upon the melody, determined—for once at least—to outdo the prodigious violin.

We proceed into what we call 'the chase'—he taking the melody first and following in Rimsky's traditional meter for the violin solo; me picking it up as he leaves off, scaling through the full range of notes on the flute while he lilts behind in the background; he picking it up again as I leave off, lilting behind—and then over and over, back and forth we 'chase' one another until, all laughter now entirely forgotten, our tormentors burst into a thunderous round of applause.

"Keep going, keep going—simply pick it up again!" Nikolai commands, quickly stowing away his prized Guarnerius and bounding over to the cello. "I'm going to accompany, just as in the arrangement. You will have to bear with me, I've still not built up enough stretch in my fingers. Come, Sasha—continue along with the melody, don't lose the momentum!"

In response, I dash back into Sheherazade's adventurous song again—and the high notes of the flute begin to soar out in triumph above the cello's steady tones of plaintive harmony.

The applause showered upon us afterwards indicates no doubt of our success. "Yes!" shouts Father with an approving roar. "Now, that is what I call music, talent, and gift! Lord in Heaven, boy—you may have no heart for your studies this year, but wait until the next! Oh, stop scowling as if I'm a nagging old mother—I can tell how much you love to play." His chuckles blend in with Vliny's and Nikolai's as all three of them burst out with another round of applause for my bravado with the flute. "Indeed, Aleksandr Sekovsky!" Father exclaims again, pointing across the room with a knowing wink as I attempt to subdue my grin behind cover of the piano's music stand. "You cannot convince me that music's passion no longer stirs your soul! Oh, no—I think this winter my Sashenka will be certain to recover his old aspirations and find his way to one of those Imperial Orchestras yet!"

* * *

"Sasha?"

The spell of night claws upon a fringing vacuum—as if a voice, a chorus, all sound on earth had suddenly met death. I seize the hand held out, grip the shoulder steadying my shoulder, and cower away from the hollow rasps of breath, the drenched beads soaking the sheets stone cold: the sweat, the panting, both of which are mine.

"Sasha?"

"Did—did I scream?"

"Yes."

Oh, God. The fifth time in as many nights.

"Oh, forgive me, Papa! I did not mean to awaken you. Again."

From behind, Father starts fussing about with the fur throw, wrapping it up about my heaving shoulders. "Everything is perfectly all right," he calls to the doorway—where Marnya and Vliny, their faces half-hidden in flickering murky shadows, await with a couple of candle tapers held up to the dark recesses of the walls.

Marnya pulls away first. "I'll go mix up some o' the sleepin' tea," she mutters, covering her head with her crocheted shawl.

"No!" I protest, pointing after her—but she saunters off down the stairs anyway, entirely ignoring my pleas. "Vliny!" I cry insistently. "Please, go and stop her from taking the trouble."

"Might do you some good," Father suggests. "You know how that woman has a brew for every ailment and then some. Certainly steered me through many a rough night after your mother—"

He stops abruptly, harsh words trailing off into the old chasm of memory and regret.

At last regaining some control over the trembling, I attempt to shirk off Father's weighty protective embrace, insisting: "Please, will you stop? I am quite all right!"

"Indeed? If that be the case, then why can you scarce recover your breath?"

Such observation boasts considerable merit: still hacking away, I grip both hands to my chest while emphatically shaking my head back and forth in response to his berating expression.

"It's the smoking," he declares, making another critical survey of the cigarette case on my nightstand. "Most people can tolerate tobacco, Sasha—"

"Yes, I know—'but others have no business tearing through twenty-five in a day.'" Again I shake my head—over the past two days, his concern about my indulging has been our most frequent topic of conversation. Snatching up the cigarette case, I stuff it into his hand. "You are right, I have got to stop—especially if I expect to continue managing a woodwind. Go ahead, get rid of all of them; more are in my coat pocket downstairs. Throw them into the stove. You are right, Papa—you, Nikolai, everyone is right."

Corners of his lips turning upward in satisfaction, Father at last rises from the bed, tucking the cigarette case into his nightshirt pocket. "Too bad your cousin is no longer here to see this. Every time you let off smoking, he near jumps for joy."

Instead, I am most profoundly relieved that pressing matters at the Conservatory dictated Nikolai's departure for Petersburg early this morn. Only for one night, at least, was my cousin subjected to my screams.

"Are you certain you are all right?" Father asks, his doubtful frown lingering from the doorway.

"Yes, yes!" With impatience, I wave him off, huddling back far down into the bedclothes.

But once he leaves, I can summon no peace, nor wrest back even a meager semblance of sleep. The old hauntings only well up in renewed torment: again, from the other witch's stake, that still unrecognizable lover, his desperate fingers stabbing out for mine in life's last caress as the flames sear up high around us, the scene finally evaporating off into visions of charred hell. The ghostly Melissa's sad eyes of love and cooing words of comfort then hover over at the window—until she fades away into strange memories of little black-haired Zhenya and her temperamental mother, Lyubov. Who both melt, as always, into hated emerald walls and the lurking eyes of the ever-greedy, insatiable Pierre . . . .

In the kitchen, I find her, huddled like the quintessential babushka she is at the samovar over her favorite copper teakettle, frantically stirring an old wooden ladle into the brew she has whipped up as pungent, steamy fumes of chamomile laced with honey and horsetail grass drift upward toward the unsuspecting rafters. "Akkh, dumplin'," she mutters, nodding approval as I grope over to the table. "Some o' this blessed drink'll have ye back sleepin' like a tiny babe in no time."

I down two glassfuls of the tea she brings before stopping her on her way back to ladle up a third, seizing hold of her arm and rasping out: "Matushka—"

"Yaa! An' what is it that ye be in need of now, my blessed angel dove?"

When I duck away in shame, hiding my head down before her in both hands, she starts to run a fond, gnarled old finger through my tangled hair, urging me closer, her tongue snapping away in grandmotherly clucks of tenderness: "Akkh, dumplin'—ye're *never* too old! Never too old fer the likes o' yer old Matushka—now, are ye?"

Stifling a sob, I throw both arms around Marnya's waist and crush my head in against her heavy bosom just as during days long ago when I was a small child.

"Give it time, my dove," she whispers, her voice a breath of cool song against my ear as she gently starts rocking the both of us back and forth. "Give it time, an' all the hurt an' pain o' whatever it all was'll go away, my love. All hurt and pain eventually goes away. Ye jest got te give it time. . . ."

The tears begin then at last: first one by one, then a veritable floodgate unleashed unto the ringing depths, unquenchable and uncontrollable—and I try to do it as quietly as possible, so as not to arouse Father yet again from his badly needed sleep; and I thank the Saints once more that Nikolai was forced to start his journey back to Petersburg early this morn, because if he saw me like this I would be mortified unto death; and I clutch my arms around Marnya fiercely as if onto my final hope for salvation, which in a way she is, because deep down she is Novgorod: old innocence and home, a birthright almost forever lost, which I now reclaim wholeheartedly to prize as my revered own forevermore. Because no matter the praise, the rounds of applause in drawing rooms innumerable for my so-called 'gift,' I know I can never return to that fickle Petersburg world of concerts, operas, recitals, and waiting in the wings with hopes of perhaps being discovered as 'the next Tchaikovsky'—despite Father's promise to resurrect our discussion about my studies soon enough next year.

For my fate lies now solely in Novgorod, where—hopefully—Sheremetev is certain never to find me.

CHAPTER FIVE

Europe by Storm: Diaghilev's *Ballet Russe*

Shading my spectacle rims from prickly whorls of the dancing snow, I jump from the troika just as the train's wheels grind to their steamy halt, its whistle sounding a triumphant blare out across the whitewashed wooden roofs of old Novgorod Station.

"Shall I take us out an' around, Yer Honor?" Rolfe calls to me, hurriedly snapping up the reins, his gestures behind toward another troika driver urging the man to curb his bellows of impatience.

"The sideyard will be fine! We'll catch up with you," I call back, waving him off. "My cousin Nikolai Petrovich is always game for a good brisk walk."

"Very good, sir!"

Perplexed, frowning, I grip up my cane and watch the troika bells jangle off into the snow shower, hard put to fathom why Rolfe—and near everyone else of late—insists upon deferring to me with such overbearing formality.

"Pardon us, Your Honor—and good day!"

"Certainly! And good day to you in turn; pardon me." Nodding to the ladies, I move aside to allow to pass the traveling group of townsfolk from the troika behind ours while mumbling to myself sardonically: "The same way they insist upon addressing Father—Heaven's Name!"

Shaking my head with incredulity, I fall in behind them and head for the station platforms. With scarce a week until the *Maslenitsa* pre-Lenten festivities, the rail yard is filled to capacity with scores of people either coming or going, as crowded as Novgorod Station ever becomes save for the week before Easter, when travel proves even more harried—although even then, this junction in our small provincial town remains dwarfed as a mere rural outpost when compared to the bustling tumult of railway stations in St. Petersburg.

At the platform, across the profusion of jostling fur and felt hats of others awaiting arrivals from the train, I once again shade my spectacles in anticipation and search amongst the debarking passengers for sight of Nikolai's familiar black sable coat. Suddenly, a collective gasp tears across the crowd, and I crane back my head, attempting to pinpoint the cause of the commotion. Sure enough, it is a woman: an exceedingly lovely woman clad like a fairy snow maiden from head to foot in sumptuous, stylish blue fox. Several gentlemen simultaneously take great pains to assist her down from the steps of the rail coach. With an embarrassed smile, she drops her eyes demurely before the crowd's enthusiastic perusal, clutches her hatbox fast to her side, and proffers her hand back toward the coach, apparently searching out her escort.

Who turns out to be none other than Nikolai.

Catching my breath, I press into the crowd, wondering what sort of mischief my debonair cousin might be up to. Upon reaching him and his conspiratorial, knowing wink, I stop short in my tracks, my jaw dropped, my voice sputtering out with all the awkwardness of a country oaf: "Dear L-Lord in Heaven! It can't be! *Anna?"*

"Oui, M'sieur Sekovsky," she replies, laughing, tucking her daintily-gloved hand down into my own.

I kiss it hurriedly. "My word, Anna! Er, pardon me—Anna Petrovna—you look positively marvelous!"

"Merci, Aleksandr Mikhailovich," she replies with a batting flutter of eyelashes.

"Dear Lord help us!" Nikolai snorts, rolling his eyes.

"Oh, poo!" Anna cries, shooting him a glare—but before she can smack him with her hatbox, he wraps an arm through hers and plants a fond kiss into the furry brim of her hat, murmuring affectionately: "Look at her, Sasha—grown up and beautiful!"

"Indeed, far too much so for words!" I reply, once more tipping my hat. Near unto two years has it been since my last encounter with my cousin Anna, during those fateful days in the Zhukovskaya townhouse before the summer of my abduction to Moscow. "Uh, I see that an extended stay in the Crimea effects a cure far better than any ten dozen tonics," I manage to say at last, groping desperately to come up with some sort of witty observation.

"And I see an extended stay in Novgorod bestows benefits of marked tangibility as well," says Anna with an approving nod, nudging

Nikolai. "Look at him, Kolya!" she exclaims. "He has become taller, and so handsome."

"You only flatter me, M'mselle," I blurt out, flushing.

At this, Nikolai breaks into a devilish grin, snatching toward my hat. "Well!" he proclaims fiendishly, "at least our country cousin's head has finally grown up past our Uncle Misha's shoulder."

In reply, I stick out my tongue at him.

"And," he raves on, going wide-eyed and closely scrutinizing my face, "is it truly so? Yes, indeed—our own Sasha has finally begun to shave!"

"Nikolai!"

As Anna bursts into a peal of shrieking giggles, I ram my fist for his ribs. "Oww! Oh, stop, Sasha!" he chokes out, laughing. "For love of the Saints, must you always take such offense at every joke?"

"Humph!" Although I crossly glare him down, in the end, I cannot forestall a smile. Heartwarming it is to find Nikolai back up to his old teasing antics, for so long was his brooding silence after last summer's death of the great maestro, Rimsky-Korsakov. To lose his revered mentor scarce within two years of his beloved cellist father seemed almost more profound a blow than my cousin could bear, and for the longest time, I worried over whether he would ever recover. A lengthy detour in Paris, fortunately, intervened with remarkable healing prowess—just as a long stint in the Crimea seems to have miraculously rid Anna of her baffling illness. And not only that—but transformed her from the clumsy, yelping girl burdened with the oversized hat into a poised, sophisticated beauty. "So, Anna Petrovna," I venture, nervously unable to dispense with the formality as I bow yet again in her direction, "you felt well enough to travel all the way to Novgorod? In the midst of a snowstorm? With the object of turning every head in the station?"

Anna leans into my arm, seizing my hand up warmly, her china-blue eyes dancing with bewitching merriment. "To see you, anything, *mon chéri* Sashenka!" she exclaims. "But seriously, I find myself not only completely cured, but as a result of my experience, have developed an interest in medicine. I chose to accompany Nikolai this trip in order to speak with Uncle Misha about my intentions."

"Interest in medicine?" I reply, cocking an eyebrow. "You mean you wish to become a nurse?"

"Oh, heavens, no," she gasps out, waving her hands with disdain. "The Saints forbid! I intend to become a doctor."

Head thrown back imperiously, Anna then waltzes out from between the two of us and proceeds down the station platform, acknowledging nods from several young gentlemen who eagerly tip their hats and scurry to assist her.

Dumbfounded, I stare back to Nikolai, who shrugs and mutters: "Yes, I am afraid she is entirely serious."

After casting another doubtful glance toward Anna, I pull out my watch. "Well," I say, pointing across the yard, "Rolfe took the troika over behind the stationhouse because so much traffic started backing up, so I'll go and—"

"No, I'll run and fetch him," Nikolai interrupts. "You stay here—I know how that leg plagues you when it becomes this cold. And we certainly cannot have Miss Blue-Fox-Regal-Highness trudging off through the snowy mud pack."

Laughing, I call after him: "Nikolai! How serious is Anna in this pursuit of hers?"

He turns and fixes upon me with a meaningful nod, replying: "Not to worry. She intends upon spending several hours querying Uncle Misha about possibilities for the Medical Academy. We shall have our chance alone."

"Good. Because—"

"Yes, I know. We have a great deal to discuss."

* * *

"Diaghilev!" I burst out.

"Shhh!" Finger pressed to his lips, Nikolai peers across my head toward the door to the drawing room, from which the voices of Father and Anna can be heard conversing enthusiastically about various medical matters in French.

"Nikolai," I whisper across at him, "I have the bulk of your letters from Paris right here!" Scarce able to contain my irritation, I point to the stack of his correspondence lying atop the orchestration notebooks strewn about the kitchen table. "You specifically stated that it was Maestro Tcherepnin who had organized these concerts."

"What I wrote was that Maestro Tcherepnin was involved in the production, along with many other notables from the Conservatory. Rimsky himself conducted his *Snow Maiden* the season before last at the *Opéra Comique*. But the actual organization, the impetus of the whole enterprise, began with M'sieur Diaghilev—and his close associates."

I roll my eyes. "You mean the Pickwickians? Oh, for God's sake, Nikolai!"

"Sasha, it is not what you think—"

"Not what I think? Might I inform you that I happen to know about the so-called *World of Art* staff: Lev Rosenberg, Shura Benois, Dima Filosofov—is not Filosofov also Diaghilev's cousin? You scarce have to tell me about their little group—and all the snooty groups that sprouted up in their stead, the legacy of May's Academy!" I groan sarcastically. "Lord, how many of these damn groups were there? The Pickwickians, Edwardians, Draconians—everyone always dreaming up some outlandish new banner cause."

"The only reason you are still fretting so about any of it is because you were never included!"

"Humph! I noticed you kept not with your snobby Edwardians for very long."

"I decided early on that one has no business succumbing to such frivolity when one has sold one's soul to—and therefore must spend near unto all of one's waking hours playing—a violin. Sasha, look—"

"No, you look—"

"Blast it! Can't you do me the courtesy of listening through an entire sentence?" Nikolai slams his tea glass down onto the table so abruptly that it cracks into several snapping, jagged pieces right within his hand.

"Akkh! No makin' o' glassholds like they used te, now is there?" From her high-backed stool behind the stove, Marnya bustles over with a ready replacement.

"Forgive me, Marina Ivanovna."

"No bother, no bother!" Overjoyed at the chance to fawn yet again over the two of us, Marnya makes a grand show of fetching Nikolai more of the spicy cinnamon tea steeping away aromatically in the copper kettle atop the samovar. After refilling my glass as well, she pauses with squinty-eyed, questioning perusal made toward my left leg, which lies propped up under several hot packs on another kitchen chair. "Akkh, dumplin'—how is the achin' tendin' now?"

"Much better, Matushka—thank you. I believe I shan't need any more warm towels for awhile. Remember, Father said not to overdo."

Clucking with motherly approval, Marnya scoops up the cracked teaglass pieces and wanders back over to her cozy cook's alcove and basketful of crocheting set behind the chimney of the stove.

Nikolai stares after her and switches in a hushed voice back to English. "She cannot understand what we are saying at all, can she?"

"Naught but the curse words, for a certainty!" I reassure him, following his gaze with a grin.

Grinning back, Nikolai ostentatiously plants a broad sugar lump in between his front teeth and starts sucking his tea through it in the atrocious Russian way, while I warn him: "Tradition or no, you'll fetch a tidy scolding should Papa catch you doing that!"

"Oh, I suppose you're right—is truly a vermin plague to the teeth, yes?" he observes, munching down the sugar lump in acquiescence. "I suppose I also should have had a doctor for a father. Anyhow, Sasha," he continues in all seriousness, "in speaking of the Pickwickians, it was scarce my intention to dredge up old wounds."

"I know, my friend—forgive me." Again I roll my eyes. "Still I suffer far too overly much from my memories as a provincial outcast at school. But Christ, Nikolai—Diaghilev?"

"Is an organizational genius, Sasha! Oh, stop looking at me so! You were not in Paris this last season; I *was*. You should have seen the *Godunov* production Diaghilev and his group put together at the *Grand Opéra*—although it was a shame they took out the tavern scene with the drunken monks—but still, eight performances, mind you, and the thing was a virtual overnight sensation! And I swear, as a result, Russian music has become the busiest topic of conversation in every salon of good taste in the city."

"I know that. You think I never catch a glimpse of the society pages? Russian music has been gaining popularity on the Continent ever since Chaliapin began his regular tours of Monte Carlo." Wistfully, I stare into my tea, ever envious of the famous basso and his incomparable voice.

"Sasha, I am telling you, this is different!" Nikolai continues excitedly, banging his fist with emphasis onto the stack of old *World of Art* magazines tucked beneath his elbows. "And do you know what Diaghilev and his friends put on in Petersburg the year before last? *Le Pavillon d'Armide*—with Pavlova herself in the role of Armida, mind you."

"The ballet?" I gasp out. "Diaghilev and his chums have become involved in the ballet?"

"Yes! And I heard it was just as sensational as the *Boris Godunov* showing turned out in Paris. So that is what they are planning to take there this season."

"The ballet? To Paris, of all places? But I thought you said this was to be a staging of opera."

"They are going to stage both opera and ballet, an interspersion of the two."

"Then they are insane! Everyone knows Parisians have no taste for the prissy *pas de deuxes* of ballet."

"Sasha, this is ballet as you have never seen it, believe me! Oh, damn—you'd know what I mean if I could simply convince you to stay in Petersburg for more than an occasional one-day visit and take in some performances with me."

Frowning, I start drumming my fingers across the table. "You say that this group of performers—with Diaghilev in charge—is that what I am to assume? You say this troupe is in need of musicians?"

"So far, they have everyone necessary for the basic orchestra. It is alternates they are attempting to round up now. You know how it can be if somebody gets in a tiff or decides to step out—the orchestra needs to have a list of competent back-ups to call on in a pinch. And Boris assures me—"

"This is Boris Timofeyevich?" So many cousins proliferate on Nikolai's father's side that I can barely keep them all sorted out—but Boris, probably in his early twenties now, was memorable several Christmastides ago at the Zhukovskaya townhouse on account of his musical expertise. "The one also from the Conservatory? Who has studied French horn?"

"Yes. It was through dear M'sieur Rimsky—God rest his soul—that my cousin came to be acquainted with Tcherepnin, who has so far been the conductor for the Diaghilev group. About a month ago, Borya made mention to me of their need for alternates—and after spending last summer on holiday in Paris and taking in what was transpiring, I felt more than enthusiastic! So last week, I met Borya and Maestro Tcherepnin for a quick breakfast, and assured them they could count me in. Whereupon they provided the preliminary orchestrations, and also said that if I knew of anyone else who might be interested in signing up as an alternate—particularly woodwinds—to pass on the word. And so," he concludes, glancing back toward the pile of correspondence, "I wrote to you."

"During which you mentioned not a word about Diaghilev!" Again I frown, shaking my head.

"Precisely because I had no doubt of your reaction!"

Idly, I begin tracing my fingers along the wood-block Russian letterings and flowery cherub-faced illustrations gracing an old 1900 edition copy of *Mir Iskustva,* or *The World of Art,* the controversial journal once edited by Diaghilev and his wayward group of friends. For whatever reason, Nikolai felt possessed to bring the copy and several other later editions along from Petersburg for my inspection. "Look, Nikolai," I say finally, catching his eye, "despite the fact that his friends in their heyday helped start up those snobby groups at school, I personally have nothing against Sergei Diaghilev."

"Yes," Nikolai replies with a sigh, his wary glance cast past my head toward Father's low monotone still humming from beyond the door to the drawing room, "but as we both know very well, somebody else does."

* * *

I stuff my fists down into the furry pockets of my ermine coat, throw back my head, and drink in another frosty, exhilarating breath. For as far as the eye can see, snow puffs glaze off endless boughs of pine and birchen forest flanking Lake Ilmen's crystal-white surface. Scarce but a verst down shore, several groups of skaters, with boisterous, laughing shouts, continue twirling about upon the thick mantle of ice.

"Such a shame about your leg," says Nikolai, shaking his head and idly kicking away at snow drifts. "And you always such a fine skater."

"Ahh, no matter," I reply, shrugging off only a twinge of remorse. Long in coming has been my reconciliation to infirmity—but as I stare off across the wondrous boundaries of my father's lands—*my* lands—all residual self-pity dissolves within the abundance for which I have become forever thankful. Never does a day go by—sometimes never does an hour go by—when I do not bless the stars, and praise my Uncle Ned's exceptionally tuned sixth sense and cunning in effecting my rescue from Sheremetev and that life of certain hell in Moscow near unto two years ago.

Yet still, of late, as the sun has lengthened each eve into gradual glimmers toward spring, I have been unable to elude a growing sense of restlessness, yearning so to once again pursue my wanderlust forevermore forsworn during those lonely November days following my return.

"Is not the story wholly exaggerated?" Nikolai inquires in a doubtful tone, nudging me back to more current musings with his elbow.

"You mean about Diaghilev? Ha! Must be, for a certainty—you know Vliny, the man thrives on embellishment. Was only when Father near murdered me for attending that exhibition with all of you that I came to believe the part about him chasing Diaghilev down past the carriage house with the shotgun. Can you imagine?"

Nikolai lets out another incredulous laugh. "I can scarce fathom Uncle Misha becoming so angry!"

"Well, the way I heard it told was—oh, what was this, five years ago now? Lord! Of course, Marnya was the one who let Diaghilev into the house—and even from the vestibule, the wealth of family portraits we possess is obvious. So by the time Father shuffles down the stairs, Diaghilev is shouting: 'It is a gold mine! A veritable gold mine!' And so he explains to Father about this exhibition he intends to put on, in the Tauride Palace in Petersburg of all places, no less! And about how he has traveled all winter everywhere about the countryside, scrounging up old portraits from every noble family he can find—sometimes out of barns and old wine cellars even—and could he requisition some of ours, which appear so fine?—et cetera. Of course, Father immediately refused: 'I'll be damned for visages of my proud Novgorodian forebears to be strung up in some decadent, two-bit art display!'—ha! Can't you *hear* him shouting that? But Vliny told me afterward that Father might have been more agreeable, had Diaghilev simply shut up, and let Father squeeze in a couple of edgewise words."

Wiping at my eyes, I stumble into Nikolai, who catches my arm and wipes once more at his own eyes, the both of us heaving out rings of frosty, hooting laughter. "In the end," I go on, "ha! Diaghilev simply would not leave! And next thing you know, Father roars out of the house after him with the shotgun, discharging two or three times into the air—and Vliny said he even took a shot at the canopy of Diaghilev's coach and missed—which must have been on purpose, because as you well know, Father never misses anything. But I guess that was enough to convince Diaghilev, who high-tailed it out of here faster than a cat with its feet on fire! Oh, Lord Jesus help me, Nikolai! You don't know how many times I have wished I had been here, and not at school in Petersburg when it happened!"

Rummaging through his coat pockets, Nikolai searches for his handkerchief, and unable to find, it borrows mine, dabbing at his eyes and seizing up my arm as—once again gone awry with my cane between my laughter and the shifting snowpack—I struggle for balance. "No wonder Papa became so cross with me for bringing you along with us to that exhibition!" he exclaims. "For years, I never could fathom his reticence about the matter."

"Oh, I knew Uncle Petya would never have allowed me to tag along with all of you if he learned of Father's forbidding me to go."

"The irony," Nikolai observes, at last getting a hold on his laughter, "is that it turned out to be such an enormous success. They took the exhibition to Paris the following year, you know—lined twelve halls of the *Salon d'Automne* with Russian pictures. I happened upon a second chance to view it when I was there that summer. Exactly like the *Godunov* enterprise—an immediate overnight success."

"Sasha!"

I turn sharply to encounter Father—clad in naught but in his rolled-up shirt-sleeves—glaring down at the two of us from the wide open doors of his study's balcony. "You march your duff back into this house this very moment, young man!" he shouts, emphatically waving out his fist. "What in the devil's name do you think you are doing out there in this weather with that leg the way it's been?"

Through cupped hands, I shout back at him: "Taking a walk, and you should try it sometime, Papa! It's invigorating!"

"Invigorating, my ass! Don't you know you're courting rheumatism in that leg, boy? Get back in here!"

Instead, grinning, I stoop downward and start scrunching up snowballs.

"Hey!" Father yells, pointing back a fierce warning.

Nonetheless, my first snowball hurls through the air, shattering apart as it hits the iron railing of the balcony—but the second plows straight into Father's ear.

"Oh, Lord Christ!" I gasp out, appalled. "I scarce meant to hit him!"

Retribution explodes in duly abrupt order, Father bellowing triumphantly: "Humph! I may be old, but I'm not dead!" Then such a torrential shower of icy snowballs begins pelting upon us one after another in quick succession from the balcony that—past our hysterical, roaring laughter—Nikolai and I barely have a chance to stoop down and scrunch up any counterparts for defense.

"Oh, no, you don't!" Father commands, pointing down at me past a warning grin as I finally start packing an icy-hard stinger inside my glove. "That's enough frivolity for one day—you two march back up here! It's high time for supper, and you'd best indulge yourselves of plenty of roasted grouse before the advent of Lententide."

As the study doors slam shut behind him, we amble our way

obediently back up the pathway toward the house. "You and Uncle Misha seem to be getting on quite well these days," Nikolai observes with a fond glance up toward the balcony.

"As I recall, we have managed rather few disagreements of late. I suppose spending so much time together on my studies forces us into an easy tolerance of one another's company. He is—" I clear my throat, and my voice chokes low. "He is a good man."

"Well," Nikolai goes on, "as you know, Anna and I must depart for Petersburg come the morn."

"Oh, yes. And I wanted to tell you—"

"I understand, Sasha," he says abruptly—and when I search his face in response, he continues on with obvious disappointment: "I can well understand if, despite my invitation, you choose to forego signing up with Tcherepnin as an alternate."

We stop short in the midst of the path, and I hold his stare, reading in his expression's somber shadow the inward struggle with which we both have been wrestling so unceasingly for the past two days.

"You have a decent life here," Nikolai goes on, sharply looking away. "I suppose had I an old estate like this coming to me in not so few years, I too would catch a yen to take up farming."

"I do not farm, Nikolai."

"Well, to mind the ledger books as you do, then. But in some respects, it is such a pity, Sasha—you have the most splendid gift for music. Although I know you have felt compelled to remain near home after, uh, whatever it was that occurred two summers ago when you were in Moscow."

Feeling my face darken, I keep my gaze fixed solidly down upon the handle of my cane.

"So, I shall inform Maestro Tcherepnin—"

"That if he will have me," I interrupt him, "I would be honored to follow along with the Diaghilev enterprise as an orchestral alternate."

Nikolai's jaw drops. "You're serious?"

"Oh, yes." Over the past two days, there has been no mistaking how earnestly my cousin desires this end. And in this last year and a half that I have kept myself cloistered like a hermit-monk at Lissushka, Nikolai has been faithful to his word, carving precious fragments from his sparse free time to visit at every possible accord. And when abroad, he has and enhanced my musical horizons with his lively, informative correspondence. Only the least it is that I can do, in joining up with the Diaghilev undertaking, to repay my cousin the favor. "After all,"

I tell him with a wink, "for years, now, you have been just itching for the two of us to tour Europe together—yes?"

Letting out a yelp of joy, Nikolai throws both arms around me in a wrenching bear-hug, shouting: "You will not regret it, Sasha—I promise! Oh, bless the Saints! Come spring, we shall have ourselves the grandest time in Paris!"

"Yes." Staring past him, I feel my smile fade and let out a long sigh, watching snowflakes flutter away in wispy warning snatches from the rails of Father's balcony.

Nikolai haltingly follows my gaze. "What are you going to tell him?"

"Hopefully," I answer with another long sigh, "as little as possible."

"You know he will eventually find out."

"About Diaghilev? Oh, yes. If not from the society pages, then certainly through the correspondence he has been so regularly maintaining these days with his many old friends in both Petersburg and Paris."

Our eyes meet yet again, and Nikolai returns my nod with reluctant acknowledgment, saying: "A pity that Anna happens to be here."

"Which is precisely why I want the two of you to board the morntide train back to Petersburg just as planned. I'll follow on the late eve run."

"Well, I could send Anna along first—and stay behind to help you explain to Uncle Misha."

"No, Nikolai. Please, do as I ask, and leave come the morn with Anna. I need to face Father on this alone."

Tinged with regret, Nikolai's hollow-gray eyes again meet mine in a knowing hold, and he nods, murmuring: "As you wish, my good friend."

And as we both glance back toward the empty reminder of the balcony, my cousin grips my arm with firm resolve, as if attempting to impart some extra bulwark of strength against the impact of the inevitable explosion.

* * *

"You want to *what?"* gasps Father, staring up from a book of ledger pages, his pipe slamming down onto the desk with an ominous, ringing bang.

"It will most probably only be for the summer, Papa." Nervously, I seize up my cane and fling it out in a sweeping arc to emphasize my point. "Only f-for a few months," I stammer on. "I had thought I would stay on in Petersburg after *Maslenitsa*—and through Easter—to join in the rehearsals. The Paris season should begin about the second week in May."

My father remains sitting in cold, stunned silence, his dark eyes fixed upon me in a scathing hold as the corner of his mouth gradually begins to twitch.

"Papa! The journals are all caught up; I have seen to it that every one of the payables accounts has been brought current. Surely you cannot object to my taking leave of the farm for a few short months?"

I stop, letting out an exasperated sigh, exclaiming: "Good grief, Papa! Say something."

Instead, Father jumps up from the desk with such a ferocious burst that his chair topples back onto the floor behind him. "You want me to say something, Aleksandr?" he roars.

Defiantly, I cross my arms, holding his stare as torrential heartbeats begin hammering away in my throat.

"You damn well better believe I am going to say something!" he shouts on. "What about your graduation examinations for school?"

With a shrug, I glance down to the floor, telling him: "I had assumed I could complete them upon my return."

"Oh, did you? Assumed you could merely waltz in and complete exams whenever you felt like it? God's teeth, boy! Haven't you any idea how many niceties I've had to parlay out, how many arms I've near been forced to break in half with these bedeviled intricate arrangements? May's Academy rarely ever grants credit through correspondence! Months have I spent haggling and pleading, attempting to convince the Board that my son is indeed qualified to sit for the examinations! And this is the way you choose to repay me? By traipsing off on some foolhardy lark to Paris?"

"It is scarce some foolhardy lark!" I shout at him, fingers clenching into fists at my sides.

"Oh, *no?"* Jabbing into his letter-file, Father extracts several thickened envelopes and storms around the corner of the desk. "Don't you think I've no inkling of what foolishness has been taking place of late in Paris!" he shouts, waving the letters back and forth in front of my face like a pile of courtroom evidence. "And don't you think I don't know who happens to be behind it—none other than Diaghilev! One Sergei Pavlovich, yes? The former editor of that garish pinnacle of decadence, *Mir Iskustva?* Who fancies himself some kind of impresario of the arts? That simpering, bloated, brazen son of a fool born right near here over in the Selistchev Barracks, who sauntered into my house one day as if he owned the whole blessed estate, demanding that I remove all portraits from the walls and entrust them every one unto his care? That crafty-eyed, underhanded, scheme-plotting rabble-rouser dismissed from the Crown Service under no less than the vestiges of Paragraph Three, mind you—employed only in cases of embezzlement and dishonorable conduct? It is indeed this very same Diaghilev who is behind this venture within which you now think you want to get yourself involved? *Yes?"*

"Papa, for Christ's sake!" I cry out, stung by the irony that my father, after his long tenure in Siberia, shows so little tolerance for another individual also embroiled in an apparent misunderstanding with the Tsar. "It is a chance to follow upon my aspirations, Papa! To play in an orchestra."

"If you wish to play in an orchestra, Aleksandr, then why can you not pursue something respectable?" he shouts back. "Like studying at the St. Petersburg Conservatory!"

"What is so damn unrespectable about going to Paris and playing for Diaghilev's troupe?"

In retribution, he waves the letters out again in front of my face, sorts quickly through the envelopes, and snatches out one of the scribble-hewn sheafs of paper. "Are you at all aware why this group of charlatans Diaghilev has been leading around has been forced to confine their rehearsals to the beer halls of the German Club on Ekaterinsky Canal?"

When I only stare back at him in stunned amazement, he rants on: "Oh, by the devil's balls, Sasha! You mean you neglected to even ascertain where these people have been rehearsing?"

"I've not yet inquired as to the particulars!"

"Oh! The boy intends to fly straight away," Father declares, pointing me down with a self-satisfied smirk, "and somehow—ha!—become a sophisticated man-of-the-world! By investing his fate in a troupe of fat-winded ne'er-do-wells—without even inquiring as to the particulars?"

"I had intended to check about rehearsals upon arrival in Petersburg! For love of the Saints, Papa! How on earth do you ever manage to learn of such sundry details?"

Gloating triumphantly, Father waves out a fat letter from his old friend Count Orlov, bellowing: "Diaghilev and his rag-tag ensemble had to move over to the German Club because they were forcibly expelled from the Hermitage Court Theater! Forbidden to use the stage by official order, mind you—on account of indecency!"

Flushing, I counter: "Oh, Father—I swear to God! You and Orlov and all those other old buggers are all little better than a bunch of gossipy old babushkas!"

Infuriated, I turn on my heel and march for the door.

Father storms after me, roaring: "You have not been excused!" In a wrathful, swiping wave, his stack of papers heaves down, slamming flat into the handle of my cane.

Which spins clattering against bookshelves and settee tables all the way to the farthest corner of the study.

Eyes riveted to the floor, I shift my balance over to my right leg and attempt to catch my breath, bracing a tentative hand out for leverage against the door.

Grumbling, Father stomps after the cane, hurriedly shoves it back beneath my fist, and then stands looming vindictively over my head, his mouth working furiously bare inches away from the bridge of my nose as he orders in his most vehement of tones: "I will *not* have you trooping off to Paris like this, Sasha!"

"Might I remind you that I am near unto eighteen years old? And scarce any longer a child to be ordered about to-and-fro however you please!" At last I glare up at him, inwardly wincing from the harsh sting of brandy caught all over his breath. "Now, may I be excused? *Sir?"*

Without awaiting an answer, I shove past him and out into the hall.

"Eighteen years old, my ass! You think you've become a man by now, boy, you have one helluva lot to learn!"

"I've learned more in my time than you should ever care to know about, Papa!" I yell back over my shoulder.

"Damn you, Sasha—get back in here! Dammit, I will *not* have my son following Diaghilev to Paris! *I will not!"* he rages out at the top of his lungs, his voice carrying like a cannon boom across the entire breadth of the house.

Grasping hold of the doorknob to my room, I whirl around, glaring him down in silence.

"Very well!" he goes on, his face darkening livid red with rage. "Go then—go on off with those no-good decadents, those infernal fireside talkers! Go and leave your papa after all he has done for you these past two years—in all your years—if that is how you choose to show your appreciation! Enjoy your youthful fling in Paris, boy—because God knows how much I desperately need each and every hand I can manage to keep around this aging farm, ledger clerks and plowhands alike. Every day, I lose more peasants to the damn stinking factories in Petersburg and Moscow. Every day, any hope of turning a decent profit from crop yields diminishes near unto entirety! Better you thank the Saints that our winery investments in Cologne and Bordeaux have performed so handsomely in recent years—otherwise, I'd be forced to withdraw principal monthly for us just to live! But go ahead—run off to Paris like some fleeting pied piper with nary a care in the world! But I am warning you, Aleksandr Mikhailovich Sekovsky: if you do go to Paris, then just don't you bother to come back!"

In response, I slam my bedroom door shut behind me, but he shouts against it: "Did you hear me? I said not to come back! *Ever!* Because this is the last straw—do you hear? At seventy-seven, I'm scarce getting any younger, you know! And am definitely becoming far too old for this continuing nonsense! But God forbid if you should bother worrying your flighty, winsome little head about an old man and his wretched provincial farm!"

And then, against a torrent of curses about the Devon-Tyler English treachery, his study door slams shut at last.

Swallowing hard, I make a quick recheck of the piccolo stuffed within my boot and of the silver *Boehm* one packed in along with the flute before heaving the long leather instrument case up over my shoulder, grasping up the handle-strap to my trunk, and heading for the stairs.

As I button up my coat with quavering fingers down in the hallway vestibule, Vliny—whom along with Marnya has surely been listening in this whole time from the foot of the stairs—pounces without the briefest pause for mercy, sandwiching hold of my arm, pleading: "Sasha, jest hold off a little while, fer God's sake! Let me go up an' talk te Misha. The man can act like such a dodderin' old fool. . . ."

Shaking him off, I pull on my thick ermine hat, adjusting it to a jaunty angle in spite of, or perhaps because of, everything, and reply coldly: "Please go and tell Rolfe to fetch the troika from the carriage house."

"Sasha! It's been a rough day around here agin—there was another incident with them strikers from town stirrin' up trouble down at the warehouse early this morn. Ye know how it's been! An' yer papa's taken up the drink agin, of late. He don't mean none o' what he jest said up there!"

Stare kept to my hands, I slip off my spectacles and dust over the lenses with the ends of my handkerchief; slip the spectacles back on and duck past Vliny's continued whining protests toward the kitchen, where Marnya—past guilty glances spied in my direction—has busied herself once again with washing up the supper dishes.

"A bit o' apple *kisel's* jest warm from the oven, dumplin'" she offers. "If ye might want te wait."

"Thank you, but I must reach the railway station before nightfall, Matushka. As I told you this morn, I have decided to travel into Petersburg to celebrate *Maslenitsa* with the Zhelanovs." Squeezing her shoulder, I plant a fond kiss upon her weathered cheek and tightly shut my eyes, breathing in the musky scent of her embroidered kerchief and her hair, my heart torn to shreds, my voice loath to affirm the bleak truth of my impending absence—which will most assuredly now be for a much greater length of time. And perhaps forever. "Goodbye, Matushka. I—I love you very much."

Achingly, she turns to spear a look at Vliny, who again bursts out: "Sasha! I am tellin' ye—the man scarce means a word!"

In response, I level my gaze squarely against his, reminding him: "Valenti Apollonovich, certainly, after all these years, you are aware that my father—" My voice breaks then in stilted rasps upon the word, and I continue low under my breath: "That my father rarely speaks without the most earnest intent. Now, I would appreciate if you would go and tell Rolfe to fetch the troika."

* * *

"Bless you, M'mselle!" I gush out, tipping my derby for the near twentieth time. "Thank you so very much!"

"Certainly, M'sieur—and a pleasant journey to you. And good luck with the Company!"

Toying with the brim of her stylish feathered hat, Tamara Karsavina winks at me again before stepping back into the enclave of dancers and musicians clustered around Maestro Tcherepnin and the great basso Fyodor Chaliapin and his faithful Chinese manservant. Once more everyone in the crowd bursts into giddy fragments of conversation, no one person able to contain his excitement or stick to reasonable coherency for more than a flighty sentence. So long awaited, dreamed of night after night and planned for day after day, our departure is now imminent, and against the heightened chatterings of young people, even the staid bastion of Baltic Station seems to shine beneath a shower of vibrant springtime intensity.

Fondly, I stare down at the treasured keepsake carried in my billfold for so many years, a picturegraph from one of the prima ballerina's earliest appearances as a pearl-strung, chiffon-layered nymphet in *The Little Humpbacked Horse*, performed at the Maryinsky when I was but a boy of twelve. Across the wrinkled, shaded image of her far-flung pose, she has hurriedly scrawled: 'To Sasha—best of luck, always! Tamara Karsavina.'

Promptly, several boisterous guffaws erupt behind my back. Boris Timofeyevich—Nikolai's fair-headed, fat-cheeked cousin—along with a couple of snickering compatriots from the brass section of the orchestra, survey me with snide amusement from their covert behind a pile of travel trunks. "Just what do you find to be so bleating funny?" I demand of Boris. "The woman is legendary!"

"No, Pavlova—now there's legend for you," retorts Anton Leonidovich—Boris's best friend—with an impudent, dismissing wave. Upon which Boris follows with: "Oh, cheer up, Sekovsky! Can't you take a little joke?"

Shooting them a warning glare in reply, I tuck the photo back inside my waistcoat pocket and turn sharply away, scanning out with impatience across the crowded station concourse for some sign of Nikolai.

Who has disappeared again, and small wonder. First, it was Aunt Sophie, fawning about with a flood of prying motherly reminders, her regrets acute that an appointment for tea out at Tsarskoe Selo would keep her from seeing off the train. But barely had she scurried away to her coach, than were we simultaneously accosted by Magdalina Vasilyevna Vorontsova and Klavdiya Semyonovna Polinskaya—two buxom, fluttery-eyed brunettes—about neither of whom Nikolai has ever mentioned a word. And neither of whom, apparently—up until that very moment—knew anything at all about the other, although each had been accorded identical gold-cast locket necklaces obviously procured from the haughty auspices of the House of Fabergé. Needless to say, sheepish explanations fell upon not a single sympathetic ear, and much to my entertainment, Nikolai, in dodging away from the combined fury of the two young women, has been tearing repeatedly up and down the station platforms ever since.

"Psst! Sasha—over here."

Cocking an eyebrow, I wander nonchalantly over toward another group of stacked trunks. "You rang, M'sieur?"

"Oh, very funny!" Crouched behind a baggage lift, Nikolai points across the top-most trunk to the stack's opposite end. "Quick! Stand over there on that side before she sees me."

"She? I thought there were two of them."

"Well! The Saints smiled upon me—Klavdiya got taken back into tow by her mother."

"You know what you are, Nikolai? You are what they call a rake!"

"Blast it, Sasha—will you simply hush up and stand over there?"

Grinning across at him, I whisper back through my teeth: "Not a chance."

"Oh, no, you don't!" an outraged feminine voice then shrieks from behind my ear. "Don't you think I don't know how you've been carrying on this whole time behind my back, Nikolai Petrovich Zhelanov—"

"Magdya, darling! Angel, please!"

"—you villainous, two-timing cad!"

Bursting past me, Nikolai chokes back: "Remind me to accord you a ready favor sometime, Sasha!"

"You'd best hurry up and marry her—the train leaves in fifteen minutes!" I call after him, laughing as Magdalina hurls out her parasol in red-faced, swiping fury, sending Nikolai trotting once more down the length of the platforms.

This time, he disappears behind a growing group of ballerinas and choir singers gathered about the Company's tall, black-haired artistic director, Mikhail Fokine.

A rake if there ever was one: all the women in the troupe are in love with him, and he knows it. Despite this, the man transforms from a smiling purveyor of compliments and baiting dinner proposals into a complete raving tyrant at every rehearsal—sometimes ordering the dancers, and therefore the orchestra as well, to repeat a piece up to twenty times or more in a sitting. Naturally, it was Diaghilev himself with whom I had expected to encounter difficulty, on account of the shotgun incident five years ago at Lissushka. But upon our brief introduction, the man scarce seemed to possess any recollection of my father's outrageous behavior, and instead immediately turned me over, with best wishes, to Maestro Tcherepnin and the temperamental Fokine.

My reference letters from my old tutor and a respectable rendition of the flute solo from the *Les Sylphides* score's *Grand Valse Brillante*—in front of the entire company upon his demand—eased Fokine's doubts about my lack of formal credentials, and secured me the flute alternate position without further adieu. Much to my satisfaction—for Fokine, as dictatorial as he is, possesses superb artistic flair and a knack for improvisation that lends sheer brilliance to the ballet choreography. From the moment I first caught sight of what was transpiring through the doors to Ekaterinsky Hall, I found the dance solos just as intriguing as Nikolai had described, and yearned to join the Diaghilev enterprise more than anything. The rehearsals, however, have yet been grueling—even though, as alternates, Nikolai and I follow a much more improvised schedule than regular members of the orchestra.

Interestingly enough, Diaghilev makes an appearance only on occasion. Apparently distracted with the intricacies of business arrangements, he says little about specific production details, leaving such trivial matters over to the more adept hands of Fokine and his old friends Lev Rosenberg—or Leon Bakst, as the daring artist now prefers to call himself—and the talented Shura Benois.

Diaghilev, though, definitely likes men. And not women.

That undeniable fact is apparent yet again as I stare across the concourse toward the famous impresario's impeccably dressed, plumpish figure. For half-an-hour without pause—although heavily involved in a gesturing conversation with several tophatted businessmen—Sergei Diaghilev's piercing gaze has wavered not one speck away from Vaslav Nijinsky's.

And as if wholly immune from the chaotic, noisy rush of excitement buzzing through the railway station, the great Nijinky remains standing dutifully aloof aside Fokine amidst the group of chattering ballerinas and singers, his eyes dropping once more to the ground and his derby held stiffly between his hands, as quiet and reticent a figure as always and so strikingly different in real life from the majestic spirit-demons he conjures up so skillfully on stage. But every few moments, plaintively, he glances upward, his eyes locking back upon Diaghilev's with that passionate, knowing hold.

Although a year-and-a-half tenure at Novgorod under my father's watchful eye may have precluded any such physical liaisons on my part, torrid memories of those scarce precious nights in Vyborg with Volodya have never, within my thoughts, reduced me to the chastity of a hermit-monk for very long—artistic admiration for goddesses like Karsavina notwithstanding. From across the safe haven of stacked trunks, I peek once more over at Nijinsky, and inadvertently manage to catch his eye as he once again looks away from Diaghilev. His barely perceptible, lingering nod—and the faint smile curling about his lips—indicate that he can tell I have deciphered the truth of his and Diaghilev's secret longings—and at the same time, that he can quite plainly see the entire truth about me.

Flushing, I look sharply away, wondering with mortification if anyone else nearby can so easily gauge my preferences with so slight a glance.

"Sasha!" cries Nikolai, stumbling up from behind a scheduling board in a breathless rush, "I just saw three bear handlers out on Voznesensky Prospekt!"

"Voznesensky Prospekt! What the devil were you doing all the way back out there?"

"I conned Magdya into a *drozhki!* Paid ten rubles; told the cabby to take her for a joyride up to Griboyedov Canal."

"For God's sake!" I shout beratingly as he bursts into uproarious laughter. "And what if she was here with her mother, or someone?"

"Oh, hell—she'll scold the oaf into turning around soon enough. But hopefully, not before Trinity Cathedral—I told him to at least take her that far. By which time, we should be long departed."

"Up to your old tricks—eh, Kolya?" Boris exclaims loudly, sauntering up behind and clapping Nikolai on the shoulder.

"And please will you refrain from calling me 'Kolya?'" Nikolai replies with a playful slapping punch. "And I have not been up to any tricks!"

"That's not what I hear from the ladies."

"Since when have any ladies taken you into their confidence, Borya?" Nikolai retorts, snickering, elbowing a pointy jab into Boris's ample paunch.

"Humph! Perhaps you'd best ask your cohort Sekovsky there about the one who recently got taken into his."

"Indeed?" Nikolai peers over at me.

Reluctantly, I extract the photo from my pocket and show him the autograph.

"Oh! M'mselle Karsavina!" Nikolai and Boris gasp out in unison with wide-eyed, mocking leers.

Scowling at them both, I hurriedly slip the picturegraph into my billfold, snapping in a flush of irritation: "And will you two nitwits stop horsing around? The young lady in question happens to be standing right over there."

With a sudden frown of concern, Boris points across at two porters surveying a baggage lift, upon which are stacked several strapped-up hampers, our own trunks, his French horn, and Nikolai's cello and violin. "Well—I believe, dear cousin," he urges Nikolai, "that we'd best rescue our instruments before they load."

Nikolai hurries after Boris, barking: "No one touches the case to that Guarnerius but me! Sasha—you've hung onto your flute, yes?"

"Never without it," I call after him, patting my leather shoulder case.

"Hey, Sekovsky!" Boris shouts back at me. "No hard feelings, eh?"

Laughing, I wave him off. So reminiscent of portly, studious Uncle Petya, Boris is such an agreeable fellow that I could never hold him at a grudge's length for very long.

Watching them lazily, I lean back against a lamp post and catch in a last whiff of the fragrant spring air. But as the porters begin loading the baggage lifts, again I cannot refrain from somewhat sinful envyings of Nikolai—whose father would have thrilled to see him traipsing off to Paris on some avant-garde musical adventure. A master cellist, Uncle Petya charmed dozens of salons from Lisbon to Salzburg during extended ventures abroad as a youth.

While I, on the other hand, have been ordered never to return home.

I had thought, for a certainty, that he would come to his senses by Easter, that he would surely have reconciled himself to my decision due to the necessity for making the Petersburg journey. Save for that horrible year of my abduction, every Easter ever since I can remember, whether at the ancient Sofiya Cathedral in Novgorod, or within the massive dome of St. Isaak's in Petersburg, Father and I have always together attended Midnight Mass—where he has always lit his candle to my candle before passing on the flame. No matter how wide any rifts between us at any time, he has always solemnly held my gaze while lighting his wick to mine, as if we were partners sharing some ancient shrouded mystery, bound together in a sacred rite of triumph: *I bestow this unto you, my flame to become your flame; I, your father, to you, my son . . . .*

But this Easter, he never even came! *Oh, God! How could he so completely abandon me? How could he not even bother to come?*

"Sasha!"

I jump, startled, as Nikolai grips hold of my arm, murmuring: "Oh, forgive me—I see you were lost in thought. Are—are you all right, my friend?"

"Of course!" I choke out, quickly shading my hand across the upper rims of my spectacles.

"Well, they are readying to board."

Biting my lip, I stare out longingly across the long platforms of Baltic Station—foolishly wishing, deep down, only to instead be standing in the familiar Nikolayevsky.

"Sasha," Nikolai goes on in a lowered tone, "if you are having misgivings—"

"No!" I say harshly. "No misgivings, no regrets! And no more of your pleas for going back and attempting to persuade some meager blessing from Father's senseless, stubborn old head! This is my life, and my choice." Forcing up a smile, I check my ticket and fall into quick step with Nikolai toward the open doors of the nearest first-class coach, telling him: "We are going off on a grand adventure, *mon cousin!* Upon which we shall have the time of our lives! We are going to Paris! . . ."

* * *

Paris!

Like a horde of wandering Gypsy vagabonds, we descend upon the rows of quaint hotels dotted along the *Boulevard Saint-Michel*—in which from that point on, in some strange pique of nationalist fervor and despite almost everyone's apt knowledge of schoolyard French, naught can be heard spoken anywhere but Russian. Unabashed, our shouts continue all eve long and half into the night, coursing up and down the halls and across the alleys between the balcony tiers. By morntide following, the tumult of gaiety even seems to have infected the dour-faced chambermaids, who begin shouldering their laundry baskets with whimsical smiles while scurrying to-and-fro past groups of dancers practicing pirouettes in the lobbies. Bowing and blowing and calling to one another through the open doors of their rooms, pockets of musicians gathered on every floor shout back and forth noisy opinions about particular phrases of the scores.

The following afternoon, Nikolai and I happen upon a photographer while out upon a stroll about the *Quai d'Orsay,* and we chalk up fifty francs for him to take a picturegraph of the two of us standing in front of the Eiffel Tower with our arms interlinked and our derbies tipped at rakish, jaunty angles. Come evetide, we accompany Amaliya Vasilyevna and Felitsiya Denisovna, two charming understudy ballerinas from the Maryinsky School, to dinner at the ritzy *Restaurant Viel* on the *Boulevard de la Madeleine,* celebrating boisterously with much champagne until long after midnight. After seeing the ladies safely to their rooms, we at last stumble back down the hall toward our own—only to encounter Boris pacing glumly outside our door. "Sekovsky—Zhelanov!" he exclaims, red-faced. "You two bumbling goats! Where the devil have you been all night? Haven't you heard?"

"Heard what?" Nikolai blurts out upon a hardy belch, blinking his eyes and quavering upon my shoulder with tentative grip as, shaken from head to foot with laughter, I attempt to lend him dubious support.

"Blast you two!" Boris rants on, "this is serious. The Company has been forbidden use of the theater!"

In answer to our abruptly sobered gasps of disbelief, Boris explains: "Since the French learnt of the inclusion of ballet in this season's repertoire, they have outright denied us use of their revered *Grand Opéra*. They refuse to see it reduced to the so-called 'banality of a mere dancing hall.' Can you imagine?"

Fortunately, Sergei Diaghilev, entirely accustomed to dealing with the throes of controversy, proves equal to what at first seems an insurmountable task—and the next day, everyone is promptly ordered to report to the *Théâtre du Châtelet,* a musty, weathered building previously utilized only for the staging of second-rate melodramas. "They must be joking!" exclaims Nikolai, wide-eyed, clutching his violin case protectively to his chest as we both stare, dumbfounded, at the army of hammering carpenters ripping out plank after ratty plywood plank in attempts at enlarging the paltry orchestra pit before the stage.

"I think not," I reply, spotting Tcherepnin waving to us from behind a high pile of crates stacked by the stage entrance door. With a shrug, I nudge Nikolai with my elbow, adding: "Well! You said it was going to be an adventure."

And an adventure it indeed proves itself to be—for if Fokine seemed overly given to outbursts of temper back in the comfortable, airy German Club in St. Petersburg, now—with all the banging and hammering of the renovation going on nonstop behind every single rehearsal session for two straight agonizing weeks—he becomes a literal raving maniac, trying even the normally subdued patience of Maestro Tcherepnin the day before the opening. "Throw out that pianist!" I hear Fokine's voice thunder all the way up into the rafters, as—apprehensive already on account of my being late—I hurriedly fit together the joints of my flute while hiding behind a partition.

"You—you cannot do that!" Tcherepnin counters in an amazed, gawking fluster.

"By God's word, throw him out, I tell you!" Fokine storms on. "I will not tolerate such incompetency in my productions—out with him, I say! Throw that pianist *out!"*

Poor Pomerantzev, the pianist, angrily storms out one of the side doors.

"Dear Lord!" I whisper across to Boris. "What happened?"

Crouched in front of me with his French horn at the ready, he possesses a better vantage point, but says: "I have no idea; I just arrived myself. Sweet Jesus, I swear the man has become a lunatic! May the Saints only smile down and somehow guide us all safely through opening night."

Mercifully, salvation descends at last: opening night.

In Paris, the dress rehearsal is ofttimes considered even more important than the actual *première,* and Diaghilev and his business manager, the ever-crafty Gabriel Astruc, have obviously made due note of such circumstance, and filled the theater balconies row after row with sumptuously beautiful women, haughty society ladies, and a bevy of artistic celebrities, the sculptor Rodin and composers Ravel and Saint-Saëns included amongst the audience in boxes prominently visible to the stage. Incredibly, the chaos of the renovation has produced within two weeks naught but a miracle in the nick of time—for the *Théâtre du Châtelet* has been transformed from its former musty staleness into the utmost pinnacle of discerning taste, with flowers and twining plants hung all about the entrances—while the floor, the passages, even the stalls themselves have been generously draped with smooth red cloth as if in direct rebuttal to similar showy trappings of the renowned *Paris Grand Opéra.*

"Did you see what they are calling it on the playbills?" I say to Nikolai as we peer out across the heads of the swelling crowd from the perch of our corner seats. "The *Saison Russe."*

"Yes, I know—damn!" he cries, glaring about with a frown of irritation. "Wish we could have gotten into the balcony."

"We were lucky to acquire seats at all," I remind him.

"Indeed—bless Tcherepnin and his gracious conniving." Dour-faced, Nikolai continues fuming about morosely. Only all too aware of his jealousy of Boris, with whom we were trading quips just moments ago from the partition separating the audience from the orchestra pit, I press a reassuring squeeze to my cousin's arm. "Perhaps we will have our chance to play," I remind him. "Most assuredly, someone will later decide to drop out."

"Well, I suppose one can hardly expect any no-shows during the first performance, humph!"

"Heavens!" I gasp, "they're starting." Against the crowd's collective silenced hush, the curtains begin to rise and the lights slowly go dim.

The program begins with the Maryinsky ballet, *Le Pavillon d'Armide.*

Espousing the princely courtliness and antiquated chivalry of Eighteenth Century France, the set has been arrayed in a wash of muted pink and green pastels, and like an apparition coaxed out of the enclave of Louis XV, Nijinsky wanders out onto the stage wearing a high silk turban and silvery costume trimmed with ruffles, festoons, and ermine tails, his plain face transformed—as always during a performance—from the bland drudgery of everyday reality into a vision of lofty enticement. Wholly absorbed with attaining naught but the height of perfection in the execution of every prancing, graceful step, his presence dominates the stage from wing to wing like a grand ghost from some netherworld of abstract physical symmetry, a spellbound wraith playing to an audience of its own imagination while scarce seeming to realize that its manifestation is, indeed, a human—dancing in a large theater hall filled to the brim with expectant, critical-eyed people.

"How does the story go again?" I whisper over to Nikolai.

But his hand shoots upward, and I wait, for the strings have erupted in full force. As is our mutually obliging habit whenever graced by the performance of any orchestral score, if either strings or flute happen to predominate, we both wait the passage out and tune in sharply pricked ears, delaying any unnecessary conversation.

At last the violins subside, and he whispers back: "I think it is an old libretto: the Vicomte enters the pavilion of the evil wizard and then falls asleep—"

"Wait," I interrupt—but Nikolai has already stopped talking, for the flute soars out above the orchestra in a plaintive watery cascade, and we both instinctively crane our heads, noting the poignancy of the innuendoes.

"So, where was I?" he asks finally, nudging my arm as the horns at last proceed to take their turn.

"Oh! The, uh—the Vicomte falls asleep—"

"Oh, yes. Then, in a dream, the Vicomte sees an enormous tapestry come to life, full of goblins and other-worldly gnomes. From this tapestry, Armida and her entourage descend like a heavenly host, casting their spell upon him with a dance—"

Again we both stop—but this time, our attention has been seized away not by the music, but by none other than the electric presence of Nijinsky, who has elicited a stunned gasp from the entire audience with his spectacular leap across the stage.

"Blessed Lord!" Nikolai blurts out. "Did he try that in rehearsal?"

"I—I can't remember," I reply, wide-eyed, my attention stolen straight away from the orchestration. "We never caught much chance to watch, you know," I mutter disjointedly, only half-hearing my own words. "Always so absorbed with trying to stave off Fokine's touchy temper."

"Well—anyhow," Nikolai goes on, "then, upon awakening in the pavilion, the Vicomte discovers a shawl left upon the ground in the exact spot where Armida had left hers in his dream."

And once more he stops—for Nijinsky flies across the stage in the same fashion once again, inspiring yet another collective wholly astonished gasp.

"By the Saints!" I cry, seizing hold of Nikolai's arm. "He could never have tried *that* in practice; I would have taken notice. He flies like a angel!"

Karsavina, in the role of Armida, then comes on, along with her group of dancing maidens, the ladies followed somewhat later by the talented Rozai in the part of the evil wizard—but the entire remainder of the troupe seems merely a requisite and ineffective distraction of attention away from the astonishing Nijinsky, who—every time he reappears—continues soaring out across the stage like some far-flung, human bird.

"Lord Jesus!" Nikolai and I exclaim in the same shortened breath, jumping near from our seats as Nijinsky plies his magic before the stunned theater yet again.

From that moment on, Nikolai's narration of the libretto dwindles away, forgotten by us each without regret. Spellbound by the exits and entrances of Nijinsky, we continue to watch, enthralled, the both of us—for perhaps for the first time in our lives, during any kind of peformance—wholly oblivious to the music.

The audience, entranced as well, also remains glued upon the sight of Nijinsky, the rest of the performance rolling on in an awe-struck, silenced hush. Stealing the show away from all the others every time he returns upon the stage, the man spins off again and again into the air, his leaps astounding, death-defying, absolved of the very laws of physics as he seems to hover, weightless and ethereal, high off from the floor before each returning toe-point—culminating at last in a startling, magnificent *pas de trois* in which he leaps—to the gasping shock of everyone—straight into the wings right from the stage!

After a numbed rush of silence, the whole building erupts into thunderous applause.

"I cannot believe it!" Nikolai shouts across the roar into my ear. "I knew the fellow was good—but had no idea at all that he was *that* good. . . ."

Everyone one ends up standing, shouting, applauding—the "Bravos!" seeming the shake down into the foundations of the building as the cast returns repeatedly to take their calls.

Scarce have we a chance to catch our breath, but the curtain rises again on the Polovetz Camp scene from Borodin's opera, *Prince Igor.*

From the French Eighteenth Century, we have been transported far eastward to a desolate medieval expanse of Scythian steppe fading off into an eerie sky of mottled gold. Crimson-gray tent flaps of nomads flutter in the foreground as slave girls pour out from either wing of the stage in a creamy fluttering wave, bursting into song and swaying back and forth around the campfire in an erotic pagan dance.

Cocking an eyebrow, Nikolai grins over at me, snickering, whispering: "And I wonder what the snooty French *patrons des arts* are going to think about this?"

I cannot help grinning also, for already, hints of disapproval have begun to glimmer down from several staid elderly faces occuping the box facing our row of seats—and dozens of pairs of opera-glasses spring up in successive order, fastened upon the stage in rigorous inspection.

But upon the finale, the opera-glasses promptly drop back down into the laps of their matronly owners, for as the slave girls bid a sinuous retreat, warriors of the Polovtsy nomads burst out upon the stage.

Whirling around the adventurous Adolph Bolm, who has been aptly cast in the role of the Khan, scores of sooty faces, gleaming eyes, and brightly splashed, colorful red-green coats charge back and forth in a rush of warring bows and arrows—stomping, kicking, and spinning en masse to the triumphant, pounding chords of Borodin's melodic score.

"What you must remember," Nikolai whispers over to me excitedly, "is that we have grown up with our flashing saber dances, our stomping, our balalaikas, our Borodin, our Mussorgsky, our Rimsky-Korsakov. But the French have most probably never seen anything quite like it."

Indeed, it certainly seems that they have not—for the tension mounts, increasing moment by each quivering, anxiously gaining moment, the whole audience hunched forward and poised upon the seats of their chairs all through the captivating, spirited remainder of the *Prince Igor* segment. At the end, another thunderous collective roar of applause erupts from the crowd, half of whom then jump for the aisles and swarm forward on a wave of enthusiastic shouts, literally attempting to overtake the stage!

"Holy Lord in Heaven!" Nikolai and I blurt out at each other simultaneously, breathless and amazed.

The gendarmes then march in and start shouting: "Order! Order! May we have order in the theater, ladies and gentlemen, please!" Their commands, however, can scarce be heard above the clamoring uproar. Everyone in sight seems to be pushing forward—clapping, calling, whistling, and shouting: "Encore! Encore!" Meanwhile, the dancers, still taking final curtain calls, attempt to defend their costumes—and the sanctity of their persons—from the overtly threatening onslaught of rose bouquets that from out of nowhere seems to suddenly have engulfed the entire theater.

"It is a success!" I shout into Nikolai's ear. "An absolute, unqualified success!"

"I told you it would be worth it!"

"How right you were, *mon cousin!"*

"And this only the dress rehearsal—my word! Just wait until the night after next! Wait until the *première!. . ."*

Two nights later, after the *première,* the reaction from the French is virtually the same. Although forced, due to Tcherepnin's unflappable sense of fair play, to relinquish our seats to another couple of compatriots from within the ranks, our euphoric mood remains unfazed as, with several other alternate musicians and understudy dancers, we witness an exact repetition of the audience's wildly astonished enthusiasm from just outside the entrance to the theater.

"Look at these!" I cry, waving out clippings from several newspapers that I have been collecting all day. "Already they are calling Karsavina: 'poetry *en forme!'* And Nijinsky: 'the genius, the dancer divine!'"

Impressed, a group of ballerinas swoops upon me excitedly, snatching the clippings from my grasp.

"What did I tell you?" Nikolai exclaims with grinning approval, hooking both thumbs up imperiously into the armholes of his waistcoat.

"We have aligned ourselves with a grand, triumphant success! Ladies!" he then calls over to Amaliya and Felitisiya, who both eye us coquettishly from the talkative group of dancers. "Perhaps you would both again be so kind as to grace my cousin, Count Sekovsky here, and myself with the pleasure of your company? The night is young! We must go out on the town and celebrate!"

* * *

After the dinner, the dancing—and far too many bottles of heady Bordeaux champagne—Amaliya and Felitsiya are properly returned to their rooms. Whereupon, like a couple of prowling, resurgent felines, Nikolai and I comb darkened Parisian avenues with cocky, appraising glances, and quite promptly procure two other 'ladies' willing to fulfill our prospective yearnings for the night—for with Nikolai, one can never embark on any celebration without eventually winding up at a *maison de rendez-vous.* Or as they say so decorously in Paris, house of assignation.

And already, the banging of the headboard against the wall from the adjoining room testifies to my cousin's having yet again divined blessed physical solace.

"You always carry a pistol, M'sieur?" the girl demands of me with widened eyes as she slips out of her chemise.

Setting my spectacles down beside the Webley on the bureau, I reply in French: "Why don't you stop worrying your pretty little head about such things, and finish taking off your clothes?"

"Oui, M'sieur!" She proceeds to do just that: the corset, stockings, pantaloons—eveything—sliding down in a crumpled lacy heap upon the floor.

I take a good amount of time staring: long dark hair. Slightly built, with small breasts and firm, slim hips. Which was why I took such fancy to her.

"You like, M'sieur?"

"Oui."

"Well!" she replies, laughing, delighted. "Perhaps you will like even more if I do this."

Whisking breathlessly over from the bed, she throws her arms around my neck and sinks like a curling snake against my body, our lips finding one another's in a draining kiss.

I crush her, devour her—and then, gasping, break away—but she seems to understand, murmuring: "Here, allow me to help."

Her fingers dart all over for the buttons, easing me out of my trousers and my shirt. "Oh, *oui!* M'sieur does like," she cries again, giggling, her hand wrapping down around my swollen penis.

"Just—just get into the bed, will you?"

"Oui, M'sieur."

As I stumble in after her, she makes a grab to shove me inside her, but with an angry scowl, I fling away her hand. "Wait, will you? Please!" I gasp out, flushing.

"Oui, M'sieur?"

"Simply kiss me." Trembling, I wrap my arms down around her tiny waist; entirely enfold her whitened shoulders, my lips searching out hers with preying desperation. We tumble across the bed, she hanging on as I roll atop and then hoist her around on top of me and then roll on top of her again, turning my head one way, turning it the other as I kiss her . . . although it is not she, but my thoughts within which I become hopelessly lost as the surging moments whirl by. Idly, I begin wondering what I would look like to Nikolai should he happen to come and stand over at the door—if I might look just as hedonistic to him as he did to me that dark night so long ago in Murzhinsky's when I hid behind the partitions, watching. . . .

Old memories then begin flooding back in querulous, haunting snatches of incongruity: Katya—wondrous, delectable little Katya and our ill-fated tryst out in the dairy barn, which has haunted me with confusion about my urges ever since; and Lyubov—perplexing, ofttimes unapproachable Lyubov—who, save for Marnya and now this French girl, is the only other woman who has ever seen me naked—and under circumstances which were so strangely different. If only I could somehow forget her . . . just like someone else I cannot forget: dark-haired. Just like this girl . . . *oh, God! If only this girl would kiss . . . just like him . . . .*

"M'sieur!" she moans out against my mouth, her hand easing nimbly downward and once more grasping its way around my bobbing penis. "M'sieur, really! Any moment now, you are going to—"

Abruptly, I let loose of her and push up to my knees on the bed.

Staring at me with eager, questioning eyes, the girl once more breaks into a ready smile, and starts spreading apart her legs.

"No!" I blurt out, impatiently shaking hair out of my face and mopping a river of sweat away from my brow with the back of my hand. Then, horribly embarrassed, I start gesturing, pointing down at myself, and whisper across to her: "Please, with . . . w-with your mouth."

Frowning, she backs away with a marked expression of distaste.

"Please!" I nearly shout, grabbing outward for her head.

"But, M'sieur!"

"Look! An extra, uh—hundred francs, *n'est-ce pas,* M'mselle? *Please."*

Finally, with a shrug, she decides to acquiesce—and crouching down before me, murmurs: "As you wish, M'sieur."

I shut my eyes—and then heaven molds itself around me *at last!* Seizing her head, I take care to cradle it between my hands with a gentle grip, run grateful fingers through her hair, and start thrusting blindly into her reluctant, quivering throat—while shuddering with ecstasy and drowning in the mire of all my forbidden visions, that voice I can never recognize rasping out upon the steeliest, sawing edge of hoarseness: "Oh, yes! Oh—oh, God! *Yes . . . ."*

* * *

"Well?" Gray eyes sparkling, his cheeks imbued with a glowing flush, Nikolai grins as we climb into the cab, muttering out low under his breath: "And now I can see that my little cousin finally has."

Wordlessly, I take the cigarette he makes such a show of offering and light it up and start blowing out haughty rings of smoke.

"So," he snickers, jabbing me in the ribs as the motor car chortles its way down the narrow, windy *Rue Lepic.* "And did my little cousin like it?"

I reply with a silent grin.

Laughing, slapping at his knee with near-tearful mirth, Nikolai seems at last to have found satisfaction with my answer, and lights up a cigarette himself, then to stare off with bemused contentment into the creamy, resplendent warmth of the approaching dawn.

I sigh also—with relief, blessing the decadent propriety of Paris. At least for an hour, one can rent a decent room with a door.

To prevent watchful eyes from reckoning the truth.

* * *

But the truth, I am reminded soon enough, is more evident to some than to others.

"Will merely be an intimate little *soirée,"* Klementi Filippovich says with an encouraging sidelong glance. "Woodwinds and such, you know."

Klementi, a tall, engaging fellow with expressive, laughing eyes, plays bassoon in the regular orchestra, and is well acquainted with most of the other musicians. Courting his friendship can only sharpen my chances of someday being taken in from the alternates. "Very well," I reply, nodding with an amiable smile as we stroll together down the long fifth-floor hotel corridor. "I shall inform my cousin."

"You mean—Zhelanov?" he snorts out derisively. "Akkh!"

"He is an excellent violinist!" I exclaim, stopping short in my tracks.

"Oh, everyone knows that—I've heard Zhelanov solo at the Conservatory back in Petersburg. A more accomplished violinist one can seldom find, I daresay. But is not your Nikolai Petrovich also a real rover? Courting one ballerina while eyeing another twenty at the very same time? Scarfing up all the prettiest ones—while leaving you, his cousin, always with second best—as he forever strings you along in his shadow? Come, Aleksandr Mikhailovich—wake up!"

"That is not true!" I retort. "Nikolai does not string me along in his shadow, nor leave me with second best!" In a huff, I snatch up my cane and barrel past him, striding on down the hall with as much haste as my limping gait will permit.

With a loud sigh, Klementi trots after me, snatching for my arm, pleading: "Oh, come now—I meant no offense!"

Glaring him down in reply, I pull to a halt in front of the door to my hotel room shared with Nikolai.

Klementi glances over his shoulder and lowers his voice. "Look, Sasha," he says—and then, coloring, adds: "May I call you 'Sasha?' Look, let us be frank with one another, Sasha, my friend. This little *fête* I have been telling you about is for 'Woodwinds.' Understand? A select group of us will be getting together to celebrate in the Blue Room at the *Le Doyen* on the *Champs-Elysées*. Why don't you wiggle out from under your cousin's wing for awhile and join us after the performance? You know what I mean when I say 'Woodwinds,' don't you? Well, surely you do! Because, Sasha—and again, I am speaking frankly—you do not truly mind so much that your cousin always swipes all the prettiest girls right out from under your nose—now, do you?"

And then, with a crafty wink, Klementi turns on his heel and strides back down the hall without another word.

* * *

After spending the entire afternoon pondering upon, and then deciding that I have read too much into, Klementi's bold insinuation, I make apologetic excuses to Nikolai later before he leaves yet again for the *Rue Lepic*. After all, I explain both to him and to myself, spending near unto twenty-four hours a day together might come to strain the limits of our friendship. There is, for a certainty, scarce ill to be thought of waning away one's remaining evetide hours after a performance with solitary pursuits.

Yet, from the moment I wander into the *Restaurant Le Doyen,* solitude becomes life's most remote probability. Everyone is wildly celebrating the grand success of the ballet *Les Sylphides* and the arrival of the incomparable Anna Pavlova. Despite my preference for the unassuming demeanor of Karsavina, Pavlova's feet, I will admit, are exquisite, unlike those of any other mortal in the world. As I pass by table after noisy, gesturing table, praise for Diaghilev's production of *Les Sylphides*, and adoration for Pavlova, continue gushing forth, literally drinkable. And not without merit—for while Nijinsky seems to defy the very breath of air, Pavlova appears to tiptoe upon unseen clouds like some heavenly porcelain doll. From every corner in the restaurant, people continue poring over the playbills adorned with the artist Serov's silvery front-cover rendering of the famous ballerina clad in demure long lacy tutu, a shining tiara crowning her jet-black hair.

The Blue Room, however, boasts its own peculiar type of celebration—behind cautiously monitored doors, unbeknownst to any of the boisterous dinner patrons clustered just outside.

Diaghilev himself is there, although he promptly leaves with Nijinsky in passionate, wide-eyed tow. Even before I reach to remove my derby, it is unmistakable just what kind of a party this is. There are no women—anywhere—although cushioned two-seater divans have been strewn with profusion between tables of steaming appetizer trays and the scores of sterling iced champagne buckets dotted in strategic positions all about the room.

"Well, Sasha!" Klementi calls gaily from behind me. "So! You decided to join us."

But I scarce hear a word he says—for instead, my attention is abruptly drawn to the room's center divan, upon which—oblivious to and hardly noticed by anyone else—the two oboe players, Alekseyev and Pazinsky, are necking.

I attempt to swallow, but cannot feel my tongue in the back of my throat. Ever since the German club rehearsals in Petersburg, I have entertained the suspicion that they were lovers. Alekseyev is also alternate flute behind me should the need ever arise, and so by necessity, I had caught some chance to know him. But until now, I was not entirely certain of his relationship with Pazinsky.

Following my gaze, Klementi lets out a loud guffaw. "Oh, never mind those two," he bellows with an approving snort. "They never bother at all with the food; always start clawing for one another the moment they're past the doors. So, Sasha, my friend," he goes on, nudging me and shoving a crystal goblet into my hand. "Some champagne?"

Numbly, I stare into the well of rose-colored liquid sloshing around in bubbly circles along the rim of my glass.

"Is something amiss?" Klementi then inquires in a lowered tone. "I thought—I mean, earlier this afternoon, while we were speaking in the hall—I was quite certain you knew what I meant by the word 'Woodwinds.'"

"If you would excuse me," I interrupt, "I think it is, uh—simply a tad of indigestion! Perhaps too much rich French food . . . ."

Like a tornado, I dash back out of the room and from the restaurant. Past an angst of impatience, I struggle with my cane up the twittery boardwalk of the *Champs-Elysées*, catch a cab, and finally stumble back into the hotel, where I curse the slowness of the elevator lift until bursting with relief back into the desolate sanctuary of Nikolai's and my room. But as much as I cower upon the bed and try to stuff a fat pillow across both roaring ears, I cannot help but at last admit with horror that there are *many* others—who merely have to steal one glance at me to know.

But worst of all is my livid jealously of those two oboe players necking down there on that divan, and the truth and violence of my own cravings, fraught now with near-overwhelming temptation: to banish my qualms, jump off the bed, re-comb my hair, and rush back without another second thought for the Blue Room at *Le Doyen*—intent upon joining in.

* * *

Nurture me with longing—Kindle me with tears—I will love you always—In a hundred-hundred-years . . . .

The stake—the fire—*nooo! Oh, please, God—Jesus, help me! I don't want to be burned alive . . . !*

I bolt straight up in my bed—at the foot of which, engulfed in an enormous flowing wave of white chiffon, stands Melissa.

Oh, dear God! . . .

"You will brave the threshold presently, my darling."

Her hand shoots upward, triumphant benediction upon the eerie ringing echo of a bell. The golden triangle whirls in metered flashes atop her head. . . .

Calling my name, Nikolai jumps from his bed and stumbles across the floor, coming to crouch before me in the darkness. "Sasha—for God's Sake!" he cries. "You look as if you've just seen a ghost!"

As my fingers stab out in panic, he grips hold of my arm, shaking me, exclaiming: "Snap out of it, Sasha! Naught at all is amiss, I tell you. We're in Paris, in the hotel! Oh, God in Heaven—don't you remember?"

"W-What was it?" I choke out at last. "Did I scream?"

Nikolai's brow creases with his familiar worried frown, and he stares a long while before answering. "No," he answers at last. "Not this time. You simply bolted upward so abruptly, it startled me awake."

Relieved, I press hold of his hand. In the past year, the dreams have not plagued me such as they once did, but occasional bad nights have bid due sleepless torment since my departure from Novgorod last February, apprehension about my fitful spates of sleep only worsening with spending so much time bedded down in the company of my cousin. "Forgive me," I say to him, flushing with shame. "I scarce meant to awaken you."

"Oh, never mind." Breaking into a gentle smile, Nikolai moves in closer, slipping his arm about my shoulders in a protective brotherly grasp. "Perhaps I should crawl in with you like I used to when we were children, eh?" he jokes, squeezing me and laughing. "Remember how scared of the dark you were for those couple of years—and how mean I was, forever teasing you? Oh! And remember how, once we became older, we'd still snuggle in beneath the covers together—one of us sneaking in the oil lamp; the other, whatever raunchy book it was that neither of us could put down at the time. Soon Maman would start pacing back and forth out in the hall, near tearing out her paper-rag curlers and chiding us to no end: 'For the twentieth time! You two boys put out that lamp, put that book away, and go to sleep!'"

Grinning at my cousin in fond reply, I poke into his ribs with my elbow. "Ha! And remember that time we set the sheets afire?"

"Lord be Praised! Remember how I used my new jacket to put it out, and then couldn't explain away the scorch marks on the sleeves afterward?"

Bursting into laughter, we stifle our mouths with our fists, ever conscious of the slightest sound carrying through the hollow walls of the hotel. "What is the time?" I whisper out, glancing for the wall clock—but unable, with my ever-worsening vision, to focus upon the numerals.

"Dawn in another hour or so, it appears." Rising from the bed, Nikolai pauses to stare down at me with concern, asking: "Are you sure you are all right?"

"Yes, my friend." Warmly, I reach up and again press his hand. "Forgive me for waking you. Was naught but a dream."

Grateful for another hour of sleep, I sink back down into my pillows, and through heavy-lidded eyes, watch as Nikolai flicks straying strands of his blond hair out from under the collar of his nightshirt as he shuffles back to bed. Dashingly handsome my cousin has come to be—a pity for the long line of broken female hearts strewn from here to Petersburg. "Hey!" I chide him, pointing across with mock accusation, "and haven't you become near as careless as I about tending regularly to the barber's! Yes?"

Grinning mischievously in reply, Nikolai swipes up my spectacles from the bedside table and slaps them onto his face, assuming a sinister, beady-eyed expression—then to shake out his pale mane and proclaim in a haughty, bloated-up voice: "Long-haired, foul-mouthed, bespectacled hoodlums of the *Intelligentsiya!*"

Howling with laughter, I toss a pillow at him—which he promptly hurls back, commanding: "Oh, go back to sleep, you wayward fool! And only pleasant dreams, now—do you hear?"

Still snickering, I turn over on my other side, the cue of song in my mind's eye softly repeating the last of Nikolai's words: *only pleasant dreams . . . and not a memory . . . .*

My eyes shoot open and I seize the covers, hacking for breath.

In an eerie flash, the vision of the burning stakes suddenly returns: only this time, in lieu of struggling against the blistering pull of the ropes, I find myself not held captive at all. Instead, from some distance away upon the crest of a hill, I view the whole violent, grisly scene in its entirety, seeing myself, with my same slight build and dark red hair, lashed to the stake—and the other man tied behind me, his hands grasping outward so desperately for mine—until the flames shoot upward, engulfing the two of us unto oblivion. Barely audible, quavering echoes of Uncle Ned's voice then relate the answer to my lifelong question in letters searing across the murky latticed papering of the hotel-room wall: *the difference between a dream and an actual past life memory is that, when you experience a memory in lieu of a dream—you will know.*

Shuddering, I pull the sheets up over my head, twisting the ends into sweaty, tightened knots. No wonder it is so profound, my acute sense of isolation from the majority of men who seek out solace in the arms of women. No wonder the party at the *Le Doyen* was so tempting; no wonder observers of like mind can spot me at a moment's glance! Does basic sexual bias ever change with death? And were not aberrant men and women, long ago, once sentenced to die as heretics? Condemned in medieval times to the same illustrious fate as many a witch?

But, then—who was the man tied behind me at the stake—that love a song still echoing so real? Could it have been Volodya? But no—even from that far distance, although I could scarce make out his face, I know I saw a head of sun-washed, lightened hair . . . musing idly upon the question, I turn over in bed again—only to end up gaping over at Nikolai.

My heart drops, thundering, in my chest. *No—oh, no! That is impossible!*

Turning over roughly, I stare back at the wall—which melts away into the blazing ghostly vision of Melissa again, and once more I cannot block out the ringing pronouncement of her voice: *You will brave the threshold presently, my darling. . . .*

"Sasha?" Nikolai pushes up on his elbow. "What is wrong?"

But at last, thank God, she fades away. . . . "I said it was nothing, for the Lord's bloody sake!" I bark crossly at Nikolai in reply. "I'm sorry I woke you yet again—go back to sleep. I've simply not been sleeping well at all of late. You know how it is with the pressure, the constant hours of practice."

"But, Sasha—"

"Dammit, Nikolai!" I snap over my shoulder, taking pains to avoid facing him. "Will you stop fretting like such a mother hen over me all the time? Go back to sleep!"

* * *

Summer, which used to drag on so endlessly beneath my yearly load of book work on the Novgorod farm, and which wore my patience to its fitful limits during those months of imprisonment in Moscow, has flown by now in a heady whirlwind, dotted with gay luncheons or festive late-night suppers at *Larue's* or the *Café de la Paix,* the pursuit of gluttony followed into each morn's wee small hours by much dancing on Nikolai's part, and much merry drinking and talkativeness on mine, in celebration of the triumphant success of the ballets. For it is the ballets, once so snubbed by the French, that daily continue dominating the front pages of the papers, despite Chaliapin's imposing performances, glittering historical ensemble and all, in Rimsky-Korsakov's operatic masterpiece, *Pskovityanka,* better known in Paris as *Ivan the Terrible. Le Festin,* danced to a menagerie of compiled scores by Rimsky, Glinka, Mussorgsky, and Tchaikovsky in an attempt to imbue a taste of Russian nationalistic flavor into the productions, proves a rather tame affair, unless one focuses strictly upon the music. In the end, it becomes quite easily outdone by the exotic spectacle of *Cléopâtre,* an expanded version of the Maryinsky ballet *Nuits d'Egypte*, which is based upon Arensky's music, but to which several other impromptu borrowings, including Glazunov's spellbinding *Bacchanal,* have been added. Leon Bakst's sumptuously appointed purple sets have become the talk of the town, along with Ida Rubenstein, whom Fokine has placed in the role of the imperious queen. With her haughty beauty, the lanky Ida has even upstaged the great Pavlova, not only in footwork, but also in receipts—for the rumors flying from balcony to balcony and across floors in the hotels for two days straight now are that *Cléopâtre* has brought in the most money.

This is welcome news, because the dancers are always paid first, and high receipts at least assure payment of some portion of our stipend. But as I step away from the gilded doors of the *Pavillon de Hanover,* an ancient, lavish building where Astruc, who manages Diaghilev's financial affairs, retains his office, I stare into my wrinkled envelope of francs while doing quick calculations in my head, and again realize that it is not going to be enough. Once more, by the end of the week, we will be depleted of funds, and either I or Nikolai will be pressed again to wire Barclay's of London or the St. Petersburg Commercial, or perhaps both, to make small drawings out of our respective inheritances. "Damn!" I grumble, frowning down glumly into the envelope before roundly cursing the growing stuffiness of the summer heat and fidgeting with my tie in a spate of impatience. Pulling the brim of my derby low to my brow beneath the lancing glare of the noonday sun, I begin to wander, aimless in thought or purpose, back down the bustling *Boulevard des Italiens.*

At the corner, I come upon the sight of Nikolai shouting out my name and running toward me full speed from the opposite end of the avenue. Past dozens of irate ducking heads, he keeps waving out one of the theater playbills like a frantically possessed demon.

"Wait!" I cry as he barrels up to me. "Slow down—I cannot make out a single word you have said!"

"The orchestra!" he bellows out again in a breathless, joyful rush, throwing his arms around me and swinging us both all the way around. "I have been taken in!" he shouts on. "A second section chair it may be, but you'd damn well better believe I'll covet it fanatically—and they want me there for the *Les Sylphides* performance tonight! We're saved, Sasha! No more dipping into the reserves; now, we shall see some honest wages!"

"That's marvelous!" I gasp, still struggling to believe my ears.

"Oh, yes! Feodorov—you know which one he was: like a frigging Cossack with all that curly black hair? He and Fokine wound up in a terrible row one night last week, and Borya said he heard Benois and Tcherepnin talking about me to Fokine right afterward, and that I had better be on the ready for it. Sure enough, Feodorov packed his bags today and checked out of his hotel. I've just come from a meeting with Tcherepnin; I must hurry back to rehearsal, they're about to start in another fifteen minutes—but I had to come find and tell you! Oh, Lord, I am so thrilled! And later tonight, we will go out again and celebrate—oh, don't you look at me like that! We're guaranteed stipend, you know, if we perform. And this is permanent, Sasha—so stop worrying your finicky bookclerk's head so about money. Oh, I must go—wave to me later when you arrive at the theater, and then we will dance the night away again with Amaliya and Felitsiya at the *Viel!* This time, the champagne is on me!"

As a consequence of my cousin's bounteous luck, during the two performances attended out of the remaining four, I watch the ballets alone from our corner seats, the extra ticket given over each time to one of the hopefuls in the pre-performance crowd always lingering just outside the *Chàtelet* doors.

And our high living and gay parties continue unabated up until the very end of summer, and straight through the twelfth and final performance of the Company, now regarded across Paris as a breath of fresh air from the mysterious lurking East, and dubbed unanimously throughout the city's bustling streets and fashionable salons as Sergei Diaghilev's *Ballet Russe.*

Ducking away from the boisterous back-slapping of the crowd of dancers and musicians lingering in *Larue's,* which boasts a Russian chef who knows, for a change, how to whip up decent *bliny* with red caviar and capers, Nikolai and I ease our way back over to our table and settle down with more champagne. "You know," he murmurs thoughtfully, eyeing me with some trepidation, "I scarce meant to act like a doltish, insensitive oaf."

"Oh, Nikolai—stop talking like a fool," I reply, immediately sensing his gist. "I am only far too aware of the odds—a couple dozen violins versus two or three flutes in an orchestra. For a certainty, I knew you'd get taken in before I ever did on account of the better chances alone. And I knew it would be you—over any of the others—due to your extraordinary talent."

Flushing with embarrassment, Nikolai stares off toward the restaurant's clamoring horn and saxophone band, his eyes scanning with a mournful glimmer over the jostling patrons and hoisted champagne bottles before coming to fix upon me once again. "Well, I simply wanted to let you know that I had not meant to one-up you in any way. During these last two performances, I swear I have never seen you more glum."

"Nikolai, I could never harbor jealously of you. Actually, it's all a bit sad, for everyone. The glowing reviews are long past; everyone is talking about future plans. I have been wondering how you and I intend upon spending the winter."

Nodding in agreement, Nikolai scoots his chair over closer toward mine and takes slow, reflective sips of his champagne, saying: "I too have been giving that matter more than mere idle thought. Earlier, I spoke with Rasskazinsky—you know, Konstantin Nikolayevich."

"The clarinetist?"

"Yes—we struck up a conversation in the pit during the intermission. He was telling me that the Company is breaking up until next year's Lenten rehearsals. Diaghilev and his circle of intimates are going to holiday for awhile in Venice, or so I heard, to start planning next spring's repertoire. And several others are departing for the seacoast. Konstantin made mention of an ensemble he is forming with the intent of wintering together in Cannes. With the crowds flocking there as the weather cools, there is work to be had: *soirées*, weddings, and such. He asked if I wanted to join in; said that they've decided to include a violin. And he also told me that two days ago, he invited you to join them, as they still need a flute—but that you had as yet not given any answer."

"Nikolai, mustn't we consider return unto Petersburg by the time your autumn term begins?"

"Oh! I had meant to tell you: I have no intention of continuing studies the St. Petersburg Conservatory. For a considerable length of time, I've been contemplating upon this decision, and now that Fokine has taken me on permanently, I see no reason to return."

"Have you wholly taken leave of your senses?" I exclaim in outraged, indignant response, slamming my fist down onto the table. "You cannot throw away three and a half years of composition study to simply pack off with some rag-tag ensemble!"

I stop abruptly, realizing—with acute embarrassment—that I sound exactly like my father.

"Look, it would be different were Rimsky still alive and still teaching!" Nikolai declares, near shouting the words into my ear. "But never have I gotten on in any decent way with that foppish old fart Auer, even if he has been violin maestro there for over forty blessed years. And I am sick unto dreary death of the damn political meandering that keeps mounting at the Conservatory with never any end. I assure you—the leave of absence, the long trip I took here to Paris last year was not solely on account of Rimsky's death. Blast it, the primary pursuit should be the study of music, not the furtherance of revolution! But still we hear naught but laments about old Bloody Sunday, even after these four and a half years, and the supposed suffering of the peasants and the working class! Have they no idea that the arts in our country continue to blossom in such triumphant wake only at behest of the Tsar? Who funds at least a half-dozen orchestras, dammit—and the Imperial Ballet School, and the Maryinsky, and near all the other theaters, mind you—out of his own privy purse, with no hope of any repayment ever, save for his own altruistic satisfaction?"

Avoiding Nikolai's gaze, I manage a quiet nod. Although jokes about the *Intelligentsiya* we may banter back and forth in good-spirited, roguish humor, God save the poor soul who ever entices my cousin into an earnest political debate. Borne of a long line of dutiful, upstanding Zhelanov princes, Nikolai has inherited, along with many others of the Petersburg aristocracy, a vested economic interest in the staunch conservatism inspired by Tsarist autocracy—and his opinions rankle forth about the subject much like those of his kind, but ofttimes politically overbearing, late father. "Very well," I answer noncommittally, near pinching myself as I bite back all temptation for rebuttal. "Then I suppose we shall travel together to Cannes."

"Unless you wish to return to Petersburg for a short while," he then suggests, breaking into a grin and rolling his eyes. "Maman keeps writing without end about how she misses me so terribly. And," he goes on with a shrug, "we could make a side trip back to Novgorod—to give you a chance to make amends with Uncle Misha."

Again I slam my fist onto the table—while Nikolai seizes up my fingers in an iron-like hold, leaning sharply forward, imploring: "Sasha, for God's sake—he is your father! Have I not told you how I would trade places with you in an instant to have my father awaiting my return trip to Russia? Uncle Misha wants to apologize—Maman says so in every single letter!"

"Are you finally going to force me into packing my things, into requesting another room?" It is the same threat I have made all summer long, each and every time my cousin has attempted to drag me into another pointless discussion about reconciliation.

"No," he murmurs, disappointed. "Of course not."

Pushing up from the table, I down the remainder of my champagne in one hurried gulp, telling him: "I will go search out Konstantin Nikolayevich and inform him that you and I will join up with his Cannes ensemble. But I am not going back to Novgorod, ever!" I remind him again before leaving, unable to resist it. "Because I no longer have a father."

* * *

In September of 1909, we celebrate my eighteenth birthday, and in November, Nikolai's twentieth. Come advent of winter, like a couple of wayfaring minstrels, we tag along with Konstantin's barrelhouse woodwind-brass-string-piano ensemble—named, after a night of much joking amidst free flowing beer, *Joie de Russe.* Though the pay is scant, the times are rushed and boisterous, for the rattly, syncopated cadences of Ragtime bands from American New Orleans start to invade the entire French seaboard, while the coast is overtaken by a whirlwind of parties for the autumn season on the heels of the Diaghilev ballets. Starving musicians, if able somehow to drag themselves away from their drunken seafaring revelries, remain in regular demand, especially in the dark bars grouped in close proximity to the Monte Carlo casinos. Yet by Christmas, when even the beaches of sunny Cannes lie hidden beneath murky clouds of white-edged fog, the longing for home, for hearty, filling food, and for the stiff bite of a true Russian winter drives us both near to the brink of despair. Having broken with our compatriots—who set out for Monte Carlo yet again with ribald, chiding taunts regarding our misdirected foolishness—we stumble at last, exhausted and bereft of any yen to ever taste French wine again, into Baltic Station and the delighted awaiting arms of Aunt Sophie. "Oh, I have been looking forward to this for so long!" she wails, tears streaming down both cheeks as she throws her arms around Nikolai for what must be the hundredth time. "Do not either of you entertain even a single worry! I have set all the servants on double-duty, and two rooms of the townhouse are readied for the both of you."

"Maman, Sasha and I have spent considerable time discussing this," Nikolai tells her in a softened tone, grasping her shoulder and shaking his head with firm insistence in reply to her anguished expression. "And as I told you in my last letter, we have sublet from our friends who have stayed behind in Monte Carlo a flat situated quite conveniently near the Ekaterinsky Canal. It is much closer to rehearsals, and we shan't need to pay much for cabs."

Aunt Sophie catches her hand to her throat. "But, Kolya, darling! The house is all ready!"

Her breath cut short with a sob, she stares over from Nikolai toward me. "Oh, Sasha!" she gasps out, her hands trembling noticeably within her enormous sable muff. "Good Heavens, will you come to your senses? It is Christmastide! And your father longs to see you."

Icily, I hold her gaze. "I assume you have not forgotten that when I departed Novgorod last February, my father ordered me never to return?"

Aunt Sophie nods reluctantly, biting her lip.

"You may tell him I intend to take him at his word."

"But, Sasha!"

From Aunt Sophie, I stare back to Nikolai—who, as expected, reconfirms agreement with the faintest nod. In the past months of living together through thick and thin, through nights of over-imbibing and days of surviving, at the best of times, off fresh-caught shellfish, and at the worst, off soup of naught but onion skins and other paltry vegetables washed down with stale crusts of bread, we have found that although we may not always see eye to eye politically, or agree about the situation with my father, our camaraderie in the quest of music remains as solid as ever. Several unfinished collaborations—on everything from the first movements of a full-fledged symphony to a pitiful little wedding march begun to the taunts of Konstantin and the others on a drunken lark—still require our strictest attention. With the German Club rehearsals in Petersburg starting up again after the first of the year, spare time will be at the utmost premium. "Aunt Sofiya," I say, addressing her quite formally, "Nikolai and I have lived these past months in studied thriftiness and parted only after a great deal of thought with four months rent to sublet the flat over by Ekaterinsky—in which we intend to live until departing once more for Paris come next May. There is no longer room on anyone's part for negotiation."

And by staying far across town from the Zhukovskaya townhouse, little chance for crossing paths with Father will present itself during these upcoming four months.

"I see," says Aunt Sophie at last with a weary, saddened sigh, seeing us both firmly set upon our decision.

"Thank you for understanding," I reply, piqued with myself inwardly for my tone of voice, sounding so rude and terse. Attempting to shrug off my acute flush of discomfiture, I snatch up my cane and the handle-strap to my trunk, leaving the two of them to follow behind in subdued familial whisperings as I stride toward the flickering gaslamps on Voznesensky Prospekt, my eyes searching out the throngs of troikas and sledges tearing through the icy slush for some sign of a cab.

* * *

"Boris! Look, they have granted it," I shout, wildly waving out the diploma as the streetcar lets me off just west of the Anichkov Bridge. "Boris, where did Nikolai go? Hey, Boris! Wait up!"

But instead, after yelling back for me to stop tarrying, Boris charges off like an overwrought steam engine, barreling westward past all the shops for at least two blocks down the broad walkway of Nevsky Prospekt.

Sighing, I tuck the diploma inside the pocket of my light woolen coat and follow after, snapping my umbrella up again. For the past three days, rain has been pouring down in a near wintery-like torrent—in spite of Maytide's hurried passing and summer's looming advent. Violet hues of daylight lengthen far into every vibrant eve now, while all the trees in Petersburg have blossomed out in glorious, fragrant wake across the city parks and palace squares. "Boris!" I cry with irritation, trudging up behind his lumbering form as he finally stops short before a barber's shop. "Hey! Where did Nikolai go? I must tell him about my diploma."

Boris whirls around. "You finally obtained your diploma from higher-school?"

Triumphantly, I fetch it out from my coat pocket for his inspection. Four months of juggling German Club rehearsals between rigorous study for final examinations; four months of pleading with Forostenko, the grumpy headmaster at May's, for permission to complete the tests a month early—a feat close to a Saint's miracle! "A year late, perhaps—but better than never," I cry, beaming from ear to ear as I point to my name affixed with the graduate's seal.

"Well! Then your late-night studying paid off—yes, Sekovsky?" he bellows, clapping me on the shoulder before turning back around again in haste.

"What are you staring at?" I squeeze in beneath his larger umbrella and peer across his shoulder—to encounter the sight of Nikolai, huddled down just past the corner with Sadovaya Street. Bereft of his coat and hat, he stands sheltered—for the moment at least—beneath the umbrella of a red-faced, strikingly blonde young lady, who continues glaring at him with pursed lips and an expression livid with furious accusation.

Nikolai's hands dart around in all directions as he attempts to coax the young woman back into his favor.

"Oh, she'll let him off," Boris declares with a nod. "That's Sonya Ilynichna—you know, that lead contralto from the choir. She's been after him for the past three months, head-over-heels in love. I saw the two of them together yesterday, batting eyes at one another for an hour straight past the bookshelves in Smirdin's."

"Ten rubles says he winds up as good as rubbish." I hold out my right hand.

Boris's eyebrows shoot upward. "Hell, I'll take you up on that one, Sekovsky!" he cries, laughing, his hand fiercely clasping mine. Pointing back toward the girl, he reminds me with conviction: "I am telling you, this is Sonya Ilynichna!"

Together, we crane our heads past a flood of noontime browsers bustling along the quaint shop-rows of Nevsky Prospekt—to see Sonya, who appeared for the briefest moment to be melting somewhat toward Nikolai's grovelings of apology, suddenly screw up her eyes, fling out her arm, and slap him across the face.

After which she turns on her heel, storming off northward down Sadovaya, umbrella and all, leaving Nikolai stranded with the rain soaking over his head.

To the dismay of several aged matrons debarking from a cab that stops behind us, Boris lets out a piercing whistle, while I yell down the street through cupped hands: "Hey, Zhelanov—you pitiful, lovesick fool! Recall you not the fate of Mozart's *Don Giovanni?*"

Nikolai replies in due kind by signaling us with the ecumenical obscene gesture—and then sprints off down Sadovaya, shouting: "But, Sonya!"

"Ah, bloody crap," mumbles Boris, stuffing a ten-ruble note into my hand.

"Oh, never mind. I'll spring for luncheon," I tell him.

"Very well. But first, I must post a letter."

"Fine, then let us meet at Donon's in half an hour. I want to check over that new shop back by the Fontanka before we return to Paris, and see if I can find something for my cousin Anna's birthday."

Boris waves me a jovial salute and bounds off for the next eastbound streetcar, while I follow after on foot for a short block, turning then from Nevsky northward onto the juncture with Theater Street. Past a bevy of grocers and noisy balalaika cafes, far down the avenue at a confluence of carriage lanes leading off toward the Fontanka Canal, I happen at last upon the tiny shop about which I have heard so much from our enthusiastic landlady.

Indeed, the place proves worthy of its reputation: despite the peeling paint and dowdiness of its outer facade, the interior is stocked to the hilt with the latest European fabrics and accessories for ladies at fairly reasonable prices. In a front-end counter, I find a calfskin billfold boasting a slide-out mirror-glass within its two-way change-case, the perfect practical gift for Anna, who is now always so pressed for time, ever dashing about to-and-fro from her studies at the Medical Academy. "How much?" I inquire of the salesgirl.

Busy with another customer, she glances over. "Seven and a half rubles, if it please you, sir."

Nodding, I finger Boris's ten-ruble note in my pocket and take my place in line.

Never one to tolerate idleness for more than a moment, while waiting, I decide to make a quick scan across the counter, taking note of any other unusual items for future gift-giving reference—until my survey comes to an abrupt halt, my eyes fixing upon an apparently deformed black-gloved hand.

Standing with his back to me, behind the salesgirl, the man saddled with such sorry plight continues speaking in low murmurs into the shop's telephone-box, his hand drumming with impatience across the glass-beveled top of the counter in the same way that a person would drum his fingers across a table or a desk—except that this man has no fingers, at least not past the knuckles, for the ends of the glove have been sewn in almost straight across like a child's mitten, keeping the fit of the leather taut and snug, a seam even being sewn straight across the thumb . . . .

"Oh—yes, sir," the salesgirl says, taking the ten-ruble note from my hand just as the man hangs up the earpiece to the telephone and turns around.

His startled dark eyes meet mine as I gasp for all escaping air.

Package in hand, I tear out of the shop and down the closest carriage avenue—but after the briefest pause, the salesgirl bursts out of the shop as well, giving chase in a flurry of petticoats, her shouts of: "Sir! Sir!" remaining in hot pursuit despite the turn I make at the first corner, and the next, and then the next, where she finally catches up with me in an alleyway just a block west of the Fontanka Canal. "Sir!" she cries out, panting and shoving an envelope into my reluctant hand. "Your change!"

And after a polite nod, she fetches up her skirts and hurries back toward the direction of the shop.

With shaking fingers, I extract bills and coins from the envelope—along with a calling card, on which is printed, in addition to the shop's telephone exchange number: *Vladimir Denisov, Proprietor in Taffeta, Silks, Light Woolens, and Distinctive Accessories for Ladies.*

And on the back of which is written, in stilted, back-handed script, the address of a flat on Vasilyevsky Island.

* * *

The door opens, he looks at me, and I look at him—and then he steps away from the door, I step inside, and he shuts it, the little bolts clicking like rifle shots into the latch of the lock, the thousand bullets screaming through my head that this is naught but stupidity, sheer madness! I should simply turn around and march back out of here right now, this very moment, this very second, *dammit!* But no matter how ruthlessly I try to force myself away, my feet forsake my head for my heart—for in the breadth of that hanging moment, he slides his arms around my neck and kisses me, his triumph assured, my torment over. My legs melt to jelly, my arms mold to lead around him as I rub my cheek against his face and feel the coarse, scraping prickliness of the both of us, unshaven since the morn, and as our lips meet once again, I keep telling myself how wrong this is, that I am not supposed to *want* to kiss another man—that it is the consummate blasphemy, the most heinous abomination, the ultimate unpardonable sin! But—abomination tastes like sweet forbidden fruit; blasphemy burns into my loins ancient bonds of serpentine power. And sin? *Oh, God!* Sin is why I *want to!* . . .

Low chuckles lancing the tenor of his breath, Volodya pulls away at last, his fingers groping urgently through strands of my hair as he whispers: "I knew that you would come."

* * *

Searching out the flat on Vasilyevsky was daring the height of folly. Going to bed with Volodya again was more foolhardy than anything else I have ever done. But this—*Jesus God! This is total lunacy.* . . .

"Try to muster up a little interest, will you?" Volodya snaps, elbowing me again.

Begrudgingly, I cross my arms and renew my attempt to pay attention.

Granted, I suppose matters could be worse. For instance, Volodya's clothes do not hang on me so much as they once did. A precaution, he said, insisting upon my changing into his dark worker's trousers and flannel shirt before we left, pointing out that I could hardly attend a meeting of his beloved Socialist Revolutionaries while yet clad in my waistcoated suit and Scottish derby.

But still, as I continue blinking beneath a harsh glare of bare light bulbs, the back of my neck remains hot with perspiration, chafing away in an angry rash as I groan inwardly that no man should ever be beholden to the promises he makes to another in bed!

The downstairs of the dress shop hangs in dingy light, the bolts of winter fabric and scattered remnants stored along the walls amongst a film of musty cobwebs. But at least the floors have been scrubbed clean, the odor of bleach and fresh tallow soap permeating throughout the dark reaches of the cellar. Upon first glance, one would hardly think of these people—mostly men with a few dour-faced women scattered amongst the group, all of them sitting with tranquil faces in neat rows of high-backed chairs—as a group of revolutionaries. To a fault, each appears as humble and scrupulously polite as the most trusted palace servant, dark caps and patched scarves twisting between studious, work-worn fingers. From up in front, the gray-haired speaker maintains his strict hold on their attention, bellowing on: "The peasant lives for the land, yearns for land! Exists only for the glory of the land! From time immemorial has the *muzhik* sewn his bonds to Mother Earth, which no holder of any worldly title, whether it be landlord or crown of state, can take away in God's righteous wisdom. And this must be our quest, our cross, our ultimate triumphant destiny," he continues on breathlessly with a wave of both hands. "To seize the land away from the evil industrialists, to take the heart of bread back from the hated yoke of the nobility, and return it whole and square to the peasant *muzhik* who knows deep down that earth belongs to none but God and those who sow land's seed! This is our trust—we, the working people, guardians of the faith, soldiers of the cause—to bring to the peasant of Mother Russia his final rightful due. For this, each and every one of us must be willing to give our time, energy, faith—and yes, perhaps even our lives. Never forget the martyrs of the *Narodnaya,* the People's Will! Never forget the dead heroes of our People's Revolution! . . ."

"Humph!" I mutter, whispering toward Volodya: "As if we've made no concessions. As if we've granted no peasants any leaseholds at all—"

"Shut up and listen—will you, Sasha?"

Groaning, I reluctantly do so—until after for what seems an eternity, the man finishes his wordy address, and to a round of hearty applause, steps down from the makeshift podium. Obligatory rounds of small talk ensue, during which Volodya nods and trades affectations with several fellows before we at last file one by one back out through the narrow cellar door. With quivering fingers, the crusty old speaker begins passing out bunches of pamphlets—some of which I take dutifully, not wishing to arouse anyone's attention. But I shove the stack into Volodya's arms once we ascend to the darkened street.

"But you must help with passin' them out!" he insists, pushing the typewritten slogans back into my grasp.

"Oh, for God's sake, Volodya!" I cry, whitening, appalled. "Is it not enough that I came along with you to your infernal meeting?"

"And only after I near dragged you behind kickin' and screamin'," he retorts, shoving his gloved fist angrily down into his trouser pocket.

"Well, what do you expect? 'Return all land to the peasants'—Lord Christ! Such would only bring on total anarchy, I tell you! How would the grain ever find its way to the mills? How would the city populace ever eat? Such matters require governmental organization! And had it never occurred to you that yours truly here would have the Ilmen estate to lose if you and these motley people ever succeed with your pitiful revolution?"

"And rightly so!" he counters, turning on me underneath the dim yellowy glow of a gaslamp. "Why should the aristocracy be singled out for favor? Why should only one faction in all the Empire hold wealth, while countless others starve? Leave off your peaceful boyhood memories of Lissushka in Novgorod, my dear Count Sekovsky!" he exclaims sarcastically. "Don't tell me you never caught sight of conditions in Vyborg when you were stayin' with me those three years ago, that you never took note of the factory workers trudgin' home in rank exhaustion!"

"Anyone rendering service unto the Tsar can elevate his status in the world!" I storm back angrily. "Why, one can even achieve hereditary nobility, mind you—by properly traversing through the Table of Ranks."

"Oh, the Table of Ranks," Volodya sneers, tossing his head. "A shenanigan, a charade! A ploy only for the rich."

"Indeed, the Table of Ranks!" I storm on. "Nobility is a status *earned,* and rightly so. My great-great-great-great grandfather, Mikhail Dmitryevich, was naught but a lowly bee farmer and sometime architect—until he, like so many others, rendered service unto the Great Tsar Peter in the construction of this fine city. And in accordance with the Table of Ranks, the Tsar made him a count."

"Spare me the reminder of your illustrious forebears, will you, Sasha?"

I bite back my next retort not so much at Volodya's urging as at that of the next corner copper we pass, whose gaze narrows in upon us with beady-eyed suspicion as he ducks back under his kiosk to avoid a renewed shower of rain, his survey of our bundles of pamphlets heightening alarmingly until we stuff the copies away inside our jackets.

Once we shy out of the copper's sight, the dispute between us continues unabated. For half an hour, we wrangle on nonstop about politics, shouting each other down from one streetcar to another until we again cross over the Neva and reach the apartment on Vasilyevsky. Once there—faced with either the prospect of changing or returning home in Volodya's clothes—I pull off his worker's cap and throw it across the room at him, while he continues to scoff at me, watching in cold silence as I whip off the shirt.

From the shirt, it is the trousers—and from there to my skin and his hands—and from there to the iron-posted bed, again—where I curse myself beneath our hot drench of sweat and every glorious, shuddering touch. . . .

"I shan't be back tomorrow," I say, my stare held to the floor as I finally button back on my own shirt and fumble with retying my tie.

Coloring, I attempt to shrug away my guilt for the past two nights of vague excuses that I have been making to Nikolai back at my own apartment.

Still in bed, Volodya leans up against the bars of the headrest and peers across the room, studying me with pursed eyebrows as he lights up another cigarette. "You'll be goin' back to Paris?" he then inquires with a knowing grin, flicking the ash carelessly down onto the floor. "With the Diaghilev Ballet?"

I glance at him, startled. "How did you know?"

"I have my sources."

Quickly, I clap on my derby.

"Uh-huh. Simply lovely when you're all riled up," he then says, sighing, again flicking away the ash. "In fact, I think you've grown more beautiful than ever. And perhaps a little taller. Not near so many bloody freckles. But I swear, Sekovsky—you're still fuckin' gorgeous!"

Without reply, I snatch up my cane and hurry for the door.

Still unclothed, Volodya bounds up from the bed and stumbles out in front of me, grinning beneath a florid haze of smoke. "If I know you," he murmurs softly, tossing away the cigarette butt as he grips for my shoulders, "you'll be back."

Slamming shut my eyes, I try to harden my lips shut from his—but in the end, I simply *cannot*. . . .

"Oh, maybe not tomorrow," he whispers, pulling away at last. "And maybe not next week. But mark my words, Sasha dearie," he goes on with insistence, pointing the stump of his severed index finger into my face. "Soon enough, you'll be back for kisses—and more."

Stooping for the floor, he retrieves some of the revolutionary pamphlets from his jacket pocket and shoves them into my hand. "And when you return, we'll add onto your 'education' with another meetin'! And fetch more pamphlets for you to—"

"I am not passing out this rubbish to anybody, Volodya!"

"What's a'matter, Sasha? You chicken? 'Fraid of all the coppers?"

Ears blazing, I snatch up a couple of pamphlets on the way out and slam the apartment door shut against the squall of Volodya's sarcastic laughter. *Damn him!* This time—so I tell myself again and again all the way down all three flights of steps—this time I am staying away for good!

* * *

Nikolai stops bowing abruptly and glances over at me. "Your delvings into the occult," he says in lowered voice, "are scarce of the most typical nature—true, Sasha?"

I follow his gaze to my bedside table, where lies Uncle Ned's book, *The Science of Numbers*, again open to the page where last night I had let off reading. "I suppose that depends on what you mean by 'typical,'" I reply, looking downward to make idle examination of the flute's headjoint pitch. "Seances, palm readings, *Ouija* boards, yoga meditation—the current decadent pastimes proving all the rage of Petersburg? I suppose such phenomena have their place in the vast realm of things. But my interest is, I feel, far more rooted in simple practicality."

"And how would you describe this interest of yours?" Nikolai inquires, cocking a critical eyebrow.

I shrug. "It is very simple: every manifestation in the universe reduces to a solitary number."

As he casts another frown in the direction of the book, I decide to risk elaboration: "Dates reduce to individual numbers when the digits comprising them are added together. Every letter in every alphabet, no matter what the language, reduces to a specific number—beginning with the number 'one' for 'A'; the number 'two' for 'B', for example. Therefore words reduce to solitary numbers when the numbers assigned to their individual letters are totaled. And numbers have various meanings. The numbers one through seventy-eight derive occult significance from the ancient science of the Tarot. The digits of numbers exceeding seventy-eight are added, reducing them to smaller numbers to fit back within the Tarot paradigm."

"And this is how you calculated the numbers in that chart you showed me a couple of years ago? That you said was based upon my birth date and my name?"

"In a manner of speaking, yes."

I watch with trepidation as Nikolai sets his violin down on the divan and approaches the bedside table. Still frowning, he picks up the book and starts leafing through it. "Would you mind if I borrowed this?" he then asks with a wry smile. "I think I should like to read it."

"Well, certainly!" I reply, amazed.

"And I take it that you believe in reincarnation," he then observes.

Astonishment pounds me a swift kick in the chest, but I manage to reply: "The only qualification I'd make to that statement is to have wholly done with the word 'believe.' After all," I go on, again shrugging, "it seems ridiculous to say that one 'believes' in something so obvious in the course of nature."

Nikolai nods. "Yes," he murmurs, still staring intently down at the title page of Uncle Ned's book. "I too find the tenets of Theosophy appealing to my sense of logic."

"You do?"

"Oh, yes."

After tucking the violin back into its case, he curls up contentedly on the divan with my book.

Still stunned, I cannot help but steal glances at him. Conservative as he tends to lean politically, Nikolai still never has wholly embraced the Orthodoxy. Nor, up to this point, any other creed, for that matter—at least not as far as I know. One day in the school-dorm a few years back, when so enthused about numbers that I attempted to engage him in a full-fledged metaphysical conversation, he scarce showed any interest. Even when, in a renewed burst of enthusiasm, I showed him his numerological chart two winters ago in Novgorod, he was not at all taken with it, much preferring a return to our discussion about Bach and counterpoint theory instead.

I continue peeking at his bent head as I clean my flute, curious as to what catalyst could have inspired such drastic change.

The lid to the case snaps shut beneath my fingers just as a chorus of voices erupts outside in the hall—not an unusual occurrence these days in a Parisian hotel stuffed full with boisterous young Russian musicians. But still, I snatch up my cane and hurry for the door, intent upon investigation.

Angry shouts cascade up the stairwell through velvety layers of the warm June air: "What do you mean, you don't remember which room he's in? You were the one who said you knew, you addle-brained, rum-guzzling nitwit!"

"Akkh! And as if it's even any of my business at all, you whimpering son of a fool! Might I remind you that *you* are the one who thinks he must get married."

"Which is why we must find him, now! Before Fokine has my head on a platter and serves it tonight as an appetizer to all of Paris! Which room is he in? We have got to find him!"

I peek out the door to encounter the flushed faces of Ignati Pavlovich, who plays second flute in the regular orchestra, and Nikita Adamovich, who in third chair usually plays piccolo. The two of them practically pounce upon me and burst into a simultaneous roar of: *"Sekovsky!* Do you know *Sheherazade?"*

"On piccolo?" Nikita wildly goes on, waving out both arms as if my answer dictates a matter of life and death.

"Of course I know piccolo for *Sheherazade."*

"Oh, thank the Saints! Then you will cover for me tonight? And for the next two to three weeks? You are flute alternate, and obliged to, yes? Oh, please, say you'll do this for me, Sekovsky—or dear God help me! Alekseyev has to stay on oboe, and there simply is no one else! I am telling you, the young lady will not be put off any longer! It must be tonight, or else I fear that she will never speak to me again! The young lady has given me the strictest, most final ultimatum!"

"Wait a moment, Nikita Adamovich!" I interrupt. "What is this all about? What young lady?"

Ignati rolls his eyes and jabs his elbow into Nikita's arm. "This mumbling idiot is intent upon getting himself married tonight!" he bellows out, laughing.

Nikolai, who has come up behind me, lets out a low whistle.

"Say you'll do piccolo for me, Aleksandr Mikhailovich!" Nikita grovels on. "I must go pack so I can catch the train for Nice that leaves in an hour! You will do the piccolo, yes? *Please?"*

"Well, of—of course!" I stammer out.

Overjoyed, Nikita lets out a screeching yell, throws both arms around me, kisses me three times upon each cheek in rapt succession, and then barrels off for the fifth floor elevator lift, shouting back: "And don't forget to tell Maestro Pierné that you're taking my place!"

"No need to fret," says Ignati, grinning and shaking his head. "I'll go inform the conductor and Fokine, I'm on my way over to the rehearsal room right now. Lucky you, Aleksandr Mikhailovich—*Sheherazade* and *Carnaval* are premiering tonight! Rehearsal's in another hour, then we'll head right into performance—as you know, Nikolai Petrovich—so you'd both best fetch a bite to eat if you can. See you at the theater."

Ignati hurries off as I gape after him, open-mouthed.

Nikolai grabs me by both shoulders. "This is it, Sasha!" he cries joyfully. "My Lord in Heaven! You are going to play!"

"Oh, my God!" I gasp out, stumbling in a stupor back into the hotel room. From the *Boehm* case, I snatch out my piccolo, my hands chilling around it like two hardened balls of ice.

"Sasha!" cries Nikolai, gauging the look on my face. "There is scarce any need to panic! You have been in faithful attendance at every single alternate rehearsal."

"You do not understand!" I retort shrilly. "You're in the string section, there's a couple dozen of you. All you need do is blend in! But in this orchestra—oh, Lord God!—I will be the *only* piccolo!"

"And well deserving of the chair!" Hurriedly, Nikolai extracts his violin and bow back out from their case—and then bounds across the room into a flurry of rosin and manuscripts, papers flying out everywhere from the desk until he locates the bound-up set for *Sheherazade.* "Come, *mon cousin,"* he urges, his hand closing around my numbed arm and yanking me along with him to his music stand. "We'll do our 'chase'—remember how well we performed two winters ago in Novgorod? I think we have just enough time to play through the entire score if we leave out Part Three, as Fokine has done for the ballet. Here, Sasha—begin right here on the first page, the opening *Largo,* remember? First we'll do Part One as the Overture; on Part Two the curtain to the ballet rises; Part Four culminates in the finale. You play from the score as written for piccolo; I'll improvise as well as I can for accompaniment. Here we go—down into haunting low overtones of the Sultan's wrath, now—remember?"

Nikolai slides his bow across the strings in a dark, low moaning 'E'.

I bring the piccolo up to my mouth with trembling fingers.

In forty minutes, we manage to play through the entire score.

"Excellent, nary a single mistake, I am telling you!" he exclaims, laughing and clapping me on the shoulder after we finish the finale. "Come now, everything is going to be just fine—you are going to be marvelous! This shall to be a night we will both long celebrate and remember! And I'd say it's about high time we dressed for the theater and made for rehearsal, don't you? Now, where did I put my tie?"

* * *

The baton dances: up and down, back and forth, pummeling across the depths of the universe and arching at last upon a waving, windswept flourish as every sound extinguishes and every breath catches in every throat. The conductor's final cue is followed by that moment, that instant, that harrowing pause capping heights of glory in every musician's secretive, nurtured dream—the scantiest, shortest lull of silences far too fleeting to taste, far too tenuous to ever hold—lasting only for the faintest second before the crowd bursts into an avalanche of applause.

The lights are put back up and Gabriel Pierné, who has temporarily replaced Maestro Tcherepnin as conductor, turns and makes his bow to the audience before motioning for the orchestra to stand and take its proper due as well. The clapping and tempestuous roars of approval are for the ballet *Carnaval,* set to Schumann's piano suite as orchestrated by Konstantinov. Naturally, however, the applause is not so much for the music as for the dancers: Nijinsky, still death-defying in his aerial leaps and magnificent tonight as the looming black-faced Harlequin, and Karsavina, fluttering forth blue and white lacy calico in the role of the coquettish Columbine. Both of them continue taking bows upon the stage above us as they catch hold of the inevitable onslaught of rose bouquets. Interwoven with dramatic narrative bevying up its showcase of dance, *Carnaval* portends to become a standard in the repertoire, a ballet audiences will not soon forget. My heart, however, continues lagging near unto an hour behind, still mesmerized by the astounding spectacle of *Sheherazade.* To judge by the reaction of the audience to the sets alone—which was a standing ovation even before the dancers came on—all Paris will be talking of *Sheherazade* for years. The renowned *Grand Opéra,* that turgid, legendary bastion of the snooty *patrons des arts,* that specter of endless theater boxes framed with Grecian colonnades and draped with gold-fringed red curtains—from which the Diaghilev troupe was expelled last year, and to which, this year, we have been auspiciously promoted—was tonight transformed by the designer Leon Bakst into the glittering decadence of a medieval sultan's harem, the stage swathed in stark purple and orange settees and bathed in monstrous green and shimmering royal-blue hangings. Such was the backdrop for an orgy the likes of which the public has rarely seen, the scores of feisty dancers leaping through the air, their billowy pantaloons and cascading ropes of pearls caught against the outlines of bare, perspiring flesh. Into the grisly culmination of the death scene, the massacre to end all massacres, every one of the unfortunate nymphets spun, helpless and pliant beneath the flash of sabers and sting of the soldiers' knives as the Sultan expunged his mighty wrath amidst the climactic, sweeping overtones of Rimsky-Korsakov's atmospheric score.

I will never, in my entire life, forget it for as long as I live—even though I was watching the conductor like a hawk and caught only brief glimpses of the ballet—just as, likewise, I will never forget having played during the actual *première!*

For the thousandth time, I bless my good fortune that Nikita Adamovich felt possessed to run off to Nice and get married tonight—and I attempt to stifle a giddy sigh as the orchestra takes its second bow to the audience. Ever since learning during the rehearsals back in Petersburg that Diaghilev had set his sights upon making a ballet out of *Sheherazade,* Nikolai and I have both felt such excitement, he certainly more so than I, for Rimsky was indeed his composition teacher, and the famous symphonic poem is my cousin's favorite above all favorites. Now, as he winks at me from his chair in the second violins from the opposite corner of the orchestra pit, I can see that he too is musing not over the applause for *Carnaval*, but over Rimsky's incomparable triumph.

"Bravo, Aleksandr Mikhailovich!" Ignati exclaims with a hearty nudge from beside me. "I believe you have filled our Nikita's shoes and then some."

"Thank you, Ignati Pavlovich! You are very kind."

Trasinketov, who plays first flute, and who has always remained rather aloof over the magnanimous Ignati, steps over and offers congratulations also—to be followed by Alekseyev and Pazinsky, the two oboe players, and Klementi Filippovich with his bassoon, and then Konstantin Nikolayevich, the clarinetist with whom Nikolai and I tagged along last year in Cannes and Monte Carlo. "Thank you, all—but honestly, was scarce so extraordinary!" I gasp out, neck reddening beneath my starched white collar as the woodwind players clear the way for the conductor himself, who approaches and shakes my hand, commenting in French: "Excellent job on short notice, M'sieur Sekovsky! Continue with the good work."

"Thank you, Maestro! I sincerely appreciate the opportunity to play."

The group around me then disperses, heading for the anteroom along with the rest of the musicians. Once more I peer across the rows of seats in search of Nikolai—to find him as the lone remaining person in his section, standing awkwardly beside his empty chair, his violin and bow grasped together stiffly in his hand as he stares at me in studied silence. "What the devil has come over you?" I cry, shaking my head at him in bewilderment.

It is the barest glance he makes—upward, to the wall separating the front row of audience seats from the orchestra pit.

Up beyond the wall, tall and strikingly white-haired, his broad form superbly clad in an elegant black evening tux with tails, his hands clapping, his dark eyes burnished with the most profound glow of admiration, stands my father.

I stare at him, stung for breath. I stare back to Nikolai—who bolts away, purposefully avoiding my gaze, his shoulders rigidly squared as he marches off toward the anteroom.

Again I stare back to Father. In silence, he merely continues clapping and nodding down at me, a lone audience of one hovering above the wall to the orchestra pit in the now emptying theater.

Turning on my heel, I swallow into a burning desert of parched sand and storm off after my cousin.

Whom I find tucking his violin into its case far too hurriedly, as if attempting to avoid me, fully intent upon escape.

"Dammit!" I shout, forcing him around roughly by the shoulders. "You *knew!* That he was here!"

In response, Nikolai silently stares me down, bitter throes of death lancing forth from those eerie, hollow-gray eyes—before he elbows me away with a decisive shove.

Two steps at a time, he bounds up toward the doors to the rotunda, while I continue shouting after him: "Damn you, Nikolai Petrovich Zhelanov! You knew that he was here—and said not a single, solitary word!"

Ears steaming, my wrath blazing for revenge, I snatch out my handkerchief and swab out my piccolo with furious stabbing motions while trying to decide what to do.

The exit from the orchestra pit in the *Grand Opéra* leads through a narrow pair of doors opening out unto the magnificent rotunda graced by a grand marble staircase branching upward toward the many rows of theater boxes. Of this circumstance, Father has apparently taken due note—for when I finally venture upward, I find him waiting just beyond the doors at the foot of the stairs, his eyes twinkling, his right hand graciously extended. "Aleksandr," he says, nodding toward me, "my congratulations—and my apologies—are, I believe, in order."

Fiercely, I shove past him, striding out into the high echoing space of the rotunda dome—but I stop midway, wholly ashamed of myself amidst the throngs of chattering theater-goers strolling past. *Blast it, Sasha—the man has traveled all the way to Paris; has stooped unto attending one of the Diaghilev ballets! What more of an apology could you ask?* Unable to move forward or backward, I remain riveted to the floor, my gaze fastened guiltily downward unto the tiled ivory hues beneath my feet.

Father pauses beside me. "Have you taken supper?" he murmurs.

I hedge a glance upward. "As a matter of fact, no."

"Good! I made a reservation over at the *Viel.* Let us go and talk, Sasha."

After giving the growlings in my stomach due consideration, I reply: "Very well."

Not only has Father reserved a table, but—far away from the second-class booths Nikolai and I must always frequent when dining at the *Restaurant Viel*—Father has been accorded one of the very best tables, in a little alcove with a splendid view overlooking the evening lights of Paris and grand banks of the Seine. In the course of our sumptuous meal of *papillote* shellfish, which I attempt to keep from wolfing down ravenously, famished as I have been since the afternoon, I find that Father not only knows the maitre d', but the head chef of the restaurant as well—who materializes like an old Army friend to offer his congratulations, to both Father and myself, on account of my performance at the theater.

"You are staying at one of the hotels?" I murmur over our dessert—in half an hour, the first words I have said.

Father laughs boisterously—saying, as if he makes the journey each week: "Oh, no! I am staying with the Comte de Ronsard, with whom I always lodge when in Paris. He keeps a charming little chateau over in Palaiseau, a bit to the south of the city. Somewhat of a drive, but worth it for the peace and quiet. He and I are old compatriots ever since the War, you know."

"Uh, and just how long have you been in Paris?"

"Two days."

"And what about matters on your 'wretched provincial farm?'"

"Certain matters have come to be of greater import to me than even the farm, Sasha. Like at long last making peace with my son."

The earnestness of his tone sounds more than ironic after the torrent of rage exchanged when we last embarked upon this discussion. "Well, how the devil did you manage to acquire tickets to the ballet in a mere two days?" I go on, scarce able to contain my irritation. "Without any operas this season, I understood near all the performances were long ago sold out."

Father shrugs, and replies with another hearty laugh: "Oh, the Comte has long been a patron of the *Grand Opéra,* and maintains a loge."

To my further amazement, Father then enthusiastically begins lavishing glowing praise upon the Diaghilev ballets, admitting his previous error in judgment, saying: "Sometimes, it takes young eyes to spot potential for success in larks at which one's elders only scoff. I now have an entire trunk at home filled to the brimming with letters and news clippings from my old friends here in Paris. All during last year, the reports continued without pause: that this Mikhail Fokine of yours had finally given choreography its rightful due, making music the foundation of the dance patterns, and not vice versa, which was always the case with old Petipa at the Maryinsky, and why I finally washed my hands of such Petersburg charades. They even forced Tchaikovsky to add in extra notes during one scene of *The Sleeping Princess*, in order to accommodate the time it took to trail backcloth draperies off the stage, for God's sake! Anyhow, I admit that I judged this Sergei Diaghilev far too harshly, although you must realize that he did act like a complete nincompoop that day he came sniffing around for family portraits. But I—ahem! Uh, what I am trying to say to you, is that, I—well. I admit I was wrong, Sasha."

I set the spoon down into my empty parfait dish, staring down at it.

"Sasha," he goes on softly, "I am trying to apologize."

"You threw me out," I whisper, not looking at him. "You ordered me never to return."

Father shifts uncomfortably in his chair. "I am an old man, Sasha," he murmurs, his hand brought upward to his face as if in reminder, his fingers stroking along a deep, wrinkle-folded crevice. "I will turn seventy-nine this year, as a matter of fact. I think sometimes you, at a mere youthful eighteen, tend to forget that. And like many a doddering old man, I ofttimes say things that I later cannot remember. Words that I certainly scarce mean."

"St. Isaak's," I interrupt him. "Easter. Last year. You never came—and you always light your candle to my candle, always!" I harp on, glaring at him, my voice rising up shrilly above the background din of the restaurant.

"No, of course I came!" he insists. "But I could not manage to arrive there until half past midnight."

"Half *past* midnight?" I gasp.

Father rolls his eyes. "We had a carriage accident—plowed into one of those damn speeding *drozhkis*, myself and Count Orlov."

"Count Orlov?"

"I stayed with the Orlovs last Easter. I—to tell you the truth, Sasha, I was just too bloody embarrassed to intrude upon you at the townhouse on Zhukovskaya. I wanted make my apologies to you at the cathedral, during the candle ceremony. I thought it would be most poignant. But when I finally arrived there, Nikolai said that you had already gone."

"Well, of course I left, Father! God help me—I thought you had refused to come!"

"What time was it when you left St. Isaak's that night? Do you remember?"

Shrugging, I glance out the restaurant windows helplessly, and shake my head. "I—I don't know! A quarter after? Perhaps twenty after midnight."

"Well, then it appears we missed each other by a scant ten minutes. I went this Easter, also: early, and stayed the entire time. But of course, you were nowhere to be found. Dear Lord, Sasha—I told Nikolai to inform you about the accident last year, to tell you I had come."

Morosely, I stare out toward the glittering lights of the Eiffel Tower. In the past year, each time Nikolai has attempted to broach even a word about Father, I have shouted him down, totally unwilling to hear.

"I take it you would not listen," Father says, grinning across at me.

As he catches the incongruity of my frown against his smile, he murmurs: "Just like your stubborn old papa."

With a chuckle, he then starts fidgeting in his waistcoat pocket for his tobacco pouch, and takes a long moment with lighting up his pipe. "And," he adds with a bemused expression, "just like another haughty firebrand I used to know." Ruefully, he shakes his head.

"I beg your pardon?" I say, at long last looking fully up at him.

"Just like Liss," he says with a nod. "Your mother."

Then, to my astonishment, he does something that—in all the years that I have known him—he has never, ever done.

He starts talking about her.

"God's teeth, boy!" he exclaims, laughing, once more shaking his head. "When you glare at me like that—the same way you have so many times over the years—I swear to God, that expression likens you so to Liss. Just like the day she talked me into taking her on the picnic."

"The picnic?" I mutter, amazed.

"Would you perhaps care for more dessert?" he then offers, indicating my empty parfait dish with his pipe.

"Uh, no. No, thank you, Papa—I'm fine."

"Well. Yes, then, the picnic," he goes on, sighing. "Let me tell you a story, Sasha. About an old man, nearing sixty in his years, and an old sixty, at that. Let me tell you about a bitter, disheartened stump of man hardened to the cruel ways of the world after spending thirty long years in a Siberian prison camp. Until a young Englishwoman came along and made that old man young again, one day at a picnic."

Still stunned, I settle back into the cushioned recess of my chair, at last offering calm, undivided attention.

A dreamy expression overtakes Father's face as he puffs away on his pipe, his gaze drifting out the window toward the lapping reflection of the Seine. "Actually, I was nearing fifty-eight that year," he says. "In 1889. As was Vliny—although he was happy. But, I? Perhaps my problem was that by that time, I had accomplished everything I'd so long wanted: two years before, my petition to the Tsar had been granted, and I'd been accorded back my lands and title, the family's honor had been restored. By Easter of 1889, the Ilmen grain take was actually yielding a profit at the mills, and the beekeeping operation was again in full swing. I had just hired Pavel as overseer the previous winter, and seeing how competent he was at running the farm, I had no qualms about leaving him in charge, while I left for Europe. In partnership with several old friends, I had invested heavily during the previous year in the Bordeaux wine country and in the Rhineland vineyards in Cologne, in Germany, and was eager to inspect the wineries themselves and evaluate operations. I also wanted to take Vliny to Europe. Save for Irkutsk and the journey there, and of course for Novgorod, the poor soul in all his life had never been more than a few versts outside of Pskov, where he was born—and you know how tiredly provincial Pskov is! At Easter, he and I were together in Petersburg, his first time there, and he was having a high-rolling time of it, I daresay. Anyhow, we set out for Berlin, and from there went to the German wineries, and then to Bordeaux, before we finally ended up in Paris. As I said, Vliny was having the time of his life—but, as I look back, I still cannot fathom what had come over me that spring, and must admit to having been in a rather glum state of mind when, in Paris, I was reunited with your Uncle Ivan and Aunt Vera.

"They had both immigrated to England when I was in Irkutsk, and I had seen neither of them since I was a young man, so it was quite a reunion: talk about the finicky old spinster and the foppish old bachelor, that was your Aunt Vera and Uncle Ivan. What a pair! They had lived together—quite harmoniously, I came to understand—in

Southampton for about twenty years at that time. Toward that Maytide, they were attending a Paris conference of the Russian Historical Society, of which they were both members. I had not intended to travel with Vliny to England; having been there once in my youth, I'd not much cared for the gloomy climate. But your aunt and uncle were so taken with showing off their little townhouse with its view of the port that I finally agreed to go. And Vliny was game for anything, so we boarded the ferry along with Vera and Ivan when they set out on return for Southampton.

"During the crossing, Vera started telling me about a woman she knew, one Marie Devon-Tyler—a descendant of the lordly Willoughby's on her mother's side, but whose father was in actuality a Zhelanov, from Pskov, a first cousin to the Petersburg Zhelanovs. Lady Devon-Tyler was also a member of the Historical Society, and she and Vera had kept up a lively correspondence for quite some years concerning matters of heraldry and such. Lady Devon-Tyler had mapped out an extensive Zhelanov family pedigree, and apparently was now eager for information on the Sekovsky line, having learned that Uncle Petya had married your Aunt Sophie, and that we were long from Novgorod, with its prominent old history.

"After Vliny and I visited at the townhouse in Southampton for a few days, Vera asked if I wished to accompany her to the coast, for she had received from her friend a standing invitation to the Tylers' summerhouse at Devonbury. Your Uncle Ivan had business in London, or so he said. He and Vliny had hit it off swimmingly, and I knew that, although Vliny would scarce admit it, he was simply dying to go with Ivan to take in the sights of London. So I warned them both to watch themselves with the drink and the ladies, which, of course—ho! ho!—fell upon entirely deaf ears. Then, along with Vera, I caught the train for the coast.

"We arrived at Winnebar at four o'clock on a lovely afternoon—almost like late summer it was, and I could scarce believe the bounteous climate of Cornwall. The Baronet, Sir William, and his wife, the Lady Marie, were wonderfully gracious hosts. At this time, Ned had just graduated with honors from Oxford, and they were raving on about him as proud parents will. That particular afternoon, the young man was said to have taken his sister out riding, but we were let to know that the young people would be back to make our acquaintance by dinner. Anyhow, I proceeded to settle our bags into the guest quarters, while Vera was visiting with Lady Marie, and was washing up when, from outside, I suddenly heard a terrible row: the children, apparently, yelling out their living daylights at one another. Suspecting wryly that the eve might hold a bit of entertainment, I finished up my toilet with all due haste, and made my way downstairs.

"My first glimpse of your Uncle Ned was of him bursting in through the side doors and shouting at the top of his lungs: 'Lissa has sprained her arm, I say! Send to town for the doctor, and hurry!' Whereupon an outraged feminine voice immediately shrieked back: 'I have not sprained my arm one bloody speck, you worm-brained, obstinate fool!'"

The young lady in question remained stubbornly hidden from view outside, still shrieking her heart out, and I lingered in the hall, smoking and checking through the newspaper, not wishing to intrude. Vera hurried in from the study with Lady Marie, who immediately began ordering the two young people to have done with their quarrel on account of the guests. From her tone of voice, it was obvious that Lady Marie was entirely accustomed to her son's and daughter's exchanges of words. This I found rather amusing, as young Ned was then twenty-three and hardly a child, by any means. Naturally, I assumed the young woman to be near the age of her brother.

"When she finally stepped through the door, I remember that I glanced up briefly, intending to offer a polite nod and then return to the article I was scanning over regarding the current commodities market. Instead, upon first sight of her, I stood gaping like a complete tongueless idiot, unable to utter a sound. I may never have been much the man about town, but I knew what beauty was—and this Melissa was astounding, ethereal, the stuff of which legends were made! Of course, at my age, I certainly had not the slightest audacity in regarding her as would a suitor. I merely stared as any fully-blooded man will, no matter how advanced in years, in aesthetic appreciation. Well, what was even more unnerving was that, Melissa Tyler stared right back.

"Without taking her eyes away from me! She simply stood staring, open-mouthed, like a shock had hit her. In place of a habit, she was wearing riding breeches like a man, with her hair bound up behind her and pinned onto the back of her head in one abundant plait, wispy tufts sticking out untidily about her lovely face. Amber-colored the hair was, like rich dark honey, setting off her doe-like brown eyes. I got the sense that everyone, even the passing servants, could not help but note how intently the girl and I were exchanging glances. Fortunately, Melissa was the first to regain her composure, and jumped furiously back into the debate with her brother about the alleged sprain.

"While rolling his eyes in exasperation, Sir William interrputed: 'Well! Count Sekovsky here is a doctor. Perhaps he might settle the dispute. . . .' Whereupon I dutifully obliged and approached to examine the young woman's arm.

"'You are Russian,' she said as she slipped out of her jacket—a statement rather than a question—and as I nodded and watched her roll up her sleeve, she demanded: 'Say something to me in Russian!'

Still tongue-tied, all I could manage to utter—like a bumbling fool—was: *'kak ochen krasivaya'*—'how very beautiful'—scarce able to fathom anything else! Fortunately, I mumbled the words, and Lady Marie and Vera were standing too far away from us to hear. When Melissa asked for the meaning, I merely told her that I had said she was quite charming, but from the way she grinned, I could tell she believed not a word, and she kept eyeing me with mounting interest as I examined her arm.

"According to Ned, she had been thrown from her horse, and therefore was very lucky, because her arm was not sprained, only bruised. I instructed her to keep a cold compress on the spot during dinner. She thanked me profusely—mostly, I thought at the time, because she had been correct about the diagnosis over her brother, who stood there furiously red-faced, while she gloated at him.

"Of course, as you know, at the Tyler household, everyone dresses for a formal dinner—and Melissa was stunning and knew it, despite the modest gown she chose with simple tucks and high lace neckline. From the outset, I had assumed her to be only a year or two younger than her brother, a prospect which now appeared confirmed by her upswept hair and stylish manner of dress, as well as by her obvious maturity: she was articulate on everything from archeology to horse racing to the latest scandal in the House of Commons, and joined in the dinner conversation with fervent gaiety. I found such forward behavior in a young woman quite refreshing, actually—and was flabbergasted, I think even more so than when I first saw her, when I later learned that she was only seventeen!

"Melissa also possessed an interest in heraldry, and spent a good deal of time over the following days cloistered in with her mother and your aunt as they went over family history, and I rarely saw her, save for the dinners. However, each night at table, she kept eyeing me so boldly that I could not help but be flattered, although I attributed the girl's interest to her fascination with everything Russian. Certainly, I never entertained the notion that she saw in me anything other than a grandfatherly old doctor who had—so to speak—'helped' her to outwit her elder brother about the contested matter of the sprain.

"That spring, the Tylers were hosting the annual Maytide Ball, a grand affair to which droves of people came from miles around. Out of politeness, I made what I had intended only to be a brief appearance, and stood off in a corner with bemusement, eyeing the many dashing young couples turning about the floor. Suddenly, from behind me, I heard Melissa's voice: 'Mikhail Sergeyevich?'

"I turned in surprise, for up until that moment, she had addressed me only as 'Dr. Sekovsky,' and I had not even realized she had been told my name. Then she said: 'That is the correct Russian manner of address: first name and then patronymic, is it not?'

"I affirmed this, to which she said: 'You have not allowed me to accord you proper thanks for seeing to my arm.'

"'My dear,' I told her, 'such a brief survey as I made of it scarce requires any special recognition.'

"To my consternation, Melissa replied by laughing at me outright—and then, before I realized what was happening, she snatched hold of my hand and literally dragged me out behind her onto the dance floor!

"I stood there, staring at her dumbly, as she insisted that we dance.

"My embarrassed protests were to no avail. Later, I was to learn that no one protested against anything upon which Melissa had set her heart. Feeling like a fool out in front of all the young people, I struggled to finish the waltz into which she had led me, intending then to accomplish a much hasty exit. However, she simply would not allow me to leave, insisting willfully upon dancing again and again! When at last I pulled it all to an abrupt, ungracious halt and began to scold her, she merely seized my hands again and dragged me off into yet another waltz! By this time, her parents, and your Aunt Vera and Uncle Ned, along with a large row of other people standing about the walls, were watching us and whispering. So finally, rather unjudiciously, I stomped away from the dance floor—with Melissa still clutching onto my sleeve—in order to put a end to the whole affair.

"'Why will you not dance with me more? The night is young!' she cried, glaring at me—that infamous glare—as once more I shook away her hand.

"'Lady Devon-Tyler!' I stormed back, 'One token waltz I perhaps can understand, but the night is half over already! And this is hardly proper!'

"'You do not recognize me?' she then said, and stood staring at me wide-eyed, as if—for once—she had lost all of her steam. And suddenly I realized that, no matter how ridiculous the notion might sound, the girl truly was quite taken with me—that somehow, I had become much more in her young eyes than a mere stodgy, highly unsuitable old Russian doctor.

"So I left her standing alone—and after making embarrassed apologies to the Tylers, I hurried upstairs, packed my things, borrowed a horse, rode into Devonbury, and spent the night in town. Vera had offered to accompany me, but I already felt as if I had near ruined everything enough, and fortunately, convinced her to stay and finish her visit with the Lady Marie. The following morn, I caught the train back for Southampton.

"To this day, I do not know how the girl managed to beat me there—she never would tell me—but at the Southampton railway station, I debarked in nervous haste from the first-class coach to find her waiting next to one of the ticket booths, wearing a large hat and simple homespun gown suitable for traveling without raising much notice. To her bosom, she clutched a small portmanteau that had obviously been hurriedly packed. 'Mikhail Sergeyevich, I must speak with you!' she implored, again clutching those prying fingers onto my sleeve.

"Totally amazed, and seeing that there was naught else to do but let her have her say, I dropped my bags right in the middle of the platform and bellowed out: 'God in Heaven, my dear! Just what in the world do you want of me?'

"'A proposal!' she exclaimed.

"'Of *marriage?'* I gasped in shock.

"'Yes!'

"'That is absolutely preposterous!' I told her.

"'Age means not a thing!' she insisted. 'My mother is fifteen years younger than my father.'

"'Fifteen years is not the same as *forty!'* I replied.

"'And why not?'

"At this point, infuriated, I began stumbling over my words, and she interrupted: 'Do you still not understand? Every mortal soul has a long-lost mate! So many aeons have I been searching for mine.'

"'That is naught but childish schoolgirl drivel!' I shouted back—whereupon, instead of countering with a barrage of protests as I had expected, she quite promptly burst into tears.

"I scarce knew what to do. I was standing in the Southampton railway station with a wailing seventeen-year-old girl who had followed me, unescorted, half across England! I could not believe it! To my great relief, your Uncle Ned then appeared—apparently, by whatever means she had managed to journey there, he had been not much farther behind. Of course, they argued—but when she started talking to him about this 'soul-mate' business, he quieted down and listened while continuing to eye me with glowering suspicion. Urgently, I appealed to him to take the girl back to Winnebar, said that it was nonsense for her to have become so infatuated with me, and begged for him to understand that I had in no way meant to encourage such behavior. But Melissa only cried more loudly with each word that I uttered—and it was to her that Ned listened, and not to me. Finally, when she calmed down enough, he asked what she wanted us to do.

"'I want Mikhail Sergeyevich to return with us to Winnebar and take me on a picnic.'

"By this time, I had thought that nothing else Melissa might say could any further amaze me, but this seemed such a mundane request, that again I stared back with my mouth gaping. 'Properly chaperoned of course!' she assured me. 'By my mother. Merely a picnic. Simply give me one day, Mikhail Sergeyevich, please! Please?'

"And then, of all things—while Melissa crossed her arms and glared as if I was the world's most heartless heel—Ned took me aside and urged me to comply with her request.

"I decided that, save for rudely turning my back upon the both of them, there was naught else to do but comply. Inwardly, I hoped that—perhaps upon seeing in the true light of day that the man upon whom she had lain her affections was truly naught but a bitter old fool—the girl would leave off this lunacy of infatuation and talk about a marriage proposal.

"Lord God—what can I say about the picnic? I was fully prepared to act as mean as possible and do whatever else I could to rebuff the girl—resolutions that melted away upon first sight of her in her yellow springtime dress and luxuriant bouffant hair. She was so beautiful, Sasha, I—I simply could not take my eyes away from her! As promised, her mother accompanied us like a dutiful shadow, lingering behind always at the most proper distance for that entire day that we spent together on the beach. We ate braised chicken and lemon pie, and took off our shoes and walked in the waves—and the next thing I knew, she had her arm linked through mine, and we were murmuring with our heads tucked down together like a couple of schoolyard sweethearts, and I felt as if I, not she, was the one who was only seventeen! I'd not realized until then that I had fallen in love with her, probably from the very instant I first heard her cursing at her brother and caught sight of her clad in those riding breeches. We talked. Sasha, I am telling you, I felt as if I had found my most treasured, long-lost friend! And the Lady Marie, with a strange half-smile curved upon her lips all day long as she surveyed the two of us, somehow seemed to understand.

"As the sun began to fade, I knew that, along with Melissa, I had cast all qualms regarding the age question off to the four winds. So, holding her hand, I asked if she still wanted that proposal, and she said: 'Yes!'

"I agreed on one condition: that the marriage be approved of by both her parents.

"The Lady Marie became our ally, and quietly acquiesced. Ned—in a state which was to indeed follow for several years—seemed at odds with himself over the whole idea, sometimes greatly for it, sometimes greatly detached and disapproving. But your Grandpa Will simply would not hear of it.

"For four days, I tried my utmost to stay out of sight, remaining sequestered with Vera in Winnebar's guest quarters while listening to Melissa shout her father down endlessly through the walls. Finally, I think the poor man simply could no longer tolerate the shrieking feminine abuse—and he agreed to permit the marriage, if we would wait until Christmas. In the meantime, I was to return to Novgorod, whereupon Melissa and I could correspond. Needless to say, I myself could see the good sense in allowing some time for a proper courtship.

"When I returned to Russia with Vliny at last, I found I had the devil to wrest with: second thoughts all over again about the age question, once I was back home alone. At first, I entertained the notion of discouraging Melissa by not replying to any of her letters, but once they began to come, I *had* to answer. Our love grew with every single one. I still have all of them—she was a marvelous correspondent! She also set herself to learning Russian quite determinedly—and in December, instead of my returning to England as we originally had planned, Melissa insisted upon journeying with her whole family behind her—some in quite reluctant tow indeed at the prospect of greeting the Russian winter! But come she did, and a week before Christmas, we were married in Novgorod in our blessed St. Sofiya Cathedral."

At last Father stops talking.

"So—it was an Orthodox ceremony," I say haltingly, my eyes closely following the motions of his fingers as he begins emptying his pipe into his crystal parfait dish.

"Oh, yes. She converted—in name, anyhow. Truthfully, though, Melissa always was much inclined toward mysticism, and such outlandish beliefs as your Uncle Ned's." Grinning, he reaches his hand across the table and pats my arm. "Good heavens, boy!" he then exclaims with a quick check to his pocket watch. "Here I have been talking your ears off, and you probably already long worn out after that performance."

I press cold fingers into the bridge of my spectacles, squinting in agreement. "Actually, Papa," I say, glancing up at him, "I just feel rather, uh, numbed. You've never spoken to me of her before. Not like this."

Again he pats my arm. "Perhaps we shall speak of your mother further in the days to come, Sasha."

The sharp nod of a waiter catches my attention, and I notice that beyond us, the lights have been dimmed. Save for two or three other tables of stragglers, the bulk of dinner patrons have long since taken leave of the restaurant. "You will return tonight to Palaiseau?" I ask Father.

"Oh, yes. Let me give you a lift back to your hotel. The Comte has lent me his motorcar. I swear the damn contraption still tickles my fancy to no end!"

It is in silence that I ride along in the Comte's cumbersome black Model T Ford, rolling my eyes at Father's atrocious driving and musing through a heavy, yet gladdened weariness over all he has revealed. At last, as we wander down the fifth-floor hotel corridor and approach the door to my room, I turn to him and warmly extend my hand—but he brushes it aside and throws both arms around my neck instead, pulling me close in a fierce, rough embrace.

Which I cannot return. No matter how hard I try, I can barely force my fingers to graze his shoulders. Finally, I let my arms fall limply back to my sides while he continues crushing his around my back.

"It is all right, Sasha," he murmurs with a wink, letting loose of me at last. "I know you are still furious with me for my outburst when you last left Novgorod."

I turn away sharply, biting my tongue with effort, desperately stifling the yen to shout him down in a blistering torrent of rage, to confirm to him just how correct he is. Instead, politely, I say: "You will attend tomorrow night's performance?"

"Will be roosted right up in that same loge," he replies, grinning and pointing to my flute case. "With my opera glasses trained all night upon that piccolo."

* * *

Father remains true to his word, scanning the orchestra pit each night with rapt anticipation and applauding from the tier of the Comte's loge through further renderings of *Sheherazade*, *Carnaval*, and the quaint love scenes of *Giselle*—a ballet which, like most older people, he greets with greater enthusiasm than the critics, who yet thirst for sensation while allowing *Giselle's* dated Nineteenth Century romanticism only tepid mention in the papers. At the *première* of *L'Oiseau de Feu*, or *The Firebird*, on the twenty-fifth of June, in which Fokine himself takes the leading role of Tsarevich, and Karsavina, in a gown of feathery orange and white, plies the stage with her usual poetic charm, I perform for the final time before the return of Nikita Adamovich. Somewhat to my dismay, relief, not regret, colors my mood as I once again assume my happenstance tenure as an alternate. Although many of the musicians remain enthused with the *L'Oiseau* score and its young author, the son of a well-known Maryinsky opera baritone whom Diaghilev and his group of friends have taken in as one of their cloistered own, I myself cannot see what promise this Igor Stravinsky's talent holds. Neither can Nikolai, whose complaints about the favor showered upon Stravinsky have been adamant ever since Petersburg. "Naught but a veritable menagerie of anarchic dissonances!" he reminds me yet again one day with his nose thrown to the air. "And they have the gall to compare his music with Rimsky's!"

Rivalry, I realize, plays some factor in Nikolai's opinion, for Igor Fedorovich was also one of the great maestro's pupils. "Perhaps Stravinsky will improve under Diaghilev's tutelage," I offer, although rather doubting it.

"Not if he keeps near attempting to demolish the piano at every rehearsal!" Nikolai snorts, shaking his head. "And not if he only continues borrowing yet again from old peasant melodies and tavern songs. It's ludicrous, I tell you, that they compare him with Rimsky! Positively ludicrous."

Father, who studied piano for some years during his youth, heartily agrees. "It was entertaining, I grant it that. The colors, the costumes," he says, with a shrug, of *L'Oiseau de Feu*.

"I think Diaghilev—or Benois, or whoever it was—could have been much more true to the old folk tales with the libretto," I reply, sighing.

"And the music?"

I roll my eyes, and Father bursts out laughing.

"Well, if you are free of Stravinsky's shackles for the afternoon, Aleksandr," he says, winking at me with a jaunty, fast twinkle in his eye, knowing fully well that today Fokine has cancelled all rehearsals due to the glorious weather and lull in scheduled performances until the morrow, "perhaps you and I should pack ourselves a lunch and venture out for another spin?"

It has become our favorite summer pastime: winding through crooked back streets and shrub-strewn French country roads in the Comte's rattly, chortling motorcar. "That," I tell him, meeting his expectant gaze with a grin, "would be delightful!"

And again, upon a checkered cloth spread out beneath a willowy copse of trees, as we wolf down two loaves of sourdough bread along with Brie cheese, black caviar, and one of our own well-aged bottles of *Cabernet Sauvignon*, Father continues with his story of Melissa and their love.

"She convinced me to go skiing with her, of all things!" he cries, laughing, relating further details of their honeymoon tour of the Alps made in the year following the marriage.

"You are joking!" I exclaim, mirthfully imagining him attempting to ski.

"Absolutely not. Oh, I must take you to see with your own eyes all of Lissa's and my old haunts. You and I shall go to Stuttgart and stay in a castle belonging to the Baron von Schlegel, another of my old friends from before the War. Oh, yes! We shall make a grand tour of it, as soon as your stint with the troupe this season ends, Sasha, my boy! Then, a'traveling we will go. . . ."

* * *

Once another summer of the *Ballet Russe* draws to a giddy close, go we do. Amidst the renewed fanfare of stark Eurasian colors overtaking all the fashion and jewelry houses in Paris in the wake of *Sheherazade*, Nikolai departs for Budapest to play by invitation in one of several popular string quartets, and to continue his study of cello. Meanwhile, I traipse after my father through endless vineyards, touring the wineries in Bordeaux and Cologne before whirling with him through

Stuttgart, Munich, Vienna, Prague, Berlin, Hamburg, and Copenhagen, tracing over virtually every step he and Melissa made in their first joyous, carefree year. As the weeks wane on, we at last huddle together up on the windy deck, shading our eyes and hanging onto our hats, the steamer groaning its way from Stockholm through Finland's rocky Gulf and finally turning us due eastward toward Petersburg and home.

Father subsequently insists upon concluding the journey unto its original end, just as he and Melissa once had done twenty years ago. So in September—despite my misgivings about the harvest, which he shrugs off with laughing impatience, as confident as during his days long ago with Melissa in Vliny's and Pavel's abilities at managing the farm without his supervision—we speed straight past the Chudovo rail junction, temporarily swearing off our claim to Novgorod's homeward realm of taiga forest land. Instead, elm and maple, linden and oak begin to predominate ever southward in mixed hues of orange and ruddy autumn gold—before giving way at last unto lush black earth and the rolling plains of the Ukrainian steppe as the train flies southward toward the jutting mountaintops of the Crimea.

Come our fifth morn in the sleeper coach, I stumble from my berth in a bleary daze, cursing myself for having overslept. The previous eve of attempting to sort through countless orchestrations and other papers has taken its toll, for my head begins to ache once my eyes focus, and I encounter the mess. Over the opposite side of the tiny squared table, Father hovers with his unlit pipe dangling between lazy fingers, his bemused stare intent upon a couple of frayed sheets sticking out from my ratty, stacked heap. "Well!" he exclaims, pointing to the fading typewritten copy, "I see that you have scarce been confining your affairs to the sole pursuit of music."

"I beg your pardon?" Rubbing at my eyes, I pull my robe closer and don my spectacles, peering across the table toward his impatiently tapping pipe—to recoil in a gasp of horror upon sight of the pamphlets, once tucked at Volodya's insistence so hastily within my jacket pocket the night of the Socialist Revolutionaries' meeting.

I stand fixated, motionless—the chugging of the rail coach wheels hammering poundings of reproach into my heart.

To my amazement, far from evincing outrage, Father merely proffers the two pamphlets across the table with an impish nod. "Best probably to put these somewhere a bit less conspicuous, Sasha," he murmurs. "We scarce want to get you arrested, now, do we?"

Then, chuckling, he shakes his head and trudges over to the velvet-cushioned easy bench, where he proceeds to curl up with his three-day-old copy of *Birzhevye Vedomosti*, the financial newspaper.

"Papa!" I blurt out, still mortified. "I can explain! Was not anything in which I was seriously involved! Was naught, indeed, but the merest lark!"

"You needn't make any excuses to me, Sasha," he replies with a wave of his hand.

"Then—you are not angry?"

"Oh, no." He shrugs and glances upward briefly from the headlines, explaining: "I was a young man once, full of fire. Assume not that you are the only fellow ever to suddenly find himself at some so-called 'meeting.'"

As I continue crouching by the table, staring at him in amazement, he adds: "This coming from a man who nursed plenty of ill once toward a certain Tsar, humph! But," he goes on, again indicating the pamphlets with his pipe, "probably best to put those away. And in the future, for you to exercise bit more care with such literature."

"Y-Yes, sir!" In a flurry, I snatch up the pamphlets and bury them far down at the bottom of my travel trunk.

Later, after our return from breakfast in the dining coach, he pauses by the table as I continue sorting through more papers. "So," he says in a lowered tone, "you believe there is going to be a revolution?"

I glance upward past the rims of my spectacles with a cautious frown, murmuring: "May I speak plainly?"

Father eases into the chair opposite mine. "Please do."

Nervously, I make a survey of the train windows, satisfying myself that—past the grinding hum of the axles and crunching of the wheels—it would be impossible for anyone in the adjacent first class sleeper to hear. "I perhaps have not kept as abreast of politics as would have been prudent," I tell him with a shrug. "My days lapse always into the evetide hours scarce before I realize, ever dwindling from rehearsal to practice to always more rehearsal. But from the drivel that escapes the censors and does make its way into the papers, one cannot help but gain the impression that the Tsar is naught but an inept fool. And . . . people talk. Still of Bloody Sunday, in 1905; still of the *Narodnaya* in the eighties—and even sometimes still of 1825 and the original Decembrists. It appears to me that a revolution in our country—of some sort—is probably inevitable."

Frowning, Father draws deeply from his pipe. "I, too," he murmurs after a long moment, "although in many ways yet hating to admit it, have come to that conclusion as well."

"The easiest transition," I go on, encouraged, "despite the staunch protests of my cousin and his compatriots in the conservative right-wing, would probably be toward constitutional monarchy. To allow the Duma to assume full political power. If the Tsar would only permit it."

"Not likely," Father replies.

"Perhaps, as time goes on—punctuated by further terrorist bombings, which are only certain to continue to occur—the man might be persuaded."

Father sighs. "In any case, eventually—whether the Tsar, or we, or anyone else likes it—certain concessions will have to be made to the peasantry. After spending more than twenty years overseeing a Russian farm, that, at least, is what I see as inevitable."

"Yes," I admit. "I suppose you are quite correct."

"Sasha, I have been wanting to discuss this with you for some time. Thanks to the wineries, matters on the farm now affect your future to a far lesser degree than they once did. Of the proposal I have in mind, you may not entirely approve: I want to allow our peasants to take back the land."

I stare to my fingers, frowning. "You mean—forfeit Lissushka?"

"Oh, by no means the estate house, God forbid!" he cries. "I would retain the estate house, the apiary, and perhaps two or three surrounding desyatins as our vested interest in the land. And allow the peasants all remaining fields, to divide up as they will. Lord knows, I've already forgiven all the leases, anyhow, under the latest land reforms—and I believe it only a matter of time before the land-owning class will be pressed for even further concessions. As you say, there continues to be considerable resistance to change from right-wing quarters. But as we both seem to sense, the turning of the tide away from the old feudal order and toward a more equitable system is probably inevitable. I am apprehensive because, without further grants to the peasants soon, matters could become ugly. We witnessed some potential for trouble a few years back, with those infernal demonstrations after Bloody Sunday. The repression carried out in the countryside ever since then has certainly only worsened, not eased tensions as everyone had hoped—and a sorry business it is also, I daresay! Some of the rumors I hear are downright dastardly: mass village hangings, shootings, and other unthinkable atrocities carried out by the Tsar's agents and those insufferable, fool Black Hundreds. Novgorod—the whole northern region, in fact—has indeed been lucky, compared with those poor souls to the south in such places as Saratov and Voronezh. Bless the Saints, there has scarce been any trouble at all on Lissushka since the time you left last year—although, I admit, we still sometimes have to chase off outside agitators. I want things to remain relatively quiet—and to promptly nip in the bud any future flare-ups—by giving the farmland over to the peasants soon."

"Could we financially survive?" I ask, searching his face.

"As you know, the winery receipts the past two years have been most favorable," he assures me. "I see no reason why you and I could not continue to live as we always have. As for your future—I will contact my broker in Berne, and have your name formally added to mine in joint ownership, so that you also may freely draw upon the Bordeaux and Cologne accounts. And naturally, the entire lot of it will revert to you upon my death. And of course, in addition, you have some accumulated funds at the Petersburg Commercial, from your summers of toil in Pavel's office. And—oh, yes!—you also you have the ten thousand pounds from your mother's inheritance, to draw upon should the need ever arise."

I nod, but quickly avert my eyes. Twice already, we have spoken of my mother's dowry, and of Uncle Ned's relinquishment of the account. Of course, I have purposely neglected to inform Father that, thanks to Sheremetev, only a mere pittance beyond the original amount remains. "Father, I have no objection to you disposing of the farmland however you wish," I tell him in haste, eager to change the subject. "Certainly, I have never been one with any inkling for the plow. Nor," I add with a grin, "with any yen at all for keeping bees."

"I was hoping you would not object," he murmurs. "It is, after all, your birthright. Our family has held those seventeen desyatins for so long that in some respects, considering forfeiture approaches sacrilege! But I am becoming far too old for tearing out my hair over yields, tax appropriations, and busy ledger tallies. Particularly when it was over the farm that—that I so foolishly spent over an entire year estranged from my son."

Reaching across the table, Father squeezes hold of my arm—and again, in shame, I stiffen, and stare downward. Through the long months of at last learning to rest at ease in his company again, through the heady nights of his beaming smiles upon each of my ascents from the orchestra anteroom at the *Paris Opéra*, through the warm sunny days of listening enraptured as he has told of further carefree adventures with my mother—a closeness that I have craved from him all my life—still, I cannot bring myself to return his embraces. The anger etched into the black prism of my soul in the months following our last terrible row at Novgorod still lies deep. As does my fear that something else said, or suddenly suggested, could again provoke from him such an outburst of rage. "Excuse me," I say abruptly, rising, snatching up my cane and jacket and hurrying for the compartment doors. Without further explanation, I slam them soundly shut and leave him far behind, his eyes following in sad weariness from the table.

And as I have so many times in this long summer of our wanderings, I head alone again for the dining car—there to crouch morosely at the farthest corner booth and sneak a cigarette in between hot sips of strong black tea. And through the windows, I gaze toward the wide rolling grasses of the level steppe—although yet seeing nothing beyond the rattling pane but the still-churning depth of my inconsolable hurt.

* * *

I awaken with a start, blanket clutched up to my chin, my ears pricked for the sound. But it is only the continued chugging drone of the rail coach wheels speeding toward the mountaintops through the lonely blackness of the night. From the shelf, I snatch up my watch and squint down at its shiny face: three A.M. *Nothing*, I tell myself. From the adjoining berth flows Father's heavy breathing. *Nothing. You heard nothing. Go back to sleep.*

Bare of another moment passes, and I hear the sound suddenly again—tortured stabs of breath, hacking and uneven. Throwing my robe up over my shoulders, I whisk back my berth's curtain and stumble outward, muttering: "Father?"

The anguished stabs rage on. Sliding back the curtain of his berth, I find him hunched over on his knees, his nightshirt clumped in sweaty twists about his legs. "No!" he moans out, cupping one hand across his face while waving out at me with the other.

"Papa!" I gasp, raw spikes of terror seizing me. "Oh, my God—what is it? A heart spasm? Oh, Jesus—Papa!"

The berth curtains and my robe go flying out behind me as I rummage through the compartment like a demon possessed until recovering his medical bag.

Shoving it down beside him, I unhook the clasp with violently shaking fingers, the grip of fear clouding away all previous primers in first aid and good judgment: *oh, dear God—no! Not now, not yet—not when we were at last becoming close again—God, please!* "Papa!" I shout into his ear. "There are all kinds of medicines in here! Surely there is something that might help?" Desperately, I begin groping around inside the bag. "Papa, answer me, for God's sake!" I cry, shaking his shoulder. "Tell me what you need!"

"No!" he thunders out, his fist smacking at my arm. "N-Nothing is wrong, dammit! J-Just go back to bed."

And then I realize that, far from suffering through a deadly heart spasm, or any other threat of bodily angst, he has instead—apparently for some length of time, now—been shaking from head to foot with sobs.

"Papa?" I set the bag down on the floor and move in beside him, easing my hand across his, whispering softly: "Papa—what is it?"

But he shakes his head at me furiously, barking out: "Blast it, Sasha! Simply go b-back to bed—will you?"

Tears then begin drenching in a stream down over his stiff, clutched hands, dripping one by one onto the small object shielded within his grasp. After considerable prying, he at last surrenders it: a tiny gold-cast locket containing a picturegraph.

Of Melissa.

"Oh, Papa," I murmur, fending off shivers from the cold as I slide both arms around him. Whereupon he breaks down completely, the berth-frame rattling noisily against its adjoining windowpanes with his each anguished, choking sob. "Was all my f-fault, everything!" he sputters out after long moments, once more attempting to hide away his face.

Fighting to control my own hold on emotion, I gently wind my fingers through the mussed strands of his blanched white hair, then find his handkerchief within the sheets, and tuck it into his hand. After blowing his nose endless times, he seems to regain some composure—but remains crouched over the locket possessively, shielding it away as if I had meant to take it from him, his widened eyes staring down at Melissa's faded image, while the gold chain dangles loosely between his fingers. "C-Couldn't get you turned 'round," he at last murmurs hoarsely, sniffling. "Oh, God—Lissa! Forgive me, my own cherished, beloved little Lissa! . . ."

I throw both arms around him once again, crushing him to my chest, murmuring: "Don't—"

"Lissa, where are you?" he rants on. "C-Can you hear me? Lissa! Where are you now?"

"Papa, stop it!"

"W-Why did she have to die? Why *her*? W-What happens to people when they die, Sasha? D-Do you know?"

Biting my lip, I clutch onto him fiercely, desperate to do anything to quell his agony, desperate to keep my own heart from breaking in two.

"H-Have you any idea what it was like, Sasha?" he goes on in a tortured whisper. "I had to abandon her . . . so young and beautiful, and so very full of life—a precious, laughing wisp of a girl! But I had to bury her smile away forever! Inside—inside a b-box in—in the g-g-ground . . . ."

And again he erupts into a torrent of sobs, his fingers clawing into my shoulders, his tears washing down between the two of us and soaking our nightshirts into chilly, dampened clumps—tears at last mixing with silent, halting ones of my own.

"Will do neither of us any good, Papa," I choke out into the darkness. "Such carrying on . . . ."

"Was all my fault!" he wails on, unhearing. "I should have prevented it, should have gotten you turned 'round! Dear God—I'd done it with near unto fifty babes by then! Why couldn't I do it with you? Blast it to the very horns of the devil, I am *supposed* to be a doctor!"

"Papa, what happened to Lissa could not have been helped!" I shout, shaking him by both shoulders. "Do you hear me? What happened to Lissa was *not* your fault!"

My harsh tone seems to quiet him down at last, and he leans back into the pillows, wiping over his eyes in shame, trembling like a child. "I—I am sorry," he rasps out, peeking up at me. "Forgive me—I did not mean to cause such a commotion. Nor to awaken you—"

"No, Papa—I am the one who is sorry," I tell him earnestly. "To have ever brought into your life such terrible grief."

"Oh, Sasha—no!" he exclaims, lurching outward and pulling me close to him yet again. Shuddering, he presses his cheek into my neck while struggling once more for control of his voice. "Sashenka, I would not trade you for anyone else in the universe!" he whispers with urgency. "Even could I turn back time and somehow bring Lissa back—you must believe me! You are so dear to me! Oh, Lord—I am naught but a senseless, bile old fool! Sasha, I beg you from the bottom of my heart: please forgive me for all those years, I have hardly been the best of fathers—no, I have been the *worst* of fathers! How—how could I ever have struck you? And repeatedly? And all over some inane folly one night in a darkened hall—and then, toward what did it all lead?" he cries, moaning, his hand pointing downward toward my bad leg. "Dear Jesus Christ in Heaven! What a heartless monster you must think me to be! . . ."

As Father gropes downward, his trembling fingertips rubbing across the whitened ribbons of my leg's old scars, I shove his hand quick away. "Papa! Was all naught but an accident, that night with the window. You scarce intended for me to fall out! I have come to understand that. And had it not been for you, and your expertise and patience—and those long months of fending off my filthy peasant curses—I know I would never have walked again, ever, upon my own leg. Save for how you helped me through the worst of it, Papa."

In response, Father's hands clasp grateful hold of both my own, all ten of his fingers interlacing tightly through all ten of mine—and we cling onto one another in the humming shadows until his breath slows and becomes even once again. When he finally speaks, his tone, greatly calmed, brims with the warm affection I have come to cherish over the last few months. "I never told you how very much Liss wanted a child," he murmurs, letting up on my hands and leaning back once more into the pillows of the berth. "The wedding was scarce over, but she began planning for the family we would have! But I had my misgivings. Some women with a particular type of bone structure should simply never bear children. I became apprehensive about the matter even during our courtship, and on our wedding night, attempted to convince her that perhaps we should wait awhile before considering sharing a bed—after all, she was so young! Of course, Lissa would not hear of it, and cried and carried on so when I refused to bed her, that finally—after lying for hours in the adjoining room with my anguished thoughts—I simply could not help but give in to the poor girl's demands. I mean, what can you do when the woman is banging without pause upon your door, begging for kisses while at the same time cursing up and down and calling you a heartless, foolish cad? Finally, I let her in, and then we—well—we loved each other so much. Although I suppose I was a bit shy of the prospect of starting a new, young family at my age. But Liss wanted children terribly—we would build us a dynasty, she said! For a year, though, our embraces came to naught. Then she sought me out one day when I was airing out the apiary just a couple of weeks before the *Maslenitsa* fairs began. I glanced outside the door to see Liss babbling on with such delight that I could scarce understand a word she said—until I realized that the date we had been watching for had come: she was a whole two weeks late again, and so hadn't borne her menses at all since late November. Well, I felt tall as the sky, like any proud man would feel. And she was overcome with joy, Sasha! She wanted you very much."

"Papa," I whisper over to him, "you do not have to tell me such things—"

"Oh, but I want to! And also, that—"

He stops abruptly, screwing up his eyes and peering through the shadows into my face. "You Turkish renegade!" he then bellows out, ruffling his hand through my hair and letting out a gruff laugh. "Still takes a fair bribe to lure you into any barber's chair at all!"

Playfully, I make a swipe back at him—but he seizes firm hold of my hand, and once again his expression darkens seriously, his stare cast downward. "Had it not been for you," he murmurs in a lowered tone, "I swear I would have thrown myself straight into the lake after she died, Sashenka. Everything was so devastating. But I knew deep down that I was rich, blessed, lucky beyond all compare! Because I had you—"

"Papa—"

"Have you any idea how proud I have been, seeing my son playing at the *Paris Grand Opéra* night after night in the orchestra of the *Ballet Russe?"*

Flushing, I remind him: "I am only an alternate, Papa."

Past hearty chuckles, he warmly presses my hand. "Oh, please forgive an old man his childish excess, my boy," he then says, reddening. "I was trying desperately to have done with my fit of lunacy and not awaken you. I've had great trouble sleeping of late. More often than not, I'm like a bear—but all this talk of Lissa day after day so stirs my memory of her that, when the nights come, I simply cannot calm my thoughts."

Elbowing back to the opposite wall of the berth, I scan across Father's face with some concern: indeed, along with redness now from the tears, heavy, darkened rings have swollen up beneath the lids of his eyes—and I chide myself for my selfish preoccupation, for taking scant notice over the last few days. "Well, Papa," I tell him, grinning, "I know of an ideal remedy for lack of sleep." Swiftly, I climb from the berth—and return with the flute.

"Oh, yes!" The taut lines about his brow ease a bit as he pulls the blankets back upward to his chin. "Now, that might just be the perfect tonic for quieting an old man's busy mind."

"I will play very softly. I scarce think it will awaken anyone in the adjoining coach. What is your pleasure, Papa?"

"Gluck's *Dance of the Blessed Spirits*," he says without hesitation.

"Indeed? I never knew you favored that piece."

"Oh, yes. It reminds me of you."

"Me?"

Father scrunches back farther in the berth, making room for me to slide in beside him. "Yes," he goes on, nestling down into the pillows and closing his eyes—but pressing one fist, as if for reassurance, against my side. "Of course, anything played on the flute reminds me of you—but particularly Gluck's *Dance*. Remember when you were four or five, or thereabouts? I took several trips to Paris in those two years—and every time I returned home, you were such a shy little soul, hiding away behind Marnya's heavy peasant skirts. But it never failed—oh, yes, I was a wily sort! Always I brought back presents: a carved toy pony, or a colorful ball, or some such keepsake. Finally, you would be lured to my chair, begging to climb up, insisting upon my telling you a story, usually the Sadko story. Or ofttimes one of the many I would make up about the Great Nevsky—your mother insisted all during the time she carried you that you be named for the Great Nevsky, you know. But you—ho, ho! My little warrior, namesake of the Great Nevsky! You near always fell fast asleep smack in the midst of my stories, and Marnya would be clucking merrily away as I would carry you up to bed and gently tuck you in—"

As I wince at the memory, Father pokes me, grinning, and urges: "Play Gluck's *Dance* for me, my Sasha. It reminds me so of those days long ago when you were small . . . oh, yes—heaven! Lord, you are so very talented, my dear boy—it sounds like a cascading waterfall! Oh, I am blessed by your blessed spirit, my Sashenka . . . indeed, I am *so* very blessed. . . ."

* * *

Come the morn, I find his berth vacant, and on the table a hastily scrawled note: *At breakfast.*

At the farthest corner booth in the dining coach, he sits with his back to everyone, and offers hardly an upward glance as I slide onto the opposite bench. "Were you able to sleep?" I inquire, nervously clearing my throat and flexing clammy fingers upon my knees underneath the table as I stare into his plate of virtually untouched mushroom *kasha* and sausage.

He nods, eyes budging not one speck from the *Birzhevye Vedomosti* headlines now four days old, as if they were still fresh news.

Of course, in his place, I too would cringe with embarrassment. For his sake, I find I must make a dogged effort to keep from blushing near to my toes throughout the remainder of breakfast. The train wheels grind on through the stiff tension for an hour, punctuating the stern silence between us with predictable chug-a-lug jabs until the dining car empties out of patrons, the clink and rattle of trays and china dishes from the kitchen compartment gradually replacing the lull of carefree early morning conversation. Finally, I set my fork down with resolution upon my empty plate and make some attempt to catch his eye—still to be met with frosty, silent response. "Father," I at last murmur. "Father, I—"

But he glares across at me furiously, an adamant contortion of raised eyebrows, the newspaper pages drifting down onto the tabletop with ironic lightened ease—as if instead, against a torrent of force, he had actually slammed them.

I look quickly away, gulping back thick swallows of hurt. *He wants us both to act as if it never happened—as if he never cried out in the night; as if I never came to offer comfort and play him softened melodies.* As he returns to his perusal of the paper, I order another glass of strong tea, stirring my spoon around long after the sugar lump dissolves, my heart ravished with vacancy. *Dammit—must he always play the stoic patriarch, the staunch master over all emotion—his and mine? Why can he not let me love him now as he did last night? Why will he never let me?*

Downing my tea in near one frantic gulp, I attempt to keep my eyes focused through the crimsoning blur, paying no heed as he rises from the bench. But instead of turning on his heel, as I had expected, he pauses—and after making a prolonged show of coughing, his face flushed to the earlobes, he steps over and squeezes his hand upon my shoulder.

Overcome with a rush of joy, I grip quick hold of his fingers. Then he grins down at me, and says: "Did I ever tell you about your Grandfather Sergei's ties to the Decembrists?"

"Good God!" I gasp, delighted. "No!"

"Come, my Sashenka," he goes on with husky laughter, urging me upward and throwing his arm around my shoulders. "There are many more tales that your old papa wants to tell you."

And as we amble slowly back again through the aisle of the dining car, I laugh and shake my head in amazement as he begins relating the dubious revolutionary adventures of my Grandfather Sergei.

* * *

"You are a poet!" he exclaims from over my shoulder.

"Jesus Christ!" I blurt out, crumpling up the paper. "God in Heaven, Papa—you scared me half out of my wits! I thought you were still outside collecting seashells on the beach—"

"Small wonder you've been sorting through so many stacks of paper," he bellows, ignoring my protestations. Grinning, he points across at the crumpled wad within my hand, again proclaiming: "You are a poet!"

"I am not!"

"But I saw what you were doing! You have been writing!"

"Oh, for God's sake, Papa! And just how long have you been standing there?"

"Long enough! Now, let me see what you were writing—"

"No!"

Undeterred, he sticks his tongue out at me, and then makes a beeline for the trash basket.

"Papa! What do you think you're doing?" I yell, stumbling after his crouched form as he sends scores of crumpled sheets spewing outward from the pile of rubbish.

"Look at this!" he declares, triumphant, squinting downward and flattening one of the pieces of paper out upon the table. "My son is a poet! Listen to this:

"Behold another eerie sunrise
"Has wrought red fury in skies of gray,
"Behold a heightened snow yet falling
"To chill this land another day . . . ."

"Give me that!" I bark, swiping for it.

"Oh, you needn't get so riled up, boy—this is marvelous! Stupendous!" Waving me off, Father whirls determinedly away, ducking into the bright light of the window and holding the sheet up out of my reach, his voice barreling on:

"Again this cold, this frozen country
"Crawls astir with revolution's fire!
"Hearken here, my revolution!
"In whirling wisps past ancient spires . . . ."

"Will you just *give* it to me?" I yell, at last wrestling the paper away from his hands.

"You are a poet!" he exclaims again with an awe-struck, worshipful stare.

"Oh, for the love of God! I am not any kind of poet, Father! Now, will you just have done with such carrying on? That was naught but a page of schoolboy drivel written years ago at May's on a dare! Lord God! You act as if you just met Maksim Gorky—"

"Humph! Save that our Gorky is naught but a smirking, opportunistic horse's ass. But, you—*you* are a poet! And one apparently refusing to admit his avocation—even to himself."

"Papa, I am no poet, I am a musician!"

"All right! A poet-musician, then."

"Are we going to venture out for our usual walk upon the beach?" I interrupt. "Or do you intend to spend the entire afternoon blabbering on about such nonsense?"

Answering with a affirmative nod, Father shuffles noisily in his leather sandals back toward the open back doorway of the bungalow. "This whole last week on the train," he says with a wagging finger, "you have been sorting through pages of poetry stuffed in between those mounds of musical manuscripts!"

Lividly glaring him down in reply, I collect the crumpled papers from the floor and once again stuff them into the trash basket. Then I search out my cane and Panama hat, roll up the cuffs to my trousers, kick off my shoes, and trudge past him out the door into the moist black sand.

Father's continued mutters of: "My son, the poet!" trail after me without shame as I wander from the small cluster of beach houses toward the shimmering turquoise mirror of the Black Sea.

Rays of the September sun, burnished high overhead in a tangy golden glow, gently warm our shoulders, the scent of wisteria, lilacs, wild roses, and pungent nectar from the nearby currant berry shrubs teasing at our nostrils through the summery air. Flowing cooly but not overly so, the water laps about our feet with every delicious windswept rush of the surf. "Beautiful, it is, this place," Father murmurs, linking his arm through mine, his head thrown back toward the breeze with a sigh of appreciation. "Liss also thought as much of the Crimea."

"I remember summers here with the Zhelanovs," I tell him with a smile. "The sand fights Nikolai and I used to have. The way we'd go traipsing off for hours on end through the trails in the hills."

Father pauses, shaking his head. "I must admit," he says, "that for some time, I was furious with your cousin for dragging you off with him to Europe. But not anymore."

In reply, I pinch a fond squeeze to his arm.

"Sasha," he then says, "when we return to Novgorod, I think that we should definitely consider airing out Melissa's room."

Nodding, I stare downward at our bare toes sunken in the sand. "That," I tell him, "would be a fine idea, Papa." But then my voice breaks away, reduced to raspy shavings in my throat, and I sharply catch his hand. "What?" he cries, frowning. "What is it, my Sashenka?"

Whether it be for the fact that I have become older, or he wiser—or both—somehow, it seems that never again could there be angry blows or harsh words between us, that never again could I choose to be at odds with my dear old papa. *Dear Lord—I know he has already been blessed with such a long fruitful life, but please—grant him to me for a few more precious years.* "Papa, I merely wanted to say," I go on haltingly, "that, uh, I mean, Papa, I wanted to say that, for a long time—a very long time—I, uh, have been, uh, meaning to tell you—"

"Yes, my Sasha," he replies close into my ear, his voice humming low. "You know, I love you, too."

* * *

Emerging from his study at last, Father presses into my hand the key to Melissa's room.

"I can scarce understand why you are fretting so!" I cry, frowning at him again—but once more he pounces upon my arm, hanging on as if unto the last dwindling shreds of dear life, exclaiming: "Wait! Where is everyone?"

"Father, no one is going to come up here this time of day! Marnya is down in the kitchen frying up *syrniki* fritters. You know how the house would have to be literally burning down to budge her away from the stove before she gets a whole four trays of them done. Tereza is helping her. Eva is at Bulya's and Natasha's, trading toddler stories. Vliny is out in the carriage-house with Rolfe, they're putting those new runner-blades on the small troika. For devil's sake!"

"All right, then! Hurry up and put in the key, will you?" he bellows, his hand impatiently indicating the bedroom door.

But as I do so, he again latches onto my arm, moaning: "Oh, no—we *mustn't!* My God, I know it's foolish! I know it's *impossible*—but I tell you, Sasha, *she's in there!"*

"Dammit!" I yell. "Once and for all, I am going to prove to you that Melissa is *not* in this room!"

I slam the key into the lock, wrenching open the door.

Thick filmy layers of cobwebs drift downward from the ceiling. I shove through the mess with my hand, dragging Father behind—despite a flood of renewed protests—and point toward the elaborate four-poster bed. "See, Papa?" I tell him, urging him to take a look. "The room is simply full of cobwebs and old dust, and no more. There is naught to be afraid of in here. Melissa has long since—"

I stop in mid-sentence, my jaw dropping as the quilted coverlet begins rising upward from the bed as if a gigantic bubble was being blown beneath.

Father grapples onto my arm: "Oh, dear God!"

The sheets roll back, tossed by a whitened dainty hand—to be followed by a tumble of braids and the impish glance of her amber-golden eyes. Her lips part in a radiant smile upon utterance of the word: "Misha?"

Like two tornadoes, Father and I rush back out of the room and slam shut the door.

"Shit!" I blurt out, scrunched up to the hallway wall, palms flattened stiffly back against it.

"Oh, dear Jesus Christ and all the Saints in Heaven!" Father moans out in agreement, pushing in beside me. He begins crossing himself profusely while uttering repeated, lengthy prayers unto the Virgin.

Fingers shaking, I cross myself as well—despite the fact I have avoided so doing in perhaps three or even four years.

"Shit," I mutter again. Without another second thought, I rush off into my room, where I begin rummaging through my travel-trunk—which I have still not entirely unpacked—until finding the cigarette case.

"I thought you gave that up!" Father exclaims, glaring with a disgruntled frown as I emerge enveloped in a heavy, acrid cloud of smoke.

"Well, I did! And I will again, when the time is right—which is certainly not now, for God's sake! So stop scolding me already.

"Humph!"

"Lord Jesus God!" I go on, pressing a still-quivering fist unto my brow. "What did we just see in there?"

"Liss. Exactly like I told you."

Muttering a slew of curses against the utter improbability of it all, I drop back once more with him against the wall.

"Well," he ventures after a long moment, "at least now you believe me."

"All right." I finish off my cigarette in haste and crush the butt out against the handle of my cane. "As I see it, Papa, there is only one course left for us to take."

Knowing the time to be short before I completely lose my gumption, I whirl around—and again grasp hold of the doorknob as Father shouts out at the top of his lungs: "Sasha, *nooo!"*

The door flies open, slamming with a splintering crunch against the wall. Melissa duly awaits us again—although no longer does she lie in bed, draped in a flannel gown and luxuriant bevy of braids. Instead, this time she hovers just above the floor, before the window, larger than life and identical to the ghostly apparition encountered so many times in my dreams.

"Oh, L-Lord—oh, *Lord!"* Father makes another turn to run.

"Papa!" I cry, seizing hold of him. "Tell me: what do you see?"

"See? *See*? It—her! She—it—it—"

"Totally enveloped in white, her long hair streaming loosely to the floor?"

"Yes! Yes—"

"And do you see the golden triangle blinking above her head?"

Clinging onto me in wide-eyed terror, he nods his head up and down frantically in agreement.

"Melissa!" I call across the room to the apparition, raising my voice with effort, "it is time for you to leave now. The time has come for you to go home."

"I know, my darling," the vision replies in a softened lilt. "I was merely awaiting the appointed hour. To watch you brave the threshold."

And then, in a whirling hail of light, she abruptly disappears.

Father and I stand dumbfounded, staring at curtains fluttering in a phantom breeze before an unopened window.

"My Lord!" Father gasps in shock. "You made the ghost disappear! Sasha! You finally broke the spell!"

Only half-hearing him past the thunder of my heartbeats, I continue staring at the window, still stung with total disbelief myself.

"Good God, Aleksandr!" he then blurts out, taking a step backward and slowly looking me up and down. "It *is* true! What they used to whisper in the village—you *are* of the *volkhvi!*

"No," I hear my voice telling him in calm reply, "I am not of the *volkhvi*. I am an initiate."

And then I near collapse beneath the roaring weight of an avalanche: Melissa appears all over again—a hundred times, a thousand times—and yet it is not her that I truly see, but instead merely the golden triangle flashing above a myriad of visions far too luminous for approaching any sense of form. I watch the eerie panorama in awe-struck silence, feeling torn with the strangest poignant hunger, an ache as old and endless as the shifting sands of time. "Sasha!" I finally hear Father shouting. *"Sasha!"*

"It—it is all right, Papa. I was—merely thinking." After patting his arm and offering murmured words of reassurance, I leave him to his inspection of Melissa's antique mahogany four-poster and stumble off to my room.

There to virtually rip Uncle Ned's numerology book apart. Trembling from head to toe, muttering over and over the words "Initiate, initiation," I search everywhere: the covers, the index—even my handwritten notes within the back pages and the margins—for something, anything, a hastily scrawled footnote, a forgotten underlined clue. But there is no hint anywhere—not a single mention of either word.

Soon I hear Father out in the hall, shuffling back and forth, talking to himself—and then finally talking to Eva, who has apparently come home. Together, they proceed about the task of sweeping up the cobwebs. I hear them both rummaging through the wardrobe-cupboards, he telling her about it being such a shame, that he should have given away all of Melissa's old gowns years ago, when the bustles and frilly thick skirts were still in the height of fashion and someone could have made decent use of them. At last I catch a glimpse of the two of them bringing out the old bedclothes and carrying fresh ones back in. Possibly, Father intends to sleep in the old four-poster bed tonight in lieu of his divan in the study which has sufficed for so many years. But despite the fact that the hall becomes blanketed in a torrent of noise as Marnya finally stomps upward in an authoritative flurry to join in with all the primping and cleaning, I continue staring at the mirror-glass on the wall above my bureau in a state of shock, watching the spectacles slip down upon the bridge of my nose over a course of time that seems to melt into untold hours, the words *initiate, initiation* droning on without mercy in my skull, over and over.

At last, with shaking fingers, I clutch up a pencil and small scrap of paper, scrawling out over the roughened corner edge: *initiate? initiation? Initiation: forbidden journey, cup of resolution, obligatory pilgrimage, dark night of the soul . . . .*

"Sasha!" Father calls merrily from the doorway. "We have swept the room fit and clean, you must come and see! Oh, and by the way," he says with a contented sigh, pausing and leaning back against the doorjamb, "what were you talking about, about being—oh, now, what was it that you said? Oh, yes—about being 'an initiate?'"

Still staring at my image shrouded within the confines of the mirror-glass, I attempt to wince away the wash of cold tremors tingling up and down my spine, answering softly: "I—I don't know."

* * *

The winter of 1910 to 1911 proves hectic, our rehearsal schedule intensified in preparation for a stopover in Monte Carlo before the springtime Paris debuts. Beyond the usual fawning acclaim of the French *patrons des arts*, during the new season, the *Ballet Russe* at last attains an international artistic following with the unparalleled success of *Petrushka*, a charming reenactment of carnival scenes and puppet dances from the long Russian tradition of pre-Lenten *Maslenitsa* fairs. Thanks to Stravinsky, who continues to insist upon writing for such large orchestras, and to the preponderance of my fellow wood-winds for jaunting off to-and-fro on holiday, I finally play both flute and piccolo in more performances during the summer of 1911, my tenure having been upgraded to the paradoxical status of 'regular alternate.' Father again spends the summer in doting attendance at near every one of the ballets, the nights and days flying by on a whirlwind of gay parties and lavish suppers in the wake of *Sadko*, *Narcisse*, *Le Spectre de la Rose*, and a sumptuous re-staging of the ever popular *Sheherazade*. In honor of King George's coronation, the Company is invited to perform at the Royal Opera House at Covent Garden in London, where—much to my delight—Tchaikovsky's *Swan Lake* is revived also in triumphant, glittering finale. All too soon, busy rounds of autumn rehearsals begin again in Petersburg in frantic anticipation of the new year, during the first three months of which we at last set out upon a full-fledged European tour. In Dresden and Berlin, droll places never much inclined toward the ballet, audiences remain stoically lukewarm, but are quite handsomely outdone by the overwhelming reception we receive in Vienna, Mozart's splendid citadel of music, its tranquil old Opera House so closely resembling our beloved Maryinsky and other St. Petersburg court theaters. Budapest also provides fertile ground for the Diaghilev innovations—for the Hungarians, in their love of flamboyance and riotous spectacle, have always been well matched in musical soul to we Russians. Boisterous drinking parties and celebratory excursions with scores of new-found friends continue flush unto our train departure time—whereupon, in April of 1912, we once again divert for a short reprise in Monte Carlo before the *premières* scheduled for the upcoming summer season in Paris.

In Monte Carlo, I leave the others behind for a brief while and return to Petersburg, for despite the nuisance of making an extra trip, springtime would not be complete without first joining Father for another of our carefree, talkative journeys back across the Continent. Nor indeed would spring be manifest in true earnest without me first wandering into the same bustling middle-class quarter on Vasilyevsky Island dotted with yellow clapboard houses and quiet tenements into which I always wander at least once, each and every year, just prior to the festivals of Maytide.

"Oh, yes!" Volodya murmurs huskily into my hair, his hands slithering up and down my back as I press pliant kisses against his throat. "Uh, huh—again you came back for more of me, Sasha, my love. Every year right after the plum trees bloom, you come trottin' on back, always. Just like a bloody bitch in heat."

Spinning back in a choke of outrage, I slam my fist for his jaw, but my balance gives way to furious, pitiful stumbles as Volodya throws back his head, howling with laughter. "Akkh! Oh, come, Sashakins—don't take it all so mighty personal! Was naught but a joke, I tell you—ha, ha!"

"Which I scarce find much amusing—at all!" Fetching up my derby and my cane, I stomp, infuriated, for the door—there to be wrestled roughly back into Volodya's sinewy, cat-like arms. "Oh, come," he insists, still gloating with mirth and kissing me again. "You don't honestly want to leave."

As I bristle to the hilt in reply, Volodya takes a step backward and begins slowly looking me up and down, his dark Armenian eyes widened with mocking perusal, his grin again taking on its inevitable sarcastic leer. "So," he declares, "my old summertime playmate out by the dairy butter churns, sneaky little pick-lock thief of Pavel's safe, the scaredy-cat leech always stealin' combs out from the honeybee hives—my own Sasha . . . oh, pardon me! My dear Count Sekovsky—has turned before my very eyes into a dashin' gent all of the age of twenty years! God in Heaven! And a fine two-score it is, at that—with those still-sultry looks of yours, darlin'. Ha! You red-headed devil, you."

"Humph!" Crossing my arms, I stare sullenly to the floor.

"Oh, akkh! An' what's a'matter with you anyway, Sekovsky? You've found no good suck-off chums to help wile away your lonely hours in Paris?"

I turn away, flushing hotly. Far from the those first days in Paris so long ago and my halting inner quandaries, the midnight 'Woodwind' suppers at the Blue Room at *Le Doyen*, the stolen feats with total strangers in the dark recesses of backroom walls at such haunts as the cabaret *Enfer* and *Bar Maurice* have long since become familiar domain. As have the affections of Klementi, whom of late has become much more in both my thoughts and passions than a mere distant purveyor of bassoon. "You ever going to shut up?" I demand, hedging a stiff glance back toward Volodya's smirking face. "Or do you intend to continue blabbering on like some harebrained fool all night long?"

"Oh, I'll shut up right now, my love—and we will proceed as you wish." From behind, Volodya slaps both arms down around my hips and pulls me back against him, the taut grip of his own desire hardening against my buttocks, his eager fingers unhooking the clasp to my belt.

I shut my eyes, moaning out against the rapturous surge: "Dammit! Why do I always come back here?"

"Because, dearest," Volodya whispers back, nuzzling into my neck and inching his hands deep down inside the folds of my trousers, "'spite of all your fancy airs, in truth, you're naught but a ruttin' little fag. You come back to me each and every year without exception 'cause you simply cannot help it. . . ."

* * *

This time, scarce within moments of our arrival, the revolutionary meeting disintegrates into a furious shouting match about the proper role of art in life—which finally culminates in, of all things, a session of poetry reading.

"Pale Horse!" one of the debate's loudest leaders keeps bellowing without pause from his seat in the back. "Nobody can outdo Bryusov's *Pale Horse!"*

"What is he yelling so about?" I whisper to Volodya. "What 'pale horse?'"

"Bryusov."

"What?"

"Shhh! Just hush and listen—"

From the opposite side of the room, somebody else then launches into a tearful, passionate tirade about some woman 'of purest Virgin glory' named Akhmatova.

"Who is Akhmatova?" I whisper again to Volodya.

"Oh, for God's sake!" he exclaims in shock, rolling his eyes. "You mean to tell me you've no idea who Akhmatova is?"

"No—"

"And Bryusov? And Bely? You mean you pray tell've never heard of any of them, neither? Oh, Christ, Sekovsky! You been too overlong in Paris with your head stuffed inside your friggin' flute and ribbony ballet shoes! Akhmatova and Bryusov and Bely and Blok are poets, you fool."

"Aleksandr Blok?"

"Yes."

"Well!" I cry in flushed defense, "I have heard of him."

"Shhh! Listen—"

The room erupts then into a volley of hand-clapping and foot-stomping, the bellows of *"Pale Horse!"* and "God bless Pushkin! Our national soul! God bless all poets in his wake!" drowning out staunch protests from a disgruntled faction of iron workers grouped over by the far cellar wall. "All right!" a portly bespectacled fellow wearing a worn doorman's uniform yells out at last. After many loud, prolonged pleas, he actually manages to retain everyone's attention. "It'll be *Pale Horse* by Bryusov that we'll be readin', then—and the rest o' you nitwits can waltz back on out o' here and go each your merry way if our Bryusov's not good enough for the likes o' you, that you can!"

More shouts assail him in furious retribution, but finally, the more resistant hecklers begin to take their leave. Then the mood of the room simmers down into tense expectation as the bespectacled doorman moves up behind the podium and pulls from his jacket pocket a crumpled, greasy sheet of paper.

"Excerpts from Valery Bryusov's *Pale Horse,"* he announces, loudly clearing his throat, his gaze sweeping the room from one end to the other with solemn, prayerful intent. "And I beg forgiveness, comrades! My version's not complete. This is all I've got of it written down:

"Behold a pale horse: and his name
"That sat on him was Death.
"The street was as the wind,
"And lo, before all reared up the Knight of Flames.
"Thunder quivered to an echoing burn,
"The instant mourned in stricken glances
"As unfurled from the Rider's scroll
"Letters afire borne in the name of: Death . . .
"Sumptuous threads ablaze.
"Magnificence dimmed then unto the vault of heaven,
"Frantic footsteps tapped distantly away,
"Only a whore from a brothel and a deranged
"Madman
"Yet reached bare hands
"Toward escaping apparition. . . ."

The whole room erupts into violent applause as the doorman concludes his reading, eager shouts of "Encore! Encore!" following from the gleeful crowd. In response, several other young men proceed in rapid succession to take the stand, filling in from memory the gaps missing from the doorman's version of the poem—while others from various groupings of seats wrangle on between themselves with added lines of their own improvisation. Finally, one by one, students—workers—three or four pale young women with pouting lips and severely short-cropped hair—the old gray-haired gentleman whom I remember for the sincerity, if not the eloquence, of his speech during my very first of these meetings—all ascend to the podium, reading from crumpled papers stuffed into pockets or shafts of boots some sparse few lines of Gorky, Bely, Blok, or Akhmatova, taken—apparently—from the latest underground magazines. But upon many others, who admit their readings as original work of their own, is showered even more enthusiastic applause.

Even Volodya, after considerable urging and loud, laughing guffaws from a couple of his scroungy friends, eventually takes the stand, bellowing out in a sing-song voice with dramatic hand motions:

"There is
"A moment gone!
"Never to be experienced
"Again."

Despite the utter inanity of Volodya's contribution, I end up clapping in worshipful awe right along with everyone else, and as the meeting finally appears to be drawing to a close, I crouch gripping the underside of my chair with sweaty palms, my body chilled, my mind numbed. At last the progression of podium speakers trickles away, the audience lets loose with a boisterous round of final applause, and everyone bursts into a flurry of small-talk and friendly self-congratulation. Nervously, I wind my way in between the scores of worker's caps, searching out the bespectacled doorman who was the first of all of them to speak.

"Er—pardon me, sir," I say, catching his eye with a nod. "That poem you read, Bryusov's *Pale Horse*. Would it trouble you greatly if I wrote myself a quick copy of it?"

"Not at all, Comrade. Hey, Alyosha!" he calls across the room to a friend. "You got a fountain pen? How about a piece of paper? Hey! Anybody here got a piece of paper for this young fellow with the cane, now?"

Back outside beneath the hovering yellow glimmer of a gaslamp, I stare transfixed at my hurriedly scrawled words: *Letters afire borne in the name of: Death* . . . .

"I take it—for a change—that you were impressed," snickers Volodya, coming up from behind. But his eyes darken reverently once he glances down to my paper, and he adds: "Moved even, I'd say."

"By Bryusov—yes." Carefully, I tuck the copy into my pocket and trudge off southward toward Nevsky Prospekt.

"Perhaps you should spend more time in Petersburg, my dear Count Sekovsky," Volodya mutters with a shake of his head, falling into step beside me.

"Perhaps. And for God's sake, will you stop calling me 'Count Sekovsky' all the time?"

"Sorry, Sasha," he replies, shrugging.

"Does that happen often?" I then ask. "Do your meetings often turn into impromptu poetry readings?"

"Poetry readins? Ha! That was scarce any kind of readin', my friend—just a bunch of fired-up rascals spoutin' off steam after a hard day's work! You want to hear poetry, you should fetch yourself an invite into—oh—someplace like the old Potemkin palace. You know, over by the Tauride? That's Slava Ivanov's place: 'Ivanov's Tower' they call it, on the top floor. Three whole flats he's got to himself up there, supposedly, and a view to beg for, or so I hear. Richest, most decadent of all the salons in Petersburg! Gorky, Mayakovsky, and other notables show up there come every Wednesday eve, or so it's said. Ha! Well, I'm certain they'd be tickled to let in a gent like you, especially with your fancy title that you'll never let me call you by, ha! Well, well—so, Count Sekovsky," he goes on sarcastically, "just what got you so suddenly tweaked about poetry, anyway—after scarce knowin' until tonight about the latest work? You got some special interest? Know somebody who writes, or somethin'?"

I fasten my gaze rigorously onto the outline of a watchmaker's sign dangling from a cornerpost three buildings down, murmuring derisively: "Humph! No, I do not know anyone who writes poetry, Volodya. Not at all."

* * *

Squeezing in between the groups of stylish loiterers crowded at the entrance of the *Viel*, I crane my head past tall feathers of ladies' hats and scan across the rows of restaurant tables. The entire place—all of Paris, in fact—remains in a violent uproar over *L'Après-midi d'un Faune*, Nijinsky's eight minute choreographic debut three nights ago, which almost literally set the theater on fire, prompting a visit by a squadron of police and frantic double-page headlines in the papers come the following morn. Whispers of "Outrage! Indecency!" and "Perfectly obscene!" continue rebounding in passionate droves as I pass by table after table involved in lively discussions of the ballet. At last, with a sigh of relief, I spy the crown of Father's head beyond an oriental screen strung with a generous row of hanging plants.

"Oh, yes, Nikolai," I hear him say, laughing uproariously and slapping his hand upon on the table. "I wholeheartedly agree with you. All this furor over *Faune* is naught but idiocy! But I am beginning to suspect that our Diaghilev rather relishes the taste of provoking a scandal—after all, what else inspires such copy in the papers? Not to mention that the theater has been packed full to the walls every night ever since. Why, calling in the *gendarmes* was probably even Diaghilev's own idea!"

His wineglass held out with jaunty abandon, his ankle crossed casually upon his opposite knee, Nikolai tosses back his head, his sun-washed hair—paled near to whiteness beneath the softened glow of the dining room lamps—provoking repeated glances of admiration from several nearby ladies clad in feathery stoles and beaded earrings. In response, my cousin coyly smooths his hand back over the long flaxen strands and begins fingering his moustache, which he has grown back again, before winking at two or three of the smiling, red-lipped *demoiselles*. Then he proceeds about pouring more wine into both his and Father's glasses, his expression warm with affection, his chuckles echoing forth raucously again as he catches wind of some remark made across the room about Nijinsky, onto which Father immediately latches with an amply verbose, opinionated declaration of his own.

Straightening my lapels for the third time, I cast my eyes down to the floor, desperately willing the lobes of my ears not to burn as I approach their table.

"Sasha!" Father exclaims, clasping my arm. "Finally, thank goodness. We were near ready to order dinner."

I glance across the table with a pang of hope, aching to be met with that familiar rakish grin—or at least with a faint smile of acknowledgment. But Nikolai, his glassy-eyed stare already resumed, offers only the merest nod in my direction and promptly turns his attention to the menu.

"Forgive me, Papa," I tell Father. "Nikita brought in that old Flemish piccolo, from his uncle's antique woodwind shop in Brussels. We were all looking it over. I am sorry for having kept the both of you waiting."

"Never you mind. The whole restaurant is aflame again over this so-called 'scandal' about Nijinsky's *Faune*. Listening to these old buffoons carry on so has been providing me vast quantities of entertainment!" he declares in a booming voice, pointedly eyeing several other scoffing nearby patrons. "Now, shall we order dinner?"

We do so, and he and Nikolai again return to their discussion—and every time I attempt to join in with any remark or even a laugh, my cousin glares across the table as if I had rudely interrupted him, his eyes lancing me with harsh accusatory spears before he resumes—gaily—conversing once again with Father.

Accordingly, throughout the remainder of dinner, I suffer through mute restraint, my fingers caught atremble in spite of myself each time I lift my fork and once again return it to my plate. By the time dessert is served, I can no longer court any claim to success as an actor, and fraught with confusion, only end up glaring at Nikolai in due turn, heart pounding, my skin tingling, my tongue torched as a match in the back of my throat. Even Father, despite his preoccupation with outdoing the noisy elderly gentleman at the adjoining table with his own intricate knowledge of ballet choreography, at last takes note of something amiss between myself and my cousin.

He taps my arm, as if wishing to say something aside to me about it, when the waiter finishes serving us with coffee.

"Oh, for Lord's sake, Sasha!" Nikolai then bursts out—stunning Father and I near straight from our seats. Pointing across at me, his eyes flashing poisonous gray barbs, he snarls: "*Must* you insist upon holding your cup in that manner?"

Angrily, I throw up my free hand. "Must I insist upon holding my cup in *what* manner? This is the exact same way I have always held my cup! Heaven's Name, Nikolai—just what is irking you so?"

In response, Nikolai leaps from his chair, slamming his own cup back down and sloshing its entire remaining contents into the saucer. "Excuse me!" he exclaims, hurriedly buttoning his evening jacket, both arms stiffening down to his sides. "And thank you very much, Uncle Misha. For dinner."

Shoulders hunched, he then storms past the paper screens and rows of hanging foliage—and presumably, from the restaurant.

"What the devil was that all about?" Father cries, his eyebrows shot toward his hairline.

Shrugging helplessly, I moan out: "Lord, Papa—how I only wish I knew!"

"Oh, I see." Nodding, Father stirs an extra dollop of cream from the engraved silver pitcher into his cup of coffee, murmuring: "You two caught up in another of your little spats?"

"Well, if we are, I wish someone would inform me as to the provocation! I thought we had both long since had done with such foolishness. Lord God, he and I have been living together on and off in countless hotel rooms for over four years—practicing together, encouraging one another—ever the greatest of friends! But of late, it seems I can do naught to please him—"

"Oh, stop fretting so, Sasha. You know how closely Nikolai takes after his father. Sofya sometimes used to swear she was going to murder your Uncle Petya over the man's dark moods."

Praying for him to be right, I shake my head, taking slow, thoughtful sips from my coffee.

"Besides," Father goes on with a wave of his hand, "I'm certain Nikolai will settle down once Sofya and Anna arrive come Saturday. I know he would probably rather die than admit it, but I think your cousin misses his mother almost as much as she misses him. The two of them always were very close, you know."

"Humph! Well, I suppose you could be right. Certainly, the amount of time he spends composing letters to Aunt Sophie testifies to that. But I am telling you, Papa, this awkwardness between the two of us is only worsening by the hour! Each night, I battle a fit of nerves upon return to our hotel room."

"Oh, he'll get over it. Perhaps he is simply apprehensive, wanting so to make a good impression upon Anna and your aunt. After all, Anna's a doctor, now—and I'm tickled-proud of her myself, I daresay! Thank goodness she and Sofya are finally going to come—I know they will both fall in love with these ballets. Oh, by the way—is the troupe confirmed yet for next month at Covent Garden?"

Nodding, I tell him: "So I hear. I received Uncle Ned's reply to my inquiry just this morn. We can all stay together at the London townhouse for as long as we wish."

"Well, I hope he realizes the visit will not be that terribly lengthy. Anna has her budding practice to consider, and Sofya will never be parted from her charity work and lady friends back in Petersburg for very long. And I—well." He pauses, staring out dreamily toward the glittering view of the Seine. "I must admit that I still abhor the dreary weather in England—and also, I suppose, that the place still simply holds too many memories. In any case, I have decided to return home with Anna and your aunt after the London *premières*. I may no longer have a flax harvest to worry over, but I do have hives that need readying for the winter again, and other kinds of odds and ends long put off after spending so much time these past two summers in Europe."

"I'll miss you," I tell him with a sad smile, warmly squeezing his arm. "Tell me—are you afraid the peasants have let more of the land back to the marsh?"

Father rolls his eyes. "Crazy fools! If I see one more desyatin go back to marsh, I think I'll tear out my hair! Vliny and I both kept warning everyone all last winter that they had better stop fighting over who should get what, and till some of that land come Maytide—but you saw how the situation was there just before we left, the bog retaking more of it every day with everyone still squabbling to no end."

I nod in agreement—my thoughts, however, dwelling not so much upon the problems in Novgorod as upon the return of the *Ballet Russe* to London and my impending reunion with Uncle Ned.

It is then that, from across the room, I catch the briefest glimpse of Klementi.

Unfazed, his eyes pass across our table as if seeing straight through me and into the wall. I also offer no nod, nor glance of recognition, as if he was merely of my slightest acquaintance, little more than a distant fellow member of the orchestra. His parents are here, a fact of which I am keenly aware, taking dinner as I so often do with Father. Secret passions, consuming as they are in the bed of night, in public are best left chasing their own shadows when the object of one's affections happens to be of one's own gender. Ever since our affair began its on-again, off-again course last year, the one constant observed dilgently between the both of us has been a silent pact of the utmost in discretion.

Indeed, I have been careful—ridiculously careful—even to the point of following Nikolai, from a distance in a closed cab, up to the entrances of countless brothel-hotels all about Paris, ever intent upon ascertaining his plans for the night before proceeding with my own at *Le Doyen* or the *Enfer.* And fortunately—far beyond my guilty wandering avenues of sin—Father still insists ever upon staying at Palaiseau, on the city's southern outskirts, in order to partake of lengthy visits with the Comte and other old European friends. Yet, fearful still of my own eyes somehow betraying me in some cruel trick of fate, I hedge another glance toward him with a renewed gulp of trepidation—only to find him once more immersed in a heated discussion with someone at another table about the merits of Nijinsky's choreography. *Blast it, Sasha! Will you stop stewing yourself clear unto early death? Neither Father nor Nikolai will ever find out—you cover your tracks cunningly, like a damned detective! Neither of them is ever going to know!*

But as I finish my coffee, I cannot help but stare off—with a growing sense of unease—toward the exit through which Nikolai last disappeared.

* * *

"Sekovsky!"

The music dies away, and everyone—woodwinds, brass, strings, even the harpist and both percussion players—stare straight at me as I blink the culprit tears away again, cursing myself to high heaven.

"Oh, all right!" storms on Monteux, the conductor, after a glance at his pocket watch. "Enough rehearsal for everyone today, then. Out, out with all of you!" he bellows on, the movements of his upper lip near obliterated beneath the heavy strands of his dark handlebar moustache. "Until two o'clock tomorrow. And not to be late, not a single one of you!"

Along with the others, I take up my instrument and make a beeline for the anteroom door—but Monteux yells out my name again, and I stop cold amidst the angled groupings of orchestra pit chairs, watching everyone else trail out beyond the tip of the French conductor's adamant wagging finger. "One more time, Sekovsky," he roars, "and you are out—*terminaison!* Do you take my meaning, young man?"

"Yes, sir!"

"Because he who cannot retain his composure in rehearsal might just as well lose his head during performance."

"I understand, sir!"

In the anteroom, as I shove the linen cloth up the pieces of my flute with the end of the cleaning rod, Alekseyev—one of the ever-amorous oboes—saunters up and elbows me, snickering: "What's a'matter, freckle-face? You and Klementi wind up in another little tiff again last night? Or is it your time of the month?"

"Blast it!" I choke back at him in a furious whisper. "What are you trying to do, get me found out?"

"Oooh! Sorry!" he cries, swishing both hands at me in coquettish, mock-eyed fear.

"Alekseyev, go suck on a snake's head, will you?"

"Darling, I intend to go suck on something much more tasty than that right now," he whispers back with a knowing grin. To my profound relief, he wanders off in search of his obliging companion in lust, Pazinsky, as I swab down the joints of the flute and tuck the three pieces into their velvet troughs in the instrument case.

"You are scarce the only one," I hear Nikolai say in a low tone from the doorway once almost everyone else has filtered out. "I find Debussy just as stirring, Sasha," he goes on with a shrug.

"Do you? But at least you've not ended up with tears streaming down your face in the midst of rehearsal!"

"No—but sometimes, almost."

"Humph! Well, the difference between 'almost' and physical tangibility may soon enough cost me my employment."

"Sasha, Monteux has had your name on his favorite serving platter ever since last year, when—"

"Yes, yes—ever since last year in London, when—two hours before the revival *première*—I broke up even worse over the overture to *Swan Lake.* You needn't remind me, Nikolai. I've not forgotten the storm Monteux made about my problem then, also—and in front of everyone."

"As I recall, he did admit that your intensity was admirable."

"But also that causing such commotion can disrupt the entire orchestra, and is inexcusable—I know! I am sorry! What am I supposed to say—to him, you, to everyone? I cannot help it! Sometimes, Tchaikovsky—Debussy—*music*—so moves me."

Nikolai breaks into a sympathetic grin. "Oh, you'll manage well enough, *mon cousin*," he murmurs, chuckling. "Never mind Monteux—that paunchy lout ought to more often heed his own heart's whim! And remember—you are not the only one possessing such profound passion. For music."

I respond with a long sigh as he tucks his violin case under his arm and nods for me to follow him up the steps.

Out in the rotunda, we shy away from the remainder of loitering musicians and duck out by the stairwell foyer for the *Opéra's* closest exit into the street. The June sun, blazing high overhead and bathing all of Paris in a brilliant shower of light, spurs Nikolai into an animated discourse about the joys of the French countryside in the summer, but brings little solace to my mood. The heady commotion involved with the family reunion, Aunt Sophie and Anna both being so filled with gaiety and talkative news ever since their arrival over a week ago, has only seemed to inspire heightened susceptibility to emotion on my part, in addition to a sorry lack of wit. Then, intending to travel back over to London with us on the ferry, Uncle Ned and Aunt Mary showed up on a lark bare of a day later—strange behavior for my uncle, ever the meticulous, careful planner. Several days of watchful scrutiny have, however, imparted possible motive for such hasty frivolity: Uncle Ned does not seem well.

It is merely the subtlest change in pallor, the barest tightened strain about the eyes—so imperceptible yet, that even Father and Anna, trained as they both are in matters of health, have taken not the slightest notice. But between my uncle and myself, it remains an unspoken confirmation. Along with that other unspoken confirmation.

For nightly, his silent nods continue in response to my excuses as I slink away from his omniscient stares. Just as I have intuitively surmised his tentative hold on health, so has he unmistakably discerned the character of my lecherous foibles of the night.

In our hotel room, I shrug off Nikolai's invitation to join in the walk he and Anna have decided to take in the park, although not without earnest words of thanks. At least Father's wisdom seems to have prevailed—my cousin's dark moods of late have much diminished, our exchanges again approaching the old cordiality, the symptoms of his homesickness seemingly placated by Aunt Sophie's and Anna's near constant companionship in between the scheduled ballet performances. *See, you silly fool? Nikolai has scarce learnt a thing about your dreadful passions! There was no need to fret so.*

Such relief, however, proves short-lived. After peeking through the curtains to watch Nikolai meet Anna out on the street, I begin thumbing listlessly—as I have every afternoon during this whole long agonizing week—through my second most prized possession after the flute, Uncle Ned's book on the science of numbers. And yet again unchecked, my mind continues racing through the reams of metaphysical questions that I now no longer feel able to broach. *Dammit, life is not fair! Why can I not be who I truly am—in front of Uncle Ned; indeed, everyone—and not be ashamed? Why must I be forced into leading this secret double life?*

But the answer to that question is horribly simple: because what would the rest of my family think about country cousin Sasha if, like Uncle Ned, they entertained even the merest suspicion of the truth?

* * *

Perhaps wisely, *L'Après-midi d'un Faune* is omitted from the Covent Garden program, and of the newest ballets, only *Thamar* is performed in London, but the troupe plays to full houses for the remainder of the season nonetheless, the Britons ever remaining such faithful aficionados of theater and dance. Come the late summer of 1912, we return from London to the French coast for the opening of the new watering resort in Deauville, and from there move on through Germany again in the autumn, touring Cologne, Frankfurt, Munich, and Berlin. Finally, December finds us again in delightful Budapest, her arms straddling the snow-swept, hilly banks of the Danube as if thrown wide in gracious welcome, our gay parties and drinking escapades with old Hungarian friends starting up again as if there had been no pause from the revelries of the previous winter.

A couple of weeks before Christmas, in one of the more risque 'for gentlemen only' tavernhouses nestled inconspicuously within the quiet villas of Gellert Hill, I wander in between rows of dimly-lit, cloistered booths, and happen upon a dour-faced Klementi.

"You neglected to leave me a note," I say, throwing back my head and glaring down at his shoulders hunched so morosely over the table.

"I scarce cared to," he replies curtly, sipping his beer, not returning my glance.

"You could at least have the courtesy to be polite."

"You could at least have the courtesy to be honest!"

Crossing my arms, I stare off toward the direction of the merrymakers whooping it up out in front with the lively accordion band.

"Sit down, Sasha," Klementi then says—and when I make no move to do so, he slams his fist upon the table, ordering ferociously: "Dammit—*sit down!"*

With reluctance, I slide in across from him on the bench and begin fidgeting with, staring at my hands.

"Where were you last night?" he then demands. "I waited for over an hour."

Shrugging, I glance out once more toward the beer taps and the music.

"You conniving little slut!" he cries, yanking hold of my arm. "More likely, I should ask *with whom* you were—the oboes again, indeed *both* of them! *Yes, Sasha?"*

"So—what if I was?" I gasp out, laughing, shoving his hand away.

"Why! You insufferable—"

"What's a'matter, Klementi? Squeamish? Ha! Still no stomach for a little *ménage à trois?"*

Shuddering away as if I had tried infecting him with the plague, Klementi gropes clumsily out of the booth, seizing up his beer tankard and yelling down at me: "You are drunk!"

Again I stare down to my hands, and shrug.

"I do not care to see you anymore!" he shouts on, his voice trembling upon its breaking edge, his tall form looming through the shadows in pitiful boyish awkwardness.

"All right, fine! Because I no longer care to see you."

"All right, fine! Because I've been watching you for the past ten minutes, ever since you waltzed in on here all chummy with Alekseyev—again! Humph! And ever since, I've been watching the way you've been batting eyes at that swarthy Gypsy with the earring! So—go have him, why don't you? Or perhaps a couple more dozen like him, as crowds so seem to suit your fiendish taste."

As he storms off, I shout after him: "All right, fine! *Fine!*"

Grumbling curses, I stare off toward the music again, debating whether I truly am drunk, whether I honestly no longer want to see him anymore, and then whether I should leave. But at last I order another beer, and once more begin attempting to snare the wandering eye of the swarthy Gypsy with the earring.

Just as I do so, two lumbering forms crowd into the booth behind me, shaking the tufted back-panel vigorously above my head, and I hear someone who sounds remarkably like Sergei Diaghilev admonishing with low laughter to his companion: "I am telling you, Kolya—no man is faithful, and no woman ever pure. . . ."

With interest, I prick up my ears, listening in past the mounting blare of accordion noise as Diaghilev continues doing all the talking. The latest whispers have it that Nijinsky has fallen for a woman again—another false rumor, perhaps, heaped upon the dozens that hound the poor soul everywhere he goes, helpless captive as he is to stardom's whims. Still, it is notable to encounter Diaghilev in one of these tavernhouses; his preference for avoiding such 'barter markets of the flesh' is well-known to those of us within the 'Woodwind' circle. Like a frumpy old matron, Diaghilev remains astutely faithful to whatever lover he has taken at the time—in this case, for the past four years, none other but Nijinsky.

"This seat taken?" says a roughened voice in halting French.

I look upward to meet the hooded eyes of the swarthy Gypsy with the earring.

"No."

He scoots in beside me, orders a beer, and grins, saying: "You are very beautiful."

"Am I?" I look away and light a cigarette, offering him one.

He takes it, replying: "Indeed! Never have I seen such fiery, darkened hair."

With bold assurance, he reaches his hand outward, brushing his fingers across my cheek and smoothing a loose strand of hair back behind my ear.

"You remind me of someone," I tell him, thinking yearningly of Volodya. I catch my breath as his hand brushes across my cheek again.

"You have a name?" he whispers.

"Does it matter?"

"No."

I stub out my cigarette just as quickly as he stubs out his, our fingers winding together underneath the table and slowly sliding up one another's thighs—and in trembling haste, I snatch off my spectacles, tucking them down into my pocket. "Kiss me," I whisper into his ear.

As his lips find mine, I seize both arms around his neck, my mouth devouring his with violent, selfish greed, remnants of my voice escaping in harsh, low moans.

"Perhaps we should go somewhere," he murmurs at last.

"Yes, perhaps." But I latch onto him again, groping through the dark solely for the blind quest of the moment, sad hunter of a thousand touches ever only sated with the glory of fresh kill.

"Humph! Sounds like someone—or a couple of someones—are certainly having a high-rolling time behind us," I hear Diaghilev's voice blurt out with amusement from the booth behind.

Against my back, their coats rustle noisily as he and his companion proceed about taking their leave—but without care as to what anyone may think upon passing by, I go on ravenously kissing the Gypsy.

"Well, I must say, Kolya," says Diaghilev as he rounds the wall with his quiet friend, "was indeed a privilege, hearing you solo last night. Thank you for obliging me on short notice. Certainly, there can be no further question about moving you up to—uh, Kolya? Is something amiss?"

The other man, halting up short next to Diaghilev in front of our booth, lets out a horrified gasp of shock.

"Someone you know?" the Gypsy says to me, pulling abruptly back, while I wonder with irritation: *And does not this fool friend of Diaghilev's realize this is a 'Woodwind' bar?* Angrily, I stare up past the Gypsy's face.

Straight into that of my cousin, Nikolai.

Beyond the accordion music, the walls crash about us in a ringing, silent roar that no one else can hear. Nikolai, his jaw dropped, his eyes totally astounded, continues staring, saying not a single word as I stare back in horror, the Gypsy's voice grating on between us in comical, sing-song repetition: "Someone you know? Eh? Someone you happen to know? . . ."

I move first, seizing up my coat and cane in a whirlwind and barreling out for the front—while the Gypsy whines after me: "No, wait, fiery-headed one!" Diaghilev's voice then blares out like a trumpet above all others, protesting to Nikolai in a brusque, business-like tone: "But, Kolya! I thought we had not yet finished our discussion of the particulars. . . ."

Into the first cab outside I scramble, shouting at the driver in broken Magyar while waving out a wad of bills: "To the Hotel Duna across the bridge—and fast, by dammit! *Fast!"*

Barely lit, the street flies by in a rush of darkened cobblestones and stately old stucco houses. From the side window, I catch the barest glimpse of Nikolai stumbling out the front tavern doors—and also procuring a cab—just as mine rounds the first corner.

It is all I can think of: to get back to the hotel. *Get back to the hotel, fetch your things, and simply get out as fast as you can—oh, dear God! He knows! Christ in Heaven! What on earth am I going to do now?*

Gasping for breath in ragged heaves, beads of sweat pouring down my face and soaking into my collar, I burst like a madman into the hotel, shout for my key at the desk, soundly curse the elevator lift operator, although the damn contraption's slowness is hardly due to any fault of his, and finally—past a sighing wave of relief—jam the key with shaking fingers into the lock of my room's door.

There to be grabbed by two furious fists and thrown, head first, into the opposite wall.

Nikolai slams shut the door behind him with a menacing growl and bounds back for me yet again, wrenching me upward by my collar. "Goddamn it, get up!" he roars.

"H-How—" I mumble out, "how did you ever get back here so fast?"

But as he once more flings me headlong across the room, I recall—cursing inwardly—my cousin's familiarity with the city of Budapest, and probable ken to a quicker route through the back streets. Two years ago, he spent the autumn here, playing in a quartet and studying cello during the months that I was journeying across Europe and the Crimea with Father.

"Get up!" Nikolai shouts hoarsely again, both his hands closing this time around my neck.

"Stop it, blast you! You're choking me!"

"Only for starters! What I ought to do is rip you limb from limb! *Just what the hell were you doing in that bar?"*

At last he lets up enough to allow me to swallow—but all I can do is stare numbly back at him.

"Goddamn you, Sasha!" he then shouts, the brunt of his hand slamming into my face.

As I protest in pitiful, gasping squeals, he wrenches me upward again, banging my head with a heavy thud back into the wall. "No, don't tell me!" he rants on. "I saw perfectly well what you were doing in that bar! Jesus living Christ! And to think that I have spent *months* in delusion, like a gullible fool, talking myself out of all the obvious clues, ever denying the rumors, the snickering back-room whispers made about you—and Klementi Filippovich!"

His fist crashes into my face again.

"Stop it!" I yell, somehow managing to plow my left hook up into his jaw.

Stunned, Nikolai stumbles back and away. Papers, clothes, and reams of orchestrations then spin out wildly from the table as I overturn it in my desperate lunge for the door—but he clamps onto my left ankle, forcing me downward in a scream of pain before landing flat on top of me.

"Not *my* cousin—that's what I told everyone!" he shouts on, shaking my shoulders. "Told them no way possible could such outlandish rumors be true about *my* beloved, favorite cousin! Tell me," he then whispers down torridly into my face, "did you like it? When that faggot was kissing you? Huh? Did you like it—*faggot?"*

"Dammit—*get off me!"*

"Did you like it?"

"I said get off!"

As we start rolling, I manage to jam my elbow into his ear, and stumble up to my feet, making a quick stab into my coat pocket before he can grapple me once more to the floor. Panting like a hyena, I whirl around, my fingers closed upon the butt of my gun.

"Ha!" Nikolai mutters out sarcastically as I cock the hammer, "you needn't resort to such a dramatic gesture on my account, *mon cousin!* I know fully well how you carry that trusty Webley of yours with you everywhere."

"Then you know fully well that it's loaded—now, *dammit!* Don't you take another step toward me!"

"You are not going to kill me—" He inches forward.

"You want one of these shells shattering into your kneecap then, Zhelanov? I told you to get back!"

Halting up short and squinting—as if trying to fathom whether I really would shoot—Nikolai at last decides to let up on the assault, crosses his arms, and glares across the room at me in hateful, stony silence.

I suppose, deep down, I had always known that someday, somehow, he would find out. Shock on his part I had expected; to his disgust, I had shamefacedly resigned myself—but in no way at all had I ever been prepared for encountering from him such a seething outburst of rage. As I struggle, in the tense lull between us, to catch my breath and recover my thoughts, and as I stare into his furiously jealous eyes, the dawning horror of the true reason for such a show of anger—the *real* reason for him surrounding himself, all these years, with endless dozens of dollymops like so many tarnished fire screens—begins to seize in upon me, the melted droplets from truth's icicle slowly creeping under my every nerve. I go cold to the rigid bone, my fingers quavering upon the gun's trigger-guard as I gasp out in amazement: "M-My God! Perhaps you should tell *me*—just what the hell *you* were doing? In that bar?"

"Me?" His eyebrows shoot upward in surprise—and upon gauging my expression, he bursts out: "Oh, Lord God! You think I'm like—like you? Diaghilev wanted to talk business—I let him choose where. Humph! And you think I've never been in a faggot bar before? Nor seen faggots pawing over each other? It's worth a laugh once in awhile, you know."

"Is it—"

"Yes, indeed!"

"—Kolya?"

Nikolai's lips turn stark white, his eyes honing in with the yen to commit murder.

"It was *you* he was so addressing—yes? *Kolya?"*

"Oh, Blessed God—you disgust me!" he rasps back, pointing a stiff, accusatory finger at my face. "Seryozha insists upon calling all close associates by their common nicknames—"

"Seryozha!" I burst out. "You call him *Seryozha?* While to the rest of us, he is still M'sieur Diaghilev—or at the very most, Sergei Pavlovich? You call him Seryozha, now? *Do you? Kolya?"*

"Bloody Christ in Heaven!" he shouts back, flushed to the teeth with rage. "How dare you have the gall to make such an insinuation!"

"And how dare you throw me around this room like I was naught but a stinking gunnysack, calling me a fag—"

"I intend to do a whole helluva lot more than that, once I get my hands on you again! You treacherous little—"

"—when you have naught but just as much a faggot heart *yourself!*"

Letting out a thundering roar, Nikolai leaps toward me again as I whirl back and shove the gun straight for his face, screaming: "Get out, damn you! Get out of here—*now!*"

"You—you are not going to get away with such accusations! You sickened, perverted little—"

"Apparently, I am not any more perverted than you! Now, blast it—*get out!*"

"—it's—it's been not months, but *years*, Sasha—yes?" he then exclaims with a shrill, incredulous gasp. "Ha! Oh, my God—what a fool I've been! And—and just how long have you been fucking around with all the other boys, anyway, then, Sasha? Huh? Since you were fifteen? Sixteen?"

"Shut up!"

"Is that why you disappeared the summer of 1907?" he shouts on. "Was that your first little tryst, Sasha? *Was that what all the mystery was about?*"

"Goddamn you, Nikolai—shut up and get the fuck out of here!"

Flinging open the door, he turns around one last time, choking out between clenched teeth: *"I—I hate your stinking, filth-ridden guts, Sekovsky!"*

Without looking back, he strides furiously away—and I stumble out the door, screaming after him down the hall for all the world to hear: "Goddamn it! *Nobody calls you Kolya!*"

Several other hotel room doors crack open in response to the commotion, wary faces peeking out as I nervously pocket the gun. Mopping the drench of sweat from my brow with the sleeve of my coat, I watch Nikolai disappear through the doors to the elevator lift; watch the lift as it slowly creaks down its rickety wrought-iron shaft, descending to the lower floors.

Near blinded by tears, I then grope my way back into our room, slam shut the door, and start packing.

CHAPTER SIX

White Magic, Black Hole

I emerge from my walk in the woods to find Father bent over a hive-body box just outside the back porch, his face covered with the wire veil, the smoke-pot in his hand steaming vigorously down into the combs. "You'd best stay out of there if you value your life," he says as I hurry for the kitchen door.

"Knew I smelled rum syrup," I answer, grinning. "And besides," I add as he lifts one of the crawling bee-covered combs out from the hive, "looks like, if I value my life, that I'd best get out of here instead."

"Naught but a few bees, Sasha," he counters, laughing. "Remember what Pavel always told you? 'Fear of bees is only the demon queen dancing in the eye of your fettered mind—'"

"Uh-huh." Shaking my head, I slip in quietly through the kitchen door.

The coast is clear: low murmurs of feminine voices rattle distantly from the door to the servants' quarters down by the woodroom. Taking care not to thump my cane upon the floor, I sneak across the kitchen toward the luscious rum-soaked cake that for half an hour has sorely been tempting my nose—and like a precocious ten-year old, stick my finger into the icing.

"Akkh! Sasha—git out o' there!" Marnya duly descends, whacking furiously at my hands.

"Oh, come, Matushka! Just a little taste—"

"Stay out o' it, I tell ye! That's made special fer tonight's Maytide supper, ye thievin' robber bandit!"

"But, Matushka!" Reaching above her head, I poke my finger out for the cake once more, lancing a second sugary dollop as she hollers out: "*Akkh!* And will ye never grow up, lad? Now ye quit pokin' like the devil hisself at God's fruits o' my labor, an' git out o' here!"

Laughing, I stumble back for the porch as she starts threatening me with her broom handle. "All right, Matushka—all right! See? I am going."

"Said you were risking your life," Father reminds me, grinning up from the honey bucket, the lid now snapped back onto the hive-body box and the wire veil removed from his face.

Before I can needle him with a joke in reply, we both prick up our ears to the sound of hoofbeats closing in from the estate house road. "That'll be Vliny back from town," says Father.

"With the mail—Lord be praised!" I cry, spinning around in a fluster. "Oh, I hope . . . ."

Back in the kitchen, Marnya has disappeared, the rum cake presumably removed to a safer haven. Nervously, I start pacing back and forth in front of the table, wringing my hands. Sipping from his glass of tea and licking stray dabs of honey from his fingers, Father eyes me from his chair, asking: "You think the letter would have arrived so soon?"

"I was told this week, for a certainty."

Amidst an uproar of wild feminine commotion—Tereza and Eva both pouncing upon him for their requisite items from town—Vliny at last appears in the kitchen doorway with Marnya clucking affectionately at his heels. "Ahem! Fer one Count Aleksandr Sekovsky!" he bellows out, waving an officially stamped letter. "From the—ahem! Maryinsky Theater of Opera and Ballet—"

I seize the envelope from his hand and rip it open, my eyes scanning double images in my excitement. "Yes!" I gasp out, overjoyed. "Oh, Papa—I got it!"

"Well, read the letter to us, Sasha!" Father cries insistently.

"Well, ahem! It simply says:

"Dear Count Sekovsky:

This notice is to confirm your appointment as third chair flute with the Maryinsky Theater Orchestra. As you know, rehearsals for the autumn pre-season festivities commence the first week of June. . . .

"And then it simply goes on with relevant details. It bears the signature of M'sieur Teliakovsky himself as Imperial Theaters Director—oh, Papa! All those interviews and auditions—throughout long months that I was certain I had not a single chance. Everyone, so the rumors go, *must* be a graduate of one of the Conservatories! The Maryinsky is—oh, deep down, what I have always wanted, ever since I was a child, once you enrolled me at May's. That was when I first caught chance to frequent Petersburg theaters . . . Lord, this is glorious, marvelous beyond compare!"

"Well, congratulations, Aleksandr." Breaking into a fond grin, Father reaches up to shake my hand.

"Yaa, and our Sasha will take grand Petersburg fer a composer's whirl yet!" Vliny exclaims in a booming voice, thumping his chest imperiously after handing over to Father the remainder of the mail.

The bottom of the stack yields an oversized package which, after a hesitant glance upward, Father holds out toward me.

"From whom?" I demand, frowning. "I was not expecting any parcels."

"Looks like from Paris," he replies with a shrug.

I freeze, staring down at the familiar stylish script of Nikolai Zhelanov.

"I do not want it! Throw it into the stove," I tell him brusquely, snatching up my letter and bounding out for the drawing room.

Father barrels after me, exclaiming: "But he has written quite plainly: *contains musical score*—look, right here beneath the address! That must be why he sent such a large package. Oh, for God's sake, boy—Sasha!"

Crossing my arms, I glare out past the drapery sheers of the drawing room windows, attempting to ignore Father's pleas.

Five months. Five months of no letters, not even a note—nor any hint that our prior closeness ever existed. As if all the years, the hopes, the dreams, our fervent youthful desires spouted off in nightly exchanged whispers never were shared. As if the many jaunts to Paris, the wonder of the Diaghilev ballets, our joy at securing seats within the orchestra—as if none of it ever occurred. As if our past anchored far into the earliest years of boyhood romps and bold discoveries now was naught but a hollowed-out slate.

"Well!" Father bellows at me in irritation. "Sulk, then—but the Saints help you! Lord, must it always be feast or famine with you and Nikolai? Either lifelong brothers barely parted, or else forever clawing at one another's throats! And usually over naught but some inane little spat—"

"Papa, this is more than a mere spat!" I shout, turning upon him.

"Oh, Sasha—give it up!" he fumes back at me. "Still I must make endless guilty excuses to your aunt about last Christmastide, about Easter—"

"You yourself admitted to enjoying the Liturgy both times here in Novgorod at St. Sofiya's."

"Well—like it or not, young man, your newly acquired position at the Maryinsky will hail you straight back to the Zhelanovs' Petersburg."

"And as I told you, I fully intend to retain a flat of my own, far from the Zhukovskaya townhouse."

"Oh, God's balls, Sasha!" he cries out in exasperation. "Four years ago, you hid yourself away like a mole on account of me. Can't you see you're following the same course now all over again with your cousin?"

"Papa, stay out of my business, will you? This is different—"

"No, it is not! And I am telling you, Aleksandr Sekovsky—someday you are going to wake up and regret all your months spent cold-shouldering members of your own family. Humph! Now, if you refuse to accept this package that your cousin has taken such trouble to send you from Paris, I intend to open it myself!"

Warily, I hedge a glance at his resolute expression. The months of Nikolai's silence have, at least so far, disproved any malicious intent on my cousin's part to inform Father as to the peculiarities of my escapades. Deciding it best to be the first to encounter any sudden revelations, I shuffle back across the room and reluctantly take the package from Father's outstretched arms.

True to the labeling, the parcel contains a complete musical score—with one hastily scrawled note tacked onto the outer cover:

*All right. I know you are still furious with me, and quite frankly, I am still incensed beyond all mortal measure at you. But no matter what else has come between us, I still respect you as a musician. Months have I let pass through the rehearsals, but in good conscience, I could no longer continue without apprising you of Stravinsky's latest monstrosity. I mean, my God, Sasha—*look *at it!*

The première *is set for May 29th (Paris calendar). I can acquire tickets for you and Uncle Misha if you so choose.*

Sincerely,
N.
Paris
April 20/May 3, 1913

Sighing, I stare down at the piece's wood-block printed title: *Le Sacre du Printemps*.

"*The Rite of Spring*?" Father asks behind my shoulder.

"Yes. Nikolai declares it Stravinsky's 'latest monstrosity.' And—" At last, my interest piqued, I begin leafing through the music—my breath catching in my throat upon sight of the very first measures, my heart coming near to a standstill, my voice halting out in a stunned murmur of: "Oh, my God . . . ."

Eyebrows raised, Father bustles in behind me as I yank the sheets apart and begin laying them out one by one for comparative survey across the top of the piano. "Jesus God in Heaven!" I cry at last, staring from one end of the piano top to the other, astounded by such travesty. "I cannot believe it—*look* at this!" Waving frantically between all the ghastly, careening notations, I attempt to explain to Father my acute dismay: "Is all naught but—but the pure sublimity of Nikolai's laments about Stravinsky's anarchic dissonances! Each measure is blatantly percussive . . . my God, the entire score is rhythmically unbalanced! He constantly changes the time signatures—look at this! And see how he only occasionally weaves in a bare snatch of melody? And fathom the size of the orchestra he wants for it: eight horns, five trumpets, three trombones, two tubas, and . . . quintuple woodwind! For God's sake, the flute section with *two* piccolos—Jesus, they'll sound like a roost of screeching birds! My God—and Diaghilev expects to perform *this* in Paris? After the furor that broke out over Nijinsky's *Faune?"*

"Well," Father observes with a shrug, "that had more to do with the erotic dancing than with Debussy's score."

"And exactly what kind of pirouettes are the ballerinas supposed to perform to this?"

Thoughtfully fingering the close-clipped hairs of his beard, Father peers down at Nikolai's note. "A shame your cousin neglected to include any layouts for the choreography," he murmurs. And then, an impish grin stealing across his face, he looks up and makes a deliberate effort to catch my eye, saying: "But he did say that he could acquire tickets."

"Oh, no!" I burst out at him, wagging a warning finger. In a huff, I gather up the scoresheets and slam them down in one stack atop the piano, muttering: "Oh, no, you don't, Papa."

"But, Sasha . . . ."

For all the remainder of the afternoon, and then through supper, he hounds, pleads, whines—cavorts on with polemics like a pumped-up firebrand entrenched in the heat of an impassioned political debate—

to the point where I even lose all interest in Marnya's rum-soaked dessert and finally throw up my hands, stomping away from the table without begging the least polite excuse.

Outside in the twilight, past the woodroom, I wearily take a seat on a rotting stump and pull off my boot, glowering up at Father yet again as he follows. From my pocket, I then pull out the small flattened pinewood knob which I have spent all winter honing with my penknife, fashioning the grain of the wood down to velvety smooth perfection. Once again I peer across its surface with a critical eye before tucking it under the arch of my left foot and pulling back on my boot.

"That was one ingenious idea," Father observes, watching from the doorway as he lights up his pipe.

"Yes, at least it allows me to move about for a time without assistance." Leaving the cane and my spectacles on the stump, I snatch up the axe and head for the wood pile.

"Sasha, why don't you come to your senses?" Father prattles on, ambling out from the doorway, his smoke rings drifting off in tangy, pungent rifts against the cooling night air. "There is no sufficient reason in all the world for you to be harboring such ill will toward Nikolai—"

"I do not want to talk anymore about why I am angry at Nikolai! *All right?"*

The axe slams down, splintering apart the log.

Father rolls his eyes, muttering: "Humph! Like Father, like son! Dear God in Heaven, save us both."

"Papa! Will you just go back into the house? *Please?"*

Again the axe slams down.

I chop wood in silence, while he watches in silence, the dusky sunset melting its way toward cover of starry darkness. At last I pull off my shirt, mopping my brow with it before throwing it at him and once more vehemently ordering him back into the house.

Acquiescence proves most short-lived. He promptly returns with Nikolai's letter, waving it out with tenacious renewed enthusiasm. "You know you want to go," he insists, ducking down and peering up at me with a knowing grin.

Again the axe slams down. "Papa, for God's sake! Get out of there before you start catching splinters in your eyes—"

"Blast it, and will you stop chopping this damned wood? All winter have you been chopping away like a madman. We've enough stacked up now to last us half into next year. Besides, you'll ruin your hands, you foolish oaf! You want to show up at the Maryinsky with blisters plaguing those prize fingers?"

"Papa, I am not going back to Paris!"

"Oh, yes!" he bursts out with a dramatic, grinning flourish. "None like the banks of the Seine in the springtime—admit it, you want to go near as much as I do!" Waving Nikolai's letter in under my nose, he forces me to hold up on the axe. "You love those avant-garde ballets! And I know you'd scarce mind seeing a furor break out over Stravinsky's music."

Exasperated, I throw down the axe and plant my hands on both hips, glaring across at him through fading echoes of the twilight. Inside, the windows start to light up one by one as Marnya hurries from room to room, setting the oil lamps.

"Well, what have we?" Father bellows out, gleefully triumphant. "About two weeks before the *première?* Then another couple to return in time for your Maryinsky rehearsals? Well, God's teeth, my boy—don't just stand there gawking at your old papa! Put that axe up, get back into the house, and start packing! . . ."

* * *

A low hush sweeps across the crowd as the lights go dim and the curtain rises on the primitive, foliage-strewn sets of *Le Sacre du Printemps*.

On the stage, about forty dancers, all garbed in barbaric tribal kaftans, the women sporting patterned headbands caught over loosely flowing hair, the men crowned with garish angular fur hats, begin not dancing, but convulsing—as eerie, pounding chords from the shuddering rhythm of their feet begin to fill the *Théâtre des Champs-Elysées* from end to quaking end. Then, squalling out in a higher register than I had ever imagined possible, the notes of a lone bassoon shear through the air in a slate-scoring, chalky caw—as I clutch my palm up to my brow and scrunch down low in my seat, muttering: "Oh, my God . . . ."

"What did I tell you?" Father gasps with delight, seizing onto my arm.

If an entire row of cannon volleys had been fired from point-blank range, the sound could not be more deafening. In an instant, every person in the hall seems to spring out from every respective seat, the entire audience appearing to have taken *The Rite of Spring* experiment as a directed affront. Together with upper loges, the whole main floor erupts at once into a hail of noise lanced with boos, hisses, and furious shouts, hoots and catcalls abounding from every corner of the theater and escalating in a gradual punitive climb until, incredibly, even the orchestra can scarce any longer be heard above the uproar! Craning my neck to see, I catch a glimpse beyond the pit partition of the back of Maestro Monteux's dark brunet head shaking back and forth in panicked spurts in his attempt to signal someone in the wings. The noise begins to abate slightly when the lights are suddenly put back up—but once lowered again, the whole pandemonium only breaks out with freshened caustic vigor. As the music mounts ever upward into a dissonant clash of flute, bassoon, and oboe trills, gentlemen from both above and below begin jumping up and down upon their seats, haranguing each other, Diaghilev, Stravinsky, the dancers, and the orchestra without the slightest pause for mercy.

"Papa, come!" I cry, snatching hold of his arm. "We must try to find our way out of here—"

"Not on your life!" he bellows, shaking me off. "Hey you!" he then calls in an angry huff to three tophatted upstarts baiting each other with torrid shouts in the row before ours. "Sit down and watch the ballet, you lard-brained, loudmouthed numskulls! Sit down!"

Without cessation, the tumultuous uproar continues: row by row, people cup their hands around shouts, stomp their feet, and wave their arms, slamming hats, pocketbooks, and fists both stern and dainty onto armrests, their paper playbills scattering to the floor in a voluminous tidal flurry of protest. From the wings, Diaghilev himself finally appears in his dapper black evening tux, and after waving at Monteux and the orchestra to continue playing no matter what, he cups his hands about his mouth and shouts down to the audience: "Listen first! Whistle afterward! *Afterward!"* Then, as if on prompted cue, all heads in our section turn abruptly upward toward the loges to watch an elegant *demoiselle* adorned in yards of chiffon and boa feathers stand up and slap across the face the gentleman hissing so loudly in the box adjoining hers—which prompts her escort to provoke a heated confrontation culminating in an exchange of cards for a duel!

"Dear Lord God in Heaven!" Father bursts out, wide-eyed. "This is even better than that whole queue of belly dancers that time in Sevastopol! . . ."

"Belly dancers?" I shriek out, aghast.

"Never you mind!"

"Papa, we have got to get out of here! This is naught but a full-scale riot!"

"Oh, Sasha—calm down. Hey, you!" he then thunders out, stomping his feet and wildly waving along with everyone else. "Get down so I can see! Yes, you—up there! Get down, I say. Get down!"

Across the floor, a man with a seething, reddened face proceeds to snatch up his cane and pummel it down into the bobbing top hat of his neighbor—after which, to my blanched astonishment, Father flings his arm across my lap, seizing up my cane while yelling: "Give me that!"

"Papa—what on earth are you doing?"

"Get down, all of you!" he roars, jumping up and swinging the cane out in a wide, circling flourish that topples several hats and barely misses near to a dozen heads.

"Papa! *Have you lost your mind?"*

Enraged, I grapple him and the swinging cane to a furious stop, shouting down his clamor of protestations while at the same time apologizing profusely to the sudden mob that descends upon us: "No harm intended! No offense meant—please, I am very sorry! Gentlemen—surely we can be reasonable? Forgive my erring old father! He is eighty-two years old, and ofttimes rather addled in the head. . . ."

Somehow, I manage to drag Father with me past the undulating rows of theater patrons—and at the outside aisle, as the theater lights suddenly start flashing on and off repeatedly, we launch into our own exchange of shouts. "How dare you patronize me like a doddering old man!" he roars.

"I patronize you like a doddering old man because you *are* a doddering old man!" I shout back, shaking both fists at him blindly. "My Lord, Papa—what if you had hit someone? For God's sake, you are a doctor! Surely, you more than most of us know what damage such a blow on the head can impart!"

Paling, Father ducks away—but shrugs off my remaining scoldings with an imperious grasp to his lapels. "Humph! Well, might I remind you that I do not turn eighty-two until November!"

"All right! You do not turn eighty-two until November!" I shout back into his face, glaring him down in a quivering spate of rage.

In reply, Father glances back at the crowd, his face breaking into an impish grin.

"And just *what* is so bleating funny?" I exclaim in exasperation.

"You. Me. All of this!" he cries, laughing—then to add with a quick wave of his hand: "I mean, my God, Sasha! *Look* at these people."

Past his fingers, I stare out toward the bustling main theater floor, the whole span of it filled to the brim with outraged Parisian *patrons des arts* all yet stomping, hooting, and carrying on like a band of savage gorillas in some fabled African wasteland. Unable to help myself, I also break into a slow grin.

"You know," I murmur to Father, my hand shielded across my mouth, "it is rather amusing."

"Amusing, my ass!" he retorts. "This is positively hilarious! Ha! And for what better revelry could I insist upon dragging you across the Continent? Imagine! A bunch of grown people."

From that point on, we never do return to our seats, but instead prowl around between one aisle exit and another, slowly working our way as close as possible toward the stage, intent the both of us upon obtaining the best views of both ballet and audience. Nudging me and guffawing with immense enjoyment, Father starts poking fun at various couples. "Look at this lout with the twisted yellow cravat and fat jowls of a bulldog!" he exclaims, pointing across the rows of seats at yet another arm-waving gentleman. "And God save us from his wife in all the tassels! Look at her: tassel headdress, tassel earrings, tassel fringes down to her toes . . . ."

Nodding with only half an ear, I stare beyond Father toward the stage. From the wings, Nijinsky can just barely be seen, standing up on a chair and shouting out the rhythm toward the dancers, who seem to be having difficulty staying in time to the music, which we ourselves can still barely hear above the commotion. And yet it is the nuances of this music, strange and wild and like nothing that I have ever before encountered, which suddenly seize upon me with a grip of tingling awe—for this is no simple Maytide affectation, no transitional rite of traded yearly pleasantries, this behemoth concoction of Stravinsky's. Instead, this is a spring borne of raw, primordial lust, blood-wet and kicking, a holy avatar shuddering into the world past screams of agony from the crown of ancient power. "You know," I murmur to Father, "perhaps I was overhasty in my first judgments of the score. I am beginning to sense Stravinsky's underlying motive—and some of these movements are not wholly unlike the oriental innovations of Debussy."

"What, have you gone daft, boy?" Father retorts, laughing. "This is the most outrageous farce I have ever seen! Oh, yes—always leave it to Diaghilev. . . ."

At the scene change, the *gendarmes* troop in and begin ejecting demonstrators, but the furor only continues to mount rampantly, and soon enough, Igor Stravinsky himself, his jaw grimly set, his head thrust angrily downward, marches on out of the theater. Despite Monteux's still desperate glances from the pit and the fact that many of the women dancers appear near ready to succumb to tears, the orchestra continues playing and the ballet goes doggedly on: the young girls rush in a magic circle around the Chosen Virgin, followed by an awkward series of ritual dances led by the old men of the tribe. Then all surround the Virgin, dress her in the sacrificial robes—and to appease the Mighty Lord of the Seasons, the girl mounts her flower-laden altar, where she proceeds to whirl around in a frenzy of hysterical, jerking movements, image of the agony and the ecstasy dancing herself straight to death.

After half an hour, it is all over. We stay behind the departing crowd in order that I might pay proper respects to my old adversary, Maestro Monteux. Afterward, when we wander out through one of the airy vestibules, Father pokes his finger with glee into my arm, declaring staunchly: "Believe, me, Sashenka! Someday, you are going to tell your grandchildren stories about this! . . ."

I turn to upbraid him with a teasing remark—but my smile fades the moment I catch sight of Nikolai.

Impeccably dressed, his violin case tucked beneath one arm—and the gloved hand of a fluttery *demoiselle* wrapped within the other—he stands beside one of the exit doors, watching for us from the corner of his eye, while throngs of theater-goers jostle past him.

"Uh, I believe I'd best go round up the Comte's Model T," says Father abruptly.

"No, Papa—wait!"

But he waves me off, abruptly vanishing within the heads of the crowd.

Slowly, Nikolai and his lady companion inch their way in my direction. With his usual ease, he keeps her immersed in conversation, smiling down and bestowing clever winks while hanging upon her every word.

I stare to the floor, bristling one more time against the casual manner he has affected in my presence with such perfect compulsion during these last two days, ever since Father and I first arrived. In no way at all does he seem to have suffered as I have during our separation: five months of tortured, sleepless nights. And of poring—word by awful, accusing word—over our fateful confrontation. Only to be met with dark confusion and growing spells of doubt: over whether I might have been horridly, foolishly wrong—over whether, in the heat of the moment, I jumped to the most obvious of conclusions, and was in fact gravely mistaken about my cousin's relations with Diaghilev—and indeed with other men. The manner in which he continues fawning so affectionately over the girl seems to make paramount the truth of my misjudgment—but despite the evidence, a vague sense of unease still pervades deep within my soul, inscrutable and unfathomable as the call of a bell in the fog. Of course, over the years, I too have stood many a time with a woman—usually one of the understudy ballerinas—on my arm, countless little charades always kept up for the sake of appearances. Watching Nikolai, I cannot help but recall the pandemic words of Klementi during one of our better times: 'Akkh! We're the lucky ones, you know. Some gents take years burying themselves in hundreds of floozies before ever admitting they'd eye another man. . . .'

Yes, dozens of times have I watched or heard Nikolai with women in whorehouses. At just what point is the line traversed? Does such a relentless pursuit of women ever evolve into a longing for men? *Blast it! Is my cousin like me or not? Why can I still not tell for certain? And why, during these long months, have I been so obsessed to truly know?*

"Sasha," Nikolai says, nodding.

Politely, I nod back as he adds: "Allow me to introduce Elena Feliksovna Trebytova, a new understudy just taken on by the Company. My dear, allow me to introduce to you my cousin. . . ."

At last, the pleasantries dispensed with, the girl spies her parents waving from the crowd and wanders off after making much gushing, talkative excuse.

Upon which Nikolai and I stare one another down, our eyes locked in a silent hold of challenge as continued droves of people swarm past us and out from the theater.

"Well—again, congratulations on your appointment to the Maryinsky," he says finally, extending his hand.

I shake it hurriedly, looking away. "Again, thank you." With deliberation, I neglect to make any inquiry regarding the atmosphere down in the orchestra pit during the performance—although for a certainty, I am still dying to know how on earth everyone managed to retain their concentration amidst all the commotion. "So," I say with a toss of my head, "I suppose, after the season ends here, that you will once again be off with the Company to London?"

"Yes, indeed. Despite our tenure there during Lententide, the famished Britons are already clamoring for a reprise."

"And from there, I hear, you are all voyaging to South America?"

"Oh, yes—a great stroke of luck! For years, I have been eager to try the ocean liners. And it shall be most fascinating to see Rio. Were you not now obliged to the Maryinsky," he then says loudly, "I'd urge you to come along." Breaking into a strained grin, Nikolai begins trading nods with his cousin Boris and an attendant group of players from the brass section, all of whom pass by within close earshot. "The woodwinds, I believe," he adds with a shrug, "are still short a second alternate."

He is, of course, only elaborating for the benefit of decorum in front of colleagues.

"Yes, well," I reply. "Thank you once again for procuring the tickets. Father greatly enjoyed the performance." Coloring in spite of myself, I extend my hand.

He shakes it hurriedly.

And we stand staring at one another's toes as Elena Feliksovna, with her parents in tow, returns full of breathless plans for a grand dinner at the *Viel.* After another lengthy round of introductions, Nikolai sends her on ahead with them—and again we succumb to a mutual shoe inspection. The remainder of the crowd continues funnelling out, at last trickling down to stragglers first in groups, then in pairs, then to only one or two here or there, their tapping footsteps mimicking our heart-beats in violently quick staccato across the crisply snapping tile.

"Well." Finally, Nikolai breaks the silence with a forced nod. "As always, best of luck to you in your professional endeavors, *mon cousin.*"

Abruptly turning on his heel, he strides off for the doors.

"Nikolai!"

He stops—shoulders squared, his fingers flexing, his chin caught sharply to the air. And then it is only the briefest glance backward that he makes, but telling in its anguish: the mask expunged, an overwhelming crush of sorrow churning from deep within those pensive gray eyes. Tearing his gaze away from me with a gnashing grimace as if severing some sort of invisible psychic cord long strung between the two of us, he then bolts on out through the doors, flinging them forward with a resolute shove—and without once looking back.

I clench my fists, grit my teeth, shut my eyes. *Goddamn you, Sasha—run after! And apologize! Whether you be right or wrong—whether his inclinations mirror yours or no—swallow your stubborn pride, run after him as fast as you can, and apologize!*

But I simply cannot. No further hesitation on his part bequeaths like inaction on mine; it is over. Fifteen years of constant friendship—that long has it been since the *Maslenitsa* festivals when I was six and my cousin eight, and he first began to include me in the curbstone street games outside the Zhukovskaya townhouse, then allowing me to tag along with him to the puppet shows and snowy carnival rides at the city fairs. Fifteen years of coincident natural instincts and camaraderie amidst the lofty innuendoes of our one true passion and lover above all others, man or woman: *music*. Fifteen years now lost—forever—within the charred vortex of those last murderously shouted words: *'I hate your stinking, filth-ridden guts, Sekovsky . . .'*

The Maryinsky now seems only the faintest consolation. It is all over—before it ever had a chance to begin. . . .

* * *

Oh, God . . . .

The overture portends only a hurried poetic hint of that which is to come, and fades off as the curtain rises toward a collection of more mundane plyings: the quick tempo for the celebration of the Prince's coming of age; the lengthy *pas de trois* followed by the solos in two/four and six/eight time; the Coda, the waltz, the little comedy *pas d'action;* and finally the symphonic conclusion with the merry *Danse des Coupes*. And then it starts: mournful, plaintive hauntings of that lone oboe cascading upward in a willowy majestic climb, followed by harp, strings, and horns—and then my heart bursting near into a thousand jagged pieces—until at last I breathe out a sigh of relief, thanking dear God in His wisdom for the intermission between the First and Second Acts.

But even after a whole ten minutes in the anteroom, gulping through prana breathing exercises as Uncle Ned once taught me, my pulse still threatens early death; my bowels remain hung in twisted, grinding knots. Back out in the pit, polite applause echoes in due course from the tiers of the audience; the overture to the Second Act begins. My fingers harden to ice, the piccolo caught atremble within their grasp. As the oboe climbs again, I ask myself through a flood of pain how I can expect to survive much longer; I ask why the music, the glory of these notes never seemed so profound with the many lights blazing overhead during our sessions at rehearsal. I tell myself that I am a professional, whatever the devil that is supposed to mean; I tell myself that I *will* be calm and composed, *dammit!* And somehow, on the outside—despite the upsweep of violins into their orgiastic thrill of glory—somehow I manage to remain rigidly in control of my emotions simply because I keep telling myself that I am. But on the inside—on the *inside*—my soul is churning apart. Because the sound keeps mounting, and I keep dying, worse each time: bitter phoenix aching toward rebirth within its fiery ashes; helpless captive of twisted fate and impossible, secret longings; lonely wanderer ever so desperately yearning for the touch of true hearth, true home. Again I peek over toward the second violins, but he is not there. No, he is far away—in Paris. Or probably in London by now—and the more I think about the hopeless distance, both in miles and misunderstanding, strewn between the two of us, the more I fear I will never be able to bear this moment, this night, the entire rest of my life. Two years ago, when I broke up over this very music in Covent Garden; last year in Paris, when I did the same thing in rehearsal over Debussy, he—out of all of them—was the only soul who understood.

Fortunately, the overture ends and the curtain rises upon the Second Act. But no sooner am I breathing easier, no sooner am I settling down and beginning to concentrate fully, like I am supposed to, upon the piccolo's upper-page measures, than a gasp of awe emits from the audience. Odette, the Swan—of course—has appeared. Throw me the crossbow from the stage, and I will gladly shoot her! But there is no rescue, no justice, no devil's advocate of recompense. Holy and ethereal, she proceeds to capture the heart of the unwary Prince—then persuading him along with her toward their famous romantic *pas de deux*. Which is accompanied by that famous romantic solo of the violin.

How many times have I heard him play it? And not only this, but all the solo pieces: Rimsky's quavering *Sheherazade* voice in triplets; Massenet's *Meditation* from *Thaïs*; Mendelssohn's *Allegretto non troppo*; Wieniawski's *Romance*; Tchaikovsky's haunting *Concerto in D Major*—and the countless others with which he once so continually enthralled me? How many times have I watched him, his whole being strung to the bone with fierce concentration—oblivious to me, time, space, everything else in the world—while focused solely upon the strings and the bow, his fingers dancing upon the wood of the neck like magic, his perspiration dripping into the groove of the chinrest like water, his hair flying through the air and teasing at his face, his collar, his eyes, at the quivering lobes of his ears? *Oh, goddamn you, Nikolai Zhelanov! Why don't I simply break free of all constraint and finally admit it? Why can I not stop—not stop!—l-l-loving you? . . .*

Again I tell myself that this, status and fulfillment—and not idle, offhand chances to play on hurried notice in an ever-changing flux of foreign cities—is what I wanted. This *is* what I have always wanted: to work every day at the Maryinsky! To bask each and every eve within this theater of theaters' creamy blue velvet hues strung aloft past gilt bas-reliefs adorning every rococo wall, a delicate hot-house aroma from potted ferns lingering about every corridor, the soul of Russia imbued within this very earth once wooed by the great Tchaikovsky himself in glittering pinnacles of ballet. This, yes, is what I have *always* wanted. . . .

Father, of course, hovers in a box up above, his seat procured from an old friend in the Tsar's Horse Guards, his opera glasses trained in the usual direction. And the thought of his constant scrutiny is the only strength that saves my sanity and manages to guide me shakily through the remainder of the Second Act.

Later, I become calmer: Acts Three and Four have always seemed by comparison anticlimactic. It is only the famous Act Two of *Swan Lake* which casts upon me such a bitter, merciless spell. At the end, when we are motioned to rise, I bow along with my fellow musicians, although due to my flighty concentration, I scarce feel deserving of applause. Then we file out. I clean my piccolo. I become the perfect masked harlequin, accepting compliments and trading quips with possible new friends. Finally, at the padded withdrawing room, where I ask for my gloves and hat, Father saunters gaily down from the stairs.

"Stupendous, I tell you! It was—oh, my heavens, *Sasha?* Are you all right? My Lord, boy—you're white as a sheet!"

"Simply nerves," I say, forcing a smile. "You know how very hectic has been the schedule. So—did you enjoy the performance?"

"Oh, immensely! Of course, during the *pas de six* in the Third Act, I would have considered a few adjustments. . . ."

He continues commenting on the choreography, while I slip on my gloves and stare toward the entrance doors. And then I catch sight of someone who causes my guilty envisionings of Nikolai to shatter like so much frail glass.

Volodya.

Yes, Volodya. His bearing regal, his manners flawless, his sinewy form clad to the hilt in pressed black evening tux, white waistcoat, wing-tipped shoes, and fashionably jaunty top hat. Strolling past the loiterers filling the lobby of the Maryinsky as if a patron of an Imperial box ever since he was weaned, he spins around the brass handle of his walking stick, fingers his pencil-thin moustache with debonair flair, and gallantly eyes several ladies while droning on in a somber, business-like tone to his companion.

Sheremetev. One Ilarion Pavlovich.

The breath of ice still torturing my fingers from the ballet begins, like poison, slowly flashing up my veins and dripping down into my chest. I stand staring, unbelieving, both at the incongruity and the implications, as Volodya eases his way past the nodding doorman and out the main theater exit. But Sheremetev turns at the last moment to light up a cigar—and looks straight at me.

With total recognition. And as if he had fully expected to see me standing just a bare twenty feet away from him. As if he had known, all during these past few moments, of my presence lingering so near to his.

Effigy of politeness, he proffers a gracious nod, his eyes sweeping me up and down with only the faintest flick of emphasis. And then, calling after Volodya in an impatient huff, he too disappears through the doors.

Father interrupts his discourse on the choreography, following my gaze. "Someone you know?" he inquires.

Without hesitation, I pull on my hat, snatch up my cane, and grip hold of Father's arm, leading him with me toward the doors. *In no way must he realize that anything is at all amiss.* "No, indeed, Papa," I reply with a shrug, shaking my head. "I suppose, perhaps—despite feeling a bit off tonight—that I might have been of some notice within the orchestra. But I have never made acquaintance of that particular gentleman. At all."

* * *

"Sasha!" Father yells out at the top of his lungs. "Will you stop and think about what you are doing for five precious, clear-headed minutes? By dammit, boy—come to your senses!"

Ignoring him, I snatch up the cleaning rod from the table and wave it about, mumbling: "Did you see where I put the piccolo?"

"Sasha, blast it—*listen* to me! And will you stop waving that thing around in the air like a stray hearth poker? It scarce matters if the rod has a blunt end! Is still dangerous, someone could get hurt."

At last spying the wooden piccolo atop the bureau, I shove the cleaning rod down into it and then stuff the piccolo inside my boot. "Go ahead, Papa, and talk, while I pack," I tell him, staring around the room in a fit of distraction.

Still close upon my heels, he follows as I begin flinging clothes, books, and papers into my travel trunk, his indignation roaring on: *"Sasha!* How can you forfeit your position at the Maryinsky?"

"Was all very simple," I reply. "I merely handed in my letter of resignation."

"That is *not* what I mean! Here you go for months, railing back and forth endlessly between Novgorod and Petersburg, for countless interviews and auditions—and now you intend upon *giving it all up?"*

"I told you: Nikolai said Monteux was still short a woodwind alternate. If I leave now, I might manage to catch the troupe at the end of the London season."

"But you said you were fraught unto exhaustion with the traveling! I thought that was why you rushed home so suddenly last Christmas—"

"Well, I have changed my mind."

"Sasha, the *Ballet Russe* intends upon sailing for South America, half a world away! You said you took the Maryinsky job so that you and I might spend more time together—"

"Have you seen my straight razor? What did I do with my razor?" Mumbling to myself, I wander past him and out toward the lavatory.

"Oh, dear Jesus Christ!" Father desperately throws up both hands, stomping after. "Sasha, *listen* to me! . . ."

He continues bellowing on as I scour back through the study of the Zhukovskaya townhouse, packing, again thanking the stars that I neglected to deposit earnest money on that little flat I had been eyeing over near the Redeemer Church on the northeast end of the Moika.

"Sofya!" Father exclaims, dragging her—past a flurry of embroidery linens and round wooden hoops—in from the hallway as I latch the lid onto my trunk. "Help me talk some sense into the boy, please!"

But Aunt Sophie only shrugs and wags a knowing finger up at Father's flustered face. "As I recall, Misha Sekovsky, there was never any swaying your mind once you had set it upon something."

Downstairs, he attempts to recruit Anna toward the same end—but she only smiles at him fondly while tucking her stethoscope into her medical bag and pulling on her dark, mannish jacket over her long skirt. "Oh, Uncle Misha—Sasha must simply feel that the stuffy Maryinsky no longer suits him! I myself would scarce mind another whirl through London, had I the time. Lord! We were all so gay there last year during the ballets. . . ."

Adieus to my aunt and cousin affectionately bestowed, my coat and trunk in hand, I finally hurry outward toward the curb, check my watch, and call out with an impatient wave: *"Drozhki!"*

"For love of the Saints, Sasha!" Father rants on. "You cannot do this—you *cannot!"*

When a cab pulls up, and I climb in, he remains standing awkwardly out on the curb, glaring at me with exasperation and raking his fingers through his hair. "Well!" I cry out through the open door. "Do you intend to stand there grumbling for the rest of the night, or will you come along and see me off?"

All the way to Baltic Station, he lectures, hounds, pleads for me to change my mind—all to no avail. "Sasha, please—stop and reconsider! It surely cannot be too late for you to retract your resignation letter from the Maryinsky . . . Sasha, I am asking you to do this for me as your father! I am begging you to at least take a few days, a week, perhaps—to stop and think everything over!"

"One way to Paris via Berlin," I say at the ticket booth.

"Sasha!"

With luck, I have barely managed to make the evetide train's scheduled departure time. As a dusky chill starts settling in over the city, I pull on my coat. From close in the distance, the hovering dark blue cupolas and high golden spires of the Trinity and St. Nikolai Cathedrals dwarf the many baroque-style apartment buildings clustered along the city's lower west end, and to the far north, the golden dome of St. Isaak's glitters up like a jeweled saucer as the sun's hues alighting upon its surface begin to fade. . . .

"For God's sake, Sasha—will you stop your appraisal of the view for once, and listen to me?" Father roars—again—into my ear. "Oh, the Saints help me!" he then moans out beseechingly, wearily rubbing at his eyes. "My boy, I do not think I will ever understand you!"

The train chugs in, wheels grinding to their steamy halt, followed by the flood of noisy passengers pouring out the doors and onto the platform. "Papa," I say, turning with some effort to face his gaze squarely at last, "you'd best not ever try to understand me."

As he grips my shoulder, I throw both arms around him and kiss him warmly, three times one cheek to another, murmuring: "Papa, I—I love you very much."

"Oh, Sasha! . . ."

To my vast relief, they call out for boarding, and I snatch up my trunk, tell him to be good to himself, and then hurry off for the open rail coach doors.

"Blast it—and you write to me!" he shouts after through cupped hands.

"Of course!"

Deliberately, I take a berth on the opposite side to those with windows facing the station platform, thereby avoiding Father's anguished image as the train pulls out.

And with my fist pressed to my chin, eyes focused in a vacant blur, I sit staring straight ahead for hours.

* * *

Conspirator of vengeance, the schedule cooperated with perfect timing. In another hour, my train leaves the railway station, bound for the Cornwall coast. In a few more moments, their ship departs the Southampton docks, bound for the other side of the world. As expected, I did not arrive soon enough to watch the troupe board the regal steamer *S.S. Avon*—much to my preference. Still, I have taken considerable precautions, attempting to remain within the shadows—while walking, despite the discomfort that it causes upon each increasing step, with the wooden knob stuffed inside my boot and without the cane, my hands stuffed deep within the pockets of my belted coat, my hair tucked back inside my upturned collar, my dark fedora's brim drawn far down to the rims of my spectacles. Being spotted by anyone familiar would only result in too many pointless, awkward questions.

He is up there with them. I cannot pick him out at this distance, but surely he is up there, probably amidst a group of gaily chattering ballerinas. Probably he is grinning rakishly, as always, his hands looped with casual ease over the bars of the rails. Probably his hair, sun-washed after another long draught of summer, is dancing about his face, tossed in all directions by the steely kiss of the wind.

Uncle Ned is the only person who knows about the awful 1907 Sheremetev affair, and therefore the only one with whom I can discuss the matter, and it is toward Winnebar that I have been journeying with such urgency, intent upon obtaining some harshly needed answers. In spite of what I told Father in Petersburg, I never meant to sign on again with the *Ballet Russe*. But spurred on by the wily pivot of coincidence, which has afforded me this precious hour to spare, I could not help but venture down to the docks to see them off.

Because for a few brief moments, he and I—he, that one up there leaning on one of the rails, his violin case tucked beneath one arm and a cello strapped somewhere back on a baggage lift; he, that one for whom I have never dared utter or admit lust's wayward urges, even unto my most private, secret self, up until this last harrowing week—for a few brief moments more on this brisk September day in 1913, he and I will once again breathe from the same cloud of air. Ever the romantic fool, I have come for this bon voyage only to end up jostling against rude shoulder-bumps in the giddy, scarf-waving crowd while wincing distastefully at the noise. I have come only in order to torture myself. I have come because I am naught but a true masochist.

I watch a little longer. I breathe in our last shared strata of life for a little longer. I choke back my agony of silence and all the reverent, tender things that I wish to God I could say to him—for just a little while longer. And then, before the ship weighs anchor, I wrench up mine, ripping my heart away from every last fleeting thought of him like a bloodied, dead placenta.

And once more turning for the quay, I march off toward my awaiting cab without looking back.

* * *

"Uncle Ned!" I shout, again pounding my fist against the front doors. "Uncle Ned? Aunt Mary?"

Whipping off my gloves, I stare with a frown back at the driver, who continues struggling with my trunk from the rickety motorcar-overhead. "Uh, just a moment!" I call to him. "Hold off with that, will you please?"

Something is wrong. Howell, the butler, usually answers with a studied bow upon the first or second ring at the latest. But I have been ringing and pounding for over two minutes now. And still, nothing.

My check of the grounds fuels further suspicion: the lawns lie ragged and untrimmed; at the trellises I find tomatoes rotting on every vine, unpicked; blackened apples and half-eaten cores languish beneath several fruit trees. Aunt Mary, ever the tender sower, would swoon at finding her harvest in such disarray. And, ardent lover of the sea, Uncle Ned never leaves Winnebar before November, if then; ofttimes, he even insists upon remaining to storm watch all through the winter season.

Granted, I did not send a cable, assuming they would be at home. Granted, my uncle could have been called away to London or Plymouth on business, as ofttimes occurs—but the servants and my aunt usually remain behind. As I trudge back around from the side of the house, staring at clumps of weeds sprouting up greedily amidst prize rose bushes, my sense of foreboding deepens profusely: something, indeed, is terribly wrong. . . .

The driver, a former miner just moved up to town from Penzance in the south, can yield no information. Neither will the two nervous, wide-eyed stable hands left behind to tend the stud horses and Sunnyrae and her new foal.

With apprehension, I bid the cab to drive me back into Devonbury.

Mr. Nigel C. Fordham, a sometime law partner of Uncle Ned's, I find fortunately remaining open for some late afternoon business in his second floor office facing out with wide windows toward the bay. When I disclose my identity and inquire as to my family's possible whereabouts, he lowers his eyes and bows his head toward the floor in a respectful pause while squeezing hold of my hand. "Ahh, Mister Shekovsky," he murmurs. "We are all so deeply saddened. By—by your loss . . . ."

Oh, no . . . *oh, nooo!*

At the main estate house at Plymouth, Aunt Mary, wan and exhausted and draped from head to foot in widow's black, rushes out across the lawn with outstretched arms. "Oh, Sasha! How good of you to come. . . ."

The funeral, or rather memorial service following cremation, is the next day. Numbed, I join my aunt and everyone else in the family pews. To my immense relief, my Uncle John—Uncle Ned's elder half-brother, the son of my Grandpa Will and his first wife, who died of the smallpox—continues supervising all details with a ready, patient ease. The service is poignant; the flowers are beautiful; the weather cooperates with a glorious burst of day-long sunshine just as my uncle would have treasured. Decorously, I manage to exude a gallant front: bowing, nodding, shaking and kissing hands throughout introductions and well-meaning murmurs proffered along with endless silver trays filled with tiny finger sandwiches. But deep within, the storm only rages renewed—for just as during the *Swan Lake* agony in Petersburg, and just as during the gloomy *Ballet Russe* ship send-off at the Southampton docks, I only continue to perish unceasingly both night and day. . . .

To Winnebar, we take the ashes, and after more tears and ceremony, cast them off into the surf, there to dance forever within the ocean waves that my uncle so dearly loved. To Plymouth, we return for the reading of the will:

> *"My holdings at the estate compound in Plymouth, of course, revert back in entirety to my brother, Sir John Devon-Tyler, Bart., who is also trustee of those funds set up to provide for the care of my dear wife, Mary, and her widowed sister, Mrs. Elizabeth White, of Long Island, New York State, America. As this trust contains the bulk of my assets and appears for such needs prescribed to be entirely adequate, my remaining scattered holdings and vested interests in capital stock, in addition to my London town-house in Bexley District, and my beloved seaside residence Winnebar at Devonbury township on the southern Cornwall coast, I wish to bequeath without encumbrance to my nephew, the son of my dear departed sister, and a Russian by birth, Count Aleksandr M. Sekovsky. . . ."*

Jolting upward from my lengthy study of patterns in the Persian carpet, I gasp out ungainly protestations until noting row after row of hooded eyes nodding in my direction without demurral upon the obviously expected news. "But, Aunt Mary!" I choke on, nonetheless. "I cannot possibly accept—"

My aunt warmly presses her hand into my arm, assuring me: "It was what our beloved Edward wanted, Sasha. Of you, he always was so terribly fond. Oh, never mind about me—I intend to join my dear sister, who lives in America. . . ."

* * *

The ocean. Once more it sweeps past in a monstrous tempest as Sunnyrae and I traipse in wayward patterns through the sand, the two of us followed upon close heels by her pattering foal.

Shivering, I pull down the brim of my cap, button my scarf into my high jacket collar, and stare out toward the crashing waves. Of course, he knew I shared his intense love of the sea. He knew I would have exulted in possessing this house for my very own. His sealed letter, two months old and awaiting upon the study's desk when I arrived, brimmed with affection:

> *I know naught of how much time remains, and there is so much I wish to say . . . you have given me more than you*

can ever know, Sasha . . . you are, indeed, the son I never had. . . .

Such avowal only perilously deepens the crevasse of my aberrant guilt. In secret, I have been childishly, selfishly furious with my uncle for choosing to leave this worldly sphere just when I felt so in need of his counsel. And without question, I know he continued to deplore the manner in which I conduct my private affairs. I also know that he had great hopes for our relationship which never met fruition. Frequent letters from him during my sojourn with the *Ballet Russe* begged for a visit, no matter how brief, saying how we would talk far into the nights again and skip together each day through the splashing waves; how we would make another of our summer solstice journeys to Salisbury Plain and the towering, eerie ruins at Stonehenge . . . .

But only when the troupe arrived in London, or when he visited in Paris, did I ever venture near him. And then only with reluctance, and always in the company of others.

At first hours, then days wane by, as I begin to wander in spells of brooding melancholy throughout the cluttered enclaves of the house, seeing and speaking to no one save for Howell, the maid, or the French cook—along with a new gardener and the stable hands, the only servants I have retained. From there, days start slowly progressing into weeks, and I find last captured solace within the scattered writings on Theosophy gracing the dusty shelves of Uncle Ned's massive library. Finally, I even begin taking my evetide meals at his ancient rolltop desk, the room enveloped always in a haze of cigarette smoke past my long hours spent scouring through various translations of, and commentaries on, *Solomon's Song of Songs,* the *Tao te Ching*, the *Bhagavadgita*, and *The Tibetan Book of the Dead*. Still thirsting for answers, I plunge into a study of Helena Blavatsky's *Secret Doctrine*, poring over the massive volumes in a famished hunt as I attempt, without much success, to decipher their abstruse mysteries. Into wee small hours encroaching upon a flux of twilight dawns, I ponder over veiled images brimming through the literature of the Christian mystics. One late sunset, just as fading rays of the sun hover low and golden-orange through the wide bay windows out upon horizon's heady ocean waves, the summation in a passage from the writings of Meister Eckhart—about the begotten Son becoming reborn in God as the soul's Son—practically leaps out at me from the very grain of the page, shooting through my heart like a pillaging arrow of fire, and I slam my fist down onto the desk, gasping:

"This is it! This is what is meant by the initiation—the forbidden journey, cup of resolution, obligatory pilgrimage, dark night of the soul . . . ."

Eagerly, I glance upward, again half-expecting to encounter some quavering visage of Uncle Ned, watchful Master at last arrived to lift away my torturous burden of questions. But as always, the curtains merely flutter back and away from the heady salt-air breeze. Doing so, as always, before an open window.

And still, all I have are euphemisms, and questions that continue hounding into my brain without a second's pause: *Is an initiate, then, the same as a white magician? A follower of the numbers, as Uncle Ned himself was; as I myself have for so long been striving to become? If so, then why can I still not comprehend the true meaning of this 'initiation?' And what is meant by the paradoxical phrase 'harmony through conflict,' which keeps shocking me awake from my dreams? Does it mean music, poetry—what? Why must the great teachings ever be shrouded in age-old obscurity? What, for instance, is the true significance of the triplicity, the 'one becoming three and three becoming one,' as Uncle Ned so often related during our discussions? Is this 'three becoming one' the Father becoming the Son-soul becoming the soul's Son? Is the three-tiered ranking system of the Freemasons a deliberate earthly manifestation of this same triplicity archetype? Is becoming a 'Master Mason' the same as becoming Meister Eckhart's soul's Son? And how does numerology pertain to this 'initiation', to this mysterious 'dark night?' Are the numbers thirteen and its multiples—the so-called 'Holy Numbers' in Uncle Ned's writings—most properly called 'initiatory numbers?' Is this why the words 'Master Mason' reduce to thirty-nine, the third multiple of thirteen? And what significance lies in the fact that the letters for the words 'Entered Apprentice'—the first ranking amongst the Freemasons—reduce to sixteen, my destiny number? And just why does this sixteen, ever dreaded harbinger of the Tower, continue to haunt my every Tarot reading no matter how adroitly I cut the cards? And why are my cousin's and my outer path numbers exactly the same? Can this possibly be only a result of coincidence? The odds are remarkable! And just what* is *coincidence? Was it coincidence that my Uncle Ned passed away just as I was journeying to see him at long last? Was it coincidence to encounter Sheremetev so abruptly in the Maryinsky? And was it merely coincidence that Nikolai happened to be the other person sitting in the booth behind mine that fateful night in Budapest?*

Or were all these events meant to occur—and if so, why? Is there, in truth, any such actual phenomenon as coincidence? Or are we all simply chasing our own shadows about the globe within some preconceived master-plan, beholden to no free-will, to no happenstances of coincidence save for those devised by God alone? And just what is *God? The grand director of reincarnation, creating symphonies of coincidence meant to foster in us this process of initiation, this becoming Father of the Son, who is fathered by the soul? And how can the Son have two fathers, both the Father and the soul? And for what purpose? And just what then* is *the purpose, the reason behind my life, other lives, everything—fate, history, the world? Why can I not banish this 'initiation' question from my mind, suffering without end from such yearning unfulfilled as if infected with a potent drug? Why do I continue devouring books by Eastern masters day after day, only to find so little peace? And why, beyond everything else, can I not stop the torment of all these damned questions?* . . .

Biting my lip, I reach for the pack of Tarot cards one more time, withdraw my Significator, the Knight of Cups, shuffle the cards, and gingerly cut the pack twice before setting my Significator down upon the desk. Then I lift the top card from the deck, which turns out to be the Nine of Swords. *Interesting—the 63/9—same vibration as both Nikolai's and my outer path numbers.* I set the Nine of Swords atop my Knight of Cups—this covers the Knight, and suggests the heart of the matter to be revealed in this reading. *All right.* Shutting my eyes, I lift off the next card, turn it over, and set it down crosswise over the other two cards. This second card crosses the Knight of Cups, either for good or for evil. . . .

Just barely do I squeeze open my eyes, and peek down at the card crossing the Knight of Cups.

The Tower. *Ever and again only the Tower* . . . .

Exhausted, once more I throw up both hands, slam down the cards and the latest library volume of my penitence, and collapse upon the entire heap, wearily shaking my head.

October brings strange haunting images toward Hallowmas, by the Russian calendar just two days before that of Nikolai's birth. One afternoon, I swear I see him dash in through the library doors, exclaiming: 'I rushed back to Petersburg from Rio! Uncle Misha said you had come here . . . I could not bear being parted from you for a moment longer . . . you are the one behind, at the fiery witches' stakes, shared phantom of my lifelong dreams . . . I have loved you forever, Sasha! . . .'

But the vision fades into a blur, my hope dashed into shards of jagged, scarring glass, my heart burned away into cinders yet again.

In November, the rains come, and by December, when the snow starts to threaten, my leg can no longer tolerate the ocean dampness, aching so some nights that I struggle to keep from moaning out in pain. Spent with my studies of the craggy rock formations out on the bluff and exhausted from endless library readings and my perusal of Uncle Ned's vast collection of notes, I wish Howell well, leave him and his family to watch over Winnebar as grateful caretakers, and make for London.

In four months in vibrant, ecstatic, bustling London, I write scads of awful poetry and tear it all up; attend no less than seventeen performances of Handel's *Messiah*; undertake a wealth of astrological and Christian mystical studies with the Rosicrucians; search out bi-monthly meetings of the Hermetic Order of the Golden Dawn; become a First Degree Mason; swear off the ingestion of meat, fish, and fowl forever, thereby to exult in the lucid meditations of ascetic vegetarianism; swear off the yoke of my lust with humbled, repentant anguish and take five different oaths of celibacy before promptly breaking them five different times. At last giving up in entirety, I take yet again another lover—though a lover he can hardly be called, fiendish lust, not love, forever the prevailing motivation. But by March, I am tired of the escapades, tired of the meetings, tired of the rain, and hounded to no end by twice-weekly letters urging the prodigal son to return home. Happening upon a decent lessee for the townhouse, I attempt to assuage Father by hedging a tad closer—this time to that Garden of Eden blessed about every park, square, winding cobblestone road, and luxuriant, vine-wrapped garden path with the lingering call of Mozart's mystic innuendoes.

And come the spring of 1914, I head for Vienna.

* * *

His name is Erich—an Erich blond and blue-eyed, but when the light is right, truth dims toward muted blendings of illusion; he could be a wintertime towhead. His eyes, warm and expressive, could very well be slate gray.

When the light is right, I sin, and presume shamelessly upon the persons of poor hapless fellows that I barely know, whispering a thousand endearments to the violin in my long ago and far away—who loves me every night and every day in a tortured a ruse of fantasy.

Buttoning on my trousers and my shirt, I watch as Erich combs his hair, his back to me, his upturned profile—haunting visage of another striking upturned profile so long familiar and now so long-lost—caught in dusky silhouette within my bureau's oval mirror-glass. "Might I ask you a question?" I inquire, struggling once again with the German. Scarce pursued beyond old rote classroom drills, my fluency, although improving somewhat of late, yet leaves much to be desired.

"Certainly," says Erich, turning, grinning, holding out his arm with his sleeve pinched tight.

I help him with his cuff links as he plants soft kisses across my brow. "I was just wondering," I begin in a hesitant tone, "if you'd not mind telling me the date of your birth."

With a shrug, he does so—and I add the digits together in my head and reveal to him the number of his life lesson.

"It is called numerology," I go on in a rush. "You see, every manifestation in the universe reduces to a solitary number—"

Nodding, Erich stares down toward the table, where books and papers lie stacked one upon and between another in careless, ratty heaps. "You are English?" he says, glancing down at the top sheets strewn with my back-handed cursive writing.

I sigh and stop talking. Again no one shows the slightest interest in the mysteries of my numbers. No one, that is, save for Nikolai—with whom I had been immersed for months in endless lively discussions of the subject before the disaster of a year and a half ago in Budapest.

"No," I tell Erich. "Actually, I am Russian."

As he stares down toward the papers with a perplexed frown, I add by way of explanation: "But my mother was English."

Still, Erich continues eyeing the papers—and me—strangely. "Well," he says with another shrug, appearing markedly uncomfortable, "perhaps we shall see one another again at the cabaret."

"Yes. Perhaps."

As he leaves the building, striding up the alley with his head tossed back and arms swinging out in rhythmic spurts, I watch from the window of my tiny flat, drinking in the sight of his pale hair and wondering if his sudden haste to leave was genuine, or simply some trick of my imagination.

Warm and sultry, rays of temperate morntide judgment then begin to course in past the curtains. Yawning, I struggle with effort to remember what month it is—July, perhaps. Perhaps even August, by now. Outside once again a torrent of shouting erupts. Apparently, a group of hooligans have begun demonstrating up ahead out in the main thoroughfare—probably another band of Serbian nationalists, or those wretched Swiss fools forever preaching world revolution, or some other such harebrained nonsense.

Listlessly, I let the curtains fall back. In the close to ten months since my departure from Petersburg, I have ofttimes seemed to hover upon the verge of every answer after which my heart has ever burned—while during other empty, harrowing hours, I fear I tread no closer to solving my inner dilemma at all. To Vienna I came to take a figurative vow of silence, to wrest my integrity unscathed through the cave of fire, the cave of water. But far from attaining the scepter of beauty, the coronet of wisdom as promised in Mozart's *Die Zauberflote*, or *The Magic Flute*, I have instead become haunted day and night with revenants of apocalyptic forewarning from the finale of his *Don Giovanni*, the dead commander ever returning to hasten my ascent toward redemption's fiery furnace. And never do I shake off Mozart's torments, even for a few trifling moments of peace, before Handel descends once more with arias from his triumphant *Messiah*: vowing to break me, purified oracle of the Sons of Levi; to dash me to pieces like a potter's vessel; to rend me soul and sinew apart into an offering of righteousness . . . .

Each eve in the risque tavernhouses, amidst the piano music, free flowing beer, and eager arms of endless eager lovers, I continue seeking solace. Never to find it—that is, not wholly. Nor holy. Unchecked, the inner questing symphony continues ringing unabated in my head no matter how desperately I try to drown it out by venturing close to the noisy saxophone bands. And, so long ago forgotten, and now probably only inspired by my brief encounter with Sheremetev, glaring visions of Melissa's amethyst crystal have become another nightly torment. Along with the strange dreams.

In the dreams, I suffer from the same poignant inner thirst that began its plague near unto four years past during the night of the freeing of Melissa's ghost. Every night, the man comes, whether I sleep with a friend or no; every night the same man—imbued, I know somehow, with the countenance of an angel, but garbed in a brilliant white shroud that obscures all but a hint of his face. And every night, I yearn, pray, *beg* to clutch that true face and whole man to me as if a lover, friend, father, a wise one come at last with every subtle answer, my ship in the night striving for his homing beacon, my heart drawn by the sound of his call, my strings tuned to the sound of his voice. Every single night, he holds out his hand, and every single night, I struggle yet again not to take it. Once I take the hand, it will all be over: I will be absorbed, completed, purified, redeemed; I will have taken the initiation. Upon which I will be compelled to climb the dreaded pathway toward the Tower.

Where I will meet Death.

And every morn, when the light of dawn begins to peek in between the curtains and etch reassuring, sunny little slatted patterns across the floor, I wonder whether taking this 'initiation' involves not the selling of my soul to God, but to none other than the very devil himself.

Sighing, I slip on my spectacles and huddle down once more to face the heap of old transgressions awaiting upon the table. Underneath my stack of notes, with several markers in it, lies Mikhail Kuzmin's novel *Wings*, which Volodya gave me as a present two years ago after the poetry reading session with his revolutionaries. *Wings* is about a man who accepts his desire for other men without apology or remorse, and who at last finds a true love, with whom he then lives in harmony and bliss.

Harmony and bliss—and a happily-ever-after that never was: four long years of stealing glances over bobbing bows of the orchestra; four long years of peeking across at the wrapped cocoon, at that bare arm stretched out across white sheets in the room's adjoining bed. Four long years of naive confusion, inner lies, and secret, impossible dreams. Guilt again nudges at my slain torment from behind, and I cannot help but glance upward toward the high brick mantle—adorned with the picturegraph taken after our first arrival in Paris in the spring of 1909. Arms interlinked, our derbies tipped in playful, sideswept abandon, we both stand grinning rakishly beneath the massive girders of the Eiffel Tower out on the *Quai d'Orsay*.

And—once again—I swallow pain and bury my heart away, staring forlornly down into the hollow dustiness of the fireplace ash.

Beneath Kuzmin lies *Cor Ardens*, poetry by Slava Ivanov, the same Ivanov about whose salon Volodya kept badgering me with such persistence the same day he gave me Kuzmin's novel. And beneath Ivanov are tucked two other booklets of tawdry verse, *The Chiming Pines* and *Brotherly Songs*, both by Nikolai Kliuev, whose bold, startling images evoking the thrills of love caused even me to blush.

If only I could know their secret—and somehow extract it, concentrate it into a potion, and inject myself with its heady, dulling comfort.

If only I could accept my own base desires without guilt or shame, and with the same carefree ease as all the Kuzmins and Kliuevs and Ivanovs.

But always I return to the lingering disapproval of my Uncle Ned, stalwart watcher ever frowning with distaste from his steady perch upon my shoulder. Always I return to the still, small voice sounding within my head and urging me ever onward and upward toward ascension of a higher path. Always, naked and ashamed, I return to my maker—to the man in the whitened shroud—his outstretched hand pointing down to the stained, crumpled sheet marked in my back-handed script with the words to Valery Bryusov's *Pale Horse*:

As unfurled from the Rider's scroll
Letters afire borne in the name of: Death . . .

On a separate sheet, I have written that sentence out at least fifty or sixty times, one line after another—appended, at the bottom, with the opening stanza from the Gospel According to St. John:

In the beginning was the Word, and the Word was with
God, and the Word was God . . .

After which I have scrawled hatefully:

Forbidden journey, cup of resolution, obligatory
pilgrimage, dark night of the soul . . . goddamn it!
Harmony is not conflict—and I am NOT A POET!!!

Then Bryusov's ending words, eerie and prophetic, lash out once more from the bottom corner of the page:

Only a whore from a brothel and a deranged
Madman
Yet reached bare hands
Toward escaping apparition. . . .

Wrenching up from the chair, I clutch my head in both my hands, once more attempting escape: from the demons of the scriptures, from the warnings of Bryusov, from the constant harsh tolling of my inner bell. *Blast it—stop! No more hounding, urging, pushing, forcing me ever onward toward the heights, past skyward summit, and beyond— my God, I simply cannot touch Your troth! Nor assume such fiery balance leveling at perfection . . . .*

Flailing for self-preservation, I begin snatching out papers, one by one, from the stack. All are torn in halves or quarters save for the very last piece lying at the very bottom of the heap, composite of my agony forged together from all the other torn-up sheets like some deathly mirage culled from quarried stone:

Threshold

Paradox
(Midnight Sun)
Opposite poles
Two sides
One
Indivisible
Shades of black and shades of white
Shades of left and shades of right
Ancient battle
Hollowing into the gray matter
Sevenfold gestation
Desperate elation's breath
Caught on the night's chill
Clinging to sunrise
Creates the madness
Unmasked
Eyes petrified

Swift panting thrashes out across the room, remnants of tortured breath at last escaping in ragged, hurtful spurts cheered on by the panicked crush of heartbeats, my cold phantom of the pen ever courting ironic denials against tender kisses of another Erich in the moonlight, in the dawnlight, in the hazy, sunny glow of wakened morn.

From the alley below, life—normalcy—smatterings of voices echo: several bicycles steer off to a sudden halt just below my window. Laughter caws up between traded barbs and whispers of the latest news. Someone calls out prices; someone else buys flowers; somebody else smacks a friend in the head and a heated, scuffling fight ensues. From the balcony of another of the apartment houses farther up the alley row, an infant can be heard squalling, while his mother bargains with a vendor down in the street below about the price of a bottle of milk.

I smear my hand up across my brow, dredging off the mask of sweat. Everything is in a name: letters. Numbers.

Bryusov's letters afire are ringing from the sum total of my name in a grail of numerological prophecy—and pointing straight toward the Tower. And his escaping apparition is opening unto the path of the deranged madman. . . .

Jolting upward from my chair past a slew of bloody oaths, I grip hold of my last whole sheet of paper and promptly rip the *Threshold* poem into a flurry of shreds.

After which I follow suit with all the other torn sections of paper, at last slamming the whole heap vengefully down into the trash basket.

Relief, however, proves short-lived, the puppet strings of life intervening once again in pervasive reminders. From the bureau, Father's letters beckon, the last two still unopened. Of late, I have been neglectful, only dashing off hurried excuses to his continued pleas to return home. The scent of home, of course, also beckons—shuffling numbly through each day from morn until next descent of the evetide ghosts does exact due toll. But day after day, lethargy propounds procrastination, and other beguilements of iniquity remain: hiding in a strange city amongst strange people who speak a strange language prevents prying questions. And the need for explanations. And near all further possibilities of fateful turns of coincidence—with family, friends, old associates. Nikolai. Sheremetev.

Further evidence of neglect escapes from the oval frame of the bureau mirror-glass: a sight wildly disheveled, unbathed, unshaven for two days, a shirttail hanging down in limp testimony to newly acquired sloth of habit gleaned from heedless nightly fornication with the poet's muse. Again Father would tease me without mercy, my hair untrimmed since perhaps even the early spring, long strands brushing girlishly at my shoulders.

Seizing upon at least the chance for physical redemption, I make staunch promise for visiting the barber's come later in the afternoon, and trudge into the lavatory. But just as I turn the faucet handle to begin running water for a bath, a barrage of heavy pounding sounds from out at the door.

However, instead of my hopes opening to Erich returned for yet another passionate tussle in bed, I rather come face to face with an impatient messenger boy from the telegraph office. Bearing a wire from St. Petersburg.

"Oh, dear Lord!" I burst out—and almost forget to tip him, at last grappling clumsily with my change. Once I slam shut the door, I rip away the envelope in panic, muttering: "Oh, my God—Papa, please! Nothing could have happened! . . ."

The cable, however, is not about Father, but from him, couched in furious words:

Foolish idiot, come home! Read not one of my letters? Situation critical—probability of war!

M.S.S.
St. Petersburg
14/27 July 1914

"War?" I gasp out, stunned.

At the bureau, I tear away the envelope from his letter of two days prior in frantic haste:

Sasha, my God! Have you taken leave of your senses? Have you not been reading any newspaper reports at all? *I know you sometimes think your doddering old Papa sticks his nose far too much into your business, but this is serious! Franz Ferdinand's assassination last month at Sarajevo has turned into much more than just another socialist gamble. My friend Orlov is convinced the Austro-Hungarians are going to attack Serbia on account of the damn foolishness! If they do, the Tsar will honor the alliance with Serbia—and the Pan-Slavic sympathies of those conservative devils in his blasted government—and retaliate against Austria-Hungary. If we move against Austria-Hungary, Germany will rouse up to her aid, whereupon Britain and France are obliged to come to ours. Sasha, don't you see? This could be war like none in the last fifty, perhaps even one hundred years! Sasha, I am begging you! Come home—before you get yourself trapped over there! Orlov tells me Franz Josef's gendarmes have begun snooping for possible spies, assassins, ne'er-do-wells—that any Russian might become suspect. . . .*

I stare, transfixed, at the letter.

Hands shaking, I wrench open his unopened letter of a week prior—my heart thundering battle ramparts as I pore over the words, the underlines, the frantic jabs of fatherly exclamation . . . .

I stare, transfixed, at this second letter.

And then, in a desperate, blinded whirlwind and without another second's hesitation, I begin heaving clothes, papers, and books one after another into my travel trunk.

* * *

Nervously, I stand in line to board the train. Two burly policemen and a steely-eyed army colonel, his chest smothered in decorations, continue surveying all passengers. With the women and children, they seem not overly concerned; of the men, they are demanding names, and occasionally requesting papers for closer scrutiny.

Be calm, I tell myself—but I cannot help scanning past the intricate Gothic facades of the stationhouse buildings with a mounting sense of unease. Solitary uniformed officers continue marching off in every direction; large queues of troops have begun amassing at both front and rear . . . *oh, Lord Christ! How could I ever have been so blind to this threat of chaos brewing all around me? Blast it—try to act perfectly normal, like a traveling businessman, for God's sake! Simply try to remain calm. . . .*

I pull a last drag off my cigarette and crush the butt out beneath my heel as the two policemen and the colonel, pricking up their ears at the sound of a Slavic name, single out the man standing four places ahead of mine.

Also a Russian. Who immediately launches into a fierce debate with them and refuses to surrender his papers.

Shouting ensues, and they grapple him over to the sidewall of a ticket booth; the colonel punches in his face, and at last peels the papers from the man's jacket pockets. Reddening with embarrassment before the sombered row of stylishly dressed men and women waiting to board, one of the policemen assists the man up to his feet. The man, the two policemen, and the colonel then continue their squabble—until finally, after much examination, the colonel returns the man's papers and motions him to proceed and board the train.

Then the two policemen and the colonel return and resume waving on the women and asking for all the men's names. Just as I reach the head of the line, a marching band that has been assembling down by the far end of the stationhouse pipes up in full force with Haydn's *Kaiserhymme*, the Austrian national anthem.

"Your name?" the colonel demands, checking his pocket watch with a snarl of impatience.

Catching in my breath, I stare downward. *All I want is to board, to go home! I don't want any trouble. . . .*

"Your name!" the colonel barks out again, fists flung to his hips.

"Devon-Tyler," I say, not looking at him. "Alexander."

The colonel's eyes narrow. He glances toward each of the policemen, and once again back at me—and then spreads out his hand, demanding: "Your papers."

Oh, shit! . . .

"Your papers!" he yells, signaling, with a snap of his fingers, for the two policemen.

Before any of them can cause a scene, I whip my Russian traveling passport out from my jacket pocket—and gulp back a rock, murmuring: "Look—I, uh, can explain. . . ."

The office door slams shut behind us and they throw me onto a stool; flick on the bright overhead lamp. My trunk, coat, my small satchel filled with notes and books, my flute case, and my cane all topple to the floor. The colonel seizes off my hat, peering down into the crown and swiping his hand around inside it before pummeling it soundly to the floor as well. Then he punches me in the shoulder and glares down into my face. "Who are you and what is your business in Vienna?" he roars, fingering the holster to his gun.

"Sir! I—I said I could explain—"

"Are these falsified papers?" he yells, waving my passport outward.

"No, sir!"

"Then why did you declare another name?"

"I merely wished to avoid—bringing on—any type of an incident—"

One of the policemen starts snickering.

"Oh, shut up, Nebinger!" the colonel blares at him. "And will you two loafheads quit standing around, and get to searching the little bastard's bags already, dammit?"

"I—the name I gave you was, in fact, my mother's," I go on sheepishly, wincing as one policeman yanks open my trunk, the other my satchel.

"Se-kov-sky!" the colonel bellows out with relish, peering down at the yellowed folds of the passport sheets. "Alek-san-dr Mik-hail-o-vich!

Ahh, hey! Hey, Getz—look at this!" he calls over to the second policeman. *"Count!* A frigging Russian nobleman, no less! Humph! Filthy terrorist Slavophiles—"

"Sir! I humbly beg to apologize—"

"How long have you been staying in Vienna?"

I wring my hands together; clench my fists; unclench them. "Uh, four months, sir."

"Four months, eh? Humph! And exactly what has been the nature of your business here in our fair city for the last four months, now? Hmmm?"

The high sill of the office window starts fluttering up and down before my eyes in a dancing double image; beads of sweat begin fringing at my brow. "Uh, for four months, I have, uh, been working, sir—"

"Working, have you?" Glowering at me, the colonel strides past from my right side to my left; paces back from left to right again. "Working for whom?"

Nervously, I swallow, and attempt to loosen my tie. "Er, uh, I have been working for—for myself, sir—"

"Oh, indeed? Well!" he grunts back toward the two policemen. "And we all know plenty enough about gents who work for themselves these days, now, humph! All right, Herr Russian Count: just what kind of sleazy dealings have you and your conniving terrorist friends been brewing up in our fair Vienna ever since your arrival here four long months ago? *Hmmm?"*

"Actually, I have been, uh—"

"Yes?" he cries impatiently.

"Uh, writing. I suppose what I have been doing is writing. Sir."

At this, the colonel lets out an exasperated sigh, while Nebinger, the policeman, once more breaks into snickers, shaking his head. "Oh, a writer!" the colonel rasps out with groveling, sarcastic delight. "Ha! A correspondent! And what kind of frigging garbage would some Slavic slime like you happen to be printing up these days in Vienna? Editorials to incite the Bosnians against the Crown? Communiques to glorify Russian socialist hyenas?"

"No, sir—by no means! I have been writing—"

"Yes? Yes?"

"Uh, poetry. Poetry. Sir."

This time, Nebinger bursts out laughing, and mumbles: "Aww, let 'im go—" But the colonel once again orders him to shut up. Then, with a leer, he demands: "Humph! All right, poet—if you *are* telling the truth—then in just which periodicals have you been publishing your work?"

Bristling beneath my collar, I let out my own exasperated sigh. "Actually, sir, I have never published in any of the periodicals."

"Oh, ho! Never published, he says! Ha! And this young gent calls himself a poet, a writer! And yet has never published in any periodicals!"

Itching to inform him that it appears one must go through hell first as a prerequisite, I manage instead to hold my tongue.

"And what d'ya write about, sonny?" Nebinger demands, nodding over from his inspection of my trunk with a toothy grin.

"Metaphysics," I snap out, immediately regretting it.

"Oh, metaphysics!" the colonel roars, laughing. But when he glares down at me again, his eyes are blackly serious. "Why have you spent only the last four months in Vienna?" he snarls.

"Previous to April, I was staying in London, sir."

"London! Oh, well! Looks as if what we have here is a traveling gentleman—"

"I happen to own a townhouse in London, sir—"

"—an honest-to-God, genuine, wandering mystic poet! Ha! And just who the hell do you think you are? *Rilke?"*

"*No*, sir!"

"How do you maintain your living?" he then demands.

"I have an independent income, sir."

"Humph! And how do you explain this?"

Wrenching up the case, the colonel shoves it open to expose my flute.

"I have, for some years, worked as a musician, sir."

"Musician? Oh, Jesus the Christ! First the man's a poet, now a frigging musician! I never heard such a half-assed story in all my life! You think they could manage a pipe bomb out of one of these?" the colonel then inquires, waving the open flute case out toward Nebinger.

"Sir, please!" I gasp out, whitening. "Do not allow the pieces to fall out—it is an 1877 *Boehm!* A delicate instrument."

"So just where were you employed as a musician, then?" he snarls, once again glaring down into my face. "With one of the symphonies? At the Opera House? *Where?"*

I sigh loudly, staring down to my hands. "Lastly, on the Continent, in Budapest with the *Ballet Russe*, sir."

"The *Ballet Russe?"* the colonel roars. "You mean that decadent Russian ballet company ever dallying about half-naked trollops in harems? Humph! The same group for which the Czechs demonstrated against the Crown in Prague last spring?"

Flushing, I push up on the rims of my spectacles. "I know naught about any such demonstrations last year in Prague, sir."

From behind, Nebinger taps the colonel on the shoulder. "There's nothin' suspect in either bag—just books, papers, and a bunch o' wrinkled clothes," he informs him. "So all we got on the lad is these two English Webleys, one he was carryin' inside his vest, the other inside his coat," he adds, handing the colonel the guns.

"Why were carrying these weapons?" shouts the colonel, waving both outward.

"For self-protection! Sir."

"Humph!"

"Aww, come on, Colonel," Nebinger blurts out. "This one's no assassin type! Actually, looks more to me like the fellow's 'bout as scared as a sittin' duck ready to take a crap."

The colonel elbows him off, still unconvinced. "If you are a musician, prove it, then!" he demands, shoving the flute case down into my lap and pointing at the pieces. "Else you and I are going for a walk down to the magistrate's office—to discuss whether one of these pipes might be thick enough for you socialist scum to be packing your explosive charges around in, humph!"

After staring between him and Nebinger with some bewilderment, I shrug and begin piecing together the joints of the flute.

One Mozart sonata later, I am at last on the train—albeit a much later run than I had originally intended to board—my eyes clamped shut, my flute case clutched up to my chest, my fingers forming the sign of the cross in shaking gratitude as I murmur upward to the heretofore unhearing, ever Unsung God: "Thank You! Thank You . . . ."

* * *

Innumerable delays, two missed connections, and a forced eighteen hour stopover in Warsaw have frazzled raw nerves to the core. Six-and-a-half days it has required me to traverse the Continent in a journey that normally requires only two, the massive influx of troops mounting everywhere across Austria, Poland, the frontiers of Russia; the legions of frantic wanderers, like myself, all desperately racing for home.

But at last at Baltic Station on August the second, or July twentieth per the Russian calendar, Father's embraces are crushing and prolonged.

Then he steps back, and in solemn silence, unfolds the front pages to the last several days' copies of both *Birzhevye Vedomosti* and *Utro Rossii*, the financial and morntide newspapers.

The day following my departure from Vienna, the Emperor Franz Josef declared war on Serbia; the day following that, Austro-Hungarian shells began pounding into Belgrade. The day following that, both the Emperor and the Tsar ordered full mobilization. As a result, the Kaiser, bound by his pact with Austria-Hungary, declared war on Russia, began to mobilize on both his eastern and western frontiers, and yesterday invaded Luxembourg in a stab against France, Russia's ally. In retaliation, the Tsar has just declared war against Austria-Hungary and Germany.

"Lord God," I mutter, staring, wide-eyed, at the headlines. On every page: *'VOINA! VOINA! VOINA . . .'*

The Russian word for war.

"They just announced the declaration over at the Winter Palace," says Father. "Thousands packed into the square to hear Liturgy before the icon of the Virgin of Kazan. When the Tsar appeared, all sank down upon their knees, shouting 'God Save the Tsar!' I haven't seen such fervor since the rally in 1904 over that damned travesty with the Japanese. Jesus in all of Heaven help us! Yesterday, everyone's a revolutionary; today, a patriot."

"I don't understand it, Papa," I tell him, shaking my head. "I did happen to buy a newspaper the day after Sarajevo. Granted, people in Vienna were somber, but friends told me no one's grief was so profound as that following Crown Prince Rudolf's tragic, romantic suicide back in 1889. I mean, Franz Ferdinand was known as stiff and cold, an unpopular relic; everyone was always complaining about his uppity commoner wife."

"These hostilities are over much more than merely the Archduke's shooting, Sasha," Father replies with a sad sigh. "Pan-Slavic separatist sympathies; the secret protocols; the way the Germans have been itching to the teeth for a fight. Dozens of factors, I am sorry to say, seem to have brought events to this ugly head."

Grumbling, he folds up the newspapers and throws his arms around my shoulders once again, crushing me to him in a fierce embrace. "Bless the Saints you made it home in time, my boy," he rasps out, wiping at his eyes. "And dear God!" he then exclaims, stepping back. "You look positively wretched, I daresay. Of course, I suppose I too would turn no heads after spending six days cavorting across the Continent like a refugee. But Christ help the both of us, Sasha! Do you never trim that hair?"

Again I attempt to slick it back, and tug low the brim of my fedora. "Papa," I moan out, "must you needle me so? Can't you see I am fraught near unto tears with exhaustion?

"All right, come, then; let us see if we can manage to commandeer a cab and find our way back to Zhukovskaya through these mobs of fools flooding the streets. . . ."

Indeed, everywhere—lining Voznesensky, Nevsky Prospekts; all up and down the broad avenues, the small side streets; in alleys, court-yards; in every haven park and regal open square—Saint Petersburg is jammed to sheer overflowing contagion with soldiers, marching bands, and crowds waving the Tsarist tricolor and shouting slogans upon the tide of nationalist songs. "Thank God they've let stand the exemption for first-born sons," Father declares loudly, crossing him-self and solidly patting my knee as he settles in beside me on the seat of the cab.

I close my hand tightly over his fingers. "They'd never take me in any case on account of the leg, Papa," I tell him. "If things were different, and there had indeed been such chance, believe me, I would have traveled straight away back to London."

"Well, were that the case, we would have bought a replacement, humph! Damned I'd be to have *my* son traipsing off into this senseless folly! God in Heaven, look at all these gaping uniformed fools," he cries, pointing toward a noisy contingent of sailors grouped beyond his window as our cab veers around a corner. "Eager eyes, ready grins on their faces. All the joviality of the tide will extinguish soon enough, I can warrant you that. I've seen war: blood and guts and naught but much else! I've been one of the sorry louts had to sew those poor lads back together."

Sighing, he clutches his head down into both hands with a genuine moan of grief, and in an attempt to lend comfort, I begin rubbing my palm out across the sagging heave of his shoulders. He is eighty-two now and beginning to fully look it: the dark rings have widened beneath his eyes, and scores of tiny new wrinkles frame the whitened hairline of his beard on both heavy cheeks. "Don't worry your head so about it all, Papa," I urge him.

"Worry? Ha! And speaking of *worry*—at last I have my primary cause of worry in life seated next to me right here!" he thunders out. "And just what the hell were you doing all that time in Vienna?"

His parental lecturing continues nonstop all the way along our slow-paced route following the path of the Fontanka canal—until, in spite of my love for the man, and unbridled joy in seeing him once again, I throw up both hands in irritation, barking out: "Papa, *please!* It is none of your—"

"—business? Of course it is! It is most definitely my business when my son forsakes his lifelong dream of playing in the orchestra at the Maryinsky Theater of Opera and Ballet! And then charges off full steam across Europe for close to a year—to end up hiding himself away like a Tibetan hermit in some squalid little Viennese flat. And without answering over half of my letters—God's balls, Sasha! I was terrified unto death that you'd not even heed the cable! And near set out for Vienna to come fetch you myself. Just what in Christ's name were you doing all that time? Laying bets on cards? Horses? Squandering my money away on drink and bawdy flophouse women?"

"No, Papa—of course not!"

"Well! Then, *what?"*

"Writing!" I burst out scarce before even fathoming the import of my words. *"Poetry!"*

Upon a sharp intake of breath, Father draws back in his seat and begins regarding me with widened eyes. "You were spending all that time in Vienna writing poetry?"

"Yes, blast it!" Wearily, I press at my brow and lean into the tufted pads lining the side of the coach. "Now, are you satisfied?" I snap, shooting him a glare. "And could we, for a few moments at least, leave off with the many questions, Papa? *Please?"*

"You were writing poetry in Vienna?" he gasps out again in amazement. "Oh, let me see some, Sasha!" he goes on, hunching forward with his elbows to his knees, his fingers groping eagerly for the clasp to my satchel. "Let me see some of your poetry."

Loath to reveal that I tore every single sheet of it up, I shake my head—and once more, not without some merit, attempt to thwart his thousand questions by pleading my exhaustion. At last, with a grin and playful, nabbing pinch to my cheek, he agrees to postpone his insistent survey of my so-called labor, although in no way whatsoever can he seem to refrain from talking about it—and it is with a mixture of anxiety and bemusement that I watch his beaming face as he starts rattling on to the driver in a booming voice: "Yes, my son! The poet . . . ."

When we at last debark at the Zhukovskaya townhouse, I once more find chance to pity Nikolai's familial plight as Father informs me that all five of my cousin's elder sisters, including Natasha with her diplomat husband and the wayward Nina just arrived from a long stint with some obscure theater company in Spain, are gathered within. "Would be the perfect time for celebrating a family reunion with all of us here, save for this damned war," Father mutters, shaking his head gloomily as we trudge together through the elegant front doors.

After proper introductions to Tatyana's and Eugenia's husbands, each of them outfitted in the crisp red-pressed uniforms of the Semyonovsky Guards, Aunt Sophie conducts us past the two girls, who continue nestling between them Tatyana's squalling babe, her twin toddlers following ever about in ready tow. In one of the upstairs rooms, where Father has been bedded down, I splash cold water on my face and hurriedly change my shirt. Flavored vodkas and lemonade are being served in the drawing room prior to dinner, and our presence is, of course, expected.

Father and Anna launch into a medical discussion as we meet her on our way down the stairs. Quietly, my eyes cast downward, I follow behind in their footsteps, quickening my pace with steady thumps of the cane and glancing upward only once we enter the noisy drawing room. Which is when I see him.

At the sofa, standing. Talking. And grinning rakishly, as ever. With a snifter of vodka lolling about in one hand and some kind of map grasped within his other—which he proceeds to fold up and return to Natasha's husband, the American diplomat, before continuing their amicable discussion about geography.

I wince back a flush, take Aunt Sophie's offered glass from the buffet table with murmured thanks, and turn away to begin an intense study of the carpet. Despite the fact that Father said that everyone was here, it had not crossed my mind that *he* would be. Of course, the future pursuits of the *Ballet Russe* are most probably just as questionable as everyone else's upcoming plans against the chaotic, looming specter of the war.

Choking back shame, longing, lust, love, fear, I edge toward him slowly. Some polite words between us, some simple indication that our relationship continues now, indeed, as it always has, is due in front of my aunt, Father, my other cousins. As I approach the sofa, he spots me, and offers silent acknowledgment with a brief, testy meeting of the eyes and a forced nod. Then he turns and says something to the woman seated behind him down upon the sofa cushions.

Following his gaze, I immediately avert my stare. Bloated up like a walrus, the woman is huge with child—ready to drop the babe any day now, from the looks of it. Frowning with distaste, I slosh down two burning gulps of vodka while attempting to place the sudden familiarity of her face. *Paris? London? No, Paris—surely. Oh, yes—and did he not introduce me to her one time? Another from amongst his growing entourage of understudy ballerinas?*

"Sasha," he murmurs, nodding in my direction yet again before glancing once more down to the woman—after which he looks abruptly back up at me, stating: "I believe you've met my wife."

Wife? *Wife?*

I freeze, heaving for air as the whole room tips into a contortion of precarious angles, my fingers curling thickly around the beveled crystal stem of my glass, his words: "My dear, you remember my cousin, Aleksandr? Yes, Mikhailovich—yes, from the *Le Sacre première* in Paris . . . ." swirling into my head and down around inside a blackened, draining hole as I blurt out: *"What?"*

Whether it be due to the tone, or the urgency in my voice, I know not, but suddenly everyone—*everyone* in the entire drawing room—ceases all conversation and turns to stare straight at us.

With a jolt, I snatch my hand upward and jam the lower rims of my spectacles into my cheek with my fist. *Lord Jesus God, you plodding fool! Do you want everyone in the entire world to know?*

"Pardon me, Elena Feliksovna!" I manage to rasp out finally, thanking the stars for my stroke of luck in recalling her name. Once I sweep down to plant the expected kiss upon her offered fingers, the buzz of voices begins afresh behind us, a wealth of curious stares at last giving way. "I—please, again, pardon me for my outburst! I have just spent six days hopping trains in escape from Vienna, and suppose am still much more distraught than I had cared admit. Oh, yes—the soldiers were everywhere; close to two days was I forced to spend in Warsaw merely to secure a seat. Yes, it was, indeed, quite an adventure. Yes, such a pity—it looks as if we are, unmistakably, bound for naught but hostile conflict. Oh, yes—it is indeed a such a pleasure to see you, also, once again. And—and my congratulations to you both, I certainly had no idea . . . ."

What I learn at dinner compounds heartache with a swell of irony: on account of Elena's condition, Nikolai has long since quit the *Ballet Russe*, and taken a cello position at none other than the Maryinsky.

As we retire later to take port and cognac in the study, while the ladies fuss in the drawing room over the children, I manage to corner Father at last:

"Why did you make no mention of Nikolai's marriage?" I demand in a lowered voice.

Father glances up from filling his pipe with a grunt of surprise. "No mention of Nikolai's marriage?" he cries, astounded.

In response to my glare, he grasps firm hold of my arm, insisting: "Oh, Sasha—I know I mentioned it in one of my letters." Pausing, scratching at his head, he then mumbles: "Uh—surely I did?"

"No, Papa. Not at all, not a word—"

"Oooh!" Emitting a long moan, Father claps himself soundly on his head with the brunt of his hand. "Heaven help us both, my boy! I humbly apologize, I am terribly sorry! For a certainty, I thought I had mentioned it—oh, dear. Small wonder you were so surprised when speaking with them earlier. Please forgive me—I am afraid your doddering old papa is becoming much more of a senile menace to the world than he should ever dare admit! . . ."

Sighing, I roll my eyes and down a long sip of my cognac. "All right, Papa—so tell me, then," I go on. "When was the wedding?"

"Well," he continues more quietly, "I suppose that was, perhaps, why I failed to promptly mention it." Leaning toward me, he whispers in a conspiratorial tone: "Can you imagine? They married not until just days prior to *Maslenitsa!*"

"Indeed?" I gasp, wide-eyed.

"Oh, yes."

So—late January. Only bare of six months past.

Unable to banish from my mind the thought that my cousin could certainly do naught else but marry the woman—assuming that the child she carries is his—I continue watching him with guarded glances, while the other gentlemen talk business, horse racing, geography, politics. At last, as everyone finishes their refreshment and begins easing back toward the drawing room to rejoin the ladies, I stop him cold at the doorway.

"Might I have a word with you?"

Hands shoved down into his trouser pockets, Nikolai shrugs and nods back toward the study's desk. "Well, certainly—"

"No, I mean privately."

Eyeing me with narrowed suspicion, he blurts out: "Look, Sasha, I, uh, hardly think it fitting to—"

"Please."

In response, he lets out a harsh sigh, his brow furrowing as he reconsiders with obvious reluctance. "Oh—very well," he murmurs finally, taking care to avoid my hardened gaze. "Upstairs, then, in Papa's old library. But only for a moment, I beg you! And first let me check back upon Elena once again. You must understand, she's due any day now—the babe is late, and we're rather worried. I'll be up in a moment."

In Uncle Petya's library, past watchful, knowing eyes of so many long-lost printed friends of years gone by, I pace until he slips through the door; stop short as he shuts it softly behind.

Turning, leaning back against it, Nikolai regards me with a steely, defensive glare. "Yes?" he then says. "There is something you wish to discuss?"

I wrench hold of my cane with a grip leveled near to crack brass. "Rather," I tell him, "there is something I wish to ask. Simply one question." My eyes hone in, wavering for not one second away from his.

"Yes?"

"Do you love her?"

Flushing, Nikolai drops his gaze to the floor. "The—the woman is carrying my child, Sasha—"

"My God, Nikolai," I rasp out in vexation, "don't you think I can bloody well see that?"

"Look," he goes on forcefully, "if your dragging me up here has something to do with Budapest, I care not for any part of—"

"Do you love her?"

Fist clenched, he slams it into his other, exclaiming: "Oh, Jesus Christ! This conversation is obviously pointless!"

"Pointless?" I snap, bounding across the room toward him as—shoulders backed to the wall—he attempts to slink away. "Is that what you call my concern for you, Nikolai?" With emphasis, I wave out my arm, pointing at him; at me; at the gulf of space long awash between us. *"Pointless?"*

"Sasha, I happen to be quite capable of managing my personal affairs! And you have obviously had far too much to drink—"

"Fifteen years of friendship!" I choke out, flinging my arm out again and lancing him down in livid, shaking accusation. "Friendship, Nikolai: do you recall the true meaning of the word? It's about camaraderie and pranks in school dorms, blood-brother gashes made in our fingers, the late night talks in shabby rooms of countless European hotels—and our time spent in the orchestra of the *Ballet Russe*—my God, if you hadn't been there to coach me before I had to go on in the *première* to *Sheherazade*, I honestly don't know what I would have done! And now, all of that means nothing to you? You think that everything we ever went through together is *pointless?"*

"You are the one who made it all pointless, Sasha—a year and half ago in that sleazy barhouse in Budapest!"

"I did naught in that sleazy barhouse in Budapest but force you to face the God-honest truth!"

Whitening, Nikolai whirls around, grasping hold of the handle to the door.

"Oh, yes!" I holler after him. "Go on, run away! *Goddamn you, Nikolai Zhelanov!* I should have known you'd never stay in this room for more than five fucking seconds to hear me out! That you've not the guts to face me like a man—"

"Shut up, Sasha!"

"Do you love that woman you married six months ago? That you had to marry simply because one night you got careless?"

"Goddamn it, shut up!"

"Do you love her?"

I see his fist coming, and duck my head just in time—but catch the blow, with a grunt of pain, in the hollow of my neck, before lashing back savagely for his jaw. Which I miss, my fist shattering instead into his elbow—which slams for my face as I smash into his ribs with my other fist, evoking from him a muffled roar—and fed with the inner demons, fueled by the outer storm, our blows continue flying out headlong and unabated in all directions. Finally, bereft of the support of the cane, which makes clattering descent to the floor, my leg gives way, and I knuckle under—but not without making a cursing effort to take him with me, my fingers gripped like talons to the back of his collar and forcing him around in a spin on his heel before he topples down against me and we both land, with a resounding crash, back against the rows of bookshelves.

Pants of two wild animals then lash out in torrid spurts, the bouquet of the wine stung on his breath and bite of cognac still lingering on mine, and we stare one another down in furious, blinded rage, the fencing match committed now to burrowing irises and molten pupils spewing out fiery, volcanic pellets of hate. Past each side of our heads, Uncle Petya's books begin tumbling out one by one from the assaulted library shelves and onto the floor.

And then, everything changes.

Echoes of infant squalls and the droning buzz of feminine chatter drift up from the drawing room just down the stairs—and Nikolai hovers up above me, close. Very close. Staring into mine, his eyes begin to widen in a dawning grip of panic, two wayward sentinels at last struck down and baring in one naked, revelatory flash a soul swept helplessly beyond every last limit of mortal pain. Then, as if of its own accord—as if no longer bound by any tenet of his earthly will at all, save for the earthly, God-honest truth—his head begins inching downward; his mouth begins inching downward, closer and closer, his lips trembling, shaking visibly, and parting just as I part mine—which begin trembling, shaking visibly, yearning in agony for the taste of his. His hand, sliding back from its resting place upon the shelf, cradles itself with a tender, lingering caress about my throat, his thumb sliding upward and brushing a loose strand of hair back from my cheek as I crane back my head . . . *oh, my God—dear God! He—he is! He is going to kiss me! . . .*

And then like a thunderbolt, he wrenches himself away.

I bump down clumsily shelf by shelf, swiping out for the last one to catch my fall—while Nikolai stumbles back, staring at me aghast, his expression horrified, unbelieving, his words garbled and unintelligible and escaping in a sickened moan as he flies blindly for the door.

"Nikolai, wait!" I shout, chasing after.

Out in the hall, his heels crash quaking stabs of fear into every resonant pinewood board.

"Nikolai, please!"

But against padded squeaks in the runner carpet, his footsteps resound—defiant and final—one by one down every step until he disappears past the foot of the stairs.

From the corner of which, Anna then emerges—apparently having started up from the ground floor vestibule just as Nikolai hurried down to the second story. Glancing toward the smoke of his angry trail, she then glares back up at me, sadly shaking her head and muttering: "Oh, good heavens, Sasha! Will you and he never make up about whatever on earth it all was?"

In response, I manage to bite back an avalanche of curses and stomp off for my room, there to slam shut the door with a furious, thwarted cry of vengeance.

After scrawling a hasty message for Father and running a quick comb through my hair, I snatch up my cane and hat and make for the nearest tavernhouse on Liteiny Prospekt, which I find engulfed in a violent merrymaking uproar. Rumor has it that the Tsar will soon declare general wartime prohibition.

"Drink up, laddie!" the barkeep bellows, sloshing a generous tankard of vodka into my grip. "Best do so while ye got the chance, eh?"

From all sides, shoulders bump and laughter coarsens into shrieks and hollers—the dribbling liquid from bottles of vodka, the foaming heads off mugs of *kvas* chafing with bitter, pungent whiffs through the smoky, song-filled air.

But I stare straight ahead, my eyes vacant and unmoving, my attention drawn solely toward the rickety bandstand stage. There, sticks of flame continue enticing the imagination as two wise fools of the ages—emulating, unbeknownst, the poet's lofty, forlorn call—begin, upon the count of three, searing their throats with seething rivers of fire.

* * *

The following day, I take considerable pains to avoid crossing paths with either Nikolai or his wife, make endless excuses to Father about the poetry, and come evetide, escape again to the same tavernhouse—where I drink the same vodka, watch the same fire-eaters, and torment myself to no end with the same inescapable questions regarding the contrivance of coincidence.

Consider, for instance, the plight of one Gavrilo Princip—a nineteen-year-old Bosnian wise fool of the ages if there ever was one. According to the newspaper reports through which I have been scouring over the last two days, he looked *away* from his intended target before hauling out his Browning and firing twice: striking the Archduke Franz Ferdinand, heir to the Austro-Hungarian throne, fatally; striking the Duchess of Hohenberg, wife of the Archduke, fatally; and striking, without even realizing it, the jugular vein of political harmony and plunging Europe's vast empires and their allies into tides of a war the scope of which is as yet barely fathomable. *Was this coincidence?*

Why? Why is God playing games with the world? And why—dammit!—is He playing games with me?

Again I take a deep drag off my cigarette, again down more vodka, again ponder over my own peculiar dilemma of circumstance now parlayed by the crafty Unsung Dealer's hand. *Why, in the ultimate parody of coincidence, did Nikolai happen to secure employment at, of all places, the Maryinsky? Where I could still be playing, had I not run off to Europe like such a harebrained fool! Whether or not my cousin will admit that what lies between us could ever be more than brotherly friendship, at least I could see his face; watch him play! Cello, violin—I do not care, if only to be near him! Oh, goddamn it—why do I never listen to Father? Why in Christ's name did I rush out of here last year without even pausing to think?*

Oh, yes—the beauty, the glory, the music: *Swan Lake.* Volodya bucking it up like a regular high-roller out at the main theater doors. *With Sheremetev.*

Sheremetev, one Ilarion Pavlovich. And how long have I been running away, burying myself in work, denying the scars in pride, the loss of self-respect, the sheer nightmarish hell of those four long months of memories in 1907? Because of my fear of somehow encountering Sheremetev's greedy ghost within the realms of this vast city, I forsook all chance for studying at the St. Petersburg Conservatory, as Nikolai once so wanted. Had I done so, how differently would recent matters have resolved themselves? Perhaps by the time we traversed Europe together with the *Ballet Russe*, Nikolai would have been the one longing for my kisses instead of endless faceless Gypsies in countless sleazy bars all the way from the London docks to Budapest. Perhaps my cousin could have borne my love had we spent more time together when younger—had I not been so withdrawn and full of nightmares, had I not shrunk from his every embrace given in genuine brotherly affection. *Goddamn Sheremetev*—what right did he have to barge in and *ruin my life* bare before it even began? And then the bastard shows up again, if on cue, with Volodya in the Maryinsky! *Was this coincidence?*

"Shit!" I mumble out, signaling the barkeep for another tankard full of the tavern's now diminishing supply of vodka.

Beside me, a shabbily-dressed postman perched upon the adjoining stool bumps my shoulder, begs my pardon, pays the barkeep, and throws down the thick string of twine with which he has been lazily weaving cat's cradles for the last half hour.

Absently, I snatch up the twine, loop it through my fingers—and through two more tankards of vodka, begin stringing out my own vengeful cat's cradle ribbons while muttering on and on beneath my breath: "Goddamn him! *Goddamn Sheremetev . . . .*"

* * *

"Well, well!" exclaims Volodya, throwing open the door with a grinning flourish. "And let's get a high sight o' you, now—whew! I swear to God, frumped up just like old Gorky himself: Cossack shirt, cotton breeches, your old peasant boots from the farm! What'a'ye been up to, Sekovsky—swaggerin' through the barhouses, tryin' to charm the pants off half the Guards regiments before they ship out for the front? I'm surprised you don't got six or seven of 'em chasin' you right now like a herd of starved bulls, after waltzin' down the streets with that red hair flyin' loose, ha! Hey, and just where you been, anyway, huh?" he cries, clapping his hand onto my shoulder. As the door slams shut behind us, he bellows, laughing, into my face: "It's July, you luscious, cheatin', sweet taste of ass, you! You're over two months late—hey, wait a minute—*holy shit! . . ."*

The cane clatters to the floor, and my left hook, ever dependable, makes quick work of Volodya's jaw—for he doubles over, gasping and spitting blood. "Shit, Sekovsky! What the hell has come over you?"

I wrench him up by his collar; deck him again—and again; dodge two retaliatory blows and take his third in the ribs without much pain or loss of momentum as I deck him yet again . . . .

"Sekovsky! *Have you lost your mind?"*

"You lied to me!" Once again I wrench him roughly upward.

"Lied? Jesus! And how the devil are you managin' to strut around like that without your cane? *Lied?* I—I don't know what you are talkin' about—"

"This." As he flails out, half-staggering and full of protests, I grip hold of his wrists and drag him over toward the iron posted bed.

"Just what in hell do you think you're doin'! . . ."

In silence, I lash the stiff pull of twine around his arms and begin tying him up to the bedpost.

"Sekovsky! If this is your idea of a little joke, I am *not* humored!"

"Oh, this is no joke," I tell him, snapping the loop knots tight.

"Oww! Shit!"

"No, this is no joke at all. You see now, Volodya—baby-darling-precious-love!—now, my friend, you and me, we are going to play a little game."

"Christ! Just what *in hell* have you been drinkin'? Torchburners over at Murzhinsky's?"

"And the reason we are going to play this game is because it's the very same little game that *he* used to play."

"What—who are you talkin' about?"

"This—him." Snarling under my breath, I reach around, and with a kicking shove, force Volodya face down on the bed. Then I unclasp his belt and begin yanking down his trousers.

"Sekovsky! What the fuck—"

"Oooh! You're smarter than I thought—the swarthy beekeeper just uttered the first magic word!" Furiously, I heave down on top of him; slide my hands in over his bare skin and begin making thrusting motions against his buttocks.

"Sekovsky! . . ."

"You know what the *second* magic word is, Rykazian?" I shout down into his ear. *"Do you know what the second filthy, disgusting, God-awful magic word is?"*

"Goddamn it, get off me!"

"Rape!"

The silence, in a portent of horror, hangs above our heads—until I slide off the bed and whirl around to face him.

Panting out a slew of curses and yanking his wrists against the knots in the twine, Volodya scoots off the bed and slides down onto the floor, attempting—none too handily—to hike his trousers up around his haunches. "How dare you burst in here and tie me up like this!" he shouts wrathfully up into my face.

"And how dare you *lie* to me!" I storm back, pointing livid accusation down at him. "Goddamn it, Rykazian—I saw you! During autumn pre-season last August—with Sheremetev at the Maryinsky!"

Blanching, Volodya stares upward, wide-eyed and open-mouthed—and then tucks his head down upon his bound-up hands, muttering: "Oh, *shit . . . .*"

"You are *still* working for him!"

"Sasha, look—"

"Blast it, *stop lying to me!* You are still working for Sheremetev—and *have* been, all this time that I've been coming to see you, ever since those four years ago when we ran into one another again at the dress shop! All during the revolutionary meetings, the poetry readings—you have been, and still *are*, working for him! Even though you *swore to me* when I first started up with you again that I was never in any danger, that you were not and *never* would work for Sheremetev again, *ever!* But it turns out that you are naught but a filthy, bloodsucking *liar!"*

Volodya catches in his breath, shaking his head at me in mortified, sheepish bursts. "Sasha!" he blurts out. "Let me try and explain—"

"Goddamn it! Don't you recall who Sheremetev is to me, Rykazian?" Dropping to my knees and facing him on the floor, I grip tight hold of his collar, snapping his neck forward hurtfully, and rasp into his face: "Sheremetev is the fucking swine who—night after night, seven years ago in Moscow—played this little game! He tied me up to the posts at the end of my bed and raped me!"

"Sasha! Sasha, look—"

"Do you think women are the only ones ever forced against their will, Rykazian? Huh? Shit! Bloody-fucking shit!"

"Sekovsky, look! Granted, I did make a delivery for him once—well, perhaps twice—since I saw you last, but I swear! I've not seen Pierre since—"

"Oh, shut up, goddamn it—you stinking yellow-bellied Armenian sonuvabitch! My God, I can hardly believe you're still working for him—the man ordered your fucking fingers cut off, for Christ's sake!"

Ears steaming with rage, I start pacing back and forth across the room, and while Volodya mumbles on with his blustering excuses, I light up cigarette after cigarette and crush out butt after butt.

"All right, Sekovsky!" he shouts out at me angrily at last. "You've bloody well made your point! Now, blast it—my back end is gettin' cold! So, untie me—"

"Rape," I say aloud for at least the hundredth time, continuing to ignore his every plea as I pace. "You know, I've never even been able to admit it to myself, nor utter that filthy, wretched word, before tonight—"

"Look, dammit!" Volodya whines on, "I must have apologized for it all at least a dozen times by now. You know I never meant for Pierre to charge in there and kidnap you!"

"And it was scarce enough," I go on, ignoring him, "for the bloody bastard to force himself upon me night after night. Still, he had to keep me locked up in his goddamn fucking glass palace, never allowing me out for even a momentary breath of fresh air! Then, on top of that, he took away my mother's amethyst crystal—and then my inheritance! Two hundred thousand *fucking rubles*, Rykazian!"

"Sekovsky, dammit—will you simply bury it all already? Jesus, now untie me! Years ago I thought we went all over this."

I stop short in front of him and peer down disdainfully, demanding: "When did you last see him?"

"Huh?"

"When did you last make one of your godforsaken 'deliveries' to Sheremetev, Rykazian? Last week? Yesterday? *When?* Goddamn it, you spineless turd of a pig's ass!" Dropping down again, I seize him by both shoulders and start shaking him ferociously, shouting: "Answer me!"

"Stop it—oww! L-Let go—!"

"Answer me! When was the last time you saw Sheremetev?"

"All—all r-right, all right! T-Two—"

"When?"

"—two days ago, *shit!* Jesus!" he moans as I let go.

"Then he's in Petersburg?" I gasp, still gripping hold of his arm.

"Yes!" Furiously, Volodya tries to elbow my hand away. "Yes, blast it! Now will you untie me?"

"No. Not until you tell me where he is."

"What? Oh, crap! How—how in hell am I supposed to know where Sheremetev is?"

"You're *lying!"* I yell, slamming my fist once more into his face.

"Agghh! J-Jesus, Sekovsky! . . ."

"You tell me where he is!" Again I shake him blindly by the shoulders; again begin pounding blows, one after another, into his face.

"Stop it—you go to fuckin' hell, Sekovsky!" Volodya shouts back defiantly, glaring up at me in between punches.

"Goddamn it, Rykazian! You tell me where he is!"

"No!"

"You see this?" I shout, brandishing a fresh-lit cigarette up in front of his face. "You want it crammed up your ass, Rykazian? Now—you tell me where he is!"

"Humph!" Volodya chokes out. "You filthy little bastard's bitchin' *whore!* You—you scarce have the bloody guts!"

Staring at the red-glowing tip of the cigarette, I sigh in reconsideration, murmuring: "I suppose you're right."

And then I crush it flat into his neck.

"Jesus fuckin' Christ!" Volodya screams out, wrenching his head back and forth wildly as the ash extinguishes in a quick pungent wisp.

"You tell me where he is!" I shout again.

"You go to hell!"

"You tell me where he is!" Another cigarette I light—and extinguish in the same dastardly manner yet again.

"Oh, all right—Jesus bloody shit!—take it off, take it off!"

Bristling for revenge, Volodya's eyes sear up at me as he mutters beneath his breath: *"Goddamn it!*—and—and how I thought I cared for you, you dirty little doe-eyed *snake!* I swear to God, you are goin' to pay plenty well for this!"

"Where is Sheremetev?" I ask pointedly, sneering down and holding out between us another fresh-lit cigarette.

"If not yet departed for Moscow, at his townhouse."

"Where?"

"I—I'm not so certain of the address—"

"Liar!"

"Goddamn it, Sekovsky, it's the bloody truth! You poke me in the neck again with one of those, and I swear I will come find you, and I will kill you!"

"Where is Sheremetev's townhouse?"

"He just leased it, just moved in! I—I don't know! I think somewhere over in New Holland district, near Moika Canal."

"Under his own name?" Abruptly, I pull to my feet.

As Volodya averts his eyes and ducks his head away, I roar down: "Blast it, Rykazian! *The truth!"*

"All right, all right! Under, uh, Pavlovsky—that's the name, I think, that he's been usin'—"

Turning on my heel, I march straight away from the apartment, leaving the door ajar with purposeful, humiliating intent as Volodya screams after: *"Goddamn you, Sekovsky!* You are goin' to pay for this! . . ."

* * *

"He calls himself 'Piccolo,' Your Honor—and will not give any other name. And he's very insistent, refuses to be appeased, to leave without seeing you—"

"Well, I scarce care how bloody insistent the lad is! Is growing late, and I happen to be quite pressed for time."

"Shall I ring for Yevgeny Ivanovich, Your Honor?"

"Do whatever you must, Timosha! I tell you, I haven't the time!"

The butler scurries back out from the room. Following him, Pierre, his cigarette dangling from within its mother-of-pearl holder as he fidgets with his gloves, sees me and stops cold in the hallway.

Then Yevgeny Ivanovich—the same massive dishwater-haired henchman who first wrestled me from the pantry in Volodya's old Vyborg flat; the same belligerent oaf who used to trample in half-drunk every few nights to slice apart my wrist bindings those many years ago in Moscow—stomps up from the downstairs. Upon spying me, he roars: "Humph! I'll throw the vermin out, Yer Honor!"

"No—wait."

Pierre makes of pointed show of easing off his gloves while scanning me up and down. In seven years, his advance in age is evident—the hair sparser, grown white at the temples, his mouth, brow, and cheeks furrowed now with deep-set lines. But his eyes, limpid and owl-like as ever, begin sparkling with youthful amusement once recognition curbs his hurried impatience. "Piccolo, did you say?" he murmurs to me in French, nodding affably. "Ahh, yes—*Piccolo . . . .*"

Holding his stare, I clench both fists to my sides and swallow hard, attempting to even out my voice's sarcastic edge as I declare, also in French: "I should like to have a word with you, Ilarion Pavlovich."

In reply, a grin. "Regarding?"

"Regarding a—a certain piece of jewelry of mine that you have retained in your possession," I stammer out. "And regarding a certain two hundred thousand rubles."

At this, Yevgeny, who appears to understand the comment about the money well enough, lets out a warning grunt, but Pierre shrugs him off with a swishing flick of his hand. "Oh, Ivanovich, get your ass back downstairs and see to the damn casements, will you? I hardly believe the young man intends any trouble." To Timosha, the butler, Pierre then turns with a questioning glance—to be met with the sight of my smaller Webley pistol displayed for his perusal in the man's outstretched hand. "Oh, very good—yes, put it out on the foyer table for the young man to pick up when he leaves. Do understand," Pierre then says, turning to me, "that our long-standing policy is to search everyone; you are not being singled out. Now, then—please." Standing back, he indicates the open door to the room from which Timosha just fetched him.

I watch the butler scurry away, while Yevgeny trudges in a grumbling mood back for the downstairs. Ducking through the doorway into a book-lined study, Pierre urges me to follow, although in so doing, I keep a safe distance between the two of us. "Well, come in, Piccolo!" he exclaims with a hearty laugh, tossing his gloves down onto the desk. After inhaling a deep drag off his cigarette, he turns swiftly to face me, murmuring: "Or perhaps I should say—Count Sekovsky?"

I stare to my feet, heart pounding in my ears, all breath gone icy-numb.

"Oh, really, darling!" Pierre cries, guffawing. "Are you so naive as to think that by now I did not know? After watching you play *Swan Lake* last year, I did some checking—and certainly, I pay Rykazian enough to dredge out the truth no matter how childishly in love with you the poor fool thinks he is! Yes, indeed, Count Sekovsky—and just how old must you be by now, my sweet? Twenty-two? Twenty-three? And a fine young man have you grown into, at that. I must say, you cut quite a dashing figure that night we exchanged glances at the Maryinsky! Let me see," he goes on thoughtfully, scratching at his chin, "last year, briefly, you played with the Maryinsky Theater Orchestra, but were previously associated—for some years, I understand—in Paris and elsewhere with the *Ballet Russe* of Sergei Diaghilev, that avant-garde troupe doing such wonders for the reputation of we Russians abroad! Yes, yes—now, what else did I manage to learn about the Sekovsky family? Oh, yes—a most ancient line hailing from the environs of Novgorod. Lissushka, is it not called, your father's estate lying on the northeast shore of Lake—Lake Ilmen, is it, now? The estate named after your mother, I believe? And your mother—God rest her soul—was not, as you once suggested, a mere governess, but indeed of noble English birth, and quite the legendary beauty, or so it is still said. And yes, your father, one Mikhail Sergeyevich—a man now certainly getting up there in his years, yes? Your father is the one, is he not, who spent a long sentence in a Siberian prison camp at the Tsar's whim for some tepid, blundering little offense—of which, of course, the poor man was later exonerated in entirety, we must point out! But such brief blight scarce diminishes the honor borne through prior generations of the Sekovsky family line: one of your great grandfathers made a count by the Great Tsar Peter himself, so it is said! And prior to that, I understand your forebears' exploits can be traced back past scourges of the Awesome Ivan, and unto the glory days of your own patron saint, Aleksandr Nevsky himself—to the time of the proud Novgorodian Republic, its practice of free trade and ties to the Hanseatic League coupled with the fierce independent thinking of its boyars—while we poor souls in pitiable Muscovy, in tormented Kiev suffered such burning and pillage under the monstrous Tartar yoke in the 1200s. Ahh, yes—so interesting it all is—lineage, heritage, history—to a man like me, who is, you see, not legitimately entitled under the law to ever lay proper claim unto his own. So, Aleksandr Mikhailovich," he goes on with a deliberate, patronizing grin, "or perhaps you would prefer that I call you 'Sasha?' You and I are, after all—or at least have been—on rather intimate terms, *n'est-ce pas?* So, Sasha, my dear—I am your humble servant! What, again, was your request?"

Forever transpires unto death until I find my voice. "Seven years ago in Moscow, you appropriated from me a gold-set amethyst quartz crystal," I rasp out. "Which once belonged to my mother. I should like it back—along with the two hundred thousand rubles, paid from my inheritance, that you stole to impart my freedom."

"Oh, now just a moment! I never *stole* a kopek. That sum was paid for services duly accrued and the value of tangible market goods—"

"I am *not* and *never* have been a goddamn market good!"

"Perhaps," Pierre cries breathlessly, waving out his hands, "we might be able to come to some kind of mutual understanding, some gentlemen's agreement, young Aleksandr! Now, neither of us want any trouble, agreed? Nor—ahem!—any abruptly started rumors? *N'est-ce pas*, my young friend?

Shaken from head to foot with rage, I slam both fists into my pockets, desperate to keep my temper within check—and after a long pause to catch my breath, reply at last with a forced nod.

"Very well!" says Pierre, grinning again and stubbing out his cigarette behind him in a large marble ashtray sitting atop the desk. "Come, then!" Elaborately, he throws open both doors leading off to an adjoining room and waves for me to follow while mumbling to himself: "Now, about that crystal . . . ."

At a highboy jewelry armoire, he starts rummaging through drawer after tiny drawer, while I stare about uneasily. Like the outer rooms of the small townhouse, the bedroom appears not so richly adorned as my hated emerald-green prison cell in the gaudy Moscow mansion, but bears every embellishment of good taste. Two diminutive lavender-tinted chandeliers offset the lightened hues of fringed draperies at the high windows, and brocade tapestries of mauve and orange striping cover the bed and mahogany Queen Anne chairs. "This is what you were wishing back?" Pierre says dryly, still searching through the armoire drawers in a state of distraction as, without looking upward, he flings out Melissa's amethyst crystal, the chain draped about his fingers.

"Yes!" I reply, taking a step toward him, but halting up abruptly. "And?" I demand. "The money?"

"First things first, Sasha, darling," Pierre snaps with impatience, waving out the crystal. "Do you want this trinket, or no?"

Biting my lip—and inwardly barking back the thousand voices in my head screaming for me not to do so—I edge toward him with caution, at last snatching the crystal away from his hand.

Only to then drop it—just as his hand clamps like a vulture's claw around my wrist. "No!" I gasp. "What are you doing! . . ."

As I scream out, Pierre shoves me around and twists my arm behind my back; slams his other hand flat against my chest and pinions me against him, his chin rubbing up against my ear as he whispers: "My God! All these years—and you have grown more fetching than *ever—"*

"Stop it, damn you!"

"—don't you realize, Piccolo—Sasha—*darling!*—had I known indeed what true treasure I possessed, I would never, *ever* have let you go. . . ."

My cane slams down across his left shin, forcing out a cry from him as he lets up on me, and I whirl around and heave it again for his shoulders in a double-fisted torrent—before he flails out angrily, deflecting it to the floor with a barreling swipe.

"Goddamn you!" I shout, flushed livid with rage. *"You filthy, stinking son of the devil!"*

"Ha! And still you remain as full of fight as ever, *n'est-ce pas?"*

"Shut up, goddamn it! How dare you lay your putrid hands on me again!"

He sees my knife flying upward as I snatch it from my boot, and seizes onto my wrist. Each struggling for the blade, we tumble onto the floor, rolling over one another, kicking, shoving, and knocking into chairs, his low laughter grating against my furious curses—until the knife spins away from the both of us, clattering across the room to land at the bricks of the hearth.

The door from the hallway then slams open as we both scramble to our feet—and the henchman Yevgeny, fists slung to his hips, stands glaring down at me before eyeing Pierre with a somber, questioning glance.

"Oh, get out," Pierre snaps.

"But, Yer Honor—"

"Get out, I said, Ivanovich! Can't you see I'm simply having a bit of fun? Go, dammit—out, I say! Get yourself down again to the tavernhouses before they exhaust the last of the damn vodka—"

"But, Pierre! *Sir!"* Frowning darkly, his beady eyes screwed up in his face, Yevgeny peers at the knife lying on the floor.

"Go!" Pierre shouts, glowering at him. *"That's an order!* And take Timosha along, will you? The damn fool's always meddling, sticking his nose into . . . into my little affairs . . . ."

Reluctantly, Yevgeny draws back and disappears through the door, slamming it behind—and upon echoes of his footsteps, I pounce for the knife—but Pierre bursts out in front of me, wagging a warning finger. "Now, wait a moment, Sekovsky—hold it right there!" he yells sharply. "Take a deep breath—yes, dammit! Stop and take a deep breath, young man, and listen to me! Now, Sekovsky—*Sasha*—you and I both know that you are just itching like the devil to have it out with me! And there is nothing I enjoy better than a fair fight—yes, a fair fight! You may be hampered by that shortened leg, but I have thirty-five years of age on you, much to my discredit—I'd call it a fair fight. So, the stakes are this: if you win, if you can best me—if you can leave me crumpled in a heap begging for your mercy—then I'll grant you back your two hundred thousand rubles, with—oh, say, seven years accrued interest at six percent. I'll grant you that amount without further dispute, if you can best me! But—should I win—well, ha, ha!" he rasps out in a lowered tone, lewdly eyeing me up and down. "Then we both know what my prize will be—*n'est-ce pas?"*

"You—you filthy, whoremonging bastard!" Through gritted teeth, I seethe at him; through heart-pounding rage, I peel off my jacket, hurling it to the floor. My cap duly follows as I flex both fists and start rolling up my sleeves.

"Good, good!" Laughing, Pierre darts around and snatches up the knife, brandishing it out between us with a baiting leer—before throwing it into the bowl of ash in the hearth and soundly clamping shut the fire screen. "As I said, sweetest," he whispers, shrugging, "a fair fight—"

Letting out a blistering yell, I lunge for him in a blinded heave, seizing hold of his arm before he can duck around the footrest of the bed for cover—and vengefully, murderously, I start throwing punches left and right for his face, chest, and ribs, slamming the air out of him and forcing up a slew of sputtering coughs until he finally shoves me off and staggers away. "Dear Lord!" he blurts out, doubling over, wide-eyed. "Whence the agility, Sekovsky? You've had your boots built up, a—a lift cobbled onto the heel?"

"Something like that." Again I loom in upon him and back him into the nearest corner, my blows glancing into his neck, chest, and flailing arms, my hound's instinct primed to the sweet scent of ready, waiting blood.

Letting out a gleeful shriek of triumph, Pierre then whirls back around—his leather switch slicing for my face, its knotted ends catching hold of my spectacles and flinging them off through the air. "No, wait!" I cry, blinking—but his fist plows into my lower jaw, and I stagger back with a moan as he trips me up, toppling me to the floor, his laughter gloating above my head in cackling, shrewish bursts.

"Goddamn it!" I shout up at him, pointing. "You said a *fair* fight!"

"All's fair in love and war, my sweet!" Again the leather switch smacks down—cracking into a spray of carpet fibers this time as I elbow out of the way, roaring: "Fuck you to hell, Sheremetev! I'll show you what's fair!"

At the fireplace hearth, I wrench the screen back to snatch the knife from the ash pile just in time—and slash out wildly for his throat as he banters forth a siege of taunts and snide barbs, the leather switch whacking in all directions. "You are naught but a despicable, lying cheat!" I shout, heaving for breath and mopping at my brow as beads of boiling sweat drench down both temples to my neck.

"And you are naught but a naive, trusting little fool!" he shouts back, grinning evilly and attempting to back me toward the bed.

Once we reach it, I spin around, stabbing for his chest—but the switch lashes snug around the blade of the knife, snatching it away from my grasp—then to be flung entirely across the breadth of the room.

"No!" I scream as he grabs for my wrist—the cord from the long end of the switch, grasped in his other hand, mocking a length of rope. Blindly, I jab out for him—cursing, punching, rolling beneath him, and then shimmying back on top as we land upon the bed. But despite my effort, he again gains the upper hand, forcing me downward and murmuring close: "Oh, yes! Now, I am going to have you once again, Sasha, my little black-eyed dove. . . ."

I thrust upward savagely—landing the blow squarely into his jaw and forcing out a pitiful squall—just as the switch again slashes down, searing its fiery row of topknots across the nape of my neck.

"Goddamn you—*nooo!"* I shout as he wrenches apart the clasp to my belt. "I will never give in to you again, ever!"

"As I see it, dearest, you'll soon enough have scarce little choice!"

Then his fist crashes dully into the side of my head, and the room blackens; whitens. Blackens again. Moaning, my head reeling, I gasp for air as he starts tying up my wrists with the switch. "Hush, darling, and enjoy it," I hear him murmur into my ear. "You know, deep down, that you always did before . . . ."

"Nooo!" Somehow, I manage to yank my right arm free—and my fingers stab downward for my boot, grasping for anything, and clamping hold of the old cleaning rod from within the piccolo. In desperation, I swipe it outward.

"Ha!" Disbelieving, Sheremetev's laughter blasts down into my face. "A flute cleaning rod, of all things? Ha! And exactly what, precious fool, intend you to do with that?"

"Precisely this!" I roar, ramming it upward. "Never will I give in to you again, Ilarion Pavlovich Sheremetev! By dammit, do you hear me? *Never, ever again . . . .*"

My shouts catch to a numb stall in my throat as his grip slackens abruptly upon the leather switch—his eyes widening, cheeks blanching, a long breath emitting in a rattling moan from his lips. "I, uh, think I might j-just have underestimated y-you," he mumbles—and then topples clumsily downward, rolling to land face up beside me upon the bed.

Another long breath fans out as his eyelids flutter; as they droop to a waning close.

And then, silence.

Stunned, I pull my left wrist free and stare, gasping, downward.

There to find the old flute cleaning rod no longer within my right hand's grasp, but instead sticking straight up of its own accord.

From his chest.

"Oh, my God!" I exclaim. "Pierre? Il-Ilarion Pavlovich? I scarce meant to—oh, my God! *Pierre?*" In a fluster, I begin gently slapping at his face, attempting to restore some glimmer of consciousness—but his eyes remain stubbornly closed, his muscles slackened and benign to every touch upon my probing. "Oh, *dear God!*" I cry. "Ilarion Pavlovich, *please*: bat an eye, move a muscle, say something, anything! I promise I'll go straight away, or—or send someone for a doctor . . . ."

But as the darkness of night seeps in past the glow of the room's only lit lamp, so does the eerie, judgmental pall of silence—and my dawning realization.

Praying for it not to be true, I stoop downward; set my ear close to his nose.

No breath. No breath at all.

"Oh, Jesus Christ!" Hands shaking wildly, I snatch hold of his arm, check his wrist; then, his throat.

No pulse.

"Oh, shit!" I scream out. *"Holy fucking shit!* I can't have—he can't be—my *God!* If—if he *is,* then just where—where the hell's the *blood?"*

All over my shirt, all over my right hand—having apparently seeped from the wound stabbed into my palm without my knowing when I lashed out at him with the cleaning rod.

Fingers still shaking so that I can hardly manage it, I reclasp the buckle to my belt while vaguely recalling something Father once mentioned about the dryness of deep puncture wounds. As my heightened senses slowly begin to level back down to normalcy, the throbbing in my palm makes itself felt in earnest, and I rummage through my pockets for my handkerchief; bind it up about the bloodied wound. "Shit!" I mutter out again—staring, wide-eyed, at Pierre's wan face. From some distance, the sound of a slamming door then echoes upward, and a surge panic grips me cold . . . *oh, motherfucking shit! I have got to get the hell out of here!*

However, the cleaning rod—indispensable flutist's tool glinting silver-bright with a ready show of evidence—remains deeply embedded within his chest. *Shit! Oh, shit—what the devil have I done? J-Jesus living God!*

Wincing, I start prying the rod outward. *Oh, Christ, here it comes!*—and once I pull it free, blood starts spurting, and I back off with a nauseated heave, smearing clumped droplets from the rod into my handkerchief and taking care to prevent any more tell-tale red stains from soaking into my clothes. "Oh, Christ's blistered balls in Heaven!" I mutter to myself, shuddering violently from head to foot. "Holy fucking God! . . ."

Like a banshee possessed, I tear through the bedroom, flinging back on my jacket and cap. From various spots upon the floor, I recover my cane, knife, Melissa's amethyst crystal, and my spectacles, from which one lense has been knocked loose. Fortunately unshattered, it lies close by, and with quaking fingers, I snap it back into the metal frame, praying to all the Saints for the thing to hold as I whirl about frantically, sweeping the room once again from end to end, attempting to recall if I might have left behind anything else.

Just barely do I remember to retrieve my Webley pistol from the foyer table before bursting out through the street entrance with a sigh of relief. The sleepy-eyed doorman, betraying not a hint of suspicion, murmurs his respects as I murmur wary reply and attempt to wander nonchalantly past him. Whereupon, from just down the street, what do I encounter but the sight of Volodya stomping over the closest Moika bridge, a blaze of self-righteous thunder at his heels, his wrath set with murderous, avenging purpose straight toward the townhouse row.

Oh, shit! Before he can spot me, I plead forgetfulness with the doorman of some personal item, and duck back inside, tearing through the lower stairwells until I reach the kitchen, where a cook—and to my horror, none other but the butler, Timosha—interrupt their conversation to gawk at my wild, panting rush and blood-stained handkerchief with raised, questioning eyebrows.

"Uh—excuse me!" I blurt out, shoving past the two of them and out the courtyard servants' entrance.

Where I slam shut the door behind me and then run like bloody hell.

* * *

"Papa, it's all right—it's me! I—I know it scarce looks at all like me—but I promise you, it truly is your Sasha! Papa, it is all right!"

At four A.M., my tiptoeings through the halls and stairwells of the Zhukovskaya townhouse have been met with shrouded cover of darkness, Father's room holding no exception: naturally thinking me a prowler, he has dived for his revolver on the bedside table, coming up with it cocked and ready before he at last stops struggling, his muffled screams evaporating underneath my hand as I finally lift it away from his mouth.

"M-My God, Sasha!" he stammers out. "You near stopped my heart stone cold!"

"Papa, please keep your voice down!" I whisper frantically, crouching down on the bed beside him and gripping urgent hold of his arm. "No one else in the house must hear us, nor know that I am here—I am telling you, Papa, it is a matter of life and death!"

Eyeing me warily, Father returns the gun to the table and scoots upward on his elbows. "And just where the devil have you been for an *entire week?*" he whispers back with an angry, flashing glare. "We have been searching for you everywhere, Sasha! And just what in God's name are you doing dressed up as a woman? Did I not know better, I'd swear you were none other than Liss!"

Indeed, the long chestnut braid does much more justice to my mother's shade of hair than to my own, which has fortunately grown long enough to be kept pinned back out of sight beneath the kerchief knotted tightly about my head. With a grunt of impatience, I yank up the folds of the heavy cotton skirt, revealing my trousers and boots still worn underneath. "Papa, I know this is hard to explain, but—"

"Hard to explain, my ass! How did you ever get past the night doorman looking like that?"

"I stole in through the courtyard, through the servants' entrance—yes, I have a key! That's how Nikolai and I used to sneak out nights when we were younger."

"You and Nikolai used to sneak out nights? Through the servants' entrance?"

"Papa, dammit—that is not important now! Will you please simply listen to me? A terrible thing has happened!"

As he stares at me, frowning, I burst out: "Well! Why else would I traipse around dressed as a damned country *devushka?*"

Rolling his eyes, Father sighs heavily, and says low beneath his breath: "After two nights without you coming home, we went to the police. *They* were looking for you, too."

Oh, God! Moaning, I duck my head down into trembling hands. Day after day have I chased through the crowded mazes of Haymarket stalls; night after night have I stolen through countless alleys in the rat-infested Vyborg workers' slums, catching only the barest snatches of sleep, the quickest nibbles of food—while ever trying to elude the fury of Volodya and escape the wily net of the police. "My Lord, Sasha!" Father whispers, his fingers squeezing into my arm, "just what kind of trouble have you gotten yourself into?"

I bring my head upward through a choked veil of tears. "Oh, God, Papa!" I rasp out. "I have done a terrible thing!"

"Is that why the police are looking for you?"

Nodding, flushing, I stab at my eyes with the heel of my hand.

"Well, Sasha, *what* has happened?"

But again I cannot face him, and bury my head downward, moaning in a grip of fear.

"Sasha," he goes on softly, staring with concern toward my still-bandaged right hand, "whatever has happened, is it serious enough to send you to jail?"

"Oh, God, Papa!" I gasp out in desperation. *"W-Worse!"*

Father catches in his breath, murmuring: "Oh, my Lord. Serious enough to send you to Siberia?"

Through the darkness, we stare at one another in a crush of silence, and at last I nod helplessly, throwing up my hands and blurting out: "And possibly worse!"

Steadying strong fingers upon my shoulder, Father avoids mention of the morbid alternative. "The police," he whispers after a long moment. "When we went to the station, they too were inquiring as to your whereabouts, and wanted to know if you had ever been acquainted with a certain Moscow businessman, one Pierre Pavlovsky—"

I slam shut my eyes as he concludes: "—who was found, on the night of August the third—the night of your disappearance—stabbed to death in his apartments over in New Holland district. Sasha—please

God!—correct me if I have mistakenly drawn the easy, over-obvious conclusion—"

Never in my life—at least for very long—have I been able to deny my father's probing stares and penchant for ultimately discerning the truth behind my many blunderings. Resigned to the omniscient axis of fate, I meet his gaze fully as he murmurs out: "Oh, Lord Jesus . . . ."

"Papa! What did you tell the police?"

"Well, what else was I supposed to tell them? But the truth: that my son is a flighty, temperamental poet ofttimes given to melodramatic disappearing acts with scarce a moment's mention to his poor old papa! And I also told them that, to my knowledge, you had never been acquainted with any such person as this merchant Pavlovsky—and that my son would be the last man in the world to commit a cold-blooded murder! Sasha, my *God!* Just who *was* this Pavlovsky? And how did you ever manage to become involved in—"

"Papa, I assure you—what transpired between myself and Pavlovsky was not without cause! But beyond that, I cannot elaborate. I risked coming here tonight so I could say goodbye, for I could not bear the thought of leaving without seeing you one last time. I intend upon heading north of Vyborg tonight, then to attempt hopping the morntide train. Hopefully, by this time tomorrow, I'll have made it across the border into Finland."

"Go straight to Oslo," he orders out emphatically, snatching up pen and paper from the bedside table. "Here, this is the address of the Janissons there. Olaf is an old friend from my Sevastopol days—we still correspond monthly. I know they will be glad to put you up until I can follow."

"Oh, Papa, no!" I cry. Already have I wrested harrowingly enough about abandoning Mother Russia, dear home and domain of my ancestors for over a thousand years. In no way possible could I insist that Father, on my account, do the very same—but he grips hold of my arm, his lips curving upward in a tender, knowing smile. "Sasha," he murmurs, "no matter what folly you have committed, you are still everything to me. If you are fated once again for foreign exile, then this time, my boy, I am coming along! I will not again be long parted from you."

In response, I cannot help but throw both arms about his neck and crush him close, fresh tears seeping from the corners of my eyes.

"Besides, perhaps it is for the best," he goes on in a solemn tone. "The Tsar's policy of charging full on into this war is naught but strident lunacy! When the excitement and fervor of the last week and a half dies down, the old problems will not have gone away. I am certain that the revolutionary yearnings, the prospect of further peasant unrest will only continue to mount—and I have been thinking long and hard this past year, particularly with you so long in Vienna, about whether wisdom might dictate following in your Uncle Ivan's and Aunt Vera's footsteps. Oh, I know it sounds callous, treacherous, unpatriotic to want to emigrate, to leave. But I think you have forever spoiled me, my boy, with those gala ballet *premières* in Paris! In any case, despite Vliny's protests from back home in Novgorod, I had thought to stay this year until Christmastide—perhaps even Easter—here in Petersburg. But small difference does it make, at my age, whether I enjoy city life here, or in Oslo."

"All right, then, Papa. After we have worn out our welcome in Oslo, perhaps toward next summer, we could make our way back to England. The London townhouse, you recall, is airy and spacious, just as suits your taste. And of course, there is always Winnebar."

"Oh, yes! Would bode me well, after all this tiresome confusion, retiring to sunny Cornwall. After all, you and I have not taken cure of the salty ocean breeze since those four years ago in the Crimea, remember?" Patting my arm, he pulls back and starts surveying me up and down, letting out a gruff, incredulous laugh. "Well, I must say, Sashenka," he murmurs, "your new outfit is certainly—uh, convincing! I near thought Lissa's ghost had returned to haunt me."

In fact, the disguise has served me almost too well. Once I baffled Volodya and the police, who appeared to give up all chase last eve toward sundown when Aleksandr Sekovsky disappeared, and I emerged from behind a market seller's stall freshly shaven and demurely clad in the kerchief, skirt, shawl, and trailing chestnut braid, countless devil-eyed swains then began, to my acute chagrin, a wholly different vein of pursuit—as they would after an attractive young woman!

Reddening, I fumble my spectacles outward from my pocket. "Papa, have you any idea how to repair these? I've not been wearing them much in any case because of the disguise, but the lens keeps falling out, and without the spectacles, it is much difficult for me to read."

As he looks them over, I go on hesitantly: "Uh, and also, Papa—I sincerely hate to ask you this—but of course I have scarce had chance to visit the bank. Have you any money?"

Grinning, he replies: "Consider it your lucky day for spoils, Aleksandr—I made a withdrawal this morn. Here."

From his billfold, he hands over near unto three hundred rubles, and then tends to the wire frames—while I scour about the room, packing some of my clothes, books, and personal items up into a sheet taken from the other guest bed. At last, flute case slung over my shoulder, I thank him profusely as he returns my spectacles, fastened up near tidy as new with a bolt pinched from an old snuffbox. Father then pulls on his robe and starts fussing absently over my injured hand, murmuring: "You are going back down through the servants' entrance?"

"Actually, Papa, I think I'd best scale down from the balcony fire escape. I would hate to run into one of my cousins up for a late-night snack and have to explain why the devil I look like this! Oh, and that reminds me—would you tell Nikolai, that—"

That *I'm sorry*... and then, in reply to the onslaught of prying paternal questions, I would simply tell Father that my cousin would know what I mean. The day of the murder, Father, like the mother hen that he is, pressed relentlessly for details after hearing from Anna that Nikolai and I had, the previous eve, quarreled once again. *I'm sorry*... yes, scant apology only can I offer through the voice of another—two common, simplistic little words peeled from the mountain of confessions growing within my heart: *I am sorry, whether right or wrong, for all the angry things I have ever said; I am sorry that you cannot—cannot love me as I love you*....

But instead of launching into fresh interrogation, as expected, Father stares gloomily downward, wringing his hands and muttering out: "Oh, dear God!..."

"Papa!" I cry with a jolt, squeezing his arm, "whatever is distressing you so?"

"Lord help me, Sasha!" he exclaims in exasperation. "I near forgot all about the entire foolish business... you see, Nikolai is no longer here. Yesterday—oh, dear Jesus, I hate to have to be the one to tell you this! Yesterday, your counsin's unit shipped out for the front—"

"Unit?" I gasp. *"The front?"*

"He became so distraught, he simply—"

"You—you mean Nikolai volunteered? For the *Army?*"

"Yes, I am afraid so. And apparently pulled some strings over at General Staff—you remember your Uncle Petya's many right-wing politcal chums? Anyhow, our Nikolai managed to secure himself a junior officer's post in some damn Lancer regiment! Second Army. Assigned to Fifteenth—no, actually, I think the Thirteenth Corps—"

"Good *God*, Papa!" I exclaim, scarce remembering to check the loudness of my voice. "Has he gone *insane?* Junior officer's post! He is a musician, not a soldier! The damn fool will more than likely get himself killed!"

"Such, indeed, was exactly what I tried to tell him as well. But would he listen? Oh, no! Sometimes, Sasha, I swear your cousin is even more stubborn-headed than you."

"But, Papa, *why?* My God—he too is first-born, and scarce required to—"

"Oh, Nikolai is fully aware of the law! And hardly courting patriotism—instead, I think he's running away from grief. Elena Feliksovna gave birth to their child two days after you disappeared. A son. Stillborn."

I grasp my hand to my mouth. "Oh, *no*—"

"For some time, of course, we had suspected that she was over-due," Father goes on, wiping a wearied hand to his brow and sighing with heavy remorse. "Although, as many children as I have brought into the world over the years, it is still sometimes quite difficult gauge the precise length of gestation—one can never be entirely certain. But that afternoon, Anna ran in searching for me in a state of panic, said she could no longer detect the heartbeat through the womb with the stethoscope. I started administering balsam drops by the hour, hoping to induce labor, but only when I decided to risk cutting away the water sac did the birth pains finally begin. And then the poor girl's time was long and difficult, and at the end, when the worst of our fears became confirmed, she launched into blind hysteria—and what is worse, has remained there. Elena will not accept that the child is gone—believes herself still carrying him, and that she is due any day now, as if the whole day and a half of torment never occurred! I am hoping that she will soon come to her senses, and accept the truth, and go on. Nikolai took the news as he always takes bad news—silently—before holing up in his father's library and seeing no one, not even Elena, save for the dreadful scene following the birth, and one dutiful time thereafter. At last, of course, he was forced to emerge for the funeral—and the day after, came and informed me dryly that he had taken the Army commission. Now, as you know, Sasha, your cousin's marriage was a rather—ahem!—rushed affair. But in these last months, I know Nikolai truly began to want the child. He fawned over Elena and saw to her every comfort, no matter how trivial. And come every evetide when we would take a smoke together in the study, he was forever bursting full of plans for his new family—for his son, he always said. Nikolai, like many a young man I have seen pampering an expectant wife, was convinced beyond all doubt that his child would be an heir."

Softly, I murmur: "Pyotr Nikolayevich? After his father?"

Father nods. "Yes, that is what they ordered engraved on the headstone."

"And so, now," I go on, "to escape new demons, my cousin has flown to the front."

"It appears so."

"Shit," I mutter, ruefully shaking my head.

Again sighing, Father once more grips his hand to my arm, his eyes drawn with reluctance toward the balcony windows. "Will be light in another hour or so," he says.

"Yes. For a certainty, I must be going." My bulky old shawl, tied in a knot down the front, has well masked the tell-tale flatness of my chest, and now once more I wrap it on—while Father, amused, laughs again and shakes his head. After pulling the flute case and knotted sheet up over my shoulder, I hold out both arms to him—and he crushes me fiercely, stray tears seeping from both eyes once he lets go. "In Oslo," he chokes out, wagging a staunch warning finger, "I want to see you back in trousers, young man!"

"You have my word, Papa," I reply with a grin. "Oh—and I would offer condolences to Elena Feliksovna—and to my cousin, were he here—but under the circumstances—"

"No one will know of your visit, Sasha," he assures me. "On that, you have my word. That is," he murmurs as he unlatches the balcony windows, "provided that you can climb down this rickety old thing without entailing mishap."

Despite the cumbersome folds of the skirt, descending the fire escape ladder proves less difficult than anticipated. Once down in the courtyard, I pause to wave up at Father, while he barks down gruffly: "You crazy fool, go! Every moment that you linger, you remain in danger!"

Nodding agreement, I steal back to the shadows. From high above, the sound of the locks catch as Father pulls shut the balcony windows.

Cautiously, I then begin to make my way, window-row by narrow window-row, along the perimeter of the courtyard toward the alley link-up with the main thoroughfare. High overhead, a late-summer band of storm clouds burns across the sky in a veil of slow, evolving motion, masking the upper ocean's starry depths and coloring scant hoverings of light into an eerie mix of blue and gray against the townhouse's inner courtyard coating of wan yellow paint. At my feet, piles of compost and unwanted trash threaten ambush from end to darkened end of the large square spread of cobblestones, pairs of rats darting in and out here and there in beady-eyed, unnerving gluttony from behind rusted barrels or old broken milk crates. To my vast relief, however, there are never so many as in Vyborg, and all scamper away with fright the closer I draw near.

But still, I cannot help but fend off a queasy shudder, and quicken my steps with nervous haste—until the barest movement from the rearward alleyway, much larger than that of a rat—catches my eye, and I stop up cold.

Dammit! Noting the faint whiff of cigarette smoke laced through the air, I flatten back once more against the wall, whipping my gun out cocked and ready. *But it is impossible—no one could have followed!* For an entire hour before I ever dared sneak in through the servants' entrance, I combed through the courtyard and both the front and back alleyways, searching up and down like an obsessed fool—to make positively certain that no one had tailed me. *Could I have been mistaken? Was it naught but foolhardiness, risking a last visit home?* Heartbeats shattering into my ears, I again start hedging my way, step by aching step, along the side of the building, my every pore stretched for the sting of breath, every muscle tensed for awaited ambush.

But the figure, once emerged into a peek of moonlit waverings, becomes only a stooped beggar wrapped up in an old priest's cassock, moaning out hoarsely for kopeks.

Hissing him off, but then thinking better of it, I fish into my pocket, toss over some coins, and send him on his way with a grumbling, wary wave of the gun. For several moments thereafter, I stare toward the rearward alleyway after his trailing shadow; stare until long after it disappears. At last the heavy cloak of silence returns, blanketed with the faint cooing hum of the night sounds: scampering of the rats; trickling of water drop by drop from a gutter somewhere close by; from Liteiny Prospekt, another block to the west, the crunch of carriage wheels echoing in tired, distant monotony. Breathing in a sigh of relief as I at last shoulder up to the forward alleyway, I release the gun's hammer with a quick flick of my thumb and slip around the corner leading out toward the airy, far less potentially hazardous vista of Zhukovskaya.

"Drop it," a thick voice orders abruptly, rifle barrel plunged hard into my ribs.

Oh, shit! . . . freezing, I sneak a glance out the archway. Yevgeny Ivanovich, Pierre's massive, ever-faithful henchman, looms within in towering menace, a cigarette butt clamped between his teeth. "Drop it, Sekovsky!" he growls, wrenching up the trigger-guard with an angry, self-assured fist.

Panicked, I do so—wincing as my pistol clatters noisily across the reach of cobblestones—and then I whirl around, full bent on naught but a course of flight or death—and run straight smack into—*oh, God! No, please! Not—Volodya!*

Grinning evilly, beggar's cassock flung to the ground and the butt of his Browning raised high in an arc of triumph, my old adversary mutters out: "And now—*Sasha-darling-precious-love!*—now, my friend, the time has come for you to take a little bitty nap."

"Nooo!" I shout, arms flailing for cover—but the butt of the Browning crashes into the side of my head—

And then the night goes w-white, t-the world goes b-b-b-black. . . .

* * *

"Wake up, darlin'—"

Oh, God! My head . . . .

"Yes, indeed—I'm sure it smarts somethin' terrible. But time's come for you to wake up, and for us to have a little bitty talk. You see, your little games are done with, baby-dear. Uh-huh—that's it, *wake up*. No, you're no longer dreamin', my friend. This is all very real."

Moaning, I bend to my knees and clutch both hands to the back of my throbbing head. Vapors coalesce, and the room fades into gradually descending focus: early dawn slatted through faded, mismatched curtains; the stark glare of four white-washed walls; the iron-barred footrest of the bed, Volodya's tenement apartment, Vasilyevsky Island.

"I am tellin' you, it was this!" he roars above me, and I moan out again, ducking down into the grip of nausea and near-convulsion.

Across the room, Yevgeny snorts derisively and slams a vodka tankard down onto the table. "Akkh! Impossible!" he bellows, the scent of his match torching the air as he lights up a cigarette.

"I am tellin' you, it *was* this!" Volodya shouts on. "He used the thing for swabbin' out his piccolo when he was livin' with me over in

Vyborg. This *is* what you used, yes?" he blares down again, this time wrenching hold of my arm.

Oh, God! My head . . . .

"Sekovsky—damn you! Answer me!"

"J-Jesus Christ! W-Will you stop yelling so loud, already?"

"So answer me! This is what you used?"

Above me, he stands waving out my old flute cleaning rod.

Oh, God! "I—I don't know what you are talking abou—"

In response, Volodya's open palm rams up under my chin, banging my head back to the wall in between the iron posts of the headboard. "Now, you listen to me!" he rasps out, dark eyes blazing, his breath slicing venomous fury into my face. "Ivanovich and I both know that you are the one who did it!"

"Blast it!" I choke out. "Was—was naught but an accident! I scarce meant to *kill* him!"

"Humph!" Satisfied, Volodya releases his grip and storms angrily away.

Hand clutched to my throat, I hedge only the barest glance upward as he returns with a glass of steaming tea. "Here, drink this," he orders in a quieted tone. "The brew's laced with feverfew. It'll help your head."

Gratefully, I cup both hands around the sides of the glass and gulp down every drop of the granular greenish liquid without pausing for breath. Then, although still wobbly, I heave both legs onto the floor, pull off my left boot, and fish out the wooden knob, worn almost without pause during this last week, but not without infliction of its own painful price: my heel throbbing constantly, tendons aching all the way up my calf into the back of my knee. "Humph! So that's how you been gettin' around easier," Volodya mutters, moving beside again as I yank the boot back on.

Grunting acquiescence, I hunch over on my elbows and begin massaging the lump swollen at the back of my head, demanding: "So? And why haven't you two brutes turned me in to the police?"

From the table, Yevgeny lets out a low guttural laugh, and Volodya joins in with ready chorus, mischief dancing in his eyes. "Oh, I sure enough meant to!" he exclaims, slapping his hands together and sneaking a conspiratorial glance back over at Yevgeny. "Believe me, I was certain tweaked enough for the way you singed me with them cigarette butts! But then you showed up in this skirt—" Snickering, he waves out the long chestnut braid, my head kerchief now tied about its end in a gaudy bow. "—and," he goes on, "I got me one helluva spankin' idea."

Again I stoop downward and clutch, moaning, at my head. "Rykazian, dammit! Simply get to the point."

"The point, darlin'," he says, "is rubles. Oh, no—not what you think, not Pierre's rubles." Affecting a sigh, Volodya casts another wink back at Yevgeny. "No, no—pity, but the man's incredible rich fortune goes to some old maiden aunt in Tambov province. You see, even Pierre had his sentimental side. But as far as business operations, the Petersburg market's still bustlin' to burst—and up here, me and Yevgeny are Pierre's main men."

Eyeing him warily, I push off from the bed, limp across the floor to the cracked ceramic pitcher set upon the bureau, and splash stale water on my face, mopping it off with the cuffs of my sleeves. "So?" I say finally, turning to Volodya.

"So—whether Pierre's dead or not, matters scarce a crappin' whit. Business is still business. Between a load of rich client names, and our city-wide contacts, we got more than enough demand. And," he goes on, guffawing loudly along with Yevgeny, "we certainly been roundin' up plenty of decent supply!"

Sighing, I stare between the two of them in bewilderment, demanding: "And what the hell do such plans have to do with me?"

In a bolting clatter of chair legs, Yevgeny jumps up from the table and slams down his vodka tankard, the pocket of clear liquid sloshing around in a wavy, concave circle inside the bottom of the glass. "Because," Volodya says, edging toward me, "we think that you—with that mop of red hair and those luscious eyes of yours, darlin'!—would be worth a whole lot more to us if we decided *not* to turn you over to rot away the rest of your life in some stinking Tsarist prison."

Instinctively, I begin backing up, watching from the corner of my eye as Yevgeny, thumbs latched into his belt, his lips curving upward in a toothy sadistic grin, begins sauntering toward me. "Just what are you proposing?" I demand of Volodya, who snickers again, and then—in one deft, side-swiping movement—forces me back with him flush to wall.

"Is not exactly what you'd call a proposition, darlin'," he murmurs close into my face. "Because, as we see it, you've no more choice! 'Specially as you brought this whole idea on, what with the way you been struttin' your pretty little ass around in a ruffly bitch's skirt—"

"Only as a disguise!"

Shoving Volodya playfully aside, Yevgeny grabs me around the waist—while I punch out at him, shouting: "Stop it!"

"Oh, no! Ye see, Sekovsky—there are certain kinds o' men who like certain kinds o' whores—"

"Stop, damn you!" But he shoves in closer, his hand sliding in beneath the skirt and up my leg along the rumpled folds of my trousers. "Uh-huh!" he goes on in a breathless rush, "ye see, some men, what they like is—ha! Sneakin' their hands up a skirt like this and grabbin' fer themselves a mincy little faggot set o' balls—"

"Goddamn you, let go of me!" I scream out at the top of my lungs—but his fingers, with gleeful, squeezing tenacity, shove straight up into my groin. "You fucking shithead!" I blast into his ear, plowing my fist for it. *"Let go!"*

Yevgeny catches my blow, but stumbles backward with amusement, guffawing and red-faced. Then he throws his arm around Volodya's shoulders and they both burst into peals of uproarious laughter. "Akkh! But not te worry, Sekovsky!" Yevgeny goes on with an elaborate wave of his hand. "I'm scarce any bloody faggot cocksucker."

"But," Volodya chimes in, shaking off Yevgeny and once more cornering me back against the wall, "I *am.*"

"Dammit, Rykazian—you take your hands off me!"

"No! No, Sekovsky, you see, from now on, I will put my hands wherever the fuckin' hell I want, and you know why? Because your days in the big grand orchestras are all over, my friend! From now on, you are workin' for us—because, once we get you dressed up, you and your bewitchin' fairy eyes are sure to bring in one heady amount of cash."

"The Grand Duke'll fancy him fer sure," Yevgeny remarks.

"Oh, I'd already thought of that," Volodya tells him, nodding backward. "The fool's a sucker for redheads."

"You—you two are *mad!"* I shout, furiously elbowing off Volodya. "I will never be party to any of your damnable prostitution schemes!"

"Oh, no?" Volodya yells back. "Then we *will* turn you in to the police!"

"Then you just go and—and do so, by dammit! I'll brave Siberia's every frozen depth any day over the hell you two would put me through in one stinking night!"

"Will be not Siberia, but the fuckin' gallows, Sekovsky! What you did to Sheremetev entails a sentence for *murder—"*

"Then *fine!"* I shout back. "Because you've got the wrong man, Rykazian! I am not afraid of death."

At this, Volodya and Yevgeny exchange raised eyebrows, while I shove past them both for the door.

Volodya storms after. "No, but all your spooky metaphysical *shit* is scarce goin' to save you from the one thing in life that you *are* afraid of, Sekovsky!"

"Humph! You think you can intimidate me into your filthy, sordid dealings, Rykazian, you are wrong, dead wrong!" Shouldering him off, I yank my cane out from between the knots of the bundled bed sheet lying upon the floor and whirl around, steadying my footing with knuckles stretched wrathfully over the handle. The bundle itself I then snatch up, and my flute case as well, throwing both over my shoulder.

"You hold it right there!" Volodya yells, wrenching hold of my arm. "You are not goin' anywhere!" To Yevgeny, he says: "Go down to the telephone box—it's in the center hallway, one flight down. Look in the directory under 'Zhelanova.' It's listed 'Princess Sophie,' I think. But the one you want to ring up is the old man, Count Mikhail Sergeyevich. He and his musician son—of whom, we must all remember, he is so very *proud*—always stay with his sister's family when visitin' in Petersburg. Uh-huh, told you it was no wild hare chase, Ivanovich. The old Count's the one our loyal little Sasha went to pay a goodbye visit to last night before tryin' to hop the border. Because that was your next move, Sekovsky—*yes?* Uh, and what you want to tell His Excellency," Volodya goes on to Yevgeny—though his eyes, narrowed, remain fiercely holding mine, "or rather, what you want to ask him, Ivanovich, is—is if he has any idea just how many cocks his faggot son has sucked in the last four years, all the way from here to bloody Paris—"

"You go to hell, Rykazian!" I burst out, whitening.

"Don't think I've no stomach for spillin' the bloody beans, darlin'!"

"You—your bluffing!"

"*Bluffing*, am I? You want to see how fuckin' much I am *bluffing*, Sekovsky?" Volodya shouts angrily—and waving Yevgeny off, he orders: "Ivanovich—go!"

In a haze of smoke, Yevgeny stomps past and heads down the stairs, while I turn once more on Volodya: "He—he'd never believe it! Not coming from you—and certainly not coming from that peasant oaf down there! He'd thoroughly denounce such lies coming from anybody!"

"Such lies? Such lies happen to be the blessed truth, Sekovsky! Which'll probably be dead obvious to the old man once someone simply takes the trouble to point it out to him! Ha! Then he'll wonder how he could have let pass so many years—without seein' what a ruttin' faggot his son truly is! Oh, you think your illustrious old papa's somehow blind to the dark passions between men? Jesus, Sasha—the man's been in prison!"

From downstairs, Yevgeny calls up: "What name did ye say? Zhelanova?"

Volodya brushes past me to the doorway. "Yes, Ivanovich! And hurry it up, you damn cross-eyed Bolshevik, will you?" Turning back to me, he grins, murmuring slyly: "Think your old papa will be the one to answer, Sasha, love?"

I clench both fists to my sides past a torrential quaking roar, yearning to strangle him. *Of course Father will be the one to answer! He'll jump from bed and run down two flights of stairs, if need be, in order to answer! Ever since our first days in Paris, from motorcars to telephones, the man has been enthralled to no end with every next newfangled gadget anyone happens to think up!*

"It's ringin'!" Yevgeny calls from downstairs.

Volodya again ducks out the doorway, shouting: "And make certain to tell the old Count that from now on, his son is naught but a stinkin' faggot whore—"

"All right, all right!" I scream at him. "Stop him—goddamn it, *stop him!* I'll—I'll do whatever you want—"

"Hang it up, Ivanovich!"

"Somebody just picked up—"

"Never mind! Hang it up." Turning back to me, Volodya holds out a triumphant, expectant hand.

Flushing, I surrender the bed sheet bundle and flute case, both of which he tosses back down to the floor. Then he begins digging into his pockets, from which he withdraws a tailor's measure-tape. "And so begins our partnership in business, Sasha, my love," he murmurs with a shrug.

Crossing my arms, I glare to the floor as Yevgeny trudges back up. "I'm goin' out te start rounds fer the takes," he tells Volodya. Lumbering past the both of us, he hurriedly downs the last gulp from his vodka tankard still set upon the table.

"Fine, then I'll take him over to the bathhouse," Volodya replies, pursing his lips and eyeing me with a long wince of distaste. "Jesus, just how long's it been, Sekovsky—a week? Well, no matter. We'll flush some hot steam into those pores, and you'll be squeaky good as new. Then we'll get our newest charge here properly outfitted for tonight."

"So—the dress shop, ye want me te meet ye?" Belching, Yevgeny rams the tankard back down, snuffs out his cigarette right on the table top, and slaps on his cap.

"Uh-huh, give us about an hour. Oh, hey! Remember that auburn fall Pashka brought in the other day from the barber's? From another idiot woman went and chopped off all her hair? I bet spruced up with a bit of henna, it'll be a fine match for his. And what'd'ya think 'bout this one, Ivanovich?" Volodya goes on with a sarcastic wink, pointing at me. "A 'Katerina?' A 'Dmitra?'"

"Akkh! Ye call him whatever the devil ye want, Rykazian."

Volodya, the measure tape looped now between his hands, frowns in thought and orders out to me loudly: "I want to get a few measurements before we go over to the baths. Take off your clothes."

Frozen motionless, I attempt to swallow and cannot; keep my stare riveted to the floor.

Face darkening, his lips curling in a glowering snarl, Volodya stomps over and wrenches hold of my arm, forcing me roughly around to face him while barking out: "I said: *take off your clothes!*"

My hand seems to alight upward of its own volition, pausing; then grasping up the first buttonhole at the neck of my shirt and unfastening it; pausing at the second and unfastening it; pausing at the third . . . while Volodya snatches out his pocket watch and checks the time, his foot tapping with steady, metered impatience upon the floor. Yevgeny shoves past with a muttering grunt and stomps out once again for the stairs as I stare after, watching the door slam behind—whereupon the walls close in and the noose knots up, the cruel, twisted tongue of fate—Karma—coincidence—clamping its wily stranglehold shut, forever, around my future.

CHAPTER SEVEN

Rendezvous with the Blonde Gypsy

From the opulent expanse of the Grand Armorial Ballroom, subtle gossipings drift toward mirrored-ivory perches of the upper balconies. Giddy, swift kaleidoscope of uniforms, taffeta, and silk, the flotilla of dancers sweeps once more across the inlaid parquet floors of the Tsar's massive Winter Palace. The orchestra plays on: Tchaikovsky's *String Symphony in C*, one of the great maestro's finest pieces, its poetic love song of the violins evoking long-lost days and happier memories: of young roguish faces far more plentiful, their uniforms more dashing and varied, their talk less fraught with worry; of young girlish glances far more sweet and less prone to moody, saddened pauses; of dire Petrograd once as bustling, cosmopolitan St. Petersburg—when a German name still befit this most European of Russian cities, and the Empire had not for near unto a year been engulfed in this hateful travesty of war. But war has proliferated, ruthlessly, not only at every cragged Carpathian mountain pass and gruesome littered Polish trench, but also across the scores of remaining battlegrounds at home, the frequency of power outages only every hour increasing, the prices at the bakeries doubling, tripling, and then quadrupling week by week due to the middlemen's ready stead of greed. And rumor's cesspool continues breeding forth further panicked rantings daily: that the insufferable Huns have torched Lvov; are gaining ground on Pskov; will scale the very outskirts of Petrograd itself upon first glimmers of tomorrow's morn—or surely the day after. Or perhaps the day after that. Which is why the musicians play along, and the dancers keep whirling about in such an intoxicated ritual of abandon, every last one of them a helpless pawn sworn to grand inevitability's sorry plan, every last one of us a last bosun on a sinking ship, staving off drowning, the fear.

Toward the string section, I gaze with longing; toward the woodwinds, with envy; toward the dancers, with an apathetic sigh—although I struggle to play my part judiciously, to stay in tune along with everyone else. Ever the hawk in dove's clothing, again I renew staunch effort to conceal my truest inner soul, pride, honor, and self-respect—behind the skirts of the woman standing up above at the southeast face of the ballroom balcony.

Up there, beyond the haloes of blazing crystal chandeliers and rows of spindly gold-cast rails grasped in many a happier, long-lost time by many a statesman, a Grand Duke, a powerful Russian Tsar—up above at the southeast face of the ballroom balcony, stands a woman more beautiful than sin. Clad in creamy folds of silk, long auburn tendrils escaping lengths of pearls wound in the latest neo-Grecian mode throughout her upswept hair, she hovers high above the common earthly patter of the dance floor, a stunning apparition from some strange and secreted world apart, her doe-like eyes remaining pinned in watchful rapture upon the orchestra. But after some moments, upon confronting the widening bevy of male stares cast in her direction from the ballroom floor below, she lets out a gasp and flicks her fan upward, shielding it across the lower half of her face, her eyes cast demurely downward and averted from the perusal of the impromptu downstairs audience.

"Oh, yes—you're attractin' attention again, my love," says Volodya with a rueful smile. "But really, darlin'—we must hurry along in any case," he goes on, nudging me. "Will not do, bein' late for His Imperial Highness."

"Please, just another moment." Again I hunt wistfully, face by face, through the string section of the orchestra.

"No." Volodya seizes my elbow and shoots me a warning scowl, the usual frowning reminder not to cause a stir. Nor to attract anymore undue attention.

Sighing, I snap the fan shut and slip my arm through his offered one, my feet—shod in laced kid-suede and aided on the left side with a specially cobbled lift—falling into halting, though measured stride beside his, the rich silk of the long slim skirt swishing in ever unnerving reminder about my ankles.

"You look ravishing tonight," he murmurs in my ear as we turn through the balcony doors.

"Yes, yes," I reply, feigning interest over apathy.

"Please, darlin'," he urges in a patronizing tone, again leaning close. "A little smile for the Grand Duke in the boudoir, hmmm? You know he pays quite well for you."

"Yes, yes." Behind us, my beloved music fades to distant echoes of futility as we pass from the balcony doors into a connecting hall and then into the long open archway leading past the somber, darkened Gallery of the War of 1812 lurking just below. A quick rightward turn brings us to one of the dozens of red-carpeted marble staircases leading to the upper palace wings. Volodya nods in polite greeting to other passing gentlemen, to several talkative bejeweled ladies, and to the occasional harried doctors tramping through from the nearby Palace hospital quarters—set up benevolently by the Tsarina since the onset of the war. Meanwhile, I toy between flirting and with attempting to fend off the bold, lusty—and none too wise—stares from various passing groups of young officers.

The subdued elegance of the suite to which the steward directs us literally puts the showy trappings of Sheremetev's Moscow palace to shame. As usual, the Grand Duke has not yet arrived.

At Volodya's insistence, I powder my cheeks and chin again as he fusses over the lacy folds at the neck of my gown and the precise placement of the many pearl strands woven within my hair. At last satisfied, he withdraws to the doorway and doffs his derby, setting it down atop his leather portfolio case. Then he begins inspecting his suit jacket lapels, picking off shreds of lint with a testy eye before snatching his watch out from his waistcoat pocket. Repeatedly, he checks the face, and starts pacing the floor with a frown of impatience.

I hedge a glance away from the window. "A family character flaw," I remind him. "I hear that each of Their Imperial Highnesses tends toward arriving anywhere a tad late."

Red-faced, Volodya glares at me from across the room, again pointing to his throat and ordering out in a whisper: "Higher!"

Rolling my eyes, I repeat the same words in my sorry excuse for a falsetto.

"Humph! Well, better, I suppose." Nodding, Volodya resumes his frantic watch-checking and his pacing, leaving me free to stare once again out the window toward the silvery shadows of Palace Square.

Bereft of my spectacles, I struggle to take in the panoramic eastward view, dark violet outlines from the Redeemer Church's cupolas quivering through the faint cover of arctic night. Just below us, past the majestic skyward stretch of the Aleksandr Column, the grand triumphal archway of the massive yellow and white General Staff Building throws wide its two long arms of busy government office rows, embracing like a lover the square's immaculate cobblestoned vastness. Once more I choke down a heady gulp upon taking in the overwhelming sight, pride in my heritage flooding throughout every humbled recess of my heart—but soon enough, the chills running up and down my spine matter nearly for naught, the haze of Tsarist monuments fading off into immediacy's blur. Abruptly, the Grand Duke—a youthful, strapping man nearing his fortieth year of age, one of the Romanov stalwarts close in line of accession to the Russian throne—abruptly, His Imperial Highness saunters on through the door, and slams it shut behind. Reflections from the overhead chandelier glint showily off the double rows of shiny buttons adorning his bright scarlet uniform, his harsh words of warning immediately pouncing upon Volodya's defensive fluster. "Blast it, Denisov!" he shouts, flinging out an emphatic pointed finger. "I am telling you—this time it had damn well better be Dmitra."

Breathlessly, Volodya indicates my presence as, eyes again cast downward, I nod with the expected show of reverence toward the Grand Duke.

"Excellent!" he cries, his frown melting into a gracious smile. "Definitely much more to my taste—and lovely as ever, I might add. But such a shame, my dear, that you are becoming so dreadfully popular!" Turning once again to Volodya, he snaps: "Well, Denisov! As I related this afternoon when I rang you up about it, this time I must insist upon the full two hours. . . ."

They haggle over the time, the money; the Grand Duke pays it, and Volodya leaves—although he merely retires to a nearby anteroom, there to occupy himself—ineptly—with the book work from his portfolio case. Later, he will remind me that he loiters behind only to assure my protection homeward past any lurking thugs. But the true reason is that, due to my value in weekly receipts, Volodya rarely—save, of course, for the actual 'assignations'—ever allows me out of his sight.

"Oh, yes—enchanting, as ever," murmurs the Grand Duke, moving in close behind me, his arms winding around my shoulders, a kiss pecked at my pearl-studded ear.

Flushing, I turn to face him—whereupon the kisses begin in raw earnest, tearing into my mouth . . . although after a moment, it is not without honest pangs of desire that I meet them. For I would be a liar to deny the double-crossing carnal surge, the beady drops of sweat that begin fringing across my brow, my eager gasps as the Grand Duke's hand slides in beneath the rustling folds of the silken skirt, inching its way upward along my thigh in search of its now-stiffened prize. One by one, the rows of pearls fly out from my hair, every costly strand cast unheeded to the floor. The long auburn fall, spraying forth dozens of hairpins, tumbles off—followed by the dress, chemise, pantaloons, and then the wire-boned, padded corset betraying its diabolical sheep's lungs bosom. At last stripped naked, I am set free—and urge the Grand Duke off with his own clothes, returning his swarms of kisses passionately as we collapse together upon the bed, thrust meeting thrust, his insistent fingers sliding back over the cool moons of my buttocks past hoarsened stabs scraping out beneath his breath: "Oh, *yes*—and again the little girl . . . becomes *such* a little boy . . . ."

All of this is the fault of that poet Bryusov and his damned *Pale Horse*. Ever those intractable, eerie words about letters afire borne in the name of death; ever my shadowy, haunted dreams about the host of unwary souls left long behind in the ghostly lamplit street, all seeing naught of the escaping apparition save for those lone two: he, from the madhouse; she, from the brothel. Yes, Bryusov—Guardian of the Tower, Master of the Count, Teller of the Round—omniscient shaman of my wayward, self-fulfilling prophecy: first, I became your madman. And now . . . now I have become your whore. . . .

* * *

Home is a large one-room apartment near University Quay on Vasilyevsky Island. Yevgeny Ivanovich and Tanya Feodorovna—a diminutive, curly-haired peasant girl who smiles a great deal but says very little—share our kitchen and water closet and live in the adjoining flat. When at last Volodya and I arrive just before dawn, Yevgeny's shouts resound above several other angry voices converged upstairs. "Oh, crap," Volodya mutters out, rolling his eyes. "Not again!"

"I think you could blame the flux in tempers this time on the sweltering July heat," I tell him, taking advantage of my 'Dmitra' guise and fanning myself profusely with the fan. "I swear, all night the whole city's been like an oven again."

"Are you certain you retrieved all the pearls?" he demands for the fifth time since debarking the cab.

"Yes, yes." Despite the aid of the lift in my left shoe, by this time of the night—or morn, rather—my ankle has begun to throb, and the stairs prove torturously difficult. Volodya bounds up two at a time, while I pause halfway up and wait until he reappears from the apartment, several other of the whores stomping out in indignation flush upon his tail. "Blast it, Ivanovich!" Volodya yells back behind him. "Can't you ever settle these disputes yourself?" Whirling around, he tosses down my cane, shouting downward: "Are you all right?"

"Yes, dammit!" I snap back. "Just hurry in there and shut everybody up, for God's sake! Or the landlady is certain to have another fit."

Upstairs at our apartment, I hobble in to find Volodya waving his arms placatingly amidst the noisy group of whores. Some remain clad in their evening jewels and ballgowns; others sport everyday cotton trousers and low-brimmed worker's caps. Several I recognize, several I do not—as is usually the case. Georgi Samsonovich, wearing a grotesquely large blonde wig crowned with a tiara of sapphires in his guise as 'Lortitia,' preens around twice to show off his new gown, and I shake my head in earnest disapproval, muttering out: "Oh, no—far too much blue for your complexion, Gorushka."

"That's exactly what I told him!" wails out Dmitri Andreyevich, with an excited torrent of hand gestures, from across the room. "See?" he calls over to Georgi. "Khulinov's got the best damn eye for color—even over Rykazian."

Then Vasili Sergeyevich—who puts my own German and Italian fluency to shame, but who cannot tell the minutes on a watchpiece to save his life, waves his cap at me in desperation and shouts out over everybody's heads: "Hey, Khulinov! Do you have the—"

"Ten to six," I call back to him as I make a beeline for the water closet.

The arguing, of course, stems from the weekly squabble over their percentages of the takes. By the time I pull on my shirt and trousers and rinse all the powder and eye-paint from my face, the noise has simmered down to a hum of low grumbles, and I emerge from the water closet to find over half the group gone, the stragglers conversing with Volodya in insistent undertones, while he drones on in irritation: "Of course prices have soared everywhere! Well, what do you expect? There's a war on; I suppose taffeta goes up right along with the cost of bread. Of course I'll give you all a discount! Come in on Monday—"

Slapping on my spectacles, I shove past the squabble and corner Yevgeny over by the door, demanding: "Did you stop by the apothecary and pick up my aloe cream?"

"Shit, Khulinov," he mutters down at me, not bothering to glance upward from picking dirt out from his fingernails. "Don't ye hear what Rykazian's been sayin'? There's a war on."

"Fuck it, Mrenitsev!" I retort hotly. "You try shaving twice a day with skin like mine and see how it tears up your face."

"All right, all right! I promise, tomorrow."

"And my matches?"

"Awww, shit—tomorrow, Khulinov! God, why can't ye jest use 'em fer lightin' cigarettes, like everybody else?"

"Humph! Well, you'd best have my aloe by tomorrow, too," I warn shrilly from over my shoulder, "or else His Imperial Highness might very well scoff at paying for a razor-burned face. And we both know whose pocket that'll all come out of! Eh, Mrenitsev?"

"Shit!" he roars, storming after me as I waltz away in triumph. "Ye know what ye kin do with yer smart mouth and yer smirkin' ways, Khulinov, ye little twit?" he shouts, his heavy boots closing in fast upon my heels. "Ye kin go an'—an' eat a pile o' shit, that's what ye kin do!"

"Ha! Well, Mrenitsev, in return, you can go inhale a puked-up pile of shit—and then rim my ass."

Predictably, the blazing warrior yell erupts full steam across the space of the apartment, and I clear the doorway to the kitchen just in the nick of time—there to encounter Tanya, the very picture of blue-eyed innocence and long dark braids, standing over the stove kettle and hurriedly ladling up the soup. "Good morning, Tanya Feodorovna," I say with a gallant bow, nodding and returning her ready smile.

Bursting through with Volodya's arms clamped fast around his shoulders, Yevgeny waves out the fireplace poker like a cattle branding iron, shouting: "I swear te God—I'll—I'll carve him up in a thousand tiny pieces! . . ."

With a gasp, Tanya chases for the opposite apartment door and duly disappears beyond it. Smacking and shoving at Yevgeny, Volodya lunges repeatedly for the fireplace poker, shouting: "Ivanovich, you crazy lamebrained fool! Put the thing down!"

Heaving in a walloping deep breath, Yevgeny screws up his eyes, glaring at me and sputtering out a stream of curses before finally slamming the fireplace poker to the floor.

"Goddamn it!" Volodya then roars between us in exasperation. "Must you two go for each other's throats like this every single morn? *Without exception?"*

In response, Yevgeny and I both point fresh accusations across the air, yelling out in unison: *"He* started it!"

"Shut up, both of you!" Volodya rants on. "Ivanovich!" he shouts, waving out, for emphasis, his diamond-studded money-clip stuffed full with thousand-ruble bills, "you got your goddamned three whole cases of shells—*and* all your fucking Mausers—yes?"

"An' I am telling ye!" Yevgeny blares back heatedly, "I don't give a devil's shit 'bout the money no more! 'Cause fer a whole stinkin' year, I been cursin' the very day ever since ye took this little vermin on! All the damn whores we got fer yer own bed, Rykazian—and the one ye choose has te be a goddamned witch!"

"Ivanovich, you just *shut up!*" Volodya orders, shouting him down. "And you!" he then exclaims, whirling about upon me, "he will fetch you your goddamned jar of aloe cream tomorrow! *All right?"*

Shrugging, I slide into a seat at the table and start dabbing into one of the bowls of cabbage soup. "And my matches," I insist, glaring over at Yevgeny.

"And your goddamned matches!" Volodya shouts out at the top of his lungs, his fingerless gloved fist shaking high up into the air.

The sight of him caught in such a purple-faced huff near inspires me into a burst of laughter—but I manage to subdue my mirth within another spoonful of soup. Yevgeny, biting back curses, stomps past the other doorway, calling in sheepish apology to Tanya.

Letting out a weary sigh, Volodya plops down to his own portion of soup and warmed bread, muttering out after a long moment: "All right. So what in hell did you say *this* time? To make him so tweakin' mad?"

Without returning his glance, I take my sweet time with fetching a glass of tea from the samovar positioned in the center of the table, mumbling finally: "Merely asked for my aloe."

Sighing again, Volodya murmurs: "Well, next time, Sasha, do you think you could try to ask Ivanovich just a wee bit more civilly?"

Again I shrug, and before diving once more into my soup, I turn around and start sorting through the kitchen drawer positioned just behind my chair, which in lieu of towels or utensils lies filled with a collection of my books. From the stack, I pull out my English-language copy of the *Bhagavadgita*, and bend in rapt concentration over the pages while sipping from my soupspoon.

Volodya steals glances—and finally says: "Is your leg better?"

Ignoring him, I keep my eyes glued to the book without reply.

Doggedly, he persists, declaring: "It's been botherin' you much more than you've let on, Sasha! Don't you think I can see plain day? Ever since last winter—yes?"

Glowering with impatience, I slam the pages of the book shut and stare down at its worn cloth cover. "Not to worry, M'sieur Denisov," I tell him tersely. "With a little sleep, your prize ravishing harlot will again be in fine form for this coming evetide's revelries."

"Dammit, Sasha—that is not why I am askin'!"

"Oh, yes, it is." Cursing him to high heaven, I snatch up my book and my cane, and past an angry clatter of flatware, storm away from the table.

"Sasha! You come back here and listen to me—"

Just as I shove past the door into our own flat, he clamps a stranglehold onto my shoulder. "Take it off," I say icily.

"Sasha—"

"Take your filthy, stinking hand off my shoulder, Rykazian!"

Volodya snatches his fingers quick away, his gaze faltering morosely to the floor.

Again cursing, I trudge away to the room's farthest corner beyond the bed, where I have erected upon the floor, as a makeshift haven, a wide board supported by two stacks of books and draped with a violet silk scarf. Upon it rest various keepsakes: my deck of Tarot cards, Uncle Ned's treatise on numerology, and my mother's amethyst crystal; the picturegraph of myself and my cousin in Paris; a stack of Father's letters; my icon of the Great Nevsky and namesake, Saint Aleksandr; my great-great grandfather's Star of the Order of Saint Vladimir; an old wooden *kovsh* ladle treasured by our family for over three centuries; a seven-tiered candelabrum. The candelabrum I grasp up tightly in my fist, lighting one by one the sacred flames, each with a fresh match. Then I scoot down to the floor in the lotus position, facing the whole array of sacred objects, and begin piecing together my flute.

"Couldn't you try to be a bit more thrifty with the matches?" asks Volodya from behind.

"No. It is imperative that each of them be a vestal virgin," I tell him loudly—although in truth, that is naught but a load of hogturds. The only reason I insist upon lighting each taper with a fresh match is simply because it irks the hell out of Yevgeny.

"Couldn't we talk a bit?" Volodya then ventures.

In response, I test out a shattering scream of notes upon the flute's highest octave, and flow straight into the eerie, oriental tones of Debussy's *Syrinx*.

Yevgeny then bursts through the kitchen door to make his regular morning complaint about the flute—while Volodya, ever steadfast, stammers out barbs and curses at him and waves him off. Without the slightest twinge of guilt, I continue playing, aware that I have not been unmindful of others in entirety, for by now the fresh morn sun has brightened in through the windows and most other of the building's tenants—students and college bookclerks—have long since made their way to class or to their offices of employment. I might have been forced to change my name to stay afoot of the police; I may have had to resign myself to complacency with Volodya's underworld schemes—but for fifteen years, I have played this flute every single day, and Yevgeny damn well knows that I am not stopping now on account of anyone's protests, particularly his.

On the wave of Debussy's haunting legacy, my inner incantation drifts softly upward toward the awaiting heavens:

I plight my troth unto the Seven-Stringed Lyre of Apollo,
Intoning Harmony through Conflict
And Numbers through Name
Toward the Voice of Sound,
Unto which I make this Forbidden Journey,
Take this Cup of Resolution
And walk this Obligatory Path . . . .
Hear me, Lords of Flame.
In honor, I bend to the Divine Will,
Which is Power
And Omnipresence in the Universe.
Acknowledge this seeker—small flicker, thy
progeny, this name—seeking
First Cross of the Seven Crosses,
First Path of the Seven Paths,
First Light of the Seven in Darkness,
And entrance,
Into the Halls of Wisdom,
Who accepts his Tower without, true Wands within,
One Sword above, and now
This lot he has been cast,
Karma's bidding upon the Diminished Seventh Chord . . . .

Later, in bed, he reaches for me, and I freeze against his touch, and again he snatches his hand away as if I had singed it, and I hear his struggle with a mountain of unsaid words until he at last turns over—roughly—in the morntide light, yanking more than his proper share of the covers with him. Of course, he's still not entirely beyond forcing me against my will. In the beginning, he forced me to grovel to his every whim, constantly—in the middle of the night, in the middle of the day, in public places, in private—partly, I think, to prove his mastery, his control; rude fulfillment of his oath to, whenever he chose, put his hands wherever he wanted. Naught could I do in the awful end each time but wearily succumb—he is taller, stronger, brutal at times, and always doubly wary now of my sneaky left hook. But of late, he seems loath to force me anymore. Ironically, it appears he has fallen in love with me over these past few months; ironically, I know I was in love with him years ago, at the very beginning, in Vyborg. I know I fell in love with him all over again for awhile after our chance encounter at the dress shop those five years ago. Little does it matter now; everything I ever felt for him dissolved into bleak ashes of hate the day he made me into one of his whores. If he truly cared, he would let me walk away—but he loves money more: three times he let up his guard; three times have I run off for the railroad yards in daring attempt at escape. Always, cunningly—and endowed with rare free reign—he sends Yevgeny straight after.

* * *

The door creaks open, and Volodya steals in through a film of shadows atop the dress shop's cellar stairs. Briefly, he catches my eye; then, stepping down, he turns around and extends his hand behind, murmuring in a subdued undertone: "Watch your step, Your Excellency."

Father scoffs at Volodya's offer of assistance, and shoves down the steps in an impatient huff, his eyes pulled to a wrinkly squint as they attempt adjustment to the murky cellar light. Upon sighting me, he opens his mouth as if to say something, but quickly shuts it again, glowering for a long moment back up toward the head of the stairs, until Volodya—with an embarrassed cough—turns on his heel and slams the cellar door shut behind him.

"Sasha!" Father then cries, his arms outstretched wide.

I fly into them, a torn breath escaping my lungs. Eyes clamped shut, I nose into the pearly-white hairs of his beard as his stocky warmth closes all around me. Like a child I sigh, dearly wishing to the dearest

God that I could only somehow, some way, turn back the cruel clock of time—to the long winters before the warm fire within those wondrous, misty Novgorod woods when he would pull me into his lap and tell endless silly stories into my sleepy ears. How I would give anything to retrieve those lost years of my childhood and my youth, to begin anew with my old hopes and tentative dreams; how I would pay any price to once more face the world without fear while bearing my true and rightful name. But of course, my proud name, my youthful caprices, my sleepy toddler's comforts in my papa's chair now lie lost forevermore to this gloomy shroud of penance. I knew he would be frantic with worry upon learning that I never reached Oslo, and after much haranguing, it was Volodya who called at the Zhukovskaya townhouse, then arranging our weekly secret meetings. A plausible explanation was called for, and Father is aware that I have been coerced into some crafty underworld scheme involving high stakes and soiled money, although he believes the blackmail stems solely from Volodya's knowledge of my hand in the 'Pavlovsky' murder. I tell him that I mostly assist with the book work, which is partly true. Were he ever to learn the whole of it, I would surely want to die.

Since then, aeons have marooned us apart, long ages dwindling in between our every chance to stand crushing one another near unto death every Sunday eve in the cellar of the dress shop. Each of us ever bitterly decrying the angst of separation, in the scant hour granted, we always attempt to make up for every lost moment forever gone, and for all the lost moments yet to come.

When at last he pulls away, Father forces a grin, and from beneath his arm, hands over another of my books from the collection we have been gradually transferring, one by one, week by week, from the Zhukovskaya townhouse. Then, with genuine glee, he begins his usual bantering about my hair, which meets only occasional trimmings these days, the length needful for securing the auburn fall for my 'Dmitra' guise. Flushing, I make another of my excuses and poke a playful fist at him, murmuring: "You are not overworking yourself too greatly again at the hospital, are you, Papa?"

"Humph! I'm fit as a fiddle!" he declares loudly. "Feel not a day over sixty-five." But then, his brow coarsening in weary, angular furrows, he adds: "Which is more than I can say for those poor lads they keep bringing in from the front."

I step back, my eyes searching his; his, mine—and we hold one another's stares through a deathly pause of silence, the unspoken question already broached, the unspoken answer already proffered. Nonetheless, he confirms it in a saddened whisper: "I checked the boards outside once more right before I left. Still no change."

Biting my lip, I turn sharply away and grip both hands onto a narrow bolt of fabric, woven fibers of olive serge twisting into sweaty knots between my fingers. In spite of myself, the register of casualty postings—massive tally of the Battle of Tannenberg's hundred thousand sacrificial sons—begins to haunt my every next thought with the same precise, awful clarity as that first day, close to a year ago, when I decided to risk a jaunt into the busy hospital corridor, intent upon scanning the long alphabetic list with my very own eyes. And there his name was, printed neatly in a row right along with the endless tragic rows of all the rest of them: *Zhelanov, N.P., Second Lieutenant—missing and presumed dead* . . . .

As I fling the bolt of fabric clear across the breadth of the room, Father's arms lock around my shoulders from behind, clamping me fast unto his chest, his head buried into my neck, his silence imparting temperance, urging restraint as I struggle fiercely against his hold, moaning out over and over: "Goddamn him to bloody-fucking hell! Jesus God—Jesus, *why?* How could he ever have been fool enough to run off to *war?"*

At last, when the shaking quells, when my heartbeats flutter back to a low rhythmic lull and the torched sweat finally begins to burn once again ice cold, Father releases his hold, a sympathetic squeeze caught to my hand as he whispers: "Sasha, I know you loved your cousin very much."

Both fists whitened over the handle of my cane, I swallow hard and ease down beside him on one of the benches in between the high stacks of remnant pieces and scattered bolts of winter fabric. "And Aunt Sophie?" I say finally, struggling to keep a hold on my voice.

Sighing in exasperation, Father rolls his eyes. "Still, she's convinced he's somehow alive—and is as determined as ever to set out for Paris, to continue her search for him from there. Although I keep telling her that such will most likely come to naught. Even were there some chance that he survived—which, as Colonel Dubensky tells me, most of them did not—but even *were* there some chance, in Paris, they know little more about the prisoners than we do here. And yes, I have warned her that any kind of voyage these days is too risky, but the woman refuses to listen! Three more days, and God willing, she sets out for Stockholm.

I'm afraid there's naught I can do to stop her—damned infernal, stubborn Sekovsky temper!"

I nod mutely—and then we huddle together in placid silence, each of us mulling over our thoughts and longingly soaking in the other's physical closeness—until at last I inquire after the other news. Far too graphically for my sheltered taste, Father begins relating various details of his and Anna's current caseloads at the Anglo-Russian Hospital, located nearby on the southeastern embankment of Nevsky Prospekt and the Fontanka Canal. And then he extols for me the latest grievances of Marnya, who has ever been denouncing hers and Vliny's enforced exile from Novgorod unto the Zhukovskaya townhouse, despite the ailing health of them both. Safety, however, prescribed retreat unto the city, its outskirts more heavily defended than the rural provinces against any sudden stealthy Hun advance. Morosely, I try to imagine the apiary without hives, the kitchen chimneys bereft of their billows of rolling smoke, and the Lissushka estate house boarded up across every window from the outside in a haste of pounded nails, chains and heavy bolts strewn across its regal front double doors.

After more or less an hour, Father checks his watch and stretches upward with a reluctant groan. "Well, I suppose I'd best return upstairs and make my requisite purchase," he says, smiling and shaking his head—and he hands over his 'purchase' of the prior week, a bundled packet of facing and thread. "As that devil Rykazian says," he goes on, "best to continue the charade and err on the side of caution. Bless the Saints, though, my boy—the police, I am certain, have finally given up their watch over the townhouse."

From Volodya's cash box on the table, I hand over a ten-ruble bill for him to exchange upstairs for some other paltry, miscellaneous item. Which next time he will bring back and exchange for another ten-ruble bill, the whole cycle—maintained to confound any tailings of him and any stray snooping over the dress shop by the police—only to repeat itself again another week hence.

I laugh as he holds out the inevitable chess paper, and berate him with loving, teasing soreness upon noting his castling in response to my latest move. "Papa," I then go on in all earnestness, "please do not allow the hospital to deprive your needed rest." As we embrace again, only all too evident is the roughened, chapped touch of his hands, the odors of lye soap, of acid of carbolic, and of pungent asafoetida resin lingering about his clothes and hair. "You are becoming far too old for such worry and tireless day-and-night doctorly ministrations, Papa!" I scold on. "Might I remind you, you are near unto eighty-four? When you started, you promised—only half-day shifts would you work, no more than three times a week. And now, look at you."

"Nonsense!" he bellows back, puffing out his chest. "I'd say you're the one looks to need some rest, my boy! But me—why, I'm fit as a fiddle. . . ."

As the cellar door finally clicks shut upstairs behind him, and I stand staring after my last sight of his beloved broad-shouldered form, a swift voiceless prayer emits from my lips with hallowed reverence: *Lord bless and keep you, my dearest Papa. How I love you so very, very much. . . .*

Thoughtfully, I steal a glance across the room toward the cellar door. Padlocked shut, of course—although had I a mind to, I could probably pick the damn thing open. But aside the cash box on the table, a pile of book work—filled with hurried errors ever begging for a studious, corrective hand—awaits with a crooked finger, and I settle down to work like a dutiful dog, bemoaning my listless sense of resignation. In any case, the stairs from the cellar door up to the street outside lead right past the front windows of the dress shop. Volodya—or more likely Yevgeny—would be in easy pursuit barely moments after.

My cluttered tonic of calculations, however, affords the mind little solace—for again the vision looms up in a ghostly squall before my eyes: that blond head thrown back, the lithe, youthful form garbed proudly in its dapper weave of muted gray—the shade of his new suit, the one so matched to the soulful hue of his eyes that he wore that Christmastide in Novgorod, just before we learned the news of Bloody Sunday from Petersburg. Time elapses—and I see him taller, older, moustached, and ever plying any and every audience into his magician's spell with a rakish, self-assured grin. Back and forth, the bow still flashes; up and down, the strings still sing; inward and outward, the quest still resounds, lofty and mysterious and as mesmerizing as ever—and again, over and over in my tortured mind's eye, I watch him spinning out that haunting melody from his utmost favorite, cherished piece, the cascading triplets from *Sheherazade* . . . .

True moron for punishment, from my pocket I slip out the 1909 picturegraph of the two of us standing with our arms locked, derbies tilted before the Eiffel Tower in Paris. And one by one, I choke back the welling pods of tears. *Oh, God! I cannot bear that I will never see that face, will never touch that hand—that I will never hear the sound of that violin . . . ever, ever again . . . .*

"Uh—are you all right?"

Gasping, I near jump straight out of my chair; whirl around to face the frowning visage of Volodya.

"Jesus Christ in hell!" I shout, infuriated. "J-Just what the fuck do you think you're doing?"

"I simply—I called you from atop the stairs. Twice. You must not have heard." Reddening, he sets another ledger notebook down beside the one lying open beneath my hands, his glance—irretrievably—drawn to sight of the picturegraph.

I snatch it back into my pocket and lunge for his collar, shouting: "You vile, unconscionable scum!"

"Hey, Sasha! Let go—"

"How dare you sneak down here! And—and *spy* on me!"

"I was not spyin' on you at all! I merely—"

"Get out, Rykazian!" I roar, shoving him toward the stairs.

"But I wanted to tell you—"

"Goddamn it! *Just get the fucking hell out!"*

Beating a hasty retreat to the stairway, Volodya turns to make an affronted show of dusting off his jacket lapels, muttering: "Andreyev cancelled—your first mark for tonight. So you've a little more time. So I wanted to tell you; so I brought down another ledger; so do the postings if you want—or don't do them, and I'll do them later. *That* way you can spend all eve long sulkin' up to high heaven's glorious ass, if you want! Jesus! I don't care."

Three at a time, he storms up the steps; angrily slams shut the door behind.

Glaring after him, I let out a blistering yell and slam the ledgers, cash box, pencils—everything—into a shattering crash upon the floor. Then I bury my head down into my arms upon the desk, torn sobs rasping out in a steady, hopeless stream: "Forbidden journey, obligatory pilgrimage, cup of resolution—cup of *despair!* Oh, *Lord!* Strike me blind, senseless, dead; by the dear Saints, *anything!* But t-take this c-cup f-from m-me . . . the whoring, Volodya, Yevgeny . . . Nikolai . . . *oh, God! Nikolai! . . ."*

* * *

"Later!" Volodya cries with annoyance, pushing me through the doors of a Sadovaya Street teahouse.

"Rykazian, you promised!" I shout, inspiring scores of raised eyebrows cast in our direction from patrons at the crowded rows of tables. "Only once a week do you allow me a free night," I remind him again. "And you promised we would go!"

"Sasha, can't you ever hold onto your temper, for bloody God's sake?" he yells in reply, wrenching hold of my arm.

"Humph!" Sullenly, I stare to the floor as he shoves me toward the closest vacant booth.

"Oh, so go and eat straw already!" Volodya mutters, shooting me a glare as he slides in upon the bench. "The place don't open 'til midnight, anyhow. We got over an hour to take a little tea, munch down some bread sticks."

"But I want to go to the Wandering Dog—"

"And we *will* go to the Wanderin' Dog!"

"Good! Because I want to—"

"—'hear the poets speak!' Yes, I know!" With a sly grin, he leans forward across the table and whispers: "Is that what you been jottin' down in that sorry notebook full of English scribbles that I cannot read? *Poetry?"*

"Shut up, will you?" Glowering at him, I yank my cap low to my brow, push my spectacles up on the bridge of my nose, and begin an inspection of the teahouse.

Generally, I remain skittish of every place we ever go—shops, squares, tea and tavernhouses—particularly those on the Nevsky side. Vyborg, filled with faceless hordes of shabbily-clad workers, and Vasilyevsky Island, ever overrun with impoverished students and an army of harried government bureaucrats always hurrying to-and-fro, both prove far less threatening. But at any moment along Nevsky, or along any one of the quaint little bridges spanning the Moika or Fontanka canals, some well-to-do gentleman from one of my many entanglements might happen to pause and struggle with a pang of recognition, unkempt and unshaven though I remain on one of the scarce precious nights Volodya grants me freedom from my so-called labor. Or some musician, conductor, or other old acquaintance might pick me out from the *Ballet Russe* or the Maryinsky days, then to pause and chat and parlay the usual polite questions that would only be torture to answer. Of course, the Wandering Dog, although little more than a drafty, run-down cellar, is frequented by many notables; Karsavina, it is said, ofttimes dances there, although I have never caught chance to see her. And perhaps just as well. Sojourns to the Wandering Dog are simply something I dare risk. Week by week, one week after another, the story at the Wandering Dog plays out the same: always we sit in the back, in the dark, flirting with the shadows, there to sip stale lemonade or the watered-down pineapple juice they serve and reminisce in grumbling undertones about the old carefree, legal vodka days. And then always, one by one—in declarations of outrage strung in flagrant, bold defiance of accepted meter, rhyme, cadence, and style—always, without pause, rage forth the decadent, bitter platitudes about War and Fate and Death. One reputed Petrograd name after another, the poets arise to speak: Akhmatova, Bely, Mayakovsky, others—each and every one forever prostrated to the oath, sworn unto the secret order, beholden to the ephemeral guise of Gorky's Luka, while cast to the supernal quagmire of his *Lower Depths*—each and every one of the poets pledged unto the fatal gambit of verse's inviolate surety, their call betraying tellers of lies through truth, of truth through lies.

"I still don't see why you're so taken with that mournful group," Volodya observes. "Had I my fancy, we'd hoof it on over to the Firemen's Club and stake some chips on a little Twenty-One."

"Shut up, will you?"

From the background, melancholy balalaika strummings start fluttering through the air as a barmaid fetches us tea and a small plateful of bread sticks. Distractedly, I stare about, while Volodya begins lauding the merits of some Gypsy fortune teller. "I tell you, she's good!" he insists, thumping his fist with emphasis onto the table. "And I hear she's in tonight—always takes one of the booths in the back. They call her 'Gypsy Moth.' She read for me a couple years back. Near all of what she said soon came true."

"Forget it, Rykazian," I reply, scowling at him in irritation. "If I want to know my fortune, I'll read my Tarot cards myself."

Shrugging, Volodya bites off the end of a bread stick and spends an inordinate amount of time chewing while continuing to closely eye me. "You know her," he then murmurs, his lips curling upward in a mischievous grin.

"What? Oh, piss on it—Jesus!" Shaking my head, I glare away, muttering: "Ha! As if I should know any women."

"Well, this one you do."

"Oh, indeed? All right—so just who is she, then? Huh? Some former ballerina? God, Rykazian—what kind of heartless devil are you turning into? You know I'd abhor crossing paths with anyone from those days."

"No, no! Nothing like that."

With a cocked eyebrow, I meet his glance across the table. All day, he and Yevgeny have been caught up in the worst raging tiff about politics—in addition to their usual heated words exchanged over me. "Just what are you up to, Rykazian?" I demand, frowning suspicion at him.

Grinning coyly, Volodya attempts another innocent laugh. "Nothin'!" he exclaims. "Simply thought you might want your fortune told, is all. Besides, Sasha," he urges on in a lowered tone, again leaning toward me across the table, "there's time before the Wanderin' Dog. And this 'Gypsy Moth' is good. And like I said, you know her."

Exasperated—and my curiosity more than a little piqued—I finally roll my eyes and blurt out: "Oh, all right!"

Five ruble bill in hand, I stride off toward the booths grouped along the wall at the back end of the teahouse. The woman is not difficult to spot—draped, typically enough, in scarves, earrings, and bracelets, a thick blonde braid dangling across her shoulder, she sits hunched over at the farthest booth, reading cards for a nodding ironworker. Checking my watch, I debate whether to shuffle back toward the front—but my glance toward the tables reveals Volodya, all winks and suggestive debonair gestures, conversing gaily with an elegantly suited gentleman—a prospective mark—and I decide better of walking in on any negotiations. Momentarily, the fellow with the girl withdraws from the booth—so, shrugging, I make a wary approach.

"You the fortune teller?"

"Yes." Bent over a parcel on the seat beside her, the woman indicates the opposing bench with an impatient flick of her hand. "Sit, then—will be five rubles."

Handing over my bill, I slide onto the bench across from her—there to gulp back my next inquiry the moment she faces me fully across the table. Framed in brightly patterned scarves, adorned with earrings, slathered in eye and lip paint, the face might be older and softened somehow, the hair blonder and more thickly evident—but beneath her nose, through the powder, lingers the faint outline of an unmistakable birthmark. Stunned, I stare across at her, wide-eyed, rasping out: "Missy? I—I mean, Lyubov?"

At first squinting at me, she then breaks into a smile and points across with her finger, sighing and shaking her head in embarrassment, as if attempting to recall a name.

"Sasha," I tell her.

"Oh, yes! Was bare on the tip o' my tongue—"

"Dear Lord!" I gasp on, still astounded. "What has it been? Eight years?"

Abruptly, she frowns. "An' I thought ye cared not fer speakin' te me! At least, that's what Ivanovich said."

"Yevgeny Ivanovich! Why, I've asked him of you countless times. He said when he came to Petersburg—Petrograd, I mean—that you had moved back to Smolensk."

"Smolensk! Oh, by the devil's arse—I was wonderin' jest why ye'd choose te shun me. When I first heard ye was working in Rykazian's group, I must've told Ivanovich 'til his ears wanted te fall off: 'Tell Red te look me up in the teahouse sometime!'"

"Damn him! Oh, pardon my cursing, Lyubov Ivanovna, excuse me, please! It's just that I—I would have loved to have known you were in Petrograd long before now."

Grinning with pleasure, Lyubov reaches her hand across the table and pats mine. "Oh, don't mind Ivanovich. Ye know, he complains about ye all the time! I s'pose he was again tryin' te git back at ye. . . ."

I listen with interest as she goes on to tell of her life since moving to Petrograd. Although older, perhaps near unto thirty by now, Lyubov Ivanovna has blossomed out like a desert rose from that awkward waif of a girl I remember from those long miserable years ago in Moscow. Imbued with a rounded, gentle softness, her face becomes increasingly more animated as she speaks, particularly when it is of her daughter, now almost thirteen and a prize pupil in school. Almost sheepishly, Lyubov explains away her fortune telling as mere pastime folly, and describes in detail her comfortable apartment located near the southwest end of the Fontanka Canal, insisting with obvious pride that her brother provides quite handsomely for both herself and Zhenya. Of Sheremetev, she makes a passing remark about 'some nobleman' having engineered his death, and I sigh, relieved that Yevgeny has at least refrained from telling her everything he knows. To her questions, I make vague references to my years of tenure with the ballet in Paris, and tell her that owing Volodya a substantial sum of money continues to keep me, to my great chagrin, bound so tightly under the man's thumb.

"It did take me by surprise, te hear ye was working fer Rykazian," she observes, nodding. "I don't know, in spite o' yer looks, ye jest scarce seemed the type."

"Yes, well. I suppose, ultimately—no matter how bizarre it is—a man simply does what he must do." Frowning, I peer back out toward the groupings of teahouse tables, murmuring: "I wonder why he sent me back here, anyhow?"

"You mean it was Rykazian sent ye back here te me?"

"Oh, yes. Although he neglected to tell me that it was going to be you; he merely said to seek out the fortune teller. Hmmm . . ."

Lyubov begins shuffling through her deck of Tarot cards, and after a moment glances up at me, asking: "Ye think Rykazian's got his nose up te some foul business behind our backs?"

Nodding as I become further convinced of it myself, I tell her: "He and Yevgeny Ivanovich have been shouting down the walls all day about their difference in opinion as to what constitutes proper 'socialist ideology.' Ivanovich was so riled up earlier, he near stabbed out another windowpane with the fireplace poker. I wonder—" Leaning on my elbows toward her across the table, I go on in a hushed undertone: "You think Volodya sent me back here to see you with the intent of somehow getting back at your brother?"

Laughing, Lyubov casts me an affectionate wink, her heavy earrings jangling forth festive agreement as she says: "Could be. Wily devil I hear he is, that Rykazian."

Thoughtfully, I begin drumming my fingers upon the table, my mind sorting through various probabilities—until Lyubov hands back my five-ruble bill, saying: "Ye want yer fortune read? I'll do it fer free."

"No, actually—" Upon catching her eye, I cannot resist my breaking grin. "Lyubov," I cry, reaching across the table and grasping hold of her hand. "I think that, if we wanted, we could play a horribly mean trick on Volodya! Would you care to?"

Through a spiel of giggles, she replies: "Sasha, my old friend, mean tricks are the very staff o' life! I'll help ye trip up Rykazian's fun any way ye want. Name it."

"Well." Once more I peer back toward the tables—and just barely spot Volodya, now alone again and sipping at his tea. "Knowing him," I tell her, "he'll shove off in a few moments and come back here looking for me. Anyhow, I—uh—I scarce know why I happened to think of this, but I—well. Somehow it simply seemed it would be hilarious if—if Volodya came back here, and saw us—" Pausing, I gauge the willingness of her nodding, expectant face. "Look," I go on, reddening, "I hope you'd not think this too forward of me, Lyubov Ivanovna! Will all be naught but a joke, truly. Because you see, if Volodya happened to wander back here to see the two of us—well, uh, necking—I know he would become positively furious!"

Letting out a delighted shriek, Lyubov slaps her hand to her thigh. "And sure 'nough, he'd tell Ivanovich—and the big ole lug is always stickin' his nose into my business. Talk about givin' him meat te chew on!"

Hurriedly tucking away her cards inside her pocketbook, Lyubov scoots further in on her bench, patting her hand down upon the seat. After I move over beside her, we both peer back across the teahouse floor, attempting to stifle our mirth, until—sure enough—Volodya makes a check of his watch, stands up, and slowly begins ambling in our direction. "Very well!" I cry, easing both arms around Lyubov's back as she slides her hands up around my neck. "Now, the only trouble is, we must be convincing, Lyubov Ivanovna. So I hope, again, that you'll not think me too forward—"

"Oh, no, no!" she cries gaily. "I love a good joke, Sasha! Ye kiss me however ye want—"

Kissing her however I want proves a bit awkward at first, especially as we both keep bursting into laughter—but at last we crush one another fiercely, our eyes clamped shut, our mouths molded into one as Volodya's footsteps finally tap near.

Abruptly, the footsteps stop short—and we hear the incredulous gasp, the stumbling, the coughing and loud guffaws—before he stomps angrily away. From Lyubov's embrace, I finally pull back, while she peers out beyond me and bursts into a gale of snickers. "Oh, my Lord!" she exclaims. "His face is red as a bloody torch!"

To make it appear truly authentic, we kiss a little while longer—and then, when she tells me he has scampered back to his table like a dog with its tail tucked between its legs, I scoot back out from the booth and plant earnest kisses of gratitude upon both of her hands. "Thank you, Lyubov Ivanovna!" I cry, shaken from head to foot with mirth. "I tell you, I've not laughed so good and hard like this in the longest of times!"

"Listen," she says, her grin stretched from ear to ear, bright devious sparks flashing deep within her violet-blue eyes. "Don't ye stop by the dress shop every night with Rykazian jest before ye go out on yer rounds? Ye want te keep this little joke up fer awhile, act like we're havin' an affair? I tell ye, Sasha, I'd love te git back at Ivanovich fer always lordin' it over my life. . . ."

* * *

The following eve at dusk, as planned, she waltzes on into the dress shop at the appointed hour, just as I tuck a stack of receipts back down behind the front counter.

"Sasha!" she cries, flinging off her wide-brimmed hat and running toward me.

"Lyuba!" I shout back, catching her in my arms and whirling her around into a torrid, languishing kiss.

After a long moment, we pull away from one another to face a barrage of guffaws and amused snickers from several patrons loitering in the dress shop—along with Volodya's dropped jaw and venomous gasp.

"Excuse us!" I then declare in a booming voice—and with my arm clasped about her shoulders, I escort Lyubov toward the back doorway leading to the cellar stairs.

"Now, just one minute!" Volodya shouts after, his hand shoving the earpiece back into the telephone box with a ringing bang. "Sekov—I mean, Khulinov!"

We slam the door shut in his face, laughing, and stumble downward, reaching the foot of the stairs just as he bursts in. "Hey!" he shouts down, infuriated. "I know what you two are up to—and it fails to amuse me one bit!"

"Amuse you?" I retort, pointing mirthful daggers of accusation back up at him from the bottom of the stairwell. "God, Rykazian! You think every happening in the world revolves solely around you?" Rolling my eyes, I throw both arms once more around Lyubov, priming to sweep her off into another daring, passionate kiss.

"Oh, give it up already, Sasha!" Volodya yells down in obvious choked-filled dismay. "You—you turd-head! I figured it all out after last night—Christ, just what do you take me for? I saw you two fools laughin' your bloody hearts out afterward! Oh, my God—and will you quit pawin' over that woman like that? You and I both know you're naught but a mincin' fag at heart, Sasha Khulinov! Sasha—*hey!* Now, you two just stop that—Lord by the Saints! *Sasha!* You and I both know that you scarce mean any of it!"

Pulling once more away from Lyubov, I glare up at him, taunting: "Humph! You think I scarce mean it when I kiss a woman like this?"

Whereupon I crush her to me and begin tearing into her mouth like a rabid wolf.

"Oh, for Christ's bloody sake!" Volodya roars out—then to spin around in a flush of jealous disgust and promptly slam shut the cellar door.

The room shudders to a stop as Lyubov at last peels her lips away from mine—but she moves back only by the barest hair's breadth, and her smile edges upward—moistened, trembling. I stand staring dumbly as she starts running her hand across my cheek, and after a moment, she brings both hands up and gingerly eases off my spectacles, which she lays down with care behind us on one of the bolt tables—before throwing both arms back around my neck and pulling me off into another devouring kiss.

"No!" I gasp. "Lyubov Ivanovna, wait! What are you—what are we doing?"

"I—I don't know!" she moans. "J-Jest *keep* doin' it!"

"But, Lyubov!"

I try to struggle away, but without aid of the cane—from the first, also left behind on the bolt table—the floor quickly slips out from under my toes, and it is all I can do to seize onto her for balance as she greedily forces her way back into my mouth past moans of searching torment. *"Lyubov!"* I shout, finally wrenching myself away. "M-My God!"

Undeterred, she clamps both hands onto my collar and yanks me close to her again, her violet-colored eyes gone luminously beautiful and staring sparks of passion into mine. "Ye kiss good," she murmurs, strands of her hair tickling against my chin, her cheek pressing a dewy film of face powder against my jaw. "Ye know how te kiss *real* good—"

"Stop it, Lyubov, don't! Don't do this—"

"Ye kiss so bloody good, ye—ye make me want te feel a man again, Sasha."

"Lyubov Ivanovna! Was all supposed to be naught but a joke! A *joke*, I tell you! You scarce know what you are saying!"

"Ye ever been with a woman, Sasha?" she then whispers with a lilting tease in her voice. "Hmmm?"

"Oh, *shi*—no! I mean, *yes!"* I stammer out defensively. "Of course I've been with a woman! W-With women—many, many times! In, uh, Paris—"

My explanations die in thin air, for again she seizes onto me before I can manage to elbow away, her arms clamping fiercely about my neck, her lips finding mine and parting the sweet blood of life back into them with continued raptured persistence. Above us, the room darkens; whitens to the oblivion of a steamy, benumbing cloud; countless bolts of fabric fade off into a forged blur of unanimity, and voices from the shop upstairs, from the street outside start droning into a hum within my ears, the poundings within my heart shattering fluid pain across my chest as my mouth yearns across the miasma, my arms yet clutching for heady embrace, my knees finally giving way on top of hers.

Once down on the floor, I briefly regain my senses, gasping: "No, Lyubov! W-We—we *mustn't!*" But despite all dire, fading warnings of common sense, it is all I can do to fight away, scarce able to help myself, not an ounce of will remaining to thwart such insistent, burgeoning desire from anyone—whether it be man or woman. No longer does anything else in the world matter; someone *wants* me—not on account of fancy gowns, nor ropes of pearls, nor the perverse mockery of my sorry looks. Someone wants me simply for *me*. . . .

So, I surrender, gasping for breath, pummeling on top of her, no longer caring about anything but . . . *this one thing* . . . both hands I dig up under her skirts, and one by one, I start snapping open the garters, my fingers peeling down the silky touch of her stockings, my hands caressing up over her shins, knees, thighs . . . she lets forth another heaving moan upon this whole crazy spell's vast torrent of heaving moans and slowly begins sliding apart her legs, her fists clenched like two knots across my back and pulling me to her with an urgent squeezing hold, her pelvis thrusting up against mine . . . I suck her mouth, chin, throat; pick open the tiny seed buttons down the front of her blouse and slide my hand in under her chemise, there to brush trembling fingers over each of the rounded, nippily peaks . . . her hand finds my hand finds my fly, and then we let the monster out . . . black, *black* devil which has always consumed me . . . and now—in the most unlikely situation, against all odds in the world!—now, that devil is set upon consuming me unto my own angst of destruction yet again . . . *oh, God! Unto a vise of agony . . . winter's sting of elation* . . . I thrust out beside her . . . I thrust up against her . . . shakily, gently, I part the folds . . . and burst inside! . . .

The barest moment, a thousand hours, a hundred years—first, it seems that I come instantly, but then, not at all—and then a dull, thudding wave slowly lowers back reality's bitter, calming layer as my breath, sight, and senses finally start to return. The roar all around us screams to a jolting stop, the street noises and dress shop dronings gradually burrowing their way back in. I gasp in suffocation and fight the fear of drowning in hair: hers, tumbled out between us in an untamed golden river. With caution, I elbow upward and reach my hand to brush the tangles away from her eyes. And at that very moment, her stare catches hold of mine—in a mortified blanch of horror.

Nervously, I clamber upward on wobbly footing and extend my hand to assist her—but she scurries quick away, seeking refuge on the opposite side of the fabric bolt table, her face gone florid with shame. Gaze riveted to the floor, I fumble with my fly and buckle back my belt while daring not so much as a peek in her direction, the blunt ferule of awkwardness slamming down with a spinsterly whack of disapproval to rudely sever apart our bond of closeness shared only the moment before. Flushed to my toes, fraught with confusion, the room still spinning blank edges around me, and a gnawing ache pounding at the base of my skull, at last I turn—sheepishly—to face her once again, my hands wrung together, my mind racing across all bounds for some comforting word or attempt at explanation. Both wither unsaid as—glaring at me coldly—Lyubov yanks the veil down low on her wide-brimmed hat, pulls her capelet up close about her shoulders, snatches up her drawstring bag, and bounds for the stairs in a haughty rush of silence.

"Lyubov Ivanovna, wait—please!" The cane trembling visibly worse beneath my grip with each halting step, I stumble after as her steps thunder furiously upward one by one.

"I—I am sorry!" I shout out.

Shoulders squared, she pauses to catch her breath at the utmost step.

"Look," I go on in haste, "forgive me, please! Was all my fault—I never should have encouraged you into this! Was scarce supposed to turn out this way, Lyubov!"

Without looking back, she stomps on through the doorway, slamming it shut resoundingly behind.

Clutching my head, I lean back into the nearest wall, cold brickwork clamping a frozen claw of death against my back, my voice murmuring out over and over in anguished, ragged bursts: "Oh, my *God!* What have we—what have I *done?"*

* * *

Three months of tortured, galvanizing crisis of identity. Three months of reaffirming my lust for swollen trouser flies and taut male asses; three months of gauging my reactions to women everywhere—at the shop, in the street, inside the palaces—and noting, with relief, naught but my mere passing clothier's interest in rounded hips and ample bosoms. Three months then of ceaseless, pointed questions stabbing for nonexistent answers in the middle of the day, the night: *why, then? Was it curiosity, a passing fancy, protest, vexation—what? Some thwarted sense of the old affection felt for her during the Moscow days gone wholly and pitiably awry?* Long after she left that night, I spent hours gazing through the window, the fullness of the moon hung aloft through the cover of the cloudy darkness like an eerie, grinning premonition—and I wondered how many murders would be committed, how many more unexplainable incidents would transpire; I wondered if, perchance, the simple waxing and waning of sweet Luna's monthly daredevil spell could have been the sole cause for so losing my head.

After three months of such penitent ponderings, come a stormy eve in late October—the sleet gushing down outside in miserable, slashing torrents and the wind banging with a riled cleric's vengeance upon every shuttered dress shop window—roguery's sad consequence duly descends. Head wrapped in a mountain of woolen scarves, her eyes cast to the floor, her pace toward me set with grim resolve, Lyubov Ivanovna Mrenitseva finally reappears—for the first time since our encounter—through the doorway of the dress shop.

"I'm with child," she says once we retreat downstairs.

Swallowing a gulp the size of a boulder, my gaze drawn toward the thick buttoned folds of her coat, I try—ineptly—not to stare. "You mean," I gasp out, pointing a petrified finger between the two of us, "you mean, as—as a result of—"

"Yes, fer love o' the Saints!" she retorts, bristling at the implied question. "Oh, by God, Sasha! In spite of what ye may think o' me, I do *not* fall into bed—nor onto the floor—with every man I meet like some strumpet tart from one o' them filthy taverns in Vyborg!"

"Lyubov Ivanovna, I scarce meant that! I—I just—"

"Well! By sacred oath, Sasha, I promise ye, there's been none other, not fer ages before! And none since."

"All right! I understand. It's just," I go on in a fluster, "my God—I can hardly believe it! I mean, it was only *one* time."

"Well, ofttimes is all it takes!" Perturbed, she glares away toward the cellar daylight windows, pulling her arms up tight across her bosom. "Look," she goes on after a moment in a softened tone, "I don't want nothin' from ye, Sasha. But I thought ye should know."

Then, after impatiently winding back on her woolen scarves, she turns on her heel and hurries for the stairs.

"Lyubov," I call after her, "wait!"

But stubbornly, the woman ignores me altogether, bolting upward in a flush of shame and rushing back out through the upstairs door. Only with considerable effort—my cane hammering upward step by step and then banging in a noisy, splintering chorus across the pinewood dress shop floor—do I tail her, tearing coatless and hatless out into the torrent on Theater Street. The foul weather, however, does naught to dampen my resolve; distasteful a prospect as it may loom, no question remains in my mind as to what I must do. Shivering as the rain soaks into my hair and through my clothes, I start off doggedly across the slush, but cannot match her pace. Finally, as she starts disappearing into bobbing heads of the bustling walkway crowd, I shout out after her at the top of my lungs: "Lyubov Ivanovna! Will you marry me?"

In curiosity, near unto half of the passing browsers pause up short to stare, and I push, jostling, through a sea of shoulders and elbows until at last catching up with her stiffened form, her stance held rigid and motionless as death at the steet corner with Nevsky. "Ye—ye needn't make such speeches te impress me!" she exclaims, scarce admitting a sidelong glance.

"Blast it, woman!" I rasp back, shaking a fist at her, "do you think all this is truly any easier for me than for you? My motive is hardly chicanery! Do you, or do you not, wish to secure the well being of the child?"

As her mouth drops in astonishment, I angrily seize off my spectacles, attempting to fling the rainwater from them while barking at her in irritation: *"Well!* Do you want to marry me or not?"

"Oh, fer the Lord's sake!" Lyubov exclaims, rolling her eyes. "Look at us—look at *ye*—don't ye got no sense at all under that fiery carrot-top? Why didn't ye fetch yer coat before chasin' on out here after me, ye crazy romantic fool! My God, ye're gittin' soaked clear unto yer death." Protectively, she throws one of her woolen scarves up around my neck and urges me with her toward the closest shop overhang. "Look, Sasha," she goes on once we duck under, her mitten-shod hands grasped to my icy ones and pressing them for warmth, "I know I'm the one, like a little hussy, that led ye on that night."

"And as if I could not have left whenever I so chose! No, honestly, Lyubov—please listen to what I have to say. I have spent the past three months mulling over this, while feeling guilty as the devil himself!"

"Well, that's not half so guilty as *I* feel! No—now, ye jest listen, 'cause I got a confession te make. I been terrible lonely on account o' someone. That I love 'til I want te die, and wrongly, perhaps. Jest as he loves me—ye see, he's my blooded uncle, Sasha, my father's own younger brother. An' he's in Siberia, or prison—even God himself scarce ever knows where, it changes so much all the time! But wherever he is, he's with the woman who's always been his loyal helpmate in every one o' life's affairs but true love. His wife."

For a long moment, I hold her gaze—and then nod with a sad, empathetic smile. "You know," I tell her, "there's someone I love, too. But he's—" Clearing my throat, I rasp out in a whisper: "Lost in the war." And my ears twinge hotly as her hands again close about mine, her glance full with sympathy. "Guess we're jest a couple o' misfits, yes?" she observes, shaking her head.

"Lyubov," I go on with conviction, "my intention for the marriage would be to provide the child legitimate name. You—you know what I am. Believe me, I'd never presume upon your person ever again! And of course, I would provide diligently for you and Zhenya, along with the new babe. I was reared in a family prided upon responsibility, upon honor, Lyubov. I promise you would never want for sustenance, nor for a roof over your heads."

Gratefully, she presses close to me and stares off toward the throngs of bundled people, the passing cabs and chortling motorcars, the queues of grinding, horse-drawn carriages vying for wheel space past the many chuckholes and puddles down Nevsky. "M-My Lord, Sasha!" she gasps out at last, breathing in a long sigh of relief. "Truth is, I been scared unto my death at the thought o' bringing another tiny babe into this world all by myself. I mean, Ivanovich helps. But sometimes, he's no better than a big, worthless lug."

"Long ago, I said I'd marry you, Lyubov Ivanovna," I reply with grin, nudging her. "Remember?"

When she laughs, I tell her: "Besides, I owe you for far more than one sorry little caprice down on the dress shop cellar floor—I owe you for Moscow, in 1907. There was a woman called 'Gypsy'—who concealed her face—who told the man working for my uncle about the auction. Without her help, I doubt I would soon have escaped that sordid life—Pierre's men took far too much care with gagging, tying me up. The 'Gypsy' was you—yes, Lyubov Ivanovna? You, the fortune teller known as 'Gypsy Moth.'"

When she ducks her head down in embarrassment, not deigning to answer, I murmur across to her: "So? What is the answer going to be, my good lady? Or do you intend to force a poor fellow to catch his death out in the rain while awaiting your pleasure? Will you marry me?"

"Humph!" she blurts out, playfully poking a finger for my ribs. "Eight years later, an' I swear by the dear Lord—the lad's not changed! Still full o' lofty, grand ideas up te his carrot-topped ears. . . ."

* * *

"Marry!" Volodya exclaims, his eyes swollen to saucers. "My God, Sekovsky—I mean, Khuli—oh, whatever! Are you out of your *living mind?"*

"And will you please stop yelling your guts out at me?" I cry, wincing away from him. "Lord! As if I haven't enough troubles: Ivanovich near tried to strangle me after she told him."

"And how the devil did you ever get the woman with child, anyway?"

"Well, I don't know! I mean—shit!—I *do* know, dammit! But I scarce know why it happened! You saw us. We simply went down into the cellar, one kiss led to another—"

"I thought it was all supposed to be naught but a joke!"

"Well, it *was!"*

Hands tearing wildly through his hair, Volodya rants on: "But, *marry!* Sasha, you cannot marry Lyubov Mrentiseva—"

"Oh? Well, I am marrying her, Rykazian, and you've no call to say a word about it—I am not your lifelong slave! The woman is going to bear my child, and I will secure her welfare however I see fit."

"That is not what I mean! Sasha, for God's sake—the woman is a Bolshevik!"

My retort catches in my throat, while Volodya points, with sweeping accusation, toward the kitchen doorway—and the direction of Yevgeny's apartment beyond. "Well, you know he is!" he reminds me with high-pitched emphasis. "I am tellin' you, they both are!"

"Well, it—it makes no difference."

"But, *Sasha!"*

"Dammit, Rykazian—aren't you a muddle-headed Bolshevik yourself, to whomever's counting?

"No!" he retorts, affronted. "I am a proud member of the Socialist Revolutionary Party of Viktor Chernov—a benevolent, insightful leader concerned with fairness for all—especially when compared to that tiresome fool's ass Lenin, and his groveling *Bolsheviki.*"

"Oh, Christ save me!" I shout back at him, "forget the political rhetoric you and Ivanovich chafe over night and day without pause, will you? Jesus! And exactly what difference will it make in the end? Revolution is revolution."

"Well, calm yourself, dear Count Sekovsky!" he snaps back, glaring me down. "It appears there'll be scarce much revolution in our near future. Perhaps your child might live to see it, humph! Goddamn police! Everybody in jail, our meetins all shut down for months. . . ."

"I notice that stops neither you nor Ivanovich from hoarding guns," I observe, casting a tentative glance toward the foot of our bed—and the generous cache stashed in wads of blankets underneath. Carbines these days come near precious as gold, and the police would think they had struck it filthy rich could they but snoop out these two apartments. Then we would all be promptly arrested and locked away in the Kresty Prison—or far worse, in the dreaded Peter and Paul Fortress itself—with the other revolutionary scum Volodya complains about missing so much all the time. I allowed the situation to bother me terribly at first, so much so that I lost tons of sleep and near suffered a heart spasm each and every time anyone knocked upon our front door. Now, my only course for maintaining a hold on sanity is to continually banish all thought of the guns—and every other clue of Yevgeny's and Volodya's underhanded dealings with some fellow named Yurenev—away from my mind. It is toward the stockpiling of guns, after all, for which goes the major bulk of money that funnels in from the whoring operation.

"Oh, there'll be revolution," Volodya murmurs glumly to himself, his gaze hung heavy toward distant horizons through our bedroom window. "Revolution will triumph in our land someday. . . ."

Within two minutes, however, the highbrowed glory of revolutionary socialist change succumbs to renewed protests over my marriage. "Dammit, Sasha!" he blares on. "Is only because I care about you."

"Care?" I roar back. "Fuck care! You care for me no better than you would a dog."

"Oh, no—now there you're wrong! And if you marry that woman, she'll only bring you trouble for a lifetime, I can guarantee it, Sasha! Will you just *listen* to me?"

"Go to hell!"

Blabbering on like a lovesick hyena, he tails me into the kitchen, follows me back out, and hovers behind in stubborn, cursing vexation as I down my tea and return to my makeshift altar on the floor. "Shut up, goddamn you, Rykazian—and just leave me the fuck alone!" I shout back, both hands cupped over my ears. "My God, can't you even smell the truth lying on a bed of thorns in the light of day? If you cared for me only half a whit as much as you keep saying you do, you'd *not* force me to whore."

Volodya finally stops yelling, and shifts his weight between his feet as if my words had truly tipped his balance in the physical sense. Lingering upon the altar, his eyes waver not an inch from my collection of keepsakes spread over its surface until he murmurs out: "All right."

Stunned, I glance up at him.

"You want proof of how much I care for you, Sasha Khulinov?" he goes on. "You want not to whore anymore? Fine, all right—consider yourself again a mere book clerk," he declares, shoving his hands down into his pockets with a flourish and adding sarcastically: "My dearest love."

My eyes locked onto his, I push slowly upward to my feet.

"Well!" he spouts on, "and what the hell good does it do, dollin' you up as 'Dmitra' when you can scarce manage that leg of yours anymore without the cane, even with your special shoes? See? I *do* care—I been watchin' you a whole lot closer than you know! And that leg's been worsenin' again as the cold weather sets in—and, besides! Business has been slackin' away, I can't keep up with so many blasted whores in any case. The novelty has worn off, all the old gents been goin' back to their mistresses, their wives—"

"Oh, thank you very much, M'sieur Denisov!" I shout in furious reply. "So what am I supposed to do now? Attempt to pick up where I left off? My God, after all this travesty you've forced me through, I could never hope to show my face in any orchestra or ensemble in this wretched city ever again!"

"Particularly on account of the police—correct? M'sieur Murderer?"

As I glare across at him hotly, he shrugs and says: "But you can keep up my books for me. You know what a sorry fool I am at figurin' accounts. And durin' the days, you can keep an eye over the dress shop. Ivanovich is pitiful at it—scarce precious gentility for courtin' so many timid lady customers."

With a grunt of acknowledgment, I edge over beside him as he moves back to the bedroom window, and follow his stare to the street below, sighing with profound relief. So far, I had been fortunate while in my 'Dmitra' guise, never encountering anyone of acquaintance from my former, more legitimate life. And then last night, into the Palace bedroom where I stood calmly awaiting a new mark, waltzed none other than Semyon Bulyarin—elder brother of my old ledger compatriot, Bulya, and son of Ilya Isayevich, the prominent village elder and laureate of the Novgorod *zemstvo*. As a youth, Semyon worked as a stable hand for Father, and taught me how to ride when I was a but a small boy. Last night, I learned that Semyon's interest in boys—younger and older—was far more than passing: reveling in my acute discomfiture, he insisted that we proceed unto the glorious end with the act for which he had paid such an exorbitant sum of money.

"You say I could merely see to the dress shop—and to the books—and that's all?" I say to Volodya, hedging a sidelong glance toward him.

Still peering dreamily out the window, he murmurs: "If you'll assure me you'll not fly headlong for the Finnish border, yes."

"Lyubov is going to have my child. You know I'd never leave now."

"I hardly thought so."

"And I am going to marry her."

"Oh, good God, Sekovsky!" he yells, whirling upon me once again. *"Why?"*

"Because, Volodya! It is the honorable thing to do."

"Oh, honorable!" he echoes, widely rolling his eyes, his sigh waning at last toward a hint of resignation.

Then, without warning, Volodya abruptly lashes outward, seizing up my arm and pulling me to him in a rough embrace. "Hey!" I shout, shoving at his hand. "Damn you, stop it!"

"No, Sashenka, dearest—because, besides keepin' the books and watchin' over the dress shop, there is, uh, one other service you can provide me. On a daily basis—"

"No!" I shout, punching for his jaw.

Ready for it, he deflects the blow and pinions my arm behind my back in a grip like an iron vise, forcing me with him over onto the bed.

"No, Rykazian—you dirty, scheming fucker!" I shout, punching out with my other fist, kicking at him as he scoots around on top of me.

"Oh, shut up—you whinin' little tart!" he retorts, yanking back a fistful of my hair and diving into an eager kiss. "I remember days when you used to beg me for it often enough. . . ."

Murderously, I keep fighting him, but to no avail—just as during most of the other times when sheer brute strength has tilted the odds in his favor. "G-Goddamn you, Rykazian!" I choke out, cursing him voraciously in between his greedy, smothering kisses.

"Oh, I suppose I can't blame you for despisin' me, Sekovsky," he whispers at last, easing back upward and meeting my glare with a saddened frown. "And God forbid if you ever could have loved me back in the old days—not our pretty red-haired Sasha, the one who was already bloody well taken—body, heart, and lofty metaphysical soul—even from the very first time I ever kissed you. Because *he's* the only one you've ever truly loved." Without hesitation, Volodya's gaze hones down toward the picturegraph of myself and Nikolai set upon the altar.

"You go stuff a fire poker up your ass, Rykazian!" I shout, lunging for his throat—but he punches me off, hollering back: "You've loved him ever since that first time I caught you starin' at him buck naked in that tavern in Vyborg—"

"You shut up!"

"—and you've kept lovin' him, even durin' each and every time you've been with me! Blast you, stop denyin' it—I see the way you idolize that picture day and night! Jesus, Sasha—why are you still fawnin' so over a man who cares nary a lick about you? And just where the hell *is* your snooty cousin these days, anyhow? Still stunnin' rich Conservatory crowds with his showy antique violin?"

"No, by dammit—he's probably strewn out in ten bloody pieces on some godforsaken battlefield in East Prussia!"

Volodya's next words spill into a snuff of air, and he stares across at me, open-mouthed, while I storm back over to my altar and collapse down onto the floor before it with an anguished moan, my gaze drawn solely toward the picturegraph.

Crouching down on his haunches beside me, Volodya whispers: "You mean—he volunteered?"

"Yes," I whisper back.

"When was he listed? . . ."

"Tannenberg."

Sighing, Volodya eases up to his feet, murmuring: "I—I'm sorry, Sasha."

His steps shuffle away, the kitchen door creaking to a close behind him. Numbed to the bone, I stare back to the altar, and after a long moment, match by match, I light my candle tapers. Word by word, I recite my morntide prayer out three times over in a rasping, voiceless stutter; piece by piece, I take out my flute, and fit the joints together. Note by note, I test the scales. And then I play Debussy until it claws the walls like pain. . . .

* * *

On a foggy morn come the first week of November, 1915, Volodya and Yevgeny look on beneath glimmering votive candlelight in the St. Andrei Cathedral, while Lyubov and I, both nervous and embarrassed, suffer through the blessing and exchanging of the rings, the wearing of the golden crowns, the shared sipping from the cup of wine sanctifying the Holy Rite of Marriage. Soon afterward, loaded up in one quick trip with my books and other scant possessions, I move into the small study tucked behind the kitchen in her second floor walk-up apartment south of Pokrov Square. Tanya Feodorovna, pleading homesickness—amongst other tearful excuses—deserts Yevgeny Ivanovich the following month, and by the brisk, icy days of Christmastide, at Lyubov's insistence, Yevgeny moves into her apartment as well, taking for himself the sewing alcove upstairs. Volodya—faced between Yevgeny's portion, and the wave of price hikes that continue plaguing the city to no end—with triple the rent from the year before, promptly forfeits the flat on Vasilyevsky, first for a sorry, run-down hole still on the island, but several streets far too tiresomely distant from either the Nikolayevsky or the Palace Bridge. Due to the sudden erratic scarcity of cab service in the city throughout the dreary stronghold of the winter, he at last succumbs to bleak necessity and carts his things over to the dress shop, storing most of them in the cellar and spending the nights beneath stacks of furs on a mat near the iron stove upstairs. In the streets, the shops, the palaces—across the gossip columns of the breathy society pages—the new year rings in upon a wave of hopeful good intentions, but business for us, both legitimate and otherwise, only continues doggedly tapering off, particularly in the dress shop, as supplies dwindle in the wake of mounting shortages everywhere on account of the war. "I hear merchants all up and down Nevsky are starting to hoard," Volodya tells me one day, ruefully shaking his head.

"Hoard?" Up to my elbows in paperwork, I glance over from my tallies of payables with a distracted frown. "Why?"

"For prices to climb up even higher—why else? Remember your wife and all her complainin' in here the other day about the butcher? I'm tellin' you, that guzzlin' old fool's got meat to spare in his shop—probably a whole side of beef packed in ice down on his cellar floor, waitin' out a few more days so the swine can squeeze out every last kopek he can."

Volodya, however—in a odd impasse of morality that leaves me both baffled with amusement and enamored with a begrudging new respect—refuses to hoard. Anything. With the result that, within weeks, the dress shop starts running out of everything from facing to button fasteners to delicate batiste which cannot be worn for months until the summer weather arrives in any case. "It's not good," I tell him late one January eve after we lock up, the both of us huddled down closely over open ledgers. "If we keep selling off fabric at this rate, Rykazian, you'll be drawing on old inventories from downstairs by the second week of next month."

Warnings about the upcoming tax allotments fresh upon my tongue, I turn to continue the conversation, but find him staring, thoughtfully, no longer at the scrawled stack of ledger pages, but at me. "Did you hear what I said?" I ask, nudging his arm with my elbow.

In reply, Volodya leans in close and presses a gentle kiss against my temple, murmuring: "No."

Heart beating wildly, I forget the figures, the books, the problems—my hand searching across the table to grasp up his. Since the night I told him about my cousin's fate—near unto three long months ago—Volodya has made no more advances toward me, nor I toward him. Nor, save for a couple of quick late-night *tête-à-têtes* at the bathhouse—and yes, one or two hurried ones at the Villa Rode—have I made any serious advances toward anyone else. "Volodya," I say softly.

"Yes?" Planting another hopeful kiss against my temple, he tucks the stubbed knuckles of his mangled hand down into my open palm.

I squeeze hold of them fervently, murmuring: "Why don't you come home with me tonight?"

"Humph! And what about your wife?"

"Oh, come—you know the marriage was only in name. Besides," I go on with a shrug, "I asked her the other day about you staying with us. She said she'd not mind. I think one of the reasons that woman married me is because the more people she has living under her roof, the happier she is."

"You are asking me to come and live with you?"

Reddening, I reply: "Well, face it—you're freezing your duff to the bitter bone every night in this damn shop. And I—I've been worried about you."

Nuzzling into my throat, he whispers: "Worried? I thought you hated me."

"I scarce hate you." Months ago, I would never have admitted it, but now, I cannot help but know that some of my old feelings for him still linger true. For so long have Volodya and I been sometime companions, sharing together a common life, laughter—and yes, I suppose, love. At least in our own peculiar way—and it is with a long sigh over such brimming memories that I slide both arms up around his neck and begin running my fingers through the wealth of graying strands peppered throughout his hair. Worry, for a certainty, has been tearing at him of late far more than it has at me; endlessly, he has been upbraiding the clerks, stalking the counters, pacing the floors—ever since the autumn, when profits began to turn. "You'll do better with a warm place to sleep," I urge, pressing to him close.

Abruptly, Volodya pulls back to face me with a questioning frown. "Look," he murmurs, "I know you been furious at me, for a long time. And I—well—I was plenty sore at you too, after tyin' me up and burnin' me like you did with them damn cigarettes. Maybe for gettin' back at you with the whorin', I went a bit too far. But looks to me like, right now, we both need each other. Don't you think?"

Nodding, I move into his embrace and kiss him fully on the mouth, easing away only after a long moment to whisper: "Friends?"

"Friends!" he replies with a broad smile, squeezing my hand.

As a result, I soon enough hear Zhenya telling a classmate, with breathless, giddy detail, via the kitchen telephone box: "Well, see—first there's my mama, and I'll have a new baby brother or sister come advent of spring. Then there's Uncle Yevgeny Ivanovich—he's gone in the sewin' room upstairs. Uh-huh, he's the one always goin' to the meetins with Mama, when they can. And then there's my step-papa—he's married to my mama, but he keeps to the downstairs, 'cause he's—he's—well, you know. His friend Vladimir Denisovich just moved in, and he sleeps with him. Yes, in the same bed. Well, I don't know! Mama says it don't bother her none at all, and that I'm not supposed to fret about such matters. Well, I don't know why she married him, then!

Mama says it was due to a 'accident.' 'Cause when Uncle Grigor and Aunt Olga finally come back, naught's goin' to change—that stuffy old biddy Aunt Olga is supposed to come in with me again, and Uncle Grigor will go back in with Mama. Yes—Aunt Olga and Uncle Grigor are married to each other. Well, I don't know! That's the way it was all the times before. See? I told you my family's even more impressive than yours. Is *so*, Tanya—we're ten times more odd and impressive a family! But Mama says if Uncle Ivanovich happens to find himself another woman by then, and moves out, then if I want, I can take the sewin' room—"

Not wishing to startle her, I latch the front door shut with a cautious hand and slip past the kitchen wall into Volodya's and my room. So far, Zhenya has remained quite the enigma. Little do I seem to know of what to say to, or inquire of, a lively thirteen-year-old girl. Likewise, from me, the child stays warily distant, but watchful, as if forever sighting me out—although she remains painfully polite, her mother ever insistent upon proper manners.

On the other hand, under Lyubov's continual chiding, Yevgeny Ivanovich begins to become less of an enigma—or at least starts to become less adversarial, occasionally doling out bits of conversation about the traffic, the weather, the best picks of any of the nearby tavernhouses with secret stills that have been cranking out home-brew. As the February *Maslenitsa* festivities come and go, and I stare out across the terrace windows day by day toward the dawning hope of spring, life for all of us does seem to ease—and yet for me, without cessation, a lone pall of melancholy remains. Week after agonizing week, Nikolai's name never disappears from the casualty rosters toward any spark of life or demise of total certainty. Economic and political turmoil only continues to heighten in intensity, for higher and higher the prices daily climb, coupled with an increased scarcity of goods in the grocer's shops and bareness of shelves in the bakeries. Day and after day without pause, the papers report further juicy bits of scandal about the Tsarina and that shameful peasant *starets,* Grigory Rasputin—the plotting, decrepit holy man taken on, to the angst of all Court society, as closest Imperial adviser. Monthly, the government flounders through new epochs of war-weariness and social intrigue, everyone wondering who will be the next Agriculture, the next Interior, the next War Minister. Nightly, rumors of impending disaster loom up vibrantly afresh upon the tips of wagging matron's tongues—the latest, that all the Russian generals are naught but a troupe of German spies, and were it not so, we would long since have won the war. And as the weeks, and then months, wane by, and I gain amicable ground with my newfound family—Lyuba, Zhenya, Volodya, Yevgeny—I yet lie staring awake into each night's darkness with a gnawing sense of foreboding. For every one of Mother Russia's dire wartime ills, whether merited or no, the blame increasingly is being laid solely upon members of the aristocracy.

Which imparts a growing sense of urgency to my weekly meetings with Father. "Oslo?" he gasps out incredulously one starlit eve. "Why on earth should I care to travel to Oslo now, in the dead of winter—without you?"

"Well, Papa—I simply thought that you might wish to consider—"

"Aleksandr! I will be damned unto hell if I am ever leaving this country without you! You tell that devil Rykazian to let up his noose's hold on your freedom, and then we'll both go."

Ironically, now, with Volodya's and my friendship tentatively restored, and my illicit activities of the night resigned to the bitter trance of memory, I cannot help but wonder, were I to broach the question reasonably enough, if I might indeed be permitted to leave. But of course, travel constraints these days stem no longer from my predicament with Volodya, but from my obligations to Lyubov—and of her, I have told Father nary a word. Moderate political thinker though he is, were he to learn I had wedded a peasant woman, I fear he would attempt to tan my hide! 'Never step beneath yourself—always remember who you are, whence and from whom you have come,' was his constant advice—in person and in countless letters—regarding women during my *Ballet Russe* years. An admonition always duly followed by long lectures about our pride in bearing the nobility and stories about various outstanding 'matches' made by Sekovsky forebears. Although of course, whenever I asked if he would have married Melissa had she not been descended of the English gentry, his only reply was ever a knowing smile. And never an answer.

With the advent of the Lententide season toward the dawn of spring, the babe starts showing unmistakably through Lyubov's clothes. "Perhaps you should sit down for awhile," I tell her one eve in the kitchen as she hovers over the soup pot.

"Ye want te eat, or no?"

"Well, of course I do. But I think I can stir soup just as well as you."

"Nonsense! Jest what d'ye think, Sasha Mikhailovich? That women give off all o' their chores on account o' carryin' a babe? My God, the whole hungry world would come to a whinin' stop! Besides, ye're the one's been workin' all day an' half the night in that dress shop, not me. Go on, git back there, sit down."

Sighing, I settle down once again at the table, but watch her with a pensive frown. Sometimes, I cannot help but feel as if I married the mother I never had. Lyubov is, after all, near unto five years my elder—and months of living with her have proven her complaints about Yevgeny 'lording it over her life' to be entirely unfounded. Instead, it is she who orders him—and everyone else—around, continuously. But the call of mothering, I suppose, well suits a woman whose very name rhymes synonymous with the Russian word for 'love.' Certainly, those many years ago in Moscow, she took splendid enough care of me when I truly needed a tender hand. Then she always laid out my meals with a tidy, smiling flourish—and as she does so again now, I watch her from the corner of my eye, pondering upon just what kind of a mother this woman will make for the babe to come—because for all of her attentiveness and motherly scoldings, Lyubov's priorities yet remain subject to a strange dichotomy. Often enough have I watched her fawning over Zhenya, only to see her check a clock, throw up her hands, and dash off through the door to another supposed 'meeting'—leaving her poor tearful daughter with her hair only half pinned up. Often enough have I wandered into this kitchen, or into the apartment's small cozy parlor, and interrupted three-way murmured conversations between Lyubov, Yevgeny, Volodya. The rebuff is always icy, their glares silent, as if upon my approach, an axe had fallen through the floor. None of them ever start up with any of it again until after I leave. Volodya, of course, occasionally mentions a few words here and there about a 'drop-off,' or some other such obscure, underhanded dealing with this or that person. As ever, I banish all details from my mind, praying that the less I know about any of the whole clandestine operation, the better.

Although, conversely, I attempt shore up any and every tidbit conducive to any future ends. Come March and the night of the Feast of the Annunciation, our bellies full, our passions—for the moment—sated, I tuck my head onto Volodya's shoulder and draw up the covers close about our chins, murmuring: "What have you told her of me?"

"Hmmm?" Sleepily, he glances upward as I press on: What have you and Ivanovich told Lyubov? About the murder; about me—Novgorod, Father, all of it?"

"Well," he replies, "to protect you from the police, I've said not a word to Lyubov Ivanovna, and long ago, I swore Ivanovich to secrecy. He knows your real name, but I neglected to tell him much more. Certainly, naught of Novgorod; both of them still believe that story you made up years ago about your mother bein' an English governess. I thought it best to leave well enough alone. After all—pity the poor day, my love, when your little wifey Lyuba learns she is married to a count."

"So—you think she would not take the truth very well, then?"

"The woman is a Bolshevik, Sasha. They all detest the aristocracy to high hell. I tried to warn you of this before you married her."

"I know, I know."

So—it is as I thought; the course is set. My child—brimming progeny of that proud, cherished Novgorodian line that ever lives on in my heart—will never know his true name. Unless, of course—someday—I tell him of it in secret.

Austere Bolshevik though she supposedly is, Lyubov remains, however, true woman at heart—much to Zhenya's consternation, the poor girl's screams shuddering in wave upon frantic wave down the stairwell on the sunny springtime morn of Branch, or Palm Sunday, Eve. "Step-papa!" she wails on, near splitting my eardrums in half. *"Step-papa!"*

"Yes, yes—I am coming!" My leg still slowing me to no end despite the daily promise of more temperate weather to come, I grunt my way up to the head of the stairs, my heart pounding into my throat. Another week, for a certainty, before the babe comes due, so the midwife said—but Lyubov's time is still pulling treacherously close, and again I gulp back tough splinters of apprehension as I stumble toward the upstairs lavatory, muttering to myself: "Oh, God, please! Not now, not yet! Let someone else be here—Volodya, Yevgeny, *anybody*—don't force me to face this alone, and—and forgive a poor fool his loathsome cowardice, dear Lord God Jesus in Heaven, because that is precisely what it is! Oh, for God's sake—what has come over me?"

Once again Zhenya screams out: *"Step-papa!"*

I burst through the door of the lavatory only to be met by a walloping splash.

In the oversized claw-footed tub, Lyubov lies soaked up to her neck in frothy perfumed bubbles. Upon spying the look of mortification on my face, she throws back her head and howls with laughter, sputtering out: "Oh, no—ye poor blitherin' idiot! *That's* not what it is!"

Zhenya, her dark skirt and pressed white schoolgirl's blouse soaked through to her skin, pulls herself up from the far end of the tub—but just as soon again, collapses back over it, also gripped from head to foot with mirth. At last, sheepishly, she glances up at me and flicks a stringy wet dark hair away from her face. "Step-papa, I am sorry to be yellin' so. It's just that I can't—"

And then once again they both burst into a torrent of hysterical, shrieking laughter.

Fiercely, I glare between them, but at last cannot thwart my inching grin. "You mean—you cannot get your mother out of the tub?"

In response, another gale of affirmative, rib-cracking howls.

"Lyubov, for God's sake!" I tell her, going wide-eyed. "Stop laughing so much or you'll bring on the birthing pains!"

"Step-papa," Zhenya says, "you'll have to help me get her out."

Pointing down at Lyubov with a wagging finger, I blare on: "And did you not bother at all to stop and think about how you were going to find your way out of there before you climbed in?"

"Humph! Might I remind ye that the one luxury the dear Lord permits these weary, achin' bones o' mine is this bath in this tub overflowin' with water and bubbles. I'd've got in here this morn even if this babe was comin' today! You know the one reason Ivanovich fixed me up in this apartment—"

"Yes, I know! Not on account of the Fontanka view, nor the large kitchen, nor the quaint parlor, but because of this gigantic claw-footed tub. Well," I go on, chuckling and shaking my head, "I suppose we should see what we can do about lifting you out."

Each of us grasping hold of one of Lyubov's arms, Zhenya and I awkwardly manage to hoist her up out of the mess of soapy bubbles, both of us blushing beet scarlet upon the sight of her swollen, protruding belly. "Oh, like neither o' ye never seen me naked before!" Lyubov bellows out, laughing as if at a couple of children as she towels off and pulls on her robe.

In truth, I never have seen her totally naked before—but I neglect pressing the point as I follow her haltingly toward the door of her room, demanding: "Are you going to be all right?"

"Why wouldn't I be? Oh, an' what are ye all the sudden so tweaked about—'cause I couldn't git out o' the tub?"

"Well, yes—"

"Oh, poppycock! Git off with ye, already!" she exclaims, waving her hand. "Ye were jest on yer way to the shop, yes? Well, git goin' then—else how's this babe I'm carryin' goin' te eat? Oh! An' Sasha," she goes on in a lowered tone, "will ye bring me a couple o' them ribbons fer the pussy-willows? Zhenya's got te have some nice branches fer tomorrow's Sunday o' the Palms."

At the shop, it is only with effort that I banish the thought of Lyubov's great heaving belly from my mind. But the day's business quickly interrupts with blessed distraction: our supply shipment arrives, as always just in the nick of time. All morn long, I spend logging boxloads of odds and ends into the books, and toward early afternoon, the tables lie spread generously full with ribbons, scarves, and tiny remnant pieces. Business picks up in brisk succession as housewives, schoolgirls, and austere society matrons arrive in bustling droves in search of keepsakes for Palm Sunday branch decorating. Pavla, the morning clerk, stays on to assist Ida, who normally remains all day, and toward closing time, even I become coaxed out from my bookclerk's cubbyhole at the back to help add up purchases during the last minute rush. Caught up in holiday spirits, Pavla and Ida fish out a couple of pussy-willows stored in the umbrella bucket behind the counter, and each stifling grins, they tie remnants of silk around the branches and start thrashing out at one another—and then at me—until I put away my abacus and thrash back, laughing, with a branch of my own. Although the customers begin dwindling out, a glow of gaiety still pervades all around as Georgi Samsonovich—always amongst the friendliest of Volodya's assortment of whores—saunters in through the door, clad in shabby worker's street clothes in lieu of his gaudy nightly disguise of blonde wig and glittering blue sapphires. Graciously, he tips his cap to every lady in the shop before cornering me over at the farthest counter beside the telephone box.

"Beatin' slugabeds early, yes, freckle-face?" he demands with a sly grin, grabbing for my branch.

I whack him with it soundly. "I beat thee not, the rod beats!" I quip, laughing. "And just what brings you in here, anyhow, Gorushka? Vasya stopped by earlier and snatched up some of the best ribbons for both of you. I thought, by now, you'd be readying for the procession."

"Akkh! We got hours yet—everyone says the churches'll be half-empty tonight anyhow, on account o' the war."

"Yes," I reply, sighing at whimsical childhood memories. "I suppose none of us celebrates like we used to."

"Well, these days we all got loftier pursuits on our minds," Georgi declares. "And speakin' of lofty," he goes on, eyeing me knowingly, "guess *who* I saw the other night out on the drag with that swarthy devil Rykazian—"

Grinning, I stare off toward the windows; then roundly bat my eyes at him, and shrug.

"—ha! *Indeed!* The most gorgeous little red-headed tramp ever blazin' her way and turnin' officers heads through the Menshikov Palace halls! Um-hum—'Dmitra' herself it was, decked out from head to foot in ropes of pearls and that creamy flood of silk."

"Shhh!" I warn him, laughing, my finger pressed to my lips. Surreptitiously, I nod toward several watchful matrons staring at us with raised eyebrows.

"Humph! Small wonder you balked at sellin' me the dress," Georgi raves on. "I swear to God, darlin', in that outfit, you shame that fool's twit Yusupov clear to sour tears! One of these nights, we oughta fetch you away from Rykazian's pawings long enough to go show you off over at the Bear, or the Aquarium, or another of the cabarets."

To such acclamation, I feign modesty, but cannot stifle a smug grin. Prince Feliks Yusupov, heir to the vastest fortune in all the Empire, remains eternal darling of Petrograd's palace parties and decadent salons, prickly thorn though he is in the side of the Imperial inner court with his marriage to the Grand Duchess Irena, niece of the Tsar. For years, the striking, pouty Prince has shown up on regular occasion at various city nightspots, ever parading his blonde wig laced with diamonds and his flowing risque gowns procured from Madame Brissac, haughty *couturière* to none other than the Tsarina herself. Comparison with the willowy Yusupov imparts a certain sense of power—as does, indeed, whisking through the aristocracy's highest echelons in my elegant silk dress and long auburn fall as the beauty so many men—both knowingly and unknowingly—covet to throes of distraction. Increasingly, of late, 'Dmitra's' naughty little larks have beckoned all the more tempting now that Volodya no longer insists upon me taking money for such favors.

Now, if only I could shirk off glum thoughts each night of my proud Novgorodian forebears all turning in their graves.

"So?" Georgi whispers on. "Just when you comin' back?"

"What? To whore? Oh, no—I scarce think so."

"Humph! Oh, so that's it—think you're too good for all of us, 'Dmitra,' sweetie? Hmmm? She's too good for us!" he blurts out with a loud, swishing flourish, pointing his thumb down at me.

"No, 'Lortitia,' you knave!" I cry, reddening. "And will you mind? There are still customers in the shop! It's simply that," I go on, searching helplessly for excuses, "it's—uh—too exhausting, that's what it is."

"Well," Georgi prattles on, "according to Rykazian, it must not be the sex."

"Shhh! No, you fool! It's the infernal busy schedule. Lord, can't anyone understand? If I play available again, it'll be work around the clock—here, at the palaces. Oh, I know the money's good, Gorushka! But I need time to write."

"Write!" Georgi's eyes narrow, his interest pouncing upon the subject. "I never knew you wrote!" he gasps out with a reverent stare. "Oh, my goodness—that bear Rykazian never said a word about it—oh, I shall flay him! What do you write, Sasha? Poetry? Plays?"

Fortunately, his friend Vasili Sergeyevich then waltzes on in through the doors and to my rescue. "Ice-breaking on the Neva!" he shouts to everyone gaily, sweeping his arm out in a grandiose wave.

Amidst a collective gasp, half the customers swarm the counters to make payments, while the other half throw their prospective purchases down and tear out of the shop. "Vasya, you lughead!" I bellow at him, glaring. "Is probably naught but another false rumor!"

"No, this one's true," he declares, pointing to the northwest facing window. "They're starting to line up the sledges, the troikas, everything out on the Neva ice."

"Oh, come! That's the same as I heard last eve over in Filippov's Bakery."

"But this time, it's true, Sasha," he cries insistently. "And hey!" he yells on, his gaze narrowing in upon the face of the wall clock above our heads. "Sasha, Gorushka—do either of you two have the time?"

"Why don't you come with us, Sasha?" Georgi urges, his hand pressed unto my arm. "Forget the procession! We'll just all bundle up in a troika and ride out on last ice."

"Oh, no, truly—I mustn't," I tell him, glancing down at a stack of receipts tucked underneath the counter. "I still have books to balance—"

"Naught but excuses, four-eyes! You always have books to balance!"

Wistfully, I sigh, shaking my head at him. Similar to the Palm Sunday Eve processions, ice-breaking on the Neva these days simply pales in comparison to the glittery festivals celebrated in the years before the war. "What's the point?" I tell Georgi. "No chance anymore to catch even a glimpse of the Tsar—they say the man's still at the front.

And even were he here, he'd probably stay hiding away like a hermit at Tsarskoe Selo."

Both Georgi and Vasili then launch into a wordy campaign to convince me along troika riding with them—until, worn down, I finally agree, and emerge from the office with my coat thrown over my arm. Then Yevgeny—capless, his hair mussed, his face stark white, his beady eyes stunned wide with fear—bursts like a tornado through the doorway of the shop. "Khulinov, dear God—ye got te come!" he roars out, terrifying several women customers near into fainting spells. "We can't find the midwife!"

"The midwife?" I gasp. "You mean—Lyubov! You mean she's—"

"Yes, by the Saints!"

"Oh, my God! . . ."

He has a cab waiting, and we fly over to Nevsky and then full length down Sadovaya before cutting south as if through a hailstorm for the canal at Pokrov Square. At home, a shrill scream pierces the air just as we clear the front door. "You are certain you cannot find the midwife anywhere?" I demand of Yevgeny for the near hundredth time as we bound up the stairs.

"I'm tellin' ye, I looked on every floor. I think the whole damn building's jest plain plum gone! Well, what with Branch Eve procession startin' up an' all. An' I heard it, too—tonight, I think they *are* goin' te break the ice."

Upstairs, we find Zhenya foraging through the wardrobe-cupboard for fresh linens, and Lyubov kicking her legs impatiently between bedsheets soiled with a watery brownish fluid. "Oh, wonderful!" she exclaims, throwing up her arms and glaring with exasperation at the both of us as we stumble in. "Jest what I need on my hands right now—*two* worthless, hysterical men! Yes, yes, I jest broke the water—blast it, *one* o' ye go an' find the midwife! An'—*ahhhhhh!"*

Down the building vestibule hall and up another flight from our front door, the midwife's apartment remains locked, and from within, no answer responds to our poundings. "I'm tellin' ye, I tried it four times already!" Yevgeny shouts down at me, shaking his fist. "They must either be headin' for the ice, or off to the procession!"

Cursing as I face yet another struggle with a stairway, I snatch up my cane and groan out: "And here we thought ourselves so lucky with a midwife in the same building!"

Worse, save for the sleepy-eyed doorman—hardly any help in this situation—the remainder of the building appears entirely deserted also.

Again I groan up and down more flights of demon steps as Yevgeny bellows out hysterically: *"Khulinov!* What're we goin' to do?"

Desperate for advice myself, once back in our apartment, I throw open the door to my room—and find the bed blankets yet freshly folded, untouched from the early morn. "And just where the devil is Rykazian?" I demand, whirling upon Yevgeny.

"Well, I dunno! Thought he was in there, too."

Friday and Saturday morns it is not usual for me to awaken and find Volodya still not come to bed; toward the weekends, business ofttimes demands his all-night attention. But generally, he soon enough wanders in, toward noontime at the latest, and attempts to snatch some sleep. "Lord Jesus Christ!" I yell up at Yevgeny. "You mean on top of everything else, Volodya has not been home since yesterday morn? And nobody *knew* it?"

Before he can answer, Lyubov's screams duly interrupt us again.

"Fer God's sake, Sasha!" Lyubov bellows as we rush back in. "Will ye jest *find* the midwife?"

In a fluster, I attempt to explain to her—but more screams promptly drown me out, followed by fierce shouts: "Sasha, if ye can't find the midwife, go an' git somebody else te help me then, fer the love o' God! *Ahhhhhh! . . ."*

"All right, look," I go on when she at last quiets once again. "I do happen to know someone who—who might be able to come and help. A doctor—"

"Well! Doctor, nurse, midwife—I'm tellin' ye, *I don't care!"* she yells back. "Unless ye're the one wants te drag this babe hollerin' into the world, ye'd better go an' find somebody! . . ."

"Ivanovich!" I bark out, whirling upon Yevgeny. "Don't just simply stand there gawking—get down into the kitchen and start boiling up water! Then bring all the clean towels you can find up here, and help make the bed ready. Zhenya," I go on more gently, catching her eye, "have you ever seen a babe born before?"

Solemnly, she nods. "Once, Step-papa."

"Well, that makes two of us. Stay here with your mother and try to help however you can. Hopefully, I will return soon enough with someone quite apt in bringing babes into the world."

Outside, I work my wedding band from my finger with some effort and slip it into my pocket; then, soundly cursing each and every one of the stops, I manage to catch a lift on one of the day's last streetcars, traversing up the harried length of Sadovaya yet again. At last, still straining against the cramp burdening my leg, I drop off to hobble up Nevsky and over its Anichkov Bridge toward the Prospekt's southeast corner with the Fontanka graced by the garish, baroque-inspired facades of the palace belonging to the Grand Duke Dmitri. Inside, the wards and halls of the Anglo-Russian Hospital, situated within, teem overflowing with sunken faces, hollow eyes, bandaged heads, and shriveled bodies caked in blood and pus. Cane thumping into the floorboards, I stare downward as the silent trail of eyes follows, although I nod to the shy nun-like nurses, who—apparently on account of the limp—all appear take me for one of the war's wounded own. Finally, on the second floor, after asking for directions for the third time, I round a corner and spy the pasted-on number to his office just ahead. But before I can venture any farther, the door to it pulls wide open and shuts behind again—and I come face to face with none other than my cousin, Anna.

With a sharp gasp, she jumps back, paling near to the shade of her stained white laboratory coat, her eyes focusing in upon me with a hateful, singeing glare.

Flushing, I doff my cap and stare to my feet, my tongue caught in my throat. Little by little has Father imparted the reaction of various family members to my fugitive status from the law. Aunt Sophie, of course, always sends love tinged with sadness. But to certain of the sisters, I seem to have become a perennial black-sheep, the wayward prodigal son who can do naught in life but bring his father endless trouble and grief.

Particularly Anna—now with her hair caught tightly at the nape of her neck to make her appear so severe that I scarce recognize her as the same beauty in blue fox who once dazzled Novgorod station, nor the laughing, playful girl sparring kisses that heady night nine years ago just before another ice-breaking, when we all sped in troikas down the icy Neva. "Is he here?" I ask after moment, at last fully meeting her gaze.

"Just what do *you* want?" she hisses back with loathing, her teeth bared, both eyes narrowed into frosty blue slits.

"Anna," I whisper with urgency. *"Please."*

"Oh—oh, all right!" As if I might try to snatch it from her, she grasps her clipboard up closer to her bosom and taps her fingers back upon the door, calling: "Doctor Sekovsky?"

From within, a mumbled: "Yes, Doctor Zhelanova?"

Hesitantly, Anna eases open the door. "Pardon me, once again, for delaying you, Uncle Misha," she says in a lowered tone. "But this—

this *person* out here—apparently wishes a word with you." Lancing me with another furious glare, she then turns abruptly on her heel and storms back off toward the direction of the wards, muttering: "Stinking revolutionary scum . . . ."

Through the crack in the doorway, Father emerges with his heavy ermine coat half pulled on. Eyes meeting mine with surprise, he glances off toward Anna's disappearing form; stares back at me. "I take it this is urgent," he murmurs, nodding. "Considering the risk."

"Indeed. Can you come? I know that there are many wounded."

"Well, I meant to step out to take some supper. My shift's long done for the day. You have an emergency?"

"A friend. The, uh—the woman from whom I rent a room. The birthing pains—we cannot find the midwife. . . ."

To my overwhelming relief, Father borrows the motorcar of a fellow doctor, and within moments, we speed past the haze of pinkish-yellow buildings dotted up and down the long length of Sadovaya. "Well, Sashenka," he says, head thrown back, his hair flying out gaily as it catches the frosty stream of dusk-chilled air blasting through the window vent, "I suppose, by now, it is perhaps not so foolhardy as it once would have been for you and I to tag along together in public. It appears the police have more than enough on their hands with containing this latest rash of ironworkers' strikes. As I told you some time ago, no officers ever question at the townhouse anymore—and in any case, I believe you are no longer the sole suspect. Apparently, this wayward merchant Pavlovsky had many enemies."

Before he can pursue further remarks about 'Pavlovsky,' I interrupt in a somber murmur: "Did you hear what Anna said to me as she left?"

Sighing, he replies: "Yes. Anna seems to have formed her own opinion as to the motive behind your shortcomings, my dear boy."

"And you let her go on thinking such?"

"Well, what else am I supposed to do?" he answers, shrugging. "Tell her the truth?"

At the apartment, we hurry upstairs to find Lyubov straining under the bedclothes and screaming to high heaven, Zhenya hovering over her, peaked and frantic, and Yevgeny looking ready to faint. "This is Doctor, uh, Mikhailov, from the hospital," I tell them all quickly, avoiding Father's questioning glance. When I introduce Lyubov under her maiden name, he assumes Yevgeny to be her husband—and in the rank excitement of the moment, neither of them seems to note my attempt at subterfuge. Only when Zhenya calls me 'Step-papa' do I find myself in a quandary for explanation, murmuring to Father as I pat the girl on the shoulder: "Oh, the little sweetheart always calls her mother's boarders that."

Fortunately, scant time remains for anyone's attention to dwell upon the particulars. "Well, little lady," Father says, winking and grinning at Zhenya with his old affable charm, "I think you should stay right here by your mother's bedside and assist me with my bag should I happen to need a hand." To Lyubov, he goes on in a soothing tone: "Now, now, my dear—calm yourself. Simply lie still, breathe in and out deeply, and try to remain calm. Yes, I know how very difficult it is when the pains twist up like veritable devil's knots inside you, but I assure you, I've been bringing babes into this world off and on for—heavens, near unto sixty years! Why, before this hateful war, the Good Lord's blessed events ofttimes accounted for my sole practice of medicine—save for an occasional accident, or if one of the peasants on my farm happened to take sick, you know. I promise you are in the best of hands, my dear. However, it appears, indeed, that I have arrived just in the nick of time. Yes, my dear—let's move your legs up a bit more like this. . . ."

I help bring upstairs the pans of boiling water, and upon Father's frowning signal, usher the deathly pale Yevgeny down into the kitchen, set him at the table in front of the samovar, and force down some strong, hot tea.

"God in Heaven's Bowels!" he mutters out, squeezing fast hold of my arm. "Never in my life thought I'd be glad te see the likes o' ye, ye blessed little bastard! By the devil—thought sure enough ye weren't comin' back at all, that I'd have te bring the babe out myself!"

Ears pricked to the rising chorus of screams from the upstairs, I mumble scant reply and nervously slosh down my own glass of tea. Then the front door bangs open, and spewing curses, Volodya wearily stumbles in.

Both eyes blackened, his nose bloodied, he shoves past the two of us and ducks his head full under the kitchen tap, splashes of cold water soaking into his shirt collar and his hair. "And what the devil happened to you?" I cry in amazement, bounding upward from my chair.

"Oh, shut up!" he snarls back. "And don't neither of you say a bloody word, Jesus! Don't ever get caught in fuckin' Vyborg playin' cards with your pants down. Yes, of course I mean without enough cash!

Shit! And what is all the damn screamin' about—is that Lyubov Ivanovna? She droppin' the brat, finally? And what the hell'd you do with all the blasted towels?"

"Listen," I insist in a whisper, seizing hold of his arm. "Don't say anything! About 'Doctor Mikhailov—'"

"Doctor Who? Jesus, Sasha—just what are you blabberin' so about?" When I glare at him, finger pressed to my lips as I nod toward Yevgeny, he blurts out: "All right, well, fine—so just bring me a damn towel, already!"

As I fetch him one from the laundry bin, the screams from upstairs shatter down in an escalating torrent, and Yevgeny's face goes stark blank, his eyes rolling up into his head as he passes out.

"Oh, for God's sake!" I groan. Shaking my head, I commence a search through the kitchen drawers for the smelling salts as Volodya, dabbing the moistened towel at scabs beneath his nose, peers down at Yevgeny with a sarcastic grin.

"Stop enjoying it so much!" I tell him, shoving the salt bottle into his hand. "Here, see if you can get him to come to. I should go call up the stairs and see if Father needs any help."

"Father?" he cries.

"I mean—shit! I meant: 'Doctor Mikhailov.'"

"My God, Sasha! You brought *your father* here?"

"Well! We could not find the midwife! Just what else was I supposed to do?"

"Oh, Jesus!"

"And," I go on, pointing at Yevgeny, *"don't* let them know."

"Well, of course not!"

"And act like the babe's Yevgeny's, will you?" I go on. "I don't want Papa to know, either—" Abruptly, my words dwindle into obscurity beneath a renewed avalanche of Lyubov's screams. Wincing, I crease my fingers into my brow—just as a piercing infant's squall wafts down from a sudden breath of stillness and whimpers and quiet.

"Well, sounds like your moment of triumph's finally done come," Volodya mutters out with relief. "Praise God for savin' my ears!"

Ignoring him, I strain against the doorway for any further sound from the upstairs, my emotions juggling between the strangest mixture of elation and fear as I down two more steaming glasses of tea. Still uncertain whether Lyubov would yet welcome my presence once more in her room, I begin to pace the floor, attempting to allow them time for awaiting the afterbirth; time for the cleaning up. Finally, Volodya, crouched down upon the floor beside Yevgeny with the bottle of smelling salts, grumbles out: "Well, for Christ's sake, Sekovsky! Stop torturin' yourself, man, and go up there."

Back upstairs, Lyubov, appearing wan but relieved, cradles a small bundle within her arms, while Zhenya leans over the bedside doting over the two of them with excited affectionate murmurs. In a basin dish, Father rinses his hands; smiles up at me. "Well!" he cries. "And just where is the proud—"

"I am afraid Yevgeny Ivanovich passed out cold on the kitchen floor," I tell them all hurriedly.

"Step-papa!" Zhenya urges, pointing toward the bundle. "Look!"

Lyubov pulls the coverlet back to reveal a wrinkled, ruddy little face and totally bald, dark little head. Two murky blue eyes stare up at me, a row of tiny fingers curled about its mother's index finger.

Speechless, I feel the cold wash tingle down my spine; swallow back a lump. Gingerly, I press my hand onto Lyubov's shoulder, asking: "Are you all right?"

"Now," she murmurs back. "Now."

Father begins packing his things back into his bag. "And have you decided upon his name, my dear?" he inquires idly of Lyubov as my heart leaps into my throat again: his. *His! M-My God! I—I have a son. . . .*

"Ivan, o' course," she replies, her eyes swiftly catching mine. "After my father."

Fingers toying with the wedding band in my pocket, I stare to the floor. Perhaps I have been presumptuous. Never had I doubted we would name a son after my father: this giant among giants in proud stature now standing before us and calmly fumbling with the buttons of his overcoat—while not even fathoming that he has already held, in his very own arms, his very own grandson.

But—he *cannot* know. *Dear God!* How would I ever tell him?

"Ivan," I murmur softly in reply to Lyubov. "Of course."

Just then, I find Father staring between myself and the babe with the strangest expression on his face—and in haste, I reach to pull the coverlet back up close about the child's head, murmuring: "Congratulations, Lyubov Ivanovna! If you would excuse me, I think I had best now assist the good doctor back out to his motorcar."

Downstairs, Volodya appears to have made himself scarce, and Yevgeny huddles over the sink, dousing his head beneath the tap. To Father's tidings of congratulation, he mumbles confused reply and waves us off. "Not overly tickled about the child, I daresay," Father remarks with a cocked eyebrow as we step out the front door.

Out on the street, I thank him profusely for coming to our aid—and then we lean together up against the side of the motorcar to take a smoke, gradually shifting our conversation, as we always do when together, back into English. "Oh, granted, it's a decent enough apartment, Sasha. But must you room with such peasants?" he demands, his brow furrowed, his nose wrinkled with distaste.

"It provides anonymity," I tell him with a shrug. "And it's cheap."

"I see."

"Oh, Papa—must you always fret so about the places where I live, the things I do?"

"Well! Truly, I had always wanted far better for you in life, Sasha."

Sighing, I stare off at the long, icy vein of the Fontanka Canal boasting numerous spans of quaint wrought-iron-railed bridges, although rows of run-down, flat-roofed tenement apartments mar grand horizon's beauty just beyond. *No, I was right. He would denounce me utterly, decry me forever for marrying into a peasant family . . . for a certainty, he cannot know about the child, nor about Lyubov and me. . . .*

"And why the devil did you call me 'Dr. Mikhailov' back in there?" he then demands.

"I think it wise," I tell him, "to continue some precaution against the police. Yevgeny Ivanovich once overheard my true name, and I thought it best not to chance any reminders."

"Oh, yes. Of course."

Together, we continue to smoke while surveying bundled throngs of passers-by, everyone heading in a northerly direction, mostly toward St. Isaak's Cathedral for the start of Branch Eve procession. "Not near so many as there used to be," Father observes with a sad sigh, smoke rings from his pipe drifting out in lacy whiffs through the frosty air. "But we shan't let it ruin any of our fun, shall we, my boy?" From his pocket, he snatches out a small pussy-willow branch, and—grinning—begins flailing it into my arm, while bellowing out: "I beat thee not—the rod beats!"

Laughing, I attempt to seize it away from him—with no luck. "Humph!" he goes on, affecting an affronted glare. "And how many times, come Palm Sunday morn, was I awakened by a little redheaded terror with sharp willow branch in ready hand, jumping all over my bed."

"Papa, I permit you your recompense," I declare, bowing toward him with a grin. "Smite me please! Until the branch turns bloody—not thee, but the rod beats!"

In response, he jabs me a quick one in the ribs with his elbow and lets out a hearty roar, ruefully shaking his head.

Naught, however, can sever the impenetrable seriousness of mutual concerns yet binding us together past such holiday frivolity. "Any word from Paris?" I venture, daring—against hope of all hopes—to fuel my hopes up somehow yet again.

"Only the same, I am afraid," he murmurs, once more sighing. "Sofya writes that she will stay there searching for him—or for some final, definitive word of his fate—even if it takes the rest of her life. However, I am afraid my last letter's old by now, over a month and a half. You know how it's been with the mail. Who knows? Perhaps with the next one, we shall receive better news."

As he tucks his pipe away at last, I stifle an inward moan, wishing so that circumstances were different. How I would exult in chasing with him through the Parisian countryside again, in sharing dinner with him at the *Viel* as we did so often those many years ago. The days at home in Novgorod, the nights in Paris and London during the ballets, now loiter only terribly far in the distance of soft, blurred memory, intangible keepsakes locked within each of our hearts, cherished and precious as gold. But his hurry now—despite his earlier comments—is obvious, his concern mounting as, for the third time, he questions the wisdom of our standing together in such obvious companionship out on the street. "Tomorrow, at the dress shop, we shall have our full hour to talk, Sashenka," he says, patting my arm and pulling open the latch to the motorcar door. "I assume the usual time?"

"Of course, the usual time. And, Papa?"

"Yes, my boy?" Settling in upon the seat behind the wheel, he smiles up at me, his expression softening with the old bemused, tender fondness.

"Next week," I go on haltingly, "at Eastertide, when we attend Liturgy at St. Isaak's, can we meet again just as last year? You know, you stood a bit past the farthest southeast entrance, between the two most rightward malachite columns of the iconostasis wall, watching until I arrived—"

"Oh, yes. By the malachite columns, watch I did, indeed—"

"—so that we knew each where the other was during the whole of the Liturgy. So that, as the flame was passed, I was able to edge through the crowd—and as it came up toward you, I just happened to be the person standing beside, with my unlit candle."

Father breaks again into his widened, wrinkly grin; reaches upward and presses firm hold of my hand. "Yes, I will wait within the wing of the southeast entrance, near the malachite columns—all night if need be, my boy. And upon once spying you, I will merge behind into the crowd and follow after . . . yes, my flame will always be lit to the wick of your Easter candle, my Sashenka. Yes, I promise—I will be there. . . ."

* * *

"Vanya," I whisper, bouncing the tiny gurgling bundle up from my knees. "Say 'Papa,' Vanya! Go ahead, I know you can do it: 'Pah-pah . . . .'"

At three months, the poor babe can scarce be expected to say 'Papa'—but I simply cannot resist any and all encouragement. Letting out a shriek, he squints his wrinkly, stark-blue eyes and grins down at me, a wizened little toothless wonder. "Say 'Papa!'" I go on, hugging him close. "Oh, I love you so much, Vanya! And I know someday, soon enough, you will say 'Papa' for me—and then perhaps come running out across the kitchen floor! Yes, you'll say 'Papa,' all right, Ivan Aleksandrovich. . . ." Slowly and selfishly, I utter the words, relishing the sound of my name within his name. Then I sneak a glimpse back over my shoulder; Lyubov's and Zhenya's voices still echo in low conversational murmurs from the kitchen, far enough off. "Sekovsky!" I go on to the babe in an emphatic whisper. "Remember it well: Sekovsky, not Khulinov, is your true name! And a proud and ancient one at that, Vanya; derives from the word for beehive, you know. I will tell you about my adventures, and why we must hide away our truth from everyone in, say—well—perhaps fifteen years from now, my boy. Let's see, that would be in—oh, Lord help me! In 1931 . . . ."

Through the kitchen door, Zhenya then hurries in, and I greet her with a warm smile. Of late, I seem to have gained not only a son, but a daughter as well. Intelligent and precocious, the girl has hounded me to no end since learning, in the wake of Vanya's birth, about my mother, the 'English governess.' Nodding, she smiles and holds out both arms, saying: "Mama wants him back now, Step-papa."

Again I squeeze the child to me close, and let out a harsh sigh. At first, I thought my imagination running rampant with pettiness—but in these past few weeks, Lyubov's jealousy over my time spent with my son has grown obvious. "Tell your mother I shall bring the babe in to her presently," I say to Zhenya. Closing my eyes, I nuzzle my nose against Vanya's ear as the little arms swipe out, latching firm around my neck, his fingers tugging at my collar.

"Now, Zhenya!" Lyubov shouts from the kitchen.

"Step-papa!" Zhenya pleads.

"Go, Zhenya—and tell her I shall bring him in to her myself. In a moment."

"But—she says it's his feedin' time, Step-papa—"

My sparring with Zhenya dissipates soon enough as the door slams open, and Lyubov storms in like an avenging angel. "Zhenya Grigoryevna!" she yells, eyes livid and her face bristling, stray blonde hairs sticking out untidily from beneath her kerchief. "Blast it, girl—I got work te do! When I tell ye te bring that child back in, ye do it right then—understand?" Looming in upon the three of us, Lyubov roughly swipes Vanya out from my grasp—and then hauls off and slaps Zhenya across the face.

"Lyuba!" I shout, reeling up from the chair. "That was uncalled for!"

"Ye stay out o' this, Sasha Mikhailovich, do ye hear? This is 'tween my daughter and me, and not *ye—"*

"You scarce had to slap her, for God's sake!"

"I'm tellin' ye, stay out o' it! Lord Almighty, as if I would have ye—or any man—tellin' me how te raise my children! Who do ye think ye are, keepin' him from me?"

"In case the fact has slipped your mind, Comrade Khulinova," I retort sarcastically, "I happen to be the child's father!"

"Well, la-dee-da! An' it happens te be yer child's feedin' time, ye dolt! I s'pose, as the child's father, ye expect ye kin manage that?"

Biting back curses, I glare after her as, triumphantly, she stomps off with Vanya back through the kitchen door.

Zhenya, having stood between us the entire time biting a pouting lip, abruptly bursts into sobs.

"Oh, Lord!" I gasp, flushing near purple with guilt. "Honey, I'm sorry." Mindful of the mass of dark curly ringlets and ribbons cascading down her back, I ease an arm about the girl's shoulders and pull her to me close, begging: "Sweetheart, please, don't weep! I tell you, was all my fault—I promise, next time I'll hand your brother over the instant you ask. Here, Zhenya—yes, my handkerchief is clean, feel free to use it. Oh, honey, don't weep so! Here . . . ."

Together, we ease down onto the sofa, and I hold my arm fast around her as she whimpers softly against my shoulder. Only after several moments does she at last quiet, but then she seems so content resting beside me that I make no move to shift away, save for reaching for the book I had been reading an hour past before Lyubov brought in Vanya. The moment I open it back up, Zhenya cranes her head and begins examining the title on the cover. "Step-papa!" she exclaims, pointing at the print. "What is this?"

"This?" With a shrug, I tell her: "Well, it is called the *Bhagavadgita*. Meaning: *Song of the Blessed Lord.* It is from the *Mahabharata*, a collection of poetic writings espousing Hindu philosophy. From ancient India." When she merely continues peering with a studied frown at the title on the old cloth cover, I go on: "You see, the story is an old one: the disciple Arjuna must reconcile his earthly duty with spiritual calling—"

"No, Step-papa," Zhenya interrupts, pointing. "I mean, are these English letters?"

My response in the affirmative provokes such an outburst of shrieking delight that I stab my hand out in pointed warning toward the kitchen, fearing another confrontation with Lyubov. "Oh, the Saints help me!" Zhenya gushes on, unheedful of my protest. "It is so impressive, Step-papa, that you speak English! Ever since I can remember, I've wanted to learn it—for all my life, I've had such dreams about England!" Barely able to contain herself, she continues scooting excitedly about upon the sofa cushions, begging: "Step-papa, say something! Say something for me in English!"

Wholly taken aback at such adulation, I ponder long before replying: "Well, how about: '*It is a far, far better thing I that do, than I have ever done; it is a far, far better rest that I go to than I have ever known. . . .*'"

Then for five full minutes, I quote Dickens, Keats, Hardy, Shakespeare, Milton—and practically everyone else I can think of who has ever written in the language—until Zhenya drops down to her knees before me on the floor, for the third time this week begging me to teach her to speak English.

"Zhenya, really! I—I've never taught anyone how to speak a language! I'd scarce even know where to start."

"Oh, but, Step-papa—they'll not start us on any languages in school until next year. I cannot wait until then—that's forever! And you are so smart—Mama, Uncle Ivanovich, everyone says so—you must know so much more than those old-biddy teachers, and I'm certain I could learn it ten times faster from you. Oh, please, Step-papa—it would be so impressive, to learn to speak English! Perhaps then I could understand my dreams—about mad highwaymen! And those dark, windy moors . . . ."

Chuckling, I tell her: "Well, my dear—sounds more to me as if you're simply a bit too enamored with the books of the Bronte sisters."

"Humph!" bellows Volodya, swaggering into the parlor, his cap still pulled low to his brow and a rumpled sheet of paper clutched between his fingers. "And it sounds to me as if another poor soul we know has been writin' a bit too much poetry! English, eh?" Frowning in perusal, he holds the paper out in both hands, inspecting it at arms length.

"Rykazian!" I retort. "Is that mine? If it is, you'd best return it immediately."

"You want some English, dearie?" he says to Zhenya. "Here—is all your uppity 'Step-papa' ever writes his lofty verses in—"

"Volodya!" Swiping outward, I snatch the paper from his hands as he leers down at me, grinning with amusement. Indeed, the page does turn out to be one of my poems. "Where did you find this?" I demand hotly, glaring up at him.

"'Neath the bed—"

"Oh, Step-papa!" Zhenya pleads, "may I see?"

At first, I snatch the paper back possessively—but as Zhenya can hardly as yet distinguish the meaning, at last I allow her a look at it. "Rykazian, you knucklehead!" I snap up at Volodya. "You simply leave my papers alone from now on!"

"Humph! You write it all in English 'cause you're just plain chicken, that's what you are."

"Chicken!" I cry. "Why, you—"

"Well, sure!" he quips back, laughing. "That way, you wiggle out of it so easy every time I rib you about tryin' your luck durin' 'Stand-Up Night' over at the Wanderin' Dog. Why, I bet that poem could get read at the Wanderin' Dog and even get a decent hand—"

"You don't even know what it says! So shut up, will you?"

"No—this time I will not shut up! I think I take your poem writin' even more seriously than you do. So why don't you translate this into somethin' I can read, already, you nitwit! In fact—you should do that with all those poems you got stacked up in the bureau drawer. I bet you got enough now to publish a whole crappin' book."

"Volodya!" Shooting him a pained glare, I nod toward Zhenya's bent head, admonishing sharply: "Will you kindly remember your language in here?"

"All right, all right! But don't you try changin' the subject on me, Sasha Khulinov, you cunnin' little rascal. I say you should write this poem out in lofty Russian words."

"And will you, for once, mind your *own* business?"

"Well, by God, this *is* my business!"

"Translation scarce proves easy, you know, Rykazian! I'd lose meter, nuances, all the rhyme—"

"Oh? Not to gain any back?"

To this, I have no ready answer, and sit gawking at him mutely as Zhenya slips the paper back into my hands.

"Oh, come, Sasha!" Volodya badgers on, again pointing down at the poem. "Be doubly creative! Frankly, I scarce think it so difficult—I can translate a decent bit of French myself, you know. You're just making up excuses—"

"Shut up, Rykazian! *Will* you?"

"—well, for Christ's sake!" he bellows on. "The poem is only all of ten lines!"

In response, I fold the paper up in a tiny wad, shove it into my pocket, and storm angrily away from the sofa, while Volodya bellows after: "Chicken! That's what you are if you'll not at least try your hand at somethin' you could read over at the Wanderin' Dog. . . ."

All the rest of the day, I fume at him; all the rest of the night, I cannot sleep, my mind jostling between English, Russian words. All the next day at the dress shop, I can hardly do my work, cannot shut reams of possibilities from my mind. It is not until far late into the following eve, long after my hour spent with Vanya, and then with Zhenya for her first English lesson, that I finally steal away some scarce precious time alone, for once blessing Volodya's penchant for gambling, and therefore his absence. And I stare at my words:

Passions hidden,
Love forbidden . . . .

When I was growing up, my father never failed to impress upon me his disdain for spoken Russian as the coarse tongue of our country's illiterate peasant culture, my conversations with him—then, as now—transpiring almost exclusively in English. At May's boarding school in

Petersburg, French was most often the toil of choice, although of course, English conversation and writing were taught, along with the fundamentals of Russian prose. But unlike my cousin Nikolai—who near always wrote his many letters to me in rambling French laments spiced with Russian proverbs and obscenities—to English, I have always returned for my private written work, favoring perhaps some continued tangible link with my British heritage beyond long-lost memories of youthful summers spent in sunny Cornwall far off upon the high seas. Hence, the rendition of the bulk of my poetry in English.

And conveniently, the continued propounder of excuses against reading during 'Stand-Up Night' at the Wandering Dog.

Sighing to the inevitable, I ponder over my verse again—which, translated strictly to the Russian, will lose its rhyme. But the meter remains intact enough with a thoughtful choice of adjectives, and I scribble out hurriedly:

Strasti tainiye,
Lyubov zapretnaya . . . .

And the title, *To See in a Dream,* even translates into a common Russian expression:

Vidyet vo Snye . . . .

* * *

"To See in a Dream," I say in Russian, at last braving a glance at the many heads in the crowd over the rims of my spectacles.

And my heart freezes. Typical of a Saturday night, the Wandering Dog Tavern stands filled wall to wall with loud people, sharp laughter, thick layers of smoke, and the clinking of glasses. Scarce a third of the onlookers even feign so much as a glance toward the podium, nor make any attempt to listen. Nervously, I once again forswear the July heat and poke a finger into the collar of my cotton tunic, buttoned too high and too tight. Upon my upper lip, prickly beads of sweat begin to fringe; beneath both armpits, I feel soaked in ashen buckets of fear. *Jesus God, Rykazian!* I moan inwardly, glaring over at him. *How the hell did I ever let you talk me into this?* What was I, drunk? *Crazy?* One matter it is to play lone piccolo—the woodwinds, the strings, the brass section of the orchestra still grouped in comforting fraternal reassurance all around. But *this*—standing all alone before a literal sea of faces, sole master of the podium—*Lord God Almighty!*—this is *really* solo wind! *Oh, my God! . . .*

As I stand staring, the impatience of the crowd ripens. Feet begin to tap, and throats are cleared, the balloon of expectancy rising in the air, poised for ready striking. Behind his table, Volodya sits perched at the farthest rim of his chair, his face frantic, his waves sharply signaling me to proceed. Biting my lip, I stare between him, the crowd, the bar, the piano. *Goddamn it, Sekovsky—simply read off the lines! What other course is there, you insipid, gullible fool? To duck off like a whimpering child, after merely reciting the title?*

"Come lad, let's git out with it!" someone then calls from the crowd.

"Yaa! 'Stand-up Night'—there's others want to read!"

More shouts follow upon a flood of hoots and whistles. Squaring my shoulders, I throw back my head, peering disdainfully at them all, and clear my throat, again reciting loudly: *"To See in a Dream . . .* a poem by Aleksandr Khulinov . . . *Passions hidden . . . ."*

At last they quiet down. Presumptuously, I start it all over, mindful of Volodya's admonitions for slow, deliberate enunciation of each and every word:

"To See in a Dream:

"Passions hidden,
"Love forbidden.
"Pauses,
"Whispers.
"Haunted shameful glance,
"Stolen trembling kiss,
"Darkened winter night,
"Resonant sleigh-bells softly
"Pierce the star-lit snow."

I hedge a glance upward into a gulf of silence. Then a flurry of nods follows upon slow smiles and grunts of agreement; florid whistles spew forth, all beckoning with approval. And about half the crowd bursts into a round of applause.

Stunned, I mumble out faint words of thanks; ease my way down from the podium as the next reader mounts to take my place. Volodya's fingers pinch like claws into my elbow, and I hear him jabbering on into my ear without pause, piling up the praise. But it is to the back, across the darkened shadows, that my gaze drifts, searching—and when I finally spy the outline of his whitened head, I break into a joyful grin—and nod across the throng of people and the noise; sense him nodding back. Surely tomorrow—somehow, somewhere—he will find some poor soul whom he can corner for at least an hour or more, to laud on endlessly about: 'my son, the poet . . . .'

Even if, most probably, it is only Vliny or Marnya. Even if, during these lonely days when I must shoulder a loathsome alias, and tread like a forgotten shadow upon the proud name that was once mine, it is only in his own dreams.

* * *

Autumn of 1916 brings renewed problems for the dress shop, for the workers, for the revolutionaries, the nobility, everyone. Basic everyday staples start to go on ration; for three days straight, Zhenya and I comb through bare shops on Nevsky and Sadovaya, searching for sugar, and for charcoal for the samovar. Come October, strikes break out in the rife, surly pockets of Vyborg, scores of workers swiftly inducted into Army garrisons as punishment. Then on November second, handbills appear on near every street corner, one or two rubles each for a copy of Pavel Milyukov's fiery speech given at the convening of the Duma the previous day: *'Chto eto, glupost ili izmena?'*—*'What is this, stupidity or treason?'* ringing out in defiant, stunning refrain in charge after open charge against the Tsarina, against Rasputin, against the blundering hypocrisy of the government.

"Perhaps," Volodya observes with a cocked eyebrow when I show him the fresh typewritten copy, "our revolution will come into its own sooner than I'd supposed. Bold accusations, in any case . . . ."

Bold accusations, somber warnings—and soon, even open shouts in the streets without fear any longer of reprisal from the Tsarist police—mount daily as Christmastide's ironic boughs of old tradition begin to beckon in. Rumors fly everywhere that on December sixth, the Tsar's name day, a true constitutional government with direct vested power will be granted at last. But nothing happens. Then the Grand Dukes Nikolai Nikolayevich, the Tsar's uncle, and Mikhail Aleksandrovich, his brother, are heard to be plotting to usurp the throne. Then Mikhail Rodzyanko, President of the Duma, surfaces as the latest contender. But still, nothing happens—until December seventeenth, when literal hell breaks loose throughout the city as news flies like wildfire across Petrograd's gray-wrought, dusky skies that a group of noblemen have killed Rasputin.

"A bunch o' hated *dvoryanye*, no less!" Lyubov wails on, "gunnin' down our savior, our soul, the worthy peasant *starets*, the only simple *muzhik* ever able te bend the Tsar's simperin' ear—"

"Oh, for God's sake, Lyubov!" I shout in bristling reply. "Your *muzhik* was naught but a drunken lout! One time when I was with Volodya at the Villa Rode, that Rasputin climbed right up on the stage and started fondling the Gypsy dancers—"

"Lies—only lies!" she shouts back.

"Not to mention that your beloved peasant *starets* has almost single-handedly undermined the Tsar's government! Small wonder we are losing the war."

"Humph! An' as if ye don't sound like one o' them snipin', higher-than-thou *dvoryanye* yerself! It's the Tsarina—and that money grubbin', self-servin' group o' noblemen she always keeps gathered 'round, not the blessed holy man Rasputin—who've been runnin' this country into the ground like a barnyard o' fools! Ye mark my words—the peasants, the workin' people'll square off soon enough with the *dvoryanye,* bring 'em all te their just deserts."

"Oh, must we argue about Rasputin like this to no end?" I cry in exasperation. "And for God sake," I go on, pointing to the rows of burning icon lamps, the profusion of carefully angled hand mirrors she has scattered out, in vigil for Rasputin, all over the parlor floor. "I thought you *Bolsheviki* held no store in these arcane peasant rituals! Nor, for that matter, in any god."

"Blast it, Sasha Mikhailovich! Will ye jest leave me alone?" Tears coursing down her face, Lyubov shoves me from the room and angrily slams shut the door.

Incensed, I storm into the kitchen, yelling down at Volodya: "You want some advice? God! Don't ever try to understand women. . . ." Through cupboard after cupboard I then ransack vehemently before whirling back upon him and shouting out in frustration: "Dammit! And are we out of bread again?"

Solemnly, Volodya snuffs out his cigarette and stares up at me from the table. "Everywhere they are runnin' out of bread," he murmurs, nodding toward the window.

"What do you mean, *everywhere?*"

"Every shop I passed on the way home had only two or three loaves stuck back on its bakery shelves."

"Well, surely they'll receive more by the morrow."

"You'd better hope."

More bread does appear upon the morrow—and by Christmas Eve; New Year's Day. Supplies dwindle to meager scarcity again in the weeks soon following—and every morn, on my way to work, I watch felt boots trudging through the ice and slush, the women's faces grimaced in the frosty, bitten cold. In lines formed in ever-increasing queues throughout the city's bakeshops, the grumblings each day begin to turn more bitter. At newsstand corners, hack poets start to gather, preaching anarchy in the face of doubt; on the street-cars, I prick up my ears: every second whisper is of revolution. Jostled in between shoulders, I stare to my fingers grasped about the pole in their sparse weave of tattered gloves, while nervously avoiding meeting glances, and any attempt to be drawn into casual conversation. And as the threat of menace grows steadily each and every eve, told through expressions on countless angry faces—as the fists clench down beside me each next morn, low and hidden into quarries of new resolve—I begin, in earnest, to worry.

January ninth, the twelfth anniversary of Bloody Sunday, brings scattered demonstrations. Yevgeny and Volodya spend the entire day in Vyborg, passing out Bolshevik leaflets. Both return in sour moods, complaining of some print shop having been raided by the police. "You have gone over to them," I accuse Volodya coldly. "You have gone over to the *Bolsheviki,* Rykazian. Yes?"

Shrugging, he averts his gaze, and mutters out: "You ought to read *Chto Delat?*, Sasha. It may enlighten some of your opinions." Then he tosses Vladimir Lenin's theoretical treatise, the infamous *What Is To Be Done?,* down on the kitchen table.

Over the next two days, I scan through Lenin's book and start to worry more, *much* more—upbraiding myself for political ignorance, for not sooner making investigation of the veiled edicts, the blatant suppositions lurking behind the Marxs, the Lenins, the Chernovs, and Martovs of the *Bolsheviki,* the *Mensheviki,* the Socialist Revolutionaries. "'Critical freedom approbating falsehood?'" I demand of Volodya, waving flying *Chto Delat?* pages out in front of his face. "'Prohibition of demeaning socialist ideology, of undermining it even to the most minute degree?' And just where the hell do the hands of your relentless, disciplined 'professional revolutionaries' turn their perfected energies once the cause is, indeed, accomplished? Into another enclave of the Tsarist police, an *Okhrana* differing only by name? My Lord, Volodya—it sounds like naught but the worst nightmares of Tsarist autocracy simply couched in tepid rhetoric!"

"I am not defendin' all of Lenin's ideas, Sasha!" he yells back, reddening. "I simply said to read it, to take into consideration . . . Vladimir Ilyich does pose some solutions, plausible ones, for structure of the new order."

"Have you gone over to the *Bolsheviki,* Volodya?"

"No!" he shouts—but once more he glances furtively away, muttering beneath his breath: "That is, not yet."

That night, as usual, we make love—unbridled passion displayed on his part, taut reserve on mine. I fall asleep fitfully, tossing and turning for hours upon the gnawing precipice of forewarning. At three A.M., I jolt out of bed in a numbed sweat, and stumble into the downstairs water closet. There, in the cabinet mirror, the glass barely reflects back my image; all I can see, in a vast parody of reprisal without compassion and with never any end, is the fury of the peasants, the storming of the Bastille, the rounding up of the gentry—the narrow roadways of eighteenth century Paris littered with blank faces and doomed souls, women and even young children crowded like common cattle fodder along with their men into rattly, open carts. The guillotine smashes down, countless bloodied heads dropping into buckets, one after another. . . .

"I want you to *go,"* I tell Father emphatically, my gaze riveted to the dress shop cellar floor.

"Out of the question."

"Father, please! I am begging you—"

"Without you?" Vengefully, he turns upon me, his dark eyes livid, his jaw set with a furious, determined grimace. "You expect me to leave behind," he shouts on in a huff, waving out his fist, "everything I have ever known, all that I have ever worked for and strived after? You expect me to forswear my heritage and what remains of my lands; you expect me to relinquish your birthright in an entirety that would be *final?* You wish me to abandon Holy Mother Russia—earth of my forefathers' earth, bones of my ancestors' bones, hallowed bastion of our family honor and glory for near unto a thousand years? And you expect me to do all of this, and then to depart for Oslo—*without you?"*

"Father!" I implore meekly, seizing hold of his arm, "two years ago, after the murder, you were perfectly willing to go—"

"For your safety, Aleksandr," he roars back, shaking me off, "I would go to the farthest ends of the earth, whether desert hell or arctic cold, I swear! But I am *not* leaving Russia without you!"

Sighing, I collapse back against several fabric bolts by the wall and throw up both hands, pleading: "Dammit, Papa! You stubborn old hog-headed mule! Will you simply listen to me? You know this concern of mine is more than trifling: each day, the bread lines worsen, the protests mount, the threat of chaos only inches closer!"

"And I say you are exaggerating! But if they indeed want to blame the nobility, then let them blame us, by dammit! Blasted, gullible peasants, taking up with every bearded, long-haired firebrand ever catching their ears at a curbstone kiosk! Don't they know that *we* have been the ones—in the military, in the ministries, in the grimy, blood-soaked hospitals, for God's sake!—we, the nobility, the upper classes, have been the strength holding this country together tooth and nail throughout this wretched war—"

"Papa!" I interject, yelling him down, "I tell you, I have been reading Lenin—the man is ruthless, without morality! If the revolutionaries have their way, scores of lives will end in a senseless bloodbath, I simply *know* it!"

"I will be damned to *hell* before leaving for Oslo without you!"

"Papa, you know I have a forged passport, falsified identity papers. My connections—through Rykazian, through others—would surely shield me from any danger. But you, Papa, your safety—with each passing day—is only becoming more doubtful; my God, you are still Count Sekovsky! And when this pent up bottleneck of a revolution, when this furious, raging torrent from the last fifty, one hundred years finally breaks free of the Tsar's weakened hold at last—heads are going to fly, Papa, the nobility's heads! I know it, I can feel it!"

Letting out a harsh sigh, Father leans back beside me against the fabric bolts and wearily creases his fingers into his brow. "Sasha," he says with forced patience, "think you not that you might simply have spent a little too much time of late sitting in the cinema house? Oh, just what is that latest picture called, all about the French Revolution—*Madame du Barry?*"

"Papa, I am not talking about any moving picture! In fact, I've scarce had chance to stop by the cinema house in months."

"Well! I hear no one else sounding such alarm bells of panic! Yes, I remember our long conversation about it all years ago, on the train to the Crimea. Of course there will be revolution. The question is, when? Surely not now, while we're caught in the midst of this hellish war. Even the peasants have more sense than that! And Lord help me, my boy—were the current situation as urgent as you insist, I know my old friend Orlov would duly inform me. The man boasts a number of contacts in the Duma."

When I remind him how dubious one's faith in the Duma should be these days, he mutters out further excuses and turns away from me, glowering and grumbling as he fidgets out a scant pinchful of tobacco for his pipe. After considerable prodding, only begrudgingly has he been willing to admit the ever increasing extent of his and Anna's and Vliny's and Marnya's own discomforts during these past few months, the servants all dismissed now for lack of ability to feed more than a few people with the meager supplies on hand, the large airy rooms of the Zhukovskaya townhouse plagued with bitter, chilling drafts for lack of furnace coal and fireplace wood.

"Papa," I tell him with resolve, "if you will not believe the portents of the bread lines now, then simply wait a few more weeks. I tell you, matters are only certain to become far worse. . . ."

Another few weeks near prove me a seer. The Feast of the Presentation graces Petrograd with memories of carnivals and puppet shows and ice slides and *bliny* cakes layered high with whipped sour cream and waiting to be stuffed in glorious mouthfuls clear up to children's ears—but this year, scarce joy, little frolic, and barely any preparations for the yearly festival greet the prospect of another *Maslenitsa*. By mid-February, hardly a loaf of bread can be had in the shops of Petrograd.

Nor can hardly any flour, nor any meat—the shops lined up and down Nevsky one after another hurriedly tacking up signs into their windows: *Muki Nyet, Myasa Nyet*. But the worst, by far—in bakeshop after bakeshop—is the benediction for bread: *Khleba Nyet, Khleba Nyet* . . . .

Within moments, protests against the absence of life's basic sustenance soar across the city in organized battle cries shouted down across every walkway, through countless courtyards and alleys, from tenement terraces . . . .

Desperate until our Sunday meeting, I feel I can no longer afford to wait, and take the risk of cornering Father in his office at the hospital. There, it is his revelation, not mine, that drives us fast into one another's arms, each of us choked for tears. "Sashenka," he murmurs, "I did everything for her that I could."

"Oh, God," I rasp on, again burying my face into the thick, comforting well of his shoulder. "My old Matushka! Dear Lord—my metaphysics, my philosophizing—it utterly fails me at times like this, Papa. Why is death always so hard?"

"Death is hard because it kicks us a swift one in the bowels, and forces us each to stop, and think, and someday face a death of our own."

Only two months past, on Christmastide eve, under foggy cover of night, I stole into the townhouse for a long-awaited visit with Marnya. Her health had been improving; weeks before, he had felt certain of the fever's demise. She had even gained back a good deal of her weight. . . . "You did not impart how close she was," I say at last, pulling back and searching his face.

"No, I chose not to. Of late, you seem to have been plagued with more than enough troubled thoughts. I saw no reason to burden you further until her actual passing. Truly, there was naught that you—nor I, nor anyone—could do, Sasha. When one's time comes, I am afraid it simply comes. But do know that seeing you at Christmastide heartened dear old Marnya's soul greatly. . . ."

"Please!" I beg moments later, my head once again bowed low before him, both fists clenched in supplication. "Papa, for your safety—for my sanity!—will you please consider, if only temporarily, leaving for Oslo?"

This time, he does not answer, but stares out the window, his brow furrowed in pensive thought. I need not even look to see; on my way to the hospital, group by group, I passed them: more vast lines curled about the bakeshops, the meat stores. "You honestly believe this situation to have become that drastic, Sashenka?" he says at last.

"Papa, you are the last person I need remind of my premonitions."

Lips curling upward in a faint smile, he nods and bemusedly shakes his head. The summer in Novgorod a year after my return from Moscow, our dock caved into the lake. Two weeks earlier, I had warned him; begged him to stay away from it. Defiant of orders from a mere seventeen-year-old, he ignored my pleas entirely, waving off any and all protests after making due inspection of the planks. When the dock finally did collapse, just as I had said, he fell clean off it and into the water, provoking much laughter but sorely bruising his shoulder in the process. Other incidents over the years—most notably the freeing of Melissa's ghost—having proven the validity of my intuition, have forced both of us to consider, with all serious import, the voice within my head through which fate ofttimes speaks, the still, quiet, paramount voice within my voice.

At last, to my relief, he acquiesces. "All right, Sasha. I will consider a short journey to Oslo. But first, I would appreciate if you would answer me one question."

"Anything, Papa!"

"Why do you insist on staying behind?"

When I afford him no response save for a stare to the floor, he turns upon me with his hand outstretched, arguing: "Oh, Lord God, boy—by the Saints! Long ago, you told me you'd settled your differences with Rykazian, that he's no longer been forcing you into so much of his shady business. Would he tip off the police now, were you to try to leave?"

I bite my lip, murmuring: "No, Papa. I scarce think so."

"Then why will you not come with me?"

Turning for his office door, I struggle with indecision only long enough to force back a hard swallow, then grasp hold of the knob and pull the door wide open, lifting back my head to squarely meet his gaze. "All right, Papa. Another concern does, indeed, preclude my leaving. Can you come with me?"

"Now?"

"Yes, now—if you could. Come with me—and I will show you."

* * *

"Father, you remember Lyubov Ivanovna?"

Lyubov stares at me with an astonished gasp; Father, with blank bewilderment. Politely, he reaches for her hand and brushes it with a kiss. "Well, certainly, my dear," he says after a moment, shrugging. "And how is—"

"I'll fetch him," I interrupt, elbowing quickly past Lyubov.

Recognition grips Father's face the moment I bring the child in. Vanya, at ten months, has become an energetic, hefty little blue-eyed toddler, already champion of his first steps lumbered across the kitchen floor into his papa's awaiting arms. And the hair growing out in stray, wispy tufts from the burnished, fuzzy crown of his head is strewn as lanky and red as mine.

"Oh, my God," Father utters out in a whisper.

"Yes," I reply, nodding. "Lyuba is my wife, Papa. And Vanya, my son."

Father's gaze fixes wholly upon the child, his mouth working feverishly without further utterance. At my urging, he retires to the sofa, cautiously enfolding Vanya within his arms. "J-Just like you!" he chokes out after a long moment, the heel of his hand stabbing tears from trembling eyelids as he bounces the child upon his knee. "Lord God in all of Heaven, Sashenka, he looks *just* like you! I can scarce believe it! This is my *grandson?"*

I cannot help but smile. "Yes, Papa."

"Well, have a look at you, young man!" Father bellows on to Vanya. "Why, I remember bouncing your papa like this when he too was naught but a gurgling little soul in bunting clothes! Precious treasure! And I daresay, you look just like my little Sashenka when he was your age!"

"Actually, Papa," I tell him with a chuckle, "of late, I have begun to think the boy much more favors you—"

"Sasha Mikhailovich!"

I turn to meet Lyubov's glare, ablaze with silent fury. With a nod, she indicates the kitchen, and turns on her heel, storming through the door without a backward glance.

"I take it," Father murmurs in a lowered undertone, "that this is not a marriage made in heaven?"

"This," I reply tersely, my gaze not wavering one speck away from the kitchen door, "is a marriage made for the sake of the child. I—I will return in a moment, Papa."

In the kitchen, her accusations pound ready and fierce: "This man," she hisses out under her breath, pointing back toward the direction of the parlor, "kindly ole doctor that he is, I grant ye that—*this* man, who I jest heard ye call 'Father,' who calls my son his grandson—is obviously a landed gentleman, a man o' rank, a—a *dvoryanin!"*

"Yes."

"You liar!" Her hand flails out, plowing across my cheek.

I slam my cane to the floor; jump for her and wrench hold of both her wrists, forcing her—past her furious shriek—back against the wall. "Now, you listen to me!" I rasp into her face. "Yes, I kept the truth from you—just as you hide away your backhanded *Bolsheviki* secrets from me. And we can bang each other black and blue about this all night long if you so choose, the moment after he leaves. But while he is here, I *will* have propriety, I *will* have decorum and manners—and most of all, *respect*—observed in this household! *Do you understand?"*

Gasping, Lyubov pushes away, emitting a string of muffled curses as I release my hold. Chasing across the kitchen floor, she fumbles awkwardly with tying on her apron and begins banging the supper dishes, with clanging thuds, into the basin.

"Why did ye bring him here?" she demands from over her shoulder in another angry hiss, her eyes kept rigid over the soapy, splashing water.

"I am attempting to convince him to leave for Oslo. For his own safety. He refuses to depart without me. I think now, he will understand why I cannot accompany him."

"Ye said yer father was long gone before ye was born, that ye were a—"

"Well, as you can see, I am not."

"Humph! So, ye are this man's legitimate son, then?"

"Yes."

"An'—his heir?"

"Yes."

"Oh! An'—an' I s'pose ye got some grand estate, all o' hundreds o' desyatins strong, somewhere—"

"For your information, Lyubov, our estate lands have been deeded—through my father's generosity, mind you!—back to the peasants who have tilled them all their lives. The only holdings we retain are the house, an old bee apiary."

"Oh, humph! An' pray tell then, which glittery mansions, which corniced palaces do ye own—here? In Moscow?"

"None, Lyubov."

"Humph! An' Khulinov? Mikhailov? Which is yer true name?"

"Neither."

"Oh!" she screams out, her words tripping one upon another in a wrathful torrent as she lashes out toward me from the basin with a soapy ladle in her hand. "Jesus in Christ help me! Ye filthy, cheatin' *liar!* Ye marry me te give yer child a name, an' then—then it's not even yer *own?"*

"No."

"Lord by the Saints! As if ye was one o' our very own comrades in arms, hidin' away from the law!"

"Lyubov, I would appreciate if we could continue this discussion later—"

"Humph! An' yer mother? Why'd ye not invite her into my humble parlor room, too? Or is she too high-landed a lady, dressed in diamonds and pearls, makin' every round o' the court balls?"

"Lyubov, my mother is dead."

"Humph! An' as if, after all yer other lies, I'm even s'posed te try te believe that! Or any o' those stories 'bout that English governess!"

"My mother was English, yes. But no governess."

"Oh, no—o' course not! 'Stead, she was a high-born English lady, yes? What, a baroness? A duchess? Blast you, Sasha—*what?* Lord God Almighty, I can't believe I married into the shameless, two-faced, back stabbin' *nobility!* Into the plague o' all this dear country's wretched ills for all the lives o' my fathers—an' yes, whether ye'll admit it or no, fer all the lives o' yorn as well—Baron, or Count, or Prince Sasha whoever-ye-are! Oh, curse ye straight te the bristlin', fiery guts o' hellfire—*how dare ye lie te me about this!"* A plate then escapes her tremulous grasp, and crashes down onto the tiled floor. Miraculously, it remains intact, circling around between us in an ringing, punctuating echo.

Letting out a long sigh, I retrieve it and return it to the counter, murmuring: "You wish a divorce?"

She shakes her head, choking off words, biting back tears. "I—I don't know, jest *get* out! *Will ye?"*

As I head for the kitchen door, she gasps back heatedly: "Sasha Mikhailovich! Ye value yer skin, ye say not a word 'bout this te Ivanovich! *Do ye hear me?"*

"Lyubov Ivanovna," I reply, not looking backward, "I will do whatever you wish."

Back in the parlor, I can barely meet his eye, and duck away in a flush of shame from the bewildered expression on his face. "My God, Sasha!" he moans out. "Why did you not tell me?"

"Papa, your opinions have always been adamant regarding intermarriage between nobility and the peasants—"

"But Christ's toes, boy!" he exclaims, once again fondly eyeing Vanya. "You could have told me of *this."*

My further explanations only pour out sounding foolish and shallow. Of course, I should have told him. I simply scarce knew how. . . .

"And your wife?" he asks. "Will she not accompany you to Oslo?"

With harrowing reluctance, I meet his gaze. "Lyuba and her family," I tell him, "are committed, both in word and deed, to naught but revolution. She would never leave Russia behind now, I know. Particularly, on my account."

"I see. Might I remind you," he goes on, stealing a glance—with marked distaste—toward the kitchen door, "of the old proverb: that he who plies his trade with wolves soon enough finds their lair his own?"

Wringing my hands, I turn away—and as his fingers catch unto mine, I shake my head emphatically, whispering back: "Papa! No matter what you may think, nor what you may ever hear, you must believe me: I am not a revolutionary! I promise you that on the lives of all our forebears, upon my most solemn, sacred oath, Papa! I may have little choice now but to see whatever happens through to the end; I would hardly steal a suckling child away from his mother. Vanya's future now dictates my responsibility, Papa."

"Sasha, I have absolutely no dispute with that," Father replies, pressing my arm with a firm, reassuring squeeze. "Above all else in life, you must now see to the welfare of your son. No other choice would I condone—you know that."

With Vanya, he lingers until the clock strikes nine, until it strikes ten—while in two hours, I smoke more cigarettes than I have in the entire past month, stubbing out the butts one after another in an old jar lid set upon the fireplace mantle. Relentlessly, I pace back and forth across the floor, my cane thumping steadily to ticks of the hallway clock. At last Lyubov insists, rightly enough, on the child's bedtime, and Father pulls on his coat and tall ermine hat with a weary sigh, his solemn dark eyes fixing once again in silent acknowledgment upon mine. Helplessly, I stare back, praying that I convey—in the pure veracity of gesture, in the naked window of a glance—that which I cannot now seem to impart in words: my love, overflowing and unbounded; my respect, pride, and honor deeply felt to have been born his son, to have borne his name; my immense gratitude for all he has ever done for me. At last a sad smile inches upward about his lips, his nod meeting my nod. And he wraps an arm around my shoulders as we both trudge silently back down the stairwell and into the pristine night toward his car—our final test together now only far too imminent upon fate's forked trail of inevitability.

* * *

"I'll stay with the cab," says Volodya as we round the last turn off Liteiny Prospekt into Finlandsky Station.

I climb out first, and huddle beside the trunks, while Father and Vliny hurry off to secure berth tickets. Beating my hands together, I attempt in vain to warm them as another long gust sweeps in from the frosty slate of the Neva. Brisk snowflakes tease at the fur of my high coat collar and the brim of my ermine hat, and the wind bites sharp and cold, lashing across my face, ice crystals forming upon the rims, the nosebridge of my spectacles. Rumor has it that the trains are running sorely late, if at all. Earlier, more shouting assailed the squares, the streets, the alleyways, particularly in Vyborg; more shaken fists, more dangerous, sullen glares have been laying siege to the shaky veneer of public order by the hour, joining in fierce rebuke against the new ration quota for bread, a pound a day. The news from the front remains mired in hopelessness; one wonders which will overtake the Empire first, the Germans, or revolution—for as of today, the twenty-first day of February, 1917, one must stand in line all night to buy bread in Petrograd.

Cheeks chapped shiny red, his nose blistered by the chill, Father returns with Vliny and burrows in beside me, sliding his gloved hand around my arm. "And now," he says, his gaze following mine across the station yard and down the long rows of platforms lining the railroad tracks, "we wait."

"They could not tell you at all how long it will be?"

"No. They have no idea."

Solidly, his hand remains. I press my own to it, nodding once again as he questions, in a furtive whisper, about the fit of the jacket worn beneath my coat.

Last night, I forsook all remaining caution and stole into the Zhukovskaya townhouse to help him pack. Last night, we talked for hours as we sorted through the paperwork, reconciling our bank accounts and tallying his investment ledgers. Earlier in the day, he had made his final trip to the St. Petersburg Commercial. From the residue, divided up between us, I packed my knapsack full with rubles and old silver coins, while within the portmanteau he stuffed pockets of his shirts and trousers full with Swiss francs and English pound notes. And last night, he made me a gift of his old lightweight hunting jacket—the elegant, tailored one worn so often beneath his coat on doctoring trips away from home when I was a youth. For my build, the fit would still have been far too ample, save for the new double-lining—the jacket's innermost layer embedded now with dozens of carefully tacked stitches caught in rugged outlines about the earbobs, rings, and necklaces—pearl and amethyst, sapphire and diamond. Silver and gold. All once my mother's. 'Perhaps, someday,' he explained, pointedly meeting my gaze, 'you will need use of the jewels.'

Last night, he also bestowed unto me a pouch of dirt from Novgorod. 'Earth of our forefathers' earth; bones of our ancestors' bones,' he said—and then entrusted me with the book, its broad covers, from end to end, near as large as a breakfast serving tray, line after line of its Old Slavonic letterings etched onto the brittle parchment paper within. Written in hands both legible and faded, it is the register where the names of the *pasechniki*, the hive keepers, have been recorded. Ever since the time of Ivan the Awesome One, in the Sixteenth Century, have those names in our book seen to the bees, has that blood of our line kept the wealth of honey flowing along our northeast shoreside of Lake Ilmen. And since long before even that perilous age—aloft of any written records, rooted in the oral traditions of the *byliny* tellers, the storysingers—exploits of even more venerable Sekovsky forebears abound amidst the paintings of the icon schools, in the legends of the fur trade, and in accounts of battles with the Tartars lost and won during the glory days of the Great Nevsky and the old feudal Republic of Novgorod. 'Keep it well, my Sashenka,' he told me, pressing the book into my arms, the pouch close into my hand. 'Never, never forget.'

Last night, I clung to him with more desperation than I have ever known, our embraces testing moments, dragging into escaping hours, while I greedily drank in the scent of old Carpathian tobacco laced always in such familiar reminder about his beard and his whitened hair. At last he pulled away, winking—indeed, he had saved back two small glassfuls of his *Napoleon* brandy in the crystal carafe; must have been stashing it ever since the onset of the war. We drank a toast to one another and to everything we have ever shared. And I swore to him that I would *never* forget.

"Lord Almighty," Vliny mutters out, hand shading his brow, his eyes squinting off into the riddled snowy distance. "Train comin' fer sure, Misha," he says with a sigh. "Straight up ahead."

My heart sinks . . . *oh, God!* Why now, of all times, must the railways coast ahead of schedule? *Oh, Lord—this is the hardest, bleakest, most difficult task of my entire life; my heart is breaking, I cannot bear this. . . .* "Well, Papa," I blurt out, forcing a grin—but breath by breath, the chill air catches like a claw at my throat, and my voice lisps forth in a shrill girlish lilt, a veritable war of heartbeats pounding upward as I joke: "I'm twenty-five now, Papa. I suppose we'd best finally give off all hope that I'll ever grow any taller." With the heel of my hand, I measure off my height through the air, jabbing playfully up against his neck.

Eyes unmoving from the distant train, Father snatches up my fist into his gloved one, his fingers crushing mine as I shut my eyes, biting back another rush of panic as fate's voice harps on, small and tinny, yet fraught to towering anguish deep inside: *oh, dear God . . .*

"Merely a short journey to Oslo," he whispers hurriedly, again pressing my arm close.

"Yes, of course, Papa!" I gasp. "Merely a short journey. After all, is high time you got your health back, for a certainty! Grown far too old for such harried dashing about to-and-fro at the hospital. Yes, I'd say you're quite due for a short trip, Papa, for your health. Merely a—a short journey to Oslo . . . ."

At last the train grinds into the station, its engines steaming, tall smokestacks belching out hoary black soot across the stationhouse's delicate sheeting of virgin frost. Upon the wheels, the fat gears bleat forth in gluttonous, wrenching torment, the burnt stench of coal and oily odor of pulley grease pungently souring the air. From the influx of debarking passengers—another vast throng of government soldiers, more potential keepers of the peace streaming into Petrograd from the outlying provinces—I avert my eyes, and stare past them just to the left of the open rail coach door. Painted beside, the striking white Russian 'P'—for *poezd*, the word for train—precedes a set of smaller printed serial numbers, lonely docket testifying to a naked, narrow fate against its widened background of black, forbidding morass. Shuddering, I grit my teeth, wincing back the sudden sense of grime in my mouth: *a thick coating, the taste of tar* . . . with effort, I fight back queasiness, the urge to retch. To scream. Abruptly, Vliny pinches fond fingers onto my shoulder; leaves his hand resting upon my arm for a long moment—as if through the closeness, and our warm affection so long shared for one another, to somehow impart the character traits I so dourly lack: courage, strength, determination, resolve. With a nod to Father, he then wanders off to see about loading their larger trunks into the baggage section.

"This," Father murmurs low in my ear, "I now want you to have."

He removes his gloves, and from his right hand, works off the ring. Engraved with a beehive, with the relief of a lakeshore, and with 'M.D.S.'—the initials of my great-great-great-great grandfather, Count Mikhail Dmitryevich—the ring has been handed down, father to eldest son, death upon death, one generation to another, ever since the time of the incomparable Great One, Peter the First.

Struggling for words, I cast off all as inadequate and simply take the ring; work it onto my right middle finger, the fit closing snug and perfect as if custom-made. Then I gulp back pebbles, marbles; soon enough, tough chunks of stone—and from my pocket, fish out the keys.

"These . . . ." Harshly, I clear my throat; stare downward as I rasp out, pointing, with a shaking hand, to each key: "These, uh, t-this is the set for the townhouse. In London—"

Nodding away from me, Father presses a fist fiercely into his mouth, as if swallowing pain.

"—which, as I told you," I go on, "should now be vacant. My latest lessees were to have moved back to Essex by last Christmas. And this," I continue in a grating whisper, "t-this . . . is the set. . . for Winnebar . . . ."

Moaning, I pull my head up sharply, my voice trailing out in another pitiful whine: "Howell should still be there, Papa. W-With his wife, the maid. And—and their tiny daughter—"

In response, Father clamps both his hands onto my shoulders in a roughened hold, pulling me square to face him. "Chin up, lad!" he orders out in the deep, decisive baritone of a crusty old army commander, his voice cutting richly across the groaning hubbub of train noise and inane chatterings of other boarders gathering in the station. "Naught but a short journey only, I tell you!" he rasps on, gulping for air. "To Oslo . . . ."

Arms seized around his neck, I cling close and fast as a child, while he chokes into my ear: "You are everything in the world to me, my dearest, my blessed, precious spirit Sashenka . . . s-simply say the word—*beg* me to stay! We'll have those bags back off that coach in a moment—"

"No, Papa."

They start calling for boarding, and we wrest free of one another once Vliny returns. To him, I extend my hand in the humblest bow of gratitude. Near unto sixty years have the two of them been together, and there had been no question whether he would accompany Father to Oslo, even—as he had quipped with such laughter last eve—were he forced, under differing circumstances, to drag Marnya along kicking and screaming. "Valenti Apollonovich," I murmur, grasping warm hold of his hand. "I cannot tell you how relieved I am that Father is not leaving Russia alone—"

"Oh, akkh!" he bellows back at me, grinning and puffing out his wrinkled, reddened cheeks. "Fer God's sake, Sasha, leave off the crap, will ye?" Guffawing, he yanks me close into his arms and kisses me three times one cheek to another as I kiss him back, murmuring: "You have been my second papa, Vliny."

"An' as second papa, I intend te duck my tail onto that train, thereby making more rightful time fer yer first. Goodbye, Sashenka. May the Saints always smile upon yer way, an' keep ye strong and fed and warm in these here wretched times. Ye have been a blessin' te all o' us, boy—yer name was last before my own on my dear old Marina's lips. I will remember ye all o' my days."

Without awaiting reply, Vliny trudges off to join the growing line of travelers filing toward the second-class rail coach doors, the only available. He does not look back as the conductors sound the second call.

"P-Papa," I whisper, turning back to him.

"Now, you listen to me!" Letting out a snort, Father squares his shoulders and glares down at me imperiously, barking: "Chin up, I said, young man—chin *up* and head held high! Yes, that's right. Now, you listen up your ears, young man—and this time, I'll not be taking any smart-nosed back-talk, nor filthy peasant curse words in reply."

I roll my eyes and cannot resist a short laugh as, hands again resting tenderly upon my shoulders, he grins down into my face, announcing: "That's better!" But again his expression mellows to seriousness, and he continues on in a lowered tone: "You take care of that boy of yours, now, you hear? You take care of yourself and him. For me. And when the time comes—when you feel him at last old enough—I implore you, Sashenka! Consider what we discussed. *Please.* Bring the child with you. To Winnebar."

"I—I will consider it, Papa."

"Aleksandr," he goes on with a long sigh, "I am the last person in the world who should be telling you how to live your life." Chuckling wryly, he then mutters out: "Oh, Lord—and that is precisely because I have always been the first person in the world telling you how to live your life! But all that aside, I have not lived for near unto nine decades on this earth without learning a few things. Promise me that you will give thought to my advice—"

Abruptly, the whistle blows; the conductors sound the final call for boarding.

Swallowing hard, I hold his gaze; crush his hands. "Of course, Papa! I—I always give thought to your advice—" My voice snuffs out, breaking into scraping fissures of hoarseness as he throws both arms fast around me, as I seize onto him again, whispering: "I love you, Papa!"

"And I love you, my son—with all my heart." Hurriedly, he kisses me the same as Vliny, three times one cheek to another in the old peasant way. Then he presses a kiss unto my brow; one to my nose; at last a long, tender, grandfatherly one to my mouth. "You do this country proud, my boy!" he then rasps on. "Whatever should happen, you and your son, you both remember whence you have come, the noble blood which you both bear. And you both do Mother Russia damn proud!"

One arm still wrapped around me, with his other he hoists up his old doctor's bag, and together we stumble for the rail coach. Before he mounts the step, one last embrace: finally, searing, hot tears escape, stinging from the corners of my eyes. Angrily, I choke them back, sniffling, coughing in a heave as he bellows: "Now, now—chin up, I say!"

"Y-Yes, sir!"

"And you *write* to me!"

"Oh, you know I will!"

"As 'Doctor Mikhailov,' remember—we want to keep this city your safe haven. And whatever should happen," he goes on, quickly grasping up my hand, "when the time comes, you give your own son this family ring."

"Yes, sir! Oh—oh, Papa! . . ."

"All aboard!" the conductor shouts down between us with a glower of impatience.

Father crushes me close; tears himself away and squeezes up my hand. Ducking downward, he presses a quick kiss upon the fingers of my glove, murmuring: "Never forget!"

Bare in the nick of time, he clambers up the steps of the rail coach doorway and wedges himself in behind the conductor. The train starts to move, and I hurry along with it as far as I can, struggling with my cane across the platform through its fresh, thin layering of ice. "Never forget, Sasha!" Father implores again, shouting this time, his arms waving frantically above the conductor's head. "And most of all, your name, my boy! *Always* remember your true name. . . ."

"My name," I shout back after him through cupped hands, "is *Sekovsky!"*

I wave for as long as I can see him—and then stand shivering, watching for as long as I can yet pick out the sight of his coach, remaining wholly frozen, stilled unto my place, caught in the silent warp of time until the train winds off into a fuzzy blur, then a shadow, then into a lean black speck smoking its way into the distance. Once it disappears, I shut my eyes, holding fast onto his beloved essence, my heart aching after the fading sound of his voice, my mind reciting back and forth every one his last uttered words. But despite his admonishments to stand tall and proud and hold my head high, sharp, hurtful breaths begin burning back into my lungs from a sudden rush of chilled winter air, and blackness—utter blackness—finally descends from the vacant gulf within.

"Come, let us go," Volodya murmurs, catching my arm.

Snarling curses, I smack out at his hand and glare away, continuing to stare off after the disappearing train.

"Sasha, for God's sake!" he urges, pointing back toward Liteiny. "The cab's still waitin'! I swear, this is costin' me a small fortune—"

"I hate you!"

Reply yet poised unsaid upon paled lips, Volodya stops cold in his tracks; steps gingerly back away from me and thrusts his hands down into the pockets of his heavy sheepskin greatcoat, his gaze faltering downward.

"I hate you!" I spout on, whirling upon him. "Because *you* are the cause of all the grief, misery, and misfortune I have ever encountered! Had it not been for you, I'd never have been kidnapped by that devil whoremonger Sheremetev! Nor taken against my will to his hideous Moscow bordello—and none of what occurred afterward between me and him, there or here in Petersburg later, would have! And I'd never have met that shrewish bitch I married, and instead of standing here facing black death inside, I'd be on that train right now with my father. Where I am *supposed to be!"*

"Sasha—"

"Goddamn you, Rykazian—you cocksucking, bloody-fucking son of a whore's jackass! *Sonuvabitch!* Everything that happened is because of you! God, how I *hate* you. . . ."

Heart spewing malice of the most livid, treacherous sort, I spit straight down at his feet, bile foam of saliva welling into a greasy wash of snow. Then I turn on my heel and leave him long behind, trudging off with a slew of further sputtered curses for the waiting cab.

Once in it beside me, he shoves a flask into my hand, muttering: "Here. Drink this."

Vodka. I ask not where, nor by what means he obtained it; merely begin sloshing it down, gulp after mindless, fiery gulp, one gulp after another, straight unto nirvana. Oblivion . . . .

Now, there is no one. Each night, when I seek escape from thought of the bread lines, from the nagging burden of book work, and from the barbs of my quarrelsome, angry wife, I return to my long-lost orchestra world, mounting the grand carousel in drowsy abandon to share once again in recitals and balls, to bask for another heady night in glorious, shattering applause for the ballets. But now, none are left to remind me of that world. Father is gone; Nikolai is dead. Even my old Matushka, God rest her soul, has passed on along with so many weakened elderly others chained this last cruel winter unto the barest brink of health in bitter, breadless wartime Petrograd. To the warm arms of my true mother Novgorod, and to that iridescent, laughing halo—the gaiety, the frolic, the charms of my phantom Lady Petersburg as she once was so long ago—I would return at once, could I but reverse the squall of time. But from time, from inevitability, there is no turning back; only a plunging forward—into which I, Count Aleksandr Sekovsky, now struggle scared and alone. . . .

* * *

"Well, my word, dear me! Think you then that you shall have been delivered it by Tuesday, M'sieur Khulinov? I declare! My daughter next week is marrying a young officer, mind you, a captain from the Preobrazhensky Guards. You can understand how important this is to us, yes? And save for you—and dear, *dear* M'sieur Denisov!—one can scarce entertain any hope these days at laying one's hands upon Belgian lace."

"In all honesty, Madame Vorontsova," I reply, "I cannot be held to any guarantees. These disruptions plaguing the city have done much to affect our good business reputation for punctuality, just as with many other of the shops lined about the Prospekt. But our regular shipment is due early Monday morn, and should it indeed arrive on time, I promise I shall ring you up about the lace without delay."

Vaguely satisfied with my answer, Madame Vorontsova—the long feathers of her stylish winter hat bobbing up and down about her ears—nods and snatches up her beaded pocketbook, trailing back out from my office and from the dress shop in a fluttery, perfumed huff.

With relief, I reshut the payables ledger, tuck my abacus back down into the drawer, and begin pulling on my coat. Then Zhenya—pert nose cast into the air—defiantly saunters on through the front dress shop entrance. "Good afternoon, Step-papa!" she calls out with a laugh, skipping up to my office door, her two long dark plaits trailing out coyly from the new sable hat that I just yesterday made her a present of, her deep blue eyes testily meeting mine.

I let out a long sigh and plant both hands upon my hips, barking: "And why do I even bother to ask? All right, young lady: and this time, does your mother have the faintest idea where you are?"

Shrugging nonchalantly, Zhenya stalls for time by sorting, piece by piece, down through the remnant box set upon the table beside the door, finally mumbling out: "Well, no—"

"Zhenya," I harp on, shaking my head, "you know you were told to come straight home! I was forced to sit through the entire exchange myself this morn in the kitchen, taking my breakfast with a good deal of noise, mind you! Now, you know your mother ordered you to go directly home from school."

"Humph! Well, she didn't say I couldn't see Masha."

"Directly home means no stopping off to see any Mashas, to see any Sonyas—to see anyone, Zhenya."

"Oh, Step-papa!" Zhenya's gaze catches mine in a plaintive hold as she tosses a thick remnant wad back down into the box. "And did you never sneak away to see friends when you were in school?"

Biting my lip, I stare downward—but at last cannot prevent the wry smile from overtaking my face.

"Ha, I knew it! Gasping with delight, the girl bounds across the floor in two quick strides, stopping up breathlessly before me. "Oh, that is what I like about you so much, Step-papa!" she exclaims, waving out her hands. "You've not yet grown so old and frumpy that you cannot remember!"

"Humph!" Fondly, I shake my head once more and gaze down upon my stepdaughter's impish face. Of late, the mounting discord between Zhenya and her mother continues tearing through our household with a predictable nightly regimen of chaos—the bickering, the accusations, the torrential weeping spells waning on always far past suppertime, and ofttimes clear unto midnight. The profanity may be absent, and the tactics much more aptly veiled in subterfuge, but so much does it all remind me of my querulous youthful years with Father, that my sympathy forever drowns out bidings of good sense. "Oh, all right, Zhenya!" I say, tweaking a playful pinch upon her ear. "And now, I suppose—no matter how I shall protest—your mother will blame me for your absence as well."

"Oh, but you've become so deft at telling her off, Step-papa!"

"Humph! So? Why didn't you stay at Masha's, then?"

"Well," Zhenya explains with a sly grin, "Masha caught a horrid scolding! I swear, the poor girl will be chained to that pressing iron for hours: three whole basketfuls of fresh-washed linen. Can you imagine? And, oh, Step-papa—I simply could not stay to help her, although she begged me to, and guilty as I felt about it, because—

oh! It is simply all so impressive!" Pointing out toward the front shop windows, she gushes on in a rush: "Everyone is saying there's another simply monstrous demonstration starting up in Znamenskaya Square—"

"Oh, no!" I interrupt with a fierce wave. "Oh, *no*, you don't."

"But, Step-papa!"

Exasperated, I throw up both hands. My worries over Father's safety at last assuaged, new troubles now constantly nip ready ulcers at my heels. In the four days since his departure, the weather has turned—the skies glowing full with the pinkish promise of spring, bright sunshine peeking through at intervals, ice in places thawing from the windowpanes. Such permutation seems to have inspired the strangest sense of gaiety amongst the now near-constant street crowds, everyone decrying the lack of bread in laughing, caroling choruses as if all were out from work or school on Christmastide holiday. Caught up in similar spirit, the Cossacks, bereft of their whips, their sabers sheathed, have done little when called out but flex their gold-fringed epaulets and banter back and forth jokingly with strikers always parting for any line of intruding mounts without hesitation and without the least fear of reprisal. At first, I questioned whether overreaction did indeed preclude my good judgment in the rush to muster Father off toward Scandinavia on the train. But come this morn, the old gnawings of foreboding gained fresh merited ground: news funnelled in that grocers' shop windows had been smashed, bands of looters clearing whole stores on Vasilyevsky Island and on the Fortress side. And this following in the wake of two days of nonstop demonstrations in tribute to International Women Worker's Day—Thursday, the twenty-third. By that afternoon—two days ago, now—the bread lines erupted into battle cries of frustration, and the massive Filippov Bakery on Bolshoi Prospekt—the largest in Petrograd—was thoroughly ransacked by scores of angry women and a mob of striking workers from the Putilov Ironworks. Declaring they valued their lives, the police made no attempt to interfere. Since then, the entire city, it seems, has taken to the streets. Usually bustling on a Saturday, today our dress shop business has dwindled down to next to nil, groups of prospective customers instead chasing to-and-fro in the excitement of the growing tumult outside. At some street corners, red flags have appeared, mounted up high above the shop advertisement signposts; in scattered intersections, long banners have been unfurled, demanding bread, or calling for conclusion to the war. Although this last hour Vasya came in, and declared both only false rumors—

perpetrated in the hope of urging the crowds homeward—earlier, I heard from Gorushka that all gaslamps will be shut off tonight come dusk, and that by morntide tomorrow, even the water plants will close down for lack of workers. On Sadovaya, it is said most streetcars have stopped running; on Nevsky this afternoon, one can no longer even find a cab. Indeed, scarce a *droshki* stood in evidence anywhere even early this morn; only a pause of luck secured my ride across town to work on the running board of a passing motorcar. But worse than any inconvenience is the fact that, amidst all the commotion, a good deal of the time I have no idea where my wife is—which means I have no idea where my son is, for Lyubov straps him onto her chest in a gunnysack secured with long burlap ties around her back and shoulders, bouncing the child along with her from demonstration to demonstration. When she finally does return home, the nightly tirade of screaming only begins renewed between her and Zhenya. . . .

"Oh, Step-papa, please!" Zhenya pleads on, clinging to my hand. "Everyone in school was off to that demonstration! I must go—if not, the others will poke fun of me come Monday morn in geometry class."

Again I sigh, unable to help recalling when I was fourteen: 1905. Following Bloody Sunday that year, to near dozens of just such demonstrations did Nikolai and I sneak off together, although we never ventured farther than the cover of a shaded doorway, or the perch of a nearby balcony. Despite such precautions, the soreness of our backsides long testified to the dire consequence of later confrontations about such matters with the headmaster of May's Academy. "Oh, all right, Zhenya!" I mutter finally, wincing as, overwhelmed with delight, the girl starts shrieking out at the top of her voice. "But only on the condition," I add in a stern tone, "that you practice your English phrases with me as we walk along."

"Oh, yes, Step-papa!" With enthusiasm, Zhenya starts rattling off our latest English study phrases: "The cake was been baked by Mama; no, no—the cake was *being* baked by Mama; the book was *being* read by me. . . ." But as I pull off my boot and stuff in the wooden knob, she switches for a moment back to Russian, demanding with a curious stare: "Does that spare block of wood truly aid with your walking, Step-papa?"

"Not near so well as it used to. The rheumatism, I am afraid, has been gaining on me sorely these past two winters. See, my dear?" I tell her with a wink, "your 'Step-papa' is in truth far more old and frumpy than you first imagined! But for a certainty, the pain has diminished somewhat with this turn in the weather. Perhaps a walk in the fresh air will do us both good," I say with a smile, offering her my arm.

Once out the door and up the street onto Nevsky, I stop short in surprise: a far vaster throng than any evident over the past few days has entirely overtaken the walkways, groups of hearty, banner-waving souls—with arms linked or fists hoisted high—trailing through soiled, half-melted clumps of the curbstone snow. Every one of them, without exception, continues surging eastward. Undaunted, Zhenya drags me out after her across the pack of ice, and as we start to pass by an elegant old row of bakeries and delicatessens and some of Nevsky's best finery shops, I fall reluctantly into step with the girl, warning her not to stray nor let loose of my arm lest we become separated from one another in the swelling tide of people. Just before we ascend the Anichkov Bridge, I glance across the street toward the white-columned palace of likened name—home of the Tsar's mother, the Dowager Empress Mariya Feodorovna. From the windows, two stories up, groups of servants can be seen eyeing the street from behind cover of delicate lace draperies. Once we cross over the Fontanka Canal, and pass by the red-painted, baroque-inspired facades of Father's old haunt, the Anglo-Russian hospital, freshened ranks join into the crowd at such a quickened pace that one can scarce avoid a jostling from the walkways, and the farther east we venture, the more retail shops on either side of the Prospekt appear entirely shuttered up for the day, their owners apparently having given off any hope of further afternoon business. Past the Liteiny Prospekt crossroad and ensuing groups of closed-up watch repair shops, empty restaurants, and a burgeoning array of cinema houses, Cossacks begin materializing increasingly from behind each next courtyard alley-way—sometimes singly, sometimes in mounted lines of two or three—all with sabers still sheathed, some with carbines strapped loosely to their saddle gear. But still, infused with a jovial atmosphere, the crowd seems to take little note of the weapons, several stout-voiced fellows hoisting up their banners with brazen shouts while waving the troops along to join in the procession. Only when we finally begin across Ligovsky Prospekt's wide intersection with the Nevsky to close in upon the outskirts of Znamenskaya Square do I at last start paying due heed to my misgivings. Southward, over at Nikolayevsky Station, I immediately glimpse—gathering before all eleven white rounded stationhouse archways—an ample line of mounted city police, their eyes critically surveying the growing crowd, whips tucked in gleaming evidence beneath the arms of their gray-pressed uniforms. As Znamenskaya's massive monument to Tsar Aleksandr III edges fully into our view, I pull Zhenya aside in a flurry of haste, urging: "Sweetheart, I think perhaps we should consider turning back. This is a far vaster number of people than I'd ever imagined would be gathered, and the square is literally swarming with Cossacks and police—"

"Oh, Step-papa, please! Don't fret so over the Cossacks—everyone at school said it would be just like yesterday, that the troops have orders not to interfere." Glaring down my further pleas for prudence, the girl seizes hold of my arm with both hands and drags me insistently behind her into the growing throng of onlookers.

One after another, impromptu speakers climb up upon the lower pedestal hosting the Tsar's snow-capped equestrian monument: workers, shopkeepers, students. All cavort in quick succession over a wide range of current political topics: the crisis in the food situation; the follies of 'the German woman,' meaning the Tsarina; the havoc in the ministries, and the incompetency, in particular, of Interior Minister Protopopov; the war. Feigning patience, I continue checking my urge to flee—while Zhenya, with a rapt, dreamy-eyed expression, listens to the contents of the speeches. Over five—then ten—then twenty long, almost unbearable minutes, a souring shift of mood starts to become evident in the square. As I peek glumly over the rims of my spectacles toward the railway station, scores more Cossacks and mounted police begin filtering their way from that direction into the fringes of the crowd. With an eye not only toward sensible precaution, but also toward Lyubov's usual afternoon supper preparations, I nervously start glancing between the high blue stationhouse clock tower and my pocket watch as the hands on both begin inching upward toward three P.M. "Zhenya," I whisper into her ear, "I think we have heard far more than enough of these speeches for today. Oh, yes, we have, my dear—Zhenya! Now, be sensible—I obliged you by coming here. I think, now, you can be good enough to oblige me back—"

"But, Step-papa!"

Abruptly, the speaker standing up before the monument bites off his last word as one of the Cossack units—at least twoscore strong, its captain barking a strident string of orders—closes ranks and begins pulling forward. Upon a spreading fan of murmurs, the crowd parts for the riders across the entire breadth of the square as the Cossacks cross it from one end to the other; then, unfazed, throngs of people simply close in once again behind the horses. Loud guffaws emit from several boisterous types; two or three banners shift up even higher into the air upon sets of defiant shoulders; the speaker up at the statue calmly resumes reciting his speech. "See, Step-papa?" Zhenya argues, pointing. "No one intends any harm. Why, it's much more peaceable than yesterday, everyone moaning all afternoon over those ransacked grocers in Vyborg—"

Without warning, a piercing bugle blast then rips between us, snuffing out any remainder of Zhenya's words. Jumping near from our skins, we dart about to find ourselves caught amidst a substantial group of onlookers hemmed in by a full-ranked squadron of the mounted police. "Lord God!" I mutter, seizing my arm around Zhenya's shoulders as the second, then the third trumpeting to arms barrels out—followed by the unmistakable, voluminous discharge of a shot.

"Run for your lives!" someone shouts behind us; hoofbeats thunder in a clash across cobblestones, and a collective roar wafts upward, all nearby bodies turning tail and breaking into headlong runs. "No, Step-papa—no!" Zhenya wails, snatching onto my arm and pointing backward.

"Blast it, girl—don't argue with me now!" I yell, piloting my cane for balance with effort while dragging her from behind. "Come along!"

"It was the constable, Step-papa, the constable of the police! The Cossacks shot the constable! Look! Now they are waving their caps!"

Briefly, I glance over my shoulder—and indeed, the Cossacks farther along in the square are waving their caps—the crowd's cheer of support bantered up behind them in what appears to have become an apparent standoff between Cossacks and mounted police. Still, upon the heels of numerous other doubtful souls yet fleeing the crowd, I continue to run northward down Ligovsky Prospekt while fiercely yanking Zhenya along behind. With a group of frenzied others, we dash into the second alleyway across the street from the Actors' House Hotel—there to stop up short within the courtyard to our every last man, woman, and child in a wide-eyed, gasping line—as two units of the mounted police, their grimaces dark and surly and rank with malicious intent, pour in behind us and pull into formation, blocking all path to escape.

Determinedly, they then raise and cock up their carbines.

Screams peal through the air; feet scatter in all directions, and as I whirl about with the rest, my cane flies off beneath the kicking jumble of panicked feet. Cold and hard I hit the icy cobblestones, near flat atop my bad leg, fighting back a swelling crush against the wind in my lungs. "Step-papa!" I hear Zhenya scream out as I struggle dully back to my feet. Up ahead, several of the policemen lower their rifles, but the captain and a group of his officers—glowers of affronted rage yet coarsening their faces—hold true to their aim, following as I attempt to limp away after other stragglers. "Zhenya!" I shout at the top of my lungs, realizing—with a cold wash of terror—that the girl has entirely disappeared. Wrenchingly, a burst of pain then enflames the joints of my ankle, and I know that any further attempt to run will only meet probable failure despite the aid provided by my wooden heel lift. "Step-papa!" Zhenya screams once more—before she plows into my side in such a sudden burst that I almost topple back over again in surprise. Into my hands, she thrusts the handle of my cane.

"You—you silly, stupid girl!" I choke out, yanking her to me close. "I told you to stay right with me!"

"But, Step-papa! You needed your—"

Hoof-clatter abruptly silences our tongues, and we whirl about to once again encounter the angry police captain and his patrol of officers—their taut expressions bent on meting out proper justice, their heavy carbines still shouldered upward, aimed and at the ready.

"Get behind me!" I order to Zhenya, shoving her around as—for once—the girl counters with no protests and huddles in behind exactly as told.

Swallowing, I grip up the handle to my cane and stare upward into the glowering snarl of the police captain. Other fugitive renegades from the crowd have long since vanished back through the various courtyard alleyways, and Zhenya and I appear to remain as sole culprits for any and all venting of the man's rage. Respectfully, I doff my ermine hat in his direction, and as I do so, the officer at his side stares me up and down in long perusal, apparently apprising the rich fur pile of my ermine coat, sharp in contrast to the mundane felt and sheepskin coverings more usually worn by the common people. "Please," I say both to him and to the captain.

I risk saying it in English—loudly—and then, still holding their stares, I continue on in English, saying again: "Please—we simply panicked along with the others, and certainly never meant to become involved in any such demonstration, I assure you, gentlemen! My daughter and I were simply out for an afternoon stroll."

Nodding, the officer just beside the captain mutters out: *"Dvoryanye."* Pointedly eyeing the others, he shrugs and lowers down his weapon.

Two other officers lower their carbines as well—and then finally the remainder follow suit the moment their captain does, although with the rifle barrel, the man gruffly indicates the street entrance through the alley. "Go, then, Your Honor!" he barks out at us in annoyance, his English lilt as crisply enunciated as mine. "And from now on, keep the likes of yourselves away from these infernal warring platoons of ironworkers! I daresay, this is no place for either you or the young lady. Well! Can't you hear me? Don't simply stand and gawk—the both of you go! *Go!*"

Hurriedly, we nod grateful thanks—and then, hands clasped, we dash off for the alleyway, while I mince back raw curses against the pain in my leg. Once we stumble together back onto Ligovsky, a renewed flood of demonstrators surges past us, and we shove our way through a formidable wall of bumping shoulders until happening upon safe haven within the archway of the next closest alley to Nevsky. The moment we stop, Zhenya throws both arms around my neck, and I crush her close as she gasps out: "Oh, Step-papa—thank the good Lord that you grew up speaking English! And that you are of the *dvoryanye!* I don't care what Mama says."

Nose pressed into the soft brim of her sable hat, my fingers caught in an escaping tendril of her curly hair, I wrap Zhenya fervently in my arms and breathe out a grateful, exhausted sigh. But my relief over my step-daughter's safety remains cruelly short-lived; beyond her head, Nevsky Prospekt looms up southward into the scant corner of my vision like a poised thundercloud of doom—a Nevsky Prospekt as I have never known it. The First Peter's Great Prospective Road—this historic avenue of avenues sworn to the countenance of the patron saint for whom I too bear proud Christian name—treasured, renowned, preciously familiar Nevsky Prospekt, this lifeline from the snowy outskirts crowned by a tiara of shimmery blue canals, this citadel of pale palaces and enchanting storefronts heretofore always breathing sweet life into my winsome Lady Petersburg's veins—Nevsky Prospekt now lies bereft of streetcars and cabs, and therefore of any means by which my step-daughter and I might find our way home. And in lieu of the usual Saturday afternoon shoppers, the wandering browsers, the bead-draped, feather-coiffed madames staring down, through old lorgnettes, groups of roguish young men sporting ties and derbies and calling out to one another past rude insults and affectionate, teasing barbs, Nevsky Prospekt continues filling up near across its entire massive width with warring legions of demonstrators shouting out revolutionary chants and waving forth red flags. Our chance clash with the mounted police may have been temporarily averted. But my misgivings have been valid: before us, the threat of true violence now appears imminent, ominous. . . .

* * *

Eight o'clock P.M.: winter's dark, hovering chill again whistles over the city, a brisk wind off the nearby river ice slashing at our noses and ears. Near unto four hours has the paltry distance of approximately four and half versts from Nevsky Prospekt cost Zhenya and I along treacherous, icy walkways refrozen from the brief morntide thaw. Only stubbornly have I been willing to admit to the sprain in my ankle, apparently encumbered during the fall before the mounted police. As I struggle with my cane in through the vestibule and up our own apartment stairwell at long last, with Zhenya guardedly flanking my back to prevent another mishap, the pain rages forth renewed in such a searing, torturous burn that I almost collapse back on down the steps. "Only three more, Step-papa; now, only two more steps—you can do it!" she urges on, both her arms pressed close to my side, the warmth of her breath etching lacy patternworks through the frosted slant of air.

Once up on the porch, I let out a groan of profound relief. But when we try the front door, the lock holds fast, and I cannot help but emit a string of muffled curses despite the proximity of the girl's tender young ears. Lyubov, by all indications, is furious—and probably frantic unto tears by now as well, with her daughter tardy by so many waning hours. With apprehension, I begin preparing, as the party responsible, to accept the certain brunt of maternal wrath, and my stiffened fingers quiver in anticipation as I fumble with poking my key into the tiny slot of the lock. The task is made all the more difficult because the woman has neglected to switch on the outside bulb, leaving the key slot barely visible. And spite, not necessity, appears the reason—because so far, contrary to the earlier rumors, all structures close by appear to have retained an ample grasp upon electrical power, tiny specks of light peeking out from behind numerous neighboring apartment windows. Fortunately, from Nevsky to the Fontanka, and then along every step of our hapless foot trodden route, such trusty window sentinels and the quaint old gaslamp rows dotted across the Canal's many wrought-iron railed bridges remained steadily aglow to light our way across the slippery pathways of ice.

"You know, Step-papa, not even any of the inside lamps appear lit," Zhenya observes, pressing her nose up to the glass of our front hall window and attempting to peer beyond the draperies inside.

"Humph!" Sardonically noting that the unlit porch bulb provides me an excuse to plunge into my bath of fire on the offensive, I finally wrench the key in and fling open the door, shouting: "Lyubov!"

A hollow, ghostly echo rebounds in answer from across the apartment as the door bangs open against the foyer wall. Together, Zhenya and I stare into the long hallway and a gulf of total darkness.

"Oh, Lord by the Saints!" I blurt out. "Lyubov, for God's sake! Yes, I am the one with whom Zhenya's been all eve long—and yes, I know you are furious with me about it! But must you sit sulking in the darkness?" Grumbling, I stumble inward and pull on the nearest switch cord.

Zhenya lets out an incredulous gasp—while my fingers remain clutched around the switch cord to the hallway lamp, another irate spiel melting unsaid upon my tongue. Jaw dropped, I stand staring in disbelief at the wrecked shambles that was once our apartment.

"Oh, dear *Lord!"* Zhenya chokes out, wide-eyed, covering her mouth with both hands.

From my inside coat pocket, I whip out my gun, cocking the hammer back as—cursing my left-handedness—I hurriedly switch hands with my cane, the pain in my leg muting to numbness in my sudden grip with shock. Everywhere—from the torn, feather-strewn parlor sofa cushions, to littered books toppled from high rows of shelves, to shattered glass panels from several curio cabinets—our apartment appears to have been ransacked by an invading army of thieves. "Lyubov?" I call across the empty reaches of the hallway. "Volodya? Yevgeny Ivanovich?"

From the parlor, the kitchen—the upstairs wings—no answer returns at all.

"Stay here," I order Zhenya, indicating the doorway.

"But, Step-papa!"

"Blast it, girl—I said *stay* here!"

"Y-Yes, sir."

Trembling from head to foot, Zhenya crouches back against the wall within the front hall foyer—while I limp with a dogged, cursing effort, my cane thrust beneath my arm, my pistol kept to the ready and quick checks made over my shoulder with every next cautious move as I begin an inspection for intruders. In my own room behind the kitchen, the bedclothes lie tossed into a heap upon the floor, the mattress having been turned over and split open down its entire length, as if a search had been made within its fill for some kind of illegal contraband. All cushioned furniture in the parlor appears to have suffered similar fate. In the kitchen, every cupboard drawer has been yanked out, the glass and porcelain tableware lying in splintered shards of destruction upon the floor. Surprisingly, though, a case of silver-plated serving implements remains virtually untouched, along with a gold-inlaid set of saucers, one of Lyubov's dearest treasures. At last satisfied that no thieves yet remain lurking behind the draperies, I signal Zhenya to venture inward once I reach the stairwell to the upper rooms. "Once again, my dear," I tell her, gripping an arm fast about her shoulders, "I am afraid you must assist your now rapidly aging step-papa upstairs. Why today—of all days on God's earth—I had to sprain my ankle, I shall never know. Now, listen," I go on in a lowered tone, "once we reach the head of the stairs, I want you to remain there. Do not, under any circumstances, follow me into the rooms until I tell you everything is all right. Understood?"

"Y-Yes, sir."

It seems to take near unto an hour for us to scale our way up the steps, although in truth, I know that only scarce moments slip by, magnified out of proportion by pain. "Now, you stay here," I remind Zhenya again emphatically. Then, fighting to catch my breath, I sponge a river of sweat from my brow with my handkerchief and once again cock up my gun, praying in desperation that I do not happen upon Lyubov and Vanya and Yevgeny all with throats slashed ear to ear, lying dead cold in their beds.

Instead, what I do encounter leaves me close upon speechlessness: smashed lumber, everywhere—in the sewing room, in Lyubov's and Zhenya's rooms—all beds tipped high up against the walls, chiffoniers and bedside tables toppled one upon another down into a rough-hewn trough of naked floorboards, as if caught in a violent cave-in. "Zhenya!" I call back to the stairs, at last motioning toward her. "Come and have a look at this."

Upon sight of the shambles made of her bedroom, Zhenya lets out a horrified shriek, and I again wrap an arm about her shoulders, attempting to soothe the shock. "Zhenya, hush—this is important," I admonish her, pointing downward. "Sweetheart, remember what it all looked like before? Now, listen carefully: do you recall any of the floors in the upper story as ever lying quite this low?"

Still choking back sobs, the girl stares after my pointing finger. After a long moment, her grimace softens toward a wary frown, and she shakes back and forth her head. "Why, no, Step-papa," she murmurs in confusion, dabbing at her eyes with the hem of her sleeve. "Now that you mention it, no. The floors up here never seemed quite *this* low."

"My God," I whisper, a cold chill lancing up my back as I stare around again at the mass of broken lumber. "False floors?" I then mutter out in amazement. "But, dear Lord—why on earth would anyone want to go to the trouble of building in false floors?"

Abruptly, the answer hits me with the full force of a runaway wall of ice: of course. *The guns*.

Volodya never told me where Yevgeny's stash of Mausers ended up; I never learnt where the boxes of rifles had been rehidden once the three of us left behind our original apartment on Vasilyevsky. Certain crates in the dress shop cellar have always been off limits to my inquiries, and naturally, I had assumed firearms and other revolutionary implements to be stored within. Apparently, I assumed wrong. Far wrong.

Apparently, much more than an oversized, claw-footed bathtub induced Yevgeny to set his sister's household up in this particular apartment.

However, not a single carbine nor revolver now lies anywhere within close sight. Which means that this apartment—far from suffering, this fateful eve, a thorough raiding by mere ordinary thieves—has instead, more than likely, been searched from end to end by none other than agents of the *Okhrana*.

The Tsarist police.

And arrest, no doubt, accounts for the absence of Volodya, Yevgeny, and Lyubov.

Although such assumption offers nary a clue—unless infants are also taken into custody—as to the whereabouts of Vanya. And as I think of him, my heart pounds to blind thunder.

Also unexplainable is the absence of my flute. Once back downstairs, it is the first item I search out, but nowhere in the dire shambles made of my room am I able to locate its faded leather case. My Paris picturegraph with Nikolai, my icons, my Tarot cards, Melissa's amethyst crystal—even Father's hunting jacket with the jewels sewn into the lining—all remain scattered about in various heaps of the disarray, and once again I become convinced of the unlikelihood of common thieves. The flute, however, cannot be found—and as I pull on Father's jacket with stiff resolution to never again be parted from it while stuffing my precious keepsakes hurriedly within its bevy of inner pockets, a swell of tears crushes at my heart: *my God, why? Why on earth would the Okhrana want to take my flute?*

"Step-papa!" I then hear Zhenya exclaim; in a fluster, she bursts in from the kitchen, pointing behind her. "Someone's knocking out at the front door!"

Once again I cock up my gun. "You hide in here," I insist, pushing her toward the wardrobe-cupboard.

"But, Step-papa! Perhaps it is simply the police! Yes, the police come after the thieves."

"Sweetheart," I tell her reluctantly, "the police may well indeed be the last visitors we should presently wish to encounter. I am beginning to think that this whole disaster might very well be, in God's honest truth, some devious work of the *Okhrana.*"

"The *Tsarist police?*" Zhenya gasps. "But why would the police want to tear up our floors?"

"Zhenya," I cry, my ears pricking up toward the sound of renewed knocking at the front door, "there is no time to explain! Now, listen," I tell her past the wardrobe door just before shutting it between us, "whatever happens, make not a sound, do you hear? And if I do not come back, I want you run out of here straight away; go ask for help from the neighbors. You remember the midwife, Yelizaveta Nikitichna, upstairs? Ask her to take you in for the night—tell them that your mother is gone, that we appear to have been robbed, and that you've no decent place tonight to sleep—"

The knocking at the front abruptly changes to pounding, and with little clue as to what else to tell the poor girl, I simply plant a kiss upon my finger and press it affectionately to the tip of her nose, whispering: "Remember, shhh!" Then I shut the wardrobe door softly, and limp out to the foyer.

To my surprise, the lone figure revealed through the front hall draperies—although sporting thick sheepskin greatcoat, long trousers, and a dark low-brimmed worker's cap—appears to be a woman. Pistol still gripped to the ready, I crack open the front door by only the barest slit, murmuring: "Yes?"

"You are Aleksandr Khulinov?"

When I make no reply, the woman continues in a hushed undertone: "Comrade, please! With the lamps burning so brightly now through the windowpanes, you and your step-daughter remain in grave danger. The police could still be keeping watch—"

"Who are you?"

"I am Martova. From the Petrograd Committee."

Frowning, I demand: "Of the *Bolsheviki?*"

"Yes. I have come to take you to your wife."

* * *

"Zhenya!"

"Mama!"

Mother and daughter burst into a flurry of embracing arms and cling together weeping and stroking one another's hair, exchanging endearments not proffered by either one to the other in the longest of times. Past them, Vanya grins at me from a sofa, and I sweep him up joyously, nuzzling into his neck as he lets forth a delighted squeal. "Say 'Papa,' Vanya!" I whisper into his ear. "Pah-pah . . . ."

"Paht-pah!" the boy shrieks, beating at me soundly with both fists.

"Close enough, by God!" Blinking back tears, I crush him close and murmur thanks to God, the stars, providence, the world. . . .

"Zhenya," I then hear Lyubov say behind me, "take yer brother from yer step-father fer a moment, will ye?"

In a blaze of righteous fury, I whirl about upon her—my flood of curses immediately bitten back, my waving fist unclenching to a tremor of astonishment. With outstretched arms, Lyubov holds out my flute.

"Oh, Lord bless you, Lyuba," I gasp, handing Vanya quickly over to Zhenya and seizing both arms fast around the old leather case.

"I knew ye'd be lost without it," Lyubov murmurs, nodding. "When the police left, it was all I could think o'—te take that, an' some clothes. I was scared they'd be back, that they'd change their minds. The only reason they balked at draggin' me off too was cause o' the babe. They told me they'd already got the two o' ye, *both* o' ye, earlier at the dress shop. Thank God, Sasha, that ye were the one out with my girl, an' that ye were both so frolickin' terrible late in comin' home."

"Then Volodya? And Yevgeny?"

"Arrested, both of 'em. Taken te Kresty Prison, we think, or the Fortress. We're not sure."

Benumbed, I nod and stare around. Martova's apartment, situated two blocks to the northeast of ours along the span of Sadovaya Street, stands brimming full near wall to wall with talkative, excited people, a considerable number of women and children amongst them. "Others that had their men arrested," Lyubov explains, following my gaze.

Glancing toward a group of men huddled together over in a corner—who all appear to be arguing over a layout of a city map—she adds: "Others runnin' from arrest. We'll all be beddin' down here tonight. They brung in lots o' extra blankets."

"When can we go back home?" Zhenya pleads, hanging upon her mother's arm. "All my schoolbooks—"

"We're not te be frettin' about school nor books very soon, honeysweet," Lyubov tells her. Turning back to me, she says: "Comrade Martova says best te wait a few days before we try goin' back."

"Lyubov," I say, nodding once again down toward the flute, "thank you for fetching this. It—it means everything to me."

My intention only a grateful squeeze, I reach my hand for her shoulder—but scarce before I know it, Lyubov ducks full into my arms, sliding both of hers up around my neck. Awkwardly—as her braided hair nestles softly against my ears, her warm bosom molding itself against my chest—I stand, in actuality for the very first time, holding my wife, while at the same time struggling with pangs of confusion and the strangest protective, paternal sense. Pulling back at last, Lyubov stares long and hard into my eyes before inching forward to plant a shy kiss upon my cheek, whispering: "Bless God that ye're both safe and all right."

Dismayed, I stutter for reply; yield instead to her chiding motherly pull toward a chair: "But ye're scarce walkin' te race the wind, are ye, Sasha Mikhailovich? I saw the way ye limped on in here, a whole lot more worse it seemed than usual! So, let me have a look at that leg."

Greenish-purple bruises and a thick, swollen lump at the ankle joint readily confirm the sprain. "Ye're goin' to have te keep off it, period," Lyubov declares. From the kitchen, Zhenya brings in a thick pack of ice, which Lyubov wraps about my ankle, and I sink back into the cushioned chair, moaning with relief. "Tomorrow, when we go out fer food," she says to Zhenya, "you an' me'll try te hunt him up some crutches."

The wrap of ice soothes the pain deliciously; after some moments, Lyubov eases it away, and with a tender touch, binds up my ankle in a snug bandage. Martova then sets out a soup pot on her kitchen table; for all who are hungry, *borshch* and day-old rye bread are served up in bland, though filling, abundance. Wholly ravenous, Zhenya and I stuff ourselves—and afterward, fraught with exhaustion, I scarce notice as Lyubov darts about, retrieving empty supper dishes. Tiredly, I mumble thanks as she tosses a woolen blanket across my lap, her fingers fastidiously tucking its ends down around within the cushions of the chair.

Tunic collar unfastened and my spectacle earwires gripped up tightly in one hand, my warm ermine coat thrown loosely atop the blanket, I scarce even realize having been asleep until I awaken, a pale hint of dawnlight glimmering through the windows. All about, the floor lies covered in bodies, with scores of children huddled in one beside another, sweet rhyme of their young breath whisking out in oddly tempered, rhythmic unison from beneath scattered rows of pillows and furry blankets. In the kitchen, several adults, crouched over steaming bowls of *kasha*, whisper morntide greetings in friendly low undertones. As I blink and begin rubbing at my eyes, a squeeze of warm fingers settles upon my shoulder. "Look what we squandered up fer ye, Sasha Mikhailovich," Lyubov murmurs, proudly displaying out a pair of mismatched crutches.

"Good heavens," I reply softly, mindful of the sleeping children. "You've already been out?"

"Step-papa!" Zhenya whispers, her face brimming to the hilt with excitement, "the streets are already filling up with people! . . ."

* * *

All morn long, the streets fill with people; as the day wears on, Martova's apartment comes to resemble naught but the busiest wayside rail stationhouse, its three sparse rooms ever afloat with talkative women, whining children—and hordes of men, some clad in coveralls and the grimy dark-brimmed caps of the workers; others sporting staid ties and tailored suit jackets of the poshest business elite. In and out continuously, the mob streams all day from neighboring apartments and from the street outside, and amongst a steady, solid core of intellectual mumblers always huddled down together over the kitchen table, the arguing wages on, unabated, for hours: is this the time, the chance, for the revolutionaries to seize governmental power, or no? The die-hard *Bolsheviki* amongst them negate the import of the street riots with sneers of cynical contempt; the Social Democrats and Pavel Milyukov's centralist Kadets—or Constitutional Democrats, as called in the Duma—call for that same body to assume full legislative and judicial control; Volodya's leftist SRs, the Socialist Revolutionaries, pull one way, then another, first toward the radicals, then toward the moderates, then toward the radicals again, the rise and fall of sharp voices from the various factions lashing about all day long in heated debate past the gurgling of the samovar and bubbling of the soup pots. From the apartment terrace windows, however, the view of the street below proves that whatever might be decided in harried kitchens here or wherever else, the course of events transpiring before us in greater Petrograd ranges far beyond any one person's ability to grasp and entirely above any one political party's sphere of domination: for versts at a stretch, Sadovaya has been transformed into a smothered, swarming sea of humanity, vast platoons of striking workers chanting slogans and waving forth caps, red flags, and tar-painted banners. "Lord help us both, little fellow," I murmur against Vanya's cheek as, in bewilderment, I nestle him up close to my chin and gaze out through the windows yet again. Just below us, the tide in the street parts briefly as another fat munitions lorry draped in red bunting rolls on through, groups of demonstrators shouting cheers after it, the hordes of soldiers crouched on board waving out rough clapboard signs and roaring down to the crowd: "Death to the Huns—down with the hated German war! Death to the monarchy—down with autocracy and all them bloody leeches in the Tsarist government! Death to imperialism—power to the people, we say! *Revolutsiya! Revolutsiya* . . . ."

As afternoon presses forward, Lyubov and Zhenya, unable to resist the excitement, both wave off my frantic pleas and once again wander out together; much to my consternation, for not within an hour, nor then two, do they return. Kept by the sprain from pacing off my anxiety, I end up moping in the easy chair, and start telling Vanya stories. Soon enough, other children become drawn in, and with lilting pauses of emphasis from my flute, I begin rattling off old seasoned favorites: tales about Maryushka, the blessed firebird; Marinka, the frozen sorceress; Ilya, the just bandit; and Sadko, the holy fool. One after another, I top off the endings with outrageous embellishments just as Father used to do so many nights by the warm drawing room fire when I fell asleep upon his knee those long years ago in Novgorod. Once the stories become old, the children start nodding off toward noontide naps, Vanya within my arms, while the remainder of the group begins stretching out before us upon the carpet. "We bless yer soul, Comrade," one young *molodka* with babe in arms says to me gratefully, offering, in Lyubov's absence, a ladling of cabbage soup and hunk of rye bread. "All couped up like this," she goes on, "and the ruckus blarin' away outside, these little mites have been drivin' us mamas half-mad—"

Her lamentation stops short as three young men in porters' uniforms, their faces flushed and adamant, burst in through the front doorway, shouting: "The troops have opened fire! At Kazan Cathedral!"

Everyone in the apartment rushes to the front window terrace, and past a crush of shoulders, I spy the mass of demonstrators down in the street below, their ranks breaking, whole rows of placards swiftly pulling down, while shouts quiet to a sudden pall of confusion. "They too must just be hearin' the news," observes Martova, sadly shaking her head.

Within the next hour, more people stream in and out through the apartment doors, and a barrage of contradictory testaments wages forth unchecked regarding the supposed shootings. In the kitchen, I catch the fringe edge of one story about the Kazan Cathedral events as related by a young porcelain smith: "Not only shootin', but *mutiny*—amongst the Pavlovsky regiment, the Tsar's own troops, by love o' the Saints! Said their orders was to clear the Nevsky—meanin' naught but chasin' out every last one o' the demonstrators. We turned high tail and ran for our skins just as they started mowin' 'em down with carbines: women, children even, I tell you! Next thing you know, same uniforms, *same regiment* marches up the rear, sounds one call, and starts firin' back on their very own!"

Sighing, I hobble back to the window and again stare forlornly down to the street. Below, the strikers have begun reconvening in pocketed groups, some marching off in defiance toward Nevsky; others, away from it. But as far as I can see, still no Zhenya. No Lyubov.

Settled down in the chair again, I cuddle Vanya close, churning through a tortured maze of worried thoughts—until an affable nod catches my attention. Of course, ever since last night, I have been eyeing him: ruddy complexion; wiry, yet muscular build; hair and moustache neatly trimmed in golden-amber blond; warm, generous smile. Ever since last night, he has been eyeing me back with the same lustful, devilish thoughts betrayed in every stolen glance. "You are Khulinov," he says, nodding once again as if confirming my identity to himself. "The poet."

Astonished, I let out a gasp and regard him mutely, my mouth going agape as, laughing, he continues: "Oh, last summer—the Wandering Dog. Notable I thought it. Whenever I like them well enough, I copy off the verses, write down the readers' names. Now, let me see—just how did that one go: *Passions hidden, love forbidden? . . .*"

Flushing, I nod and lower my gaze. But after a moment, I cannot help but again meet his eye in a studied mutuality of appraisal.

"Perhaps, when this uproar has subsided," I suggest, "you might care to join me in a comfy little booth somewhere to guzzle down a couple tankards of *kvas?"*

"Indeed." Returning my smile, he snatches out paper and pencil from his shirt pocket, and scribbles down his name and a telephone exchange number. "You really should publish," he then urges me, warmly extending his hand. "A pity not to, with work of such promise, Comrade Khulinov. I could put in a word with Gorky, if you ever choose. Ofttimes, I do sketches for *Novaya Zhizn*. You know, his magazine."

"Oh! Well, thank you. I'll keep that in mind—" Quickly, I stare from the worn sketch-pad tucked beneath his arm down to his name written on the piece of paper in my hand, murmuring: "—Anatoly Lukyanovich."

My exchange with Anatoly—or Tolya, as he immediately insists I call him—meets premature end as a vast group of women barrels through the front apartment door, all shouting atop their lungs about the shootings on Nevsky. Despite piercing effort with the crutches, I bound upward in a fit of haste once I spot Lyubov—bareheaded, and with her braids half undone—trailing up the rear of the group as one of the last stragglers. Straight into my arms she shoves Zhenya, just as the poor girl bursts into tears. "Oh, as if ye've never seen a little blood before, child!" Lyubov exclaims in exasperation. Deftly, she starts unwinding her kerchief from her bloodied arm, taking the bandage offered by Martova, while bellowing at me: "Jest grazed, I tell ye, hardly a scratch. Lord save us all, ye should o' seen the others! I got past the carbines quick as a bird, was one o' the lucky ones—"

"Lord Jesus God, Lyubov!" I roar out above her. "Have you entirely *lost* your senses? And how could you lead Zhenya into such danger—*by the blessed Saints, woman!* We just heard about shooting over at Kazan Cathed—"

"Shootin' indeed! There, an' at Znamenskaya. I swear, must o' been more than a hundred souls all lyin' about killed or hurt, stiff as bumps on a log—"

"Oh, Step-papa!" Zhenya interrupts breathlessly, grinning past another stream of tears. "It was all *so* impressive!"

"Oh, impressive by the devil's arse!" Lyubov spouts on. "But you was right, Sasha Mikhailovich—it was same exact as you two saw yesterday: Cossacks turnin' with the people against mounted police." Still wrapping the bandage, Lyubov waves off my further panicked upbraidings and bounds off full length across the floor toward the apartment's rearward terrace, there to fling open wide both glass-paned windows, while shouting outward with a shaken fist: "Cossacks turnin' with the *people!* Do ye all hear me down there, united workers o' Petrograd? *Cossacks with the people! Revolutsiya . . . !"*

"Lyubov, for God's sake!" I yell, stumbling after her. "Will you get yourself back in here before someone takes a mind to—"

From the street, a lone rifle shot shatters full blast into the left side panes of the window, a shower of shards and splinters flying out toward us just as I manage to grab Lyubov to safety by the back of her collar. Screams erupt across the apartment, Martova's shrieks blazing out fiercely above the rest: *"Everybody down!"*

Ruthlessly, the volleys continue—one after another, soon enough shattering apart the right side window panes as well. At last, when the shots finally abate, I poke my head upward with care to glimpse in the street below scores of demonstrators wrestling down a lone uniformed rifleman. "Looks as if it's all right, everyone," I call out across the buzz of murmurs and terrified children's whimpers. "They appear to have downed the sniper—it's all right."

"Comrade Khulinova, that was uncalled for!" Martova shrieks at Lyubov—and as everyone else gropes to their feet, the two women hustle each other back into the kitchen, their voices escalating furiously past the clanging of dishes and pans.

Several snickering fellows see to the glass clean-up and repair of Martova's terrace windows—while I fumble upward, grateful for Zhenya's assistance, and head back with her for the cushioned chair. We snuggle in together along with Vanya, his head finding the crook of her arm, hers my shoulder as she begins relating breathless details of hers and her mother's exploits of the morn: "Oh, Step-papa, it was so exciting! Everywhere, gaslamp poles were plastered with posters calling for order and banning meetings, but the demonstrators simply kept tearing the posters down! And a whole group of ironworkers I saw had their own guns! And I even saw this one fellow with a grenade! . . ."

Fortunately, Zhenya soon enough exhausts herself from talking, and I ease down onto the floor beside her feet as she begins dozing off in the chair with Vanya. Lyubov—the dispute in the kitchen apparently, for the moment, settled—then marches back in, and noting the children, exclaims in a whisper: "Lord by the Saints, Sasha Mikhailovich, I think ye saved my life! Jest what caused ye te grab me so quick away from the window? Some kind o' hunch?"

"Not so much that," I whisper back, "as yesterday in Znamenskaya. Not for a moment since have I been able to stop thinking about the potential for violence—there, here. Everywhere."

Shaking her head, Lyubov kneels down beside me, her fingers gingerly picking away my ankle bandage as I fight off a wince. "Still," I tell her, "the pain is much improved over last night. I surmise I took not really so severe a sprain."

"Yes, ye were lucky, looks like," she agrees, taking in sight of the much-lessened swelling. While rewinding the bandage, she begins in curiosity a further inspection of my leg up along the calf's old whitened, withered scars. "Never looked at these all that close before, even them days back in Moscow," she observes. "Ye almost lost this leg once, yes?"

As I relate the story of my unfortunate accident, Lyubov gapes in disbelief. "Your father threw ye out the *window?"* she gasps. "That sweet, charmin' old man?"

"Oh, but you should have heard how I provoked him!" I tell her, laughing, a wealth of old memories flooding back in precious chastisement. But my grin extinguishes to an aching sigh as I murmur, more to myself than to her: "Ofttimes, I fear I shall never see him again. Ever."

With my ankle bandage once again pulled snug, Lyubov nods and settles down cross-legged upon the floor, wrapping her arms up about her knees. This time, her gaze alights behind me, toward the flute case tucked into the chair cushion aside the folds of Zhenya's skirt. "Jest how long ye played that flute o' yers, anyhow, Sasha?" she asks softly, her lips curving upward in a gentle smile.

"Well." Staring downward, I poke my fingers into the fibrous weave of the worn carpet, and shrug. "I'd always had a piccolo," I tell her, "ever since I was six or seven. Been piping out tunes on old wooden recorders ever since I was about four. At nine, I started on a student flute. This particular one Father brought back after a trip to Munich when I was ten. Silver flutes cost dearly then, just as now—he complained endlessly for years to come about paying all of fifteen hundred marks for it. We, uh, had begun having considerable difficulties with the flax harvests that summer, at least so I found out later. The yields, he swore, were so poor, that the seed was scarce worth sowing."

"I take it," Lyubov goes on, "that this here estate o' yer father's was no grand affair sprawlin' out in all directions fer hundreds o' desyatins?"

"No. Even during the heyday of my family long ago, our landed holdings always remained meager in comparison with grants achieved by the court nobility, Lyubov."

Nodding, Lyubov stares downward, and follows my example by beginning to pick idly into the carpet weave herself, drawing circle patterns around and around with the tips of her fingers. "They said," she continues on in a lowered tone, "that Sheremetev was killed by one o' his own kind. A *dvoryanin*, a nobleman."

Swiftly, I look away—but the bright flush crimsoning my ears betrays the truth well enough, and she prods on: "So, that's why ye changed yer name?"

"Lyubov Ivanovna! I would honestly prefer not to discuss—"

"Oh, but it's all right, Sasha," she interrupts, catching hold of my arm. "I hated that schemin', vicious, snake-eyed scoundrel o' the no-good devil's filthy kin!" Eyes narrowing, her lips curling back in a frightfully soured grimace, Lyubov whispers on: "Them years ago in Moscow, things went peaceful enough fer awhile, an' I s'pose fer a long time even after ye left, I still kept lookin' the other way—past everythin'—until that monster, that filthy, low-down beast of a man, decided that he—that he wanted—"

Lyubov's words trail off, and near shaking with rage, she glances behind me toward the dozing Zhenya.

"Oh, dear God," I murmur under my breath.

"Yes," she goes on. "That was why Yevgeny moved us up into our own place here in Petrograd. So, what ye did te that man, Sasha, te that 'Pierre Pavlovsky'—humph! What I'm tryin' te say is, I bless ye fer it. An' will with all o' my heart fer the rest o' my days. An' I bless ye fer what ye been doin' fer my girl ever since, too. Ye see, my little Zhenya never truly had a father, not 'til now."

"Oh, Lyubov," I protest, once again flushing—but unable this time, in spite of myself, to help my grin. "I am no honest father to the girl, hardly!"

"Oh, yes, ye are—an' a good one at that. An' te yer son, also. An'—I thank ye fer worryin' over my own feelins as well, an offerin' te leave if I wished it, ever since that night ye brought Vanya's grandpapa te see him, an' we had our words about it out in the kitchen. But, I don't want no divorce from ye, Sasha Khulinov. I want ye te stay—*dvoryanin* or no—if it's what ye want, also."

"Lyuba," I tell her, squeezing earnest hold of her hand, "I, too—above all else—now want only what is best for the children."

The best prospect for the children, however, does not, from my wife's point of view, include any forthcoming journeys to Oslo, or anywhere beyond. "Lyubov, please!" I beg, groveling down before her and wringing my hands. "I promise we'd not live like common refugees, destitute without any means, nor a roof over our heads! I've retained my British stock investments, and I own two houses in England. One's massive, Lyuba, over a dozen rooms! It's in Cornwall, on the Atlantic coast, set on a bluff by the seashore. Vanya and Zhenya would love it—"

"I cannot leave my homeland, Sasha," Lyubov murmurs with a slow shake of her head, her gaze gone sad before me but yet held solemnly defiant. "Forgive me my life, and my loyalty, but I jest cannot leave certain comrades behind. Not now."

And once again, upon an advent of renewed shouting from the kitchen by several women considering a second foray up to Nevsky, Lyubov begins preparing to venture out—as once again I beg unto futility for restraint: "Lyuba, please! What if it's worse than a grazed arm this time? Lyuba, blast you, listen to me! You said you'd seen people killed out there today—I'll not have Vanya growing up without his mother!" But in the end, she only acquiesces to wearing my ermine coat and packing along my gun and spare case of shells—while I moan after the whole group of women in a gnarled fit of worry as they leave, watching helplessly as, shoulders squared, her kerchiefed head held high and proud, Lyubov marches out with fist-waving, slogan-chanting purpose on the heels of the others.

Three hours torture my thoughts this time until their return—all of them fortunately untouched by, but rife with, stories of the cross fire: "Naught but a bloody war in Znamenskaya! An' soldiers everywhere still firin' back on their own. . . ."

Taking me aside from the others, Lyubov bites her lip, pausing for a long moment before murmuring under her breath: "The dress shop. All the windows smashed; looks like looters took away all they could carry."

"In truth," I tell her with a long sigh, "there was scarce much left for them to take. And I can't say that, since yesterday, I've not been expecting such."

Only long enough to wolf down some supper with us does Lyubov stay. Then, although forbidding Zhenya's tagging along, and at least still packing along my coat and loaded pistol, she marches back out with the enthusiastic, noisy group of protestors once again.

To my relief, our vigil this time proves most brief—within moments, all the women rush back in. "I think they must o' brung in some loyal troops," she tells us. "Folks said barricades was goin' up on the Nevsky—and the shootin', this time, came far too close, even fer me. . . ."

Through Martova's new terrace windows—both, by all appearances, hastily absconded from two very different sources, and tacked up in piecemeal fashion with squeaky ill-fitting hinges—I stare downward. Night's chill of uncertainty hovers its way inward as darkness starts to descend upon Petrograd with a wary hold, draping a numbed lull of silence over the city. Just below us, hordes of gray-uniformed troops loiter about down on Sadovaya, and the air both outside and in begins burning with pungent whiffs of smoke from their torches and scattered bonfires. To all gaslamps this eve, the power has obviously been cut, the only street illumination emitting from the constant eerie flash of a single searchlight mounted, apparently, atop the spire of the Admiralty just to the north on Nevsky. "Them soldiers are settin' in fer the night, all right," Lyubov observes, following my gaze with a worried frown as she eases in beside me. "God save us from what they may decide about doin' te everybody come the morn."

Nodding, I wrap my arm around her, pulling her close to my side as her hand reaches up to my shoulder, squeezing it from behind.

The evening flies by on wings of renewed debates and a flood of fearful rumors: that two amply munitioned garrisons of loyal Tsarist troops have been amassed in secret at the Admiralty; that, called up from the front and from the provinces, even more soldiers will take to the streets by early morn; that bands of extremist right-wing Black Hundreds have been leading the pillage and looting of Nevsky's shops and palaces, intent upon later placing blame upon the people; that everyone found to be involved in the demonstrations will soon enough be arrested, put on trial for treason, and sentenced to hang . . . .

Solace I attempt seeking in a corner away from the others, hunched over my Tarot cards. Interestingly, one reading after another, I pluck down the deck's twelfth card—the Hanged Man—ever a puzzling countenance veiling the lesson of reversal. *He who in all things walks contrary to the ways of the world,* according to the written discourses of my Uncle Ned. Of late, such obscure portents have been chasing my meditations. Twelve is the sum total of the letters of my most intimate name, *Sasha*—at least as spelled out in the English—and lends comfort to my thoughts as I continue, reading after reading, to lay the cards down upon the floor. But scarce before I know it, my old demon Tower readily returns—grim, forbidding path of its sixteenth lesson always landing in dominant position over my prevailing future—leading me to reshuffle the cards beneath another inward flurry of curses. Little difference does any attempt at manipulation make; with a harsh sigh, at last I lay them out once more. And once more my lifelong nemesis remains in hot pursuit, peeking upward in a gleeful spat of triumph, its snarl bared through ready, waiting teeth, famished as a rabid wolf's: *the Tower. Ever and only the Tower* . . . .

"Yer not pullin' that one up each time on purpose, are ye?" Lyubov inquires, surveying the spread with widened eyes as she passes by with Vanya bouncing upon her hip.

"No," I murmur in quick reply, "but I wish I was." Stare drawn toward the pot in the kitchen warming a nightly nursing bottle, I watch my wife and child through a weary daze, whispering to myself: "Then, I would know it not to be fate. . . ."

Upon the approach of midnight, Vanya and Zhenya curl up together in the cushioned chair, and as I stretch out beneath their feet upon the floor, Lyubov—without a word—settles in beside me. Before drawing up the blankets, she pulls my arm in snug about her waist. Too tired to protest, I shut my eyes and nuzzle in with a long sigh to the fragrant scent of her loose-bound braids, basking in her warmth and in a hollow ache forgotten for the longest time. Not since my days of imprisonment in Moscow, when I think she and I both cared for one another more than either of us knew, have I felt such regard for a woman. Again I wonder in awe at the strange bond of friendship and adversity that seems to bind us one to another—anchored, perhaps, in the dusty annals of some lost and forgotten pair of lifetimes intertwined in marriage centuries long ago. But comforting as are such romantic, indolent thoughts, still I cannot sleep—for yet simmering from the whirling torrent of this day's events, the quiet of night proves transitory, illusory, its cloud naught but the briefest quell from apprehension before the apocalypse lying surely dead ahead. For with each passing breath against the comfort of my wife's hair close within the darkness, my fears only continue mounting unbounded—of what, past the anarchy in the streets, the coming morn, and the future, now holds—for us; for the fate of our children . . . .

* * *

Early morntide ushers in renewed rumors of fear, news of police spies combing through the city in search of the 'safe houses,' the *Okhrana* said determined to snuff out every last fugitive of the revolutionaries and bring them—this time along with wives and children—to the jails for arrest. Unable to sleep along with Zhenya, I lean back against the chair beside her knees and grasp up her trembling hand, pressing my fingers unto hers in a feeble attempt at reassurance as, each wide-eyed and silent, we listen to the murmurs and haunted whispers of the others from across the room. "Oh, stop frettin', both o' ye," Lyubov mumbles out, her eyes opening from a dreamy sleep as she glances upward from my lap. "I'm tellin' ye both—git them sorry pouts off yer faces. Well! I don't know—I jest can't help but feel that everythin' is goin' te turn out all right."

At our breakfast of *kasha*, however, Zhenya and I both pick glumly. "They'll not actually hang people—will they, Step-papa?" she whispers to me once out of earshot of her mother.

"Of course not, sweetheart!" Once again I pull my arm around her close—but avoid her gaze, and stare off in nervous silence toward the windows.

Armed once more with my Webley pistol and clad in my ermine coat, Lyubov readies yet again to take to the streets with the other women. "Don't go," I beg her, *"please."* Struggling with effort upon the crutches, I follow behind as, dour-faced, Zhenya escorts her mother to the door. Vanya, despite his sister's bouncings, will not be placated; arms seized outward toward Lyubov, he continues squalling out at the top of his lungs, tears and runny sniffles coursing down his face. "Sasha, I have te do what I have te do," Lyubov insists, pausing with a fond smile to kiss both children as she pulls her gloves onto her hands. "Jest give Vanyushka the bottle I warmed fer him, an' I'm sure he'll be fine."

Rank with anticipation, the noisy, talkative group of adults streams out, leaving behind many other children who require soothing and warmed bottles as well. Zhenya and I find ourselves watching over the whole lot, about fifteen in all left behind in our charge by various rebel mothers and fathers. Only as the late morntide sun begins climbing high do I escape for a few moments from the flute music and the stories to check on the scene in the street outside. Once again Sadovaya lies engulfed across its entire breadth with hordes of shouting, fist-waving demonstrators, whom into their midst have swallowed up all remaining enclaves of soldiers, last eve's oppressively looming force now appearing wholly bent toward fraternization in an atmosphere of merry bantering. "Step-papa, what does it all mean?" Zhenya ventures in a somber tone, fetching me some hot tea as I lean up against the terrace windows.

My answer, confused and only halfheartedly uttered, defers within seconds to the onslaught of shouts and 'hurrahs' that volley through the front entrance of the apartment: "Mutiny! Mutiny in the barracks! The Volinsky, the Preobrazhensky regiments firin' back on their own officers! The core o' the Tsar's troops now standin' with the people! . . ."

"Three whole regiments!" Lyubov gasps, scarce able to contain her excitement, her face flushed as a beet, her voice torn with gleeful breaths as she grasps hold of my arm. "The Volinsky, the Preobrazhensky—an' then the Litovsky Regiment, Praise God in His Glory!—all firin' back on their own officers! Happened early this morn, and then soldiers joined up with the very folks demonstratin' out on the Nevsky and Liteiny, Sasha! Oh, Lord bless! An' some troops even led the way with their own marchin' bands! . . ."

"The Arsenal on Liteiny!" Martova chimes in beside her. "Soldiers everywhere were helpin' the crowds; broke into the Arsenal just an hour past, we heard! Thousands of rifles and revolvers they found; took back all the guns we lost in the raids Saturday night, and then some—"

"Everybody, *look!*" Zhenya calls suddenly from the terrace windows.

To the northeast, a thick column of smoke starts billowing upward, while from our front doorway, a stout, grinning fellow bursts forth through the wall of bumping shoulders, near tripping over his own feet as he yells out in giddy explanation: "It's the court buildings, the jail up on Liteiny—the House o' Detention, I tell ye! A group o' lads in the crowd said they was headed up there next! And now," he roars on, waving high his fist, "onward, everybody! To the palaces!"

"To the palaces!" everyone else echoes—all once again streaming out behind. "Death to the Romanov monarchy and its hated German war! Death to the *dvoryanye!* Onward, to the palaces! *Revolutsiya . . . !"*

All afternoon, intermittent sputters of rifle fire tear above the shouting on Sadovaya, and I watch through the windows as more columns of smoke bloom upward one by one from various palaces and office buildings across the city. And all afternoon, I continue murmuring in silence a grateful inward prayer: *Thank God, Papa! That we got you out in time . . . .*

Toward four o'clock, Tolya wanders in, and shows me some of his sketches. "It's the District Court Building, all right, and the big

House of Detention up on Liteiny Prospekt," he says, indicating the outlines of several structures drowning through his drawings of the flames. "I'd been perched at a window on that corner there ever since it started up late this morn; the crowds wouldn't even let through the firehoses. Was all still burning away like a bloody inferno twenty minutes ago when I left. And up the street, on the Aleksandrovsky Bridge, you could see groups of loyal troops on the Vyborg side trying to keep back the rebels, but without much luck. Last I heard, we'd broken across, and Finlandsky Station's now supposed to be caught firm in the hands of the revolutionaries. . . ."

On his way back out, Tolya urges me with him into the tiny water closet alcove sandwiched behind the kitchen—where we share a cigarette, and then steal a kiss. "Soon enough, my new friend," he whispers with a husky laugh, "you and I shall sneak away from this rampant foolishness to that comfy little tavern booth and our shared tankards of *kvas.*"

As he leaves, I stare after him with a lustful sigh, noting the boyish blondness of his hair, the nimble cockiness of his gait, the supple outline of his buttocks molded through the seat of his trousers . . . Zhenya then stumbling in and yelling for me twice—loudly—before even thwarting my attention.

Once sunset finally begins glimmering upon the horizon, Lyubov returns with the others at last, once again flushed unto overflowing with exuberance, and this time proudly brandishing a Beretta carbine. "Thousands o' troops fer as far as the eye can see!" she announces, waving out the rifle barrel with both fists arched high in triumph over her head. "We saw 'em all surroundin' the Tauride palace, swearin' they was with *the people!* Folks said they was waitin' fer arrival o' the Duma!"

Convincing her to relinquish the rifle takes some doing, but finally I extract it from her grip just as Martova elbows toward us, her face aglow with fresh news. "Lyubov Ivanovna!" she cries with an eager smile, "did you hear?"

Stuttering for reply, Lyubov merely grins back, nodding past an abrupt rush of tears.

"Lyuba!" I cry. "What is it?"

"Happiness!" she chokes out joyfully. "The jails—and Kresty Prison, too, we heard—all been stormed to every last filthy, leechin' cell by soldiers and the demonstrators! Which means our comrades will soon be released."

"So, that means Volodya and Ivanovich—"

"Should be on their way here, yes. They know Martova's is first safe house past our apartment."

All gaiety aside, supper for everyone proves a rather meager affair, our much-thinned ladlings of *borshch* and cabbage *shchi* topped off with dried crusts of old rye bread. As darkness takes fast hold, more revolutionary stragglers wander in from their adventures of the day, some begging for food, others sporting ripped-up shreds of Tsarist tricolor flags and painted wooden emblems of Imperial double-headed eagles broken off from the facades of public buildings. The dinner mood livens up noisily upon the sight of such battle trophies, especially when several stout fellows heave in upon their shoulders six whole crates full of stolen vodka. Instantly, the bottles start making rounds across the room. News then breaks of the speech given by the War Minister, Aleksandr Kerensky, bare hours earlier at the reconvening of the Duma: "That, fer good o' the people, the Tsar must be forced from the throne—*forced from the throne*, Kerensky said, mind ye!—an' by the bombs o' revolutionary terrorists, if need be! The Tsar from the throne at the biddin' o' no less than one o' the Duma ministers, by God! By will of the people, fer the good o' the people—*the Tsar from the throne!*" And once again a ready chorus peals upward, echoed by toasts, the clinking of glasses, and more boisterous roars of: *"Revolutsiya!"*

Elated, Lyubov keeps waving out her fists and shouting along with the others; Zhenya, dazed and caught up in the excitement, shouts along also; Vanya, warm and content within his mother's lap, gurgles out: "Relusa!" after everyone and claps together his hands. From a crate shoved in beside me upon the floor, I fetch out another bottle of vodka, uncap it, and begin gulping in a frenzy, the burn cool and stinging deliciously down my throat. And I smile and nod agreeably along to the bellows of defiance and spiels of revolutionary chants—although in furtive pauses, I continue glancing down toward the Sekovsky family ring still caught snug about my middle right finger. And the stark pain of loss continues searing through my heart with each renewed call to rebellion that continues assaulting my ears, a cold knot of torment twisting in my bowels with each tattered emblem of the Tsarist order that every next straggler troops viciously in. Everything—every hope, ideal, attainment of Imperial honor, status, and pride that my father—that *all* of my forefathers—ever strived after, the mobs are now burning up and tearing to shreds. . . .

As triumphant singing starts up to the tunes of the *Marseillaise*, to *Dubinushka*, and to the classic revolutionary 'heave-ho' refrain from the *Song of the Volga Boatmen*, throngs of weary, dirtied men clad in tattered prison garb begin wandering through the open apartment doors. Shrieks burst forth from the women and dozens of joyful reunions immediately ensue, people throwing their arms about one another, kissing and dancing with loved ones and children. Soon enough, Volodya saunters on in, and I catch him eyeing me, but turn my attention straight away back to my vodka bottle, quickly downing another fierce gulp. Perhaps with justifiable reason, since my outburst near unto a week ago at Finlandsky Station, my old sometime-friend, sometime-foe has avoided me like the plague, sleeping either away from home, or on the sofa in Lyubov's parlor. But still, as if for old time's sake, he at last ambles over; meets my nod and then slouches back against the wall, his thumbs caught disdainfully in his trouser pockets, his grin teasing, yet derisive. "And don't you look the worse for wear, twinkle-toes," he observes, surveying with a laugh and a shake of his head the crutches and bandage wrapped about my ankle.

"Humph! And I daresay, you could use a shave," I quip back with a wry smile, tossing him up a bottle of vodka.

Still nestling Vanya, Lyubov lets out a delighted howl and throws her free arm up around Yevgeny. "Akkh, woman—ye're smotherin' me clear te my death!" he bellows, laughing and playfully attempting to shove her away, an uncapped vodka bottle already caught tightly in his grip. "Akkh, Missy—cut that out! Humph! Ha! An' how ye doin' down there, Mikhailovich?" he says to me, nodding downward with an amicable grin. As I nod back, he waves up his bottle and shouts out: "A toast, everybody! Let's give our good workin' selves another hootin' toast in celebration!"

"Revolutsiya!" Volodya calls out to everyone in a booming voice, his bottle brandished with a high, swinging flourish—and the whole room joins in once more to the chime of bottles, the clinking of glasses.

Lyubov, however, stops short with her half-filled goblet held up in midair as a second group of capless, smudge-faced men tramples through the front doorway. Their leader, a dark-haired fellow endowed with a thick, swarthy face, stands near head and shoulders taller than all the rest. Upon first glance of him, I struggle at a loss with the strangest pang of recognition; discard my first impression only to—upon a spare glimpse of Zhenya—sharply catch in my breath.

"Lyuba," the man cries hoarsely, his arms outstretched.

Her goblet spinning to the carpet, near straight into my face Lyubov shoves Vanya. Chiding her, I nestle him down into my grasp to see her literally fly across the room and into the swarthy man's embrace. Desperately, tenderly, he slides his arms up her back, his lips pressing through a rush of tears unto her throat, chin, and ears, his arms rocking her gently back and forth as if about the most wondrous treasure in all the world. Their kiss is primordial, mesmerizing—and the wild singing trails off as everyone in the room quiets to watch it, all heads bowing, not in shame nor embarrassment, but in hushed pauses of respect—for here, undeniable for every eye to see, is a great love, a bond beyond all others spanning glory in time and space, a quest of two hearts lasting through centuries, lifetimes—lifetime after lifetime. Along with the others, I cannot help but stare in awe. Scarce times across the riddle of life, one happens to chance upon such fortunate pairs—true star-crossed, soul-mated lovers sharing more depth in a single glance, exchanging more physical passion in one feathery, winsome touch than other couples not so blessed can hope to mutually beckon over the course of months, or even years—for it is a holy, sacred thing, this incomparable mating of two souls. 'Into some incarnations,' my Uncle Ned would say, 'such sacred pairs venture ofttimes separate and alone unto tests for fostering individual growth. Then, during other lifetimes, the blessed two join together once again in holy unison upon their mutual destiny, and it is beauteous, wondrous, my boy—an astounding, mystical thing, this shared pinnacle of joy, this bonding between such a sacred duo.' Of my father, it was—and Melissa—that my Uncle Ned was, at the time, speaking.

But of course, my uncle's unspoken assumption remained steadfast: that such lucky pairs always and only mate male to female. Which leaves pariahs like me marooned somewhere out on the interstellar gangplank of obscurity—and again I bemoan the gall of those who, judging so harshly, try so little to understand. Just as I bemoan once more the fate of myself and my own one true and only beloved—he, that ever-cherished song on a bow strung now only to the beleaguered dust of memory from the sad countenance of his last stand upon some godforsaken battlefield in Prussia. Now Nikolai Zhelanov finds form's embraces only within the quiet lines of desperation written nightly in my poems, taking true love's flight for himself only within the snowy sleigh rides of my dreams.

Sighing with an envy only the poet can know, I tear my eyes away from the sight of Lyubov's dramatic reunion and murmur to Zhenya: "This man is your father?"

Gaze remaining locked upon the still-embracing twosome, Zhenya hisses out vehemently: "Humph! That man has never been any father to me."

Casting a frown at her, again I turn my attention back to Lyubov and the tall, swarthy man—and with a shock, the memory hits: Moscow, 1907—the emerald palace—my last walk through its whore-lined, marbled hallways toward the room of the awaiting auction, my way there led by the man who had last taken me from the room with Lyubov, his glower sarcastic as, upon my cheek, she had planted an affectionate goodbye kiss. That same man with the swarthy face, dark curly hair, and wiry pocketed pince-nez began, just as we reached the doorway, whispering about his misgivings of conscience—and about revolution . . . .

Several dour-faced women in ragged skirts follow in upon the heels of the men, and Zhenya points to one of the last to venture beyond the doorway—a severe, purse-lipped matron with hair caught back in a tight black chignon, her expression devoid of any hint of emotion as she joins everyone in watching the continued display of passion between the embracing couple. "Aunt Olga," Zhenya informs me with a sneer. "His wife. You see, Grigor Fokimovich is my mother's uncle," she whispers on, still glaring with disgust across the room at her parents. "The man is my mother's father's own younger brother—and according to his fancy, I am not supposed to have happened. As far as he cares, I do not even exist."

When I glance back at them again, it is straight to me that I find the man staring—questioningly, his eyes darting between myself, Vanya, and Lyubov—who, shaking her head, gasps out in explanation: "Yes, Grishka, the child is mine, and yes, he—" Pausing, only by the barest nod does she defer to my direction, murmuring on: "—yes, he is the father. But it changes none at all between us, Grishenka—I promise ye with all my heart!"

Warily, I set my vodka bottle down upon the floor, fully expecting some backlash of jealous fury—but Grigor Fokimovich only tenderly wraps Lyubov once more within his arms, murmuring: "Yes, of course—naught will be ever changed between you and I, my dearest love."

After another kiss, he at last pulls away, although yet clinging fast onto her hand as he exclaims to the roomful of onlookers: "Comrades! This eve, the Duma has reconvened in defiance, after strictest orders of dissolution from the Tsar!" Upon a chorus of cheers, he continues on: "At the behest of rebel soldiers, the Tauride palace—the entire seat of the Imperial government—now lies in revolutionary hands! As of this hour, by majority vote of the workers, the Petrograd Soviet of 1905 is hereby fully reinstituted! All power to the Soviets!" he shouts, waving high his fist.

"All power to the Soviets!" the crowd shouts back, more toasts and cheers roaring forth again upon chants of: *"Revolutsiya!"*

Turning back to Lyubov, Grigor's eyes again melt toward her in reverent, loving regard, and he grasps up each of her hands, enfolding them within his own, his words bounding joyfully outward—to her, to everyone: "We have taken over the telegraph lines, and now have custody of the railway stations, the jails, the printing presses; we are yet at this very moment gaining over all remaining strongholds of Imperial power! This night, the people surge yet untamed and wildly chanting through the streets, more ranks of soldiers breaking and joining with them even as I speak! Give heart, comrades—there will be no more slaving to the German war, no more standing in the bread lines, no more bending beneath oppression's cruel whip, no more groveling to favors for the rich and privileges granted only the *dvoryanye!* Tonight," he thunders on with a generous sweep of his hand, "talk is of naught but the Tsar's impending abdication! Which is everything we have hoped for through these many long banishments to exile, sentences unto imprisonment, and condemnations to death; this has been our ultimate common goal over these many wretched years!" At last bowing down low before Lyubov, Grigor kisses her hands and once more briefly holds her gaze before triumphantly throwing back his head to gasp out—as if still hardly able to believe his own voice: "My God, Lyuba! *It's the Revolution! . . ."*

CHAPTER EIGHT

Revolution: This Time It's War

For near unto a thousand years, we have been tempting fate with revolution. Nay, it has been even more than a thousand years—for what is beginning, origin, genesis; what is the apex of desire, the quickening of seed, the agony of birth, but revolution? In the year A.D. 862, the tribes called *Rus*—the fair-headed, red-headed ones from beyond Finland's icy gulf—scattered their way southward through the marshy taiga forest lands, and bare north of a lake called Ilmen, their chieftain, Ryurik, settled and began his rule. This—the founding of a dynasty, the forging of a nation, the fashioning of destiny for centuries to come upon the heels of some tired old wanderer's long-forgotten dream—was our dawning essence, our first Russian revolution. By the following century, Ryurik's *Rus* had driven southward to the plains of Kiev, and in 988, Prince Vladimir ordered baptism for all, both high- and low-born, into Byzantine Christianity. Enamored, however, by their rituals, incited by their pagan *volkhvi* priests, the Slavic peasant folk clung tenaciously to their ancestor worship and old mythic ways, only the lull of ensuing centuries yielding their conversion unto Eastern Orthodoxy. The next revolution occurred three hundred years later upon siege from three separate antagonistic sides: the Teutonic Knights to the west, the Golden Mongol Hordes to the east, and the savage Swedes to the north. Aleksandr, Prince of Novgorod—in the battles for which he was forever after hailed as the Great Nevsky and later canonized a Saint—fought off all gallantly in the name of free will and democracy. Yes, free will and democracy once existed in Russia: in the feudal principalities of Novgorod, in old Vyatka, and in proud Pskov, self-rule once existed; in the meager, barren hinterland of the northern *Rus*, a world founded upon elected government once thrived. Beneath the strict tow of our headstrong people, local princes faced the threat of expulsion upon any dire deeds, answering always to the councils of the *veche*, or town assemblies, which stood freely elected one vote to each head centuries before the Reformation, centuries before the Enlightenment, centuries before the American colonists thought to lay down such grand principles of self-governing in their own fledgling constitution. For this privilege, the fierce, independent peoples of the northern taiga lands would pay their price in blood and revolution against further sieges from Lithuanians, Swedes, and other warring Slavs; against further threat of annihilation from heathen hordes of slant-eyed Mongols; and finally, against the encroaching rise of what would later become their most feared enemy of all: Muscovy, dreaded harbinger of doom looming up across the horizon from the south-to-the-southeast.

In 1328, upon his coronation as Grand Prince, Muscovy's Ivan Kalita brazenly stole away the seat of the Orthodox Patriarch, moving it westward from the holy city of Vladimir. A century later, his great-grandson, Ivan the Third—*veliki*, the Great, they call him—declared himself 'Tsar and Autocrat' over all the Russian lands. In 1472, this Third Ivan conquered Novgorod, carting off the *veche* bell, and exiling the plucky Marfa Boretskaya—widow of the town's mayor and herself acting as such—unto a nunnery. Soon thereafter, the Tsar abolished the office of *Tysyatsky*—elected commander of the town regiment. By 1494, the city's depot for the Hanseatic League was permanently closed down, ending five hundred years of free trade, free influx of Western thought, and cherished independence. Over the next century, Novgorod fought back with tempered disgruntles of revolution—only to finally be near-fatally crushed in the awful terror of 1570 carried out by the drunken, bullying *oprichniki* of another Ivan—the Fourth Ivan, known to history as Awesome, the Formidable, the Terrible One. That year, sixty thousand of our people he vengefully condemned to torture and ruthless slaughter—three quarters of the population of the province.

But in the heart of the downtrodden—of Novgorod, of Pskov, of the growing rebellious Volga lands in the southern part of the Ukraine—revolution lived on, culminating, most rightfully, in the extinction of Ivan's dynasty. In 1598, Boris Godunov became Tsar upon commencement of the 'Time of Troubles.' Poles occupied Muscovy, burned it to the ground, murdered Godunov, and set up a series of 'pretenders' upon the throne—only to be forced back by the determined guile of the people. Two people, in particular: one, a nobleman called Pozharsky; the other, a hapless butcher named Kuzma Minin—who together almost single-handedly raised up a mob and wrested the city back into Russian hands. In 1613, Mikhail Romanov was crowned Tsar in magnificent

Russian triumph. To the south, however—against whomever might rule—swept further spirit of revolution. First, in Tula, Ivan Bolotnikov inspired uprisings of bondsmen against their masters, and in his wake followed the growing legend of the fiery and fierce Don Cossack horsemen, brawny bands of free and independent thinkers escaped from shackles of serfdom in the north—who like the Novgorodians, elected their own leaders. In the flamboyant, poetic guise of Stenka Razin, the Cossacks rallied about a common standard-bearer after decades of Volga River unrest, welcoming him two hundred thousand peasants and soldiers strong when he marched victoriously into Simbirsk in 1671. Against the greater strength of Muscovy, the cause was sorely lost—but before the Tsar's troops caught and quartered him alive, Stenka struck a chord deep in his countrymen's souls with the romance and glory of revolution. Songs of his daring would live on through further exploits of other Cossack rebels: Kondraty Bulavin in 1708, during the rule of the Great Peter; Yemelyan Pugachev in 1773, during the reign of the haughty Catherine the Second—and fifty-two years later, toward the end of 1825, following the death of Tsar Aleksandr the First, simmers of discontent had even spread upward to the sacred echelons of the nobility itself, the long-suppressed ideals of free thought and Western liberalism infiltrating into restless ranks of Russian officers following their retreat from Europe during the Napoleonic Wars. *Dekabristy*—the Decembrists—the new revolutionaries came to be called. The *coup* failed miserably, its leaders caught and condemned unto execution; the more lucky of the group wandered their way into Siberian exile—which further fanned the flames of revolution. Tsar Nikolai the First brutally tightened the Imperial vise, only to have it loosed again upon his death by his own son, Aleksandr the Second, the Great Tsar Liberator—who in 1861 freed all serfs at last from their eternal, silent bondage to the land. Reform, however, came too little too late to satisfy grumblings of the ne'er-do-wells in the countryside and shouts of the radical Populist upstarts in the cities. In the 1870s, peasant riots finally broke out openly, and arson fires seared in pockets of protest from St. Petersburg to scores of towns lined up and down the Volga. Finally, through the auspices of a small band brandishing the name *Narodnaya Volya*—the People's Will—the Tsar met due and just death for every last Tsar before him upon the explosion of a terrorist's bomb along Petersburg's Griboyedov Canal quay in 1881.

In retaliation, Aleksandr the Third, and subsequently, his son, Nikolai the Second, swore to quash forever the threatening fire of revolution. Yet, in 1905, it was not only the officers, not only the peasants, but all classes of people who rose up in Bloody Sunday defiance—although they did so reverently, timidly, marching with demands for constitutional rights behind robes of an Orthodox priest in respectful religious procession toward the Winter Palace in St. Petersburg—there to be mown down with rifle fire and silenced with the butts of guns. A powerless Duma was offered, but another twelve years had obviously taught the government little, and forged over to the people, everything—for one year ago, in the spring of 1917, the tide rose up again—unquenchable, insurmountable, this time. The city became the people's pride, at last; the revolution spoke the people's will, at last; the Tsar's abdication belonged to every ecstatic soul who rose up and cheered in shivers upon the news! But—someone had to govern. Who? Since then, hopeful names have proliferated—Lvov, Kornilov, Kerensky; months passed by, but not one took for himself firm hold. The leftists ventured even farther toward the left; the rightists ventured even farther toward the right; the war did not end and bread lines only grew longer; the Duma never agreed inside or outside on anything and everything; the Soviets gained day by day and man by man in radical Bolshevik strength—and that brief glimmering light, that faint hope for democratic rule beckoning once again in Russia's starry eyes after these many violent, chaotic centuries—that light faded away forever four months ago. Because four months ago, Vladimir Ilyich Ulyanov—or Lenin, as the swine prefers to call himself—wrenched apart the people's revolution and twisted it into his own.

"Madness, I tell you, naught but sheer insanity!" shouts Volodya, his fist waved high at Grigor Fokimovich, his teeth clenched, the rise of rage flushing into his cheeks. "They are moving the seat of the government to *Moscow?* Just like that?"

"Comrade Rykazian!" Grigor bellows back, the red armband tied about his coat sleeve flashing in a satiny glow beneath the bare bulb light of the overhead lamp, "might I remind you—again—that your remarks could be construed as highly counter-revolutionary!"

"Counter-revolutionary, the fuck . . . !"

Volodya Rykazian: forever an upstart and a devil. *God bless your soul, Volodya.* He and I may no longer share a bed, but over these past few months, we have indeed reached a much closer affinity of political opinion. Contrary to my suspicions, he never did join the *Bolsheviki*—and it was he who patiently pointed out to me last summer, after much discussion, that naught but senseless Tsarist repression caused my father's sentence to thirty miserable years of exile in a Siberian prison. A day later, on a dare, Volodya escorted me through the Putilov Ironworks, and past row after row of shanties in the Vyborg workers' slums, revealing the squalor, the filth in which such people must work and live. *From each according to his ability, to each according to his need . . .* in the end, I could do naught but acquiesce, agreeing with him—and with Lenin, I suppose—on the equity of this one socialist principle. To make good my word, I offered, after considerable debate, to join not Volodya's left-wing SRs, the Socialist Revolutionaries, but Pavel Milyukov's party of revolutionary, although still democratically-minded, Kadets.

That was mere hours before Lenin declared the Kadet party a subversive 'tool of the bourgeoisie,' its leaders 'enemies of the people' subject to arrest and trial before a Bolshevik revolutionary tribunal.

"Does Lenin care not a whit for the fate of Petrograd's citizens?" Volodya roars on to Grigor—and additionally to Lyubov, her sleeve also sporting a shiny red armband—for into the fracas she too has joined aside the protective arm of her lover and uncle. "Do you hear me, Mrenitsev?" Volodya shouts out at the top of his lungs. "This so-called 'peace treaty' Trotsky has rigged up with Germany is not worth the rag it's printed on, you blind, heel lickin' fool! Rumor has it the Kaiser's troops are now near upon Petrograd's western gates! What good for any of us does Lenin think he can bring by tuckin' his tail between his legs and haulin' the government off to Moscow?"

"Vladimir Denisovich!" Lyubov barks back at him. "Quiet yerself before ye frighten the children. We all believe Comrade Lenin is doin' the best he can te protect Red Petrograd."

"The only thing your 'Comrade Lenin' has done for Red Petrograd is fill the streets with blood! With Red terror!"

"Enough, I am telling you!" Grigor roars out above them both. *"Enough!"*

Out of breath, the three of them pause, glancing in unison over toward my corner sanctuary at the table—where I crouch forward in a chair, huddled up in my coat. My felt one—for we are all bundled up, past cold, aching shivers, in our coats and scarves and fur hats. To the children for their bed I have long ago given over the ermine, and would not take it back even could I wear it safely in the streets without Red Guards hacking me down in a test for survival as if they were slaughtering a dog for his skin. In the same way, they have murdered near every other last rich or formerly well-to-do fool unfortunate enough to have been left stranded behind in this godforsaken city under this godforsaken 'dictatorship of the proletariat.'

At the window, the gray wind whips up, slashing across the panes. Today is March 11, 1918—a cold, silvery, silent March in Petrograd, where there is no wood to be split for fires, no coal to be found for furnaces. Nor is there much bread—nor flour, even—to be bought in most of the shops. We have survived only by slowly hawking away on the black market, ruble by contraband Tsarist ruble, my dwindling stash from my father's inheritance hidden away in the wardrobe-cupboard. Quick, cunning hold it was that Lenin gained over the Workers' Soviets last autumn—by promising his followers everything: prosperity, an end to the war. The problem was, all the poor gullible fools—the hot-headed peasants and illiterate foot soldiers serving in the lower ranks of the Army—listened. They listened to Lenin without studying his writings; they joined the party of the *Bolsheviki* while scarce knowing what Bolshevism truly means. An end to the war was their utmost demand—but none ever bothered to look beyond the horizon toward what, after an end to the war, might come.

In silent rebuke, Mother Wind continues to sternly whip her hand at us against the panes of the window. Staring back at Grigor and Lyubov and Volodya, I study each of them in critical turn, and then in like silence, grasp up my vodka bottle and slosh down another fiery, mindless gulp.

"He's right, ye know."

Now, it is Yevgeny who speaks—for he has ventured into the squabble, Bolshevism coming apart at the seams right here in the wrecked parlor of our old Neva apartment. Defiantly, he moves in against his sister and his uncle, standing firm to his convictions beside Volodya.

In response, Lyubov's hysterical shriek pierces through the air: "Ivanovich, my God! Ye harebrained fool—ye want te bring a *Cheka* watch down over this house, over my children?"

The *Cheka. The All-Russian Extraordinary Commission for the Struggle against Counter-Revolution and Sabotage.* Created by Lenin last December. Yes, Lenin—that insipid, whining little man. Such courage he has, this Lenin of theirs, cheering on wars and phantom revolutionary undertakings during the Tsarist years from his neutral comfort of Swiss exile. Such fortitude he possesses, this legendary Lenin, burying himself away in some Finnish marsh—fishing—while Leon Trotsky spearheaded the disorganized, rabble-rousing, so-called *coup* that brought the *Bolsheviki* into power last November. And now, to further insulate himself from his revered, faithful proletariat, the almighty Lenin has created the *Cheka*—naught but the very same as the Tsarist *Okhrana* spelled with different initials, its motives shrouded behind hypocritical assurances. All couched in tepid rhetoric.

Once more Volodya and Yevgeny, Grigor and Lyubov pause in their arguing to cast stares in my direction, almost as if I had taken the trouble to verbally utter such blasphemies. So again—disdainfully—I shrug, glaring at them all: *blast it, I told you so! I told you all so* . . . and I heave my bottle up, gulping more vodka down.

And again, as if to chide us, brisk chill-wind whips her hand in stiff rebuke at the window.

Storming across the room, Volodya waves out a tattered copy of the now-outlawed *Peasant Izvestiya*, the leftist SR newspaper. "Even the Tsars," he begins, attempting to lower his voice down to an evenly reasonable tone, "never had such nerve as to shut down a newspaper permanently! Not without allowin' it press under a differin' name and editor the next day, or in another week or two at the most!" Shouting to the doorway with full intent, he bellows on: "Oh, the Saints take it—I don't care *who* hears! Let your bloody *Cheka* agents come and arrest me then, by God! Centuries of oppression have we toppled over, and this is s'posed to be our revolution, with a government by and for the people! Yet, now—again—a man dares not speak his mind even in his own home! And might I remind you that your revered Vladimir Ilyich Ulyanov was the first to call for freedom of the press, but these days, any paper, any magazine the man takes offense at, he promptly shuts down—just like he shut down the Constituent Assembly in January!"

Oh, yes, indeed. *How greatly I respect you, Rykazian, you old Armenian guttersnipe whoremonger, my old friend—yes,* do *bring it up:* the Constituent Assembly. Russia's first congress of freely elected, truly democratic leaders since the time of the ancient *veches* in Novgorod, in Pskov, in old Vyatka. On January fifth, the long-awaited Constituent Assembly finally convened. Volodya's Chernov spoke with eloquence for the SRs; Skobelev, at length for the Mensheviks. Along with many others—but the following day, Lenin turned the Assembly on its newborn heel and promptly shut it down as if he was doing naught but swatting away an irritating fly—first by issuing a formal government decree condemning as counter-revolutionary any attempt by any person or body of persons at exercise of state power; then—on the strength of his muscle-flexing, carbine wielding Red Guards, and backed up by an order of the Soviet of People's Commissars—by merely locking every last one of the Assembly delegates out of the Tauride Palace. And since then, terror; since even before then, terror: on New Year's Eve an attempt was made on Lenin's life. Scores of arrests followed. The jails stormed in such triumph bare unto a year ago have been filling up again with 'comrades in arms' ever since.

"I am warning you both," Grigor hollers at Yevgeny and Volodya, "to come back to your senses! The Government of the Soviet of Workers, Peasants, and Soldiers' Deputies will not tolerate—"

"Oh, bullcrap!" Volodya shouts back as Lyubov lets out an incredulous gasp.

The torrential shouting I bring to an abrupt halt by slamming my empty vodka bottle down onto the table, the hollow echo of glass-against-wood reverberations splitting across the air. Over the past few weeks, at least vodka we have been made ample supply of; I suspect Lenin's intention to subjugate the proletariat purely through a regimen of drunkenness. Casually, I uncork another bottle and stare down at the week-old Moscow newspaper, *Znamya Truda*, lying in prominent position amidst the clutter of empty bottles and other newspapers littered upon the table. Volodya, Yevgeny, Grigor, Lyubov—and now Zhenya and Olga, from the doorway to my old bedroom where, with Vanya, they have both been attempting to snatch some sleep—all follow my gaze. Because this coveted copy of *Znamya Truda* straight from Moscow contains, in full rendition, the lines of Aleksandr Blok's poem, *The Twelve*. Although *The Twelve* can scarce be called a simple poem. Oh, no—*The Twelve* is a *sensation:* about twelve Red Guards looting, raping, killing, destroying—twelve Red Guards who fancy themselves akin to the Twelve Apostles with vengeful, bleeding Christ at their head, marching their way through the streets of Red Petrograd toward socialist victory via the glory of revolution. Fitting, somehow, that such stark, idealistic images should be scratched out by some symbolist Bolshevik sympathizer tucked safely away in a tavernhouse in Moscow. *Damn Blok his stupidity, his guile; damn him as both a genius and a fool.* Pointedly, I raise up my vodka bottle once again in a toast of mockery; catch Lyubov's, then Grigor's and Olga's, then Volodya's eyes—and rasp out under my breath: "All Power to the Constituent Assembly . . . ."

A direct quote, it is—from the sixteenth line of Blok's poem. And my sarcasm is lost on no one.

"Stop it, Sasha," Lyubov demands, scurrying across the room with her hand muffled to her mouth in embarrassment. Without success, she attempts to wrest the sloshing vodka bottle from my grip.

"Blasted wallowing poets," Grigor mutters from behind her, casting me a dubious, disgust-filled glance.

"Aww, let him drink himself to death, if that's what he chooses!" Volodya rages after them both. "The way the whole world's goin' off its filthy. stinkin' end, he might just be the wisest amongst us all."

And then, as if a switch had been tripped, the shouting furor starts up once again between the whole lot of them—with Olga joining into the fray this time—over politics.

From the table, I pick up my larger Webley pistol, break it open and load three fresh shells into the empty cartridge slots in the chamber. Snapping the gun shut, I slip it into my pocket and grasp up my cane, while my coat collar and old woolen scarf I draw up close in double folds about my neck.

"Where are you goin'?" Lyubov darts out from beneath Grigor's arm and runs to the front doorway, cutting off my path.

"What do you care?"

Her arm seizes forward, her eyes holding mine fast and plaintively, and her voice, beginning with an insistent whisper, raises upward with each word to countermand the shouting in the background of Olga, Volodya, Yevgeny, and Grigor. "Ye watch out fer snipers," she implores me, squeezing stiffened, chilblained fingers into my hand. "An' fer them murderin' cutthroats in the alleys."

"Uh-huh."

Elbowing past her, I slam shut the door behind and limp down the steps to the street entrance, my thumb resting ready on the hammer of the gun in my pocket. Little does it matter whether I told her; she knows where I always go when they all start ranting on at one another each and every eve unto no blessed end. Like the overbearing, wise mother that she is to the children—and to me—Lyubov knows fully well my chosen avenue of escape when the truth becomes too unbearable, the sadness too impenetrable—when vodka's grand illusion tempts so utterly amidst night's bitterness fraught cold with despair. My wife knows fully well that, short of a Red Guard scuffle for robbery or murder of me on my way there, I am going to where I always go.

Tolya's.

* * *

"The name is Tolya!" he hisses out at me with a furious gasp. "Tolya! *Anatoly!* Not *Nikolai!"*

"I—I know, I know! F-Forgive me—I am sorry! . . ."

I draw the sheet up about my chest, shivering naked in the cold; watch as he bounds out of bed, hurriedly pulling on his underdrawers, trousers, flannel shirt, and bulky overhead sweater, then his coat and wrap of woolen scarves. After a moment, I do the same, making awkward, fumbling work against the many chips in my buttons. Barely do I plunge my arms down into my coat sleeves before he pounces from behind, whirling me about roughly to face him, his voice a raging whisper as he attempts to thwart any eavesdropping by his mother and widowed sister, both hopefully still asleep in the next room. "B-By damn you, Sasha!" Both his fists spring for my collar.

"Tolya! Stop—"

"Who is he? *Who is he?"*

"Tolya, is *not* what you think!"

"Oh, yes, it bloody well is!" he roars. "You've been seeing another man behind my back!"

"No, I have not!"

At last he stops shaking me and lets loose his hold. But the assault continues in rude bombardment from his anguished hazel eyes—his gaze piercing, harrowing, utterly devastated. "Then why," he rasps out softly, a taut finger of accusation slashing out across the air to point me down, "did you whisper out his name? And not for the first time, Sasha!"

"Tolya, I—"

"So—has this whole past year been for naught between us? I tell you, I cannot bear your calling me by another man's name! *I simply cannot bear it!"*

I swallow hard, choking back tears, and watch him shuffle toward the window with a listless, weary tread, where he stares blankly outward into the blackened night, his chin sinking to his chest, lanky blond hairs peeking up about the folds of his woolen neckscarf. "I thought this was different," he whispers without looking toward me as I move in cautiously aside him. "I thought you cared—"

"Tolya! I *do* care. . . ."

Indeed, that is the whole point. This *is* different—more so than anything I have ever known; this is special, wondrous . . . this is not the same as some Friday night tryst in a bathhouse or tavern water closet with another obscured face to be cast off blindly after the thrill of the moment, never to be met again. Tolya is a man of enormous sensitivity and feeling—an artist of the heart as much as through any pencil or pen, a poet through images as much as I am through words—a fellow, kindred spirit-wanderer, who not only laughs at my jokes and soothes away my cares, but who possesses an ear for music as I share an eye for color, who adores Tchaikovsky the same way I revere Van Gogh . . . and this whole past year, he has been my heart, my joy, the basking gaiety of my life. Following return to the theater season last spring—and up until just before the hated Bolshevik takeover in November—plays, ballets, and concerts we took in together constantly, ravenously, night by night, week by week at the Maryinsky, the Aleksandrinsky, the Maly Theaters—staying up and talking for hours afterward about the sets, the scores, the costumes, and librettos . . . this, yes, is more than a mere passing fancy in the night, a brief quenching of desire; this is caring, warmth, empathy, affection . . . love . . . .

"Get out," he whispers hoarsely, his eyes yet glued upon silent targets at the window. "I never want to see you again."

"Oh, Tolya—no!" I gasp. *"P-Please!"* Earnestly, I seize hold of his arm—but he flings me quick away, barking: "I said get out!"

"Tolya, you do not understand! He—he is dead—long dead, I swear to you! Lost in the war—"

"Oh, well—at least the bloody truth at last!" he snaps, whirling around. "And so that is what I have been struggling against all this time—a ghost, then? Dear Lord, don't you see that makes everything even worse? Not a living, breathing foe in the flesh do you give me to butt heads with, Sasha, oh, no—you have to come up with a lofty, quivering ghost! Oh, God! And how many more years will it take for you to forget him? How many more times must I bear your utterance of his name, while I hold you in my arms and whisper to you my endearments? How can I ever expect to win you over from someone who has so obviously stolen away your deepest heart—without leaving even the tiniest shred untouched for a later fellow like me to come and try to woo away for his very own?"

His glare of wounded pride burns into the core of my soul, shame's hot flush searing across my ears. Shaking my head in affirmation, in denial—in humble affirmation yet again—I once more latch both hands about his arm—begging, pleading—but once more he shoves me fiercely away. I bury my face into my fingers; he slams his fist onto the windowsill, choking out under his breath: "Please get *out!"*

Through a tunnel of numbness, I grovel my way to the bedroom door, pausing before I turn the knob to pull on my scarves and button up my coat; pausing against all hope for one last reprieve—one unwary, desirous glance—from beyond the harsh pronouncement of his words. But he continues facing away, presiding in brooding, silent judgment before the frosted pane of the window, his jaw set with the grim resolve of finality. My voice grinds off to a brittle sob as I whisper back at him: "All right, then! Goodbye, Tolya. I—I am sorry."

"Just please *get out!"*

At the adjacent bedroom door, lamplight shines from beneath the crack, and I can tell that his mother and sister—tolerant ladies, though they are, of his choice in intimate companions—have arisen from bed again. Probably they are both standing side by side with ears cupped against the wall, listening—as he has said they inevitably do—in delight and dismay. Reddening yet again in embarrassment, with my cane I take care not to thump too loudly against the parlor floorboards, and let myself quietly out the front entrance of the apartment.

Upstairs and down two doors lies Martova's; his neighborly acquaintance with her caused his joining into the 'safe-house' crowd during those first days of the Revolution. Oh, yes, those first days—that first breathy kiss of ours stolen back by the water closet in her apartment—and after that, the first knee-rubbings, the first thigh squeezings—the first tentative, lusty hand-holds . . . that first passionate, tearing time we shed our clothes in entirety and tumbled one upon another into his bed . . . during those first heady, romantic days of the Revolution, when all of Petrograd spun wild with an ecstatic buzz of promise, spring fever brimming upon the sunny, glowing horizon of each new day, solemn, hopeful dreams spinning out before the majestic cover of every magical white night . . . .

Now, Sadovaya, as I hobble westward down its lonely ice-encrusted avenue, frowns dimly through a mourning veil of stillness, a widow's face scarred in time, her former laughing buoyancy framed with shreds of old posters from the first days of the Revolution peeling from gaslamp poles and old news placards. The stench of litter and refuse piled up in slush at the curbstones and at barred and locked shop doors wafts upward with the burnt odor of old ink and kerosene; hollow windows of hollow buildings gutted out by the torches of angry Red Guard mobs stare back upon my trail like so many hollow, hurt, questioning eyes. Back toward them, I blink in my own confusion, unable to offer explanation, cast adrift myself for answers—and soon enough, I hoist my cane beneath my arm past a sharp intake of breath, my fingers gripping tightly around the butt of the gun in my pocket as my ears prick up to a sudden burst of predatory footsteps matched unto my pace from the corner down the street. Fortunately, the threat this time fades off in the opposite direction. Back toward the windows—and my Lady Petersburg's darkened, glassless eyes—I stare again, gauging her emptiness through my own emptiness. And as the moments slowly pass by one by one, I slowly find my way once more back toward the Fontanka Canal and Lyubov's apartment. Inside, everyone lies fast asleep, and on my mat in the hallway beyond the kitchen, I burrow down in my clothes, doffing only my coat to throw atop the blankets. The walls then start closing stealthily in, and I clamp shut my eyes, crushing my fist into my mouth as night's cocoon twists its dank, dampened hold around me. But even as the sobs start welling up in my throat, I know that—deep down—none are for Tolya. Instead, my pent-up tears are for the priceless treasure slipped out from the pocket of my jacket, the old picturegraph worn and tattered at the edges now, its image faded, but no less unmistakably poignant: of two cousins out on a lark in Paris in 1909 . . . .

Indeed, Tolya was most prudent to throw me out of his apartment and out of his life, was wise to forswear ever seeing the likes of me again. I have been using him—just as I have used every single last lover, stranger in the night, and warm affectionate friend that I have ever had—without exception—unto my own selfish ends. Even Volodya have I used, even as early as 1907—scarce before I had come to the faintest grips with my true romantic feelings. Even then, when Volodya was kissing me, sucking me, loving me during our every heated rendezvous at his old Vyborg apartment, the one for whom I desperately yearned was Nikolai. With Tolya at the concerts, the ballets, the plays, and during our animated discussions afterward, I made continual comparisons, testing to see if he would watch, laugh, or comment as would have Nikolai—who is hardly dead. Oh, no—in my poems, in my dreams, in my thousand dark wayward fantasies groped to hot, guilty fruition within cover of my bed in the night, my dear cousin lives on—and *on . . . no, it is not for you, Tolya, my friend, that I will now surely lie awake into the wee small hours again, entirely beside myself like some silly, mooning schoolgirl. Instead, it is all for naught but an unconsummated mythical dream—a love that might have been, but never was. Oh, dear Jesus! Help me to survive another night of agony, another day of torment that I can scarce bear without the sight, sound, nor the touch of him! Oh, God—all my tears, my every prayer, such lonely thoughts only serve for condemnation unto the depths of Dante's bitter, flaming hell, with never any hope of reprieve! Even after all these years, my sacred love is still solely for Nikolai. . . .*

* * *

Up all night again, like some silly, mooning schoolgirl . . . perhaps I am only garnering my just and proper due—for I am a fool, clinging so to a love that might have been, but never was. Chances are, he never would have loved me in any case—chances are that he was far from my pledged brother-soul for whom I have for so long been searching. Chances are, we would have fought terribly, bitterly, just as in the old days. And then he would have left me long behind, crushed and devastated. Yes, we would have fought—he was ever so moody, inscrutable at times, caught up in a world of inner visions and beholden to that lofty plane of his own peculiar gifted temperament. A forceful, magnanimous individual, to be sure—but he never would have loved me. Of course, had Tolya cared in earnest, would not sympathy have quelled anger in the end? *Fool! Tolya never loved you; Nikolai never would have, either* . . . and now, all night again, I have been up in mournful torment, wondering if anyone *ever* will . . . .

Morntide. I grope my way to the kitchen table and huddle in upon a chair, quivering from head to toe. From the parlor, I can hear Zhenya chasing Vanya back and forth in a gleeful game of tag. Upstairs, Yevgeny and Volodya appear to have already started work on the hammering in the second bedroom; the first one, where Lyubov and Grigor now sleep, has only recently been renovated, our supply of wood and nails ever remaining so scant. The rest of us have taken for ourselves various spots across the downstairs until the extra rooms can be made ready. Dolefully, the hammers pound, a few more nails retacked into a corner here, some more plastering board remounted onto a sidewall there. Again I wince against the pain the sound causes to my aching head as if the sun had burned into my eyes, although outside, the world of Petrograd yet looms fetid and sterile, its skies harboring an unfathomable gray gloom. From all appearances, someone has already ventured out to hunt for food, for a fat hunk of bread lies upon the table before me in offering to whomever might want it, gaping holes already torn from its crispy heel. I reach for a tiny piece, but snatch my fingers back, shuddering from a queasy lack of appetite, and wrap my arms up across my chest to hold in the warmth as Zhenya and Vanya scurry in, both shrieking and howling with laughter.

"Oh, Vanyushka, go!" Zhenya exclaims wildly. "Or my horsies will win the game! My horsies will catch your horsies—and then you'll be a puddin' face, Vanyushka, ha, ha, ha!"

Wailing at the top of his lungs, his red hair flying, Vanya barrels back into the parlor at full speed, while Zhenya doubles over in laughter, clapping her hands after him and urging him on with frantic mirth. "Oh, Step-papa!" she cries, pausing to catch her breath. "Vanya has become so—"

Her words halt abruptly short, her grin fading as her eyes widen in upon me. *"Step-papa?"* she gasps. "Are you all right?"

Reddening, I lower my gaze to the table, push my spectacles back up on the bridge of my nose, and run a shaking hand through my hair: untrimmed since December, uncombed ever since last night, and probably sticking out now hilariously in all directions. When I attempt to utter some reply of reassurance, its intent sticks hard in my throat, another torrential avalanche of sobs threatening to overtake my childish hold on emotion yet again. In shame, I cower away as she squeezes a hand onto my arm; as, crouching down low beside me, she again inquires with a worried frown: "Step-papa?"

Her arm burrows through mine and she pulls up a chair, her breath whisking cool and fresh against my brow as she murmurs: "Step-papa, whatever is troubling you so?"

Shaking my head in negation, I attempt to duck away, but she presses doggedly on: "Step-papa, I have never seen you so distraught—my word! Did you know that your eyes are all red? And puffy? Oh, my heavens—have you been weeping?"

Barking at her to hush, I snatch up the vodka bottle from the table, the picturegraph flying out from beneath my elbow as I sullenly slosh down my first morntide gulp.

From the floor, Zhenya retrieves my treasured keepsake, and grasping it between both hands, her lovely blue eyes focused intently down upon its image, she gasps out with amazement: "This is *you?"*

When I nod, she laughs in total incredulity, exclaiming: "But, my Lord! You look so young!"

To this, I roll my eyes, perplexed, my sigh filtering off into a heavy moan. "It—it was taken in Paris," I manage to choke out at last. "N-Nine years ago. I was only seventeen."

"Well, and how I should love to visit Paris!" she exclaims with a laugh. "Praise the dear Lord, what could ever be more impressive? And who is this young fellow in the picture with you, a friend? Oh, my—but he is so *very* handsome."

"Y-Yes."

"So? Who is he? You know, he resembles you a good deal, Step-papa. Could practically be your brother—"

"He was my cousin, Zhenyushka."

In response to my tone, the girl glances upward with a questioning pause, and I stare away, whispering: "He—he was lost in the war."

Nodding, her dark curly-haired ringlets bobbing coquettishly about her ears, Zhenya murmurs: "May God rest his soul then, Step-papa." And as she crosses herself with a tender sway of three solemn fingers, her eyes dropping down to her lap afterward in thoughtful, prayer-like reverence, I cannot help but marvel at how very much like a grown woman my little step-daughter has in the past months become, so poised beyond her years in temperament and grace, although only just turned fifteen.

Of course, then she quite promptly riddles to holes my lofty estimation by blurting out: "Is that why you were weeping so?"

Glaring at her, I snap back: "And aren't you the nosiest little she-devil in town this morntide!"

"Step-papa! I simply meant—"

"Humph! And will you scoot yourself back into that parlor this very moment, young lady, and find out just what the devil it is that your brother has chosen to holler at with such unbridled velocity? *Please?*"

"Yes, sir."

When she returns with Vanya—now happily tucked within her arms and ready for a nap—I ask after the whereabouts of her mother and Grigor.

"Mama and 'Uncle' said they heard of candles for sale down at Pashninkov's. So, that is where they have gone with snooty old Aunt Olga—whom, mind you, I am sick to death of sharing a room with! And whether any of them ever sets foot back through that front door again, I scarce care."

Again I roll my eyes. Her ease with most adults aside, Zhenya still picks nightly battles with her mother—and still shuns the company of her natural father, provoking continual fits of irritation by addressing him—pointedly—as 'Uncle.' Despite the fact that, over the past year, the man has steadfastly been attempting to make amends for his many exiles and imprisonments—and therefore his lack of presence—in his daughter's early life.

"That was not the only reason," she insists again as I point such out to her. "Might I remind you of the shame I bear—incest, illegitimacy? Ugh! And even when he *was* around to bounce me upon his knee those few years he lived with us in Moscow, it was only because she forced him. To this day, he's embarrassed and ashamed of me, just like everyone else in the entire family!"

"Zhenya, believe me," I warn her with a sigh, "no matter what the reason, one mustn't hold grudges against one's parents. You'll live to regret it, I assure you. I know I have. If you only knew how much I wish I could steal back some of those precious years in Paris when I seventeen, and foolishly cold-shouldering my own father—"

"Oh! Speaking of your father," she cries, reaching for a stack across the table, "this came in the mail, while you were sleeping."

With a start of joy, I note the beloved familiar script of 'Dr. Mikhailov' from Oslo at the space for the return address, and tear open the letter—only to have my hope dashed to pieces. Whole paragraphs this time have been blacked out by the censor. From what is left, I glean the poor state of the Norwegian weather, the robust hardiness of his health, and his worry over my absence of correspondence.

"Damn," I mutter to myself, rubbing my fist to my chin. Each week, faithfully, I have written since he left; up until last Christmastide, he regularly received the letters. And since then, apparently, none have gotten through, although I have made myself a regular nuisance at the Post Office, even sending the most recent under special delivery.

Once I return the letter to the envelope, Zhenya duly pries back my attention: "Step-papa, tell me again about those years you lived and worked in Paris! Are the croissants there as truly marvelous as they say? Is this cousin in your picturegraph the same one who used to so grandly play the violin? Oh! And did you two play in the orchestra for M'sieur Diaghilev in England?"

For the first time in ages, it seems, I cannot suppress a grin; the girl's enthusiasm remains ever so infectious. "And now, I suppose," I observe with a wink, "we shall launch into another discourse about England? All right then, young lady—but *pa-anglisky,* I implore you," I insist, switching over to English. "We must both endeavor to keep ourselves in practice."

After only a year and a half of study, Zhenya's fluency is now fast approaching mine, and as I watch her rattling on in the most properly clipped of accents like a young duchess or baroness about the many places she would deign to visit upon her wishful journey to England, I cannot help but recall my Uncle Ned's observation about such people who find themselves so inexplicably, irrevocably drawn—to the near throes of distraction—unto a foreign country. 'A past life—or ofttimes many past lives—lived in that particular place,' he would say, smoking his pipe and staring about in bemusement at the many souvenirs from America lining his study.

My exchange with Zhenya in her beloved English, however, snaps to an abrupt halt once the door bangs open and Grigor, Lyubov, and Olga amble in, stomping the snow from their boots.

Throwing her nose to the air, Zhenya clambers upward and saunters off in a huff, spiriting Vanya away into the parlor the moment her mother pokes her head past the kitchen archway.

"Don't matter, girl—I heard ye!" Lyubov bellows after her, then whirling upon me to demand: "Ye quit stuffin' such uppity bourgeois ideas—as I know ye have—into my child's head, Sasha Mikhailovich!"

"We were simply talking!" I counter, throwing up both hands. "Oh, for heaven's sake, Lyuba—when will you see clear sense? All right—yes, of course Russian is the national language, and we must encourage patriotism, I know and support that—oh, yes, I *do!* But as your Lenin presumes himself head of state, think you not that someday the man might request aid to converse, perhaps, with Prime Minister George? Or with President Wilson?"

"Humph!"

From behind Lyubov, Olga's eyes narrow in upon mine with her severe, distilling gaze. "Perhaps, Comrade Khulinov," she states, casting a quick glance off toward Grigor, "when teacher postings are assigned for the autumn term, you can be called upon to offer services unto the schoolchildren of the proletariat as an instructor in languages?"

My eyes drop to the table, my heart thudding into my throat as Grigor echoes behind her: "Indeed—listen, Lyuba, and learn. Comrade Khulinov's viewpoint is well professed and a strong one. One must remember always that World Revolution is at hand, and for aiding our comrade workers in the British Isles and the United States, a knowledge of their language can prove of the utmost value. Thanks to the efforts of her step-father, our little Zhenya might someday find herself an international ambassador of goodwill, a true helpmate for the bringing in of the Worldwide Socialist Order."

"French, I believe, you also speak?" Olga goes on pointedly. "Or at least read, yes? Comrade Khulinov?"

Obviously, I have not taken near enough care with keeping my many books sequestered into the makeshift shelf in the hallway aside my bed mat. "Y-Yes, ma'am," I blurt out, flushing. "Er, I mean—Comrade Mrenitseva."

In weighty silence, Olga and Grigor exchange glances once again—but seem satisfied for the moment, and start conversing together in low undertones as they head upstairs with several sheafs of papers and a bag of candles.

Once they are out of earshot, I immediately corner Lyubov, exclaiming: "Lyuba, they cannot be serious! I could never teach languages in a Soviet school!"

"An' why not? Seems as if ye've done a fine enough job teachin' my Zhenya."

"That is not what I mean." In consternation, I follow her about the kitchen and then across the rugless parlor-room floor as she sets fresh candles out upon the sideboard, the tables, the fireplace mantle. "Lyuba," I go on in a grating whisper, "the authorities would surely make a very thorough check of my credentials before posting me to teach in any school, yes?"

"Well, I s'pose—"

"Then they will learn of my true background! Don't you see? The higher school I graduated from was May's Academy."

When she fixes a complete blank upon me in response, I tell her: "May's was a school for the well-to-do, for sons of the nobility, Lyuba. Rykazian never forged me up another diploma. We never thought I'd happen upon any need for it."

"Oh. Well, I'll try to talk 'em both out o' it, then. Oh, quit worryin' so. Ye know I've not told anyone a word—nor will, ever! I promise ye again, Sasha—yer secret's safe 'tween us. Much as I love Grigor," she goes on, lowering her voice unto a whisper, "ye know I'll not have him learnin' 'bout somethin' that could harm the children. An' what in the devil's name is the matter with ye this morn, anyway?" she harps on more loudly. "Yer eyes are all puffed up an' red—have ye taken sick? What is it, nose sniffles? A head fever?"

Her hand glides cool and soft across my brow, the hot sweat I have broken into sufficing well enough for explanation. Clucking her tongue, Lyubov drags me back into the kitchen, forces down some hot broth, and demands when I last ate. Afterward, I find myself tucked back into my hallway bed, shivering with a fierce chill despite the wealth of covers drawn up snug about my neck. "An' ye *stay* there, Sasha Mikhailovich— an' try te fetch back some rest. I hear this grippe has been makin' the rounds house by house all along the Canal. . . ."

In a few moments, out in the kitchen, I hear her discussing with Olga my dubious morality, my tendency toward drunkenness, my poor promise a mentor to 'proper Soviet youngsters.' Beyond them, both hammers keep banging away in irksome clarity from the floor of the second bedroom overhead, but all I can hear in my ears is a pounding chorus not of tools, but of words: first, Rykazian's, from last night. About the daily battle with the grim reaper of fear these days, even within the confines of one's own household.

And then, my father's—about the subtle dangers, indeed, of plying one's trade with wolves.

* * *

Wolves . . . surrounded, we are surrounded! The pack keeps closing in—panting, salivating, carnivorous, rabid—lusting for bloodletting, lusting for revenge—oh, God! They're cornering us, they'll kill us! The pack keeps closing in! Closer and closer . . . .

"Sasha! Sasha Mikhailovich, it's all right! I'm here now. Ye jest lie still an' try te rest. . . ."

"God, Lyuba! They'll tear us to bits, they'll eat us alive!" Gasping for breath, grasping at straws, I clutch my fingers for the ruffled cotton sleeve of her blouse. "Wolves, Lyuba! Everywhere! Naught but a fiendish, snarling pack of wolves! . . ."

"Shhh! Hush, now—*hush*, I said! Ye must sleep. . . ."

Sleep . . . night . . . again I drift away into old Vienna before the war, resolving myself unto a vast wandering journey of the night, an endless, shadowy longing for the dark unknown . . . *hallowed, forbidden journey in the dark, dark night . . . of the soul . . . .*

Sacred shroud . . . I uncover my face to bathe in a pool of light . . . I become light; am light . . . I am . . . that I Am . . . I am That and That I Am . . . the white shroud peels away at last from . . . my own face . . . and beside me, stands another . . . Nikolai! It—it is *you! Oh, yes—I love, worship, adore you, Nikolai . . . pledged forever and evermore . . . yes, I will share this cup with you, Nikolai . . . with thee, unto God, I stand . . . with thee, unto God, I raise this cup . . . of resolution . . . .*

Dawn, silvery morning dawn . . . coughing myself awake, I twist around upon the bed mat, wrinkling my nose against the sweaty stench of the blankets. Across the apartment the sun shines in slatted haloes upon the pinewood floor; into my lungs, a cool breeze tickles in delicious, icy whispers. Above, Zhenya looms like an angel from heaven, her smile tender, her dark curls bunched and twisted atop her head very *au mode* and secured with a large tortoise-shell comb that she must have found or been given by someone. From the cup in her hand, she fills the spoon with broth. I lift up my head; sip obediently. "Vanyushka took sick, too, Step-papa," she tells me. "Oh, no—do not fret. He is much better—hollering, already, even. Got over it lots quicker than you, though Mama's yet keeping him at bedside. She said you should try to stand up and walk about a bit if you could finish the broth. Would you like some bread?"

At the terrace, sipping tea and munching down rye hardtack spread with a tasty mash of herring, I blink against the high noon sun, wrap the blanket close about my shoulders, and peer out the windows into the wash of spring air. From below, ice floes in the Fontanka can be seen breaking up and slowly melting their way toward the Neva. April, it is already mid-April. I have been sick for over a month.

Passing through the parlor, Olga nods to me in her stiffened, spinsterly way. Yevgeny and Grigor then hurry in from the kitchen, their hands shuffling papers, their voices rattling on nonstop about the war. *War*. Everywhere, it seems, the talk is of naught but war—or rather, two wars. The first, of course, remains humming along as ever with the Germans, despite Trotsky's so-called 'no-war-no-peace' Treaty of Brest-Litovsk. By terms of the treaty, Soviet Russia has surrendered away her Baltic provinces—Estonia, Latvia, and Lithuania—in addition to Poland, much of Byelorussia, and a good part of the western Ukraine. Scanning further easy territorial pickings, the Germans, however, have scarce made any retreat; instead, have continued gearing up for renewed military offensive at our every border. Because to the south, to the east—and aligned hand in hand with the mounting German muscle in the west—has coalesced a sprinkled gathering of malcontents called White forces: former Tsarist officers, ministers of Kerensky's Provisional Government, and many of the ousted SR and Kadet delegates to the Constituent Assembly; former members of the bourgeoisie and the disenfranchised nobility; bands of disgruntled Cossacks, monarchists, anarchists, and provocateurs; legions of peasants sworn to avenge with blood the forceful seizure, by armed Bolshevik troops, of grain from Petrograd's and Moscow's outlying provinces . . . .

Civil war . . . as early as last November, the railroad and telegraph unions, the Soviets of workers, the numerous Petrograd infantry and artillery garrisons—everyone decried the possibility: *four years have we spent fighting the godless, greedy Huns! We will not take up arms against other Russians! We will* not *fight our fellow Russians. . . .*

* * *

Before the doorway to Tolya's apartment, I stand hesitating with my fist poised in the air, sighing against a wealth of churning inner butterflies. Three nights have I been up tossing and turning with thoughts, finally, of him, and by so coming here, I hope to make amends. To at least allow us an amicable parting—after all, I *do* care about him. Not, perhaps, with the same fated bond of passion that I feel for Nikolai, but my friendship and affection remain strong for Tolya. War—and therefore uncertainty—is again looming upon our every horizon; after all we have shared together, should he not at least be good enough to allow the two of us to part as friends?

At last I knock, and his sister answers. "Yekaterina Lukyanovna," I say, doffing my cap, "good day. If you would be so kind as to ask Tolya—"

"Tolya is not here," she replies gruffly, pushing shut the door.

Quickly, I wedge my foot in against the jamb—while she glares at me, her arms crossed in a defensive hold up over her bosom. "Yekaterina Lukyanovna, please," I implore her through the crack. "I know Tolya does not wish to see me, and admit that he has good reason. But if you would simply convince him to come to the door for a moment—"

"Let him in," another gruff—though feminine voice—barks from beyond the doorway.

With reluctance, Yekaterina pulls back to allow me inside.

Between twisting fingers, I nervously grasp my cap, staring between Tolya's sister and his mother. After a moment, she appears to recognize me, her lips parting in a sad, wistful smile before puckering stodgily inward once again. "Aleksandr Mikhailovich," she murmurs, nodding acknowledgment, "you must believe it true when we tell you that Tolya is no longer with us."

From the bureau—in tight-lipped silence—his sister retrieves a wooden box.

In it, one of his suit jackets, hastily folded—and bloodstained at the shoulders and collar. Along with his pocket watch. Also a tie-pin; the amber-inlaid ring he always wore. A scuffed pair of shoes.

"My little brother was arrested two weeks ago," Yekaterina whispers, crossing herself, and shakily adding: "May God rest his soul."

Shoving her fist into her mouth, she then turns away, succumbing to quiet sobs, while her mother—again meeting my gaze with her saddened one—crosses herself also.

Numbly, I follow suit, my mouth parching dry as sand. Again I stare into the box. *So much blood . . . stained throughout the jacket's shoulders, the collar . . . .*

Which portends only the latest rumors, verified; the inexorable requital of the *Cheka*, swift and sure, and by this evidence, graphically confirmed. A bullet, they say, shot straight into the back of the head. The current touted fate for all state enemies. . . .

Still speechless, I bow down before Tolya's mother and grasp up her hands, plant kisses upon them both, and finally rasp out: "I—I am sorry . . . forgive me for having intruded upon the both of you! I am so terribly, utterly sorry. . . ."

Out on the street, I storm in a blind fog back up Sadovaya, seething with rage, struggling with powerlessness, searching for reasons. Of late, Gorky's newspaper has come under increasing political fire, the great playwright himself—although long a Bolshevik sympathizer—at last seeing the light and attacking in print Lenin's devilish, strong-armed hypocrisy. Tolya had not only been submitting lampoons and caricatures, but ever since the first of the year, also some very defiant articles—to *Novaya Zhizn;* to other papers, many now long since shut down. We were commensurate of political opinion, Tolya and I—it was one of the reasons why we took so well to one another. An Aries he was, my old friend Tolya: the fire-headed, fist-wielding Ram. He possessed no fear of speaking his mind, and damn the consequences. Apparently, the consequences caught up with Tolya far too soon—he was only five months my elder, just barely turned age twenty-seven. . . .

Red terror, Volodya calls it. *Lenin is scouring the land with an unholy, bloody crucible of Red terror. . . .*

The closer I draw back to the Fontanka, the more the sky seems to darken with my every step, flocks of pigeons huddling away in silent mourning, spring's brief promise lying fallow now unto the stagnation of a harvest moon. The gloom pervades even more so once I round the last corner toward home—there to happen upon the scowling grimaces of women crouched behind one another in shop lines snaking down the walkway. Lines I pass at three separate shops, two of them bakeries. Lyubov, for a certainty, will chide me without pause once I arrive home. Anymore, if one encounters a line, prudence dictates joining into it without a second thought; little does it matter whatever is being offered for sale. A line means that some precious, scarce commodity is actually available, and one should make the effort to buy up as much as possible of the awaited item, whatever it is—for God knows when more bread, candles, or tins of canned herring or sturgeon will arrive, if at all. But today, I cannot bear to stand in line; today, I will not honor the memory of my dead friend by stooping to an exercise of mundane triviality. No, today, I must simply be alone, with myself, with God—today, I must take my flute to one of the parks, or perhaps Pokrov Square . . . today, yes, I must find some budding trees or sprouting flowers, and play for an hour, or two, or three—in honor of Tolya's memory. Today, I must play for *all* of my dear ones' memories. . . .

The moment I edge past the apartment door, Lyubov descends in justifiable housewifely vengeance: "There's lines out there—*yes?* Well, I can see 'em from here! So why didn't ye get yerself in one? Lord, do I have te do *everythin'* around this half-torn-down apartment? Can't ye see I'm tryin' te keep from taking sick myself after waitin' on the two o' ye hand an' foot fer near unto a month?"

Brushing past her, I make a beeline for my bed mat, and from its side with the wall, grasp up the case to my flute. It is then that—although only half-listening—I catch the urgent gist of Volodya's and Yevgeny's conversation filtering in from beyond the kitchen archway.

"All the manor houses?" Volodya gasps.

"Yes, all. By now, them raidin' devils are s'posed te be in full retreat from Gatchina. All they're savin' fer themselves is the grain stores, an' some o' the better lookin' women, humph! Past that, they're burnin' whatever they can: towns, peasant huts. An' the manor houses, when they find 'em. If it's anarchists, they're doin' it jest fer spite; if it's Whites, though—like I s'pect it is—they're doin' it te keep the Reds from gettin' their hands on any kind o' property or goods that'll later be useful. Them Whites, they got a 'if we can't have 'em, ye can't have 'em type thinkin'. Uh-huh. Well, they're s'posed te be skirtin' the main cities, but the little towns—and especially the old estates o' the nobles—they're goin' straight fer, guttin' 'em out one by one. More than a hundred versts south, Yurenev said they'd got—in fact, one o' the other fellows said that band o' White

Guards was probably all of a hundred-fifty versts south o' Petrograd by today. So, where would that put the latest pillagin'? Luga? Novgorod?"

My flute bangs to the floor, silencing them all, including Lyubov, who stops in mid-sentence with her harping on about the shop lines. When I glance back upward from retrieving the instrument case from the floor, I find Volodya gauging my horrified expression with widened eyes, his head shaking in near imperceptible negation, his Adam's apple working violently at the hollow of his throat. "No, Sasha!" he finally exclaims in a frantic whisper, shoving up from the table. "No, by God—don't you dare!"

Past Lyubov, I charge in a frenzy, banging open the door to my old room now shared by Zhenya and Vanya and Olga.

Barely do I snatch out my old portmanteau from the wardrobe-cupboard when Volodya seizes onto me like a bear from behind. "There is naught that you can do!" he shouts, grappling for my arm once—twice, thrice—while I shake him off. "Sasha, listen to me! It is not even your house anymore, remember? Lenin's decree on land last December—which wholly abolished all private holdins, handed the old estates over to the rural agrarian committees that are bein' set up . . . Sasha, my God! What the hell do you think you're *doin'?* I'm tellin' you, it's no longer your house!"

"The hell it's not my house, by dammit!" I roar back at him. "My father built that house with his own two hands!"

"What house?"

Yevgeny, it is, who speaks. Feet solidly straddled across the doorway, he continues puffing away on the short stub of the cigarette stuck in between his teeth, his brows knitted together in a frown of suspicion, his eyes searching first mine, then Lyubov's, then Volodya's. "What's he talkin' about, Rykazian?"

Ignoring him, Volodya whirls upon me again, yelling: "They'll not allow you to board the train, I'll guarantee it! Two, three weeks it's said to take—at least—after making application, mind you! To receive a Soviet traveling passport."

Only for a moment do I stare him down before dragging out my old riding knapsack. Between it and the portmanteau, I start switching contents while muttering: "Then I'll gladly trade away cushioned seat for horse and saddle—"

"Have you completely *lost your senses?"* Volodya counters, his arms flying out wide. "It's—it's a hundred and sixty fuckin' versts!"

"At the end of which stands my house!" I storm back. "And I am telling you, nobody—anarchists, Whites, or whoever what the hell have you—is going to pillage or burn down my house! Unless it's over my dead body!"

From the kitchen, Yevgeny's voice then erupts between us in a hailstorm of shouts: "Ye know, don't ye? Blast it, woman—I can tell ye know plum good and well what Mikhailovich is carryin' on so about!"

Fending him off with blustery, snarling threats, Lyubov soon enough charges through the bedroom doorway. "Sasha Mikhailovich!" she yells, stumbling toward me, "ye can't go out ridin', ye jest spent a whole livin' month in sickbed! Will ye listen te yer wife fer once? And not go stormin' out o' here like some pig-headed fool?"

"You *shut up!"* I rage back, my fist arching out in warning. Hurriedly, I shove past her and make my way into the kitchen—where I start stuffing the knapsack full with hardtack, cans of fish, and any other food I can find. "Oh, by the Lord's arse!" Lyubov hollers, her nails digging with a frightening lack of sensation into my arm. "Where are ye goin'? Rykazian, ye nitwit!" she then yells, turning upon Volodya. "Stop him!"

"Yaaa—an' just where is he so set on goin'?" Yevgeny demands, seizing hold of Volodya's collar.

The reply issues forth in stunned amazement: "Lissushka. Lissushka on Ilmen—on Lake Ilmen, near the village of Watery Forever—"

"An' where the devil is that?"

"Novgorod. Southeast of Novgorod."

To this, Yevgeny's mouth drops, his cigarette trailing in a spew of ash down to the floor—while Lyubov, ducking her face into her hands, mutters out: "Oh, Lord God—"

I take advantage of their continued ranting with Volodya to fit the wooden knob down into the heel-well of my left boot; then into its shaft, I slip my knife. And recheck, in my right boot, placement of the old wooden piccolo. Deep within my pockets, I finger the Paris picturegraph, Melissa's amethyst crystal, my family ring, and various other assorted items, while in the lining, the hidden necklaces and other jewelry yet lie securely tucked and stitched; ever since the *Okhrana* raid on the apartment so long ago, I have never ventured far without Father's jacket and my most precious keepsakes. Again shouldering off Lyubov's protests as she corners me once more, I reload both my Webleys and stuff them also into my pockets. My light felt coat and ermine hat, I sweep up under my arm; the knapsack, I hoist up over my shoulder, followed by the flute case on my way to the front door. As Lyubov wrenches one last hold upon my hand, I squeeze hers in response and press a kiss upon her fingers, murmuring: "Tell Zhenya and Vanya that I love them both. Terribly. And that I shall return as soon as I can."

"Sasha Mikhailovich!" she screams after, "ye twitterin', harebrained fool! Ye're goin' te catch yer death out there come nightfall, ridin' in the freezin' rain—winter's not past all the way yet, ye know! Sasha Mikhailovich, do ye hear me? Ye get right back up them steps and in this door this minute! *Sasha!* Oh!" As I cross down through the vestibule to the street entrance, I hear her shrieking back into the apartment at Volodya and Yevgeny: "Well, don't jest stand there gapin', ye two lug-addled, good-fer-nothin' numskulls! If ye can't stop him, go with him then, fer the love o' God! Before he stows away on some train an' gets himself arrested fer it! Or—or somethin' even worse . . . !"

* * *

All the remainder of the day, then into the night, we ride—on three horses and armed with three Mosin-Nagant rifles bartered away from a group of wayward Cossacks at Gatchina in exchange for my mother's sapphire necklace. Perhaps not Volodya, but Yevgeny—or the both of them together—could certainly have dragged me back to Lyubov's insistent quarantine, had either so wanted. Instead, Yevgeny seems intent upon satisfying his curiosity about my erratic behavior, while Volodya—his doubts long since cast aside to a flask of vodka, and that familiar wily gleam once again sparkling in his eye—is, I know, chasing after me solely in pursuit of adventure. Their low murmurs continue reaching my ears with only an occasional recognizable word or phrase as they keep up an hourly pace with my hoof tracks from behind. To my relief, the weather remains clear and brisk, bright stars and an eerie fan of moonglow lighting our way once nightfall descends in chilly hold. The further inland we venture, the more the snow and ice lie stiff and cold yet well within winter's grasp, which proves not a hindrance, but beneficent, for in another week or two, with the thaw, will come the bane of the dreaded Russian spring muds, churning to so much lumpy mush the pathways through the forest bogs and ruts of the old country roads.

All the way south, we follow the ancient Moscow roadway lying roughly parallel to the railway tracks, ducking our mounts off into thickets of birchen and high pine forest here and there upon sightings of scattered patrols of Red Guards. One such skirmish just past the rail platform at Tosno—after refusal to stop and surrender forth our papers for inspection—results in several volleys of shots fired after us into the air, but little else. During the forest diversions, my memory serves us well, for en route to Chudovo, and from the Chudovo junction all the way southward, the sleepy river crossings, the gently sloped rises and lonely wooden platforms of the old rail stop landmarks stand as preciously familiar as in my boyhood days, when either by myself or accompanied by Father, I took this same journey so many times by train.

Morn's dawn, however, proves a sad fate for many other more distantly remembered sentinels, for once we can see our way clear unto the hazy, broadening horizon, scores of burned-out churches abound in every village we pass clear up unto the northern gates of Novgorod. There, though, to my vast relief as we pause to scan a quick view of the kremlin gates once again from the high eastern banks of the River Volkhov, the Holy Cathedral of St. Sofiya yet looms as tall and proud in a wealth of shining gold as she has for near unto nine hundred years, the winged dove still aloft upon the height of her grand central dome, old Lord Novgorod the Great remaining true to his people's heart, mind, and soul—Revolution or no Revolution.

Beside me, Volodya sighs bemusedly as well and nods in my direction. Half-Armenian my old arch-companion may be, but he was born at Watery Forever, his mother the daughter from a long-biding peasant family there, and Novgorodian pride, I know, runs within his veins just as thoroughly as in mine.

Once clear of town, however, the news proves far worse, for more churches lie in ruins at Gorodishche and at Kholinya, their windows gutted out and canvasses of old icon paintings trampled in the slush, vestments, censers, and chalices all smashed to bits with pieces lying scattered about in the snow and along the byways. In Bronnitsa, the same fate holds in an ugly testament of smashed window glass for the roadside Transfiguration Church, and also for the solitary Chapel of the Presentation looming up soon to our right upon Bronnitskaya Hill. "Bastards," Yevgeny mutters, scowling at the sight of the wreckage, his faith, ironically—along with Lyubov's—ever remaining steadfast in the Orthodox rituals despite his Bolshevik political ties. "No good'll come o' it, Rykazian, I tell ye!" he storms, glaring righteously around when we make a stop at a peasant well at the south end of the village to partake of water for ourselves and the horses. "What do them Red Guards think they're out te gain, sacrilegin' the Church up an' down the countryside like such mindless beasts? Peasant folk livin' on the land'll never give up God's ways, no matter what Lenin tries te tell 'em."

The rampage in Bronnitsa spurs us on to a quickened pace, and within the next hour, the hillside chapel's pale blue dome and high bell tower shrink slowly behind us into the snow-capped horizon, and finally disappear as we find ourselves trotting three abreast down the narrow, bumpy dirt road leading toward Watery Forever and Lissushka. The sight of the old familiar trees and spry tufts of withered grass sprouting up through the slush past wearied tread-markings seizes me fast in a grip of near physical pain: *Dear Lord, how I wish I could have brought the children here to live in this wondrous, special haven in the woods, no matter about the ongoing threat of war, or what would have been Lyubov's objections.* Fending off a mounting wave of regret, I feel my heart quickening into my throat the closer we draw toward the estate house. But as we near the final bend in the road, the double chimneys swinging into view at long last above a swelling rise of trees, my nostrils start to quiver against the stench of smoke, my ears pricking up abruptly to sounds of shouting in the distance. Squinting, I gaze out ahead: far up along our path, lying dead center ahead in the roadway, a black metallic splotch shines ominously through a cradle of snow. "What is it?" demands Volodya, shading his brow with his hand. "An old scythe? A harrow left behind from the fields?"

I reach it first—to stare down in disbelief at an angled Orthodox cross from one of the tombstones, my voice cracking out: "Oh, my God—the *cemetery!"*

Through the woods on my mare I fly like a madman, rifle shouldered at the ready. Voices through the trees begin to reverberate distinctly, and as I burst out into the cemetery clearing, several elderly men with shovels, their mouths going agape, all stare back in fright as I shoot off a volley into the air, roaring: "Just *what* in hell's name do you people think you are doing?"

Wildly, I take in the sight before me: the fence enclosing the cemetery perimeter torn down all around in a mangled heap of wood and wrought-iron, half the graves lying open as fresh mounds of shoveled dirt, several missing or befit only with smashed remnants of their angled Orthodox crosses. While Melissa's marble headstone has disappeared in entirety. *"My God!"* I shout, recocking the rifle and aiming straight for the closest of the diggers. "What madmen, *what monsters are you?* This is a cemetery—holy, consecrated ground! This is—"

I stop as one of the eldest of the men throws his shovel to the ground and doffs his cap, bowing low toward me in humble, trembling reverence. "Blessed Virgin, Sasha Mikhailovich, I—I mean, Yer Honor! We meant no harm," he exclaims. "Fact, we came to clean up the mess them hooligans left behind."

The rifle I lower slowly to my side, at last gasping out: *"Pavel?"*

Indeed, it is him—Father's old overseer of the Lissushka farm. "Yes, Yer Honor," he mutters out, bowing low again while waving forth his cap in greeting. "Good te see ye once again, Yer Honor, Count Sekovsky, Aleksandr Mikhailovich, sir! Them, uh, bands o' hooligans dug up half these graves, that they did. We had te wait 'til they left te keep from gettin' our own heads shot off, but fer the last hour, we been shovelin' and diggin', square on settin' things here proper once again."

"Ye're old Sekovsky's son, then?" one of the other men—with a surly, hostile glare—pipes up gruffly from behind him.

In silence, I dismount the horse, snatch my cane out from the saddle cinch, and storm into the cemetery, the group of elderly men gathering behind Pavel as I approach Melissa's grave. "This one they dug up, too?" I demand, staring down in a froth of rage at the fresh mound of dirt.

"Yes, Yer Honor—but has all been made right an' proper again now, Aleksandr Mikhailovich, Yer Honor, sir! We promise ye—"

"But would scarce be made right by a kopek!" the surly one snaps, shoving out from behind Pavel and planting both fists in a blatant show of defiance upon his hips. "Nuh-uh—we'd o' done no diggin' nor shovelin' without pay here at all—*Yer Honor,"* he goes on sarcastically. "'Cause we hold no grit fer *dvoryanye* leeches any more around here! But, old Sekovsky—well, the old man did give his land over te us, that we'll grant him—and long before the Bolshies came along an' forced others in these parts te give their holdins free an' clear back unto them whose it should o' been in the first place! An' *that,"* he spits out with venom, *"Count,* is the only reason we come up here te shovel these *dvoryanye* caskets back into these open graves."

"For that, I thank you, then," I whisper, glaring back at him. To my knees I then sink, my head bowed low over Melissa's mound. Countless times I cross myself, my lips forming at inept, unspoken words, my rage threatening to blow in a geyser unchecked out the very drums of my ears. *I am sorry, dear Melissa—my own mother whom*

I never knew, and yet who lies so beloved like a special friend close to my heart . . . I swear . . . I will kill the fiends who defiled your hallowed grave! . . .

Pavel has brought with him some withered trestle boards, a few nails, an old rusty saw—and over the following few moments, he and I proceed with erecting an Orthodox-fashioned cross to replace Melissa's missing headstone. Into the soft, dampened grain of wood, I carve with the blade of my pocket knife our family name, Melissa's first and maiden names, the dates of her birth and death. Then into the soggy mound of earth we hammer my mother's second beacon of finality, and I bow down low again at the foot of the grave, whispering further prayers as the men continue watching—some without much interest, others reverently, silently. Only when Volodya's hand, squeezed firm and strong upon my shoulder, imparts renewed urgency do I at last arise to my feet—and only then, against a sharp turn in the wind, do I once more inhale the full assault of the smoke. "I am sorry, Yer Honor," Pavel chokes out abruptly, hanging his head and wringing his hands, "that we couldn't keep 'em away from—that we couldn't do more te save—the house—"

The house!

"Sasha, no!" Volodya shouts, wrenching hold of my arm. "Listen to me, dammit! You do not want to see . . . will be better if you simply remember the old estate house the way it was—"

"Let me go!"

Another anguished ride through the trees—another traversing of forever's bridge suspended in a single quivering breath of time—but I have arrived too late: *oh, my God! Chimneys, I see the chimneys, but—oh, dear God! Where is the cupola? Oh, God, no!* Where *is the house?*

Into the clearing at last I tear, gulping back frantic, ragged heaves of breath. Reining in the mare past a gasp of astonishment, I whirl around in a circle to find one building after another scorched clear unto the ground: in the distance, the apiary, gone; even farther back, all the farmhouses, gone; up closer, Pavel's old office, where I toiled for so many tiresome hours on the ledgers with Bulya, gone; and the house, the chimneys—*oh, dear God!* The house, the place where I was born—my sweet haven in this ancient spot of woods that my father built upon model of the Kizhi Island churches with his own two loving, studious hands—only the chimneys remain . . . *there is no more house . . . there is no more fleck-carved wooden cupola. . . .*

To where the front doorway would have been, I drift toward on my mare, the rifle shaking within my grasp. Only the stone chimneys remain intact above a smoking bed of ash, every other last solid inch of the house having been torched clear unto the ground, thick embers yet glowing in places atop bare mounds of dirt. On the masonry above the former drawing room fireplace mantle, where Father stood so many a time wrathfully shouting me down, someone has painted, in thick, ugly globs of tar, a black cross.

"Who did this?" I scream at Volodya and Yevgeny as they approach in wary silence. Blindly, I shake out at both of them both with my rifle, roaring: *"Who on earth would be insane enough to do this?"*

"I'll tell ye who did it, laddie."

The three of us whirl about to encounter, closing in from the south shore with the woods, a tall, striking fellow sporting a white eye patch and red armband. Confidently mounted astride a black Arabian stallion and flanked by a heavily armed group of companions, their carbines all aimed for us at the ready, he grins and twirls his fingers down about his thick handlebar moustache.

"Did you do this?" I demand, aiming for him in turn, unheedful of the cocking of their guns. "Are *you* the one to blame for this ungodly, senseless pillage? Because so help me to *bloody God!* If you are . . . ."

In response to my threat, the man merely grins nonchalantly, and points with a knowing hand off toward the chimney masonry. "Was scarce me and my band that burnt up yer house, laddie. We ride after the folks who set the damned torchins—on that, ye got my solemn word. An'," he goes on, pointing to the chimneys and the tar-painted cross, "before yer eyes, ye got the evidence. See? Only Makhno's men got the stomach gall te pull this kind o' rotten business."

"Makhno's Greens?" Yevgeny blurts out. "But I thought that band's not s'posed te be near this far north."

"You've *heard* of these people?" I cry, turning upon him.

"Yaaa, Mikhailovich. Anarchists. Anarchists, Makhno's men are—"

"Greens it was, all right," says the fellow with the eyepatch. "An' Black Hundreds with 'em again, looks like," he adds, again indicating the chimneys. "Ye can tell by that cross."

"By God," I mutter under my breath, "Greens, Black Hundreds—I'll kill them all! Every last blessed one!"

"Then ye'll do well to fall in with us, laddie. 'Cause we're goin' after Makhno's men the very same as ye, 'till we sinker our bayonets into 'em all."

"Who are you?" insists Volodya, frowning across at him.

"Zorshenko. Commander of this proud Regiment o' Bolshevik Guards, at your service, Comrades! As Bolshy Guards, we stand united with all Kadets an' SRs fer free socialism against all Whites, Greens, Germans, and Communists!"

At this, I eye Volodya, who shrugs, muttering across in a lowered tone: "Ever since Lenin ordered the provincial grain seizures. Some folks in the countryside—uh, some even in the cities—refuse to recognize both Communists and Bolsheviks as bein' one and the very same."

"That's damn right!" Zorshenko echoes on boisterously. "Them Commies came in an' kicked out the November Bolshies, who promised us a free press an' land fer all the peasants! So them Commies we Bolshy Guards are goin' to mow down te their bloody death, along with filthy house-burnin' Greens—hey, boys!"

At his whistle-sound, about thirty more men on horseback, all sporting red armbands, their carbines pointing for us, materialize into view—one by one—from behind cover of the trees.

"And now," exclaims Zorshenko, nodding with another sly, yet affable grin, "ye three young fellows with yer fine-bred mounts'll be comin' along with us." Emphatically, he cocks up his own carbine, joining with the others in aim against us and adding with a shrug: "'Cause we Bolshy Guards need all the men we can get."

* * *

Makhno's men . . . over the next hours, my fury curdles on in a volcano of rage unchecked against both real and imagined atrocities of Makhno's men . . . it scarce matters that Zorshenko forces Yevgeny and Volodya and I to swear undying loyalty to his rag-tag Bolshevik band, on penalty of facing their firing squad for daring any attempt at escape. It scarce matters to have caught no sleep in near unto two entire days, our meals boasted of little more than crumbs of stale hardtack, nor that my thighs keep chafing raw with saddle sores, my hands blistering against the pull of the reins. It scarce matters at all because *all* I can see, hear, taste, and smell, beyond my own seething froth of outrage, is the zeal for glorious cold-blooded retribution—its swift sword to be dashed without pause for mercy against the scourge of bandits razing the countryside: Black Hundreds and Makhno's men . . . .

The first rout takes hold some forty versts to the south from the sight of Lissushka's haunting spoils, the victors gathered in a lakeside clearing and discussing without shame nor pretext another potential target for their ungodly mischief: Kolinsky's farm, lying bare ahead through a willowy copse of trees. "See the green ribbons pulled sidewise 'cross their chests?" Yevgeny whispers into my ear. "It's fer the mix o' blue an' yellow Ukrainian colors. Makhno himself's Ukrainian, from Gulyay-Polye district in the Donets basin, they say he hails. An' the black armbands," he goes on with a derisive snort, "shows these fellows here have joined up with them infernal Black Hundreds bandits. Jest like Zorshenko said."

Grimly, Volodya and I nod in reply, and with rifles tensely shouldered to the ready, we peer once again up ahead at Zorshenko's arm, held high aloft over heads of the others.

With the signal, the arm waves abruptly downward. The cocking of carbines rattles into the stillness and our swarm of bayonets flashes through the air, the forward mounts rearing up in the excitement of the charge as all fifty of us dash full speed off after Zorshenko into the clearing.

Shouts, curses, and volleys of bullets greet us in a thundering torrent of reply. Cautiously, Volodya and I pull back along with Yevgeny, the three of us mindful to each pick out for ourselves one target man in the enemy line to pound with a steady barrage of rifle fire. The ploy is aided by Zorshenko's band's obvious strength in numbers; outmanned two to one, the Greens turn high tail in a course for flight, and we charge blindly after them into the trees. Charging ourselves straight into an ambush—for there, more Greens await behind their horses and begin their own barrage of gunnery. Jumping from our saddles to take cover, we pound back at them, cursing and waving out obscenities, the light snow-cover churning to gray slush beneath the trampling of our feet, the mossy forest floor soon lying littered everywhere with the casings of spent shells. Finally, everyone starts wanting for fresh ammunition, but no time ensues to reload; upon a fierce battle cry, a daring group from Zorshenko's forefront sprints straight into the Green stronghold, losing four men in the process, but amply spooking off the cover of the horses. Then it all turns into a savage, thrusting battle of bayonets, metal clanging in hollow wails against the crash of metal until meeting at last the shear of skin, bone, blood. Into my ear, I hear Volodya's call of warning, and whirl about to find myself caught in a fencing match unto the bloody death with a tall Ukrainian towering near unto a foot over my head. Lack of height, for once, proves an advantage; as he wings his blade for my chest, it grazes my upper arm instead—just as I plow my own bayonet into the folds of his coat. Caught in a silent, pivoting scream, he topples downward into a bed of ferns, grasping his girth with both hands as red blood oozes out across the black and white of the earth and the snow. Snarling in rage, I kick him about to face me, his head reeling backward, his eyes focusing into and then holding mine for the briefest split second in a numbed schism of panic. But mercy proffers not the slightest thought of restraint; gritting my teeth, I slash the bayonet down—again and again into his stomach as his screams peal through the air; again and again I continue slashing even once the screams finally abate, the blade hacking into his groin, chest, arms, and face, the blood spurting out bright red everywhere just like the blood from the towering, bloody flames—blood-red flames spurting out from every corner of the earth and engulfing my life, land, home, honor, memories—everything that I ever held dear, everything that I ever lived for . . . .

"We took 'em, men!" Zorshenko yells out across our heads as we gain ourselves clear into the upper hand, the Greens at farthest fringes of the tumult extricating themselves without apology to their fallen comrades and galloping off on frightened horses through the woods. "Praise God!" Zorshenko gloats on, waving his carbine high through the air in triumph. "We just 'bout got 'em all!"

Back through the clearing, I wander my way with others of the band through piles of the Green's bodies, my own blood draining in a growing trickle down to my jacket's ripped elbow; the Ukrainian's drenched in dirtied smears across the lower shafts of my boots. Already returned to the horses, Volodya meets my gaze with a solemn nod and says nothing, tossing me a bandana to make use of as a bandage. Grinning as if we all have just done naught but trump our bets at a tavernhouse, Yevgeny saunters on up with an armful of bedrolls and other supplies squandered from the Greens' abandoned horses. From my saddle gear, I snatch out my canteen flask, and unheedful of my spectacles, start splashing icy water across my brow and into my hair; icy water I splash across both of my hands—which will not stop shaking in violent spasms seeming to match, in intensity, the perilous hacking of my breath, the frantic tremors tearing at every beat of my stunned and vacant heart.

Mumbling something about a bad leg never stopping anybody with a mind to fight, Yevgeny slaps me on the back; so, later, does Zorshenko. Yet, victory's taste soon enough proves sourly short-lived. As we finally leave the bodies behind and fall into trot with one another, taking the lakeshore route south away from the ravaged clearing, I hear many of the men conversing together—with a hatred not unmatched to mine—about Makhno and his fierce legendary Greens; I hear derisive whispers of Makhno himself—who was nowhere near this group we slaughtered today—and of his followers, numbering literally in the thousands strong, their fearsome sorties raising riot across the plains and through the hills for up to thousands of versts all the way from here to the southern Caucasus.

* * *

First, we pursue further conquests to the south, and then veer gradually westward, for Zorshenko's grievances stand not solely against the tell-tale raids of Makhno's Greens, but as related during our first encounter at Lissushka, continue fanatically against White counter-revolutionaries, Red Communists, and German gadabouts as well—in other words, against anyone who attacks or attempts to infringe in even the slightest manner upon the freedom of him and his roving band. For a fortnight, I follow along with the others readily enough. But after a dozen or so more skirmishes following our first entanglement with the Green group near Kolinsky's, my anger begins to cool down toward a solidified core of resolution, my pent-up rage over Lissushka's fate dissipating itself in blood. The letting of which, I will admit, does not suit my taste for sustained daily fare as on ongoing prospect—much as I çan, to my vast surprise, hold my own against an assault. Thus it is that my thoughts begin dwelling increasingly upon the family in Petrograd to whom I should, by all respects, return. When I finally happen upon Zorshenko aside the campfire one glowing golden eve to find him in a reflective mood, I take the opportunity to start telling wistful tales of my children—and he agrees, although with some reluctance, to allow my departure from the band. "Will be a shame, though, laddie. Spite o' yer size an' that limp, ye fight 'em off like a mean little rat when ye have te, an' do fine with a rifle fer a city fellow. But yer two friends seem te want te stay on with me well enough—an' mustered-up, determined fightin' men is what I need. Go ahead then, if ye got pressin' family needs back in Petrograd—do what ye feel ye must."

A doleful-eyed Rykazian I meet on my way to saddle up. "We rode south at night, I can find my way back up north at night," I tell him, glaring off his protests. "We're scarce a few versts east of Pskov. I know the railway tracks from here to Novgorod well enough. Remember the many summers I headed this way with Bulya to pick up the Pskov market ledgers? God, Rykazian, what are you, my mother? Well, I don't care—do whatever you choose! You and Ivanovich want to tag along with this Zorshenko and have yourselves the grandstanding adventure of a lifetime, it's fine enough by me."

"Sekovsky, you do *not* understand. Ivanovich!" he yells across my head, cupping his hands. "Over here!"

Yevgeny brings along a hefty, bearded fellow named Yakovlev, with whom he's become friendly over the past few days. What Yakovlev shows me is the latest copy of the Moscow *Izvestiya*—which indicates that Trotsky has been officially named War Commissar. And into the Communists' latest brain-child—the Red Army—full-scale conscription has been mandated, compulsory for all workers and peasants who do not hire labor. In view of the increasing threat of hostilities from White counter-revolutionary forces in the south, the exact length of service for inductees has not yet been specified.

"Whether ye got young'uns or no, don't matter lad," Yakovlev tells me with a sad shake of his head. "I got young'uns, too—jest three and five years each, they are—two sons, an' their sweet little *matushka* ever takin' sick all the time. But I took off straight away from Moscow last week with a whole bunch o' others as soon as them damn Communists started makin' the rounds house te house, lookin' fer any men o' fightin' age. Whole groups o' workers I saw them soldiers draggin' off into the streets right from their beds, goadin' 'em awake with bayonets. Only way I escaped at all was on account o' jest sneakin' back from a tavernhouse. Group o' fellows I was with had heard o' rovin' bands up north here past the hills, so this way we come. Decided we'd jest as soon fight fer a scraggly lot like this than fer them godless, bloody Reds. An' don't think that leg o' yers'll fetch an exemption, neither. I seen all kinds of limpin' fellas, war injuries from the German front. If they can walk, Trotsky's takin' 'em in every one."

"If you don't believe him, Sasha," urges Volodya, "just look at how many more have joined up with Zorshenko over the last week."

It is true. In the past week, as we have inched our way slowly westward, the band's numbers have swollen to near double. Cautiously, however—as the bonfire glows its way down to red-tinged embers and the men finish gnawing off their bits of smoked fish and roasted whole potatoes, I begin asking around—and story after story not only confirms Yakovlev's somber warning, but tells of similar recruitment nightmares taking place as little as two days past in Petrograd.

Yevgeny catches up with me as I hoist the saddle down from my mare's back. "So. Ye're stayin' then?"

Sighing, I meet his eye, and nod. My promise to Lyubov to always provide sustenance for her and the children I have never taken lightly. But I did leave behind the entire remainder of my stash of Tsarist rubles, still near valuable as gold in the black market alleys these days against Lenin's worthless influx of Soviet bills. And for her safety, for her peace of mind, Lyubov will always have Grigor—who would care for her children well, I know, in spite of his distasteful feelings for me. It was he with whom both Vanya and Zhenya were out—on their daily walk to the park—the afternoon that Volodya and Yevgeny and I rode off. "I suppose I've no choice but to stay—yes," I tell Yevgeny. "I'll be damned if I'll be dragged away, once I reach home, to fight for Trotsky and his stinking Communist Reds."

"Me neither. Think I rather take a likin' te callin' myself a Bolshevik—but not a Communist."

Bolshevik, Communist—little will it matter soon enough. On my way back to inform Zorshenko of my change in heart, I pass by two fellows drawing a map with sticks in the dirt, their frowns worried, the tones of their voices ominous: "Yaa, to the south we got the Ukrainian Rada fightin' under colors o' the ataman Kaledin. An' ready te join up with 'em any day now is General Anton Denikin an' his bloodthirsty, Commie-hungry Whites—the Volunteer Army, folks say they call it. An' mad, they all are—naught but a bunch o' highbrowed nobles an' old Tsarist officers, all stinkin' mad 'nough to spit on the damn Revolution. While due north in Petrograd, the Commies are hangin' on by a scarecrow's thread, but they're entrenched fer a long one. So too in Moscow—them Reds are in charge o' the streets, the Kremlin, everythin'. Then all along the rail-line connectin' the old capital with the new capital, there's scores o' Makhno's Greens pullin' raids on trains. Them torchin' Black Hundreds're are ridin' along with 'em, an' both groups are full hell-bent on pushin' their way te the west. While te the west, we got Poles—an' then more Germans, jest te the west o' the Poles, than ye can shake the devil at, both groups pushin' due east. An' guess who's stuck in between?"

The point of his finger on the hand-drawn map is unmistakable—northwestern European Russia. The whole region from Lake Ilmen's eastern shore to the Estonian and Latvian borders just west of Pskov.

Us.

* * *

War . . . . we soon find ourselves trapped as wanderers at bay amidst the blood lust of Lenin's desperate battle for supremacy. Day by day, week by week as the melt of springtime slowly whimpers its way forward into summer's radiant, basking warmth, we regroup again and again in hurried posturings of attack and retreat to maintain hold on our line of defense, battling nightly unto throes of exhaustion against the intractable monster—the devil that transforms sane men who once would have taken tea with one another into ruthless, murdering beasts. For unlike the Tsar's territorial skirmishes with the Japanese in 1905; unlike the mawkish foolishness carried on with Germany ever since August of 1914, this war bids forth consequences far more devastating than any before it and perhaps more than any other since or hence—for this is the war to end all wars, the final benediction, the reigning Golgotha supreme. This—in the stark, brutal countenance of father against son, brother against brother, peasant against bourgeoisie, and White counter-revolutionary against insurgent Communist Red—is truth arisen from the dire warnings, our fate incarnated thirstily alive from the Revolution's earliest dissident fears. This is the way, the path, the light shown shining pure and clear, Blok's bedraggled Twelve Apostles guiding forth Christ's thorny visage from the ashen mount of Hell; this is naught but inevitable, unconscionable, unholy *civil* war. . . .

For a time, ever straining to stay a fair distance from both the encroaching Bolshevik Red Army and the Polish, who continue heightening their push for independence from Germany's wavering yoke, we squeeze into a cramped vise along heathery river fronts in Estonia and in the eastern pastures of Latvia. But Makhno's and other raiding parties forever add fuel to the fire, keeping us on constant move and preventing any permanent encampments. Farther to the south, once the Germans occupy Kiev, the Ukrainian Rada proclaims its homeland an independent People's Republic. In Kharkov, however, a Soviet regime gains fast hold against dwindling opposition, the Ukraine's borders then taking on a continuous mutability in their partition between Communist east and Nationalist west. Meanwhile, seizing opportunity, the Japanese swarm into the far eastern port of Vladivostok; British, French, and American troops take up air and artillery strongholds at Murmansk, at Arkhangelsk, and in the Crimean peninsula, all in Allied support of the White General Denikin, who begins his massive northward advance with the Volunteer Army after forging tough new alliances with Don and Kuban Cossack atamans in the heart of the Volga basin and the Caucasus. At about the same time, to the east in the Urals, a legion of Czech prisoners some forty-thousand strong—held over after their surrender from the Austrian side in the war—clamors for revolt. Against the Moscow government's attempted assertions of power, the Czechs launch throughout the summer into increasing offensive, finally taking for themselves—in the name of counter-revolution—string after string of Siberian towns: Chelyabinsk, Novo-Nikolayevsk, Penza, and Omsk, amongst others. As a result, monarchist plots begin simmering forth upon the seedy lips of rumor, for the Tsar—far from having been evacuated to England, as everyone had previously thought—is, in June, sighted in Yekaterinburg, a week after the disappearance—and supposed shooting by Red Guards—of his brother, the Grand Duke Mikhail Aleksandrovich.

The following month, Lenin's Communists respond in due kind to eager monarchist hopes and counter-revolutionary rumor—and to the last surviving tenets of any human decency—by executing in cold blood the Tsar, his wife, his young son, and four teenage daughters.

Thoughts of the Tsar's five dead children torment me night by night far into the remainder of the summer, sabotaging away any hope for decent sleep. Thoughts of the war, the fighting, the vendettas, the ruthlessness hound me day by day as, along with the others, I spearfish for sturgeon in shallow beds of the rivers and dig up half-rotted, woody turnips in countless abandoned farm fields. And guilt and remorse rend to thorny tatters my code of honor and family pride when, with no other means of obtaining fodder for our horses, we converge again and again at gunpoint upon groups of helpless, pleading peasants and ransack their storehouses of all remaining grain. At night, God rains upon us His just and aptly metered punishment: the curse of open warfare waging on across the land—mercilessly, endlessly, never pausing for a moment's lull, the machine-gun and artillery fire forever rattling a sputtering, grisly hum throughout cover of the darkness. As much as I shut my mind and attempt to keep hold on some semblance of sanity, my eyes clamped tightly shut as I curl up shivering each eve upon my fraying bedroll, the roar never ends, the poundings never cease, the pockets of burnt flashes from the tireless tolling of the guns chase across every last reach of the starry sky, flirting with the light of the moon. . . .

And as autumn's beckonings begin squaring their approach upon summer's hazy horizon, true Red Terror—spelled now with a capital 'T'—begins in earnest. As we continue our routs with other roving bands and crisscross back and forth over the western Russian frontier in hapless meandering attempts to stay clear of Red and White exchanges of fire, the destruction visited upon any estate houses lying in harm's way begins to take on a much more grisly, violent character, proving Lissushka's fate to have been, in actuality, a necessary act of mercy. My own house I would choose to see burned down; to my own birthplace, I would have set the torches ablaze myself in attempt to forestall such desecration as we encounter after scores of apparent Red Guard raids: sliced paintings, smashed mirror-glasses, antique furniture hacked into a thousand bits and scattered into yards, roads, the surrounding forest; rugs and floors soiled unto the stinking height of disgust, strewn throughout every ransacked room with dried pools of piss and mashed piles of horse and human dung. Across doorways, eaves, and high glass cathedral windows, hammer-and-sickle emblems drip in triumphantly painted strokes of blood; family members—even babes and tiny young children—are found shot to death in their kitchens, on their sofas, within the blankets of cradles, and in large four-poster beds—or at the most, lie spooned together outside in battered heaps within shallow common graves. Lenin, yes, is keeping strict word to the promises brandished with such cunning, veiled ability in the tepid pages of his *Chto Delat*. His cohorts are fulfilling my prophecies of doom cast in dreams of guillotines and visions of rabid wolves, for the Red Guards are hunting down and murdering all remaining members of the Imperial family, along with waging slaughter upon the Empire's former noble and middle classes, gunning down untold scores of people like so many worthless, common dogs. . . .

Although, over a common dog, I sometimes wonder if I am any better.

For day after day, dog that I am, naught I have done but plod on like a dog, one death-defying, dogged foot slapped down once again dully before the other, my limbs never focused past the immediate moment but only upon each next prospective movement, my thoughts centered solely upon each muddied, filthy, animal-like step, my throat succumbing ever to thirst, my body, again, to hunger. . . .

I lean back against a fir tree and watch. The brisk hint of autumn pours cool and clear, tingling down my throat against desire's pliant pull, the taste of the air as light and sweet as sparkling, white spring water. Scarce twenty feet away, Zorshenko and the others are all having at it again. No one remembers where the girl came from this time: another refugee; another wide-eyed tag-along garnered up since we passed by the last deserted railhead; another orphan left adrift to care for her none-to-adept-self in this wild, chaotic world bound by no more rules, nor chivalrous acts of male heroism. She made a mistake—they would have let her be, otherwise. But she became friendly, and parlayed a few kisses with a couple of the blue-eyed, burly peasant youths—the fellows with the broad grins and heavy, muscular arms of stout young farmhands who always hold such firm sway unto Zorshenko's forefront ranks whenever we ride. Again they are all riding—and laughing, and grinning—although now in an entirely different manner: the girl's skirts and petticoats, torn apart and stained with blood and muddied splotches, have been thrown up over her quivering bosom. Her legs—stark bare against the moist bed of grass and brush—lie white and still as the mask of death, giving way to neither a twitch nor the slightest bend as yet another of the men finishes, pulling himself out; as yet another of them falls down at once unto his knees and then upon her, thrusting himself inside. Snorts and grunts of satisfaction emit once more from the group gathered around watching, the flasks of vodka making further rounds. Vedinsky, the current perpetrator, inspires a chorus of boisterous shouts and low whistles of envy by staying firm inside the girl for a full ten fucking minutes. Then he pushes back up, bowing ceremoniously to all nearby as they slap him heartily on the back. And then another of them hunkers on down.

Yevgeny, who has already gone once, is waiting with Zorshenko to try a second round. He looks in my direction and shrugs.

Again I stare down toward the bare legs of the girl, again breathing in the eerie, pulling drift of the air—*so crisp, clear, and clean; so firm, hot, moist, wet—like the undulating, engulfing mouth of the river; so high and far and long and deep, like the glorious, white parting span of the sun; the air so cool, light, and fresh . . . like sparkling, sweet spring water . . . .*

"Hey, Carrot-top!" one of the sandy-haired peasant youths yells over at me. "What about it, eh? Like te come over an' chance a bit o' desert before yer supper? C'mon along with the rest o' us—this little bitch is still tight as maidenhead!"

Rykazian has been watching me, and from the corner of my eye, I catch his probing stare once more. But away from the girl, I cannot tear my attention; away from the bare skin spread out in the dirt, tiny trickles of blood seeping down her naked thighs like so much dark cranberry icing . . . away from the whole disgusting, humid scene, I cannot shear my heightened senses . . . away from the cool air, I cannot wrest apart raw lust. . . .

"C'mon, Laddie Red—quit stallin'!" Zorshenko shouts this time upon a rash of jokes over the backs of two other fellows—the first withdrawing out from the girl, the second shoving his way down in. "We can tell ye want her," Zorshenko quips on, laughing and pointing over at me. "Uh-huh, everybody can tell—even all the way from here!"

The groups erupts into snickers as, reddening, I inch my head forward just enough from the trunk of the tree to glimpse the bulge growing down the front of my trousers. Then I come eye to eye square with Rykazian again. He ducks away, and shoves his hands into his pockets, stomping off toward a group of abandoned farm buildings lying southward through the woods.

Following after, I take the cigarette which I have lit, but not smoked, and smash it to the ground, ignoring the laughter and gleeful insults of Zorshenko and the others—who continue pounding away without pause at the blank-eyed, motionless girl.

The door to an old tool shed I find ajar; the moment I step in, he slams it shut behind. I toss away my cane and plunge my fingers into the long, graying strands of his hair; he seizes both hands about my neck and our kisses melt together in a frantic spin as we wrap arms and legs about one another in sighs of relief, kneeling our way for the ground. Once there, I shimmy myself on top, thrusting unto his thrusting, moaning into his moans and crushing my mouth into, then out of; again into, then out of, his . . . finally, he bolts away and mops his sleeve up across his brow, thick beads of sweat coursing down his temples, while I fumble with the knots in the strips of cloth used to keep my spectacles tied on, at last flinging the wire frames away from my face in a breathless angst of impatience. Long and hard we stare into one another's eyes, aware of no need any longer to make apology for the past, nor offer any explanation for the present. Our fingers then intertwine, groping their way downward to pick away each tier of buttons straining firm against swollen flies . . . and then our two centers of the world we hold aloft in the palms of trembling, eager hands to fondle and stroke and lick and kiss . . . and then I suck him . . . and he sucks me . . . .

Afterward, we keep to our silence, and avoid meeting each the other's gaze. He wanders out, and I hear him peeing into the bushes; hear him lighting a cigarette as he ambles slowly away. Back through the open doorway, I finally stumble, short of breath, and lean into the post. And again I watch—for through the woods, the men are only continuing their heartless ravishment of the girl. Soon enough, they will tire of her—just as they have of all the others—and for sport, one of them will pull out a revolver and shoot her dead, leaving her there spread-eagled as she lies.

Intervention on my part would prove wholly futile; the next bullet shot would sound for me. In wartime, no woman should ever allow herself to get taken in by a wandering band of men—where no man, no matter how greatly he might wish to, can defend her honor. Or his own.

Indeed, my own honor I cannot even any longer recognize; my precious, guarded integrity has all along been naught but a shambles, a ruse, a lie. Long ago, I put my hand into one outstretched from the indiscernible, hallowed depths of my dreams; long ago, I pledged my inner self unto the holy white light, and therefore unto a higher calling of morality—a standard of conduct which equates all intention with action. *For that which is created in thought by one who deems himself a Knower, is as much created in form—one and the very same.* Yes, the man in the whitened shroud has taught me many lessons, and taught them well. Again unto the Tower's precipice, I shall once more unconditionally surrender; again into the Hanged Man's noose of irony—the walking in all things contrary to the ways of this awful world—I must lay down my neck and bind the knots with repentant, humble fingers. One gem of truth beyond all others have I taken to heart well: whatever little forays I might indulge in with Volodya—or with any other *willing* partner—matters naught, in truth, to the Higher Powers that be. But solely in my simple, naked wanting, in my mere passing thoughts of rapacious lust for the girl, I have proven my discipleship as yet remaining flawed, my evolvement crude, my earthly vessel as yet unworthy to glimpse the light, tread the path, grasp the hand unto which I am ethereally bound. Of course, within God's cup of resolution, the way ever remains open to one who seeks, for final culmination stands always at the end—which is said to be only the beginning of dark night's mysterious, forbidden path. And there, ultimately—for all serious errors of intention—one dies a thousand deaths for one's sins. . . .

* * *

Winter . . . it is the apocalypse of which Tolstoy wrote, the adversary from which Napoleon fled in history's deadliest march after the ravage of the battle of Borodino. None save those who have heard it, none save those who have felt its ache sawing rifts into the marrow of their bones can know the blind fury of the Russian *burya* wind, its chill loosed in fierce, whistling contagion from icy gulfs of the northern

White and Kara Seas—without a mountain across the vast tundra plains to stem the squall of its rampant flow, with nary a hill throughout the dense spread of taiga forest land to hold back the swell of its bristling tide. None save those who have withstood its rigors can know the impact, the meaning, the horror of this arch, frozen hell we call Russian winter. . . .

Winter means ever a crust of icicles tickling up beneath the tip of your nose and upon your dry, cracked lips with each haggard, halting breath that you take. Winter means the constant hunt for shelter away from the hail of high storm winds and raining ice; winter means foraging with knives and the long sabers of bayonets for remnants of autumn's potato crop in countless stiff and sickly fields. Winter means pushing and shoving against those with whom you once rode as friends in order to stand closest to the fire, to the soup pot, to the occasional span of railway tracks lying scarce visible beneath greasy layers of crusted snow and warmed since the last smoking engine with its paltry string of refugee cars coursed past. Winter means scavenging like a vulture through pile after pile of wounded foes in desperate search for fresh cartridge clips, for spare hardtack—and ultimately, for a warm coat; it means peeling that coat off the arms and back of a dying man who spits in your face and calls you a bastard, who cares not a whit that you've found no speck of luck with the corpses, on whom the curse of the weather, the icy stiffness of death's pall has already duly set in. Winter, indeed, means corpses, everywhere—across every hill and vale, and within every darkened, menacing cluster of birch and pine. This awful winter of wartime has spawned naught but a deluge of corpses and rotting parts and pieces of bodies throughout the land, everywhere: arms, legs, hands, toes, feet, and fingers—the hands some still wearing gloves; the fingers some still bearing rings; the feet, the legs some still stuffed partway within wraps of leggings or warm leather boots—which you pry off, if time permits, just in case they might fit. Winter. Fighting war in winter means consigning oneself to the doubtful spoils of survival fraught with the vile countenance of the anti-Christ, the devil's dark, evil vantage masked within one's own vacant eyes. Winter in wartime proves the naked shame of the animal that man is, that all men are. It means admitting the animal one has become . . . .

Throughout the winter, all straggling clues from Makhno's green-ribboned raiding parties finally disappear from the Pskov-Novgorod region. At last seeking a more constant supply of food over confrontation with anyone—Red, White, or Green—we move gradually southward, and more and more, Zorshenko's band becomes awkwardly embroiled in fending off lures of partisanship with the Communist Reds while fighting back the growing infringement of the counter-revolutionary White resistance. And more and more, the old ways in the countryside fall victim to wartime's pervading tomb of obliteration: at Christmastide, my heart aches at the sight of more desecrated churches, the air long bereft of the wondrous treble peal of their bells. The new year of 1919 dawns bearing swift remuneration for the many dire deeds of ourselves, of the Reds, the Whites, of Makhno's, and whoever else's men: the grippe and flux cost Zorshenko between a quarter and a full half of his numbers, and appears to dole out unto our enemies their fair share of torturous grave digging also, because for near unto three entire months—January through the ides of March—a good part of the fighting lulls. Incredibly, I manage not to take sick along with the rest; incredibly, as spring begins edging her way slowly toward new horizon's dawn and routs with the Whites, and especially with lingering German gadabouts, commence once again, I continue to hold my own with the others in the band, all of us yet intent upon man's primeval instinct borne against the brunt of the uncertain future since the very dawn of time: to simply, somehow, eke out a bit of sustenance from the barren morass of a war-torn winter; to simply, somehow—against all odds—survive . . . .

Grumbling, shivering, and yet struggling to survive, jabbing elbows and beating our hands together, we huddle about our iconostasis, our graven image, our blessed and cherished holy altar divine—the soup pot, an old tin wash bucket suspended on a rod above the campfire between branching trunks of two trees. Again beneath my arm, I grip the buttstock of my Mosin-Nagant, slung over my shoulder; everyone else, too, keeps closely nursing their rifles at the ready. Three times in one day, the Whites have hemmed us in with fire from their scouting patrols. According to the latest sightings, the bulk of General Nikolai Yudenich's Northwestern White Army, backed up by a volunteer division of Germans, is once more pushing this way, chasing after a regiment of Reds. Who once again have scurried eastward, retreating back to within Russian territory just east of the Latvian border.

And once again Zorshenko's band has been left abandoned to the naked brunt of open warfare between the two sides, our position holding nebulously, hour by hour, just a few versts in between.

The soup—a watery, thin gruel of fish bits strewn with scanty pieces of potatoes—we wolf down greedily once finally warmed. Shivering, I keep my hands held snug about my tin cup; keep my lips pressed against it, sighing against the ebbing warmth as the fellow beside me bumps my arm again and mumbles: “Don’t ye want te fetch ’nother look?”

Still, they are passing around a picturegraph taken three days ago by Tverinikov, a refugee on his way to Riga, who came through shouldering, of all things, a photo-camera and darkroom equipment. After much pleading on his part, with stiffened lips and shouldered rifles, we all stood in a group, while he fidgeted about endlessly with the tripod and the cords. Finally, after a two-day hiatus sequestered away in his tent, he produced the image over which all the band has been gloating ever since. “Take ’nother gander at us, Carrot-top,” the fellow beside me urges again, his smile hooked in satisfaction as he passes over the picture.

“Shit,” I mumble in disgust, turning away. *As if I should even care to see myself so dirty, rag-clad, probably lice-ridden and reeking like a barnyard pig . . .* shaking my head, I desert last visions of the picture and the warmth of the fire without further thought, and once again seek out Rykazian.

“Our turn,” he says without looking at me, gulping down the remainder of his soup and striding off for the horses.

Nodding, I surrender my cup and spoon to the snow to wash them out; stuff both back into my knapsack, and trudge after. By the time I catch up, Vedinsky and Yakovlev have already ridden back in. “Watch yerselves,” Yakovlev warns, crossing himself and shaking his large, brow-creased head with weary emphasis as he dismounts his horse. “Them White bastards are combin’ ’cross the forest ridge again—an’ll be on us for certain in full numbers by nightfall. Zorshenko’s goin’ te have no choice but te either give into ’em, or move eastward again.”

“Yaa,” chimes in Vedinsky with a snort. “Eastward, the Reds’ll force us over to their godless side fer sure. Westward, the Whites’ll give us a high-laughin’ time ’gainst their Mausers and them damn machine-guns they been luggin’ along behind. Humph! Yaa, ye both better watch yerselves extra careful,” he goes on, pointing with a grin between the two of us. “They spot them two Commie coats o’ yers—an’ that red-star cap ye been sportin’ all this week like such a lout, Rykazian—they spot ye two, an’ Yudenich’s bootlickers might jest take ye both sure fer a couple o’ Reds.”

Glowering at Vedinsky, I sputter out: “Oh, shut up. You know these were the only warm coats we could find. Fuck, more than half the men in the band have stolen themselves Red coats.”

"Ahh, yes," drawls Volodya, doffing his red-star cap with a sarcastic bow. "The blessed perils of sentry duty—"

"Humph! And why don't you do me a blessed favor, Rykazian, and shut your yap up, too?" Angrily, I shove my cane and rifle into the saddle cinch.

"Shit, Sekovsky," he snaps back. "You know, I am sick and tired of havin' to 'shut up' around you all the time! In fact, I am gettin' plumb irked at you and your preenin' little ass. . . ."

Swearing back at him in turn, I hoist myself into the saddle—only, once up, to let out a searing gasp as I plow my leg down far too abruptly into the left-side stirrup.

"Oh, hell!" Volodya exclaims. "What is it?"

"Nothing."

"That damn rheumatism still plaguin' your leg?"

"Blast it, Rykazian—I said it was nothing! Now are we going to cover sentry? Or leave the damn flank unguarded?"

"All right, all right."

None too soon for my disgruntled comfort, we start winging our way quietly through the forest, skirting through snow-covered ferns and around blackened moats of peat bogs as we close in upon perimeter of the westward ridge. "What the devil do you mean," I demand of Volodya, once my thoughts clear as the pain in my leg subsides, "'preening?'"

"Well, Jesus!" he replies, shooting me a pained glare. "The way you insist on spoonin' your soup, Sekovsky—when everybody else simply drinks theirs! And I never to God in my entire life thought I'd see you haul off and eat potatoes—when we can find 'em—with a blessed fork! And I sure as hell never thought I'd see anyone act so damned finicky about shavin' out here in the mucky wilderness."

"I was brought up to observe proper table manners," I snap in reply, "no matter what the circumstances. And as far as shaving, for me, a week's full long enough! God, Rykazian—you look simply grand with that stubble growing out all over your face. Me, I look like a girl with a beard."

"Oh, you do not."

"Was you and the farmhands all used to tease me near unto fits about it—remember? Endless insults, everywhere I went, every single summer—said, come winter skating time on the lake, I'd be the next fairy princess."

"Oh, by bowels of the Saints! Are you still sore at me over that? Christ, Sekovsky—that was years ago! Might I remind you that you've grown up? And are a whole lot—well—older lookin' now than durin' them years on the farm. And—why the devil are we fightin' like this, anyway? I thought we made up since last summer in that tool shed—we been sneakin' suck-offs past these yokels in the band every chance we can find ever since. Oh, all right—I'm sorry for what I been sayin' about your fork and spoon and your shavin'—shave all you blessed want to then, my dear, fastidious Count Sekovsky! Even if we are stuck out here in the middle of a reekin' hellhole. And if you want, I'm sorry for whatever else I said—which I can scarce remember, mind you!—them years back at Lissushka. I'm sorry for whatever else I've said that might have stung that damned sensitive pride of yours in all the years that came after. *All right?"*

At his tone, I cannot subdue my chuckles, and he throws up both hands, bursting out: "And what is so goddamned funny?"

"Speaking of looking older—"

"Don't you start in again about my gray hairs!"

Shaking my head, I pull out two cigarettes, light both, and hand one over to him as he finally breaks into a grin. "God, Sasha," he mutters ruefully as we ease within sight of the widest lookout point upon the ridge. "What the hell are we doin' out here, stuck God-knows-where in the middle of fuckin' Latvia?"

With a long sigh, I stare out for any sign of White Guards and pull my ermine cap low to my brow. "Next month," I tell him, "my son will turn three years old. I wonder if he even remembers me."

Volodya answers only with a nod, and we both drag off our cigarettes in listless silence until tossing the butts away, when he catches my eye with a solemn glance, murmuring: "They say there's starvation in Petrograd."

"So I've heard."

"That's according to Medvedev," he goes on. "You know—that big bear of a fellow who joined up last month? Of course, he's probably just another Red infiltrator.

"So I've thought."

"Uh-huh. Ivanovich says most all the one's we've took on since last Christmastide are naught but a bunch of Red infiltrators. Says the Commies know full well how to win over the forest bands from the inside out, 'stead of fightin'. Vedinsky told me the other day that Zorshenko's even thinkin' of goin' over. Says more than half the rovin' bands from here to Pskov have gone over to the Reds; it's better than facin' slaughter at hands of the Whites—who'll scarce give the time of day to anybody, unless they spit out each word with proper syllables like a damned *dvoryanye* blueblood. Uh, no offense meant by that personal, Sasha, my old friend."

"And you think the Reds would mete out any fairer treatment—or terms of surrender—than the Whites?"

Volodya shrugs in reply. "The Reds need men—they'd take us in. But the Whites—once they catch up, they'll simply hack us to bits. That's what I've heard from every fellow I've talked to who's ever run in with them."

I nod in silence, again torn between separate loyalties over the war. The Whites, after all, comprise the bulk of my former peers: members of the aristocracy and the upper middle class, the group Lenin so derisively terms the *bourgeoisie*. But the Reds—by last account, at least—are still protecting Petrograd. And therefore, the welfare of my wife, my children . . . .

Sighing against such reflective thoughts, Volodya and I light up two more cigarettes, and near complete our round through the forest when, from beyond the ridge, the faint sound of voices picks up our attention. "Not ours," Volodya whispers, emphatically shaking his head.

"Are you sure?"

"Not from Zorshenko's band, no. But I'm damned well going to find out who," he adds, frowning and cocking up his rifle.

"Perhaps we'd best head back to the clearing. Bring some of the others with us—"

"No, I want to go check this out myself. You stay here and cover my back."

"Dammit, Rykazian—you be careful. Don't you go pulling any heroic capers!"

"Oh, darlin'—I'll be back to kiss you 'nother sweet goodnight quick as a lick!" he quips back, laughing and puckering up his lips.

Bristling in reply, I watch with unease as he throws back his head and trots off past the bog toward the muffled sounds in the distance.

Up ahead, the ridge hovers invitingly within view. Below it, upon riding close enough, one would happen upon a sloping gray descent unto a wealth of rolling pasture and scattering of some of the scores of serene little lakes that weave their way back and forth across fertile rivers of the Baltic heartland. Sighing, I check my watch; at half past four, the light will hold for some time yet, each day of late gradually lengthening, the span of nightfall ever shrinking shorter and shorter. A full year now it has been, almost, since the three of us rode off like such inane adventurers that night from Petrograd; a full year now since I have, in the wake of Lissushka's memories, reverted back to use of my true and legal name—a prideful, and in these times, perhaps wholly rash thing to do. The only good that can transpire from such wielding is that if I ever find my way safe back to Petrograd, the children would be disassociated from me—and protected, if the Communists win their war, from my aristocratic-blooded truth. Nonetheless, regret tears at me once again as I steer my mare away from a muddied sandbog—regret for all the foolish, selfish stunts, the hasty decisions I have made in my life with scarce a second thought for Father, Vanya, Zhenya, for so many others. If only I could repay them all their kindness, love, and patience. If only I could somehow know what the children are doing now, right at this very moment: is Zhenya in school, studying English? Chemistry? Is Vanya talking in full sentences yet and yanking like a little hellion at Lyubov's skirts? If only I could somehow know where and how Father is: did he sail for England once the Armistice was signed last November between the Allied and Central Powers, as he had for so long been staunchly promising to do?

"Damn this war," I whisper to myself, wresting in a further ache of regret with such thoughts that near fill to overwhelm my heart, just as they have for months. But as I stare around, taking note of tiny green sprouts budding out from the willowy branches of bare linden trees tucked here and there in between the rows of slender, scented pines, earth's yearly miracle of fresh life arising anew from her war-torn shackles somehow begins imbuing a strange, resigned sense of peace. I can only hope that the return of the rooks and the starlings, the advent of spring back home—despite the awful rumors about the war's toll on the city—holds such refreshing promise for the future of my little Vanya, and for Zhenya.

Smashing my cigarette butt to the ground, I let out a long sigh and fish out another—just as, from over the ridge, a hail of voices erupts into a volley of shots.

"Oh, Rykazian, you damn fool," I mutter out, cocking up my rifle.

Coat flying in a pair of tails out behind him, Volodya reemerges at a runaway gallop just past the summit of the ridge. "Go, by dammit!" he yells, swinging around in the saddle and firing behind. "Warn the others!"

Rearing back, I blast off three quick shots into the air—the prearranged signal for any trouble—and fall into a gallop a good fifty feet ahead of him, ducking as scores of bullets whiz past my head. "How many?" I yell back behind my shoulder.

"God, close to a whole fuckin' regiment!" he shouts, piloting his rifle in volley after volley back behind. "Jesus, what were Vedinsky and Yakovlev doin' at their turn on patrol, sleepin'? I swear there's a hundred—maybe even up to hundred-fifty—"

Once we clear the bog and duck into the deeper part of the woods, our pursuers pull back—but only, by all appearances, to briefly regroup and talk it over, for within moments, the shots pour after us in a storm once again, only dwindling off as Zorshenko and a guard of about twenty meet up with us at the break to the clearing. "How many?" he demands, the jaws of the men mounted beside him locking in determined grimaces to the cock of their carbines.

No time remains to answer, because the next hail of bullets sends each of us scattering for our lives, Volodya yelling: "Shit! Machine-gun fire!" Whereupon Zorshenko hollers out at the top of his lungs: "Fall back—that is the order! Ye value yer skins, ye damn well better *fall back!"*

In the clearing, the camp breaks up in a shambles, saddles, knapsacks, and soup pots flying. "No, wait!" Zorshenko then screams in an apparent switch of tactics. "Hold the line, hold the line, I say! *We've got no time!"* Another deadly barrage of machine-gun bullets hails past as he continues barking out orders to return fire in lieu racing off with our horses. "Otherwise, they'll cut us down to ribbons with them damned German man-killers!" he calls in hurried explanation. *"Shit!"*

Behind an embankment of bushes, Volodya and I tumble from our saddles and start fishing in our pockets for fresh cartridge clips. "Sure wish we had more than a mere five rounds to each magazine," he says to me, his hands shaking along with mine as we both proceed to reload. "God fuck the Germans for comin' up with a killer gun that can pick off twenty, thirty men at a head."

My answer meets the thick muffle of dirt and trampled snow as I flatten down, another gruesome volley rattling nonstop across our heads.

"I'd still think it wiser to try a run for it on the horses," I reply finally, snapping my chamber shut and spewing off with my own volley of shots once the incoming machine-gun discharge clears. "Sometimes, Zorshenko's not all the sly fox everyone takes him for, Rykazian—don't you think?"

When my observation merits no answer, I sneak a quick peek beside me—to find Volodya slumped over upon the buttstock of his rifle, the chamber still open, two clips of shells lying limply within his outstretched hand. "Oh, by the Saints alive!" I exclaim, gripping onto his shoulder and wrenching him roughly backward. "What the devil has the come over you?"

Glazed and stunned, his eyes meet mine—and I stare in horror at the well of blood seeping out from the midriff of his coat. "A bit too close, looks like," he blurts out with a shrill, fading laugh.

"Oh, *God*, Rykazian!"

"Fall back—fall back after all!" Zorshenko then hollers out wildly from some amount of distance. "Fall back, I say—*fall back!"*

"Shit!" Shouldering my rifle, I seize an arm quick around Volodya, muttering: *"Damn* him! Will the man ever make up his living mind? Jesus! Well, in any case, Volodya, we—we need to move you out of here, away from the line of fire. . . ."

Men lugging saddles and men already mounted on horses surge past me in all directions as I drag Volodya off toward a higher cover of trees and brush. "G-Green ribbons," he mumbles out, waving his arm and pointing back toward the mounting onslaught from our attackers.

"Rykazian, what the hell are you talking about? Jesus, I swear, you are bleeding *everywhere—"*

Blood unchecked has begun seeping through his fingers from the wound, and as he nods, a trickle starts oozing out from the corner of his mouth. "Makhno's men," he stutters on emphatically, inclining his head toward the barrage of fire. "When I was up on the ridge, I caught a glimpse . . . whole swarm of green ribbons . . . ."

Hands shaking, I fumble like wildfire through my knapsack in search for some bandaging cloth. "Rykazian, you've simply gone daft on account of the wound. You know we've not run in with any of Makhno's hooligans since last summer. Most of them rode south to help keep the Communist threat from the Ukraine—"

"With Whites," he gasps on. "Green ribbons I saw for a certainty, Sasha . . . mounted with bloody crappin' Whites!"

"How many times are you hit?" I demand, tearing open his coat and shirt. "Oh, *God—"*

"Twice, I think. Sasha, it's a gut wound. You—you're goin' to have to leave me. G-Get out with Zorshenko and the others—"

"Dammit! I am not leaving you behind."

In reply, his lips quiver upward in an attempt to smile; his hand, bloodied from the ragged hole of the wound, brushes lightly toward my face, his voice dropping low with emotion as he murmurs: "I always kept a soft spot in my heart for you, too, Sasha, my old f-friend . . . who whittled thirty lashes d-down to eighteen . . . ."

"Sekovsky!"

I glance behind to spot Yevgeny crouched past the next farthest grouping of pines, firing up a frenzy in order to cover us. "What the hell are ye two nitwits doin'?" he shouts, spitting out his cigarette and glowering at us with an incredulous stare. "Zorshenko said te high-tail it back on out o' here!"

"He's hit!" I shout back, pointing to Volodya.

"Awww, *shit—"*

"G-God . . . !" Volodya then moans, "I'm hot!" Wild-eyed, he grasps a rigid vise onto my sleeve. *"So hot*—burning *everywhere!* B-By the *Blessed Mother . . . !"*

"Volodya!" I urge back, attempting to calm him, "it's still naught but bloody freezing winter! You're not hot—here, look—see? Your hands are cold as ice, and your back end's probably gone numb by now, too. No, Volodya, no one is trying to burn you! We're both stuck out here in the middle of a goddamned snow patch—"

"Sekovsky!" Yevgeny yells again—and then lets out a stream of curses as his rifle empties of all ammunition.

I toss him mine, and watch him shimmy for it across the snow beneath a hail of whizzing bullets, while I shout through cupped hands: "Ivanovich! You're going to have to cover me while I try to drag Rykazian over there—"

"Well, God blast it, Mikhailovich! Hurry it up!"

"This is probably going to hurt like hell," I tell Volodya, shoving both hands up under his arms.

"Sasha Sekovsky, y-you damned sentimental fool!" he chokes back. "Just l-leave me! Save yourself . . . just leave m-m-me . . . ."

But no sooner do I push up from my knees, than to topple back upon them in a heap once again, the air crushed from my lungs, my face smashed into the dirt as an explosion rips all sound, thought, scatterings of dead leaves, trails of wispy ferns, and pieces of straying, scraggly brush off into a booming whirlwind throughout the clearing.

"G-Grenade—" mumbles Volodya.

Spears of shrapnel, indeed, I spot flying out everywhere as I peek upward. Of Yevgeny—still swearing out a florid stream of peasant oaths—I just barely catch a glimpse as he dashes full speed back through the trees.

"Ivanovich, you *bastard!"* I shout after him.

"Sasha!" Volodya cries, catching my arm at the sound of hooves.

From my holster, I wrench out my pistol—only to have it blown straight from my hand. "Get 'em in the air, or you're a dead man, you bloodsuckin' Commie sonuvabitch! Both of 'em up high over your head—*now!"*

The horseman—clad in a gray Tsarist uniform, a wealth of medals and both green and black ribbons drawn sidewise across his chest—sneers at me and once more cocks up his carbine.

"All right, don't shoot!" Reluctantly, I thrust my arms into the air, telling him: "My friend's hurt—"

"Shut up!"

A score more horsemen then thunder in from the wooded glen just behind him. "Oh, ho!" the leader shouts out with a hearty, triumphant wave. "And catch a decent sight, men," he bellows on, "of what we've managed to corner for ourselves: couple Commies they left behind for us to shoot up execution style . . . ."

With a gasp, I lurch for my knapsack—and my other Webley pistol—only to have both wrenched roughly away as the group of the riders dismounts in a flurry of kicking boot heels. "Stop it, please!" I beg them as several pounce for Volodya. "No! Can't you see he's hurt?"

Bare before I see it, the rifle butt plows into my ear, my knees reeling under upon a barrage of further grunts, curses, kicks, and shouts. "Over here!" one of them yells—and I see my knapsack being torn apart, my cup, fork, and spoon, my stash of hardtack, extra cartridge clips, and bundles of rags and rope flying out from it. And both long since devoid, in the sake of brevity for riding, of their old protective instrument case, pieces of the flute and *Boehm* piccolo tumble to the ground—while the White officers gloat in admiration: "Look at this! A true orchestra piece, pure silver—why, the mouthpiece plate, some of these keys, even faced with gold! God, the murdering little Communist thief!"

"You take your filthy hands *off* my flute!" I roar against another pounding, savage thrust from another rifle butt.

"Execution style!" their leader then gruffly orders out once more. "Come on, let's have on with it. . . ."

Volodya they drag away first—forcing him up to his knees, ordering him to keep his hands held stiff behind his back as he attempts to stifle his moans. "Y-You bloody-fuckin' White counter-revolutionary scum!" he finally rasps out with effort, glaring up at them.

The slap hammers down, crushing into his face; again and again the White officer slugs him, while the blood continues coursing down into his trousers from the stain of the wound; unchecked, blood starts to pour in a stream from each side of his mouth. "You damn Commies are due to get just what your godless, terrorizing *Cheka* imparts unto our own!" the officer shouts. Forcing Volodya up to his knees again, he whips out his pistol and saunters behind, aiming the barrel point-blank into the back of Volodya's neck.

"Nooo!" I scream out, ducking away from another vicious pounding from a rifle butt.

"Revolutsiya!" Volodya shouts out defiantly, his eyes awash with both pain and fury. "Long live the new socialist order, long live Marxism-Leninism! *Russkaya Revolutsiya . . . !"*

The shot rings out, and he slumps down. The group gathered around then bursts into self-satisfied grunts of congratulation and laughter—and without mercy, nor any shred of decency, they start gouging him into the snow and dirt with rifle butts and the bloodied toes to their boots.

"And now, him!" the leader roars, whirling about and pointing over at me.

The same thing: upon my knees they force me, hands shoved in behind my back. "You are naught but a league of savages!" I rasp out, cringing away from the slap—and then from slap after slap. "To shoot an unarmed, wounded man in cold blood! W-What he said about you was t-true—"

"Shut up, fucking little Communist pig! We'll teach you and yours a bit of truth about your Bolshevik hyena Lenin and his filthy, stinking *Revolutsiya."*

"Y-You do not understand—"

"This is for my wife, for my twelve-year-old daughter!" the leader snarls back at me from behind. "The dear Lord again bless their souls, both raped and gunned down on the front steps of our home by your bloody, God-smearing *Cheka!"*

Wrenching me upward by my collar, he shoves his pistol into the back of my neck . . . *oh, God! This is it . . . hear me, Lords of Flame . . . acknowledge this seeker, thy progeny, this name . . . oh—oh, God! Yea, though I walk through the valley of the shadow of death, I will fear no evil. . . .*

"Hey, Colonel! Wait a moment."

The speaker, a crusty-eyed second-in-command, steps forward and yanks a hold of my hair.

"Borisovsky!" the Colonel shouts at him, enraged. "What in hell are you up to?"

"Colonel," Borisovsky pleads, "will you simply wait for one blessed moment? I mean, take a look at him."

The colonel, too, yanks me up by a tuft of hair, roaring: "Take a look at *what?"*

Upon Borisovsky's urging, the whole group gathers closer around—while I shut my eyes, cringing from the pulls, prods, and yanks, praying to God that they would simply finally have done with it. . . .

After a long moment passed between snickers and meaningful, squinty-eyed stares, Borisovsky grins down into my face; grins back up at the Colonel. "Once cleaned up, would be pretty as a picture," he declares, forcing my head back upward again with another hurtful yank. "Yes?"

"By the devil!" another of them blurts out, laughing in agreement. "Old Borisovsky's right! Look at this little Commie baggage—face like an angel. Ha! Pity not a girl—"

"Humph! Girl or no," Borisovsky declares with a wink, "we can make better use of the little swine than this quick foolishness—eh?"

"Shit, Borisovsky!" the Colonel growls in adamant, pistol-waving reply. "Why don't you just shut up and let me shoot the bastard's head off!"

"No. I'll give you, say, five hundred—all right, then, a whole thousand rubles for him."

"Whatever the *hell* for?"

"Colonel!" Borisovsky protests, "by God, will you simply pause for a moment—sir—and *look* at him? You take my meaning? He's not much more than a bare willowy lad. And I swear to God, I've never seen such eyes—"

"'Doe-eyes,'" the fellow beside him adds, nodding. "Like in the old fairy legends. Black Russian 'doe-eyes.'"

"And such hair," Borisovsky lauds on. "Lord, red as fire—"

"So a Red Commie has red hair!" the Colonel hollers back, coloring stark purple in the face. "Holy Jesus, Borisovsky! Just when the fuck did you go and turn bloody *faggot* on us?"

"Is not for me that I want him, Colonel!" Borisovsky insists loudly, shrugging. "It's on account of Petrov—and the debts at cards I owe the filthy bastard—and, yes, dammit, on account of him saving my life! Twice, in fact. But most of all, because I hate being so beholden to that cocksucking, highbrowed sonuvabitch—"

"You bite your words, Borisovsky!" one of the other officers demands with a low growl, whipping out his pistol. "Captain Petrov's proven himself damn worth his salt in the field—"

"I'm not denying Petrov's been smart enough to bring us through scores of routs with nary a man hit," Borisovsky counters, reddening. "And the bastard can outshoot both me and *you*, Zanisky! But nobody, by God, *nobody* standing here can deny that Captain Petrov is naught, deep down, but an ass-licking fag—Jesus, you've seen him with the recruits! And Colonel," he goes on, lowering his voice once more to a respectful tone, "I tell you, I've had full enough of the swine and those steely-eyed stares of his up to here! And I'll wager he'd leave off pressing for my gambling debts, and make peace about the rest of it, if I brought him this little Commie tart."

Sly grins meet this declaration; grunting acquiescence, the Colonel finally withdraws the gun from the base of my skull, while another of the men chimes in: "Hey, Borisovsky—why let only Petrov have him? Why not all the rest of us, too?"

"Well, well!" the Colonel groans with a roll of his eyes, "you turning your ass up on us, too, Rulenitsov? Lord God Almighty, I never took you for a gutless, mincing fag—"

"Can't find a woman in these parts," Rulenitsov complains. "Shit—all blessed winter, we've not caught us a single one to bed down, willing or otherwise. Might as well take up with the next best thing."

"Ha!" the fellow at his side grunts, laughing. "For a certainty, then—let's take this freckle-faced Bolshy back to camp, and have ourselves a bit of fun. . . ."

The gist of their conversation I begin to glean fully only once the shock from the blows, the thought of the gun thrust behind my neck finally wears off—when confrontation with the sinister intent upon their faces renders placid, by comparison, my prior kneeling plight of inner death throes. *Oh, God—no! Better that they shoot me to death like a dog! But not this . . . !* My thoughts, in stark admonition of terror, finally escape unto the realm of voice, my shout of: *"Nooo!"* pealing out across the clearing and through the woods unto every last reach of the fading sky. Desperately, I pitch forward into a blind run past the whole lot of them—and with bootheels slipping in the snow, I limp past Volodya's body; almost, in my burst of fright, make it into the saddle of one of their horses—but then another rifle butt slams down, the blow toppling me into a hellish yawn. The reins slip from my grip, my foot from the stirrup as rattled breaths of protestation sink in helpless rebuttal against outer hootings of the soldiers' laughter, the small voice whimpering on over and over within the swollen confines of my dizzy, reeling head: *too late! Oh, dear God! T-T-Too l-late . . .*

* * *

I come to to find myself hog-tied over the bare rump of a horse; once the knife slashes through the knots, I tumble into the slush, spitting against a mouthful of ice and soggy pasture grass. Shouts assail my ears, pain drills into every bone in my skull, and I stumble my way upward against the burning yank of the ropes, my eyes blearing back and forth into and out of focus. Like rabid wolves, they start to gather around—jeering, snorting, laughing, whipping out pistols and placing bets—near unto fifty White enlisted men, many sporting black and green ribbons intertwined together across the breasts of their gray Tsarist uniforms. "Bring Petrov!" they continue shouting out in boisterous unison as I cringe against a dozen rough hand grips that pinch hard; that shove me about, abruptly, to face them. Then slowly they part, one by one, to make way for an arrogant, haughty stride brushing past all to respectful murmurs of: "Captain." And as they step away from him, I feel my face blanch in horror, jaw dropped, my eyes widening in a reeling pall of fear—for the gaze piercing back at me is like none other that I have ever beheld on earth. Save for one.

Now, that gaze—that one gaze once so familiar and so long now so distant within my starry, forgotten dreams of another place, another world, another time; that one gaze cherished far above every other like precious gold within passion's mournful, chaotic depths—now, that gaze descends once more at long, harrowing last, inscrutable and unyielding and fraught to perfect distillation upon cruelty's gleaming, razor-honed edge. For now—without the least spark of compassion—those haunting hollow-gray eyes I once thought I knew and loved so well narrow in on me for the kill, his face coarsening in the glower of a frown, his upper lip curling back from shiny white teeth in an embittered, taunting sneer. Shaking my head, shaking from head to foot—shaken to my utmost core of reason—I sink down to my knees and stare back up at him, cold, silent shouts of disbelief tearing scars of pain deep into the well of my throat: *my God, my God! I am dreaming—I am imagining—I am shot dead and brought back to life's screaming lie in some mythic, backward mirror of hell! It is impossible, incredible, it simply cannot be! Resurrection is not that simple, coincidence is not that powerful—dear Holy God! It can't be him! . . .*

CHAPTER NINE

Phantom of the Opera, Phantom Wolves

Still gaping in astonishment, I can scarce take my eyes away from him. He scarce takes his eyes away from me. Still beholden to the phantom of my memories, I marvel at how little five years has changed him—noting how lithe, how tall, how devilishly handsome the man still is, his beard grown out now full and neatly trimmed, much like my father's; his jaw set squarely resolute with a stern, familiar haughtiness borne against my father's countenance also. His gait as he strides through the parting throng of soldiers invokes a rein of taut command, the mark of aristocratic prominence felt in the regal, authoritarian lift of his every step. His hair, falling past his collar, gleams blonder than before, the strands caught lanky-fine as if paled already with the gentle wash of the sun, although we linger nowhere near the smile of any such pleasant, faraway days of forgotten summer. His eyes appear no less; no, in fact, seem even more penetrating—and stare back fringed now with a hardness, a remoteness, a mask of brusque indifference clipped short upon the scathing edge of temper. All around, scores of unfamiliar scarecrow lines frame his brows and his sparse brown lashes, his temples bearing ragged, wealed scars that I know were never manifest during the years that I knew him. As he peers at me with those scars whitening, the set of his mouth tightening—and those eerie hollow-gray eyes of his scanning the red-star trim of my Bolshevik browncoat with naught but a virulent glare of hate—I catch my breath once more in a stab of fear, seeing, without any doubt, that he has changed. This man standing before me may look, walk, and throw back his head disdainfully just like my cousin Nikolai Zhelanov, but no matter what truth my sight imparts, and despite all that my heart yearns to tell me, this 'Captain Petrov' sporting two ribbons of black and green wound in sinister testament to Makhno's loyalties across the belt and buttons of his gray Tsarist uniform; this White officer boasting a fiendish black kerchief tied about his arm as an obvious Black Hundreds' standard; this silent, wary stranger stamping his tall German boots with brooding impatience into the mix of grass and dirt and trampled snow is not, in his own heart, the same. Because—even after our lengthy pause of silence, and long after the soldiers gathered around once more start in with the hoots and hollers of their brutal plans, those piercing eyes harbor back at me not the slightest hint of recognition. At all.

But—the sear of lust, they do.

"What say you, Petrov?" Borisovsky insists for the third time. "You let off my seven thousand rubles—and the rest of our squabble, dammit!—for this little Commie prize? God, have a heart man! I already paid a thousand to the Colonel."

Still without flinching one speck away from my gaze, Nikolai reaches out toward the group of enlisted men, who have been jostling elbows and trading threats with one another beside him. He snaps his fingers and holds out his right hand wordlessly, the palm lying open, waiting.

Past a chorus of groans, the men surrender into that hand my set of wire spectacles—although not without protestation: "But, Captain! We was just parlaying around a bit of fun—"

In response, he allows them to keep my ermine hat, but stashes the spectacles, after trying them on himself, inside the breast pocket of his jacket. Then of Borisovsky, he demands: "Seven thousand rubles?" Pointing down at me with a gasp of contempt, he adds: "For *this?*"

"Better deal than you'll ace out tomorrow night, Petrov, you cunning bastard," Borisovsky sneers back, his fingers tapping the holster of his gun.

Turning abruptly on his heel, Nikolai marches straight away, muttering: "Draw on whatever call you damn well please whenever you think you're damn well good and ready, Borisovsky."

Instead, Borisovsky trudges after him, pleading: "Awww, shit—Captain! Wait . . . ."

Ten feet away, Nikolai halts as Borisovsky latches onto his arm, whereupon they both erupt into a heated burst of accusations. Finally, Nikolai whirls around and charges back toward me—and as I cringe away from him, he yanks up a fistful of my hair, bellowing out this time: "Seven thousand rubles you want me to forfeit over? For *this?*"

"Captain," one of the enlisted men offers, elbowing his way in and grinning between the two of them, "if you don't want the little Bolshy lad, then we do."

Shoving him off, Nikolai blares on to Borisovsky: "A prize was what you offered me—a *prize*, you weasel-brained, good-for-nothing cunt! And not," he shouts, wrenching hold of my coat collar and dragging me upward alongside him, "a whore." Whirling around, straight down into my face he then stares, whispering hotly under his breath: "Because naught but an ass-laid whore is what you are—yes?"

I slam shut my eyes, my heart stung cold as death as he shouts on to Borisovsky: "Yes, yes—another pretty face, naught but another mincing whore. Especially this one—God, *look* at him! Bet he can't get a shot off a rifle worth a fucking damn; bet the Bolshies only been dragging along the likes of *this* little feast for their own tawdry jests! Humph! Well, at least it proves that some of them are still human."

"Captain!" the same enlisted man pleads again, "we'll bargain for the carrot-headed tramp if you don't care for him."

At this, Nikolai pauses as if to reconsider, and Borisovsky takes the chance to nudge him once more from behind, muttering with a snicker: "Akkh! Quit with your damn vexations, Petrov! You scarce fool me one bit. All right—five thousand rubles then; I'll fork up the other two. Hell, I know you want him—we can see the way you been looking at him! Everybody knows about our Petrov's yen for red hair."

Cursing at Borisovsky, to the enlisted man Nikolai then demands: "And you fellows think you want him? Humph! Yes, always the same story: takes a preening city whore to inspire more eclectic taste in those of unlike persuasion . . . oh, all right, Borisovsky: the five thousand, then—kiss it back, if you want. In truth, I don't fucking care. Hey, you men!" he then calls out above the anticipatory ruckus rising all around us. Roughly, he seizes onto my shoulder, inclines his head in my direction, and announces: "Yes, we'll all grovel for our bit of fun with the Bolshy lad—but one thing's set damn square about it all straight off: I nail him first."

And again he turns to me, a chilling smile graced upon his lips, the stark glow of passion lanced within his eyes as he once more stares me down head to toe and back up again. "Yes, indeed, little carrot-topped Bolshy," he murmurs, leaning in close with a searing brush of breath to my ear. "And then we shall discover what kind of filthy whore you are—just as soon as we get back from the vodka wagon."

Back toward him, I stare in agony and hatred: *y-you are not my cousin! No matter about this war, the Revolution, our former differences—my own cousin would never will upon me such a fate! G-Goddamn you! Whoever the hell you are, whatever monster you have become, you are not my cousin! . . .*

Only his mirthful sneer replies to my glare of silence—his chuckles filtering out seductively, evilly.

Once he strides away, the men pounce for me in unison, the one called Rulenitsov tearing at my coat and muttering: "Well! And let's have a peek at what you look like underneath them Red Bolshy colors—"

"You take your filthy hands off me, you bloody-fucking White bastard!" I swing up with both bound wrists, smashing into a wall of arms before jolting backward—along with the rest of them—as the air splits forth with the hollow blast of a shot.

Across the pasture, Nikolai stands with his pistol smoking in the air, growling: "Rulenitsov, I said I was first."

"Yes, Captain, sir!" Gallantly, the man salutes him in reply—but once Nikolai marches away again, Rulenitsov continues on to me in a whispered grumble: "Damn highbrowed sonuvabitch—and me second lieutenant to him, humph! Well, no matter, little Carrot-top," he says, fishing into his coat and inching forward once again—this time with a knife. "We'll all have ourselves a merry enough rout with that pretty face of yours after Petrov fucks his stinking faggot fill, yes?"

Again I slam shut my eyes, gulping down ragged heaves of breath as he traces the blade of the knife down the line of my jaw and into the hollow of my throat, his voice sputtering on over and over: "Yes? Yes?"

Finally, he too turns on his heel and storms away—but then the others converge in a mob, and with playful, teasing prods and pushes, force me with my back up against a tree. "What's your name, little Bolshy?" they shout, bursting into laughter. "Hey! Where'd you come by such a pretty face? Your daddy fuck himself the most gorgeous whore in all of Moscow? Riga? Paris? Petrograd? Ha! Sure you're not more like a girlie maid 'neath them buttoned trousers? Ho, ho!—but he's got whisker-shadow, fellows—oww!—humph!—and a spry couple fists smacking back at us, now, ha, ha! Hey, don't get him too riled up, boys! We'd best leave behind a bit of spunk for the Captain. Hey, what's your name, little baggage? Lord, what long red hair . . . hey! Simmer down, freckle-face! You've no call to run scared of us. . . ."

One after another, I punch away at them; from one tree to another, I drag myself desperately, the knots of the ropes lashed about my ankles tripping me up and pinning me down, the pain in my bad leg shooting up my calf in a stinging spray of arrows, the fear in my heart raging on in a torrent unchecked as I fumble to no avail toward the shaft of my left boot for the last chance salvation of my knife. But my wrists, bound too tightly, cannot reach far enough to the side; my gait, faltering, cannot match such a pace of pursuers. Finally, the shouting over my head mounts into a climactic squall as one of the men manages a hold onto the collar of Father's jacket, worn underneath my coat. As the fabric tears, they all lunge for me in a stampede, and I butt out at them with my head and arms, my own screams pealing above their avalanche of screaming. As I tumble into the dirt and snow, praying for it all to end, five or six of them latched upon me and every one of us shrieking out bloody oaths, the anarchy shatters to a dead, thundering halt beneath the roar of an explosion.

"Red partisans!" erupts the call from across the field. *"Red partisans!"*

In a frenzy, the enlisted men stumble upward, plowing into one another, trampling over me, the bugle calls to arms blasting ramparts across the field, the dash to combat posts galvanizing scattered ranks into a marathon of chaos. Explosion after explosion hits supply wagons, artillery batteries, and officer's tents, the field of green and soggy pasture and scattered trees lighting up against the fall of dusk in a smoky dance of flames. Shout after shout screams outward the dreaded warning: "Red partisans! Red partisans!" bullets tearing soon enough in torrential sprays across the field to confirm the danger omnipresent and true.

Grateful for any reprieve, I shove back for cover behind a tree, grappling in a haze to regain some sense of balance—when a rough hand forces me upward to my knees. And faces me square upon the gleaming blade of a knife.

Rulenitsov's face twists above mine in a triumphant, cruel grin. "And now, little Carrot-top," he whispers into my ear, "let's see how we can carve up your pretty throat—"

"Drop it, Rulenitsov."

Past the tree, Nikolai—clad now in his dark sable hat and long-skirted officer's greatcoat—cocks up his gun.

"Fuck it, Petrov! You go eat fucking shit—"

Two shots fired this time land one hit, a double-solid blast ripping apart the mortar noise with reverberations mounting in a whirlpool gone awry through every quivering, tremulous branch above our heads. Arms plunging down around me, Rulenitsov lets loose his pistol and wilts into a wrinkled heap, his mouth gone agape, his hat spinning off, a pool of blood gushing out from the socket into which the bullet was aimed—apparently, straight for his right eye.

Casting off the body in a shudder of disgust, I whirl about to find Nikolai looming in upon me with the blade of the knife, then to hack a quick slash through the ropes binding my legs. Cocking up his pistol once more, he seizes hold of my arms and shoves the barrel hard into my neck, barking out: "One false move, you filthy Bolshevik traitor, and I'll blow your fucking head off. Understand?"

Numbly, I nod.

"All right. Let's go."

The pasture behind us lights up like a flash in a pan afire as he drags me off at breakneck speed through the length of the woods. Helplessly, I struggle to keep up, my wrists still bound and thereby slowing my progress, my bad leg mustering brunt after brunt of wrenching pain, my head reeling in a squall of dizziness, my breath catching in my throat, burn by ragged burn. At last, through a clearing, I spot a mounted officer guiding another fully saddled, riderless horse. Straight to him Nikolai leads us and gratefully extends up his hand. "Zanisky, my old friend," he murmurs, nodding.

"Godspeed, Captain," Zanisky replies, the warmth between them evident as he catches Nikolai's grasp within his own. "Pray tell—you are going to need it."

"Again, I thank, and salute you."

Toward the saddle—and left-side stirrup—Nikolai then shoves me as I gasp in protest: "No, wait! Please! I—I cannot mount from the—"

"Goddamn it!" he rages into my ear. *"Get up there!"*

My leg hits the stirrup and the world strikes black with pain; dazedly, I lumber up, grasping shaken fingers onto the horn as he plows behind me into the saddle, snarling out with the gun once more jammed up to my head: "You sniveling little Commie slut! Not so much as another godforsaken peep out of you if you value both our lives!" Zanisky he then waves off, and the reins he seizes up, the horse whipping around past his fierce yanks and blistering oaths of impatience as his voice barrels out: *"Yaaa!"*

* * *

Wild rides I have indeed charged off on before, but never anything like this. Particularly not with Nikolai Zhelanov—gay ladies' rogue, premier violinist, once ever the ubiquitous citified dandy—who, save be it in an upholstered troika or amply cushioned country sledge, I could rarely ever convince along with me for an afternoon of daredevil races or equestrian jumps during his many visits long ago to the Lissushka farm. Now, he guides the horse as if he was born on it: charging into the wind, tearing past the trees, forging into the rivers with grunts of riled abandon like some saber-flashing Kuban Cossack . . . .

Dusk falls, and I can scarce see how far we have gone; night descends in chilly, rattling hold, and I cannot tell how long it has been; thirst and hunger stab into my throat and gut as the stars peek out one by one from the darkness, the distant hum of artillery fire fading farther away the higher the still moon climbs aloft above our heads. Wisely, he keeps to the beds of the rivers, or continues skirting the gravelly banks thereon, following tributary after slushy, ice-floe beladen tributary, an obvious ploy to foil any trackers—for now, without a doubt, he is as much the fugitive as I. But in the lonely hours that pass, not one word drifts its way in explanation or condolence between the two of us, my hesitancy founded upon his earlier warnings; his bearing, by all appearances, willed solely and resolutely upon the path of our trail without any pause for rest. In the darkness, in the silence—upon the constant up-and-down jolting undulations of the horse's back—I wrestle with teeming questions, wondering whether this indeed be rescue, or abduction. After the passing of what seems a thousand hours, I incline back my head, desperate for some water—but his angry snarl dissuades my yearnings, and again I shut my eyes, leaning back numbly into the strange, protective well of his arms enclosed about my elbows as he manages his hold on the reins. After a time, railroad tracks begin to appear up beyond the riverbank, and he keeps us warily aligned to their edge, watching, I know, for patrols—Red or White—and for roving bands of scouts or pockets of snipers. As the night presses forward, and still we ride—exhaustively, murderously—on into the wee small hours, I marvel at his sureness, his daring, his seeming ken of every little inkling stone or pot-bellied hole or next threatening nuance in our path. Uncannily, it is almost as if he knows exactly where he is going.

Finally, an old etched sign we pass reading 'Daugavpils.' From its eastward-pointing arrow, we veer away, winging back from the railway tracks into a darkened cover of woods. Here and there, vacant buildings slowly begin looming their way into much more haunting evidence than before, the many farmhouses, old silos, and wooden windmills all gutted out and long since abandoned by local inhabitants. Toward one of these—an old barn with its door gaping half-open off the hinges—he slows the horse at last, just as I realize that he has long since given over to me his sable hat, the flaps tucked down securely about my ears, and that as I have been shivering, he has long since been holding me close within the cradle of his arms, attempting to coax back warmth. Yet, as we finally ease to a halt, and he dismounts, he drags me off behind him with another bitter snarl of contempt, although this time taking care to land me to the ground upon my right foot over the left. "Into the barn!" he orders, pointing with his revolver toward a hole of darkness looming past the creaky, swaying wood door.

Numbly, I limp off as told, making an effort not to trip over the scores of old dung-encrusted, overturned buckets and scattered farm implements—hoes and scythes all lying in piles, most with the wooden handles broken off. Into a mound of hay I settle, watching as, against the glow of a lit candle, he drains water into a trough, unsaddles, and then fodders down the horse. Clearing my throat, without meaning to, I catch his eye—upon which, grumbling, he stomps over and shoves his canteen into my face. Gratefully, I start sloshing water down my parched throat, still gulping ravenously as he yanks the canteen away. Of course, I know fully well that too much at once after a such a long dry spell can induce retching, but still I glare after him, cursing under my breath, incensed at his severity, his rudeness, at his continual preponderance of rage fixed upon me with every next watchful sidelong glance cast in my direction. Finally, the horse tended to, he at last returns with the canteen, his knapsack, a bedroll, and oddly enough, a balalaika. Tossing them into the hay, he then pauses above me—holding out, in the grip of both hands, a long wooden board.

"Stretch your legs straight out," he orders tersely. "Both of them."

Going stark white, I stare up at him in horror. As he barks out the order yet again, I tuck both knees under and start scooting away instead, shaking my head back and forth, my previous glares of retaliation reduced to whimpered pleas for mercy: "N-No! P-Please—"

"Dammit—I said stretch out your legs!"

"Nikolai!" I rasp on. "I—I mean, Captain P-Petrov—*please!* Don't break my legs—"

"Oh, for God's sake!" he exclaims, widely rolling his eyes. "I am not going to hurt you, blast it! God, far from that! It's simply that I don't want you to hurt me. Now, come—stretch out your legs."

Reluctantly, I finally comply, wincing as he rests the board down across both of my ankles, his one palm pressed unto it firm and steady. Into the shafts of both my boots, he then slides his other hand, fishing out, from one, my piccolo, and from the other, my knife. "Uh-huh, thought they missed it—damn inept bastards," he mutters, ducking out of range of my feet as he snatches back the board.

"You give back my piccolo!" I snarl through gritted teeth. "They already took away my flute! I've not seen my flute since they hit me over the head in the clearing—"

"Shut up!"

In response, I whack off his sable hat with both bound hands and throw it at him, stuttering obscenities, while he shouts me down—ordering me, this time, onto my knees.

With the knife, he towers above me, bellowing out as I blanch again in fear: "Oh, Christ Almighty! Dammit, you want those ropes about your wrists sliced off or not?"

Sullenly, I stretch out my arms, again wincing as he slashes apart the knots.

My spectacles he then hands over, and I slap on the wire frames, glaring at him through a scraggly muss of hair, my wariness gauged against his tempered own as he settles into the hay aside me with the pistol still cocked in his hand. Once more he aims the barrel into my neck. "I'll not hesitate to tie those ropes back on—nor to use this," he declares, waving the gun and eyeing me with a disdainful snort as I rub against my chafed wrists and massage trembling fingers down against the now steadily burning ache in my leg. "Jesus God!" he then mutters out in disgust, staring me up and down. "Look at you—"

"Where are you taking me?" I demand, seething at him with a clench of both fists.

"Yalta."

"Yalta? In the *Crimea?"* I stare at him aghast, in disbelief. "W-What are you? Half-mad, Zhelanov? . . ."

"Yalta in the Crimea is where we are headed, Sekovsky."

"I cannot go to Yalta in the Crimea—"

"Yalta is where we are going, by dammit!" he counters back, slamming his fist down into scatters of hay. "Because from now on, *mon cousin,"* he goes on, pointing up at me, *"you* will go where *I* say."

Still stunned, I watch, entirely beside myself, as he starts gulping from his canteen. "Nikolai, I—I cannot go with you to Yalta," I tell him, lowering my voice toward some attempted semblance at normality. "If I am going to head anywhere, it must be back to Petrograd."

"Petrograd? Oh, God—then it is true!" he roars, both hands this time seizing up about the butt of his gun. "Everything that Anna said! For the love of Jesus, you *have* become naught but a godless, ravaging Bolshevik!"

Once more down the barrel of his revolver, I find myself staring, swallowing hard as he burns up red in the face, his voice choking out in a torrent of fierce words tripping fast one upon another: "I'd never have believed it—until I saw you! I told Anna dozens of times that she was wrong, mistaken, that she had utterly lost her senses! And then, lo and behold, you turn up straight out of the starry blue—in a fucking Bolshy browncoat! My God, have you any idea what it was like for me, to finally return, after all I have been through, to the city where I was born—only to find that Lenin and his pillaging Red Guards have shorn it into naught but a stinking hellhole I can scarce recognize?"

"Nikolai—"

"I cannot believe that you, of all people, would consign yourself to this Revolution!" he bellows on. "I cannot believe that you—a musician, an artist!—would throw in your lot with the godforsaken *Bolsheviki!* My God, naught but the reigning monarchs supreme at thievery, raping, killing, plundering, torture! Ha! Oh, yes—torture: one hears of your notorious *Cheka* and the handy little hatchet job they use to snip a man's pecker off in the bat of an eye—their primary method of persuasion against captured White officers! Ha! I understand you bomb refugee trains, that you herd women and children into old barns, houses—even hospitals, goddamn it!—and lock shut the doors, then setting both buildings and people afire—"

"Nikolai!"

"—and the men!" he goes on shakily. "Our own men we've found caught in the field—tied up to trees, their gullets slit sternum to navel, all the entrails sucked out to the ground out in a ring of bloody glory—"

"Nikolai, stop it—my God!" I burst back at him, clamping both hands flat over my ears. "I have neither seen, nor done any of those things! Whatever Anna told you is not true—I am *not* a Bolshevik!"

"You were with Zorshenko's band!" he shouts back. "Oh, yes—we know all about Zorshenko, and about the number of Red Guards he's been taking on of late! True to his Bolshevik leanings—"

"And," I holler in reply, "White uniforms or not!—you were riding with a band of those infernal Black Hundreds sympathizers pledged in alliance with Makhno's Greens! Goddamn it, don't deny it—I saw the black armbands you and those other officers had tied on! I saw the green ribbon wound across your chest—"

"Let's you and me get one thing clear right now: I've only been moving under Makhno's colors to achieve my own ends."

"They were the ones who destroyed my house, Nikolai—they burned Lissushka, dammit! All the way to the ground!"

As I nurse the ache growing up my leg, the events of the past year begin spilling forth from my lips in a halting stutter of allegory—and after listening with a glare of impatience, he bellows back: "Oh, for God's sake—you naive, pitiful fool! More likely than not, it was Zorshenko and his rag-tag group of hellions who set fire to your house—"

"Oh, no, it was not! We found Greens ready to throw torches again forty versts south at Kolinsky's!"

"Humph!" Still glaring, he passes over the canteen; hands me some hardtack and a cold cooked potato. "Eat!" he commands with a begrudging wave of the gun. "And save us a spare bit of water for the morn, will you? The spring's out back past the barn, and a fair walk yet."

In silence, I break apart my potato; watch him eat his—ironically, with a fork. Past his knapsack, I eye the balalaika with a pang of hope, but continue watching him with narrowed, wary suspicion. Just as he continues eyeing me, his guard up firm against enemy fire. "I am not a Bolshevik!" I tell him for the near twentieth time, sighing in exasperation as he again waves me off. "Nikolai, you must believe me!"

"Humph! The last time I believed you, I got my heart blistered through the pit of hell."

Drawing back, I frown at him for a long moment. "And exactly what is that supposed to mean?"

"Nothing." Lowering the gun at long last, he makes a check of his watch. A wristwatch—the first one I have ever seen, save for a drawing in an apothecary advertisement—its small round dial secured onto his arm with a narrow, buckled leather band. "Five hours, at the most, until daylight," he says, reaching for the bedroll and loosening its ties. "Best fetch some sleep. We've a long ride ahead of us."

"Nikolai! I cannot go to Yalta—"

"We'll talk about it come the morn, Sasha—*all right?"*

As my name departs his lips, an odd slant hits the air—as if, with the speaking of it, the old bond had suddenly been renewed between us. For the first time since our terrible reunion of the afternoon, the unflinching grip of authority seems at last to escape his strident hold, his color darkening in a heated flush, his eyes becoming tinged with wounded glimmers. Yet only for a moment does he lapse into such a pause of vulnerability—before the mask promptly casts itself over his features yet again. "Sleep," he again insists gruffly, throwing the bedroll out sideways across the both of us. "We both need it."

The gun, I note, he at last uncocks, but keeps held firm at his side, his fingers cradled to the trigger-guard once he blows out the candle.

Sleep at first proves grievously futile beside the familiar up-and-down rising and falling of his breath, the silvery glint of his pale hair caught by cracks of moonlight spilling through the rent barn boards above. Only through sheer exhaustion do I finally doze off into a restless, busy hinterland of scattered past and present dreams—to be prodded rudely awake far too soon, in the dark and coldness, by the urgent inevitability of nature's call. Groaning, I force myself onto my elbow, but gasp into a halt—for in bumping Nikolai ever so slightly, I cause him to jolt upward with the bellowing roar of a lion and pounce upon me with the gun.

Eyes fixed upon me wildly, he stares back through the window of time known only by those who have cultivated lightning response. It is something that my father, possessed of the ability himself, explained to me once—having perfected the talent to bolt awake with gun in hand upon even the slightest, most feathery touch of provocation after his many years spent under the yoke of prison guards in exile. Without moving, without breathing, I shiver back a gulp against the blunt barrel of the revolver thrust into my throat. "Please," I whisper out softly. "I—I need to pee."

Ducking low before me, Nikolai swallows hard, shuddering, his fingers darting up across his brow past a runny rim of sweat. At last he lowers the gun, muttering apology and indicating the barn door with a nod of his head.

Outside, I do not venture far, and on the way back, scarf up an old broken branch to make use of as a cane. With my every step, the harsh chill of the night air seems to seep with even further demonic predication into my aching joints. Once back through the barn door, I cannot help but emit a moan of weariness, the tree branch trembling across the bare dirt floor with my every step as I thump it heavily down.

Over at the mound of hay, I find my piccolo waiting in my place aside the bedroll—and Nikolai propped up on his elbow, peering at me past the light of a flickering candle.

"You're in pain," he says as I ease my way back down beside him.

He says it in English. Reverently, I relish the sound—so long now since I have heard it spoken—of the other half of my heritage. Relish it as I whisper in reply: "Yes."

"I am sorry. About the stirrup, forcing you to mount from the left. I had entirely forgotten about your leg. It—it has been so long."

When I proffer only an affirmative grunt in reply, he fishes into his knapsack, fetching out a small jar. "Here—take it," he says softly. "Use all you want. It's balm of eucalyptus."

Hesitantly, I take the jar from his hand, flushing at the lingering touch of his fingers upon mine. The glance I sneak at him then, past fluttery black-and-white tiltings of the candlelight, stirs my heart with both relief and a crush of poignant irony—for again the mask of the stalwart White officer has been dredged wholly away. Staring back at me with naught but a mournful softness harbored in the depths of his clear gray eyes, I find only my cousin—my childhood story time bedmate, my prankster accomplice in the school halls of our youth, my best friend from the gay Paris and old Petersburg days. "I am sorry," he utters out once more, his breath this time caught bare above a whisper, his eyes dropping down to the gun lying between us—now tucked within its holster—in the hay. "Forgive me, please. I scarce meant to corner you like that. When you bumped me—"

"I know."

The balm, in delicious, soothing tingles, I smear across the old whitened scars of my leg, while he watches. "And—I am sorry about the flute," he says after a moment, wringing his hands and peering down at them with a long sigh. "I heard the Colonel had taken it; went to him, and he denied it. There was naught else I could do but see to saddling my horse—we had *no* time. I would never have let them harm you, not without first fighting to my death in attempt to prevent it—but to save us both, I had to play along for a little while, or they might have suspected. I had but ten minutes from the time they brought you in unconscious on the rump of that horse, another five after I left you on the field. My doing sounded that call of 'Red partisans.' With help of some trusted others, I stirred up the diversion; they set off grenades to the tents and supply wagons, while Zanisky and I hid and let go with machine guns like a couple of bloody Huns, hoping everyone would think it was real."

"Then—you are not a White officer?" I gasp in astonishment.

"Oh, I am a White officer," he replies with a crooked laugh. "And now a deserter—if they find us, they'll hang me. But they have their own problems—and I think will not deign to chase this far south after us. As to their cause: yes, I believe in what they are fighting for; yes, I want them to win, and hope they do. But, I doubt they will."

"Then—you risked your life—and everything you believe in—to save me?"

"Perhaps. Perhaps not—I hardly think absenting myself from the ranks of Yudenich's army will, in the end, make any difference. The Reds control Petrograd and Moscow—and therefore the industrial, the communications, the transportation bases. The war's going to rage on whether I fight in it, or no. And to be honest with you, Sasha, I have reached a point in my life where I am weary unto death of fighting wars. The only reason I had stuck with the Whites thus far was that I found it the quickest way to get myself to Petrograd."

"Petrograd!" I exclaim. "I thought you were going to Yalta—"

"I am. Now."

"Nikolai, I do not understand!"

"You will."

Confused, I cap the lid onto the jar of eucalyptus balm and hand it back over to him. But in lieu of taking it from me, he instead grasps hold of my hand, his fingers curling gently around mine. "I am sorry about the flute," he says again, straining to catch my eye. "I know what that flute meant to you."

"No one," I rasp out bitterly, staring down into the hay, "knows what that flute meant to me."

"I do," he whispers, at last reaching up with his left hand and extracting the jar of balm. Although—still—his right hand he keeps held to mine in the firm grasp of a handshake. And then his thumb he begins edging back, ever so slowly—in a crooked, pointing stab—against the hollow between mine and my index finger.

Unmistakably, naught but the secret hand grip of the Freemasons.

I shut my eyes; let out another gasp—and as we stare at one another once again, his arms fly around me; mine around him . . . with a moan of relief, I sink against his embrace, sighing in rapture at the well-scrubbed scent of him, wincing in amusement against the scratchy pocket flaps of his Tsarist uniform jacket . . . *this is rescue then, and not abduction! Oh, God bless you, my one and only true, brave, daringly courageous cousin! Bless you—thank you!—Blessed, Blessed Lord* . . . .

Infinity seems to pass far beyond our many years of shared memories as we cling together chest to chest, smoothing our hands up one another's backs, caressing our palms each down the other's arms. Finally, I drag myself away, staring across into his smoky eyes, my voice choking out near unto a squall of tears: "I—I thought I'd never see you again . . . I thought you were dead. . . ."

In response, his hand—after the slightest pause of hesitation—cradles its way up behind my neck, urging me to him closer; his mouth—parting in the barest, most fleeting of anticipatory tremors—inches slowly downward toward my own.

And then we arch together tentatively, boyishly: a little brush of the lips here, a tiny lick of our tongues there—like a couple of gawking innocents playing at a schoolyard lark, only to find it luring, lethal—until our hesitancy shatters apart, lurching into respective seas of torment. Once again I throw my arms back around him; once again he winds his fast around me—and then I open my mouth fully beneath the full, fierce, gentle parting of his mouth, and we kiss . . . and *kiss* . . . .

I always thought that only past the ruse of death would I ever feel this—that someday, after my ascent from the dreary sorrow of this present earthly path, I would find him once again, awaiting me out in a little wooded glen hidden somewhere in the purplish, hazy depths of the astral-fringe world—that only then and there could we at last consummate, in our higher ethereal forms, this long, awful yearning. Now, as the aching seed so long nestled deep and buried within my heart blossoms forth into its violent, whipping tongue of reality at last, I can scarce believe it, shuddering against him in an elation past all knowing, warm tears squeezing out from the corners of my eyes and running down each side of my face, my fingers shaking as I run them through his hair and wind them into his beard and brush them across his brow with aching sighs of delight, my heart bursting against gasps searing down my throat as my kisses melt into his again and again in a fury rending, a longing unending—and a life only now, at this startled, spinning moment in time, beginning. After awhile, his soft laughter tickles down against my chin, then up upon my nose, back along the earwires of my spectacles—and finally, he eases his head away, staring back at me with fire in his eyes and joy upon his face, both his hands stroking into my hair. And then, as if the pinnacle of all happiness had not just been met—as if the utmost strata of heady bliss in the entire grand, sparkling glory of the universe had not just now been gripped unto vibrant fruition within every quivering fiber of my being—*then* he whispers out, in a bare rasping choke caught against the well of his own brimming tears: "I love you, Sasha. I—I have *always* loved you."

* * *

Tears of wonder, ecstasy—and then, pain . . . raggedly, they course down my face as I hold him; silently, they drop one by one onto the crown of his head as I press unto it once again my trembling, fervent lips blanched white as death. "Oh, G-God!" I whisper, rocking him back and forth like a child as he clings to me, his eyes held vacant unto long years put behind him in the battle-ridden distance. Dawn brims closer by the moment, and with each next ruddy, telling influx of morn's light, the scars slashed in such brutal testament all over near every inch of his body only show forth more clearly and awfully, each a thousand times worse than I thought any of them could possibly be when I first touched them in the mask of dark with my eager, exploring fingers. "Sasha, don't," he utters out, pushing upward and drawing me once again into his embrace, his kisses doting at my temples. "You mustn't fret about it so—"

"Why did they do this to you? *Why?* My God! H-How many beatings, how many slicings? How many lashes with the bullwhip was it, Nikolai?"

Sighing without answer, he urges me closer. Against his left hand, I brush my cheek; press more tearful kisses unto his wrist—where a ridge of bone sticks out gruesomely from the break that never healed. Because it was obviously never properly set. "The Germans did this to you?" I insist again, easing back to face him. "Why, Nikolai? Why, for any call on God's earth?"

"For trying to escape," he murmurs softly, his eyes again cast away, beyond me, to the mirror of memory. "From prison."

I duck my head again onto his shoulder, sniffling loudly, and blurting out: "My God, then—how did you ever manage to find your way here? How did you ever get away?"

Turning to face me again, he holds my gaze in his distant own, replying after a long moment: "I escaped."

With awe, I stare away, pondering upon what courage it must have taken to attempt it a second time after suffering such brutal reprisal from failure of the first. "Prison," I say then, leaning back against his warmth—and gently, worshipfully, I trace a finger once again down his bare arm, scar by ragged, wealed scar. "After Tannenberg, then? We heard it was a bloodbath—over one hundred thousand men all dead or taken prisoner."

"All night, we stayed up with those four guns," he whispers in reply. "Four howitzers we'd captured from a German battery. Exhausted, we were—and half-starved, the whole lot of us. But all night, we stayed up shooting; all night, the Huns fired back. All night, the bodies fell; one had to keep kicking them out of the way. Finally, somebody staggered in and told us there was naught else to do but surrender. We were stranded—the last of the whole bloody Thirteenth Corps . . . ."

As his voice fades off, I latch onto him again, yet tracing my fingers over other scars, yet choking back renewed threat of tears. "Oh, Sasha," he cries earnestly, crushing me close. "Don't, please! I'll not have you tearing your heart to pieces so—it is over, all of five years gone. Since then, I've dredged most of it from my mind. I never would have taken off my clothes, had I known you'd become so distraught—"

"I cannot bear the thought of you being hurt!"

"Shhh!" Cradling back my neck again, he pulls my mouth unto his—and again we loll against one another in a flurry of kisses, caresses, soft sighs, and rapturous moans. The bedroll and the coats which have been serving us as blankets we once more pull over the both of us, and I shut my eyes and sink against him, still awash in the bliss of his nearness, still agog over this lingering taste of heaven. "That's better," he whispers into my ear, tempering back a laugh. "Much better to think about the here and now, not the then and there. Here and now, you are happy, yes?"

"Oh, God! So happy, and so in love with you . . . ."

Above us, he stares up toward the light peeking through slats of the missing barn boards. "We'll need to move soon," he murmurs, winding his fingers lazily through strands of my hair as I ease my head upon his shoulder. "In any case," he goes on with a wink, "perhaps we should consider putting on our clothes. God forbid if any damn Huns or Poles—or Red or White scouting patrols—might happen upon the two of us lying in here like this unarmed and buck naked."

"Nikolai," I say, pressing another languishing kiss across his lips, "I want to sleep buck naked with you for the rest of my life."

"I know."

As he pushes up to his feet, he pulls me along—protesting—with him, and again we sink against one another in a heady wrap of arms and legs, moans and lustful kisses. "Although sleep," he insists, edging away from me with a laugh, "I would scarce call it."

Reluctantly, we start retrieving our clothes—but even as we dress, neither of us can take his eyes from sight of the other. "You are very beautiful," he says, eyeing me yet again with fires ablaze from across the mound of hay. "All the way to your toes. Yes, even with that leg. You always have been, and I have always thought so. God, how I'd like to suck you away to the heights again right now—"

Flushing, laughing, I hike up my trousers and throw his uniform jacket at him as he adds: "God, I wish I'd not been such a fool. In Paris . . . in Budapest . . . ."

"Budapest," I say, staring down the shaft of my boot.

And then, the questions return—in the dozens strong, all still teeming, and most yet unanswered. "Budapest," I say again with a studied pause as I wipe over the lenses of my spectacles with the tail to my shirt.

"Certainly, you recall," he answers, peering at me closely and buttoning on—with pointed one-by-one deliberation—the fasteners to his jacket, "a certain wild chase we made hot on each other's heels one night across the river to the Hotel Duna."

Going cold to the bone, I pull on my boots, shirt, belt. Fasten the buttons down the front of Father's old hunting jacket. When I stare back at him, I find myself come face to face with the imperious White officer again, his eyes narrowed, judging me from an inscrutable, haughty distance—exactly like yesterday in the pasture. Although now, bold lust has demurred to a boiling froth of jealously. Telling myself that he is certainly not the only one prone to such feelings, I throw back my head, glaring at him across the hay as I burst out: "Ah, yes—Budapest! Indeed, I do recall, now that you happen to mention it, a certain little wild ride across the river to the Hotel Duna. So, tell me, Nikolai Petrovich—dear cousin, my good friend!—and were you physically intimate with Sergei Pavlovich? You know—M'sieur Diaghilev?"

Immediately, I know I have said the wrong thing—but I stand my ground stubbornly, yet awaiting an answer as he belts on the holster to his gun with a snarl and strides straight to me past the hay. "Is that what you want, Sasha?" he demands, shoving both hands onto his hips and glaring me down. "Is that what you insist upon, pray tell, to finally clear the air between us—an itinerary? A year by year, date by date accounting? Of lovers? Is that what you want from me? Naught but a roster, a list?"

"I have always thought," I spout back, fiercely holding his gaze, "that any relationship—particularly romantic, and—and particularly with someone with whom I would choose to sleep buck naked for the entire rest of my life—should, above all else, be founded upon honesty."

"Agreed. So let us divvy up your half of this sacrosanct honesty pie of ours right now, shall we? Dmitra?"

I scarce know from where the bell sounds; then I realize that naught at all has sounded but the panicked, hollow roaring in my ears. On my heel, I whirl around for any chance at escape—but he will permit *no* escape, his arms looming, then locking in upon me, his hands snatching for mine as I punch away from him in a scathing frenzy, my awkward stumbles making mincemeat piles of the hay as I try to limp for cover while thrusting back at him, kicking him, my mind cringing beneath his furious, deafening demands for explanation. Against the onslaught, my fear pounds to steam, my heart to thunder, and savagely, I continue lashing out at him, every attempt foiled—until at last my wily hook slams upward into teeth of triumph: straight into his jaw, halting the bombardment of accusations and sending him reeling backward.

And then an explosion—vaster than a quantum howl from hell—an explosion like naught but a bloody, booming grenade blast rips off from the angry brunt of his hand.

Face smashed into the ground, blood seeping from the corner of my mouth, I lie choking into the dirt, while he roars above me: "A Zhelanov born in Petersburg I may be, but my mother is blood of your father. You, in half, are blood of me—as I, in half, am blood of you. Blood of a thousand years, pride of a score of generations runs through our veins from the old *pasechniki* wanderers of Novgorod. The blood of farmers, yes; the blood of toilers, yes; the blood of tradesmen, yes—but never, by dammit, *never the blood of a whore!* You have brought disgrace upon me—you—upon all of our family!"

Turning on his heel, he then stalks off across the barn and out the door, wrenching it shut behind him.

Shakily, I wrest up to my elbows and fetch hold of my spectacles, lying upside down at arm's length away from me in the dirt. Wince by wince, I drag myself over to the nearest wall, collapse against it, run my sleeve up to stem the flow of blood from my lip, and watch Nikolai storm back in with the dripping canteen. Retrieving a set of saddlebags from the gear, he charges back step by authoritative, haughty step across the barn, pulling to a halt before me and peering down with hooded eyes. Without speaking, he then drops to his knees and reaches over; begins dabbing at my face with a moistened handkerchief.

Snatching it from him, I shoot him a florid glare, barking: "Where in hell did you ever learn to hit a man like that?"

Easing down beside me with his back scrunched to the wall, he sighs and fishes out a cigarette, lighting it, murmuring: "In prison."

"Blessed motherfuck!" I reply, jamming the handkerchief into my lip.

"I went to the Villa Rode one night," he then says, letting out a long, withering ring of smoke. "With a whore. He called himself 'Loretia' or 'Lorelia'—something like that. Real name was Gorushka, I think. Very appealing, very stunning—sapphires sprayed in a blond wig; tempting little fruit basket poking out beneath his blue silk skirt to my under-the-table pawings. Fooled all the burly types, the stiff-necked bureaucrats, the one's who never suspect. Anyhow, another of Gorushka's 'marks' happened upon us at our table. The conversation started out congenially enough; the gentleman—sporting a Bolshy lieutenant's uniform—simply wanted to know where 'Sasha' was. Naturally, I thought naught of it—not in Petrograd, which only boasts a million-thousand 'Sasha's'—and went on with my drinking. Until this fellow in the Bolshy uniform started describing this particular 'Sasha:' red hair, freckled face, doe-eyes. Still, I maintained my composure—until he claimed that he *knew* you; until he started describing—in perfect detail!—the layout plan of the Lissushka farm buildings; until he began recalling, with snide remarks, his employment there in his youth as a groomsman, when your father had been boarding more Arabians. Until he starting bragging, with lurid relish, about fucking himself to high heaven this same pretty little Russian count turned whore—"

"Oh, God," I mutter out, hanging my head in my hands.

"I shot him on the spot," Nikolai goes on, passing me over the cigarette. "Simply whipped out my revolver and plowed a shell into his chest right then and there without even thinking. Of course, things had become rather rough by that time in Petrograd; this was a bit past Eastertide last year, near unto six months after the Bolshy revolution. Shootings, outright murders in the streets—and, yes, in tavernhouses—were no longer uncommon. I bribed the barkeep, and no one else nearby seemed to think much of it. But still, it was a damn foolish thing to do. Especially as the poor man was speaking the truth. Yes?"

Letting out a long sigh, I drag off the cigarette and pass it back to him—but keep my stare fixed straight ahead, murmuring: "What do you want from me, Nikolai?"

"What I want from you," he says in fervent reply, "is what we had, what we *have*. What's been between us ever since last night. Buck naked in my bed, for the rest of my life. But not without honesty, *mon cousin*. Most of all, I want honesty from you."

"Honesty, humph!" Fiercely, I turn upon him, stuttering out: "All right, Nikolai Zhelanov—you want honesty from me, then here it is, the whole reeking, carnivorous truth: during that Easter week when I was fifteen and you were seventeen, when you brought me yet again to watch you fuck women all night at Murzhinsky's whorehouse, I happened to run in with someone I had known from the farm. He name was Volodya Rykazian. . . ."

I tell him everything: about my first night with Volodya, about the abduction, Sheremetev's palace in Moscow, my rescue by Uncle Ned; my meetings with Volodya later, during the *Ballet Russe* years; my run-in with Sheremetev later, when I finally joined the Maryinsky. I tell him about standing on the dock in Southampton the day he sailed away for Rio; I tell him about Uncle Ned's funeral and Winnebar and London and Vienna; I tell him about the murder. With abandon, I tell him about every single lover I can think of that I have ever had, including the Grand Duke; I tell him about running fugitive from the law, about working in the dress shop, about changing my name, about changing it back again. Finally, I end off with a recounting of my charging off from Petrograd in the middle of the night. "See? I am naught but a fool," I tell him, backing my head onto the wall and gulping from the canteen yet again as he hands it over. "Everything I have ever done has been absolutely without any forethought. Always have I endeavored to avoid turmoil—only into turmoil to become hopelessly embroiled! Yes, like a fool, I lowered myself unto the shame Rykazian insisted upon—but reluctantly, mind you! They dialed Father up on the telephone line, Nikolai! They were going to tell him about the affairs I've carried on with other men. God, if he had found out, I—I scarce know what I would have done!"

"Hush," Nikolai murmurs, easing the canteen away from my grasp and moving in close, his arm cradling about my shoulders. "It is all my fault, this horror you went through."

"Your fault?"

Once more he takes the handkerchief, and dabs it to the corner of my mouth, his lips lingering softly afterward in a kiss. "Yes. It was I, after all, who first took you to Murzhinsky's."

"Y-You don't hate me, then?" I whimper out, warily seeking his glance.

"To love is to forgive, Sasha."

"Then—you still love me?"

"Always, *always*. And I'm sorry I hit you."

"I—I'm sorry I hit you, too."

"I suppose, after a time, we will have done with our apologizing to one another over every blessed nagging thing—past or present."

"Yes. I suppose."

From the saddlebags, he fishes out some hardtack and an apple, which he slices up, handing me half. "Lord—it truly is all my fault," he goes on after a moment, shaking his head. "No, indeed, it is, Sasha! I am the one who's been naught but the fool. I know it sounds fiendish, but I—I should never have taken up with any women. I should simply have talked *you* into joining me in one of those cubbyholes that night—all those nights—in Murzhinsky's. It certainly could have saved us both a fair amount of heartache—"

"You mean," I gasp, "you wanted me? Even then?"

"Oh, yes. I've wanted you ever since I can remember."

I stare at him incredulously as he goes on: "Well! Recall you not the night we took in *Godunov?* During that same week, at the Maryinsky?"

To my shrug, he exclaims: "'Breathtaking!' Was what you kept whispering, over and over, again and again as we sat through the entire tenor aria: 'breathtaking!' And all the while you kept latching onto my sleeve with such enthusiasm. I thought I would tear out my hair, so desperately, so passionately I wanted to latch back—and to hold, to kiss you—to tell you that what was truly breathtaking was the face I beheld, so near to mine, yet so far; the cheek I longed to touch, but that I *dared* not. And then—even when I stormed out into the water closet in an attempt at escape, you followed after, haunting me!"

"Nikolai, good Lord!" I gasp in amazement. "Why did you not simply tell me?"

"Tell you? Oh, my God! And what would you have done had I tapped you upon the shoulder: 'Er, pardon me, *mon cousin*, but I long to kiss—hold—fuck you madly?' Straight away from me you would have run, just as you did at first from your friend Rykazian! Tell you! Lord, I was afraid, even with keeping secret my wicked desires, that I'd yet corrupt you beyond all imagining—you, my young cousin, my little brother in everything but name, for whom I was always urged to set proper social example. Difficult enough it was, attempting to deal with my yearnings, with my guilt over all the little under-the-table hand-holds at school. Oh, yes—I was dallying around with the other boys, even then. But it was only you I could think of. I suppose that, in my way, I attempted to tell you surreptitiously. Remember that book I gave you, the one from Paris? You know—about the faggot brothel? Oh, now what the devil was it called—*Victorian Platitudes?*"

"Oh," I reply, meeting his grin with one of my own as I bite off another slice of apple. "Yes."

Washing down a chunk of hardtack with a swig from the canteen, he murmurs on: "I suppose I'd been trying to tell you ever since I'd kissed you."

"Kissed me?"

For a long moment, he holds my gaze; then, his cheeks crimsoning in a flush, he stares awkwardly down to his hands. "You do not remember, do you? About the one time I did kiss you? You were twelve; I was fourteen—"

"Nikolai, we must have kissed one another hundreds of times as children."

"Of course we kissed hundreds of times! Yes, yes—the usual cheeky, 'oh, I've-not-seen-you-in-ages-darling-cousin!' boisterous, friendly Russian kiss! I am not talking about that! I am talking about a kiss like this."

The demonstration proves his point amorously enough; just as during our first breathtaking time last night, I can barely tear myself away. "Nikolai," I whisper against his mouth, peeking up at him, "when on earth—in the old days—did you ever kiss me like that?"

"You were twelve. I was fourteen. . . ." His voice trails off then, and as he stares into the silence, the words return only slowly—softer, lower than before, tinged with tremors of regret. "Fresh out of Dostoevsky," he begins, clasping firm hold of my hand. "It was dark. And winter. We took a troika to Peterhof. Just you and I alone—we had let Anna and Eugenie off back at the townhouse. From the open doorway, I remember we could hear the lull of Papa's cello from the upstairs library. Maman stood out at the curbstone with a wagging finger, but with a smile upon her face, scolding me, warning me not to keep you out too late. I'd made off with another bottle of champagne; I paid the driver an extra five rubles. And we rode to Peterhof."

"I scarce remember that," I murmur, leaning against him close. "Was only the second time I'd ever been to the Great Peter's 'Versailles' palace. So beautiful—"

"Yes, we rode to Peterhof. Where we lingered long through all the lush lower parkways before taking higher to the bluff to view the palace flanked end to end by cathedral spires, everywhere golden statues sprung up amidst sumptuous rows of fountains. Bells jangled gaily from the troika, and we laughed and drank champagne, and after a while nestled one against the other for warmth within cover of the high-piled furs. As we turned at last for home, you rested your head in upon my shoulder, and fell asleep. I kept staring down at you; you had grown so beautiful. And were growing up—no longer the pudgy little yapping nuisance ever chasing me about the school halls. No, you were growing up very quickly, indeed—and every day, I was falling more and more in love with you. And now, here you were with your body molded to mine, your head lapping against my shoulder, your lips parted slightly with sweet breaths of sleep, only bare inches away. You never saw how I flushed in embarrassment, nor how I peeked endlessly at the driver—his back stooped forward, unflinching, uncaring, a man simply bent upon completing his task, his glance never even once stealing back upon the two of us. And as the moments hurried by, and the flickering of the city lights began to fall upon your face, I knew we were nearing home, and that my only chance would soon be lost forever. And I—well, I could not help myself. And so leaned down and kissed you.

"I kissed you for a good long time. Then you blinked suddenly awake, and I pulled back in horror, terrified that I had been found out. But you simply laughed at me, and blurted out: 'What?' as if I had done naught but simply ask you a question. By that time, we were passing by the Narva Arch, and hemming in upon the southern city boulevards. Composing myself, I told you that we would pull home soon, that it was time to make ready.

"That was fifteen years ago—this month, in fact. Fifteen years have I been living with my guilt. And—for fifteen years have I been longing for you ever since then night and day, Sasha."

Squeezing his hand, I stare off into the mute depths of the barn, chills of awe lancing up and down my back. "Passions hidden," I begin softly, turning to face him, "love forbidden. Pauses, whispers—haunted shameful glance—stolen trembling kiss—darkened winter night—resonant sleigh-bells softly pierce the star-lit snow."

Holding mine, his eyes widen in delight, the corners of his lips edging upward into a smile. "Dear Lord in Heaven!" he exclaims, shaking his head. "Is that a poem?"

"Yes."

"About our sleigh ride? Then—then you remember!"

"Well, in truth, Nikolai," I stutter back, embarrassed, "I don't. Not, I think, consciously. All I can recall about Peterhof was its beauty, and then you nudging me awake. But—I suppose I must have remembered. Somehow, deep down."

Pressing kiss after kiss against my cheek, he whispers joyfully: "My Sasha is a poet!"

In response, I throw both arms around his neck—and once again our kisses sink together, passionate and reckless as two tempests scaling a storm at high tide. "Oh, God," he cries against my ear, "everything will be all right, now—life is glorious, wonderful! Sasha, my dearest heart, my holy love—I was heading back to Petrograd sworn unto my dying breath to find you. After the Revolution, the Germans let us out from the camps; recruited all Russian prisoners into what they called the White Russian Northern Corps. They planned to set us against the Bolsheviks. Thus it was ironically by courtesy of the Germans that I last year found myself in Estonia. Sensing the time was right, I rode off from my unit one night as a scout; simply never returned. Instead, I high-tailed it straight to Petrograd. Found the Zhukovskaya townhouse ransacked and gutted out; found Anna living in her office in that hellhole of a hospital where she'd been working. We cabled Maman in Paris; told her we would set out for the Crimea and then to Europe via Constantinople. The plan was perfect—except that, after combing through the city like a madman, checking every haunt I knew, I could find not a trace of you. Anna could not recall your assumed name, nor where, nor with whom you lived. Four times I wrote to Uncle Misha in Oslo, but the mail was erratic; I never received an answer. When I tried to cable him, we could not get through. Then the Bolshies started in with their massive Red Army recruitment drives; I knew I had to get myself and Anna out. Under the name of Petrov, we managed to obtain papers. We were lucky, used Anna's jewelry to bribe our way past the growing numbers of White Guards and Cossack patrols converging on the front lines, and made it through to Yalta before the war set too far in. Maman had caught a steamer there, and was waiting for us at the station in Simferopol with Tatyana and her three children, who had been staying at the Yalta bungalow ever since the February Revolution. Maman wanted to set sail back for Europe on the spot, but I swore I'd never leave Russia without you. So—anxiously, I must say—they are waiting. To find my way north again, I skirted through the outlaw bands—that's how I took on colors of Makhno's Greens. And finally, of Yudenich's army. Ever since last summer, my whole life has been centered solely upon one purpose: to return to Petrograd, to find you—and drag you back out kicking and screaming, if need be. But now, the blessed hand of fate has intervened, and I can forget all that in entirety, for I have found you! We have found one another at long last, Sasha!"

Crushing his arms around my shoulders, he again squeezes me to him close, murmuring into my ear: "So—now, we must make all haste back for Yalta—"

"Nikolai, I cannot go with you to Yalta."

I stare into the aftershock of a fired cannon shell, those deep gray eyes widening upon me in astonishment. And then—after long, gleaning perusal—narrowing in with venomous loathing.

Hardtack and apple shavings crumble to the ground as he lurches upward, his teeth gritted, his fists clenched, heels of his boots hacking tufts of oblivion into the hay as he whirls upon me and roars: "You promised me—you *swore* to me—that you are not a Bolshevik!"

Barely managing to stumble to my feet, I shout back: "And what I told you is the truth! I am not a Bolshevik!"

"Then why *the hell* is it so damned important for you to return to Petrograd?"

"Because I have a son!"

Shattering to silence, our echoes fade around us, waning into the quiet stillness of the warming morn as we stare adrift at one another; as we each, slowly, turn away. Over within its makeshift corral, the horse snorts at us goodnaturedly, chomping on oats. I swallow hard and bite my lip, glancing back to see his rigidly squared shoulders, his stiffened back, his pale hair whitened beneath the wash of slatted light. As I step once more close beside him, he makes not a move, takes not a breath, only continues staring straight ahead toward the dense, flat void of the barn wall. "And?" he utters out finally, his voice scraping just bare above a whisper. "Your wife?"

I grasp hold of his hand and press my head unto his shoulder, murmuring: "Married—to the Revolution. Nikolai, my true and only love, I promise, I *swear* to you, she cares naught for me. For years, the woman has long been sharing conjugal bed with her blooded uncle. It is she who is the Bolshevik, not I."

"Well, Lord God, Sasha! What in hell's name possessed you to marry such a woman?"

"The same notion that possessed you to marry Elena, dammit!" I shout back, holding his glare.

"Oh."

"Was all supposed to be joke!" I go on, shrugging. "A lark, a little frolic we were playing on Rykazian. But before we both knew it, the kisses went too far . . . anyhow, Vanya will be three next month. And then there is Zhenya, Lyubov's daughter by Grigor. The girl would be sixteen now—and has taken to me as if I'm her own father, despite the mere eleven years between us. I scarce know what it is; there must be some kind of Karmic entanglement, I think, between myself and Lyuba and Zhenya. In any case, I cannot simply leave them there, Nikolai. I cannot run off with you to Yalta—although it is what I would otherwise choose. More than anything."

Sighing, Nikolai slides his arm in around mine, and together, we lean back against the wall. "I suppose only one fool can understand another so well," he says sheepishly, grinning and pressing a kiss into my hair. "And no one, after all, is worse fool than yours truly here—tossing his life into the trash basket in the name of glory and running off to war."

Despite the hurtful flutter that pinches down my throat, I ask after a moment: "Is Elena waiting for you in Yalta, also?"

"No. Elena, at behest of her parents, is in Zurich. In a sanatorium. Still thinks she's with child, due any day now. The poor dear never did recover from the stillbirth."

"I see. I am sorry," I then whisper earnestly. "About your little Petya."

"Yes, so am I. Still. You can't know how much. I suppose I thought war would provide me due escape. From everything—or at least, assuage the pain. Of course, part of it was that I was so discontented with playing cello at the Maryinsky; I hardly know what possessed me, my heart has always been for naught but violin. But also—as far as Elena—family, lineage, heritage has always held the greatest importance for me. Without ever any doubt, I always intended to marry and carry on my father's name. When Uncle Misha told me the child had never breathed, I was devastated. And felt so guilty. For two days, I had been going through hell as it was: you had disappeared—again. I knew it was all my fault—again. For two days, all I had been able to think of was my tussle with you in the library—about you lying back against those shelves amidst those toppled books, and the way you looked up at me, so clearly wanting a kiss! I thought I would lose my mind with the hauntings I had of you that week, with the hauntings I had always been having of you. I asked myself a million times what went wrong in Budapest—another instance of my insufferable temper, of my acting naught but the fool. How many years had I been gazing at you in secret—in Paris, London, Vienna, everywhere!—all the time as you slept, as you ate, as you sat across from me in the pit of the orchestra . . . when I realized the rumors about you and that bassoon player were true, I near blew the top of my head off. When I saw you kissing that Gypsy in that tavern booth, I wanted to kill him. And you. I was *that* jealous. When we squared off in the hotel room, fortunate it was indeed, my friend, that you, not I, were the one toting the gun.

"Later," he goes on, "in prison—left unto exhaustion, starvation, degradation—I found time to think. And began to realize, to accept the way I was, the way I always had been, in my thoughts—with men. Despite all the women I've bedded over the years in my attempts to prove otherwise to myself. In prison, faced with so many dark harrowing hours, I was forced to come face to face with the true faggot swain I had always been longing to be. And I began to think about you no longer with guilt; instead, with hope. Because I knew, Sasha—ever since that time in the library, when you stared up at me,

I—I knew you loved me. I knew you always had. During the beatings, the lashings—the endless days moaning into weeks of solitary confinement—it was the image of your face staring up at me from those library shelves to which I held my every thought. Ofttimes, I think it was the only thing in the world that kept me alive."

Pierced to my soul with a shudder of pain and love, I move in close and kiss him again; squeeze his hand as he pats it to my arm. And then we lean together, pressed side to side against the boards of the dank barn wall, our thoughts muting unto quietness and resolution, a dwindling at last of the many questions and explanations seeking form in the long rift of years torn between us. Finally, he squints at the light peeking through the barn boards high above and scarfs up the saddlebags from the ground, winking at me, urging: "What say you we head out for the stream to wash up and take a breath of air?"

I search out my branch-cane as he once again waters down the horse; then I follow him outside, watching as he throws back his head in that cocky, imperious way of his. Watching as he exults like carefree youth in the warmth of the sun basking down upon the two of us. "Looks like the thaw's ebbing early!" he cries, kicking at the slush all around and grinning back at me.

"Humph! We'll catch another cold snap, be damn sure," I reply with a laugh. "Simply proved lucky for us, this sun. Today. Yesterday."

"Indeed. I was attempting to avoid lighting a fire. Smoke's a dead-sure giveaway."

"So I thought." Once again, warily, I prick up my ears to the rattling hum of artillery fire in the distance.

At the stream, we pause to pee—and I drop back aways to do it, closely surveying him; flushing to scarlet as he turns to closely survey me, his voice barreling out in a hearty roar: "Oh, come, English! You needn't keep so shy about me now." Then he cups his hands down into the icy water and starts splashing it back at me, while I holler at him, laughing and bristling at the same time as he shouts out yet again his pet name for me during our May's Academy years: "English! *Anglais! Anglisky!"*

"Nikolai, you turd-brain!"

"Da, eisayki! By *drozhki*, I take ye all the way back down the Nevsky—fer only five rubles, I take ye, Meester *Eisayki—"*

"Eisayki?"

"Cabby jargon for those stuffy *angliskis* in the bowlers. Well! You know how them dapper, proper English like to talk. All the spitting image of your Uncle Ned: *I say!* By jove, good fellow! *I say*, good fellow! *I say, I say, I say . . . .*"

With my own well of water, I splash a torrent back at him, while he lets out a howl of laughter, again splashing back at me. Finally, as I stoop down and loosen my shirt, grinning and shaking my head, he ambles back toward me, picking the buttons open down his jacket and tossing up and down in his other hand a bar of soap.

Gratefully, I catch hold of it as he throws it. "God bless your soul," I tell him, lathering up my hands and sighing in delight at the clean, stiff scent. "Over a week since my last tallow slivers gave way."

"Pity the sun's not a tad warmer," he replies, staring out at the floes breaking up in the midst of the stream. Scooting down beside me, he starts splashing water and soap upon his face; down his chest. "And pity that the days are not more lazy for us, my love. The stream's near high enough to wade. I'd not mind taking a dip."

Dropping to my knees, I whisk off my spectacles and dunk my whole head down into the water; pull up to take the bar of soap from him again, which I start lathering into my hair. Cropped short last summer to impede the lice, it has since grown out again—into a bushel, as it ever grows out, and crying always for cleanliness against the rigors of outdoor living's scaling, itchy patches. "We'd best hurry, English," Nikolai says with a squeeze to my shoulder, his tone gone solemn as he glances off toward the woods, the distant rattling hum of the artillery growing by the moment.

"Yes, I know." Once again I dunk my head down, shivering against the shock of the coldness and the ice.

As I climb back up again, toweling over my head with the end of a saddle blanket, I find him crouched upon his haunches a few feet away from me down the stream, the water lapping about the toes of his boots, his elbows rested upon his knees, his stare hung wide and vacant to the flowing, gurgling eddies of water. "So," he says, sighing and biting his lip, "you will return to Petrograd? To your wife and children?"

I limp back to the rocky bank, just clear of the water, and ease down upon a flattened boulder, staring to my feet, murmuring: "It—it is my responsibility."

"And mine," he replies—his stare yet held to the water, "to return to Yalta. To make certain that my mother and sisters find passage safely out. Before the Reds swarm in there."

"Yes."

Hurtfully, I swallow; press my fist unto my mouth. I sneak a glance over at him, and still he remains crouched by the edge of the stream, a warrior victorious and yet defeated, his face pensive, his quest silent now against the encroaching stranglehold of inevitability. Thirty years of age he will turn this November, and looks it; looks, in fact, even a bit beyond it, the crow lines deepened in with spidery furrows against weals of scars slashed at the corners of his eyes, tiny white strands peeking up through the chin of his beard and the trimmed side-whiskers at his cheeks. But along the back of his collar, the brushed hair glints like a wreath of harvest gold against the spray of morn's fresh light. And his mouth—although now set grimly—yet quivers with the lingering memory of my touch, the sweet bruises of our long night's passion lurking upon his lips in ruddy, glowing evidence. "I love you!" I burst out, seizing my hands together and thrashing them, uselessly, against my knees. "Oh, my God! Perhaps there is an alternative—"

"Is there?"

At last he turns to fix his gaze upon me—his eyes hollowed unto the depths of stark winter's mourning, resigned to the will of fate—and yet holding back to a question, grasping at any last offered straw, daring to hold out hope against hope's every last fading glimmer.

"I—I don't know. . . ." Shuddering, I wrestle, in a clench of fists, with my demons.

He nods; stares back to the water. "That man I shot," he murmurs after a moment. "What was his name?"

"Semyon Bulyarin."

"Oh, yes. Yes, his father, I hear, was rather influential, during the old days, in the Novgorod *zemstvo*. And is now a Bolshevik. A commissar in Lenin's government, in fact. That's the second reason why I fled Petrograd with Anna in such a hurry. The man wants my head."

So—it is dangerous for him, even more so than I realized. Dangerous for him amongst the Whites here in Latvia. Dangerous for him amongst the Reds back in Petrograd . . . .

He stands up then, eyes lowered to the ground, and walks toward me. I reach for my cane to aid my way upward from the boulder, but he shakes his head and drops down onto the gravel before me, scooting in close, his arms winding around my back, his head pressed, ear to ear, against mine. Nosing into his hair, I shut my eyes, squeeze my knees up close about his hips, and clamp my arms back around him fiercely, straining against all odds to hold him forever—to never allow him to go, nor to permit us to be parted . . . except that all of forever, could I but count it unto the end of time, would not be long enough to hold him, to stay and breathe and live and love with him, scarce ever letting him out of my adoring sight . . . "I l-love you," I choke out again, shuddering back tears, my panicked scream. "Oh, G-God, Nikolai Zhelanov! I love you *so much. . . .*"

I edge back then, striving to say more, the words trembling pitifully half-uttered from my lips—but he presses a finger to my mouth, shaking his head, whispering: "No, no—shhh! I know, *I know.* Hush—not another thing, dear heart. Not a thing else, we've already said more than enough words. Not another blessed, painful thing . . . ."

And then he crushes his lips to mine, and it is exactly like the first time—and tears renewed start seeping, one by one, once again from the corners of my eyes, and I quiver against him, devastated unto the core of my heart, fearful that, of all the kisses, this will be our very last. . . .

Finally, he shoves upward, smoothes his hands along the creases of his trousers, and peers down at me, asking: "You suggest another alternative?"

Struggling to regain hold of my voice, I shrug and stare helplessly into the depths of the lapping water, whispering: "I—I am not sure."

With innate understanding, he nods. "I'll be back at barn." Glancing to his wristwatch, he adds: "But as I said before, we'd best move, and soon. I am not the only one ken to this little haven of ours with its hidden stash of oats and easy watering trough for a horse."

Mutely, I nod in reply—luxuriating for one last time in the wealth of his smile as he chucks two affectionate fingers up under my chin. Then he turns on his heel, marching away in long, purposeful strides, his hands jammed into his pockets, his head lowered in thought as he follows the foot path through the woods back to the barn.

From the boulder, I return to the stream, kneel down upon its bank, and clamp my hands tightly together. My reflection wavers back at me, countenance of a heart torn asunder unto raw, bloody pillage. I stare down at the image of my face in the water—and again beg for insight, grasping desperately for any staff of guidance. None emits save for that already ensconced deep within my inner knowing soul, and against what I must do—against what I *have* to do without any further question—I shut my eyes, waging in battle with all my will. Then I dip my right hand down into the water and cross myself in the old way from brow to heart and shoulder to shoulder with three solemn fingers, whispering: "God forgive me . . . ."

I find him out front of the barn door, again the formidable White officer clad in long-skirted greatcoat, his wary, distant eyes and pale locks peeking out from beneath the brim of his black sable hat. The horse, beside him, saddled and ready, awaits my decision. I slip my arms into my own coat bearing the brightly embroidered star of the Bolshevik Red Army; take my knife and slip it into my boot once he hands it over; take, with murmured thanks, the spare Luger pistol and box of cartridge clips that he offers from the outer pocket of his knapsack. "Semi-automatic," he says, nodding. "Loads straight up the butt. Eight-round magazine." Resting his fist high upon the saddle horn, he then scans the horizon from north to south, east to west, sighing, murmuring: "Well?"

Without another moment's hesitation, I load a clip up the butt of the Luger, snap shut the catch, and turn to meet his stare, uttering out decisively: *"All right.* This is my plan. . . ."

* * *

Heads bent upon our purpose, we stride down Sadovaya, the fog lending an eerie glow to the rise of Petrograd morn air. "Get along, you lazy, good-for-nothing souse!" Nikolai barks again, shoving at me with the butt of his pistol, playing his part to the hilt. Clad in the trim brown greatcoat and peaked red-star cap of a Red Army colonel, he continues, with those tunneling eyes of his, inspiring gasps of fear from near unto every cautious pedestrian we pass. Groveling in response, I squeeze up close about my neck the collar of my old felt jacket and tip the brim of my worker's cap, muttering out from the side of my mouth: "Darling, we have got to stop meeting like this! I hate stealing clothes off corpses."

"Indeed. Evil times necessitate evil deeds." Once more he glares down passers-by; once more, like an imperious dragon, spews out a stream of smoke from his cigarette.

Watching him, I cannot contain my grin, nor a snide comment: "Least I had not the gall to reoutfit the poor dead lout in my gray-spanking White captain's uniform."

"Evil times," he replies—perfectly straight-faced, and still nudging along at me with the pistol butt, "necessitate approaching life with a sense of humor."

Past Pashninkov's apothecary, we halt up beside the alley. "There, there, and there!" he orders, pointing with the pistol to the walkway.

Dutifully, I take the push broom I have been making use of as a cane and start sweeping.

Half a block ahead of us, the number twenty-nine streetcar pulls to its dutiful five-minute-late halt. Two elderly babushkas debark, muttering loudly into one another's deafened ears. To be followed by that vibrant, impish young woman I know so well, a gay spring caught to her step, her sable hat tilted at a stylish angle upon her head, long curly braids cascading down her back intertwined with ribbons.

"That her?" asks Nikolai.

"Um-hmm. Hope you've thought up a good line." Burrowing my stare back down to the walkway before me, I keep sweeping.

"Dearest heart," Nikolai intones in reply, whisking the cigarette butt out from his lips and flinging it to the ground, "you simply leave matters to Petrovich when it comes to squiring the ladies."

"Be kind," I say as he struts off, his head thrown back, his boot heels tapping hearty drumbeats of a mission pursued down the walkway.

I linger long enough to watch him pause and tip his cap to her; to hear his repeated, glowing plaudits of *'devushka;'* to watch him break into a rakish grin—and watch her respond, coyly, flattered. Then I quickly sweep my way past the apothecary and turn in through the alley.

Straight into a Red Guard patrol. "Hey! You there—halt!" From the opposing alley of the building's littered courtyard, two browncoats hustle toward me—one eagerly, the other with overwhelming red-faced reluctance, begging: "Akkh, Captain! Ye'll not see the likes o' this chance again! I tell ye—it's Sonya, Captain! An' Natasha!"

From beyond the back alley, giggles erupt in a lingering, teasing torrent.

"Smirnov, shut up! Hey, you!" the captain barks again, stomping with blustery importance across the length of cobblestones and angrily pointing me down. "What is your business here?"

"Fifth Sanitation Detail, Comrade, sir!" I shout back, saluting and tipping my cap.

"Huh?"

From my jacket, I drag out a scraggly, mismatched ream of papers. "Fifth Sanitation Detail!" I shout at him again. "Ordered up by Comrade Mrenitsev hisself, at six o'clock this morn! Yes, sir—bright and early they woke us up to join the upstandin' work o' the proletariat, sir! Covered my beat from Griboyedov Canal and the St. Nikolai Cathedral to here since then, sir! In spite o' fog so thick, I could scarce see the gaslamps—kept bumpin' my back end into 'em pole by pole, without missin' nary a one! An' in spite o' my leg," I tell them, pointing down and woefully exaggerating my limp. "Near blew that foot off 'gainst the Whites last month at Narva! But the doc, he sewed me up near whole again—"

"All right, all right! Fifth Sanitation Detail? Humph! Let's see them papers."

"Yes, sir!" Shoving the pile at him, I let go clumsily before he can latch on a hold, and send the whole mess scattering across the cobblestones of the alley. "Oh!" I gasp, waving out my hands in a fluster. "Pardon, forgive a poor fool, sir! F-Fifth Sanitation Detail—"

"Captain!" exclaims Smirnov, nudging him. "Ye sure ye want te pass up Sonya? An' Natasha? Fer this nonsense?"

"Shut up! You!" the captain roars, snatching up papers along with me. "You show me on these papers where it says 'Fifth Sanitation Detail!'"

Quizzically, I stare down at the first piece of paper thrust into my face. "Uh, 'scuse me, sir! Jest took te learnin' o' my letters bare o' two months past, Comrade, sir! Uh, yes, now—let's see here," I mumble, turning the paper upside down. After much deliberation, I point to the uppermost row of letters, demanding: "Uh, is this a 'P'?"

"Oh, for God's sake!"

"Captain!" Smirnov snorts again, elbowing him, "the women!"

"You!" the captain bellows, shoving Smirnov aside and pushing me, vengefully, back toward the broom. "You pick up every single damn one o' these papers you spilled! And sweep this whole courtyard, blast it—and the alley, too, clear back out to Sadovaya, 'til it shines like crystal! Do you hear?"

"Yes, sir! Fifth Sanitation Detail!"

"Aww, shut up!"

Blessing the fancy that turns most young men's heads come advent of spring, I scavenge after papers and sweep up in a flurry, peering over the rims of my spectacles as the two browncoats stomp off hurriedly to the back alley, disappearing beyond amidst a rash of breathy feminine giggles.

Footsteps then resound upon my back from the direction of Sadovaya. Snatching up the broom, I dart across the courtyard and press against the building beside the front alley entrance, peeking around and holding my breath, waiting.

Nikolai and Zhenya emerge arm in arm, twittering along together in the height of flirtation—until he suggests she accompany him into the alley, at which she pauses to reconsider. But he convinces her by lavishing compliments, and she hangs close into his arm, giggling and gazing up at him in wide-eyed rapture. "Silly little girl," I mutter out, chuckling under my breath. "Soon enough, I suppose, you'll learn it pays naught to throw your heart away to debonair cads. Especially that one."

Once they clear the alleyway into the courtyard, I step out from the building's shadow and doff my cap.

Letting out a gasp, Zhenya stops cold with her smile frozen upon her face. Lunging for her, Nikolai seizes her into his arms and clamps his hand across her mouth. "It's all right, sweetheart!" he says into her ear. "I am not going to hurt you in any way. Now, listen very carefully: I know it must be a terrible shock to see your step-father so suddenly once again, but please—we cannot have you scream. Do you understand me? *Do not scream*—nor cry out, nor squeal with delight—anything. *Please.* The streets are teeming with Red Guard patrols, making this atrociously dangerous—for him; for me. Now, for you. Understand?"

Slowly, he then eases away his hand.

Uttering out "Step-papa!" in a stifled whisper, Zhenya stumbles forward and throws her arms wide, collapsing into mine.

"Yes, sweetheart," I murmur against the furry brim of the sable hat that I so long ago bought her as a present. "Yes, it truly is me."

Pulling back, she chokes out tearfully: "Oh, Step-papa! They said you were dead! . . ." And again she throws her arms around me, shaking her head in disbelief, her words rasping away into sobs.

Beyond her, I catch sight of Nikolai nervously eyeing Sadovaya through the alleyway, his frown urging us to hurry.

As I proffer my handkerchief to help her wipe her tears, Zhenya turns to steal a glance back at Nikolai—and stares between the two of us several times, squinting up her eyes. "You—you are the man in the picture," she says to him at last. "In the picture of the Eiffel Tower in Paris. With Step-papa."

Nodding, he again glances beyond her to me, urging all due haste.

"Zhenya," I say, swallowing hard, "how fare your mother and Vanya?"

"Humph! Mama remains as much an old biddy as ever! But especially without you, Step-papa—oh, I have missed you so much!—but since you went away, Vanya has become my joy. Though I fear Mama yearns to ring his trouble-making neck sometimes, I bless the day you gave me a little brother." Turning to once more regard Nikolai in confusion, she goes on: "He is the one who is your dear violinist cousin?"

"Yes."

"My Lord, Step-papa! If he was lost in the War, then how in the world? And why did you simply not come home? Why are we hiding away from the Red Guards like this in a courtyard?"

In response, I earnestly grasp up her hands, answering: "Zhenyushka, my beloved little girl—who has always been like mine, although in truth, not so at all—Zhenya," I go on, my throat parching dry to the brittle bone, "do you remember the many times that you told me how you so wished to someday travel to England?"

* * *

"Hoofbeats. They're coming," he says, urging us to hurry.

"Are you certain?"

"Yes."

Oh, God. I cannot help but marvel at his calmness, his sureness, while my own heart is quaking. Pensively, he frowns down yet again, making a final check over the seals and signatures affixed to our forged papers: *Count Nikolai Sekovsky; his wife, Aleksandra; his children, Zhenya and Ivan* . . . . My wire spectacles, set square upon the bridge of his nose, lend a dignified air, as does the Scottish derby, the outmoded frock coat, the silk-tied cravat, the blue serge trousers. Shorn of his beard now, with weals of scars ridged in evidence about his cheeks and lower jaw, he appears older, almost middle-aged—but as he glances up at me, that rakish smile breaks through once again, and he lets out a hearty laugh, his eyes teasing, his barbs stabbing quips at me as if we were about to embark upon naught but one of our old dormitory larks. "Oh, keep that chin up, English," he murmurs out at last, nodding reassurance. "It will be *all right.*"

"Step-papa, hold still!" Zhenya orders, dabbing onto my mouth a finishing touch of lip paint.

"Zhenya!" I bark back. "If we intend to slip past them like this, you are going to have to stop calling me that!"

"Yes, sir!" she gasps, catching in her breath at my scolding. But then—upon eyeing me up and down once more—she bursts into another helpless peal of giggles.

Between both her and Nikolai, I shoot blazing exasperation, snapping at him gruffly: "All right, Zhelanov—blast it! I know you have been simply itching for me to ask you, so I might as well oblige, and let us have done with what you so gleefully intend to say! How do I look?"

"Ravishing!" he declares, again fixing me with that grin.

"Oh, shut up!"

His laughter filters off abruptly; the papers he tucks down into the pocket of his waistcoat, murmuring: "Make ready. Here they come."

Once more I pin into my hair the crown of the feather-laden hat and pull the thickly knotted shawl up close about a neckline of lacy ruffles and my tissue-paper bosom. As I edge back toward Nikolai, I cannot help but wince once more in annoyance against the pleated folds whipping about my legs from Zhenya's borrowed petticoat and skirt. A pair of laced women's shoes, the left retaining a heel, the right made devoid of one, aids against much conspicuousness of the limp. "Praise God that all the women have been cropping off their hair in such droves," I say, rolling my eyes. "And that I have always been so testy about taking a shears to mine."

"It looks perfectly fine—wonderful, in fact. You look fresh out of Paris," Nikolai assures me, fondly smoothing a long auburn lock down into the well of my throat as I ease in beside him.

"Did I buff enough powder onto my chin, my cheeks?"

"Dear heart, you look grand as a belle at a ball," he replies with another sidelong grin. "Will you manage without a cane?" he then asks with concern, taking my hand and sliding it through his arm.

"For a time."

"Step-papa!" Zhenya whispers, heaving Vanya along upon her hip. "What, then, shall I call you?"

"Simply 'Sasha,' sweetheart. As if for 'Aleksandra.'"

"But that seems so disrespectful!"

"No, it is not—we *are* family. But remember, I am supposed to be your step-*mother*. And your last name, now, is Sekovskaya—"

I clip my words up short, shaking my head against Zhenya's further whispered questions as the patrol of White Guards charges into view up ahead through the trees. Glad at least that under such a guise my closeness to Nikolai will no longer seem improper, I lean into his arm, squeezing it with nervous fingers while he croons into my ear: "It will be *all right. . . .*" But should any one of the officers scrutinize him closely enough in recognition, nothing will be all right ever again, and for the rest of my life, I shall want to die, knowing we should have stuck to my original plan, with him going on for Yalta, and me following thereafter with the children—not with him accompanying me back to Petrograd like such a vain, lovesick fool who would hear of naught else! *Oh, God!* No, they cannot take him away and hang him, not when we have been separated for so long in time, only to have reunited just scarce more than a brief month past. Never will I let anyone, or any force is this world, take him away from me, ever again. . . .

"You, there—all of you! Halt!"

A dozen White Guards converge, their shouts of heated orders mimicking foibles of the ridiculous: huddled up against the trees, sporting foppish clothes and two old battered portmanteaus lashed upon our horses' backs, we are obviously naught but another group of estranged nobility on the run. And to them, naught but another wayward family of refugees.

"Humph, refugees!" sneers the captain of the guard, signaling back to his men to hold their fire. "Lord, help us all!" the man cries, rolling his eyes with distaste and scanning us over. "And how many more of you poor fools are left out there in the woodwork? Don't you know these forests are teeming with Red bandits? How did you ever find your way past the firing lines—and with two children yet, ye gods! All right, let's see your papers. . . ."

I strain to watch as the man snatches the stack out from Nikolai's hand and begins leafing through it with a weary sigh of impatience. Holding her breath, Zhenya slips her fingers into mine, and I squeeze them fiercely, again blessing the girl's admirable proficiency with her father's typewriter. Decorously, quietly, Nikolai begins conversing in low undertones with the man—ascertaining, after some prying, that Yudenich's defensive line against the latest Red infringement has indeed held solid, all the way from Narva, on the northern Estonian coast, to

Pskov, which now lies before us about seven versts or so through the woods. Only a miracle has seen us this far on horseback from Pulkovo without any mishap or injury, one Red Guard patrol after another firing at us, missing always by bare inches; the groups of partisan bandits hot on our trail in shouting pursuit all the way from Luga, and only dropping back once we made straight for the White lines. And straight into what could be Nikolai's doom.

My fears for the moment prove unfounded: in relief, I attempt to contain a loud sigh as the forged papers elicit no more than the usual bored affectations, the captain soon enough wrinkling the stack back into Nikolai's grasp. "Yes, yes, we'll escort you to the railway station then, Your Honor, for requisition of the horses. Yes, well! Don't mind, sir, toasting along a sip of brandy if you've a flask, don't mind if I do! Yes, the Baltic ice has finally broken up; yes, indeed, spring's long overdue since Maytide. You could hear the Bolshies' six-inch guns back in Petrograd? We'd been told they shipped the fleet out, but the Brits are coming back up at 'em from the Estonian coast, and hard, I might add. Indeed, yes, Your Honor—well, thank you again!" the man lauds on, swigging down another generous gulp of brandy. "And might I add that you have a very lovely young daughter there, sir. And—well! If you don't mind my also saying so, not to mention a very beautiful wife."

While I glare to the ground, biting back curses, Nikolai escorts us toward our own horses. Zhenya—flushed with joy at the captain's compliment, and fussing coquettishly with the brim to her close-crowned hat—he assists upward first into stirrup and saddle.

And then turns to me.

And the air quivers between us, his mouth parting bare inches above my own, so close. Momentarily, he lingers, staring down into my eyes, almost swaying upon his feet—the world, the war, the patrol of White Guards forgotten unto infinity. Staring back, I swallow hard and hold his gaze; hold it until he tears himself away and reaches down for Vanya, gathering him up into his arms with a gentle, teasing quip. Head lowered, I then lead the way around to the right side flank of the horse—where, with his free hand, Nikolai assists me upward into stirrup and saddle.

Fumbling with my skirts, the petticoats, the stockings—and hoping that my trouser legs remain hiked up far enough underneath—I settle into the saddle behind Zhenya amidst reverent nods from the gathered group of White Guards. At least there can be no doubt that 'Count Sekovsky' loves his 'wife.'

"Ladies," the captain calls out as he passes, grinning and doffing his cap.

Grasping up the reigns, I moan into Zhenya's ear: "Something tells me this is going to be a very tiresome journey."

"Oh, Step—I mean, Sasha!" she gushes out in reply. "This is the grandest time I've had ever since I can remember!"

The grandest time ever since Zhenya can remember culminates one half hour later at the Pskov railway station—the same junction where the Tsar abdicated his crown two years and two months past—although the field artillery grinds on, yet booming in rampant testament to unresolved conflict in the distance. We surrender our horses to the White Guards and join into the crowd of refugees—the wanderers, the lost and homeless ones. The people to whom, for over a year—although encountering them everywhere—I have struggled not to pay due mind. Now, retribution descends in swift numbers: swarmed into the station, scores of watchful, fearful, apathetic souls crowd across every platform and post and wooden step, the smell of dried urine permeating thickly across the air through the stench of swaddling clothes from babes toted about in the arms of numerous wide-eyed, frighteningly young mothers. Discarded shells of walnuts and pits from apricots, peaches, and other fruit litter the platforms and stationhouse walkways in putrid, crunchy abundance everywhere one steps. The ticket booths, boarded up, display large signs reading 'Stationmaster' with arrows pointing both to a nearby office door, at which a line of about two dozen has formed. The remainder of people continue loitering about the station, but make no attempt to join in. "Looks like bribery time," Nikolai murmurs into my ear. "Watch yourself and the girl—joining the line shows the others we have valuables. Your pistol still ready?"

"Full clip loaded in my pocket, darling," I reply, my falsetto rasped out bare above a whisper, one hand clasped firm unto Zhenya's shoulder and the other about the butt of my gun.

After more than an hour's wait in the line, passage to Ostrov—a scarce fifty versts southward—costs us one hundred paper rubles and one three-inch link of a ruby necklace. "God bless dear old Uncle Misha's heart," Nikolai says as—past a rash of sullen glares from the crowd of watchful vagabond eyes—we crowd into another long line awaiting the next train just beyond the stationmaster's office.

"And Melissa's," I add in a whisper. "God rest her soul."

It takes two more hours until a train pulls in, and far from the days of sleeping berth compartments and continental dining service in first class, only third class coaches remain available, ours sharing with the coach before us a sorry, stinking little water closet. The two standard rows of cushionless benches face one to another, each chipped and marred with gashes, the handrails either missing or entirely broken off. Our two portmanteaus Nikolai shoves in beneath a dirt-strewn bench aside the farthest back window. "Only to Ostrov?" I ask in a lowered tone, easing down close beside him. "And then we must pay again?"

"All the way from here to Yalta, looks like, my love," he replies with a cocked eyebrow. "Pray to God your jewels last. And not only that," he goes on, "but military and armored trains have priority. Which means we could find ourselves shunted off on a siding for hours. A whole day, even."

"I remember when one could reach Yalta in five or six days, at the most, from Petrograd."

"Yes," he replies, nodding. "It appears this journey will take a wee bit longer."

With trepidation, I eye the growing line for the water closet, pondering upon how many more hours I can safely remain 'Countess Sekovskaya' without a shave.

As the steam whistle blows and our coach lurches forward, Zhenya hungrily breaks out the sausage and pastries purchased from a vendor during our wait in line. "Oh, come, Vanyushka—it's good!" she exclaims, picking off tiny pieces of meat to wave out in front of his face. "Juicy just as you fancy it . . . ."

But only after much coaxing on his sister's part will the child eat. Just as his every other response to our any and every prodding as to his bodily necessities has, over the past three days, been coaxed out only after near throes of prostration from Zhenya—and no one else. The heavy bangs from his bowl-cut hair hanging down into vacant blue eyes, my son slowly stares around—first between the three of us, then to the portmaneaus, and then to the chattering droves of other families scooting in upon other benches—his glance at last settling once again, in confusion, back upon me as he whimpers out: "J-Just w-want m-my mama . . . ."

"Zhenya," Nikolai suggests, "perhaps the time has come to take your little brother for a trip to the water closet."

"Yes, Nikolai Petro—I mean, Papa."

Fist crushed unto my mouth, I stare down the aisle after the children as they amble away—and then shut my eyes, shuddering, rasping out: "Oh, God! What have I *done?"*

Nikolai grips my arm, murmuring: "Absolutely, positively the best thing—"

"The best thing? I have stolen the child away from his mother! Oh, dear God!"

"Sasha, dear heart, keep your voice *down."*

"I know, I know! I am sorry—I just—oh, God! Three days now, and every time the boy looks my way, he stares as if knowing me to be the one responsible! I am telling you, Nikolai—at first, I thought this to be the best thing. Now, I don't know."

"They will both have a better life, Sasha," he reminds me in gentle, patient reply. "Both Zhenya and your little Vanya will have a far better life with us in England, than if they stayed living here under the Red Terror of the Bolshies—"

"Lyubov is not a bad woman, you know, Nikolai. Despite Zhenya's harping complaints—and despite, I know, your own opinion of her political leanings—Lyubov Ivanovna is *not* a bad woman. And when I think about what this must be doing to her, I don't know how I am going to live with myself!"

"Do you wish to go back?" he replies earnestly, catching a hand to my shoulder. When I hesitate in answer, he continues on in a rush: "Do you wish to take the children back, Sasha? Do you feel *that* strongly about it? If so, we'll—we'll turn right around soon as we reach Ostrov, I promise. If you truly cannot live with yourself, if you think that the only just, proper thing for us to do is turn straight around and take the children back to their mother, then that is what we shall do. To my utmost, I will help you however I can."

Overwhelmed, I turn and meet his solemn gaze, again searching the face I know so well; again appraising this thoughtful, generous stranger that I am yet only beginning to come to know. Back upon me, he exudes a patient watchfulness, his ready, listening ear. And such empathy. "No," I tell him after a long moment, resolutely shaking my head. "You are right. We must do this, no matter how painful. They will both have a far better life in England."

"Sasha," Nikolai whispers, leaning close unto my ear. "The boy is as much your child as he is Lyubov's. Never forget that. And Zhenya is almost grown, will find herself a spry young fellow to run off with in a couple of years. Better in England, than here—where everything is naught but war and death."

"Yes, my love, dearest love. You are right."

Once Zhenya returns with Vanya, Nikolai and I both glance up toward her with the unspoken question, and with a nod back toward the water closet, she rolls her eyes and lets out an embarrassed laugh, muttering: "Yes, believe it or not, he finally went!"

And again the boy clambers up straight into his sister's arms once they sit back down, clinging onto her with his tiny head buried deep into her bosom, wholly ignoring, this time, her baitings with the sausage.

Nikolai squeezes my arm, whispering: "He will get over it. Will simply take some time."

With a long sigh, I nod and lean back into the hardened bench of my seat. "Ostrov," I say after a moment. "And from there?"

"From there, the tracks head southwest."

As he swallows, I can see his Adam's apple working. "To Rezekne," he adds. Then, forcing nonchalance, he reaches down into the portmanteau and fishes out a newspaper.

Across his arm, I glance to the blur of printed pages before peering back up, long and hard, into his face. Drawn by the force of my wordless perusal, after a moment he catches my eye and nods, murmuring: "It will be *all right.* And I love you, too."

His pinch to my hand comes firm and reassuring, but comfort escapes me, and I succumb unto the blight of despair, watching forlornly out the window as lindens, pines, and ferns roll by. *Oh, God!* Due southwest. To Rezekne—and directly into the jaws of the wolves! In Latvia . . . .

* * *

Two hours later, in Ostrov, to our vast surprise, the stationmaster merely waves our train on after a brief stop made for loading coal into the tender. "Perhaps this will not cost us as dearly as I had thought," Nikolai observes, shaking his head in befuddlement and returning to the newspaper.

As everyone in our coach settles down to their evening meals of sausage and stale bread and *vatrushki* cheese tartlets bartered away from noisy peasant vendors through the windows, I pounce upon the chance to steal back into the water closet for a few moments with razor and face powder and aloe cream, where I make quick work of my shave with one eye peeled upon the rattly door and its useless broken lock.

Just barely do I whisk onto my cheeks and chin a second layering of powder when a squealing little tot bangs his way in from the outside, the door swinging open and his mother abashedly snatching it shut again with red-faced murmurs of apology. Upon return to the coach, however, I find my ministrations well worth the effort, for at the next junction—not a scheduled stop—the train halts up without a moment's warning, and a contingent of near unto a dozen White Guards boards, carbines snapping fist to palm at the ready, their boots pounding echoes of foreboding across the floorboards as they comb, coach by coach, throughout the train in search of recruits. Those traveling with families in tow are let alone unto their business, but any unencumbered men of fighting age are promptly escorted from the train, none to return. "All-volunteer army, my ass," Nikolai mutters under his breath, again pulling my arm close into his and burrowing back behind the newspaper as yet another of the beady-eyed officers saunters past.

With the approach of nightfall, the train moans to a stop once again and shifts over onto a siding sounding not far from the airy, splashing sounds of a river. "They'll not continue until morn?" I ask, frowning and peering through the window at canopies of budding birch trees.

"So it appears," Nikolai replies, breaking into the portmanteaus and fishing out rolls of clothing for us to make use of as pillows and blankets.

Together, Zhenya and Vanya curl up on the opposing bench, while Nikolai stretches out down upon the dirt-ridden floor, shaking his head up with a grin of amusement when I burst forth in protest. "My love," he insists again, "I shall be perfectly comfortable down here, I can sleep anywhere. No, we will not trade off for the bench night by night. Would not be deemed appropriate at all, remember? Dear, darling, little wife?"

Sighing, I resign myself to my pillow of wrinkled clothes and stretch my arm down to him, catching hold of his hand—while Zhenya, glancing between the two of us with wide-eyed, conspiratorial enthusiasm, stifles continued giggles, still assuming our exchanges of affection as naught but part of the act. "She might as well become accustomed to it," Nikolai murmurs up to me once the girl nestles down beside Vanya and starts drifting asleep. "And the sooner, the better."

Not without discomfiture have I, too, noted Zhenya's lengthy stares held upon my cousin's face in between her endless busyings with Vanya, ever since that first day in Petrograd. "So," I whisper down in reply. "You think you've struck her fancy?"

"Humph! You know I always have the most peculiar effect upon women," Nikolai groans upward with a grin. "They like me."

Stifling a laugh in response, I smack my hand down at him—which he catches up in his own, pulling my fingers unto his lips and brushing them with kisses, murmuring: "But I love only you."

"Nikolai," I say, again basking in the warmth of his gaze alighting upward so wistfully, "how are we going to arrange matters, once we reach Yalta? And then, England? The children, of course, must stay with me, but so must you—I shan't hear of us living apart. But how will we manage such an affair without—well, you know. Without Father, Aunt Sophie, your sisters learning of the truth?"

"Will prove difficult," he admits, sighing. "You say Zhenya's privy enough to the way affairs were between you and Rykazian?"

"It appears so."

"Anna, I am afraid, has her own suspicions about me. Lord knows how she found out—I have taken diligent care with concealing my escapades, but I swear that woman has the damndest gift for delving beneath the surface. The night before we departed Petrograd together, she finally confronted me openly, demanding flat out whether I was a—" Here, he stops, and glances over to ascertain that Zhenya and Vanya remain, indeed, fast asleep, before mouthing up to me in the barest whisper: "—a homosexual. Of course, I hardly admitted such to her," he goes on, rolling his eyes, "and marched, instead, straight from the room in shock, scarce able to believe that my own sister had uttered such a thing, much less thought it! Our price to pay, I suppose, for allowing the women out of the kitchens and into the realms of business, government. Medicine."

"Do you think she has told anyone?" I ask, appalled.

"I doubt it. My mother, my other sisters have long lived more sheltered, ladylike lives—and would not, I am certain, even discern the meaning of the word if she did tell them. And Anna would die before causing any hurt to Maman. She knows I would, too. So, my hope is that my nosy doctor sister will keep her suspicions to herself."

"Why must everyone think our love so wrong?" I ask in frustration, inching my hand out from his to stroke my fingers along his cheek.

"And did you not think it wrong yourself, at first?" he answers back softly, grasping up my wrist. "For men to love other men?"

"I suppose. I can't recall when I changed. But I'd be a liar not to admit continued shame. Not of the love I feel, nor the way we express it, but of what others think of us, with such horror—or what they would think, if they knew."

"Yes," he agrees, nodding, "pity that only in this little masquerade of ours can we trade such obvious affections while crowded onto a train full of people running away from a war. War . . . God! Indeed, naught but war harbors such bane of prejudice against those such as you and I, dear cousin. Perhaps someday, dear heart, wars will come to their rightful, holy end, and two poor souls like you and I shan't ever again be forced to desperately flee across the ravaged countryside, and men who chase off to fight will at last make truce with one another and themselves, allowing men who choose to love one another to simply carry on with their lives."

"You are a dreamer," I whisper in reply, smiling down at him.

"Which is why I am on this train with you," he whispers back. "And no longer fighting in the war."

Mouthing words he can scarce hear, but that I know he well understands, I hold his gaze for a long while, and then settle back onto the bench against my makeshift roll of pillows, falling asleep with my arm draped over the side, my hand grasped in his.

Before the first trystings of dawn's light, I force myself awake and steal away for my shave in the water closet. Afterward, my tiptoeings back up the aisle past rows of slumberers curled upon the benches prove futile in intent, for once I reach our back window, the train lurches forward once again with a steaming scream to the air, jolting everyone awake amidst yawns and mumbled curses. Behind my back, I hand off the straight-razor and aloe cream to Nikolai for him to pocket until his own trip to the water closet. "Vanyushka, we are on holiday, a joy-ride, an adventure!" Zhenya pleads with effort, rocking the boy back and forth in her arms past a bevy of whispered endearments in helpless attempt to thwart off another morntide burst of tears and pleas for 'Mama.'

Sighing, I slide back down beside Nikolai, acknowledging his squeeze to my shoulder with one back to his hand as I stare in silence out the window.

Soon enough, at yet another unscheduled junction stop, the train halts up again, and once more a surly-faced group of White Guards boards and begins combing, bench by bench, throughout the coaches—dredging out this time two more youthful charges apparently overlooked in the search made yesterday. With a sigh of relief, Nikolai returns to the newspaper once the last of the soldiers stomps back outside—but glances upward as, with a gasp, I seize hold of his arm, my attention riveted upon the scene transpiring just outside the window.

The first young man, like the score of others forced off yesterday, disappears past the line-up of horses, but the second fellow several White officers drag up to the switching tower, a noose already wound about his neck. "Oh, dear God," I moan out under my breath.

With shouts urging the train passengers to watch and take due note of the fate of deserters, they promptly mount the man on a horse, throw the rope high up over the tower-boards, and shoo the horse out from under his legs.

Gasping, his limbs jerking about crazily in all directions for a moment far too gruesomely long, the man finally swings limp and still as a grain sack, a flow of urine darkening in a damp black stream down the front of his trousers.

Several ladies in our coach, fraught unto tears, cling against their husbands as the train starts forward once again. Crushing Vanya's hand close into hers, Zhenya gawks down at her feet, for once at a loss for words. Nikolai, blanched white as a sheet, continues his survey of the newspaper, which I know he is not reading, uttering out dryly: "Some of them they merely shoot."

Two hours later, we cross the border into Latvia.

And then the stations—the villages—all cities large and small held by ample, obvious garrisons of White Guards—we fly by wholly without incident. At Rezekne, at noontide, they force us to debark and line up to pay bribes to the stationmaster, which assures us passage to Daugavpils—where, as the sun begins hanging low off the western horizon, we again pay yet another bribe. Past the town's outskirts the train stops once more for the night, pulling up to a siding in a screech of rusty gears as another group of White Guards signals it to halt. This time, however, they do not board; instead, after much conversation held through the windows between them and a group of passengers two or three coaches down from us, the whole train seems to literally burst apart with excitement, shouts of 'Hurrah!' and 'For Faith, Tsar, and Fatherland!' tearing up and down the rail line.

"I am going to find what it is all about," Nikolai says, pulling on his frock coat in haste and tilting his derby low to his brow.

"Nikolai," I warn him, catching his sleeve. "Wait! The White Guards—"

"I know. I'll be careful."

Within ten minutes, he hurries at a trot back up the aisle to us with the news. "Baron Peter Wrangel!" he exclaims breathlessly. "You've not heard of him? Of German-Russian extraction, he's General Denikin's right arm in the Caucasus. Some upstarts even insist the man—an able strategist—should hold supreme command over Denikin, save for the inevitable politics. Anyhow, it appears he's scored a brilliant victory with his cavalry at Velikoknazheskaya, east of Rostov. The entire Red Tenth Army wiped out almost to a man, save for near unto fifteen thousand taken off as prisoners. The Whites are regrouping along the southern flank, driving straight up for Tsaritsyn and Kharkov. If they can keep that kind of pressure on Trotsky and cut up the Red retreat, everyone is saying naught but that the Whites could find themselves in Moscow by Christmas!"

"Then," I stutter in amazement, "the Whites will have won the war."

"Yes, that is the import."

Searching his face, I murmur softly: "But even should the Whites win the war, such will bode not much better for us—for you—than if the Reds do."

"That," he replies, "I think, will depend. The Whites have aid of the Ukrainian atamans and their armies in the south—there, I've heard, recruitment is not such a factor. They possess, for the moment, enough men. As to whether, ah, punishment is meted out so fiercely, we will simply have to wait and see. But in any case," he goes on, shrugging, "one victory alone does not a victor make. As I said before, the Bolshies still control the bulk of industry, communications, transportation. The tables could easily turn again. Even news such as this latest about Wrangel could be wrung dry by now, no longer holding much sway in the larger scope of things. Who knows what tricks for retribution that devil Trotsky has waiting up his sleeve?"

Dreading myself any run-in with Trotsky's—and the Reds'—particular 'tricks,' I seize upon the opportunity to make a suggestion: "Perhaps," I say to him, "we should reconsider about heading south. Could we not rail westward instead, across the Continent? You could cable Aunt Sophie and your sisters once we reach Vilna, tell them to go ahead and sail, to meet us in London. Would comprise about the same traveling distance—"

"No!" he snaps back abruptly, his ears crimsoning in fury. "Absolutely not—I will be damned to contend any more than I already have with those stinking, insufferable Huns! Yes, yes—I know they're in league with the Whites, and the Ukrainians. But only because they've taken the krauthead-holier-than-thou attitude that—in spite of the armistice with the West—they've certainly not lost the war in the East, Treaty of Brest-Litovsk, or no. Jesus! No, railing across the Continent is out of the question, Sasha. I promise you, naught is the same as when we used to dillydally so lightheartedly across Europe to Paris, Budapest, Vienna. As Russians, we'd be stopped and questioned—even searched, perhaps—at near every junction the Huns hold from here to the Rhine. Indeed, these long years of conflict have changed everyone, and everything. I only hope, in pursuing our way southward through the Ukraine, that you and I and Zhenya and Vanya can manage to stay afoot of the fighting from all directions. . . ."

* * *

Through the window, I survey the sights as we pull into Vilna, Lithuania, blessed with sweeping groves of dark lush trees and square stately buildings set wide over a wealth of space much like our own sprawling Petrograd. From Daugavpils, a week it has taken us to cover less of a distance than that entailed in our two days journey to that same township from Pskov, the White Guards halting the train three, four, sometimes five times in a day and ordering the engineer to shunt us off onto sidings for hours at a time in order to make way for military transports and armored trains. "And they say will be the same story south to Lida," Nikolai moans, rolling his eyes and leaning back into the bench, his gaze fixed overhead. "Or possibly worse. That old fellow I was speaking with, remember the last junction? He said that to the south, the engineers are contemplating a strike for higher wages in such perilous times. Oh, well—I suppose I should stop burdening you with complaints, my friend. At least so far, we've managed to avoid being shot at, eh?"

With a pat to my shoulder, he pushes up from our bench to stretch his legs, and when Vanya starts squalling at Zhenya in agitation, he reaches down and swoops the boy up into his arms, telling him: "Oh, come! I shall take you this time, Vanyushka, little soul. Let us permit your sister a spell of peace."

Together, they march off toward the inevitable queue for the water closet.

Staring after the two of them, Zhenya gushes out: "Oh! Nikolai Petrovich is so very thoughtful, Sasha!"

"Yes."

"And so very handsome!"

Intermittently sipping water from the canteen, I take another swig and stop with the spout rested upon my lips, watching as Zhenya pokes another loop-stitch down into her rounded frame of needlework. Smiling across at me, she goes on in a lowered tone: "You love him so much more than you ever did Vladimir Denisovich, yes?"

My last gulp of water, caught halfway down my throat, explodes upon the impact of her words; heaving forward, I start choking in a frenzy—so much so that, with concern, she tosses her sampler aside and darts over from her bench, shoving in beside me, her fist pounding upon my back. "Forgive me, Step—I mean, Sasha!" she cries. "I meant not to startle you so! Are you all right?"

Staring at her aghast, I mumble back ineptly: "Y-You mean—you can tell? About us?"

"Well, of course I can. It is obvious how you and he love one another."

"God, the Saints help me!" I gasp below my voice in reply—mindful, as ever, of the need to hold to the disguise. "Lord God, Zhenya! I thought you thought all that was simply part of our act."

"Oh, I know that's what you thought I thought. But I could tell how things are between you and Nikolai Petrovich ever since that first day back in Petrograd. Simply from the way he looks at you, the way you look at him."

Flushed to my teeth, I duck my head down into the well of my hand, moaning in amazement: "And this does not trouble you, Zhenyushka?"

"Oh, no. Why should it?"

As I plug the stopper back into the canteen, I remind myself that Zhenya, budding neophyte in life though she is, yet was reared from early on in Sheremetev's palace in Moscow, and has probably seen things that would set me—despite my own years of carousing—on my ear. "So then, you are not taken with Nikolai yourself?" I ask after a moment, sneaking a sidelong glance at her.

"Oh, no." With the combs binding up her hair, Zhenya begins to fidget back and forth, tucking up stray tendrils, while she rattles on: "Oh, perhaps at first I was a bit daft for your cousin, I must admit. Who could blame me, after the way he enticed me into that alley? He is, after all, so terribly handsome, even with those scars. But then I saw the way you were together, and I realized immediately, especially after I recalled the picture you showed me of the two of you, and remembered how sad you were."

Still shaking my head in amazement, I tuck the canteen back down into the portmanteau and squeeze a fond hold of her arm, telling her: "Zhenya, my dear, you are a very perceptive—and what would, in some circles, be called a very modern—young woman."

Scooting back to the other bench, Zhenya lets out a long sigh and clasps her hands together, uttering out in a dreamy lilt: "Well! I only hope that once we reach England, I too will find someone to love. Oh! And how impressive should he have shiny, coarse black hair! And fierce eyes, like Emily Bronte's Heathcliff . . . ."

At the main railway station in Vilna, we debark, and at the telegraph office, Nikolai sends a cable through to Aunt Sophie. "Yes, I told her about Zhenya and Vanya, and added that it looks as if it might be the end of May, or even the first part of June, before we will arrive. And Lord help us, even to make that fair of an amount of time, we'll be damn lucky, with the way everything is going."

Within moments, it appears that the end of May or first part of June is naught but a highly over-optimistic estimate. "Grodno!" he shouts out at the stationmaster. "I scarce intend to journey to Grodno, that's straight into the heart of Polish territory! To Lida I said I desired passage, for four people—blast it man, can you not even hear? What do you mean, through Grodno is your only open route south to Baranovichi?"

Quickly, I escort the children out of the way as he fumes on—to finally stomp back over to us from the stationmaster's office with steam literally venting from his ears. "Through Grodno is the only route south to Baranovichi. Permitted for refugees," he tells us tersely. "And not for six to seven hours yet. We may as well take the time to catch a meal and stock up on provisions while we're here."

We take brunch at a little cafe not far from the stationhouse and then head for the open-air market—where he continues glaring about, seeing naught of the ample fruits and vegetables, the fried meat pies, doughy pastries, and bargain tables filled with linens stretched out before us, his whole countenance etched in preoccupation. "Nikolai, what is irking you so?" I ask, clutching up his hand that now, uncharacteristically, stiffens in response to mine.

"Nothing."

At a tiny wayside park rimmed with trees and geese winging for a plot of space at the bank of a tiny pond, we pause on the way back for luncheon, and for the first time since the commencement of our now two-week old journey from Petrograd, I note a smile brightening across Vanya's face as Zhenya pushes him back and forth on an old tree swing. But Nikolai keeps bent unto himself in a gloomy spate of reflection, only grunting reply to my many proffered observations regarding the town, the sights, the fairness of the summer-like weather. And he remains inviolable unto distraction once we again board the train; remains so even as Vilna slips slowly backward from our range of view, the rail tracks looming ahead unto the rich expanse of broad, open pasture leading southward toward the Byelorussian border.

After two entire days of feeling spurned by his silent withdrawal inward, I learn the reason upon our approach to Grodno. And chide my heart for selfishness.

The chattering and children's shrieks normally abuzz throughout the coach snuff out to a collective gasp of silence as, without warning, we wind through a thickened cluster of spruce before pulling into a open gray field suddenly devoid of any trees, grass, shrubs, water, buildings, people, or any trace of life at all.

Instead, crusty embankments etched unto phantasms from some godforsaken lunar dream stretch out for as far as the eye can see, littered everywhere with tangled barbed wire, abandoned fortifications, chunks of shrapnel both large and small, and bodies and pieces of bodies.

Skeletons, most of them. A number still garbed in the faded dark gray of their old Tsarist uniforms.

"Russian soldiers," says Nikolai without so much as a glance stolen toward the window, his nose buried within the newspaper.

"My God," I gasp out, scarce able to believe my eyes. "From Tannenberg?"

"No, First Army. From the pursuit the Huns made afterward through the Masurian Lakes region in Poland."

To our relief, the battlefield testament lasts no more than a few tense, silent moments. Once into Grodno, where we again pull onto a siding for the night, blessedly, the trees, life, and sanity return.

Sleep, however, proves far from anyone's grasp, the passengers, the children only settling down after much uneasy restlessness. Zhenya arises to take Vanya to the water closet two weary times once the darkness blankets its cover upon us in totality and snores of the others begin. Sighing, I watch the young girl and whimpering three-year-old boy tiptoe their way yet again down to the creaky coach door; watch them return and meet her nod of relief once he finally agrees to climb back up with her upon the bench. Then I nestle down into my rumpled pillow of clothes, attempting to silence my thoughts and dismiss the horror of the battlefield visions—only to toss and turn, it seems, for hours. Until awakening to the pungent aroma of a cigarette.

Down on the floor, I see him crouched in the darkness, his shoulders flattened up against the window baseboard, his stare held straight ahead, his breaths caught harsh and shallow, the cigarette brought up to his lips, its tiny orange stalwart beckoning again and again—his hand, his fingers shaking about it uncontrollably.

"Nikolai," I whisper, reaching downward.

When he moves not a muscle in response, I push off from the bench in an impatient fumbling of skirts, scooting down to the floor beside him upon my knees. "Nikolai," I whisper out once more, my fingers clutched to his sleeve, "please, *talk* to me."

Instead, he seizes out a wrenching hold and crushes me up into his arms, his cheek shoved into mine, his hands gripped fast around my shoulders, his heartbeats caught deep into his throat and thundering against my ear.

I wind my arms around him and linger down to caress his back—and he pulls me with him up against the window baseboard, settling us both in with an aching moan, his whispers coming forced and uneven. "F-Forgive me, Sasha, my lifelong love," he chokes out. "For my behavior over the last few days—"

"Nikolai, never you mind—I understand now!" Edging back a little, I run my hand up over the scars upon his cheek, urging: "Perhaps if you would simply talk about it?"

When he shakes his head, shuddering in reply, I lean in closer against him, sighing. Only once has he spoken directly about the war, following our first night together—that one stray comment about the howitzers and the surrender of the Thirteenth Corps. And since then, nothing. "Nikolai," I whisper into his ear, "I thought you said it had been five years. That you had put this behind you—"

"That is what I must repeat to myself every day within my head—in order to try to forget."

He reaches upward then to retrieve my makeshift pillow from the bench, slides it in behind my head, and covers us both with the old coat he has been making use of as a blanket. "Sleep down here with me," he murmurs, brushing a gentle kiss against my temple. "Will not seem improper, my little countess," he jokes. "Please, remain here upon the floor and hold me, sleep with me—I have missed your touch, your scent, the whisper of your breath against mine in the stillness of the night . . . oh, God, Sasha! How I still long for you *so* much. . . ."

Come the morn, I awaken within his arms, and find those smoky gray eyes of his ebbed down upon me with the tempered glow of warmth, love, gratefulness.

South of Grodno, we encounter in the train's path yet another charred, empty field strewn with wire and ruins, bodies and pieces of bodies. This time, however, he slips his arm through mine when we pass by, his shoulder leaned in close to my own, while I press his hand for comfort, murmuring reassurance.

And only then does our true adventure begin: over another five grueling days, we struggle onward in our roundabout route from Grodno to Baranovichi, the train continually turned from the tracks and shunted onto sidings at the order of—at various times—White, German, and then Polish soldiers. And so for hours we sit, or talk, or doze, or play *poddavki*, a game of draughts, or venture off a little ways to stretch our legs and take a whiff of fresh air, the adults' faces ever drawn with worry and irritability, the children grown restless and cranky against the uncertainty of our journey's haphazard on-again, off-again course. And so it goes: upon arrival at last at Baronovichi, we learn that no refugee trains are allowed through from there to Lvov by way of Luninek and then Rovno, the route Nikolai had so meticulously planned. So again we rumble on eastward toward the Polish border—this time to Brest-Litovsk, covering with the detour over twice the distance that we would originally have traveled—until finally, mercifully, we press onward toward Kovel in the Ukraine.

In the Ukraine, nationalist partisans take the upper hand in shunting refugee trains off onto sidings, intent upon making way for their own armored locomotives and supply transports—while junction by junction, the stationmasters start to become exorbitant in their demands for bribes. From Kovel, the rail stops and tiny towns drag by in a daily churning press of weariness: Turisk to Ustilag, Ustilag to Ivanchi, Ivanchi to Soka, Soka to Gornyak, Gornyak to Kamenka. Finally, during the second week of June, we grind at last into the bustling ancient principality of Lvov. Where the Poles are on the attack—warring against Germans, against Ukrainians, and against both Red- and White-aligned Russians. Narrowly, we escape one of their bombardments just as the train pulls out from the station. "Lord God help us!" Nikolai cries, grabbing me with one hand and the children with the other and forcing us all down onto the floor.

"Did you get the cable off to Yalta?" I ask of him above the booming noise. "That queue at the telegraph office looked as if it would take a person hours—"

"Indeed, correct. So, no, I scarce got the cable off. But I think it should be apparent to them by now that we will hardly arrive there by the first or second week of June."

Nor even the end of June—for that is how long it takes us to reach the northeastern Romanian border and junction leading southward toward the coast through Bessarabia. Where conditions only worsen: food begins to become scarce, the days of peasant vendors hawking wares with such bargaining enthusiasm at the train's windows long left behind in the Baltic provinces and Byelorussia. In silent agreement, Nikolai and I start rationing our own portions of cheese and fruit and long-stashed hardtack, intent on making certain that enough remains for feeding the children. And my disguise finally proves beyond any more managing, for in amazement, the four of us stand gawking open-mouthed at the flat-roofed cattle cars—without benches of any kind; without a water closet save for a holding tank aside a piss-bucket shielded by a flimsy stained curtain. And again the stationmaster shrugs his shoulders, insisting that, for refugees, such is the only transport available. "Ugh!" Zhenya exclaims, making a face and balking—despite the many hardships encountered so far—for the first time since beginning our journey.

I catch Nikolai's eye, and he nods. Since Vilna, the White Guard recruiting squadrons have abated in entirety; since Lvov, he has let off shaving, allowing his beard to grow back in, while to forestall the fierce headaches that plague me so when I shun them for too long, I have taken back my spectacles. And although I have, along with Zhenya, long traded my stylish hat for a simple knotted kerchief, continuing the ruse further under such conditions of deprivation—without running water and brief bouts of privacy to steal a shave—will indeed prove impossible. So I take the portmanteau containing my clothes, disappear into the stationhouse lavatory, and reemerge—not without relief—moments later as my old self in trousers and boots and Father's worn old hunting jacket. "Welcome back, Count Sekovsky," Nikolai murmurs with a grin, handing me over a long-handled cane and plopping a straw-brimmed fedora down upon my head.

"Where did you happen upon these?" I cry, delighted.

"Last junction. When you were off stretching your legs with the children. No, they scarce cost that dearly! You still retain your old papers, I hope? Humph, so at least one of us can consider himself an honest man. I suppose, from now on, should anyone ask, we can tell them we are brothers."

Smiling back at him, I reply with a toss of my head: "But in truth, we are brothers, yes?"

In response, a wink, that rakish laugh, and his whisper of: "In a manner of speaking. Particularly German. *Warm bruder.*"

Well aware, from my time in Vienna, of such endearments traded by young men who court one another's fancy in that fair city, I wink back at him. Then I hungrily suck in a breath of the rich summer air—warmer here than in northern Russia, and laced with the sweet scent of vineyards and maize and giant sunflowers bursting out in rounds of golden petals all about the curving, dirt-clogged roadways. Green and fertile, the land shimmers with the promise of a good catch to be had in the streams and ample spreads of shade for summer picnickers beneath the boughs of vast draping trees. After some moments, it is all I can do to tear my eyes away from the rolling vista and set them back upon the business at hand: the greasy, crowded drollness of the railway yard. Where I find that Nikolai's gaze, too, remains hung to the horizon upon a wish for easier days, his pale locks grown out now and caught gently to the breeze, his attire simpler than when we first embarked—a faded farmer's jacket, white peasant shirt, dark cotton trousers. His tall German boots and a straw-brimmed hat similar to mine. "And how long, dear brother, do you think, to Belsy?" I ask him with a sigh, knowing all too well that again he will be forced to only guess at any answer.

Shrugging, he replies: "Praise God we reach Odessa by the end of summer. I'll be damned to be gallivanting out across the open country like this when the *burya* wind blasts down here come October, November."

"Step-papa," Zhenya cries, hurrying over from the stationhouse water spigot with Vanya, "it is all right now, if I call you that once again?"

"Zhenya, my dear," I reply, laughing, "you may call me whatever you wish."

"Are they honestly going to force us onto that awful cattle car?"

With reluctance, I stare back over at the train; watch as the whistle sounds, the throng of refugees—perhaps fifty to sixty strong—making for the doors in an elbowing rush. "I am afraid so, my dear," I tell her, trading another glance with Nikolai—to watch him also wrinkle up his nose in distaste.

On board, they squish us in upon the floor like herring in a can, the odor of sweat upon bodies mingled with the scrubbed sting of disinfectant to permeate throughout the coach, the only fresh air lofting in from rows of venting windows high above. "Oh, God," I moan, pulling out the canteen and moistening Nikolai's, Zhenya's, and then my own handkerchief, which we all shove up under our noses. "Listen to me, both of you," Nikolai intones softly, instructing us to close our eyes. "One can put his mind in a separate place. One can transport his consciousness to a different time. Listen to me: you are both lying on the seashore in Yalta. The sun is glowing and the gulls are flying high overhead, the air brisk with salt of the sea. You are burrowed into the sand, warming in the sun beside a cool, sparkling pitcher of lemonade. You are not here and now—you are then and there—*soon*—in Yalta. Listen to me and concentrate only upon my words, and you will grow more and more drowsy by the moment—and more comfortable, and finally find yourselves lying content and serene upon naught but the dark, sandy beach in Yalta . . . ."

From station to station, we concentrate upon Nikolai's meditation. Junction by junction, we halt up to pay yet more bribes to stationmasters; town by town, we find the Bessarabians becoming openly hostile to Russian refugees. Blessedly—or perhaps not so blessedly—the shuntings off to sidings decrease, but the train still grinds along at a literal snail's pace, and we do not make Belsy for another entire week; Rybrika, a week and a half after. Then, once past the border and finally back into Ukrainian territory, the nationalist soldiers return in full force, again shunting us off onto a siding—and this time requisitioning the train's locomotive, leaving hundreds of people stranded in the open country without transport of any kind. Dumbfounded, we stare down the length of the tracks as other refugees, without a second thought, heft up their belongings and start walking. "Will there be another train?" I ask Nikolai anxiously, falling into step beside him and wincing against the sudden tremor of pain that claws its way up my leg.

"There has got to be, Sasha," he moans, pulling the brim of his hat low and shaking his head in disgust. "Dear Lord Jesus! There has *got* to be . . . ."

Until nightfall we press on, and still—save for two armored transports that rush unceremoniously past—not another train stops for refugees. Along the rail tracks, old abandoned boxcars proliferate, all obviously seeing long and battered use as makeshift shelters for the night. "We'll need to stake one out for ourselves," Nikolai says to me as I struggle, in panting desperation, to keep up. "Sasha," he then murmurs low into my ear, "we will only go as far as you feel you can."

The majority of refugees have long since disappeared farther up the railtracks, obviously making better time. "I cannot understand it!" I burst out in frustration, groaning against the pain once more in spite of myself. "The rheumatism scarce plagues me so, save come the winter. Even this last year when I was riding forever out in the open, I suffered not greatly from it until near unto spring. Lord, why now?"

Squeezing my shoulder, he urges me to slow up. "It will be dark within moments. Let's take that old boxcar up ahead, the one through this cluster of trees. You hear water gurgling? Yes, so have I—for the last ten or fifteen minutes, bless God. There must be a spring nearby."

Exhausted, we approach the boxcar, and Nikolai leads the way around its corner—to halt up abruptly, with a sharp gasp, against the cocking of a gun.

Beyond the boxcar, a portly gentlemen sporting heavy whitened moustaches and side-whiskers, silk cravat, and a large monocle fitted up into his right eye from a chain at his waistcoat pocket brandishes out his pistol, barking: "Halt right there, you thieves!"

Behind him, a woman and two children huddle down beside a pile of wood and kindling made ready for a fire.

In response, I whip out my Luger from the pocket of my jacket and take due aim—but Nikolai, setting his portmanteau down to the ground, raises up both arms in submission and nods back at me to lower my gun. "Pardon us, good sir," he murmurs with respect. "We meant not to intrude. We shall find another boxcar."

As he lowers his hands and takes up the portmaneau again, we turn away—but the man with the monocle shouts: "Wait!"

Across the silence, we glance back toward him, while he slowly stares us up and down. Then—in properly clipped English—he demands: "You speak and look—although just barely, I daresay!—like naught but fellow members of the nobility. Is this so?"

After a pondering moment of hesitation, Nikolai nods his head, replying also in English: "Prince Nikolai Zhelanov of Petersburg, at your service, sir." Then he turns to me, and I tell the man: "His first cousin—Count Aleksandr Sekovsky, of Novgorod. These are my children, Zhenya and Vanya."

Pompously, the man lowers his gun, removes the monocle, and bows low in reply. "I am Baron Feodor Dolgurukov, of Petersburg myself! Well, now—Zhelanov, why does that ring such a bell? Oh, yes! Nikolai . . . Petrovich, then, yes? Your father was, indeed, the concert cellist?"

"Yes!" Nikolai cries in delight, glancing back at me—while with a wry smile, I pocket my pistol.

The Baron introduces us to his wife, Anastasiya Pavlovna, and to Mariya and Oleg—the girl about eleven or twelve, the boy lanky-tall upon the verge of manhood, and both children pale and raven-haired in the willowy image of their mother. "Join us please, all of you, if you wish not to trudge farther on tonight in search of another box-car," the Baron insists with a gracious sweep toward the wood pile. "Especially with the look of that leg, Count Sekovsky."

"Aleksandr Mikhailovich, please," I tell him warmly, extending my hand. "No, I am afraid it is an old injury, incurred when I was a youth. Yes, hopefully another train will happen along to rescue us come the morn. . . ."

While he lights the fire, the Baron tells us his latest hearing of the news: "Yes, the Whites have taken Kharkov. And obliterated three Red armies in doing so, praise God—and now, the line stands firm from there to Tsaritsyn. Ufa, however, in Siberia, has fallen to the Reds—where Kolchak's Whites have turned unto retreat. But General Denikin is holding good to his word to make the push for Moscow by Christmas, his army split into three sectors: Wrangel, coming up north from the Volga, Sidorin, north from Rostov, and Mai-Mayevsky, north from Kharkov. *Za veru, za Tsarya, za rodinu*—for Faith, Tsar, and Fatherland!" he shouts on, his arm raised upward in salutation to his wife. "Yes, my dear—only a Russia Great, United, and Indivisible will we take back!"

"The Cossacks will test you to the limits on that last one," Nikolai tells him with a grin. "One hears they're only in this fight in exchange for their own autonomy."

"Bah! We shall triumph gloriously and send the Cossacks back to turning turnips. What good have Cossacks done our dear Tsar's legacy? Always playing like children with whips along the Nevsky, forever flashing sabers about like naught but trumped-up dandies . . . ."

Over the fire, the Baroness whips up in a steel cook pot a delicious smelling mix of *kasha*, sunflower seeds, and small white beans. Just beside in a pie plate, carrots simmer in a light coating of oil, and we volunteer our own hunks of smoked fish, hardtack, and bunches of celery and radishes toward enlivening the meal. Zhenya and Mariya soon enough start fussing about breathlessly with one another's hair, while Oleg fishes out for Vanya a tiny wooden horse from one of the Dolgorukovs' portmanteaus of belongings. "He may keep it, if you wish, sir," the young man says to me with a smile as Vanya dashes about with the toy.

"Oh, no," I protest. "I'd not think of taking one of your keepsakes."

"But is not a keepsake, truly, sir. Simply an old toy we found at the last station. Masha played with it for awhile until she became bored."

"What is this?" I say in Russian to Vanya, smoothing my fingers over the toy as he thrusts it gleefully into my hands.

"Horsie!" he bursts back in English—while, astonished, I stare with my jaw dropped as he snatches it back from my grip, hollering out—still in English: "Horsie you give back, Sasha!"

"Well, of course I have been teaching him," Zhenya informs me a moment later when I corner her about it. "With you away for so long, I had to practice on somebody, and the one I'm with the most is him. Actually, I'm surprised he's not said any more until now, although he's only resumed talking at all over the last few days. Of course, he's still so young, but before we left Petrograd, I had been teaching him the letters. I think he might be able to rattle off the first five or six or so for you, if you ask him loud enough."

"Can you say your letters, Vanya?" I say loudly in English, bouncing the boy up upon my shoulder.

Toy horse waving out in triumph over my head, the child shrieks back: "A—B—C—D—E!"

"G-God bless you!" I choke out in reply, seizing him downward and crushing a tearful kiss upon his cheek. "And God bless your dear, talented sister!"

Dinner proves delicious, each of us making due with our mismatched tin plates and cups and remnants of utensils. "Again I apologize," the Baroness insists with a blush. "Never had I cooked a meal in my life until the Revolution. Small wonder my husband decries the take-over of the *Bolsheviki.*"

"Nonsense, my dear—delicious it is!" the Baron assures her with a tender glance. "The one blessing for which I owe the Bolshies due kind. For is it not a wonder, indeed, what this woman has learned to do with carrots?"

As night's chill cools in, the stars beginning to peek out overhead, we help with the cleaning up, wash up ourselves in the nearby spring, and return to gather once again about the fire—one of scores of fires, many visible now in clear evidence from other distant abandoned boxcars scattered up and down the rail-line. Fishing into the portmanteau, Nikolai brings out his balalaika, motions me to join in with my piccolo, and we both start playing—while everyone else sings along to—tunes of old folk melodies: *Troika Whirling Away* and then *Beyond the Island*—about that legendary scoundrel, Stenka Razin—and then at last *Abundant Peterskoy*, which Nikolai strums with adoration, staring across at me and joining in loudly with everyone to the words of the refrain: *"Come and kiss me, dove; come and kiss me, love; another kiss, another kiss . . . ."*

Then the Baroness begins humming out a Chopin tune—and drags the stuttering, frumpy old Baron up to his feet with her and convinces him, after much begging and prodding, to join into dancing the mazurka. Letting out a gasp of delight, Zhenya catches a hold of Oleg's hand—much to the poor young man's blanch of mortification—and whisks him along with her into the fray. After the first few turns, no one appears any longer reluctant or embarrassed, the four of them tossing back their heads and dashing about and kicking high their heels, their elbows set akimbo to wrists flattened back against their waists, their voices rising boisterously with each stirring round of the chorus. "Is not fair! Mama! Papa!" shrieks Mariya in a whiny pout, her gawkish half-child's, half-woman's form huddled down across from us beyond the fire. "Mama!" she wails again. "I haven't any partner with whom to dance!"

"Like I said," Nikolai tells me with a laugh, handing off his balalaika, "you simply leave it to Petrovich when the time comes for charming the ladies."

Chuckling, I start strumming out the few chords I know and watch him stride over to Mariya, where he bows gallantly before her and offers out his hand. Overjoyed, the girl leaps upward with such a start that she jolts him clear off balance, but making light of it, he snatches up her wrist and pulls her along with him into the rounds of the mazurka.

I cuddle Vanya close to my side and whisper into his ear: "Watch, Vanyushka. Watch them, and remember. So when we set away—far away—upon the ocean, you can take our precious dances with you. And folk songs so easy to forget."

"You my papa?" Vanya asks suddenly, gazing up at me with a solemn, widened stare.

Uncomfortably, I shift my weight on my haunches and nod. "Yes."

"Zhenya say so. W-Where Mama?" he then pleads, his reddened lips puckering inward. "Where Mama go?"

Letting out a long sigh, I tell him—in a phrase gleaned so painfully over the years from my own childhood: "Well, Vanyushka, your mama had to go away."

"Why?"

Unable to bear the probing of his eyes any longer, I set the balalaika aside and gather him up close into my arms, urging him to hush and watch the dancing as I stress into his ear: "Papa loves you, Vanya. Always remember—your papa loves you with all his heart. . . ."

As he yawns and starts to doze off, I turn my attention back to the dancing again—to see the women now standing off to the side, shrieking and clapping, while the Baron, Oleg, and Nikolai twirl about in a frenzy, repeatedly attempting to outdo one another with hand-abouts, jumps, and high Cossack kicks. "Daggers up, Nikolai Petrovich!" Oleg shouts, fetching a knife out from the shaft of his boot and jamming it in between his teeth. Guffawing at him, Nikolai showily does the same. Then the Baron joins in, and in addition to the stamp of feet and flailing of palms across dirt and grass, the knives soon start flying out everywhere in metered unison, to be snatched up and thrown yet again as the dance whirls frantically along. "Zhelanov, you idiot!" I mutter under my breath with a laugh, shaking my head at the rambunctious foolishness of it—while at the same time pausing to marvel at how unequivocally Russian my cousin is. Hailing, as he does on his father's side, from a long line of musician-artisans much sought out, in the old days before the Great Peter's time, for their intricate carvings of wishing wells, Nikolai's blood remains undiluted by my *Eisayki* temperance, his soul deeply rooted in the earth, legacies, and proud traditions of this lusty land where ofttimes, although borne of the soil myself, I have stood divided unto my prim English traits, an outsider ever peeking warily in. "Pretty lousy, city boy!" I yell at him, laughing. "Volodya and his plowhands could have showed you a step or two on the farm!" But such barbs only spur him on to reattempt his wild leaps with an abandon testing the bounds of recklessness, his blade flying, his voice shouting, his taunts barreling out in rank vexation against my own.

Finally, hair hanging into his face, beads of sweat streaming down his throat, he stumbles back over and collapses beside me, his fist clamped to his chest as he heaves gratingly for breath. "That Oleg's a bit too spry for me, I'm afraid!" he gasps out, shaking his head. "Lord! I must be getting old. . . ."

The fire at last glows down to embers, and amidst dwindling conversation, we finally retreat to the boxcar, staking out places for our respective families on either side. "Godspeed and a good rest to you all," the Baron cries with a hearty laugh, grasping up and shaking both Nikolai's hand and mine once more, and then trading cheeky kisses with every one of us before retiring—after a last wary check about the doors with the monocle—for the night.

"How kind of them to share their supper with us. And their company," I whisper to Nikolai as we burrow back into a corner with the children nestled, for safety, between us.

"Yes. This great land of ours thrives on such kindness and high spirits. However, in these times, it's still best to keep your gun within easy reach. The Baron told me he'd heard reports of bandits in the area—who are more than privy to *dvoryanye* refugees like ourselves with jewels sewn into linings of coats."

Nodding, I notice him fishing out his Luger, and do the same with mine, falling asleep with the pistol held to the ready within my grip.

Morntide brings news of a train. "About three or four versts south, we heard, near the next junction," the Baron informs us. "Full to a tilly of empty boxcars just waiting to load up poor souls left stranded along the rail tracks."

Hurriedly, we munch down hardtack, see to our necessities, and break camp. "Another train, thank goodness!" Zhenya moans. "I thought we were going to have to walk all the way to Odessa."

"The Dolgorukovs keep a summer house there," Nikolai says to me as we start along the tracks once again, the four of us following behind the Baron and his wife and children. "Which is where they are headed," he adds. "Pray only that the Reds have been chased back out."

"Are the stories true," I ask him with a cocked eyebrow, "about the evacuation made by the French?"

"After they were based there last winter, yes. The Whites held the city until spring, with French aid. Then come this last April, in scarce two days time, without explanation, the French decided to pull out, and the Whites could not hold Odessa without them. Added to this was a shortage of coal, stranding many ships in the harbor. Hundreds of refugees, it is said—having fled to Odessa to escape the Red advance—jammed the docks. Some of the rumors I have heard seem too ghastly to believe: people pulling out pistols, when they could not book passage, and shooting themselves and their families to death right there at dockside. Others flinging themselves into the water to drown. Since then, the city has gone back and forth, into and out of both White and Red hands."

"And now?"

"From what I hear, the Reds currently maintain their hold on the outskirts. But the Whites, as the Baron said, have been pushing forward in that heavy three-pronged advance. With as long as it is taking us to find our way southward, by the time we arrive there, the Whites should not only hold the city, but also be well on their way to the north."

"We could run across some fighting on the way then," I say, eyeing the children with concern.

"Possibly."

After a time, the train brims into our view from up ahead. The Baron and his family quicken their pace in pursuit of it, and Vanya, in yet another sudden burst of energy, charges off after them in a blinding run for the third or fourth time since the early morn. "I'll fetch him," says Nikolai, patting Zhenya's arm and trotting off after the boy, while again I roll my eyes, wordlessly cursing my ineptitude as a father. "Step-papa, simply slow up!" Zhenya insists, latching onto my arm as once again I nurse a spear of pain down my leg. "Rheumatism in the summer!" I bellow out in disgust, shaking my head. "Whoever heard of such nonsense?"

"Step-papa, look!"

At her urging, I glance upward to spot winging toward us through the sky the largest, darkest bird I have ever seen—only, upon detecting the faint rumble of engines behind it, to sharply catch in my breath and gasp out: "My God! It's a—"

"A flying machine!" Zhenya exclaims in wonder, clapping her hands. "Oh, my word!"

"L-Lord God Almighty," I stammer in awed reply. "To think that a man can go up in one of those contraptions and soar through the clouds like a bird—" I stop short abruptly upon the sight of Nikolai—with Vanya caught up into his arms—rushing toward us and yelling out at the top of his lungs: "Get down! *Get down!*"

"But, Nikolai!" I protest, pointing upward. "It's a—"

"By dammit, I know what it is! Now, for the love of God, *get down!*"

He tumbles in upon us, taking us both into the dirt with him as, from down the line, a coach from the train explodes in a shattering crash—the earth rumbling, the air vibrating in a roll of thunder, the blasts pounding quakes of horror into our ears as the airplane swoops down, its visage no longer a harbinger of lofty beauty, but one of death.

"My God!" I choke out. "They're attacking the train!"

"I told you," Nikolai shouts across at me, "that they bomb refugee trains!"

"Then—it's the Reds?"

"Yes! Look—red star insignia on the fuselage."

"Oh, dear God!"

"Looks like a Spad," he goes on, peeking upward at the plane as yet another harrowing crash booms down. "Or perhaps an Albatros—"

"A *German* airplane?"

"Uh-huh. Captured by the Red Army."

Screams split forth in a chorus from the train as the airplane soars low and scores another direct hit. Again we burrow down as close as humanly possible to the ground, Nikolai hunched over the sobbing Vanya, myself over Zhenya's head as she wails from beneath my arm: *"Nooo!* Oh, S-Step-papa! *I'm scared!"*

"Hush, sweetheart!" I tell her helplessly, shaking from head to foot myself. "Shhh, it will be all r-right. . . ."

"Look!" Nikolai exclaims, pointing over toward the train.

Past it, a contingent perhaps one hundred strong of nationalist soldiers gallops at a breakneck pace, rifles hoisted upward and blasting in unison for the airplane—which, after dipping its bi-leveled wings downward in a showy spin, promptly turns tail and soars off northward through the clear blue sky.

Letting forth blustery cheers of triumph, their blue and yellow colors and fluttery green ribbons waved out high upon the ends of rifle barrels against retreat of the plane, the Ukrainians congratulate themselves, turning back to regroup with their horses up near the locomotive of the train. Then they start seeing to disconnecting those boxcars shattered to pieces by the bombs.

"Oh, L-Lord, Step-papa!" Zhenya sobs. "I never want to see any of those flying machines ever again!"

It takes us some moments to calm the children and start once again back up the rail-line—there, to our despair, to our horror, to encounter the Baroness and her two children, crouched all of them over the

Baron's supine body, his head dashed onto the railway tracks, blood spilt out in a crimson fan over the wooden crossties.

"He merely stepped back and looked upward," she sobs, clamping both hands onto Nikolai's arm. "Oh, by the dear Saints! It all happened so fast—"

Oleg, teeth gritted and his fists wrathfully clenched, flails upward from the tracks with a wrenching animal moan, shouting out: "I will kill the vermin, the scoundrel who brought this fate upon my father!"

"The vermin who brought this fate upon your father," Nikolai says to him, "was the Red Army."

Again crushing Zhenya close, and attempting placation against her sobs, I tell her: "Sweetheart, take Mariya. Do not venture far—other airplanes could be in the area. We'll need rocks, as many as you both can carry." Turning to Nikolai with a sigh, I then ask: "What have we to dig with?"

The Baroness kneels down and watches over Vanya as—with the steel cookpot from the night before, the pie plate, and two tin cups—Nikolai and Oleg and I begin digging a shallow grave a short distance from the railway tracks. Up ahead, others of the refugees appear to face similar predicament, especially nearer the rail coaches where the dead can be seen to be laid out in rows upon the grass. "At least it looks as if the Ukrainians are lending a hand," Nikolai observes tersely, eyeing several horsemen up ahead who dismount to join into the digging with blunt-ended shovels.

It takes near unto an hour, as the July sun begins beating down its wrath upon us, to create a decent place of rest for the Baron. Nikolai and Oleg finally lift the body and lay it down into the shallow cocoon of ground. With dirt and rocks, we cover him over, while the Baroness, having thus far bravely bitten her lip, finally succumbs to open sobs. Oleg arises to reach his arm about his mother's shoulders, and motioning everyone to gather around, he snatches off his hat and intones solemnly: "For Faith, Tsar, and Fatherland—for birthright and my long-held heritage—for the future of Mother Russia, and of my children, and of my children's children—I swear that my father's death will not be in vain, and will be avenged!"

Crossing ourselves, we dazedly replace our hats—Nikolai meeting my eye as, understanding immediately, I reply to him with a nod. "Baroness," he then murmurs with a respectful bow toward the woman, "my cousin and I must insist upon taking the responsibility to see you and your family safely unto Odessa."

Gratefully, she grasps up his hand. "Nikolai Petrovich, Aleksandr Mikhailovich—you are both very kind."

With a party of seven then, we make for the refugee train, passing upon our way scores of wounded bound in wraps of old clothing and bloody bandages, the most dire cases tended to by the Ukrainian soldiers. Beyond a sea of stricken eyes all staring about dumbly, dimly, lost in the shock of sudden violent death, the grasslands harbor grave after freshly mounded grave. The cattle car—yet another reeking pigsty with open latrine and rusty water holding tank—seems a haven of bliss after our long foot trodden journey. Moaning, I settle down upon the metal floor, crowding in against the others with a sigh of relief. But just as the sliding door slams shut upon us, it bangs rudely open once again, and one of the nationalist soldiers—standing down upon the ground outside—peeks inward with a sheepish grin, shrugging his shoulders and mumbling in a mix of broken Russian-Ukrainian: "Sorry, folks! We be takin' the engine off again. Order o' the Colonel! Fer transport requisition."

So once more we stand staring down a stretch of railway tracks laid bare through the open country, bereft of any locomotive to take anyone anywhere. "The junction is only another verst or two up ahead," Nikolai says with an anxious squeeze to my arm. "They said for certain that another refugee train would be there awaiting all of us."

Again hunching downward to grasp hold of my leg—the pain shooting up my calf in a riddling spray—I shake my head, groaning inwardly: *oh, God! How much farther? How much longer . . . ?*

* * *

Two months . . . near unto two grueling months does it take us to cover, on foot, a distance not much farther than that from Lissushka to Petrograd. Wandering always southward along the rail-line, we pass countless little Ukrainian villages each boasting a simple blue-domed Orthodox church accompanied ofttimes by small Roman Catholic chapel; one market stall each for fruits and vegetables, one for potatoes, and one for bread; one travelers' inn, all rooms forever filled unto capacity. And one road—the timber-framed peasant huts ever set close upon it, or edged along the banks of slow, lapping rivers. Each day, artillery fire hovers never far distant, and the Red bombing squadrons flex their muscles at us in repeated rounds with terrifying overhead presence. Every so often, we happen upon a cattle car with an engine; most other times, not. Ofttimes, we go hungry, squirreling away provisions for the children. Meanwhile, we trudge diligently onward in the face of mounting exhaustion—to cover one more verst, to make one more junction, to find one more scuttled boxcar in which to spend another chilly, uncertain night. And then at last, a week into September, a passenger train finally pauses to offer us blessed respite, picking up group by weary group of refugees as we descend the hills close upon the coast. *Two months*—and dear God, fast in the echo of Zhenya's words!—two months, and we have literally *walked* our way to Odessa . . . .

Upon reaching the city, we find it ravaged, only a week past fallen into White hands from the grip of the Reds. But the Baroness finds her stylish house on French Street blessedly intact, her married daughter awaiting us with husband and toddlers in tow. "From Kharkov we came," the young woman tells us solemnly. "Lord, you'd not believe the pillage of those murdering Bolshy thieves. . . ."

At insistence of the Baroness, we consent to stay for a few days, finding her guest room more than adequate and ourselves wholly unaccustomed to such appointments of luxury after spending so many nights shivering upon makeshift berths in cattle cars, our needs assuaged within dung-filled ditches of the open roads. "Two large feather beds," Nikolai cries, staring around, "a private lavatory, quilts and pillows up to our ears! No better haven could we ask in which to hide away for a few days to catch some much needed rest."

Into the large claw-footed tub, Zhenya forces Vanya, and then starts running water for both Nikolai and myself. "No, I intend to go in last, the very last!" she insists, running her fingers with a groan of dismay through the snarls and knots tangled throughout her hair. "Yes, I am going to wait my turn until after the both of you finish, Step-papa. You shall see why."

Emerging from the bath with relief and toweling behind my ears, I pull on clean clothing as quickly as I can and hurry outward, pausing outside the door once the girl scurries back in and starts running water for herself. "Is there enough left hot for you, sweetheart?" I ask, noting the run of the tap lasting twice, then thrice as long as she allowed for the rest of us.

When aching moans answer me, I start knocking worriedly upon the door. "Zhenya! Are you all right?"

"Ohh! Glorious! It is simply . . . *glorious!"* she exclaims, a walloping splash of water accompanying her words. *"Ohhh!* All the way up to my neck . . . !"

Chuckling, Nikolai eases Vanya into my arms, murmuring: "I suspect she will stay in there until suppertime. Until she wrinkles up like a sorry prune—"

"Until I wrinkle up like a sorry prune!" comes the answer from beyond the door, dissipating to laughter.

Vanya, scarce able to keep his eyes open, cuddles against me, and I carry him over to the farthest feather bed and gently lay him down, the words of the *Peterskoy* folk song lilting forth from my raspy monotone into his ear: *"Come and kiss me, dove; come and kiss me, love; another kiss, another kiss . . ."*

Kisses meet his temples, nose, cheeks, and tiny chin, and I scoot down beside upon the bed, leaning over to sing the refrain of the song once again, while he yawns up at me sleepily, murmuring out in a mix of English and Russian: "Papa, tell me 'nother story!"

"Well, Vanyushka—this afternoon, we've already been through so many stories! Oh, all right, perhaps one more: once upon a time, there lived a beautiful maiden named Maryushka, known far and wide for the lovely hangings she sewed with bits of golden thread, each one more perfect than ever the eye could see. And one day, disguised as naught but a mere lad, an evil sorcerer came into the village, plotting to steal away Maryushka's hangings by means of a magic trick. . . ."

Gazing down fondly, I watch as my son's eyes at last droop to a close, the tiny breaths starting in deep and steady, his one small hand clamped firm about my fingers, the other caught about the toy wooden horse that Oleg made him a present of during our first boxcar encampment so many nights ago.

"Sasha," Nikolai whispers.

Turning, I find him seated upon the opposite bed—holding out toward me, with questioning eyes, his jar of eucalyptus balm.

Extracting my fingers from Vanya's, I limp over with effort, set aside my cane, and grasp up my cousin's hand as he urges me to lay out flat across the bed. With a deep sigh, I sink back into the pillows and comforters; watch as he reaches downward, rolling up the cuff of my trousers from my left ankle. "Oh, that feels marvelous," I moan out as he starts spreading on the balm. "Near as glorious, I think, as must Zhenya's high-necked bubble bath."

I almost doze off, scarce realizing when he finishes—until I feel him sliding in to sit aside, facing me, upon the bed, his hand slipping once more into mine. "I would have done anything," he whispers, leaning down close, "could I have—by some spell, or wild magic of my own—brought on a train sooner, dear heart."

"I know." Instinctively, I reach my arms up about his neck and crane back my head, eager for a kiss—but he shies away, glancing between Vanya's sleepy, motionless form and the lavatory door, yet fraught beyond with delighted spiels accompanied by splashes of water. "We mustn't, my love," he murmurs, reddening. "The children."

"Y-You—you are right," I stutter in reply, tearing myself away. "We mustn't. The children—"

But then, as if of its own volition, his palm winds its way around my neck, once more drawing me to him close—and again I melt against the pull—but force myself back with a start, murmuring disjointedly: "No! We mustn't! The children—"

"Oh, God," he whispers then. "If you only knew how jealous I once was. When the others spoke of you. During rehearsal, before curtain time—all during the years of the ballets: 'How about that red-haired piccolo? Plays like a dream, no? Naught but an artist, he is! A genius—'"

"No one ever said *that!*" I protest, muffling a laugh.

"Oh, but is true," he goes on in all seriousness. "In the hotel corridors, I heard such. Remember the time you broke down during the *Swan Lake* rehearsal, and sent Monteux into a royal tiff? And the way you lit up like a fire afterward, playing the hell out of the piece? 'Passionate, exuberant!' everyone started saying about you then. Words that rang in my ears; words that haunted me unto distraction as, later that night—later so many nights—I watched you play, my eyes glued upon the rhythm of your fingers. How I yearned to touch—to hold—to caress those fingers then. God! Sometimes, when we were warming up in the pit—sometimes even smack in the midst of a performance!—I'd almost entirely forget what I was about, in my intensity upon watching you in between my glimpses toward the conductor. And I was so jealous unto rage—could scarce bear to hear the others speak of you, to have your name falling so casually from their lips. If you only knew," he continues on, his voice dropping low unto a whisper, "how many times—in God knows only *how* many hotel rooms—I watched as you fell asleep. Every night. If you only knew how I longed to tiptoe over to your bed . . . how many times I finally *did* tiptoe over, how many breathless, agonizing moments I stood fighting myself, desperate to reach out and brush the hair from your face with my fingers . . . ."

Slamming shut my eyes, I grip hold of his hand and crush it within my own, smothering it palm to wrist and back again a dozen times with kisses. When I peek upward, I find him again leaning close, his gaze ravaged with that same awful longing—that same unquenched fire burning through my own pounding heart. "Forbidden love," I say softly, no longer able to stop myself from seizing my arms up fast about his neck. "Passions hidden, love forbidden . . . ."

I sink in a gasp against the parting of his mouth, and the world spins out in a chasm of tumult from underneath the both of us. Moaning, I caress everywhere, worshiping his elbows, arms, ankles, his thighs, his chest down the open buttons of his shirt, the fresh-scrubbed scent of his loose, lanky blond hair. "You drive me mad, Nikolai Zhelanov!" I whisper torridly against another crush of his lips, urging him to move aside with me all the way onto the bed.

"Very quietly," he whispers back, grasping his hand into my crotch.

"Oh, God—y-yes! We—w-we can do it very quietly. . . ."

He rubs me off, and then I do the same for him, near fraught to tears with the emotion of it as he finally collapses against my chest, heaving in searing rasps while attempting to keep his voice down. "D-Do you think she heard?" he sputters out at last, catching hold of my hand and flushing scarlet to his ears.

"No—like I told you, she knows about us. Not that I'd wish for her to see, nor hear us—God forbid! But, she could scarce have heard us—she's still sunk up to her neck in that tub and splashing water to her heart's content like a nymphet mermaid. Will take quite some while, I think, for her to finish washing all that hair."

"I love you, Sasha," he murmurs hard against my throat. "I don't give a damn about how wrong anybody says—or has said—or will say that it is. All I want for the rest of my life is to kiss you, fuck you, love you. . . ."

Dinner the Baroness and her married daughter put on for us grandly, considering the bleakness of the times. Sampling naught but the pinnacle of baked chicken Kiev, *halushky* dumplings, fresh garden greens, and a heavenly strawberry mousse for desert, we sit about the table properly clad in fresh-pressed linen shirts, our waistcoats, jackets, and ties. Zhenya, her mass of hair swept stylishly upward upon her head, beams the entire time under Oleg's grinning attentions; at my side, Vanya laughs and screeches up a storm. But across the table, I glance yet again in the direction of those smoky eyes—and beneath us, upon the carpet, the toe of his shoe touches mine; keeps touching it throughout the remainder of the meal—while I gaze back yearningly in reply, willing telepathy, wanting so for him to hear my every unspoken word: *Nikolai Zhelanov, I love you more than ever. . .*

* * *

"Bad news and good," he says, whisking off his new gray fedora and crouching down before me.

Upon the parlor sofa, I ease my leg to a more upright position and grasp hold of his hand. "The bad then, first," I tell him. "Please."

"No coal," he informs me. "Still. So, every vessel remains stranded at harbor. Will take some time, they say, before commercial supplies can be replenished. The Whites have only been here for two weeks, with their own reinforcement requisitioning over which to worry. Which, of course, has priority; which, of course, should, considering that the Reds—in some outskirts—are not all that far away. Because as you know, the White power base remains solid only in the east—at Rostov, Yekaterinoslav, Kharkov. Only by the skin of their teeth have they managed to take Odessa from the Reds again—and yes, are moving on northward. Have marched even as far north as Kiev, in fact, if my latest news is correct. But even there, the stronghold is a day by day proposition; Denikin's reserves on his western flank remain spread out to their farthest limit. And are not near as firmly entrenched as they are to the east, north of the Crimea, the Caucasus."

"So. The city could possibly switch hands again?"

"That is my concern, yes."

"And without coal for steamers, no one can obtain sea passage—anywhere. Including us. To Yalta."

"I am afraid so, Sasha," he murmurs, sighing and peering long into my eyes, his fingers pressing firm unto mine.

"And?" I reply tightly. "The good news?"

Nikolai pulls to his feet and stands before me holding out his hat, the railroad schedule visible in his jacket pocket, the morntide newspaper folded in beneath the crook of his arm. "As I said before," he goes on, "farther east, the Whites are better entrenched. Firmly, they hold Nikolaev and Kherson, and much territory well to the north of there. And of course, the Crimea they have dominated—even over the Sevastopol, the Simferopol Soviets—ever since the onset of the Revolution."

Clamping both fists forward about the handle to my cane, I force myself upward shakily from the sofa, and hobble with measured steps toward the bright, open expanse of the parlor window.

"Should you be walking on it?" he asks after a moment.

"If I do not keep my weight to the leg," I snap impatiently, "then I shan't be able to later. Muscles will weaken."

In response, he bites his lip, his glance falling to the floor.

"So," I go on, staring out at Vanya and the Baroness's grandchildren all frolicking together in the yard with gay, shrieking abandon, "our choice is either to remain in Odessa, or—"

When I pause, Nikolai offers not a word—and the laughter of Zhenya and Oleg, filtering in from the nearby drawing room, splits harshly across our silence. "Or," I continue finally, turning to face him—and to stare, without another moment's hesitation, at the railroad schedule, "to travel again over land."

"Sasha," he intones softly, "you are the one has to live with the pain in that leg—"

"Purchase tickets for Nikolaev, then," I tell him. "There is no question but to risk train travel again—and yes, the possible shuntings off to sidings; yes, the possible requisitioning of locomotives. Yes—again, the dire possibility of walking. Because I will not rest until I see my children unto territory safe from the Reds! And I cannot tell you how I deplore the Baroness's own lack of concern. If the White hold upon this city indeed remains as tentative as you say."

Nikolai stares at me mutely, watching as I hobble, panting and with teeth gnashed into the effort, over to the piano, easing down in relief upon the bench. "Sasha," he says at last low under his breath, "we both know that, under no circumstances at all, can you walk across the open country again on that leg. Not from here to Nikolaev. Not, by God, from there to Yalta—"

"Purchase the tickets, Nikolai," I say, not looking at him, my stare held to the window.

* * *

Gulping for breath, I jolt awake to be met with the roaring rush of the train and the lap of quiet water trickling from the slopes of the mountains, the grunt of double engines once again scaling a steep, hilly incline. Across from me in the darkness, Zhenya lies sprawled out upon the opposite bench, her breath rising and falling in soft, bleating snores,

Vanya cuddled up within her arms. As the wheels chug on, heads everywhere shift back and forth upon their makeshift pillows of clothes or bundled coats, keeping time with the rattly, swaying movements of the coach.

From the floor, Nikolai reaches upward and catches hold of my arm. "Wolves again?" he whispers, peering up at me with concern.

Hand still trembling, I crease cold fingers into my brow and nod.

"Move down here with me," he then urges, scooting up against the window baseboard. "I cannot stay asleep either; the climb through the mountains is playing havoc with my ears."

Gratefully, I vacate the bench and huddle down beside him, reveling in the arm slid so tenderly about my shoulder, nurturing the hand grasped warm to mine beneath the cover of his coat. "How much longer until Simferopol?" I ask, peering around and discerning, moment by moment, the lift of darkness as it slowly dissipates its way toward the glow of dawn.

"Perhaps another hour."

Another hour. Incredible, it seems, to finally near the end of our long journey. And after only two and a half short weeks from leaving Odessa. Incredible, it has been, to find trains actually running at night, to encounter coaches lined with benches again and vendors hawking foodstuffs at the junctions. From Odessa to Nikolaev, from Nikolaev to Kherson, from Kherson to Dzhankoy, the shuntings off to sidings, it is true, have yet remained a fact of life. But eventually the trains would start running again, the requisitioning of locomotives only occurring twice, and then within easy walks of junctions and other waiting transport. Although the crowds waiting to board such have been ample—and rude and self-serving, the bribes of the stationmasters peaking all the more exorbitantly the farther south we have come. Of all of Melissa's earbobs, necklaces, and bejeweled bracelets that Father stitched with such painstaking care into the lining of his old hunting jacket, we retain only one tiny five-inch strand of emeralds. At least this last leg of our journey has proven hospitable by comparison, fraught more with competition for rail lines caused by a growing influx of hospital trains—for wounded White soldiers—than with danger of overhead bombing raids by the Reds.

"Tell me about your dream," Nikolai whispers, leaning in close—close enough for a kiss. Close enough for another passionate, open-mouthed kiss, should I but turn my lips upward toward his. But of course, I do not; we do not. Not—with the days of my disguise long past and buried—while on board this crowded train of people. Even if most are asleep.

"The same dream," I tell him, fending off a shudder, my fingers once again whitened to my brow. "Terror of being eaten alive, surrounded by a pack of snarling wolves."

"The one that has plagued you off and on now for a couple of years?"

"Yes."

"Am I in it?"

Only with the greatest reluctance do I turn to face him, murmuring softly: "Yes."

"I am with you when you are surrounded by the wolves?"

"Uh, yes."

"Hmmm. Do we manage to escape, then? To get away?"

"I—I do not know," I tell him, shrugging. "I always awaken once one of them lunges for my throat."

I neglect to tell him the rest of it: about the dark caverns, the heavy iron doors, the pools of blood—ankle-deep—in which we both, at the end, find ourselves standing. Instead, I shrug off his further questions, ask if he wants to share a cigarette, and make comments about the havoc the climb through the mountains is, indeed, wreaking upon our ears. I avoid telling Nikolai how forebodingly the dream lingers—like one of those old, eerie premonitions . . . .

* * *

Exhausted, elated, we at last stumble into the crowded railway station at Simferopol, and like ourselves, scores of refugees stand about gawking dully, attempting to gauge the means by which to continue various journeys southward. "Aunt Sophie's cable said someone would pick us up, correct?" I ask Nikolai as he stares around in consternation.

"That they would 'send transport,' yes. I told her we could continue on to Sevastopol, since it's the railhead, and closer. But she insisted that we stop here, and take the loop way around. I wonder why on earth—"

"Step-papa—look!"

The instant Zhenya finishes speaking, a blaring squawk peals across the length of the station—as if from the throat of some strange animal attempting a sense of humor—in a gritty refrain of: "Ahh-ooo-gah! Ahh-ooo-gah!"

Breaking into a grin, Nikolai catches sight of Anna, who waves at us, proud at her perch behind the windshield of a shiny black motorcar.

The woman whom I kissed so impetuously while upon our Neva troika ride twelve years ago—the matronly doctor who only three years past, within the Anglo-Russian hospital corridors, appeared so rampantly hostile and severe—has now bobbed her hair, the blonde ends flipped to tease about her chin, her blunt-trimmed bangs wetted to her brow in wispy ringlets. And she has—of all things!—taken up smoking, an amber-inlaid cigarette holder spewing forth a hazy stream between her manicured fingers. While Nikolai and I, both positively aghast, stop short and gape outright at her, she saunters toward us flaunting the most garish shade of red lip-paint that I have ever beheld, a jet-black stole of boa feathers wholly engulfing her neck and arms. Looped about her left ankle, I spy a golden bracelet, her black-seamed silk stockings adorning noticeably shapely calves, the hemline of her flounced black and white polka-dot skirt draped bare unto a decent level of propriety just below her knees. "Welcome back, Petrovich—you old heartbreaker," she intones with a husky laugh, pecking a seemingly much-forced kiss upon her brother's cheek. Both arms then thrown wide to the children, she sweeps each up into a friendly embrace, exclaiming: "This must be Zhenya and Vanya! And how would you two like to go for a gay, windy ride to Yalta in that shiny black motorcar over there?"

Coloring to blazing scarlet fury, Nikolai pinches a roughened hold of Anna's arm, forcing her to a halt beside him, his disgust rasped into her ear: "Since when did you take to traipsing around like some cheap Parisian harlot?"

"One can look the harlot. But others play the part, *n'est-ce pas?* Dear, darling, little brother? Aleksandr Mikhailovich," she then says to me, extending her hand.

I take due note of the formality, and bend to proffer the expected kiss in response, murmuring: "Anna Petrovna."

"Come!" she urges the children. "Maman expects to set luncheon out by noontide sharp! We mustn't keep her waiting."

In the motorcar, Nikolai slips into the front with Anna; the children and I, into the rearward seat—while Zhenya gushes breathlessly on and on: "Oh, Step-papa! As soon as we reach Yalta, I am going to bob my hair! And cut off my skirts, and wear silk stockings! Just like Anna Petrovna—"

"Oh, no, you are *not.*"

"But, Step-papa!"

Up in front, glaring at Anna as she straps on her driving goggles, Nikolai switches heatedly from English into French, choking out under his breath: "See? Humph! And a fine example you set, parading about like a circus harpy! In front of such a young girl—"

"Did you travel here from Petrograd intending to do naught but chide me about my manner of dress?"

"Well, my God, Anyuta! Could Papa but see you—I swear by the dear Lord!—he would turn you over his knee—"

"Shut up, Kolya."

"Step-papa," Zhenya whispers to me. "What are they saying?"

"Shhh! Never you mind. We shall discuss it later."

"Will you teach me to speak French next, then? Please?"

"Yes, Zhenyushka, sweetheart—of course, if you wish. But for now, let us try to sit back and enjoy the ride."

Despite the irate bickering from the front seat, Zhenya's excited prods into my ear—and despite the fact that Vanya knocks his head up against the window-pull of the door and launches for several moments into a blood-curdling, sniffling bout of hollers—I do enjoy the ride immensely, head thrown back to the wind, my nostrils quivering to the clean, fresh scent of the high blue mountains. Soon enough, as the roar from the engine intervenes to drown out his feud with Anna, Nikolai glances back toward me with a roll of his eyes and throws up both hands, but upon spying the three of us gazing about with such ruddy-cheeked contentment, a faint smile starts to play at his lips, and he casts me an affectionate wink, his expression softening upon view of the scenery, his eyes squinting up against the high curve of the sun and his hair whipping out about his face in a fan of carefree tangles. The motorcar chortles on, the road winding and curving its way upward about precarious, treacherous bends, snaking high above the valley of the Salgir River as we make our way for the pass. After awhile, the magnificent, towering precipice of the *Chatir Dag*—Tent Mountain—looms up to our right in a wash of deep forest green and hovering purple highlights, graced at one turn-off by a quaint little roadside inn nestled upon the edge of a steepened crag. "Step-papa, I never thought there could exist such splendid mountains!" Zhenya yells across to me, gaping about in wonder.

"Indeed! Only the Alps beg for comparison. And wait until you see Yalta. . . ."

Yalta . . . a haven where hills tier upward in lush green bands from the sandy shore exactly as I remember, the shimmering turquoise water crashing forth upon the beach in wave after heady, inviting wave . . . .

The reunion is touching, heartfelt. Three years of futility Aunt Sophie spent in Paris, searching out every record, transcript, and last scrap of information she could abscond on Russians taken prisoner after Tannenberg. As she and Nikolai cling together, tears overtake the both of them, and he rocks her gently within his arms, his nose buried into her hair. "I thought I had lost you all over again!" she sobs out, kissing him frenetically. "That you'd scarce survive a second chance at return—oh, Kolya! You noble, daring fool!"

Tatyana, clad in a dark gown draped demurely to her ankles and her hair caught back in a breezy bouffant, throws her arms about me as if naught but a day has ebbed between us, and showers me with kisses. In a breathless rush, she introduces her children: the twins, Dunya and Darya, both age twelve, as blonde as their mother, and also grinningly precocious; and Petya, five years old and desperate for a playmate. "Vanyushka!" he cries, seizing up my son's hand. "After Gran-Maman serves us luncheon, we shall go and build castles in the sand!

To the girls, Zhenya takes a ready liking, and soon all are off in the boudoir, fussing over petticoats and hair. "Your step-daughter is very lovely," Anna says to me, pausing to assist once Aunt Sophie starts fetching drinks for everyone from the bureau. "My condolences, Sasha, about your wife."

Nodding, I avert my eyes, content to let the matter rest with her assumption.

"Tatyana only recently lost Ivan Feodorovich, her husband," Anna goes on in a huff. "Mortally wounded in the battle to take Kiev. Although at least she caught chance to board the hospital train, and see him once before he passed on."

The reference, laced with sarcasm, is of course to Eugenia, and uncomfortably, I murmur likened condolences and thank Anna for the glass of cognac she hands me. Very little has Nikolai spoken—save to break the news to me during our time in Latvia—of his one sister killed, along with her husband, in the street riots during the February Revolution. "Lord rest her soul," Aunt Sophie whispers, smudging back a tear as we each cross ourselves in respect to mother's utterance of daughter's name, our stares drawn sadly toward the missing member from the Zhelanov family portrait hung atop the fireplace mantle. "Nina," Aunt Sophie goes on, "bless her wayward heart, had the good sense to keep put in Lisbon with her theater company throughout the whole affair. And Natasha—praise God, with a brood of five now!—remains in Montreal, where that diplomat husband of hers has been assigned."

I remain standing with them for as long as politeness dictates, and then grasp up the handle to my cane, easing my way over onto the sofa with a wince of effort. "Let me have a look at it," Anna insists, dropping to her knees before me upon the floor once I sit down.

"No—Anna!—please—"

Despite my protests, she promptly rolls up the cuff to my trousers, her fingers poking and prodding about the whitened scars on my leg. "Uh-huh. Naught but osteo-rheumatism," she announces, shaking her head. "You'd have done better to have let Uncle Misha saw this leg off years ago, Sasha."

Fixing her with a fierce glare in reply, I yank my trouser leg back down, chafing beneath an embarrassed flush once she backs away. "And always have I abhorred the casual ease," I tell her sharply, "with which those who have taken an oath to do no harm refer to the disposition of appendages not their own."

None too easily put off, Anna remains towering over me, her finger wagging, her tone adamant as she orders out: "You must revert back to crutches for awhile—"

"I scarce need any crutches."

"I think I'll drop over to the hospital and bring a pair back for you after luncheon. I need to make another check on my rounds in any case."

Throughout luncheon, over conversation brimming about the war—the latest White advance having been confirmed unto Kursk—I tangle with Anna over the necessity for crutches. "By dammit!" she finally shouts across the table, throwing down her flatware, bolting up from her seat, and vengefully glaring off the widened eyes of all of us, shocked to hear a woman swear. "Kolya said you did naught, Sasha Sekovsky, but *walk* most of the way from the Bessarabian border to Odessa, you stubborn-headed fool! Small wonder you're hobbling about now like some rheumatoid invalid! Oh, you'll stay to the crutches, just as I say—or see that leg amputated yet."

Then, cigarette yet again spewing forth a stream of smoke from its holder, she stomps off in a clatter of heels and perfumy whiff of boa feathers through the door and outside to the car.

"And you condone this?" Nikolai demands of his mother, his hand waving out in incredulity toward the swinging screen door of Anna's trail.

"No, I scarce in any way condone your sister's outlandish behavior," Aunt Sophie replies with a roll of her eyes. "But—heaven help me, Kolya! Anna is no longer a teenage *ingénue*. I can scarce tell a thirty-one year old doctor, a professional woman in the community, how to act, or dress. So, what else am I supposed to do?"

Toward Nikolai, I stare with some concern as he answers with a grimace and then plows his spoon back down into his dish of fruit salad. Ever since our arrival, he has begun stalking the rooms, agitation adamant in his every glance, save for the few moments spent in the embrace of his mother. Worriedly, I scan his countenance yet again as we finish with luncheon, and stare in amazement as—apparently bent upon seeing unto conclusion all awaiting tasks—he even deigns unto helping afterward with the washing up of the plates. Finally, after seeing Aunt Sophie and Tatyana and I and the children out unto the sandy back-yard beach for an afternoon of sand castle-building and lazy chasing through the surf, he disappears inside the bungalow once again, slamming the door shut behind and leaving me stranded forlornly at my seat upon the chaise lounge.

Generous to a fault is the dose of self-pity I begin nursing into my shot of cognac—until I prick up my ears to a faint sound emanating from the inside: the tone of the 'A' struck upon a tuner. Followed by that long-vanished, ever-so-familiar bite of horsehair bow against strings.

"Oh, sweet Jesus," I mutter out, feeling the true insensitive dolt, my palm whacked to my brow. "The Guarnerius!"

Quickly, I make another check of the beach: Vanya, half-buried into mounds of sand along with Petya, continues laughing his little heart out; Zhenya and the twins bound yet again upon shrieking, wild chase into and out of the waves. Aunt Sophie and Tatyana, with contented smiles, remain watching over the entire brood from their checkered blanket spread beneath cover of a wide beach umbrella. Satisfied that the situation appears under control, I hoist upward and limp—attempting to keep halfway quiet about it—back inside.

Once I veer into the main room, he stops his tuning cold, the bow caught to the air, his eyes tearing away from the strings and fixing—glowing and feverish—upon me, their perusal harsh with severity against slats of bright afternoon light peeking in past the window blinds. "I—I am sorry," I blurt out, stopping short to choke back a wave of disappointment as he makes not a move in reply, the clock upon the mantle ticking the silence out between us. "I scarce meant to interrupt you, Nikolai," I say at last. "I shall return outside—"

"No—*stay.*"

Glancing back, I find him impatiently snatching up a glass of water and downing most of it in three quick gulps, then to slam the goblet back atop the bureau, his pointed index finger motioning for me to sit down. "Stay, if you wish, Sashenka, dearest heart," he murmurs. "Of everyone here, especially you. And forgive me, today, my preoccupation. It has been near unto a year, before I turned straight around for Petrograd again, after bringing Anna with me here. And then, my chance was so brief. Before that, it had been clear unto before the war—"

"Nikolai," I interrupt loudly, "*play* your violin."

Without further adieu, he snaps up the bow again, and completes his tuning as I take a seat upon the sofa, the cane eased down aside my lap.

And then the clarion of ages stirs within my soul.

Seven long years have waned away since I have heard that gift, save for the phantom echoes intoned to memory. Over a year has passed since he has knelt to worship the instrument of his peace, although to listen, one can scarce tell the missing of a day. Again I ask myself when I first fell in love with him, only to know that it must have been when he was playing something like this: like a tempest, he launches into Lalo's *Symphonie espagnole*—a deep, tragic melody of old Spain, the very pinnacle of fantasias for a virtuoso—and I moan aloud to hear such passionate shimmers of sound. Lifting unto vibratos of glory, the call to arms issues forth, and one can almost picture, galloping across a russet span of Moorish plain, the visage of a Don Quixote triumphant and transformed: his rags melded unto armor, his nag bred into a steed, his madness pledged wholly unto the true and just cause of eternal knight-errant. At painted dusk upon Atlantic shore, he pursues his quest of love for the ephemeral Dulcinea, her siren's form twirling atop the waves in the rapid, fiery heeltaps of the flamenco—while his ocean bow he tenderly caresses to her strings. Tenderly, yes, lovingly—and then wrathfully, desperately—that bow seduces, bites, churns, and tears into those four pliant, quivering strings, acting out the tale of love in a teasing farce of dramatic poses, the sweet song mounting forth double-stopped, triple-stopped, peaking unto the height of brilliance; lolling downward repeatedly into passages of dazzling chords; trilling upward bemoaned in rapture, aflame with ecstasy—then to trickle down from solo loft and drop back with nary a nuance missed into periodic joinings for the entire orchestra—as Nikolai, my beloved cousin, focuses into his fate like a madman possessed solely by the strings and the bow, again assuming his rightful cloak of naught but magician *extraordinaire* . . . .

Swept into the tumult, his pale locks fly about his brow, all color blanching away from his face. Tiny beads of perspiration moisten up at his hairline and begin to trickle down: temple to cheek; cheek to chin, and into the whiskers of his beard; chin to throat, or to the handkerchief stuffed as a pad upon his shoulder. Faster than flicking strobes of light, his fingers dance across the instrument's slender wooden neck, his wrist flexed behind again and again, utterly impervious to the unset break made years long past in the bone. Abducted from reality, his gaze fastens onto a mirror-glass hung in echelons far and fleetingly distant, a vast ringing panorama of the ages that my own eyes yet cannot detect, but toward which my ears and heart unquestioningly surrender, heeding the poignant call—and I bow my head low in reverence, worshiping sound, worshiping gift, worshiping all that I love in him and everything about his talent that, beyond my humble ken, remains inured in mystery.

Once he dashes off the finale to Lalo's wild Spanish cadenza, the sun starts to pull high, the air chafing into the room warmly, and moments blend into an hour—then two—as he tears off into various other favorites of his repertoire: all twenty-four of Paganini's *Capricci*, and then, with a wink over toward me, the *Dialogue for Two Lovers*. Followed by a menagerie of excerpts from further works for violin and orchestra, including his old standards from Wieniawski, Mendelssohn, Schumann, Sibelius, Elgar, Dvorak—and Tchaikovsky, the haunting *Concerto in D Major*—at which he pauses, another glance cast in my direction, encouragement offered to follow. I lift the piccolo out from my boot and echo him on a few phrases, but finally cannot continue to play, so enraptured am I with watching, with listening, with simply bearing witness. "Bravo, Maestro!" I choke out in a whisper as he dashes off the last bow-stroke with emphasis, the goblet of water again seized up with a flurry of impatience and then slammed down once more atop the bureau.

But this time, the violin he lays lovingly back into its case, and bow still in hand, he bounds over in a rush of excitement toward the sofa, dropping down beside me. "Power!" he declares, waving forth the bow, his eyes ablaze and locked onto my own. "It is as in the old folk tale—so much wisdom in the old folk tales," he rasps out. "A soldier returns to his native land following a war, comes face to face with the devil, and sells him his soul—in exchange for a magic wand that will bring peace, resolution, love, and happiness forevermore." Pausing, Nikolai holds the bow aloft high unto the air, and gazes, enraptured, upon it, his voice trailing on in a low murmur: "Paganini, it was said, sold his soul to that same devil in exchange for such a wand. Like him, I've done naught but the very same—sold my soul in exchange for power, Sasha—for this violin that my great-grandfather brought back from Florence over a century ago after hearing Paganini play one bearing likened name. In exchange for this bow, this sound, this power, I have surrendered my soul, but—oh, God! I *must* have this power. . . ."

Frog-end of the bow yet gripped between his fingers, he ducks his head down into both arms, shuddering from head unto foot. "Nikolai," I whisper, stretching my arm about his shoulders, "you have not sold your soul—no, not at all. Instead, my love," I say softly, "you have truly gained it."

"Oh, do you honestly think so?" he cries in desperation, bolting upward and seizing back upon me with stricken, questioning eyes.

"Nikolai, you poor fool!" I mutter with an incredulous laugh. "To do what you do—to capture such power, to wield such majesty as, I swear, I have *never* heard—you have not sold your soul to the devil—but offered it. Unto none but God."

"But—so enthralled I become, so utterly possessed!" he goes on mournfully. "As if the devil himself has taken me up by the throat—or, more aptly put, by the strings, both the violin's and my own—my every movement guided with perfect forethought as if I were naught but a puppet at the fair! If this be God, Sasha, and not some devil behind my musical lust, He is scarce the God whom other people see."

"True God," I tell him with conviction, "is scarce the God other people see."

Swallowing, Nikolai holds my gaze for a long while; at last sets down the bow and grasps up my hand, murmuring: "We must speak more of this. And at length."

"Yes."

"You know," he goes on bare above a whisper, "when I used to whip out a piece like that Lalo concerto past my twenty minute exercises at school, old Maestro Auer would storm about for clear unto a week, declaring me naught but another 'grandstanding prima donna.' But—you understand! Thank you—oh, bless God for bringing you back to me!"

His arms fly about me then, and the kiss comes sure and long; exhilarated and horrified, I linger far beyond any dictate of good sense, and only tear myself away upon the warning grumble of an engine pulling up outside the front window. "Oh, Lord Jesus!" Nikolai gasps, peering back beyond my head to ascertain that Aunt Sophie and Tatyana and the children yet remain safely far enough from view out upon the beach. "Sasha," he exclaims in frustration, smacking his fist with a loud snap into his opposite palm, "forgive me! *God!* How foolish—"

"It's all right," I whisper back, unable to quash a grin as I say into his ear: "I love you, too."

Through the front door, the tyrant doctor of the house then marches, proudly brandishing a pair of crutches. "Please," Nikolai urges, nodding as Anna resumes rattling on about osteo-rheumatism, "take the crutches Sasha—if only for a little while. She is merely seeing to your best welfare."

"And for your best welfare, dear cousin," says Anna, "I am right now going out to speak to Maman about delaying our departure for a couple of weeks. In my opinion, you are scarce in any condition to travel."

"But, Anna!" I burst out.

"Oh, poo!" she shrugs back in reply. "Small difference a couple of weeks will make. Will, in fact, give the children some chance to enjoy the beach for one last time. And I have yet to sell the car, which will take a few days. My replacement at the hospital does not arrive until the first week in October as it is, so I cannot turn in my resignation until then. Oh, have done with your fretting, Sasha—my Lord! Here you have been cavorting across the country for near unto five months—allow yourself some peace in the sun, by God. Take a little time to rest."

"I'd rest easier," I tell her, "were not the Reds yet infringing upon White reserve flanks at Odessa, at Kiev."

"Sasha," Nikolai implores, again grasping hold of my hand, "since we left Odessa, the Whites have taken Kursk—over two hundred versts to the north of Kharkov. Praise God, we may indeed see 'Moscow by Christmas' yet! In any case, for the moment, I assure you, we are quite safe in Yalta."

Only after a long moment of gauging his earnestness, his own lack of concern over the situation, do I finally acquiesce. "Well," I admit with a sigh, "after everything we have been through, a couple of weeks of lolling about lazily upon the beach indeed sounds rather appealing."

Regarding the two of us with a frown, her glance lingering first over Nikolai, and then myself, Anna blurts out abruptly: "You two have—indeed—settled your differences about whatever it all was. Yes?"

Taken aback at the strange bent of her tone, Nikolai and I glance at one another—and then back up at her as, her expression stiffened, she shoves the handles of the crutches down into my grasp. Without another word, she then saunters away—kicking off her shoes and peeling off her stockings unceremoniously at the back screen door—before striding out onto the beach.

"We must take much more care," I say, my gaze held rigid upon Anna, and Nikolai nods in agreement, cautiously easing his hand away from mine.

* * *

Two weeks lapse into three as I heed Anna's bidding about recuperation, weeks that I come to wish could last forever. The children, rambunctious and elated, begin to brown upon their arms and the tips of their noses beneath daily exposure to the sun, the days filled from morntide to sundown with frolics of sand fights and castle building and giddy turns through the waves. Long conversations I have over tea with Aunt Sophie about Father. Robust and ornery as ever, he has finally made the journey to Winnebar, and after our first few days in Yalta, a letter even arrives from him, which I pore over for hours—laughing, crying, relishing unto memorization his barbs of wit and wordy observations. Afternoon naps I take with Vanya, delighting in the joy I find aglow upon my son's pudgy face, the child exulting in the warmth, the sunshine, his playtimes with Petya and the love of Aunt Sophie, Tatyana, and her daughters always gathered all around. A few spats I find myself involved in with Zhenya, particularly after Aunt Sophie presents the girl with several old tattered copies of *La Vie Parisienne*. The crux of our dispute: the shortness of skirt hemlines, the necessity for silk stockings, the possibility of bobbing her hair. But finally one afternoon, after an outing with Anna, my step-daughter waltzes in triumphantly with the mass of curls clipped off up to her chin, and wisping not unattractively about her cheeks and ears—and I find myself with little else to say about it. Never in any case could I remain piqued with her for long—nor with anyone else, for that matter, as the lazy hum of days continues to drift on by. Notwithstanding the crutches, endless ambling walks I take up and down the beach each morn and afternoon with Nikolai, relishing every moment spent with the man for whom I have for so long carried my lofty, romantic torch. About life's grand profundities, we talk: literature, music, art, the theater, the ballet;

God and metaphysics; democracy and socialism; war and the mystery of death. And about precious, mundane little things we carry on for untold hours: flashes of childhood memory, types of foods that strike our mutual fancy, the daily peculiarities of the weather, all the while basking in one another's company and enamored with the time—after these recent harrowing months—to at last simply talk without the press of worry, desperation, and exhaustion ever so beset upon us.

With the advent of October, news from the front proves surprising and encouraging: on the sixth, Denikin's forces take Voronezh; on the eleventh, Yudenich's Whites, fanning in from Estonia in the north, capture Yamburg on the Luga River, less than one hundred-fifty versts from Petrograd. On the twelfth, Chernigov falls into the hands of the Volunteer Army; on the thirteenth, Orel. From there, White advance guards begin their approach upon Tula, and the refrain 'Moscow by Christmas!' resounds again like wildfire throughout the town and for versts afar up and down the beach. "They say they threw a noose around that Lenin's neck and hanged him from atop the Kremlin!" says old Count Byelov, our elderly neighbor, his striking blue eyes caught afire beneath a bristle of white hair, his laughter tickling at us through the barrier of currant bushes.

"Not true—that rumor can in no way be true," I say to Nikolai once we wave our afternoon tidings to the old man, the two of us peering after him as he shuffles off, shaky cane in hand, back through the door of his bungalow.

"Why not?" Nikolai says to me, his grin still lingering long with affection after old Byelov.

"Because that scoundrel Lenin would put a gun to his head before allowing White soldiers to capture him, that's why."

"Hmmm. Most likely, you are right. Still, old Byelov intrigues me, Sasha. Last year, when I was here, the afternoon before I left, I sat down and had a long talk with him, and he began laying out precise predictions for Denikin's troop movements. I swear to God, near every one of them later turned out to be right on the nose. I tell you, there's more than meets the eye about old Byelov."

"Might I remind you," I interrupt with a roll of my eyes, "that old Byelov is also the one who claims to be three hundred years old?"

The old Count's outrageous contention has indeed long been a standing joke around the neighborhood. "Well?" Nikolai tells me with another sidelong grin. "Perhaps that's the reason he seems such a wise old man."

Laughing, I poke my cousin an elbow in the ribs, and follow his gaze once more out unto sea, the quiet and peace of ages foaming back upon us from the shore, wave by crashing breakwater wave. "I love this place," I rasp out, my voice going low, my hand seeking his behind safe cover of the bushes. "Will be difficult to leave it behind."

"Yes," he murmurs close into my ear, his lips brushing against my hair. "I know."

Despite the progress in the war, however, our plans to leave we doggedly pursue. "Naught is left of Petrograd, Maman," Anna insists to Aunt Sophie during another bout of hesitations. "Even if the Whites win, that slime Lenin and his Red Guards have ransacked the city hideously. Years of restoration would it take to bring back our old St. Petersburg you so fondly remember."

"Indeed," says Tatyana. "And even were our own St. Petersburg to bloom again, I'd not choose to return. Too many memories. Poor Eugenie—"

"Yes, darlings, I know," Aunt Sophie admits in reply, sadly grasping up both daughters' hands. "Still, not so easy is it, my gems, to leave behind us our thousand-year-old legacy."

With resolution, Anna pats her mother's arm and pushes up from the table. "I, for one," she declares with smile, "long again for Paris! Remember how happy we were while together there upon holiday?" Glancing toward Nikolai and myself, the both of us lounging back against either side of the kitchen archway, she rambles on: "Those years when you two played with the ballet were some of the most joyous I can remember! Oh, by the way, Kolya—your old friend Diaghilev has kept his concern going strong, you know. Perhaps again you could secure work with the *Ballet Russe* orchestra—"

"Let us fret over only one matter at a time, shall we?" Nikolai replies curtly, brushing past me and then making, head lowered, his fists jammed down into his pockets, once more for the beach.

After ducking out from Anna's curious stare with a shrug, I follow after him—to find him waiting out in the sand for me to catch up. And for us to again begin hashing over our continued dilemma: Father is at Winnebar, and adores the place. To Winnebar, I have promised to take the children. Tatyana, enthralled with beachside living, intends also upon taking her children to Winnebar. But Anna and Aunt Sophie will not think of living anywhere but Paris. Hence, the rift: how, bound by loyalties tearing us in opposite directions—and without anyone discerning the truth—can Nikolai and I stay together? Which, to each of us, is the most paramount matter of all?

Nonetheless, happenstance as they are, our plans proceed: Anna resigns her post at the hospital and sells her car; Aunt Sophie begins auctioning off the furniture, various other possessions, and informs Count Byelov next door that she will not be renewing the five year lease, which comes due on the bungalow upon end of the month. Then on the twenty-second of October—while Zhenya and I, crouched down upon the floor, practice French grammar lessons in between packing delicate knickknacks into a box—Nikolai returns from a walk into town white-faced and tight-lipped, the back screen door banging shut ominously behind him. "My Lord! What is it, Kolya?" Aunt Sophie bursts out, a china plate near sliding from her grasp upon the sight of his woeful expression.

"They have lost Orel," he rasps, lancing us with a blank-eyed stare. "The Whites have lost Orel. And none but the dreaded crack cavalry of Semyon Budyonny has recaptured Voronezh. It appears Denikin spread out his reserve units far too thinly along the entire front. For a certainty, now, he hasn't enough men. The Reds, I am afraid, are coming."

Within a day, peaceful Yalta turns tumult into a wild uproar, panic spreading contagiously over news of the White retreat and impending advance by the Reds—and the sudden somber forewarning of rumors about a lack of coal. "That's it—we will book our passage today!" insists Anna, meeting Nikolai's nod as he seizes up his hat and follows after her. "The Italian-Lloyd line," I hear her say to him as they charge together out the door for town. "Yesterday, I heard a steamer pulled in from Novorossiysk, bound for Constantinople. . . ."

The news they return with is devastating. "A thousand percent inflation on steamship tickets!" Nikolai shouts in disbelief. "A thousand percent inflation in only one day—I tell you, it's ludicrous, appalling!"

Later, with the others, I stare numbly at our collection of viable currency—English pound notes, French francs, old Tsarist rubles—spread out in a pile upon the kitchen table. Basically, after hours of counting and recounting—and even including in the tidy sum gained from the sale of Anna's car—our total fortunes amount to only enough to purchase steamship tickets for seven people.

Over the next few days, everything else we possess, we then proceed to sell—dishes and platters, punch bowls and tea serving sets, gold and silver flatware; the women, their jewelry; Nikolai, cuff links and other keepsakes once belonging to his father; myself—while bemoaning the fate of my flute and its precious silver—the hapless little five-inch strand left of Melissa's emeralds. But after haggling with the moneylenders for hours on end, after counting every coin painstakingly and juggling all remaining contingencies in a frantic angst of desperation, the sum we finally arrive at still is not enough.

Violin case in hand, out from the house he charges, while I bound on my crutches through gritty sprays of sand, swearing, screaming after him: "My God, you *can't! You can't!* Nikolai, by dammit to bloody screaming hell, *listen* to me! *Nikolai . . . !"*

But without a backward glance, he strides off far down the length of the beach, making toward the direction of town.

And two hours later, to my overwhelming relief, he returns—with the violin—in a rage. "No label!" he storms, gulping down the last of our cognac in a frenzy and stalking about in a panther's gait as the rest of us sit gathered together in shock, our stares drawn dumbly toward the Guarnerius placed at center of the table. "I shouted it until they must have heard me up in the hills!" Nikolai rages on. "I repeated tirelessly: of course, no label! Everyone who knows anything about these violins knows that the Master—del Gesu, Guiseppe Guarneri—kept not always so stringent about engraving any label! And that fool moneylender had to gall to say back to me: 'If this be prize violin, you show me label!' Oh, my God—I cannot believe it! 'The make is 1737,' I told him again and again. 'Was full unto eighty years old when my great-grandfather brought it back from Florence in 1817!' But would he listen? Oh, no—instead, the fool only scoffed at me, and said: 'No prize violin? These days, wood and strings alone not worth so much—fifty francs, I pay you then, no more.' God holy Jesus—fifty francs! As if he was merely itching to dole out insult! *Fifty francs—Jesus blessed Christ!* Scarce more than the cost of a light supper for two over at the Cafe Yellow Parrot! Dear God, I—I simply cannot *believe it! . . ."*

Smashing his hat back onto his head, Nikolai lets out a murderous groan and once again stomps off through the back door, sand kicking up behind his heels and in through the mesh of the fly screen.

"One ticket," Aunt Sophie murmurs, sighing. "All we need is enough currency for one more ticket. But scarce help, I am afraid, can be lent by a paltry fifty francs."

I find him hunched out upon the sand—and shuffle my way cautiously toward him upon my crutches. At the tilt of my shadow, he glances upward and rises to his knees, reaching to assist me down, and drops back to the sand himself, his fingers hacking at and picking out black pebbles, then to toss them, one by one, out toward the splash of the waves. "In truth, Sasha," he says at last, his gaze caught far to the horizon, "I am not so angry, as I am relieved."

Nodding, I bite my lip and search his face in earnestness as he murmurs on: "I cannot go to any more moneylenders, nor risk one of them seeing in the Guarnerius its true value. I—I cannot sell that violin."

"I know."

"See? I told you I had sold my soul to naught but the selfish grip of the devil."

His voice breaks then, and he casts off the pebbles with a forlorn shake of his head, his lips pursing inward. "We have enough, save for one ticket," he rasps out, avoiding my eye. "I will stay behind—"

"No!"

"Yes! My God, what are you—blind? It is the only way, the only course which makes any sense—"

"I will not leave you."

"Sasha," he goes on gently, "listen to me. You, my friend, have no choice about whether to leave or to stay. You have the responsibility of your children."

"I will *not* leave you!"

"Goddamn it!" he snaps back. "Don't you start wallowing in sentiment, blast it! Nor choose to vent that infernal Sekovsky stubbornness on me now!"

"We will *both* stay!" I cry insistently, smacking my fist into the sand. "The children can go on with Tatyana to Winnebar—"

"You cannot abandon your children!"

"I would scarce be doing so! Might I remind you that Father is there? And Tatyana has literally taken Zhenya and Vanya into her own brood—"

"You are mad!" he rages at me in disbelief.

"I will not leave you!" I shout back, seizing off my spectacles and flinging them out, with emphasis, toward his face. "Either both of us go—or *neither*, Nikolai Zhelanov! *Period!"*

"And what of your son?" he counters back, glaring me up and down. "You expect to send him away—torn from a parent? *Again?"*

"Stop it!"

"And what if you and I cannot find passage out later?" he goes on. "What if we *never* manage to find any passage out? You expect to see your father raise the child? For the boy to grow to manhood in England without you?"

"Nikolai!" I roar back, "were they your children, and were I the one insisting to stay, would you leave me?"

His mouth drops then, his stare lingering upon me, half-uttered words dissipating from his lips. Finally, he turns back to the sand, catches hold of a stick, and starts digging randomly about with it. At last shakes his head. "No," he whispers out, a hard swallow carved down his throat. "Even—even were they my own children, neither would I leave you, Sasha."

His hand I grasp hold of first—and then his arm—finally, his shoulder as I swear off whomever might be watching, sighing in relief against the strong crush of his embrace. "I—I could never leave you," he chokes into my ear, pecking a shy kiss upon the lobe, his chest trembling in a heave against mine. "Oh, dear God forgive me!"

"So," Anna blares out like a fire horn above us, "it is all settled then? You are both staying?"

Mortified, we bolt away from one another and gape upward—to find her sneering down at us, her eyes widened with shock, her tone strung with the height of contempt as she utters out: "Humph! Just as I thought—that you two have, indeed, been lending naught but new credence to the old adage 'kissing cousins.'"

Nikolai shoots up to his feet scarce before I can catch in a breath, his hand strangling for her arm, his teeth gritted in rage. "Y-You—you smirking little smart-mouthed bitch!" he shouts at her. *"How dare you!"*

"Oh, not to worry, Kolya!" she snaps back, her eyes screwed up in loathing upon the both of us, her laughter gone sarcastically shrill. "Your filthy little faggot secret is safe enough with Doctor Harpy."

Whirling about on her heel, Anna marches off in triumph back for the house—and Nikolai, charging after, halts up with a flurry of curses as I lunge out prone into the sand and clamp both hands fast around his ankle—pleading, begging with him: "Don't, please! Simply let her go, Nikolai. I think she's known ever since the first day, after you played the violin, when we ended up kissing like a couple of lovesick fools while sitting upon the sofa. I think she must have caught a glimpse of us through the window when she pulled up out front in the motorcar. It is all my fault—I should have insisted we stop, should have heeded caution. Please—let her go. If you follow after and make a scene in the house, she may decide to tell everyone."

Spewing out obscenities in a torrent beneath his breath, he stands trembling, fuming, glaring after her for what seems ages; finally, shoves back down with a grunt into the sand beside me. "Blast it," he mutters out, hanging his head into his hands. "Yes, English, you are right. Indeed, better it will be—for them, to leave. For us, to stay."

"Yes."

Meeting his nod with a sad one of my own, I slip my spectacles back on and grip my fingers close around his arm; ease away again after he squeezes my hand in his. And together, we gaze out once more toward the breakwater of the Black Sea, each of us resigned to our mutual tide of inevitability.

* * *

"Ohhh!" Zhenya sobs against me. "Step-papa!"

I crush them both fiercely again—Vanya, sniffling and whining within my grasp without knowing exactly why; Zhenya, soaking tears into her handkerchief with a flood of abandon and stuttering out for the near thousandth time: "Step-papa, how I wish to God you were coming along!"

Toward Nikolai, I glance again—to see him yet gripped fast within his mother's tearful embrace. Up and down the dockside, the story is the same: families clinging together, their lives soon to be torn asunder, some members destined to leave, others choosing or forced, for whatever reasons, to stay behind. "Zhenyushka," I murmur against my step-daughter's short-cropped hair, "Nikolai and I will find passage out as soon as we can. My father intends upon liquidating the remainder our stock holdings, and will cash in everything he can from his winery investments, and then will send on the money. No doubt will we all be together again very soon."

The boarding whistle blows, and people start breaking away from one another, making in reluctant steps toward the stretch of gangplank stairs. Hurriedly, I set Vanya to the ground, squeezing hold on his hand while digging through my jacket pockets. "Zhenya," I say, bidding her to wipe her eyes as I draw out the amethyst crystal, "some keepsakes I simply could not impart unto the moneylenders. This pendant belonged to my mother. I want you to have it."

"Oh, Step-papa—it's beautiful!"

"And a miracle I have been able to keep it safe and whole for so long," I murmur to myself with a sigh.

"Oh!" Zhenya gasps on. "I shall wear it always!"

"And this," I continue, taking from my pocket the old ring engraved with the beehive and my great-great-great-great grandfather's initials, "I want you to keep for your brother. And if it turns out to be a long time before I ever reach England, when Vanya grows old enough, and the ring fits him, he may wear it. Tell him that it came from his father—and from the long line of his father's fathers that ever lived before him. Tell your little brother never to f-forget, Zhenyushka—"

My voice breaks then, and I seize them bóth up once more, crushing my arms about each as the second whistle blows. "Come along," I choke out, urging her away, my hand clamped onto her shoulder.

We return to the Zhelanovs—to find them, too, all clinging to one another in a rush of tears—even Anna, the sneer of contempt vanquished from her face this morn, and replaced by the strangest glimmer of benevolence as she has stared between myself and Nikolai. Whether we could have purchased one more ticket soon enough became a moot point, the steerage passage booked for the eight of them amounting to simply that—passage only. So, even more money had to be squandered up: for food, for 'accommodations'—a berth with a blanket—while upon the journey. "Kolya," Aunt Sophie says to Nikolai, "we will cable funds to you from Paris—"

"But I want you settled first," he insists again. "And not in some fleabag flophouse on the *Rue Lepic,* Maman—you promise me! Sasha and I will get along swimmingly, and will follow after as soon as we can."

The third whistle finally sounds, French crewmen in white blousoned shirts and bright red berets sweeping through the dockside with outstretched arms, urging ticketed passengers toward the gangplank stairs. I kiss and embrace Aunt Sophie, Tatyana, her children—and haltingly, Anna—before seizing up Zhenya again. Then for one last time I throw my arms around my son, whispering a slew of endearments into his ear and bidding him: "Never forget, Vanyushka—your papa loves you! Never forget . . . ."

Struggling with wobbliness on the crutches, I pull close to Nikolai and lean into his side as we watch them board, the brims of their hats pulled low, their coats thrown over their arms, their trunks thudding with effort upon each plodding step across the stiff wooden boards of the gangplank stairs. Wordlessly, he slips his arm around my shoulders, while with his other hand, he waves—until they all disappear through a companionway into the lower decks, guided there by crewmen who seem much impatient with hurry, the days of streamers and balloons and grand bon voyages at steamship rails long put behind us in the expediency required in times of war. “You care to watch it pull out?” Nikolai says to me once they start weighing anchor, his voice rattling deep with emotion in his throat.

When I shake my head, he loops his arm through mine and guides me along with him—and somehow, past the terminal, the warehouses, the fishing wharves, and the span of quaint little shops, hotels, and rows of dockside cafes, he manages to flag down a cab. As the motorcar chugs along, I stare through the shiny glass windows numbly, watching a city basking in sunshine, but yet spun adrift in mounting rumors of doom. Everywhere, people’s faces remain drawn dourly as they amble along the streets, the old regulars gathered at cafe corners shaking their heads, young women gawking about with frightened stares as they walk their toddlers and push along their infant carriages. Budyonny’s cavalry, it is said, continues tearing south, cutting up the White resistance, leaving entire towns ravaged in the onslaught, innocent civilians slaughtered unto the thousands by fierce legions of Red Guards possessed of no mercy once territory changes hands. Against the news, I shut weary eyes—praying, wishing, desperately willing for the whole damnable nightmare to end—for the war, the fighting, the death, the bloodshed to somehow simply *stop* . . . .

After awhile, Nikolai’s hand slips through mine, and low on the seat, hidden away from the perusal of driver or outside passers-by, I grip onto his fingers as if unto my last lifeblood on earth—for the whole remainder of the way home.

I had thought that once behind closed doors, I would break down in entirety and give way to a hacking ocean of tears. Instead, despite the crutches, I pace, wandering numbly from room to room. Count Byelov pays a visit, speaking with Nikolai in low undertones about the lease on the bungalow. Madame Rosenberg inquires as to whether Aunt Sophie and the others made safe departure. Once the neighbors take their leave, Nikolai asks whether I desire luncheon—to which I shake my head. But I follow outside to sit with him in the sand, and find him choosing to do naught but stare numbly also—at bushes, trees, sand, the deep crystal-blue waves of splashing water. And our afternoon begins in silence. Once, he pushes upward, and wanders his way back in; returns after a few moments with tumblers and a cold pitcher of lemonade, which he sets down between us. Once, I push upward and return inside as well, venturing outward again with some dried fruit and stale crusts of bread. The beach umbrella I pause to fetch up from beneath the porch overhang as I make my way back, although the brim of my hat I yet again draw low to my brow, cautious ever, with my pigmentation, of catching a burn. And afternoon mourns on. While I sit munching bits of bread, content to sip now and then from my tumbler of lemonade, he wolfs down in scarce two or three precious bites the currants and crusts I offer him; downs an entire glass of juice in near one long thirsty gulp—and fishes about the sand in agitation, pebbles picked out here, sticks and bits of shells snatched up there and tossed about in the palm of his hand, then shunted back once again unto their gritty, layered world of oblivion. But his eyes remain, like mine, spellbound by distant images lurking in the crash of every wave—our stares each betraying souls stretched bone-bare, two companion psyches mutually rended.

Finally, as the sun begins ebbing low, he scrambles upward again, sets away the umbrella and pitcher of lemonade, and returns to cradle hold of my hand and urge me inside. The stove in the kitchen he then lights, stuffing logs of driftwood and shreds of old newspaper and bits of kindling down into its iron belly. Vegetables and butter and bits of seasoning he starts ransacking out in a flurry of enthusiasm from the icebox, throwing the whole lot into Aunt Sophie's old cast iron skillet. Bits of broccoli, red onion, white cabbage, and Chinese celery dance about in colorful array as he mixes in with them a little leftover rice and some canned chickpeas. "I scarce knew you could cook," I say to him, easing down to the table with a sigh, my thoughts centered upon the whorl lines etched into the flesh of my thumb, my mind adding up, in precise calculation, the amount of nicks and chips caught in the stem of a bent tin camp spoon.

"Cook?" he replies, shrugging, his face lighting up—just ever so briefly—with that familiar grin. "In truth, I never have much, until now. So—dine at your own risk, *mon cousin,*" he declares, setting down upon the table one plate of rice, vegetables, and beans before us each.

The meal proves not only palatable, but tasty—suddenly, I find myself wolfing down eager mouthfuls in response to latent pangs of hunger. But once I scrape the plate clean, the window's lurking ocean depths recast their silent spell, introspection without thought or purpose regaining its stranglehold upon me, my perusal scanning a horizon decades, even centuries far distant.

The dishes Nikolai rinses over and stacks in the sink before pausing beside me. "Come," he whispers, latching hold of my arm.

Save for the one bed left in Aunt Sophie's old boudoir, no furniture remains, only crates and raggedy cushions littering the front room of the bungalow. The crates he stacks up, fashioning a sort of table, while the cushions he plumps out firm against the wall. "Sit," he urges, gently helping me downward as I pay due heed to my stiffened leg. "Comfortable?" he asks finally, sitting down beside.

"Enough."

"The bad news or the good?" he then murmurs, straining to catch my eye.

"The bad news or the good," I say blankly. "Well, the bad, I suppose, then," I tell him with a sigh. "Please."

"Well—we've little food left, dear heart. And scarce any money. I am afraid that, come the morn, we shall be forced to consider taking on some sort of menial labor. Can you still balance ledgers?"

"Oh, for a certainty, if need be," I assure him. "In my sleep."

"Good. But I want you to stay here—no, I'll not hear of you trooping about town with me. You know Anna said for you to stay on your crutches for at least another month. I'll inquire in town for you, and see whatever work I can bring back."

"And you?"

"The restaurants, the tavernhouses," he says, eyeing the case of the violin lying beside him upon the floor. "As long as soldiers crowd them, there are women to woo. And for musicians, the prospect of business."

"And?" I go on, turning to him. "The good news?"

Throwing back his head, he lets forth a hearty laugh and rolls his eyes, blurting out: "We have finally rid ourselves of the troupe of nagging females who insist upon calling me 'Kolya.'"

Tempering back a chuckle of my own, I ask him: "And why do you so despise that nickname, my old friend?"

"Ugh! My father, as you might remember, never addressed me as such—always called me 'Nikolai.' I suppose I simply came to prefer it."

"My father only called me 'Aleksandr' whenever he was speaking with the utmost gravity. Or if I had irked him in some way."

"Which was plenty often enough, yes?" he retorts, laughing, jabbing me with his elbow.

"You allow Count Byelov to call you 'Kolya,'" I remind him, jabbing back.

"Oh, but one must humor Count Byelov. The man is, after all, our landlord. And three hundred years old," he adds, chuckling again. "In any case," he goes on, "I meant to tell you that the kind old gent has consented to renew the lease. Even without payment of the money."

"Indeed? But—for how long?" I ask, searching his face.

"Oh, I think long enough," he says, leaning close. "We'll dig up some money in a few days, pay him part of it, and everything will be fine. Because the final good news is—the *best* good news of all, Sasha, my love—is that we are finally alone."

That sudden realization jolts new life into my veins. No longer, indeed, must we hide out behind the bushes to touch hands or trade shy, watchful kisses. No longer must we check our passion, stifle the longing, guard the open tenderness of our stares. No longer must we sleep apart, two gazes locked above the children's heads in silent, fiery yearnings of the night. Devastating, harrowing, it is, to love someone in secret—furtively, deceptively—loath always to share the fact with others, one's hallowed core of inner truth forever hidden away in shame from friends and closest kin—that truth spawning a love felt so deeply, so immeasurably . . . .

Breaking into a smile, I throw my arms around Nikolai's neck and run fond fingers up through strands of his lanky blond hair, while he grins back at me—and then our kiss comes swift as a falcon sentinel of first light. Once he draws away, I ease back from him with a shudder of awe, yet finding myself so in love with those fervent, smoky gray eyes. "Oh, yes," I rasp out, scarce yet fathoming the import, "we're alone, Nikolai! Without, for the moment, Red or White—or God pray tell whoever else's patrols—to shoot at or hide ourselves away from. Without the prospect of another long struggle across the open countryside greeting us upon tidings of tomorrow's morn. And we even have a secure roof over our heads—for the time being." Melting once again into his eager embrace, I meet renewed tremors of his lips, our next kiss ignited by whispers: "We're all alone, Nikolai Zhelanov! At long, glorious last! . . ."

CHAPTER TEN

Love of the Hundred-Hundred Years

From my canvas-board, I glance up to spy the gull again. Always the same gull—once more alighting in a long, lazy swoop down onto the headrest of the chaise lounge, there flapping its wings about and regarding me with the most patient stare of curiosity, its head turning around on its neck every which-way like metered tickings on the face of a clock. Smiling, I turn back to my paints and canvas, forswearing the temptation. If I toss a crumb to the damn bird, a legion of greedy beaks will descend upon me within the moment, and none too tidily. "Shoo!" I call out, laughing, waving out my hand until the gull flies away.

To the sea, I gaze out once again and sigh. As ever, its rolling waves elude my call to compose, define, create. No, not Yalta with its fresh-plucked splendor do I paint, no vast stretches of black sand nor pale water dance upon my crochety hemp canvas. Scarce justice can I do the seascape—nor the grapes, the strawberries bursting forth so fat and juicy upon their vines, nor the cypress and magnolias, nor the hefty stalwarts harboring their greenish, never-ripening bananas. No, Yalta provides inspiration only for oceans laden with birch and pine, grim reapers towering high above a godforsaken land bleakly masked with ice and the cover of marshy forest bogs, feathery long shadows of the trees gracing a cupolaed wooden house that once was, but is no more. But as I scan over my third rendering of Lissushka done within four weeks, satisfaction proves tenuous, and talent sorely lacking. Letting out another sigh, I take down the canvas-board and start setting away into their lacquer case Tatyana's old set of watercolors. "Mediocre painter, mediocre musician," I mumble to myself, shaking my head. "It appears, Sasha Sekovsky, that you are destined for naught in life but mediocrity."

But the artwork, however feeble, remains treasured creation. With care, I grasp up my cane and take the canvas-board into the safety of the bungalow to dry. The paints, the crude wooden easel—hammered together one day on a lark—I fetch inside also. In the kitchen upon the stove, my vegetable soup simmers along in Aunt Sophie's old steel kettle, the air throughout the bungalow tinged warm and moist with the scent of creamed spinach, cucumber, scallions, and fresh-cut sorrel leaves. Pausing on my way back out, I sip a steaming spoonful yet again; add in a dash more salt, and throw another couple of driftwood logs to the fire churning away in the belly of the stove. Then, after pondering for a long moment, mindful of my two recent tumbles taken within thick billows of the outside sand, I switch my cane reluctantly for my worn pair of crutches, pull low the brim of my hat, and start out once more for the beach.

All the way to the breaking edge of the water, I amble and then pause, staring outward, marveling at the lack of a chill, the warmth of the sun so pleasant here like Cannes in the Mediterranean, although March remains sown just bare unto the advent of spring. Staring far and long unto the frothy depths of the ocean waves, I bite back my worries over the war—purging from my mind all thought of the chaos, and willing myself to bask only in this sun, this peace, this sparse bit of heaven's harmony caught within the eye of the storm. And then I catch sight of him.

From down the beach. Early. And lancing me with that rakish grin, the violin case tucked beneath his arm as he saunters along. Flirtatiously, he tosses back his head, his hair catching pale highlights of the sun and tumbling loose and long to his shoulders. From his suit jacket pocket, his tie flutters out in a trail of carelessness, although the legs of his good linen trousers he has rolled up against assault of the sand, his feet lolling through the dark grains white and bare, his shoes tied together at the laces and lapping over his shoulder. Again he grins at me, but once he pulls close enough to gauge the earnestness of my expression, that grin fades to a gentle nod, and he downs a visible swallow, his eyes raking me from head to toe—as, with mine, I rake him.

I swallow hard also, conscious suddenly of what a sorry sight I must appear: shirttail hanging out, paint splotched into my trousers, shirt-sleeves, and the ends of my hair. Little does it matter; Nikolai starts forward again at a much quickened pace, his head inclined emphatically toward the bungalow. I turn about on my crutches and start back for it, peeking from the corner of my eye as he turns in from the breakwater and starts across the beach himself. Like a hawk, I gauge his every movement as he wings in closer; watch with my chest tightening in anticipation as he catches up and falls into step beside me, the taut pull of silence binding us, our tension fraught to a twang of bone as we hurry toward cover of the house. From next door, Madame Rosenberg can be seen peering through the curtains of her kitchen window, measuring her suspicions of us with her spyglass. "There she goes again," I tell him, scarce glancing sideways.

"Uh-huh."

"You're early," I then say. "No work?"

"It's Monday," he says in explanation, shrugging.

Vaguely, I note him bereft of any ledgers, also. But little does that, or anything else in the world matter, once we stumble past the back screen door and into the bungalow.

He drops his shoes; snatches his gun out from his belt and sets it down, along with the violin, upon the kitchen table. My crutches I shove in with impatience behind the door. "The soup smells good," he murmurs, reaching for me.

"Uh-huh." I toss away my hat and spectacles and fly into his arms, moaning against his moans, kissing unto his languishing, open-mouthed kiss—a kiss just like the very first time, near unto a year ago, in Latvia; a kiss just like this heady morn, scant hours ago, before he left—no trace, in the interim, of familiarity having bred diminishment, the same excitement and intensity, the same poignant, forbidden lust yet ravaged as ever between us. Gripping my fingers across his shoulders, letting out ecstatic sighs, I hollow out my mouth again and again—yearning and begging; striving for pressure, succulence, dominance, ravishment, more . . . *more* . . . . "I love you!" I rasp out, teetering against him precariously as he starts to half-carry, half-drag me toward the boudoir. "Dear Jesus God in Heaven, how I love you, Nikolai Zhelanov! *Tebya lyublyu . . . je t'aime!* Forever and evermore will I love you! . . ."

Once we tumble onto the bed, he rolls atop me, kissing, sucking, hacking at me like a banshee, our tongues rolling, clamping, slathering together, fluttering apart, testing lips, inner cheeks, the smooth, wet glassiness of our teeth. "Tonguing, they call it, yes?" he cries out, laughing. "Your naughty little woodwind secret!"

In response, I seize hold of his head and kiss him furiously again, my tongue thrusting deep inside his mouth to aptly illustrate the point.

"You drive me out of my senses," he then whispers, rolling down beneath as I hoist around on top of him. "All day," he mumbles on in between kisses, "I can scarce work. Can think of naught but *you.* Lunchtime, was playing Schubert; made four mistakes in the twenty-ninth *Andante*, all in a row. All your fault, English! Could think of naught but last night, *every* night. In bed . . . !"

As I start unbuttoning his shirt, he starts unbuttoning mine, shoving atop me again in a mountain of dizzied moans. Dazedly, I thrust up against him to meet his fierce thrustings downward against me; desperately, I seize my hand in for his crotch and roll back atop him as he seizes under for mine—and then we both stop, fingers frozen to guilty rifts at our plyings. From out in front, pounding again sounds in a torrent upon the door.

"Come along, you two lovebirds!" old Count Byelov shouts out for all the neighborhood to hear. "I know you're both in there—and I know what you're up to! But—dinner first."

Atop Nikolai, I hover bare an inch away from his mouth before sinking down to steal a last kiss, muttering out: "Damn."

Throwing back his head with a laugh, he pulls me close once more, murmuring: "Well, he'll not let up, you know. Until we allow him in."

"And must he dine with us every night that you cannot find work?" I say with a groan, forcing myself upward.

"Oh, Sasha, have a heart. The man is lonely—"

"And I'm selfish!" Pushing off from the bed with reluctance, I reach down to assist him upward—and he grasps my hand unto his lips, kissing my fingers and murmuring placations. And then we stand before one another hurriedly rebuttoning our shirts, while I gaze longingly up into his eyes, rasping out under my breath: "I want you!"

"I know." A tender, brotherly kiss he this time pecks upon my brow. "Patience, English," he whispers, chucking two fingers up under my chin. "In a little while."

Still grumbling with irritation, I wander out into the kitchen to check my soup as Nikolai opens the front door to admit Count Byelov. And again I learn the value, indeed, of patience, for again the old man has brought us loaves of bread, a canister of tea, and several bunches of fresh vegetables from his garden. And once more he has fished out from his attic more records for his Victrola, which so graciously he has allowed us to borrow. Winking at me, Nikolai sets on our favorite love song, Debussy's *Clair de Lune*, and I lean back against the kitchen archway, holding his ardent stare. And as he nods and smiles again toward Count Byelov, I smile at last also, blessing the old man for his generosity and tolerance. Without him, we would surely starve, for in this small seaport teeming with thousands of penniless refugees, Nikolai cannot find work on any consistent basis; myself, even less so. And still, after all these months—in addition to providing at least half of our food—for lease of the bungalow, the old Count charges only what we can afford to pay, week by frugal, scrimping week. At first, I was stunned at his ken to our situation, but from scarce the day after Aunt Sophie and the others left, he began calling us the 'love-birds' with fondness and nary the bat of an eye, accepting as completely natural our linkings of arms and holdings of hands, our lustful glances cast toward one another while in his presence. "You were painting again today, eh, Sasha Mikhailovich?" he asks, his eyebrows shooting upward, his bristly hair standing out all on end and making him appear, both at once, impish and most fearsome.

"Attempting to, in any case, Makar Serafimovich," I say, bowing in respectful reply. "And," I go on, "for your pleasure, *botvinya* vegetable soup, from my old Novgorod nanny's recipe, I have attempted to conjure up tonight. Although I fear without the sturgeon. But with ample crab meat—I pray you will fancy it. And might I fetch you some tea?"

And so the evening goes: the three of us breaking bread, downing tea, slurping soup; the old Count telling stories of his days in the Crimean and Turkish wars, and spieling out outrageous tavern jokes; Nikolai playing the violin, dashing off favorite cadenzas and following *Clair de Lune* along on the Victrola—while I devour him with a reverent gaze, aching, thirsting, lusting so for him inside, and taking in every secreted smoky-eyed glance stolen my way as well as he thirsts, lusts back for me. Finally, long after the descent of darkness, long after the many anecdotes begin to wane, and long after two rather boisterous, noisy games of cards, the old Count loudly guffaws, decries any wearing out of his welcome with a widened grin, and bids us adieu. Whereupon the soiled plates we toss into the basin, forgetting them until the morrow; the Victrola plays until its stylus catches over and over within the record's end grooves. And at last, with candles lit all about upon the boudoir floor, we tussle naked in bed—kissing, stroking, moaning against one another in rapture. After an onslaught of it, runny beads of sweat smear with semen between our two phallic hand-holds thrusted shaft to shaft and grappled head to swollen, leaky head—while he purrs like a mighty lion tamed into mussed strands of my hair: "Devil . . . shameless little devil-whore! God, how I love you! . . ."

"Nikolai," I whisper against the hollow of his throat, coveting every precious, beloved syllable of his name. "Ni-ko-lai . . . !"

Worshipfully, I yawn kiss after hungry kiss across the close-clipped hairs of his beard, and then start to suck my way downward—lolling slowly, inching teasingly from his chest to navel to lower belly as he trembles against me with a scathing moan, his fingers clawed into my shoulders. Then I acquiesce—kissing, sucking, swallowing his penis in elation—until he begs me stop, forcing me insistently upward, around, backward—and collapsing in a heave to do naught, unto me, but the very same. Finally, when I, when he can no longer bear another feverish instant, he reaches over, and from the old crate serving as a table aside the bed, hands me the jar of olive oil.

Rasping raggedly for breath, I mix cool oil into the milky froth coated across my fingers, slather it between the both of us, and then poke into him gently, tenderly, taking slow, deliberate care—until sliding in all the way as he pulls my arm through his, his fingers intertwining with mine. Against the nape of his neck, I lay my cheek and breathe in the sweet scent of his hair—while below, divine fire consumes me, and I start thrusting inside him. Slowing down, I try to last, grip onto his hand more tightly, and burrow my knees into the hollow well of his bent ones. "You are a devil," he whispers, squeezing my fingers close. "But in truth, God's devil. Pity the poor fools," he goes on breathlessly, "who never in their lives get ass-laid, who never search afar this other locus leading to—oh, *God!*—to ecstasy . . . ."

Moments later, after plunging my sanity away and scaling the sheerest heights of the cosmos, I lay within a drowsy, contented buzz to myself pity such poor fools as he prods inside me—first his fingers, and then glory. Opening unto diffusion with a rekindled sigh, I seize his hand up from behind, rounds of icy shivers tingling at my loins, chest, throat. "You, my love, are the one who is pure devil," I whisper back against his cheek. "And such a lusty devil!"

"I love you, Sasha," he whispers into my ear, his voice breaking, his thrusts becoming frantic. "God! How I waited all the years of my life to sleep with you, fuck with you, love you. . . ."

Afterward, I wake up halfway through the middle of the night, scarce realizing having fallen asleep. My check of the candles finds them all blown out; the Victrola in the front room flicked off. In the darkness,

I down remaining water from the tumbler he must have used to snatch a drink when he arose. Then I stumble back to bed—where I slide back in beneath the sheets and wind my arm around him once more from behind, while in sleep, he tucks my fingers within his cradled own. And nestling against him in the darkness, I pause to reflect again upon this one aspect of my life that is not, in any sense at all, mediocre.

Is it possible to literally drown in happiness? Five months now have he and I lived together without a day less magical. Never have I wanted anyone so blindly, so profoundly, only to have him want me back with the same ferocious, unparalleled devotion, our passions attuned one against another to the harmonic strum of perfection. Never has my rapport with another mortal so aspired to symmetry upon spiritual planes of light, our nightly siege of love rivaling an act of holiness, consecration. . . .

And yet, during more quiet times, guilty gnawings peek in from the fringes. Never, for instance, have I mourned overly much for Volodya Rykazian—indeed, bare any pause have I taken over the death of the lover with whom I spent, on and off, almost twelve years. And not enough, for a certainty, have I pondered the fate of my children, shipped off so conveniently first to Constantinople, then to Paris. But I cannot help myself—never has life been fraught with such wonder! Never—for the love of God!—have I felt so deliriously *happy* . . . .

* * *

Save for my late nights and lazy morns spent with Nikolai, and our dinners joined by Count Byelov, I live like a hermit most of the time, and it suits me. But on occasion, I must venture into town to drop off ledgers, and each time, I regret it, particularly tonight. *Verné's*, a large cafe graced by airy pavilion built upon the seaside quay, and usually lively even at mid-week, stands three-quarters empty by half past eight, and I can tell that old Aleksei Lavrentyevich will again close up early due to the lack of patrons. Sighing, I nurse my goblet of sparkling water and begin tracing a finger blankly along the red and white checkered patterns of the tablecloth, my gaze caught to the bow of the Guarnerius as Nikolai moves about from table to table with Dmitri, another violinist, the two of them churning out love songs. Every other man in the place—save for ourselves, the cook, and old Aleksei Lavrentyevich—is a smirking, self-satisfied bull of a White officer; every woman, a whore. And all, without pause, are speaking of naught but the evacuation made ten days ago from Novorossiysk.

"Bloody hell's inferno!" exclaims the gruff major seated at the table across from mine. "Slaughter it was, I tell you! Budyonny's cavalry stormed down in there from the pass, and cut the poor fools to ribbons. Simply mowed 'em down with machine guns: women, children, whole families at a time—"

"Humph! And the Brits act no better," snorts the fellow beside him. "Before the fleet shipped out, they set their own gunners upon the docks."

"And had to!" counters a youngish-looking lieutenant sitting across from them. "The refugees were making to rush the gangplanks of the ships; the British had to evacuate their troops. What else could they do?"

"Scarce had to turn the guns on 'em!"

"The throng of refugees was so vast, their weight alone would have *sunk* the ships had the Brits permitted 'em to board. Was naught but crowd control, I tell you—and I bet a tough order for a man to give, too, bidding those machine guns to open fire."

"Well," says the first man sadly, "no matter who turned their guns upon whom, the news is final: Denikin has resigned his command, and sailed for Constantinople. And the Brits are pulling out—which leaves us with only Baron Wrangel, and French allies. Don't take me wrong—Wrangel's a good man: able commander, a fine strategist. But the French are scarce known for their loyalty in war; could pull out any day now right behind the Brits. And mark my words, gents—once they do, it'll be a fight to the bloody death for the peninsula. The whole sorry lot of us against Budyonny's massive Red cavalry."

To the last gulp, I drain my sparkling water, set the empty goblet down upon the table, and wipe the back of my hand across my mouth. For months now, day by day, the news has been as such, ever only growing more dismal, the war maps taped up behind town shop windows all sporting narrowing red lines of demarcation indicative of the gradual White retreat. Last October, when the popular slogan 'Moscow by Christmas!' indeed garnered viable promise, the bubble soon burst to smithereens as the Whites bore heavy losses. Then a number of Makhno's bands chose to align themselves openly with the Reds, and rode in to effectively extinguish any last hope for the White offensive by slicing up Denikin's rear, managing even an attack as far south as the General's headquarters compound itself at Taganrog. From there, the Reds tightened their hold around the noose, steamrolling southward after the diminishing White Army from Voronezh, Kharkov,

Tsaritsyn. Outnumbered, the Whites failed to hold the line, and at dawn of this new year of 1920, Novocherkassk fell, followed by Rostov and its hordes of panicked, fleeing refugees trapped upon frozen Don River bluffs and stranded across the town's lone railway bridge, murdered most of them unto the desperate typhus-ridden thousands by merciless volleys from Red gunners. The month following, in February, the front to the west collapsed, a tragic second evacuation taking place from the harbor at Odessa. Then two weeks ago, Ekaterinodar, Denikin's new White headquarters, fell. And now, come first tide of April, this news of Novorossiysk—a city situated upon the map at the same latitude as Yalta, just a scant two to three hours jaunt away by tug or steamer. So now, the Crimean peninsula, from Yalta and Sevastopol in the south to Dzhankoy and the northern Perekop isthmus, remains the only territory of the whole former vast Russian empire held within White counter-revolutionary hands.

With a icy shudder, again I recall Nikolai's dreadful forewarning of last October: the Reds, indeed, are coming.

"Aleksei Lavrentyevich told us to call it a night, English," he says to me, setting the instrument case down with care upon the table and tucking the violin and bow down inside.

Nodding, I grasp up my cane, pull low the brim of my hat, and rise up from the chair. "Did he have any more ledger work?" I ask, eyeing him.

"No. He says he's sorry."

We wander out together in search of a cab, both of us lugging in our arms my payment for previous ledger work; his for the night's performance: three sacks of barley and a bundle of other assorted food. "At luncheon," he tells me with a wry smile, "a fellow was so impressed with my *Ave Maria*, he left behind a pouch of tobacco as a tip."

"Good. We can use it."

We will not, of course, smoke it. Ages has it been since either of us has indulged in the pleasure of smoking. Instead, we will use the tobacco, along with the barley, as currency for needed commodities, the profusion of paper rubles printed by the White government long since having become commercially worthless. "Just in the nick of time," I tell him as he flags down a cab. "We're near out of candles. And butter and salt. And, uh, olive oil."

At this, Nikolai shoots me a sly grin beneath glow of the gaslamp, and I grin back, feeling my ears flush.

On our way home in a sputtering old Russian *Byents*, he tells me his all-day hearing of the news: "Yes, one after another, they talk of naught but Novorossiysk. All the passenger bookings were halted over a week past by the civilian carriers, and only warships have been kept at moorage, the whole lot of them pounding ten-inch shells up into the pass to keep the Reds at bay while the Brits hurried through their evacuation. Tanks, planes, guns, shells, artillery—all supplies, all materiel imaginable—they dumped straight into the harbor, intent upon preventing any of it from falling into hands of the Reds. And I've heard about that dreadnought's machine guns opening up on the refugees. In fact, ghastly and inconceivable as it is, I've heard the same story in such striking similarity of detail from so many fellows today, I cannot help but believe it to be true."

"My God," I utter out, fingers creased unto my brow. "Could such horror happen here?"

In response, he gives no answer; only tightly, nervously—across the breadth of the automobile seat—grasps hold of my hand.

At home, we coast silently through another late-night supper of rice and beans and vegetables, and then retire, for a change, not to the boudoir, but to the front room, burrowing down together upon our faded cushions set against the wall. "Nikolai," I whisper to him after a long lull of quiet, "we are not going to find any passage out."

Again he grasps up my hand in silence. And slips out, from his pocket, the envelope that arrived for us yesterday. Which was supposed to have come by registered post, signed for at each mail stop, sealed unto impunity. Instead, all we received was a rumpled testament of smudged ink, obviously slit open and then reglued, containing only a picturegraph.

Of the front porch at Winnebar—and of Father sporting a high top hat, his eyes dancing with merriment despite the rugged, postured set of his mouth, his arms outstretched wide about Dunya and Darya and Petya and Zhenya and my little Vanya.

My joy, of course, is immense at knowing that they made it, and that Father and the children are together at long last. But from the envelope, the picturegraph was the only token left us. No letter, no message. No bank draft. No funds with which to book out our own passage.

"Don't be sad," Nikolai implores me, nestling close to my side and brushing a lock of hair from my brow with affectionate, lingering fingers. "If our money was stolen, it must mean that we are simply not meant to go."

"And?" I ask, leaning back and peering up into his face. "For what fate, then, do you think we are meant?"

"I think we are meant," he murmurs in somber, halting reply, "that is, I think you and I have been set upon this earth at this time to—to follow a particular path. One which, by many others, may yet be called forbidden. But is only regarded so because it is forbidding, fear-ridden against the sight of prior limitations. I think that, to follow that path, we must follow our hearts—and no matter what else, stay with, and learn from one another."

"Forbidden journey," I whisper with a nod. "Obligatory pilgrimage, cup of resolution, dark night of the soul."

"Yes."

"Nikolai," I ask, still eyeing him, "how can something that is obligatory be, at the same time, so forbidding, so forbidden?"

"Well—one must consciously choose the path, I think. Up until that point, one forbids it only to oneself. See, the clue to the whole mystery is that what one forbids, one can also bequeath. The point is in the making of the choice—"

"You know *so* much," I interrupt with an enthusiastic sigh, squeezing hold of his arm. "Your prowess in metaphysics soars, my friend!"

"Oh, but it was you who first taught me," he insists, chuckling. "Remember your Uncle Ned's book on numbers, and how I scarce felt the slightest interest when you first divulged your investigations at Lissushka? And then how we pored over the theories for hours on end during our years with the ballet in Paris? Yes, long and hard did I ponder upon our many discussions—every single one—during my years in the prison camp. Long and hard, indeed."

He bites his lip then, staring to the floor. "Sasha," he says after a moment, "what if the money had come? Would you have gone to Winnebar? Could I have followed?"

When I stall in answer, he goes on in a rush: "And what if Maman can manage to send some funds from Paris? Are we both to go to Winnebar? Or—are matters simply better as they are: the two of us here, and the rest of them there, all not knowing, save for Anna?"

"You are saying that we should never seek any passage out?"

"I am saying precisely this: that if more money does come, and we are able to book passage out, I think that we should go—somewhere. Nice, perhaps. Or Cannes, on the coast. But neither Paris, nor London. And definitely, not to Winnebar."

"And what, then, do we tell them?" I gasp out, tearing away from him.

"Not a word. Ever again."

I seize my head into my hands. I stare past our swinging pendulum down into its narrow, yawning abyss—only to know that he is right. "A choice, yes?" I rasp out, my voice ground to its breaking edge. "Our path indeed chosen, Nikolai Zhelanov?"

Without answer, he winds his arms back around me, and I pull hard into his embrace, my fingers fishing out—from my own pocket—another picturegraph: of the Eiffel Tower. And him. And me. "Oh, yes," he murmurs fondly as I show him, "yes, dear heart, I remember. And yes, our choice is us—or them."

"And? What if the no money ever comes, if we can never book passage out? Only in a matter of time will the *Bolsheviki* swarm in here. What course do you suggest we follow, then?"

"We could head north," he says to my astonishment. "Yes, north. No, I am not an utter fool. When your enemy is upon you, follow the farthest course that he expects. The *Bolsheviki* wreak slaughter upon all White-occupied towns in retribution, correct? Well, my thinking is, if we can manage to get ourselves north of the lines, we could settle in somewhere. Find a little out-of-the-way village where the Bolshies have already done their dredging out. There to fade into the woodwork, become proper Soviet citizens—"

"Nikolai, that's madness!"

"Perhaps."

"By God, you are talking about attempting to sneak past Budyonny's cavalry lines! The dreaded crack troops, Nikolai! And—and what of Bulyarin?" I go on, nursing a violent rift gone clear down the pit of my stomach. "Do you suppose, after all this time, that he might still be after you?"

"Perhaps. I think also that another prospect we must consider is that your wife might probably be after you."

Neither circumstance portends well for such a plan. "I tell you, it's preposterous, Nikolai! No matter how small the village, nor how vast the city, wherever we go, there will be demands for explanations. The Bolshies will never allow anyone to simply 'fade into the woodwork.'"

"Sasha," he cries with a sigh of perturbation, "unless you have any other suggestion, this is the best plan I can come up with! Because I will be damned if I will sit here in Yalta to be slaughtered like a dog when the Reds finally march in. My God, you've heard about Tsaritsyn,

Rostov, Novorossiysk—they torched the towns, literally. Lined up women, families with young children, in front of firing squads. Mowed down with machine gun fire those still waiting after the Brits pulled out from the docks—"

"Stop!" I shout, again clutching both hands to my head.

Wordlessly, he moves back in aside me, straddling his long legs apart and pulling me close within the warmth of their embrace, both arms crushed about my shoulders. "Shhh," he whispers into my ear. "Forgive me—I know how the war news grates so sorely upon your nerves."

"Nikolai," I rasp out urgently, stifling a sob, "how could we find one another once again, with such joy—only to now face certain doom like this?"

"Doom is scarce certain," he insists, a torrent of kisses nuzzled—as if to prove so—into my hair. "If anyone can outwit the Reds, will be your daredevil cousin Petrovich. I got myself past the bloody Huns, remember?"

* * *

The sound of knocking summons me from my angst of misgivings, and I hurry across the room and throw open the front door, coming face to face with Count Byelov. "Not home yet?" he asks with a cocked eyebrow, handing me, as I thank him, a loaf of bread and large jar of apricot preserves.

"No, Makar Serafimovich, I am afraid not." The bread and preserves I deposit upon the kitchen table as I return in haste to the back screen door. But another scan of the beach, swept long through the darkness, reveals yet no sign of Nikolai.

"Well, perhaps he caught a spot of late-night work," murmurs the old Count, attempting a comforting tone.

Nervously, I check my pocket watch again and shake my head. Near all the cafes close by ten, Nikolai almost always traipsing in from the beach soon thereafter. Of course, he has struck up several friendships in town: with Dmitri, with other violinists and musicians. Ofttimes he stops off to share in musical discourse at someone's house, or at one of the seedy, run-down tavernhouses near the fishing wharves. Still, such is only on occasion, and never has he stayed out as late as half past midnight, leaving me to cringe inside at the thought of what could have befallen him at the hands, most likely, of the *Azbuka*, the secret police. Cruel and violent as behavior of the Reds is purported to be, the Whites, in most ways, prove not one iota better. Anyone even suspected of Bolshevik leanings can be summarily executed without any trial, and rumor has it that the jails are filled with innocent people accused by enemies rife at settling personal scores. And the Army, far from making any gallant defense of the population's civil rights, instead conducts itself like a force of occupation. One of the worst rumors floating around town of late tells of a young boy shot to death out in a residential street, in broad daylight, by a group of White officers coveting possession of his bicycle. And of course, our escape from Latvia portends not well for Nikolai should someone covet his violin, or should he, without knowing or so intending, rile some haughty graycoat's feathers. Yudenich's army may have disintegrated away to token nonexistence in Estonia after its retreat last November from Petrograd, but no doubt some of the officers found their way south to Denikin's, and now Wrangel's ranks. Every night, I worry that my cousin could be recognized, accused of desertion, and carted off for hanging without my even knowing of it. Shuddering at the thought, I peer out into the starry blackness and once more scan the empty length of the beach. Of course, robberies, murders by vagabonds and lowdown criminal thieves are not uncommon in Yalta, either, in these wretched times. But Nikolai, an able marksman, always keeps his Luger loaded and at ready hand. With a sigh, I let fall the curtain once more across the back door window, and turn to thank Count Byelov again for his concern and for the food, offering, in return, a jar of my cooked *borshch* already set away for him within our icebox. "Oh, you needn't worry your head so, Sasha Mikhailovich," the old man urges softly, his wizened, gnarled hand lingering long upon my shoulder. "Sure enough, your cousin simply caught himself a bit of late-night work. And will return momentarily."

Just then, the sound of a motorcar pulling into the gravelly drive outside bids us away from our lookout post at the back door, and we hurry toward the front. "Well, see?" exclaims Count Byelov. "Now, what did I tell you?"

With relief, I throw open the front door to find Nikolai thanking his friend Dmitri for the ride in from town. "Sorry, English!" he calls to me with a sheepish grin, waving. "I know you were most probably tearing out your hair."

"You can say that again," I mutter, raking icy fingers through a sorry tangled fistful in reply.

With some effort, Nikolai carts in from the motorcar, with the violin case set atop it, a large wooden-crated box.

At the kitchen table, he sets it down, and the old Count hovers about us in curiosity, lingering to inspect the contents. "Merry Christmas!" Nikolai cries with a laugh, stepping back from the box and urging me, with a gentle push in its direction, to open the lid. "Or perhaps, more accurately, my love," he goes on, noting the calendar tacked up on the wall, "Merry Easter."

"Christmas in April?" I reply, meeting his wry grin.

"Christmas anytime for you, dearest heart."

"And? What did you do?" I ask with suspicion, smiling at him, my hands sliding in beneath the lid of the box.

Inside, I find a gift that little delights; rather, horrifies me profoundly: a stack of paper, close to a hundred precious sheets. And beneath it, an English-language typewriter.

"Oh, dear," Count Byelov utters with a gasp, staring between Nikolai's tremor of anticipation and my gaping, dropped jaw.

In the shock of silence, the old man then wisely makes a beeline for the front door, bids us quick good night, and lets himself outside as we scarce take notice.

"Have you *taken leave of your senses?"* I shout out at last, mustering up ragged, trembling protest.

"I—I thought you would appreciate the gift," Nikolai replies, taken aback, his eyes widening upon me in surprise.

"A-Appreciate?" I sputter out, incensed. "By God!—how did you ever get your hands on a *typewriter?* And *paper—"*

"Only," he tells me with emphasis, "after considerable trouble."

"Oh, Jesus God!" I storm off into the archway, bemoaning his foolhardiness. Everyone knows of the shortage of paper—the newspapers can scarce even obtain any on the black market, and depend for their sole supply upon the press offices of the White government—which only obtains paper after expending valuable foreign currency in Constantinople, or in Europe. Everyone knows about the shortage of paper because it is the specific reason why the newspapers, and all other publications, remain sworn to rigid obedience, any derogatory accounts about the government, the Army, the current campaigns against the Bolshies shorn to bits by Wrangel's reactionary watchdog censors. *"Have you entirely lost your wits?"* I shout again, whirling back around upon Nikolai. "How many nights in the black market alleys did you spend in acquiring so much paper? My God, Nikolai! The White Guards shoot speculators just as well as Bolshy sympathizers!"

"I am well aware," he interrupts curtly, "of the priorities observed by the White Army."

"And a—a *typewriter!"* I go on, aghast. "My God, *my God!* Y-You stole it, yes? You could never have purchased a typewriter—we haven't any money!"

"I made a deal, Sasha."

"So—you are denying that you stole it?"

Clearing his throat, he rasps back in low, grating reply: "We, uh, for the time being, are merely, uh, 'borrowing' it."

"Oh, dear God!"

Collapsing in a chair by the kitchen table, I watch, mortified, as he lifts the paper out and extracts the typewriter from the box. "Put it back!" I demand, glaring at him, pointing to the box. "You put that typewriter and that paper both back inside that box, and take it *all* back—the paper, typewriter, everything. Tomorrow!"

"No!"

I glance upward to find his eyes narrowed in upon me, seething with fury, his pointed finger dashed down toward the typewriter as he chokes out under his breath: "It's your Christmas present, dammit! Because I've a feeling the Bolshies will be here by then, that we'll not ever have chance for another Christmas! I wanted to give you something special and meaningful, something you would treasure forever—"

"And what in hell's *name,"* I bark back at him, "makes you think I would treasure paper and a *typewriter?"*

"The chalkboard!"

Before I can wrest upward one speck with my cane, he charges off into the boudoir—while I struggle after him, cursing to high heaven. "No, Nikolai—please," I beg, springing for him as he reaches down deftly beneath the bed, whisking out his old childhood chalkboard. "Uh-huh, fresh again!" he declares, rubbing tips of his fingers across the smooth black surface and sniffing from them an abundant yellow dusting of chalk. "Fresh like this every damn day without exception!" he goes on loudly, turning to find me blanched white and gripping my cane with both hands. "What?" he cries out, shaking the board into my face, "you think I cannot smell it, Sasha? That I am not well aware of how you spend your time when I am gone? Oh, I know—you think I think that you're painting, that you're cooking, that you're playing your piccolo. But none of that is what you truly do—or honestly are, Sasha!"

When I hold stiff without an answer, he pulls in close, looming over me, the chalkboard falling limply from his hand onto the bed. "Take the typewriter," he whispers, his breath lanced cool as ice against my brow. "Take the paper—and by dammit, Sasha Sekovsky!—be a poet."

In response, I dash out from under him and struggle back into the kitchen in a flurry of disgust, muttering out: "God! *Shit!* Hedge a bet during 'Stand-Up Night' in a tavernhouse, manipulate a few little verses, everybody thinks you're the next goddamned Pushkin!"

"For God's sake, yes!" he blares after me, storming in close upon my heels. "And was not Pushkin himself," he shouts on, reddening in the face, "naught but another unknown hack hedging bets in a tavernhouse until he *tried?* Until he paused long enough in life to look himself squarely in the eye, to embrace hold of his true calling?"

"You go to hell!" I shout in panicked defense, flailing out at him with my fist.

He catches it up, roaring back: "No, hell is where *you* are going—over the edge! Should you never deign to give yourself a chance—"

"Then I will take my hell and bask in it gloriously, Mr. Pokes-His-Nose-Into-Everybody-Else's-Blessed-Private-Business, thank you very much! *Jesus!"* I gasp out, once more appalled at sight of the typewriter. "Take it back!" I insist again, wrenching my hand away from him with a groan. "I do not want any paper, nor a typewriter—*do you hear me?"*

"And *why* not? For God's sake, Sasha—and will you stop whacking at me so! Lord, just what are you so goddamn tiffed about? Huh? Just what are you so cold blasted *afraid* of?"

"Possession!"

The word resounds thickly throughout the bungalow. Finally having uttered it, I sink down into a listless heap at the kitchen table, and close my eyes into my hands. This is the first time my cousin and I have been at odds over anything since last October, when he suggested that I go on to Europe with Aunt Sophie and the others. This, in truth, is the first serious falling out between us at all since our fateful reunion of a year ago in Latvia. Having lashed out at him so fiercely, I hang my head in shame, yearning only to thank him for his intent in bringing such a gift, aching so to tell him again how much I dearly love him beyond my anger fraught only with worry from the danger of the times.

But his avoidance of my eye, his hurt over my reaction remains obvious as, letting out a plaintive sigh, he turns away abruptly to the icebox, fishing out for his supper some *borshch*, cheese, and a thick hunk of bread. Taking a seat across from me at the table, he begins munching from the crust of rye while casting wary glances my way in between sips from his cup of cold soup.

Deriding myself soundly, I stare off to the mirror of darkness glazed across the kitchen window. Where lurks, from shadows of my mind, the phantom of his image—accompanied, as ever, by the strings and bow. Forever his muse haunts me; ever his quest in playing continues to astound me. Never does he stop, not tiring when I would long have set aside my flute or piccolo for a spell of rest. On the days when he cannot find any work in town, he instead churns out improvisations from sunup clear unto midnight, and of late, has composed several entirely new works, music strung on a symphonic scale of such daring and flamboyance as I have never heard, masterworks imbued with passionate stirrings gleaned, I well know, from the glories of Debussy, Tchaikovsky, and his beloved Rimsky-Korsakov. "I have watched you of late," I say at last, breaking the dense silence settled like a coat of ashen dust between us. "At your composing."

When he opens his mouth to reply, I cut him off with a wave of my hand, murmuring on: "And I have watched you become utterly, intractably possessed—as never before, my friend. Hours pass, and you scarce realize the time. I wander in and out of the rooms past your bare notice of me. And I have marveled at the tenacity, the steadfastness, the pure intention of your quest to do naught but become sound, to so constantly, unanimously create. And—it is the path, the way for you, Nikolai. But—not for me."

Regarding me with solemnness, he replies bare above a whisper: "Is not the devil that has me, Sasha. I swear to you, I was wrong—you were right. Is just as you said—it is truly God."

Wanting so to grasp his hand, instead, I clutch my own together, shaking my head in negation. "And as I said, for you, my love, such is the true light. But for me—"

"For you, creation is naught but the true light also, Sasha. But will you never understand? I was born to caress a violin. But you—no, not a paintbrush. No, not even flute nor piccolo, the practiced competence achieved thereon yet held wholly at your disposal, I do not deny. But the gift—that rare, beauteous thing, that inextinguishable, creative breadth of true light—to find yours, Sasha, I think you must take hold of a pen. Chalk, a typewriter—"

"But I am terrified to give myself up unto such possession!" I counter raggedly, again blanching unto a morbid, pale rendering in coward's cloak. "Will *you* never understand? *Years* have I spent running headlong away on heels of fire from becoming a bloody poet! And why, you ask? Because I know, once I heed that call, that never again shall I breathe free. Then I will be like you—possessed! But not by music, Nikolai—by words! *Atrocious words!* Which prove not so sweet and floating like your clarion call; instead, are burdensome, cumbersome, dense as stones, for so awkward a fool I am with them still, like a mason scarce learnt at his craft!"

"Sasha," he whispers back in gentle reply, "have you not given in to your words, however awkward and dense you imagine them to be, already? Have you not already surrendered unto your light, your path, your way? With my old schoolboy's chalkboard?"

Again I duck my face down into my hands. With another long sigh, he finishes off the last of his *borshch* and bread and cheese, grasps a tender hold to my shoulder, and pecks a kiss unto my clammy brow, murmuring: "Dear heart, I must go to bed before I drop right here in my shoes. If you still do not want the typewriter come the morn, then I will take it back. Whatever pleases you. You have my solemn promise."

Nodding, I stare after him in a blur; listen as he brushes his teeth and pees within the water closet; listen as he finally blows out the candles set in the boudoir and peels off his clothes, settling down beneath the sheets and bedclothes to retiring breaths of sleep.

Past waning flickers of candlelight, the inevitability of the typewriter stares me back naked in the face. From a drawer, I fetch out another candle and light it, then pull the damn thing before me at the end of the table. And I peer down in befuddlement at the center row of black-plated, gold-rimmed keys: *a, s, d, f, g, h, j, k, l.* "Lord God!" I exclaim to myself in a whisper, widely rolling my eyes. "And could they not have simply arranged the letters alphabetically? Who the devil ever thought up this sorry contraption? And why am I even sitting here gawking at it like this? Oh, shit . . . ."

The paper *would* have to slide in easily enough with only one reluctant, cautious turn of the knob. I hover for a wealth of heart-pounding moments with my left index finger poised above the *t* key—

until finally, after spewing out a long, anxious stream of breath, I type out, in one stab after another with my two index fingers: *T-o S-e-e i-n a D-r-e-a-m.*

And below it: *P-a-s-s-i-o-n-s h-i-d-d-e-n . . . l-o-v-e f-o-r-b-i-d-d-e-n . . . .*

When I finish typing the ten lines of the poem, artistic possession has warped my soul for all time, exactly as predicted. Mesmerized, enthralled, I sit staring my first token of creation—the troth plighted, the sword taken, my devil's passion looming sated and triumphant. Never before have I had occasion to see any of my writing in print. Tolya, of course, urged me to submit some pieces to Gorky while in Petrograd, but I never took the chance on account of the murder, still fearful of the police, of drawing undue attention to myself. Now, I wish I had submitted something, anything: to Gorky's, to any of the other newspapers. I wish I had not delayed so many years to see this—by God! *My poetry in print . . . !*

With impatience, I stuff in another sheet of paper and start typing, this time the old poem Father happened upon me scribbling out years ago within in this very bungalow in Yalta, the one called *Revolution's Fire.* The child's chalkboard, of course, has been the vehicle by which I have been prodding old memory of the many poems left behind in a ratty stack in Lyubov's apartment in Petrograd. Day after day, ever since last November, a few more lines have I etched out one by one upon the chalkboard, perfecting counts of syllables and polishings of the nuances stanza by stanza upon page by lengthy, memorized page. Now, after near unto five months of cramming, scores of poems lurk like festering embryos in my head, bursting for validity, recognition, *print* . . . after two hours, I whip out three long, mistake-smudged pages entitled *Revolution's Fire*—and scarce able to catch my breath, stuff in another sheet of paper . . . .

Three days and three nights it goes on, with bare any rest partaken, little food ingested for sustenance. Nikolai wanders in and out, smiling at me blandly while murmuring wordless encouragement. Count Byelov visits in the afternoons to drop off vegetables from his garden, but ever seems content to sit and watch me without speaking, a bemused expression caught to his impish, wizened face, his nods ever beckoning approval. Out in the vast, chaotic reaches of the Red and White world, the war rumbles on, but I scarce pay it any more heed, gripped without cessation by my war within: to snatch the thoughts unto words; to cast the words alive upon sheets of typewritten paper;

to then stack the papers, one after another, into miraculous, tangible, evident reality . . . .

Finally, on the third day, toward late afternoon, I stand staring at a near inch-high stack. A small book, possibly, of poetry: about Lissushka, Father, Russia, about being Russian though born both English and Russian; poetry about old St. Petersburg and Paris in the *Ballet Russe* days; long accounts about my affairs with Volodya and Tolya and Lyubov; poetry about my children, about revolution and redemption, about God and the universe, about metaphysics and passionate, awe-struck love. "Power!" I gasp out at last, staring from my wealth of creation to both fists clenched high over my head in the air. *"Yes!* This is what Nikolai meant, exactly, unquestionably! Oh, I *must* write—I *must! I must have this power. . . ."*

To ascertain that it is, indeed, Monday, I find it necessary to check the calendar twice—and then, sure enough, my scan down the beach reveals him sauntering toward home from afar down wanings of the warm black sand, apparently bereft of any work for the eve once again. My crutches, my hat I snatch up in a rush, bounding outside, and as I hobble along, I know I appear more a sorry sight than I ever have before, unbathed, unshaven now for three entire days, and clad still in the cotton shirt and old flannel trousers worn the night he brought home the typewriter. But again little does it seem to matter, for once he spots me, his greeting bursts forth in a hearty wave, and he breaks off into a run, dashing toward me with the sand kicking back at his heels, his shoes and violin case caught together in the grip of one hand. And against the roaring, salty spray of ocean surf, we tumble in upon one another right within full spanking view of Madame Rosenberg's kitchen window and her trusty spyglass. I let my crutches fall one to each side and throw my arms around his neck, while he swoops me joyously up into his embrace, swinging the both of us all the way around until landing me back with care upon my feet, our lips meeting in an unabashed kiss. "God bless you, my love!" I gasp out, wrenching myself away to tell him in humble, earnest gratitude: *"Thank you!"*

"A virtuoso, my friend," he murmurs back upon tilt of his rakish smile, "must have his instrument."

* * *

"Creation?" old Count Byelov barks out heartily, his blue eyes squinted into startling, wrinkly slits and steadied in long perusal upon the both of us. "Oh, yes," he goes on, a slow smile overtaking his face, "such is, indeed, indicative of ascension of the path."

"See?" Nikolai whispers into my ear. "I told you."

Squeezing his hand, I snuggle closer beside him upon Count Byelov's old wingback sofa, my gaze drifting about the musty room cluttered all about with tattered books and a wealth of intricate porcelain knickknacks. Summoning effort, I attempt to recall exactly how we managed to steer the conversation onto the topic of metaphysics, but then the old Count draws my attention once again with his meandering discourse.

"Individually inspired creation," he continues on, his voice dropped low in reverence, "issues from the pure self, the soul—although not the soul as most other men would so describe. Your web of light attached to your corporal form—the visage of the dear departed hysterical widows ofttimes claim to glimpse at funerals—is not, contrary to much mention made as such in sensational literature, your soul. More aptly put, it is the means of transmission by which the soul contacts the corporal form. What you must both understand is that one's web of light is merely another aspect of physical manifestation, the confluence of intellect and emotion, if you will—and is the part of a human being that, attached both earthward and heavenward as it is, discerns life's duality, and ever yearns for return unto its source during the time trapped in corporal form—that source being, properly called, the soul. For what, after all, is man's basic instinct?" he goes on with an emphatic stabbing of his finger. "Self-preservation! The love, the guarding of the self above all others, correct? To ask what this means ethereally, *not* corporally, is to begin to understand the yearning for ascent of the pathway toward the soul. The soul is one's flame of light, connected through the nest of love eternal wrought in higher vibration unto the flesh of one's earthbound lower self. Man's duty is to become the agent, the vehicle, the hands on earth of his own higher source, the instrument of his upper being, the sound note of his own distinct hovering essence—which is both the individuality and totality of God at one and the same time, both the smaller and greater of the universe, the microcosm and the macrocosm manifesting in one eternal, pulsing point of light. Only with an earnest regard for true self can a man then love others altruistically, and become a force in the world for ultimate good. Much is revealed in paradox: he who understands self-love loosed of selfishness, esteem emanating from selflessness, is attempting ascension of the path. Sooner or later, such a seeker becomes an apprentice in artistic creation—or in scientific endeavor, in world politics, or in business acumen, such as whatever his soul's inclination and natural talents may be. He strives always for improvement, betterment, perfection—both in the defining of his work and in the building of his character—until the day comes when the path is ascended upon, the corporal body and heavenly soul united fast unto becoming indivisible, never to be rent by the veil of separateness again."

"Even upon a new incarnation?" I burst out, near ready to fly from the sofa in my excitement.

"So that," joins in Nikolai, "one remembers one's past life? Or—even all past lives?"

"Well!" replies Count Byelov with another hearty laugh, his hand slapping down upon his knee, "always there follows a sort of—oh, how can one say?—adjusting period. Ofttimes, the soul takes considerable time in the entering of a new corporal body. Why, look at me! All of a hundred twenty-five years flew by, until 1738, when I finally woke up, and realized where the devil I was."

"And up until then, you were asleep?" I ask, casting at him a most doubtful glance.

"Oh, not physically asleep, Sasha Mikhailovich. Simply dazed, dumbfounded, I suppose you could say. Then one day, it was as if I suddenly 'woke up.' And I realized what I was supposed to be about, and set to my work. But worry not—you and your cousin each appear much more expedient in your respective quests than I," he goes on with a thoughtful nod. "Ascension of the path means leaving the dust of the earth behind, casting away illusion in exchange for reality. Dust, however, can scar one's eyes as one attempts to purify them of its murky essence. Earth's illusions are many, and tempting. Turning one's back on all in pursuit of the path of light is never easy."

"Then," Nikolai asks, "you think that Sasha and I are each followers upon this path? Upon this ascension to our own respective souls?"

"Oh, definitely—the very fact that we are sitting here carrying on this conversation, and that you have even broached such a question, proves so indicative. And—it might be comforting to both of you to know that pledged soul mates invariably ascend the path together."

Nikolai and I stare at one another, open-mouthed, while Count Byelov lets out a loud snort and downs a sip of his tea. "Then," I venture finally, "you believe that soul mates blend not necessarily always male and female? That they can just as well issue of the same gender?"

"Well, now—and is that not wholly evident?" he cries out with a guffaw, pointing between the two of us. "I mean, *look* at you two lovebirds! And think you that this reunion of which you told me, the way that you happened upon one another again so miraculously last year in Latvia, was naught but an accident? Oh, no! When it comes to such sacred pairs—pledged twins, whatever you choose to call yourselves—fate acts her part as regent in the name of coincidence. Oh, and fret not over that inane hogwash you hear touted either, about men such as yourselves actually posed as naught but females taking their required opposite. Yes, it is true that, during the long centuries of incarnations, one usually takes on a corporal form of the opposing gender at least once. But in most cases, the task is fulfilled early in the evolution, and during the remainder of lifetimes, one follows one's natural inclination toward one gender or the other. Remember always the old maxim: 'as above, so below.' Yes, sacred pairs can indeed plight their troth as two males, or two females, although this proves not so usual in the upper realms as the customary conjoining between male and female souls. Just as couples such as yourselves turn up not so commonly in the corporal scheme of things, correct? But—it takes a *man* to love a man," he then says pointedly. "Yes?"

While the Count winks at us, we grin back at him and lean toward one another across the high headrest of the sofa, our lips meeting in the barest brush of a kiss.

"Now, how do you go about conducting your meditations, Kolya?" the old Count abruptly demands, his tone gone harsh with the criticism of a stern old schoolmaster.

"Well," Nikolai replies, reddening, "I've not held to the traditional methods in the longest while, I must admit, Makar Serafimovich. Actually, most of my insights I obtain while playing the violin."

"And you?" Count Byelov demands of me.

I feel my own ears redden as well, and cannot thwart a sheepish shrug. "I, uh, at one time attempted most prudently to follow my uncle's instruction in the way of Yoga, studying always in the lotus position," I tell him. "But as a youth, I ever would reach for my flute while doing so, continuing my meditation while playing. But now, insights come to me all the time: I can be writing, or lying down, or slicing vegetables, or merely staring out the window. No matter—I always seem able to fall back into that quiet state rested upon inner consciousness."

"You know," murmurs Nikolai in agreement, "I must attest to such experience, also. Even while walking along the streets in town, the damndest theories will come to my head straight out of the blue."

"Good," declares Count Byelov. "Then you are both well set upon your way."

"You mean," I ask, "that one needn't take strictly to the centered stillness, or hold to the position of the lotus? To ensure proper benefit from meditation?"

"Oh, for a certainty, the position of the lotus can aid the seeker, and a spell of quiet time reserved for reflection each and every day proves most beneficial," replies the old Count. "But proper meditation strives for cultivation of the inner state of consciousness *all* the time, from dawn of morn awakening unto evetide sleep, and during all of one's daily tasks. Which is what you both seem to be well accomplishing."

As Nikolai and I trade thoughtful, studious glances, Count Byelov embarks upon the subject of dietary moderation. "What is best," he says, "although most people find the regimen somewhat difficult, is to attempt to hold throughout the entire year to strictures of the Lenten season, with the exception that butter or oil, and on occasion eggs, may be taken."

Again we nod in agreement with the old Count. Never did we even discuss the forswearing of meat and poultry; simply, over the past few months, by some unspoken, mutual agreement, began to banish all animal flesh from our table. Along with wine, vodka, and favorite sweet liqueurs, expensive as spirits have become anymore in these troubled, inflationary times. "And what of fish, Makar Serafimovich?" I ask with concern. "You suggest holding to the Lenten strictures, but is not a sturgeon or a crab, or any other creature of the sea, an animal in as much the same sense as one of land?"

"One must always remember," advises the old Count, "above all else, to observe tenets of simple common sense. Should you find yourself trapped in the wilderness with naught but a squirrel to eat in lieu of going two-days hungry, by all means, roast the squirrel! Man's ultimate responsibility is to equip his physical body by the most prudent means, for without physical well-being, the spiritual tasks can prove most laborous. The Lenten strictures merely hold forth an ideal: the more purified the body, the more purified the mind; therefore, the more approachable through daily meditation is one's corporal form to the soul. As for fish, such are not animals in the same sense as those that walk and thrive beside us upon land. Eat all the seafood you desire, Sasha Mikhailovich. Of course, there are those who, in the wielding of certain encumbrances, take asceticism one step further, and deign not even unto the partaking of fish. Should this for you ever seem tantamount, ponder upon the prospect with earnestness, and the correct choice will be indicated in your heart's knowing though your meditation."

"Makar Serafimovich," Nikolai then says, "everything you have told us seems to center upon the individual, himself, making the choice—whether about meditation, or diet, or whatever the aspect in life. Which leads me to conclude that a man is directly responsible, spiritually, only to his own soul for his choices."

"Yes, Kolya, that is correct."

"So," Nikolai goes on, "I would deduce that, when people say that God talked to them, or Jesus talked to them—or some Saint, or whoever—that what such people are actually hearing is the voice of the god in their own heart—the sound note of their own souls."

"In such so-called 'religious' experiences," murmurs the old Count with a smile, "ofttimes comes the first glimpse of the soul, the first taste of truth over illusion. After many lifetimes, the man finds himself standing alone with the One in the dark night, the same One as the I Am. Remember the scripture: 'Before Abraham was, I Am?' That is the whole quest of the path, Kolya. To come face to face with one's soul, which is one's own 'I Am.' To do so is to embrace the 'I Am' wholly, to become the 'I Am'—and at last to make the supreme ethereal allegation: 'I Am That.'"

Nodding in silent agreement, I stare downward, pondering with reverence upon my dreams of the man in the white shroud, whose hand I have so long ago since taken. Which has become as my very own.

"The Christ, then," Nikolai goes on, "was the first to ascend this pathway to the soul?"

"And so became example for all men," replies the old Count with another reverent nod.

"And if the soul," Nikolai continues on in a rush of inspiration, his eyes lit afire, "springs from God, then we are *all* sons of God . . . we are the instruments in an orchestra playing the symphony, which is God. Without the music, we, as instruments, experience no vivification. Without us as instruments, God, by definition, ceases from manifest existence. And yet, what does it mean to be a composer, a player, an accompanist, but to *become* the music, God with One and One with God?"

When he stops abruptly, letting out an exhilarated sigh, I add in a low murmur: "So—we are all inexorably bound, ourselves and God, then. For the truth, past all illusion, is that ultimately God is us, and we are God. Man can become as the God ideal—the Christ, long ago, being the first to embark upon ascension of the Godly path."

Nodding in satisfaction, as if we each have more than aptly passed his first test of expectations, old Count Byelov at last arises from his wicker chair, his gnarled fingers gripped about the handle of his cane, his bright blue eyes yet glimmering with humor, but also fading quick unto weariness. "Yes—now, come," he orders, motioning about with his free hand, "up, up, the both of you! Enough talking has this been for one carefree, starry night. More opportunity for such discussion will present itself in the coming days, I assure you both. In the meantime, an old man steadfastly requires his sleep—while young men must steal away for serving passion's end, yes?"

Back inside our own bungalow, Nikolai and I shut the front door and pull to one another close, our kiss lengthy and fervent. "Told you there was more to old Byelov than meets the eye," he murmurs against my lips, adding: "Connected heads, twin hearts, paired lovers, sacred vows, pledged souls."

"And do you think," I venture, searching his eyes, "that we have been together before? In previous incarnations?"

"Oh, I know it."

"When?"

"I—I am not sure."

I stare away, disappointed, reluctant to confess to another—even my Nikolai—his possible previous lifetime's death. Retreat to safety I find in the subject of old Count Byelov and his fantastic claim of having lived for three hundred and six years—the old man's past proving a much easier topic of conversation than our own.

* * *

"No, you are correct, Sasha Mikhailovich," says Count Byelov the following day when I decide to risk broaching the question upon visiting him alone in his garden. "As much as you love your cousin," he goes on, his wizened old hands yanking out from his asparagus patch weed after ratty, offending weed, "you are correct in the assumption that one must never take upon himself the detailing for another of his possible previous death. That Kolya has not yet spoken of it—and that he still seemed so reluctant to pursue the topic when you brought it up after leaving here last night, as you say you did—indicates that he has not yet come to terms with the matter himself."

"Then—you do think he and I have been together before? That the man behind me in my burning stake dreams might indeed be him?"

"Pledged soul mates," the old Count replies with conviction, "spend many lifetimes both together and apart, learning to vibrate to one another in harmony. Such unity with another being is a great privilege, Sasha Mikhailovich. Have patience with your cousin—remember, his Sun lies in the sign of Scorpio, the task before him immense. And fraught, in all probability, with mortal peril."

"Mortal peril!" I exclaim, bolting upward from my help with the weeding as he adds: "Oh, fret not, Sasha Mikhailovich. To truly embrace as one's own law the theory of reincarnation, each of us must ever remember Van Gogh's admonition to his dear brother Theo in his letters: upon any train, one can travel to a French town. But it takes death to reach a star."

"But, Makar Serafimovich!"

Waving off my continued dismay, the old Count abruptly returns to ordinary daily matters—the current progress in the war, the latest infringements of the weather—his head bent down, his concentration pinned with determined relish upon the weeding of his vegetable patch. For awhile I stay, observing politeness, until he loads me up with an armful of greens and a bucket full of potatoes, urging me homeward. Once I retreat inside our bungalow, soaped shirts beg for a rinsing in the laundry tub, and my typewriter, loaded with a blank sheet of paper, awaits my next inspired keystrokes. But my every afternoon task I shift through in a daze, unable to help brooding over the old Count's haunting reference to Van Gogh's words.

* * *

Summer brings us, in an abundance of warm, lazy days, further opportunities for philosophical exploration under the guidance of Count Byelov—and incredibly, favorable news of progress in the war. In June, General Baron Wrangel, now commander-in-chief, thrusts northeastward with a bolstered force through Dzhankoy and the northern reaches of the Crimean peninsula, intending a link-up with Kuban and Don Cossack armies rallying to the east, for rumor has it that though the *Bolsheviki* may have reached the sea and plundered Rostov and

Novorossiysk, the populations of the Caucasus yet remain resistant, undermining through raids of their partisan bands all Red efforts to secure hold upon the region. "They say Wrangel is gearing up for a vast offensive!" I stutter out excitedly one day to Nikolai, bounding in upon him as he sits huddled in thought upon the floor cushions in the front room, the violin aside him and rested upon his hip, the frog-end of the bow grasped within his hand. "That the Cossacks will join the White Army again," I go on with a flustered waving of both hands. "And that the Reds, over-preoccupied with the Polish war to the north, haven't the men to fend off a renewed attack from the south—"

"Best not to let your hopes run away with you, Sasha," comes the quiet reply, my cousin's eyes held before him to his own lurking wall of inevitability.

"Well!" I spout back. "It *is* good news."

"Yes. I suppose."

Good news remains tentative, teetering day by day, alternately, upon rising and sinking expectations, over the next two months. In July, Wrangel lands two detachments, said to be each over a thousand men strong, upon the northern coast of the Azov Sea—and for a month, they hold the line fast, managing even to penetrate inland from Taganrog, until giving way to defeat. But the move buys time, sure enough, for Wrangel's well-planned offensive launched thereafter into the Caucasus: fifteen hundred White soldiers landed at Novorossiysk; near unto three thousand at the Taman peninsula. Yalta hums suddenly abuzz with a flurry of excitement for two entire weeks, fresh war maps appearing by the hour each day within the quayside shop windows, for if the *Bolsheviki* possess not enough men at the seacoast to prevent a landing, and the Cossack populations continue rallying up in fury against the Reds, the Caucasus could be taken, the war rekindled, the old slogan 'Moscow by Christmas!' possibly bantered in the streets yet once again. But then, on August twenty-second, the Ninth Red Army advances and dashes our hopes back to despair, forcing the Whites into full withdrawal by September the first, and into another large scale evacuation from Novorossiysk on the seventh. "I suppose you were right again, my friend," I say dolefully to Nikolai, dropping down beside him upon the cushions. "I should never have allowed my hopes to range so high."

"Pity this had to occur the week of your Birth Day," he says, squeezing hold of my hand. "And—pity I could not find for you a more suitable gift."

More suitable gift? *Lord God*—only the rarest, most precious of commodities has he bequeathed unto me: paper, another twenty or so sheets. "No finer gift could I ask, dear love," I tell him with heartfelt gratitude. "I can scarce imagine how you succeeded in laying your hands upon such contraband."

Cocking an eyebrow, he casts me a humorous wink in reply, murmuring: "As I said before, only through considerable trouble."

Considerable trouble, indeed. In town—in fact, throughout the district—the Whites have dispensed in entirety with the notion of a volunteer army, and resorted to conscription round-ups again, much as we encountered last year during our journey through Latvia. And so for weeks, now, danger has lurked before my cousin's every step on any venturings into town to seek work. "I suppose," he observes wryly, "I could give them my name as 'Sekovsky'—which I have been using in town anyway ever since we arrived here, simply to play it safe. And I suppose, in all actuality—and to appease my own troubled conscience—that I should simply break down and volunteer, and have done with this running and hiding. But," he goes on, a tender glance cast in my direction, "I could never leave you. Call me selfish, self-serving; blame every misfortune of this hopeless war on the thousands of lovesick louts like me who'll not fight in refusal of being torn away from their loved-ones. Especially not now."

His eyes alight upon the crutches then, which duly rest at my side upon the floor, for once more have I been driven to rely upon them from morntide unto near every eve without pause, the rheumatism this year plaguing not only the joints of my ankle and lower calf, but also, in orbs of aching torment, the bones of my kneecap. "Forgive me," I tell him with a sad shake of my head. "For becoming such a burden unto you."

In response, an abrupt grip to my shoulder, his glare searing to silence my sheepish glance as he cries out fervently: "You are never a burden unto me, Sasha-Sashenka! Dearest heart of my life!"

"But I will be," I go on adamantly. "When the Reds finally ride in. When, should we choose to follow the course you have suggested, we must take to the hills."

"Perhaps the Poles in Minsk and Warsaw will keep the Reds busy for awhile—"

"And?" I counter. "What if they make peace, as goes the current rumor? Then the Reds will no longer be diverted in their attentions, and in full force they can—and will—concentrate an attack upon the south."

When he stares to the floor, not deigning to reply, I go on with resignation: "We have not much time left here in our peaceful lovers' abode in Yalta, Nikolai."

"No." Tenderly, he squeezes up my hand.

That night, I sleep fitfully, tossing and turning upon visages of guilt and remnants of old dreams: Father's florid variety of expressions haunting me, Lyubov's nagging voice cackling in my ears, Vanya's pleas for stories mounting by the hour. Darkness then settles in at last, masking their faces into a trailing blur—until the black tower rises above, its bottomless dungeon widening out in a forest thick with brambles and dusted over with a fresh layering of winter snow. Through it, we stumble helplessly, our breath tearing ragged in our chests, stark fear nipping at our heels—while in foaming snarls of triumph, they descend out from cover of the trees, sharp fangs lunging for us, massive jaws sprung wide for our throats . . . .

I bolt awake, screaming, and Nikolai latches upon me an anxious hold, gently rocking the both of us back and forth while crooning over and over into my ear: "Sasha! It—it is all right. . . ."

Out at the kitchen table, I spy the hands of the clock striking toward three A.M., and sip down the tea he has warmed, the cup yet caught atremble within my grasp. "I—I am sorry, my love," I tell him, woefully shaking my head. "To awaken you so. God, will it never end?" I go on. "No, of course not—such is the lesson the Tower, the dreaded number sixteen of the Tarot. Forever has it been my haunting muse, this terrifying looming path of my destiny—"

"Sasha," Nikolai interrupts, settling down into the chair aside mine, his crocheted blanket pulled up closer about his bare shoulders, "since when is the sixteen your destiny number?" Impatiently, he stretches his arm out across the table, his fingers fishing about for a piece of scrap paper in between the typewriter and my ratty manuscript stack. "Can I use this to scribble on?" he asks, waving out a half-sheet covered on both sides with typewriter print and my handwriting, scarce endowed from top to bottom and side to side with any white margin left.

"There's a cleaner piece over there—yes, right beneath the stack," I tell him, then demanding: "But what the devil are you doing?"

"Calculating your numerology," he says, his head and shoulders bent down to the task. "Now, let's see: per the Russian alphabet, *'A'* is one; *'L'* is four. . . ."

"Nikolai! No matter how you manipulate any such calculations, the total is scarce going to change!"

"No—but I have true doubt as to whether your destiny number is sixteen in the first place."

"Not sixteen?" I cry in amazement. "But—why else did I literally take leave of my senses while in Vienna? And why else do I continue to suffer from such horrific dreams? For years have I lived upon assumption that sixteen is the number of my destiny. . . ."

I go on sputtering out protestations until he holds up into my face his own numerological rendering, showing my destiny number to be not sixteen, but eighteen—derived from ninety-nine, the sum of thirty-six and sixty-three, my soul and outer path numbers—taken, respectively, from the totals for the vowels and consonants of my name.

"Impossible!" I shout, snatching the paper from his hand.

"Well!" he cries, pointing. "Add it up yourself."

I do so—only to prove him quite correct. "I—I cannot believe it!" I gasp, tearing a hand up through my hair. "You mean—all this time, I have been basing my life's pursuits upon an erroneous numerological assumption?"

When he shrugs, grinning in answer, I rant on: "But I am the fool who scrapes by his living with mundane plyings of ledger work! Lord Christ in Heaven, I am supposed to *know* how to add up numbers! Oh, for the love of God . . . !"

Near unto an hour I spend writing out the complete Russian alphabet and assigning it, stringently, from *'A'* to *'Ya'*, the numbers one to thirty-three just as my Uncle Ned taught me. Then over and over, in close scrutiny of my name written out in my cousin's hand upon the paper, I proceed about adding and re-adding the figures. Nodding mutely, Nikolai hovers about me, ever quick to refill my glass of tea. "Well, I'll be damned!" I exclaim finally, sneaking a most humbled glance at him. "And don't I feel like a mindless, incompetent fool."

"Anyone can make a mathematics error, Sasha."

"Yes, but from something so simple? Thirty-six and sixty-three obviously add up to ninety-nine; one needn't even impart the figures onto paper! Lord, a child's primary school exercise! And here I wile away so many years, torturing myself with visions of the Tower and awesome forewarnings."

"You know, even the sixteen itself proves not necessarily an evil number," he points out. "It does, after all, reduce to a seven, the most holy delineation of priests or priestesses, those consecrated unto God. Perhaps the Tower, in its overpowering rent image, stands for the

Temple of God—which of course, is the Temple of Man. But in any case, one must always bear in mind that all numbers, all vibrations share equal potentialities for both good and evil, Sasha—depending upon how one makes use of them in one's life."

"You are beginning to sound much like Count Byelov," I observe, surveying him with a fond grin.

"Yes, we have learned a great deal from the old fellow, my friend."

In the coming days, I ponder from morn until night upon the implication of my true destiny number, the eighteen—the number of the Moon, and the final nine manifesting within the Major Arcana in the Tarot. "Makar Serafimovich," I say one morn out in the garden to the old Count, "my astrological Moon, as listed by your ephemeris charts, is posited in the sign of Leo?"

"Yes, I believe that is correct, Sasha Mikhailovich."

"And my cousin's, I remember you said, is posited in a most similar position?"

"Yes—I think that, also, to be correct. In fact, I seem to recall that your two Moons conjunct one another within less than a degree."

Small wonder that Nikolai and I sing so attune with one another on planes both emotional and spiritual. "Indeed, an interesting combination," Count Byelov observes, shoving into my arms a fat bunch of green-topped radishes. "One always chooses the interplay of signs within which one will incarnate," he explains. "As for pledged souls, it is the ultimate challenge: compromising birth number dates; choosing the best interplay of planetary aspects with which to complement love's energies."

I stare after the old Count with fondness, nodding my head. "And did you not say also, dear old friend," I murmur in grateful reply, "that there are many like you? Who have lived far past their allotted span in years, and who roam the earth, teaching, imparting wisdom?"

"Did I say that?" he cries, ducking his head upward and lancing me with his wrinkled grin. "Well, indeed—I suppose one may presume that where there is one, others, perhaps, may follow."

"Three hundred and six years *truly?*" I demand, closely eyeing him.

To this, he pulls out from his waistcoat—to show me for the third time in this last year—his baptismal certificate, which is written in old style Slavonic letterings and dated the thirteenth of March, 1613. "Oh, yes," the old Count then exclaims, rolling his eyes. "And of course, the young man begins rationalizing to himself that the document is simply a forgery, or the like!"

Shaking my head, I grin at him again, and bend once more to assist with the weeding of his radishes.

"The choosing, between soul mates, of complementary planetary aspects," states Nikolai thoughtfully, later, over luncheon.

"Yes." Upon spooning more fruit salad into my bowl and his, I glance upward to note the sparkle in his eye, his mind obviously darting aloft over reams of questions.

"Of course, I suppose we must acquiesce to the superior accuracy of the modern calendar," he observes, wrinkling up his nose in disdain.

"The only reason you detest the new calendar, my friend," I tell him with a laugh, "is because it was the *Bolsheviki* who instigated the change."

"Humph! Oh, perhaps. But in truth, I admit that modernizing the calendar is a worthwhile contribution of 'socialist ideology.' At least we no longer lag near unto two weeks behind Europe in our dates. And the new style, as you say, indeed proves more astrologically accurate. So, in any case: I was born two days after old-style Hallowmas; add twelve days for the Nineteenth Century, and it makes my Birth Day November the fifteenth. In numerology, that reduces to a lesson number of fifty-two—compared to your twenty-nine. Actually, though, I would think our kindred hearts stem more from the striking correspondence of our astrological Moons. Plus the fact that, numerologically, our outer path numbers are one and the very same—which outer paths, though varied in events, have, despite seemingly insurmountable obstacles, yet led us into one another's arms—yes, dearest heart?"

After I meet his eager kiss in reply, he grasps hold of his fork, and with absent, pensive motions, begins waving it about in mid-air. "However, my birth lesson number," he goes on, "is the fourth multiple of thirteen—that number, according to the writings of your Uncle Ned, being one of the sacred hallmarks of initiation."

When I nod in agreement, he causes me to start suddenly upward by uttering out with a breath of force: "The Death Card!"

But when I fix him with a horrified stare, he merely breaks into another smile, murmuring: "Oh, worry not, English! Is not so much death, as the thirteen of the Tarot implies, but transformation."

"Transformation," I whisper in reply, watching in a grip of numbness as he begins picking up our empty plates.

All afternoon, I cannot shake off visions from the wolves dream, nor my worries over our fate once the Whites lay down their arms unto the Reds. Struggling to calm myself, I lie down for awhile in the boudoir, attempting to snatch some sleep, but soon enough, my attempt proves of no use, and I wander back out into the front room listlessly, the crutches thumping with effort into each step. There I find Nikolai dozing in his usual spot against the cushions upon the floor, the violin rested at his side. He awakens with a yawn, his gaze melting in fondness as he sweeps over me with a long head-to-toe glance—before his eyes pierce in with the strangest burrowing exactness, gray as flint and holding fast and rigid to mine.

Can you hear me? his voice then echoes, without so much as the slightest movement from his lips—and when I stop cold in my tracks, gaping at him, muttering incredulity, he goes on: *Shhh! Do not attempt to speak, my friend—simply nod. Can you hear me?*

Astounded past all comprehension, I sink back in a helpless blanch against the wall, nodding mutely, my tongue caught in my throat.

Good. Then let us attempt a little experiment. Glance toward the kitchen, will you, my love?

Numbly—after casting at him a dubious stare—I glance in the direction of the kitchen.

Good! Now—glance toward the front door.

Again I follow suit, and open my mouth to comment, but swiftly he brings a finger to his lips, urging quiet. *No, Sasha—do not say anything aloud. Rather, say it in your head. Talk to me in your head. No, no—don't ask how! I cannot explain how, except to say that it is very simple—all you need do is concentrate. Think of it as an invisible cord, the bond of love that binds us, which can never be broken. Now, come, dear heart—talk to me in your head.*

After several seconds of floundering, of tossing about over choices of words like an inept fool, I calm my mind enough to ask across to him: *Can you hear me?*

He nods.

My God! Going weak in the knees, I sink down to the floor and stare across at him. *Dear God, Nikolai! It is naught less but true telepathic communication! . . .*

Yes.

Holy Lord in Heaven! This is astonishing, incredible!

Oh, yes!

Did you learn how to do this from Makar Serafimovich?

No. I suppose I simply taught myself the skill on my own, at behest of my meditations. Listen, Sasha—I am going to walk out onto the beach. I want you to stay here, and see if you can still hear me.

Not only can I still hear whatever he chooses to say to me once out upon the beach—comments about the sweet scent of the limes and the oranges, and about several children chasing their way giddily through the black sand—but I *see* him, not in the distance, but at close range. As if hovering just bare before him, I see him sauntering along, his fists jammed down into his pockets, his head thrown back carelessly to the lift of the breeze. *I think I will walk into town*, he informs me, nodding. *Yes, I can see you, too, back in the bungalow: you're heading for the kitchen now; now, you're loading wood into the stove; now, you're stirring together the soup you've started for supper. No, I shan't be long. I simply want to test this, to put some distance between us, and see how long, how far we can maintain it.*

Maintain it, we do: I see him walk, in twenty minutes, into downtown Yalta; watch as he ducks his way in from the beach to the fishing wharves and then to the boardwalks of the city quays. Past *Verné's*, with its airy pavilion and groups of tables outside set for dinner with gleaming silver flatware, sparkling crystal, and pressed cloth napkins, he wanders, and then strolls past the wide hanging sign of the Cafe Yellow Parrot, another of the haunts at which he ofttimes plays violin. I warn him sharply once I spot a White conscription patrol, and after ducking into an alley, he thanks me in profusion, wiping beads of perspiration from his brow with the cuff of his sleeve. At last he turns back once more for safety of the beach to head for home—while in my mind, to my continued amazement, I watch his every step on the return route the entire way.

Straight to Count Byelov we both go at once when he returns—the old man guffawing, waving off our excited attempts at explanation of our new found 'power.' "Scarce remarkable," he declares, stuffing our arms each full with turnips and lush asparagus greens. "Simply another step mounted in the evolvement of two twin-mated souls."

That night, I touch my hand to Nikolai's, and it is as if my essence, his essence, bound together, elicit fire. I smooth my fingers across his cheek and murmur in my mind hallowed, reverent words—only to hear him murmur such back to me with the same aching, poetic regard. And again I cradle in my arms this man past whom, since living this last year and a half in love with him, I have wanted *no* other; the man whose touch causes me still to quiver like an innocent at ecstasy, whose voice peals ever with a bell of sweet, laughing resonance into my ears, whose scent, whose glance, whose magnificence of presence arouses me to such heights of passion as I once would have branded evil, that branding issuing forth from influences borne upon my formative years, but holding sway no more. Now, the bond is greater, bolder than bodily between us, borne instead of light, transcendence, ethereality. *I am, therefore, I love,* I impart to him, pressing my lips unto his and digging once again in joy for his mind's attentions—and then aloud, giving voice to thoughts of each of us, I whisper on: "I love, therefore, I *am*. . . ."

* * *

Over the ensuing weeks, Nikolai and I continue practice of our new-found faculties, ever struggling with the necessity to set bounds ensuring privacy, for exhausting it can be, possessing the power to probe another's mind, to have him comb yours unto its every last insignificant, meandering detail. And so, limits we gradually set up, intent upon allowing ourselves some spell of each day away from one another, both physically and mentally—only to come together again every eve in a renewed troth of joy, kisses reveled in, embraces partaken of, and our minds interacting with a force that pounds near like unto a harsh, swift kick into the lungs, the sound of it rung far upon the horizon, numbing the ears. After a time, the novelty of our telepathic-clairvoyant powers mutates into a state of normalcy between the two of us, providing the spark for much impetuous conversation, and remaining a comfort we each draw upon whenever in need of the other, the benefits of such closeness shared in our blessed, fervent moments together, and appreciated aptly in respective daily cultivations of inner silence. For, as the old Count reminds us with a wagging finger, although mated souls remain immutably bound together, each man ultimately must face his fate—and his God, and his death—alone. In pondering such, we each begin to spend an increasing amount of time in study upon old Count Byelov's many metaphysical books, amongst which I find various seasoned favorites: the Hindu *Bhagavadgita*, the *Dark Night of the Soul* by Saint John of the Cross, and the works of the medieval Christian mystic, Meister Eckhart. But even more compelling in the collection than these priceless flagons of eternal truth are the Rosicrucian tables—ephemerides, as the old Count calls them—with which we each begin charting the positions of the planets upon our respective dates of birth. And I learn that my nativity does not portend well: Uranus, the force of cataclysmic change, stands alone in my eighth house, while the Sun, Saturn, and Mercury, the Moon, Mars, and Venus hover closely aligned in the House of Partnership—in a configuration which can be, according to some of the interpretive books, an indication of early death. "But this can mean many other things," the old Count assures me, his hand patted to my arm, although when I quiz him about such 'things,' he makes a mere passing remark, and shrugs off any further elaboration.

Endlessly, then, I begin brooding upon the aspects, and not without justification—for come October, the Whites, after some surprising victories in the field, begin full retreat from their hapless offensive, the bulk of the Army streaming down through the Perekop isthmus and the northern straits of the Crimean peninsula. "On account of the Red Second, Sixth, and Thirteenth Armies," says Nikolai gloomily while loitering out at the front doorway, having paused to impart the news at the same time to both myself and Count Byelov. "And Budyonny's cavalry," he goes on with a sigh, "is expected to reach Taganrog within a week."

Then on the fourteenth of October, he returns from a trip into town for necessities to tell me that the Poles have finally signed an armistice with the Reds.

So, I observe, catching his glance. *You think the Reds will now unleash full fury upon the Crimea?*

Yes.

For weeks, we have instinctively been putting up bread for hardtack, rationing our wood, and hoarding, when we can, any commodities. Upon his trip next door to break the news, I ask Nikolai to urge the old Count to begin making such preparations as well—only to stare in amazement when my cousin returns just as immediately as he had left, telling me that old Byelov has disappeared.

"Disappeared?" I gasp aloud, stunned.

"Come out to the front porch, Sasha. Look at this."

Upon the front porch, I find myself staring, along with Nikolai, down at a large grain sack stuffed with potatoes, a wide tray of covered sun-dried tomatoes, several loaves of bread wrapped up in butcher paper, and a note:

> *Best wishes, lovebirds! You are welcome to the remainder of greens in the garden, whatever else you are able to harvest. And please do not hesitate to make good use of the ephemerides. An old man must continue his journey.*
>
> *B.*

Gulping, I say to Nikolai: "He has left us, then?"

"So it appears."

Together, we venture into his bungalow, which we find unlocked. The wide wingback sofa beckons as cozily as ever, the profusion of porcelain knickknacks coated with dust, but left undisturbed upon the tables. The closet in the bedroom remains filled with an old man's clothes. "Looks as if he's taken not a thing with him," comments Nikolai, shaking his head.

"My God," I mutter out. "Where could he have gone?"

"Or should we be asking: was he even here?"

"Whatever do you mean?"

"Was he here? Physically?"

"But—I've touched him," I protest. "Ofttimes, I'd squeeze his arm or grasp hold of his hand. He was scarce some kind of phenomenon, Nikolai—not a spirit, nor an angel, if that is what you are suggesting!"

"Sasha, I've known the man since I was bare the height of the wingback headrest on that sofa; no one would more attest to his obvious physical presence than I. But if he was, indeed, physical in the same sense that you and I are, how, then, has he managed to literally disappear from the face of the earth?"

We make another thorough search of the old Count's bungalow then, and follow through with a sweep of the man's beloved backyard garden, still turning up nary a trace of him, nor his trail. "Well," I say finally, "I hope whatever his journey is, that the old fellow finds the way well lit. And his pathway warm."

Warm as the old Count's way may be, wherever it is, ours proves not near so inviting. Upon news of the White Army's retreat, vast crowds of desperate, disease-ridden refugees—some bearing the dreaded spotted typhus—begin to swarm into Yalta, scores more stumbling in from the hills each day and setting up household many of them out upon the beach in makeshift shelters and old Tatar tents. Nightly, scavengers comb the sand for driftwood to either use or sell, and we find ourselves forced to ration our own diminishing supply, luxuriating in a hot meal only every two or three days. Then city services begin to break down, first milk, then ice for the icebox no longer proving available for delivery. In town, long snaking queues start appearing at every grocer's shop, rumor running rampant about an impending shortage of bread. I watch in my mind each day as Nikolai walks the beach into town to seek work—finding it rarer to come by as the cafes start to close down, the musicians, cooks, the service waiters all left behind stranded and empty-pocketed at the doors. Then White officers start openly venting their frustration out on the streets, and I cringe in disgust at the sights I take in: young women forced into alleys in open daylight and molested, children kicked and gouged at, motorcars requisitioned from civilian oldsters without any warning or payment. "You must stop going into town! I am afraid for you," I tell Nikolai finally, no longer able to bear the dangers I detect lurking about his every next step.

"Yes, agreed. Come, then—we must harvest what remains in the old Count's garden, dry as many vegetables to pack along as we can."

The first week of November, the weather turns frightfully cold, and by the seventh—the third anniversary of Lenin's godforsaken Bolshevik takeover in Petrograd—the sound of artillery fire begins echoing in forewarning from reaches of the far hills. Wrangel, the last commander in whom the old Tsarist guard had put their faith—the man who said he would go in league with the very devil to defeat the *Bolsheviki*—finally appears to have sold his soul for utter naught. Outnumbered four to one, the White army finally surrenders unto the Reds the last of the northern Perekop fortifications, and the exhausted, demoralized rear-flanked corps begin their ragged trek southward through Dzhankoy—and then through Simferopol. To at last make for the port cities: Sevastopol and Yalta.

At this time, incredibly, at letter manages to get through from Father:

> *I am sorry, my boy, so truly sorry, you cannot know. Per your instructions, I have sold the London townhouse, and had thought that surely we would then have enough to send on to you. But I simply had not counted upon all the expenses; five growing children make considerable demands. And I have a confession to make, for loath have I been to burden you with my own troubles. Put simply, the dilemma is this: near bankruptcy, for the Rhineland vineyards have borne a near total loss, those in Bordeaux only slightly less so. Fault of the war. I am sorry, Sasha. I have done everything I can think of to scrape up money, and can scarce believe, at my age, to find myself caught starting all over again. All we possess now is Winnebar. So, that is my question. Do you wish for me to sell the house, and send on to you the funds?*

Seized in a grip of panic, I switch crutches for my cane, dash outside, and hitch a ride into town on the running board of the first passing motorcar. At the telegraph office, after spending over an hour chomping at the bit in line, I send a frantic cable:

No! No sell Winnebar—absolutely, positively, under no circumstances!—I implore you, Papa.

S.
Yalta
10 November 1920

Back out on the street, bumping shoulder to shoulder with hordes of hysterical matrons and contingents of angry White officers all elbowing to make their way in to send their own messages abroad, I wander awkwardly with my cane until hailing another ride, during which I stare off at the careening seashore and city sights in a daze, the implication hounding me unto virulent throes of distraction: absolutely, positively—no matter *what*—Father must *not* sell that house! And it is more than simple sensibility and self-sacrifice on my part, the ensuring for my family of a place to live. That house, for whatever the reason, and half a world away as it is, yet seems essential to my survival. But the how and why of it, I cannot fathom; can only, as I bounce along on another bumpy ride upon a running board, continue to ponder.

Once home, I find Nikolai caught in one of the blackest of his black moods.

Upon the sand just outside the back screen door, he huddles cross-legged, staring blankly at our beloved stretch of beach now littered with filth and rubbish and the tents of refugees—his hands, ever so prone to fidgeting and restlessness, instead lying slackened, limp and lifeless before him. *What is it?* I question across to him—only to find that, mentally, he has put up a rigid wall, entirely blocking me out. "Nikolai," I say aloud, "what is bothering you so?"

"Nothing!" And he continues staring in numbness at the sand, the beach, the droves of people, the mournful lull of ocean waves.

For the next entire day, he wrests in silence with his demons. I make a stoic effort to stay clear of his path, but watch him with an ache in my heart, again reminded so painfully of fourteen years past, and his similar brooding descent upon the death of his father; then, two years following that, another such morbid, silent spell after the death of his beloved maestro, Rimsky-Korsakov. In such times, my cousin becomes as a Christ in the garden: alone, adrift, abandoned, bereft of even the slightest deified prod for comfort. For the whole eve and another entire day, he continues to shut me out, both mentally and physically, his eyes set hard as two jagged hematite stones, his mouth a gripped and whitened furrow. "What is it?" I venture finally, setting a bowl of soup and hunk of bread down before him as at last, toward the second eve, he finally succumbs to the taking of a meal. "Nikolai," I urge him, "talk to me, please!"

Sighing, he catches hold of my hand. "F-Forgive me for causing you to fret, Sasha-Sashenka—is simply that I have been pondering this last week over many latent matters. You have been forced to deal with pain over a good part of your life," he then says, glancing toward my leg.

While I quizzically search out his face for some explanation, he goes on in a lowered tone about 'karmic restitution,' stressing: "A man must die for his sins—remember?"

Easing down across from him into a chair at the table, I feel my spine go bone cold. "Nikolai," I rasp out bare above a whisper, "God help me! First the old Count, and now, you. What can such strange comments mean?"

Staring down into his soup, he sloshes the spoon around in the bowl, murmuring: "Of the future, Sasha, one is not always permitted to say."

Immediately, I start digging to probe his mind, but he again throws up that impenetrable shield. "No, my love—forgive me. I cannot share such thoughts, even with you—not on this matter," he whispers. "My restitution is mine to make alone; in no way is it yours. Please understand, I have much pressing, from many lifetimes, as a result of untold foolish dealings, due to my foul temper! My murder of Semyon Bulyarin was only one amongst many such serious errors of intention. And my time spent in the German prison camp, harrowing as it was, yet did not suffice. Not in entirety. I—I must make restitution. . . ."

"Nikolai," I say to him adamantly, "you are not the only man on earth who has ever killed another—"

"Your stabbing of Sheremetev," he counters, "was self-defense—you struck back when attacked. So, in like context, does one reconcile oneself to the perils of duty when at war: no ethereal trust is breached in the guarding of one's person, the protecting of one's comrades against enemy fire, even if life falls by the workings of one's own hand. Both instances differ grievously from hauling off and firing a loaded pistol at a stunned man's chest, scarce giving him a clue, nor the slightest breath of warning!"

His voice breaks then, and he clutches stiffened fingers to his brow, a shudder catching him visibly, intoned with the brittle clearing of his throat: "I—I can scarce bear the thought of being parted from you—*ever*—but for your own welfare, for your safety, you—you should perhaps consider staying behind. Perhaps the Reds will prove more merciful in Yalta than in Rostov or Novorossiysk—"

"Nikolai, by God—I said it before, and I'm reminding you again now: I will *not* leave you!"

Inhaling a lengthy breath, he nods. "All right. Together we will face my penitent quest, then. To do what I must do, all I know is, I must, as I said before, head north, follow the course the enemy least expects. Which means return unto what is now Soviet Russia."

Desperately, I start grasping at straws. "Earlier, in town," I tell him, "I noticed scores of ships in the harbor, more than I've ever seen at anchor since we arrived. They say they're gearing up, that an attack is being planned to retake Odessa—"

"Naught but rumor."

"—they—they say Wrangel fully intends upon remaining as Governor of South Russia—which includes the whole of the peninsula, as diplomatically recognized by the French. Nikolai, listen to me, please! They insist Yalta will be defended—"

"Simply what the White Army wants the local populace to believe. In order to prevent embarkation panic."

"But, Nikolai!" I gasp on, "will be suicide for us to take to the hills, I tell you. They say Makhno's bands have joined in full cooperation with the Reds. Those barbarous oafs will slaughter us simply for the food we carry, the clothes we wear—"

"Desire," he then whispers, cutting me short with a forceful wave of his hand, "must, above all else, be expunged. No, I am not speaking of desire for a caress, nor for a fuck, nor a mouthful of food to satiate one's hunger. The Orthodox prelates have twisted the meanings awry through many long centuries, have befuddled interpretation of the scriptures, wholly misconstrued prophetic intention. I am speaking of primal, ultimate desire. That which stands in the way of self-preservation ethereally—and which constitutes the final token, the last cache of earthly dust which must be surrendered in totality unto God, before true ascension of the path—in the choosing, if it be so—if—if it indeed be asked, of death. Over life. Death over life, reality over illusion, truth in exchange for the rending of desire in totality. A death, though, not by one's own hand, but—in a surrendering of the utmost humility to the will of the soul, a death only by—by God's auspices—"

In response, I bury my head into my hands and choke back tears, unable any longer to look at him, both loving and hating him at the same time for his insight and ken to secreted chords of truth. In these last weeks, Tower or no Tower hovering upon the road of destiny, my own forebodings, visions, and helpless thrashings night by night with the wolf dreams have not stopped—instead, have only intensified with the same looming sanctity of premonition.

The next day, on November the twelfth, General Wrangel, at last said to himself be present in the city, publicly issues orders, through behest of the newspapers, for the White Army to begin its evacuation of Yalta.

Late in the morn, our turnings of the soil in the old Count's garden at last complete, we meet one another's eye and nod.

The ceremony, he murmurs in thought to me.

Yes. It is time.

All former dabblings in Freemasonry and other such disciplines aside, I am not certain how we know what to do, but we do. From Count Byelov's bungalow, we borrow a five-tiered candelabrum, and add two of our own individual taper holders to make a sixth and seventh tier. From the garden, we pluck three of the whitest, purest roses we can find amidst bushes gone spindly with the recent burst of cold. Inside, we pull all blinds and draperies shut, and make an altar from an old crate box, spreading over it our best tablecloth, followed by most treasured possessions: Nikolai's violin and bow; my wooden piccolo given me as a gift by Father so many years long past; the picturegraph from Paris and the more recent one of the children from Winnebar; all letters and cable messages from Father and Aunt Sophie that we have received in the last year. Across them all we drape the three roses and then light the tapers, setting the candelabrum atop the crate, flanked by the Tarot card representing the Nine of Swords, our combined outer path. When all is ready at last, our nods once again met in solemn agreement, he wanders into the kitchen, and returns with a long handled butcher's knife. "Will have to suffice," he murmurs, shrugging. "Though hardly elegant."

Again I nod in reply, and on either side, we sink down upon our knees before the altar.

"You realize," he then says, "that once we plight our troths, swear our oaths—give ourselves up each unto the shrouds of our own individual starlit Christs—that there can be no turning back. Will be like being in the Army, all over again—although with never any discharge, nor chance for reprieve."

"Yes."

"All right, then." Before me, he reaches out with his right hand and grips up the handle of the knife, the blade raised straight upward.

I extend my left arm across the altar and grip my own fingers about the handle, intertwining them with his—and I watch him swallow, the knot caught hard as a flinty rock down his throat. I feel the like one piercing rivulets of thunder down mine.

And we shut our eyes.

I am, I am, the music I am, he vibrates across to me—his voice gone low and gentle, resonant as a holy song of the wind within my head.

In response, I catch his eye, and glimmer back in a hushed, swift mantra: *I am a story of light. . . .*

And then we hum alternately, inwardly, back and forth, with him starting: *I begin in the endings*,

I am the ending of all beginnings,
I offer myself as a lamb of sorrows,
Unto the greater good,
I will purge all Karma,
I will purge all Karma,
I surrender unto primal desire,
In offering unto the inner call of the soul,
For what is truth, but illusion,
And what is illusion, but reality,
I am, I am, the music I am,
I am a story of light,
And I take willingly, without encumbrance, this cloak of flame,
And I take willingly, without encumbrance, this cloak of flame . . . .

Then, together, aloud, our voices reverberating with conviction across the room, we repeat the invocation which, over the past few days, I have labored so painstakingly in my writings:

"I am He, Guardian of the Wand,
"I am She, Virgin of the Temple,
"I am She, Bearer of Fruition,
"I am He, Rock of the Foundation,

"I am He, Sounder of the Clarion,
"I am He and She, Union of Polarity,
"I am He, Apprentice to the Inner,
"I am He, Vestige of the Outer,
"I am He, Wanderer unto Wilderness,
"I am This, Mystery of the Future,
"I am This, Scale of the Watcher,
"I am This, Suffering unto Glory,
"I am This, Phoenix from the Ashes,
"I am This, Balance of the Silence,
"I am This, Paradox of Knowledge,
"I am This, Precipice of Illusion,
"I am This, Spell of the Ancient Wonder,
"I am This, Shroud of the Forbidden,
"I am This, Light of Logoic Honor,
"I am This, Master unto Karma,
"I am This, Image of the Holy,
"I am This, Keeper of the Secret,
"And am Thus, Son unto the Father:
"Conflict unto Harmony,
"Agent of Creation,
"Body of the Sacred Soul,
"I am That."

The moment we pronounce the last *t*, I find myself laboring for breath, and tear open my eyes to see him struggling in the same way, his stare fixed in shock upon our hands gripped together about the handle of the knife—for literal orange it glows, both the handle and our fingers burning bright as a torch in the night. "My God!" I gasp out, horrified. "What is it?"

"Shhh! Try to hang on—"

"But—"

Concentrate! Merely concentrate upon the handle of the knife, Sasha. . . .

But, Nikolai! I stare aghast as the orange glows dark unto a bloody hue of violet, then bright again into a sting of icy, hovering blue—and then a tempest, as if from the blast of a terrorist bomb, sears in full force across the room, my eyes blinded by the flash, the wind howling in my ears, Nikolai's voice ringing on and on within the confines of my head: *Hang on, Sasha! Simply try to hang on. . . .*

When the smoke clears, I find myself staring not at the handle of an ordinary kitchen knife, but at the most dazzling sword I have ever beheld, my thumb and fingers caught along with my cousin's up against the hilt of two inverted crescent moons which gleam in the sweet air like spun threads of virgin gold, the both of them fastened together at their backs by two sparkling golden knobs. And then I realize that I am no longer kneeling down upon the bungalow floor, but standing wholly erect over a long gilded altar—an altar from far away and long ago in space and in time—along with Nikolai, his face, his whole dashing, gray-eyed countenance caught with more beauty, majesty, and nobility of spirit than I can ever remember, the scars from his skin and ever other lingering infirmity gone . . . *infirmity? My God!* Catching my breath, I steal a peek down at my left leg—to find it straight and whole, unscathed as if never crushed in the fall from the window those many years ago. Instead, it sports up the calf a supple shaft of soft gray felt, while imparting from the bones and inner joints no hint of the stiffened pain with which I have so long battled; across sensations of the skin, not a trace remains of the old whitened, withered scars. I stare across toward Nikolai once again to find him clothed in the same linen garb as I, a fabric of gray flannel almost, but lighter to the touch. Tiny golden buttons diagonally trim the tunic, near like some type of uniform; fitted trousers and high felt boots swathe our legs. Cloaks of the same pastoral gray, draped in rich folds across our shoulders, are fastened at our chests with intricate golden amulets bearing the same crescent-knobbed symbol as that gracing the hilt of our sword. Then I glance beyond him—and behind myself, finding the both of us mounted atop a pedestal in a hall amidst a waiting throng of people, their raiment distinctively matching ours, all attitudes demurred before us in patient reverence. Suddenly, from billowing folds spread like curtains in the starry distance, emerge three figures, each ablaze with such glory and brilliance that we can bare withstand the strain of beholding them. The first and second come to our one side, while the foremost, brightest, most towering figure takes his place across from the others, at Nikolai's right hand and my left, his flashing, pearl-white gaze sweeping us each in acknowledgment as he raises high both hands and declares—in an obvious beckoning to all gathered within the hall: "Let it begin. . . ."

* * *

I jolt groggily awake to find myself staring up at our candle tapers, all seven yet caught in an eerie glow, the wax pods half melted down. From the floor, I push up onto my elbow, murmuring: "Nikolai?"

Upon receiving no answer, I peek around to the other side of our makeshift crate-box altar to see him also collapsed upon the floor, lying unconscious, his hair mussed into his face. "Nikolai," I say again, crawling over to him. "Are you all right? Wake up!"

He moves not a muscle as I touch my hand to his arm, and I crouch over him in worry. Then he lets out a gasp, a long ripple of surprise running up the entire length of his body, his eyes flying open. "God in Heaven," he mumbles out, rubbing at his temples with the heels of both hands. "The Saints help me! Feel as if I leapt off the dome of St. Isaak's and landed flat onto the Nevsky."

Nervously, I search his face. "Did you see the sword?" I ask him, my eyes drawn to the kitchen knife long cast away and lying between us upon the floor. "And the three towering figures? And the crowd of people?"

"Lord!" he bursts out, "was *glorious*—yes, Sasha?"

After blowing out the candles, we scoot over to the wall, easing in the both of us upon our raggedy throw cushions, and Nikolai begins relating everything he saw—not a single facet in his description deviating from mine. "After the grandest figure spoke," he goes on in a rush of excitement, "I felt filled with light, agog with light bursting in upon me to the bloody seams from every conceivable direction! But I could tell that the stream of energy was somehow being filtered by the figures standing at either side of the altar. Otherwise, I doubt if I could have withstood the full power of the force, that such light would have rent upon me utter destruction. But I absorbed enough of that holy white sun to feel such joy and peace, a contentment as I have never known . . . afterward, the gathering in the hall adjourned, and the figures at the altarside escorted us through several winding, tile-inlaid corridors to the triangle wall."

"Yes!" I concur breathlessly. "I remember the tile work lining the corridors as well—so small and intricate, and laid piece to each piece with such exacting care, the bulk of it colored a muted gray like our folded cloaks, but flecked in places with minute specks of black and white. And—the triangle wall!" I go on. "My Lord—a sight more majestic, more astounding than any I have ever beheld, a vast corridor filled from end to end with pulsating waves of light—and such colors as to defy all description!"

"Did you understand about the assignment?" he then asks.

"Yes, I think. We are to 'imbue colors.' Whatever that means."

"It means sound," he explains. "Ethereally, sound translates to color, color to sound. You and I, my love, have attained a state known as 'triangular affinity' on the soul mate level, which qualifies us to assist with the preparation of the triangle wall. With words of power," he goes on solemnly, "two, conjoined such as ourselves, may imbue triangles of light."

"But—how shall we do this?"

"Oh, you will see. To be honest, I am not entirely certain of the whole matter myself. Remember they said to take some time to pause and reflect? The answer, I am sure, will transpire soon enough through our meditations."

"And the light triangles themselves?" I then say. "They are, I surmise, a most special project? A tangible manifestation in the ethereal realms lending assistance in prayer, in meditation, for those choosing to so partake while dwelling upon the earth plane?"

"So appears their esoteric purpose, yes."

"After we left the wall," I go on, "it was almost as if we went home—to a place of both woods and beach, ocean and sky, an ethereal haven of sorts that has always been our home. And then we started talking about lifetimes—"

"Yes—also part of our assignment. Which comprises three lifetimes, our present experience constituting the first. Then, next time, I will come into incarnation, and you will hover in the ethereal realms, and we will learn to interact with one another exclusively from mind to mind. Following that, we will switch: you will proceed into incarnation, I will go out—and will hover above, ever watching over you, just as you did me. After that, at last, both mentally and physically, we will join together again."

"The triplicity," I observe, nodding. "Uncle Ned always stressed the archetype of the Godhead, of cycles occurring in threes."

"Yes."

"But—the interim between now and the third lifetime," I go on, eyeing him with concern. "Could we not avoid the separation?"

"Oh, but don't you see, Sasha? The whole purpose is to learn once and for all that, as pledged companions in soul, we are never separate—and that we never will be again. Besides, there is much work; remember what I said about this being like the Army? They have need for each of us, while we hover in between incarnations, to assist with more concentrated work upon the triangles."

Just then I blink my eyes, thinking that I see naught, indeed, but a flaming triangle of light dancing like a golden crown above his head—but just as suddenly, it fades. Once again I find myself staring about the room at mere mundane vestments of the earth, in our bungalow in Yalta.

Demurring to such notice himself, Nikolai arises with a sigh and proceeds directly to the front window, where he pulls open the draperies, allowing in the afternoon light—and I stare after him, debating whether to cast off my apprehension once and for all, and finally mention something to him about my visions of us together in the burning stake dream. But he turns away from the window, fixing upon me an expression of alarm, muttering: "My God—what's happening out there?"

Clambering up on my crutches, I follow after as he flings open the front door—and the sight is appalling, tragic: all up and down our small roadway, and along every other avenue terraced up into the hills above the town, for as far as the eye can see—in carts, old motorcars, brichkas, in every other conveyance imaginable, and on foot—black throngs of refugees push and jostle, children screaming at the top of their lungs, women shrieking in hysteria at one other, men young and old alike juggling satchels, trunks, boxes, and portmanteaus. As if in chimed unison, the voices climb, resounding in a frantic din above the grumbling, shifting movements of the crowd: *"Skoro budyet Bolsheviki—skoro budyet Bolsheviki!* Soon, it will be the *Bolsheviki! . . ."*

In silence, Nikolai and I shut the door and turn to investigate the rear side of the bungalow—there to find naught but panic pervading across the beach also, the camps of families breaking up, tents hurriedly being wrested down, vast piles of rubbish left behind as all on the beach make due west into town.

"They are heading for the docks," Nikolai says low under his breath. "For the embarkation."

"That is why the many ships remain at anchor in the harbor," I murmur. "For the embarkation of the White Army."

"Yes," he answers, biting his lip. "They'll first load officers and their families; then, the enlisted and their families. After that, of course, the dreadnoughts will accommodate as many civilian refugees as they can. But—my God, Sasha," he goes on, staring out the window mournfully. "Is exactly like last year at Novorossiysk, and Odessa the two other times: so many refugees, the sheer weight of their numbers alone would sink even the largest ships."

"We must start making ready," I reply.

"Yes."

All the remainder of the afternoon, we pack and tidy up, and cannot help but watch through windows at both ends of the bungalow the continuing influx of panicked refugees—the steady rumble of feet, the noisy tide of screaming never abating; the sound of four inch guns from Bolshevik armored trains descending at last from the hills toward descent of dusk. "Will it be tomorrow?" I ask, the pit of my stomach gripped like a fist, my voice rasping dry with resignation as I stare once more out the front windows.

"Actually," Nikolai says, "we perhaps have a couple of days. To be sure, White loyalists are most probably answering the *Bolsheviki* back with fire from their own armored trains. I hear Wrangel has seen to paying the engineers well, intent upon ensuring safety of the embarkation. Tomorrow, come the morn, I will venture for one last time into town. A gunsmith on the quay has promised me two boxes of cartridge clips for our Lugers. But I am afraid I must take, for exchange, the typewriter."

"I understand," I tell him with a nod, and without regret. My manuscript of poetry, now near to a hundred pages complete, lies packed already within my knapsack.

As the sun begins to wane low, we start a fire in the stove, and take the luxury of preparing ourselves a warm meal. For a few brief moments, I shun the misfortunes of the outside world and sigh in contentment to linger in the kitchen beside Nikolai, my arm rubbing affectionately against his as we both slice turnips and broccoli and celery greens, his smile fastened long upon me as he catches another of my glances stolen, with such passion, toward him. "Oh, and although it's early," I murmur, winking, "perhaps we'd best celebrate tonight. Happy Birth Day, my love."

"Why, thank you, English!" he replies jovially, tossing the assortment of vegetables into the skillet.

He whips around the wooden spoon with his usual dramatic flair, and within moments, we retire to dinner—mere rice and vegetables and beans though it may be—but splendid nonetheless. For the entire time that we sit at table, I tease him over turning all of thirty-one, while he shoots me humorous, threatening glares. But as we at last scrape our plates clean, I revert to a serious mood, and shyly extract from my pocket a typewritten paper.

"And what have you there?" he asks, grinning at me, elbow rested to the table, his chin perched upon his fist.

Although his Birth Day falls not until three days hence, something special have I wanted to give him before our taking leave of Yalta—in return for the joy in love he has given me. But as I stare at my paper, again I shake my head, forswearing such efforts as yet proving piteously inadequate, my long hours as having been spent wholly in vain, mere words remaining so cumbersome an artistic medium. "I—I wanted to have for you a decent Birth Day gift," I tell him, reddening, my ears cringing purple with shame.

"Well, decent enough this looks," he says, his gaze fetched with interest upon the paper. "You have written me a verse?"

"Yes." I hand it over but he waves me off, insisting: "Oh, no—please. Read it."

I draw back in consternation—but he urges on: "Yes, *read* it, Sasha. Why? Because I love to hear the sound of your voice! And who better to render his poetry aloud, but the poet himself?"

Reluctantly, I stiffen back into the kitchen chair, my tongue caught in my throat. "Well—perhaps I should explain," I tell him, reddening. "Swear it took me forever to piece this together. I longed to write something about you—me—*us*—but it is all so close and dear! Everything I ever attempted came to utter naught—until I began asking the question: 'What if?' What if, for instance, the both of us had not been such fools? What if, during the years with the ballet in Paris, we had loved one another as we do now?"

Nikolai's smile fades to a furrow of regret, his eyes seeking the distance as he murmurs: "God. So many lost years . . . forgive me," he then cries abruptly, squaring his attention back upon me. "So—this is a 'what if' poem? Do go on." Engagingly, his smile returns—and again his elbow finds the table, his chin the perch of his fist, his gaze, warmly swept, meeting mine.

"The title is *Sonata,*" I tell him.

"Sonata," he repeats, nodding. "For one or two instruments."

"Yes, my love," I whisper. "You and I." And I begin reading:

"*Sonata*—for Nikolai:

"*Spiral me around, Violin,*

"Spiral me around.
"Curved upon the ecstasy again,
"Strings of your taut bow
"Hard as rock;
"Rock-hard together, we are making music,
"Making love.
"Touch me
"With your fingers; let me
"Touch you with my fingers:
"Hands on hands,
"Notes on notes,
"Crashing apart into crescendos.
"Double me over, double me back,
"Let me echo your mountings on my silver keys,
"Spiral me around.

"Even during practice in the ensemble, I cannot
"Tear my eyes away from your face,
"Sneaking peeks across the rows of chairs,
"In between quarter-rest pauses.
"Yet, alas—duty calls, and I return,
"Thumbing through the scoresheets
"In a fluster of desperation,
"Fumbling over the phrases, trying to catch up,
"Pied piper pressing his own measured innuendoes
"Upon the dancing keyholds:
"Backing up the strings,
"Savoring the triumph,
"Lusting through the finale,
"Bursting into tears.
"And then the conductor shouts:
"'Hey, you! Flute! Third chair!
"'Get a hold on yourself, or get out of here!'
"Once more embarrassed to death,
"Once more must I beg his pardon:
"'Forgive—oh, please, forgive me!
"'It is just—the music—such rapture—
"'The wonder of the violins!'
"'Intensity is admirable,' he replies,
"Not without a wry half-smile.

"'But you have got to calm down and learn
"'To maintain control! Otherwise, the commotion
"'Upsets the entire orchestra!'
"'Yes, sir—I know!'
"Yes, I know.
"I do not tell him what my problem truly is:
"You.
"You, the one with that bow dashed out,
"Slicing up the air,
"Wreaking phantom yearnings into quiescent
"Harmony and churning sound into an orgiastic
"Synergy of pathos—
"Blinding, hounding me,
"With the sweetest, loveliest pain,
"That I have ever known or felt or heard.
"You, the one whom all the reviewers in the city
"Rave about in droves, constantly.
"You,
"Concertmaster, First Violin,
"Rakish blond lout with that devilish grin!
"Winking at me as you apply your rosin
"During the break in the concerto,
"Spiraling me around.

"We lie hot with sweat,
"We climb, we soar,
"We shudder in agony together:
"My hands on your hands,
"Your hands on my body,
"Mine all over yours.
"Kisses bruising, and ramparts
"Battling into our earth
"Until the spell of dusk, of dawn,
"Your whisperings fraught with tears:
"'Double me over, Silver Keys.
"'Let me echo you upon your mountings,
"'Let me follow you into the soul
"'Of your wind. . . .
"'Have you not heard what is said of you
"'In the corridors? Passion! Exuberance!

"'Artistry and genius! How I have longed
"'To touch, to hold, to worship
"'Your frantic, flying, beautiful,
"'Fragile fingers,
"'How long have I longed . . . .'
"My voice answers you,
"Quiet sobs lashing unto darkness:
"'Spiral me around, Violin,
"'Spiral me around . . . .'

"Our love
"Catapults through the cosmos,
"Wheels on ice,

"Song
"Of the
"Electric stars."

Upon finishing, I gaze for a long while at the paper, mortally flushed to my ears, embarrassed, chafing at such open surrender of my vulnerability, even unto him. And as the clock ticks on between us, he says not one word at all in response to my poem. Forcing a glance upward at last, I encounter his eyes widened upon me, and his pallor frightful, both cheeks blanched to the hue of death, his jaw trembling past a rigid, iron clenching of his teeth. "Nikolai!" I gasp out, lurching toward him in dismay. "What is wrong?"

He reaches out then, and thinking him to want it, I hand over the paper, but it is my hand that he grasps up insistently instead—and I land hard into his lap as he clamps both arms around me, his head tucked into the well of my neck as he starts shaking, from head to foot, with sobs. "Wheels on ice," he rasps out, fingers floating up through my hair. "No traction! Oh, dear God, Sasha—a poet, a sage beyond all earthly measure you are! My love, my dearest, blessed heart . . . !"

Never has my cousin been one given easily to tears, even in his darkest, blackest, nor in his most euphoric moments—yet now, tears stream out from him in a torrent, soaking into the collar of my shirt. "I—I meant not to sadden you," I whisper, choking back the sticky threat welling up within my own throat. "Simply wanted to wish you a *happy* Birth Day—"

"You have made me more happy than any man alive!" he cries out, throwing back his head and seizing me downward into a tremulous kiss.

We keep kissing until we near end up splayed upon the floor; keep kissing as he drags me along with him, hoisting me up with impatience full into his arms once I start paying due favor to my leg. I part my lips to devour his again and again as he stumbles with me into the boudoir, as we both land, in a heaving crash, down upon the bed—the kisses still tearing between us in heady succession as my hands, his hands dart everywhere, stripping off his, my clothes . . . .

All night, we abandon ourselves to the onslaught, making love with such violence and ferocity of desperation as we have never dared—fucking, sucking, clawing like a couple of savages at one another—until we both lie spent, exhausted, unable to lift our heads or even a finger. Then a spell of sleep rekindles lusty urges yet again, and we tumble once more upon each other with renewed devouring intent. Dawn breaks, and I struggle with myself to elbow away, mumbling distractedly against his mouth: "You—you meant to head into town. Shells for the Lugers—"

"Will wait another day."

"But—"

"Shhh! Strike that damned Virgo practicality, not now, English!" And then, in a comforting tone: "Shhh, trust me. The White trains are yet holding the line. We will have enough time. . . ."

And so all day it goes; all the following night, it goes, neither of us set to bear departing the bed. . . .

Finally, on Sunday morn, the fourteenth, I awaken with a contented sigh to hear him rustling about in the front room. When I turn to nuzzle my nose into his pillow, wishing only to bask in the delicious, lingering scent of him, I find beside me one of the white roses, a bit wilted, but none the less beauteous. "For you," he whispers fervently from the doorway, fully dressed, my poem and another piece of paper clutched within his hand.

Shoving upward, I throw my arms out wide, and as he comes to sit aside me on the bed, I fling both fists around his back, crushing him to me in delight. "And what have you there, love of my life, jewel of my heart, song of my soul, love-fucked forbidden fantasy of my whole rapturous, elated being, forever and evermore?" I whisper in a rush, moaning, sighing against him.

"Well," he answers, his lips edging upward in a hesitant smile, "I certainly could never hope to concoct a love poem such as the gem you wrote for me. But—these verses have been lolling about for so long now within my head. In truth, I scarce even think I am the one who wrote them—I think you did."

And he hands me a scrap of paper upon which reads:

Nurture me with longing,
Kindle me with tears,
I will love you always
In a hundred-hundred years . . . .

I catch my hand to my mouth and attempt to swallow, but cannot—and when I glance at him again, he nods and pulls me once more into his embrace, whispering: "You see, there is no death, Sasha. Only life. Yes, it was me. Behind you at—the burning stakes. Always has been, always will be."

To tears I then succumb, in a flood, sobbing until my nose begins to ache, my eyes reddened at the corners. "I—I longed to tell you," I say at last, choking hoarsely and leaning in exhaustion back against him.

"Yes. I wanted to tell you, too. But the responsibility—"

"Yes."

"Well, in any case, it appears we have now bared our final truth to one another, dear love."

Kissing him once more with joy abounding, I murmur: "Nikolai, what does it all mean? A 'hundred-hundred' years?"

"I think," he says, slowly and carefully enunciating each word, "that it means that you and I share an incarnation together every one hundred years."

"Every one hundred years?" I echo, going cold with awe—and as I pour through possibilities—remembrances, dreams—in my mind, I begin suddenly, as never before, to sense strange visions and quests for peace, pride, and soulful redemption all lost somewhere in the annals of prior time—but with him, always, at my side. "But, Nikolai," I go on, "what does it mean then, the 'hundred-hundred?' The one hundred mentioned twice?"

"Because, I think," he tells me, his eyes gone solemn and glinting almost as dark as my own in the murky slant of morntide light, "that when we near completion this triad, this three-lifetime project of ours, and again each manifest, at the same time, in physical incarnation, another one hundred years or so from now—that then, it will be for us, together, the one hundredth time."

To this, I shake my head in astonishment, pondering the implication of such a statement. "But one hundred multiplied by one hundred," I whisper to him, "is naught but ten thousand years!"

"And so, we are relatively young—yes, my friend?" he replies, grinning and snatching at my cheek with a playful pinch.

"Nikolai! You mustn't joke about such a thing."

"Who's joking? Imagine, if you will, dear heart, the 'hundred-hundred-hundred' years in age of someone like Count Byelov."

Nodding in reverence, I pull the blanket up across my chest, fending off a shiver—and then a wince—at abrupt unfortunate reminders from our present incarnation: the renewed drone of guns and mournful hum of doom that both of us have been attempting to ignore over the last day and a half, artillery fire from howitzers and armored trains once more picking up in ominous forewarning from the distance.

Frowning at the noise himself, Nikolai leans close and kisses me tenderly again; then presses hold of my hand, murmuring: "I am going to head into town now, dear heart, to fetch those shells for the Lugers. And to steal for us a horse."

* * *

He hands me the binoculars, and in spite of myself, I whisk off my spectacles and stare through the double spyglass yet again. To face outright the stark cruelty of man's inhumanity to man: far below us lie the city quays and Yalta harbor, its docks engulfed unto every last pitiful, creaking plank in a swarming sea of refugees. Scarce but ten ships remain, out of the dozens anchored only an hour past. As a small cargo launch bearing the name *Nadezhda*—'hope'—weighs up and finally begins to shift out, another collective scream wafts up, people throwing wide their arms, outstretching desperate hands in pleas for reprieve. Both by accident and upon intention, several tumble off the pier and straight into the water, those so doing making a swim for the stern of the ship, although to no avail. Spurts of gunfire once more start rattling across the breadth of the hysterical crowd, both men and women alike yanking out hand pistols and turning the barrels to their ears, temples, or to the insides of their mouths; some even pausing to first level lethal aim upon members of their families. Sickened by the sight,

I yet cannot tear my gaze away from the horror of watching a very proper gentlemen, clad in English derby and dark silk cravat, produce from his waistcoat pocket a hunting knife, with which he then systematically proceeds to slit the throats of his five children—all standing, to the end, lined up in mute obedience in front of him upon the dock—before turning the blade upon his wife, and then himself. "Blessed God have mercy!" I rasp out, seizing away in a cringe of disgust and shoving the binoculars back at Nikolai.

Mouth set grimly, he peers once more through the thick lenses toward the docks, murmuring: "So, it is over. The Reds can at last claim victorious their hideous Russian Revolution."

Still wincing, I slip my spectacles back on and glance at a nearby gaslamp pole, upon which flutters a fresh-printed, runny-inked evacuation directive, its blunt flag of warning pasted hastily over shreds of old mobilization posters from late 1917, the first days of the White Army. At the base of the pole, huddled down upon the cobblestones in a cocoon of raggedy skirts, sits a woman indeterminable of age, wasted and unkempt, a lost and forgotten waif of the world left behind, apparently, by whatever family to which she once laid claim. Tears streaming down her face, hands hacking up through loosened, graying hair, she continues leafing aimlessly through page after page of an old French fashion magazine—all the while bemoaning the loss of elegant gowns she once wore, the extinction of balls she used to attend, the ruin of what was once our world by the savage, godless *Bolsheviki.*

"Come," urges Nikolai, nudging me as more rumbling from the turreted guns of armored trains shakes the air above our heads. "It is all over. Let us go."

For one final time, I survey the harbor to watch the last of the big dreadnoughts, the cruisers, the cargo launches weigh out. General Wrangel himself is said to be on one of them, and must be given credit for having stayed unto the very end, for seeing personally to the evacuation of the bulk of his army, those who could make it to the docks in time past the burgeoning encampments of refugees—through which the White soldiers could find their way only at point of their bayonets. "Budyonny and his murdering thugs will slaughter these people," I say, yet riveted in numbness to the sight below us.

"Sasha," comes the gentle reply, "there is naught that we can do."

Loathing my helplessness, I nod in agreement, murmuring: "Yes, so it appears." Letting out a long sigh, I belt Father's old jacket snug about my waist, pull on my second-hand sheepskin greatcoat, and take the knapsack in which rests my typed poetry pages and the case containing Nikolai's violin. Slipping the straps on forward, I grasp our most treasured contents at my chest.

Our larger knapsack, filled with a stash of potatoes and dried vegetables, along with a scanty kit of camping supplies, Nikolai hoists up across his back. Turning once more to the mare, he pats his hand across her muzzle while whispering softened, cooing words, attempting to steady the poor creature's nerves against the mounting roar of artillery fire.

With effort, I make my way via the assistance of a long-handled cane to the horse's right side flank, slip the cane through the cinch, and hoist up into the saddle. Nikolai follows suit from the left-hand side, easing in behind me—and leans forward, his warm fingers brushing back a wisp of my hair, his lips pressed in a fervent kiss upon the nape of my neck. "I love you, Sasha Sekovsky—with all my heart," he whispers. "For the last time—would you rather chance mercy at the hands of the Reds? Do you wish to stay behind?"

"Whither thou goest, so I go, Nikolai Zhelanov," I whisper back, grasping up his hand as he slides it across my thigh. "Thy people shall be my people. Thy god, my god . . . ."

In silence, he nods and takes the reins as I hand them backward. From the weeping woman and the empty, trash-ridden streets, from the harbor nightmare of last evacuating ships and the terrified families of refugees, we determinedly turn our backs, forever forsaking our precious year of love so sweet and dear spent in sunny, beachside Yalta. The reins snapped up with a firm, decisive shake, Nikolai urges the mare off into a headlong gallop past his hearty bellow of: *"Yaaa!"*

* * *

For three days, we ride, and it is just as in Latvia—he seems ken to every nook or crevice in our path, to every next threatening rift of road or treacherous, lurking pothole; seems even to sense scattered rankings of Red Guard units, and the many coverts of Makhno's vicious bandits whom we find combing the forests of the hills. As a precaution, we scavenge through a group of corpses, and soon enough ourselves bear black and green and also Bolshy red colors wound in ribbony strips across our arms and chests. The move proves a wise one, for later, two partisan scouting patrols corner us as we attempt to slip by outer skirmishes of the front lines, the hills swarming with encroaching Reds. Nikolai suavely talks our way to safety past the whole lot of them, while I grit my teeth in earnest, panicked prayer, my fingers clutched to the butt of my Luger beneath cover of my coat. Come nightfall, we retire within rushes of the heathery mountain slopes, and alternate between one of us snatching for himself some sleep, with the other remaining awake to keep watch. All goes well until the third day, when, in the hills within foggy, faraway sighting distance of Sevastopol, Nikolai's trusty prescience abruptly disintegrates away, his wits scattered to befuddled distraction and our minds no longer able, as they have over the tiresome hours of riding, to unite in telepathic connection for the inward carrying on of conversation. "For Lord's sake, what is it?" I cry aloud, urging him to pull up. "Nikolai!" I exclaim, leaning back against him—only to sense a frightening warmth to his skin. "Are you ill?"

"No!" he blares out in ragged protest—only to slump near to the ground as he dismounts, his fall saved by the barest lunge for the mane of the horse.

I scramble from the saddle and charge around to catch him at the other side just before he finally does fall. "You *are* ill!" I gasp, biting back a renewed surge of panic as I brush tremorous fingers to his brow, finding it damp and clammy to the touch. "Damn! Tell me—what is wrong?"

"A cave," he mutters in reply, shaking his head, pointing northward. "Another verst or so, I think there's a cave. Boris—you remember my pudgy cousin, the French horn player? We rode up here one time, to bare east of Sevastopol, from Yalta. I think I was about fifteen—was just before I started at the Conservatory that autumn. I—I remember we camped out in a cave—"

Once I land him back upon the horse, shoving in behind on the saddle myself, the cave proves difficult to find, elusive for another half hour, while we skirt steepened crags and scraggly bunches of trees upon the fringe of a Red Guard patrol warily alerted to our presence. At last I take to ducking from tree to tree, hiding us behind and holding my breath against any outright glimpses of detection, while Nikolai continues slumping in front of me, complaining of headache, fever, nausea. "There!" he blurts out finally, pointing with relief. "The cave! Through that copse of trees."

The mouth of the cave proves scarce large enough to fit the mare through, and the moment we steal within, Red Guards in the dozens begin combing through the perimeter outside, their hollers to one another echoing in disdain against flat, high shafts of the mountain boulders. "Shhh!" I urge Nikolai, my hand pressed over his mouth as we huddle, both of us daring not to move, against the dank wall of the cave. "Hush, darling, dearest love—I'll fetch you some water in a moment," I go on, kissing his cheek, his temple, attempting anything to quiet his raging moans. "Yes, I know you are not feeling well, my love. I'll fetch water for you in a moment. . . ."

Finally, miraculously, the Red Guards take their leave. "Spring," Nikolai whispers, gesturing frantically toward the inner tunnel of darkness. "There's a spring far end of the cave, at the second mouth—yes, there's a second entrance. Just outside it, reach down—you can near dip your canteen into the tiny spring there, I'm certain."

From the spring, I return in due haste, my canteen dripping with water, to find him rummaging through his knapsack and fetching out from it the tin of powdered quinine. Only then do I grasp the true gravity of his state, for we had paid the druggist dearly, forswearing use of the quinine save for only the most dire of emergencies. "Mix a spoonful for me, please!" he begs, thrusting his tin cup upward with a shaking hand. "I—I can scarce even think one word clearly to the next! Oh, God . . . ."

I mix quinine and help him to drink it; help him off with his coat, loosen the collar of his shirt, and sponge a moistened rag across his perspiring brow—only to feel him yet burn up like a festering torch, his lips soon drained of all color and trembling with every next intake of breath. "Nikolai," I say to him, "the last time you ventured into town before we left, do you recall lingering near anyone taken sick? Did you perhaps happen to pause overlong in the queues? Brush aside any refugees?"

"Are you *mad?*" he exclaims, glaring rank perturbation at me in reply. "Of course I shunned any and all refugees! Last rumor had it, more than half of them were bearing full-blown spotted typhus!" Squeezing fast hold of my arm, he goes on with insistence: "Oh, for God's sake, Sasha! Is not the spotted typhus, for love of the Saints! Dmitri was down with a flux when I last saw him, on my way back, the day before we left, when I exchanged the typewriter for the Luger shells. Is perhaps only that."

He sleeps for awhile then, and I cover him over with both the bedroll and a saddle blanket, wincing at his every labored, rattling breath. The mare I then see to, fetching her a nosebag of oats from the saddlebags.

Upon my further inspection, the cave proves a pleasant abode of sorts, the spring lapping merrily at its opposite end, the floor down its center covered with beds of moss and sparse, straggly ferns. Evidence of prior encampments—by Reds, Whites, Greens, or whomever—abound in the embers of old campfires, although most such tell-tale remnants appear only after rather persistent digging through the moss on my part, attesting to a length in age of months, or even years. "Praise God," I murmur to myself, "luck was with us as this last patrol skirted by, none the wiser to such a tidy hiding place in the mountains."

Back at Nikolai's side, I crouch down as he awakens, his body caught in shivers from head to foot, his voice scraping deep in his throat as he whispers out: "M-More quinine! Please . . . ."

Two more days of sponging his brow, two more days of administering generous doses of the quinine, prove for utter naught: I awaken the third morn to find him flushed and sweating to the hilt, the fever raging higher than ever, and his arms and chest covered to near every inch with a rash of mottled red spots that drain to blood against his furious fits of scratching. "My head!" he moans out, lolling against me and clutching his brow in a fierce grip of pain. "Sasha-Sashenka, do something, help me, please! Ohhh! M-My aching head . . . ."

"Oh, God," I whisper, crossing myself. "Naught, indeed, but the spotted typhus . . . ."

After that, time melts into a vast continuum of uncertainty and desperation, the days, the nights waning by unbeknownst and unheeded as I sponge his brow, continuing to administer the quinine and forcing him by the hour to down some water. Thrashing about upon the edge of delirium, he finally can no longer arise even to munch down a bit of hardtack, or heed the rousings of nature's call. Instead, I start to catch his urine in one of our tin cups, inspecting with dismay each time the brownish discoloration of the fluid, and finally its scantiness, bare even a dribble after untold hours of prostration and my constant urgings for the taking of water. Another two days pass, and more spots manifest on his arms and chest, some appearing even on his legs; then all meld together in a thick dark rash of murky reddish-brown, and to my relief, he at last stops scratching. "Air!" he cries out in his more lucid moments. "Need air . . . ." As ever, I attempt to drag him as close as prudence will allow to the open mouth of the cave, only well aware enough myself, at behest of my father's years of doctoring, of the need for cleanliness, for fresh, pure air against such as the typhus—for a week of our presence coats the inner reaches of the cave with the reeking, putrid stench of humanity caught at its worst, and after a time, I myself can scarce eat, all appetite long diminished, the raw potatoes, the dried vegetables, the scraps of hardtack tasting thick as paste and lying lifeless and sallow upon my tongue. Each night, the *burya* wind whips up, howling through the mouth of the cave with bidings of winter, no longer broken as it was in Yalta by steep, protective shoulders of the northward mountains. Not daring to risk a fire, next to Nikolai I continue to huddle faithfully, my arms wound around him, attempting to warm both him and myself while only knowing that I risk catching the infection as well, probably already have it; that the both of us will now most likely meet our sorry end wrung dry of the rot of disease in this chilly, hidden cave. Come the morn—every morn—I struggle with pangs of conscience, watching over Nikolai as he dozes in fitful lulls of sleep. For again, once some warmth of sun encroaches, I sit back from him for a spell, pausing to reflect, to think—and to oil my gun.

Again sin beckons toward me its wily finger of temptation. So simple, so easy, so final would it be to end it all now, here, abruptly—one shell to his head, and one to mine. His suffering would be alleviated; mine averted—along with this insane quest he insists upon pursuing north—to 'blend in, to become proper Soviet citizens,' as he has said. Such, I think, is far from his true aim, for still he remains bent like an Orthodox fanatic upon making restitution, as he calls it, for achieving absolution for his murder of Semyon Bulyarin. And yet, I understand, for I too stand guilty of errors of intention—and know that ultimately, one must oblige the call of Karma by following the whims of one's heart. Nonetheless, I stare once more down at the Luger, cursing, fighting with myself, fending off a shudder, then to bite my lip and reload a cartridge clip up the pistol butt and fasten closed the catch. Reaching out arms-length, my breath searing into my lungs, I aim the sight of the gun with both shaking hands down toward Nikolai's slumbering head.

My fingers continue their trembling unto a violent squall of contagion, tears choking my last wayward breaths unto a blurry daze as I glimpse again, mussed about his furrowed brow and teasing at the notches of his open shirt collar, those blond locks I so dearly love. I try to imagine them blood-soaked. I try to imagine, as I shove the barrel of the gun hard into my left temple, if—after blowing half of his head to gruesome, lifeless bits—I could possibly pull the trigger on myself.

Fate's answer already bodes deep within my guilty, remorseful soul. Numbly, I ease the Luger down and tuck it away. Such is without doubt the ultimate taboo, the most profound of all errors of intention—the taking of one's life upon one's own egoistic presumption. Before the due working of God's auspices . . . .

On the eighth day, the fever breaks at last, his body becoming drenched in a cold, runny sweat, his headaches finally easing, but the delirium mounting with heart-rending, poignant force, his every utterance tinged with some descent into the past. Mostly, of the prison camps: "Yes, Herr Commandant!" he gasps out in broken German, while I hold him, his hands thrashing forward in jerky, stirring motions. "Yes, mein sir—yes, mein sir! I—I am mixing the mortar . . ." And I cling onto him with shudders of despair, attempting to whisper words of comfort while choking back my own tears, for as our second week in the cave begins, I watch the hands that I love—hands so gifted with the call of music beyond all mortal compare—cringing as if before a prison guard: "Yes! I am mixing the mortar . . ." Blindly, those hands toil and work, stooping to the sloth of manual labor. Hour by hour, he mixes mortar, lays bricks, rolls out wire fencing—and shrinks away from the onslaught, his teeth gnashed, eyes squinted in stoic effort against lashings from the bullwhip, bruisings from the billy-clubs, one blow after another. "No escape, no escape!" he sobs out again and again in the same broken German, collapsing onto my knees, begging unto shame for mercy. "Yes, mein sir, I promise, I swear! No more try to escape—*please!* Stop, I beg you . . . Russky soldier no more try to escape. . . ."

That night, he awakens me with a start, and begins speaking in French to someone called Emile.

"I must tell you about my cousin Sasha, Emile," he whispers, ducking his hand down across his lips—as if some towering presence, looming over with disapproval, might see. "He has the darkest, reddest hair you ever shall see—grand as the fire of garnets crowned in bejeweled gold! And the most soulful Russian eyes, Emile, the irises dark and onyx-like as the pupils. And the finest countenance, the proudest lift of the head my Sasha has—oh, Lord! So long have I berated, tortured, fought with myself in the long nights, harshly examining my motives, asking over and again if the only reason I care so for my cousin is on account of his remarkable beauty! But my feelings soar far beyond base lust, Emile—poetic the lad is, and a patron of music himself. Yes, an accomplished flutist, my Sasha is.

Although—God forgive me!—he was scarce ever *mine.* Oh, but he *shall* be—I swear it, I can feel it! Even now, I can sense his thoughts from afar. And somehow, I suspect him now living in Petrograd, for whatever the reason; most probably, he and my Uncle Misha have boarded up the Novgorod house, and moved into the city on account of the war. God . . . *damn* this war! Damn my utter foolishness, chasing off when I scarce had to! Oh, why am I ever the bumbling fool? I could see that he loved me, yet I ran straight away! Was not from Elena, nor from our poor son barely birthed and promptly buried—was from *him.* And *why?* Perhaps, because of a fear deep down, that with Sasha, it would be unlike any other love: all-consuming; blinded; a passion reeling distraught, with never any end . . . oh, but I am no longer afraid of such sharing, Emile. If only you knew how I yearn for him, how I always have! Yes, well—perhaps you do know. And after the war, you will indeed return to Paris, and again find your dear Jean-Jacques. And perhaps the day will come when I can hasten back to Petrograd, and at long last reunite with, beg forgiveness of my Sasha. . . ."

Then he begins to weep—in torrents, buckets such as I have never seen. "Will never get back!" he sobs, seizing frantic hold of my hands. "Will never find my way home now—oh, God, Emile! Is all hopeless—damn, stinking Bolshevik revolution! Now will never make it safe unto Petrograd! . . ."

"Nikolai," I whisper hoarsely, "you did make it back. Don't you see? It's *me—"*

"Help me, Emile! I swear I shall lose my bloody mind in this godforsaken German hellhole! Dear Jesus God, I live now only for one goal in all of heaven or on earth: to someday find my beloved Sasha once again. . . ."

Come the morn, he sleeps at last, and I leave him dozing and head with the canteens for the spring, there to splash a good amount of cold water upon my face and down my neck. In exhaustion, I peer out from the mouth of the cave to spot the high boulders and scraggly brush dusted lightly with snowfall, the ground below covered by about an inch. In my mind, I gauge how many potatoes we have left, debating how long it will be before I must find it necessary to waste a pistol shell on a squirrel, or hare, or some other such unfortunate creature of the wild. And as if food for ourselves was not becoming trouble enough, oats for the mare are beginning to run short . . . sighing back pain and worry, I crease my fingers to my brow, shuddering against a dull, ringing ache. But then I hear Nikolai moaning again, and hurry back into the inner reaches of the cave.

To find him staring up at me, wide-eyed, once I pull back into his view. Jaw dropping, he wrests himself up with a start from the pack of blankets tucked in behind his head, gawking at me from head to foot and muttering out in amazement: *"Sasha?"*

Letting out a heave of relief, I drop down beside him and fill a tin cup high with water, urging: "Here—no, do not try to talk—*drink.* Yes, yes, bless the Saints! Looks as if you are, indeed, much better—"

"It—it truly *is* you!" he cries, clinging onto my arm as if to never allow it free.

"Of course, love of my life, dearest joy of my heart!"

"Oh, *God!* I—I thought I had merely dreamt it—*everything!* The reunion in Latvia, our journey southward, our year spent alone together so blissfully in Yalta . . . oh, Sashenka—thank God! Then our love, it—it is all *true!"*

"Hush, darling," I whisper, smiling reassurance and pressing kiss after kiss unto his brow. "No, you mustn't arise just yet—you have been very ill. Here, pee in this other cup for me."

"What the devil are we doing here in this cave?" he gasps, wrinkling up his nose in disgust at the stench.

"We've been stuck in this cave because you have caught yourself naught but a grand spanking case of the spotted typhus, my love."

Gaze draped with sudden weariness, he stares around, the memory of the last weeks creeping back. "Oh."

Over the next few days, he recovers swiftly, his urine no longer proving so scant, and its color returning to normal. His skin clears almost entirely of the rash, and soon enough, he is bounding about upon his feet again, and venturing out, at the end of the week, to strip down partway and wash up in the spring. "We'll need to burn these clothes, once I get completely over it," he says, loath to put on his soiled shirt again. "Thank the stars we each brought an extra change along. But then we'll risk ourselves a fire and cook a grouse or something, eh?" he says with relish. Peering toward me in concern when I deign no answer from my perch crouched just behind him inside the mouth of the cave, he blurts out: "My love! Are you all right?"

"I—I feel fine!" I snap shrilly, bolting to my feet and storming back inside.

He sprints after me, and catches up just as I slump with a groan down against the cave wall, my fingers clutching at dirt pods and bits of moss, my cane teetering down to the ground. "God, y-you're burning up!" he chokes out, his hand smoothing over my brow—while I cringe against wave after wave of nausea, my fists clutched against the gnashing pain in my head . . . .

Nikolai rips open the buttons down my shirt to reveal, flushed across my chest, a rash of dark spots pinpointed each upon the skin in tiny gleaming testaments of blood.

"Oh, God," I moan out, catching his harrowing glance. "N-Naught but the s-s-spotted t-typhus . . . ."

After that, time floats, and I wander. I try to drink the water and quinine that he forces upon me, but shrug away any and all food, save for crumbly bits of hardtack. Finally, I can no longer even bear the thought of that, the nausea becoming overpowering but never welling up to the blessed retch of relief. I burrow back into pillows of saddle blankets that he keeps tucking up about me with tender care, and through nights melding into day after day, I stare up at him, sometimes knowing him and sometimes not, although ever heartened by his cooing words and admonitions to rest as, without ever taking any such pause himself, he sponges cool water across my flaming brow. Once the fever slackens, I become cold, deathly cold, and each morn and eve through the mouth of the cave, the *burya* wind howls deep into the marrow of my bones without a single moment's abatement—chilling, frightening, hounding me with scarred dreams and strange, futuristic visions. In Uncle Ned's library at Winnebar, I carry on a long all-afternoon conversation with Father, attempting to convince him that I will not be coming to England—at least, not this lifetime. And he argues with me much as he ever did, demanding explanations, refusing to listen to reason. Angered, I storm out the door—and into a hallway lit with stars, there to meet Melissa, her hair caught back in a lovely old-fashioned bouffant, her gown beaded up the neck and down the sleeves in an elegant muted gray, its hue precisely matched to Nikolai's and my uniforms worn during the ceremony with the sword. Melissa attempts to explain to me the significance of the ceremony, but just as so long ago upon her visits during my imprisonment in Sheremetev's ungodly palace, she speaks in naught but riddles that I can scarce understand, leaving me adrift with unanswered questions. Then, one after another, I make my peace with various people: Volodya, Tolya, Marnya, all to whom so much more I would have said before losing them, only given the chance. To Winnebar, I return once again, and see Zhenya from a far, windy distance: first romping through the lawns with the twins and with Vanya; later, strolling demurely, her gloved hand rested upon the arm of young man who adores her—a British officer with fierce eyes and shiny, coarse black hair—her divine paramour, her legendary Heathcliff. Vanya I then begin to follow, over a course of years: I watch him growing up, my father and Tatyana ever tending to his every need, from primary school until his university years. After which he, too, becomes a British officer . . . finally, it is to Lissushka and my youthful roots that I return—and suddenly, I am thirteen again, and it is summer, with Nikolai visiting for a week before setting off on another jaunt with his parents southward to the Crimea. Without mercy, he churns out on the violin Rimsky-Korsakov's *Flight of the Bumblebee*—while I storm about the room tearing at my hair, for all day, everyone on the farm has been goading me to no end again about my fear of bees. 'Stop it, I tell you—stop, you fiend!' I shout, throwing books at him, while he grins and darts out of the way, the bow twittering back and forth across the strings to mimic the hovering, frantic drone of a swarm of bees. 'Zhelanov, you turd-brain!'

'Fear of bees is only the demon queen, English! Only the demon queen . . . .'

"Nikolai, stop!" I choke out, grabbing for his sleeve. "I don't want to hear you bow those bees anymore! Stop making the violin sound like a swarm of bees. . . ."

"Hush, English—shhh!" Again he sponges the dampened rag up across my brow. "Here, my love—take some water. *Try* to," he urges.

Numbly, I sip down the liquid and stare around. At towering walls of a tomb caught in dank hollows of darkness, the putrid stench of the cave reeking up high within the mountains, bare east of Sevastopol.

Glancing back upward with a long sigh, I once again take in the lithe features of him whom I so desperately love—his blink gentle, his nod understanding, his smile edged with a profound glimmer of relief as he hands me my spectacles. "Yes, you will be all right now, dear heart," he murmurs joyfully. "Here, drink some more water."

"H-How many days has it been?" I ask, shuddering against the cold.

He pulls the blankets up closer about my throat, tucking them in, murmuring: "Difficult to judge. Another week and a half, I think, will be Christmastide. Some sorry holiday, eh? Now, come, dear heart—I want you to try to pee for me in this cup."

After I do so, I ask him what I said during the delirium.

"Many things," he whispers. "Many things."

Nervously, I try to imagine what I might have uttered to, or about, Tolya, Volodya.

"And I spoke of Emile," he says abruptly, obviously quite clued in upon my thoughts.

"Yes," I answer with a flush.

"In the prison camp," Nikolai goes on in a quieted tone, "after the escape attempt, they separated us. The escape was a plot—in all, with five of us involved. Two died under the beatings. The remainder, they stowed away with other prisoners, far from the Russian compound. I found myself in with a French lot. Idiot krautheads—thought they were fostering punishment by forcing us in with groups of foreigners, scarce realizing that, in my case, I could well speak the language."

"And Emile," I go on softly, "was your first lover. Your first male lover—beyond the other lads at the Conservatory. The naughty little schoolboy hand-holds—"

"Yes."

"S-So in Budapest, those long years ago," I go on, reddening in dismay, "I was completely, horribly wrong. To imply, in any way, that you had become—uh—more than merely friendly with M'sieur Diaghilev."

"Indeed, that whole meeting was solely about business," he says, nodding. "I was trying to egg my way up into a first section chair. And even hadn't it been, Sasha—everyone, faggot or no, knew Diaghilev was a one-man man, that he had eyes for none other than Nijinsky."

"I know! I'm sorry, Nikolai," I whisper earnestly, my ears flooding purple with shame. "God, what an inept fool I was! . . ." With tentative longing, I reach my hand upward and smooth it across his cheek.

Shrugging off our old feud to annals of triviality, Nikolai begins kissing, one by one, each of my fingers, murmuring: "But do you know what he told me?"

"Who?"

"Diaghilev. He told me—straight out of the blue, almost as if he had some kind of compunction to tell me—that he and his cousin, Dima Filosofov—remember, another legend from the old school days at Mays? He told me they were lovers. Before he met Nijinsky."

"Really?"

"Uh-huh. So, you see, we are not the only such two ever so passionately taken with one another, dearest, beloved heart. . . ."

Another two and a half weeks it takes for me to fully gain back my strength. A glowing amber dawn ushers in the first brisk morn of the new year, 1921, when we at last venture out from the lower mouth of the cave to a wider cleft of the stream. I kneel at the edge of the bank and shave the wreath of stubble from my face; watch Nikolai as he peers into another jagged mirror-piece while trimming short again with his barber's shears the past month's growth of his beard. Then we finally each strip down fully and bathe, the both of us shivering and berating the lancing chill of the wind and another fresh coating of snowfall dusted about the brush and the boulders. Moments later, against the warmth of a hot, stoked fire, we dry our hair and roast the pheasant he has shot, along with the remaining half-dozen of our potatoes. After eating—the both of us ravenous and sucking the meat down to the softened, gristly bones—we burn the sick clothes and the soiled saddle blankets, and make hastened preparations for departure, skittish each of us about the smoke from the fire attracting notice from Red guard patrols. As fate would have it, the mare—although Nikolai had long since set her off to forage for herself, our oat supply running treacherously low—yet returns, just as she has once or twice each day over the past weeks, checking up upon us, refusing very far to wander. "Good to see you again, too, old girl," Nikolai murmurs, chuckling and fondly patting the horse's muzzle as he saddles her up.

"So," I say, pulling on my coat and knapsack and glancing over at him. "And to where, my friend, does our journey take us from here?"

"The railhead," he replies without a moment's hesitation. "Sevastopol."

* * *

We scamper in between the caboose and the terminal boxcar, climbing up one after another onto the coupling, the both of us heaving for breath. *You all right?* questions Nikolai in silence, glancing backward.

Yes, yes!

There's only one guard.

Are you sure? I thought for certain there were two—

The other's sneaking off to the card game—look.

Sure enough, one of the browncoats we have been tailing shoulders his rifle, smiles guiltily, and shrugs toward an unseen companion—then to pull low his red-star cap and saunter off toward the stationmaster's office, where roars of the bottle-smashing, hell-raising card game in progress continue to the tunes of horns, balalaikas, and boisterous singing of the *Internationale.*

May all be die-hard Reds, Nikolai observes, rolling his eyes, *but deep down, those hearts still beat true Russian.*

Smiling wryly, I nod my head toward the boxcar just aside us. *This the one with the open door?*

Uh-huh, this and the next three up the line. Cautiously, he ducks his head out to confirm that fact once again. Then, bending low, he scarfs up a large stone from down between the tracks. *Make ready*, he warns, nodding toward my cane.

I grip it up, and with my other hand again hoist my knapsack and our saddlebags upon my shoulder—while Nikolai, his eyes once more peeled around the corner at the guard, arches his arm backward, reaching the rock high.

He throws it to opposite side of the train, duly attracting, across the switchyard, the attention of the remaining guard.

Now! he orders, motioning at me.

Juggling both his large knapsack and our dripping water gourd, he sprints for the open boxcar door. I limp after as fast as I can, wincing back moans of pain while staring widely about through the Sevastopol railway switching yard. From end to end, the place lies jammed to the hilt with locomotives both Red and captured White, some armored, some not, but all scattered amidst scores of wooden boxcars bearing the bright red-painted letters *RSFSR*—for Russian Soviet Federated Socialist Republic. Fortunately, such vast proliferation of rolling stock has provided us apt cover, shielding our sly maneuvers as I have sprung locks at two stationhouse gates to permit our entrance. Ever since, we have darted from car to car beneath the noses of the guards, lent fair enough assistance by the card party raging on so raucously in the background. *Come along!* Nikolai urges, grabbing for my knapsack and saddlebags, and then for my hands, as I seize onto him with a grimace and clamber upward through the open boxcar door.

Inside, we find naught but barrel after barrel and crate after crate filled with onions and garlic. *Oh, for God's sake!* Nikolai moans, wrinkling up his nose. *Of all the cars from which to choose in this damned switchyard, we manage to stow away in one that reeks like Italian heaven?*

Well, I reply, shrugging, unable to suppress a grin at the expressions of disgust he continues making, *you said best to hide in the last boxcar by the caboose.*

I know, I know. Quick, back here—sounds like someone's coming.

We gather our things in haste and make for the farthest corner from the door, hiding just in the nick of time behind a group of high barrels. Two browncoats promptly march past outside, although their droning conversation ambles on, and they seem scarce roused to any suspicion.

Seconds later, the whistle blows; more footsteps resound outside, and soon enough, another browncoat bolts past to grasp up the handles and slam shut the boxcar doors.

As the latch clamps shut outside, I glance down at the hatchet axe Nikolai has been lugging along in his knapsack. Our only means, once the train starts moving, of sneaking our way out.

And I stare at the water gourd, catching his eye, asking: *How long will it last us, you think?*

We will be forced to ration. A sip only when we each need it. At that, five, perhaps six days.

And then?

Then we jump the train.

* * *

Five and a half days the water lasts, but its lack burdens neither of us so harshly as the cold—for a blight such as I can never remember soon devours us unto the bleak crucifixion of each bitter, aching bone. Desperately, we huddle one against the other, ever flexing fingers within our mittens and toes within our boots in attempts at fending off the nagging threat of frostbite. "I had forgotten how cold the Russian winter can be," I say, my teeth chattering. "After our sunny year in Yalta."

"Yes," he replies, pressing against me again, his lips gone blue and trembling violently with the chill. "At least," he adds, "we can no longer smell the garlic."

"Is because it is frozen, Nikolai."

"Yes."

I want to go on, and remind him that this is sheer arcane madness—but I do not, and raise quick guard on my thoughts before he can sense their mournful gist. Instead, I duck my head down and peer out through the mesh of one of the open air vents cut in the lower wall of the boxcar. To again see naught but piles of bodies heaped in various spots along the tracks: bodies stricken down with the grippe, the flux, and the spotted typhus; bodies shot up, mangled, and caked in rivers of dried darkened blood; bodies bereft of limbs, heads, or ofttimes even whole lower trunks; bodies stripped of boots, scarves, and near all other stitches of clothing. Beyond them, across the vast open reach of the Ukrainian steppe, I catch sight in the far distance of another burned-out village, testament to so many other scores of former countryside idylls laid to senseless socialist waste. Likened to others we have noted in our few days of riding past, its peasant huts stand charred and blackened aside churches demolished unto heaps of icon scrap, its storefronts teetering torn and vacant to the open howl of the wind. "Another one?" Nikolai asks, yet shivering beside me.

I pull up and snuggle back into his arms, murmuring: "Yes."

"Will not be long, now," he whispers, pressing a kiss against my cheek. "Last stop for coal was Kharkov. At least with the Bolshies triumphant, trains are making decent time again. Soon, we'll be past the Ukrainian border, back into the heart of Russia."

He will of course, true Russian that he is, remain steadfast unto his heritage; not deign for us to abandon ourselves unto the sprawl of empty steppe in the lowly southern Ukraine. No, for my cousin of the wishing wells from the long line of musical Zhelanov princes, salvation lies only past the borders of ancient Muscovy, within the arms of the Blessed Virgin Mother—in, as they used to say of old, the endless forest lands of true Great Russia . . . .

A few hours later, true Russia's story proves the same: more burned out villages, more piles of bodies heaped beside the tracks, and the cold only lashing at us with renewed ferocity. The water in our gourd levels down to a mere trickle, and we count out between our two knapsacks only three remaining potatoes. In finality, we lock stares and throw wide our arms, wrapping fists each about the other—then to kiss torridly, savagely, as if to never allow our souls free. Forcing effort, he wrenches himself away, fondly smoothing back a stray lock of hair peeking out from the furry brim of my hat before brushing the heel of his hand up across his own cheek, cursing off tears. And from his knapsack, he lifts out the axe.

Beside the door, he chops a hole large enough to permit a man's head and shoulders through. "All right, now you are going to have to hang onto me, *tight,*" he orders. "And pray that I have no trouble unlatching the door."

I do as told, shuddering against a blinding freeze of cold and the roar of noise that blasts in from the outside—and I wince against his every grunt as he bends outward with the handle of the axe, attempting to pry loose the latch on the door. "By dammit!" he shouts at last, shoving back inward after a long toil of moments, hot sweat streaming down his face. "The bastard will simply not loosen!"

"All right, so let me try."

"But your leg—"

"My leg is faring well enough, and in any case, I hardly intend to try pulling open the latch with it. Now, come—you're tired."

We switch places, and I hang outside banging the axe handle against the latch for a good ten minutes, again meeting with no success. "Shit!" I mutter out, collapsing inside in my own stream of sweat as he yanks me back through the hole.

"All right, well—three makes good," he says, motioning me to once again hold him. "Here goes."

This time, the latch releases almost immediately, and I drag him back in with a sigh of relief. "Hope no guards in the caboose saw us," I tell him, peering toward the outside with apprehension.

"Would have by now, unless either asleep or drunk," he observes.

We gather up our knapsacks, saddlebags, the dry water gourd, the hatchet axe, some frozen onions from a crate we have broken into. "Remember, now—lest they suspect stowaways, best we both jump, both land in the snow at the same time," he reminds me before laying his shoulder full into the metal bearings to slam open the boxcar door.

The outside air blasts in upon us in a torrent, the chugging blare of the train deafening into our ears. For as far as the eye can see lies naught but a foreboding horizon of snow and frost-laced forest.

"Now!" he says, grasping hold of my arm.

We heave off through the door, and land one atop another in a bank of snow—and lie the both of us silent and absolutely motionless, not daring to move a muscle as the caboose—and whoever might lurk within to see—rumbles past.

The train snakes off into the distance, disappearing into the whispered silence of the trees.

I rub bits of snow from my face and stare around, again wanting to scream at him, fight with him, to decry unto insanity this impossible northward quest! Out in the middle of bloody nowhere we are—and stark in the midst of winter. In godforbidden, godforsaken, godforgotten Soviet Russia.

"The quieter you tread, the farther you go," says Nikolai, quoting an old proverb. Pointing toward a thickened copse of birch, he adds with insistence: "This way."

And starts heading north.

* * *

Untold hours of tramping through drifts of snow melt into one day, then into another—and we ration the onions and the remainder of our potatoes, subsisting each day each of us upon only one onion and one potato half—until only one potato remains. In my knapsack. And then I learn the honest truth about love—here, in the silent, barren, deep-blue depths of the Russian forest, I learn far more about love than I ever did at the sandy Yalta beach filled with lazy strolls, our stolen kisses, the fire in his eyes sweeping me from both near and afar, the yearnings in my heart bursting forth into line after line of the written word. No, love is not, in truth, about such lofty ease. True love hinges upon one timeless, simple predication: whether, in the straits of bowel-churning, virulent hunger, one will, with one's loved one, share one's only remaining potato.

Within such ponderings, I begin at last to sense the true objective of our journey—for certainly, deep down, despite all he says about it, this goes far beyond some noble, wayward course toward redemption for sins. No, instead, in all symbolic gravity, this is *the* journey: the pilgrimage over ages called both forbidding and forbidden, that which is naught but the lighted path, the holy way, faith's final obligation, love's ultimate test upon which one travels only with one's own paired, pledged partner in soul, Christ's grail of towering mystery awaiting in either triumph or downfall at the end. First, however, worthy such partners must prove themselves—of one another.

Come nightfall of the third day, a storm lumbers in—one of those abrupt, ghastly winter terrors, the wind hailing in upon sleet's cutting edge from the far Siberian east. Despite attempts to keep it burning, our fire extinguishes beneath the onslaught, and we huddle miserably beneath cover of the pines, the both of us shivering against hunger's blight, our noses paled to whitish-blue, our fingers frozen to stiffened lumps, our toes no longer meeting the slightest prick of sensation within our boots. After a few moments, I lift out from the shaft of mine, with a shaking hand, my long-handled hunting knife—and from my knapsack, scavenge the remainder of the onions and the potato. To cut away half, handing it to him.

His thoughts breach over words both spoken and unuttered, no enunciation necessary either way between us as he takes the potato half gratefully, his eyes meeting mine. "To the Holy Grail, then," he says, raising high the potato, as if in toast. Once he takes a bite, he attempts to chew slowly, his sigh ravenous with hunger.

I do the same, praying in silent gratitude and benediction for all the feasts, both large and small, of which I have so casually partaken in my life—and for this final token, savored now bit by bit in earnestness, humbleness, reverence. Which is, more likely than not, our last meal.

As the wind rages on through the trees, for two more hours we huddle together, kissing one another to inspire warmth. Again and again I shrink from ever allowing him to part one inch from my fervent grasp, willing to die right here, right now, in this spot, beneath these trees, if only I can hold this man, Nikolai Zhelanov, in my arms until the end. And for the thousandth time I mull over in my mind the wisdom of our departing Yalta—while his gaze meets mine in answer, his words ringing somber and low within my head: *House to house, it was said, the Red firing squads searched, once they reached Rostov, Novorossiysk. Would have been no different in Yalta, Sasha—especially for those families dwelling in the beachside bungalows, known havens of the upper classes, the former nobility.*

Of course, you are right, I glimmer back, snuggling once more against him. *In Yalta, by now, we would most probably be dead. At least here, for a little while longer, we remain alive—so kiss me, love of my life, joy of my heart! Kiss me madly without another second's pause. . . .*

At last the storm calms unto a light snowfall dusting about our heads. Scarce do we arise to our feet—still kissing and touching, our hands yet jostling eagerly within one another's coats—to jump back each of us with gasps of fear. Shrill and lonely and aching with old primordial majesty, the howling bays high up above the reaches of the woods.

"Wolves!" I cry, my stare caught stonily ahead.

Nikolai squeezes his hand to my shoulder, murmuring: "Sasha, they do not attack."

This is true, they are said not to attack unless provoked—and indeed, once the first appears, it dashes straight away upon the sight of us, obviously stricken to the core with fear.

"See?" he says, catching my glance, shrugging.

"Uh-huh." Again, within folds of my coat, I finger the trigger guard of my gun.

It takes not long after that: once we hoist up our gear and start trudging through the snow, within moments, six full-grown gray wolves, thin and scrawny and evidently famished with hunger, emerge from the trees to bar our way.

No longer glib about it, Nikolai whips out his Luger, stabbing toward them with it and shooing them away. "Your dream," he says without looking toward me.

"Yes." I whip out my gun also, but cannot manage both it and the cane—so I switch the gun to my right hand, cursing the many times I ever rampaged against Father shoving my fork into the same. "Damn," I mutter, shaking my head. "How many of them can there be?"

A chorus of howls meets us in answer, and Nikolai pulls back close to me, staring widely around, his breath caught to an icy rattle in his throat. "You never told me!" he exclaims, seams of panic ridged within his voice. "You never said that your wolves dream was a premonition!"

Several more pairs of demon eyes peek out through the trees, another six or eight wolves closing in upon numbers of the first group as Nikolai rages on: "Dammit! Why did you keep this from me?"

"Because—of the future, one is not always permitted to say."

His glance, held upon me briefly, yields understanding then. Twin souls we may indeed be—but yet owe each ultimate responsibility unto individual mastery, which is often beholden to certain dictates of silence. Unable to help recalling, in spite of my efforts to shun all such thoughts, memories of the dark caverns, the visions laced with heavy iron doors so prevalent throughout my many wolf dreams, I tell him brokenly: "The f-future ever remains a contingency, dependent upon many factors. M-Much is seen, of which cannot be spoken—"

"Yes," he murmurs, nodding. "I know." Once the wolves start encircling us, within my head I hear his voice echoing with tender remorse: *Forgive me, my love, for becoming irate with you—*

Nikolai, it is all right—

Snarls begin to beleaguer us then, and we whirl about to find ourselves surrounded on every side by the panting, open jaws of hungry wolves. Dropping my cane and switching my gun, I strive for balance upon a prayer, rasping out: "Oh, dear God!"

The first of them charges from the right-hand side—and Nikolai cuts in front of me, the blast of his Luger barreling into the still, hushed night. Into a ball the wolf tumbles, blood from the wound in its head spurting out and soaking into the snow. "I thought you said they never attacked!" I cry, both my hands quaking upon the grip of my gun. "Fucking Jesus!"

Towering above the head of the dead wolf, Nikolai begins a fastidious inspection—and then I too catch a glimpse of the whitish foam frothing out from the side of its mouth. "Not," he murmurs to me in reply, "unless they're very hungry. Or rabid."

"Oh, holy shit, Nikolai!" More shadows from the woods start to prowl in upon us then—exactly as in my dream, a looming coven of snarls, pants, and foamings at the mouth pawing through thickened brambles of twigs and snow. We start shooting, picking them off one by one. "How many more cartridge clips have we?" Nikolai calls to me, his arm flashing through the air, his eyes combing across the woods, his nostrils flared for the whiff of their hoary scent.

"One box in each knapsack—three clips each," I remind him.

"Get them out. I'll cover you."

As I struggle with the knapsacks, three more wolves converge, and three more bullet shots blast out in panicked response, Nikolai barking back at me: "By dammit—*hurry!* I've only one round left on this clip—"

I hand him another cartridge clip just in time: four more wolves charge in, the drool spewing from their mouths, their fur cleft up in hackles, fangs each gruesomely bared. His last round he gets off and hastens to reload, while I down the other wolves with my remaining three shots. Then I reload and take to his cover again while searching my knapsack for the remaining box of shells. Which I cannot find.

"What the fucking devil do you mean, you cannot *find* it?" he hollers in exasperation.

"Well, it is not anywhere in here! Are you certain you haven't the second box in yours?"

"No!"

I search through his knapsack again in a frenzy, still turning up no trace of the second box of shells. Vaguely, then, I retrace my steps back to our time spent in the cave above Sevastopol, seeing him lying again so ill in the dark hours of the typhus—while I toyed with, oiled up my gun. Could I have possibly taken the box of cartridge clips out, laid it aside, and neglected to replace it into my knapsack?

"All right, then!" Nikolai yells, "so how many *do* we have left?"

"Oh, for the love of God! One—only one clip left between us, besides what we each already have loaded—"

"Shit!" he cries out. "Motherfucking *shit . . . !*"

The pack of wolves, seeming to sense our fear, again starts crowding in closer, another half dozen leaping out in ragged, drooling sloughs from the trees. Blindly, we each start shooting, some shells downing heads, shoulders, hindquarters; some shells missing whole bodies in entirety due to our nervousness and on account of my eyesight proving far less reliable than in the years of my youth. Again he runs out first; grabs the last cartridge clip from me and jams it up the butt of his Luger, slamming shut the catch. "More, still, than we have shells," he utters out shakily, his eyes ranging across the wealth of shadows continuing to lurk against low, hissing growls throughout the woods.

Promptly, another wolf steals out, springing into attack—and then another, and another—the floor of the forest becoming littered with wolf carcasses and downed wolves snarling at us from the bridge of death as we step gingerly about their heads, each of us grappling for breath. "H-How many shells have you left?" he demands finally, grasping hold of my arm.

"One! Oh, my God—only one!"

"Two," he answers to my unspoken question. "I have two shots left."

"We can't keep fending them off!"

"No, we can't."

From a glance stolen down to his gun, he looks pointedly back upward.

"What are you suggesting?" I cry, aghast, staring from him to my own gun—and down the throat of my foolish plyings with it during those hours in the cave. Back into his eyes, I then gaze—and for the first time, see that, when I took sick with the typhus later, he too must have faced his own desperation square against hell's tempting, bitter chasm in the cave; must have paused, perhaps one morn or one eve, to play a little roulette with his gun. With a cold shiver, I try to imagine his Luger aimed at my head in the darkness; wonder if, had I noticed, I would have tried to stop him. "So—you think we should simply finish it all?" I gasp out, gulping raggedly for breath. "Now? Here?"

He opens his mouth to reply, but cringes back a grimace; flails out beyond me to loose another shell again into the skull of a charging wolf. "Now, I have but one shell left," he whispers, crossing himself, dropping down to his knees.

Shaking torrentially from head to foot, I drop down with him, uttering prayers. "G-God forgive us!" I whisper, crossing myself also.

And then for one last time I stare up into his eyes, whispering: "I—I love you—"

"And I, you. Forever and evermore."

Numbly, I raise my pistol up and ease it in against his neck, tucking the barrel just below his ear.

"No, Sasha," he murmurs gently, shaking his head. "That is not how you do it. This is the way you do it."

Wrapping his fingers around the barrel of the gun, he pokes it up into his mouth.

"Oh, *God . . . !*" I practically scream, tears coursing down my face.

His free hand he reaches up, brushing the back of it tenderly against my cheek—while with the other, he brings the barrel of his own Luger up, easing it into my mouth. Shutting our eyes, we each slide trembling fingers for the triggers.

Through the woods, baying howls and low snarls break yet again. I heave for my last life's breath as his voice rips shards of agony into the plunging depths of my soul: *All right—on the count of three: one . . . two . . . th—*

"I can't!" I shout at him, wrenching my gun away and ducking down from the aim of his—just as, with a violent shudder, he does naught but the very same. "I could never be the cause of your death, Nikolai Zhelanov! Bloody God in all of Heaven's Bowels! I—I simply *can't . . . !*"

Past my ear, another menacing form pounces. Grabbing my shoulder, Nikolai seizes me to him, the sky overhead ringing unto oblivion with his gun's final shot, the wolf falling with a lumbering thud into a bed of leaves and snow.

"Another's behind it—give me your gun," he says.

I shove it at him, and again wince against the echo of the blast, another wolf tumbling behind with a growling, snarling thud.

Nikolai again pulls me close, his hand flinging off my hat and caressing through my hair, his lips lingering downward, brushed bare upon the breath of mine. "I—I could never have shot you, either—not in a million centuries!" he whispers, tears spilling down his cheeks, his voice rasping to a halt. "Is the ultimate sin," he goes on. "Must—must always leave death only—unto—God's auspices . . . w-will not be bad, my love," he goes on with a quivering moan. "Scarce but a moment—the wolves will go for the throat first. J-Just one quick rip into the throat—"

"Oh, bloody Jesus Christ!" I rattle against him, choking back sobs.

"I love you, Sasha," he whispers fervently. "Kiss me—for one last, glorious time . . . ."

We kiss to the echoes of snarls, growls, hungry pawings in the dirt. "Here they come," he rasps out at last, tearing himself away and dragging the both of us hurriedly back up to our feet. "I'll cover you as best I can—"

From his knapsack, he snatches out the hatchet axe, and I grip my hands like talons around the long handle of my boot knife, steeling myself for snarls, blows, and the hot, ragged searings of my flesh torn asunder, to be devoured by an animal, like naught by a lowly, stinking animal . . . until the air shatters apart above our heads. Echoes of thunder pound into my ears, one shot after another blasting far beyond us to pick off or scare away the onslaught, every last straggler from the pack of wolves scurrying back to the cover of the woods.

Stunned, we both whirl about to face a flank of steely-eyed horsemen clad in Bolshevik browncoats and pointed red-star caps, their carbines cocking back up, their rifle barrels swinging around, from retreat of the wolves, onto us.

Numbly, we drop the hatchet, the knife; stare at one another. And raise up our hands.

* * *

"Who are you? Who is your friend?"

With his brass knuckles, the *Cheka* interrogator hits me again, and I slump forward, my hands cupped to each side of my mouth, catching blood, the chains from the manacles clamped about my wrists rattling up a storm. "M-M-Mikhailov!" I gasp out, pulling back up with effort—and cringing as the man's arm again arches upward, readying for another blow. "Aleksandr—"

"That is a lie." Again the solid cuff of brass crashes down, plowing into my jaw, pummeling me to my knees.

Before departing Yalta, we burned every scrap of paper—old Russian traveling passports, later Soviet document forgeries—that could possibly identify either of us as Sekovsky or Zhelanov. Upon their searches, both bodily and of our belongings—past the violin, now smashed to wooden bits across a jagged boulder; past my manuscript of poetry, now scattered to the forest's four billowing winds—the Red Guards found naught else. As agreed, we have told them merely that we are both 'Mikhailov,' Aleksandr and Nikolai. . . .

"Who are you? Who is your friend?"

I cannot remember much after Orel. South of which, the wolves attacked, the Red scouts saving our lives. Why, I do not know. Immediately, they separated us from one another, but I know from my telepathic link with Nikolai that he was with me on the same prison train, holed up somewhere in another locked berth—while they forced him, also, to down the broth and to drink the water laced with whatever drug it was that has kept us both gripped upon the edge of stupor ever since. Afterward, the cities rumbled by: Plavsk, Shchokino, Tula, Nenashevo . . . until Moscow. Our destination always, although unspoken it was, ever since Yalta. Only in Moscow could my cousin bring his grim pilgrimage to its sorry end; only in the heart of this strife-torn, ancient land of ours can a holy Russian Christ properly wield his beggar's crown of thorns—just as the Tsars have always returned, for a time, southward from the Neva's sparkling crystal waters, loyal in the end unto the Holy Mother's awaiting arms for the pageantry of their coronations. So again, I find myself unjustly imprisoned in Moscow: this time, I suspect, in the echoing dark caverns of the infamous *Lubyanka*, the *Cheka's* famed bastion of thick walls and doomed cellars, an entire world unto itself muffled away from all outside life. No need here to start up a motorcar engine out on the city streets to mask the discharge of rifle fire. What evil deeds transpire within the *Lubyanka*, no one on the sterile Soviet outside can even hear.

"Who are you? Who is your friend?" Again more blows. Again my piteous, half-stuttered answer: "M-M-Mikhailov! Aleksandr . . . ."

The interrogator, a Red Army major, pauses for a moment to wipe his hands of the blood on a towel while regarding me with an intense, disdainful expression. "Our scouts heard the both of you speakin' to each other in English," he declares loudly, towering over me, both fists set firmly to his hips. "You are Englishmen? Or perhaps," he goes on with a menacing glower, "stinkin' Tsarist noblemen?"

I shake my head in denial—only to have him growl back at me: "Liar!" Once more his fist smashes down, and this time I almost reel off the stool, save for the assistance of his silent lieutenant standing beside, who grasps roughened hold of my shoulder and forces me back upright.

"A certain resemblance exists between the two of you," the major goes on, peering into my face and nodding; then clicking together, for emphasis, his shiny black boot heels. "Indeed—a certain kinship between you and your friend burns in the fury of the eyes; a certain trust of lineage, delicately boned, betrays the prideful, rigid set of your chin and his. You are *what?"* he then yells abruptly, whirling back about, glaring downward. "Brothers? Cousins? *Disgustin'!"* he blares on. "Because our scouts heard, saw more than the both of you merely speakin' in English—oh, yes—oh, *ho! Humph!* Such a kiss as what the advance scout swore he saw stems from more than mere brotherly affection—yes, my pretty little red-haired friend?"

When I stare straight ahead, not moving a muscle in response, he laughs and whips out from his jacket pocket a crumpled sheet of paper. More incrimination in English: my poem, *Sonata*, written for Nikolai's Birth Day. The one sheet of paper kept on his person that he would not, could not burn—stained now, from top to bottom, with dark smears of his blood. "Need I say more?" the major demands, grinning evilly and crumpling up the paper in his hand.

I shut my eyes and bury my head into my hands, while he harps on: "So—he is your lover? Small wonder you've kept so set on protectin' him, humph! Because it is *him* you're protectin' so steadfastly, now, yes? Fool! Don't you see? *He* is the one we want—because a *murderer* he is, yes? Uh-huh—same as we've been seekin' out for a long, long time. But you—*you* we can just as easily dispose of. Or—let go. So, which shall it be?"

As I remain immobile, he pounces upon me with an angry grunt, grasping up a fistful of my hair, forcing me upward—and he stares down into my eyes, seeing clearly that not another word am I going to impart. "Bah!" he gasps out, snarling, signaling to his lieutenant. And then they both stomp out, the heavy iron door slamming shut behind them—the guard, posted just outside, jostling immediately with the lock, his keys jangling on his belt afterward as he marches away.

Again I shut my eyes, this time pressing both palms to each of my temples, attempting to concentrate: *Nikolai! Can you hear me?*

But once more only static do I receive in answer, as if from a faulty transmission over wireless radio: *Sasha, I—Sasha, I—ohhh!* And then I sense him, too, reeling from the blows.

But he is here. And close—I know it, I can feel it! Perhaps not more than three or four cells down. If only we could maintain our tenuous link, could somehow conquer this daze wrought by their infernal disrupting drug.

Still sponging off, licking up blood, I crawl down from the stool onto the floor and ease myself into the corner—there to grasp up the tin cup with shaking fingers, loath to drink, knowing the water yet to be tainted. And not for the first time, I debate whether to continue drinking any water at all—in lieu of simply lying back and allowing my body to die of its own bedeviled thirst. Resolution, however, dwindles with each passing moment of my throat's parched yearning. Finally, I take the cup, sip down some water, and shudder once more at the sour taste, within it, of the drug.

Then I float off into blessed sleep, but only for a few moments—for the major returns, along with his lieutenant, and two men in worker's caps bearing between them a large wooden and metal apparatus. I blanch in fear the moment I catch sight of it, and scoot farther into my corner upon the floor, but they grab hold of my arms and hoist me upward, forcing me again onto the stool. "No!" I gasp out as they yank up, past my right forearm, the cuff of my shirt-sleeve. "N-No! Please—"

To the wooden bar, poised parallel above my arm, the workmen start screwing in rows of short pointed spikes, all thin as needles. "Tell us who you are, and who your friend is," the major demands with an exasperated sigh, "and we will dispense with such unpleasantries."

"I—I told you!" I choke out at him. "He is Nikolai, I am Aleksandr. The both of us, Mikhailov—"

"You are brothers, then? Cousins?"

In answer to my tight-lipped silence, the major nods at the lieutenant, who moves in close beside the wooden device.

"For the last time," utters the major with a low growl. "Tell us who you both are!"

I shake my head.

The wooden bar slams down, ramming into my arm—and bringing with it a spray of stinging agony, the half-dozen needles set to each side of the bone piercing down into my flesh. The lieutenant declines to lift the bar immediately back upward again; instead, leaves the needles embedded and presses his own hand down upon the bar, increasing the pressure—and the pain—while the major hollers at me: *"Tell* us who you are! . . ."

For hours, it seems, it keeps up, for ages they pursue their questioning, through infinity I continue to refuse response, my whole life floating before my eyes in scattered, hazy visions. Over and over, they lift the bar back up, the needles back out; move the whole apparatus down just a fraction of an inch, and again plunge it back into my arm—while I grit my teeth, attempting with every last fiber of my will not to scream. So long ago in the barn in Latvia, Nikolai warned me, making graphic enough account of the fascination for torture devices possessed by the *Bolsheviki*. . . . "*Tell* us who you are!" the major blares on. "You want us to stop? Yes, we will stop—immediately, with pleasure! You think this any easier on us? We are not vindictive men. But we've spent over three years fightin' off a bloody civil war near unto our last man; we have a state, a populace to protect! Now, simply *tell* us who you are. . . ."

Finally, when thick clots of blood begin interfering with the effectiveness of the needles, the bruises mottling to dark purple and garish green, they lift the device away—and wheel it around to my opposite arm.

"Oh, God!" I gasp out in spite of myself, shrinking away from them.

"Well!" the major yells into my ear, obviously strung for patience. "Simply tell us, then, just what in the devil's bloody name you and your brother—cousin—*whoever* he is—were doin' out in the middle of the godforsaken wilderness! How did you get there? Where did you come from? Who are you? British spies? Or—more likely—*dvoryanye* monarchist insurgents from the south? And what the hell are you both so *damn* set at hidin' away from us?"

Just before the workmen strap the bottom board of the device onto my left arm, a knock sounds at the door outside, summoning the major.

"Indeed?" he says through the crack, nodding, then signaling the workmen to halt. "Says the missin' man matches our description? Well, send him down, then!"

To my relief, in lieu of continuing with the torture, he bids the workmen to lug the device back out, and motions to the lieutenant, who meets him outside of the door, where they both stand talking, waiting.

Cradling my arm and rubbing at the manacles scraping about my wrists, their fine-gauged metal chain rattling after my every movement, I grope from the stool back down to my chilly, darkened corner on the floor—where awaits my water cup and the one blanket they have allotted me. Hand shaking, I attempt to roll the cuff of my sleeve back down my bruised and bloodied arm, but without success, the pain simply proving unfathomable. "Nikolai," I whimper out, caught with another violent, nauseated shudder from head to foot, "whatever they are doing to you, I hope it does not hurt so much. I love you, Nikolai. . . ."

Abruptly, the door bangs open again, and I glare upward into the eyes of the major, the lieutenant—and into those of none other than my hefty dishwater-haired brother-in-law, Yevgeny Ivanovich Mrenitsev.

"Is it him?" the major demands of him with a long sigh. "Is this tight-lipped little red-headed bastard that same 'Aleksandr Sekovsky?'"

Yevgeny peers at me for a long moment without speaking, and I peer back—knowing, in my heart, that when he bolted off through the woods, leaving Volodya and I to our fate with the White Guards, little else was there that he could have done, save risk capture himself. Certainly, no malicious intent was manifest on his part. Over our years of living together in Lyubov's apartment, of fighting side by side in Zorshenko's band, a begrudging respect we had earned one for the other, long aeons away from our first adversarial encounter in Volodya's Vyborg apartment. And so I nod up at him, acknowledging such—while faintly, he nods back. "Yes," he then murmurs to the major. "It *is* him."

"And," goes on the major to the lieutenant, who glances down at a sheaf of papers, "per the old Tsarist records, this same Sekovsky is first cousin to the one we have been searchin' out? One N. P. Zhelanov?"

"Yes, sir," the lieutenant replies, nodding, saluting.

"Excellent. Hasten to inform Commissar Bulyarin."

"Nooo!" I scream, bolting upward with a bloody clench of fists.

The three of them stare at me, the major breaking again into his evil smile, and muttering: "Well, well—so the silent martyr talks at last! And we have, indeed, our confirmation."

Into a heap upon the floor, I collapse as they leave, the iron door slamming shut behind. Now, in one moment of senseless, reactionary panic, I have revealed all that they have sought. With one word, everything they have spent hours attempting to force from me to no avail I have endowed clear unto the open. *Shit! Christ's blessed, fucking shit . . . !*

Time hovers then. I sip the water one drop at a time, rationing it, for only one cup a day do they permit us, along with one spare crust of bread, and every two or three nights—twice now, since our arrival—a bowl of tepid, tasteless broth. I stare listlessly over at the piss bucket, emptied only once each day as well, and wrinkle up my nose once more against the stench. High overhead, one electric bulb hangs, bare and bright, never switched off morn nor eve, no credence given to the comfort of darkness for hours of sleep. Scarce wide as a cubbyhole the cell is, dank and cold and graced only with the scantiest source of steam heat, the vents above blasting down warm air only once every two or three hours. The walls, thick and ominous, muffle every sound, including footsteps. And other prisoners' screams.

Sasha-Sashenka! Can you hear me?

I scramble upward and concentrate with all my strength: *Yes, my love! Yes!*

Is s-some drug they have given us, befuddles my thinking—

Nikolai! I tell him in despair, *they know! They know!*

Yes, I know that they know. Will not be long now—

Is all my fault! Someone they brought identified me—

No, dear heart, is not your fault at all. None of this is your fault—is, instead, mine. Fret not at whatever you told them—the truth they would have learned in any case, was inevitable. Oh, Sasha—forgive me for bringing you here with me from Yalta. F-Forgive me for all of this—

Bulyarin they meant to tell, they said!

Yes, I know.

I keep trying to focus upon where you are, but I can see nothing—

Is the drug, my love. The drug interfering—oh, God. They're coming—

Nikolai, stay with me! Don't let loose your concentration—

I will try. Here they come. The door is opening. Oh, dear God—Bulyarin! Ohhh . . . .

And then all I hear are moans as he cringes backward, as he staggers from the blows.

Nikolai, stay with me! I beg him, grappling at the thinnest echo of his voice dissolving in the air. But to the floor myself I then collapse in a squeal of pain, wincing from every blow as their fists, bootheels, billy clubs plow into him. He crumples to the ground, glimmering back at me upon the last heels of desperation: *Sasha, I—I have to cut you off now. R-Remember the old mantra: nurture me with longing, kindle me with tears, I will love you always—in a hundred-hundred y-y-years . . . .*

And then nothing—no more words, not another thought, nor sound. Only the awful, savage pummeling of the blows. *Nikolai!* I shriek deep inside the tomb of my soul, crumpling to the floor in sobs. *D-Don't shut me out—talk to me, keep talking to me! Nikolai, please . . . !*

But he deliberately blocks me out, the force of his will sabotaging all attempts at visualization that I try to piece together of the scene—while I rage back at him to stop, to allow me through, to not try to protect me from the brunt of his hurt. No use. From my seeing him, or from hearing any part of his thoughts, he continues to throw up a silent mental shield—but the depth of his pain he cannot contain, not as it becomes overwhelming. Mercilessly, they beat, flog, and hurt him, my head reeling to squalls of anguish with every cruel, bone-shattering blow. Then I feel his manacles gripped up and wrenched apart, his arms yanked near from their sockets. To somewhere outside of his cell, they start dragging him. . . .

Within the moment, more pain shoots up the arms—my hands becoming numb as I know his are, my agony echoing every quavering nuance of his. Shivering, I grasp downward, attempting to warm my fingers—and across the walls of space and empty coldness barred between us, to warm his, to soothe some sense of feeling back into each of us through the strength of my own clairvoyant power. Still, no use. It matters little, for after that, I start choking.

I choke for air, scarce able to breathe, knowing they must have strung a noose around his neck. Both hands I clamp to my throat, trying to loosen the invisible cord—and I know that this is the end, then—that he is going to die, and me with him through the power of my own empathy. *Love, worship, adore you, Nikolai Zhelanov,* I tell him with a sob, wondering if he can even hear. *Forever and evermore will I love you. . . .*

To my astonishment, a feeble answer patters back, as if from the greatest distance: *Love you, too, Sasha-Sashenka—dearest heart, so love . . . only . . . y-y-you . . . .*

And I catch a breath of joy as suddenly the noose loosens, the flow of life returning to me, to the both of us, in a gasping rush. But then I double over again, thrashed unto a scream of fire, a torch of flame igniting every muscle, fiber, and cell in my chest, loins, gut.

"Oh, God!" I gasp aloud, collapsing blindly back onto the floor. "Oh, *my God . . . !*"

The torch burns clear up the pit of my stomach into every wall of my thudding heart; scorches into the lower base of my throat—which I clutch again, shaking my head against the savage blade of the invisible perpetrator, begging for mercy. *"Nooo! Lord Jesus God!"* I scream. *"What are they doing to him? . . ."*

But in answer, only silence. No thoughts from my beloved Nikolai, save for the agonizing, wrenching silence of his pain. No God for deliverance to anyone in these lonely, silent cellar depths of the *Lubyanka*.

Just when I think that there is naught else I can bear—not another moment, second; not another single shattered breath of such horrific pain—the door to my cell slams wide open. And *she* storms in.

Like the mother of death. "Fiend!" she shouts, pointing me down in accusation and ramming the door solidly shut behind, her dark blue eyes blazing, her blondish-brownish hair cut so short and stiff about her face that I scarce recognize her as the woman I left three long years ago. "Ye are the one who took my children!" she screams at the top of her voice, shaking both fists high into the air. *"Ye bloody, thieven' scoundrel!"*

I clamber to my feet in bare enough time to fend off her angry charge, and shove her back from me with both hands, shouting: *"What have they done to my friend?"*

"Not near so filthy awful as I intend doin' to *ye!"* she rages out, *"Count* Sekovsky!" Bursting past the manacle chain that I throw up toward her face, she lands against me and starts grappling wildly, both her hands seizing about my throat. "By God, I'll *kill* ye!" she wails. "Because I know it was *ye!* Who *else* could o' so easily lured away my Zhenya, most likely with naught but fancy talk an' starry English promises? I swear, divorcin' ye afterwards was scarce *enough!* No, by God—I'll see ye torn from limb from te limb, ye back-stabbin', child-stealin' *monster!* Where—*where* are they?" she then demands, her voice careening off into sobs.

"England."

Letting out a gasp, Lyubov releases my throat and staggers back, the flat of her hand plowing into my face.

I sink against the wall, submitting, for the moment, willfully—for this I deserve, fiend that I am, just as she has said. She is right: without telling her, without consulting her wishes or asking any permission, I used her daughter to arrange the whole affair behind her back, and indeed stole away her children, the elder not even lawfully mine. Blow after blow, I bow to my just and proper due, and even unto the bloody end would I allow it to go, bequeathing unto the poor woman some comfort in my death at her hand, as I can now give her naught else. But somewhere here, writhing in torture in some other locked and barren room, still lives Nikolai. *"What* have they done to my friend?" I burst out abruptly, catching her off-guard as I at last lash back and seize up her wrists past the icy rattle of my manacles. "Lyubov Ivanovna, I know you owe me not a favor, not a prayer in the world—but you have *got* to tell me!" I shout on at her. *"What have they done to my friend?"*

"Humph!" Glaring forth livid hatred, she smacks me soundly away and stumbles backward, hissing out: "Who? That Zhelanov? The one they claim is yer cousin? Nobody can help him now."

"Take me to him!" I demand, swaying dizzily on my feet, but again groping toward her.

She stares me up and down, and laughs. "Ha! What fer? As if I'd help *ye* with anythin'—"

Shoring up one last burst of strength, I whirl about—pouncing upon her, pinning her back with a thud against the wall, while she screams out, summoning the guard.

"Lyubov!" I roar, raking my stare into hers. "Despite all that's gone between us, you have *got* to take me to him! Lyuba, he—he is the one I told you of, for whom I yearned, of whom I dreamt endlessly, the one I thought lost in the war . . . Lyubov Ivanovna, *please!*" I beg on, crumpling into a sob and collapsing in a smear of blood against her bosom as the door bangs open, the guard stomping in.

"Comrade Mrentiseva!" he shouts. "Ye require assistance?"

She shakes her head, barking at him: "Get out! Leave us."

"Please!" I whimper on, at last sapped unto exhaustion and shuddering against her in a helpless moan before she throws me off. "H-He needs my help, Lyuba! You have *got* to take me to him—"

"Yer execution is scheduled fer fifteen minutes from now," she blurts out abruptly, making a pointed check of her wristwatch. "An' were I merciful at *all*, Count Aleksandr Sekovsky, those'd be the last words I'd say te the likes o' ye, an' I'd walk out o' this stinkin' hellhole before returnin' bloody soon enough with the Major, an' the others, for bearin' witness te yer death. But no, Sasha!" she yells, barreling forward and yanking hold of my wrist as I duck away. "Fer such vermin as *ye*, there should be no mercy!"

To my astonishment, she grabs hold of the cell door, dragging me through it and out into the darkened hallway, while I struggle to limp after, the baffled guard staring at us from behind.

"Where are you taking me?" I demand, smearing my free hand up across my mouth in a sorry attempt to stem the flow of blood still draining from my lip.

Staring straight ahead, Lyubov drags me onward, hissing out hatefully: "Te yer friend."

"But—a moment ago, you said me, you'd never help—"

"Shut up!"

Warily, I do as told, limping along beside her with my teeth gnashed into the effort, scarce able to bear my own weight anymore upon the stiff rheumatic burden of my leg. Through a darkened, winding hallway dotted with yellowish iron doors, each one bearing a numbered metal nameplate, she drags me—until finally, before an unmarked door aside a stairwell, she halts, promptly launching into confrontation with the posted guard. “Open it!” she orders, glaring him down and fingering up the pistol tucked into the holster at her right hip, of which I have only now taken notice.

“But, Comrade!” he cries. “The Commissar left strict orders—”

“I happen te be well aware o’ the Commissar an’ his blessed orders. Now, open it, if ye value yer head! I am Mrenitseva, from the District Justice Committee! I have priority clearance!”

“Yes, Comrade!” the guard cries, coughing, nodding, saluting.

Once he pulls the door open, the reek of the stench within near overpowers my senses. “Get in there!” Lyubov screams hysterically, pushing me through. “An’—an’ good riddance te ye, ’til yer judgment day in *hell*, Sasha Sekovsky!” she shouts, seizing hold of the latch herself and slamming shut the door.

Although I cannot hear them, I sense her footsteps—vengeful and vindictive—pounding off in triumph back the way we came.

Gripped with a lancing chill, I try to breathe, though almost fainting beneath the rancid power of the stench. As if from a bloody abandoned stockyard, thick bursts of death and decay smolder through a soiled, blackened curd of darkness. As my eyes struggle for adjustment to the lack of light, I reach out, attempting to steady my balance against something poking up beside me, its surface smooth and glistening to the touch. Glancing downward, I find myself running my hand up and down naught but the long length of a human bone.

My scream I muffle, both fists jammed into my mouth. In the foreground, enough dim light finally filters through to reveal a small alcove packed with old desks, filing cabinets, boxes, broken swivel office chairs—and bones, human bones and skulls stacked everywhere, from end to end, from wall to wall. “Oh, God!” I gasp out, doubling over and retching—despite my stomach’s plaguing, empty growls—into a pile of legs and feet with broken-off toes. “Oh, dear God!” At last, my inner tremors quivering toward forced, gulping calmness, I reach up and wipe the back of a shaken hand over my mouth, again staring around. Into a corridor, and then another room, the alcove appears to lead off, the way there pitch-black. Beyond, just barely, I can detect a disjointed on-again, off-again rasp that sounds far too eerily like someone breathing.

Drawn against my will, I edge my way through the stacks of bones, casting off, with sickened grimaces, one skeleton after another that falls upon me from precarious perches aside desks, chairs, tables, and old floor lamps. Past the darkened corridor of the alcove, I emerge into a large room.

Once again, every breadth of space lies scattered from end to end with bones—and also with human carcasses cursed to varying states of decay, gruesome hunks of flesh gaping up to surround me from all sides, every inch infested with the drone of flies, the cackling sluice of tapeworms, the whitish, dotted blight of maggots. Again I duck into a corner and retch, quivering throughout every pore of my being. Finally, I lumber up, dazed, my gaze once again fighting through a feathery blanket of dimmed light—to glance, through the pile of bodies encroaching all around, to the farthest corner of the room. There, strung straight up by the manacled arms, bent at the knees, chest bared, hangs another dead carcass, the man beaten and bloodied—and most horrific of all, his lower belly slit open, bands of chalky blue entrails hanging down from the fly of his trousers all the way to the floor, and there gathered into a pile to which a match appears to have been struck, smoke still wafting up from ribbons of charred, acrid-smelling human flesh. "Oh, Mother of *God!"* I moan out again, once more buckling downward and shuddering out retch after empty, heaving retch. Only, after a long moment, to bolt back upward with a blanch of horror, Lyubov's angry grumble of explanation reeling inside my head. Mortified, I gape across at the carcass in a widening shock of recognition. "Nikolai?" I gasp out, a cold sob seizing me. *"Nikolai?"*

And then, he breathes.

"Oh, dear bloody-fucking God! He's still alive!" I burst out, fists once again plunged into my mouth. "They—they've *left* him like this—he—he's s-s-still *a-a-alive! . . ."*

Through bones, carcasses, reeking smears of dung and crusted, runny stumps, I stumble my way across the room to him—to confirm my most awful, terrified suspicion, for against a peeking shaft of light, I glimpse in full the treasured familiarity of his countenance—to find his blond hair matted, soaked in a literal bucket of blood; his face bruised, broken, and bloodied also; his eyes just barely wavering open; his breaths coming slow, shallow, agonized. "Nikolai?" I whisper, halting up abruptly before the ungodly horror of the lagging entrails, stark tears coursing down my face. "C-Can you h-hear m-me?" I choke out, breaking into a sob.

Finish it! comes the urgent, desperate reply, shorn through every inner recess of my mind.

"W-What?" Shuddering from head to toe, I grapple for reeling thoughts scarce leveled to any semblance of sanity.

Finish it!

I bring both my fists upward, plunging them into my mouth, my gaze again lured, in spite of myself, to the hideous sight of the entrails. Even could I hope to break his manacle chains down from their clamps high above us on the overhead water pipes, no surgeon in the world, no miracle of medicine on God's earth could possibly piece him back together into a whole man. Numbly, I ponder over how many agonizing moments of torture it has been, how long he has spent like this; attempt to estimate, in desperation, how many more moments remain. Whereupon I hear voices, and glance beyond him—to notice a door, scarce twenty feet away. Ajar. Beyond the opening, a gruff, sinister cackle calls out: "Well, lads—make quick 'bout fetchin' that vodka fer us, will ye? We got te git on with the bloody quarterin'—uh-huh, both legs, both arms then, after that—yes indeed! Swear I'm goin' te lop the reekin' soul out o' this murderin' Zhelanov bastard. . . ."

Finish it, please! Nikolai begs back at me, his head moving by a scant breath's edge, his swallows hacking suddenly in a choke of blood up his throat, his eyes—the lids raising up just ever so slightly—pleading into mine.

"W-With *w-what?"* I gasp out, still blanched in a quarry of tears—and I search, panicked, about the room for anything that might suffice: rope, twine . . . .

The chain! he echoes at me with insistence.

"What chain?" Shattered with sobs, I cast my arms up before him, pleading helplessness—and stare, with a cold shiver, at the chain looped between the manacles.

Yes! he tells me, his head dropping, in exhaustion, back onto his bloodied chest. *The chain* . . . .

Gulping hard, I nod in agreement, all wrestings with my conscience welling up in a hurried, questioning avalanche—and at once fiercely forsworn. God can take His holy auspices and fuck them to bloody *hell!* My cousin is as good as dead, the choice before me proving not one of murder, but of mercy. Without another moment's hesitation, I stretch my arms out wide and start winding the chain around Nikolai's neck. "And I said I could never be the cause of your death!" I gasp at him, again fending off the urge to retch, to quiver away in gagging horror as the entrails, warm and watery, smear up against my own belly, soaking me with ooze and his blood. "I said never, Nikolai Zhelanov!"

I sob at him, at last pulling my wrists close together about his throat. "That I would not be the cause of your death!"

Once more the same voices resound beyond the door, echoing closer this time.

Finish it, Sasha! he moans for one last aching time. *God, please!*

Shuddering from head to toe, gulping back sob after sleeve-soaked sob—and terrified with doubt of my own strength after the torture, raw spikes of pain yet gnawing their way through every muscle and joint of my right arm—again I swallow hard, and pray. I pray that there is, indeed, a god, a soul, my one source in heaven—and assuming as much, I *curse* Him—for not letting the typhus take us, for not allowing the wolves their final triumph of slaughter. "Damn You!" I sputter out, screaming upward my furious retribution. "By dammit, I hope that *this* satisfies Your cruel wrath of Karma, Your holy auspices . . . !" Holding my breath, gritting my teeth, within my fingers, I grasp up the chain as fiercely as I can—and wrench it around Nikolai's neck.

Blessedly, the bone snaps apart on my first try—and his head slams down, lolling against his chest, a vast grateful sigh of relief filtering throughout the cosmos. Still retching with sobs, I reach my thumb in to check the pulse point at his throat—to find it deafened, silent. Then I break down and let go the full course of my tears, quavering awkwardly against his body, clinging fast hold with both arms thrown around his shoulders as I strive to keep my balance. At last, slowly, cautiously, I lift up to disengage the manacle chain, winding it back from around his neck, fresh tears spilling into my hands. "And if there truly is no death," I choke out, "t-then why can I not hear your voice singing still within my head, Nikolai? W-Why are you not talking to me now, as always? Oh, Nikolai . . . !"

A shaking hand I bring up, brushing my fingers into his blood-soaked, matted hair. Quivering against his form yet again, I plant upon the crown of his head one final lingering kiss. "I l-love you!" I whisper, gripping onto him with life's last desperation. "Death or no death, only *you* shall I love, forever and evermore. . . ."

"Well!" booms out the boorish cackle honing in directly behind me. "Lookit what the witch hunters jest brung in—how touchin'!"

I stumble back to stare, past a snickering group of Red Guards, straight into the jowly, leering face of Ilya Isayevich Bulyarin—ever an uncouth, churlish man, petty and self-serving. Once, as rumor had it, he favored the right-wing Black Hundred terrorists, while at the same time wielding rising power in the democratically-minded Novgorod *zemstvo*. Now, in a switch of sides that, knowing him, could only have been motivated by the tide of opportunism, he appears, indeed—by the look of the many medals pinned upon the chest of his Soviet uniform—to have become a commissar in Lenin's Bolshevik government. His sarcasm whitens to anger once he takes note of the blood dripping from my manacle chains, the hanging, lifeless bent of Nikolai's head. "What, ye have killed him, then—fer Mother mercy's sake? Oh, God blast ye!" he yells, pointing indignant accusation across the room. "Ye meddlin' sonuvabitch! An' how the hell'd ye ever git in here? Well, no matter!" he then cries, his eyes screwing up upon me with a renewed malicious glimmer, his hands caught in a flurry of impatience as he signals to the group of Red Guards. "Stole my amusement with Zhelanov, did ye? Then ye'll pay, by God! 'Specially as *ye're* the cause o' all this sorry business in the first place, ye filthy little faggot whore! 'Cause now, Sekovsky," he shouts, this time snatching out from the sheath at his belt a gleaming long-handled butcher's knife, "we'll be bringin' the same bloody end unto *ye—with* the quarterin'! Well, don't jest stand there, boys!" he yells with lip-smacking, anticipatory relish at the group of men. "String him up!"

They start toward me just as, beyond them, another officer—tall, dark, and bespectacled, and proudly sporting a Red Army colonel's bars, his hands gripped to whitened knuckles about the stock of a sawed-off shotgun—leans in through the door.

Viktor Ilyich Bulyarin: Bulya, as we used to call him about the farm. Bulya, with the over-large nose and protruding buck teeth; Bulya, my old studious, prudent helpmate with the ledgers; Bulya, ever so shy and gangly-awkward, that he never could have proposed to his beloved Natasha without the hapless encouragement of my Tarot card reading. Bulya, ever so clumsy about a horse that he saddled himself always with the clattering buckboard rig, crashing it duly into the barn, the apiary, even into the estate house itself once. He stares across the room at me, and our eyes meet, exchanging memories; acknowledging again his son as my namesake. With a frown of disgust, he then glances over at his father, and I can see that he has only taken a reluctant part in these ghastly, inhuman proceedings—that, Red or no, Viktor Bulyarin remains, in his heart, a decent man, forthright and honest, and following the way he sees fit as best he can—his way, as fate would have it, simply garnering to the side of the *Bolsheviki*. Back toward me, he glances again with resolution, and nods.

Imperceptibly, I nod agreement—just as old Bulyarin sees; just as he yells: “Vitya, no!” But the barrel of the shotgun springs up, aimed straight in my direction and mine alone. The men, near upon me, abruptly glimpse the threat, and scatter upon a stream of curses out of the way. “Vitya, *nooo!”* old Bulyarin screams on, the rifle shot ringing out in a hail of smoke, Bulya’s grip quick and sure upon the trigger—as I shut my eyes.

I shut my eyes and grasp hold of Nikolai’s hands upon the willowy, pliant wing of a violin dream . . . and as the cannon roar plows into my skull—as the careening whiteness saws to blackness, and the nightmare finally howls away unto its vicious, bitter end, I topple to the floor past faces I can no longer see, voices I can no longer hear—while the splatterings spell relief, the splatterings breathe mercy . . . the splatterings spill down my sleeves from the gulf of blood in my head. . . .

CHAPTER ELEVEN

Epilogue: Cornwall, 2019

You can take a train to Tarascon or Rouen,
but it takes death to reach a star.

— Vincent Van Gogh

Forever, it seems, will I hear the shot from that gun and writhe in silence, cast adrift through my memories: Nikolai's subsequent lifetime spent in Germany during the Second World War, which I watched from ethereal realms afar; mine passed largely in America decades thereafter . . . both experiences capped by haunting echoes of a Tarot card reading performed during my American years by a gifted esoteric adept. "These two," he began, his fingers alighting upon the first drawn card, his tone rung with ageless authority long before I revealed even a solitary hint about my past with Nikolai, "these two were together, *very* together. And then the Fool was cast out, and set forward upon the journey once more," he continued on, pointing to the second drawn card. "Behind was a past filled with both tribulation and wondrous contentment—whence heaven merged with earth, body with soul, these two selves one with another, and with God. Against the memory of such bliss, the woman, beneath the Nine Swords, is now sentenced unto her bed of contemplation—knowing within her heart that somehow, something yet remains missing. There will be money," he went on, indicating several further cards drawn from the Pentacles suit, "first, through the learning of its proper use through many harsh lessons. Then, in actuality, there will be a lot of money—but only in the pursuit of true art wrought through the cultivation of that rare inner magic which is sought after, yearned for, and toiled over by he who casts off alone above and beyond all yearnings for worldly attainment—toward the mountain, the stars, the holy specter of the wilderness. For the goal of this Seeker both begins and ends upon higher planes in the temple of the Holy One—as edified by this individual's predominant male principle, for here is one whose heart is true yang, whose call is the raw quest of the daring pioneer. Once the life-goal is achieved, then it will be party time," he insisted with a smile, moving along to the card depicting the lone Sun set ablaze in heights of glory—only to abruptly stop at the next card, the Ace of Wands lying upside down, its face depicting a hand emerged from a cloud shown grasping a singular fiery wand. Reaching to turn the card right-side up, the adept frowned, and changed his mind, murmuring: "No, inverted—definitely inverted. And then, there will be false starts," he went on with conviction, "or a journey will be cut short somehow. And then these two . . . these two once so passionately bound one to another—body, heart, and soul—in the beginning . . . these two will be together. Again."

True to the prophecy, days come when my cousin's beloved voice starts to mount with an ever-growing resonance inside my head, culminating at last with one of his whispered meditations: 'You are lolling about upon a long stretch of winter beach set in our own cherished north country. Yes, brisk the day is, and sandy the beach is, ocean waves crashing before you, the tall mossy bluffs towering behind. All cares and maladies of the recent past you bear no longer, dearest heart—for the middle tier you have finally left behind. The second part of our project you have accomplished well, and with the utmost expediency, my most sacred, holy love. And now . . . now, you are young again, and more healthy and free than you have ever felt before—for this is the culmination, the third and final undertaking on our grand universal journey . . . of your journey which now lies spread before you upon the open, sandy promise of the beach . . . .'

I awaken in a bed of sand. Wincing, blinking against an unseasonable afternoon glare bathing the whole westward horizon in metallic streams of light, I shiver against a faint burst of fresh chill-wind, and instinctively snatch into my shirt pocket for my sunglasses. Twenty feet away, ocean waves rebound once more in a wondrous frothy torrent, stark depths of blue glinting against a sheer height of gold, the tempestuous roar plunging beyond the most infinite voice of sound itself, earth's deluge bowing in humble reverence through every cascading crash unto her holy, unfathomable white sun. Still wobbly with confusion, not quite sure where I am, nor how I even came to be upon this beach, I grope upward, heaving into my lungs a crisp bite of the salt air. Then the waves tempt me as waves ever have, and I wander into the water unto the dire soaking of my tennis shoes and the lower hems of my jeans—only to abruptly stop short, the water yet lapping in sweet eddying pools about my feet, my breath caught hard to recognition at the sound, high across the cool gusts of wind, of someone shouting a name.

"Jonathan!" the plea sounds out again. *"Jonathan!"*

I spin about to stare upward toward a massive house perched high upon the mossy bluff. From an upstairs terrace, a smartly-dressed, strikingly beautiful woman possessed of an abundance of upswept honey-colored hair glares down at me, shaking one fist overhead—while from the other, waving out, like a flag of battle, a red vinyl baseball jacket. "Jonathan Sekoff!" she cries in exasperation, "you troop yourself back up here *immediately*, young man! Have you no bloody sense at all, wandering about upon the beach this time of year in naught but a T-shirt? And the time, Jonathan! Your father must hurry for Heathrow soon, and you know how gridlocked the A46 air lanes become in the afternoon—telly says three elevation point spinouts so far, and another simply monstrous tie-up through Wiltshire! Surely we'll not make the first Petersburg evening commuter flight, perhaps not even the second . . . Jonathan! Do you *hear* me? Well, don't simply stand down there gawking up at me like such a lobotomy—come *along!"*

With both hands, I grasp hold of the frames of my wire-rimmed sunglasses, pinning them back upon my face in disbelief, finally gasping out at the woman: *"Melissa?"*

And then I hear, in echo from so many shared and treasured lifetimes past, that generous familiar baritone booming out in a fluster from one of the rooms below: "Lyss! That boy will chase his way back home without a doubt once his stomach starts growling at him. Well! Oh, stop fussing so over that jacket. Is warm for December, and in any case, I need you more right now than he does—this infernal toner cartridge has jammed again! And you know I need my layouts! Yes, all ten of them—and complete, mind you! Before we make for Heathrow—"

"Jonathan!" the woman blares out at me again, still shaking the jacket. "Ohhh!" Turning on her heel, she marches in a huff back through the door, slamming shut a threatening rattle of glass-latticed panes behind.

Gulping, I stare long and hard up at her trail, and then at the terrace—upon which, yes, I have stood. For this, indeed, is that mausoleum strewn rife unto the overflowing, contagious hilt with cluttered halls, through which—so long ago—I have trod. "Winnebar?" I gasp out joyfully, my arms thrown wide to behold, cherish, grovel within sight of its stately, imposing vista. "Oh, my God—*Winnebar!"*

I break off into a run fed with shivers of awe; bound with the carefree, scrambling ease of youth along the old horse trail leading in a mossy-edged zigzag upward from the beach path. The side door, ever easy to sneak in through, is exactly where I remember. Panting in euphoria, I burst on past it—only to find the old downstairs parlor, once dotted with fringe-edged lamps and musty, prim Victorian chairs, transformed into the straight-planed lines of a modern computer room. Paper smudged to varying degrees of profundity spouts out from a printer in the corner, while Father—his face younger, fiftyish; his mane of thickened auburn scored with peppery streaks of gray—throws back his head and bellows out at the top of his lungs: "By dammit, Lyss—*Lyss!* I tell you, this infernal contraption is on the blink again! Well! Alyssa—sweetheart, darling, dearest love of all my life—I scarce mean to shout at you so, but will you please come down here and salvage the last shred of my sanity before this mind-of-its-own machine starts devouring that, too? And they have the audacity to call this the Twenty-First Century, humph! Damned if I'll ever swear by wristwatch-sized Japanese computer savvy—which will never print a layout faster than I could sketch it . . . *Lyssa!"*

Then he sees me—and his eyebrows shoot upward in surprise as he blurts out: "Well! Broke the three minute mile, did you, son? Dear Lord, Jonathan—your poor mother still thinks you to be strolling out upon the beach—"

"Papa!" I gasp, bounding across the room and plowing into his arms.

He catches hold of me with a startled gasp and bends his cheek in bewilderment to my flurry of kisses, muttering out with one hand still caught unto a score of spewing computer pages: "Well, heavens name, boy—calm down, calm down! Well, I love you, too—my word! And when was the last time I ever *heard* such? God's teeth, Jonathan, such a display of affection! And to think, three days ago at the airport, you scarce even gave me the time of day. What has gotten into you?

Lyssa!" he then shouts on above my head. "This mind-of-its-own computer . . . !"

"All right, Misha, darling—I am coming!" Bursting through the door, Alyssa stops short in shock, gasping out upon the sight of me embracing Father: *"Jonathan?* What in the world? I thought you still to be out upon the beach!"

I step back, and nearly fly across the room to embrace her, too—save for the scolding, her voice ringing high upon shrills of exasperation as she storms after me with the baseball jacket, yelling: "And where—*where* have you been? Lolling about upon the beach all day, while I've been fielding your nonstop phone calls? Indeed, ever since—oh, my Lord, look at the time—this morning!"

"I—I am sorry!" I stutter out, flushing in embarrassment and ducking away from her. *"Nyet, Maman-Matushka,* no! I meant not, upon intention, to worry you—"

"Don't you try to *pa-russky* sweet talk me, young man!"

"Lyss!" Father interrupts with a grumble of impatience. "Will you forget about your *pa-russky* endearments, and help me with these printouts?"

"Oh, for bloody God's sake, Misha!" she snaps at him, hurling the baseball jacket to the floor and stomping in a clicking banter of high heels across the room. "And how on earth do they bear your raving fits in Petersburg, when I am not there to coddle to your every whim?" she demands, stopping before the machine and fixing him with a pronounced glare. Deftly, she then reaches down beneath the smudged bundle of papers—still spewing, one by one, out from the printer—to fumble with a few sensors. Within no more than five seconds, the whole menagerie begins to whisk forth normally again, printed sketches inked in perfect compliance upon every page.

"The lady with the magic touch," says Father gently, grasping his hands to her shoulders with murmurs of: *"Tebya lyublyu. . . ."*

"Ohhh! If not *pa-russky* sweet talk from one, then from the other!" she rants on, yet again glaring between the both of us. But she breaks into a smile and turns back against him to meet his lips with a tender, worshipful kiss.

Reddening, and yet marveling at the sight of the two of them, I step quietly across the floor and fetch up my baseball jacket—to recall that he is now the doctor who has switched careers midstream for the lure of choreography—she, his ballerina love. And their story folds into the past, mirrors the future just as have so many other untold numbers of love stories, each so akin to every other, and also as unique in itself as a snowdrop cast to intricacy across the air. From over her shoulder, he catches my eye, smiles, and winks—and upon taking note of the trail of water dripping in such grimy testament from the soles of my shoes, he conspiratorially motions his head toward the door.

Too late. Alyssa leans around, dreamy-eyed still against the enfolding comfort of his arms—but her face goes livid white upon sight of the water puddle. "Jonathan!" she shrieks out, pointing. *"Ohhh!* By God, look at you—soaked up to your knees! Phone calls, water puddles—and must you continue to cause me one headache after another, without ever any end? Off with those tennis shoes this very moment, young man!"

I kick them off just as the sound of an ethanol motor purrs into the driveway outside. Father collects his array of sketches from the printer and pecks kiss after kiss at Alyssa's cheek in attempt to assuage her rampaging tirade about the tennis shoes. "That You-Know-Who?" he says to me past her head, an eyebrow cocked toward the front door.

"You-Know-Who?" I mutter out dazedly in reply, following after the two of them with tennis shoe laces caught up in my fingers, Alyssa hounding back behind without a second's pause for breath: "Jonathan, go change! I'll not have you soaking into my new living room furniture in those soggy jeans! And you remember to mop up the water on that computer room floor! . . ."

In a frenzy, they struggle with flight bags and rush out the front door, Father waving off my hurried embrace with the promise to return in two days; Alyssa calling back instructions about what to microwave for dinner. And then past them, upon a stream of friendly, familial 'hellos' to each, *he* saunters in.

Sporting a long blond mane streaked with garish iridiscent purple dye, duos of gold-hooped earrings pierced through the lobes of each of his ears. His dark leather jacket, faded jeans, and black T-shirt blazing down the front with an ancient *Metallica* motif overlayed with his own *Mal Lotoff* rock band logo testify to recent proclivities. Grinning at me rakishly, he drags in upon his shoulder instrument cases for an amp and an electric guitar, kicks shut the door behind, and hushes me to silence, awaiting departure of the bustling parental entourage. Once their car takes off, he bounds back across the room, gauges the look of incredulity still spread across my face, shakes his head in amusement, and sweeps me full into his arms, rasping out: *"No* death, Sasha-Sashenka—Jonathan—my dearest love! Never ever was, never will be, any such horror as death. There is only life—*life everlasting*, and love abounding beyond every last measure of time! Oh, yes—the past held pain and horror for us at the end—a test, if you will. And afterward, we scarce bore the long years of physical separation, the two intervening lifetimes—one mine, one yours—in between. Yet, so many triangles we imbued mentally during that time, so many numbers we inured, so much intricate astrological planning we agonized over, even up until the very moments of embarking upon this last pivotal adventure. All through which we have garnered for ourselves such splendid opportunity! What better way could there ever be to tell the others? So *kiss me*, you cherished little devil-whore of a hundred lifetimes! Fantasy of all my dreams . . . ."

Throwing my arms around his neck and crushing him to me with a gasp of joy, I gnaw open in a cavern for his mouth, and we consume the lights out of one another, thighs locking together, hands mussing through hair—until he inches backward, whispering excitedly against ecstatic tremors of my lips: *"Avatar!* That is what I intend to rename the band! That's it, I have finally decided."

Loring, his name is now—although he insists, just as disdainfully as ever, that everyone call him not by any conceivable nickname save for—this time—his first and middle initials. Extricating himself with some difficulty from my fierce embrace, he dashes back across the room and seizes open both instrument cases, exclaiming: "Wait until you hear your lyrical nuances against the furor of this!" Then he hooks the guitar up to the amp, plugs both cords into an outlet in the wall, and proceeds to assault the entire house from shaky ceiling down to its helpless, quivering foundations with the thundering voice of metal-wailing, rad-bad sound such as no mortal ear has never heard.

Going weak in the knees, I lean back against the wall and watch the florescent play of laser beams leaping out from the frets of the guitar beneath his dancing fingers. "Oh, God!" I gasp in elation. "I think I am bloody *in love. . . ."*

As he starts singing, his raspy tenor sparring back and forth zealously with the rhythm, everyday trappings of my current life slowly begin flooding back—and the grip of sudden realization shatters into me like a thunderbolt. Although I flaunt no purple streaks in my hair—yet—I know that I too have at last reached the same crowning solar goal, the height of achievement, the peerless summit toward which, along with him, I have been striving ceaselessly for scores of centuries. And just as during so many other times in life—through countless lives—that the bare obviousness of confirmation has struck without the slightest cue of warning, naked insight starts to render an icy thrill up and down the column of my spine, intuition's nod of promise granting, in the scantiest breath of a moment, seemingly, all for which he and I have for so long sought. "So," I whisper out—begging penance for ever cursing God, or Karma, or auspices—and finally stealing my gaze away from Loring's plyings with the guitar long enough to hedge a glance through the wide west-facing living room windows. In grand dominion, the tempest of the sea and boulders of the earth frame our call toward all music, the hallowed Lord of the orchestral stars bidding us a wry grin of welcome high upon the crimson-blue horizon's every stratospheric, painted triangle of sunset.

Although he could not possibly have heard my faint utterance in the physical sense, Loring stops playing and sets away his guitar. In another moment, I lean into the warmth of his embrace clasped about me from behind, quivering in delight beneath his every fervent kiss nuzzled across the nape of my neck. "So," I go on with a contented sigh, interlinking both my arms through his, "I suppose that this . . . *all* of this . . . ." And I stop cold, swallowing grating, chalky whispers—for such a cataclysm of love, hate, loss, pain, ecstasy, triumph, and potential—three separate lifetimes—colors the simple letterings of the three meager words 'all of this' . . . . *"All* of this," I go on with a pale, eye-widened choke of reverence, "is—is what is called the initiation?"

Punctuating the pause of silence between us, it remains a paradox of wonders, hovering on the air—unanswered, yet the answered question.

The end is only the beginning. . . .

AFTERWORD

Death to Reach a Star is a novelization of the latter half of my prior incarnation lived in Russia as Aleksandr K. (circumstances preclude public disclosure of the full surname). The dramatic turns of coincidence indeed all occurred as related, and such uncanny incidents continue peppering events of my life unto the present day. Fiction's end has been served by capitulations from mundane, intervening spans of time and by some deliberate rearrangements of happenstance, my intent ever keen upon creating a lively, readable story. Most notable diversions: (1) Devonbury is a fictionalized name for an actual town situated on the British seacoast, and (2) Tamara Karsavina was in Prague when Sergei Diaghilev's ballet troupe departed St. Petersburg in May 1909. Interspersing my earlier acquisition of the autograph with the train departure account adds spice to the narrative (additionally, one of my aims throughout has been to showcase Mme. Karsavina's career at every opportunity; Anna Pavlova always stole her well-deserved limelight). Fiction's due is further merited by other such instances of scene tightening or the elimination of sundry personal details, e.g.: I actually broke my leg a year before the Lissushka peasant demonstration; Nikolai played both cello and double bass on a regular basis in addition to violin; as well as flute, I played oboe and violin also. Rendering one's existence smoothly unto the expansive realm of demon words requires simplification/condensation if overwhelming the reader is to be avoided. One of the major physical characteristics I chose to exclude was my aggravating tendency during this prior lifetime toward stuttering. In writing this book, I had from the outset decided to shun any reference to this handicap, the story and characterization already respectively proving lengthy and complex enough. Interestingly, through entirely subconscious effort, so many repeated words, both in dialogue and narrative, made their way into the early drafts—despite all outright attempts to expunge the nagging fault from the start—that in yet another way, I had the validity of my remembered past life confirmed in my heart yet once again.

Recollection of a past incarnation is much like attempting to conjure up visions of a week-old meal—one remembers his or her mental/emotional state and particular relations with significant others at the time, but God help you to recall what you ate. The plausibility of every 'remembered' event I have attempted to verify through painstaking research, and I owe an irrevocable debt to every scholar who has ever penned a word about Russian history and/or culture. However, despite my autumn 1991 journey made to the then Soviet Union (during which my husband and I searched out and found the sight of the old Lake Ilmen estate) health impairments have cramped the extensiveness of my research quest. I have not, for instance, had the opportunity to consult with distinguished experts. Consequently, to none do I need lend credit, but likewise, any factual errors contained herein are mine and mine alone.

From the time I decided, after many years of preparation/contemplation, to at last embark upon the writing of this novel (once the Sun entered Scorpio in 1989), great assistance has come through family and friends, some whom I must thank in particular: my woodwind teacher, Mr. Dick Burley, for his perusal of and suggestions on the musical portions of the manuscript; my draft readers, Murph Gagnon, Patti Codorniz, Lorrayne Haynes, Peggy Huggins, and Dr. Lynne Stampfes, for their boundless enthusiasm and steady encouragement. To Andrei Bazdyrev I will be forever indebted for procuring from his personal collection in Russia a copy of Valery Bryusov's *Pale Horse*. The 'gifted esoteric adept' mentioned in the Epilogue nudged open the doors to the universe, and to him I remain profoundly grateful. And for his invaluable intuitive advice, for his selfless help with both the planning and production of this book, and for many hours of tireless listening, my husband James M. Gagnon has earned himself more Karmic gold stars than he knows. Of my dear maternal grandmother, Margaret Christensen Anderson Bryce Hoffer, who turns a spry eighty years of age this month, I again beg forgiveness for the many luncheon visits missed due to my being buried beneath a monolith of a manuscript for the past three years. On the Sirius side, thanks goes to The (Arts) Committee, especially to Master D., Master Ch., and in particular to 'Arnie' (Greek Master Arstphns.) for teaching me to teach myself how to write with eight words (*'Break the Rules, Feel the Pauses, Form Out'*), and also for shrugging off the brunt of the temper tantrums. Lastly, again I bless my partner in soul, to whom this work, with all the love and passion expressed throughout, is appropriately dedicated. Without him, this story in its joy and variant richness would never have been lived, nor a word of it written.

J. Maris Gagnon
Seattle, October 1992

ABOUT THE AUTHOR

J. Maris Gagnon was born in Heidelberg in 1957, and lived for several years in Okinawa and Japan before taking up the study of Russian at Arizona State University in the 1970s. Formerly employed as a legal typist, J. currently divides her time between astrological consultations and occult research, and resides near Seattle. Her poetry has found print in small press magazines, and her stories have earned national recognition. *Death to Reach a Star* is J.'s first published novel. Her *White Sun Burning*, a 'fusion between the seen and unseen worlds,' is in progress.

The author welcomes friendly correspondence and will attempt to answer all inquiries. Please address to J. Maris Gagnon in care of Twin Omega Press, P.O. Box 55697, Seattle, WA 98155.